Actors' YEARBOOK 2011

WITHDRAWN FROM STOCK

Edited by Simon Dunmore

methuen | drama

Seventh edition 2010

Methuen Drama
A & C Black Publishers Limited
36 Soho Square, London W1D 3QY
www.acblack.com

Copyright © 2010 A & C Black Publishers Limited

ISBN 978 1 408 12840 4

A CIP catalogue record for this book is available from the British Library.

The publishers make no representation, express or implied, with regard to the accuracy of the information contained in this book and cannot accept any legal responsibility for any errors or omissions that may take place.

This book is produced using paper that is made from wood grown in managed, sustainable forests. It is natural, renewable and recyclable. The logging and manufacturing processes conform to the environmental regulations of the country of origin.

Typeset by QPM from David Lewis XML Associates Ltd
Printed in the UK by CPI William Clowes, Beccles NR34 7TL

Contents

Foreword

Equity (see page 364) is a relatively small union covering a wide variety of issues – not just contracts – of importance to those working in the performing arts. Despite our size we are expert in all the issues we cover, thanks to a dedicated staff with a wide variety of specialist knowledge to support our members.

However, you, as lone actor, also have a range of other concerns that are outside Equity's remit. For instance, how do you go about finding a specialist photographer capable of capturing the essential 'you'? What unforeseen pitfalls can you expect to encounter on a small-scale tour? Which agents and casting directors are happy to receive unsolicited showreels?

The joy of this wonderfully comprehensive book is that it gives you not only detailed listings for every aspect of work-related issues, but also great insights into the experiences of seasoned practitioners. The really helpful introductions and articles are written with warmth and humour. It is a valuable companion and an essential tool for all actors at whatever stage in their careers.

Christine Payne
General Secretary of Equity

Introduction

It is well known that an actor's life is not an easy one. Those who aspire to the 'bright lights' face a seemingly bewildering array of courses, audition processes and funding methods. Drama school graduates confront a bedazzling array of agents, casting directors and production companies (in all media) to whom they could send their precious CVs and photographs. Experienced actors try to become philosophical about how secure-seeming 'contacts' they once had have been superseded by a new generation. ("There's a new bunch of schoolboys running the networks each week." Joan Collins) The art and crafts of acting are difficult enough – the prospect of navigating through 'bald' lists of services and potential employers can overwhelm all but the most determined. Those with time and money can simply blitz every agent (for instance) that they can find, in the hope that some may respond with offers of representation – this will cost several hundred pounds, let alone the time spent stuffing envelopes. And the chances of success, with this kind of unfocused approach, will be extremely limited. Judicious targeting, using the information in this book and your own research (especially on the Internet), can save a considerable amount of money and will give you a greater chance of satisfaction and success.

The aim of this book is also to make some more detailed sense of the ever-diversifying world of professional acting – from training to the wide range of companies offering work in all media, via the 'brokers' (agents and casting directors) of much of that work. In addition, you will find more details of the available services (photographers, showreel companies, and so on) so that you can make detailed comparisons before committing your precious funds. In order to help you cut your way through the 'jungle' of performing arts information, the listings are restricted to those directly relevant to aspiring and work-seeking actors. (For instance, agents who only represent directors, designers, and so forth, are not included.) Careful study of the section(s) appropriate to you at a particular moment could save you time and money through more accurate 'targeting' of your intentions – whether looking for appropriate training, whom to send your CV and photograph to, where to get your showreel made, and so forth.

This book contains details of those organisations and individuals from whom we were able to glean more full information, beyond the basic contact details. Some were prepared to provide helpful information but requested that their telephone numbers, for instance, should not be included. You'll find more organisations listed in *Contacts* (published annually by The Spotlight). Some individuals and organisations declined to contribute to this book, apparently fearful of attracting even more actor-submissions. Some simply did not respond. Some information will go out of date – new companies will start up and others go out of business – and personnel will change; this profession has a highly mobile population. However, the listings will help focus your research and enable you to 'target' more accurately and efficiently.

Actors' Yearbook is designed to work in harmony with my *An Actor's Guide to Getting Work* (4th edition, A&C Black, 2004), in which you will find much more detailed advice on how to market yourself and enhance your chances as a professional actor.

Simon Dunmore, Consultant Editor
www.simon.dunmore.btinternet.co.uk

Important note – the new postage rates

As of 2nd April 2007, postage rates started to vary according to size as well as weight. There are three basic formats (more details available from **www.royalmail.com**):

'**Letter**': A thin (less than 5mm – i.e. probably not padded in any way), just over A5-sized package, which could contain:
• a letter
• a folded CV
• a postcard-sized photograph
• a CD/DVD (in a paper or plastic sleeve)
• an sae (stamped with sufficient postage) for return of your photo and CV/DVD

'**Large letter**': A just over A4-sized package, which can be up to 25mm (nearly an inch) thick; this could contain:
• a letter
• an unfolded CV
• a 10x8in photograph
• a CD/DVD (in a paper or plastic sleeve)
• a board-backed envelope (stamped with sufficient postage) for return of your photograph and CD/DVD

'**Packet**': Any package that exceeds the dimensions of the above – or where the weight exceeds 750g.

Your submission

As most submissions will contain a 10x8in (unfolded) photograph, they will be classified as 'Large letters'. These have charge bands by weight. A board-backed envelope with a 10x8in photo, A4 CV and A4 or A5 letter weighs in at just under 100g and should therefore be fine with a standard 'Large letter' 1st or 2nd Class stamp (66p and 51p respectively, at the time of writing). If you're adding a stamped addressed envelope for return of your photo, however, this will probably push you over the 100g limit and you will need a stamp for the next band up. (At the time of writing, this is 96p for 1st Class and 81p for 2nd Class.) You'll also go into the higher band if you add a CV or DVD in a paper or plastic sleeve.

If you're sending a light, A5 padded envelope with a CD or DVD then your choice of case will affect the postage: the chunky old-style CD cases, the full-size DVD cases, and the heavier-style padded envelopes will need the higher postal rate, whereas a paper or plastic sleeve, or some of the modern, lighter-style cases, will probably still come in at under 100g. If you use a padded envelope you will probably need a 'Large letter' stamp; without a padded envelope a standard 'Letter' stamp will probably suffice.

An old-fashioned video cassette in a padded envelope will fall into the 101-250g 'Packet' charge band, which will cost £1.72 (1st Class) and £1.51 (2nd Class). Even if the video cassette weighed less, then it would still be charged at the 'Packet' rate because they are thicker than the 25mm maximum allowable in the 'Large letter' charge band.

It is very important to get the postage right on a submission, as it's the recipient who has to pay an excess charge. Many companies – fed up with people getting this wrong – will simply not accept delivery and it will be returned to you unopened ... with all your hard work and postage costs wasted.

It is also important to consider the cost of the postage on your sae, especially if you want your photograph returned intact.

Note: The larger style of envelope, unless board-backed, does not survive the postal system very well, and your photo and CV will probably arrive looking rather dog-eared. If you're sending a 10x8in photograph, then always use a board-backed envelope; if you're not sending a 10x8 then consider folding your letter/CV and using a C5 envelope (takes A5 or A4 folded once).

Postage costs usually go up each April, so if you're reading this after April 2011 then check the Royal Mail website for the latest rates.

Training
Introduction

This section is largely devoted to those who are 18 and older. This is not to dismiss the fact that there is training (of varying kinds) for those under that age. However, the field is so wide that the confines of this book limit listings only to the major organisations.

In spite of the fact that a minority of well-known actors did not formally train, it is very important for today's aspirant to do so. An ever-increasing number of people want to become actors, so those with 'casting clout' (agents, casting directors and directors) have more and more people to choose from. Doesn't it make sense to select from those who've undergone the rigours of a respected training process? It is an essential fact that the acting industry works on very tight time-scales and budgets – trained actors should be quicker, more reliable and, usually, more inventive than their untrained counterparts. For instance, an untrained voice that cracks up after a few days of live performance is time-consuming and costly for a management – only the larger productions can afford understudies. An untrained actor, who may look good on camera, will take time to learn how to work on a television set, where time spent keeping technicians waiting is very, very expensive. A fight (in a theatre or on camera) has to be staged so that it (a) looks real, (b) is safe for the participants and (c) can be seen properly by camera and/or audience – actors who've been trained in the essentials of combat will make this staging process much quicker. Moving correctly in period costumes, performing all kinds of formal dance and using microphones properly are just a few of the other time-saving skills that the trained actor can bring to a production. It is only an exceptional few who, nowadays, have the opportunity to 'learn on the job'.

For today's aspiring actor, it is important to train on a professionally recognised course. The established drama schools are the focus of such training. There are acting-related university degree courses which have a reasonable proportion of vocational training (as well as academic work) and there are numerous part-time, short-term and 'foundation' courses which will give you basic insights into the many crafts involved in acting. However, because of the intense competition, a full-time drama school course of at least a year is essential for most people.

For those who have already trained, there are opportunities to learn new skills and refine those already acquired, or simply to keep them in trim when the acting work is not coming in. The latter is very important, as you can be asked to demonstrate your skills at very short notice. Being an actor is a bit like being a fireman – without the regular salary. Also, the more you can legitimately add to the 'Skills' section of your CV, the more you can enhance your chances of finding work.

Editor's Note: It is especially important to **check for the latest information on all fees listed** under all headings in this section. *Actors' Yearbook* makes every effort to ensure that such information is correct and up-to-date, but prices are especially liable to ongoing amendment.

Training for the under-18s

It is a fact that many child stars do not succeed as adult actors. There are notable exceptions – Nicholas Lyndhurst, Dennis Waterman and Jenny Agutter, for instance – but they are the exceptions that prove the rule. I also wonder whether a childhood largely devoted to performing is entirely healthy: what about learning about life? And what about learning other essential skills in order to earn one's living when the acting work is not coming in? Generally speaking, the best thing for the stage-struck child is to send him or her to one of the numerous youth theatre groups and drama workshops that exist in almost every town and city. These are often listed in *Yellow Pages*, and many are members of the National Association of Youth Theatres – see below. Public productions are often the last priority of such groups – especially for the younger ages – but a terrific amount can be learnt by the young from what seem like simple, make-believe games. Children in such groups won't learn many of the technical skills necessary to acting, but they will learn a lot of important social skills and the fundamental business of 'interacting' that is so important to an acting ensemble – that it's not just what you can create that matters, but what you can create with other people. Some youth theatres are allied to agencies who will promote their members for professional work, but it is important to note that employment of the under-16s is very strictly regulated.

National Association for Youth Drama (NAYD)

7 North Great George's Street, Dublin 1
tel 353-1 878 1301 *fax* 353-1 874 9816
email info@nayd.ie
website www.youthdrama.ie

NAYD is the development organisation for youth theatre and youth drama in Ireland. It supports youth drama in practice and policy, and supports the sustained development of youth theatres in Ireland.

NAYD advocates the inherent value and the unique relationship between young people and theatre as an artform, and is committed to extending and enhancing young people's understanding of theatre and to raising the artistic standards of youth theatre across the country. The organisation supports youth drama in practice through an annual programme that includes the National Youth Theatre, National and Regional festivals of youth theatres, commissioning new writing, publications, resources, training and other services, as well as research and policy development.

With a membership of more than 50 youth theatres throughout the country, NAYD supports the sustained development of youth theatres in partnership with local authorities, youth services, theatres and arts centres. Its productions are of a professional standard and are cast from youth theatres around Ireland. Previous productions include: *Our Town*, by Thornton Wilder and directed

by Ben Barnes; *A Midsummer Night's Dream*, directed by Andy Hinds; *Young Europeans*, written and directed by Gerard Stembridge; and *The Crucible* by Arthur Miller, directed by Ben Barnes. For further details about NAYD's work, please refer to the website.

National Association of Youth Theatres (NAYT)

Arts Centre, Vane Terrace, Darlington DL3 7AX
tel (01325) 363330 *fax* (01325) 363313
email nayt@btconnect.com
website www.nayt.org.uk

Founded in 1982, the National Association of Youth Theatres (NAYT) is the development agency for youth theatre practice in England. The organisation supports the development of youth theatre activity through training, advocacy, participation programmes, and information services. Registration is open to any group or individual using theatre techniques in their work with young people, outside formal education. NAYT is an educational charity (No. 1046042) and a company limited by guarantee (No. 2989999).

NAYT responds to more than 800 enquiries a year from young people, teachers, parents, carers, youth workers and social services looking for information and advice about youth theatre provision or career or educational opportunities. This free service puts young people in direct contact with youth theatres.

National Youth Arts Wales (NYAW)

245 Western Avenue, Cardiff CF5 2YX
tel 029-2026 5060 *fax* 029-2026 5014
email nyaw@nyaw.co.uk
website www.nyaw.co.uk/nytw.html
NYTW Artistic Director Tim Baker (there are other
Artistic Directors with the other disciplines)

NYAW represents the National Youth Brass Band of
Wales, National Youth Choir of Wales, National
Youth Chamber Ensemble of Wales, National Youth
Dance Wales, National Youth Orchestra of Wales,
and National Youth Theatre of Wales (NYTW).

The National Youth Theatre of Wales was founded in
1976 and has since provided opportunities for
hundreds of young people, many of whom are now
actively involved with the theatre as professional
actors, directors, writers, designers and stage
managers. The NYTW is aimed at young people aged
16-21 who are drawn from all over Wales. With
guidance from its Artistic Director, the youth theatre
prepares and rehearses during the summer of each
year for a series of high-profile public performances.

In addition, the NYTW spearheads a development
programme of workshops and education activities,
designed to increase interest and participation in
youth theatre.

National Youth Music Theatre (NYMT)

2-4 Great Eastern Street, London EC2A 3NW
email enquiries@nymt.org.uk;
auditions@nymt.org.uk (Auditions);
sheena.clark@nymt.org.uk (Sponsorship & Support)
website www.nymt.org.uk

The National Youth Music Theatre exists to produce
challenging music theatre work (both major
productions and workshops) for young people of all
backgrounds as participants. It helps them to explore
new and existing works, to inspire themselves and
each other – giving them the opportunity to achieve
their highest aspirations and to realise their talent,
imagination and creativity.

National Youth Theatre of Great Britain (NYT)

443-45 Holloway Road, London N7 6LW
tel 020-7281 3863
website www.nyt.org.uk
Artistic Director Paul Roseby *Executive Director* Sid
Higgins *General Manager* Alexa Cruickshank

Founded in 1956, the NYT is the UK's premier youth
arts organisation, providing young people aged 13-21
with the opportunity for creative participation and
learning through theatre arts. Courses are offered in
Acting, Stage Management, Lighting & Sound,
Scenery & Prop Building and Costume Making at a
professional standard, which culminate in a season of
productions and community projects around the UK
and abroad, in professional theatres and site-specific
locations.

Many leading names in the creative industries started
out at the NYT, including Sir Ben Kingsley, Sir Derek
Jacobi, Dame Helen Mirren, Daniel Craig, Daniel
Day Lewis, Chiwetel Ejiofor, Timothy Spall, Liza
Tarbuck and Matt Smith.

The NYT auditions approximately 3000 applicants
each year at one of 20 audition centres across the UK.
Approximately 650 new members are recruited
annually. Successful applicants are offered a place on
one of the courses, and, having completed a course,
members are eligible to audition for the NYT's
production season or to become Peer Mentors within
the Creative Learning programme. Major
productions are mounted each year.

The NYT also has a robust Creative Learning
programme which embeds learning throughout all
projects. It runs accredited courses for those not in
education or training, as well as many open access
projects and community productions.

Scottish Youth Theatre

The Old Sheriff Court, 105 Brunswick Street,
Glasgow G1 1TF
tel 0141-221 5127 *fax* 0141-221 9123
email info@scottishyouththeatre.org
website www.scottishyouththeatre.org
Artistic Director Mary McCluskey

Founded in 1977, Scottish Youth Theatre is
Scotland's national theatre for and by young people.
Runs weekly drama classes for young people aged 3-
25, in addition to a variety of training courses,
festivals, educational workshops, youth theatre
projects and productions throughout the year. There
is no audition process to attend the drama classes,
but participants in the annual summer festival are
asked to prepare a 2-minute speech and a song. In
2003 almost 2000 applications were received and
1000 places offered. Stages at least 5 productions each
year, which in recent years have included: *Mary
Queen of Scots* and *Dying for It*. Staff are happy to
help applicants with any enquiries.

Youth Music Theatre UK

London Office 40 Parkgate Road, London SW11 4JH
tel 0844-415 4858
Edinburgh Office c/o FST, Theatre Workshop,
Hamilton Place, Edinburgh EH3 5AX
website www.youthmusictheatreuk.org

Youth Music Theatre UK, also known as YMT, is a
national charity whose principal aim is the personal
and creative development of young people through
the medium of musical theatre. Set up in 2003, the
organisation is the UK's biggest and most active
music theatre provider for young people aged 11-21.

The company provides a wide range of residential
workshops around the country, in the form of
summer productions and Studios. Each year, YMT
presents work in all corners of the UK, and works
with hundreds of young people from a wide range of
backgrounds.

Training

The charity also provides a wide range of Outreach opportunities with schools, youth services and cross-cultural groups, and is dedicated to giving an unique and memorable experience to every young person who participates.

Auditions for young performers take place around the UK from January to March, and successful applicants join the company of 8 fully staged productions at venues and festivals around the country in the summer holidays.

YMT also runs The Studio, a non-auditioned, residential summer course which allows young performers and musicians the chance to work with professional artistic teams to create a unique new musical. In 2008, YMT also introduced the Young Writers' and Composers' Course, led by professional musical theatre creators working with 15 young writers and composers to create new work with the intention of possible future development.

YMT also offers training opportunities for graduate directors, assistant directors, assistant MDs, designers and choreographers alongside its professional summer teams – check the website for details early each year.

For further information on YMT's work, visit www.youthmusictheatreuk.org.

Drama schools

Currently there is a core of established drama schools which belong to an organisation called the Conference of Drama Schools (CDS – **www.drama.ac.uk**). Most of these run courses that are 'accredited' by the National Council for Drama Training (NCDT – **www.ncdt.co.uk**); for more details, see the article on the NCDT and accreditation. At present, all courses that have 'accreditation' are provided by schools who are members of the CDS. However, there are also courses within these schools which don't have 'accreditation', and there are a few well-respected courses that are neither 'accredited' nor part of CDS schools. The reasons for these variations are too complex to explain here.

It is important to check the current funding arrangements for each course you intend applying for. Don't simply rely on what arrangements were in place last year, as things have a habit of changing. Many three-year accredited courses have 'degree' status – in spite of the fact that there is little or no written component to the courses, let alone formal, written exams. (Historically, the schools took the 'degree' route to help students get funding on the same basis as those following conventional academic courses.) Degree status actually means very little in the acting profession, and courses with degree status are not necessarily better than those without it. Some schools have been quite vociferous about not wishing to become embroiled in the whole philosophy and bureaucracy that is fundamental to degree education – believing that joining with a university would compromise the purely vocational character of their courses. One such adds: "Universities are academic institutions, and the intelligence required of an academic is different from that required of an actor. While some are blessed with both kinds, many talented and intelligent actors are of indifferent academic ability. We would not wish to exclude them." Degree status will enable you to go on to a higher degree and enhance your employment prospects outside the profession – but not within it.

Funding for some accredited one- and two-year courses is available, but not with the same frequency as for three-year courses. However, there is advice on finding funds from private sources on both the NCDT and the CDS websites, and some schools have scholarships and/or are good at helping students with this task.

It is worth spending time checking through all the courses listed below – also, read through the CDS's *Guide to Professional Training in Drama and Technical Theatre*, which is available from their website. Also, look at **www.theessentialsguide.co.uk** for a very thought-through list of what to look for in a course. (Additionally, if possible seek the opinion of those with recent knowledge of drama schools.) Then get prospectuses for any school that you feel could be viable for you – and read each one thoroughly. Important considerations include whether you could be eligible for funding for your fees (and a maintenance loan), and potential living costs – central London is significantly more expensive to live in than Manchester, for example. (Bear in mind, too, whether a degree qualification at the end of the course is important to you.) Above all, it's important to try to assess which courses you feel would suit you best, and to apply – some require application via UCAS **www.ucas.ac.uk** – to as many as you can afford the audition fees and travel costs for. Don't forget to factor in the cost of overnight accommodation, if necessary. The plain truth is that competition for places is so intense (especially for women) that you need to audition for as many places as possible. Every time you do another audition you will learn more about the techniques of auditioning than any book or class can teach you. It is important to take on board the fact that many people take two or three years of auditioning, and sometimes more, before they get places. If you are determined to become a professional actor, you have to take rejection in your stride – learn from it, and keep on trying until you succeed.

Finally, carefully check the application deadlines, funding details and audition specifications of each school to which you intend to apply – there are some considerable variations (see the Checklist on page 14). You may find it useful to read *An Applicant's Guide to Auditioning and Interviewing at Dance and Drama Schools*, which is available from the NCDT's website. Andrew Piper's website (**www.andrew-piper.com**) contains useful advice on auditioning and fundraising for drama school, as well as an account of his own first year. Auditioning advice is also available from Simon Dunmore's website (**www.simon.dunmore.btinternet.co.uk**), which additionally suggests playwrights suitable for audition material, and lists over-used Shakespeare characters.

Notes:
• For general information on funding for fees and maintenance loans, see **www.directgov.uk/en/EducationAndLearning/index.htm** and click on Student Finance.
• Places on some accredited courses are currently funded through Dance and Drama Awards (DaDAs). These were introduced in the late 1990s, and provide funding for about two-thirds of successful applicants. For more details, check each relevant school's prospectus and website – also look at **www.direct.gov.uk/danceanddrama**.

* denotes membership of the Conference of Drama Schools

The Academy of Live and Recorded Arts (ALRA)*

Studio One, The Royal Victoria Patriotic Building, John Archer Way, London SW18 3SX
tel 020-8870 6475
email info@alra.co.uk
website www.alra.co.uk
Co-directors Clive Duncan, Adrian Hall

Accredited acting courses:

• BA (Hons) Acting. A full-time, 3-year course to prepare students for a varied career as a professional actor. This course will also be available at ALRA North – further details to be announced.
• MA Acting. A full-time, intensive 1-year course to prepare students for a career in the stage and screen industries.

Consult the website for more details.

The Academy of the Science of Acting & Directing

9-15 Elthorne Road, Archway, London N19 4AJ
tel 020-7272 0027 *fax* 020-7272 0026
email info@asad.org.uk
website www.asad.org.uk
Principal Helen Kogan *Administrator* Philip Pritchard

Full-time acting courses: No public funding is available for the courses listed below, but students may apply for a limited number of scholarships. There are daytime and evening courses.

• Three Year Acting Course. Applicants must be aged 18 or over. Offers 14 places each year.
• Two Year Acting Course. Applicants must be aged 18 or over. Offers 14 places each year.
• One Year Acting Course. Applicants must be aged 18 or over. Offers 14 places each year.

The Arden Theatre School

1 Universal Square, North Devonshire Street, Manchester M12 6JH
tel 0161-279 7257 *fax* 0161-279 7218
email AMurray@ccm.co.uk
website www.thearden.ac.uk (School) or www.ccm.ac.uk (College)
Head of School David O'Shea *Administrator* Angela Murray

The Arden was established over 15 years ago, in a unique collaboration between Manchester University, City College and The Royal Exchange Theatre. The school now offers 3 BA (Hons) programmes and a postgraduate Diploma in Writing for the Stage.

Full-time acting courses:

• BA (Hons) Acting Studies (3 years full-time). Applicants must be aged 18 or over at the start of the course with a minimum of 12 UCAS tariff points. Entry to the school is by audition only; applications from mature students with relevant experience in place of qualifications will be considered. Applications must be made through UCAS and auditions run from December to June.

Training

• BA (Hons) Musical Theatre Studies (3 years full-time). Application procedures as above.

Arts Ed London*

Cone Ripman House, 14 Bath Road, London W4 1LY
tel 020-8987 6666 *fax* 020-8987 6699
email drama@artsed.co.uk
website www.artsed.co.uk
Principle/Director of the School of Acting Jane Harrison
Director of the School of Musical Theatre Chris
Hocking *Key contacts* Nicola Ramsbottom (Acting),
Vivienne Hobbs (Musical Theatre)

Part of the Dance and Drama Awards scheme.
Applications for courses and awards should be made
direct to the school. All courses are accredited by the
National Council for Drama Training or the Council
for Dance Education and Training, and validated by
City University.

Accredited acting courses:

• BA (Hons) Acting (3 years). Applicants must be
aged 18 or over.
• BA (Hons) Musical Theatre Programme (3 years).
Applicants must be aged 18 or over. In addition, the
school has a limited number of bursaries.
Applications will be accepted until the end of
February but the academy recommends early
applications.
• MA Acting (1 year postgraduate). Applicants must
be aged 21 or over.

Birmingham School of Acting*

Millennium Point, Curzon Street,
Birmingham B4 7XG
tel 0121-331 7200 *fax* 0121-331 7221
email info@bsa.uce.ac.uk
website www.bsa.uce.ac.uk
Principal Stephen Simms *Admissions Manager* Roger
Franke

Accredited acting courses:

• BA (Hons) Acting (3 years). Applicants must be
aged 18 or over with 2 A levels (grade E or above) or
equivalent.
• Graduate Diploma in Acting (1 year). Applicants
must be aged 21 or over with a university degree or
relevant professional experience.

The Birmingham Theatre School

The Old Rep Theatre, Station Street,
Birmingham B5 4DY
tel 0121-643 3300 *fax* 0121-643 3300
email info@birminghamtheatreschool.co.uk
website www.birminghamtheatreschool.co.uk
Principal Chris Rozanski *Key contact* Andrea Cobham
(Arts Admin Manager)

Full-time acting courses:

• HND Performing Arts/Theatre Acting (2 years).
Applicants must be aged 18 or over with 12 points at
A level or BTEC.
• BTEC National Diploma in Performing Arts.
Applicants must be aged 16 or over.

• Advanced Acting Diploma (1 year). Applicants must
be aged 17 or over.
• Open Access Foundation in Acting (1 year).
Applicants must be aged 16 or over.

The Bridge Theatre Training Company

Cecil Sharp House, 2 Regent's Park Road,
London NW1 7AY
tel 020-7424 0860 *fax* 020-7424 9118
email admin@thebridge-ttc.org
website www.thebridge-ttc.org
Joint Artistic Directors Mark Akrill, Judith Pollard
Company Administrator Alex Abbott

The Bridge is a non-profit organisation which
provides intensive training for a career in professional
acting. Courses include comprehensive career
guidance, and a graduating season of public
productions in London theatres, with a West End
showcase at the Criterion Theatre in front of agents,
directors and casting directors.

Full-time acting courses:

• Professional Acting Course (2 years). Applicants
must be aged 18 or over.
• Professional Acting Course (1 year postgraduate/
post-experience). Applicants must be aged 21 or over,
with a university degree or significant relevant
experience.

Bristol Old Vic Theatre School*

2 Downside Road, Clifton, Bristol BS8 2XF
tel 0117-973 3535 *fax* 0117-923 9371
email enquiries@oldvic.ac.uk
website www.oldvic.ac.uk
Principal Paul Rummer *Artistic Director* Sue Wilson

An affiliate of the Conservatoire for Dance and
Drama. All courses are entirely vocational and are
validated by the University of West England.

Accredited acting courses: The official age for entry
is 18-30, but the school frequently makes exceptions
in the case of older applicants. Applications should be
made direct to the school.

• BA Professional Acting (3 years). Recalls take the
form of a weekend school in Bristol.
• Diploma of Professional Acting (2 years).

Other full-time acting courses:
• Certificate of Higher Education in Professional
Acting (1 year).
• Professional Acting Course for Overseas Students (1
year). See the website for audition procedures.

Central School of Speech and Drama*

64 Eton Avenue, London NW3 3HY
tel 020-7722 8183 *fax* 020-7722 4132
email enquiries@cssd.ac.uk
website www.cssd.ac.uk
Principal Gavin Henderson

Scholarships/Bursaries Diana Wade Memorial Award,
Gary Bond Memorial Award, Robert Tunstall
Memorial Award

Accredited acting courses:

• BA (Hons) Acting (Acting for Stage) – 3 years.

Applicants must be aged 18 or over. Normal entry requirements are a minimum of 2 Cs at A level, a minimum of 3 Cs at GCSE, and selection by audition. Exceptionally, applicants who do not meet this requirement but demonstrate appropriate academic potential may be accepted. Applications should be made through UCAS by January.
• BA (Hons) Acting (Music Theatre) – 3 years. Applicants must be aged 18 or over. Normal entry requirements are a minimum of 2 Cs at A level, a minimum of 3 Cs at GCSE, and selection by audition. Exceptionally, applicants who do not meet this requirement but demonstrate appropriate academic potential may be accepted.
• BA (Hons) Acting (Physical and Visual Theatre) – 3 years. Applicants must be aged 18 or over. Normal entry requirements are a minimum of 2 Cs at A level, a minimum of 3 Cs at GCSE, and selection by audition. Exceptionally, applicants who do not meet this requirement but demonstrate appropriate academic potential may be accepted. Applications should be made through UCAS by January.

Other full-time acting courses:
• Alternative Theatre and New Performance Practices (qualification, BA (Hons) Theatre Practice). Normal entry requirements are a minimum of 2 passes at A level plus 3 GCSEs at grade C or above. Applications should be made through UCAS by January.

All the 1-year courses listed below are for postgraduates or actors (aged 21 or over) with significant professional experience. Applications for all postgraduate courses should be made direct to the school:
• Acting Musical Theatre
• Classical Acting
• Advanced Theatre Practice – Performing
• Movement Studies
• Actor Training & Coaching
• Acting for Screen

Cygnet Training Theatre*
New Theatre, Friars Gate, Exeter EX2 4AZ
tel (01392) 277189 *fax* (01392) 277189
email CygnetArts@btconnect.com
website www.cygnetnewtheatre.com
Artistic Director Alistair Ganley *Key contact* Malcolm Mardon

A member of the Conference of Drama Schools, Cygnet offers a 3-year, full-time training course based in its own studio theatre. Functions as a small touring company, drawing its members from all over the UK and abroad. The small number of applicants selected each year (6-8) are chosen for their flexibility, maturity, awareness and self-discipline. They are expected to work with professional commitment from the first day in this ensemble training. Financial assistance is occasionally available to third-year students.

Full-time acting courses:
• Professional Acting Certificate (3 years). Applicants must be aged 18 or over.

Other options include: Acting with Music, and Acting with Directing. People may enter straight from school, after a university degree, or as a career change. All need stamina, commitment and an ability to put the work of the ensemble before their personal feelings. This training, regardless of the option, requires serious commitment.

Drama Centre London*
Central Saint Martins College of Art and Design,
10 Back Hill,
London EC1R 5EN *(until summer 2011; new premises in Kings Cross from summer 2011)*
tel 020-7514 7022 *fax* 020-7514 8777
email drama@arts.ac.uk
website www.csm.arts.ac.uk/drama
Principal Dr Vladimir Mirodan *Acting Principal* Jonathan Martin *Key contact* Maggie Wilkinson

Trains students to become professional actors, directors and screen writers. Established 48 years ago, it is now part of the University of the Arts London, and is a member of the Conference of Drama Schools. The school awards 3 Foundation Scholarships; 1 Malmgren Scholarship; 1 Reeves Scholarship; 5 UK/EU Leverhulme Scholarships; and 2 International Leverhulme Scholarships. For detailed information on Scholarships and Bursaries, see the website under 'News and Events'.

Accredited acting course:
• BA (Hons) Acting (3 years). Applicants must have 2 A levels. Public funding is available for all UK/EU students doing their first degree. Applications should be made through UCAS.

Other full-time acting courses: Note that applicants for both MA courses must have a related degree, a diploma in dance or drama, an honours degree in another discipline supported by performance-related experience (professional, amateur or student), or significant professional experience. Applications are made direct to the school.
• MA in European Classical Acting (45 weeks). 20 places are available.
• MA Screen: Acting (60 weeks over 16 months). 16 places are available.
• Diploma in Foundation Studies (Performance) (30 weeks). Applicants must have 1 A level and a BTEC National Diploma in Performing Arts or equivalent. 20 places are available. Applications are made direct to the school.

Drama Studio London (DSL)*
1 Grange Road, London W5 5QN
tel 020-8579 3897 *fax* 020-8566 2035
email admin@dramastudiolondon.co.uk
website www.dramastudiolondon.co.uk
Principal Peter Craze *Registrar* Sue Quelch-Woolls

Drama Studio London (DSL) provides full-time, professional acting training for mature and postgraduate students aged 21 and over. A 1-year course of 44 weeks (beginning in August), and a 2-year course of 36 weeks per year (beginning in

October), are offered each year. Auditions and open days are held from November to June. For a prospectus, information or an application form, contact **admin@dramastudiolondon.co.uk** or visit the website. Some Dance and Drama Awards are available; all candidates are automatically assessed for a DaDA at recall. Successful graduates will receive the Drama Studio London Diploma, and may also take the Trinity College London National Certificate in Professional Acting, if they wish.

East 15 Acting School*

Hatfields, Rectory Lane, Loughton IG10 3RY
tel 020-8508 5983 *fax* 020-8508 7521
email east15@essex.ac.uk
website www.east15.ac.uk
Director Professor Leon Rubin *Key contact* Linda Humphreys

Accredited acting courses:

• BA Acting (3 years). Deadline for applications is June. Applicants must be aged 18 or over with A level grades EE, AVCE grades EE, or BTEC National overall pass or equivalent. (If an applicant does not meet the specific criteria, he or she may discuss the application with East 15 admissions.) Students over the age of 21 are not required to fulfil the same A-level grade criteria. There is no upper age limit, although it is unusual to admit students over 40 years.
• BA in Contemporary Theatre (3 years). All applicants must be aged 18 or over at the time of enrolment. There is no upper age limit, although it is unusual to admit students over 40 years. Applicants must hold A-level grades EE, AVCE grades EE, or BTEC National overall pass or equivalent. (If an applicant does not meet the specific criteria, he or she may discuss the application with East 15 admissions.) Students over the age of 21 have no minimum educational requirements.
• MA/PG Acting (1 year). Selection for this course is based upon experience and potential. All applicants must be over the age of 21; there is no upper age limit. Applicants must hold a BA degree (normally at least a 2:1) or have suitable previous life professional or academic experience.
• MA/PG Acting for TV, Film and Radio (1 year). Selection for this course is based upon experience and potential. All applicants must be over the age of 21; there is no upper age limit. Applicants must hold a BA degree (normally at least a 2:1) or have suitable previous life professional or academic experience.

Other full-time acting courses:

• Foundation in Acting (1 year). Applicants must be aged 18 or over with 2 A levels or equivalent.
• MA in Professional Theatre (see website for details).
• Certificate of Higher Education in Theatre Arts (see website for details).
• Foundation Degree/BA Degree in Community Theatre (see website for details).
• Foundation Degree/BA Degree in Specialist Performance Skills (Stage Combat) (see website for details).

GSA Conservatoire* (formerly Guildford School of Acting)

Stag Hill Campus, Guildford GU2 7XH
tel (01483) 560701 *fax* (01483) 535431
email enquiries@gsauk.org
website www.conservatoire.org
Director Peter Barlow

GSA was founded in 1935, and from 1964 onwards has concentrated on the vocational training of actors and stage managers. Since 1987 the Musical Theatre Course has held a leading position in the world of actor training.

Accredited full-time acting courses: Applications for the courses listed below should be made direct to the Conservatoire by the end of January.

• BA (Hons) Acting (3 years). Applicants must be aged 18 or over, with 2 A levels.
• BA (Hons) Theatre, Musical Theatre (3 years). Applicants must be aged 18 or over, with 2 A levels.
• MA in Acting (4-term postgraduate) *[subject to validation]*. Applicants must be aged 21 or over.
• MA in Musical Theatre (4-term postgraduate). Applicants must be aged 21 or over.

Guildhall School of Music & Drama*

Silk Street, Barbican, London EC2Y 8DT
tel 020-7628 2571 *fax* 020-7256 9438
email registry@gsmd.ac.uk
website www.gsmd.ac.uk
Director of Drama Wyn Jones

Accredited acting courses:

• BA (Hons) Acting (3 years). Applicants are normally at least 18 years old with a minimum of 2 A-level passes or equivalent. Applications should be made direct to the school as early as possible, and by mid-January at the latest. Student Support from the UK Government is available for most EU students.

In the final year of training, clear guidance is given on starting in the acting profession. There are regular talks and visits by regional theatre directors, agents, casting directors, income tax advisers and representatives from Equity.

InterACT Training Scheme

c/o NTC Touring Theatre, The Playhouse, Bondgate Without, Alnwick, Northumberland NE66 1PQ
tel (01665) 602586 *fax* (01665) 605837
email interact@northumberlandtheatre.co.uk
website www.northumberlandtheatre.co.uk
Artistic Mentor Gillian Hambleton *Managed by* Northumberland Theatre Company

Not a formal drama-school training, but a 44-week scheme to provide a bridge between education or training and the profession, with the aim of encouraging and retaining talent within the North of England. The training consists of a series of workshops, masterclasses and placements within professional companies. There are no fees. Trainees are awarded a modest weekly bursary, based on Equity's average annual wage for a professional actor. Accommodation, travel and theatre tickets are also provided. Minimum age is 18, although most applicants will have a degree. "All applicants *must* either originate from Northumberland, Tyne & Wear, Cumbria, Durham or Cleveland, or have trained or studied in those regions within the past 5 years. We endeavour to provide facilities and access to accommodate all disabilities."

International School of Screen Acting

3 Mills Studios, Unit 3, 24 Sugar House Lane, London E15 2QS
tel 020-8555 5775
email office@screenacting.co.uk
website www.screenacting.co.uk
Key contact David Craik

Founded in 2001 to specialise in offering full-time training specifically in television and film acting, taking a holistic approach to creativity in relation to students' personal development and fuller understanding of screen acting. No public funding or scholarships are available for these courses. The school is now accredited and will soon be included on UK Border Agency's Tier 4 list. It also offers a number of short courses – see the entry under *Short-term and part-time courses*. While the school is happy to receive applications from disabled students, there are currently significant access issues with the school's premises.

Full-time acting courses:

• One Year Full Time Advanced Screen Acting. Students should be between 21 and 35 on entry to the course.
• Two Year Screen Acting. Students should be between 18 and 21.

Italia Conti Academy of Theatre Arts*

'Avondale', 72 Landor Road, London SW9 9PH
tel 020-7733 3210 *fax* 020-7737 2728
email acting@lsbu.ac.uk
website www.italiaconti-acting.co.uk
Course Director (Acting) Chris White

A member of the Conference of Drama Schools, the Academy offers a 3-year BA (Hons) Acting Degree, validated by London South Bank University and accredited by the National Council for Drama Training. This course takes a unique approach to actor training. Based loosely on the teachings of Sanford Meisner, whose work now dominates in the United States, it trains actors to be open, responsive and spontaneous.

Accredited acting courses:

• BA (Hons) Acting (3 years). Applicants must be aged 18 or over with 5 GCSEs (grade C or above), including English, and 2 A levels (grade E or above) or equivalent.

The Liverpool Institute for Performing Arts (LIPA)*

Mount Street, Liverpool L1 9HF
tel 0151-330 3232/3116/3084/3022 *fax* 0151-330 3131
email admissions@lipa.ac.uk
website www.lipa.ac.uk

LIPA is dedicated to providing the best teaching for people who want to pursue a lasting career in the arts and entertainment industry, and offers a variety of styles of courses aimed at different age groups. It looks for more than acting talent in its students, and applicants should show evidence of versatility and trainable ability in other performance-related skills.

Full-time acting courses:

• BA (Hons) Performing Arts – Acting (3 years). Applicants must be aged 18 or over; there is no upper age limit. Educational attainment, relevant experience and interdisciplinary interest and ability will be taken into account when applying. Applications should be made through UCAS initially. If invited to audition, further information will be required.
• Postgraduate Diploma in Acting (1 year). Applicants are usually aged 21 or over, and educated to degree-level standard with some acting experience. Mature students without degree qualifications, but with considerable related professional experience, are welcome to apply. This is an intensive year-long programme enabling students to become flexible, multi-skilled practitioners.

London Academy of Music and Dramatic Art (LAMDA)*

155 Talgarth Road, London W14 9DA
tel 020-8834 0500 *fax* 020-8834 0501
email enquiries@lamda.org.uk
website www.lamda.org.uk
Principal Joanna Read *Admission Assistants* Amy Richardson, Elissa Perrau, Philip McDonnell

LAMDA is one of the oldest and most celebrated drama schools in the English-speaking world. The Academy is dedicated to helping actors, directors, stage managers and theatre technicians acquire the necessary skills and levels of creativity to meet the highest demands in theatre, film and television. LAMDA's continuing success derives from its ability to adopt its traditional teaching to match modern advances. "At the Academy, we offer classical training for the modern acting profession. Through our affiliation with the Conservatoire for Dance and Drama, the Academy strives to ensure that the most talented students can continue to benefit from the outstanding vocational training we offer, regardless of their background or financial circumstances."

LAMDA also conducts an eminent set of Speech and Drama examinations through LAMDA Examinations, and has gained acclaim in the corporate sector through LAMDA Business Performance (LBP).

There are a limited number of scholarships available for the Three and Two Year Acting Courses and the Two Year Stage Management & Technical Theatre Course. Scholarships are allocated at the Academy's discretion – there is no application procedure prior to being offered a place.

LAMDA operates an equal opportunities policy for all students, and welcomes applications from disabled students. Disabled students are encouraged to disclose their needs, in order to ensure that they are supported in the training. For more information, please see the website, or contact LAMDA Admissions (**admissions@lamda.org.uk**).

Accredited acting courses:
• BA (Hons) in Professional Acting (3 years). Applicants must be aged 18 or over. Applications should be made directly to the school; please see the website for application deadline and course fee. Song required at recall stage; refer to the website for full details.
• Foundation degree in Acting (2 years). Applicants must be aged 18 or over. Applications should be made directly to the school; please see the website for application deadline, course fee and full details.

Other full-time acting courses:
• Postgraduate Diploma in Classical Acting (1 year). Applicants must be aged 18 or over; please see the website for fees and further details.
• Single Semester Acting Course (14 weeks). Applicants must be aged 18 or over; please see the website for fees and further details.

London Academy of Radio, Film & TV
1 Lancing Street, London NW1 1NA
tel 0870-850 4994
website www.media-courses.com
Director of Courses Andy Parkin *Key contact* Estelle Burton

The school has more than 30 teaching staff; around 1200 students take one or more of its 100+ courses. It is situated opposite Euston Station.

Full-time acting courses:
• Diploma in Screen Acting. Application deadline is June. Age range: 16+. Entry is by audition: 1 modern and 1 classical speech.

London Drama School
30 Brondesbury Park, London NW6 7DN
tel 020-8830 0074 *fax* 020-8830 4992
email enquiries@startek-uk.com
website www.startek-uk.com
Key contact Sarah Mann/Michelle Newman

Established 1996. All teachers are actors, directors, writers or producers currently working in the industry. 2 bursaries are available to talented students with financial difficulties; these bursaries cover half the tuition fees.

Full-time acting courses:
• One Year Professional Acting Course. Prepares to the Trinity Guildhall LTCL Degree in Performance Arts.
• One Year Advanced Acting Course. Prepares to the Trinity Guildhall ATCL Diploma in Speech & Drama.
• One Year Foundation Acting Course. Prepares students to audition for either the course above, or for other drama schools.

London School of Musical Theatre
83 Borough Road, London SE1 1DN
tel 020-7407 4455 *fax* 020-7407 4455

email info@lsmt.co.uk
website www.lsmt.co.uk
Principal/Course Producer Adrian Jeckells
Administrator Laura Blundell

Full-time acting courses:
• Musical Theatre Diploma Course (1 year). Age range for entry is 18-35.

London Studio Centre (LSC)
42-50 York Way, London N1 9AB
tel 020-7837 7741 *fax* 020-7758 0222
email nic.espinosa@london-studio-centre.co.uk
website www.london-studio-centre.co.uk
Director Nic Espinosa *Audition Enquiries* Sarah Tudor *Head of Studies* Robert Penman

Primarily a dance college offering a BA Hons in Theatre Dance, accredited by the Council for Dance Education and Training and validated by the University of the Arts, London. The LSC also offers a 1-year full-time diploma in Musical Theatre, for those students who have completed a performing arts course elsewhere and who wish to further their training in this specialist area. Public funding is not available for this 1-year course. More details are available from the website.

Manchester Metropolitan University School of Theatre*
School of Theatre, Mabel Tylecote Building, All Saints, Manchester M15 6BH
tel 0161-247 1305 *fax* 0161-247 6875
email k.daly@mmu.ac.uk
website www.theatre.mmu.ac.uk
Course Director Niamh Dowling *Key contact* Kath Daly

Accredited acting courses:
• BA (Hons) Theatre Arts/Acting (3 years). Applicants must be aged 18 or over with 2 A levels or equivalent. Applications should be made through UCAS by January.

Mountview Academy of Theatre Arts*
Ralph Richardson Memorial Studios, Clarendon Road, London N22 6XF
tel 020-8881 2201 *fax* 020-8829 0034
email enquiries@mountview.org.uk
website www.mountview.org.uk
Principal Sue Robertson

Scholarships/Bursaries Sir John Mills Scholarship, Dame Judi Dench Scholarship, Margaret Rutherford Scholarship, Peter Coxhead Scholarship (all for postgraduate performance courses)

Accredited acting courses: Applications for the courses listed below should be made direct to the school, by March for the BA (Hons) and by July for the postgraduate diploma.

• BA (Hons) Acting (3 years). Applicants must be aged 18 or over, usually with A levels but these are not essential. Dance and Drama Awards are available for a significant number of students.

• BA (Hons) Musical Theatre (3 years). Applicants must be aged 18 or over, usually with A levels but these are not essential. Dance and Drama Awards are available for a significant number of students.
• PG Dip in Acting/MA in Performance (1 year). Applicants must be aged 21 or over, usually with a university degree.
• PG Dip in Musical Theatre/MA in Performance (1 year). Applicants must be aged 21 or over, usually with a university degree.

Other full-time acting courses:
• PG Dip in Acting – Screen and Radio (1 year). Applicants must be aged 21 or over, usually with a university degree.

Oxford School of Drama*

Sansomes Farm Studios, Woodstock,
Oxford OX20 1ER
tel (01993) 812883 *fax* (01993) 811220
email info@oxforddrama.ac.uk
website www.oxforddrama.ac.uk
Principal George Peck *Executive Director* Kate Ashcroft

The smallest of all the drama schools with accredited status. Awarded Beacon Status by the Minister for Education in 2006. Provides a significant number of Dance and Drama Awards for its 1- and 3-year courses. Also offers its own Hardship fund which is distributed each year to students on full-time courses at the school. Students not in receipt of a DaDA are prioritised for funding. The Lionel Bart Foundation and the Sir John Gielgud Charitable Trust currently support the school; in addition, students have also won the Laurence Olivier Bursary, the Henry Cotton Memorial Fund Award, the *Evening Standard*/Patricia Rothermere Award, the Alan Bates Award, and the BBC Carleton Hobbs bursary award.

Accredited acting courses: Applications for the courses listed below should be made direct to the school by May.

• Three Year Acting Course. Applicants must be aged 18 or over.
• One Year Acting Course. Applicants must be aged 21 or over.

Poor School

242 Pentonville Road, London N1 9JY
tel 020-7837 6030 *fax* 020-7837 5330
email acting@thepoorschool.com
website www.thepoorschool.com
Principal Paul Caister

The school was created in 1986 with the aim of providing high-quality acting training that is financially within the reach of all, or almost all. Training lasts 2 years and operates in the evenings and at weekends until the final 2 terms, when daytime work is involved. Since March 1993 the Poor School has owned its own theatre, the Workhouse; this is a flexible studio theatre seating 50-80.

Full-time acting courses:
• Two Year Acting Course (6 terms). Most students

are in their early 20s but the school offers many places to older and younger people.

Queen Margaret University College*

Drama and Theatre Arts Programme,
Queen Margaret University, Edinburgh EH21 6UU
tel 0131-317 3900 *fax* 0131-317 3902
email cowen@qmuc.ac.uk
website www.qmuc.ac.uk
Key contact Catherine Owen

Full-time acting courses:

• BA (Hons) Acting and Performance (3-4 years). Applicants must be aged 18 or over with Scottish Higher CCC, A level at grade E, BTEC or HNC/NC. Applications should be made through UCAS by March. Initially the core subjects of acting, voice, text and movement are taught separately; as the course progresses, they combine and focus on performance through a wide variety of productions and projects. In the past few years, highly successful collaborations with students on other courses (stage managers, directors, playwrights, etc.) have become a feature of the course. Close collaborations with professional theatre companies provide another dimension to the training.
• BA (Hons) Drama and Theatre Arts (4 years). This course is designed to develop understanding and practical experience in the broad canvas of drama. In years 1 and 2, students have classes in drama and performance and study the texts and contexts of theatre crossing between theory and practice. In years 3 and 4, students complement their studies with intensive work in a specialist area of study, including playwriting, directing, contemporary performance, producing, dramaturgy, community theatre and arts journalism.

The REP College

17 St Mary's Avenue, Purley on Thames,
Berks RG8 8BJ
email tudor@repcollege.co.uk
website www.repcollege.co.uk
Key contact David Tudor

Provides acting students with 1 year of practical education, including 14 public performances.

Full-time acting courses:

• Acting Course (1 year). Applicants must be aged 18 or over.

Rose Bruford College*

Lamorbey Park, Burnt Oak Lane, Sidcup DA15 9DF
tel 020-8308 2600 *fax* 020-8308 0542
email enquiries@bruford.ac.uk
website www.bruford.ac.uk
Principal Professor Michael Earley

Accredited acting courses: Applicants for the BA degree courses listed below must be over the age of 18 with the equivalent of a minimum of 2 A Levels at grade C or above. Applications should be made through UCAS.

• BA (Hons) Acting (3 years).
• BA (Hons) Actor Musicianship (3 years).

Other full-time acting courses:
• BA (Hons) American Theatre Arts (3 years).
• BA (Hons) European Theatre Arts (3 years).

Royal Academy of Dramatic Art (RADA)*

62-64 Gower Street, London WC1E 6ED
tel 020-7636 7076 *fax* 020-7323 3865
email enquiries@rada.ac.uk
website www.rada.org
Key contact Sally Power

Founded in 1904 by Sir Herbert Beerbohm Tree at His Majesty's Theatre, the Academy moved to its present premises a year later. In 1996 the Academy received a Lottery Grant from the Arts Council and embarked on a £32 million rebuilding programme, opening its new premises in 2000. Some maintenance bursaries are available for students to supplement their own fundraising efforts. Applications should be made direct to the school by March.

Accredited acting courses:

• BA (Hons) Acting (3 years). Normal age-range for entry is 18-30. Recalls may take the form of second audition, group workshop or individual working session; an unaccompanied song is also required. The auditions are 'lengthy and rigorous' and the process may span several months.

The course is for students who wish to earn a living working not only in the more traditional outlets, but also in the many alternative areas of theatre, film, television and radio. It is intensive, with a minimum working day of 10.00am – 6.00pm and individual classes in the evening. When public performances take place, the working day can be from 10.00am – 11.00pm.

Royal Academy of Music

Musical Theatre Department, Marylebone Road, London NW1 5HT
tel 020-7873 7483 *fax* 020-7873 7484
email mth@ram.ac.uk
website www.ram.ac.uk/mth
Head of Music Theatre Mary Hammond F.R.A.M, L.R.A.M *Course Leader* Karen Rabinowitz

Students are enrolled at the Royal Academy of Music, one of Europe's leading conservatories and a full member of the University of London. Fellow students include instrumentalists, pianists, concert and opera singers, composers, jazz and commercial musicians.

Full-time acting courses

• One Year Music Theatre Course. Aimed at graduates, mature students and professionals wishing to refocus their careers. The aim of the course is to give a thorough professional musical and dramatic training to students of postgraduate (or equivalent) level, in order to equip them for performance in contemporary musical theatre, through the integration of singing, acting and movement. It aims to bridge the gap between the 'acting singer' and the 'singing actor'.

Royal Scottish Academy of Music and Drama*

100 Renfrew Street, Glasgow G2 3DB
tel 0141-332 4101 *fax* 0141-332 8901
email registry@rsamd.ac.uk
website www.rsamd.ac.uk
Principal John Wallace

Accredited acting courses: Applications for the courses listed below should be made direct to the school by March. Public funding is available for some students.

• BA (Hons) Acting (3 years). Applicants are normally aged 18-21 but this is flexible.

Other full-time acting courses:
• Master of Performance in Musical Theatre (1 year).
• BA (Hons) Contemporary Theatre Practice.
• BA (Hons) Musical Theatre.

Royal Welsh College of Music and Drama*

Castle Grounds, Cathays Park, Cardiff CF10 3ER
tel 029-2039 1327
website www.rwcmd.ac.uk
Principal Hilary Boulding *Drama Admissions Officer* Luise Moggridge

Accredited acting courses:

• BA (Hons) Acting (3 years). Applicants should normally be at least 18 years old by the time of enrolment. There is a range of support in place to help cover the cost of tuition, the details of which will depend on where the student normally lives. Applications should be made through UCAS.
• Postgraduate Diploma in Acting for Stage, Screen and Radio (1 year). Applicants should normally be at least 21 years old by the time of enrolment. Applications should be made directly to the college.

Other full-time acting courses:
• MA in Acting for Stage, Screen and Radio (4 terms – September 2010 until January 2012). Applicants should normally be at least 21 years old by the time of enrolment. Applications should be made directly to the college.
• MA in Musical Theatre (Subject to validation; 3 terms – January 2011 until December 2011). Applicants should normally be at least 21 years old by the time of enrolment. Applications should be made directly to the college.

Training

Checklist of drama school deadlines, audition requirements, audition fees and funding systems

Only schools with 'accredited' courses are included, and postgraduate courses often have later application deadlines and funding systems.
Compiled by Simon Dunmore.

School	Definition of 'Classical'	Definition of 'Modern/ Contemporary'	Other Parameters	Audition Fee	Funding System	Application Deadline
ALRA	Shakespeare	After 1950 – to camera	No longer than 2mins each	£35	DaDA	Mid January – via UCAS
Arts Ed	Classical	Modern	No longer than 2mins each	£35	DaDA	31st March
Birmingham	Shakespearean/Jacobean (They provide you with a list that you MAY choose from)	"Last 20 years"	No longer than 2mins each; a song for the recall, with sheet music – no more than 3mins	£40	Maintained	1st March
Bristol	Classical English play (written before 1800)	20th or 21st Century	2 speeches together should not exceed 4mins; an unaccompanied song	£50	Maintained	1st March
Central	Two from supplied list	After 1960		£46	Maintained	Mid January – via UCAS
Drama Centre	Shakespeare/Contemporaries – verse	After 1830	No longer than 3mins each; alternative is to do a duologue	£40	Maintained	Mid January – via UCAS
Drama Studio	Classical	Modern		£35	DaDA	No specific deadline

School	Definition of 'Classical'	Definition of 'Modern/Contemporary'	Other Parameters	Audition Fee	Funding System	Application Deadline
East 15	Shakespearean/Jacobean – "10-15 lines only"	20th/21st century – "serious"	And a speech from a contemporary play (after 1950); no longer than 2mins each; short song with sheet music	£40	Maintained	Mid January – via UCAS
Guildford	Two Classical – ideally Shakespeare and in verse	Two modern	No longer than 2mins each	£35	DaDA (Acting) Maintained (Musical Theatre)	31st January
Guildhall	Shakespeare/Jacobean – verse	Modern	And a "lighter" speech from any period; no longer than 2mins each; a short unaccompanied song	£45	Maintained	Mid January
Italia Conti	One from supplied list	After 1870	No more than 1.5mins each	£35	Maintained	31st May
LAMDA	Elizabethan/Jacobean	20th/21st century	No longer than 3mins each and clearly contrasting; asked to sing at recall	£40 (online) £50 (paper)	Maintained	1st March
Manchester Met.	Shakespeare – blank verse	After 1970	And a contrasting speech from any published play; no more than 2mins each	£35	Maintained	Mid January – via UCAS
Mountview	Elizabethan/Jacobean	After 1945		£35	DaDA	Mid March
Oxford	Shakespeare	Modern	No more than 1.5mins each	£35	DaDA	31st May
Rose Bruford	16th/17th/18th century or Ancient Greek	After 1960 – "not verse"		£30	Maintained	Mid January – via UCAS

School	Definition of 'Classical'	Definition of 'Modern/ Contemporary'	Other Parameters	Audition Fee	Funding System	Application Deadline
RADA	Elizabethan/Jacobean	Modern	Second Classical speech may be required; a song in recall	£45	Maintained	1st March
Royal Scottish	Shakespeare – "preferably in verse"	A contrasting speech of your choice	No less than 1 min and no more than 3mins each; song	£35 (£50, if applying for 2 courses)	Maintained	31st March
Royal Welsh	Elizabethan/Jacobean	Modern	No longer than 2mins each	£35	Maintained	Mid January – via UCAS

Notes:

• When only 'Classical' is specified, this can mean anything written before about 1800.

• When only 'Modern' or 'Contemporary' is specified, you should be fine with anything written after 1945 – and speeches written between 1900 and 1945 have often proved acceptable in this category.

• 'Verse' is sometimes specified – this doesn't mean that it necessarily needs to rhyme.

• You'll find various definitions in the 'Classical' column – "Shakespearean/ Jacobean", "Elizabethan/Jacobean", "Shakespeare/Contemporaries". Strictly, these all imply slightly different (but overlapping) periods in history. In practice, anything written between about 1560 and 1640 should be fine.

• See individual schools' websites for more detailed audition requirements and advice.

• UCAS fee (where appropriate) is in addition to each school's audition fee.

• Musical Theatre courses have additional audition requirements.

• Also see *Effective audition speeches* on page 134.

Warning:

Some of these details may change for entry in future years. Please inform the Editor of any such changes at **Simon.Dunmore@btinternet.com.**

The NCDT and accreditation
Ian Kellgren

If you were going to buy electrical goods and wanted some reassurance about the quality of a particular product – making it fit for purpose, and safe – you might well look to see if it had an industrial kitemark. If you wanted reassurance about a particular vocational drama course, you would be wise to look and see if it was accredited by the National Council for Drama Training (NCDT).

This accreditation aims to give students confidence that the courses they choose are recognised by the drama profession as being relevant to the purposes of their employment. In its turn, the profession can have confidence that any people they employ who have completed these courses will possess the skills and attributes required for the continued well-being of the industry.

NCDT was formed in 1976, after a Gulbenkian Foundation report, 'Going on the Stage', recommended its establishment. There were fears then that a recent, severe increase in unemployment in the profession, coupled with a multiplication of training establishments, was leading to a critical situation for vocational drama training. NCDT was created to provide some way of judging which courses were truly vocational, and realistically leading to a career. Local authorities were the major funders of drama students, and they wanted some way of distinguishing those courses that the profession would recognise as being of value.

At that time, there were only seven universities offering drama degrees: there are now more than 2000 degrees with 'drama' in the title. The need for potential students and the current funders to have some way of knowing which are vocational is stronger than ever – not least because of the changes that have taken place since 1976.
• Equity is no longer a closed shop (although there are 37,000 members, and extensive use of Equity contracts is made by employers); the profession has undergone massive change.
• Few, if any, reps exist in the way that they did in the early 70s.
• Musical theatre is a much more dominant force, demanding a supply of 'triple threat' performers – that is, those who can act, sing and dance, all to a high standard.
• Technological advances have revolutionised the ways in which the recorded media operate, and this area provides many more first-employment opportunities.
• Local Education Authority student grants have given way to the Dance and Drama Awards and core funding from the three national funding councils, in England, Scotland and Wales, at various rates.
• In Further and Higher Education, the Conference of Drama Schools (CDS) schools are now subject to the relevant Quality Assurance requirements.
NCDT accredits courses, not drama schools. Currently, there are about 50 courses in 20 drama schools that are accredited by NCDT: in acting, stage management and technical and musical theatre. Some courses that are not currently accredited may well apply to be so in the near future, and these would have to pass stringent tests as to their 'vocationality'. If they became accredited, they would have to apply for re-accreditation after six years.

The accreditation process
The application process for both accreditation and re-accreditation is similar. This involves the school submitting documentation about the course, which is examined in detail by

specialists. The course is then visited by a panel, which talks to the staff who deliver the course and to the students who are on it, as well as attending classes. Panel members are looking all the time at the professional relevance of the programme of training.

For this, they really need to have their finger on the pulse – so that everyone contributing to the accreditation process has to have at least five years' professional experience; a good general knowledge of current practice relevant to the course, with some being subject specialists as well; and a keen interest in the development of drama training in this country. Panel members are all well trained for their tasks.

At the end of a re-accreditation visit, the panel decides if the course should be re-accredited or not. They may decide to re-accredit, but with recommendations or conditions. The Chair of the panel submits a recommendation in a report to the Review Committee; this is a group of 14 people who are current practitioners with demonstrable knowledge in at least one of the following skill areas: acting, casting, dance & movement, directing, knowledge of funding and statutory inspectorate regimes, film, musical theatre, production management, radio, representation, stage management, technical, television, vocational drama school training, and voice. The Review Committee decides on this recommendation, and passes its judgement to the Council of NCDT for formal approval.

In addition to the accreditation visits, schools are required to submit annual reports, and there is a system of show reporting. This is where professionals visit the shows or showcases of a course and complete a report for NCDT. Each year, NCDT is therefore able to decide if a particular course is still fulfilling the aim of accreditation.

Embracing change

Recently, NCDT recognised that it needed to check its operation in the light of the host of changes since its inception. A period of intense research produced a programme of reform that has now been implemented.

NCDT is a unique partnership of employers in the theatre, broadcast and media industry, employee representatives and training providers. When it began, it had three 'wings': the industry, Equity and CDS. Now under its new Chair, Sir Brian Fender, it has a more widely composed membership which, as well as Equity and CDS, includes the BBC, Channel 4, ITV, the Theatre Managers Association, the Film Council and up to five independent members.

Their brief is not only to work to safeguard the highest standards, and to provide a credible process of quality assurance through accreditation for vocational drama courses in the UK; it is also to ensure that NCDT exists to act as a champion for the industry, by working to optimise support for professional drama training and education, and embracing change and development.

The discerning shopper will want the electrical goods they buy to be not only fit for purpose and safe, but also to have benefited from development and innovation. NCDT offers such 'shoppers' a means of identifying those vocational drama courses which are based on the best practices of more than a hundred years of drama training, but which also recognise and embrace all the benefits of development and innovation.

Ian Kellgren is an award-winning theatre director. He started out as an assistant director at the Royal Court in London, rising to Literary Manager, before becoming Artistic Director of Durham Theatre Company and the longest-serving Artistic Director of the Liverpool Playhouse. Alongside his theatre and media work, he was NCDT Review Committee Chair until 2007.

Training in America
David Taylor-Sharp

In 2004 I applied to a number of British drama schools, with no clear idea of what the schools had to offer and, perhaps more importantly, what differentiated one from another. I knew that a career in film and television was my preference, and by sheer coincidence I noticed in a theatre magazine that an acting college called the American Academy of Dramatic Art (AADA) was holding auditions in London. "Why not?" I thought, "I am American as well!" Whilst I had lived all my life in England, I was born in California and had dual British and American nationality.

AADA has two campuses, in New York and Los Angeles. Given my desire to work on screen, I thought that LA would be the most appropriate. Even though the AADA course was theatre specific, it was clear that once I had graduated, the majority of acting jobs in LA would be in the 'on screen' medium. I had been offered a place at a prestigious British drama school; I was impressed by the campus, and its reputation for excellence was indisputable. Conversely, I was to audition for AADA in London and therefore would have no first-hand experience of the school or its facilities. I was going to be very reliant upon what I was told at the audition. With time to decide running out, I was faced with making a decision based on insufficient information. Of course, AADA involved a degree of risk that a British drama school did not. I had no experience whatsoever of life in America. But the prospect was exciting – very exciting. I felt as though I had the resilience and confidence to make it work.

I got into AADA and liked what I read about the school, but to this day I cannot be sure whether it was the lure of training in Hollywood, or an impartial assessment of AADA's credentials, that swayed my decision to join. However, just before my 19th birthday I moved to America. Dual citizenship with the United States meant that I had no issue with visas or green cards. I simply packed a bag and flew out to Los Angeles.

The training at AADA was excellent. The idea seemed to be to expose the students to as many different 'methodologies' as possible. My first term was spent studying the teachings of Uta Hagen, and the second studying Lee Strasberg's 'Method'; each was taught by a different tutor who was passionate about their respective style. Each term we were introduced to a new philosophy on how to act. All alongside voice, singing and movement classes, which ranged from classical dance such as ballet and waltz to interpretative modern dance.

At the end of the first year, many students were not asked to return for the second year of the programme, which is by invitation only. The knowledge that there was no guarantee of graduation certainly helped to keep serious students on their toes and ensure that a certain level of skill and effort was maintained throughout the school. I am aware that nowadays, once into a British drama school you are – almost certainly – there for the duration of the chosen course.

The second year continued the process of learning more acting techniques from various tutors. Towards the end of the year we had agents and casting directors in to discuss 'the industry' and how best to interact with 'their kind'. By the end of the final year we were encouraged and expected to take parts from all the different methods we had studied, and to develop our own technique and put it into practice for our graduation plays.

In the UK, if you complete a course 'accredited' by the NCDT, you are automatically eligible to join Equity. AADA is 'accredited' by America's National Association of Schools of Theatre (NAST), which is something to look for when enrolling at any drama conservatory in America. However, even going to an NAST-accredited school doesn't guarantee entry into any of the American unions. Certainly when I graduated in 2006 I didn't qualify for union admission – a fact that can affect your ability to get an agent and that all-important first role.

Unlike in Britain, in America there isn't just one actors' union. There is Equity for the stage, and SAG and AFTRA for the screen. One thing that British drama schools certainly do is showcase the students to the industry and give them the first push into the world of acting. Whilst the training across the pond is excellent, a student must also be motivated enough to promote themselves into the industry. In general, it is my experience that British drama schools offer far more support during the early stages of an actor's career.

So, having concluded that British drama schools have a great deal to offer, why would I choose the American route to training? Well, consider all the American powerhouses in actor training. Hagen, Strasberg, Adler and Meisner did their work in America. If one wanted to learn Commedia dell Arte, why not do it in Italy? If one wants to learn about Greek theatre, what better place than Greece? It is reasonable to deduce therefore that as I was looking for a modern acting technique that translated well to screen, America seemed the place. The debate as to which country offers the best training for actors will, I'm sure, rage on for a long time, and I sit happily on the fence of 'different, not better'.

So why else pick America over Britain? This brings into play personal as well as career reasons. There is a huge cultural difference between the two countries that people aren't always aware of. These differences put me, a young Brit, in an environment that challenged and stimulated me. I had to resolve issues on my own, in a strange country with different rules and ways of doing things. My parents, whilst fully supportive, were so far away that I only had a short window of time in which I could contact them for advice. Dealing with these situations made me grow up quickly and gave me life experience that I know I would not have gained if I had stayed within the relatively safe environment of Britain. As 'coping on my own' developed me as a person, it simultaneously furthered my acting credentials; I had far more experiences upon which to call.

Fundamental things, such as where to buy groceries, were totally new. There was no Tesco or M&S; just Ralph's and Trader Joe's. Finding an apartment in Los Angeles before leaving the UK was a logistical nightmare … after all, I wouldn't have a car, and in LA you really need one. There was a lot of trial and error. Lots of error.

Also, finding a roommate who is compatible with you is hard enough when you come from the same basic cultures and backgrounds and have at least met. But signing a lease to live with people you have never seen, from a different side of the world, is something I can't say is a safe bet. Not to mention that when things get tough, your usual support group is no longer there. Fortunately, technology is increasingly helpful on that front.

Obviously, as time moves on I look back on the calamities I faced as character-building steps in my life, and I wouldn't change them. But it is certainly important to really think about what you want. I would strongly recommend doing your research before relocating: find out how to do basic things such as setting up a bank account. A foreign national in LA needs a passport to board a train; back in Leeds I sometimes didn't even get my rail ticket checked. That significant, but almost unimaginable, difference from Britain's norm meant I was a day late for my first holiday within the States. What if that had been a train to my first film shoot?

As an American citizen, after a few months I had updated enough paperwork to ensure that I no longer had problems at train stations or with prospective employers. But believe me, those on a typical student visa should budget for not having a job, because the law is very strict on illegal work. If you don't have the budget to live without a job, think really hard before making the move.

I really hope this piece gives a balanced overview and doesn't sway too much one way or another. All I will say is that despite my many problems, I wouldn't change the decision I took from both a training and a personal perspective. Now, for personal reasons, I'm back in England. I continued my training at postgraduate level at a British drama school. The training was incredible and I wish that the two could be fused somehow. But until that day, the choice of 'here or there' is up to each individual. I hope this has helped.

David Taylor-Sharp is a graduate of both the American Academy of Dramatic Arts and East 15 Acting School. His work in film has been showcased at the International Film Festival England, and Seattle True Independent Film Festival; David also won an Accolade Award for his 2008 short film *Fun with Lesley*. He has worked in television in North America, and is the co-star of the web series *The World of Cory and Sid*. More information about David can be found via IMDb or on Spotlight Pin: 8735-7836-8465.

Training

Short-term and part-time courses

This section lists both 'taster' opportunities for drama school aspirants, and further training for professional actors.

Pre-drama-school courses

Competition for drama school places seems to be growing even more ferocious, and many applicants will enhance their chances if they go on a pre-drama-school course. You may, for example, have done A level Drama, but the actual acting training on such courses is often limited – generally geared more towards the exam-passing university entrant than auditioning for drama school. Whatever your acting background, a 'taster' course (for just a week, for instance) can give you a good idea of what further help/training you need in order to prepare you properly for drama school auditions.

Additional skills

As well as the organisations listed below, there are periodic 'one-off' workshops around the country. These are usually 'trailed', and sometimes advertised, in *The Stage*. Equity occasionally subsidises such enterprises (some, away from the major cities), so it is worth checking with your local Branch/Organiser. Actors Centres are not just places to sharpen up your existing skills and develop new ones, but also great meeting places for actors to exchange ideas and information.

The Academy of Live and Recorded Arts (ALRA)*

Studio One, The Royal Victoria Patriotic Building, John Archer Way, London SW18 3SX
tel 020-8870 6475
email info@alra.co.uk
website www.alra.co.uk
Co-directors Clive Duncan, Adrian Hall

Courses offered:

• Acting Foundation Course. A part-time, 3-term course to prepare students for full-time vocational training.
• Acting for Deaf BSL Users. A part-time, 3-term introduction to acting for TV and the theatre.

Consult the website for more details.

Academy of Creative Training

8/10 Rock Place, Brighton, East Sussex BN2 1PF
tel (01273) 818266
email info@actedu.org.uk
website www.actedu.org.uk
Principal/Director Janette Edisford *Key contact* Joanna Nash

All classes are in the evenings and at weekends to allow students to undertake actor training whilst maintaining their domestic and financial commitments. Entry onto both courses is via attendance on a 2-week intensive workshop (*Fee*:

£60) held throughout the year and designed to "enhance creativity and explore acting skills, as well as offering an insight into the training that we offer". Students embarking on the Diploma in Acting training are invited to audition for a scholarship that covers half of the tuition fees. The school operates an equal opportunities policy that includes disabled students, but there is limited physical access to the dance studio and washroom facilities.

Courses offered:

• Diploma in Acting (2 years). For students aged 18+. Course fee: £3525. *Audition requirements*: 2-week workshop, as above
• Intensive Foundation Course (1 year, 10 hours per week). For students aged 16+. Course fee: £1175. *Audition requirements*: 2-week workshop, as above

Academy of Performance Combat (APC)

tel (07928) 324706
email info@theapc.org.uk
website www.theapc.org.uk

APC is dedicated to bringing combat in any form in any media into the 21st century. "We are absolutely committed to safer, more exacting techniques than any other organisation." Please see the website for more details of courses and qualifications offered.

ROSIE STILL (PHOTOGRAPHER)

Zoe Heyes

Christopher Parker

Bella Emberg

Michael Barber

Debra Stephenson

Charlie Clements

Gabrielle Bradshaw

Mia McKenna-Bruce

Liz Fraser

John Judd

Maureen Sweeney

Chris Jarvis

*Special SPOTLIGHT prices*Student rates*Free prints*Free airbrushing*
Very relaxed atmosphere in my own South London studio
*View work instantly*Whole shoot put onto CD*

020 8857 6920 ** www.rosiestillphotography.com

WE CAN
HELP ACTORS'
CHILDREN

Are you:

- a professional actor?
- the parent of a child under 21?
- having trouble with finances?

Please get in touch for a confidential chat.

The Actors' Charitable Trust
020 7636 7868
robert@tactactors.org

TACT can help in many ways: with regular monthly payments, one-off grants, and long-term support and advice.
We help with clothing, child-care, music lessons, school trips, special equipment and adaptations, and in many other ways.

Our website has a link to a list of all the theatrical and entertainment charities which might be able to help you if you do not have children: www.tactactors.org

TACT, 58 Bloomsbury Street, London WC1B 3QT.

Register charity number 206809.

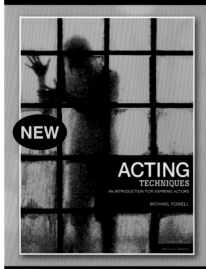

Darren Day

Jenny May Morgan

MOUNTVIEW
ACADEMY OF THEATRE ARTS

Ralph Richardson Memorial Studios, Kingfisher Place,
Clarendon Road, Wood Green, London N22 6XF

Musical
Theatre

Acting

Technical
Theatre

Stage Management · Lighting · Sound · Design · Construction

Undergraduate &
Postgraduate Courses
Plus an exciting programme of
Part-time and Summer Courses

Tel: 020 8881 2201
Fax: 020 8829 0034
enquiries@mountview.org.uk
www.mountview.org.uk

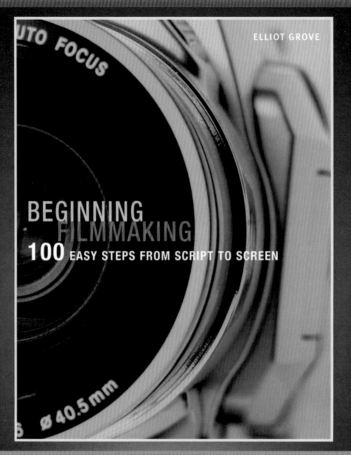

Tel: 0208 438 0303

Picture Credits Sinitta actresss and singer, Martina Miss Slovakia, Sir Richard Branson Virgin, Andy Hamilton Whitbread, Jana Hyncociva, Miss Pinto with Rat, Kate Melton actress, Elizabeth actress

Will C specialises in actors, actresses and personalities in advertising, editorial, film and television. He has been principal photographer on over 30 major films and has directed and shot 40 commercials. Actors and actresses portraits can be taken in our fully equipped film and digital studio in NW2 - just 15 minutes from Marble Arch or Baker Street.

Tel: 0208 438 0303 Mobile: 07712 669 953
e-mail: billy_snapper@hotmail.com
www.london-photographer.com
www.theukphotographerexhibition.co.uk - www.billysnapper.com

Will C - Photographer to the Stars

Pascal Mollière // Photography •

Actors Headshots Specialist
Theatre Skills
Film Stills
Performing Arts Photographer

Sami Stefanos - Actress "I had an amazing day and experience with Pascal, where I felt totally at ease and comfortable".

Jackie Lye – Actress "Pascal - Thanks so much for my photos, I love them! I will certainly recommend you to The results are fantastic, here's to lots of castings from them!"

Session Prices from just £150 when quoting The Actors Yearbook –
Studio, Outdoor or location – fast turn-around
Digital and Hand Printed 10x8's – cd, email and retouch available...
Contact Sheets – online gallery/ordering.

Tel: 020 8406 9185 07713 242948
www.pascalphoto.co.uk   info@pascalphoto.co.uk   Skype: pascalart

Freema Agyeman   Daisy Lewis

Jennie Gruner   Claire Foy

SIMON ANNAND
PHOTOGRAPHER
www.simonannand.com
07884 446 776

Paul Ritter   Josh McGuire   John Woodvine

Author of *THE HALF, Actors preparing to go on stage*
Works for NT, RSC, Royal Court, Almeida
25 years experience
Competitive rates/concs available

The Academy of the Science of Acting & Directing

9-15 Elthorne Road, Archway, London N19 4AJ
tel 020-7272 0027 *fax* 020-7272 0026
email info@asad.org.uk
website www.scienceofacting.org.uk
Principal Helen Kogan

Courses offered:

• Three Year Evening Acting Course. Applicants must be aged 16 or over. Course fee is £4160 p.a. Offers 14 places each year. *Audition requirements/fee:* see entry on page 6 for details
• Two Year Evening Acting Course. Applicants must be aged 16 or over. Course fee is £4160 p.a. Offers 14 places each year. *Audition requirements/fee:* see entry on page 6 for details
• Intensive Acting Course (33 weeks). Course fee is £1440 with 6 hours of classes per week. No audition required
• Spring Workshop (2 weeks). Course takes place in March and the fee is £500. No audition required
• Summer Workshop (2 weeks). Course takes place in July and the fee is £400. No audition required
• Autumn Workshop (2 weeks). Course takes place in March and the fee is £500. No audition required

The Actor Works

First Floor, Raine House, Raine Street, Wapping, London E1W 3RJ
tel 020-7702 0909
email ask@theactorworks.co.uk
website www.theactorworks.co.uk
Director Daniel Brennan

Full-time evening and weekend course: This course is designed for those who may:

• need to work during the day to pay for their training;
• have family commitments that prevent them from studying in the day;
• be considering changing their career and need to keep 'the day job' until the acting bug finally bites for good.

It is an intensive, 2-year vocational training, which covers all aspects of an actor's work. Subjects covered include: acting for stage, screen acting, actors' movement, speech, voice, reading, audition technique, stage combat, dance, singing and theatre history. During the course students will take part in up to 5 different productions, normally at the end of every term.

The course culminates in an agents showcase at a major theatre and a season of graduation plays on the London fringe.

Students on this course must be aged 20 +. There is no upper age limit.

There are 6 terms in all.

Postgraduate course: This course is designed for those who:

• studied drama at university and would like some more 'hands on' experience;
• have had actor training and would like to hone their skills.

This is a 1-year daytime course, which offers full actor training. Subjects covered include: acting for stage, screen acting, actors' movement, speech, voice, reading, audition technique, stage combat, dance, singing and theatre history. During the course students will take part in up to 4 different productions, normally at the end of every term.

The course culminates in an agents showcase at a major theatre and a season of graduation plays on the London fringe.

Students on this course must be aged 21 +. There is no upper age limit.

There are 3 terms in all.

Foundation course: This course is designed for younger students who:
• need guidance and support through the gruelling process of auditioning for major drama schools
• have not yet decided whether acting is for them
• want to do something productive with their gap year

This one-year daytime course is not full actor training as such, but it prepares students for what they will experience should they choose to take up acting as a career. Emphasis is placed on preparation, application and discipline. We encourage confidence and a feeling of self-worth which helps students through the audition process. Subjects covered include: voice, speech, actors' movement, audition preparation, stage combat, theatre history and reading. Students can expect to take roles in 3 different productions over the year.

Students on this course must be between the ages of 17 and 20.

There are three terms in all.

Other courses offered: Also now runs a part-time course designed for those who wish to pursue acting as a leisure interest. "You may wish to 'test the water' before considering full-time training; to improve your self-confidence in group situations; to improve your public-speaking skills; or perhaps simply enjoy a new activity one night a week." These qualifications are currently NVQ Level 3 equivalent and from 2008 count for between 20 and 65 points towards UCAS tariffs. The cost for 10 Tuesday evenings is £350. For LAMDA tuition on Thursdays, an extra £100 (plus the cost of exam – £40-£50).There is no need to audition, though "please phone us in the first instance to reserve a place, before sending payment".

Actors Centre (London)

1A Tower Street, Covent Garden, London WC2H 9NP
tel 020-7240 3940

email act@actorscentre.co.uk
website www.actorscentre.co.uk
Artistic Director Matthew Lloyd

Full membership is open to Equity members, registered graduates from the Conference of Drama Schools in their first year of registration (must hold a student Equity card), and foreign actors holding an Equity letter of exemption. Members are entitled to a wide range of subsidised classes and workshops led by experienced directors and tutors who are active in the industry, plus full use of the centre, café facilities when available and a quarterly schedule. Fees are now £55 per year and £37.50 for 6 months (£5 discount for Equity members' first membership). Associate membership is also available for £25 per year; associates are entitled to observe designated workshops but not to participate in them. Provisional membership is open to applicants whose training/experience is not as substantial as that of the majority of members; this is available on the basis of an audition and is reviewed after a 6-month period.

Regular classes and workshops include Acting, Tool Box, TV and Film, Auditions, Advice, Labwork, Voice, Shakespeare, Stage Combat, Directing, Musical Theatre and Writing. In addition, members can book individual sessions to work on singing, acting, sight-reading, Alexander Technique, dialect, voice and movement. Contact the centre for a membership form or a current brochure.

Provisional Membership is offered to some applicants for membership at the centre whose training and/or experience is not yet as substantial as for the majority of our members. Provisional Membership is offered for an initial 6-month period and entitles you to: attend a range of classes targeted to your needs; receive ongoing feedback and guidance sessions; use the Actors Centre café and bar facilities; use available studios on an ad hoc basis; sign in up to 4 guests; and receive a quarterly schedule and details of the Tristan Bates Theatre's programme. Towards the end of the 6-month period, your progress will be assessed to help us decide whether full membership can be offered at that stage. The fee for Provisional Membership is £50 per 6 months.

Associate Membership is designed to allow members of related professions (e.g. directors, writers, producers) who are not actors to observe, but not participate in, selected classes. We accept applications for Associate Membership from members of Equity or affiliated unions (e.g. Directors Guild, Writers Guild) or from anyone working in the industry who has been nominated by a member or a tutor. This membership entitles you to use the café and bar facilities and available studios on an ad hoc basis, sign in up to 4 guests, and receive details of the Actors Centre's and Tristan Bates Theatre's programmes. Applicants should write to the Artistic Director explaining why they wish to take up Associate Membership, and supply a CV that demonstrates

their professional credentials. The fee for Associate Membership is £25 per year.

All fees are inclusive of VAT.

Actors Centre North

21-31 Oldham Street, Manchester M1 1JG
tel 0161-819 2513 *fax* 0161-819 2513
email info@actorscentrenorth.co.uk
website www.actorscentrenorth.co.uk

Core provision of ongoing professional development for trained actors. Workshops for all Equity members, covering every aspect of an actor's toolbox and led by leading industry professionals. Equity members or professional actors with sufficient experience are eligible for membership. Membership fees are £30 per year or £18 for 6 months. Graduates in the first year following graduation from an NCDT-accredited course are entitled to a reduced membership.

Regular workshops include Acting for Screen, Auditioning for TV & Theatre, Beginners' Meisner Technique, Tools for Learning an Accent, and Shakespeare Surgery, Advice, Voice, Stage Combat, Directing. Members can book individual sessions to work on any chosen area.

Actors Temple

Studio Theatre, 13-14 Warren Street,
London W1T 5LG
tel 020-3004 4537
email tanja@actorstemple.com
website www.actorstemple.com
Directors Mark Wakeling, Ellie Zeegen *Key contact* Tanje McGhie

Training and production company specialising in the Meisner technique. Studio theatre in the West End.

Courses offered:

• 5-week intensive 1st term; 5-week intensive 2nd term (20 weeks each). Fee for each is £1750
• Introduction week (monthly; Mon-Fri 5 x 4-hour classes). Fee is £350

"Unfortunately there are stairs to the basement studio, so not good for wheelchair-users; we do however have a disabled toilet. We have a very open policy towards those with disabilities."

Arts Educational Schools London*

Cone Ripman House, 14 Bath Road, Chiswick,
London W4 1LY
tel 020-8987 6666
website www.artsed.co.uk

Courses offered:

• Post-Diploma BA (Hons) in Performance. Validated by City University. A year-long evening conversion course. Open to students who hold a diploma in acting or musical theatre from an NCDT- or CDET-accredited course.

Training

• Foundation in Performance (1 year part-time). Acting or Musical Theatre option. 3 evenings per week running over 3 terms, starting in September.

Part-time evening and holiday courses for 17+ years:
• Various courses in acting and musical theatre disciplines, including stage, screen, voice, dance and audition technique, are offered for varying skill levels throughout the year.

For full details on all courses offered at ArtsEd, please visit **www.artsed.co.uk**.

Birkbeck College Faculty of Continuing Education
26 Russell Square, London WC1B 5DQ
tel 020-7679 1064 *fax* 020-7631 6688
email performance@fll.bbk.ac.uk
website www.bbk.ac.uk/ce/ps

The faculty is a leading provider of part-time Higher Education courses in London. Its Performance Studies programme offers certificated courses in Acting, Dance, Opera and Concert Singing. It does not offer scholarships or bursaries. The college is committed to doing everything it can to support students with disabilities.

Courses offered:
• Certificate of Continuing Education in Performance Studies: Acting (formerly the Foundation in Acting). The course lasts 96 hours (3 hours per week) and entry is by audition. Contact the college for details of fees
• Certificate of Higher Education in Performance Studies: Acting (formerly the Diploma in Acting). The course lasts 192 hours (6 hours per week) and entry is by audition. Contact the college for details of fees

Birmingham School of Acting*
Millenium Point, Curzon Street, Birmingham B4 7XG
tel 0121-331 7200 *fax* 0121-331 7221
email info@bsa.uce.ac.uk
website www.bsa.uce.ac.uk
Principal Stephen Simms *Admissions Manager* Roger Franke

Courses offered:
• Creative Drama (30 weeks part-time). Course fee is £306 with 3 hours of classes per week
• Acting Summer School. Course fee is £510 for 2 weeks in August
• Shakespeare Summer School. Course fee is £299 for 4 days in August
• Musical Theatre Week. Course fee is £350 for 6 days in August
• Musical Theatre Weekend. Course fee is £185 for 2 days in August

The Birmingham Theatre School
The Old Rep Theatre, Station Street, Birmingham B5 4DY

tel 0121-643 3300 *fax* 0121-643 3300
email info@birminghamtheatreschool.co.uk
website www.birminghamtheatreschool.co.uk
Principal Chris Rozanski *Key contact* Andrea Cobham (Arts Admin Manager)

Courses offered:
• Professional Diploma (Evenings & Weekends). Applicants must be aged 18 years or over
• Acting for Beginners (11 weeks). Covers the basics of character creation, voice, improvisation and performance discipline for acting beginners. Students participate in all aspects of the creative process, from basic exercises to final presentations. Course fee is £79 per term; classes take place in the evening
• Creating Performance (11 weeks). Each term, students will create and perform using a variety of techniques and using both texts and devised work. All aspects of character creation and working with an audience will be explored. Suitable for people with previous experience in acting. Course fee is £79 per term; classes take place in the evening
• Pub Theatre (11 weeks). Provides students with the chance of experiencing exactly what working in a fringe theatre company is all about. Course fee is £89 per term; classes take place in the evening

The Bloomsbury Alexander Centre
Bristol House, 80A Southampton Row, London WC1B 4BB
tel 020-7404 5348 or 020-8374 3184
email bloomsbury.alexandercentre@btinternet.com
Directors Stephen Cooper, Natacha Osorio

The centre specialises in teaching the Alexander Technique. Teachers are available for private lessons, with discounts available for students and actors. There are ongoing introductory workshops and courses, as well as drop-in vocal work for actors with experience of the AT. The introductory course runs for 4 weeks (1.5 hours a week) and costs £80. The drop-in AT vocal work classes are £15 per session. *Note for disabled actors*: "Our premises are on the ground floor with one step up onto the main entrance and one other just inside."

Boden Studios
99 East Barnet Road, New Barnet, Herts EN4 8RF
tel 020-8447 0909 *fax* 020-8449 5212
email info@bodenstudios.com
website www.bodenstudios.com
Director Adam Boden

Established in 1973. A part-time performing arts school offering 1 full scholarship each year.

Courses offered:
• Acting Performance – 12 weeks, 1.5 hours per week. Course fee is £84
• Guildhall Drama Exams – 12 weeks, 1 hour per week. Course fee is £96

British Academy of Dramatic Combat
email via form on website
website www.badc.co.uk

Offers a Performance Certificate in Stage Combat at Foundation, Basic, Basic Level 2, Recommended and Advanced levels. Training is available in the following methods: Broadsword & Shield, Double Handed Broadsword, Quarterstaff, Rapier & Dagger, Rapier & Cloak, Rapier & Buckler, Smallsword, Unarmed Combat. Programmes of workshops are arranged throughout the country, and anyone with suitable venue spaces or wanting to be added to the workshop mailing list should email **workshops@badc.co.uk**.

The British Academy of Stage & Screen Combat

Suite 280, 10 Great Russell Street,
London WC1B 3BQ
tel (07981) 806265
email info@bassc.org
website www.bassc.org

The British Academy of Stage & Screen Combat was founded in 1993 with the aim of improving the standards of safety, quality and training of stage combat, and promoting a unified code of practice for the training, teaching and assessing of stage combat within the United Kingdom.

All BASSC teachers have undergone a rigorous training programme and the examining members of the BASSC are highly qualified, experienced professionals with a tradition of working in theatre, television and film productions such as *Alexander*, *Troy*, *Stardust*, *Closer*, *The Last Legion* and *The Golden Compass*.

Since its formation the BASSC has established a reputation as the invigorating driving force behind stage combat in the United Kingdom, and is respected, both nationally and internationally, as the leading provider of professional-level stage combat training.

As a result of this, British Equity, in 1997, recognised the BASSC's Advanced Certificate as a valid qualification for entry onto the Equity Fight Directors' Training scheme, and in 2001 the BASSC was appointed by the Equity Council for the training and assessment of Fight Directors candidates applying to join the Equity Fight Directors' Register.

The BASSC now has training schemes in place which allow for development from actor/combatant to Certified Teacher, as well as assessment and training of Fight Directors for the Equity register.

British Military Fitness (BMF)

Unit 7B and C, 3/11 Imperial Studios,
Imperial Road, London SW6 2AG
tel 0870-241 2517
email barney@britmilfit.com
website www.britmilfit.com
Managing Director Robin Cope *Communications & Membership* Barney Larkin

The original 'military style' training provider. Set up in 1999 and now operating across the UK, BMF offers a great way to get fit while having fun in the great outdoors. Classes take place outdoors in parks throughout the country and throughout the year. Each class lasts for an hour and is divided into groups to cater for all levels of ability.

You can attend any class at any venue at any time, to suit your schedule (Equity card numbers must be provided). *Actors' Yearbook* have negotiated corporate rate membership for all Equity members. In London this is (at the time of writing) £38 per month; other regions vary between £26 and £34. BMF offers a free trial class for anyone interested in membership. After that, payment is by direct debit or by paying for sessions in a block. Membership can be suspended in the event that acting work makes attending classes impossible.

BMF is member of the Fitness Industry Association, has the backing of Sport England, and all instructors are either former or serving members of the armed forces with recognised fitness & adventure training qualifications. To find your nearest class, please see **www.britmilfit.com** or call the office on 0870-241 2517 for a chat.

BMF also organises adventurous events such as skiing, abseiling and mountaineering, as well as charity fundraising events and corporate training.

Central School of Speech and Drama*

64 Eton Avenue, London NW3 3HY
tel 020-7722 8183 *fax* 020-7722 4132
email enquiries@cssd.ac.uk
website www.cssd.ac.uk
Principal Gavin Henderson

A selection of courses offered:

• Saturday Drama Classes (1 term). Course fee is £145, entry is possible throughout the year. For ages 6-17
• Winter Introduction to Audition Speeches (3 days, January). Course fee is £275. Separate classes for ages 18+ and 16+
• Easter Scenes Workshop (9 days, April). Course fee is £380
• Introduction to Acting (2 evenings p.w., termly). Course fee is £385, entry is possible throughout the year. For ages 18+
• Introduction to Text (2 evenings p.w., termly). Course fee is £385, entry is possible throughout the year. For ages 18+
• Working Text (2 evenings p.w., termly). Course fee is £385, entry is possible throughout the year. For ages 18+
• Working Shakespeare (2 evenings p.w., termly). Course fee is £385, entry is possible throughout the year. For ages 18+
• Classical Theatre – Level 2 (2 evenings p.w., termly). Course fee is £385, entry is possible throughout the year. For ages 18+
• Introduction to Movement for Performance (2 evenings p.w., termly). Course fee is £385, entry is possible throughout the year. For ages 18+

• Movement for Perfomers – Level 2 (2 evenings p.w., termly). Course fee is £385, entry is possible throughout the year. For ages 18+
• Introduction to Voice for Performance (2 evenings p.w., termly). Course fee is £385, entry is possible throughout the year. For ages 18+
• Introduction to Acting for Camera (2 evenings p.w., termly). Course fee is £385, entry is possible throughout the year. For ages 18+
• Directed Scenes (Saturdays, termly). Course fee is £460
• Puppetry (2 evenings p.w., termly). Course fee is £385, entry is possible throughout the year. For ages 18+
• Singing (1 evening p.w., termly). Course fee is £165, entry is possible throughout the year. For ages 18+
• Central Theatre Group (1 evening p.w., termly). Course fee is £230, entry is possible throughout the year. For ages 18+

Summer school courses:
• Combat and Stage Fighting (1 week, July). Course fee is £440. For ages 17+
• Mask (1 week, July). Course fee is £440. For ages 17+
• Devising (1 week, July). Course fee is £740. For ages 17+
• Musical Theatre (1 week, July). Course fee is £870. For ages 17+
• Summer Shakespeare (1 week, July). Course fee is £870. For ages 17+
• Directed Scenes (1 week, August). Course fee is £740. For ages 17+
• Voice and Text (1 week, July). Course fee is £440. For ages 18+
• Actors' Auditions Pieces (1 week, July-August). Course fee is £550. For ages 17+
• Youth Theatre For Actors (1 week, July). Course fee is £380. For ages 5-17
• Youth Theatre For Actors (3 weeks, July-August). Course fee is £1140. For ages 5-17

The City Lit
Keeley Street, Covent Garden, London WC2B 4BA
tel 020-7492 2542
email drama@citylit.ac.uk
website www.citylit.ac.uk
Head of Drama, Dance & Speech Vivienne Rochester

The college offers an eclectic mix of disciplines such as acting, movement, voice, musical theatre, media, mime, circus, stage fighting, magic, comedy, dance, self-presentation, debating, accents, sight-reading and pronunciation for speakers of other languages, etc. which develop vocational, social and personal skills.

A student bursary scheme is available, and as much as £2000 may be awarded to a few talented Advanced Performance Diploma students who are in financial hardship. There are various other small grants that might cover travel, books or child-care. Students may ring or come into the office for an interview between

12.30pm and 1.30pm (Monday and Wednesday) or 5.30pm and 6.30pm (Monday, Tuesday and Thursday).

The City Lit Rep Company was set up to train a company of actors to produce work of the highest professional standard, providing a platform for its members to hone their skills and display their talents. Directors, teachers and practitioners are invited and engaged to facilitate. Its members are made up of a combination of graduates from the accredited courses, or from the advanced/professional provision in the Drama, Dance & Speech department's programme, and experienced practitioners who wish to further their experience with the college. Auditions are held annually. The college has awarded associate status to a number of actors who have produced an excellent body of work with the company. All company members are eligible for the 3 productions staged each year, and are invited, if appropriate, to professional castings that are occasionally held at the City Lit. Professional Masterclasses are held throughout the year.

The 1-year accredited courses are as follows:

• Foundation course (1 year part-time)
• Access course (1 year part-time)
• Musical Theatre Diploma (1 year part-time)
• Advanced Performance Diploma (1 year part-time; professional diploma). Equity card awarded; applicants must be aged 19 or over

Entry is by audition to all the above courses.
• Stage Fighting (1 year part-time, plus a number of shorter courses). Applicants must be aged 19 or over. Entry is by interview.

A range of acting, voice, movement, TV and film, radio presenting classes and other related disciplines are also available. Courses run for 12 weeks with entry at various points throughout the year. Contact the City Lit for a prospectus and further details.

Drama Studio London (DSL)*
1 Grange Road, London W5 5QN
tel 020-8579 3897 *fax* 020-8566 2035
email admin@dramastudiolondon.co.uk
website www.dramastudiolondon.co.uk
Director Peter Craze *Key contact* Sue Quelch-Woolls

Courses offered:

• Summer Acting Course (4 weeks full-time). Course fee is £1200. Course starts in July/August

East 15 Acting School*
Hatfields, Rectory Lane, Loughton IG10 3RY
tel 020-8508 5983 *fax* 020-8508 7521
email east15@essex.ac.uk
website www.east15.ac.uk
Director Leon Rubin *Key contact* Linda Humphreys

Courses offered: All courses listed below take place in July/August:

• Introduction to Acting (1 week), fee is £220
• Approaches to Shakespeare and Jacobean Theatre (2 weeks), fee is £350

- Devised Theatre (3 weeks), fee is £500
- Audition Technique (1 week), fee is £220
- Physical Theatre (1 week), fee is £220
- Stage Combat (1 week), fee is £250 (includes BADC examination fee)

All of the above courses carry University of Essex credits. Applicants must be aged 17 years or over.

Exeter Dance Consultancy

Holly Tree Cottage, Clyst St George, Exeter EX3 ORB
tel (01392) 873683
email info@exedance.demon.co.uk

Offers 1:1 tuition in dance movement therapy for performing artists, specialist movement coaching for actors, and dance coaching for auditions. A 10% discount is available for Equity members, Spotlight members and students. To arrange an appointment, contact Jeanette Macdonald.

GSA Conservatoire* (formerly Guildford School of Acting)

Stag Hill Campus, Guildford GU2 7XH
tel (01483) 560701
website www.gsauk.org
Director Gerry Tebbutt

Courses offered:

- Singing in the Theatre (1 week). A summer course designed for students over the age of 17 who wish to improve their singing. Other disciplines relating to the voice will also be explored. Entry is in July and the fee is £299
- Musical Theatre (2 weeks). Culminating in a performance in the Bellairs Playhouse, this course is open to students aged 17 or over and takes place in July/August. Course fee is £499
- Audition Techniques (1 week). Course takes place in August and is geared towards students aged 17 or over. Course fee is £198
- Intensive Musical Theatre Dance for Beginners (1 week). An intensive course to discover what your body is capable of doing. Explore the foundations of tap, jazz and ballet and get guidance and expert advice on what you need to work on and hopefully gain the confidence to compete in a dance class situation. The course takes place in August and is open to students 17 years and over. Course fee is £295
- Acting for Camera (1 week). The course takes place in August and is open to students 17 years and over. Course fee is £295

Other summer schools: Courses are offered at a reasonable cost and provide either a stimulating refresher course or an introduction to basic theatre training. There is no audition procedure, and everyone is welcome. All courses are staffed by members of the GSA faculty.

July/August:
- Youth Theatre (9 days)

- Musical Theatre (2 weeks)
- Intensive Musical Theatre Dance (5 days)
- Intensive Musical Theatre Acting (5 days)
- Intensive Musical Theatre Singing (5 days)
- Audition Technique (2 x 5-day sessions)
- Directing a Musical (5 days)
- Acting for Camera (5 days)

For further information or to download an aplication form, please refer to the website, or telephone or email (**summerschool@gsauk.org**) for a brochure.

Guildhall School of Music & Drama*

Silk Street, Barbican, London EC2Y 8DT
tel 020-7628 2571 *fax* 020-7256 9438
email registry@gsmd.ac.uk
website www.gsmd.ac.uk
Director of Drama Wyn Jones

Founded in 1880, the Guildhall School is acknowledged internationally as a leading conservatoire for both music and drama.

Courses offered: The 2 summer school courses (Acting in Shakespeare & Contemporary Theatre; and Acting in Musical Theatre) each offer 3 weeks of stimulating and inspiring training in acting. Both will include class work or workshops with many of the school's core staff.

- Acting in Shakespeare & Contemporary Theatre. 3 weeks of intensive tuition, workshops and rehearsals. Students have craft-based classes for half of the day; for the other half they work with a director and explore short scenes from Shakespeare and contemporary plays, investigating the texts through group exercises and improvisation. The aim is to demystify Shakespeare and provide a challenging insight into modern drama. The course concludes with a presentation of work-in-progress to students and staff (not open to the public) which may take the form of a workshop or open class.
- Acting in Musical Theatre. 3 weeks of intensive tuition, workshops and rehearsals. Students have craft-based classes for half the day; for the other half they work as an ensemble with a director on a musical project, exploring a selection of scenes, songs and dances based around a theme. The focus of the course will be upon the craft of acting within the context of musical theatre. It will conclude with a presentation of work-in-progress to students and staff (not open to the public) which may take the form of a workshop or open class. The course is led by Guildhall School tutor Martin Connor, who directs the school's annual musical.

Craft-based classes for both courses include: Acting, Voice, Movement, Improvisation, Mask, Combat, Historical, Dance, Audition Technique. At least 2 visits to attend performances in London theatres are included in the fees of both courses, which are set at £1600; there is a £350 non-refundable deposit. Applicants must be at least 18 years old by the start of the course; there is no upper age limit. A good standard of English is essential. Accommodation is available. Please consult the website (**www.gsmd.ac.uk/acting/summerschool**) for up-to-date information on fees, curriculum and application procedure, or telephone 020-7382 7183 for details of the application procedure. Email enquiries to **dramasummerschool@gsmd.ac.uk**

"There is no application deadline but, in view of the limited number of places, applicants are strongly advised to book early. If the summer school is full, you will be placed on a waiting list."

Hope Street Ltd
13a Hope Street, Liverpool L1 9BQ
tel 0151-708 8007 *fax* 0151-709 3242
email peter@hope-street.org
website www.hope-street.org
Director Peter Ward

Provides training and professional development for emerging artists: actors, directors, workshop leaders, designers, composers, film makers, and production managers. The 6-month programme is led by professional artists from the UK and Europe. 4 or 5 projects are produced during the programme; these are cross-artform productions in the street, in unusual spaces and in non-traditional venues for audiences of between 150 and 30,000. Applications are welcome from anyone over 18 living anywhere in the world. No fees are payable. No training allowance is provided.

Courses offered:

• Physical Theatre (26 weeks full-time). Applicants must be aged 18 or over. Course fee is £2800. 8 places are offered each year
• Young People's Theatre (26 weeks full-time). Applicants must be aged 18 or over. Course fee is £2800. 4 places are offered each year

International School of Screen Acting
3 Mills Studios, Unit 3, 24 Sugar House Lane, London E15 2QS
tel 020-8555 5775
email office@screenacting.co.uk
website www.screenacting.co.uk
Key contact David Craik

Founded in 2001 to specialise in offering full-time training specifically in television and film acting, taking a holistic approach to creativity in relation to students' personal development. While the school is happy to receive applications from disabled students, there are currently significant access issues with the premises.

Courses offered:

• Screen Acting (3 months for 3 nights a week). Course fee is £1200. No audition required
• 'Crash Course' – week-long course offered at various times throughout the year. Course fee is £295. No audition required

• Summer Course – week-long course offered in Aug/Sept. Course fee is £295. No audition required

London Academy of Music and Dramatic Arts (LAMDA)*
155 Talgarth Road, London W14 9DA
tel 020-8834 0500 *fax* 020-8834 0501
email enquiries@lamda.org.uk
website www.lamda.org.uk
Principal Joanna Read *Admissions Assistants* Amy Richardson, Elissa Perrau, Philip McDonnell

Courses offered: Short-term courses are offered on the following:

• Shakespeare and His Contemporaries (8 weeks)
• Shakespeare (4 weeks)
• Physical Theatre (2 weeks)
• Audition Technique (2 weeks)
• English Communication Skills Through Drama Workshop (EFL – 3 weeks)
• Introduction to Drama School (2 weeks)
• EFL in Audition Technique (2 weeks)

With the exception of the Introduction to Drama School and Audition Technique courses, where the minimum age is 16, students on all other Summer Courses must be 18 years or above. For more information on all LAMDA's courses, including fees and deadlines, please visit the website.

London Academy of Radio, Film & TV
1 Lancing Street, London NW1 1NA
tel 0870-850 4994
website www.media-courses.com
Director of Courses Andy Parkin *Key contact* Estelle Burton

The academy has more than 30 teaching staff; around 1200 students take one or more of its 100+ courses. It is situated opposite Euston Station.

Courses offered:

• Acting Masterclass (1 week – 30 hours). Course fee is £695. No audition required
• Acting for Film & TV (9-week course – 9 x 3 hours). Course fee is £395. No audition required (*Note*: 2 versions of this course exist – 1 on a weekday evening; 1 on a Saturday)

London Drama School
30 Brondesbury Park, London NW6 7DN
tel 020-8830 0074 *fax* 020-8830 4992
email enquiries@startek-uk.com
website www.startek-uk.com
Key contact Sarah Mann

Courses offered:

• Saturday Drama Workshop (10 weeks). Course fee is £450 for 6 hours of classes per week, or £250 for 3 hours of classes per week
• Thursday Evening Workshop (10 weeks). Course fee is £185 for 2 hours of classes per week

• Advanced Drama Workshop (10 weeks). The course runs on Tuesday evenings for 2 hours and costs £195
• Developing Stage & TV Acting Skills (10 weeks). The course runs on Monday evenings for 2 hours and costs £225

Summer courses:
• Improvisation & Acting (July). 3-week intensive course. Course fee is £875
• Comedy & Acting (July/Aug). 3-week intensive course. Course fee is £875
• Acting & Screen Acting (August). 3-week intensive course. Course fee is £875

The summer courses run consecutively. Course fees are reduced for students taking more than one course, thus: £1575 for 2 courses; £2230 for all 3 courses. 1-year courses are also available.

Morley College Theatre School

61 Westminster Bridge Road, London SE1 7HT
tel 020-7450 1832
email drama@morleycollege.ac.uk
website www.morleycollege.ac.uk
Key contact Dominic Grant

Offers part-time acting classes which lead to London Open College Network accreditation. Classes are led by specialist acting tutors with extensive professional experience. An Access Hardship Fund and concessionary fees are available to some students.

Courses offered:
• A range of evening and part-time acting skills courses are available, including: Actors' Voice Workshop, The Acting Business, Singing for Actors and Dancers, Absolute Beginners Drama Workshop, Developing Acting Skills, Introduction to Physical Theatre, and many different styles of Dance.
• Intermediate Foundation Theatre Arts (1 year part-time). Covers Acting Techniques (including voice, improvisation, text work and scenes) and Dance Techniques (Jazz and Contemporary) leading to performances in term 3. Course fee is approximately £650 p.a. for EU students, with concessions and hardship grants available. Entry is by audition.
• Acting Studies (1-year evening school). Develops improvisation, characterisation, voice and movement skills through a series of workshops and rehearsals. Course fee is approximately £400, with concessions and hardship grants available. Entry is by audition.
• Morley Theatre School (1-year evening school). For those with ability and confidence as actors who want to consolidate their skills. Workshops explore different techniques and approaches, and lead towards performance at the end of the course. Entry is by audition.

Mountview Academy of Theatre Arts*

Ralph Richardson Memorial Studios,
Clarendon Road, London N22 6XF
tel 020-8881 2201 *fax* 020-8829 0034
email enquiries@mountview.org.uk
website www.mountview.org.uk
Principal Sue Robertson

Courses offered:
• Foundation Acting (1 year). Course fee is £1100 with 9 hours of classes per week. Entry is by audition.
• Foundation Musical Theatre (1 year). Course fee is £1300 with 9 hours of classes per week. Entry is by audition.
• Acting for Screen (2 terms). Course fee is £800 with 3 hours of classes per week. Entry is by audition.
• Professional Masterclass, available from 1 day to 1 week during spring and autumn. Fees vary. No audition required.
• Summer School Acting (2 weeks). Courses take place in July/August, fee is £550. No audition required.
• Summer School Musical Theatre (2 weeks). Courses take place in July/August; fee is £550. No audition required.
• Audition Technique (4-6 weeks). Courses take place in spring and autumn; fee is £180. No audition required.
• Perform: Acting (2 terms). Course fee is £700 with 6 hours of classes per week. Entry is by audition.
• Perform: Musical Theatre (2 terms). Course fee is £700 with 6 hours of classes per week. Entry is by audition.

Oxford School of Drama*

Sansomes Farm Studios, Woodstock,
Oxford OX20 1ER
tel (01993) 812883 *fax* (01993) 811220
email info@oxforddrama.ac.uk
website www.oxforddrama.ac.uk
Principal George Peck *Executive Director* Kate Ashcroft

Courses offered:
• 6-month Foundation Course in Acting which runs from September to March. Aimed at students aged 17 and over (most are 18-19 years old); the course covers acting methods and technique, movement, voice, singing, film and television, stage fighting and stage management. Course fee is £5,000 with 32 hours of classes per week for 22 weeks. Entry is by audition.
• 6-month Foundation Course in Musical Theatre, which runs from September to March. Aimed at students aged 17 and over (most are 18-19 years old), this course helps students develop a flexible, healthy voice, and introduces them to the range of techniques required to act through song. Course fee is £5450 plus VAT (2009/10), with 32 hours of classes per week for 22 weeks. Entry is by audition.

Pineapple Dance Studios

7 Langley Street, London WC2H 9JA
tel 020-7836 4004 *fax* 020-7836 0803
email studios@pineapple.uk.com
website www.pineapple.uk.com

Pineapple offers more classes than any other studio throughout Europe, and the widest variety of dance styles. The philosophy behind the creation of the Pineapple Dance Studios was to break down the elitist barriers surrounding dance, making it available to everyone – from the absolute beginner to the advanced and the professional dancer. All classes are open, so you do not need to book; you can just come along at any time and join a class. Everybody is welcome: Pineapple offers classes for all levels and all ages (from dancers who are 4 years of age to those in their 90s – its oldest member is currently 93!). Around 40 different varieties of dance styles are taught, at approx. 200 classes per week, ranging from classical ballet to street jazz, hip hop to Salsa, Egyptian dance to Bollywood grooves plus many more. *Opening hours*: Mon to Fri: 9am – 9pm; Sat: 9am – 6.30pm; Sun: 10am – 6pm.

The Questors Theatre Ealing

12 Mattock Lane, London W5 5BQ
tel 020-8567 0011 *fax* 020-8567 2275
email enquiries@questors.org.uk
website www.questors.org.uk
Principal David Emmet *Key contact* Andrea Bath (Executive Director)

Provides part-time training for actors in the context of a working theatre. Financial support is available from a private trust fund for a limited number of students.

Courses offered:

• Acting: Foundation and Performance (2 years). Course fee is £270 with 6 hours of classes per week. Entry is by audition.
• Introduction to Acting (1 year). Age range for entry is 17-20. Course fee is £135 with 3 hours of classes per week. Entry is by audition.

Richmond Drama School

Richmond Adult College, Parkshot,
Richmond TW9 2RE
tel 020-8439 8944
email Mark.Woolgar@racc.ac.uk
website www.richmonddramaschool.com
Key contact Mark Woolgar

Courses offered: Long-established Richmond Drama School Course incorporates an Access Course, and sends many students on to Honours Degree Courses at top drama schools, while others go straight into the profession. Up-to-date details of all courses are available from Mark Woolgar.

Rose Bruford College*

Lamorbey Park, Burnt Oak Lane, Sidcup DA15 9DF
tel 020-8308 2600 *fax* 020-8308 0542
email enquiries@bruford.ac.uk
website www.bruford.ac.uk
Principal Professor Michael Earley

Courses offered:

• Acting Summer School (2 weeks). Designed for participants over the age of 18 (16+ for non-residential students), this programme includes classes, rehearsals and workshops on voice, movement, acting and improvisation.

Royal Academy of Dramatic Art (RADA)*

62-64 Gower Street, London WC1E 6ED
tel 020-7636 7076 *fax* 020-7323 3865
email enquiries@rada.ac.uk
website www.rada.org
Key contact Sally Power

Courses offered:

• Acting Shakespeare (8 weeks). Designed for experienced actors, this course offers an opportunity to expand, explore and deepen awareness of Shakespeare's texts. Covers all aspects of vocal technique, with classes to develop the resonance and range of each student's voice. The last 2 weeks of the course are spent in full-time rehearsal for a workshop production culminating in 3 performances in a RADA theatre. Entry is deliberately restricted, and places are awarded by competitive audition. Students below the age of 18 are not normally accepted; most students are in their 20s. Course fee is £4500, which includes breakfast, lunch and refreshments Monday-Friday. Course takes place in June and July. *Audition requirements*: 1 speech from Shakespeare and 1 from a modern play, each lasting no longer than 3 minutes. *Audition fee*: £33
• The RADA Summer School (4 weeks). Based on exploring Shakespeare from an actor's point of view, this course mixes rehearsing scenes and speeches with intensive classes in essential acting skills. Students below the age of 18 are not normally accepted; most students are in their 20s. Course fee is £2560, which includes breakfast, lunch and refreshments Monday-Friday. Course takes place in July and August. No audition required.
• Skill Development through Classical Acting (3 weeks). This course explores the acting skills required to handle the complex texts of the English Classical Theatre. Each week, a director works on a different era in classical theatre: week 1 – Shakespeare; week 2 – Jacobean/Caroline tragedy; week 3 – Restoration comedy. Students also attend classes in voice and speech, movement, sword fighting and period dance. Students below the age of 18 are not normally accepted; there is no upper age limit. Course fee is £1750, which includes a light continental-style breakfast and lunch.
• Musical Theatre (5 days). This course is designed for intermediate and advanced singer-actors who have already received some formal vocal training and are intending to pursue a career in musical theatre. During the course, guidance on casting and help with audition repertoire is given. Students work with a singing tutor, director, choreographer and musical director, both in groups and individually, to develop

Training

the necessary skills required by the successful singer-actor in today's musical theatre. At the end of the course there is an informal presentation of selected pieces for an invited audience, followed by individual feedback. Course fee is £725.
• The RADA Contemporary Drama Summer School (10 days). This course provides the opportunity to work on modern or contemporary texts. Students work in groups led by a director, with support from a voice and a movement instructor. Other playwrights talk about their work during special evening sessions, describing their experience of working with actors and what they expect from them, following presentations of excerpts from their plays by RADA graduates. Students present rehearsed material and receive feedback from the director and the voice and movement teachers on the last day of the course. Students below the age of 18 are not normally accepted; there is no upper age limit. Course fee is £1250, which includes a light continental-style breakfast and lunch.

Theatre Royal Haymarket Masterclasses

Theatre Royal Haymarket, London SW1Y 4HT
tel 020-7389 9660 *fax* 020-7389 9697
email masterclass@trh.co.uk
website www.trh.co.uk/masterclass
Patrons Sir Peter Hall, Sir David Hare, Maureen Lipman CBE

Masterclass is an arts initiative which allows young people aged 17-30 to attend workshops and talks given by leading actors, directors, designers and writers working in theatre today. All events take place at the Theatre Royal Haymarket and are free of charge to young people aged 17-30. People over the age of 30 may also take part and contribute to the project by joining the Masterclass Friends scheme.

In addition to the masterclass events, the programme includes a longer-term new writing project and a series that gives career advice and support. Previous Masters have included Steven Berkoff, Simon Callow, Mike Leigh, Alan Rickman, Prunella Scales and Janet Suzman. For details of forthcoming events, consult the website.

Youngblood

Top Floor, 57 Paddington Street, Marylebone, London W1U 4HZ
tel 020-7193 3207
email info@youngblood.co.uk
website www.youngblood.co.uk

A company of fight directors and stage-combat teachers. Runs ongoing classes for professional actors in various locations around London. Also provides fight directors and trainers for film, television and theatre projects, including low-budget productions.

Private tutors and coaches

Acting Audition Success (Philip Rosch)

53 West Heath Court, North End Road,
London NW11 7RG
tel 020-8731 6686
website www.philiprosch.com

Specialises in Shakespeare; also offers expert career advice. Charges £50 per hour and gives generous extra time for free at the end of each lesson. Is happy to provide material for private students to use, and to answer minor follow-up queries. Teaches from home, about 3 minutes' walk away from Golders Green tube (bus routes 13, 82, 83, 102, 183, 210, 226, 240, 245, 260, 268, 328 and 460). "For more details about my work, the best thing is to call me so that I can explain in detail my working methods. I also send out extremely useful written information through the post." Has taught more than 1200 actors and aspiring actors over a 24-year period; is a highly experienced British-American actor (and acting tutor). Advises clients: "Truthful acting is simple, and involves just two things: how your character feels, and what your character wants. My teaching methods are highly effective in bringing actors to truthful performances."

Barbara Berkery

London N19
tel 020-7281 3139
email barbaraberkery@hotmail.com

Specialises in accents, voice and text. Details of fees and discounts are available upon enquiry. Happy to provide material for private students to use, and to answer minor follow-up queries at no extra charge. Teaches from home and/or studio, both of which are wheelchair accessible. Main teaching location is 10 minutes' walk from Holloway Road tube (bus routes 17, 43, 271 and 263). Further details are available from IMDb. Has taught hundreds of actors/aspiring actors over a period of 30 years, and possesses extensive experience both as an actress and as a director.

Irene Bradshaw

Welbeck Mansions, Inglewood Road,
West Hampstead, London NW6 1OX
tel/fax 020-7794 5721
email irene@irenebradshaw.fsnet.co.uk
website www.voice-power-works.co.uk

Specialises in audition technique, voice/production, RP and accents. Charges £40 per hour, which is a special rate for actors. Provides material for students to use, and all lessons are recorded to CD or memory stick. Is happy to answer minor follow-up queries. Teaches from home (unless a client is disabled, in which case will travel to theirs); the nearest tube is West Hampstead, a 5-minute walk. Bus routes are C11, 139 and 328.

Has taught "countless" actors and aspiring actors over 36 years. An actress for more than 20 years in film, television and theatre, she trained in the Linklater method of voice production at LAMDA with Kristin Linklater, sponsored by the Arts Council of Great Britain. Has taught at the City Lit, the Actors Centre and most of the leading stage and drama schools, as well as running her own theatre company, where she directed several plays in new writing as well as classics. Has trained numerous students for entry into drama school with considerable success, and has helped many actors find their voice.

Mel Churcher

mobile (07778) 773019
email melchurcher@hotmail.com
website www.melchurcher.com

Specialises in audition technique (stage and screen), voice (all aspects) and screen acting (teaching with camera, screen tests). Please ring or email to enquire about rates.

Teaches at home, at the client's home, or at the Drill Hall/Actors Centre. The nearest tube is Northwood Hills (home) or Goodge Street (Drill Hall). More details are available from **www.imdb.com** and from own website.

Has taught thousands of actors and aspiring actors over 22 years. Has worked as an actor and theatre director; taught at the major drama schools and at the Actors Centre; run national and international workshops; and authored two books, *A Screen Acting Workshop* plus DVD (Nick Hern Books, 2010), and *Acting for Film: Truth 24 Times a Second* (Virgin Books, 2003). Holds an MA in Performing Arts (Middlesex) and in Voice Research (CSSD). "I am happy to help with most aspects of auditioning and working in theatre and film. I can can advise on understanding the differences between film and theatre, film technique, and building confidence and overcoming nerves."

MJ Coldiron

54 Millfields Road, London E5 0SB
mobile (07941) 920498
fax 020-8533 1506
email jiggs@blueyonder.co.uk

Offers audition coaching for professional and aspiring actors; advice about theatre and performance training in the US and the UK; and coaching in acting technique, public speaking and presentation skills. Charges £40 per hour (3 sessions for £100). Occasional group workshops. Can provide material for clients and is happy to receive minor follow-up queries. Teaches from home, with the nearest rail station being Hackney Central Overground. Has taught hundreds of aspiring actors over 25 years: please make contact for more details. Advises clients: "The theatrical profession is very demanding and is not to be sought for fame or fortune. It is also very competitive and you must work hard, but if you have talent, desire and discipline I can help you to improve your technique and gain in confidence."

Jerry Cox MA BA PGCE
4 Stevenson Close, Barnet, Herts EN5 1DR
mobile (07957) 654027
email jerrymarwood@hotmail.com

Specialises in audition technique and voice. Charges £25 per hour or £40 for 2 hours. Is happy to provide material for private students to use, and to answer minor follow-up queries. Teaches from home or from the client's home. The nearest railway is Oakleigh Park/Totteridge & Whetstone – a 10-15 minute walk from the main teaching location. Bus route 383. Further details of work can be found in *Contacts*. Has taught 300-500 actors and aspiring actors over 8 years, and worked as an actor, deviser and director; lots of film, theatre, TIE and touring experience. Advises clients: "To paraphrase Bella Merlin, get the process right, and the results look after themselves."

Luan de Burgh
West London
mobile (07976) 809693
email luan@luandeburgh.com
website www.luandeburgh.com

Specialises in voice, presentation and audition technique. Charges £50 per hour for recent graduates, £60 for working actors, and £100 for business professionals. Discounts may be available; please call to discuss. Prefers to be paid by direct online transfer. Is happy to provide material for private students to use where appropriate, and to answer minor follow-up queries at no extra cost. Works from the client's home or place of work (rooms can be sourced, but this adds to the cost). Nearest overground and tube station is Victoria, 5 minutes' walk from the main teaching location. Trained at Webber Douglas, Lecoq and CSSD.

Bridget De Courcy
19 Muswell Road, London N10

Taught singing at the Actors Centre, Covent Garden for 19 years.

Jane de Florez, LGSM PGDip
London (Waterloo) SE1
tel 020-7803 0835
email janedeflorez@fsmail.net
website www.singingteacherlondon.com;
www.janedeflorez.co.uk

Specialises in singing technique, repertoire, performance, auditions. Charges £45 per hour. Is happy to provide material for private students to use, and to answer minor follow-up queries at no extra charge. Teaches from home studio, which is 4 minutes' walk from Waterloo overground and Waterloo and Southwark tubes. Bus routes are 100, 45, 63, 176, 76, 139, 243, 68 and 168. Has taught hundreds of actors and aspiring actors for the past 15 years, and now sees at least 10 pupils each week who are performers or aspiring performers. Teaches a strong, versatile technique that is suitable for all types of music. Most students go into classical, musical theatre and cabaret.

Patricia Doyle
19 Cranfield Road, Brockley, London SE4 1TN
tel 020-8691 2839 *mobile* (07941) 108942
email patricia.doyle@virgin.net

Has been teaching for more than 20 years. Specialises in audition technique and as a coach for young performers working or wishing to work in film. Offers career advice, guidance on how to approach looking for work, personal preparation for the profession, and honesty and encouragement. Rates are negotiable; cheque payments preferred. Happy to provide material for private students to use, and to answer minor follow-up queries after a lesson.

Teaches at home, at the client's home or at other locations. Brockley is the nearest railway station, approx. 4 minutes' walk away: trains go from Charing Cross and Leicester Square. Bus routes are 24, 171, 172.

Trained at RADA, an actress for over 25 years (RSC, NT, Royal Court). Has worked in film, radio and television, and as a director for professional companies and in Drama School and Dance training. Director and Co-director for Northern Ballet Theatre: the website **www.nbt.co.uk** offers links to further details and information.

Simon Dunmore
email Simon.Dunmore@btinternet.com
website www.Simon.Dunmore.btinternet.co.uk

Specialises in audition technique (primarily for drama school entry) but also expert in other aspects of 'actor-promotion' – letter- and CV-writing, interview techniques and much more. Has a vast collection of audition speeches, a large library of plays and a wide knowledge of drama schools and the profession.

"Once I get to know you in person, I can help you:
  – by commenting upon your current collection of speeches
  – find speeches that are suitable for you
  – with your choices of where to apply
  – get the best from your chosen speeches
  – with your overall presentation (believe me, this can make the difference between success and failure)."

Is happy to answer minor queries before and after meeting. Charges £40 per contact-hour, teaches at home, and lives just north of London – 20-30 minutes from King's Cross. Has taught around 1000 students over the last 15 years, in drama schools and privately. Also has 20 years' experience as a director in regional theatres, is author of *An Actor's Guide to Getting Work* and the *Alternative Shakespeare Auditions* series, and is the creator and Consultant Editor of *Actors' Yearbook*.

Diana Fairfax

62 Muswell Avenue, London N10 2EL
tel 020-8883 0817
email dianafairfax@gmail.com
website www.dianafairfax.co.uk

Specialises in audition technique. Offers "a high level of support and encouragement, always giving extra time at the end of the hour to discuss any questions arising from the session, or any acting or career issues". Charges £45 per hour. Is happy to provide material for private students to use, and to answer minor follow-up queries after a lesson.

Teaches at home, which is being made wheelchair-accessible – please enquire. The nearest tube/railway stations are Highgate and Bounds Green; a short bus ride on routes 104, 43 and 134. Has taught around 1000 actors over 15 years. Has wide classical and commercial experience in both stage and television, and has worked at the Actors Centre for many years. LGSM Drama Teacher's diploma.

Julia Gaunt

116 Nottingham Road, Selston, Notts NG16 6BX
tel (01773) 775156 *mobile* (07712) 624083
email joolsmusicbiz@aol.com
website www.joolsmusicbiz.com

Specialises in musical theatre, voice and performance; a subsidiary of Jools Music Biz. Charges a minimum of £30, and a maximum of £45, per hour, with discounted rates for block bookings. Happy to provide material for clients and to receive minor follow-up enquiries. Teaches from home, but will travel (if travel costs paid) for a company or group. The nearest railway station is Alfreton, and the house has stairs with a handrail. More information can be found on the music teachers' or LCPA websites. Has taught hundreds of aspiring actors both privately and in association with colleges and universities. Is a member of the British Voice Association and has run many workshops and masterclasses. Advises clients: "Remember the 3 Ds: Determination, Dedication and Discipline."

John Grayson

2 Jubilee Road, St Johns, Worcester WR2 4LY
mobile (07702) 188031
email jgtutor-performer@yahoo.co.uk
website www.JohnLGrayson.com

Specialises in audition technique, voice, accents, singing, public speaking and coaching. Charges £21 per hour. Can provide material for students and is happy to receive minor follow-up queries. Can teach from home or from a client's house. The nearest station is Worcester Foregate Street (there is a good service from Birmingham), from which the house is 10-15 minutes' walk. Has taught around 20 aspiring actors in about 6 years. Please see the website for more details. Is happy to advise students on how to survive when not working.

Martin Harris

32 Baxter Road, Sale, Manchester M33 3AL
tel 0161-969 1444 *mobile* (07788) 723570
email martin@auditioncoach.co.uk
website www.auditioncoach.co.uk

Specialises in audition technique and selection and direction of audition pieces. Offers group acting classes as well as one-to-one tuition for aspiring and professional actors. Also teaches sight reading and gives advice about CVs, agents and jobs. Charges £25 per hour, with a discount of 20% if the client pays for 10 sessions in advance. Accepts payment with cash or cheque, or via Internet banking.

Is happy to provide material for private students to use, and will answer minor follow-up queries at no extra charge. Teaches at home, or at the client's home (with a small extra charge). The home office is wheelchair-accessible. Sale metrolink is the nearest station, around 5 minutes' walk from the office (bus routes: 16, 18, 18A, 19, 41, 86, 99, 245, 263, 264, 266, 267, 268 and 272). Has taught more than 200 actor clients over 10 years. "I trained as an actor at Birmingham School of Acting, and have worked as an actor and director since 1995. I am the current Artistic Director of Rocket Theatre in Manchester."

Daniel Hoffmann-Gill

London
mobile (07946) 433903
email danielhg@gmail.com
website http://danielhg.blogspot.com

Specialises in actor confidence-building, improvisation technique, removing actors' blocks, audition technique, casting technique and various practitioner-centred methods such as Guskin, Meisner, Lecoq and Donnellan.

Has been a professional actor for more than 12 years, working in film, TV and theatre, and has taught actors for over 10 years. Focuses on one-to-one work, aimed at enabling the actor to do themselves and their imagination justice – also, on practical assistance in audition technique and how to do the very best you can in any casting situation, "no matter how bizarre". Uses real casting briefs and exercises, for students to try out their ideas. Currently teaches at the Central School of Speech and Drama as a guest lecturer, at the Actors Centre and for the National

Theatre, as well as for numerous London agents. References from previous students are available on request.

Charges £40 per hour, with special packages available for long-term work or working towards drama school entry: these are tailored on an individual basis, so please email for details. Works from home or from the client's home, and occasionally uses performance spaces, depending on the project. All locations used are wheelchair-accessible. The nearest stations are Wood Green or Bowes Park (bus routes 141, 329, 232 and 121). Has taught around 200 actors. Advises clients that "hard graft and positive attitude go a long way in a tough, tough industry".

Barbara Houseman
34 Shawbury Road, London SE22 9DH
mobile (07767) 843737
email barbarahouseman@hotmail.com

Specialises in audition technique and voice. Also teaches in the areas of confidence-building, presence, dealing with one's inner critic, acting, dealing with classical texts, and preparing for TV/film roles. Charges £60-100 per hour and may offer special packages for block bookings. Is happy to provide material for private students to use, and to answer minor follow-up queries afer a lesson.

Teaches at home, which is wheelchair-accessible. The nearest station is East Dulwich – a 10-15 minute walk. Bus routes are 176, 185 and 40. Has taught around 800 actors and aspiring actors over 29 years, and authored 2 books: *Finding Your Voice* and *Tackling Text and Subtext*. Worked as a Voice Coach for the RSC (1991-97) and as an Associate Director at the Young Vic. "I can advise on overcoming blocks, and becoming the actor you want to be."

Charlie Hughes-D'Aeth
22 Osborne Road, Brighton BN1 6LQ
mobile (07811) 010963
email chdaeth@aol.com

Charges £45 per hour; discounts are available for long-term students. Is happy to provide material for private students to use, and to answer minor follow-up queries. Teaches from home. The nearest station is Preston Park/Brighton (bus route 5B). Has taught hundreds of actors and aspiring actors over 18 years. Is a director and playwright, and has been a performer and musician. Also teaches playwriting.

Desmond Jones
20 Thornton Avenue, London W4 1QG
tel/fax 020-8747 3537
email enquiries@desmondjones.com
website www.desmondjones.com

Specialises in physical audition techniques and mime and physical theatre. One of the founders of physical theatre; has run his own School of Mime and Physical Theatre for 25 years, with expertise in all aspects of movement. Charges are negotiable, with various packages and discounts available; please make contact for more information. Will provide clients with occasional worknotes and is happy to answer minor follow-up queries. Teaches out of home (a 3-minute walk from Turnham Green station, bus routes 94, 27, H91, 191, 267), or the home of the client – whichever is more suitable. Has taught more than 2500 aspiring actors over 40 years. Advises clients: "Do it now!"

Lawrence Lambert
c/o The Actors Centre, 1A Tower Street, London WC2
mobile (07539) 239451
email lawrielambo@yahoo.co.uk

Specialises in audition, creating character, improvisation, text and voice. Work detail can be for beginners, professionals or individuals returning to the profession. Charges £35 per hour, with a discount for block bookings. Happy to provide material for private students to use, and to answer minor follow-up queries after a lesson.

Will teach at home, at the client's home, or at the Actors Centre; all are wheelchair-accessible. Nearest tube/railway station is Arsenal (home) or Leicester Square (Actors Centre). Bus route is 19.

Has taught hundreds of actors and aspiring actors over 22 years of teaching. Experienced in stage, television and feature film, and is an East 15 graduate. "I cater for all types of experience – from novice to seasoned professional."

Marj McDaid
Stoke Newington, London N16
tel 020-7923 4929 *mobile* (07815) 993203
email marj@voicings.co.uk
website www.voicings.co.uk

Specialises in voice (Estill method – safe techniques for shouting, screaming, etc.), character work, and accents (especially Irish and American). Charges £40 per hour; discounts can be arranged when a number of sessions paid for in advance. Prefers cash or cheque. Is happy to provide audition speeches (not songs) for private students to use, and will answer minor follow-up queries at no extra charge. Teaches from home, which is 10 mins from Stoke Newington (overground; Highbury & Islington tube). Bus routes include 67, 73, 76, 149, 243, 393 and 476. Has taught hundreds of actors and aspiring actors over 20 years.

Martin McKellan
Neal Street, London WC2
mobile (07973) 372052
email martinmckellan@yahoo.co.uk

Specialises in auditions, acting classes and all aspects of voice work (accent and dialogue a particular area of expertise). Rates are negotiable and offers are available; please make contact for full details. Is happy to provide material for private students to use, and to answer minor follow-up queries at no extra charge. Will teach from home, from a client's home or at another location. Covent Garden is the nearest tube station, 3 minutes' walk away. Has taught thousands of actors and aspiring actors over the past 15 years, and has extensive experience as a freelance acting/voice coach working in the West End and in Regional Theatre and for both film and television.

Sally Mortemore

7 Groton Road, Earlsfield, London SW18 4ER
tel 020-8576 2192 *mobile* (07973) 835292
email mortemores@aol.com
website www.sallymortemore.com

Fully qualified voice coach and professional actress; specialises in Shakespeare and is very experienced in voice, audition coaching, text and accent softening. Charges £30 per hour or £40 for 1.5 hours. Offers a free half-hour consultation for new students, and a discounted rate of £20 per hour for drama school leavers in their first year as a professional. Is happy to provide material for students to use, and to answer minor follow-up queries. Teaches from home, which is wheelchair-accessible; the nearest station is Earlsfield, only 2 minutes away. Has taught 200+ actors and aspiring actors over 6 years. More details are available from *Contacts*.

Rebecca Semark

Epping, Essex
mobile (07956) 850330
email rebecca@semark.biz
website www.semark.biz

Specialises in audition technique, voice, and singing (to student level, not professional). Charges from £25 up to £40 per half hour, depending on whether the student is a child or working adult. Offers discounts to sibling groups. Fortnightly teaching is preferred, as this gives more time to do work and allows for other commitments. Is happy to provide material for private students to use, and to answer minor follow-up queries. Teaches from home; the closest station is Epping (Central Line) – a 5-10 minute walk. Has taught hundreds of actors and aspiring actors over a 19-year period. Since 1973 has worked extensively in theatre, especially in Musical Theatre (comedy).

Ros Simmons

120 Hillfield Avenue, Crouch End, London N8 7DN
tel 020-8347 8089
email info@realspeaking.co.uk
website www.realspeaking.co.uk

Specialises in accents, voice and auditions, as well as spoken English skills for those with Englsh as a second language. Charges £55 per hour with a reduction to £50 per hour if a block of 4 sessions is booked in advance. Student rate is £45 per hour. A one-off 1.5-hour accent coaching session is also

available, at £75. Provides material for students' use, and is happy to answer minor follow-up queries. Teaches from home, with Finsbury Park the nearest tube (overground, Hornsey Station on Tottenham Lane, just around the corner from the premises). Buses to Finsbury Park tube are the W3 to Tottenham Lane or the W7 to Crouch End Broadway. Has taught around 1000 actors and aspiring actors, in drama schools and privately, over a period of 9 years. Trained as an actor at the Polytechnic School of Theatre in Manchester, and has worked extensively in theatre, film, TV and radio.

Speak Good English Well

School of Economic Science Building, 11-13 Mandeville Place, London W1V 3AJ
mobile (07976) 805976
email neville@speakwell.co.uk
website www.speakwell.co.uk

Specialises in audition technique and voice. Dialogue coach, Shakespeare, musical comedy and lyrical interpretation. Services include coaching in elocution, communication techniques and self-awareness; also the establishment of confidence and natural performance. Fee details are available on application. Offers special packages and coaching in stage, TV and radio techniques. Teaches from the Mandeville Place address, which is wheelchair-accessible. The nearest station is Bond Street underground, around 3 minutes' walk away (bus route 10). Has taught hundreds of actors and aspiring actors over 16 years. Advises clients: "Have complete faith and confidence in *yourself*. Continually work on voice and movement and penetration of Shakespeare – the greatest master teacher."

Giles Taylor

mobile (07973) 960681
email gilestaylor@ukgateway.net

Specialises in Shakespeare and audition speeches. Is a verse specialist, but works too on prose texts – classical and modern. Charges £40 per hour. Discounts are available: 3 sessions for £100, and students £30 per hour. Is happy to provide material for private students to use, and to answer minor follow-up queries after a lesson.

Teaches from home, but other locations can be arranged (please note that these may incur travel costs). The nearest tube station is Highgate and bus routes are 43 and 134. Has taught more than 100 actors and aspiring actors over 6 years. "I have been in the business for nearly 20 years, working in theatre, music theatre, television, film and radio. I am a regular teacher at the Actors Centre."

Paul Todd

3 Rosehart Mews, London W11 3JN
tel 020-7229 9776
email paultodd@talk21.com

Specialises in acting, singing, music theory,

drumming and audition technique. Charges £36 per hour. Discounts for block booking or lessons close together. Teaches from home. The nearest tube station is Notting Hill and bus routes are 7, 70, 23, 27, 28, 31 and 328. More details about services offered are available via Google search. Has taught hundreds of actor/singers and aspiring actor/singers. Extensive experience as MD, arranger, actor, musician and writer.

Genevieve Walsh

37 Kelvedon House, Guildford Road, Stockwell, London SW8 2DN
mobile (07801) 948864

Specialises in coaching for auditions and public speaking (presentation technique). Charges £30 per hour (£20 for students). Happy to help in the selection of material for students' use, and to answer minor follow-up queries, time permitting. Teaches from home (nearest station is Stockwell, a 5-minute walk away; bus routes 2 or 88). Has taught dozens of actors and aspiring actors over a 35-year period, and has extensive experience as an actor, teacher and director. "Know your material inside out and all the background to the speech. It is very basic advice, but it is essential."

Brendan Weakliam

23 Alders Close, Wanstead, London E11 3RZ
tel (07724) 558955
email brenweakliam@hotmail.com

Specialises in singing tuition – vocal technique, song interpretation and audition preparation. Charges £25 per hour, with reduced rates for low earners. Prefers students to provide their own material, but can provide songs on occasion when necessary. Is happy to answer minor follow-up queries at no extra charge. Teaches from home, which is 15 minutes' walk from Wanstead tube station. Bus routes are 101, 308 and W19. Has taught singers from all walks of life over a 10-year period. In addition to extensive singing performance and teaching qualifications, has trained

full-time as an actor and is a founder member of Aside Theatre Company. Recommends that actors auditioning for any part where they are required to sing, treat their songs exactly as they would a monologue, and look for the dramatic truth in every word.

Tessa Wood

43 Woodhurst Road, London W3 6SS
tel 020-8896 2659 *mobile* (07957) 207808
email TessaRosWood@aol.com

Specialises in physical voice including centring, alignment, tension release, breath, articulation, range, projection, tone. Also Standard English, RP and period RP, and audition technique. Fee is negotiable and there is a 20% discount for students and sometimes for actors who aren't working. Can provide copies of audition material, but generally does not lend books as they never seem to be returned. Will give minor follow-up advice for no extra charge. Teaches from home or the client's home (for an additional charge). Nearest train link is the Silverlink (North London Line) and the station, Acton Central, is 5 minutes away. Acton Town (Piccadilly/District Lines) is about 15-minutes' walk, and Acton Mainline (1 stop from Paddington) is about 10 minutes away. Many of the buses from Shepherd's Bush going in the direction of Ealing pass within 5-6 minutes of the house (route 207 plus others).

Has taught well over 2000 actors and aspiring actors over a 15-year period. Pursued a full-time acting career for 15 years, and still does some acting every year. Also directs the initial scene studios at Drama Studio London, and every year co-directs and voice-coaches an entry for the Sam Wannamaker Festival at The Globe. Has coached well-known TV presenters and actors on a one-to-one basis. "Whether or not an actor has full-time training (which I would highly recommend), they should keep up their process with classes, both one-to-one and in the form of group workshops."

An actor's toolkit

Compiled by Simon Dunmore

You need to organise the following essential items before you even get your first interview, let alone an agent and/or your first job. You should start planning for all these in good time, before the end of your training – ready for your first public production.

1. Join Equity! You can join (very cheaply) as a student member (see **www.equity.org.uk/ HowToJoin** and click on Student Membership) and, for a small extra fee, reserve your professional name: details of how to go about this are on the website.

2. A good, strong professional name. If you can't (or don't want to) use your real name, it's important to select an alternative that you're completely comfortable with.

3. Well-designed headed paper. Beatrice Warde, the passionate typography expert, said, "Typefaces are the clothes words wear." Find a typeface that 'dresses' your professional name well.

4. Secure and reliable telephone and Internet connections for professional use. *Note*: It is very important that your outgoing message and email address sound professional and not like hangovers from your adolescence.

5. A reliable computer with printer. *Tip*: Laser printers provide a much crisper quality when printing text – and laser toner is much cheaper, per page, than ink.

6. An up-to-date copy of *Actors' Yearbook*. *Tip*: It is worthwhile not only reading the rest of this book to get a feel for how different parts of the profession function, but also reading through websites.

7. A good set of photographs and sufficient copies. See Angus Deuchar's article and the introduction to Photographers and Repro Companies starting on page 375.

8. A well-laid-out and up-to-date CV. *Notes*: It's important to ensure that all spellings of proper names (directors, play titles, etc.) are correct. Also, to understand how to convert your CV into Portable Document Format (PDF) for email transmission.

9. A good standard letter that you can adapt for individual circumstances, and use in emails, etc. See Ian Liston's article *Marketing Yourself – A Producer's Viewpoint* on page 114.

10. Half-a-dozen (or more) varied audition speeches. See my *Effective Audition Speeches* article on page 134.

11. Half-a-dozen (or more) varied audition songs. See Jennifer Reischel's article *Cattle Calls and How to Survive Them* on page 143.

12. A mental list of things (not just acting ones) you could talk about in order to respond to the almost inevitable question(s), "What have you been doing recently?" and/or "Tell me a bit about yourself."

13. An entry in *Spotlight* – details at **www.spotlight.com/join**. *Note*: Entry into *Spotlight* is strictly limited to professionally trained and/or professionally experienced performers, and applications are always vetted.

14. A reasonable selection of clothes for interviews and auditions. Essentially, you need to feel comfortable and appropriately dressed for each individual circumstance … and you will face a wide variety of such circumstances.

15. A budget. The costs of the above can accumulate quite quickly – before you've earned

a penny. And there are many other minor things not listed: postage (see Postage Rates on page 10); Equity entry fee and annual subscription; subscriptions to *The Stage* and other professional publications; travel costs to interviews, and so on. All the above items can easily add up to much more money than you might think: you need to calculate your potential professional expenses and budget for them. *Notes*: Although many of the above are allowable against tax (see Philippe Carden's article *Tax & National Insurance for Actors* on page 408), don't forget to include your potential tax bill! Also, at the outset of your career, consider carefully the cost-effectiveness of items like personal websites, showreels, etc. These are only worthwhile if you have sufficient high-quality material that makes you look 'professional'. Also see Nancy Bishop's article, *Marketing and the Internet: maintaining your online presence* on page 372.

16. Sources of non-acting income that are flexible enough for you to drop at 24 hours' notice. At an educated guess, only about 10 per cent of the profession earn a living *solely* from acting. And, even for those, incomes can be incredibly variable – £200 one year to over £20,000 the next, to quote just one example (see Andrew Piper's article *Between Engagements* on page 415).

17. A working knowledge of the nation's transport systems (especially London's): you will often not know where you might be required for audition/interview (even work) until very late in the day. *Tip*: As a general rule it is wise to double your estimated travelling time to allow for the almost inevitable foul-ups.

18. A great deal of patience, persistence, determination, cunning and resourcefulness.

19. A stoical source of solace for the bad times. *Tip*: Find another activity that absorbs you as much as acting does.

20. A copy of my *An Actor's Guide To Getting Work* for reading on the loo (published by A &C Black).

General points:

(a) Can you organise yourself? Acting can be an instant business. For days/weeks/months/years nothing happens, and then a few minutes/hours/days/weeks/months/years later it can *all* be happening. You must always be ready, but not constantly on tenterhooks. In spite of the popular image of the chaotic, dizzy actor, you have to be personally organised or you could significantly harm your employment prospects.

(b) As an actor you are your own business. You are not only your own work-force, but also your publicity and public relations office, accountancy division, transport manager, and – above all – your managing director. Of course, you may well have an agent, an accountant, etc., but none of these people can do anything unless you give them clear direction. You are finally responsible for your success or failure in the business.

Simon Dunmore has been directing productions for over 30 years – nearly 20 years as a resident director in regional theatres and, more recently, working freelance. In that time there have been more than 200 productions (of all styles, colours, shapes and sizes), most recently several Drama School Showcases, Maugham's *Home and Beauty* and new plays about sex, WB Yeats' up-and-down relationship with Maud Gonne, one set inside a pyramid, and another about Bismarck. Past favourites include: *The Promise* (Alexei Arbuzov), *Antigone* (Jean Anouilh), a seven-handed version of *Antony & Cleopatra* and too many others to mention. He also teaches acting, and has worked in many drama schools and other training establishments around the country. He has written several books: *An Actor's Guide to Getting Work* (now in its fourth edition), the *Alternative Shakespeare Auditions* series, and is the Consultant Editor for *Actors' Yearbook*.

www.simon.dunmore.btinternet.co.uk

Agents and casting directors
Introduction

Actors have probably existed since before the invention of writing; actors' agents have only been around since the invention of the telephone, just over a century ago. Prior to this, work-seeking actors had to make themselves known in person to potential employers – for instance, certain hostelries in the Covent Garden area of central London were well-known 'talent-spotting' haunts. Actors would also 'catch a ride' with one of the touring companies in the hope of proving themselves to the manager – and then being put on the payroll. Others would pay managers to let them play small parts, in the hope of being noticed. All this meant a lot of hard work and/or expense (let alone the time needed to earn his/her living by other means) for the pre-electronic-age actor. The invention of actors' agents seemed to fill a vital gap.

In the 1970s, a number of actors, dissatisfied with the (by then) traditional agent system, formed the first co-operative agencies (see page 78). This apparently simple idea – with all members taking turns to 'man' the office – took a while to become established. Like many 'simple ideas', the pioneers found that there were more complications involved than they'd initially envisaged, and employers were slow to accept the idea. Nearly forty years later, the best 'co-ops' have as much professional credibility as their conventional counterparts.

It used to be the case that only the biggest companies used casting directors. The administrative burden inherent in running such a company (let alone directing productions) meant that assistance in the casting process became essential. The 1990s saw a rise in the use of casting directors and in the number of freelancers working on short-term contracts: most of the latter work in a wide variety of fields.

The simple fact is that a significant proportion of properly paid acting work is 'brokered' by casting directors and agents.

Agents and casting directors have very distinct functions – see the articles. The term 'casting agents' is used to describe walk-on agents who take the responsibility for casting walk-ons/extras in television and film. They have client bases comprising lots of different types, and on request can supply a suitable crowd for any occasion. Thus they fulfil the roles of both agent and casting director for non-speaking parts that don't need to be auditioned.

Agents

A good agent understands contracts, knows the current rates in every field of work and – most importantly – has plenty of professional contacts and access to far more casting information than most individuals can ever possess. Directors and casting directors rely on the agents they know and trust to help with the filtering process of whom to interview. A good agent will work hard at promoting each of his/her clients; in return, it is not unreasonable that they charge commission on every contract they negotiate for you – generally, 10-20 per cent (plus VAT, if appropriate). A good agent will also (a) have only as many clients as they can reasonably handle, and (b) ensure that they have a good range of ages and types of actors in order to cover as many casting opportunities as possible.

When you are seeking representation, it is advisable to contact agents by post in the first instance – unless specifically informed otherwise. It is a good idea to include a separate 10x8in (25x20cm) photograph, and it is important that all your enclosures give your name and the best way to contact you (not a long list of confusing alternatives). Agents receive many requests for representation, and photographs can become separated from their accompanying letters and CVs, so proper labelling is essential.

Use the listings that follow to (a) target your submission as accurately as possible (for example, by writing to a specific, named person), (b) check for any details that could inform the content of your letter, and (c) find out whether each would be interested in any extras, like a showreel. Time spent checking such details can save money and enhance your chances of being noticed more than the next person. Unless you have a good collection of professional credits, it is generally best to write to agents when there's an opportunity for them to see you performing in something.

If you are invited to meet an agent, that is often a good sign. You should approach the occasion in much the same way as you would an interview for a production. The major difference is that you should be prepared to ask (reasonable) questions – rates of commission, for instance.

When seeking representation, it can be a good idea to target only those agencies that you think might suit you. For instance, might you feel lost in a large agency, but feel more comfortable with a smaller one? On the other hand, some larger agencies have huge 'clout' and can be the first 'port of call' for the casting of prestigious productions.

When you've been taken on by an agent, it is important to establish how your working relationship will function. Be clear about any areas of work that you don't want to be suggested for, discuss your availability for auditions and interviews, agree how much promotion you should do for yourself, and so on.

These listings only contain agents who represent adult actors – there are many others who represent children, models, extras and so on.

21st Century Vaux Casting
The Corn Exchange, Fenwick Street,
Liverpool L2 7QS
tel 0151-258 1679 *fax* 0151-231 1067
email mail@21stcenturyactors.co.uk
Key personnel David Williamson

Established in 1991, the agency represents 20 actors.
Areas of work include theatre, television, film,
commercials, corporate and voice-overs.

Will consider attending performances at venues in
Greater London and the North West with at least 1
week's notice. Accepts submissions (with CVs and
photographs) from actors previously unknown to the
company sent by post or email. Will also accept
showreels, voicereels, and invitations to view
individual actors' websites. *Commission*: 7.5%

A&J Management
242A The Ridgeway, Botany Bay, Enfield EN2 8AP
tel 020-8342 0542 *fax* 020-8342 0842
email info@ajmanagement.co.uk
website www.ajmanagement.co.uk
Managing Director Jackie Michael *Key
personnel* Joanne Michael, Hannah Liebeskind

Established in 1984. 3 agents represent actors. Areas
of work include theatre, musicals, television, film,
commercials, corporate and voice-overs.

Will consider attending performances at venues
within Greater London with a minimum of 2 weeks'
notice. Accepts submissions (with CVs and
photographs) from actors previously unknown to the
company if sent by post. Invitations to view
individual actors' websites are also accepted.
Commission: 15% plus VAT

June Abbott Associates
Bowling Green Walk, 40 Pitfield Street,
London N1 6EU
tel 020-7729 7999
email jaa@thecourtyard.org.uk
website www.thecourtyard.org.uk
Agent June Abbott *Assistant Agent* Tanya Parkin

Established in 1994. 2 agents represent 50 actors.
Areas of work include theatre, musicals, television,
film, commercials, corporate and voice-overs.

Attendance at performances is dependent on
potential client submissions/interviews. Accepts
submissions (with CVs and photographs) from actors
previously unknown to the company if sent by post.
Enclose an sae if a reply is required, and for the
return of CVs and photographs. Showreels and
voicereels should only be sent on request. Actors
should only apply if they have training, and will only
be contacted if the agency is interested. Recommends
the photographer Peter Simpkin (see entry under
Photographers and repro companies on page 386 for
further details). *Commission*: Theatre 10%; Voice-
Over and Radio 12%; Film and TV 15%

Access Artiste Management Ltd
11-15 Betterton Street, Covent Garden,
London WC2H 9BP

tel 020- 7866 5444
email mail@access-uk.com
website www.access-uk.com
Manager Sarah Bryan

Established in 1999. Areas of work include theatre,
musicals, television, film, commercials, corporate.
Also represent musical directors, composers and
playwrights.

Will consider attending performances in Greater
London and elsewhere with 1 month's notice.
Accepts submissions (with CVs and photographs)
from professional actors previously unknown to the
company. Showreels, voicereels and details of
individual actors' websites should only be sent upon
request. Welcomes enquiries from disabled actors.

Acting Associates
71 Hartham Road, London N7 9JJ
tel 020-7607 3562 *fax* 020-7607 3562
email Fiona@actingassociates.co.uk
website www.actingassociates.co.uk
Agent Fiona Farley

Established in 1988. 1 agent represents 45-50 actors.

Will consider attending performances with 1 week's
notice. Accepts submissions (with CVs and
photographs) from actors previously unknown to the
company if sent by post. Recommends the
photographer Catherine Shakespeare Lane (see entry
under *Photographers and repro companies* on page 375
for further details). *Commission*: Theatre 10%; Other
15%

Actors International Ltd
The White House, 52-54 Kennington Oval,
London SE11 5SW
tel 020-3268 0023
email mail@actorsinternational.co.uk
Agents Kay Potter, Ruth Robinson

Established in 2008. 3 agents represent around 80
actors. Areas of work include theatre, musicals,
television, film, commercials and corporate.

Will attend performances within Greater London
given as much notice as possible. Welcomes letters
(with CVs and photographs) from individual actors
previously unknown to the company, sent by post or
email. "Our office is at the top of a building with no
lift, so it is inaccessible to anyone with walking
difficulties. We would consider representing actors
with disabilities that would not prevent them from
coming to the office." *Commission*: Theatre 10%; TV,
Film and Commercials 15%

Actors Ireland
165 Ormeau Road, Crescent Arts Centre,
Belfast BT7 1SQ
tel 028-9024 8861 *fax* 028-9024 8861
email actorsireland@aol.com
website www.actorsireland.net

Established in 2001. 2 agents represent 90 actors.
Areas of work include theatre, musicals, television,
film, commercials, corporate and voice-overs.

Agents and casting directors

Will consider attending performances at venues in Northern Ireland. Accepts submissions (with CVs and photographs) from actors previously unknown to the company if sent by post. Will also accept invitations to view individual actors' websites. *Commission*: Theatre 5%; TV 10%

Actors World Casting

13 Briarbank Road, London W13 0HH
tel 020-8998 2579
email katherine@actors-world-production.com
Agent Katherine Pageon

Established in 2005. 1 agent represents 70 actors. Areas of work include theatre, musicals, television, film, commercials, corporate, voice-overs.

Will consider attending performances in Greater London with at least 2 weeks' notice. Notices of performances should be sent via email. Accepts submissions sent via email (with CVs and 1 photograph only) from actors previously unknown to the company. Invitations to view individual actors' websites also accepted, and follow-up calls welcomed – as are enquiries from disabled actors. *Commission*: Theatre 10%; Other 15%.

Actual Management

The Studio, 63A Ladbroke Road, London W11 3PD
tel 020-7243 1166 *fax* 0870-874 1149
email info@actualproject.com
website www.actualmanagement.co.uk

Established in 2002. 2 agents represent 50 actors. Areas of work include theatre, television, film and commercials.

Will consider attending performances at venues in Greater London with at least 2 weeks' notice. Accepts submissions (with CVs and photographs) from actors previously unknown to the company sent by post or email. Will also accept showreels, voicereels, and invitations to view individual actors' websites.

AFA Associates

Unit 101A, Business Design Centre, 52 Upper Street, London N1 0QH
tel 020-7682 3677 *mobile* (07904) 962779
email afa-associates@hotmail.com
Agent Rhiannon Mosson

Established in 2009. Works in theatre, film, TV, commercials, corporate, musicals and promos.

Welcomes performance notices within the Greater London area if given at least 7 days' notice. Accepts approaches from actors by post and email, and welcomes showreels and invitations to view individual actors' websites. Represents actors with disabilities.

The Agency

47 Adelaide Road, Dublin 2 Eire
tel 353-1661 8535 *fax* 353-1676 0052
email info@tagency.ie
website www.the-agency.ie
Directors Teri Hayden, Karl Hayden

Established in 1982. 2 agents represent 80+ actors in film, television, theatre and voice overs.

Welcomes performance notices for shows in Dublin and London with 2 weeks' notice. Welcomes representation enquiries (with CVs and photographs) by post or email. Happy to receive follow-up calls, showreels, invitations to view individual actors' websites, and enquiries from disabled actors. *Commission*: 10%

Alexander Personal Management

Pinewood Studio, Pinewood Road, Iver Heath, Bucks SL0 0NH
tel (01753) 639204 *fax* (01753) 639205
email apm@apmassociates.net
website www.apmassociates.net

Casting and Personal Management. Established in 1989, and representing British and International actors, singers, dancers and presenters with extensive film, television, commercial, voice-over and theatre credits. Will consider submissions with CVs and photographs.

All Talent – Sonia Scott Agency

Unit 325, 95 Morrison Street, Glasgow G5 8BE
tel 0141-418 1074 *mobile* (07971) 337074
email enquiries@alltalentuk.co.uk
website www.alltalentuk.co.uk

Established in 2005. 2 agents represent 50-60 actors. Also represents other skills within the profession.

Will consider attending performances in Central London and Glasgow with at least 2-3 weeks' notice. Accepts submissions (with CVs and photographs) from actors previously unknown to the company; postal submissions preferred. Invitations to view showreels or voicereels and individual actors' websites also accepted, and follow-up calls welcomed. Welcomes enquiries from disabled actors. *Commission*: 15%

Anita Alraun Representation

5th Floor, 28 Charing Cross Road, London WC2H 0DB
tel 020-7379 6840 *fax* 020-7379 6865
Sole Proprietor/Agent Anita Alraun

1 agent represents a varying number of actors. Areas of work include theatre, musicals, film, television, commercials, radio drama, corporate and some voice-overs.

Attendance at performances is dependent on potential client submissions/interviews. Accepts submissions (with CV, photograph and sae – essential for reply) by post only from trained/experienced actors previously unknown to the company. Emailed submissions will not be considered. Showreels and voicereels should be sent only if requested, following interview. *Commission*: Radio 10%; Theatre 10-12.5%; Film and TV 12.5%; Commercials 15%

Alvarez Management

33 Ludlow Way, London N2 0JZ
tel 020-8883 2206 *fax* 020-8444 2646

Established in 1990. 2 agents represent 55 actors. Areas of work include theatre, musicals, television, film, commercials, corporate and voice-overs.

Will consider attending performances at venues within Greater London with 3-4 weeks' notice. Accepts submissions (with CVs, photographs and sae) from actors previously unknown to the company if sent by post. "When you are on the phone, please introduce yourself." "Have a really decent photograph taken." *Commission*: Theatre and Radio 10%; Film and TV 12.5%; Commercials 15%

ALW Associates

1 Grafton Chambers, Grafton Place,
London NW1 1LN
tel 020-7388 7018 *fax* 020-7813 1398
email alw_carolpaul@talktalk.net

Established in 1977 as Vernon Conway Ltd. Sole representation of 35 actors. Areas of work include theatre, musicals, television, film and commercials.

Will consider attending performances at venues within Greater London and occasionally elsewhere with 1 week's notice. Accepts submissions (with CVs and photographs) from actors previously unknown to the company sent by post or email. Also accepts invitations to view individual actors' websites. Showreels and voicereels should only be sent on request. *Commission*: Theatre and Radio 10-12.5%; Film and TV 12.5%; Commercials 15%

Amber Personal Management Ltd

28 St Margaret's Chambers, 5 Newton Street,
Manchester M1 1HL
tel 0161-228 0236, 020-7734 7887 *fax* 0161-228 0235
email info@amberltd.co.uk
website www.amberltd.co.uk
Principal Agent Sally Sheridan *Agent* Jasmine Parris
Associate Agent Estelle Jenkins

Works in theatre, musicals, television, film, commercials, corporate and voice-over. 3 agents represent 90-100 actors. Recommends the photographer John Nicholls (868online@googlemail.com). Will consider attending performances in Manchester, Leeds and Liverpool if given a minimum of 2 weeks' notice.

Welcomes letters (with CVs and photographs) from individual actors previously unknown to the company if sent by post. Does not welcome email approaches or follow-up telephone calls. Encourages enquiries from actors with disabilities. Will accept showreels, voicereels and invitations to view individual actors' websites. *Commission*: Recorded Media (TV/Film/Commercial) 15%; Theatre, Musicals, Corporate 10%

The American Agency

14 Bonny Street, London NW1 9PG
tel 020-7485 8883 *fax* 020-7482 4666
email americanagency@btconnect.com
Agent Ed Cobb

Areas of work include theatre, musicals, television, film, commercials, corporate and voice-overs. 2 agents represent 80 actors.

Will consider attending performances within the Greater London area. Accepts submissions (with CVs and photographs) from actors previously unknown to the agency if sent by post, but not by email. Invitations to view individual actors' websites, showreels and voicereels are also accepted. Welcomes enquiries from disabled actors. *Commission*: Theatre 10%; Other 15%

Susan Angel & Kevin Francis Ltd

1st Floor, 12 D'Arblay Street, London W1F 8DU
tel 020-7439 3086 *fax* 020-7437 1712
email agents@angelandfrancis.co.uk
Director Kevin Francis

Established in 1976. 3 agents represent about 75 actors (including 1 disabled actor) and 6 major TV/film casting directors. Areas of work include theatre, television, film, and commercials.

Will consider attending performances at venues within Greater London and occasionally elsewhere (e.g. Leeds, Bristol, Manchester) with 2 weeks' notice. Accepts brief postal submissions (with CVs and photographs) from actors previously unknown to the company. Emailed applications are not considered, due to the volume of mail. *Commission*: 10-12.5%

Christopher Antony Associates

The Old Dairy, 164 Thames Road, London W4 3QS
tel 020-8994 9952 *fax* 020-8742 8066
email info@christopherantony.co.uk
website www.christopherantony.co.uk
Agents Chris Sheils, Kerry Walker

Established in 2005 and represents about 35 actors. "We represent a small and diverse list of artistes in all areas of theatre, television and film."

Accepts submissions (with CVs and photographs) from actors previously unknown to the company, sent by post or email. Suitable clients will be contacted to arrange a meeting, or will be invited to attend a workshop audition "to select the right clients with whom we are confident we can work closely and creatively. If you require your details to be returned, please enclose an sae".

APM Associates

Pinewood Studios, Iver Heath, Bucks SL0 0NH
tel (01753) 639204 *fax* (01753) 639205
mobile (07918) 166706
email apm@apmassociates.net
website www.apmassociates.net
Managing Director Linda French

Established in 1989. Represents around 65 actors. Areas of work include theatre, musicals, television, film, commercials, corporate and voice-overs. Also represents actor-writers, presenters and directors.

Will consider attending performances at venues within Greater London with 2 weeks' notice. Accepts submissions (with CVs and photographs) from actors previously unknown to the company if sent by post with sae. Will also accept showreels and voicereels. Will consider looking at websites only if an actor's CV is of interest. Welcomes applications from disabled actors. *Commission*: Brochure available upon offer of interview

Argyle Associates
St John's Buildings, 43 Clerkenwell Road, London EC1M 5RS
tel 020-7608 2095 *fax* 020-7608 1642
email argyle.associates@virgin.net
Director Richard Linford *Key personnel* Geraldine Pryor

Established in 1995. 2 agents represent 30 actors. Areas of work include theatre, musicals, television, film, commercials and corporate.

Will consider attending performances at venues in Sussex and Surrey (e.g. Eastbourne, Brighton, Guildford, Dorking, Windsor) with 2 weeks' notice. Accepts submissions (with CVs and photographs) from actors previously unknown to the company if sent by post. Invitations to view individual actors' websites are also accepted. "Be clear about what you think you have to offer the agency – your type and roles. Your photograph should look like you and be a high-grade holiday snap." *Commission*: Theatre and Radio 10%; TV 12.5%; Commercials, Film, Corporate and CD Rom 15%

Asquith & Horner
The Studio, 14 College Road, Bromley BR1 3NS
tel 020-8466 5580 *fax* 020-8313 0443
website www.spotlightagent.info (view PIN 9858-0919-0728)
Senior Partner Anthony Vander Elst *Partner* Helen Melville

Established 1989. 2 agents represent 70 actors. Also represented are directors, choreographers, presenters, singers, dancers and commercial models. Areas of work include theatre, musicals, television, film, commercials, corporate and voice-overs.

Will consider attending performances at venues within Greater London and elsewhere, but requests as much notice as possible. Accepts submissions (CVs and photographs) from actors previously unknown to the company; also accepts showreels and voicereels, and invitations to view actors' websites. "Unsolicited enquiries should always be accompanied by an appropriately stamped and addressed envelope for return of answer, photo, voicereel, etc." Email applications are discouraged.

Associated International Management (AIM)
Fairfax House, Fulwood Place, London WC1V 6HUT
tel 020-7831 9709 *fax* 020-7242 0810
email info@aimagents.com
website www.aimagents.com

Key personnel Derek Webster, Stephen Gittins, Lisa-Marie Assenheim, Amy Jenkins

An international management established in 1984. 3 agents represent around 90 actors. Areas of work include theatre, television, film and commercials. Also represents directors.

Will consider attending performances within the Greater London area with at least 3 weeks' notice. Accepts submissions (with CVs and photographs) from actors previously unknown to the agency if sent by post, but not by email. *Commission*: 12-15%

BAM Associates
Benets Cottage, Dolberrow, Churchill, Bristol BS25 5NT
tel (01934) 852942
email casting@ebam.tv
website www.ebam.tv

2 agents represent 60 actors. Areas of work include theatre, musicals, television, film, commercials, corporate and voice-overs.

Will consider attending performances at venues within Greater London and the South West, but requests as much notice as possible. Accepts submissions (with CVs and 10x8in b&w photographs) from actors previously unknown to the company if sent by post. Welcomes enquiries from disabled actors. *Commission*: Theatre 10%; Mechanical Media 15%

Gavin Barker Associates Ltd
2D Wimpole Street, London W1G 0EB
tel 020-7499 4777 *fax* 020-7499 3777
email katie@gavinbarkerassociates.co.uk
website www.gavinbarkerassociates.co.uk
Managing Director Gavin Barker *Associate Director* Michelle Burke

Established in 1998. 2 agents represent 55 actors and a handful of creatives. Areas of work include theatre, musicals, television, film, commercials, corporate and voice-overs. Also represents directors and choreographers.

Will consider attending performances at venues in Greater London given at least 3 weeks' notice. Accepts submissions (with CVs and photographs) from actors previously unknown to the company if sent by post. Follow-up calls are not welcome. Happy to receive showreels and voicereels. "We do not currently represent any disabled actors, but would consider each applicant on a case by case basis." *Commission*: 10-12.5%

Olivia Bell Ltd
189 Wardour Street, London W1F 8ZD
tel 020-7439 3270 *fax* 020-7439 3485
email info@olivia-bell.co.uk
Managing Director Xania Segal

Established in 2001. 2 agents represent 90 actors. Areas of work include theatre, musicals, television, film and commercials.

Will consider attending performances at venues within Greater London with a minimum of 1 week's notice. Accepts submissions (with CVs and photographs) from actors previously unknown to the company if sent by post. Invitations to view individual actors' websites and showreels or voicereels are also accepted. *Commission*: 12.5-20%

Audrey Benjamin Agency

278A Elgin Avenue, Maida Vale, London W9 1JR
tel 020-7289 7180 *fax* 020-7266 4580
email a.benjamin@btconnect.com
Director Audrey Benjamin

Established in 1985. Works in all areas; represents around 45 actors.

Will consider attending performances within Greater London, given 2-3 days' notice. Welcomes letters (with CVs and photographs) from individual actors previously unknown to the agency if sent by post, but not by email. Encourages enquiries from actors with disabilities. Does not welcome follow-up calls, showreels, voicereels or invitations to view individual actors' websites. *Commission*: Theatre 10%; Film, TV, Commercials 15%

Better Chemistry

1st and 2nd Floors, 20 Stansfield Road, London SW9 9RZ
tel 020-7737 5300 *mobile* (07905) 259060
email info@betterchemistry.co.uk
website www.betterchemistry.co.uk
Director Paul L Martin

Agency dedicated to cabaret, burlesque, circus and variety acts. Corporate work, private parties, etc. for already existing self-contained acts.

Jorg Betts Associates

Gainsborough House, 81 Oxford Street, London W1D 2EU
tel 020-7903 5300 *fax* 020-7903 5301
email agents@jorgbetts.com

Established in 2001. Areas of work include theatre, musicals, television, film, commercials and corporate. Also represents directors and presenters.

Accepts submissions (with CVs and photographs) from actors previously unknown to the company if sent by post.

Billboard Personal Management

Unit 5, 11 Mowll Street, London SW9 6BG
tel 020-7735 9956 *fax* 020-7793 0426
email billboardpm@btconnect.com
website www.billboardpm.com
Agent Daniel Tasker

Established in 1985. 1 agent represents 55 actors. Areas of work include theatre, musicals, television, film, commercials, corporate and voice-overs.

Will consider attending performances at venues in Greater London given a minimum of 2 weeks' notice.

Accepts submissions (with CVs and photographs) from actors previously unknown to the company if they are currently performing. *Commission*: Commercials 16%; Film and TV 13.5%; Other 11%

Bishop Burnett Agency & Management

47 Dean Street, London W1P 5BE
tel 020-7734 9995 *fax* 020-7734 9996
email lara@mcslondon.com
Key personnel Keith Bishop, Lara James

Areas of work include theatre, musicals, television, film, commercials, corporate and voice-overs. 3 agents represent 35 actors. Also represents models, presenters, reporters, celebrities and celebrity hairdressers.

Will consider attending performances within the Greater London area with at least 1 month's notice. Accepts submissions (with CVs and photographs) from actors previously unknown to the company (include an sae). Invitations to view individual actors' websites, showreels and voicereels are also accepted. Welcomes enquiries from disabled actors. *Commission*: Theatre 10-15%

Rebecca Blond Associates

69A Kings Rd, London SW3 4NX
tel 020-7351 4100 *fax* 020 7351 4600
email rebecca@rebeccablondassociates.com
Agent Rebecca Blond

Established in 1991. 2 agents represent around 60 actors in all areas of acting work; also represents directors.

Welcomes performance notices for shows within Greater London with two weeks' notice. Welcomes representation enquiries (with CV and photograph) by post or email, as well as showreels and invitations to view individual actors' websites. Does not welcome follow-up calls. *Commission*: Varies

Bloomfields Management

77 Oxford Street, London W1D 2ES
tel 020-7659 2001 *fax* 020-7659 2101
email emma@bloomfieldsmanagement.com
website www.bloomfieldsmanagement.com
Director Emma Bloomfield

Established in 2004. Areas of work include theatre, musicals, television, film, commercials and corporate. 2 agents represent 40 actors.

Will consider attending performances anywhere, given at least 2 weeks' notice. Accepts submissions (with CVs and photographs) from actors previously unknown to the company if sent by post, but not by email. Invitations to view individual actors' websites, showreels and voicereels are also accepted. Welcomes enquiries from disabled actors.

Sandra Boyce Management

1 Kingsway House, Albion Road, London N16 0TA
tel 020-7923 0606 *fax* 020-7241 2713

email info@sandraboyce.com
Agent Sandra Boyce (MD)

2 agents represent 70 actors in all areas of acting work; directors also represented.

Welcomes performance notices if given at least 2 weeks' notice, and is prepared to travel within the Greater London area. Happy to accept letters (by post, not email) with CVs and photographs from individuals previously unknown to the company, but does not welcome follow-up calls. Encourages approaches from disabled actors. Also welcomes showreels and voicereels.

BROOD

High Street Buildings, 134 Kirkdale,
London SE26 4BB
tel 020-8699 1757
email broodmanagement@aol.com
website www.broodmanagement.com
Director Brian Parsonage Kelly

Established in 2003. 1 agent represents 40 actors. Areas of work include theatre, musicals, television, film, commercials and corporate. Also represents models.

Accepts submissions (with CVs and photographs) from actors previously unknown to the company if sent by post. *Commission*: Theatre 10%; Film 15%

Jeremy Brook Ltd

37 Berwick Street, London, W1F 8RS
tel 020-7434 0398 *fax* 020-7287 8016
email info@jeremybrookltd.co.uk
Partners Jeremy Brook

Originally Jean Clarke Management established in 1995. 1 agent with an assistant represents 65 actors. Areas of work include theatre, musicals, television, film, commercials, corporate and voice-overs.

Will consider attending performances in Greater London with at least 2 weeks' notice. Accepts submissions (with CVs and photographs) from actors previously unknown to the agency. Will only accept showreels and voicereels if they have been requested. Follow-up calls are not welcomed. *Commission*: Theatre 10%; TV/Film 12.5%; Commercials 15%

Valerie Brook Agency

10 Sandringham Road, Cheadle Hulme,
Cheshire SK8 5NH
tel 0161-486 1631
email colinbrook@freenetname.co.uk

2 agents represent 25 actors. Areas of work include theatre, musicals, television, film, commercials and corporate role-play.

Will consider attending performances at venues outside Greater London with 2 weeks' notice. Accepts postal submissions (with CVs and photographs) from actors previously unknown to the company. Invitations to view individual actors' websites are also

accepted. *Commission*: Negotiated with clients individually

Brown & Simcocks

1 Bridgehouse Court, 109 Blackfriars Road,
London SE1 8HW
tel 020-7928 1229 *fax* 020-7928 1909
email mail@brownandsimcocks.co.uk
website www.brownandsimcocks.co.uk
Partners Carrie Simcocks, Kelly Andrews

Established in the 1970s; 2 agents represent 65-70 actors. Areas of work include theatre, musicals, television, film, commercials and corporate.

Will consider attending performances within the Greater London area, given 2-4 weeks' notice. Accepts submissions (with CVs and photographs) from actors previously unknown to the company if sent by post. Unsolicited emails are not welcome. *Commission*: 10-15%

Brunskill Management Ltd

Suite 8A, 169 Queen's Gate, London SW7 5HE
tel 020-7581 3388 *fax* 020-7589 9460
email contact@brunskill.com
website www.brunskill.com
Agents Aude Powell, Geoff Stanton, Roger Davidson

Agency represents more than 100 actors. Areas of work include theatre, musicals, television, film, commercials, corporate and voice-overs. Also represents producers, directors and musical directors.

Will consider attending performances at venues in Greater London and occasionally elsewhere, but requests as much notice as possible. Accepts submissions (with CVs and photographs) from actors previously unknown to the company if sent by post. Emails are not encouraged, particularly if they include large attachments.

Bronia Buchanan Associates Ltd

1st Floor, 23 Tavistock Street, London WC2E 7NX
tel 020-7631 2004 *fax* 020-7631 2034
email info@buchanan-associates.co.uk
website www.buchanan-associates.co.uk
Director Bronia Buchanan *Agents* Daniel Albert,
Laura Justice, Ben McDougall, Ben Totty

Sole representation of approximately 25 creatives and 150 actors. Areas of work include theatre, musicals, television, film and commercials.

Will consider attending performances at venues within Greater London and elsewhere, but requests as much notice as possible. Accepts submissions by post or email (with CVs and photographs) from actors previously unknown to the company. Showreels and voicereels are also encouraged. Recommends the photographer Chris Baker (020-8441 3851). *Commission*: 10% plus VAT

Burnett Crowther Ltd

3 Clifford Street, London W1S 2LF
tel 020-7437 8008 *fax* 020-7287 3239

Agents and casting directors

email associates@bcltd.org
website www.bcltd.org
Agents Barry Burnett, Lizanne Crowther

Established in 1965. 2 agents represent 140 actors.

Will consider attending performances at venues within Greater London, with 3 weeks' notice. Accepts submissions (with CVs, photographs and sae) from actors previously unknown to the company if sent by post. *Commission*: 10-12%

Jessica Carney Associates

4th Floor, 23 Golden Square, London W1F 9JP
tel 020-7434 4143 *fax* 020-7434 4175
email info@jcarneyassociates.co.uk

Established in 1950. Areas of work include theatre, television, films, commercials and musicals. Also represents technicians and directors.

Cannot consider actors for representation unless they can be seen in performance (not showcase) at a venue within Greater London (requires 2-3 weeks' notice), or possess good mainstream TV credits. Accepts submissions (with CVs and photographs) from actors previously unknown to the company if sent by post; an sae must be included if a reply is required. Emails should only be sent with a sensible-sized photo and CV attached. *Commission*: 10%; Commercials 15%

Casting Couch Productions Ltd

213 Trowbridge Road, Bradford-on-Avon, Wiltshire BA15 1EU
tel (01225) 869212 *fax* (01225) 869029
mobile (07932) 785807
email moiratownsend@yahoo.co.uk
Key personnel Moira Townsend

Established in 1991. Sole representation of 25 actors. Areas of work include theatre, musicals, television, film, commercials, corporate and voice-overs.

Will consider attending performances at venues within Greater London and elsewhere, with 2-3 weeks' notice. Accepts submissions (with CVs and photographs, clearly stating age and nationality) from actors previously unknown to the company, preferably by email. An sae should be included for the return of hard-copy CVs and photographs. Actors will only be contacted if the agent would like to meet them. *Commission*: 15% across the board

See entry under *Casting directors* on page 95 for further details.

The Casting Department

277 Chiswick Village, London W4 DF
tel 020-7384 0388 *fax* 020-7736 2221
email jillscastingdpt@aol.com
website www.thecastingdept.co.uk
Key personnel Jill Searle

Agency representing about 250 actors and models. Areas of work include television and commercials.

Accepts submissions (with CVs and photographs) from actors previously unknown to the company if sent by post.

CBL Management

20 Hollingbury Rise, Brighton BN1 7HJ
tel (01273) 321245
email enquiries@cblmanagement.co.uk
website www.cblmanagement.co.uk
Agents Claire Carpenter, Beth Eden, Linda Edwards

Established in 2008. Works in theatre, musicals, television, film, commercials, corporate and voice-over. Directors, choreographers and musical directors also represented.

Will consider attending performances if given 2 weeks' notice. Welcomes approaches by post (with CVs and photographs) and by email; also accepts showreels, voicereels and invitations to view actors' websites. *Commission*: Theatre 10%; TV/Film & Commercials (below £500) 15%; Commercials (above £500) 20%

Chapman Agency at Birmingham School of Acting

The Link Building, Paradise Place, Birmingham B3 3HJ
tel 0121-262 6807 *fax* 0121-262 6081
email agency@bssd.ac.uk
website www.bsa.bcu.ac.uk/Graduates/Chapman_Agency

An agency representing Graduates of Birmingham School of Acting until they have their own independent agent.

Cinel Gabran Management

PO Box 5163, Cardiff CF5 9JB
tel 0845-066 6605 *fax* 0845-066 6601
mobile (07958) 583718
email info@cinelgabran.co.uk
website www.cinelgabran.co.uk
Managing Director/Agent David Chance *Agent* Sioned James

Established in 1988. 2 agents represent 65 actors. Also represents presenters, singers who act, and actors who write. The company has a London client list, although 60% of clients are Wales-based and 75% bilingual. Works in both English and Welsh-language production.

Will consider attending performances at venues in Wales and Central London with 2 weeks' notice. Accepts submissions (with CVs and photographs) from actors previously unknown to the company if sent by post. An sae should be included with CVs and photographs. *Commission*: Varies

Clic Agency

Rhoslwyn, Rhos Isaf, Cernarfon, Gwynedd LL54 7NF
tel (01286) 831001
email clic@btinternet.com
website www.clicagency.co.uk
Proprietor Helen Pritchard

Established in 2006. 1 agent represents around 50 actors in all areas of work.

Accepts submissions (with CVs and photographs) from actors previously unknown to the company sent by post or email. Encourages enquiries from disabled actors and welcomes showreels, voicereels, follow-up calls and invitations to view individual actors' websites. *Commission*: varies, but not more than 15%

Cloud Nine Agency

96 Tiber Gardens, Treaty Street, London N1 0XE
tel/fax 020-7278 0029
email email@cloudnineagency.co.uk
website www.cloudnineagency.co.uk

Established in 1995; 2 agents represent around 80 actors working in theatre, musicals, television, film, commercials and corporate role-play.

Will consider attending performances in North London and the West End given 2 weeks' notice. Accepts submissions (with CVs, showreels, photographs and sae) from actors previously unknown to the agency if sent by post. Will also accept invitations to view an actor's website. Follow-up telephone calls and emails, however, are not welcomed. *Commission*: 20%

Elspeth Cochrane Personal Management

16 Old Town, Clapham, London SW4 0JY
tel 020-7819 6256 *fax* 020-7819 4297
email via form on website

1 agent represents 40+ actors in theatre, musicals, TV, film, commercials and corporate work. Welcomes performance notices as far in advance as possible, and is prepared to travel to most venues in Greater London. Welcomes letters (by post or email) with CV and photograph from individuals (including disabled actors) previously unknown to the company. Also welcomes showreels. *Commission*: 12.5%

Cole Kitchenn Ltd

212 Strand, London WC2R 1AP
tel 020-7427 5680 (Switchboard)
tel 020-7427 5681 (Personal Management)
tel 020-7427 5682 (Production Department)
fax 020-7353 9639
email info@colekitchenn.com
website www.colekitchenn.com
Theatre/Creatives Agent Stuart Piper *TV/Film Agent* Paul Martin *Assistant* Jo Fell

The agency is a team of 4 representing a select list of actors and creatives, from directors and choreographers to designers and musical directors.

Welcomes performance notices within Greater London given 2-3 weeks' notice. Happy to receive letters and emails (with CVs, photographs and showreels) from new actors, but prefers not to receive follow-up telephone calls.

Shane Collins Associates

11-15 Betterton Street, Covent Garden, London WC2H 9BP
tel 020-7470 8864 *fax* 0870-460 1983
website www.shanecollins.co.uk
Agents Shane Collins, Polly Andrews

Established in 1986, the agency represents around 85 actors working in all areas of the industry.

Will consider attending performances within Greater London given as much notice as possible. Accepts submissions (with CVs and photographs) from actors previously unknown to the company; however, follow-up telephone calls, emails, showreels, voicereels and invitations to view an actor's website are not welcomed. Photos, CVs and showreels will only be returned if the actor includes a stamped, addressed envelope.

Collis Management

182 Trevelyan Road, London SW17 9LW
tel 020-8767 0196 *fax* 020-8682 0973
email marilyn@collismanagement.co.uk
Agent Marilyn Collis

Established in 1992. 1 agent represents 60 actors working in theatre, musicals, television, film, commercial and corporate work.

Will consider attending performances within the Greater London area with 3 weeks' notice. Welcomes letters, emails, showreels and invitations to view websites from actors previously unknown to the company, but not follow-up calls. *Commission*: 10-15%

Conway Van Gelder Grant

3rd Floor, 8-12 Broadwick Street, London W1F 8HN
tel 020-7287 0077 *fax* 020-7287 1940
Agents Jeremy Conway, Nicola van Gelder, John Grant, Liz Nelson

4 agents represent actors working in all areas of the industry.

Will consider attending performances within Greater London and occasionally elsewhere, given 3-4 weeks' notice. Accepts postal submissions (with CVs, photographs and sae to ensure reply) from actors previously unknown to the agency, along with invitations to view an actor's website. Showreels and voicereels should only be sent if requested after initial contact has been made. Follow-up telephone calls and emails are not welcomed. *Commission*: Varies according to contract

Howard Cooke Associates (HCA)

19 Coulson Street, London SW3 3NA
tel 020-7591 0144
Managing Director/Senior Agent Howard Cooke
Associate Agent Bronwyn Sanders

2 agents represent 40 actors. Areas of work include theatre, musicals, television, film, commercials and corporate.

Will consider attending performances at venues within Greater London and elsewhere (if within easy travelling distance) with 3 weeks' notice. Hard-copy applications (with CVs, photographs and sae) from actors previously unknown to the company are welcome, but email submissions are not accepted. *Commission*: 10-20%

Clive Corner Associates
'The Belenes', 60 Wakeham, Portland DT5 1HN
tel (01305) 860267
email cornerassociates@aol.com
Key personnel Clive Corner, Duncan Stratton, Bill Upton

Established in 1988. 3 agents represent 75 actors. Areas of work include theatre, musicals, television, film, commercials and corporate.

Will consider attending performances at venues within Greater London if given 3 weeks' notice. Rarely prepared to travel elsewhere. Accepts submissions (with CVs and photographs) from actors previously unknown to the company if sent by post. Showreels, voicereels and invitations to view individual actors' websites are not accepted unless requested following receipt of CV/photograph. *Commission*: Theatre and Radio 10%; TV, Film and Corporate 15%; Commercials 20%

Coulter Management Agency
PO Box 2830, Glasgow G61 9BQ
tel 0141-357 6666
email coultermanagement@ntlworld.com
Agent Anne Coulter

Areas of work include theatre, television, film, commercials, corporate and voice-overs.

Will consider attending performances at venues in Scotland with 3 weeks' notice. Accepts submissions (with CVs and photographs) from actors previously unknown to the company if sent by post. Showreels and voicereels are also accepted. *Commission*: 7.5-15% (sliding scale)

Covent Garden Management
5 Denmark Street, London WC2H 8LP
tel 020-7240 8400 *fax* 020-7240 8409
email agents@coventgardenmanagement.com

Established in 2002. The agency represents around 30 actors. Areas of work include theatre, musicals, television, film, commercials, corporate and voice-overs. Also represents directors.

Will consider attending performances at venues within Greater London with 2 weeks' notice. Accepts submissions (with CVs and photographs) from actors previously unknown to the company if sent by post. *Commission*: 10-15%

CSM Artists
Honeysuckle Cottage, 93 Telford Way, Yeading, Middlesex UB4 9TH
tel 020-8839 8747
email csmartists@aol.com
Proprietor Angela Radford *Agent* Carole Deamer
Personal Assistant Anthea Francis

Personal management established in 1984. Sole representation of 40-50 actors. Areas of work include theatre, musicals, television, film, commercials and corporate.

Will consider attending performances at venues within Greater London with 3 weeks' notice. Accepts submissions (with CVs and photographs) from actors previously unknown to the company if sent by post. An sae must be included. *Commission*: 15%

Curtis Brown Ltd
Haymarket House, 28-29 Haymarket, London SW1Y 4SP
tel 020-7393 4400 *fax* 020-7393 4401
email info@curtisbrown.co.uk
website www.curtisbrown.co.uk
Agents Grace Clissold, Mary Fitzgerald, Maxine Hoffman, Lucy Johnson, Sarah MacCormick, Grant Parsons, Sarah Spear, Kate Staddon, Olivia Woodward

One of Europe's oldest and largest independent literary and media agencies. Established over 100 years ago, there are now more than 20 agents within the Book, Media, Actors and Presenters Divisions, 5 of whom represent actors. Also represents writers, directors, playwrights and celebrities.

Submissions should be sent by post and addressed to 'Actors Agents'. They should include a covering letter with email address, CV, photograph, showreel (if actor has one) and sae for the return of the showreel. Tries to respond within 4-6 weeks. Does not meet potential clients before viewing their work. Does not accept email or faxed submissions. *Commission*: 12.5-15%

David Daly Associates
586 King's Road, London SW6 2DX
tel 020-7384 1036 *fax* 020-7610 9512
email agent@daviddaly.co.uk
Manchester office: 16 King Street, Knutsford WA16 6DL
tel (01565) 631999 *fax* (01565) 755334
email north@daviddaly.co.uk
website www.daviddaly.co.uk
Agents David Daly, Louisa Clifton (London); David Daly, Mary Ramsay (Manchester)

An established actors' agency bring 30 years of experience to the entertainment industry.

Chris Davis Management
Tenbury House, 36 Teme Street, Tenbury Wells, Worcestershire WR15 8AA
tel (01584) 819005 *fax* (01584) 819076
email info@cdm-ltd.com
website www.cdm-ltd.com
Agent Kerry Foley

Areas of work are theatre, musicals, television, film, commercials and corporate. 2 agents represent 80 actors; directors, choreographers, designers and musical directors are also represented.

52 Agents and casting directors

Agents and casting directors

Will consider attending performances within Greater London and elsewhere, given as much notice as possible. Welcomes letters (with CVs & photographs) from actors previously unknown to the agency, sent by post or email. Does not welcome follow-up calls. Accepts showreels, voicereels and invitations to view individual actors' websites. Encourages applications from actors with disabilities.

Will consider attending performances within Greater London and elsewhere, given as much notice as possible. Welcomes letters (with CVs & photographs) from actors previously unknown to the agency, sent by post or email. Does not welcome follow-up calls. Accepts showreels, voicereels and invitations to view individual actors' websites. Encourages applications from actors with disabilities.

Davis Bishop Associates

Cotton's Farmhouse, 28 Whiston Road, Cogenhoe, Northamptonshire NN7 1NL
tel (01604) 891487
email admin@cottonsfarmhouse.freeserve.co.uk
Agents Lena Davis, John Bishop

Established in 1986. Areas of work include theatre, musicals, television, film, commercials, corporate, voice-overs. Also represent other skills within the profession.

Will consider attending performances in Greater London with plenty of notice. Accepts submissions (with CVs and photographs) from actors unknown to the company. Follow-up calls and email submissions are not welcomed. *Commission*: 10-20%

Caroline Dawson Associates

125 Gloucester Road, London SW7 4TE
tel 020-7373 3323 *fax* 020-7373 1110
email cda@cdalondon.com

3 agents represent 60 actors.

Will consider attending performances at venues within Greater London with 3 weeks' notice. Accepts submissions (with CVs and photographs) from actors previously unknown to the company if sent by post. Showreels, voicereels and invitations to view individual actors' websites are also accepted. *Commission*: Variable

Felix de Wolfe

Kingsway House, 103 Kingsway, London WC2B 6QX
tel 020-7242 5066 *fax* 020-7242 8119

3 agents represent 100 actors. Areas of work include theatre, musicals, television, film, commercials, corporate and voice-overs. Also represents directors and producers.

Will consider attending performances at venues within Greater London and elsewhere, given 10 days' notice. Accepts submissions (with CVs and photographs) from actors previously unknown to the company if sent by post. *Commission*: Variable

Dealers Agency Belfast

22 North Street Arcade, Belfast BT1 1PB
tel 028-9031 1075
email info@dealersagency.co.uk
website www.dealersagency.co.uk
Agents Patrick Duncan, Philip Young

Established in 1997 and represents about 250 clients.

Lisa Dennis Management Ltd

Lisa Dennis has joined The Narrow Road Company Agency. All contacts for actors and casting should be directed to **Lisa@NarrowRoad.co.uk**.

DP Management

Argyle House, 29-31 Euston Road, London NW1 2SD
mobile (07837) 138892
email danny@dpmanagement.org
Agent Danny Pellerini

Founded in 2005, 1 agent represents 60 actors for all forms of acting work.

Welcomes performance notices with as much notice as possible. Welcomes letters (with CVs and photographs) from individuals previously unknown to the company, including disabled actors. Welcomes showreels and invitations to view individual actors' websites. *Commission*: 10-15%

DQ Management

Suite 2, Kingsway House, 134-140 Church Road, Hove, East Sussex BN3 2DL
tel (01273) 721221 *fax* (01273) 779065
email info@dqmanagement.com
website www.dqmanagement.com
Senior Partners Peter Davis, Kate Davis

Established in 2003. Areas of work include theatre, musicals, television, film, commercials and corporate. 2 agents represent 40 actors.

Will consider attending performances within the Greater London area and elsewhere with at least 2 weeks' notice. Accepts submissions (with CVs and photographs) from actors previously unknown to the company if sent by post. Invitations to view individuals' websites, showreels or voicereels are also accepted. Welcomes enquiries from disabled actors. *Commission*: Theatre 10%; West End 12.5%; TV/Film/Commercials 15%

Simon Drake Management

9 Golden Square, London W1F 9HZ
tel 020-7183 8995
email admin@simondrakemanagement.co.uk
website www.simondrakemanagement.co.uk
Agent Simon Drake

Established in 2007. Works in theatre, musicals, TV and film. Unsolicited approaches should be made via email only, giving Spotlight PIN.

Bryan Drew Ltd

Mezzanine, Quadrant House, 80-82 Regent Street, London W1B 5AU
tel 020-7437 2293 *fax* 020-7437 0561
email bryan@bryandrewltd.com
Managing Director Bryan Drew *Personal Assistant* Mina Parmar

Established in 1963. 2 agents represent 40 actors. Areas of work include theatre, musicals, television, film, commercials, corporate and voice-overs. Also represents writers. *Commission*: 12.5-15%

DS Personal Management

St Martin's Theatre, West Street, London WC2N 9NH

tel 020-8743 7777 *mobile* (07711) 245848
email ds@denisesilvey.com
website www.denisesilvey.com

DS Personal Management represents performers in
theatre, musicals, television, film, commercials and
corporate work. Also represents directors, MDs and
lighting designers.

Welcomes performance notices and is prepared to
travel within the Greater London area with at least 1
week's notice. Welcomes representation enquiries
(with CVs and photographs) from individuals by
email, but does not accept unsolicited showreels or
invitations to view actors' websites. *Commission*: 10-
15%

Also runs a production company called Cahoots
Theatre Company from the same address. See entry
on page 165.

Kenneth Earle Personal Management

214 Brixton Road, London SW9 6AP
tel 020-7274 1219 *fax* 020-7274 9529
email kennethearle@agents-uk.com
website entertainment-kennethearle.co.uk

Established in 2000. 1 agent represents 10-15 actors.
Areas of work include theatre, musicals, television,
film, commercials, corporate and voice-overs.

Will consider attending performances at venues in
Greater London and elsewhere with 1 week's notice.
Accepts submissions (with CVs and photographs)
from actors previously unknown to the company if
sent by post. Follow-up telephone calls and
invitations to view individual actors' websites are also
accepted. Showreels and voicereels should only be
sent on request. *Commission*: 10-15%

Susi Earnshaw Management

The Bull Theatre, 68 High Street, Barnet,
Herts EN5 5SJ
tel 020-8441 5010 *fax* 020-8364 9618
email casting@susiearnshaw.co.uk
website www.susiearnshawmanagement.com
Agents Susi Earnshaw, Melissa Gillespie, Jessie Tsang,
Robin Parsons

Established in 1989. 4 agents and bookers represent
30 adult actors, 60 child performers, and various
tribute bands. Areas of work include theatre,
musicals, television, film, corporate, live
entertainment, dance videos, radio and commercials.
Prefers submisisons via email (with CVs and photos).
Commission: Theatre 10%; TV, Film and
Commercials 15%

Debbie Edler Management

Little Friars Cottage, Lombard Street, Eynsham,
Oxon OX29 4HT
tel (01865) 884203 *fax* (01761) 436631
email info@demagency.co.uk
website www.demagency.co.uk
Directors Debbie Edler, David Edler

Established 2005. 2 agents represent 200 actors. Areas
of work include theatre, musicals, television, film,
commercials and corporate.

Will consider attending performances in Greater
London and elsewhere with plenty of notice. Accepts
submissions (with CVs and photographs) from actors
previously unknown to the agency. Follow-up calls
are not welcomed. See Representation page on
website for details of what is required. Welcomes
enquiries from disabled actors. *Commission*: 5-15%

EPMC Talent

30 Great Portland Street, London W1W 8QU
tel 020-7299 3555 *fax* 020-7299 3558
email enquiry@epmctalent.com
website www.et-nik-a.co.uk
Managing Director Aldo Arcilla

Established in 2000. 3 agents represent 80 actors.
Areas of work include theatre, musicals, television,
film, commercials, corporate and voice-overs.

Will consider attending performances at venues
within Greater London and occasionally elsewhere
with 1-2 weeks' notice. Accepts submissions (with
CVs and photographs) from actors previously
unknown to the company if sent by post. Invitations
to view individual actors' websites are also accepted.
Showreels and voicereels should only be sent on
request. *Commission*: Theatre 10%; TV and Films
15%; Commercials 20%

June Epstein Associates

62 Compayne Gardens, London NW6 3RY
tel 020-7328 0864 (main number) or 020-7372 1928
fax 020-7328 0684
email june@june-epstein-associates.co.uk

Established in 1973; represents approximately 40
actors working in theatre, musicals, television, film
commercials and corporate role-play. Recommends
the photographers Jonathan Dockar-Drysdale (**fact-
d@lineone.net**) and Peter Simpkin
(**petersimpkin@aol.com**).

Will consider attending performances within Greater
London given 2-3 weeks' notice. Accepts postal
submissions (with CVs and photographs) from actors
previously unknown to the agency. Welcomes
voicereels from singers, follow-up telephone calls and
showreels, but prefers not to receive emails.
Commission: 10%; Commercials 15%

Ethnics Artiste Agency

86 Elphinstone Road, Walthamstow,
London E17 5EX
tel 020-8523 4242 *fax* 020-8523 4523
email info@ethnicsaa.co.uk
website www.ethnicsartisteagency.com
Managing Director Pauline Oni

Founded in 1997. 2 agents represent 60 actors in all
areas of acting work. The company represents
multicultural and international performers and

Agents and casting directors

artistes from across the globe, including actors, singers, dancers, musicians and martial artists from Asia, Africa and Europe, and performers of ethnic-minority British origin. Specialises in representation of performers of colour and those with fluent foreign-language skills.

Welcomes performance notices 2-3 weeks in advance; will consider travelling to shows within Greater London. Welcomes letters (with CVs and photographs) from individuals previously unknown to the company if sent by post, but not by email. Welcomes showreels, but not invitations to view individual actors' websites. Welcomes representation enquiries from disabled actors.

– see entry under WIS Celtic Management on page 77

Stephanie Evans Associates (formerly Vocalworks International)

Rivington House, 82 Great Eastern Street, London EC2A 3JF
tel/fax 0870-609 2629
email steph@stephanie-evans.com
website www.stephanie-evans.com
Director Stephanie Evans

Established in 2003. 1 agent represents 60 actors. Areas of work include theatre, musicals, television, film, commercials and corporate.

Will consider attending performances in England and Wales with at least 1 month's notice. Accepts submissions (with CVs, photographs and showreels) from actors previously unknown to the company if sent by post. Invitations to view individual actors' websites are also accepted. Welcomes enquiries from disabled actors. *Commission*: 10%

Evolution Management

Studio 21, The Truman Brewery Building, 91 Brick Lane, London E1 6QB
tel 020-7053 2128 *fax* 020-7375 2752
email info@evolutionmngt.com
website www.evolutionmngt.com
Development Directors Loftus Burton, Henrik Bjork

Founded in 1999; 3 agents represent around 30 actors working in theatre, musicals, television, film and commercials. The agency also represents directors, make-up artists and presenters.

Welcomes performance notices within Greater London and occasionally further afield, given a minimum of 2 weeks' notice. Also accepts letters and emails with CVs and photographs, showreels and voicereels. Always provide an sae if you wish your material to be returned. Advises actors to have monologues prepared when coming to see the agency – especially if agents have not had the opportunity to see their work beforehand. *Commission*: Theatre 10-15%; Commercials 20%

Paola Farino – Representing Actors

109 St George's Road, London SE1 6HY
tel 020-7207 0858

email info@paolafarino.co.uk
website www.paolafarino.co.uk

Established in 2007. Sole agent, works in theatre, musicals, TV, film, commercials, corporate and photography. Will consider attending performances within Greater London. Prefers to receive performance notices and all other approaches by email – include Spotlight View Pin. "Check website first to see if there is anybody else represented with a similar MO."

Feast Management

1st Floor, 34 Upper Street, London N1 0PN
tel 020-7354 5216 *fax* 020-7354 8995
email office@feastmanagement.co.uk
Agent Sadie Feast

3 agents represent actors. Areas of work include theatre, musicals, television, film, commercials, corporate and voice-overs.

Will consider attending performances in the London area if plenty of notice is given. Accepts submissions (with CVs and photographs) from actors previously unknown to the company.

Colette Fenlon Personal Management

26 Hope Street, Liverpool LL1 9BX
tel 0151-707 7703 *fax* 0151-706 0838
email collettefenlon@hotmail.com
Director Colette Fenlon

Established in 1989, the agency represents 10 actors working in theatre, musicals, television, film and commercials.

Will consider attending performances within Greater London and beyond, given as much notice as possible. In general, does not welcome representation enquiries from actors unknown to the agency. *Commission*: 15-20%

First Act Personal Management

2 St Michaels, New Arley, Coventry CV7 8PY
tel (01676) 540285 *fax* (01676) 542777
email firstactpm@aol.com
website www.spotlightagent.info/firstact
Agent John Burton

Established in 2003. 1 agent represents 25 actors. Areas of work include theatre, musicals, television, film, commercials, corporate and voice-overs.

Will consider attending performances in England and Wales with at least 2 weeks' notice. Accepts submissions (with CVs and photographs) from actors previously unknown to the company if sent by post. Invitations to view individual actors' websites, showreels or voicereels are also accepted. Welcomes enquiries from disabled actors. *Commission*: 10-15%

Sharon Foster

15A Hollybank Road, Birmingham B13 0RF
tel 0121-443 4865 *fax* 0121-224 7677
email mail@sharonfoster.co.uk
website www.sharonfoster.co.uk

1 agent represents around 40 actors working in theatre, musicals, television, radio, film, commercials and corporate role-play.

Will consider attending performances given sufficient notice. Accepts submissions (with CVs and photographs) from actors previously unknown to the agency sent by post or email. Follow-up telephone calls, showreels, voicereels and invitations to view an actor's website are also accepted. *Commission*: 10-15%

Julie Fox Associates
tel (01628) 777853
email agent@juliefoxassociates.co.uk
website www.juliefoxassociates.co.uk
Agents Julie Fox, Corrine Murray, Jill Harmer (responsible for children and young performers)

Julie Fox previously worked with Tim Kent Associates, and when the agency disbanded in 2008 she continued under her own name. Agency works in all areas of live and recorded media. 2 agents represent 50 actors; directors and casting directors also represented. Accepts email approaches only (letters, CVs, showreels or links to Spotlight). *Commission*: 10% (Theatre, on work under £300); 12.5% Other

Fushion
27 Old Gloucester Street, London WC1N 3XX
tel (08700) 111100 *fax* (08700) 111020
email info@fushion-uk.com
website www.fushionpukkabosh.com
Key personnel (London office) Lawrence Endacott, Judy Oliver (New York office) Ron Nixon, Sarah Cornish

Fushion was established in 1998. It merged with Pukka Bosh in 2004 to form a sole management agency with offices in London and New York, and an intimate portfolio of 25 artistes and 5 recording artistes.

Hilary Gagan Associates
187 Drury Lane, London WC2B 5QU
tel 020-7404 8794 *fax* 020-430 1869
email hilary@hgassoc.freeserve.co.uk
Assistant Shiv Coard

3 agents represent approximately 100 actors. Areas of work include theatre, musicals, television, film, commercials, corporate, voice-overs. Also represents directors and choreographers.

Will consider attending performances in Greater London with at least 2 weeks' notice. Accepts submissions (with CVs and photographs with name on back of photograph) from actors previously unknown to the agency (include sae). Invitations to view individual actors' website, showreels and voicereels are also accepted. Follow-up calls are welcomed, as are enquiries from disabled actors. *Commission*: 7.5-15%

Galloways One
15 Lexham Mews, London W8 6JW
tel 020-7376 2288 *fax* 020-7376 2416
email hugh@gallowaysone.com
website www.gallowaysone.com
Directors Hugh Galloway, Jill Moore *Personal Assistant* Isabelle Desrochers

Established in 1971. Agency represents 150 actors. Areas of work include television, commercials, corporate and voice-overs, with the primary focus on commercials.

Will consider attending performances at venues within Greater London and occasionally elsewhere, given as much notice as possible. Accepts submissions (with CVs and photographs) from actors previously unknown to the company if sent by post. Enclose an appropriately sized sae for the return of personal details. *Commission*: TV 10%; Other 18%

Gardner Herrity
24 Conway Street, London W1T 6BG
tel 020-7388 0088 *fax* 020-7388 0688
email info@gardnerherrity.co.uk
Key contact Andy Herrity

Areas of work include theatre, television and film.

Will consider attending performances within the Greater London area with at least 3 weeks' notice. Accepts submissions (with CVs and photographs) from actors previously unknown to the company if sent by post, but not by email. Also accepts showreels, voicereels, and invitations to view individual actors' websites. Welcomes enquiries from disabled actors. *Commission*: 10%

Garricks
Angel House, 76 Mallinson Road, London SW11 1BN
tel 020-7738 1600 *fax* 020-7738 1881
email megan@garricks.net
Key personnel Megan Willis

Established in 1981. Areas of work include theatre, television, film, commercials and corporate. Also represents directors and presenters.

Will consider attending performances at venues within Greater London and elsewhere with 2 weeks' notice. Accepts submissions (with CVs and photographs) from actors previously unknown to the company, sent by post or email. Invitations to view individual actors' websites are also accepted. *Commission*: TV, Film and Theatre 10%; Commercials 15%

Gilbert & Payne Personal Management
Room 236, 2nd Floor, Linen Hall, 162-168 Regent Street, London W1B 5TB
tel 020-7734 7505 *fax* 020-7494 3787
email ee@gilbertandpayne.com
Director Elena Gilbert *Key personnel* Elaine Payne

Established in 1996. 2 agents represent 50 actors. Areas of work include theatre, musicals, television, film, commercials and corporate, with a particular emphasis on musical theatre. Also represents choreographers.

Will consider attending performances at venues in Greater London with a minimum of 1 week's notice. Accepts submissions (with CVs and photographs) from actors previously unknown to the company if sent by post. Follow-up telephone calls are also accepted. *Commission*: Theatre 10%

Global Artists
23 Haymarket, London SW1Y 4DG
tel 020-7839 4888 *fax* 020-7839 4555
email info@globalartists.co.uk
website www.globalartists.co.uk

A personal management company representing professional actors and actresses. Areas of work include theatre, musical theatre, television, film, commercials and corporate. Also represents a limited number of theatre designers, choreographers, directors and musical directors.

Accepts submissions from actors previously unknown to the company, sent by post or email. Does not welcome telephone enquiries.

Grantham-Hazeldine
Suite 605, The Linen Hall, 162-168 Regent St, London W1B 5TG
tel 020-7038 3737/8 *fax* 020-7038 3739
email agents@granthamhazeldine.com
website www.granthamhazeldine.com
Partners John Grantham, Caroline Hazeldine

Established in 1984. 2 agents represent 75 actors. Areas of work include theatre, musicals, television, film, commercials, corporate and voice-overs. Also represents writers and stunt co-ordinators.

Will consider attending performances at venues in Greater London and elsewhere with 1 month's notice. Accepts submissions (with CVs and photographs) from actors previously unknown to the company if sent by post. Will not accept showreels and voicereels at the initial stage of contact. *Commission*: Theatre and Radio 10% plus VAT; TV and Film 15% plus VAT

Darren Gray Management
2 Marston Lane, Portsmouth, Hampshire PO3 5TW
tel 023-9269 9973 *fax* 023-9267 7227
email darren.gray1@virgin.net
website www.darrengraymanagement.co.uk
Managing Director Darren Gray

Established in 1994. 2 agents represent 60 actors in both England and Australia. Agency mainly represents Australian actors, the majority of whom come from Australian soap operas. Areas of work include theatre, musicals, television, film, commercials, corporate and voice-overs. Also represents directors, producers, writers and presenters.

Will consider attending performances at venues within Greater London and elsewhere at whatever notice possible. Accepts submissions (with CVs and photographs) from actors previously unknown to the company, sent by post or email. Showreels, voicereels and invitations to view individual actors' websites are also accepted. Welcomes enquiries from disabled actors. *Commission*: 10%

Joan Gray Personal Management
29 Sudbury Court Island, Sunbury-on-Thames, Middlesex TW16 5PP

1 agent represents a small number of actors. Areas of work include theatre, musicals, television, film, commercials, corporate and voice-overs. *Commission*: 10%

Grays Management Ltd
Panther House, 38 Mount Pleasant, London WC1X 0AP
tel 020-7278 1054 *fax* 020-7278 1091
email grays.man@btconnect.com
website www.graysman.com
Agent Mary Nelson

2 agents represent approximately 90 actors working in theatre, musicals, television, film, commercials and corporate role-play.

Will consider attending performances within Greater London given 1 week's notice. Advises actors to contact the agency only when currently appearing in a production, as the agency does not welcome general representation enquiries. *Commission*: Theatre 10%; Screen 15%

Katherine Gregor Associates
Colombo Centre, 34-68 Colombo Street, London SE1 8DP
tel 020-7261 9466 *fax* 020-7261 9466
email agent@katherinegregorassociates.co.uk
website www.katherinegregorassociates.co.uk
Key personnel Katherine Gregor

A personal management agency representing actors and directors. Areas of work include theatre, musicals, television, film, commercials and corporate. Accepts applications for representation by email only (please send CV, photo and covering letter). *Commission*: 12.5% for actors

Sandra Griffin Management Ltd
6 Ryde Place, Richmond Road, East Twickenham TW1 2EH
tel 020-8891 5676 *fax* 020-8744 1812
email office@sandragriffin.com
website www.sandragriffin.com
Key personnel Sandra Griffin, Howard Roberts

Established in 1989. Represents actors in theatre, musicals, television, film, commercial and corporate work.

Welcomes written enquiries from actors seeking representation (with CV, photograph and sae to ensure reply), but does not accept unsolicited demo tapes, DVDs or showreels. Will consider seeing potential clients in current theatre productions, if in easily accessible locations. *Commission*: Varies according to contract

Louise Gubbay Associates
26 Westmore Road, Tatsfield, Kent TN16 2AX
tel (01959) 573080
email louise@louisegubbay.com
website www.louisegubbay.com
Managing Director Louise Gubbay

Founded in 2006. Works in theatre, musicals, television, film, commercials and corporate. 1 agent represents 40 actors.

Will consider attending performances within Greater London given 2 weeks' notice. Welcomes letters (with CVs and photographs) from individual actors previously unknown to the agency if sent by post; encourages enquiries from actors with disabilities. Does not welcome unsolicited approaches by email. Accepts showreels, voicereels, and invitations to view individual actors' websites. "LGA is an Associate Member of The Agents Association." *Commission*: Varies

Hall James Personal Management
PO Box 604, Pinner, Middlesex HA5 9GH
tel 020-8429 8111 *fax* 020-8868 5825
email info@halljames.co.uk
website www.halljames.co.uk
Directors Sam Hall, Stori James

Established in 2006. Areas of work include musicals, television, film, commercials and corporate. 2 agents represent around 50 actors; also represents theatre directors and choreographers.

Welcomes performance notices and letters (with CVs) from individual actors previously unknown to the agency, as well as showreels. *Commission*: 10%

The Harris Agency Ltd
71 The Avenue, Watford, Herts WD17 4NU
tel (01923) 211644
email theharrisagency@btconnect.com
Agent Sharon Harris

In association with The Harris Drama School. Evening acting workshops for all clients and actors seeking representation. Established in 1977. 1 agent represents around 50 actors.

Welcomes performance notices within Greater London, and elsewhere (seasonally, for example at Christmas) given at least 1 week's notice. Welcomes letters (with CVs and photographs) from actors previously unknown to the agency, sent by post or email. Also accepts follow-up calls, showreels, voicereels, and invitations to view individual actors' websites. Encourages enquiries from actors with disabilities. *Commission*: Theatre 10%; TV, Film, Commercials 15%

Hatton McEwan
PO Box 37385, London N1 7XF
tel 020-7253 4770 *fax* 020-7251 9081
email info@thetalent.biz
website www.thetalent.biz

Established in 1988, the agency represents actors working in theatre, musicals, television, film, commercials and corporate. Other clients include directors, composers and designers.

Will consider attending performances within Greater London (but rarely elsewhere) given 4 weeks' notice. Accepts submissions (with CVs and photographs) from actors previously unknown to the agency sent by post or email. Showreels, voicereels and invitations to view an actor's website are also accepted, but follow-up telephone calls are not welcomed.

Cheryl Hayes Management
85 Rothschild Road, London W4 5NT
tel 020-8994 4447 *mobile* (07767) 685560
email cheryl@cherylhayes.co.uk
website www.cherylhayes.co.uk

Established in 2008. Works in all areas; sole agent represents actors and writer/performers.

Will consider attending performances if given 2-3 weeks' notice. Welcomes approaches from actors, with CVs and photographs, by post or email and will accept showreels, voicereels and invitations to view individual actors' websites. *Commission*: 15%

Henry's Agency
53 Westbury, Rochford, Essex SS4 1UL
tel (01702) 541413 *fax* (01702) 541413
email info@henrysagency.co.uk
website www.henrysagency.co.uk

Established in 1995; 1 agent represents 35 actors. Areas of work include theatre, musicals, television, film, commercials and corporate.

Will consider attending performances at venues within Greater London with 2 weeks' notice. Accepts submissions (with CVs and photographs) from actors previously unknown to the company if sent by post. Emails are accepted if attachments consist of Word documents or small jpeg files. Follow-up telephone calls, showreels and voicereels are also accepted. Recommends the photographer Ash (**ash@ashphotomedia.com**). *Commission*: Varies

Edward Hill Management
Teddington Film and Television Studios,
Broom Road, Teddington, Middlesex TW11 9NT
tel 020-8614 2678 *fax* 020-8614 2694
email hill@management.freeserve.co.uk

1 agent represents 40 actors. Will accept submissions (with CVs and photographs) from actors previously unknown to the company if sent by post. *Commission*: 10-15%

Elinor Hilton Associates
BAC, Lavender Hill, London SW11 5TF
tel 020-7738 9574 *fax* 020-7924 4636

email info@elinorhilton.com
website www.elinorhilton.com

Represents actors for film, TV, radio and theatre. The agency was established in 2003, and currently has 60 actors.

Offers representation only after seeing an actor perform. This can either be in a theatre production or a showreel. Will consider attending shows with at least 2 weeks' notice. Showreels are accepted by email or post. Submissions to the agency are preferred via email, although postal applications are also considered. Welcomes enquiries from disabled actors. *Commission*: 12.5% across all disciplines

Dee Hindin Associates

9B Brunswick Mews, Great Cumberland Place, London W1H 7FB
tel 020-7723 3706 *fax* 020-7258 0651

Established in 1991. Represents 15-20 actors. Areas of work include theatre, musicals, television, film, commercials, corporate and voice-overs. Recommends the photographer Chris Baker (020-8441 3851). *Commission*: 12.5-15%

Liz Hobbs Group Ltd

65 London Road, Newark, Notts NG24 1RZ
tel 0870-070 2702 *fax* 0870-333 7009
email casting@lizhobbsgroup.com
website www.lizhobbsgroup.com
Managing Director Liz Hobbs MBE *Agent* Harriet Robson

2 agents represent 50-60 actors. Areas of work include theatre, musicals, television, film, commercials, corporate and voice-overs.

Will consider attending performances at venues in Greater London and elsewhere with 1-2 months' notice. Accepts unsolicited CVs / head shots, but not unsolicited showreels or voicereels. *Commission*: 10-15% depending on the type of work

Hobson's Actors

62 Chiswick High Road, Chiswick, London W4 1SY
tel 020-8995 3628 *fax* 020-8996 5350
website www.hobsons-international.com
Drama Agent Christina Beyer *Commercial Agent* Linda Sacks

Areas of work include theatre, musicals, television, film, commercials and corporate.

Will consider attending performances at venues within Greater London given 2 weeks' notice. Accepts submissions (with CVs and photographs) from actors previously unknown to the company if sent by post. Showreels are also accepted.

Hamilton Hodell Ltd

Fifth Floor, 66-68 Margaret Street, London W1W 8SR
tel 020-7636 1221 *fax* 020-7636 1226
email info@hamiltonhodell.co.uk
website www.hamiltonhodell.co.uk

3 agents represent 80 actors, working in leading roles in film, television, theatre and radio productions.

Jane Hollowood Associates Ltd

Apartment 17, 113 Newton Street, Manchester M1 1AE
tel 0161-237 9141 *mobile* (07801) 432842
email janehollowood@ukonline.co.uk
Agents Jane Hollowood, Charlotte Reeve

Established in 1998; 2 agents represent approx. 75 actors working in many areas of the industry.

Will consider attending performances within Greater London and potentially elsewhere, depending on diary commitments and provided that 2-3 weeks' notice is given. Accepts postal and email submissions (with CVs and photographs) from actors previously unknown to the agency. Showreels and voicereels should only be sent on request, and follow-up telephone calls are unwelcome. *Commission*: Theatre 10%; Radio, Role-play and Voice-overs 12%; Television, Film and Commercials 15%

Amanda Howard Associates

21 Berwick Street, London W1F 0PZ
tel 020-7287 9277 *fax* 020-7287 7785
email mail@amandahowardassociates.co.uk
website www.amandahowardassociates.co.uk
Agents Amanda Fitzalan Howard, Mark Price, Darren Rugg, Kirsten Wright *Voice-over Agent* Annette Parnell

5 agents represent around 100 actors working in theatre, musicals, television, radio, film, commercials, corporate role-play and voice-overs. Other clients include writers, broadcasters, designers, directors and composers.

Will consider attending performances within Greater London given 2-3 weeks' notice. Welcomes submissions (with CVs, photographs, showreels, voicereels and sae) from actors previously unknown to the agency if sent by post. Does not accept email applications or invitations to view an actor's website. *Commission*: 10-15% depending on the medium

Hunwick Hughes Ltd

Suite 2F, 45A George Street, Edinburgh EH2 2HT
tel 0131-225 3585 *fax* 0131-225 4535
email maryam@hunwickhughes.com
website www.hunwickhughes.com
Agent Maryam Hunwick *Assistant* Amanda Stewart

Personal management agency established in 1999. One agent represents actors in all media including several BAFTA and BIFA award-winning stage, screen and television artists.

Will consider attending performances at venues within Greater London and in Scotland given 4 weeks' notice. Accepts submissions (with CVs and photographs) from actors previously unknown to the company if sent by post. Will also accept showreels. *Commission*: Theatre 10%; TV and Broadcast Media 12.5%; Commercials 15%

Icon Actors Management
Tanzaro House, Ardwick Green North,
Manchester M12 6FZ
tel 0161-273 3344
email info@iconactors.net
website www.iconactors.net
Agent Nancy Lang

Established in 2000. Areas of work include theatre, musicals, television, film, commercials, corporate and voice-overs.

Image Management
The Media Centre, 94 Roundhill Crescent,
Brighton BN2 3FR
tel (01273) 695290
email mail@imagemanagement.co.uk
website www.imagemanagement.co.uk
Agent Adam Campbell

"We are always interested to hear from experienced actors who are seeking new representation. However, in order for us to market you effectively, it is essential that you have the following: a current Spotlight page; a recent showreel on DVD; good quality, recent 10x8in b&w headshots; recent professional feature film or terrestrial TV credits; and voice clips on MP3 or disk. Hard copy (only) applications should be sent to the address above. We treat each application with the utmost discretion. If you would like your material returned, please enclose an sae."

Imperial Personal Management Ltd
102 Kirkstall Road, Leeds LS3 1JA
tel 0113-244 3222
email katie@ipmcasting.com
website www.ipmcasting.com
Managing Director Katie Ross

Established in 2007. 4 agents represent 30-50 actors working in television and film; also has a subsidiary company, IPM Crew. Recommends Imperial Photography (**info@ipmcasting.com**).

Welcomes performance notices within the Greater London and Northern areas (within 50 miles of the company's postcode), and prefers 1 month's notice if possible. Welcomes letters (with CVs and photographs) from individual actors previously unknown to the agency, sent by post or email. Accepts follow-up telephone calls, showreels and voicereels, and welcomes invitations to view individual actors' websites. Encourages enquiries from actors with disabilities. *Commission*: 10-15%

Independent Talent Group Ltd (former ICM, London)
Oxford House, 76 Oxford Street, London W1D 1BS

11 agents represent actors. Areas of work include theatre, musicals, television, film, commercials, corporate and voice-overs. Also represents directors, writers, technicians and presenters.

Will consider attending performances at venues within Greater London. Accepts submissions (with CVs and photographs) from actors previously unknown to the company if sent by post. 10x8in photographs are preferred. *Commission*: 10%

Inter-City Casting
Portland Tower, Portland Street, Manchester M1 3LF
tel/fax 0161-238 4950
email intercitycasting@btconnect.com
website www.iccast.co.uk
Agent Caroline Joynt

Established in 1983. 2 agents represent approximately 60 actors. Areas of work include theatre, musicals, television, film, commercials and corporate.

Will consider attending performances at venues in Manchester and Liverpool. Accepts submissions (with CVs and photographs) from actors previously unknown to the company if sent by post. Showreels, voicereels and invitations to view individual actors' websites also accepted. Recommends the photographer Michael Pollard (see entry under *Photographers and repro companies* on page 375). *Commission*: 10-12.5% plus VAT

International Artistes Ltd
4th Floor, Holborn Hall, 193-197 High Holborn,
London WC1V 7BD
website www.intart.co.uk

7 agents represent approximately 220 actors. Also represents producers, directors, casting directors, presenters, light-entertainment artists and comedians. The company has a separate voice-over department. (Artists are represented by a total of 11 agents.)

Will consider attending performances at venues within Greater London and occasionally elsewhere, given 4 weeks' notice. Accepts submissions (with CVs and photographs) from actors previously unknown to the company if sent by post. Showreels, voicereels and invitations to view individual actors' websites are also accepted. *Commission*: 10-12.5% plus VAT

International Theatre & Music Ltd
Garden Studios, 11-15 Betterton Street,
Covent Garden, London WC2H
tel 020-7470 8786 *fax* 020-7379 0801
email info@it-m.co.uk
website www.it-m.co.uk
Managing Director Piers Chater-Robinson *Personal Assistant* Claire Lloyd *Assistant* Emma Brown

A team of 3 with musical backgrounds representing 70 actors and creatives. Areas of work include musicals, theatre, opera, TV and commercials. All artistes must have exceptional singing and/or instrumental skills.

Will consider attending performances at venues in Greater London and occasionally elsewhere, given as much notice as possible. Accepts submissions (with CVs and photographs) from actors with the requisite skills if sent by post. Will also accept voicereels/CDs of singing voices. *Commission*: Theatre 12.5%; Film and TV 15%

Alex Jay Personal Management

8 Higher Newmarket Road, Newmarket GL6 0RP
tel (01453) 834783 *fax* (01453) 834783
email alexjay@alex-jay-pm.freeserve.co.uk
Director Alex Jay

Established in 1992. 2 agents represent 30 actors. Areas of work include theatre, musicals, television, film, commercials, corporate and voice-overs.

Will consider attending performances in Greater London and elsewhere with 2 weeks' notice. Accepts submissions (CVs and photographs) from actors previously unknown to the agency. Encourages enquiries from disabled actors. Welcomes showreels and invitations to view actors' websites. *Commission*: 12-20%

JB Associates

4th Floor, Manchester House, 84 - 86 Princess Street, Manchester M1 1DN
tel 0161-237 1808 *fax* 0161-237 1809
email info@j-b-a.net
website www.j-b-a.net
Proprietor John Basham

Established in 1996. 2 agents represent 60 actors. Areas of work include theatre, musicals, television, film, commercials, corporate and voice-overs.

Will consider attending performances at venues in the North and occasionally within Greater London, given 3-4 weeks' notice. Accepts submissions (with CVs and photographs) from actors previously unknown to the company if sent by post. Will also accept showreels, voicereels, and invitations to view individual actors' websites. *Commission*: Theatre 10%; TV 15%

Jeffrey & White Management Ltd

No. 2 Ladygrove Court, Hitchwood Lane, Preston, Hitchin, Herts SG4 7SA
tel (01462) 433752
email info@jeffreyandwhite.co.uk
Partners Judith Jeffrey, Jeremy White *Key personnel* Laura Elgar

Established in 1986. 3 agents represent 85 actors. Areas of work include theatre, musicals, television, film, commercials and corporate.

Will consider attending performances given as much notice as possible. Accepts submissions (with CVs and photographs) from actors previously unknown to the company if sent by post. *Commission*: Theatre, Film and TV 12.5%; Commercials 15%

JGM

15 Lexham Mews, London W8 6JW
tel 020-7376 2414 *fax* 020-7376 2416
email mail@jgmtalent.com
website www.jgmtalent.com
Director Jilly Moore

Established in 1997. 3 agents represent 100-150 actors. Areas of work include theatre, musicals, television, corporate and voice-overs. Also represents directors, musical directors and choreographers.

Will consider attending performances within Greater London with at least 3 weeks' notice. Accepts submissions (with CVs and photographs) from actors previously unknown to the agency (please include sae). Invitations to view individual actors' websites are accepted, as are showreels and voicereels. Welcomes enquiries from disabled actors.

JLM Personal Management

259 Acton Lane, London W4 5DG
tel 020-8747 8223 *fax* 020-8747 8286
email info@jlmpm.co.uk
Agents Janet Malone, Sharon Henry

Established in 1978. 2 agents represent 80 actors. Areas of work include theatre, musicals, television, film, commercials, corporate and voice-overs.

Will consider attending performances at venues within Greater London given 2 weeks' notice. Showreels and voicereels should only be sent on request. Welcomes letters (with CVs and photographs) from actors previously unknown to the company, including disabled actors. Does not welcome approaches via email. *Commission*: Theatre 10%; TV 15%

Johnston & Mathers Associates Ltd

PO Box 3167, Barnet, London EN5 2WA
tel 020-8449 4968 *fax* 020-8449 2386
email JohnstonMathers@aol.com
website www.johnstonandmathers.com
Key personnel Dawn Mathers, Suzanne Johnston

Established in 2001. Areas of work include theatre, musicals, television, film, commercials and corporate. 2 agents represent 65 actors.

Will consider attending performances within the Greater London area with at least 1 month's notice. Accepts submissions (with CVs and photographs) from actors previously unknown to the company if sent by post or email. Invitations to view individual actors' websites are accepted, as are showreels and voicereels. Welcomes enquiries from disabled actors.

KAL Management

95 Gloucester Road, Hampton, Middlesex TW12 2UW
tel 020-8783 0039 *fax* 020-8979 6487
email kaplan222@aol.com
website www.kaplan-kaye.co.uk
Key personnel Kaplan Kaye

Established in 1982. Sole representation of approximately 25 actors. Areas of work include theatre, musicals, television, film, commercials, corporate and voice-overs.

Will consider attending performances at venues within Greater London given as much notice as possible. Accepts submissions (with CVs and photographs) from actors previously unknown to the company if sent by post. Showreels and voicereels should only be sent on request. *Commission*: Theatre 10%; TV 15%

Roberta Kanal Agency
82 Constance Road, Twickenham,
Middlesex TW2 7JA
tel 020-8894 2277 *fax* 020-8894 7952
email roberta.kanal@dsl.pipex.com
Director Roberta Kanal

Established in 1972; 1 agent represents approximately 30 actors working in all areas of the industry.

Will consider attending performances within Greater London and occasionally elsewhere, given sufficient notice. Accepts submissions from actors (able-bodied or disabled) who have previously checked that it is appropriate to do so. Follow-up telephone calls, emails, showreels, voicereels and invitations to view an actor's website are not welcomed. "Take a simple approach: phone first; send a CV if requested, with a clear letter and one photograph, along with an sae for their return. As with casting directors, only use email if requested. Unsolicited items will be ignored due to the growing number of applications becoming impossible to handle."

Karushi Management
Estilo, Unit 10, Wenlock Road, London N1 7SB
tel 0845-900 5511 *fax* 0845-900 5522
email victoria@karushi.com
website www.karushi.com

Areas of work include theatre, television, film, commercials, corporate, voice-overs.

Will consider attending performances in Central London with at least 2 weeks' notice. Accepts submissions (with CVs and photographs) from actors previously unknown to the company, sent by post or email. Invitations to view individual actors' website, showreels and voicereels are also accepted. Follow-up calls are not welcomed. Welcomes enquiries from disabled actors.

Keddie Scott Associates
Studio 1, 17 Shorts Gardens, Covent Garden,
London WC2H 9AT
tel 020-7836 6802 *fax* 020-7147 1326
mobile (07786) 070543
email fiona@ks-ass.co.uk, anna@ks-ass.co.uk,
alex@ks-ass.co.uk
website www.ks-ass.co.uk
Managing Director Fiona Keddie *Associate Agent* Anna Loose *Welsh Rep Agent* James Owen *Scottish Rep Agent* Paul Michael *Agents' Assistant* Alex Beuselinck

Keddie Scott Associates Ltd has been established since 2003 and became a member of the Personal Managers' Association in 2007. Deals in practically every area of the performing industry, including TV, Film, Commercials, Theatre, Musical Theatre (Small/ Mid/Large Scale) and Corporate Assignments of every nature. Please note that KSA operates on a Personal Exclusive Management basis.

Details for Welsh Book (KSA-Wales) and Scottish Book (KSA-Scotland):
Wales: Address c/o Head office (above)
tel 020-7836 6802 *fax* 020-7147 1326 *mobile* (07917) 272298
email wales@ks-ass.co.uk
Scotland: (0/1) 430 Tantallon Road, Langside, Glasgow G41 3HR
mobile (07980) 121728
fax 020-7147 1326
email scotland@ks-ass.co.uk
website www.ks-ass.co.uk

Kelly Management Ltd
11-15 Betterton Street, Covent Garden,
London WC2H 9BP
tel 020-7470 8757
email assistant@kelly-management.com
website www.kelly-management.com

Established in 2006. 2 agents represent clients in musicals, theatre, television, film, radio and commercials. Recommends the photographer Steve Lawton (**www.stevelawton.com**). Will consider attending performances within Greater London, and at Repertory theatres nationally or Number 1 touring venues in the South East, given 4-6 weeks' notice. Welcomes letters (with CVs) from individual actors previously unknown to the agency, sent by post or email; showreels, voicereels and invitations to view individual actors' websites are also accepted. *Commission*: Theatre 10%; Corporate & Radio 12.5%; TV & Film 15%

Steve Kenis & Co
Royalty House, 72-74 Dean Street, London W1D 3SG
tel 020-7434 9055 *fax* 020-7287 6328
email sk@sknco.com
Agents Steve Kenis, Tessa Glover

Founded in 2000. 2 agents represent 14 actors, as well as directors and technicians. *Commission*: 10%

Kew Personal Management
PO Box 679, RH1 9BT
tel 020-8871 3697
email info@kewpersonalmanagement.com
website www.keypersonalmanagement.com
Company Manager Kate Winn

Works in theatre, musicals, TV, film, commercials, corporate, voice-over and presenting.

Will consider attending performances in the Greater London area. Accepts letters (with CVs and photographs) from actors previously unknown to the company, but email is preferred. Accepts showreels, voicereels and links to Spotlight pages. Happy to accept submissions from disabled actors.

Agents and casting directors

Keylock Management

85 Rupert Avenue, High Wycombe, Bucks HP12 3NF
tel (01245) 321638
email agency@keylockmanagement.com
website www.keylockmanagement.com

1 agent represents 60 actors working in TV, film, commercial, theatre and corporate.

Will consider attending performances, given sufficient notice. Accepts sumissions (with CVs and photographs) from actors with professional training and previously unknown to the agency, if sent by post with sae. Showreels are also accepted.

Adrian King Associates

33 Marlborough Mansions, Cannon Hill,
London NW6 1JS
tel 020-7435 4600/ 4700 *fax* 020-7435 4100
email akassocs@aol.com
Agent Adrian King *Assistants* Caroline Funnell, Ruth Mayo

Established in 1989. 2 agents represents 48 actors. Areas of work include theatre, musicals, television, film, commercials and corporate. Also represents presenters and directors.

Welcomes showreels and letters from actors, as well as invitations to view individual actors' websites. May attend performances within the Greater London area, given 2 weeks' notice. *Commission*: 10%

Richard Kort Management

Midlands Office, Moat Farm, Norwell Woodhouse,
Newark, Notts NG23 6NG
tel (01636) 636686 *fax* (01636) 636719
email richardkort@dial.pipex.com
website www.richardkortassociates.com
Director Richard Kort

Established in 2005. 1 agent represents 50 actors. Areas of work include theatre, musicals, television, film, commercials, corporate and voice-overs. Also represents presenters.

Will consider attending performances within Greater London and elsewhere, with at least 2 months' notice. Accepts submissions (with CVs and photographs) from actors previously unknown to the agency; showreels, voicereels and invitations to view individual actors' websites are also accepted. Welcomes enquiries from disabled actors. *Commission*: 15%

Ladida Management

Ladida Group, Cambridge Theatre, Earlham Street,
London WC2H 9HU
tel 020-7379 6199 *fax* 020-7379 6198
email m@ladidagroup.com
website www.ladidagroup.com
Agent Jimmy Jewell *Assistant Agents* Eva Willis, Neal Wright

Established in 2005. Main areas of work are theatre, musicals, television, film and commercials. 2 agents represent 70 actors; also represented are directors, choreographers, musical theatre writers and musical directors.

Will attend performances in London only, if given at least 2 weeks' notice. Welcomes letters (with CVs and photographs) from individual actors previously unknown to the company if sent by post, but does not accept unsolicited emails, follow-up calls, or invitations to view individual actors' websites. Welcomes showreels and voicereels, and actively encourages enquiries from actors with disabilities.

Laine Management

131 Victoria Road, Salford M6 8LF
tel 0161-789 7775 *fax* 0161-787 7572
email info@lainemanagement.co.uk
website www.lainemanagement.co.uk
Company Director Samantha Greeley

Areas of work include theatre, television, film, commercials and corporate.

Will consider attending performances at venues in Manchester and the surrounding area with 2-4 weeks' notice. Accepts CVs and photographs from individuals previously unknown to the agency, but emails, showreels and invitations to view individual actors' websites are not welcomed. *Commission*: 15%

Langford Associates Ltd

17 Westfields Avenue, Barnes, London SW13 0AT
tel 020-8878 7148
website www.langfordassociates.com
Key personnel Barry Langford, Simon Hayes

Established in 1987. 1 agent represents 40-45 actors. Areas of work include theatre, television, film, commercials, corporate and voice-overs.

Will consider attending performances at mainstream venues within Greater London, given 2 weeks' notice. Accepts submissions (with CVs and photographs) by post or email. Email submissions should include no more than 1 small image (emails with multiple attachments will be deleted unread). 'Name' actors seeking representation may ring and speak to Barry Langford in complete confidence.

"I am always happy to receive details by post and I regularly meet with new actors. When writing, please include an sae if you would like your details to be returned. Please do not send unsolicited showreels. I prefer to receive 10x8in photographs, and would suggest that you use a good photographer and update your photo at least every 18 months. Make sure you are listed in Spotlight, as this is a prerequisite for all professional actors."

L'Brooke Personal Management

7 Malt House Place, High Street, Romford RM1 1AR
tel (01708) 723883 *fax* (01708) 723883
email lbrooke@btopenworld.com
Director Nancy Walker

Established in 2002. 1 agent represents 20 actors. Areas of work include theatre, musicals, television, film, commercials and corporate.

Will consider attending performances at venues within Greater London and elsewhere, given 2 weeks' notice. Accepts submissions (with CVs and photographs) from actors previously unknown to the company if sent by post or email. Showreels, voicereels and invitations to view individual actors' websites are also accepted.

Anna Lee Garrett Personal Management

24/26 Arcadia Avenue, Finchley Central, London N3 2JU
tel 020-8144 1142
email contact@annaleegarrett.net
website www.annaleegarrett.net
Agency Director Anna Lee Garrett *Associate Agents* Sandra Hughes, Nick Allan

Established in 2005. 3 agents represent 30-40 actors. Areas of work include theatre, musicals, television, film, commercials, corporate. Recommends the photographer Johnny Ball.

Will consider attending performances in Greater London with at least 2 weeks' notice. Accepts submissions (with CVs and photographs) from actors previously unknown to the agency. Follow-up calls are not welcomed. Welcomes enquiries from disabled actors, and older actors as well as up-and-coming talent. *Commission*: 10-15% (depending on whether theatre, film or commercials)

Lee Morgan Management

Cameo House, 11 Bear Street, London WC2H 7AS
tel 020-7766 5234 *fax* 020-7839 1900
email leemorganmgnt@aol.com
website www.leemorgan.co.uk

Established in 2005. Represents clients working in musicals, television, film and commercials.

Welcomes performance notices in the London areas, given 2 weeks' notice. Is happy to receive letters (with CVs and photographs) from individual actors previously unknown to the agency, sent by post or email. Accepts showreels and voicereels, and encourages enquiries from actors with disabilities.

Jane Lehrer Associates

100A Chalk Farm Road, London NW1 8EH
tel 020-7482 4898 *fax* 020-7482 4899
email janelehrer@aol.com
Sole Proprietor Jane Lehrer *Agent* Caz Swinfield

Established in 1986. 2 agents represent 80 actors. Areas of work include theatre, musicals, television, film, commercials, corporate and voice-overs. Also represents presenters.

Will consider attending performances at venues in Greater London with 2-3 weeks' notice. Accepts submissions (with CVs and photographs) from actors previously unknown to the company if sent by post. An sae must always be included. Showreels and voicereels should only be sent on request.

Mike Leigh Associates

37 Marylebone Lane, London W1V 2NW
tel 020-7935 5500 *fax* 020-7486 5886
email mail@mikeleighassoc.com
website www.mikeleighassoc.com
Agents Mike Leigh, Janie Jenkins

Established in 2007. Works in all areas except voice-over. 2 agents represent 60 actors; also represented are presenters, comedians, DJs and writers. Recommends the photographer Steve Ullathorne (**steve@steveullathorne.com**).

Will consider attending performances within Greater London given 1 month's notice. Welcomes letters (with CVs and photographs) from actors previously unknown to the agency if sent by post, but not by email. Will accept showreels, voicereels, and invitations to view individual actors' websites. *Commission*: 15%

Leigh Management

14 St David's Drive, Edgware HA8 6JH
tel 020-8951 4449 *fax* 020-8951 4449
email leighmanagement@aol.com

Established in 1989. 2 agents represent 75 actors. Areas of work include theatre, musicals, television, film, commercials and corporate. Also represents presenters.

Will consider attending performances at venues within Greater London given a minimum of 1 week's notice. Accepts submissions (with CVs and photographs) from actors previously unknown to the company if sent by post. Follow-up telephone calls and invitations to view individual actors' websites are also accepted. *Commission*: 10-15%

Lime Actors Agency & Management Ltd

Nemesis House, 1 Oxford Court, Bishopsgate, Manchester, M2 3WQ
tel 0161-236 0827 *fax* 0161-228 6727
email georgina@limemanagement.co.uk
Director Georgina Andrew

Established in 1999. 1 agent represents 70 actors. Areas of work include theatre, musicals, television, film, commercials, corporate and voice-overs. Also represents musical directors.

Will consider attending performances at venues within Greater London and elsewhere given 4 weeks' notice. Accepts submissions (with CVs and photographs) from actors previously unknown to the company if sent by post. Follow-up telephone calls, showreels, voicereels and invitations to view individual actors' websites are also accepted.

Linkside Agency

21 Poplar Road, Leatherhead KT22 8SF
tel (01372) 802374 or (01372) 378398
fax (01372) 801972

Established in 1986. 2 agents represent 40 actors. Areas of work include theatre, musicals, television, film, commercials, corporate and voice-overs.

Will consider attending performances at venues within Greater London given a minimum of 2 weeks' notice. Accepts submissions (with CVs and photographs) from actors previously unknown to the company if sent by post. An sae should be included for the return of CVs and photographs. Showreels and voicereels are also accepted.

Eva Long Agents

107 Station Road, Earls Barton, Northants NN6 0NX
mobile (07736) 700849
fax (01604) 811921
email EvaLongAgents@yahoo.co.uk
Key personnel Eva Long

Established in 2003. 1 agent represents 40 actors. Areas of work include theatre, musicals, television, film, commercials, corporate and voice-overs.

Will consider attending performances within the Greater London, Midlands and East Anglia areas, with at least 1 month's notice. Prefers to receive submissions (with CVs and headshots) by email, rather than by post. Showreels, voicereels and invitations to view individual actors' websites are also accepted. Welcomes enquiries from disabled actors. *Commission*: 15%

Longrun Artistes Agency

Marylebone Dance Studios, 12 Lisson Grove, London NW1 6TS
tel (07748) 723228 *fax* 0871-522 7926
email gina@longrunartistes.co.uk
website www.longrunartistes.co.uk
Director Gina Long

Established in 2006. Areas of work include theatre, musicals, television, film, commercials, corporate and voice-overs. Recommends the photographer Phil Conrad (**phil@ambercom.net**) for dancers and movement.

Will consider attending performances in Greater London with at least 10 days' notice. Accepts submissions (with CVs and photographs) from actors previously unknown to the agency. Follow-up calls are sometimes welcomed. Invitations to view showreels or voicereels and individual actors' websites are also accepted. Welcomes enquiries from disabled actors. *Commission*: 15% for up to and including 31 days; 10% for 31 days plus

"In January 2008 we took on business partner Irene Wernli, who is doing a great job specifically for actors. She can be contacted on (07983) 742022 or emailed at **irene@longrunartistes.co.uk**. We continue to take on a number of actors, and have more than 50 on our books. Commission is now 20% for all television work; other commission remains the same."

Louise Dyson at VisABLE People

PO Box 80, Droitwich WR9 0ZE
tel (01905) 776631

email louise@visablepeople.com
website www.visablepeople.com
Agent Louise Dyson

Founded in 1994, VisABLE is the UK's first agency representing only disabled people for professional engagements. It represents artistes with a wide range of impairments and in every age group, including children. 1 agent represents around 50 artistes in all areas of acting, including presenting.

Does not welcome performance notices: "Sorry, usually no time to get out and see them; existing clients only." Happy to receive other enquiries (with CVs and photographs) from disabled actors via email only. Showreels should always be accompanied by an sae for return. Also happy to receive invitations to view individual actors' websites. Recommends the photographer Simon Donnelly. *Commission*: 10-17%

Lovett Logan Associates

40 Margaret Street, London W1G 0JH
tel 020-7495 6400 *fax* 020-7495 6411
email london@lovettlogan.com (London);
edinburgh@lovettlogan.com (Edinburgh)
Scottish office: 2 York Place, Edinburgh EH1 3EP
tel 0131-478 7878 *fax* 0131-557 8787
website www.lovettlogan.com
Agents Dolina Logan (London), Pat Lovett (Edinburgh)

Established in 1981. Areas of work include theatre, musicals, television, film, commercials, corporate and voice-overs.

Will consider attending performances at venues in Greater London and Scotland (handled by Scottish office) with 2-3 weeks' notice. Accepts submissions (with CVs and photographs) from actors previously unknown to the company if sent by post. Invitations to view individual actors' websites are also accepted.

LSW Promotions

181A Faunce House, Doddington Grove, London SE17 3TB
tel 020-7793 9755 *fax* 020-7793 9755
email LSWpromos@hotmail.com
website www.londonshakespeare.org.uk
Executive Director Bruce Wall *Development Associate* James Croft

Established in 1998. 2 agents represent 20 actors. Areas of work include theatre, musicals, television and film.

Will consider attending performances at venues within Greater London and elsewhere, given 2 weeks' notice. Accepts submissions (with CVs and photographs) from actors previously unknown to the company, sent by post or email. Invitations to view individual actors' websites are also accepted. *Commission*: 10% donation to charity (LSW Prison Project)

Dennis Lyne Agency

503 Holloway Road, London N19 DD
tel 020-7272 5020 *fax* 020-7272 4790

email info@dennislyne.com
Agent Dennis Lyne *Associate* Sharon Levinson

Established in 1995. 1 agent represents 50 actors. Areas of work include theatre, musicals, television, corporate.

Will selectively consider attending performances within Central London, given at least 2 weeks' notice. Does not welcome submissions from actors previously unknown to the agency – unless they are appearing in something. *Commission*: 10%; Commercials 15%

MacFarlane Chard Associates
33 Percy Street, London W1T 2DF
tel 020-7636 7750 *fax* 020-7636 7751
email enquiries@macfarlane-chard.co.uk
website www.macfarlane-chard.co.uk
Agents Theresa Hickey, Eamonn Bedford, Derick Mulvey

Founded in 1994. Works in all areas. 3 agents represent 120 actors, as well as directors, writers, producers, technicians and authors.

Will consider attending performances in Greater London, given as much notice as possible. Welcomes letters (with CVs & photographs) from actors previously unknown to the agency if sent by post, and encourages enquiries from actors with disabilities. Does not welcome follow-up calls, invitations to view individual actors' websites, or unsolicited approaches by email. Will accept showreels and voicereels. *Commission*: Varies

Magnolia Management
136 Hicks Avenue, Greenford, Middlesex UB6 8HB
tel 020-8578 2899 *fax* 020-8575 0369
email mail@jaffreyactors.co.uk
Proprietor Jennifer Jaffrey

Established in 1982. 2 agents represent 55-60 actors. Areas of work include theatre, musicals, television, film, commercials, corporate and voice-overs.

Will consider attending performances at venues within Greater London and occasionally elsewhere, given as much notice as possible. Accepts submissions (with CVs and photographs) from actors previously unknown to the company if sent by post. Photographs should have the actor's name written on the back, and sae(s) enclosed for the return of personal details. Follow-up telephone calls should only be made if the agency has shown an interest in the actor. Showreels, voicereels and invitations to view individual actors' websites should only be sent on request. *Commission*: 10-15%

Management 2000
11 Well Street, Treuddyn, Flintshire CH7 4NH
tel (01352) 771231 *fax* (01352) 771231
email jackey@management-2000.co.uk
website www.management-2000.co.uk

Established in 2000. 1 agent represents 40 actors. Areas of work include theatre, musicals, television, film, commercials, corporate and voice-overs.

Will consider attending performances at venues within Greater London and elsewhere, given at least 1 week's notice. Accepts submissions (with CVs and photographs) from actors previously unknown to the company if sent by post. Follow-up telephone calls, showreels and voicereels are also accepted. *Commission*: 10-15%

Marcus & McCrimmon
1 Heathgate Place, 75 Agincourt Road, London NW3 2NU
tel 020-7485 4040 *fax* 020-7485 5030
email info@marcusandmccrimmon.com
website www.marcusandmccrimmon.com

Founded in 1999. Main areas of works are theatre, musicals, film, commercials and voice-over. 3 agents represent around 60 actors; also represents presenters.

Will consider attending performances within Greater London given 4 weeks' notice. Welcomes letters (with CVs and photographs) from actors previously unknown to the agency if sent by post, but not by email. Encourages enquiries from disabled actors, and accepts showreels, voicereels and invitations to view individual actors' websites.

Markham & Froggatt Ltd
4 Windmill Street, London W1T 2HZ
tel 020-7636 4412 *fax* 020-7637 5233
email admin@markhamfroggatt.co.uk
website www.markhamfroggatt.com
Key personnel Pippa Markham, Alex Irwin, Stephanie Randall (Agents), Millie Chadbon (Voice-over and Commercials Agent)

Works in theatre, musicals, television, film, commercials, corporate and voice-overs.

Markham & Marsden
John Markham and David Marsden have decided to close Markham & Marsden and form independent companies. David Marsden has formed Sainou (**www.sainou.com**), and John Markham has formed the Markham Agency (**www.themarkhamagency.com**).

Ronnie Marshall Agency
66 Ollerton Road, London N11 2LA
tel 020-8368 4958

Established in 1980. 1 agent represents 25 actors. Areas of work include theatre, musicals, television, film, commercials, corporate and voice-overs.

Will consider attending performances at venues within Greater London with 2 weeks' notice. Accepts business-like submissions (with CVs and photographs) from actors previously unknown to the company if sent by post. Photographs should be a good likeness. Enclose an sae for return of personal details. Follow-up telephone calls and invitations to view individual actors' websites are also accepted.

Commission: If instigated by client, 10%; otherwise 20%

Scott Marshall Partners
2nd Floor, 15 Little Portland Street,
London W1W 8BW
tel 020-7637 4623 fax 020-7636 9728
email smpm@scottmarshall.co.uk
Agents/Company Directors Amanda Evans, Suzy Kenway, Manon Palmer

Areas of work include theatre, musicals, television, film, commercials, corporate and voice-overs. Also represents directors (theatre and TV) and sound designers.

Will consider attending performances at venues within Greater London if given as much notice as possible. Accepts submissions (with CVs and photographs) from actors previously unknown to the company if sent by post. No email submissions.

Cassie Mayer Ltd
5 Old Garden House, The Lanterns, Bridge Lane,
London SW11 3AD
tel 020-7350 0880 fax 020-7350 0890
email info@cassiemayerltd.co.uk
Agents Cassie Mayer, Jayne Billington, Annalisa Gordon

Established in 1985. 3 agents represent 50-60 actors. Areas of work include theatre, musicals, television, film, commercials and corporate. Also represents directors, presenters and designers.

Will consider attending performances at Equity venues within Greater London if given 3 weeks' notice. Accepts submissions (with CVs and photographs) from actors previously unknown to the company if sent by post or email. All artists' applications will receive an answer. Commission: PMA-recommended rates

MBA
Concorde House, 18 Margaret Street,
Brighton BN2 1TS
tel (01273) 685970 fax (01273) 685971
email info@mbagency.co.uk
website www.mbagency.co.uk
Key personnel Derek 'Bo' Keller, Andrea Todd, Stephen Holroyd, Alan Kite

Established in 1964. Sole representation of 85-90 actors. Areas of work include theatre, musicals, television, film, commercials and corporate.

Will consider attending performances at venues within Greater London and on the South Coast with 1 month's notice. Accepts submissions (with clearly written CVs and photographs) from actors previously unknown to the company if sent by post. Photographs should be of a good quality. Enclose an sae for return of personal details. Showreels, voicereels and invitations to view individual actors' websites are also accepted. Commission: 10-17% depending on the type of work

Alexandra McLean-Williams
14 Rathbone Place, London W1T 1HT
tel 020-7631 5385 fax 020-7631 3739
email info@mclean-williams.com

Established in 2002; 1 agent represents approximately 40 clients working in theatre, musicals, television, film, commercials and corporate role-play.

Will consider attending performances within Greater London given 2 weeks' notice. Welcomes submissions (with CVs, photographs, showreels and voicereels) from actors previously unknown to the agency. Will also accept follow-up telephone calls, emails and invitations to view an actor's website.

Bill McLean Personal Management
23B Deodar Road, London SW15 2NP
tel 020-8789 8191 fax 020-8789 8192

Established in 1972. Will consider attending performances in Greater London with sufficient notice. Accepts submissions (with CVs and photographs) from actors previously unknown to the company if sent by post. Follow-up telephone calls are also accepted. Commission: Theatre 10%; TV 12.5%; Commercials 15%

Ken McReddie Associates Ltd
11 Connaught Place, London W2 2ET
tel 020-7439 1456 fax 020-7734 6530
email email@kenmcreddie.com
website www.kenmcreddie.com
Managing Director Roger Charteris

7 agents represent actors for theatre, television, film, commercials and voice-overs. Also represents directors.

MCS Agency
47 Dean Street, London W1D 5BE
tel 020-7734 9995 fax 020-7734 9996
email info@mcsagency.co.uk
Agent Keith Bishop

Established in 1994. 2 agents represent actors. Areas of work include theatre, musicals, television, film, commercials and voice-overs. Also represents presenters.

Will consider attending performances at venues within Greater London with 2 weeks' notice. Accepts submissions (with CVs and photographs) from actors previously unknown to the company if sent by post. Showreels, voicereels and invitations to view individual actors' websites are also accepted. Commission: 15-20%

MH Agency
High Street, Bushey, Herts WD21 1TT
tel 020-8421 8008 mobile (07817) 589103
email mhgancy@aol.com
website www.mhagency.com
Agent Fran Proctor Gibbs

Established in 1996. Works in theatre, musicals, television, commercial, film and cruise. 3 agents represent around 200 performers.

Will consider attending performances within Greater London and Central London only, given 1 month's notice. Accepts submissions, with CVs and photographs, sent by post, but email is preferable. *Commission*: 10% Theatre; 15% TV; 20% Commercial

Mitchell Maas McLennan Ltd

29 Thomas Street, Woolwich, London SE18 6HU
tel 020-8301 8745
email agency@mmm2000.co.uk
website www.mmm2000.co.uk

Established in 2005. 2 agents represent approximately 60 actors. Areas of work include theatre, musicals, television, film, commercials, corporate. Also represents choreographers. Recommends the photographer John Clark (see entry on page 380).

Will consider attending performances in Greater London and elsewhere with at least 2-4 weeks' notice. Accepts submissions (with CV's and photographs) from actors previously unknown to the agency. Showreels, voicereels and invitations to view individual actors' websites also accepted. Follow-up calls are welcomed. *Commission*: 10%.

MKA

11 Russell Kerr Close, London W4 3HF
tel 020-8994 1619 *fax* 020-8994 2992
email mka.agency@virgin.net
Key personnel Malcolm Knight

Founded under a different name in 1955, MKA was established under its present name in 1995. 2 agents represent 70 actors. Areas of work include theatre, musicals, television, film, commercials, corporate and voice-overs.

Will consider attending performances at venues within Greater London with 2 weeks' notice. Accepts submissions (with CVs and photographs) from actors previously unknown to the company if sent by post. *Commission*: 10-20% depending on the job

Morgan & Goodman

Mezzanine, Quadrant House, 80-82 Regent Street, London W1B 5RP
tel 020-7437 1383 *fax* 020-7437 5293
email mgl@btinternet.com
Proprietor Tanya Greep *Key personnel* Natalie Elliott

Established in 1981. 2 agents and 1 assistant represent 70-80 actors. Areas of work include theatre, musicals, television, film, commercials, corporate and voice-overs.

Will consider attending performances at venues within Greater London with 2 weeks' notice if an actor is playing a substantial role. Accepts submissions by post (with CVs and photographs), but only from experienced actors. An sae must always be included for the return of CVs and photographs. Showreels and voicereels should only be sent on request. *Commission*: 12.5%

Morse & du Fer Management Ltd

39 Ludford Close, Warrington Road, Croydon CR0 4BY
tel 020-8941 8122 *mobile* (07503) 372781
email info@morsedufer.com
website www.morsedufer.com
Director Paul du Fer

Established in 2009. Works in theatre, musicals, TV, film, commercials and corporate. Will travel all over the country to see performances, if given a minimum of 24 hours' notice. Welcomes approaches from actors by post or email, but *no phone calls*. *Commission*: 12.5% & 15%

Mrs Jordan Associates

Mayfair House, 14-18 Heddon Street, London W1B 4DA
tel 020-3151 0710
email apps@mrsjordan.co.uk
website www.mrsjordan.co.uk
Associates Sean D Lynch, Guy Kean

Established in 2008. Areas of work include stage, television, film, commercials, corporate and voice-overs. Does not represent walk-ons, extras, models or under-16s. 2 agents plus associates represent around 35 actors. Recommends the photographer Jon Campling (**photo@joncampling.com**).

Will consider attending performances, given a minimum of 2 weeks' notice. Unsolicited CVs and photographs accepted by email only, Spotlight link preferred. Happy to consider applications from actors with disabilities, on the understanding that, unfortunately, casting opportunities are very limited. Advises actors: "We have a very small client list and a strict 'no clash' policy. Check our website to see if we have a vacancy for your type before you email us. We cannot consider applicants unless we have seen a showreel or performance." *Commission*: 10-15%

Elaine Murphy Associates

Suite 1, 50 High Street, London E11 2RJ
tel 020-8989 4122 *fax* 020-8989 1400
email elaine@elainemurphy.co.uk
Director Elaine Murphy

Established in 1990. 2 agents represent 50 actors. Areas of work include theatre, musicals, television, commercials, corporate and voice-overs.

Will consider attending performances within Greater London with plenty of notice. Accepts submissions (with CVs and photographs) from actors previously unknown to the agency; showreels, voicereels and invitations to view individual actors' websites are also accepted.

The Narrow Road Company

3rd Floor, 76 Neal Street, Covent Garden, London WC2H 9PL
tel 020-7379 9598; 020-7379 9586 *fax* 020-7379 9777
email amy@narrowroad.co.uk
Agents Amy Ireson, Lisa Dennis, Richard Ireson

Established in 1986, the agency has 3 offices with each agent representing approximately 40 actors. Areas of work include theatre, musicals, television, film, commercials, corporate and voice-overs. In addition, the Surrey office represents writers, directors, lighting designers, fight directors and choreographers.

Will consider attending performances within the Greater London area, given 1-2 weeks' notice. Accepts submissions (with CVs and photographs) from actors previously unknown to the company if sent by post, but does not welcome email submissions. Showreels and voicereels should be sent only if requested. "We always try to be helpful and informative, but callers should be aware of how busy we often are." *Commission*: 10-15%

Surrey office
182 Brighton Road, Coulsdon, Surrey CR5 2NF
tel 020-8763 9895 *fax* 020-8763 2558
email coulsdon@narrowroad.co.uk
Agent Richard Ireson

Manchester office
Grampian House, 4th Floor, 144 Deansgate, Manchester M3 3EE
tel 0161-833 1605 *fax* 0161-833 1605
email manchester@narrowroad.co.uk
Agent Elizabeth Stocking

Nelson Browne Management Ltd
40 Bowling Green Lane, London EC1R 0NE
tel 020-7970 6010 *fax* 020-7837 7612
email enquiries@nelsonbrowne.com
website www.nelsonbrowne.com
Company Director Mary Elliott Nelson

Established in 2007. 2 agents represent 80-90 actors working in musicals, television, film, commercials, corporate and voice over; also represents directors and actor/musicians.

Welcomes performance notices within the Greater London area, given 2 weeks' notice. Welcomes letters (with CVs and photographs) from individual actors previously unknown to the agency, sent by post or email. Accepts follow-up telephone calls and invitations to view individual actors' websites. No showreels or voicereels. Encourages enquiries from actors with disabilities. *Commission*: Theatre 10%; TV and Film 15%

Nicola Roberts Management
149 Nelson Road, London N8 9RR
tel 020-8375 5555
email info@nicolarobertsmanagement.com
website www.nicolarobertsmanagement.com
Agent Nicola Roberts

Established in 2009. Works in all areas; 1 agent represents 45-55 actors.

Will consider attending performances with, ideally, 2-3 weeks' notice. Preferred method of contact is by email, including a covering email, link to Spotlight

CV or CV/jpeg photo attachments (small files only) and details of online showreel if available. All fully trained, experienced professional actors are considered. *Commission*: 12-15%

NJR Management Ltd
Hilltop Cottage, Welland Road, Upton upon Severn, Worcs WR8 0SJ
tel (01684) 592108 *mobile* (07767) 773735
email nikki@njrmanagement.com
website www.njrmanagement.com

Established in 2004. Works in commercials, role-play, corporate, voice-over, television, film and theatre.

Will consider attending performances in the Midlands area, given as much notice as possible. Prefers to be approached by email, including showreels and links to websites. *Commission*: Theatre 10%; Other 15%

North West Actors – Nigel Adams
36 Lord Street, Radcliffe, Manchester M26 3BA
tel/fax 0161-724 6625
email nigel.adams@northwestactors.co.uk
website www.northwestactors.co.uk
Proprietor Nigel Adams

Established in 2007. Main areas of work are theatre, musicals, television, film, commercials, corporate, radio and voice-overs. 1 agent represents 32 actors. Recommends the photographer Michael Pollard (**info@michaelpollard.co.uk**).

Will consider attending performances within the Greater Manchester area, given 2 weeks' notice. Welcomes letters (with CVs and photographs) from individual actors previously unknown to the agency, sent by post or email. Also accepts showreels, voicereels and invitations to view individual actors' websites. *Commission*: 15%

Northern Lights Management
Dean Clough Mills, Halifax, Yorkshire HX3 5AX
tel (01422) 330101
Agents Maureen Magee, Angie Cowton

Established in 1998. 2 agents represent 40 Northern and Northern-based actors. Areas of work include theatre, musicals, television, film, commercials, corporate and voice-overs.

Will consider attending performances at venues within Greater London and elsewhere, given 2 weeks' notice. Accepts submissions (with CVs and photographs) from actors previously unknown to the company if sent by post. Showreels and voicereels are also accepted. Enclose an sae for the return of items sent. Telephone calls and emails with attachments are not accepted. Advises actors that the agency is small and rarely takes on new clients.

NS Artistes' Management
10 Claverdon House, Hollybank Road, Billesley, Birmingham B13 0QY

tel 0121-684 5607 *mobile* (07870) 969577
email nsmanagement@fsmail.net
website www.nsmanagement.co.uk
Managing Director Neale Stephen McGrath *Director*
Arali Niamh McGrath

Founded in 2004, and representing 75 actors in all
areas of acting work including role-play, presenting
and training, the company also represents individuals
for writing, consultancy, design, stage management,
presenting, drama tutoring and fight arranging. "If
you have a talent in the business, even if I have not
mentioned it, then I am interested – no matter what
age, creed or colour you are, or whether you are
disabled or able-bodied."

Welcomes performance notices a fortnight in
advance; will consider attending performances
around the UK. Welcomes letters (with CVs and
photographs) from actors previously unknown to the
company if sent by post, but not by email. Does not
welcome unsolicited showreels or invitations to view
individual actors' websites. *Commission*: Theatre
12.5%; Stage Management 10%; Other 15%

Nyland Management Ltd
20 School Lane, Heaton Chapel, Stockport SK4 5DG

2 agents represent 60 actors. Areas of work include
theatre, musicals, television, film, commercials,
corporate and voice-overs.

Will consider attending performances at venues
within Greater Manchester and the North West given
at least 1 week's notice. Accepts submissions (with
CVs, photographs and sae) from actors previously
unknown to the company if sent by post.
Commission: 15%

The Offstage Agency
No. 199, 2 Lansdowne Row, Mayfair,
London W1J 6HL
tel 020-7543 7780 *fax* 020-7493 4935
email info@theoffstageagency.com
website www.offstageagency.com
Managing Director Dean Salvara

Established in 2004. 2 agents represent 40 actors.
Areas of work include television, film, commercials,
corporate and voice-overs. Also represents presenters.

Accepts submissions (with CVs and photographs)
from actors previously unknown to the company if
sent by post. Also accepts showreels, voicereels and
invitations to view individual actors' websites.
Welcomes enquiries from disabled actors.

On Screen Agency.com
No. 199, 2 Lansdowne Row, Mayfair,
London W1J 6HL
tel 020-7193 7547
email info@onscreenagency.com
website www.onscreenagency.com
Casting Agent Dean Salvara

Established in 2005. 2 agents represent around 20
actors. Areas of work include television, film,
commercials, corporate and voice-over.

Does not welcome performance notices, but letters
(with CVs and photographs) from individual actors
previously unknown to the company are accepted,
sent by post or email. Welcomes showreels and
voicereels, and invitations to view individual actors'
websites. Please note that showreels should be sent to
the address on the website,
www.onscreenagency.com. *Commission*: 15%.

David Padbury Associates
44 Summerlee Avenue, Finchley, London N2 9QP
tel 020-8883 1277 *fax* 020-8883 1277
email info@davidpadburyassociates.com
website www.davidpadburyassociates.com
Director David Padbury

2 agents represent 30 actors. Areas of work include
theatre, musicals, television, film, commercials and
corporate.

Will consider attending performances within Greater
London with at least 1 week's notice. Invitations by
email to view individual actors' websites are accepted.
Welcomes enquiries from disabled actors.
Recommends the photographer Mark Davis
(**mad.photo@onetel.net**). *Commission*: 10-15%

Pan Artists Agency
Cornerways, 34 Woodhouse Lane, Sale M33 4JX
tel 0161-969 7419
email panartists@btconnect.com
website www.panartists.co.uk

Established in 1973. Accepts submissions (with CVs
and photographs, "which must be up to date") from
actors previously unknown to the company, sent by
post or email. Postal submissions must be
accompanied by an sae.

Pelham Associates
The Media Centre, 9-12 Middle Street,
Brighton BN1 1AL
tel (01273) 323010 *fax* (01273) 202492
email petercleall@pelhamassociates.co.uk
website www.pelhamassociates.co.uk
*Agent*s Peter Cleall, Dione Inman

Established in 1993. Areas of work include theatre,
musicals, television, film, commercials, corporate and
voice-overs.

Will consider attending performances at venues
within Greater London and elsewhere, given at least 2
weeks' notice. Accepts submissions (with CVs and
photographs) from actors previously unknown to the
company if sent by post. *Commission*: 8-12.5%

Pemberton Associates Ltd
Express Networks, 1 George Leigh Street,
Manchester M4 5DL
tel 0161-235 8440 *fax* 0161-235 8442
London office: 193 Wardour Street, London W1F
8ZF
tel 020-7734 4144 *fax* 020-7734 2522

Agents and casting directors

website www.pembertonassociates.com

Established in 1989. 5 agents represent 150 clients. Areas of work include theatre, musicals, television, film, commercials, corporate and voice-overs.

Will consider attending performances at venues in the North West, with 2-3 weeks' notice, if looking for new clients. Accepts submissions (with CVs and photographs) from actors previously unknown to the company if sent by post.

PFD

Drury House, 34-43 Russell Street,
London WC2B 5HA
tel 020-7344 1010 *fax* 020-7836 9544
website www.pfd.co.uk

Please see website for latest details of actor-representation.

Frances Phillips

89 Robeson Way, Borehamwood, Herts WD6 5RY
tel 020-8953 0303 *mobile* (07957) 334348
email derekphillips@talk21.com

Established in 1983 and representing 40 actors aged 16 upwards. Member of Personal Management Association. Areas of work include theatre, musicals, television, film, commercials, corporate and voice-overs. Submissions by email only considered if Spotlight View Pin number and date of birth details are included. CVs and photos will be requested at a later date if required.

PHPM

184 Bradway Road, Sheffield S17 4QX
tel 0114-235 3663
email philippa@phpm.co.uk
Key personnel Philippa Howell

Established in 1996. 1 agent represents 80 actors. Areas of work include theatre, musicals, television, film, commercials, corporate and voice-overs.

Will consider attending performances at venues outside Greater London if given as much notice as possible. Accepts submissions (with CVs and photographs) from actors previously unknown to the company if sent by post. Enclose an sae bearing the correct postage. Showreels and voicereels are also accepted. Recommends the photographer Andrew Chapman (see entry under *Photographers and repro companies* on page 375). *Commission*: Theatre, Radio and Voice-over 10%; Film, TV and Commercials 15%

Piccadilly Management

23 New Mount Street, Manchester M4 4DE
tel 0161-953 4057 *mobile* (07930) 834891
email info@piccadillymanagement.com
website www.piccadillymanagement.com
Agent Peter Foster

Established in 1985. Main areas of work include television, theatre, stage, commercials, corporate and voice overs. Represents around 50 actors.

Welcomes approaches from actors previously unknown to the company, sent by post or email. Accepts invitations to view individual actors' websites and welcomes enquiries from actors with disabilities.

Janet Plater Management Ltd

Floor D, Milburn House, Dean Street,
Newcastle upon Tyne NE1 1LF
tel 0191-221 2490
email magpie@tynebridge.demon.co.uk

Established in 1997. 1 agent represents approximately 50 actors. Areas of work include theatre, musicals, television, film, commercials, corporate and voice-overs.

Will consider attending performances at venues in North East England with 1-2 weeks' notice. Accepts submissions (with CVs and photographs) from actors previously unknown to the company if sent by post. Showreels and voicereels should only be sent on request. *Commission*: Maximum of 15%

PPM

73 Leonard Street, Shoreditch, London EC2A 4QS
tel 020-7739 7552 *fax* 020-7739 7552
Managing Director Polo Piatti

Established in 1996. Agency represents 3 actors and works mainly in musicals/music videos.

Will consider attending performances at venues within Greater London with 3-4 weeks' notice, if complimentary tickets are provided. Accepts submissions (with CVs and photographs) from actors previously unknown to the company, sent by post or email. Showreels and voicereels are also accepted. "We will always consider actors wishing to expand into music work, including pop music." *Commission*: 15-20%

Morwenna Preston Management

49 Leithcote Gardens, London SW16 2UX
tel/fax 020-8835 8147
email info@morwennapreston.com
website www.morwennapreston.com

1 agent represents 50 actors for theatre, musicals, TV, film, commercials and corporate. Also represents some presenters and choreographers.

Welcomes performance notices 4 weeks in advance, and is prepared to travel within the Greater London area. Welcomes letters (by post or email) from individuals previously unknown to the company. Does not welcome follow-up calls. Encourages applications from disabled actors. Welcomes showreels and invitations to view individual actors' websites. *Commission*: 12.5%

Price Gardner Management

PO Box 59908, London SW16 5LL
website www.pricegardner.co.uk
Contact Sarah Barnfield

Television, film, theatre, musical theatre, commercials, radio, voice-over and corporate.

Submisions can be made via the website or in writing to the office address. Please enclose the correct postage or material shall not be returned.

Principal Artistes
4 Paddington Street, London W1U 5QE
tel 020-7224 3414 *fax* 020-7486 4668
email principalartistes@hotmail.com

Established in 1993. 2 agents represent 60 actors. Areas of work include theatre, musicals, television, film, commercials and corporate.

Will consider attending performances at venues in Greater London with at least 1 week's notice. Accepts submissions (with CVs and photographs) from actors previously unknown to the company if sent by post. Always enclose an sae bearing the correct postage for the return of photographs and CVs, and if a response is required. *Commission*: Theatre 10%; Other 15%

Profile Management
The Old Chapel, 9 West End, Ashwell,
Herts SG7 5TH
tel (01462) 743843 *fax* (01462) 742967
Agent George Perry

Agency represents 35 actors. Areas of work include theatre, television, film and commercials. Also represents physical theatre artists.

Will consider attending performances (particularly of physical theatre) at venues within Greater London and Hertfordshire, Cambridgeshire and Bedfordshire, given 3 weeks' notice. Accepts submissions (with CVs and photographs) from actors previously unknown to the company if sent by post. Showreels and voicereels are also accepted. Does not welcome telephone calls.

Pure Actors Agency & Management Ltd
44 Salisbury Road , Manchester, M41 0RB
tel 0161-747 2377 *fax* 0161-746 9886
email enquiries@pure-management.co.uk
website www.pure-management.co.uk
Director Debbie Pine

Established in 2005. 1 agent represents 40 actors. Areas of work include television, film, theatre, commercials, radio and corporate.

Will consider attending performances within the Manchester area, given at least 6 weeks' notice. Recommends the photographer Michael Pollard (see entry on page 385). Accepts submissions (with CVs and photographs) from actors previously unknown to the agency – but be sure to include an sae. Showreels, voicereels and invitations to view individual actors' websites are also accepted. Welcomes enquiries from disabled actors. *Commission*: 15%

RBM Actors
3rd Floor, 168 Victoria Street, London SW1E 5LB
tel 020-7630 7733

email info@rbmactors.com
website www.rbmactors.com
Agent Rob Sandy

Works mainly in theatre, musicals, television, film and commercials. 2 agents represent around 20 actors, and some comedians/writers.

Will consider attending performances within Greater London, given 2-3 weeks' notice. Welcomes letters (with CVs and photographs) from individual actors previously unknown to the company, sent by post or email, but not follow-up calls. Accepts showreels and voicereels, as well as invitations to view individual actors' websites. Encourages enquiries from actors with disabilities. "We advise you to contact us when you are appearing in something. We don't represent actors we don't know or haven't seen."

Randall Richardson Actors
2nd Floor, 145-157 St John Street, London EC1V 4PY
tel 020-7060 1645 *fax* 0870-762 3212
email mail@randallrichardson.co.uk
website www.randallrichardson.co.uk
Agent Juliet Fergus

Established in 2001. 2 agents represent 40 actors. Areas of work include theatre, musicals, television, film, commercials, corporate and voice-overs.

Will consider attending performances within 1 hour's journey time from London, given at least 1 week's notice. Accepts submissions (with CVs and photographs) from actors previously unknown to the agency; also welcomes enquiries from disabled actors. *Commission*: 10%

RDF Management
22 Torrington Place, London WC1E 7HD
tel 020-7317 2251 *fax* 020-7317 2245
website www.rdfmanagement.com
Head of Agency Debi Allen

Established in 2002. 4 agents each represent approximately 25 actors. Areas of work include theatre, musicals, television, film, commercials and corporates. Also represents writers, presenters and stand-up comics.

Will attend performances at venues within Greater London, but requests as much notice as possible. Accepts submissions (with CVs, photographs and, if possible, showreels) from actors previously unknown to the company, if sent by post. Follow-up telephone calls and invitations to view individual actors' websites are also accepted. *Commission*: 15%

Redroofs Associates
Littlewick Green, Maidenhead, Berkshire SL6 3QY
tel (01753) 785444 *fax* (01753) 785443
email agency@redroofs.co.uk
website www.redroofs.co.uk

Established in 1947, the agency only represents Redroofs graduates and current students. It does not, therefore, welcome performance notices or representation enquiries from actors unknown to the school. Areas of work include theatre, musicals, television, film, commercials, corporate and voice-overs. *Commission*: 15%

Lisa Richards Agency

108 Upper Leeson Street, Dublin 4
tel 353 1 637 5000 *fax* 353 1 667 1256
email info@lisarichards.ie
website www.lisarichards.ie
Managing Director Lisa Cook *Agents (Actors)* Lisa Cook, Richard Cook, Jonathan Shankey
Administrator Lorraine Cummins

The Lisa Richards Agency was founded in 1989 by Lisa and Richard Cook. Originally established as a theatrical agency, Lisa Richards now provides representation for actors, comedians, voice-over artists, authors, playwrights, directors and designers. The company employs a staff of 9 people across the different departments. 3 agents represent 90-100 actors, and there is 1 voice-over agent, 1 comedy agent, and 1 literary agent.

Welcomes performance notices if sent 3 weeks in advance, and is prepared to travel around Ireland. Welcomes letters (with CVs and photographs) from actors previously unknown to the company if sent by post, but not by email; does not welcome follow-up calls. Happy to receive showreels and invitations to view individual actors' websites. Welcomes enquiries from disabled actors.

Rossmore Management

10 Wyndham Place, London W1H 2PU
tel 020-7258 1953 *fax* 020-7258 0124
email agents@rossmoremanagement.com
website www.rossmoremanagement.com

Established in 1993. 4 agents represent 120 actors. Areas of work include theatre, musicals, television, film, commercials, corporate and voice-overs.

Will consider attending performances at venues within Greater London. Accepts submissions (with CVs and photographs) from actors previously unknown to the company if sent by post. Please include sae. *Commission*: Theatre and Radio 10%; Film, TV and Commercials 15% plus VAT

Royce Management

29 Trenholme Road, London SE20 8PP
tel/fax 020-8778 6861
email office@roycemanagement.co.uk
website www.roycemanagement.co.uk

Established in 1980. 1 agent represents 50-60 actors. Areas of work include theatre, musicals, television, film, commercials, corporate and voice-overs.

Will consider attending performances at venues within Greater London with a minimum of 1 week's notice. Accepts submissions (with CVs and photographs) from actors previously unknown to the company if sent by post. Include an sae if a reply is

required. *Commission*: Commercials 15%; All other work 10%

RPM2

Studio House, Delamere Road, Cheshunt, Herts EN8 9SH
tel/fax (01992) 893259
email info@rhinomanagement.co.uk
website www.rhinomanagement.co.uk
Owner/Head Booker J K Sands *Assistant Booker* Steve Day

Represents 72 actors (as well as 14 presenters and 10 voice-over artists) in all areas of acting work.

Will consider attending performances within Greater London and elsewhere, if given at least 1 week's notice. Welcomes letters (with CVs and photographs) from individuals previously unknown to the company sent by post or email. Happy to receive follow-up calls. Welcomes showreels, voicereels and invitations to view individual actors' websites. Welcomes approaches from disabled actors. *Commission*: Up to 20%

St James's Management

19 Lodge Close, Stoke D'Abernon, Cobham, Surrey KT11 2SG
tel (01932) 860666
Managing Director Jacqueline Leggo

Established in 1965. 1 agent represents approximately 40 actors. Areas of work include theatre, musicals, television, film, commercials, corporate and voice-overs. Actors should approach the company by letter and enclose an sae.

Saraband Associates

265 Liverpool Road, London N1 1LX

2 agents represent actors. Areas of work include theatre, musicals, television, film and commercials.

Will occasionally consider attending performances at venues in Greater London, given 1 month's notice. Accepts submissions (with CVs and photographs) from actors previously unknown to the company if sent by post. An sae should be included with CVs and photographs. *Commission*: Varies

SCA Management

77 Oxford Street, London W1D 2ES
tel 020-7659 2027 *fax* 020-7659 2116
email agency@sca-management.co.uk, scamanagement@aol.com

Established in 1980. 2 agents represent 50 actors. Areas of work include theatre, musicals, television, film, commercials and corporate.

Will consider attending performances within Greater London given sufficient notice. Accepts submissions (with CVs and photographs) from actors previously unknown to the company if sent by post. Showreels and voicereels are also accepted. All submissions

must be sent with an appropriately sized sae for reply.
Commission: 15%

Scott-Niven Associates
205 Victoria Rise, Clapham, London SW4 0PF
mobile (07505) 045757
email theteam@scott-nivenassociates.com
website www.scott-nivenassociates.com
Agents Lydia Scott, David Niven

Established in 2008. Works in all areas; 2 agents
represent 20-30 actors.

Will consider attending performances if given at least
a week's notice. Prefers to receive email in the first
instance, with links to all information; letters
accepted with hard copy reels, as are invitations to
view individual actors' websites. No follow-up calls.
Commission: Varies in line with standard industry
rates

Tim Scott
PO Box 61776, London W1V UX
tel 020-7833 5733 *fax* 020-7278 9175
email timscott@btinternet.com

Established in 1988. Areas of work include theatre,
television, film, and commercials.

Accepts postal submissions (with CVs and
photographs) from actors previously unknown to the
company.

Dawn Sedgwick Management
3 Goodwins Court, London WC2N 4LL
tel 020-7240 0404 *fax* 020-7240 0415
email dawn@dawnsedgwickmanagement.com
website www.dawnsedgwickmanagment.com
Key personnel Dawn Sedgwick, Nicola Mason-
Shakspeare

Established in 1992. 1 agent represents 10 actors.
Areas of work include theatre, television, film,
commercials, corporate and voice-overs. Also
represents presenters, comedians and writers.

Accepts submissions (with CVs and photographs)
from actors previously unknown to the agency if sent
by post, but not by email. Showreels, voicereels and
invitations to view individual actors' websites are also
accepted. Welcomes enquiries from disabled actors.
Commission: 10-15%

VSA Ltd
186 Shaftesbury Avenue, London WC2H 8JB
tel 020-7240 2927 *fax* 020-7240 2930
email info@vsaltd.com
website www.vsaltd.com

VSA has a long and very fine heritage as an agency,
having been created by the theatrical agent and
impresario Vincent Shaw back in the 1950s. Since
then the agency has maintained its position as a top
theatrical management looking after many successful
artists, including the legendary Jessie Matthews, as
well as giving many industry leaders such as Bill

Kenwright an opportunity to get started in the
industry.

Andy Charles took over the agency in 2002, after
working alongside Vincent Shaw as his head agent,
and today runs VSA with fellow agent and business
partner Tod Weller. Their combined experience of
the industry from both sides of the fence (Andy's
from his career as an actor, and Tod's from his career
in TV, advertising and commercial production)
ensures an in-depth understanding of the demands of
an ever-changing business, as well as an empathy and
insight into the daily challenges of an artist's life.
"Our continued success depends on our relationships
with our clients and our relationships with casting
professionals – relationships we nurture and never
take for granted; friendly, professional and very
personal management is paramount to all that we
do."

VSA is a member of the Personal Managers'
Association.

Shepherd Management Ltd
13 Radnor Walk, London SW3 4BP
tel 020-7352 2200 *fax* 020-7352 2277
email info@shepherdmanagement.co.uk
Agent Christina Shepherd

2 agents and 1 junior agent represent 120 actors, 1
director and 1 designer. Areas of work include
theatre, musicals (occasionally), television, film,
corporate and voice-overs.

Will consider attending performances within Greater
London given as much notice as possible. Accepts
postal submissions (with CVs, photographs and sae)
from actors previously unknown to the agency.
Showreels and voicereels will also be accepted. Emails
and follow-up telephone calls are not welcomed.

Shepperd-Fox
5 Martyr Road, Guildford, Surrey GU1 4LF
tel 07957 624601
email info@shepperd-fox.co.uk
website www.shepperd-fox.co.uk
Agents Jane Shepperd, Sarah Fox

Established in 2005 and represents about 55 actors.
Areas of work include television, theatre, film,
commercials and radio.

Claire Sibley Management
15 Tweedale Wharf, Madeley, Telford,
Shropshire TF7 4EW
tel (01952) 588951
email claire@clairesibleymanagement.co.uk
website www.clairesibleymanagement.co.uk
Director Claire Sibley

Founded in 2007. Areas of work are theatre, musicals,
television, film, commercials, corporate and voice-
over. 1 agent represents 17 actors.

Will consider attending performances throughout the
UK, given at least 1 month's notice. Welcomes letters

(with CVs and photographs) from actors previously unknown to the agency, sent by post or email, and welcomes enquiries from actors with disabilities; also accepts follow-up calls, showreels, voicereels and invitations to view individual actors' websites. *Commission*: 10-12%

Sandra Singer Associates

21 Cotswold Road, Westcliff-on-Sea, Essex SSO 8AA
tel (01702) 331616 *fax* (01702) 339393
email sandrasingeruk@aol.com
website www.sandrasinger.com
Key personnel Sandra Singer

Main areas of work are feature films, film, television, commercials and musical theatre. Also represents singers.

Will consider attending performances when looking for new clients to join the management. Accepts postal applications only with sae. No zip files, jpegs, or emails with large files unless requested. Showreels should only be sent on request. Enclose an sae for the return of material.

Spire Casting

PO Box 372, Chesterfield S41 0XW
tel 0790 051 7707
email mail@spirecasting.com
www.spirecasting.com
Agents David Gilbrook

Established in 2001. Accepts submissions (with CVs and photographs) from actors previously unknown to the company, sent by post or email. "Applicants must be members of Equity and appear in the current edition of *Spotlight*; include an sae if you want your CV and photograph to be returned."

Paul Spyker Management

PO Box 48848, London WC1B 3WZ
tel 020-7379 8181
email info@pspy.com

Works in all areas of the entertainment industry; also represents directors and choreographers. Recommends the photographer Jorge de Reval.

Will consider seeing performances given a month's notice. Welcomes letters (with CVs) from individual actors previously unknown to the agency, if sent by post or email; also accepts invitations to view individual actors' websites. Encourages enquiries from actors with disabilities.

Helen Stafford Management

14 Park Avenue, Bush Hill Park, Enfield EN1 2HP
tel 020-8360 6329 *fax* 020-8372 0611
email Helen.Stafford@blueyonder.co.uk
Agent Helen Stafford

Established in 1991. Sole representation of 30 actors. Areas of work include theatre, musicals, television, film, commercials, corporate and voice-overs.

Will consider attending performances at venues within Greater London with 2 weeks' notice. Accepts

submissions (with CVs and photographs) from actors previously unknown to the company if sent by post. Showreels and voicereels should only be sent on request. *Commission*: Commercials 15%; Other 10%

Stage & Screen Personal Management Ltd

20b Kidbrooke Grove, Blackheath, London SE3 0LF
mobile (07958) 684740
email info@stageandscreenpm.com
Agent Orit Sutton

Established in 2005. 2 agents represent 20 actors. Areas of work include theatre, musicals, film, commercials and corporate.

Natasha Stevenson Management Ltd (NSM)

Studio 7C, Clapham North Arts Centre, Voltaire Road, London SW4 6DH
tel 020-7386 5333 *fax* 020-7385 3014
email inbox@natashastevenson.co.uk
Agents Natasha Stevenson, Jennifer Withers, Pippa Godfrey

3 agents represent 85 actors. Areas of work include theatre, musicals, television, film, commercials, corporate and voice-overs.

Will consider attending performances at venues within Greater London with 2 weeks' notice. Actors should approach the company by post, enclosing an sae. Showreels should only be sent on request.

Stiven Christie Management

1 Glen Street, Tollcross, Edinburgh EH3 9JD
tel 0131-228 4040 *fax* 0131-228 4645
email info@stivenchristie.co.uk
website www.stivenchristie.co.uk
Proprietor Douglas Stiven

Founded in 1983 (and incorporating The Actors Agency of Edinburgh); 1 agent represents actors for theatre, musicals, television, film, commercials, corporate and voice-overs.

John Strange Management

Film City, 401 Govan Road, Glasgow G51 2QJ
tel 0141-445 0444
email tracy@strangemanagement.co.uk
website www.strangemanagement.co.uk

John Strange Management represents around 50 actors. Areas of work include theatre, television, film, corporate, musicals, voice-overs and commercials.

Will consider attending performances in the West of Scotland, given a minimum of 1 week's notice. Welcomes letters (with CVs and photographs) from individual actors previously unknown to the company, but no follow-up calls or email submissions. Will accept showreels and invitations to view individual actors' websites. Encourages enquiries from actors with disabilities.

Talent Artists Ltd
59 Sydner Road, London N16 7UF
tel 020-7923 1119 *fax* 020-7923 2009
Director Jane Wynn Owen

Talent Artists Ltd represents actors working in all
fields of the industry, with a particular emphasis on
musical theatre.

Tavistock Wood
Tavistock Wood, 45 Conduit Street,
London W1S 2YN
tel 020-7494 4767 *fax* 020-7434 2017
email info@tavistockwood.com
website www.tavistockwood.com
Agents Angharad Wood, Charles Collier

Represents about 30 actors and a few other directors
and writers. Accepts submissions (with CVs and
photographs) from actors previously unknown to the
company by post only – these should be
accompanied by a covering letter and an sae.

TCG Artist Management
14A Goodwin's Court, London WC2N 4LL
tel 020-7240 3600 *fax* 020-7240 3606
email info@tcgam.co.uk
website www.spotlightagent.info/tcgam

Established in 1998. 3 agents represent 60 actors.
Areas of work include theatre, musicals, television,
film, commercials and corporate role-play.

Will consider attending performances at venues
within Greater London given as much notice as
possible. Accepts submissions (with CVs and
photographs) from actors previously unknown to the
company if sent by post. Follow-up telephone calls,
showreels and voice samples are also accepted.
Commission: 10-15% depending on the job

Paul Telford Management
3 Greek Street, London W1D 4DA
tel 020-7434 1100 *fax* 020-7434 1200
email info@paultelford.net
website www.paultelford.net
Partner Paul Telford

Established in 1994. 2 agents represent around 70
actors. Areas of work include theatre, musicals,
television, film, commercials and corporate.

Will consider attending performances at venues
within Central London given at least 2 weeks' notice.
Accepts submissions (with CVs and photographs)
from actors previously unknown to the company if
sent by post. Showreels and voicereels are also
accepted. Include sae for return of material.
Commission: Variable

Tennyson Agency
10 Cleveland Avenue, Merton Park,
London SW20 9EW
tel 020-8543 5939
email mail@tennysonagency.co.uk
website www.tennysonagency.co.uk
Agents Christopher Oxford, Jane Hutchinson

Established in 2001. Works in theatre, television, film,
commercials, musical theatre, audio and voice-over
(photography on an ad hoc basis). No clients under
16. Dramatists and screenwriters also represented.

Will consider attending performances within the
Greater London area given at least 1 week's notice.
Approaches by initial letter via post or email, with
photo, resumé and web links – preferably when there
is an opportunity to see a forthcoming stage or screen
performance. Observes the requirements of the DDA.
Commission: 10% for actors

Katie Threlfall Associates
2A Gladstone Road, Wimbledon, London SW19 1QT
tel 020-8543 4344 *fax* 020-8543 7545
email katie@ktthrelfall.co.uk
Agent Katie Threlfall

Founded in 1996 as Hillman Threlfall; changed its
name in 2006 to Katie Threlfall Associates. 1 agent
represents 90 actors in theatre, musicals, TV, film,
commercials and corporate.

Will attend performances at venues within Greater
London if given 1 month's notice. Accepts
submissions (with CVs and photographs) from actors
previously unknown to the company. Welcomes
showreels and invitations to view individual actors'
websites. "Address letters correctly to the agent. Only
write in if you have a showreel, or with an invitation
to a show: we do not take on or meet people whose
work we do not know." *Commission*: Commercials
15%; Other 12.5%

Threshold Agency
186 Courtlands Avenue, London SE12 8JD
tel 020-8463 9238 *mobile* (07949) 601935
email steve@thresholdagency.co.uk
website www.thresholdagency.co.uk
Agent Steve Nealon

Works in theatre, film, television, commercials,
musicals and corporate.

Depending on the production and the actor, will
attend performances anywhere in the UK, given a
week's notice. Welcomes letters, with CVs and
photographs, sent by post and email, and accepts
showreels. Plans to represent actors with disabilities.
Commission: 10-15%

Janice Tildsley Associates
47 Orford Road, London E17 9NJ
tel 020-8521 1888 *fax* 020-8521 1174
email info@janicetildsleyassociates.co.uk
website www.janicetildsleyassociates.co.uk
Agents Janice Tildsley, Kathryn Kirton

Established in 2003. 2 agents represent 60-70 actors.
Areas of work include theatre, musicals, television,
film and commercials.

Will consider attending performances within the
Greater London area. Accepts submissions (with CVs
and photographs) from actors previously unknown

to the agency if sent by post, but not by email. Welcomes enquiries from disabled actors. *Commission*: 10-15%

Total Vanity Ltd

15 Walton Way, Aylesbury, Bucks HP21 7JJ
mobile (07739) 381788
email Teresa.Hellen@TotalVanity.com
website www.totalvanity.com
Agent Teresa Hellen

Established in 2000. 1 agent represents 50 actors. Areas of work include theatre, musicals, television, film, commercials, corporate and voice-overs. Also represents presenters.

Will consider attending performances within the Greater London area with at least 1 week's notice. Accepts submissions (with CVs and photographs) from actors previously unknown to the company if sent by post. Showreels, voicereels and invitations to view individual actors' websites are also accepted. Welcomes enquiries from disabled actors. *Commission*: 20%

United Agents

12-26 Lexington Street, London W1F 0LE
tel 020-7166 5266 *fax* 020-7166 5282
email info@unitedagents.co.uk
website www.unitedagents.co.uk
Agents Ruth Cooper (Commercial & Voice-Over), Olivia Homan, Lindy King, Duncan Millership, Joanna Scarratt (Commercial & Voice-Over), Dallas Smith, Lisa Toogood, Maureen Vincent, Ruth Young

Established in 2007. Represents about 500 actors. The agency also represents writers, directors, producers, designers and other creatives.

"We happily accept submissions by post only – *no emails*. Please mark the envelope 'Submissions' and enclose your CV with a headshot. Only those also enclosing an sae can expect a reply, usually within 4-6 weeks. We *do not* accept showreels and cannot accept responsibility for the loss of any items. Please ensure that any sae is large enough for the return of your photos."

Urban Talent

Nemesis House, 1 Oxford Court, Bishopsgate, Manchester M2 3WQ
tel 0161-834 0990 *fax* 0161-834 0014
email liz@nmsmanagement.co.uk
Key personnel Liz Beeley

Urban Talent represents 30-50 actors. Areas of work include theatre, television, film, commercials, corporate and voice-overs. Also represents presenters.

Will consider attending performances at venues in the North West with 2 weeks' notice. Accepts submissions (with CVs and photographs) from actors previously unknown to the company, sent by post or email. Also accepts invitations to view individual actors' websites. *Commission*: 15%

UVA Management

Pinewood Studios, Pinewood Road, Iver SL0 0NH
tel (01753) 652233
email info@uvamanagement.com
website www.uvamanagement.com
Head agent Wayne Berko

Established in 2004. Main areas of work are theatre, musicals, television, commercials and corporate. 2 agents represent around 8 actors; also represents presenters.

Welcomes letters (with CVs and photographs) from actors previously unknown to the company if sent by post or email, but prefers not to receive invitations to view individual actors' websites. Does not accept showreels or voicereels. Welcomes enquiries from actors with disabilities. *Commission*: Theatre 10%; TV and Film 13%

Roxanne Vacca Management

73 Beak Street, London W1F 9SR

2 agents represent 45 actors. Does not welcome performance notices, but will accept letters (with CVs and photographs) from individual actors previously unknown to the agency if sent by post. Also accepts showreels, voicereels, and invitations to view individual actors' websites. *Commission*: Film & TV 12.5%; Theatre 10%; Commercials 15%

Suzann Wade

9 Wimpole Mews, London W1G 8PB
tel 020-7486 0746 *fax* 020-7486 5664
email info@suzannwade.com
website www.suzannwade.com
Director Suzann Wade *Assistants* Andrew Simic, Martine Mercer

Areas of work include theatre, musicals, film, commercials, corporate and voice-over. 1 agent represents 19 actors.

Welcomes performance notices for London venues only (West End and Central), if received as hard copy by post and at least 2 weeks' notice is given. Welcomes letters (with CVs and photographs) from individual actors previously unknown to the company if sent by post with sae. No emails, follow-up calls or voicereels, but will accept showreels if they are sent with an sae for return. Encourages enquiries from disabled actors sent by post, and currently represents, or plans to represent, actors with disabilities.

Waring & McKenna Ltd

31 Sackville St, Mayfair, London W1S 3DZ
tel 020-7734 7555 *fax* 020-7734 5050
email dj@waringandmckenna.com
Agents Daphne Waring, John Summerfield

Established in 1993. 2 agents represent approximately 80 actors. Areas of work include theatre, musicals, television, film, commercials, corporate and voice-overs.

Will consider attending performances at venues within Greater London and occasionally elsewhere, given at least 1 month's notice. Accepts postal submissions (with CVs and photographs) from actors previously unknown to the company. Follow-up telephone calls are also accepted. Showreels and voicereels should only be sent on request. *Commission*: Theatre 10%; TV and Low-Budget Films 12.5%; Commercials and Feature Films over £4 million 15%

Janet Welch Personal Management

Old Orchard, The Street, Ubley, Bristol BS40 6PJ
tel (01761) 463238
email info@janetwelchpm.co.uk

Established in 1990. Areas of work include theatre, musicals, television, film, commercials, corporate and voice-overs.

Will consider attending performances at venues within Greater London and sometimes elsewhere, given sufficient notice. Accepts submissions (with CVs and photographs) from actors previously unknown to the company if sent by post.

West End Management

The Penthouse, 42/17 Speirs Wharf, Glasgow G4 9TH
tel 0141-226 8941 *fax* 0141-226 8983
email info@west-endmgt.com
website www.west-endmgt.com
Agents Maureen Cairns, Martin Bristow

Established in 1996. 2 agents represent 50 actors.

Will consider attending performances at venues in Scotland with 3-4 weeks' notice. Accepts submissions (with CVs and photographs) from actors previously unknown to the agency, including disabled actors – but please do not submit by email. Showreels, voicereels and invitations to view individual actors' websites are also accepted. *Commission*: 15%

Williamson & Holmes

9 Hop Gardens, St Martin's Lane,
London WC2N 4EN
tel 020-7240 0407 *fax* 020-7240 0408
email info@williamsonandholmes.co.uk
Agents Jackie Williamson, Michelle Holmes *Voice-over Agent* Sophie Reisch

Established in 2004, the agency represents 70 actors and 30 voice-over artists. Areas of work include theatre, musicals, television, film, commercials, corporate and voice-overs.

Will consider attending performances at venues within Greater London with 2 weeks' notice. Accepts submissions (with CVs and photographs) from actors previously unknown to the company if sent by post. Showreels and voicereels are also accepted with sae for their return. Emails with attachments will not be opened. *Commission*: Theatre 10%; TV, Film, Commercials and Radio 15%

Willow Personal Management

151 Main Street, Yaxley, Peterborough PE7 3LD
tel (01733) 240392

email office@willowmanagement.co.uk
website www.willowmanagement.co.uk
Director Peter Burroughs

Established in 1995. 1 agent represents more than 150 actors. Specialises in the representation of short actors (under 5ft) and tall actors (over 7ft). Areas of work include theatre, musicals, television, film, commercials, corporate and voice-overs.

Accepts submissions (with CVs and photographs) from actors previously unknown to the company if sent by post, but not by email. Showreels, voicereels and invitations to view individual actors' websites are also accepted. Welcomes enquiries from disabled actors. *Commission*: 15%

Newton Wills Management

The Studio, 29 Springvale Avenue, Brentford, Middlesex TW8 9QT
tel (07989) 398381
email newtoncttg@aol.com
website www.newtonwills.com
Managing Director Newton Wills
International Christopher Socci

Established in 1963. 4 agents represent 50 actors. Areas of work include theatre, musicals, television, film and commercials. Also represents choreographers.

Will consider attending performances at venues within Greater London and elsewhere, but requests as much notice as possible. Accepts submissions (with CVs and photographs) from actors previously unknown to the company, sent by post or email. Showreels and voicereels are also accepted. "Find out as soon as possible what an agent does. The relationship between actor and agent should be a partnership – work with your agent to develop your talents, and add new ones to your repertoire."

WIS Celtic Management

86 Elphinstone Road, London E17 5EX
tel 020-8523 4234 *fax* 020-8523 4523
email wis.celtic@ethnicsaa.co.uk
Managing Director Pauline Oni

Established in 2004, specialising in Welsh, Irish and Scottish actors. Areas of work include theatre, musicals, television, film, commercials, corporate and voice-overs. One agent represents 12 actors.

Will consider attending performances within Greater London with at least 3 weeks' notice. Accepts submissions (with CVs and photographs) from actors previously unknown to the agency if sent by post, but not by email. Welcomes showreels and voicereels, and enquiries from disabled actors. *Commission*: Varies

Edward Wyman Agency

67 Llanon Road, Llanishen, Cardiff CF14 5AH
tel 029-2075 2351 *fax* 029-2075 2444
email edward.wyman@btconnect.com
website www.wymancasting.co.uk

Managing Director Edward Wyman *Casting/Accounts* Judith Gay *Casting* Audrey Williams

Established in 1969, the agency represents more than 200 actors. Areas of work include television, film, commercials, corporate and voice-overs. Also represents directors, singers, dancers, circus performers, models, look-alikes, extras and promotions people.

Accepts submissions from actors previously unknown to the company. Actors should download an application form from the website. All submissions should be sent by post only, and should include CVs, photographs and sae. "The large majority of our work is in the Welsh language and is filmed in the South Wales area, so Welsh actors are particularly welcome." Recommends the photographer Brian Tarr (6 Bangor Street, Cardiff CF24 3LR).
Commission: OAPs 12.5%; Others 15%

Yellow Balloon Productions Ltd

Freshwater House, Outdowns, Effingham KT24 5QR
tel (01483) 281500 *fax* (01483) 281502
email yellowbal@aol.com
Managing Director Mike Smith *Producer* Daryl Smith
Consultant Sally James

A management company established in 1974 and covering all aspects of clients' career and long-term development; represents around 10 actors. Areas of work include television, film, commercials, corporate and voice-overs. Also represents radio and TV presenters and sports stars.

Will consider attending performances at venues in Greater London and elsewhere, given 2-3 weeks' notice. Accepts submissions (with CVs and photographs) from actors previously unknown to the company, sent by post or email. Also accepts showreels and voicereels. Invitations to view individual actors' websites are only accepted if sent via email. Submitted CVs should be as complete as possible, and clearly separate professional experience from student productions. Applicants should always state if they have yet to acquire a professional role.
Commission: 15-20% according to press, accountancy, and PR agreements

CO-OPERATIVE AGENCIES

Before making an approach, it is important to understand what being a member of one of these entails, and to be clear about your reason(s) for wanting to join. Many Co-ops have clear details for applicants on their websites.

21st Century Actors Management

E10 Panther House, 38 Mount Pleasant,
London WC1X 0AP
tel 020-7278 3438 *fax* 020-7833 1158
email mail@21stcenturyactors.co.uk
website www.21stcenturyactors.co.uk

Co-operative management established in 1992. Represents 21 actors. Areas of work include theatre, musicals, television, film, commercials, corporate and voice-overs. Members are expected to work 3 days in the office per month.

Will consider attending performances at venues in and around London. Accepts submissions (with CVs and photographs) from actors previously unknown to the company if sent by post. Actors requesting representation should write stating why they wish to join a co-operative, and outlining their casting type and skills. *Commission*: 10% for Theatre, TV, Commercials and Film

1984 Personal Management Ltd

Suite 508, Davina House, 137 Goswell Road,
London EC1V 7ET
tel 020-7251 8046 *fax* 020-7250 3031
email info@1984pm.com
website www.1984pm.com

Co-operative management (CPMA member) representing 27 actors. Areas of work include theatre, musicals, television, film, commercials, and corporate. Members are expected to work 4 days in the office per month unless paying commission.

Will consider attending performances at venues in Greater London with 1 month's notice. Accepts letters (with CVs and photographs) from actors previously unknown to the company, following an initial telephone call. Actors should always enquire whether the agency is recruiting before sending CVs. Will also accept showreels and follow-up telephone calls. *Commission*: 10%

Actors Alliance

Disney Place House, 14 Marshalsea Road,
London SE1 1HL
tel 020-7407 6028 *fax* 020-7407 6028
email actors@actorsalliance.co.uk
website www.actorsalliance.co.uk

A co-operative group of actors established in 1976 to advance one another's careers. Currently there are 18 members, who are all in *Spotlight* and belong to Equity. Areas of work include theatre, musicals, television, film, commercials, corporates and voice-overs. Members are expected to work in the office at least 1 day a week.

When interested, and given a minimum of 2 weeks' notice, will attend an applicant's performance in Greater London. Apply (with CV and photograph) by post only, enclosing an sae for reply. Do not send a showreel unless requested to do so. Actors Alliance is not funded from commission.

Actors' Creative Team

Panther House, 38 Mount Pleasant,
London WC1X 0AN

tel 020-7278 3388 *fax* 020-7833 5086
email office@actorscreativeteam.co.uk
website www.actorscreativeteam.co.uk

Founded in 2001, the agency has 20 members working in theatre, musicals, television, film, commercials and corporate projects. Members are expected to work 4 days in the office each month.

Welcomes performance notices for events within Greater London (inside the M25), given 1 month's notice. Will also accept letters (with CVs and photographs) and follow-up telephone calls from actors previously unknown to the agency. Does not welcome emails, showreels or voicereels. Is unlikely to look at an actor's website unless the agency has already shown interest. "Understand what a co-op is, and the financial/time commitment it involves, before you write to us. Make sure that this is the direction you want to pursue, and include your reasons in a covering letter." *Commission*: Theatre 10%; Media 12.5%

Actors Direct Ltd

Gainsborough House, 109 Portland Street, Manchester M1 6DN
tel 0161-237 1904 *fax* 0161-237 1904
email info@actorsdirect.org.uk
website www.actorsdirect.org.uk
Administrators Eilis Hetherington, Jonathan Byrne

Established in 1994. Co-operative management. Sole representative of approximately 25 actors. Areas of work include theatre, musicals, television, film, commercials, corporate and voice-overs. Members are expected to work 2-3 days in the office each month.

Will consider attending performances at venues in the North (Manchester, Leeds, and Liverpool areas) if given 2 weeks' notice. Accepts submissions (with CVs and photographs) from actors previously unknown to the company if sent by post. Also accepts showreels and voicereels. Will consider applications from trained professional actors with excellent IT and communications skills and the ability to perform office duties to a high standard. "Actors Direct is constantly striving to maintain a high professional image and to provide a first-class service to casting directors." *Commission*: 10% for members

Actors Exchange Management (AXM)

308 Panther House, 38 Mount Pleasant, London WC1X 0AN
tel 020-7837 3304
email info@axmgt.com
website www.axmgt.com

Established in 1983. Co-operative management representing 20 actors. Areas of work include theatre, musicals, television, film, commercials, corporate and voice-overs. Members are expected to work 4 days in the office per month.

Will consider attending performances at venues in Greater London, given 1 month's notice. Accepts

submissions (with CVs and photographs) from actors previously unknown to the company if sent by post. Showreels and voicereels should only be sent on request following an interview. *Commission*: 10%

The Actors File

Spitfire Studios, 63-71 Collier Street, London N1 9BE
tel 020-7278 0364 *fax* 020-7278 0364
email mail@theactorsfile.co.uk
website www.theactorsfile.co.uk

Established in 1983. Co-operative management representing 20-25 actors. Areas of work include theatre, musicals, television, film, commercials, corporate and voice-overs. Members are expected to work 4 days in the office per month and to attend business meetings.

Will consider attending performances at venues in Greater London and occasionally elsewhere, if given a minimum of 3 weeks' notice. Accepts submissions (with CVs and photographs) from actors previously unknown to the company if sent by post. Will also accept showreels. *Commission*: 12% (negotiable on low fees)

The Actors' Group

21-31 Oldham Street, Manchester M1 1JG
tel/fax 0161-834 4466
mobile (07963) 832060
email enquiries@theactorsgroup.co.uk
website www.theactorsgroup.co.uk

Established in 1980. Co-operative management representing 20 actors. Areas of work include theatre, musicals, television, film, commercials, corporate and voice-overs. Members are expected to carry out various office duties.

Will consider attending performances at venues in the North West with 2-4 weeks' notice. Accepts submissions (with CVs and photographs) from actors previously unknown to the company if sent by post. Will also accept follow-up telephone calls, showreels, voicereels and invitations to view individual actors' websites.

Actors Network Agency

55 Lambeth Walk, London SE11 6DX
tel 020-7735 0999 *fax* 020-7735 8177
email info@ana-actors.co.uk
website www.ana-actors.co.uk
Coordinator and Administrator Sandie Bakker

Established in 1985. Co-operative management representing 20-30 actors. Areas of work include theatre, musicals, television, film, commercials and corporate. Also represents role-play. Members are expected to work 4 days in the office per month.

Will consider attending performances at venues in Greater London and occasionally elsewhere, given as much notice as possible. Accepts submissions (with CVs and photographs) from actors previously unknown to the company if sent by post. Will also accept showreels. "An interest in, and commitment to, this type of agency is essential." *Commission*: 10%; Commercials 12.5%

Actorum Ltd
9 Bourlet Close, London W1W 7BP
tel 020-7636 6978 *fax* 020-7636 6975
email info@actorum.com
website www.actorum.com

Co-operative management representing 30 actors. Members are expected to work 4 days in the office per month.

Will consider attending performances at venues in Greater London and elsewhere, given 4 weeks' notice. Accepts postal submissions with CVs and photographs. "No applications by email, please." Showreels, voicereels and invitations to view individual actors' websites accepted. *Commission*: Theatre 10%; TV, Commercials and Film 15%

Alpha Personal Management
Studio B4, 3 Bradbury Street, London N16 8JN
tel 020-7241 0077 *fax* 020-7241 2410
email alpha@alphaactors.com
website www.alphaactors.com

Established in 1983, the agency represents 25 actors in theatre, musicals, television, film, commercials and corporate work. Members are expected to work 4 days in the office each month.

Will consider attending performances within Greater London given as much as notice as possible. Welcomes submissions (with CVs and photographs) from actors previously unknown to the company, sent by post or email. Will also accept invitations to view an actor's website. Follow-up telephone calls, however, are not appreciated. *Commission*: 10% with concessions for low-paid work

Arena Personal Management Ltd
E11 Panther House, 38 Mount Pleasant, London WC1X 0AP
tel 020-7278 1661 *fax* 020-7278 1661
email arenapmltd@aol.com
website www.arenapmltd.co.uk

Co-operative management representing 20 actors. Areas of work include theatre, musicals, television, film, commercials, corporate and voice-overs. Members are expected to work 1 day in the office per week.

Will consider attending performances at venues in Greater London given 3-4 weeks' notice. Accepts submissions (with CVs and photographs) from actors previously unknown to the company if sent by post. Will also accept follow-up telephone calls, showreels, voicereels and invitations to view individual actors' websites. *Commission*: Theatre 10%; Commercials 12.5%

Bridges: The Actors' Agency Ltd
St George's West, 58 Shandwick Place, Edinburgh EH2 4RT

tel 0131-226 6433
email admin@bridgesactorsagency.com
website www.bridgesactorsagency.com

Established in 2008. At present the only co-operative agency active in Scotland. Areas of work include theatre, television, film, commercials, radio and corporate. Members are expected to contribute to the running of the office, and to attend meetings; therefore all prospective members must be based a commutable distance from Edinburgh.

Accepts submissions via letters and emails: include a CV and headshot. Will also accept showreels, voicereels and invitations to view individual actors' websites. Welcomes invitations to attend performances and showcases.

Entry to the agency is via audition. If successful, a stakeholder donation of £100 is required to join the agency. Prospective members must also be registered with Spotlight. *Commission*: Non-Electronic 10%; Electronic 12%

Castaway Actors Agency
30-31 Wicklow Street, Dublin 2
tel 353-1671 9264 *fax* 353-1761 9133
email castaway@clubi.ie
website www.irish-actors.com

Established in 1989. A co-operative agency representing 29 actors. Members are expected to work 2 days a month. Areas of work include theatre, musicals, television, film, commercials, corporate, voice-overs. Also represent presenters.

Will consider attending performances in Dublin only, with at least 1 week's notice. Accepts submissions (with CVs and photographs) from actors previously unknown to the agency. Will also accept CVs and photographs sent via email. Invitations to view individual actors' websites, showreels and voicereels are also accepted. Follow-up calls are welcomed.

CCM
Panther House, 38 Mount Pleasant, London WC1X 0AP
tel 020-7278 0507
email casting@ccmactors.com
website www.ccmactors.com

Secretary David Shackleton *Administrator* Elyse Marks

Established in 1993. Co-operative management representing up to 30 actors. Areas of work include theatre, film, television, musicals and commercials. Members are expected to work up to 3 days in the office per month, and need office skills.

Members will consider attending performances, with notice. The agency accepts letters and emails (with photographs and CVs) from actors previously unknown to the membership, and will also accept invitations to view actors' personal websites. Entry to the agency is via audition, which prospective members will be invited to attend. Actors must be aware of how co-operatives work, and their role within them. Information is available from Equity and The Spotlight. A Stakeholder fee of £250 (in 2 instalments) is required to join the agency. Prospective clients must also be registered in *Spotlight*.

Central Line
11 East Circus Street, Nottingham NG1 5AF
tel 0115-941 2937
email centralline@btconnect.com
website www.the-central-line.co.uk

Established in 1984. Co-operative management representing 15-25 actors. Areas of work include theatre, musicals, television, film, commercials, corporate and voice-overs. Also represents directors. Members are expected to work in the office as and when appropriate.

Will consider attending performances at venues in Greater London and elsewhere. Accepts submissions (with CVs and photographs) from actors previously unknown to the company, sent by post or email. Will also accept follow-up telephone calls, showreels, voicereels and invitations to view individual actors' websites. *Commission*: 10%

Circuit Personal Management Ltd
Suite 71 SEC, Bedford Street,
Stoke-on-Trent ST1 4PZ
tel (01782) 285388 *fax* (01782) 206821
email mail@circuitpm.co.uk
website www.circuitpm.co.uk

Established in 1988. Co-operative management representing 20-25 actors. Areas of work include theatre, musicals, television, film, commercials, corporate and voice-overs. Members are expected to work approximately 15 days annually and attend monthly meetings.

Will consider attending performances at venues in the West Midlands, North West and West Yorkshire, preferably with 3-4 weeks' notice. Accepts submissions from actors (with CVs and photographs) sent by post or email. Will also accept follow-up telephone calls.

City Actors' Management
Oval House, 52-54 Kennington Oval,
London SE11 5SW
tel 020-7793 9888 *fax* 020-7820 0990
email info@cityactors.co.uk
website www.cityactors.co.uk

Co-operative management representing 21 actors with 1 permanent, office-based rep. Areas of work include theatre, musicals, television, film, commercials and corporate. Members are expected to work 4 days in the office per month.

Will consider attending performances at venues in Greater London with a minimum of 2 weeks' notice.

Submissions (with CVs and photographs) should be sent by post and not by email. Advises actors to contact the agency when appearing in a show, or with a showreel, as new members will not be admitted without their work being seen. Will also accept follow-up telephone calls. *Commission*: Theatre 10%/12.5% depending on income; Media 15%

Crescent Management
10 Barley Mow Passage, Chiswick, London W4 4PH
tel 020-8987 0191
email mail@crescentmanagement.co.uk
website www.crescentmanagement.co.uk

Established in 1991, the agency has 24 members working in theatre, musicals, television, film, commercials and corporate drama. Members are expected to work 3 days in the office each month.

Will consider attending performances within Greater London given 2 weeks' notice. Accepts submissions (with CVs and photographs) from actors previously unknown to the agency if sent by post. Email applications are unwelcome. Will also accept follow-up telephone calls, showreels, voicereels and invitations to view an actor's website. *Commission*: Theatre 10%; Television 12.5%; Film 15%

Denmark Street Management
Clarendon Buildings, Suite 4, 25 Horsell Road, Highbury, London N5 1XL
tel 020-7700 5200 *fax* 020-7084 4053
email mail@denmarkstreet.net
website www.denmarkstree.net

Established in 1985. Co-operative management representing up to 30 actors working in theatre, musicals, television, film, commercials, corporate and voice-overs. Members are expected to work 4 days in the office per month.

Will consider attending performances if given notice. Accepts submissions by email from actors previously unknown to the company (members of Spotlight only). Showreels and voicereels should only be sent on request. Applicants should state why they would like to join a co-operative. Ethnic-minority and older actors are particularly welcome. *Commission*: 10%, up to 15%

Direct Personal Management
Park House, 62 Lidgett Lane, Leeds LS8 1PL
tel/fax 0113-266 4036
email daphne.franks@directpm.co.uk
St John's House, 16 St John's Vale, London, SE8 4EN
tel/fax 020-8694 1788
website www.directpm.co.uk

Established in 1984 (formerly Direct Line Personal Management). Co-operative management representing 35 actors. Areas of work include theatre, musicals, television, film, commercials, corporate, role-play and voice-overs. Members are expected to work 2 days in the office each month.

Will consider attending performances at venues within Greater London and elsewhere, with 1 month's notice. Accepts submissions (with CVs and photographs) from actors previously unknown to the company, sent by post or email. Follow-up telephone calls, showreels, voicereels and invitations to view individual actors' websites are also accepted. "Please consult our website before applying. Every applicant's enquiry is discussed at a monthly meeting. We do reply, but would appreciate it if actors enclosed an sae to help reduce our costs." *Commission*: 5-15%

IML

The White House, 52-54 Kennington Oval, London SE11 5SW
tel 020-7587 1080 *fax* 020-7587 1080
email info@iml.org.uk
website www.iml.org.uk

Co-operative management established in 1980. Represents 22 actors. 2 members work in the office each day on a rotational basis. Areas of work include theatre, musicals, television, film and commercials. Members are expected to work 4 days in the office per month.

Will consider attending performances at venues in Greater London given 3 weeks' notice. Accepts submissions (with CVs and photographs) from actors previously unknown to the company if sent by post. Will also accept follow-up telephone calls. Showreels and voicereels should only be sent on request. *Commission*: 5-15% depending on the job

Inspiration Management

Room 227, The Aberdeen Centre,
22-24 Highbury Grove, London N5 2EA
tel 020-7704 0440 *fax* 020-7704 8497
email mail@inspirationmanagement.org.uk
website www.inspirationmanagement.org.uk
Key contact Applications Team

Established in 1986, Inspiration is a co-operative management representing 20-25 actors. Principal areas of work include theatre, television, film and commercials; occasionally corporate, audio and role-play. Members work 3 days in the office per month, when not engaged in professional acting work, and attend regular meetings.

Actors should apply by post only, including a CV, 10x8in headshot and covering letter with land-line number and email address if available; do not send demos or showreels initially. Members are consulted on all applications and will interview candidates wherever possible. Actors are advised to consult the website to check for casting overlaps. As at least 2 members will need to see an applicant's work, and a minimum of 3 weeks' notice is required for any forthcoming appearances. *Commission*: 10%

Links Management

34-68 Colombo Street, London SE1 8DP
tel 020-7928 0806 *fax* 020-7928 0806
email agent@links-management.co.uk
website www.links-management.co.uk
Office Manager John Holloway

Established in 1984. Co-operative management representing 25 actors. Areas of work include theatre, musicals, television, film, commercials and voice-overs. Members are expected to work 1 day in the office per week.

Will consider attending performances at venues within Greater London given 2 weeks' notice. Accepts submissions (with CVs and photographs) from actors previously unknown to the company if sent by post. Also accepts follow-up telephone calls, showreels and voicereels. *Commission*: Theatre 10%; TV and Film 12.5%

MV Management

Ralph Richardson Memorial Studios,
Kingfisher Place, Clarendon Road, London N22 6XF
tel 020-8889 8231 *fax* 020-8829 1050
email theagency@mountview.org.uk
website www.mvmanagement.co.uk

Represents actors in all areas of the industry: television, film, theatre, musicals, commercials, radio and voiceover. "MV Management is a co-operative agency exclusively for actors who attended and have graduated from Mountview Academy of Theatre Arts. Please do not contact the agency regarding representation unless you are a Mountview graduate."

North of Watford Actors Agency

Bridge Mill, Hebden Bridge, West Yorks HX7 8EX
tel (01422) 845361 *fax* (01422) 846503
email info@northofwatford.com
website www.northofwatford.com
New Applications Coordinator Chris Orton

Established in 1992. Co-operative management representing 25-30 actors. Areas of work include theatre, musicals, television, film, commercials, corporate and voice-overs. Members are expected to work 3-4 days in the office per month.

Will consider attending performances at venues in Northern locations (Leeds, Manchester, etc.) but requests as much notice as possible. Accepts submissions (with CVs and photographs) from actors previously unknown to the company if sent by post. Will also accept follow-up telephone calls, showreels, voicereels and invitations to view individual actors' websites. *Commission*: Varies depending on the work

North One Management

HG08 Aberdeen Studios, Highbury Grove,
London N5 2EA
tel 020-7359 9666
email actors@northone.co.uk
website www.northone.co.uk

Established in 1987. Co-operative management representing 25 actors. Areas of work include theatre, television, film, commercials and corporate. Members are expected to work 3 days in the office per month.

Will consider attending performances at venues within Greater London given at least 1 week's notice. Accepts submissions (with CVs and b&w 10x8in photographs) from actors previously unknown to the company if sent by post. Will also accept follow-up telephone calls, showreels and voicereels. Prefers to hear from actors when currently performing. Administration and technical skills are advantageous. Applications from non-European performers are particularly welcome. *Commission*: 10%

Oren Actors Management
Chapter Arts Centre, Market Road, Cardiff CF5 1QE
tel 029-2023 3321
email info@orenactorsmanagement.co.uk
website www.orenactorsmanagement.co.uk
Key personnel Co-operative Administrator

Established in 1981. Co-operative management representing 20-25 actors. Areas of work include theatre, musicals, television, film, commercials, corporate and voice-overs. Members are expected to work 2-3 days in the office per month.

Will consider attending performances at venues in Greater London, Cardiff, South West England and Wales given 2 weeks' notice. Accepts submissions (with CVs and photographs) from actors previously unknown to the company if sent by post. Will also accept follow-up telephone calls, showreels, voicereels and invitations to view individual actors' websites. Applicants are asked to state clearly why they have approached a co-operative. *Commission*: Theatre 8%; Mechanical Media 10%

Otto Personal Management Ltd
Office 2, Sheffield Ind. Film, 5 Brown Street, Sheffield S1 2BS
tel 0114-275 2592 *fax* 0114-279 5225
email admin@ottopm.co.uk
website www.ottopm.co.uk

Established in 1985. Co-operative management with a full-time co-ordinator, and representing approx. 45 actors. Areas of work include theatre, musicals, television, film, commercials, corporate and voice-overs. Also represents directors and presenters. Members are expected to work an average of 3 days per year in the office.

Will consider attending performances at venues in Yorkshire, the North Midlands, Manchester and the surrounding areas with approximately 1 month's notice. Accepts submissions (with CVs and photographs) from actors previously unknown to the company sent by post or email. Will also accept follow-up telephone calls, showreels, voicereels and invitations to view individual actors' websites. "We mainly recruit actors living within a viable distance of Sheffield – Leeds to the North, Mansfield to Manchester." *Commission*: 10-13%

Our Company
Room 205, Channelsea House, Canning Road, Stratford, London E15 3ND
tel 020-8221 1151 *fax* 020-8221 1167
email info@our-company.co.uk
website www.our-company.co.uk
Company Directors Euan Winson, Anna Ecclestone
Head of Recruitment Kirsty Malyon

Established in 2006. Co-operative management representing 10-20 actors working in musicals, television, film, commercials, corporate and voice-overs. Members are expected to work 4 days in the office each month.

Will accept performance notices within the Greater London area only, with a minimum of 2 weeks' notice. Wecomes letters (with CVs and photographs) from individual actors previously unknown to the agency, sent by post or email; will also accept follow-up telephone calls, showreels, voicereels, and invitations to view individual actors' websites. Encourages enquiries from actors with disabilities. *Commission*: 8% to Company; 2% to Member securing contract

Performance Actors Agency
137 Goswell Road, London EC1V 7ET
tel 020-7251 5716 *fax* 020-7251 3974
email info@performanceactors.co.uk
website www.performanceactors.co.uk
Key personnel Lionel Guyett

Established in 1984. Co-operative management representing 30+ actors. Areas of work include theatre, musicals, television, film, commercials, corporate and voice-overs. Members are expected to work 4 days a month in the office.

Will consider attending performances at venues within Greater London and occasionally elsewhere, given as much notice as possible. Accepts submissions (with CVs and photographs) from actors previously unknown to the company if sent by post and enclosing sae. Will also accept showreels and voicereels. " We only recruit new members when specific categories are required. Call first." *Commission*: 10%

RbA Management Ltd
37-45 Windsor Street, Liverpool L8 1XET
tel 0151-708 7273
email info@rbamanagement.co.uk
website www.rbamanagement.co.uk

Established in 1995 (as Rattlebag Management). Co-operative management representing more than 25 actors. Areas of work include theatre, musicals, television, film, radio, commercials, corporate and voice-overs. Many of the actors have other, additional skills. Members are expected to work a minimum of 4 full weeks within a 12-month period.

Will consider attending performances at venues in the North West (Manchester, Liverpool, North

Wales) and nationally with 3-4 weeks' notice. Accepts brief, straightforward submissions (with CVs and photographs) from actors previously unknown to the company if sent by post. Photographs should ideally be current b&w headshots. Showreels, voicereels and invitations to view individual actors' websites are also accepted. "If invited to an audition or interview, it is always best to call in with a response – whether you wish to accept or not." *Commission*: 12.5%

Rogues & Vagabonds Management

The Print House, 18 Ashwin Street, London E8 3DL
tel 020-7254 8130
email rogues@vagabondsmanagement.com
website www.vagabondsmanagement.com

Co-operative management representing 28-30 actors. Areas of work include theatre, musicals, television, film, commercials and corporate. Members are expected to work in the office 3 days per month.

Will consider attending performances anywhere, if given at least 3-4 weeks' notice. Accepts submissions (with CVs and photographs) from actors previously unknown to the company if sent by post or email. Showreels, voicereels and invitations to view individual actors' websites are also accepted. Welcomes enquiries from disabled actors. *Commission*: TV/Film 10% on first £200, 15% thereafter; Theatre 10%

Rosebery Management Ltd

Hoxton Hall, 130 Hoxton Street, London N1 6SH
tel 020-7684 0187 *fax* 020-7684 0197
email admin@roseberymanagement.com

Established in 1984. Represents 27 actors in theatre, musicals, television, film, commercials, corporate work and voice-overs. Rosebery has a full-time Lead Agent. Members are expected to work 2 days in the office per month. 10% commission on all acting work.

Will consider attending performances at all venues within Central London. Only accepts submissions from actors seeking representation if sent by post. Submissions must include a 10x8in b&w photograph, a current CV and a covering letter. Showreels, voicereels and singing reels are also welcomed.

Stage Centre Management Ltd

41 North Road, London N7 9DP
tel 020-7607 0872 *fax* 020-7609 0213
email info@stagecentre.org.uk
website www.stagecentre.org.uk

Established in 1982. Co-operative management with Lead Agent representing 18-26 actors. Areas of work include theatre, musicals, television, film, commercials and corporate. Members are expected to work 1 day in the office per week when not acting.

Will consider attending performances at venues within Greater London and elsewhere, given at least 2 weeks' notice. Accepts submissions (with CVs and photographs) from actors previously unknown to the company, sent by post or email. All applicants are advised to call asking for a specific contact name before applying. Will also accept follow-up telephone calls, showreels, voicereels and invitations to view individual actors' websites. Applicants should not apply if they are unable to provide visible evidence of their work (e.g. performance notice, showcase or showreel). *Commission*: 10-15% depending on job

West Central Management

E4 Panther House, 38 Mount Pleasant, London WC1X 0AP
tel 020-7833 8134 *fax* 020-7833 8134
email mail@westcentralmanagement.co.uk
website www.westcentralmanagement.co.uk

Established in 1984. Co-operative management representing 15-20 actors. Areas of work include theatre, musicals, television, film, commercials and corporate. Members are expected to work 4 days in the office per month.

Will consider attending performances at venues within Greater London with 2 weeks' notice. Accepts submissions (with CVs and photographs) from actors previously unknown to the company, sent by post or email. Will also accept invitations to view individual actors' websites. "We would need to see an applicant's live performance or showreel, but only after an initial meeting/audition." *Commission*: 10%

Being an agent
Howard Roberts

There are a number of unfortunate stereotypes of agents, and – particularly among younger actors – misconceptions about an agent's role. Whilst popular belief would have us all enjoying long lunches between bouts of shark-like behaviour, the truth is somewhat more akin to that of any other hard-working facilitator.

What does an agent do?

There is no definitive job description for an agent; you will find that different agents have different styles, and work in different ways. Broadly speaking, however, we can divide the agent's role into four broad aims, as follows: ·

• to maintain contacts across the industry, in order to secure work for their clients – most commonly in terms of obtaining casting information; ·

• to negotiate fees on behalf of those clients, in order to maximise rewards for the artist, and to ensure that those fees are paid; ·

• to manage the artist's diary in order not to miss the next job opportunity; and ·

• to advise the artist on their career choices and options.

Bear in mind that your agent is working for you all the time, even when you might not be earning. It is for this reason that you pay them commission for all performing work in which you are engaged whilst they represent you.

When you see agents at showcases and first nights, or when you hear that an agent is coming to your production, remember that this is usually after they have already worked a full day in the office. Attending these events is a key part of their business: it is their opportunity to network, to keep abreast of new developments and new performers, and to maintain good relationships – for example, with a casting director. The job of an agent can be immensely rewarding, but those rewards come as a result of long hours and hard work.

How do I get an agent?

Sadly, anyone can call themselves an agent, because there are no entry restrictions to the profession. In this book you will find more than 50 pages listing agents: some of them belong to the Personal Managers' Association (PMA), a body that requires members to have at least three years' trading in the industry prior to joining. However, many other established and reputable agents choose not to belong to the PMA. So take advice. Talk to other performers, to casting directors and to established industry advisers like John Colclough, and endeavour to establish a shortlist of suitable contacts.

A phone call or an email may establish whether an agency is currently considering new clients. Don't be too disheartened if they say that their list is full – persevere with other approaches. And do be careful with emailed requests: many agents now find themselves inundated with email traffic from actors seeking representation, and could choose not to respond.

If an agency asks you to send in your details, check what they require: this will usually be a current CV, a clear 10x8in head shot and a covering letter. See if they want a DVD showreel, or a CD voicereel, but be careful of sending these unsolicited. I would suggest that you always send a correctly stamped and addressed envelope with your submission, as this will make it easier for the agent to respond.

The CV should contain your relevant professional experience, details of where you trained, and any other marketable skill(s) you may possess (for example, a clean driving licence, sports at which you are proficient, languages you might speak, musical instruments you can play, whether you can safely ride a horse, and anything else that might add to your performance).

Photographs should be clear and as up to date as possible. Remember, on the Spotlight site your photo will appear slightly smaller than a passport photo, so you want the best possible definition, at the smallest size. You are in an image-led profession, and your picture is likely to be the first point of contact. Always go to a professional photographer, but be careful of spending too much money on photos until you have an agent; chances are, they might want something different. And always put your contact details on the back of your photo; in a busy office it can get separated from your letter and CV.

Keep your letter businesslike: check to whom you are writing, date the letter and spell their name correctly. Finally, ensure that you use the correct postage: it will not improve your chances if the agent has to pay a surcharge on your letter. Of course, the agent might be happy to receive an emailed submission, using your Spotlight PIN number to access your details. Always ensure that your Spotlight entry is up to date with your correct playing age, latest credits and full list of marketable skills.

Interviews

Turn up on time – never late, but not too early either. Check where you are going in advance so that you don't arrive flustered. You are going to see a busy person, who may be in a position to help your career, so treat the meeting seriously. If you fail to attend at the agreed time, they may think that you will treat castings in a similar manner.

Before 'the day', have your questions ready and prepared in your mind. How long have you been established? How many agents work here? How many clients do you represent? What are your commission rates? (It is unusual for these to be higher than 15% – and be very wary of any agency who would charge you for enrolment.) Are you VAT registered? (If so, remember that this means you will be paying VAT on top of your commission.) Where would you fit in with this agency, and would you clash with any of their existing clients?

This is all information that you need to glean – but at interview, do be careful *how* you ask your questions. Some agents might be more reticent than others; you will need to carefully judge the mood and tone of the meeting. The agent might want to make it clear that they are interviewing you, and not the other way round. Remember, agents will vary in their style and way of working: you must be sensitive and able to adapt.

Offers of representation

Agencies come in all shapes and sizes. Larger, well-established West End concerns certainly have the attraction of the star names they represent, and if they offer you a place it could work for you. They will have the first look at film scripts, and the international cachet. However, what are sometimes referred to as the 'boutique agencies' might also be advantageous: with them, you are likely to have direct access to the principal partners, and you are more likely to be important to them. Smaller agencies have the motivation to secure as much work as possible for their clients, for as much time as possible. They will not want 'passengers'.

If you do get an offer, or offers, of representation, take time to think about it, and *always* seek advice. This is an important decision. Remember that you are entering into a business relationship, not looking for a new best friend. Of course, the best sort of actor to be is a working actor, and so the agency that works best for you is the one that helps you to keep working, irrespective of its size and location or how long it has been established.

Contracts

A contract should place your business relationship on a professional basis, clearly stating not just commission rates, but also such important issues as the required notice period for terminating your agreement. Don't be afraid of being contractually committed, but neither should you ever sign a contract on the spot. Take it away and get a second opinion, be it from another performer, from Equity, or from someone with specialist knowledge.

Problems?

How often do agents hear actors complain that their agent never puts them up for anything – or that they are not seen, even though they are ideal for a part? The harsh reality is that it is a buyer's market. You face vast amounts of competition for every job, and despite your agent's best efforts, the casting director still might not want to see you.

If you really do feel that the actor-agent relationship is not working, the first person you should talk to is your agent! Try to work out if there has been any misunderstanding about your skills, or playing age, or photo; often such issues can easily be resolved by honest discussion.

If there are irreconcilable differences, then try hard to part amicably. It's a small profession, and agents do talk to one another. Attempt to secure new representation before you move, but first check any obligations you have to your existing agent in terms of period of notice, or ongoing work, or work for which you have been submitted.

And finally ...

Always try and work with your agent. Establish how proactive they want you to be. If there are areas of work you do not wish to pursue, make sure that you let your agent know. Always ensure that you keep your agent fully aware of your availability – weekends and holidays included.

Remember: actors face huge amounts of competition, and it is the agent's job to improve the odds in a client's favour. It is a very tough profession, and experience often indicates that you have to work very hard just to be lucky.

Howard Roberts MSc is a partner in Sandra Griffin Management Ltd. He has been an actors' agent for more than 20 years, initially as an assistant and then as a co-director. Prior to this he was a lecturer in Economics and Politics in Further Education. He lives in West London.

CPMA: the Co-operative Personal Management Association

Almost all actors' co-operative agencies belong to the CPMA, which was created in 2002 to promote co-op agencies in the profession, encourage the highest professional standards, and represent the interests of co-op agencies to outside bodies, such as Equity and Government departments.

Actors represented by co-operative agencies run the agency themselves, through a democratic structure, and work as unpaid agents for each other. Some co-ops employ a co-ordinator or administrator (who is not an actor). Co-op agencies are non-profit-making, and any surplus funds are put back into the business. Co-op agencies began in the UK in 1970, since when many more have been established and thrive. Co-ops access the same casting information as conventional agents and suggest actors for jobs, negotiate contracts and fees, take commission on jobs, and recommend and promote their clients to casting directors (CDs) and others. There is often a fee to join a co-op, which is refunded when you leave. Other, non-refundable, fees may be charged, and there could also be a voluntary monthly levy to cover office costs, co-ordinator's fees, etc. Co-op members work in the office (typically two to four times a month), attend business meetings (usually monthly) to discuss aspects of running the agency, oversee the work of other co-op members (often with CDs), and consider the work of applicants.

Belonging to a co-op has many advantages: ·
• You quickly learn how the industry works, which can be very useful for newcomers and those returning to the profession.
• You are in contact with many industry professionals, which could help you get work.
• You are supported by other actors in the agency, some of who will have a lot of experience.
• You know which jobs you have been suggested for, and can monitor them.
• You have more influence over how you are represented, and can be more pro-active in your career.
• You can say which type of work you will or won't do, without fear of being asked to leave the agency.
• Usually, more than one person decides whom to suggest for a job. Many CDs acknowledge that co-ops often know their clients much better, and can sell them with honesty and confidence.
• Co-ops have smaller lists of clients, tend to avoid clashes, and commission rates are lower.

However, you should be aware that there can be drawbacks to being part of a co-op. As with conventional agents, standards vary; a co-op is only as good and professional as its members. Can you be sure that other members are working as hard for you, as you are for them? Continuity can also be a problem, with so many people involved. Although co-ops with a co-ordinator may have an advantage in this respect, measures such as detailed note-taking and not changing negotiators on a contract still need to be taken. And CDs tend to send breakdowns for major TV and film roles to the top agencies in the industry – although other parts will be sent to good co-ops.

To join a co-op you need to be a good agent (not just a good actor), committed, reliable and keen to support fellow actors. You must be able to use a computer and learn the software the agency uses. You must be prepared to get on the phone, talk to CDs, and sell your clients with knowledge and conviction, making intelligent and credible suggestions for roles. Consider, too, your personal commitments, such as doing non-acting jobs to earn money, and expenses, such as travel to and from the office, and joining/training fees.

If you are thinking of applying to a co-op, first ask if applications are being considered – and if so, how they should be submitted. Many co-ops, like conventional agents, do not accept email applications. Check CVs and photos on the agency's website to identify potential gaps. Send your photograph and CV, saying why a co-op agency interests you, and stressing skills and any contacts you have which could be useful. Co-ops usually want to see an applicant's work, so send a showreel or details of the show you're in (they tend not to go to drama school shows or showcases, unless someone has expressed interest).

To find out more about the agency, talk to current and former members. You might want to know when the agency was established; if any ex-members have returned; the extent of their contacts with CDs and with theatres; the range of casting information they receive; and whether they belong to the CPMA, which has a code of conduct (Equity particularly welcomed the creation of the CPMA for this reason). If the co-op is interested in your application, you will be interviewed by all available members. If offered a place, you will usually have a three- to six-month trial period. After discussion to see how both sides feel, you may then be offered full membership.

Please visit **www.cpma.coop** for further information.

Agents and casting directors

Voice-over agents

This section lists agencies that specialise in voice-overs. Check the details of how each wishes to be approached, and refer to the 'Showreel & Voice-Demo Companies' section for more about getting a voice demo (or 'voicereel') made. Some of the larger conventional agencies have their own voice-over departments – generally for their existing clients only.

Accent Bank
420 Falcon Wharf, 34 Lombard Road,
London SW11 3RF
tel 020-7223 5160
email enquiries@accentbank.co.uk
website www.accentbank.co.uk
Director Lisa Paterson

Areas of work include TV, film, commercials, audio books, radio, corporate and training material. 3 agents represent more than 200 clients. Has in-house facilities to produce voicereels for clients and other actors. See the website for current rates.

Accepts submissions from actors previously unknown to the agency. Will also accept submissions sent via email. Voice demos and invitations to view individual actors' websites are also accepted. Follow-up calls are welcome. Will consider representing disabled actors. *Commission*: 15%.

AD Voice
Oxford House, 76 Oxford Street, London W1D 1BS
tel 020-7323 2345 *fax* 020-7323 0101
email info@advoice.co.uk
website www.advoice.co.uk
Key personnel Susan Bartlett

1 agent represents more than 100 clients working in television and radio commercials, documentaries, corporate, animations and audiobook recordings.

Welcomes letters with CVs and voice samples from new actors, but strongly recommends that an sae is included for their return. Prefers not to be contacted by email.

Calypso Voices
25-26 Poland Street, London W1F 8QN
tel 020-7734 6415 *fax* 020-7437 0410
email calypso@calypsovoices.com
website www.calypsovoices.com
Manager Jane Savage

2 agents represent 80 clients for voice-over work. Areas of work include television and radio commercials, documentaries, animation, corporate, audio books and on-air promotions.

Cinel Gabran Management
PO Box 5163, Cardiff CF5 9JB; also at PO Box 101, Whitby, North Yorks YO21 3WT

tel 0845-066 6605 *fax* 0845-066 6601
email info@cinelgabran.co.uk
website www.cinelgabran.co.uk
Managing Director/Agent David Chance

Represents actors from any ethnic background, but also specialises in Welsh-language speakers. See entry on page 49 for more details.

Conway Van Gelder Grant
Third Floor, 8-12 Broadwick Street,
London W1F 8HW
tel 020-7287 1070 *fax* 020-7287 1940
email info@conwayvg.co.uk
website www.conwayvangelder.com
Agents Kate Pulmpton, Graeme Legg

Areas of work include animated film, commercials and audio books. 2 agents represent approximately 150 clients. Client list includes some disabled actors. *Commission*: 15%

Cut Glass Voices
Studio 185, 181-187 Queens Crescent, Camden,
London NW5 4DS
tel 020-8374 4701 *fax* 020-8374 4701
email info@cutglassproductions.com
website www.cutglassproductions.com
Agents Kerry Mitchell, Phil Corran

Voice-over agent dealing with all areas of voice work – commercials, documentaries, cartoons, audio books and radio. 45+ voices are represented by 3 agents.

"We provide a voice-over showreel service at Cut Glass Productions – for our own agency and others, and for newcomers to the voice-over industry. For more details please visit our website."

Welcomes representation enquiries from actors not previously known to the agency, by post or email. "Please do not send large MP3s by email; send showreels by post." Happy to receive invitations to view individual actors' websites. Client list includes disabled actors, and further enquiries are welcome. Happy to receive follow-up calls. Prefers actors to phone before sending their voice reel. *Commission*: 15%

Earache Voices
177 Wardour Street, London W1F 8WX
tel 020-7287 2291 *fax* 020-7287 2288

email alex@earachevoices.com
website www.earachevoices.com
Agent Alex Lynch-White

Provides voice-overs for commercials, documentaries, audio books and animation. One agent represents 85+ actors. Recommends Patrick Rowland at Angell Sound (Top Floor, Film House, 142 Wardour Street, London W1F 8WX, 020-7478 7777).

Accepts voicereels by post (include sae) and via email. *Commission*: 15%

Foreign Versions

tel 0333 123 2001
email info@foreignversions.co.uk
website www.foreignversions.com
Directors Margaret Davies, Anne Geary *Project Manager* Bérangère Capelle

Works with advertising agencies for foreign markets, corporate clients, companies producing audio guides, and film and television companies.

As the agency specialises in foreign languages, all voices must be mother-tongue speakers. Voice samples should be sent on MP3 via email, together with a CV.

Hamilton Hodell Ltd

5th Floor, 66-68 Margaret Street, London W1W 8SR
tel 020-7636 1221 *fax* 020-7636 1226
email info@hamiltonhodell.co.uk
website www.hamiltonhodell.co.uk
Head of Voice and Commercials Louise Donald

Main areas of work are television, film, commercials and audio books. 1 agent in the Voice department and 4 in the Acting department represent around 124 clients in total.

Welcomes letters (with CVs) from individual actors previously unknown to the agency, sent by post only. Will accept follow-up telephone calls, unsolicited voicereels, and invitations to view individual actors' websites. Currently represents, or plans to represent, actors with disabilities. *Commission*: 15%

Hobson's Voices

62 Chiswick High Road, London W4 1SY
tel 020-8995 3628 *fax* 020-8996 5350
email voices@hobsons-international.com
website www.hobsons-international.com
Managing Director Donna Lampton *Agents* Kate Davie (Head), Tania Edwards, Linda Spinetti, Ann Dawson, Maxine Burrows, Janet Ferguson-Lees

6 agents represent 160 artists. Welcomes submissions for representation. MP3s to **submissions@hobsons-international.com**, or CDs by post.

iCan Talk Ltd

Palm Tree Mews, 39 Tymecrosse Gardens, Market Harborough, Leics LE16 7US

tel (01858) 466749
email hello@icantalk.co.uk
website www.icantalk.co.uk
Key contact Katie Matthews-Lee

Established in 2009. Voice-over agency; also manages some actors. Approaches welcome if via email with voice clips in MP3 format, CVs and photographs. *Commission*: 12-15%

Lip Service

60-66 Wardour Street, London W1F 0TA
tel 020-7734 3393 *fax* 020-7734 3373
email bookings@lipservice.co.uk
Key personnel Susan Mactavish

4 agents solely represent 80 clients and a number of foreign clients. Areas of work include television, film, commercials and audio books.

Accepts submissions (with CVs and voice CDs) from individual actors previously unknown to the company, sent by email or post. Please enclose an sae for their return.

Rabbit Vocal Management

2nd Floor, 18 Broadwick Street, London W1F 8HS
tel 020-7287 6466 *fax* 020-7287 6566
email info@rabbit.uk.net
website www.rabbit.uk.net
Founder Melanie Bourne *Managing Director* Rebecca Fuller *Agent* Lexi Cantacuzene-Speransky

3 agents represent 120 clients. Areas of work include television, film, commercials, audio books and radio.

Accepts submissions (with CVs) from actors previously unknown to the agency if sent by post, but not by email – and please always enclose an sae. Invitations to view individual actors' websites are also accepted. Represents disabled actors.

Red 24 Voices

Crown House, 72 Hammersmith Road, London W14 8TH
tel 020-7559 3611
email info@red24management.com
website www.red24voices.com
Managing Director Pam Weedon

Main areas of work are television, commercials and radio. 2 agents represent around 30 clients. Recommends the company The Showreel for the production of voicereels.

Welcomes letters (with CVs) from individual actors previously unknown to the agency, sent by post or email. Will accept unsolicited voicereels and invitations to view individual actors' websites. Currently represents, or plans to represent, actors with disabilities. *Commission*: 20%

Rhubarb Voices

1st Floor, 1A Devonshire Road, Chiswick, London W4 2EU

tel 020-8742 8683 *fax* 020-8742 8693
email johnny@rhubarbvoices.co.uk
website www.RhubarbVoices.co.uk
Key personnel Johnny Garcia

Leading UK voice talent agency with experience casting voices into all platforms of the spoken word, including commercials, continuity & promos, corporate pieces, animation, games, ADR/lip-synch and more. Represents around 90 exclusive UK and North American artists, and more than 100 foreign-language artists.

Actors seeking representation should email their CV (including any VO work to date), a photo and an MP3 showreel. Please note that the agency prefers not to receive follow-up calls.

Shining Management Ltd
12 D'Arblay Street, London W1F 8DU
tel 020-7734 1981 *fax* 020-7734 2528
Director Clair Daintree *Key personnel* Jennifer Taylor

2 agents represent 55 clients. Areas of work include voice-overs for television, film, commercials and audio books.

Accepts submissions (with CVs and voice CDs) from individual actors previously unknown to the company if sent by post. Include an sae for the return of submissions. "Please do not ring with submission enquiries." *Commission*: 15%

Speak-Easy Ltd
PO Box 648, Harrington, Northampton NN6 9XT
Voice-Overs & Corporate Agent Sarah Pickering
Television Agent Kate Moon (Director)

2 agents represent 80 clients. Areas of work include television, commercials and audio books.

Accepts submissions (with CVs and voice CDs) from individual actors previously unknown to the company if sent by post. Enclose an sae for reply.

Talking Heads
Argyll House, All Saints Passage, London SW18 1EP
tel 020-7292 7575 *fax* 020-7292 7576
email voices@talkingheadsvoices.com
website www.talkingheadsvoices.com
Key personnel John Sachs

4 agents represent 150 clients, including foreign-language voice-over clients. Areas of work include commercials, television, film, animation, corporate videos and audio books.

Accepts submissions (with CVs and voice CDs) from individual actors previously unknown to the company if sent by post. Invitations to view websites are also accepted. *Commission*: 15%

Sue Terry Voices Ltd
3rd Floor, 18 Broadwick Street, London W1F 8HS
tel 020-7434 2040 *fax* 020-7434 2042
email sue@sueterryvoices.co.uk
website www.sueterryvoices.co.uk
Managing Director Sue Terry

3 agents represent around 200 actors working in voice-overs only. Does not welcome unsolicited approaches by actors unknown to the company. *Commission*: 15%

Tongue & Groove
4th Floor, Manchester House, 84 - 86 Princess Street, Manchester M1 6NG
tel 0161-228 2469 *fax* 0161-237 1809
email info@tongueandgroove.co.uk
website www.tongueandgroove.co.uk
Producers Bev Ashworth, John Basham

2 agents represent 50 clients. Areas of work include voice-overs for television, commercials and audio books.

Accepts submissions (with CVs and voice CDs) from individual actors previously unknown to the company if sent by post. Also accepts voicereels and invitations to view individual actors' websites.

Vocal Point
25 Denmark Street, London WC2H 8NJ
tel 020-7419 0700 *fax* 020-7419 0699
email enquiries@vocalpoint.net
website www.vocalpoint.net
Agent Ben Romer Lee

Areas of work include: television, commercials and audio books. 2 agents represent approximately 85 clients.

Accepts submissions from actors previously unknown to the company. Invitations to view individual actors' websites are also accepted. Follow-up calls are not welcomed. *Commission*: 15%

Voice & Script International
Aradco House, 132 Cleveland Street, London W1T 6AB
tel 020-7692 7700 *fax* 020-7692 7711
email info@vsi.tv
website www.vsi.tv
Head of Voice-Over Department Jenny Morris *Voice-Over Project Managers* Neil Bessant, José Luis Alonso, Isobel George, Valesca Vos *Key contact* Neil Bessant

5 voice-over agents represent approx. 1500 foreign-language voice-over clients. Areas of work include voice-overs for television, film, corporate and commercials.

Accepts submissions (with CVs) from individual actors previously unknown to the company, sent by post or email. Also accepts CDs and invitations to view individual actors' websites. "We only use mother-tongue foreign-language speakers."

Voice Bank Ltd
1st Floor, 100 Talbot Road, Old Trafford, Manchester M16 0PG
tel 0161-874 5741 *fax* 0161-888 2242
email elinors@voicebankltd.co.uk
website www.voicebank.ltd.co.uk
Director Elinor Stanton

Works in all areas: musicals, television, film, commercials, audio books and radio. Represents 42 clients.

Welcomes unsolicited voicereels and invitations to view individual actors' websites. Does not currently represent any actors with disabilities, but "this would not be a barrier to joining the company".

Voice Box Agency Ltd

Laser House, Waterfront Quay, Salford Quays, Manchester M50 3XW
tel 0161-874 5741
Manager Elinor Stanton

1 agent represents 40 clients. Areas of work include voice-overs for television, film, commercials and audio books.

Accepts voicereels from individual actors previously unknown to the company. *Commission*: 15%

Voice Shop

First Floor, 1A Devonshire Road, London W4 2EU
tel 020-8742 7077 *fax* 020-8742 7011
email info@voice-shop.co.uk
website www.voice-shop.co.uk
Key contact Maxine Wiltshire

3 agents represent 42 clients working in television, film, commercials and audio-book recording.

Welcomes emails with MP3 audio samples from new actors, but prefers not to receive follow-up telephone calls or voicereels. All audio samples should contain appropriate material, and be professionally produced. *Commission*: 15%

Voice Squad

1 Kendal Road, London NW10 1JH
tel 020-8450 4451
email voices@voicesquad.com
website www.voicesquad.com
Director Neil Conrich

2 agents represent more than 70 clients. Areas of work include television, film, commercials and audio books.

Accepts submissions (with CVs and voicereels) from individual actors previously unknown to the company if sent by post. *Commission*: 15%

Voicebank, The Irish Voice-Over Agency

The Barracks, 76 Irishtown Road, Dublin 4, Eire
tel 01-668 7234 *fax* 01-660 7850
email info@voicebank.ie
website www.voicebank.ie
Company Manager Sharyn Hayden

Main areas of work include musicals, television, film, commercials, audio books and radio. 2 agents represent more than 80 clients.

Welcomes letters (with CVs and photographs) from individual actors previously unknown to the agency, sent by post only. Accepts unsolicited voicereels and invitations to view individual actors' websites. Currently represents, or plans to represent, actors with disabilites. *Commission*: Varies

The Voiceover Gallery

Paragon House, 3rd Floor, 48 Seymour Grove, Salford, Manchester M16 0LN
tel 0161-881 8844 *fax* 0161-881 8951
email info@thevoicegallery.co.uk
website www.thevoicegallery.co.uk
Agents Marylou Thistleton-Smith, Rachel Knighting

Areas of work include corporate, documentary, new media, TV and radio advertising. 3 agents representing 60 English voices and multiple foreign voices. Recommends The Showreel.com (see entry on page 397) and Cut Glass (see entry on page 396).

For all representation enquiries and instructions for submissions to the agency, visit the 'Our Services' section of the website, and click on 'Artist Services'. *Commission*: 15%

Suzy Wootton Voices

72 Towcester Road, Far Cotton, Northampton NN4 8LQ
tel (01604) 765872 *fax* 0870-765 9668
email suzy@suzywoottonvoices.com
website www.suzywoottonvoices.com

1 agent represents 46 clients. Areas of work include television, film, commercials and audio books.

Accepts submissions via email only, and invitations to view individual actors' websites. *Commission*: 15%

Yakety Yak All Mouth Ltd

7A Bloomsbury Square, London WC1A 2LP
tel 020-7430 2600 *fax* 020-7404 6109
email info@yaketyyak.co.uk
website www.yaketyyak.co.uk
Proprietor Jolie Williams

4 agents represent 155 clients. Areas of work include voice-overs for television, film, commercials, animation and audio books.

Accepts submissions (with CVs and voice CDs) from individual actors previously unknown to the company if sent by post. Include an sae for the return of submissions. *Commission*: 15%

Agents and casting directors

Presenters' agents

James Grant Media

94 Strand on the Green, London W4 3NN
tel 020-8742 4950 *fax* 020-8742 4951
website www.jamesgrant.co.uk

5 agents represent 21 presenter clients; also represents TV presenters and stage actors.

Welcomes letters (with CVs and showreels) from individuals previously unknown to the agency, sent by post or email.

Jeremy Hicks Associates

3 Richmond Buildings, London W1D 3HE
tel 020-7734 7957 *fax* 020-7734 6302
email info@jeremyhicks.com
website www.jeremyhicks.com
Agents Jeremy Hicks, Sarah Dalkin *Agents' Assistant* Charlotte Leaper *Assistant* Julie Dalkin

2 agents represent 20 clients; only presenters, writers, comedians and chefs.

Welcomes letters (with CVs and showreels) from individuals, and emails. "Our only criteria is that someone is talented and we feel we can offer them something. We do not base any decision on gender, race, sexuality or disability status." *Commission*: 15% (10% for scriptwriters)

Sandra Singer Associates

21 Cotswold Road, Westcliff-on-Sea, Essex SS0 8AA
tel (01702) 331616 *fax* (01702) 339393
email sandrasingeruk@aol.com
website www.sandrasinger.com

2 agents represent 3 presenter clients. Also represents actors, choreographers and stylists.

Will accept unsolicited CVs sent by email but not by post; showreels only upon request. Welcomes

invitations to view individual presenters' websites. Will consider representing presenters with disabilities. "When submitting showreels, remember it is you and your personality that are important. Some of the presenters that have made it in the industry submitted imaginative, home-made showreels. Above all, be original." *Commission*: 10-20% (depending on stage or television)

Jo Wander Management

110 Gloucester Avenue, London NW1 8HX
tel 020-7209 3777 *fax* 020-7209 3770
email jo@jowandermanagement.com
website www.jowandermanagement.com
Managing Director Jo Wander

1 agent represents 15-20 presenter clients.

Welcomes letters (with CVs and showreels) from individual presenters previously unknown to the agency, sent by post or email; will accept invitations to view individuals' websites.

Paul Weedon/Red 24 Management

Crown House, 72 Hammersmith Road,
London W14 8TH
tel 020-7559 3611
email info@red24management.com
website www.red24management.com
Managing Director Paul Weedon

1 agent represents 20 presenter clients. Also represents voice artists.

Welcomes letters (with CVs and showreels) from individual presenters previously unknown to the company, sent by post or email, and accepts invitations to view individuals' websites. *Commission*: 20%

Casting directors

Essentially, casting directors take on the 'nitty-gritty' work involved in the casting process – it is usually the director, and sometimes the producer, who actually 'directs' the casting decisions. The crucial thing to remember is that each one is employed – by someone else. Some casting directors are employed on a full-time basis; a significant number work freelance and can be as concerned about where their next job is coming from as you are. Therefore, if one gets you to meet their director-employer, it is important that you live up to that casting director's expectations: carefully absorb any brief that s/he gives you. If you suddenly decide to take a radically different approach, s/he will be put into a difficult position with that director-employer.

Fundamental to the job of being a casting director is a wide knowledge of all kinds of actors. Therefore a good one will have seen as many productions as possible. Like squirrels storing nuts for the winter, they keep extensive notes and are continually adding to their collections of actor-profiles. An empathetic, intuitive and imaginative casting director has immeasurable value to both actors and director.

You should approach casting directors in much the same way as you would agents: however, it's even more important that there's something they can see you in. You can keep reasonably up to date with the activities of some casting directors by looking at the website of the Casting Directors Guild (CDG) – **www.thecdg.co.uk**.

Joanne Adamson Casting

Northern Spirit Creative Casting, PO Box 140, Leeds LS13 9BS
mobile (07787) 311270
email watts07@hotmail.com

Main areas of work are theatre, musicals, television, film and commercials. Casting credits include: *Flesh and Blood* and *Nice Guy Eddie* (BBC), and *Fat Friends II* (Rollem, Tiger Aspect and Yorkshire Television).

Will consider attending performances at venues in Greater London and elsewhere given 1-2 weeks' notice. Accepts submissions (with CVs and photographs) from actors previously unknown to the casting director if sent by post, but does not welcome email enquiries. Will also accept showreels. "I am eager to arrange general meetings with actors."

Pippa Ailion

3 Towton Road, London SE27 9EE

Main areas of work are theatre, musicals, television and commercials. West End: *Porgy and Bess*; *Wicked*; *Billy Elliot*; *We Will Rock You*; *The Lion King*. Current /recent Regional and tours: *The Sunshine Boys* (West Yorkshire Playhouse); *My Fair Lady* (Denmark). *Jerry Springer The Opera*; *The Lion King* (EuroDisney). West End/London credits include: *The Enchanted Pig* (Young Vic); *Acorn Antiques*; *Simply Heavenly* (Young Vic and Trafalgar Studios); *Follow My Leader* (Hampstead); Disney's *Beauty and the Beast*; *Rent*;

Wit; *The Magistrate*; *Into the Woods*; *Annie Get Your Gun*; *Forever Plaid*. Television: *Little White Lies*; *Breaking The Code* (multi-award winning); *Witness Against Hitler*; *Space Vets*; *Hanger 17*.

Will consider attending performances at venues in Greater London and occasionally elsewhere (such as Chichester or Stratford) given 2-3 weeks' notice. Accepts submissions (with CVs and photographs) from actors previously unknown to the casting director if sent by post. Does not welcome email enquiries.

Dorothy Andrew Casting

Mersey TV, Campus Manor, Childwall Abbey Road, Childwall, Liverpool L16 0JP
tel 0151-737 4044 *fax* 0151-722 9079
email casting@merseytv.com

Casts mainly for television, film and commercials. Recent credits include: *Hollyoaks*, *Grange Hill* and *Court Room*.

Will accept postal submissions (with CVs and photographs) from actors previously unknown to the company, but unsolicited emails and showreels are not welcomed. "When writing, make your letter short and to the point. Always include a photograph (10x8in b&w) and a CV. Only send in a showreel if requested."

Ashton Hinkinson Casting

1 Charlotte Street, London W1T 1RD
tel 020-7580 6101 *fax* 020-7636 1657

email casting@ahcasting.com
website www.ashtonhinkinson.com
Casting Directors Emma Ashton, Debs Hinkinson

Areas of work include television, film and commercials. Recent credits include: *Brother* (commercial for Bacon, Copenhagen); *Galaxy* (commercial for RSA, London); *Hostel 1 & 2* (for International Production Co.).

Will consider attending performances in Greater London with at least 1 week's notice. Invitations to showcases are also welcomed. Accepts submissions (with CVs and photographs) from actors previously unknown to the company; invitations to view individual actors' websites are also accepted.

Derek Barnes CDG

BBC Drama Series Casting, BBC Elstree, Room N221, Neptune House, Clarendon Road, Borehamwood WD6 1JF
tel 020-8228 7096 *fax* 020-8228 8311
email derek.barnes@bbc.co.uk
website www.derek-barnes.com

Main areas of work are film and television. Casting credits include: *Casualty*, *Holby City*, *Doctors* (BBC Drama Series) and *Down To Earth* (Series V, BBC).

Beastall & North

41E Elgin Crescent, London W11 2JD
tel 020-7727 6496
email lesley@beastallnorth.co.uk
Casting Director Lesley Beastall

Works in commercials. Recent credits include: *Sunshine* (ITV1); *Built with You in Mind* (Thompson's Holidays); and voice-overs for The Natural Confectionary Company.

Does not welcome performance notices or unsolicited submissions by actors previously unknown to the company, but will accept invitations to view individual actors' websites. Any such approach should be made by email only.

Lauren Beauchamp Casting

34A Brightside, Billericay, Essex CM12 0LJ
mobile (07961) 982198
email laurenbeauchamp@tiscali.co.uk
Head Casting Director Lauren Beauchamp *Assistant Casting Director* Dee Atkins

Main areas of work are theatre, television, film and commercials. Recent casting credits include: *Itch* (short film; Director, Antony Gallagher for Itchka Productions); and *Bacon Sandwich* (theatre; Director, Emily North for Interact Productions).

Will consider attending performances within the Greater London and Essex areas, given at least 2 weeks' notice. Welcomes unsolicited CVs and photographs, sent by email only. Accepts showreels and invitations to view individual actors' websites.

Lucy Bevan CDG

2nd Floor, 138 Portobello Road, London W11 2DZ
tel 020- 7727 5572

email lucy@lucybevan.com

Main areas of work are film, television, commercials, pop promos and theatre. Credits include: *His Dark Materials: The Golden Compass* (New Line Cinema); *The Libertine* (Mr Mudd/Weinstein Co.); *Dirty War* (BBC Films); and *Camera Obscura* (Almeida Theatre).

Sarah Bird CDG

PO Box 32658, London W14 0XA
tel 020-7371 3248 *fax* 020-7602 8601

Casts for film, television, theatre and commercials. Casting credits include: *You Don't Have To Say You Love Me*, directed by Simon Shore (Samuelson Productions); *Ladies in Lavender*, directed by Charles Dance (Scala Productions); *Fortysomething* (Carlton TV); and *Calico*, directed by Edward Hall (Sonia Friedman Productions).

Hannah Birkett Casting

26 Noko, 3-6 Banister Road, London W10 4AR
tel 020-8960 2848
email hannah@hbcasting.com
Casting Director Hannah Birkett *Casting Associate* Shae Potter

Areas of work include television, film, commercials, idents, pop promos, voice-overs. Recent credits include: Toyota, Coca Cola, Altoids, and *Beyond the Rave* (Hammer Horror).

Will consider attending performances within Greater London with reasonable notice. Accepts CVs and photographs via email. Hard copies are usually not kept.

Siobhan Bracke CDG

Basement Flat, 22a The Barons, St Margaret's, Middlesex TW1 2AP

Main area of work is theatre. Theatre credits include: Head of Casting for the RSC (1986-91); Shakespeare's Globe for Mark Rylance; Lyric Hammersmith for Neil Bartlett; Hampstead Theatre for Tony Clark/ Lucy Bailey; Cheek By Jowl for Declan Donnellan; Chichester – *Nicholas Nickelby* for Philip Franks; *I Am Shakespeare* for Mark Rylance; *When We Are Married* for Ian Brown, West Yorkshire Playouse. Television credits include: *A Doll's House* and *Measure for Measure* for David Thacker; *Buddha of Suburbia* and *Persuasion* for Roger Michell; *Cheek By Jowl*.

Will consider attending performances at venues in Greater London and occasionally elsewhere, given as much notice as possible (preferably 4-5 weeks). Accepts submissions (with CVs and photographs) from actors previously unknown to the casting director if sent by post. Does not welcome email enquiries.

Candid Casting

1st Floor, 32 Great Sutton Street, London EC1V 0NB
tel 020-7490 8882

email mail@candidcasting.co.uk
Casting Director Amanda Tabak CDG *Assistant* Georgina Harwood

Main areas of work are television, film and commercials. Casting credits include: *Kidulthood*, *Britain's Got the Pop Factor*, and *MI High*.

Will consider attending performances at venues in central London given at least 2 weeks' notice. Accepts submissions (with CVs and photographs) from actors previously unknown to the casting director if sent by post. Does not welcome email enquiries, unsolicited showreels or invitations to view individual actors' websites.

Cannon Dudley & Associates
43a Belsize Square, London NW3 4HN
tel 020-7433 3393 *fax* 020-7813 2048
email cdacasting@blueyonder.co.uk
Casting Director Carol Dudley CDG, CSA *Casting Associate* Helena Palmer

Main areas of work are film, theatre and television. Recent credits include: *The Third Mother – Mother of Tears* (Director: Dario Argento); *Master Harold and the Boys* (Director: Lonny Price); and theatre productions for Hampstead, Edinburgh and the West End.

Will consider attending performances at venues in Greater London given as much notice as possible. Accepts submissions (with CVs and photographs) from actors previously unknown to the casting director if sent by post. Does not welcome email enquiries. CVs which are not submitted for specific projects or with reference to current shows or television performances cannot be kept for future reference. Telephone enquiries about current casting projects or progress of mailed submissions are not welcomed.

John Cannon
BBC Elstree, (Rm N223) Neptune House, Clarendon Road, Borehamwood WD6 1JF
tel 020-8228 7122 *fax* 020-8228 8311
email john.cannon@bbc.co.uk, john@johncannon.co.uk

Former Resident Casting Director for the Royal Shakespeare Company, now working for BBC Drama. Recent credits include: *The Bill* (ITV); *Presence* by Doug Lucie (Plymouth Drum); *See How They Run* (No. 1 Tour); *Hedda Gabler* (West Yorkshire Playhouse/Liverpool Playhouse); and *Yellowman* (tour for Liverpool Everyman).

Welcomes performance notices with at least 2 weeks' notice. Also happy to receive letters and emails (with CVs and photographs) from actors, as well as invitations to view individual actors' websites. Does not welcome unsolicited showreels.

Anji Carroll CDG
tel (01270) 250240
email anji@anjicarroll.tv
Main areas of work are film and television. Casting

credits include: *The Cup* (BBC); *Number 10*, political drama series (BBC R4); *The Sarah Jane Adventures*, hour-long pilot (Dr Who Productions for BBC); *Mrs Ratcliffe's Revolution* (feature film directed by Bille Eltringham); *The Bill* (Talkback Thames); four films shot by first-time drama directors (IWC Media for C4); *The Knock*, 4 x 90 minute eps. (LWT); *London's Burning*, 32 x 60 minute eps. (LWT); *Out of Depth* (feature film directed by Simon Marshall); *The Jolly Boys' Last Stand* (feature film directed by Chris Payne); various commercials for home and abroad. Theatre credits: 8 shows for the Bristol Old Vic, 5 for the Northcott Theatre, Exeter, and 1 co-production for Ludlow Festival and Northcott Theatre.

The Casting Angels (London and Paris)
Suite 4, 14 College Road, Bromley BR1 3NS
fax 020-8313 0443
Director Michael Ange
Key personnel Michael *(Big Decisions)*, Gabriel *(Announcements)*, Raphael, Uriel *(The Daily Grind)*, Lucifer *(Special Consultant)*

Main areas of work are television, musicals, film and commercials with "casting across the board". Casts for the UK and other countries within Europe.

Will consider attending performances at venues in Greater London and elsewhere, given as much notice as possible. Accepts showreels.

Casting Couch Productions Ltd
213 Trowbridge Road, Bradford-on-Avon, Wiltshire BA15 1EU
mobile (07932) 785807
email moiratownsend@yahoo.co.uk
Casting Director Moira Townsend

Main areas of work are television, film and commercials. Casting credits include: *Who Killed Tutankhamen?* (documentary) and advertisements for DVLA and Lunn Poly.

Will consider attending performances at venues in Greater London and elsewhere (especially Bath/Bristol area), given 2-3 weeks' notice. Accepts submissions from actors previously unknown to the casting director if sent by email. Actors will only receive a response if the casting director is able to attend a performance.

See entry under *Agents* on page 42 for further details of the company's work.

Casting UK
Studio 125, 77 Beak Street, London W1F 9DB
tel 020-7993 5165
email drew@castinguk.com
Casting Director Andrew Mann

Casts mainly for film and commercials. Casting credits include: commercials for Bacardi, Acuview, DFS, ASDA and Maltesers; and pop videos for Placebo, Sugababes and Busted.

Will consider attending performances at venues in Greater London given 2 weeks' notice. Accepts submissions (with CVs and photographs) from actors previously unknown to the casting director if sent by post. Does not welcome email enquiries.

Suzy Catliff CDG

PO Box 39492, London N10 3YX
tel 020-8442 0749
email soose@soose.co.uk

Casts mainly for television, film and theatre. Most recent credits include: for television, *Lifeline* (BBC1), *Empathy* (BBC1), *Silent Witness* (Series IX & X), *Blitz* (Channel 4), *D-Day* (BBC 1), and *Sir Gadabout* (ITV); for film, *Stormbreaker* (associate), *The Swimming Pool* (assistant), *Sense and Sensibility* (assistant), and *Wilde & Hackers*; and for theatre, *Life X 3* (No. 1 tour), *The Play What I Wrote*, *Ducktastic* (associate).

Urvashi Chand CDG

Cinecraft, 69 Teignmouth Road, London NW2 4EA
tel 020-8208 3861
email urvashi@cinecraft.biz

Main area of work is film. Recent credits include: *Daylight Robbery* (directed by Barry Leonti), and *Red Mercury* (directed by Roy Battersby).

Will consider attending performances within the Greater London area and elsewhere with at least 2 weeks' notice. Accepts submissions (with CVs and photographs) from actors previously unknown to the agency, by email. Showreels, voicereels and invitations to view individual actors' websites are also accepted.

Alison Chard CDG

23 Groveside Court, 4 Lombard Road, London SW11 3RQ
tel 020-7223 9125
email chardcasting@btinternet.com
website www.thecdg.co.uk

Main areas of work are theatre, television and film. Casting credits include: *M.I.T.* and *The Bill* (television). Formerly cast for the Royal National Theatre and the Royal Shakespeare Company.

Will consider agents' invitations to performances at venues in Greater London given good notice. Accepts submissions (with CVs and small photographs) from actors sent by post. Only CVs may be emailed. Showreels are accepted if they are on DVD, and accompanied by an sae and of good quality (does not welcome filmed stage pieces). Invitations to view individual actors' websites are unnecessary; ensuring that *Spotlight* entries are up-to-date is more useful. Advises actors to: "Target performance notices in accordance with the location of the recipient. Avoid unnecessary expense and disappointment by doing your research; find out what they are working on, who they are working with and if they are familiar with your work."

Charkham Casting

Suite 361, 14 Tottenham Court Road, London W1T 1JY
tel 020-7927 8335 *fax* 020-7927 8336
email charkhamcasting@btconnect.com
Casting Directors Beth Charkham, Gary Ford

Areas of work include theatre, musicals, television, film and commercials. Recent credits include: *Charlie and the Chocolate Factory*, *Silent Witness* and *The Bill*.

Andrea Clark Casting

PO Box 28895, London SW13 0WG
tel 020-8876 6869
website www.aclarkcasting.com
Casting Director Andrea Clark

Works mainly in film, television, commercials and theatre. Recent credits include: *Mutant Chronicles*, *Keeping Mum*, and *7 Lives*.

Will consider attending performances in London only, given a minimum of 2-3 weeks' notice. Welcomes letters (with CVs & photographs) from individual actors previously unknown to the company if sent by post, but not by email. Accepts showreels and invitations to view individual actors' websites. "Sorry but I am unable to return unsolicited showreels and photos. When an actor has an agent, I prefer contact to be made via the agent."

Jayne Collins

4th Floor, 20 Bedford Street, London WC2E 9HP
tel 020-7422 0014 *fax* 020-7422 0015
email info@jaynecollinscasting.com
website www.jaynecollinscasting.com

Areas of work include theatre, musicals, television, film and commercials.

Will consider attending performances within the Greater London area and elsewhere, given at least 1 week's notice. Accepts submissions (with CVs and photographs) from actors previously unknown to the company if sent by post, but not by email. Welcomes showreels.

John Connor CDG

See entry for Jane Davies Casting Ltd.

Lin Cordoray

66 Cardross Street, London W6 0DR

Main areas of work are television and commercials.

Will consider attending performances at venues in Greater London. Accepts submissions (with CVs and photographs) from actors previously unknown to the casting director if sent by post. Does not welcome email enquiries.

Irene Cotton Casting

25 Druce Road, Dulwich Village, London SE21 7DW
tel 020-8299 1595 *fax* 020-8299 2787

email irenecotton@btinternet.com
Director Irene Cotton CDG

Recent credits include: *The Bill* (ITV), *The Countess* (Criterion Theatre, London), *Panorama* (BBC), and *Caffe Latte* commercial (Home Productions). Welcomes performance notices as far in advance as possible, and is prepared to travel to performances within Greater London. Does not welcome any other unsolicited form of approach, including CVs, photographs, showreels or invitations to view individual actors' websites. Advises actors to make contact only to inform the casting director "when their work can be seen – TV, film or stage".

Margaret Crawford

92 Castelnau, London SW13 9EU

Casts mainly for television. Casting credits include: *Bad Girls* (Series 2-8), *Footballers' Wives* (Series 1-5), *Footballers' Wives Extra Time* (Series 1 & 2), *Waterloo Road* (Series 1) and *Bombshell* (Series 1).

Will consider attending performances at venues in Greater London and occasionally elsewhere, given as much notice as possible. Accepts submissions (with CVs and photographs) from actors previously unknown to the casting director if sent by post. Does not welcome email enquiries. Also accepts showreels, voicereels and invitations to view individual actors' websites.

Crocodile Casting

9 Ashley Close, Hendon, London NW4 1PH
tel 020-8203 7009 *fax* 020-8203 7711
website www.crocodilecasting.com
Casting Directors Tracie Saban, Claire Toeman

Established in 1996 with the aim of constantly accessing new faces and fresh talent. The company casts mainly for commercials, pop videos and corporate work; sometimes holds general auditions to meet new actors and models.

Jane Davies Casting Ltd

PO Box 680, Sutton, Surrey SM1 3ZG
tel 020-8715 1036 *fax* 020-8644 9746
email info@janedaviescasting.co.uk
Casting Directors Jane Davies CDG, John Connor CDG

Casts mainly for television. Casting credits include: *My Family*, *The Green Green Grass*, and *Black Books*.

Will consider attending performances of light drama, and particularly of comedies, at venues in Greater London.

Gary Davy CDG

1st Floor, 55-59 Shaftesbury Avenue, London W1D 6LD

Casts for film and television. Casting credits include: Steve McQueen's 2008 Cannes-winning *Hunger*; Nick Love's *The Business*, *Outlaw* and upcoming *The*

Sweeney; *Revengers Tragedy* (Alex Cox); Nick Cave's *The Proposition* (John Hillcoat); *44 inch Chest* (Malcolm Venville); and the comedy *Faintheart* (Vito Rocco). Television credits include: *He Kills Coppers*, *My Boy Jack*, *Sweeney Todd*, *Mr Eleven*, *Mistresses II*, and UK Casting on *Band of Brothers*.

Gabrielle Dawes CDG

PO Box 52493, London NW3 9DZ
tel 020-7435 3645
email gdawescasting@tiscali.co.uk

Gabrielle Dawes is Associate for Casting at Chichester Festival Theatre, and a freelance Casting Director.

Theatre includes: *The Norman Conquests*, *All About My Mother*, *New Voices 24-Hour Plays* (Old Vic); *Cat on a Hot Tin Roof*, *Three Days of Rain*, *Treasure Island* (West End); Rupert Goold's *Macbeth* (Chichester/West End/Broadway); *Wallenstein*, *The Grapes of Wrath*, *Separate Tables*, *Hay Fever*, *Aristo*, *Funny Girl*, *The Circle*, *Taking Sides / Collaboration* (and West End); *Hobson's Choice*, *The Waltz of the Toreadors*, *Twelfth Night* (all Chichester); *The English Game* (Headlong Theatre); *The Elephant Man* (Sheffield); *As You Like It* (Watford).

As Deputy Head of Casting at the National Theatre 2000-2006, award-winning productions included *Caroline, or Change*, *His Dark Materials*, *Elmina's Kitchen*, *The Pillowman*, and *Coram Boy*.

Television credits include: Harold Pinter's *Celebration*, and *Elmina's Kitchen* by Kwame Kwei-Armah. Films include *Perdie* (BAFTA award for Best Short Film) and *The Suicide Club*.

Stephanie Dawes

13 Nevern Square, London SW5 9NW
tel (07802) 566642
email stephaniedawes5@gmail.com

Works in television and voice-over. Recent credits include: *Blue Murder*, *Stockwell*, and *Britannia High* (all ITV1).

Kate Day CDG

Pound Cottage, 27 The Green South, Warborough, Oxfordshire OX10 7DR

Main areas of work are television, film and commercials.

Will consider attending performances at venues in Greater London and occasionally elsewhere, given as much notice as possible. Accepts submissions (with CVs and photographs) from actors previously unknown to the casting director if sent by post. Does not welcome email enquiries.

Paul De Freitas

PO Box 4903, London W1A 7JZ
tel 020-7486 5407 *fax* 020-7486 181 7
email info@pauldefreitas.com
website www.pauldefreitas.com

Main areas of work are film, television and commercials. Casting credits include: *Dog Boy* (BBC2); *Lazarus & Dingwall* (BBC2); *Bernard & The Genie* (Talkback/Attaboy); *The Princess Academy* (Weintraub Productions); and *What Larry Says* (Platypus Productions).

The Denman Casting Agency

Burgess House, Main Street, Farnsfield,
Notts NG22 8EF
Key personnel Jack Denman FEAA

Main areas of work are theatre, musicals, television, film and commercials. Casting credits include: *Peak Practice*, *Doctors*, and *Crimewatch* (television); and videos for PC World and Boots. Awarded Preferred Agents status by the BBC for supporting artists and walk-ons.

Accepts submissions (with CVs and photographs) from actors previously unknown to the casting director if sent by post. Does not welcome email enquiries. No short film enquiries.

Lee Dennison CDA

Fushion, 27 Old Gloucester Street,
London WC1N 3XX
tel 0870-011 1100 *fax* 0870-011 1020
email leedennison@fushion-uk.com
website www.ukscreen.com/crew/ldennison
website www.leedennisonassociates.com
Casting London/New York Lee Dennison, Chuck Harvey, Ram Tucker *Casting London/Paris* Lee Dennison, Will Baker, Jamie Lowe *Assistant* Dean Saunders

Casts mainly for film and television features as well as commercials and music promos. Recent credits include: *Vacancy* (Screen Gems), *Buttermilk Sky* (Charles R Leinenweber), *Echo Park LA* (Sony), *United 93* (Universal), and *Standoff* (Fox).

"As we deal only with featured established artistes, please, no unsolicited requests."

Malcom Drury CDG

34 Tabor Road, London W6 0BW
tel 020-8748 9232

Casts mainly for television. Casting credits include: *The Bill*, *Heartbeat*, *The Beiderbecke Affair* and Laurence Olivier's *King Lear*.

Carol Dudley CDG, CSA

See entry for Cannon Dudley & Associates.

Maureen Duff CDG

PO Box 47340, London NW3 4TY
tel 020-7586 0532 *fax* 020-7681 7172

Main areas of work are film, television and theatre. Credits include: *Closing The Ring* (Richard Attenborough); *The History of Mr Polly* (Granada Media); *Poirot* (several episodes for Granada Media);

and *Dancing At Lughnasa* (and several other productions for the Northcott Theatre, Exeter).

Julia Duff CDG

73 Wells Street, London W1T 3QG
tel 020-7436 8860 *fax* 020-7436 8859

Casts mainly for television. Casting credits include: *New Tricks*, *Hotel Babylon*, *Secret Diary of a Call Girl*, *Persuasion*, *Monarch of the Glen*, and *The Amazing Mrs Pritchard*.

Jennifer Duffy CDG

11 Portsea Mews, London W2 2BN
tel 020-7262 3326
email casting@jennyduffy.co.uk

Main areas of work are film and television. Credits include: *Life 'n' Lyrics* (Fiesta Productions, BBC Films, Universal), *Wallace & Gromit: The Curse of the Wererabbit* (Aardman/Dreamworks), *Macbeth* (BBC) and *Dunkirk* (BBC2, Huw Wheldon BAFTA Award 2005).

Irene East Casting CDG

40 Brookwood Avenue, Barnes, London SW13 0LR
tel 020-8876 5686 *fax* 020-8876 5686
email IrnEast@aol.com

Main areas of work are theatre and film. Casting Director for Love and Madness Productions. Theatre credits include: *Babba and Luvvie*, *Richard III*, *Fool for Love*, *Macbeth*, *Ajax* (dir. Jack Shepherd), *A Skull in Connemara*, *The Tempest*, *The Playboy of the Western World*, *Murder in Paris*. Features include: *Feet*, *A Distant Mirage*, *The Problem with Pets*, *Big Claus*, *Little Claus*.

Will attend performances at venues in Greater London and occasionally elsewhere, given a couple of days' notice. Showreels should only be sent on request.

EJ Casting

PO Box 63617, London W9 1AN
tel 020-7564 2688 *mobile* (07891) 632946
email info@ejcasting.com
Director Edward James

Casts for theatre, musicals, film, commercials and corporate work. Casting credits include: *Into the Woods* and *Sweet Charity* (theatre); commercials for AOL, Lloyds Bank, Sony BMG, Universal Music, and Cadbury's Fingers; and *Air on a G String* (film).

Will consider attending performances at venues in Greater London and occasionally elsewhere. Accepts showreels containing work that has been broadcast. Due to the overwhelming number of CVs sent, is unable to accept general enquiries. "Please only send an application if it is a performance notice or in response to a specific breakdown."

Richard Evans CDG

10 Shirley Road, London W4 1DD
tel 020-8994 6304

email info@evanscasting.co.uk
website www.evanscasting.co.uk
Key personnel Richard Evans CDG

Main areas of work are theatre, musicals, television, film and commercials. Casting credits include: *The Rat Pack – Live From Las Vegas* (theatre).

Will consider attending performances at venues in Greater London and occasionally elsewhere, given sufficient notice. Requests 1-2 weeks before the opening night for theatre productions, and 2-3 days prior to transmission for television shows. Accepts follow-up telephone calls after a production has opened. Welcomes submissions (with CVs and photographs) from actors previously unknown to the casting director if sent by post. Does not welcome email enquiries. Showreels should only be sent on request. Advises actors to: "Be specific, find out about current projects and suggest yourself for particular roles. Always ensure that the part you are playing is worth casting personnel coming to see. Offer complimentary tickets. It is worth keeping in touch as your career progresses."

Bunny Fildes Casting CDG
56-60 Wigmore Street, London W1U 2RZ
tel 020-7935 1254 *fax* 020-7298 1871

Casts mainly for theatre, television, film and commercials.

Will consider attending performances within Greater London given 2 weeks' notice. Accepts postal submissions (with CVs and photographs) from actors previously unknown to the company. Unsolicited emails and showreels, however, are not welcomed.

Sally Fincher CDG
tel 020-8347 5945
email sallyfincher@btinternet.com

Main area of work is television. Credits include: *Murder In Suburbia, Sweet Medicine, Barbara, Kiss Me Kate, Outside Edge* and *The Upper Hand*.

Janie Frazer CDG
email janiefrazercasting@gmail.com

Freelance casting director. Previously worked for many years at ITV. Casts mainly for television (drama and comedy, serials and one-offs). Casting credits include, most recently: *Candy Cabs* (comedy drama series for BBC1, filming 2010); also *Coronation Street, Vincent, Murder in Suburbia, Blue Murder, Island at War, City Lights,* and *Spaced*. See Janie's article on page 300 for advice on television casting.

Caroline Funnell
25 Rattray Road, London SW2 1AZ
tel 020-7326 4417

Areas of work include theatre and musicals. Will consider attending performances within the Greater London area with at least 2 weeks' notice.

Artistic Director of Sixteenfeet Productions (25 Rattray Road, London SW2 1AZ, info@sixteenfeet.co.uk).

Tracey Gillham CDG
Room 4018, BBC TV Centre, Wood Lane, London W12 7RJ
tel 020-8225 8648 *fax* 020-8576 4414
email tracey.gillham@bbc.co.uk

Main areas of work are film and television. For recent credits, please see *Spotlight* or the CDG website.

Nina Gold CDG
117 Chevening Road, London NW6 6DU
tel 020-8960 6099 *fax* 020-8968 6777

Main areas of work are film, television and commercials. Casting credits include: *Vera Drake*, directed by Mike Leigh (Thin Man Films); *The Life and Death of Peter Sellers*, directed by Stephen Hopkins; *The Jacket,* directed by John Maybury (Warner Bros); *Daniel Deronda*, directed by Tom Hooper (BBC TV); *Amazing Grace* and *Rome* both directed by Michael Apted; *Starter for Ten* directed by Tom Vaughan; *The Illusionist* directed by Neil Burger; and *Brothers of the Head* directed by Keith Fulton and Louis Pepe.

Miranda Gooch
102 Leighton Gardens, London NW10 3RP

Casts mainly for feature films. Recent credits have included: *True Story* and *Tooth*.

Will consider attending performances within Greater London given as much notice as possible. Accepts submissions (with CVs and photographs) from actors previously unknown to the company sent by post or email. Showreels are also accepted.

Jill Green CDG
PO Box 56927, London N10 3UR
tel 0845-478 6343

Casts for theatre, musicals and film. Casting credits include: *Jersey Boys* (Prince Edward Theatre); *The Producers* (Drury Lane Theatre); *Thoroughly Modern Millie* (Shaftesbury Theatre); *Contact* (Queens Theatre); and *Beyond the Sea* (film directed by Kevin Spacey).

Will consider attending performances within Greater London and occasionally elsewhere, given a minimum of 2 weeks' notice. Accepts postal submissions (with CVs and photographs) from actors who are currently appearing in a production, but does not welcome blanket mailings, unsolicited emails or showreels (unless an sae is enclosed for their return).

Marcia Gresham CDG
3 Langthorne Street, London SW6 6JT
tel 020-7381 2876 *fax* 020-7381 4496

email marcia@greshamcast.com

Main area of work is television. Casting credits include: *Britz*, *The Government Inspector*, *Warriors*, and *The Project* – all projects directed by Peter Kosminsky for television.

Will consider attending performances at venues in Greater London given 1 month's notice. Accepts submissions (with CVs and photographs) from actors previously unknown to the casting director if sent by post, but does not welcome email enquiries. Showreels and voicereels (with sae for return) are also accepted.

David Grindrod CDG
4th Floor, Palace Theatre, Shaftesbury Avenue, London W1D 5AY
tel 020-7437 2506 *fax* 020-7437 2507
email dga@grindrodcasting.co.uk

Casts for musicals and films. Film credits: Dance casting *Nine*, Ensemble casting *Mamma Mia!* and *The Phantom of the Opera*. West End casting: *Chicago*, *Mamma Mia!*, *Ghost*, *Hairspray*, *Love Never Dies*, *Sister Act*.

Will consider attending performances within Greater London and possibly elsewhere, given as much notice as possible. Does not welcome unsolicited submissions from actors. Casting breakdowns are released via The Spotlight, therefore actors should only write in with reference to specific productions. See also David's article *Casting for musical theatre* on page 111.

Janet Hall
3 Shaw Road, Littleborough, Oldham OL15 9LG

Main areas of work include television, film and commercials. Casting credits include: AXA commercial, and *The Sound of Music* (theatre).

Will consider attending performances at venues in Greater London and in Manchester, Liverpool and Leeds, given 1 week's notice. Accepts submissions (with CVs and photographs) from actors previously unknown to the casting director sent by post or email. Also accepts showreels, voicereels and invitations to view individual actors' websites.

Louis Hammond
6 Brewer Street, London W1F 0SD
tel 020-7734 1880

Main areas of work are theatre, television and film. Casting credits include: *Mirrormask* and *Arsene Lupin* (films); *The Bill* (TV); *Rock 'N' Roll* (Royal Court/West End); *The Member of the Wedding* (Young Vic); *The Importance of Being Earnest* (West End); and *Testing the Echo* (Tricycle).

Will consider attending performances. Accepts submissions (with CVs and photographs) from actors previously unknown to the casting director. "When sending submissions, I suggest a photograph built into the CV. 10x8in photographs may not be retained by the casting director."

Gemma Hancock CDG
North Lodge, Weald Chase, Staplefield Road, Cuckfield, West Sussex RH17 5HY
tel (01444) 441398 *fax* (01444) 441398

Main areas of work are theatre, television and film. Casting credits include: *The Bill* (Talkback Thames); Peter Ackroyd's *London* (BBC 2); *Blithe Spirit* (West End and tour); and *The Dresser* (Bath Theatre Royal and tour).

Judi Hayfield CDG / Judi Hayfield Ltd
6 Richmond Hill Road, Gatley, Cheshire SK8 1QG
mobile (07919) 221873
email judi.hayfield@hotmail.co.uk

Former resident casting director for Granada.

Polly Hootkins CDG
PO Box 52480, London NW3 9DH
tel 020-7233 8724 *fax* 020-7828 5051
email phootkins@clara.net
website www.thecdg.co.uk
Key personnel Polly Hootkins

Will consider attending performances at venues in Greater London and occasionally elsewhere, given as much notice as possible. Accepts submissions (with CVs and photographs) from actors previously unknown to the casting director if sent by post. Does not welcome email enquiries. Showreels, voicereels and invitations to view individual actors' websites are also accepted.

Hubbard Casting
14 Rathbone Place, London W1T 1HT
tel 020-7631 4944 *fax* 020-7636 7117
Casting Directors John Hubbard, Ros Hubbard, Dan Hubbard, Amy Hubbard

Casts mainly for film, television, theatre and commercials. Casting credits include: *United 93*, *The Damned United*, *Lord of the Rings*, *The Bourne Ultimatum*, and *Ben-Hur* (mini series).

Sarah Hughes
Room 4018, BBC Television Centre, Wood Lane, London W12 7RJ

Former Resident Casting Director for the Stephen Joseph Theatre, Scarborough.

International Collective (INC)
9-13 Grape Street, London WC2H 9ED
tel 020-7484 5060 (London office)
tel 0113-219 2896 (Leeds office)
email joadamson@internationalcollective.co.uk
email casting@internationalcollective.co.uk
website www.internationalcollective.co.uk
Key personnel Jo Adamson CDG, Christopher Manoe

Area of works include television, theatre, film, musicals and commercials. Recent work includes: *The War of The Worlds* (UK National Tour); *That's Amore* (UK National Tour); *Fat Friends* (ITV/ Tiger aspect); *The Bill* (Talkback Thames) and *Touchdown* (Findaway Films).

Will consider attending performances within the Greater London area, in the North of England and elsewhere, given at least 1 week's notice. Welcomes invitations to view actors' showreels and websites.

Sue Jackson
53 Moseley Wood Walk, Leeds LS16 7HQ

Freelance casting director.

Trevor Jackson CDG
1 Bedford Square, London WC1B 3RA
tel 020-7637 8866 *fax* 020-7436 2683

Casts mainly for musicals produced by Cameron Mackintosh Ltd. Casting credits include: *My Fair Lady, Les Miserables, Miss Saigon, Phantom of the Opera, Mary Poppins, Avenue Q* and *Oliver!*.

Will consider attending performances at venues in Greater London given as much notice as possible. Accepts submissions (with CVs and photographs) from actors previously unknown to the casting director if sent by post, but does not welcome email enquiries. Showreels, voicereels and invitations to view individual actors' websites are also accepted.

Janis Jaffa Casting
67 Starfield Road, London W12 9SN
tel 020-7565 2877 *fax* 020-8743 9561
email janis@janisjaffacasting.co.uk

Works mainly in television, film and commercials. Recent credits include: *The Bill.*

Will consider attending performances within Greater London. Welcomes letters (with CVs & photographs) from individual actors previously unknown to the agency sent by post, but not by email. Will accept showreels and invitations to view individual actors' websites.

Jennifer Jaffrey
The Double Lodge, Pinewood Studios, Pinewood Road, Iver Heath, Bucks SL0 0NH
tel 020-8578 2899 *fax* 020-8575 0369
Key personnel Jennifer Jaffrey *(Proprietor)*

Main areas of work are theatre, musicals, television, film and commercials. Casting credits include: *Cross My Heart, Ten Minutes Older* and *Such a Long Journey.*

Will consider attending performances at venues in Greater London given as much notice as possible. Accepts submissions (with CVs and photographs) from actors previously unknown to the casting director if sent by post, but does not welcome email enquiries. Photographs should have the actor's name

written on the back, and an sae must be included for the return of material. Showreels should only be sent on request.

Lucy Jenkins CDG
74 High Street, Hampton Wick, Kingston on Thames, KT1 4DQ
tel 020-8943 5328 *fax* 020-8977 0466

Casts mainly for film, television, theatre and commercials. Casting credits include: *Babyfather* (BBC), *The Bill* (television), *Top Dog* (short film) and *Emma* (theatre).

Marilyn Johnson CDG
11 Goodwin's Court, London WC2N 4LL
tel 020-7497 5552 *fax* 020-7497 5530
email casting@marilynjohnsoncasting.com

Main area of work is television. Credits include *Our Mutual Friend, Holding On, Murphy's Law, Nature Boy* and *Inspector Morse.*

Doreen Jones
PO Box 22478, London W6 0WJ
tel 020-8746 3782 *fax* 020-8748 8533

Casts mainly for television and film. Recent credits include: *Fingersmith, Prime Suspect, Elizabeth, The Palace* and *Wallander.*

Will consider attending performances within Greater London and occasionally elsewhere, given as much notice as possible. Unsolicited submissions and enquiries from actors are not welcome.

Sam Jones CDG
Flat 3, 56 Trinity Church Square, London SE1 4HT
tel 020-7378 0222
email samjonescasting@btconnect.com

Former Head of Casting for the Royal Shakespeare Company. Other credits include: *Journey's End* (West End and tour); *After Mrs Rochester* (for Shared Experience); *Abigail's Party* (Hampstead Theatre/ West End); *Trial & Retribution* (for La Plante Productions/ITV); and *Human Cargo* (for CBC/Force Four – nominated for 17 Gemini Awards).

Sue Jones CDG
24 Nicoll Road, London NW10 9AB
tel 020-8838 5153 *fax* 020-8838 1130

Main areas of work are film, television, theatre and commercials. Casting credits include: *The Virgin of Liverpool,* starring Ricky Tomlinson and Imelda Staunton (MOB Films); *The Sound of Thunder,* with Ed Burns, Ben Kingsley and Catherine McCormack; *The Origins of Evil* (CBS/Alliance Atlantis); *Messiah* and *Coriolanus* (both plays directed by Stephen Berkoff); *The Vicar* (BBC television); and *The Politician's Wife* (Channel 4).

Kate and Lou Casting
The Basement, Museum House, 25 Museum Street, London WC1A 1JT

mobile (07976) 252531
website www.kateandloucasting.com

Casts for commercials. Recent credits include: Tilda Rice, Macdonalds, Lotto, and Doritos.

Does not welcome performance notices. Will accept letters (with CVs and photographs) from individual actors previously unknown to the company, and unsolicited CVs and photographs sent via email. Does not welcome showreels or invitations to view individual actors' websites.

Anna Kennedy Casting

8 Rydal Road, London SW16 1QN

Welcomes performance notices, for productions within the Greater London area, with 2 weeks' notice. Will accept letters, but not emails, with CVs and photographs from individuals previously unknown to the casting director; also welcomes showreels and invitations to view actors' websites.

Beverley Keogh

29 Ardwick Green North, Ardwick, Manchester M12 6DL
tel 0161-273 4400 *fax* 0161-273 4401
email via form on website

Main areas of work are television, film and commercials. Casting credits include: *Fat Friends*, *Clocking Off* and *Second Coming*.

Accepts submissions (with CVs and photographs) from actors previously unknown to the casting director, sent by post or email.

Jerry Knight-Smith CDG

Royal Exchange Theatre, Manchester, M2 7DH
tel 0161-615 6761
website www.royalexchangecasting.co.uk

Resident Casting Director for the Royal Exchange Theatre, Manchester. See entry under *Producing theatres* on page 127 for further details.

Suzy Korel CDG

20 Blenheim Road, St John's Wood, London NW8 0LX

Will consider attending performances at venues in Greater London given as much notice as possible. Accepts submissions (with CVs and photographs) from actors previously unknown to the casting director if sent by post, but does not welcome email enquiries. Invitations to view individual actors' websites are also accepted.

Sharon Levinson

30 Stratford Villas, London NW1 9SG

Main areas of work are theatre, television, film and commercials. Casting credits include: *Two Thousand Acres of Sky* and *A Christmas Carol* (television).

Will consider attending performances at venues in Greater London and occasionally elsewhere, given 2 weeks' notice. Not currently casting.

Karen Lindsay-Stewart CDG

PO Box 2301, London W1A 1PT

Main areas of work are television and film. Casting credits include: *Sylvia*, *Harry Potter and the Chamber of Secrets* and *Cambridge Spies*.

Will consider attending performances at venues in Greater London with sufficient notice. Accepts submissions (with CVs and photographs) from actors previously unknown to the casting director if sent by post, but does not welcome email enquiries. Do not send sae(s) for replies.

Maggie Lunn

Resident Casting Director for the Almeida theatre – see entry under *Producing theatres* on page 117.

Kay Magson Casting

PO Box 175, Pudsey, Leeds LS28 7LN
tel 0113-236 0251
email kay.magson@btinternet.com
Casting Director Kay Magson

Recent credits include *Bollywood Jane*, *Twelfth Night*, *Alice in Wonderland*, *Duchess of Malfi* (West Yorkshire Playhouse), National Tours of *Singin' In the Rain*, *Aspects of Love*, *Round the Horne...Revisited* and *Dracula*, *Noises Off*, *Billy Liar*, *The Flint Street Nativity*, *The Electric Hills* (Liverpool), *A Model Girl* (Greenwich), *One Last Card Trick*, *Aladdin* (Watford), *Merrily We Roll Along*, *Importance of Being Earnest*, *As You Like It* (Derby), *The Way of the World*, *Follies* (Northampton), *East Is East* (York/ Bolton), *Rosencrantz & Guildenstern Are Dead*, *Much Ado About Nothing* (Manchester Library).

Will consider attending performances within the Greater London area and elsewhere, with at least 4 weeks' notice. Accepts submissions (with CVs and photographs) from actors previously unknown to the casting director, via email only.

Lisa Makin

Resident Casting Director for the Royal Court Theatre. See entry under *Producing theatres* on page 117 for further details.

Andrew Mann

See entry for Casting UK.

John Manning

4 Holmbury Gardens, Hayes, Middlesex UB3 2LU
tel 020-8573 5463

Works in theatre and musicals. Recent credits include: *The 39 Steps* (Criterion Theatre); *Turandot* (Hampstead); and *An Inspector Calls* (national tour).

Will consider attending performances within the Greater London area, and regularly attends regional theatre – but does request 4 weeks' notice. Welcomes letters (with CVs and photographs) from individual actors previously unknown to the company, sent by post only; will also accept invitations to view individual actors' websites.

Carolyn McLeod

PO Box 26495, London SE10 0WO
tel + 44 (0)704 4001720
email actors@cmcasting.eclipse.co.uk

Main areas of work are film, television and promos. Casting director credits include: *WMD, Starship Troopers 3, Pumpkinhead 3: Ashes to Ashes, Pumpkinhead 4: Blood Feud, The Bill* (2006-2008), and *Power Rangers: Operation Overdrive*. Promos for: Lemar, Oasis, and The Feeling.

Will consider attending performances at venues in Greater London and occasionally elsewhere, given 2-3 weeks' notice. Accepts submissions (with CVs and photographs) from actors previously unknown to the casting director, sent by post or email. Showreels, voicereels and invitations to view individual actors' websites are also accepted. Applicants should only submit their details once. Advises actors that: "As most casting directors have little capacity for storing CVs, it may be worth telephoning to check whether they are accepting submissions – though do be warned that some people may not appreciate the phone call. If you already have an agent, ask them to contact us on your behalf."

Chrissie McMurrich

16 Spring Vale Avenue, Brentford, Middlesex TW8 9QH

Main areas of work are theatre and television. Recent casting includes: the tour of *Scooby Doo and the Pirate Ghost Live on Stage*; the Ludlow Festival/Exeter Northcott Theatre production of *Romeo and Juliet*; *Original Sin, The Blue Room, A Christmas Carol* and *Cyrano de Bergerac* for the Haymarket Basingstoke; and the tour of *Thomas the Tank Engine and Friends*.

Will consider attending performances at venues in Greater London given 2 weeks' notice. Accepts submissions with performance notices (containing photos and CVs) from actors previously unknown to the casting director if sent by post. No unsolicited emails are accepted. "Please be aware of the new postage rates for A4 envelopes. Not everyone will pay the Royal Mail handling charge to get unsolicited photos and CVs."

Anne McNulty

Resident Casting Director for Donmar Warehouse. See separate entry under *Producing theatres* on page 117.

Sooki McShane CDG

8a Piermont Road, East Dulwich, London SE22 0LN
tel 020-8693 7411 *fax* 020-8693 7411

Works mainly in theatre, film and television. Casting credits include: *Rainbow Room* (Granada television);

My Brother Rob (feature film); and casting for the Warehouse Theatre Croydon.

Currently Resident Casting Director for the Nottingham Playhouse. See entry under *Producing theatres* on page 117 for further details.

Carl Proctor CDG

15 Bury Place, London WC1A 2JB
tel 020-7681 0034 *mobile* (07956) 283340
email carlproctor2@btinternet.com
website www.carlproctor.com

Casts mainly for film, television, theatre and commercials. Casting credits include: *Blood Creek* (Joel Schumacher), *Shadow of the Vampire, The Wedding Date, Mrs Palfrey at the Claremount*, and *Twelfth Night* (Trevor Nunn).

Performance notices, submissions, showreels and unsolicited emails are not welcomed. Advises that CVs and photographs are no longer kept on file as these details are available on Spotlight Interactive.

Andy Pryor CDG

Suite 3, 15 Broad Court, London WC2B 5QN
tel 020-7836 8298 *fax* 020-7836 8299

Casts mainly for film and television. Casting credits include: *Glorious 39* (a film directed by Stephen Poliakoff); and *Doctor Who* and *Life on Mars* (for BBC Television*).

Gennie Radcliffe

Casting Director for *Coronation Street*. See entry for Granada under *Independent television* on page 298 for further details.

Leigh-Ann Regan Casting Associates Ltd

Ynyslasuchaf Farm, Blackmill, Bridgend LF35 6DW
tel 01656-841 841 *fax* 01656-841 815
email leigh-annregan@btconnect.com

Areas of work include television, film, commercials and theatre. Resident casting director at Clwyd Theatr Cymru (see entry under *Producing theatres* on page 119). Recent credits include: 21 part drama series for S4C/Fiction Factory (Ypris), 4 years casting *Caerdydd* for S4C/Fiction Factory.

Will consider attending performances in Greater London and elsewhere with at least one week's notice. Accepts submissions (with CVs and photographs) from actors previously unknown to the casting director.

Simone Reynolds CDG

60 Hebdon Road, London SW17 7NN

Main areas of work are film, television, theatre and commercials. Casting credits include: *The 39 Steps* (Olivier Award for Best Comedy); *The Vicar of Dibley* and *Turning Points: Emma's Story* (both for BBC television); *Jack and Sarah* (film for Granada); *Shining Through* (film for Twentieth Century Fox) and *Quicksand* (film).

Will consider attending performances at venues in Greater London and elsewhere, given as much notice as possible. Accepts postal submissions (with CVs and photographs) from actors previously unknown to the casting director, but does not welcome email enquiries. Advises actors to: "Keep CVs clear (separate out the part from the director and venue) and keep covering submissions brief."

Danielle Roffe Casting
71 Mornington Street, London NW1 7QE

Works in film and television. Recent credits include: *The Upside of Anger*, *She's Gone*, and *Holy Cross*.

Welcomes performance notices and is prepared to travel within Greater London. Does not welcome unsolicited CVs, photographs or showreels, but is happy to receive invitations to view individual actors' websites.

Jane Salberg
86 Stade Street, Hythe, Kent CT21 6DY
tel (01303) 239277
email janesalberg@aol.com

Works in theatre and musicals. Recent credits include: UK Casting Director for Jean Ann Ryan (Cruise Musicals); *Horrid Henry Live and Horrid* (UK tour); and *The Wizard of Oz* (Royal Festival Hall).

Prefers not to receive performance notices or unsolicited submissions, but will consider invitations to view individual actors' websites.

Marie Claude Schwartz
13 Avenue de Fouilleuse, 92210 St Cloud, France
tel (33) 1 4602 9909
email mc.schwartz@assorda.com
website See http://www.assorda.com

Works in TV and film. Recent credits include: *JE "François Villon, poète voleur, assassin"*; *Comissaire Magellan*; *C'est Mon Tour*. Will accept CVs and photographs sent by email, showreels, voicereels, and invitations to view individual actors' websites.

Laura Scott CDG
56 Rowena Crescent, London SW11 2PT
tel 020-7978 6336 *fax* 020-7924 1907
email laurascottcasting@mac.com

Main areas of work are film, television, theatre and commercials. Casting credits include: *Bonekickers* (BBC TV), *William and Mary* (Series 1-3, TV), *Trial and Retribution XIV* (TV), and *The Time of Your Life* (TV).

The Searchers
70 Sylvia Court, Cavendish Street, London N1 7PG
Directors Wayne Waterson, Ian Sheppard

Casts mainly for television, film and commercials.

Recent credits include: commercials for Pepsi, Nike, Kellogg's and Royal Mail. Has worked for directors including Terry Gillingham, Tarsem and Earl Morris.

Will consider attending performances within Greater London given 1 week's notice. Accepts submissions (with CVs, showreels and photographs) from actors previously unknown to the company, but does not welcome unsolicited emails or invitations to view an actor's website.

Phil Shaw
Suite 476, 2 Old Brompton Road, South Kensington, London SW7 3DQ
tel 020-8715 8943
email shawcastlond@aol.com

Main areas of work are theatre, television, film and commercials. Casting credits include: *Deckies* (TV series pilot); *Days in the Trees* (BBC Radio); *Body Story* (BBC doc/drama series); *Romans 12:20* (short); *Winter Fiction* (NFTS); *The Turn of the Screw* (theatre); *The Last Post* (film – BAFTA nominated); and *Love and Virtue* (feature).

Will consider attending performances at venues in Central London given a minimum of 2 weeks' notice. Accepts postal submissions (with CVs and photographs) from actors previously unknown to the casting director, but does not welcome unsolicited showreels or email enquiries.

Michelle Smith CDG
220 Church Lane, Woodford, Stockport SK7 1PQ
tel 0161-439 6825 *fax* 0161-439 0622

Main areas of work are film, television and commercials. Casting credits include: *Steel River Blues* (ITV); *Max and Paddy* (Channel 4); *Phoenix Nights* (Channel 4); and *Cold Feet* (Series 1-5 – Granada).

Suzanne Smith CDG
33 Fitzroy Street, London W1T 6DU
tel 020-7436 9255 *fax* 020-7436 9690

Main areas of work are film, television, theatre and musicals. Casting credits include: UK casting for *Alien vs Predator* (directed by Paul Anderson for 20th Century Fox); *The Dark* (directed by John Fawcett for Impact Pictures); UK casting for *Black Hawk Down* (directed by Ridley Scott); and *Band of Brothers* (for television – HBO/Dreamworks).

Wendy Spon CDG
c/o National Theatre, South Bank, London SE1 9PX

Main areas of work are film, television, theatre and musicals. Until recently, Head of Casting at Talkback Thames (*The Bill*), and now Head of Casting at the National Theatre (see entry under *Producing theatres* on page 124). Casting credits include: *The Graduate* (theatre, directed by Terry Johnson); *Oklahoma* and *Oh What a Lovely War* (both for the National Theatre); and *Shadow Man* (short film).

Emma Stafford

Royal Exchange, St Ann's Square,
Manchester M2 7BR
tel 0161-833 4263 *fax* 0161-833 4264
email info@emmastafford.tv
website www.emmastafford.tv

Areas of work include television, film and
commercials. Recent credits include: *200 Magazine*,
Co-op Bank, Robinsons, *If I Were a Butterfly*.

Will consider attending performances within the
North West area with at least 2 weeks' notice. Accepts
letters (with CVs and photographs) from actors
previously unknown to the agency; will also accept
CVs and photographs sent by email, and view
showreels.

Gail Stevens Casting CDG

Greenhill House, 90-93 Cowcross Street, London
EC1M 6BF

Main areas of work are television, film and
commercials. Casting credits include: *Twenty-Eight
Days Later*, *Calendar Girls* and *Spooks*.

Sam Stevenson CDG

email sam@hancockstevenson.com
website www.hancockstevenson.com

Main areas of work are television, theatre and film.
More details are available on the website.

Liz Stoll

BBC Elstree, Room N223 Neptune House,
Clarendon Road, Borehamwood WD6 1JF
tel 020-8228 8285 *fax* 020-8228 8311
email liz.stoll@bbc.co.uka

Has worked in all areas of actor casting and has been
casting BBC1 drama for the past 10 years. Credits
include: *Holby City*; 5 series of *Judge John Deed*; 5
series of *Down To Earth*; various episodes of *Waking
the Dead* and *Dalziel & Pascoe*; *Magnificent Seven* (a
film for BBC2); *A View from a Hill* (a film for BBC4);
and 6 Afternoon Plays for BBC1.

Happy to receive performance notices at least 2 weeks
in advance, and is prepared to travel within Greater
London (sometimes further, work permitting) to see
shows. Welcomes letters (but not emails) with CVs
and photographs from actors previously unknown to
the casting director; does not welcome unsolicited
showreels, but is happy to receive invitations to view
individuals' websites.

Emma Style CDG

1 Overton Cottages, Kings Lane, Cookham,
Maidenhead SL6 9BA

Main areas of work are film and television. Credits
include: *Scenes of a Sexual Nature* (feature film),
Mansfield Park (ITV drama), *Callas Forever* (Callynta
Films, Franco Zeffirelli), *Tea With Mussolini*
(Universal, Franco Zeffirelli), *Prime Suspect V*

(Granada Television) and *Our Friends In The North*
(episodes 5-9, BBC2).

Syson Grainger Casting

1st Floor, 33 Old Compton Street, London W1D 5JT
tel 020-7287 5327 *fax* 020-7287 3629

Recent feature films include: *Children of Men*,
directed by Alfonso Cuaron; *Syriana*, directed by
Stephen Gagan; *Batman Begins*, directed by Chris
Nolan; *Troy*, directed by Wolfgang Petersen; *Snatch*,
directed by Guy Ritchie; *Spygame*, directed by Tony
Scott; and *Fifth Element*, directed by Luc Besson.

Amanda Tabak CDG

See entry for Candid Casting.

Thea Meulenberg Casting

Keizersgracht 116, 1015 CV, Amsterdam
tel (31) 2 0626 5846
email info@theameulenberg.com
website www.theameulenberg.com

Established in 1980. Works in TV, film, commercials,
corporate, print and photography. Recent credits
include: Grolsch for Worldwide; Fia for *X Factor*;
Job.TV (Swiss). Around 3000 actors represented.
Accepts CVs and photographs sent by email (also
links to TV commercials – send by email).
Commission: 20%

Topps Casting

The Media Centre, 7 Northumberland Street,
West Yorkshire HD1 1RL
tel (01484) 511988 *fax* (01484) 483100
email nicci@toppscasting.co.uk
website www.toppscasting.co.uk
Casting Director Nicci Topping

Works in television, film and commercials. Recent
credits include: AA TVC, Iceland TVC, and Global
Stories.

Welcomes performance notices within Greater
London and elsewhere (Manchester, Leeds, Sheffield)
if given 2 weeks' notice. Accepts letters (with CVs &
photographs) from individual actors previously
unknown to the agency, sent by post or email.

Moira Townsend

See entry for Casting Couch Productions Ltd.

Jill Trevellick CDG

92 Priory Road, London N8 7EY
tel 020-8340 2734
email jill@jilltrevellick.com

Main areas of work are film and television. Casting
credits include: *The Ruby In The Smoke*, *Vanity Fair*,
North and South, and *The Canterbury Tales*, *Merlin*,
(all BBC); *Primeval* (ITV); *The Queen's Sister*, *North
Square* and *The Hamburg Cell* (both Channel 4).
Film: *Fish Tank* (Andrea Arnold – 2009), *I Know You
Know* (Justin Kerrigan –2009)

Sarah Trevis CDG
PO Box 47170, London W6 6BA
tel 020-7602 5552 *fax* 020-7602 8110

Main areas of work are television and film. Recent casting credits include: work for Granada television, the BBC and Twentieth Century Fox.

Will consider attending performances given 2 weeks' notice. Accepts submissions (with CVs and photographs) from actors previously unknown to the casting director if sent by post. Does not welcome email enquiries.

Sally Vaughan CDG
2 Kennington Park Place, London SE11 4AS
tel 020-7735 6539

Main area of work is theatre. Credits include: *Porridge* (No. 1 UK tour); *'Allo, 'Allo* (No. 1 UK tour); *Dad's Army – The Lost Episodes* (No. 1 UK tour); *Sweet Charity* (Victoria Palace Theatre), *Of Thee I Sing* and *Sweeney Todd* (Bridewell Theatre); and *Anna Weiss* (Whitehall Theatre).

Vital Productions
mobile (07957) 284709
email mail@vital-productions.co.uk
website www.vital-productions.co.uk
Key personnel Melissa Waudby

Main areas of work are theatre, television and film. Casting credits include: BBC *Crimewatch* and *The Great Dome Robbery* (television).

Will consider attending performances at venues in Greater London and elsewhere, given 1 month's notice. Accepts submissions (with CVs and photographs) from actors previously unknown to the casting director. "Because of time pressure, we tend to use *Spotlight* and specific agents or individual suggestions rather than CVs and photographs submitted to us."

Anne Vosser CDG
PO Box 408, Aldershot GU11 9DS
tel (01252) 404716 *mobile* (07968) 868712
email anne@vosser-casting.co.uk
website www.vosser-casting.co.uk

Main areas of work are theatre and musicals. Casting credits include: *Zorro, Taboo, Fame, Saturday Night Fever, Footloose, Never Forget* (all in the West End).

June West
Resident Casting Director at Granada. See entry under *Independent television* on page 298 for further details.

Matt Western
150 Blythe Road, London W14 0HD
tel 020-7602 6646
email matt@mattwestern.co.uk

Main areas of work are film, television and commercials. Casting credits include: *Affinity* (ITV1), *Coup!* (BBC2), *Roman Mysteries* (2 series for BBC1), *55 Degrees North* (2 series for BBC1), and *Class of '76* (ITV1).

Toby Whale CDG
80 Shakespeare Road, London W3 6SN
tel 020-8993 2821 *fax* 020-8993 8096
website www.whalecasting.com

Head of Casting at the National Theatre 2003-06. Main areas of work are film, television and theatre. Casting credits include: *The History Boys*; *East is East* (Assassin Films/FilmFour); *The French Film* (Slingshot); *True Dare Kiss* (BBC); *Spoonface Steinberg* (BBC Films); *Wire in the Blood* (Series 1 & 2 – Coastal/ITV); and more than 40 theatre productions for the Royal Court Theatre, Out of Joint, the Almeida Theatre, English Touring Theatre and Sheffield Crucible, among others.

Tara Woodward
Top Flat, 93 Gloucester Avenue, Primrose Hill, London NW1 8LB
tel 020-7586 3487 *fax* 020-7681 8574

Main areas of work are film, television, theatre and commercials. Casting credits include: *The Early Days*, *Post* and *Hello Friend* (all for Shine/Film Four Lab); *Chasing Heaven* (for Venice Film Festival); *The Browning Version* and *Romeo and Juliet* (theatre); and commercials for Parmalat Aqua and Royal Danish Post. Has worked as Casting Assistant to Nina Gold on films including *All Or Nothing* (directed by Mike Leigh) and *Love's Labour's Lost* (directed by Kenneth Branagh).

Jeremy Zimmermann Casting
36 Marshall Street, London W1F 7EY
tel 020-7478 5161 *fax* 020-7437 4747

Main areas of work are film and television. Recent casting work includes: *Keeping Mum, The Contract, Van Wilder 2, Dog Soldiers* and *Blood And Chocolate*.

Will consider attending performances at venues in Greater London and elsewhere. Accepts postal submissions (with CVs and photographs) from actors previously unknown to the casting director, but does not welcome email enquiries. Invitations to view individual actors' websites are also accepted.

The working life of a theatre casting director

Sophie Marshall

Twenty-something years ago, when I became the first Casting Director for the Royal Exchange Theatre in Manchester, I inherited a four-drawer filing cabinet, stuffed with letters from actors who were keen to be seen by the directors. I had no idea how long the letters had been there, but soon found out that many actors had moved, others had become TV regulars, and one or two had even died. I realised then that casting is, and has to be, an 'in the moment' activity – circumstances change too much, too often.

The title Casting Director is perhaps a misnomer; s/he is more a facilitator, coordinator and encyclopaedia of information, rather than the final decision-maker – the latter has to be the director, at least in theatre. In television and film the process is much the same, in terms of selection for interview, although the readings and screen tests may often need to be more 'spot on'.

The process starts with a discussion between myself and the director about the play, from which can come a casting breakdown (which may be made accessible to actors and agents, or may be kept for us to work on in private). The director will generally have some actors in mind, or the project may be based on an element of 'lead' casting, and I will then add my own lists of ideas. About ten weeks before rehearsals begin, I will then start on all the clerical back-up work – checking availabilities, sifting through the agents' and actors' submissions, setting up interviews. This is followed by the hands-on part: being at the auditions and probably reading-in, discussing the outcomes with the director, arranging recalls, offering and negotiating contracts.

Actors and agents sometimes assume that a casting breakdown is written in stone, and will not change, but this is very often only a starting point; in the ensuing weeks, the ideas will develop throughout the audition process. When I was casting *A Midsummer Night's Dream*, we decided not to put out a breakdown; however, agents knew the production was happening, and submitted around 1000 CVs, and actors wrote too – probably about another 1000 letters. Everyone had an idea of how Oberon ought to look, how small Hermia should be, what regional accent Bottom could use. It can take literally hours to open all the envelopes, unfold the contents and read them, and it is even more time-consuming when the letters are badly typed or vague, the CVs uninformative, and the photos so bleached you can't distinguish any features.

In theatre, it is by no means essential to have an agent, and, even if you do, a letter from an actor is always interesting and the CV invariably more detailed. (In fact, it's a good idea to ask your agent for a copy of your CV, so you can see how they are promoting you. They are, after all, your representative and business partner.) When you write in for a particular production, by all means mention which role attracts you, and show a little of your personality in the letter; but your attached CV should tell all the truthful facts about your experience and skills, and your photo should look like you! The CV, photo and letter are a package, but one which should be altered according to the recipient. The CV and photo

Agents and casting directors

will most likely be constant, but the letter should refer to the particular company or project. Don't repeat your whole CV in the text of the letter, but do refer to any specifically useful points. If you no longer look like your photo, get a new one! There may be instances where you are selected for interview because you resemble another member of the cast, for instance (lots of twins in Shakespeare!) – and if you turn up on the day and look nothing like the photo, the director's reaction could be very demoralising. It's harder to write for specific screen jobs, but the process of sending details to the casting director should be the same.

Silver pen on black paper, letters in rhyme, photos of you in a school production, camomile teabags ("to soothe you as you read my letter") ... all of these make you look a little desperate. Firm facts are better, and an approach such as, "I haven't had the opportunity to be in a Shakespeare play since I was at college, but I hope my music and movement skills will be of interest to you for the role of First Fairy," is much more positive and pertinent. It would show your interest, the fact that you've read the play, and make us look immediately at your CV to see which plays you covered at college, and what special skills you have – Result!

Some of the hardest auditions to deal with are those where we know the actor is terrific, but is so well-behaved in the interview – only speaking when spoken to, reading cautiously before getting some director input, and so on – that there is absolutely no personality and no sense of this being a two-way process. When we offer you an audition, it is not a charitable act – it's because we think you are worth it. So interact, be a part of it, ask questions, say what works for you. It's not an exam, so if you weren't happy with your speech or reading, for example, say so: that way, the director knows you are aware of what you are doing. It's worth remembering that if you get the job, you will be in a rehearsal room for a number of weeks with this person, so see what you can find out about him/her, the production, the way of working.

Obviously a large part of our job is to watch shows, showcases, TV, films, even commercials. Sometimes the first half is enough – we're there for work, not fun, and may have five more nights out that same week. We sometimes hold general meetings with actors we know a little about, to discover more – especially for screen work, where you need to know more about the actor's personality, their ability to cope without much rehearsal, and so on. Our knowledge of any actor is like a jigsaw puzzle, and putting in another piece to complete the picture is helpful.

Of course, I remember some actors for the wrong reasons, such as the one who offered to knee-cap me if I didn't give him an interview, and the one who, in the course of doing a speech of adoration to a car engine, stripped down to a black leather jock-strap! I've had to cast cartoon characters, deadly sins, a statue, a pack of dogs, and the Marx Brothers, never mind all the run-of-the-mill roles. So really, there are jobs out there for all of you, if you just keep your cool and use your common sense. Good luck!

Sophie Marshall was born in Cheshire and joined the Royal Exchange Theatre Company in Manchester in 1973. She began as Secretary to the Project Manager for the building of the new theatre, and was able to see the company grow from a small, part-time organisation (producing around three productions per year) to the nationally renowned company it is today, producing work on the main stage and in The Studio. Having seen the theatre built, bombed, and rebuilt, she left in 2004 to work freelance.

Casting for musical theatre

David Grindrod

The process of producing/casting a musical can be a very long and costly affair. Everyone is looking for the next *Phantom of the Opera* or *Mamma Mia!*; years of work can go into the production you see on stage today. Workshops have now become a necessity in order to see if a show 'has legs', without spending too much money. In consultation with the producer and creative team, I will assemble a group of actors who may not be totally right for the roles but who work well in a workshop situation. If the green light is given after the workshop presentation, the casting process – in conjunction with everything else – begins.

A casting breakdown is drawn up: this consists of all the details required by agents and artists about the characters, vocal ranges, etc. plus the proposed dates of the production. Open calls are sometimes organised for specific roles, but normally the breakdown gets sent to agents via The Spotlight Link, which reaches 500 agents/representatives at the touch of a button.

There is always a 'wish list' of actors whom producers would like in their production, but the bulk of submissions will come through agents in the form of photos and CVs. Unsolicited mail is also received; sometimes it is difficult to keep all this on file due to sheer number of submissions. Either I or my associates will also attend college shows and presentations to look for specific talent.

When preparing your photos and CVs, always remember that these are the calling cards with which you promote yourself! A good photograph is not 'artistic' (i.e. showing a face half in shadow); rather, it should always present a good full face that really does look like you. Your CV should ideally be just one page stapled to the back of your photograph. It should include all relevant details (*not* forgetting contact details) to show your skills. Make this information clear and precise. If you feel that you are suitable for musical casting, be very accurate and truthful about your vocal range: don't make it complicated – basically, tenor or soprano, with the top of your range noted. We can normally tell your style by the shows you have appeared in.

The audition process normally begins with artists performing two contrasting songs that show range and personality. Make an effort to pick a song that is suitable for the show – not pop, for example, when you are up for Rogers & Hammerstein. Nerves will take over; therefore, don't sing the song you learnt yesterday, but perform something tried and tested (something you would be happy singing naked in Trafalgar Square!). When we ask, "Have you got something else?" we don't want the answer, "My agent said you only wanted two songs,"; have your book of audition pieces with you and give us the chance to choose an alternative. Actors often ask whether I have favourite songs that I like to hear – or songs that I don't: I only really mind when they come in with completely the wrong song for the production.

If an actor is successful, they will receive a call-back for a dance/movement call. This normally causes concerns, but actually it is not usually that specific; we only want to see whether a person is happy with his/her body. If the audition is for a major dance show, hopefully you will know your limitations, and either not audition at all, or be ready to throw yourself into the routine. Again, be honest: then you won't upset the creative team.

Agents and casting directors

Further recalls take place with music and script from the show: the musical supervisor or associate director normally takes these calls. If you come in for the musical supervisor, come back with music prepared and your own song. *Always* bring your own song – it's a good reminder for the team. In addition to any script you are asked to read, you may get asked for a speech: have a couple of acting pieces prepared and again, nerves will take over, so make sure you know them properly. Remember that these speeches are also to allow the director to assess how well you can respond to direction, and how readily you can take a note.

The culmination of the casting process: 'the finals' – the most nerve-wracking experience even for a highly experienced artist. Bring everything with you that you have been given. You may not get *asked* for everything, but have it just in case. You may have been asked to dress in a certain way; always put some thought into that, as directors can be blinkered at times ... I have known artists to arrive with a couple of outfits and ask me to pick one! The panel will consist of the whole creative team and the producers. At this stage I can't do any more for you – though hopefully I can keep the atmosphere in the room happy and 'up'. Stay calm, don't change anything that you have been told, and audition to the best of your abilities.

Now the wait to see if you have the role. Always remember that you have got this far in the process because you can sing and act far better than anyone else. In the end, the decision could come down to height, look, hair colour; funnily enough it may not have anything to do with your singing/acting skills at this point. And you may not get an instant answer; you may have to wait until other meetings have taken place. You may get put on 'hold': normally that means you are not first on the list, but if somebody above you declines the offer you may move up. If you are lucky, the phone call will come with a straight offer. How exciting is that ... Contractual details are then advised, and, if all that is agreed, your date for first rehearsal is given. Always remember that you are a small part of the bigger picture – a small part of the jigsaw puzzle that goes together to form: The Musical.

David Grindrod founded David Grindrod Associates (DGA) with Stephen Crockett in January 1998, after 20 years' experience in the theatre in various roles ranging from assistant stage manager to general manager. Current West End casting includes *Chicago*, *Evita*, *The Lord of the Rings*, *Mamma Mia!* (worldwide), *Spamalot*, *The Sound of Music*. Films include *The Phantom of The Opera*. DGA are also casting consultants for *On The Town* and *Kismet* at the English National Opera, and belong to the Casting Directors Guild of Great Britain.

Theatre
Introduction

Theatres and theatre companies/managements abound in all kinds of different forms, and paid opportunities for live performance are not restricted to putting on productions. The days of the permanent repertory company are almost gone, but there is a much wider diversity of work available. The larger companies/managements often use casting directors (see page 95), who should usually be your first port of call with your letter, CV and photograph. However, it can be worth exploiting any personal contacts that you may have.

For all approaches, it is important to send your submissions to the person named – unless you have a personal contact.

Some organisations have regular casting patterns – see The Casting Calendar on page 271 for details.

Marketing yourself: a producer's viewpoint

Ian Liston

Anything and everything an actor does in his or her working life is about presentation. A sloppy, badly rehearsed performance is not going to win prizes, let alone get you more work. You may have spent a couple of years or more – and invested many thousands of pounds – developing your talent with a lifelong career in mind, so why risk the good work you've done already by not marketing yourself properly? Hopefully you regard yourself as an actor of some quality, so why jeopardise your potential by failing to promote yourself in a 'quality' way?

Whether you've had formal training or never had a day's tuition in your life, it is still going to take a lot of effort and hard work on your part to find work and ensure that the time and heartache already invested has been worth it. It's inadvisable to rely solely on an agent, no matter how good they may be, to find you work. If you don't have an agent, in order to get one you will have to impress them as much as any other director or company you want to contact – and the ability to market yourself properly and create a good impression is even more essential.

Your most important asset will be your CV. Using even the simplest word processing programme makes it easy to keep this up to date. Not only will your CV contain, ideally, a couple of contrasting recent photographs, but you should also have the ability to 'drop in' a particular photograph that may be more suited to the part you are applying for.

It's worth spending as much as you can afford to obtain decent photographs. Even though you may a have a friend who knows how to use a digital camera, they're unlikely to have the skill and experience of a professional photographer, who will have the expertise to produce pictures that will get you noticed.

Published yearly by The Spotlight, *Contacts* provides many and varied examples of the work of specialist photographers; you can also find out more details about individual photographers starting on page 375 of this book. Most have websites, which can help you choose someone who appeals to you.

As with photographs, don't skimp on materials: invest in some decent paper – 100gsm at the very least. CVs usually get passed around various interested parties and, while they may arrive in good condition, for a few pence extra you can enclose them in a plastic folder to prevent them from becoming dog-eared when passed around a busy casting or production office. Most people prefer to print on white paper, but a tint or subtle colour can make your CV stand out even more, and make it easier to locate at a hectic casting session.

In terms of layout, a neat listing of your credits in chronological order is essential. As a producer, I much prefer to see credits categorised into separate sections of Stage, TV, Film, plus other relevant categories (e.g. Radio, Opera, etc.). Most actors are in *Spotlight*, which has a neat and efficient layout in its online publication that is worth adopting.

You should list the year of performance followed by the medium (i.e. Stage, TV, etc.) and then the character name, the title of the piece, the production company and the director. If the productions were at drama school or were unpaid or amateur, make that clear.

Every director / producer will look for their own 'tell-tale' clues in a CV: I put great emphasis on directors and companies with whom an actor has worked. Make sure you spell the names correctly. There's nothing more indicative of a sloppy actor than inaccurate spelling, be it a play title, director or character's name, and poor grammar. Don't be tempted to pad out your CV or fabricate plays, parts and directors, as you can be sure your sins will find you out!

You may have a wealth of leading roles under your belt before you became a professional actor: much better to list them as 'non-professional', 'training' or 'unpaid' work. Sadly there still seems to be a stigma surrounding the word 'amateur' when, in truth, much good work, comparable with the best of fringe or profit-share, is performed by amateur companies.

Let's assume that you've done all your groundwork. You will have familiarised yourself with the various casting services that are available (several offer free trials) and you are developing a network of your own to find out about the possibilities of work. You are reading the trade press (e.g. *The Stage*, which can now be accessed online on a daily basis) and you have invested in a copy of *Contacts* (and this yearbook, of course) so that you have all the names and contact addresses to hand of just about anyone who is anybody.

Now starts the slog – and it's not going to be a one-off afterthought on a Friday afternoon, after the phone hasn't rung about work for yet another week. Treat it as a business: your business. Research the market. Identify the companies whose work most interests you – or who might be most interested in you. A simple telephone call is usually sufficient to find the name of the person to contact. It could be a producer, director or casting director, but getting an individual's name will better your chances. It's useless writing to ask for a general audition or interview if the company never holds any.

To maximise your chance of success, write your short, to-the-point letter and send it with your CV to the identified contact. A brief comment to acknowledge the company's work doesn't go amiss, and gives you a better chance of engaging someone's interest ... but don't be smarmy, smart-assed or clever. There is nothing more annoying to a producer than someone who 'desperately wants to work for your company' when plainly they have no real idea of what the company does.

Avoid gimmicks. I've never forgiven the sender of the childishly folded letter which, when opened, spilled a heap of stars and glitter that took months to get out of clothes and carpet. I may not have forgotten the gimmick about wanting to be a star, but I've certainly forgotten the name!

If you're sending a photo with your CV, then you must remember to *put your name and contact details on the back of the photo*! It never ceases to amaze me how many people omit to do such a simple thing. For at least 50% of the hundreds of applications we receive each year, we have no means whatsoever of identifying the photo – so if it gets separated from a CV, as can often happen, it will have been a total waste of time and money.

First impressions count. You wouldn't (would you?) attend an audition or interview looking scruffy and unkempt. Some people do, but that's another story. Take care with your spelling and grammar and avoid using exclamation marks at the end of every sentence. A neatly addressed, handwritten letter using quality paper certainly grabs my attention:

they're such a rarity these days. Keep it brief and to the point, without being verbose. If you have 'doctors' handwriting', use simple typed labels and a neatly typed letter but, at the very least, handwrite the salutation and the signature. Mass-produced mail-shot letters are easy to spot and they usually end up straight in the bin. Unless a stamped addressed envelope is enclosed (and I only speak for myself) I would not usually offer the courtesy of a reply and the return of a photograph.

There is an increasing tendency these days to include a DVD or similar visual medium as part of the submission. This should be of the highest possible quality and capable of being played on any equipment; and it should comprise a personal introduction from your good self together with a selection of photographs / video clips from recent work. It should *not* be a replacement for the letter and CV. As with every element of your submission, make sure your contact details are clearly marked.

A major factor to get right is the postage. Since the new method of sizing, weighing and pricing for postage came into force in 2007, it's amazing how few people still bother to check they have the right amount of stamps. Too few, and your recipient will have to fork out a few pounds to get something he or she hasn't expected and will likely bin; too many and you're wasting your own hard-earned cash. Useful advice on this matter is included in Simon Dunmore's introduction to this *Yearbook*.

Email is being used increasingly as a method of contact and every recipient has their own way of dealing with it. It can be particularly useful if a potential work opportunity comes to your attention at short notice. It's faster than the post and nothing is more effective than striking whilst the iron is hot – but make sure any files you send are as small as possible. Include your Spotlight link and, if you have a website, the link to that as well.

In similar fashion, always make sure you have ready a good supply of your photographs and CVs, although it's pointless printing too many at one time, as the real worth of a good CV is the fact that it's absolutely up to date. If you're suggesting that your correspondent can look up your entry in *Spotlight*, make sure that too is up to date. In 2007 an agent suggested I look up his client in *Spotlight*; a pointless exercise since the actor's most recent credits were for 1998!

Success is so often a matter of luck. A CV / letter arriving in the right hands, just when a producer / director is looking for someone like you, can open untold doors, but it's astonishing how few actors bother to spend that little bit of extra time and effort getting it right.

Always remember the wise words of Ivor Novello, one of the most successful actor / managers of the 20th century: "If you want to be a success, look it!" – and that goes for your correspondence as well as your appearance.

Good luck! I look forward to hearing from you.

Ian Liston is an actor and producer whose career covers over 40 years' experience as an actor in feature films, on TV and on the stage. His company, Hiss & Boo Ltd, is one of the UK's leading producers of pantomime and revue, and its productions are frequently seen on the UK touring circuit and overseas.

Producing theatres

Included in this section are the national and regional building-based companies that mount their own productions – sometimes in co-operation with others, and sometimes sending out tours. (Almost all also receive touring productions.) The majority are subsidised by the national and regional Arts Councils (and use Equity's regional theatre contract), but a few are not (and use Equity's commercial theatre contract), and a few have their own contractual arrangements. Almost all have websites which can be very useful for keeping track of their activities. A little extra insight – beyond that listed on the following pages – into a theatre might just tip the balance in your favour.

In real terms, rates of pay are better than they were a decade and more ago, but they are still only 'adequate' – especially if you are incurring the extra costs of living away from home. However, rehearsing and performing a production in such a theatre can be an exhilarating experience. A well-run theatre has a wonderful 'family' atmosphere, and in the close-knit working environment you can often make friendships which sustain for many years afterwards – as well as contacts who might be useful in years to come. It is well worth checking each theatre's 'casting procedures' very carefully as there are significant variations between them. It is also worth familiarising yourself with their programmes of productions via *The Stage* and/or their websites.

Almeida Theatre
Almeida Street, London N1 1TA
tel 020-7288 4900 *fax* 020-7288 4901
email info@almeida.co.uk
website www.almeida.co.uk
Artistic Director Michael Attenborough *Associate Director* Howard Davies *Artistic Associate* Jenny Worton *Executive Director* Neil Constable *General Manager* Ros Brooke-Taylor

Production details: The Almeida is committed to staging British and international drama presented to the highest possible standards, and productions which reveal classic plays in a new light. Embraces international classics, foreign classics in newly commissioned versions, and new plays – in addition to an annual Opera season of specially commissioned operas, music theatre pieces and concerts of contemporary music. Stages approximately 6 productions each year. Recent productions include: *Big White Fog, Dying For It, There Came A Gypsy Riding, The Lightning Play,* and *Tom and Viv.*

Casting procedures: Productions are cast by external freelance casting directors on a project by project basis. Uses the TMA/Equity Subsidised Rep contract and subscribes to the Equity Pension Scheme. Actively encourages applications from disabled actors and promotes the use of inclusive casting.

Yvonne Arnaud Theatre
Millbrook, Guildford, Surrey GU1 3UX
tel (01483) 440077 *fax* (01483) 564071
website www.yvonne-arnaud.co.uk
Artistic Director James Barber

Production details: The Yvonne Arnaud Theatre is a busy producing and receiving house, creating shows in Guildford and touring nationally, with many productions transferring to the West End. On both the main stage and in the Mill Studio an eclectic mix of classical and contemporary work is staged by new, lesser-known and established writers.

The Youth and Education facility offers an exciting mix of activities for young people and adults all year round. The Yvonne Arnaud opened the 80-seat Mill Studio in 1993, to provide a venue for work that would not otherwise be seen in Guildford. It also forms the base for the Youth Theatre's activities.

Belgrade Theatre
Belgrade Square, Coventry CV1 1GS
tel 024-7625 6431
email admin@belgrade.co.uk
website www.belgrade.co.uk
Theatre Director & Chief Executive Hamish Glen
Associate Director Gadi Roll

Production details: After closure for refurbishment, the Belgrade re-opened in late 2007. Recent productions include: *One Night in November* (about the Coventry Blitz), *Scenes from a Marriage* (directed by Trevor Nunn), and 'legendary' annual pantomimes.

Birmingham Repertory Theatre
Centenary Square, Broad Street, Birmingham B1 2EP
tel 0121-245 2000

website www.birmingham-rep.co.uk
Artistic Director Rachel Kavanaugh *Associate Director (Literary)* Ben Payne *Executive Director* Stuart Rogers *Associate Director Learning & Participation* Steve Ball *Casting Co-ordinator* Alison Solomon

Production details: Stages 15 productions in the main house each year, and 6 in the studio. Also runs Outreach, Community and Education programmes.

Casting procedures: "The play's director, a casting director and sometimes a producer handle casting for all Main House and Door productions. We currently make use of freelance casting directors, specific to each production, administrated by our in-house Casting Co-ordinator."

Birmingham Stage Company (BSC)

Suite 228, 162 Regent Street, London W1B 5TB
tel 020-7437 3391 *fax* 020-7437 3395
email info@birminghamstage.net
website www.birminghamstage.net
Actor/Manager Neal Foster *Chief Executive* Philip Compton *General Manager* Sally Humphreys *Administrator* Michael Throne

Production details: Founded in 1992, the BSC stages 5 shows each year, 4 of which tour nationally. Produces a range of plays with particular emphasis on new writing, and is recognised for its children's shows, which visit 60 venues around the UK. Recent productions include: *Proof* (West End), *Horrible Histories* (UK tour), *The Jungle Book* (UK Tour), *Treasure Island* (UK Tour), *Danny the Champion of the World*. Offers TMA/Equity approved contracts and subscribes to the Equity Pension Scheme.

Casting procedures: Uses freelance casting directors and sometimes holds general auditions. Casting breakdowns are published on their website, and in *Spotlight*, *SBS* and *PCR* (see entry under *The Spotlight, casting directories and information services* on page 367). Submissions by hard copy only – no phone calls. "Do as much research as you can before submitting." Actively encourages applications from disabled actors.

Bristol Old Vic

King Street, Bristol BS1 4ED
tel 0117-949 3993 *fax* 0117-949 3993
email admin@bristololdvic.org.uk
website www.bristololdvic.org.uk
Artistic Director Tom Morris *Executive Director* Emma Stenning *Associate Director* Simon Godwin

Bristol Old Vic is a theatre company founded in 1946 and based in a complex which includes the unique Theatre Royal, opened in 1766 – the oldest theatre auditorium in the UK, which many think the most beautiful. Bristol Old Vic is also unique in its close working relationship with the Bristol Old Vic Theatre School.

The Bush Theatre

Shepherds Bush Green, London W12 8QD
tel 020-8743 3584

email info@bushtheatre.co.uk
website www.bushtheatre.co.uk
Artistic Director Josie Rourke *Executive Director* Angela Bond

Production details: Founded in 1972, the Bush specialises in developing and producing new writing to the highest professional standard. Stages 5-8 productions a year, totalling around 280 performances. Also tours productions, although the bulk of performances are at the Bush itself. Up to 6 actors are employed on each production, and the company offers TMA/Equity approved contracts. Recent productions include: *The Contingency Plan, Apologia and Stovepipe* (HighTide Production in collaboration with the Bush Theatre and the National Theatre)

Casting procedures: Casts in-house, and does not hold general meetings or issue public casting breakdowns. Welcomes letters and emails from actors previously unknown to the company. Does not welcome showreels or invitations to view actors' websites. Actively encourages applications from disabled actors and promotes the use of inclusive casting.

Byre Theatre

Abbey Street, St Andrews KY16 9LA
tel (01334) 475000 *fax* (01334) 475370
email enquiries@byretheatre.com
website www.byretheatre.com
Chief Executive Officer Jacqueline McKay

Production details: Founded in 1933, the Byre moved into a new state-of-the-art theatre in 2001, where it presented a mixed programme of in-house and guest productions. From July 2007 the Byre refocused its programme, presenting a range of touring theatre as well as co-producing with a range of partners.

Casting procedures: Please see the website for current casting procedures.

Chichester Festival Theatre

Oaklands Park, Chichester PO19 6AP
Artistic Director Jonathan Church *Casting Director* Gabrielle Dawes *Executive Director* Maggie Saxon

Production details: Consists of the main house set in parkland, the Minerva Studio, and a multipurpose auditorium. In-house plays and musicals are produced in the main house during the festival season (April-September), and family shows at Christmas. The Minerva Studio places emphasis on new and experimental work during the festival and also stages an in-house Christmas production. 4 productions are staged both in the main house and the Minerva Studio each year. Also runs TIE, Outreach and Community programmes (contact Alison Roden). Recent productions include: *The Merchant of Venice, Pinocchio, The Seagull* and Gilbert & Sullivan's *The Gondoliers*.

Casting procedures: Occasionally holds general auditions. Actors should write in December or January requesting inclusion. Welcomes submissions (with CVs and photographs) sent by post or email.

Citizens Theatre

Gorbals, Glasgow G5 9DS
tel 0141-429 5561 *fax* 0141-429 7374
website www.citz.co.uk
Artistic Directors Guy Hollands, Jeremy Raison
Company Manager Jacqueline Muir

Production details: Internationally renowned producing theatre, producing work in Glasgow and on tour as well as a pioneering year-round Citizens Learning, and TAG programme for participants of all ages. Stages 7 productions a year, and undertakes 2 tours per annum. Offers TMA/Equity approved contracts.

Casting procedures: Does not use freelance casting directors. Holds limited general auditions once a year in June, and specific casting for individual shows as and when required. Welcomes emails from actors (with CVs and photographs), which should be submitted to **jackie@citz.co.uk**.

Clwyd Theatr Cymru

Mold, Flintshire CH7 1YA
tel (01352) 756331 *fax* (01352) 701558
email mail@clwyd-theatr-cymru.co.uk
website www.clwyd-theatr-cymru.co.uk
Artistic Director Terry Hands *Associate Director* Tim Baker *Casting Director* Leigh-Ann Regan

Production details: The major drama-producing company in Wales. Although most work is presented in English, some pieces are performed in Welsh. Stages 5-6 shows in the main house, and 5-6 in the studio each year, with some mid/large-scale productions touring Wales and England. Also runs TIE programmes. Recent productions include: *Mary Stuart, Noises Off, Great Expectations* and *A History of Falling Things*. Offers TMA/Equity approved contracts and subscribes to the Equity Pension Scheme.

Casting procedures: Welcomes enquiries from actors: these should be sent to Leigh-Ann Regan at the above address. (More information about Leigh-Ann Regan can be found under Casting directors on page 105.) Will consider applications from disabled actors to play characters with disabilities.

Coliseum Theatre

Fairbottom Street, Oldham OL1 3SW
tel 0161-624 1731 *fax* 0161-624 5318
email mail@coliseum.org.uk
website www.coliseum.org.uk
Artistic Director Kevin Shaw *Administrative Director* Liz Wilson *Administrator* Joanne Moss

Production details: A traditional repertory theatre producing 8 shows each year, with additional incoming tours and one-off special events. Also runs TIE, Outreach and Community programmes (contact Jodie Lamb). Recent productions include: *Look Back in Anger, How the Other Half Loves, Return to the Forbidden Planet, Women on the Verge of HRT*.

Casting procedures: Does not use freelance casting directors. Sometimes holds general auditions. Casting breakdowns are available through postal application (with sae). Welcomes letters and email submissions (with CVs and photographs). Also accepts invitations to view individual actors' websites. Offers TMA/Equity approved contracts and subscribes to the Equity Pension Scheme. Will consider applications from disabled actors to play characters with disabilities.

Contact Theatre

Oxford Road, Manchester M15 6JA
tel 0161-274 3434 *fax* 0161-274 0640
website www.contact-theatre.org
Artistic Director Baba Israel *Executive Producer* Jon Morgan *Associate Director* Cheryl Martin
Administrative Officer Katie Taylor (casting enquiries) *Head of Creative Development* Ekua Bayunu

Production details: Since re-opening in 1999, Contact has emphasised its work with young adults (aged 13-30), putting participation at the heart of its ethos and activities. Contact is also one of the most culturally diverse theatres in the country; it was awarded the inaugural ECLIPSE award for cultural diversity, as well as the Arts Council's ART04 Award Northwest for 'outstanding achievement in the arts'.

Contact has striven to rewrite the rulebook on what 'theatre' can be. A wide range of touring theatre, music, dance and mixed-media work complements the theatre's in-house productions. The huge variety of participatory work with young people is integrated as closely as possible with the company's 'professional' programme. High quality and innovation are key to Contact's participatory work; leading companies working with young people at Contact have included: Frantic Assembly, RJC Dance, Quarantine, and Nitro – as well as a huge range of artists from hip hop to forum theatre and from verse drama to contemporary dance. Recent productions include: *Perfect* (Kaite O'Reilly and Paul Clay); *Slamdunk* (Felix Cross, Benji Reid with Nitro); *Dancing within Walls* (by Rani Moorthy with Rasa); *Dreaming of Bones* (with Red Ladder).

Casting procedures: Uses freelance casting directors and does not advertise casting breakdowns publicly. Welcomes letters (with CVs and photographs) from actors, but warns that it is unable to reply to unsolicited submissions. The theatre prefers not to receive showreels, emails and invitations to view actors' websites. Offers TMA/Equity approved contracts. Actively encourages applications from disabled actors and promotes the use of inclusive casting.

Crucible Theatre
55 Norfolk Street, Sheffield S1 1DA
tel 0114-249 5999 fax 0114-249 6003
email info@sheffieldtheatres.co.uk
website www.sheffieldtheatres.co.uk
Chief Executive Dan Bates Artistic Director Daniel
Evans

Production details: After major refurbishment, the
Crucible re-opened early in 2010. Recent productions
include: Enemy of the People, Alice, and That Face.

Curve
Halford Street, Leicester LE1 1SB
tel 0116-253 0021 fax 0870-706 5241
email enquiries@leicestertheatretrust.co.uk
website www.curveonline.co.uk
Artistic Director Paul Kerryson Associate Director Adel
Al-Salloum Chief Executive Ruth Eastwood Executive
Producer Ian Gillie

Production details: A new state-of-the-art theatre
designed by world-renowned architect Rafael Vinoly.
Has 2 auditoria, one with 750 seats and the other
providing a 350-seat flexible smaller space. "A
stunning glass façade encloses a magnificent foyer
and mezzanine walkway, with views onto the café,
bars, dressing rooms and workshop areas. The stage is
placed at street level between the 2 auditoria."

Casting procedures: Uses both in-house and
freelance casting directors. Holds general auditions;
actors may write in for casting breakdowns as soon as
productions are announced. Does not welcome
unsolicited approaches by post or by email,
showreels, or invitations to view individual actors'
websites. Offers Equity-approved contracts as
negotiated through TMA. Actively encourages
applications from disabled actors and promotes the
use of inclusive casting.

Derby Theatre (formerly Derby Playhouse)
Theatre Walk, Eagle Centre, Derby DE1 2NF
tel (01332) 594250 fax (01332) 242828
website www.derbytheatre.org
Theatre Manager Gary Johnson

Since the University of Derby stepped in to purchase
the lease for the former Derby Playhouse, the theatre
has been refurbished and the facilities improved to
welcome the public, performers, students and staff.
Further developments are planned over the next few
years.

The University of Derby's vision has been to create a
'learning theatre' where staff and students can gain
vital work experience and skills in all forms of theatre
arts. The uniqueness of the partnership between the
University and DerbyLIVE (**www.derbylive.co.uk**),
who manage the calendar of public performances, is
bringing the best professional, student and amateur
productions to this great city centre venue.

Donmar Warehouse
41 Earlham Street, London WC2H 9LX
tel 020-7240 4882
website www.donmarwarehouse.com
Artistic Director Michael Grandage Associate Directors
Rob Ashford, Jamie Lloyd Casting and Creative
Associate Anne McNulty

Production details: Independent producing house
located in Covent Garden. The building originally
served as a vat room and hop warehouse for the local
brewery. In 1961 it was purchased by Donald Albery
and converted into a rehearsal studio for the London
Festival Ballet, which he formed with ballerina
Margot Fonteyn. The theatre takes its name from
them.

In the 1990s the Donmar was redesigned. The current
theatre space retains the characteristics of the former
warehouse while incorporating a new thrust stage.
Recent productions include: The Chalk Garden,
Othello, Parade, The Wild Duck, and Mary Stuart.

Casting procedures: Casting breakdowns are not
publicly available. Offers TMA/SOLT/Equity
approved contracts. Rarely has the opportunity to
cast disabled actors.

The Dukes
Moor Lane, Lancaster LA1 1QE
tel (01524) 598505 fax (01524) 598579
website www.dukes-lancaster.org
Director Joe Sumison Theatre Secretary Jacqui Wilson

Production details: A producing theatre with an
independent cinema. Stages 5 shows each year in the
main house (313 seats) and 1 in the studio (178
seats), with a focus on contemporary drama and
outdoor, site-specific productions. Also runs a Youth
Arts programme. Recent productions include: Blue
Remembered Hills, Betrayal, Under Milk Wood, The
Accrington Pals, and Tom Thumb and Other Giant
Stories (outdoor production).

Casting procedures: Does not use freelance casting
directors. Casting breakdowns are obtainable through
the website, postal application (with sae), Equity Job
Information Service and PCR. Welcomes letters (with
CVs and photographs) but not email submissions.
Showreels and invitations to view individual actors'
websites are also accepted. Offers TMA/Equity
approved contracts. Actively encourages applications
from disabled actors and promotes the use of
inclusive casting.

Dundee Repertory Theatre
Tay Square, Dundee DD1 1PB
tel (01382) 227684 fax (01382) 228609
website www.dundeerep.co.uk
Artistic Director James Brining Associate Director
Jemima Levick

Production details: Producing theatre housing
Dundee Repertory Ensemble – Scotland's only

permanent acting company. Stages 6 shows each year in the main house. Also runs TIE, Outreach and Community programmes (contact James Brining). Recent productions include: *Peter Pan* and *Twelfth Night*.

Casting procedures: Does not use freelance casting directors. Welcomes letters (with CVs and photographs) but not email submissions. Actors should write in the spring.

Gate Theatre
Above Prince Albert Pub, 11 Pembridge Road, London W11 3HQ
tel 020-7229 0906 *fax* 020-7221 6055
email gate@gatetheatre.co.uk
website www.gatetheatre.co.uk
Artistic Directors Natalie Abrahami, Carrie Cracknell
Producer Evanna Meehan *General Manager* Cath Longman *Education & Access Manager* Lynne Gagliano

Production details: Presents new writing and undiscovered classics from around the world in original and visually imaginative productions. Stages 5-6 shows each year. Also runs a Community/Education programme. Recent productions include: *Things Of Dry Hours* by Naomi Wallace, *Ghosts* by Henrik Ibsen, *The Chairs* by Eugene Ionesco.

Casting procedures: Does not accept unsolicited CVs/submissions. "Individual directors tend to cast from their own lists – contact with the director is the best way to ensure that your application is considered. The Gate Theatre Company is committed to promoting theatre as an activity for all."

Greenwich Theatre
Crooms Hill, Greenwich, London SE10 8ES
tel 020-8858 4447 *fax* 020-8858 8042
email info@greenwichtheatre.org.uk
website www.greenwichtheatre.org.uk
Executive Director James Haddrell

Production details: Currently mainly receiving touring productions, but occasionally produces shows in-house. Specialises in musical theatre, and produces showcases, semi-staged readings and cabarets at different points of the year; these often involve professional performers. Recent productions include: *Longitude* (play with music), and *Sleeping Beauty* (pantomime). The theatre also runs a year-round programme of training for 14-19 year-olds (the Greenwich Musical Theatre Academy), including a full-time course. Offers TMA/Equity approved contracts and subscribes to the Equity Pension Scheme.

Casting procedures: Generally uses freelance casting directors. "Please don't send unsolicited applications, as we can't maintain a sensible filing system. Please do look at the casting section on the website, as we aim to provide advance information on our future productions, and answer standard questions. Most

casting is concerned with the pantomime, so the best time to enquire is between May and July. We are keen to hear from locally based musical performers and especially anyone who has experience of working with young people." Does not have a specific policy on casting disabled actors, as the stage is not wheelchair-accessible: "It depends on the actor's particular needs."

Hampstead Theatre
Eton Avenue, London NW3 3EU
tel 020-7449 4200 *fax* 020-7449 4201
email info@hampsteadtheatre.com
website www.hampsteadtheatre.com
Artistic Director Edward Hall *Creative Learning Director* Eric Dupin

Production details: Hampstead Theatre identifies and produces important new writers. It aims to challenge established writers and seek out the best international work to bring to London. Plays are sometimes provocative, always intelligent and often full of laughter. The auditorium has been built for writers who understand actors, and The Space will provide a dedicated arena for a rich and varied education and workshop programme. Presents 7 shows in the main house each year, and a varying number in the studio. Recent productions include: *Glass Eels* by Nell Leyshon; *Taking Care Of Baby* by Dennis Kelly; *Fast Labour* by Steve Waters; *On The Rocks* by Amy Rosenthal.

Casting procedures: Uses freelance casting directors; suggests that actors write 2 months before each season starts. Casting breakdowns are sometimes available by postal application (with sae) or email, depending on the director.

Harrogate Theatre
Oxford Street, Harrogate, North Yorks HG1 1QF
tel (01423) 502710 *fax* (01423) 563205
email info@harrogatetheatre.co.uk
website www.harrogatetheatre.co.uk
Chief Executive David Bown

Production details: Stages 3 productions annually in the main house; also works in Outreach and Community (key contact, Hannah Draper). Recent productions include: *Absent Friends*, *Blithe Spirit* and *Aladdin*.

Casting procedures: Uses freelance casting directors and sometimes holds general auditions. Offers Equity approved contracts as negotiated through TMA, and participates in the Equity Pension Scheme. Will consider applications from disabled actors to play characters with disabilities. "We have no resident Artistic Director, and so unsolicited approaches are not welcome. Please check the website for any casting opportunities."

Hull Truck Theatre
50 Ferensway, Hull HU2 8LB
tel (01482) 224800 *fax* (01482) 581182

email admin@hulltruck.co.uk
website www.hulltruck.co.uk
Creative Director John Godber *Artistic Director* Gareth
Tudor *Operations Director* Paul Marshall *Associate
Director* Nick Lane *Casting enquiries to*
Administration Department

Production details: In operation since 1971, Hull
Truck has established a national/international
reputation for excellence. Hull Truck moved into a
brand new purpose-built theatre in April 2009, which
houses 2 auditoria. It presents a mix of new writing,
classic adaptations and one-night comedy/music
events. The theatre also works on TIE, Outreach and
Community projects, for which Mark Rees is the lead
contact. Stages approximately 14 productions each
year, touring to more than 70 venues, including
theatres, educational and community venues.
Roughly 2-6 actors are used in each production.
Recent productions include: *Studs, Teachers,
Bouncers, Beef, Lucky Sods* and *Funny Turns* by John
Godber; *The Flags* by Bridget O'Connor; *Honeymoon
Suite* by Richard Bean; *Ladies Down Under* and
Amateur Girl by Amanda Whittington; *My Favourite
Summer* and *A Christmas Fairytale* by Nick Lane; *A
Kick in the Baubles* by Gordon Steel; *Confessions of a
City Supporter* by Alan Plater; *Every Time it Rains* by
Rupert Creed; and *Say It With Flowers* by Jane
Thornton.

Casting procedures: Casting is done in-house, and
breakdowns are advertised on the website and in *PCR*
and *The Stage*; they are also available by postal
application. Welcomes letters (with CVs and
photographs) from actors, but prefers not to receive
showreels. Actively encourages applications from
disabled actors, and promotes the use of inclusive
casting.

Key Theatre

Embankment Road, Peterborough,
Cambridgeshire PE1 1EF
tel (01733) 552437
email michael.cross@peterborough.gov.uk
website www.peterboroughkeytheatre.co.uk
Artistic Director Michael Cross *Youth Theatre/TIE
Officer* Paul Collings

Production details: Mainly a receiving house with
occasional in-house productions including an annual
pantomime and TIE tours. Stages 4 shows each year.
Recent productions include: *The Full Monty, Bad
Blood* and *Cinderella*.

Casting procedures: Does not use freelance casting
directors. Occasional general auditions. Unsolicited
communications are not advised. Casting
requirements are sometimes available through the
website, but usually through professional casting
services, Spotlight Link, *PCR* and *The Stage*. "Actors
working in the area (and especially touring to the
Key) are always encouraged to make contact with the
Artistic Director and introduce themselves.

Invitations to see artists working in productions are
always welcome, and, wherever possible, accepted!"
Offers TMA/Equity contracts and does not subscribe
to the Equity Pension Scheme. Rarely (or never) has
the opportunity to employ disabled actors.

Library Theatre Company

St Peter's Square, Manchester M2 5PD
tel 0161-234 1913 *fax* 0161-274 7055
email ltcadmin@manchester.gov.uk
website www.librarytheatre.com
Artistic Director Chris Honer

Production details: Regional producer of
contemporary drama and modern classics; also
produces a play for families and children at
Christmas. Stages 5-6 shows each year, and runs an
Education programme (contact Liz Postlethwaite).
Recent productions include: *If I Were You, Frozen,
Waiting for Godot, Tom's Midnight Garden, Faith
Healer,* and *Private Lives*. Offers TMA/Equity
approved contracts.

Casting Procedures: Uses freelance casting directors;
casting breakdowns are available from the website.
Also holds a limited number of general auditions/
interviews in the Summer. Actors requesting
inclusion in these are advised to write in March or
April. Encourages applications from actors with
disability, and promotes inclusive casting.

Note: In July 2010 the Library Theatre moved out of
its home, the Central Library in Manchester. The
company will now be producing 3 shows a year at the
Lowry in Salford, plus some site-specific work from
summer 2011, before moving into its new home, the
Theatre Royal on Peter Street in the city, in 2014. For
more information, please check the website.

Live Theatre

Broad Chare, Quayside,
Newcastle upon Tyne NE1 3DQ
tel 0191-261 2694 *fax* 0191-232 2224
email info@live.org.uk
website www.live.org.uk
Artistic Director Max Roberts *Associate
Directors* Jeremy Herrin, Paul James

Production details: New writing theatre established
in 1973. Produces 8-10 shows each year in the main
house. Also runs TIE, Outreach and Community
programmes (contact Paul James).

Casting procedures: Does not use freelance casting
directors. Welcomes submissions (with CVs and
photographs), sent by post or email. Actors may write
at any time. Showreels and invitations to view
individual actors' websites are also accepted. Offers
ITC/Equity approved contracts. Actively encourages
applications from disabled actors and promotes the
use of inclusive casting.

Liverpool Everyman and Playhouse Theatres

13 Hope Street, Liverpool L1 9BH
tel 0151-708 3700 *fax* 0151-708 3701

email info@everymanplayhouse.com
website www.everymanplayhouse.com
Artistic Director Gemma Bodinetz

Production details: The Liverpool Playhouse focuses primarily on imaginative interpretations of classic drama, from ancient to modern, while new writing forms the core of the programme at the Everyman. The theatre also hosts touring companies from around the country; runs a busy Literary Department, working to nurture the next generation of Liverpool playwrights; and has an active Community Department, which takes work to all corners of the city and surrounding areas. Recent productions include: *King Lear, Ten Tiny Toes* and *The Hypochondriac.*

Lyric Theatre

Crannóg House, 44 Stranmillis Embankment, Belfast, BT9 5FL
email neil@lyrictheatre.co.uk
website www.lyrictheatre.co.uk
Chief Executive Ciaran McAuley *Artistic Director* Richard Croxford *Theatre Administrator* Neil Edwards

Production details: *Please note that the Lyric is currently closed for the rebuild of a new £18.5m theatre; re-opening Spring 2011.* Northern Ireland's leading full-time producing house for professional theatre. Presents a distinctive, challenging and entertaining programme of new writing as well as contemporary and classic plays by Irish, European and American writers. Currently offsite whilst new theatre being built, and producing 4 productions a year as well as a full Education and Outreach programme. Recent productions include: *The Miser, The Absence of Women, The Homeplace, Be My Baby, Pump Girl, The Parker Project.*

Casting procedures: Does not use freelance casting directors. Welcomes submissions (with CVs and photographs), sent by post or email. Actors may write in at any time. Advises actors to check the website for its future programme. Offers TMA/Equity approved contracts. Will consider applications from disabled actors to play characters with disabilities.

Lyric Theatre Hammersmith

King Street, London W6 0QL
tel 0870-050 0511 *fax* 020-8741 5965
email enquiries@lyric.co.uk
website www.lyric.co.uk
Artistic Director Sean Holmes *Executive Director* Jessica Hepburn

Production details: Produces and co-produces original theatre for a wide audience. Recently completed work which redeveloped the theatre, creating 2 new spaces – a purpose-built rehearsal studio, and an education/training room. The theatre runs an extensive Education programme and focuses on working with disadvantaged communities and young people in the local area. For further information, contact the Education Administrator, Herta Queirazza. Recent productions include: *Don Juan* and *The Firework-Maker's Daughter.*

Casting procedures: Different directors cast their own productions, using freelance casting directors.

Manor Pavilion Theatre

Manor Road, Sidmouth, Devon EX10 8RP
tel 020-7636 4343 *fax* 020-7636 2323
email cvtheatre@aol.com
Artistic Director Charles Vance *Associate Director* Imogen Vance

Production details: Summer repertory theatre with a 3-month season (July-September). Stages 12 shows each year in the main house.

Casting procedures: Welcomes letters (with CVs and photographs) but not email submissions. Actors should write in February, sending application to: Summer Play Festival, Hampden House, 2 Weymouth Street, London W1W 5BT.

Mercury Theatre

Balkerne Gate, Colchester, Essex CO1 1PT
tel (01206) 577006 *fax* (01206) 769607
email info@mercurytheatre.co.uk
website www.mercurytheatre.co.uk
Artistic Director & Chief Executive Dee Evans *Artistic Director* Gregory Floy *Associate Directors* Adrian Stokes, Sue Lefton

Production details: A regional repertory theatre which opened in 1972, producing 3 ensemble shows each season. Stages 6 shows each year in the main house and 1-2 in the studio. Also runs a Community programme (contact Elaine Leppard). Recent productions include: *Wagstaffe the Wind-Up Boy, The Lonesome West, A Chorus of Disapproval* and *David Copperfield.*

Casting procedures: Each show is cast by the director from within an ensemble company, which has evolved over the past 6 years. It is preferred that actors build up a relationship with the artistic team rather than to approach by letter or email. A knowledge of the Mercury's work is essential. For all casting enquiries, please email Hannah Love (**hannah@mercurytheatre.co.uk**).

The Mill at Sonning Theatre

Sonning Eye, Reading RG4 6TY
tel 0118-969 6039
email admin@millatsonning.com
website www.millatsonning.com
Artistic Director Sally Hughes

Production details: Popular 'dinner theatre' venue, producing a range of plays for audiences to watch while eating a meal. Recent productions include: *French Without Tears, Time to Kill,* and *It Runs in the Family.*

Casting procedures: Forthcoming productions are listed on the website. Actors should send their details, along with specific casting suggestions, to the Artistic Director 2 months before each show.

National Theatre

South Bank, London SE1 9PX
tel 020-7452 3335 *fax* 020-7452 3340
email info@nationaltheatre.org.uk
website www.nationaltheatre.org.uk
Artistic Director Nicolas Hytner *Head of Casting* Wendy Spon CDG

Production details: A National Theatre was first proposed in 1848. In 1951 a foundation stone was laid near the Royal Festival Hall, and in 1962 Sir Laurence Olivier was appointed the National's first director, based at London's Old Vic Theatre. Finally, in 1976, the new NT officially opened with a production of *Hamlet*. Today, the National stages a range of classics, musicals, new plays and entertainment "for all the family". It comprises 3 theatres: the Olivier (open-stage, capacity 1120 people); the Lyttleton (proscenium arch, capacity 890); and the Cottesloe (studio theatre on 3 levels with flexible staging, capacity 300).

Casting details: The National Theatre's casting team works with approximately 10 directors a year casting NT shows. Actors known to the theatre may be approached directly, but casting is predominantly carried out through agents. The NT will first approach agents to check actors' availability, then audition a shortlist. New talent is actively sought out, and the casting team sees several performances a week within London and (less frequently) outside. It also attends drama schools' showcases and will sometimes approach other casting directors known to the NT.

National Theatre of Scotland (NTS)

Atlantic Chambers, 45 Hope Street, Glasgow G2 6AE
tel 0141-221 0970 *fax* 0141-248 7241
email info@nationaltheatrescotland.com
website www.nationaltheatrescotland.com
Artistic Director & Chief Executive Vicky Featherstone
Associate Director John Tiffany *Artistic Development Producer* Caroline Newall

Production details: The National Theatre of Scotland launched to the public in February 2006. It has no building, and instead takes theatre all over Scotland and beyond, working with new and existing venues and companies to create and tour theatre of the highest quality. This theatre takes place in the great buildings of Scotland, but also in site-specific locations, community halls and drill halls, car parks and forests. To date, over 130,000 people have seen or participated in its work. NTS has produced 28 pieces of work in 62 locations, from the Shetlands to Dumfries, and from Belfast to London. In 2007/8 NTS toured to the USA and Australasia.

Scottish theatre has always been for the people, led by great performances, great stories and great playwrights. The National Theatre of Scotland exists to build a new generation of theatre-goers, as well as reinvigorating the existing ones; to create theatre on a national and international scale that is contemporary, confident and forward-looking; to bring together brilliant artists, designers, composers, choreographers and playwrights; and to exceed expectations of what and where theatre can be.

Offers actors in-house ITC/Equity approved contracts and does not subscribe to the Equity Pension Scheme.

Casting procedures: Each casting process is led by the Director of each production, with advisory support from the NTS Artistic Team and Casting Director. When casting for specific shows, the Casting Director puts out a call to agents through *Spotlight*.

The NTS Artistic team makes every effort to see every theatrical event produced in Scotland, maximising the number of actors that NTS sees. The team also responds to individual requests to see actors' work. All actors' CVs and headshots that NTS receives are acknowledged and kept on file in the NTS office. The NTS Casting Director reviews these files at regular intervals, and Directors are encouraged to go through these files before casting their productions. In addition, NTS holds an annual 2-day casting workshop to connect with actors who have sent in CVs but whose work it has been unable to see during the year. Actively encourages applications from disabled actors and promotes the use of inclusive casting.

National Theatre Wales

30 Castle Arcade, Cardiff CF10 1BW
tel 029-2035 3070
email admin@nationaltheatrewales.org
website www.nationaltheatrewales.org
Artistic Director John McGrath

National Theatre Wales is set to create bold, invigorating theatre in the English language, rooted in Wales, with an international reach.

New Vic Theatre

Etruria Road, Newcastle-under-Lyme ST5 OJG
tel (01782) 717954 *fax* (01782) 712885
email admin@newvictheatre.org.uk
website www.newvictheatre.org.uk
Artistic Director Theresa Heskins *General Manager* Nick Jones

Production details: Purpose-built theatre-in-the-round with a full programme of in-house drama, concerts and occasional touring productions. Stages 10 shows each year in the main house. Also very active with Outreach and Education programmes (contact Sue Moffat and Jill Rezzano respectively). Recent productions include: *Sweeney Todd, My Night* with Reg, *The Duchess of Malfi*, *Kes* and *The Marriage of Figaro*.

Casting procedures: Does not use freelance casting directors. Casting breakdowns are obtainable by postal application (with sae), and up-to-date casting information is posted on the casting section of the website. Welcomes letters (with CVs and photographs), but not email submissions. Submissions should be specific and referenced to a particular role. Also accepts invitations to view individual actors' websites.

Northcott Theatre

Northcott Theatre, Stocker Road, Exeter EX4 4QB
tel (01392) 223999
website www.exeternorthcott.co.uk
Chief Executive Kate Tyrrell

After going into administration, the University of Exeter agreed to set up a new company to run the Exeter Northcott in May 2010. The new University company will operate until 31st March 2011. By then the Northcott's stakeholders – Arts Council England, Exeter City Council and the University – will know what funds they have at their future disposal following expected cutbacks in public funding by the new government. The 3 organisations have agreed to keep their funding at current levels until 31st March 2011, provided they don't suffer budget cuts in 2010 and that an acceptable programme of activity can be set out for the remainder of the financial year. The eventual aim may be to set up an independent company to run the Northcott, subject to a sustainable model for the theatre being agreed.

Northern Stage (formerly Newcastle Playhouse)

Barras Bridge, Newcastle NE1 7RH
tel 0191-232 3366 *fax* 0191-242 7257
email directors@northernstage.co.uk
website www.northernstage.co.uk
Chief Executive/Artistic Director Erica Whyman
Associate Director Neil Murray

Production details: Northern Stage is the largest producing theatre company in the North East of England. The building, formerly known as Newcastle Playhouse & Gulbenkian Studio, re-opened in summer 2006 as Northern Stage following a £9m redevelopment programme. The new building has 3 stages and presents and produces a wide repertoire of UK and international theatre. Staging 6 shows a year, the company also works on participatory projects, with Kylie Lloyd as the lead contact. Touring productions in 2009/2010 include: *Oh What A Lovely War* and *Apples*. Offers TMA/Equity-approved contracts and subscribes to the Equity Pension Scheme.

Casting procedures: Casting breakdowns, when available, are published on the website. Actively encourages applications from disabled actors and promotes the use of inclusive casting.

Nottingham Playhouse

Wellington Circus, Nottingham NG1 5AF
Artistic Director Giles Croft *Casting Director* Sooki McShane *Director of Roundabout & Education* Andrew Breakwell

Production details: Nottingham Theatre Trust was founded in 1948 and moved to its current location in 1963. Stages 10 shows each year in the main house and 3 Roundabout productions. Also runs TIE, Outreach and Community programmes. Recent productions include: *Burial at Thebes, On the Waterfront, Vertigo, Whale's Tooth, Can You Whistle Johanna?*.

Casting procedures: Does not use freelance casting directors. Casting breakdowns are available from the casting director, Sooki McShane. Welcomes letters (with CVs and photographs) but not email submissions. Showreels and invitations to view individual actors' websites are also accepted.

Nuffield Theatre

University Road, Southampton SO17 1TR
tel 023-8031 5500 *fax* 023-8031 5511
email info@nuffieldtheatre.co.uk
website www.nuffieldtheatre.co.uk
Artistic Director Patrick Sandford *Associate Director* Russ Tunney *Executive Director* Kate Anderson

Production details: A regional theatre performing a range of classic plays and new writing. Stages 5-7 shows each year in the main house, and 3-4 in the studio. Also runs TIE, Outreach and Community programmes. Recent productions include: *Bloodshot*, a new play by Douglas Post; *Antony and Cleopatra*; and *Bleak Expectations* (touring schools). Offers ITC and TMA/Equity approved contracts and subscribes to the Equity Pension Scheme.

Casting procedures: Uses freelance casting directors. Holds local auditions for actors in the Southampton area. Actors may write at any time requesting inclusion. Casting breakdowns are sometimes available through *PCR* or Equity Job Information Service. "We consider applications from disabled actors in exactly the same way as applications from able-bodied actors."

Octagon Theatre

Howell Croft South, Bolton BL1 1SB
tel (01204) 529407 *fax* (01204) 556502
email info@octagonbolton.co.uk
website www.octagonbolton.co.uk
Artistic Director David Thacker *Executive Director* John Blackmore *Head of Production* Lesley Chenery *Head of Administration* Lesley Etherington

Production details: Stages 8-9 shows each year in the main house and 18 in the studio. Also runs TIE, Outreach and Community programmes (contact Activ8 Department). Recent productions include: *All*

Theatre

My Sons; *A Midsummer Night's Dream*; *Rafta Rafta*; and *The Hired Man*.

Casting procedures: Does not use freelance casting directors. Actors may write requesting inclusion in the company at any time, and should enclose an sae. Accepts invitations to view individual actors' websites.

The Old Vic
The Cut, London SE1 8NB
tel 020-7928 2651 *fax* 020-7261 9161
email ovtcadmin@oldvictheatre.com
website www.oldvictheatre.com
Artistic Director Kevin Spacey

Production details: Under Artistic Director Kevin Spacey, and Producers Kate Pakenham and John Richardson, the Old Vic Theatre Company is now in its 6th season. Since the theatre company was launched by The Old Vic's Chief Executive (Sally Greene) in 2004, the theatre has once again become a destination as a producing house. Through Old Vic New Voices, the theatre also supports young and emerging talent; runs extensive education projects to complement the work in the season; and reaches out to the community with the aim of opening up the building to new and diverse audiences.

Casting procedures: "We're not able to accept CVs or speculative applications for employment."

Open Air Theatre
Inner Circle, Regent's Park, London NW1 4NR
website www.openairtheatre.org
Artistic Director Timothy Shaeder *Executive Director* William Village

Production details: Stages 4 shows each year in the main house, including 1 family show. Recent productions include: *Much Ado About Nothing*; *The Tempest* re-imagined for everyone aged 6 or over; *The Importance of Being Earnest*; and *Hello, Dolly!*.

Casting procedures: Uses freelance casting directors, who send full casting breakdowns to agents as required for each production. "Unfortunately we are unable to consider unsolicited CVs."

Orange Tree Theatre
1 Clarence Street, Richmond TW9 2SA
tel 020-8940 0141 *fax* 020-8332 0369
email admin@orangetreetheatre.co.uk
website www.orangetreetheatre.co.uk
Artistic Director Sam Walters

Production details: "The Orange Tree Theatre is wholly concerned with the performance of quality live theatre, and with reaching as wide an audience as possible with its work. Over the 30 years of its existence it has established a reputation for being the leader in its field, and is the only permanent theatre-in-the-round in London." Presents a mixture of new writing, classic plays, comedies and musicals.

Education and Community work forms a major area of activity. Stages 7 shows each year.

Casting procedures: Does not use freelance casting directors. Welcomes letters (with CVs and photographs) but not email submissions. Actors should write in June for the new season. Also accepts invitations to view individual actors' websites. Offers TMA/Equity approved contracts. Actively encourages applications from disabled actors and promotes the use of inclusive casting.

Perth Theatre at Horsecross
185 High Street, Perth PH1 5UW
tel (01738) 472700 *fax* (01738) 624576
email info@horsecross.co.uk
website www.horsecross.co.uk
Creative Director Ian Grieve *Administrator* Elaine White *Associate Director – Youth Theatre* Jennifer McGregor

Production details: Scotland's oldest theatre company with a mixed programme of in-house and guest productions throughout the year, including drama, musical theatre and pantomime. Produces 4 shows each year. Also runs Outreach and Community programmes. Recent productions include: *A Streetcar Named Desire*; *The Snow Queen*; *Tom O'Shanter*; and *The Mystery of Irma Vep*.

Casting procedures: Casts in-house. Welcomes submissions (with CVs and photographs) sent by post, or by email to **casting@horsecross.co.uk**. Actors should write in the spring. Also accepts invitations to view individual actors' websites.

Pitlochry Festival Theatre
Port-Na-Craig, Pitlochry PH16 5DR
tel (01796) 484600 *fax* (01796) 484616
email admin@pitlochry.org.uk
website www.pitlochry.org.uk
Artistic Director & Chief Executive John Durnin
Community and Education Director Drew Scott

Production details: Founded in 1951, Pitlochry Festival Theatre is a producing and presenting theatre located in the Perthshire Highlands. Comprises the main house (capacity 544), an extensive production facility, and Explorers: The Scottish Plant Hunters Garden, containing a number of open-air performance spaces. Between April and October each year a 20-strong acting ensemble presents a season of 6 major productions performed in day-change repertoire. Visiting theatre, music, dance, opera and other activities are presented during the winter months. Also runs TIE and Community programmes. Recent productions include: *Habeus Corpus*; *Arcadia*; *Outlying Islands*; *Whisky Galore – A Musical!*; *Good Things*; and *The Prime of Miss Jean Brodie*. TMA/Equity contracts are offered.

Casting procedures: Does not use freelance casting directors. Recruits new members of the acting ensemble each autumn and winter, with a detailed casting breakdown published each September. The closing date for applications is usually in mid-November; auditions are then held in London and Edinburgh in November, December and January. Casting breakdowns are obtainable by postal application (with sae) from September. Submissions at any other time – or not in response to the casting breakdown – will not be considered. The theatre actively encourages applications from disabled actors and promotes the use of inclusive casting.

Queen's Theatre
Billet Lane, Hornchurch, Essex RM11 1QT
website www.queens-theatre.co.uk
Artistic Director Bob Carlton *Associate Director* Matt Devitt *Education Manager* Patrick O'Sullivan *Administrative Director* Thom Stanbury

Production details: Has been a producing theatre since it was first established in 1953. Currently works with actor-musicians in a permanent repertory company model. Stages 9 shows each year in the main house. Also runs TIE, Outreach and Community programmes. Recent productions include: *A Midsummer Night's Dream*, *Jane Eyre* and *Return to the Forbidden Planet*.

Casting procedures: Does not use freelance casting directors. Holds general auditions; actors should write in April or May requesting inclusion. Welcomes letters (with CVs and photographs) from actor-musicians only.

Rose of Kingston
24-26 High Street, Kingston-upon-Thames, Surrey KT1 1HL
tel 020-8546 6983
email admin@rosetheatrekingston.org
website www.rosetheatrekingston.org
Artistic Director Stephen Unwin *Executive Director* David Fletcher *General Manager* Jerry Gunn *Director Emeritus* Sir Peter Hall *Life President* David Jacobs

The Rose Theatre, Kingston opened its doors to the public in January 2008 with English Touring Production's production of *Uncle Vanya*, directed by Sir Peter Hall. The design of the theatre was inspired by the Elizabethan Rose on London's Bankside; Kingston's Rose has the same horse-shoe shaped auditorium and an open lozenge stage, creating a sense of intimacy between actors and audiences. The Rose auditorium has a capacity of more than 850 across 3 tiers of seating, including a pit area where audiences can sit on cushions for just £7. In addition to the main space there is a studio, capacity 120, and a gallery, capacity 60. These spaces host a variety of talks and workshops led by theatre writers and practitioners. The theatre also has a strong connection with Kingston University, where it facilitates the University's MA in Classical Drama.

The Rose presents a combination of home-produced drama and received work. Since opening, it has produced *Love's Labour's Lost*, directed by Sir Peter Hall; *A Christmas Carol* and *The Winslow Boy*, directed by Stephen Unwin; and a rep season which included *Bedroom Farce* and *Miss Julie*.

Royal & Derngate Theatres
Guildhall Road, Northampton NN1 1DP
tel (01604) 626222 (Admin) or (01604) 627566 (TIE)
website www.royalandderngate.com
Artistic Director Laurie Sansom *Associate Director* Dani Parr

Recently the subject of a £15 million redevelopment project, the theatre offers 2 auditoria and 'Underground', a creativity centre that is home to the Youth Theatre and a wide range of workshops and projects for the local community. The theatre's annual pantomime is produced by Qdos (see entry under *Pantomime producers* on page 209).

Royal Court Theatre
Sloane Square, London SW1W 8AS
tel 020-7565 5050 *fax* 020-7565 5001
email info@royalcourttheatre.com
website www.royalcourttheatre.com
Artistic Director Dominic Cooke *Casting Director* Amy Ball

Production details: Since 1956 the English Stage Company at the Royal Court has focused on developing, funding and producing new writing. Productions frequently transfer to the West End and Broadway. Stages 6 productions each year in the Jerwood Theatre downstairs and 8 upstairs. Also presents programmes of rehearsed readings (contact Lisa Makin). Recent productions include: *The Seagull*, *Drunk Enough to Say I Love You?* by Caryl Churchill and *Rock 'n' Roll* by Tom Stoppard. Offers SOLT/TMA/ Equity approved contracts and does not subscribe to the Equity Pension Scheme.

Casting procedures: Welcomes submissions (with CVs and photographs) by post or email all year round. Will consider applications from disabled actors to play disabled characters.

Royal Exchange Theatre
St Ann's Square, Manchester M2 7DH
tel 0161-833 9833
website www.royalexchange.co.uk
Artistic Directors Greg Hersov, Braham Murray, Sarah Frankcom *Casting Director* Jerry Knight-Smith *Casting Associate* Katherine Lawson *Education Director* Amanda Dalton

Production details: Manchester's leading producing theatre company, comprising a main theatre and studio space. Presents 8-9 productions, on average, in the main theatre and 4-5 in the studio each year. Also runs Education and Community programmes involving schools, young people, community groups and theatre enthusiasts of all ages. Work is based around the theatre's repertoire and its unique

Theatre

building. Where possible, the department leads sessions in the theatre, and frequently works with other departments around the building to give participants an insight into how theatre, and particularly the Royal Exchange, works. Recent productions include: *The Glass Menagerie*, *Three Sisters*, *Antigone*, and *A Taste of Honey*.

Casting procedures: Has a casting department of 2, who coordinate casting for each show. Actors are contracted for individual plays rather than for a season of work. Releases advance production information to around 200 agents on the website. Detailed casting breakdowns are only available for some shows.

Will consider attending performances at venues in the North West and London with sufficient notice. Accepts submissions (with CVs and photographs), but actors should bear in mind that the department expects to receive more than 2000 CVs and photos each season – and more in the summer months following graduation at the drama schools. All submissions are considered but they are not kept on file indefinitely.

Royal Lyceum Edinburgh

Grindlay Street, Edinburgh EH3 9AX
tel 0131-248 4800 *fax* 0131-228 3955
email info@lyceum.org.uk
website www.lyceum.org.uk
Artistic Director Mark Thomson

Production details: The Royal Lyceum is one of Scotland's largest producing theatre companies with a season of in-house drama productions running from September to May. In addition, the theatre stages a children's show every Christmas. Occasionally tours in Scotland and abroad, limited hosting of touring companies, and runs an ambitious and acclaimed Education Department. Recent productions include: *Mary Rose*; *The Lion, the Witch and the Wardrobe*; *The Man Who Had All the Luck*; *Curse of the Starving Class*; and *Copenhagen*.

Casting procedures: Does not offer general auditions. "Casting depends on individual directors' choices."

Royal Shakespeare Company (Casting Department)

1 Earlham Street, London WC2H 9LL
tel 020-7845 0500 *fax* 020-7845 0505
website www.rsc.org.uk
Artistic Director Michael Boyd *Head of Casting* Hannah Miller

Production details: One of the best-known theatre companies in the world, the RSC has been operating under its present name since 1961, a year after Peter Hall was appointed director. The repertoire was widened at this time to include modern writing and classics other than Shakespeare. Over the next 30

years the company continued to expand under the artistic directorships of Peter Hall, Trevor Nunn, Terry Hands and Adrian Noble. Michael Boyd succeeded Adrian Noble as Artistic Director in 2003. The RSC is committed to an ensemble approach to theatre, with actors most often being contracted to perform in several productions for 1-3 years.

Casting procedures: Welcomes performance notices 2-6 weeks in advance, and is prepared to travel around the UK, dependent on workload. Welcomes submissions with CV and photograph of some kind – original 10x8 not required – and showreels via post, and preferably in relation to specific productions.

Salisbury Playhouse

Malthouse Lane, Salisbury SP2 7RA
tel (01722) 320117
email info@salisburyplayhouse.com
website www.salisburyplayhouse.com
Artistic Director Philip Wilson

Production details: Stages 9 productions each year in the main house, and 3 in the studio – alongside an extensive Participation programme and Theatre For Young People.

Casting procedures: Offers TMA/Equity approved contracts. Uses freelance casting directors, but welcomes submissions - by email only. Promotes inclusive casting, and actively encourages applications from disabled actors.

Shakespeare's Globe

21 New Globe Walk, Bankside, London SE1 9DT
tel 020-7902 1400 *fax* 020-7902 1401
email info@shakespearesglobe.com
website www.shakespeares-globe.org
Artistic Director Dominic Dromgoole *General Manager* Lotte Buchan *Executive Producer* Conrad Lynch *Theatre & Projects Officer* Jasmine Lawrence

Production details: A reconstruction of Shakespeare's Globe, the theatre has a repertoire which includes the work of Shakespeare, his contemporaries and new writing. The season runs from May to October with up to 6 productions staged each year. Also runs Outreach and Community programmes (contact Deborah Callan on 020-7902 1430). Recent productions include: *Othello*, *The Merchant of Venice*, *Love's Labour's Lost*, *Romeo & Juliet* – UK Tour, *In Extremis* by Howard Brenton, *Holding Fire!* by Jack Shepherd, and *We the People* by Eric Schlosser.

Casting procedures: Welcomes letters (with CVs and photographs) but not email submissions. Actors should write to the Theatre & Projects Officer in December and early January. Offers actors Equity approved contracts through an in-house agreement. Actively encourages applications from disabled actors and promotes the use of inclusive casting. The website has more information about casting procedures.

Sheringham Little Theatre
2 Station Road, Sheringham, Norfolk NR26 8RE
tel (01263) 822117
email enquiries@sheringhamlittletheatre.com
website www.sheringhamlittletheatre.com
Artistic Director Debbie Thompson

Production details: A professional seaside repertory summer season which runs for 10 weeks from July to September, comprising 5 plays which are traditional comedies, farces, thrillers and classics.

Casting procedures: Holds general auditions. Actors should write between Jan and March, sending a CV and *recent* photograph. Email submissions not welcome. "As a small venue we are non-Equity, but we do work with Equity to pay a realistic wage; we also pay for accommodation and towards travel costs." Actively encourages applications from disabled actors and promotes the use of inclusive casting.

Sherman Cymru
Senghennydd Road, Cardiff CF24 4YE
tel 029-2064 6901 *fax* 029-2064 6902
website www.shermantheatre.co.uk
Director Chris Ricketts

Production details: Stages 4 shows each year and specialises in work for young audiences. Often uses actor-musicians.

Casting procedures: Does not use freelance casting directors. Sometimes holds general auditions. Welcomes letters (with CVs and photographs) but not email submissions. Also accepts invitations to view individual actors' websites.

Soho Theatre
21 Dean Street, London W1D 3NE
tel 020-7287 5060 *fax* 020-7287 5961
website www.sohotheatre.com
Artistic Director Steve Marmion *Executive Director* Mark Godfrey *Casting* Nadine Rennie

Production details: Soho Theatre is a producing theatre dedicated to new work and presenting a year-round programme of new plays, comedy and cabaret from its own central London theatre with 2 performance spaces. It also houses the Writers' Centre, running an extensive writers' development programme of readings, workshops and other events; and a Community and Education programme entitled 'Soho Connect'.

Casting procedures: Casting is carried out in-house by Nadine Rennie.

Southwold & Aldeburgh Summer Theatre
14 York House, Upper Montagu Street, London W1H 1FR
tel 020-7724 5432 *fax* 020-7724 3210
Artistic Director Jill Freud *Co-director* Anthony Falkingham *Production Coordinator* Peter Adshead

Production details: Summer theatre with an extensive programme. Stages 5 productions each year. Recent productions include: *Arsenic and Old Lace*, *Dick Barton – Special Agent*, *One for the Pot*, *Climbing the Wall*, *Private Lives*, and 6 guest Children's shows.

Casting procedures: Does not use freelance casting directors. Holds general auditions; actors should write in November requesting inclusion. Does not issue casting breakdowns. Welcomes letters (with CVs and photographs) but not email submissions, and advises that it is not possible to see everyone who writes in. Offers non-Equity contracts. Rarely (or never) has the opportunity to cast disabled actors.

Stephen Joseph Theatre
Westborough, Scarborough YO11 1JW
tel (01723) 370540 *fax* (01723) 360506
email enquiries@sjt.uk.com
website www.sjt.uk.com
Artistic Director Chris Monks *Executive Director* Stephen Wood

Production details: Stages 6-7 productions each year with lunchtime shows, late nights, rural and national touring. Most work is new writing. Recent productions include: *Improbable Fiction*, *Playing God*, and *Villette*.

Casting procedures: Sometimes holds general auditions; actors may write at any time requesting inclusion. Welcomes submissions (with CVs and photographs) by post or email. Also accepts showreels and invitations to view individual actors' websites. Offers TMA/Equity approved contracts. Will consider applications from disabled actors to play characters with disabilities.

"Casting Director Sarah Hughes is not resident at the SJT. Casting normally only takes place 2-3 times a year. Please note that unsolicited CVs/photos/showreels will only be returned if with an sae to the same value as the original."

Theatre By The Lake
Lakeside, Keswick, Cumbria CA12 5DJ
website www.theatrebythelake.com
Artistic Director Ian Forrest *Associate Director* Stefan Escreet *Artistic Coordinator* Sophie Curtis

Production details: Each year, Theatre by the Lake produces a Summer Season of 6 plays in repertoire, an Easter production / Spring Season, and a Christmas production. Also promotes a touring programme of visiting professional work across all artforms, and runs Education and Outreach programmes. Recent productions include: *A Chorus of Disapproval*; *Blackbird*; *The Memory of Water*; and *A Midsummer Night's Dream*. Offers TMA / Equity approved contracts and subscribes to the Equity Pension Scheme.

Casting procedures: Auditions are held 3 times a year. All casting is in-house; does not use freelance casting directors. Casting breakdowns can be obtained by postal application with sae. Does not accept general submissions from actors. Further information about the casting process can be found on the website.

Theatre Royal & Drum Theatre Plymouth

Royal Parade, Plymouth PL1 2TR
tel (01752) 668282 *fax* (01752) 230499
website www.theatreroyal.com
Artistic Director Simon Stokes

Predominantly a receiving house, but produces some shows (especially musicals) which transfer to the West End.

Theatre Royal, Bury St Edmunds

Westgate Street, Bury St Edmunds, Suffolk IP33 1QR
email sharron.stowe@theatreroyal.org
website www.theatreroyal.org
Artistic Director Colin Blumenau *Artistic Co-ordinator* Sharron Stowe

Production details: Seating capacity 358. Built in 1819, the theatre is the only surviving Regency theatre in the country. Produces an annual pantomime at Christmas and 2 other shows a year – a rural tour in the Spring (2007 production was Ayckbourn's *Intimate Exchanges*) and an in-house production in the Autumn, often from or about the Regency period. Offers non-Equity contracts.

Casting procedures: Casting is done in-house by Sharron Stowe. Casting breakdowns are published via *Spotlight* only. Actors wishing to be considered for the pantomime should write to the theatre in August. (The Spring and Autumn shows are cast in January/February and June/July respectively). Only welcomes letters and emails (with CVs and photographs) from actors previously unknown to the company during these casting periods. Does not welcome showreels, but is happy to receive performance notices. Rarely or never has the opportunity to cast disabled actors.

Theatre Royal Stratford East

Gerry Raffles Square, London E15 1BN
tel 020-8534 7374 *fax* 020-8534 8381
email theatreroyal@stratfordeast.com
website www.stratfordeast.com
Artistic Director Kerry Michael *Associate Director* Dawn Reid *Executive Director* Vanessa Stone

Production details: Committed to work which portrays the experiences of different social and ethnic communities, the theatre is constantly striving to present shows which resonate with its diverse local audiences. Stages 8 shows each year. Also runs TIE, Outreach and Community programmes. Recent productions include: *The Harder They Come*, *Pied Piper* and *Township Stories*.

Casting procedures: Casting opportunities are advertised on the website. Welcomes submissions (with CVs and photographs) sent by post. Advises actors to research the theatre's work before writing, and to think carefully about their own suitability. Invitations to view individual actors' websites also accepted. Actively encourages applications from disabled actors and promotes the use of inclusive casting.

Theatre Royal Windsor

Thames Street, Windsor SL4 1PS
tel (01753) 863444 *fax* (01753) 831673
email info@theatreroyalwindsor.co.uk
website www.theatreroyalwindsor.co.uk
Chief Executive Bill Kenwright *Theatre Director* Simon Pearce

Production details: A long-standing, non-subsidised producing theatre. Shows run for 2-3 weeks. Stages 15 productions each year with some going on to tour. Recent productions include: *Stepping Out, Lord Arthur Saville's Crime* and *A Man for All Seasons*.

Casting procedures: Does not use freelance casting directors. Welcomes letters (with CVs and photographs) but not email submissions. Offers TMA/Equity approved contracts. Will consider applications from disabled actors to play characters with disabilities.

The Tobacco Factory

Raleigh Road, Southville, Bristol BS3 1TF
tel 0117-902 0345 *fax* 0117-902 0162
email theatre@tobaccofactory.com
website www.tobaccofactory.com
Artistic Director Dan Danson *Theatre Manager* David Dewhurst

Production details: Stages 2 productions a year in the theatre space, and also works with the local community. Does not offer Equity approved contracts.

Casting procedures: Casts in-house and does not hold general auditions. Casting breakdowns are available from the website, via postal application (with sae), and via *SBS*. Welcomes letters (by post and email) from actors previously unknown to the company, but does not welcome showreels or invitations to view individual actors' websites. Actively encourages applications from disabled actors and promotes the use of inclusive casting.

Torch Theatre

St Peter's Road, Milford Haven SA73 2BU
tel (01646) 694192 *fax* (01646) 698919
email info@torchtheatre.co.uk
website www.torchtheatre.co.uk
Artistic Director Peter Doran *PA to Artistic Director* Lynn Muir *Casting Director* Christine O'Reilly

Production details: Stages 4-5 productions each year. Recent productions include: *Macbeth, One Flew Over the Cuckoo's Nest* and *Blue Remembered Hills*.

Casting procedures: Sometimes holds general auditions; actors should write in June requesting inclusion. Casting breakdowns are available by postal application (with sae) and Equity Job Information Service. Welcomes submissions (with CVs and photographs), sent by post or email. Showreels and invitations to view individual actors' websites are also accepted. Advises actors to join the mailing list so they know what is being planned 6 months in advance. Offers TMA/Equity approved contracts. Actively encourages applications from disabled actors and promotes the use of inclusive casting.

Traverse Theatre

Cambridge Street, Edinburgh EH1 2ED
tel 0131-228 3223 *fax* 0131-229 8443
email linda.crooks@traverse.co.uk
website www.traverse.co.uk
Artistic Director Dominic Hill *Associate Director* Lorne Campbell

Production details: Scotland's only theatre committed to new writing. Presents a mixed programme of in-house and guest productions. Stages 4 shows each year in the main house and 2 in the studio. Also runs Outreach and Script Development programmes (contact Neil Coull). Recent productions include: *People Next Door* by Henry Adam; *Dark Earth* by David Harrower; *Iron* by Rona Munro; and *Outlying Islands* by David Greig.

Casting procedures: Does not use freelance casting directors. Welcomes letters (with CVs and photographs) but not email submissions. Actors should write in January, June or September. Particularly interested to hear from Scottish actors. Invitations to view individual actors' websites are also accepted.

Tricycle Theatre

269 Kilburn High Road, London NW6 7JR
tel 020-7372 6611 *fax* 020-7328 0795
email admin@tricycle.co.uk
website www.tricycle.co.uk
Artistic Director Nicolas Kent *General Manager* Mary Lauder

Production details: Since opening in 1980, the Tricycle has striven to produce a challenging and innovative programme of theatre, cinema and visual arts reflecting the cultural diversity of its neighbourhood – and in particular, plays by Irish, African-Caribbean, Jewish and Asian writers – as well as responding to contemporary issues and events with its ground-breaking 'tribunal' plays. The new Tricycle now comprises a 230-seat theatre, a 300-seat cinema, a large rehearsal studio, a visual arts studio for educational use, a smaller theatre/workshop space, an Art Gallery, and a new room called the Creative Space for educational/social exclusion workshops. The Tricycle maintains a comprehensive Youth and Education programme in Brent schools, and a

thriving youth theatre reaching more than 20,000 children and young people each year through access schemes and community work. The theatre stages 5 plays each year. Recent productions have included: the premières of Harold Pinter's *The Dwarfs* and Athol Fugard's *Sorrow and Rejoicings*; 2 plays about the political situation of Northern Ireland – *As the Beast Sleeps* by Gary Mitchell, and *10 Rounds* by Carlo Gebler; and a collaboration with the Royal National Theatre of Zinnie Harris's *Further than the Furthest Thing*.

Casting procedures: Uses freelance casting directors but also occasionally posts casting breakdowns on the noticeboard section of the website. Does not welcome casting enquiries and submissions from actors unknown to the company. The Tricycle does however keep files on Black/Asian actors for its own information and as a resource for others; in such cases a photograph and CV are welcome.

Tron Theatre

63 Trongate, Glasgow G1 5HB
tel 0141-559 3748 *fax* 0141-552 6657
email casting@tron.co.uk
website www.tron.co.uk
Artistic Director Andy Arnold *General Manager* Anne McCluskey *Outreach* Lisa McIntosh.

The Tron is one of Scotland's leading producing and presenting venues, delivering a vital and engaging programme of creative, popular and contemporary theatre by both Scottish-based and international artists and companies. The Tron also provides a supportive environment for emerging and established direction talent, nurturing the future voices of Scottish Theatre. Seating Capacity: Main House 230, Studio 60.

Production details: 6 productions are staged annually in the Main House (including co-productions) and 1 production is staged annually in the Studio. Other areas of work include Outreach. Recent productions include: *The Patriot* by Grae Cleugh, *The Boy's Own Story* by Peter Flannery, *Wullie Whittington* by Gordon Dougall and Fletcher Mathers and *The Tempest*.

Casting procedures: Casting is done by liaising with show director and casting directors, and using details of actors on file. Actors can write at anytime to request inclusion, as their submissions will be kept on file. Accepts submissions (with CV's and photographs) from actors unknown to the the company. Actors are employed under Equity approved contracts, and the theatre participates in the Equity Pension Scheme. Encourages applications from disabled actors and promotes the use of inclusive casting.

Warehouse Theatre

Dingwall Road, Croydon CR20 2NF
tel 020-8681 1257 *fax* 020-8688 6699

email info@warehousetheatre.co.uk
website www.warehousetheatre.co.uk
Artistic Director Ted Craig *Administrative Director* Evita Bier *Education Manager* Rose-Marie Vernon

Production details: New-playwriting producing theatre for South London, presenting a mixed programme of in-house and guest productions. Recent productions include: the *Dick Barton* series; *Femme Fatale*; *Blowing Whistles*; and *Woody Allen's Murder Mysteries*.

Casting procedures: Uses freelance casting directors. Welcomes postal submissions at any time (with CVs and photographs) with sae for reply, but not email submissions. Offers ITC/Equity approved contracts. Encourages applications from disabled actors, although the building is not wheelchair accessible.

Watermill Theatre

Bagnor, Nr Newbury RG20 8AE
tel (01635) 45834 *fax* (01635) 523726
website www.watermill.org.uk
Artistic and Executive Director Hedda Beeby *Associate Directors* John Doyle, Edward Hall *Outreach Director* Ade Morris

Production details: A producing theatre where actors live onsite. Stages 6 shows each year with runs of 6-8 weeks, and 2 Outreach tours. Recent productions have included: Shakespeare, Music Theatre, New Writing and Classics.

Casting procedures: Does not use freelance casting directors. Casting breakdowns are available by postal application (with sae), but actors should call first. Welcomes letters (with CVs and photographs) with reference to specific castings only. Offers TMA/Equity approved contracts and subscribes to the Equity Pension Scheme. Will consider applications from disabled actors to play characters with disabilities.

Watford Palace Theatre

20 Clarendon Road, Watford WD17 1JZ
tel (01923) 235455 *fax* (01923) 819664
email enquiries@watfordpalacetheatre.co.uk
website www.watfordpalacetheatre.co.uk
Artistic Director and Chief Executive Brigid Larmour *Executive Director* Matthew Russell

Production details: Producing theatre built in 1908 and recently refurbished, it currently stages 8 shows each year. The theatre presents a varied programme but with an emphasis on new plays and adaptations. Also involved in Education and Community theatre, for which Kirsten Hutton (Head of Learning & Participation) is the lead contact. Offers TMA/Equity approved contracts and does not subscribe to the Equity Pension Scheme.

Casting procedures: Uses freelance casting directors and is unable to respond to individual CVs. Will consider applications from disabled actors to play disabled characters.

West Yorkshire Playhouse

Playhouse Square, Quarry Hill, Leeds LS2 7UP
tel 0113-213 7800 *fax* 0113-213 7250
website www.wyp.org.uk
Artistic Director Ian Brown *Producer* Henrietta Duckworth

Production details: Founded in 1990, the West Yorkshire Playhouse has 2 auditoria – the Quarry (750 seats), and the Courtyard (350 seats). Works include new writing, classics, Shakespeare and musicals, as well as guest productions from incoming touring companies. Also runs TIE, Outreach and Community programmes (contact Gail McIntyre): the schools company tours 3 times a year. Stages 15-17 productions each year across both theatre spaces. Recent productions include: *The Lion, the Witch and the Wardrobe*; *Othello*; *Animal Farm*; *The Hounding of David Oluwale*; *When We Are Married*; and *Peter Pan*. Offers TMA/Equity contracts and does not subscribe to the Equity Pension Scheme.

Casting procedures: Currently the West Yorkshire Playhouse casts through agents' submissions, and works with casting directors on productions on a show-by-show basis. Replies to individual actors can only be sent on receipt of sae. Casting breakdowns are only available to agents. "The West Yorkshire Playhouse is an equal opportunities employer in relation to casting."

The New Wolsey Theatre

Civic Drive, Ipswich IP1 2AS
tel (01473) 295911 *fax* (01473) 295910
email info@wolseytheatre.co.uk
website www.wolseytheatre.co.uk
Artistic Director Peter Rowe

Production details: Mixed producing/receiving house, staging 4-5 productions a year in the main house and 2 in the studio. Also works in Creative Learning and Community Outreach; the contact for this is Rob Salmon. Recent productions include: *Angel House*, *The Glass Menagerie*, *The Doubtful Guest*, *Spies*, and *Laurel & Hardy*.

Casting procedures: Uses freelance casting directors and does not hold general auditions. Casting breakdowns are available via postal application (with sae). Does not welcome unsolicited approaches from actors, unless in response to a casting breakdown. Offers TMA/Equity approved contracts. Actively encourages applications from disabled actors and promotes the use of inclusive casting.

York Theatre Royal

St Leonard's Place, York YO1 7HD
tel (01904) 658162 *fax* (01904) 550164
website www.yorktheatreroyal.co.uk
Artistic Director Damian Cruden *Chief Executive* Liz Wilson

Production details: One of the oldest theatres in the country; seats 867 in the main theatre and 102 in the studio. Productions include classics, new writing and the famous York pantomime every Christmas. Also hosts touring companies, premières and has a partnership with Pilot Theatre Company, who are resident at the theatre. Also runs Outreach and Community programmes (contact Education Administator Jessica Fisher). Recent productions include: *The Seagull, The Railway Children, Up the Duff, Twelfth Night, The Homecoming* and *The White Crow.*

Casting procedures: Occasionally uses freelance casting directors; submissions from actors may be sent directly to Katy Nelson.

Young Vic
66 The Cut, London SE1 8LZ
email info@youngvic.org
website www.youngvic.org

Artistic Director David Lan *Associate Artistic Director* Sue Emmas

Production details: During 2005/6 the Young Vic's home in The Cut was redeveloped. From the new building, it now runs TIE, Outreach and Community programmes (contact Sue Emmas). Recent productions include: *Skellig* by David Almond (directed by Trevor Nunn); *Hobson's Choice* adapted by Tanika Gupta (directed by Richard Jones); *Simply Heavenly* by Langston Hughes (directed by Josette Bushell-Mingo); and *Cruel and Tender* by Martin Crimp (directed by Luc Bondy).

Casting procedures: Uses freelance casting directors. Does not welcome direct submissions from actors. Offers TMA/Equity approved contracts. Actively encourages applications from disabled actors and promotes the use of inclusive casting.

Theatre

Effective audition speeches

Simon Dunmore

Audition speeches may be a fundamental part of the actor's 'toolkit', but a surprising number of otherwise good actors are not very good at doing them – and many make poor choices of material to use. It's true that most castings involve a reading, but sometimes audition speeches are asked for in advance, and occasionally you'll get, "We'd just like to see something else; what can you show us?" It would be very silly to be caught out because you haven't done an audition speech since drama school.

Essentially, audition speeches should be self-contained, well chosen, well researched, well staged and well gauged for the space you are in and for whoever is watching you – just like a good production of a play. In fact an audition speech should be a 'mini-production' (of a 'mini-play') in its own right.

Essential parameters

Length

An audition piece should be no more than two or two-and-a-half minutes long (that's roughly 300 words, depending on pace). Two minutes (or less) can be very effective provided that it contains all the parameters listed elsewhere in this article.

How many?

The important thing is to have a good range of audition material so that you've got a library to choose from to suit each given circumstance. I suggest at least half a dozen.

What types?

Your collection should consist of a good variety of characters you could credibly play. They should be within your 'playing range' and appropriate to your appearance: an audition speech is not an acting exercise; it's part of your marketing portfolio.

You should also aim to find material that rarely (if ever) appears elsewhere on the audition circuit. Judging acting is a highly subjective business, so it is generally better to find 'original' material to heighten your chances of not being compared to others. I suggest that you only use material that is popular if you feel sure you can perform it (them) extremely well – on a bad day ...

Accents

If you choose to do a speech written in a regional accent, make sure you can do that accent well enough to convince a native. (It is important to have at least one in your repertoire that features your own accent if it is a strong and 'characterful' one.) Some people choose to 'translate' a speech into an accent with which they are more comfortable, and this can work. However, watch that in doing this you are not sacrificing too much of the quality of the original language.

Sources of speeches

Don't just rely on plays that you know; you should be steadily expanding your knowledge of dramatic literature. Seeing, reading, sitting in libraries and bookshops (especially second-hand ones); even picking up an audition book to find inspiration for a playwright (previously unknown to you) whom you could explore further.

Look in novels, less well-known films, and good journalism (for instance) for material that could be made into good 'drama'. For example, Shakespeare copied (almost word-for-word) Queen Katherine's wonderful speech beginning "Sir, I desire you do me right and justice ..." (*Henry VIII*, Act II, Scene 4) from the court record.

It's generally inadvisable to write your own speech(es). This rarely works, because very few actors are good playwrights. If you do decide to use a self-written piece, it can be a good idea to use a *nom de plume;* you're selling yourself as an actor, not as a playwright. You should also be prepared to talk about the whole play, even if you haven't written it yet.

Content

Too many people fail because they choose to do an indifferent speech. Even if they do it well, it somehow doesn't have much impact because of indifferent writing, lack of depth, and so on. Essentially you should go for pieces that have good 'journeys' – just like a good play.

It can be useful to find speeches that enable you to show your special skills (singing or juggling, for instance), but don't try to cram so much in that the sense is lost in a firework display of technical virtuosity. At the other extreme, avoid something that requires per-formance at one pace or on one note.

And, never set out to shock deliberately through content and/or crude language. That is not to say don't do 'shockers'; rather, don't set out with the specific idea of shocking your interviewer(s) as many people seem to intend. We've heard most of it before. I cannot describe how mind-numbingly tedious audition-days can become when peppered with such speeches.

Warning: There is now a lot of free audition material available on the Internet. Much of it is indifferently written; however, I have come across the occasional 'gem'.

Shape

Make sure that each of your pieces has a decent shape. In a sense it should be like a good play, with a beginning, middle and ending. Even if the character ends up back where he/she started, so long as he/she has travelled a 'journey' then that's fine.

Shakespeare and the classics

Traditionally you have to have at least one of these in your armoury. The fact is that most people perform them indifferently. Too many renditions seem as dead as their writers. The problem is that they are remote – in language and in content – from our direct experience, and therefore usually require much more research, thought and preparation than a modern speech.

NB It's very tedious to see comedy Shakespeare speech done in a 'cod' West Country accent. If you can genuinely do one of the many variants of this accent, then that's fine, but his language works in every other regional accent in which I've heard it done.

'Trying on'

Try reading any speech that looks good to you (on the page) out loud in front of someone else before you start rehearsing it. If you do this, you'll get an even better idea of whether each speech really suits (and 'grabs') you. It's a bit like buying clothes: you see a pair of trousers (say) that look good on the hanger; sometimes you will feel completely different

Theatre

about them when you try them on. The opposite can also occur: you feel indifferent about a speech on the page; you read it out loud and it feels much, much better.

Rehearsing your speeches
'What are you bringing on stage?'
You must bring your character's life history (gleaned from the play and supplemented by your imagination) into your performance. [As the character (i.e. in the first person), write notes of all the bits of information (big and small) that you find in order to build his/her life.] Most of what you 'bring' won't be obvious to your auditioner(s). However, it will be immediately obvious if that 'life history' is not present. Just as 90% of an iceberg is underwater, a similar proportion of a good performance is also hidden ... but must be there, underneath, to support that performance.

It is particularly important to be clear about what actually provokes the character to start speaking – the 'ignition' that kicks your 'engine' into life. Try running a brief 'film' in your imagination, culminating in the event (for instance, a statement or a gesture from someone else) that is your cue.

Your invisible partner(s)
If you choose a speech addressing another character, then it is vital that that other person (and how they are reacting through the speech) is clear to you. It is generally better to imagine an adaptation of someone you know rather than to 'borrow' someone you've only seen on a flat screen. There can be a huge difference in how we perceive others between two and three dimensions.

It's not just them (and how they are reacting); it's also important to be clear about your relationship. As well as imagining what your character's lover looks like (for instance), you must also know the feel of their touch, their smell, and so forth – and many more personal aspects.

It is also important that any other people, places and events mentioned in the speech are similarly 'clear' in your imagination.

Your invisible circumstances
You should also bring the setting, clothes and practical items with you – in your imagination. (NB I could have written 'set, costumes and props', but I believe that it's important to think of everything being 'real' and not items constructed for a production.) I believe that actors neglecting these is the cause of a high proportion of failed and indifferent speeches. It's not just the visual images, it is also what the other senses give you: the 'brush' of a summer breeze across your face, for instance. Plays are not performed in 'real' rooms (there will be at least one wall missing) and every play has at least one non-appearing character mentioned. These absences are filled by the actors' imaginations. Do the same with these 'absences' in the audition circumstances.

It isn't just the major features that you should think about, but also the apparently minor details – for instance, that mark on a wall that suddenly catches your character's eye. It can be a good idea to draw a map (or groundplan) so that the whole 'geography' of your 'circumstances' is clear for you. Then fill out your imaginary location with as much detail as possible.

Interpretation
As you are creating a 'mini-production' of a 'mini-play' (the 'child' of its 'parent-play'), I believe that it's legitimate to make changes to the given circumstances of the speech when

it occurs in the play, especially if such changes enhance your audition performance. [After all, a 'child' can never lose the genetic code of its 'parents', but he/she will evolve their own personality, which will be different.] However, be prepared to justify it – and don't get defensive. There's usually no harm in honest disagreement.

That voyage of discovery

Be aware of the 'voyage of discovery' that shapes your speech. Don't anticipate the end at the beginning. This is a common fault in rehearsal, which is easily corrected – but a remarkable number of people fall into this trap when performing their audition speeches.

It can be very useful to write out a speech with each sentence (or even each phrase) on a separate line. It then appears less of a 'block' of words on the page and more a series of separate, but connected, thoughts and ideas. It is also a good idea to leave sufficient space between each line to write notes on what the impulse is to go on to say the next thing, and the next, and ...

Beginnings

If you start your speech nebulously, your interviewer probably won't take in what you are doing for the first few seconds and may miss vital information that could make the rest of it a complete puzzle to them. You need to find a way of starting your speech that will grab their attention from the very beginning. This doesn't mean that the beginning has to be loud, simply that it should be positive and effective – almost as if the house lights were faded down and the curtain rising on ... You!

NB It can also be very useful to incorporate a simple movement to start a speech; a turn of the head, for instance.

Endings

It's also important to be clear as to why a character stops speaking after talking for two minutes. You need to be clear what your character's final thought is – crucially stopping his/her flow.

Finally

Ask yourself: "Is my speech and my presentation of it a good piece of 'Theatre'?"

Some practical considerations

Staging

Once you've done all the work set out in the previous paragraphs, you need to think carefully about how you stage each piece. Too many people seem inclined to put in extraneous moves either to compensate for the lack of the other character(s), or because they think the speech is boring if it doesn't contain enough movement. If you are properly 'connecting' to character and 'circumstances', the moves will follow naturally from each 'impulse'. However, much of the effect of your performance will be dissipated if your auditioners don't see enough of your face, and especially your eyes. In general (unless it is an address to the audience), they should be able to see three-quarters of your face for at least half the duration of the speech. To achieve this, orientate the other character(s) and 'circumstances' to suit the audition situation. For instance, place the imaginary person to whom you're talking at around 45 degrees to left or right in front of you. If your map (or groundplan) is clear in your mind, then it should be simple to angle it appropriately.

There is no point in placing a chair specifically to mark another character – or even the hat-stand which I once saw used as the object of some singular passions. If you do use

Theatre

such objects you'll usually find yourself concentrating on that object rather than your 'partner(s)'. They should be clearly lodged in your imagination so that the interviewer can 'see' them through you. Also, don't think that you have to stare at one place continually just to make it clear that he or she is there.

Chairs

A warning about chairs. There is a common variety of chair, as familiar as the bollard is to the motorway, that inhabits many popular audition venues. It can serve all kinds of functions as well as the simple one of being sat upon. However, don't rely on the well-known weight and balance of these plastic and steel functionaries for crucial elements of your well-prepared speech. You may suddenly find only chairs with arms or a room filled with wobbly ones. Be prepared to adapt to whatever form of seating is available.

Tip 1 Do a brief check on the mechanics of your audition-chair before you start your speech. For instance, you don't want to be thrown by the fact that the back is lower than that of the chair you rehearsed with ...

Tip 2 If your audition-chair represents a different type of seat (a low, backless bench, for instance), sit on the chair as though you're sitting on that 'bench'.

Props

Avoid using props. As you haven't got a proper set, costume or lighting, too much of the visual emphasis goes on to the prop and consequently away from you. It is amazing how riveting even a small piece of paper produced for one of the numerous 'letter' speeches can become.

Props can be mimed: that mime doesn't need to be brilliant. And think how much easier it is to put down an imaginary glass on an imaginary table, without making a sound at the wrong moment. In using any imaginary prop, remember not just the shape as you 'hold' it in your hand but also its weight and its impact on your sense of touch.

The only exception to this can be a prop introduced briefly and then quickly discarded. Even then, make sure its impact doesn't take the focus from the rest of the speech.

Performing your speeches

Each presentation of a speech has to have the raw energy of a first performance. Unlike a first night, where the only new factor (in theory, at least) is the audience, you have to face numerous new and possibly unexpected factors when doing your audition speech. You need to be not only well rehearsed but also well prepared for how to cope with all the peripherals that are other people's responsibilities when you are actually doing a production. You are your own stage-management, wardrobe department, front-of-house manager, and so forth.

'Act in here?'

I don't think any audition-room is entirely satisfactory. They can be dirty and unkempt, too hot or too cold, too big or too small, have inconvenient echoes, have barely adequate waiting facilities and/or be hard to find down a maze of corridors. You'll be very fortunate if the whole session has only road traffic as a background noise. You have to be prepared to adjust the presentation of your speech(es) to each context – by fractionally slowing down and enhancing your diction slightly if there's an unavoidable echo, or scaling down your movement in a small room, for instance.

It's your space

You should regard the space in which you are doing your speech as your stage with which to do whatsoever you wish – as long as you have due reverence for the fabric of the building, for your interviewers and their goods and chattels. Move the chairs if you need to, take your shoes off if that's necessary, and so on ... but don't ask if it's 'all right' to do so. It can get very tedious for an interviewer if you keep on asking permission every time you want to change something. Providing it doesn't affect your audience directly, just get on with what is necessary for your performance.

Don't ask where to stand; your actor's instinct should tell you the optimum place for what you are about to do. Especially, don't ask permission to start, even if it's only with one of those pathetic little enquiring looks – another way of undermining yourself in your interviewer's eyes. Once you've been given your cue, it's all yours and in your own time.

Natural hazards

Be aware of natural hazards in the room: for example, a low afternoon sun pouring through the windows that blinds you as soon as you happen to turn into it. Don't, on the other hand, stand in the deepest shadow; nobody wants an actor who cannot find his or her light.

Your interviewer will probably be sympathetic if the unexpected suddenly interrupts you, but it really is your responsibility to spot this kind of thing beforehand and adjust accordingly. If it is something impossible to anticipate, then aim to recover as quickly as possible and get back into your speech. After all, if something goes wrong during a performance, you don't just stop until it's put right; you continue as best you can, and 99.9% of the time nobody in the audience will notice that anything went wrong.

Explanations

Minimise explanations about your speech. Ask yourself if you need them at all. In fact the best speeches are self-contained and don't need explanation beyond the character's name and possibly the title and the writer of the play. Whatever their individual faults, most directors do know a lot of plays, the characters within them and who wrote them. Be careful not to insult directors by telling them what they already probably know. (For example, 'Hamlet from *Hamlet* by William Shakespeare.') On the other hand, make sure you know the title and writer of more obscure plays and be prepared to discuss them.

Sometimes, in the process of getting inside the character, actors forget to give these basic details. I don't think this matters (I enjoy trying to work them out for myself), but some directors have a nasty habit of interrupting actors' preparations with demands like "What are you doing, then?" If you do forget and are so interrupted, don't be so thrown that you rush into your speech.

Your interviewer as the other character

Some people try to use their interviewer as the other character for the purposes of their speech. This is not necessarily a good idea. It can work but is fraught with pitfalls.

First of all, do you need to ask permission beforehand? Politeness dictates that you should. After all, you are asking the auditioner to do the job of being in your play. He or she may say, 'Yes, of course', but has probably been asked the same question in every other session of the day; it can get very tedious. Even if it is all right, the auditioner is probably not an actor, will become self-conscious in the process, not react in the way you anticipated,

Theatre

may well want to drop out of character to write notes and consequently won't be a consistent partner.

Preparation

Do give yourself a moment to position and check your chair and to check the 'geography' of your performance in this particular space.

A pause for thought

Then, also do give yourself that moment of thought before starting a speech – a moment to immerse yourself within your character and circumstances. Almost everybody understands that it can be hard to change gear from chatting to acting. Don't think that you are wasting time; it'll only be a few seconds, and your interviewer will almost certainly have something else to write down before concentrating on you again. (For most actors a 'few seconds' feels much, much longer in these stressed circumstances.)

However, don't take too long to wind up into your speech with lots of heavy breathing or pacing about or even just standing quietly in a corner. That may be what you have to do before you go on stage, but most directors, however understanding, will begin to wonder what kind of lunatic you are and are you going to take up precious rehearsal-time with these warm-ups? Your 'pause for thought' should be as brief as you can make it without showing your inner turmoil. Properly done, this can be riveting to watch.

Starting

One of the hardest aspects of doing a speech is starting it from cold. If you are onstage at the beginning of a stage-production (especially on a first night), you'll experience an immense, and for some, terrifying, feeling of excitement and power as the audience goes quiet. You should aim to recreate this feeling just before you start your speech. It'll give you tingles up your spine and put a real 'kick' into your speech. This will 'communicate' to your auditioners and make them really look at you – even if they've had their heads down scribbling in the preceding seconds.

Tip To help stimulate this process, get the smell of dust into your imagination – it's the pervading smell of any theatre.

Communication

You may well 'feel' your speech, but are you communicating it? Just because you are in a small room with only one person watching, don't mutter your speech at below conversation-level. How do I know you can fill a stage, however small, if you are not filling the room we're in? You have to make that room your stage, the interviewer(s) your audience. Think of them as being in the best seats in the stalls (the ones reserved for the critics on a first night) and aim just beyond the limits of the space. Only a lazy actor will give a smaller performance on stage just because there is a small audience.

Don't blast your interviewer out of his seat, either. Measure the acoustics: a lot of audition-rooms are part of church-hall complexes and tend to have high ceilings with the inevitable echo.

The 'need'

There is a 'need' that drives any speech; two minutes is a long time for someone to keep on talking. A long speech is a series of connected thoughts and ideas; underneath there has to be the 'need' to talk at such length. We all know people who 'go on' too much in everyday life – the odd person is able to sustain attention because of the energy and 'need' to communicate. The same is true on stage and in the audition.

Also, remember that your character hasn't usually planned to say so much. Essentially, the circumstances provoke the 'need' for them to add more, and more, and...

Stopping

If you do need to stop during a piece – you've dried or it's started badly – do it positively and calmly, and do it without a grovelling apology. You may feel terrible but you have to get yourself out of the mess without becoming embarrassing. You can even capitalise on having handled it well. A brief (and positive) "I'll start again" or whatever won't be held against you. If you dry or make a mistake significantly into a speech, just pause briefly and find your way back, just as you would in a public performance.

Bear in mind that most interviewers do not know how acting works. So if, say, your breathing starts going haywire, that's not a reason to stop unless it really is affecting the speech badly. You have left your teachers behind at drama school.

Finishing

When you finish you should keep the final thought in your mind and gently freeze for a moment, just as you would if you're left onstage at the end of a scene in a play. Then fade the imaginary stage-lighting (and close the curtains) at a suitable rate. (That 'moment' should last about a second. If you're unsure, say a multi-syllable word like 'Mississippi' in your head.) Then – without looking your interviewer(s) in the eye – relax back to your normal self, ready to move on to whatever your interviewer wants to do next. Many find the not 'looking your interviewer(s) in the eye' difficult, and a few even think that it might seem rude. However, if you do make eye contact at that crucial moment, you'll probably start to feel very vulnerable – and give out the 'vibe' that you're unconfident about your performance. Whatever you may really feel about that performance, there's nothing else that you can now do, except wait.

There may be a silence; your interviewer(s) may well want to write notes on what you've done. Just settle down and let them get on with it. Don't be thrown by that aching pause; you should quietly wait. The 'ball' is now very definitely in the interviewer's 'court' to restart the conversation.

'Thank you' (a)

There may be a vague 'Thank you' or 'Right', even 'Mmmm' from the interviewer at the end of your speech. Don't read anything in to these vague expostulations. If you do you'll start to undermine yourself. We directors are usually thinking about what we're going to write down about your efforts. That thinking process is dominant and what comes out of our mouths is merely our acknowledgement that you've finished – an attempt at politeness that doesn't come out quite right. (I hear myself doing this constantly, but have never found a way round it.)

'Thank you' (b)

Some actors opt for a 'Thank you', or 'That's it', at the end. Sometimes this sounds pathetic; on others it comes across as sheer arrogance (watch the way some actors do curtain calls). If you've got a good enough 'ending', you've given the cue. The director may not respond to it immediately, but you should have clearly established that the 'ball' is now firmly in his or her 'court'. It's much better to say nothing.

Theatre

Switching off

It is respected that it can take a few seconds to come back to reality, particularly if it's a very emotional speech. But it's fundamental to acting that just as you can 'switch on', you can 'switch off' with apparent ease. I will never forget a woman who did a wonderfully passionate speech from Arnold Wesker's *Four Seasons* and ended up in buckets of tears. She had done it extremely well but when it was over she simply could not stop crying and had to be taken from the room and given time to recover. What would have happened if she'd had to get similarly emotional on stage and then immediately go on to do a comic scene, as can occur? This is an extreme example which exemplifies the need to look very carefully at how you change back to reality.

'Why don't you try that again? This time standing on your head'

Don't get so stuck into a way of doing a speech that you cannot do it in any other way put to you. Some directors like to work on speeches. You should understand the insides of each speech so well that you could do it 'standing on your head'.

Advice

Some directors give constructive advice. In general, take that as a compliment, even if they are critical. Nobody will waste time and energy giving notes if they didn't at least like some aspect of you and your work. However, one director's constructive notes can become another's criticisms. In rehearsal an actor will take a note and try it out. Sometimes it doesn't work, and the moment has to be looked at again. Maybe it was only half-right. In an audition there is usually no time to rehearse that note to see if it works for you. So, when you do try it, and it perhaps doesn't quite work, you have no recourse to its originator for further amplification. Take such notes as suggestions to be utilised or discarded as suits you and your speech. That's how rehearsals should be anyway.

Final note

Working on audition speeches can be a wonderful way of keeping your 'acting juices' flowing through periods of unemployment.

Simon Dunmore has been directing productions for over 30 years – nearly 20 years as a resident director in regional theatres and, more recently, working freelance. In that time there have been over 200 productions (of all styles, colours, shapes and sizes) – recently: several Drama School Showcases, Maugham's *Home and Beauty* and new plays about sex, WB Yeats' up-and-down relationship with Maud Gonne, one set inside a pyramid and another about Bismarck. Past favourites include: *The Promise* (Alexei Arbuzov), *Antigone* (Jean Anouilh), a seven-handed version of *Antony & Cleopatra* and too many others to mention. He also teaches acting and has worked in many drama schools and other training establishments around the country. He has written several books: *An Actor's Guide to Getting Work* (now in its fourth edition), the *Alternative Shakespeare Auditions* series and is the Consultant Editor for *Actors' Yearbook*. **www.simon.dunmore.btinternet.co.uk**

Theatre

Cattle calls and how to survive them

Jennifer Reischel

Standing in the same spot for hours in the cold at 7am. Listening to endless renditions of the same songs. Finally, being herded into a small studio with 50 others to try and dance a routine from *Cats* in the back row without kicking the person next to you. Sound familiar? These are all experiences you may encounter when attending the infamous 'cattle calls', also known as open auditions ...

Why are open auditions held?

These 'mass viewings' are often the only possibility for newcomers to the industry and performers without the required contacts, to get a foot in the audition system door, as literally anyone can attend. Casting directors and production teams use opens to spot those who do not have agent representation, are not fully professional (therefore not found in *Spotlight*, etc.), and those professionals they may have missed in their jam-packed audition schedule. Usually held for large-scale musicals, such as *Les Miserables*, *Phantom* or the recent production of *My Fair Lady*, most open auditions tend to take place for West End shows, although there are also examples of opens for touring productions. As an educated guess, I would say that musicals hold at most around half-a-dozen adult calls (for properly paid work), each year. Other types of open auditions include searches for children and teenagers for musicals, film and television shows, such as *Harry Potter* and *Billy Elliott* (film and musical version), as well as very occasional open auditions for adult parts in screen and stage ventures. Cruise ship auditions also tend to be open calls, as do searches for pop/rock band members and solo music artists for recording deals and similar projects.

How do I find out about when/where they take place?

Opens are usually advertised in the weekly newspaper *The Stage*, and sometimes in *PCR* (*Production Casting Report*) and other casting services such as Castweb and Castnet. Auditions for children and large nationwide searches are also often found in daily newspapers such as *The Guardian* or in local papers sold in the town hosting the audition. Common audition venues tend to be large theatres, dance studios (such as Pineapple and Danceworks in London), grand buildings such as The Welsh Trust Centre in London, and similar locations that are capable of hosting sizeable numbers of waiting and queuing hopefuls.

Cattle calls ads: what are they actually looking for?

Ads for opens in newspapers tend to be quite general and vague. "Looking for excellent singers and dancers" is a favourite, as are "come prepared to dance and sing", "young, sexy and funny", or "hip, trendy and cool". How do you judge if your particular skills are up to scratch or your look is right? First of all, be honest. Can you really hit that top C like your favourite musical theatre performer? Can you really pass for 25 if you are actually 40? If in doubt, ask an industry professional. The truth about opens is that most of the time, the panel will make up their minds within 10 seconds of seeing you walk in – based on first impressions of your appearance, general persona and whether you fit the general look of the part/show. You have very little control over this process, but you can make sure that you start your audition with the right attitude. Be open, friendly, and full of

Theatre

positive 'ready to perform' energy (a smile always helps). Make sure that your 'hello' or similar greeting is clearly audible. Just be yourself, and be proud of who you are and what you have to offer. After all, if you are not confident in your own abilities, how can you expect anyone else to believe in you?

Being recalled – the next step in the process– often depends purely on whether you have the right look or not, although singing range (which should be indicated on your CV), sometimes where you trained, and whether your dance technique is up to scratch during the few minutes they see you leaping around the room can also affect your chances. A lot of it is gut feeling, and whoever the panel feels drawn to or stands out for them at that particular moment. They usually have a pretty definite view of what they are looking for, and make decisions very quickly as lack of time forces them to do so.

NB Some open calls may involve members of the casting team going through the queue of waiting hopefuls, telling people then and there to go home/stay to be seen. This often happens if the auditions are running late or they know that they will not be able to see everyone queuing that day.

Physical and age restrictions

Some ads mention size and height restrictions. Most of the time, the panel will stick to these and you may be sent home while queuing if they see that you are not in the required bracket. There are always exceptions, of course, and sometimes an inch or two may not be noticed. Music groups tend to be stricter, especially if they are replacing band members. Children/teenage auditions seem to take height restrictions very seriously. As regards age, if you are underage and the ad specifically states that you should be 18 or over, or 16 or over, there is little point in attending this open call as the age limit has been given for legal reasons.

The procedure on the day – and how to prepare

Preparing for an open calls starts with one important point – having an EARLY night the day before. You will be up at the crack of dawn heading to the particular audition venue so you can be there at least two hours before the official start time given in the ad. If you do not turn up early, a) you may have to wait for up to eight hours or b) you may not get seen at all. For example, if the queue officially opens at 9am, get there at 7am. Some auditions will involve you literally queuing until you get seen by the panel, while other opens will give you a number and ask you to return at a specific time to audition with another 50 or so people in the queue. It is impossible to tell beforehand. While you are waiting, your CV and photo will be collected by an assistant and they may also sometimes take a Polaroid of you and ask you to fill out a form. Most open calls will tell you straight after your audition whether you were successful or not, and say that they will be in contact for any recall.

Musicals

Depending on the ad, you will have been asked to prepare to sing, dance or both. Even if the ad only asks for one of these, be prepared for both. You may turn up at *My Fair Lady* thinking you will be giving your best 16-bar rendition of 'I could've danced all night', but once you are in the building you discover that you will actually be dancing to 'Get me to the church on time'. It is best to be prepared for everything. Remember that if your open call is the 'queuing until you get seen' kind, you will not have time to find somewhere to warm up. You will have to warm up beforehand and/or in the queue, dancing and singing. Dance auditions often take place in small, crowded dance studios with anything between 20 and 50 people at a time. You are normally given about 10 minutes to learn a routine (sometimes two routines) taught by the dance captain, and then have to perform this to the panel (who will be in the same room watching as you rehearse) with the entire audition group (and then in smaller groups, usually of four or six). In terms of singing, you will very probably not get past 16 bars (I have been to opens where they cut people off after eight bars). In most cases you will be able to choose your own song and will be required to bring your own sheet music. Do NOT sing anything from the show you are auditioning for unless requested to do so in the ad. The ad will usually ask for material "in the style of the show" or to "show off your vocal range/style" – this is particularly popular if the open is for a new musical. Some opens hold both dance and singing auditions on the same day. Remember this if you are taking time off work, as if you are successful in the first part they may well require you to stay on for a second round. The panel will not excuse you or make arrangements for you to come back on another day. They are usually unsympathetic when it comes to work commitments.

Children
Auditions for child roles often require accompaniment by an adult, height measurements, and proof of age. Sometimes they may involve group auditions/workshops to put children at ease and encourage them to perform to the best of their best abilities.

Cruise ship opens
These are quite similar to open calls for musicals, although it is common to be asked to sing two contrasting songs here. It pays off to bring a selection and let the panel choose, especially for Disney cruises. For cruise ship auditions it is also sometimes acceptable to bring backing tracks instead of sheet music – to be on the safe side, bring both unless the ad definitely states which kind of accompaniment to use. Again, be prepared to sing and dance on the same day, which is common for cruise ship calls.

NB Your audition may be videotaped for later use.

Music groups/solo artists
With no existing production to refer to, these cattle calls can often be the hardest. Ads sometimes state the genre that they are looking for, e.g. "in the style of Beyonce/Michael Jackson/Sugarbabes", etc. – but most of the time you will literally have to turn up and just present what shows you and your talents/skills off best. Again, prepare sheet music and backing tracks if you can. Note that for music auditions your style of dress is very important, as image and look can be a large part of your appeal. Don't be afraid to be yourself. Don't copy anyone or try to sound exactly like anyone referred to in the ad. Use you own style and bring your own interpretation to a piece of music. Feel free to bring along a guitar, etc. if you feel that this represents you and/or the kind of band you are going for.

Plays, soaps, films, other
In this kind of open audition you may be asked to sight-read, meaning you will be given a piece of text in the queue or in a waiting room to study (not learn by heart) and then read in front of a camera and/or the panel once it is your turn to be seen. Auditions for screen productions may also involve a screen test, which simply consists of you saying your

name (and sometimes an interesting random fact about yourself) in front of a camera and turning your head from right to left so they can take shots of your profile.

The open call survival guide

• Take along a large bottle of water. You may not be able to get out of the queue for an entire day and the last thing you need is to have a dry throat and 'stick-together' lips when you finally get your 30-second chance to sing!

• Bring easily digestible food. Comfort food such as your favourite takeaway chicken tikka masala may clog up your throat and make you feel too heavy to stand, let alone dance.

• Bring a friend. They really can be lifesavers at opens. It is best if they are also auditioning, as you can share experiences of open calls or warm up together ... and most importantly, they can hold your place in the queue while you go to the toilet at a nearby M&S.

• Buy a reliable alarm clock! There is nothing worse than waking up hours too late because yours failed to wake you.

• Take something to distract you. iPods are good to drown out chatter, tears, screaming fits, family feuds and unbearable warm-up exercises by fellow queue members. If you are able to read surrounded by lots of noise, a book can come in handy.

• Remember to take a copy of your CV and photo! Keep the CV to one page, type it out and follow a professional format. Your photo should be a 10 x 8 inch black and white professional headshot if you are a professional. For children's auditions, other photos may suffice.

• Have details of your agent and personal details like your measurements, etc. listed somewhere, as you may need them in order to fill out forms handed to you.

• Take a pillow. This is very useful for sitting on the kerb when standing becomes too tiring. Or to hit annoying queue members with if their singing becomes too aggravating.

• Take your demo CD and/or a showreel. Vital for any aspiring recording artists – but also handy for musical theatre and cruise ship auditions, especially if they run out of time and simply collect CVs and photos and say they will be in touch with anyone who looks interesting.

• Choose your dance wear/movement wear carefully. *Always* bring these along to a musical theatre/cruise ship cattle call, even if dance is not mentioned in the initial ad. Remember to bring various types of dance footwear (ballet, jazz, capezios, tap, character shoes or 'heels').

• Dress comfortably. Wear a warm coat, scarf, boots, anything to keep you warm and your voice protected if it is cold. You can always take these off once you get inside the actual building. Standing outside for long periods of time can make weather seem much colder than it actually is. Don't invest in expensive make up, clothes or hair styling; it is not needed.

• Use sunscreen on a hot summer's day. You don't want to suffer burns from queuing in the blazing sun and look like a tomato when you finally get seen!

• Whatever you do, do *not* forget your sheet music/backing tracks! Have your sheet music photocopied, neat and taped together , and with any key changes, etc. highlighted. Do not bring books (especially if they are new) as these will just fall off the piano once opened and cause delays and embarrassment.

• A mobile phone with free minutes/free text messages is a must-have at an open call queue.

Do's and don'ts for cattle calls

Do ...

• Chat to other people in the queue. Everyone is in the same boat and you may meet some like-minded people and make new friends.
• Warm up physically and vocally beforehand.
• Turn up EARLY.
• Remain friendly and polite at all times. You never know who may be watching.
• Make sure your hair is out of your face so the panel/camera can actually see you.

Don't ...

• Take a family member with you (unless you are underage). Most of the time they will not understand the process and will get impatient, cold/hot, worried or embarrass you with overprotective care. This is your audition and you need to deal with it by yourself. It's part of the process of being a professional. (Not to mention the fact that an entourage of family members simply clogs up the queue even further.)
• Wait until you get into the queue to learn/choose your song. Choose and rehearse a couple of songs that are appropriate *beforehand*; take all required sheet music/backing tracks along with you and make your final choice when you get into the audition situation (think about it while waiting). There is nothing worse than an audition hopeful panicking because they have not learnt a song/learnt the words, and rehearsing it at the top of their voice for hours in the queue.
• Dress the part. You turning up in Maria von Trapps' nun's habit, Eponine's rags or the Phantom's mask will do you no favours whatsoever and only cause a lot of giggling and pitiful looks. Equally, don't dress as Britney, Snoop Dogg or a member of ABBA. This is not a fancy dress party. Very occasionally, dressing as the part is specified in the advertisement – this is the only time dressing in costume is appropriate.
• Be put off by someone singing 'your song'. The panel will probably hear the song that you selected a hundred times that day, and for opens your choice of song is not that vital as long as it suits your voice, range and the production they are casting for.
• Practise your song full blast in the queue. It's just annoying for everyone else around you and will not help you. Hum to yourself quietly after a thorough warm-up at home.

Originally of German heritage, **Jennifer Reischel** was raised predominantly in the Far East, schooled in various languages, and following her passion for the performing arts, graduated from the three-year musical theatre course at Mountview Academy in 2002. Professional experience includes musical theatre productions in London and other parts of the country, acting stage work touring the UK, cabaret and jazz solo singing engagements in London and Singapore, as well as filming a television pilot at Pinewood Studios. Born into a family of professional writers, she is pleased to carry on this tradition, having recently also completed her first book, *So You Want to Tread the Boards*, available through Robson Books. After several years of experiencing the pit falls and difficulties first hand, Jennifer decided to compile her experiences in the form of a practical, no-nonsense and to-the-point guide, including specifically advice on a career in musical theatre. She hopes her experiences and research will assist fellow and aspiring performers to create work and audition opportunities, as well as remaining financially and emotionally afloat in a difficult and uncertain industry with no rules to follow to guarantee success.

Theatre

Independent managements/theatre producers

This section mostly lists commercial organisations that mount West End and touring productions to larger-scale venues – some of which originate in the subsidised sector. Most such productions will be led by well-known actors, but they will usually need supporting actors who can also understudy those leads. (In long-running West End productions, the understudies get a chance to do their own performance – a useful opportunity to 'showcase' for agents and casting directors.) Sometimes, such a production will tour to try it out before (hopefully) coming into the West End; at others, a management will tour to 'milk' further profits from a West End success.

On tour, apart from 'Acting ASMs' (assistant stage managers who also understudy), you shouldn't be asked to do any of the graft of get-ins and get-outs – unlike on smaller-scale touring. However, if you are also understudying, you will be expected to do an understudy rehearsal every week until the last stages of the tour. This rehearsal will probably be taken by the company manager (rarely, the director) and the whole ambience will feel very unsympathetic to good acting. Despite this, it is very important to be as fully prepared as possible for the chance that the 'name' you are understudying will be unavoidably delayed one night. Touring is fraught with potential delays, and a reputation for being able to 'deliver the goods' at very short notice will enhance future employment prospects. The downside of playing small parts and understudying is that you can become stuck doing this – a good agent will be able to advise in this area.

Touring is not for everyone: long periods away from home, wide variations in the quality of digs (often costing more in holiday resorts during the 'season'), and the fact that you could miss opportunities to be seen for other work are some of the potential disadvantages. On the plus side, contracts for large-scale tours are usually at least three months with a minimum of a week in each venue, and you should have time to see some of the most beautiful sights in the UK (if not Europe and further afield).

Although not as expensive as major films, such productions do cost a lot of money to mount, and productions have been known to collapse suddenly without any warning. When accepting work in this area it is important to have a proper Equity contract.

Ambassador Theatre Group (ATG)

Duke of York's Theatre, 104 St Martin's Lane, London WC2N 4BG
Head of Production Meryl Faiers *Head of Group Casting* Neil Rutherford

Production details: ATG is the second-largest theatre owner and operator in the UK, with 22 venues (11 in the West End and 11 regionally). It produces across the UK, Japan, Europe and New York. Anywhere between 3 and 30 actors work on each production. Recent productions include: *Guys and Dolls*, *Sweeney Todd*, Matthew Bourne's *Nutcracker* and *Highland Fling*, *The New Statesman* and *The Rocky Horror Show*. Offers Equity approved contracts and is "happy to make contributions [to the Equity Pension Scheme] on behalf of any members of the scheme that we employ".

Casting procedures: Uses freelance casting directors. Welcomes letters (with CVs and photographs), but not email submissions. Actors may write at any time, but prefers contact to be made via an agent and preferably during pre-production. Advises actors against sending expensive photos 'on spec', especially if unaccompanied by a letter. Actively encourages applications from disabled actors and promotes the use of inclusive casting.

Andy Barnes Productions

5A Irving Street, London WC2H 7AT
tel 020-7839 9003
email andy@andybarnesproductions.com
website www.andybarnesproductions.com
Director Andy Barnes *Associate Producer* Wendy Barnes

Production details: Founded in 2005. Primarily a producer of new musicals with Fringe and West End experience; also produces small plays. Founder and producer of Perfect Pitch Musicals Ltd, a development network for new musical theatre. Stages 2-3 productions each year at various venues, which include arts centres and theatres. Number of actors going on tour varies, and regions covered include London, the South East and New York. Recent productions include: *When Harry Met Sally* (UK Tour); *Days of Hope* (King's Head); *Departure Lounge* (Arts Theatre & Edinburgh Festival); and *Someone Who'll Watch Over Me* (Gene Frankel, NY).

Casting procedures: Uses freelance and in-house casting directors. Holds general auditions; actors should write in March and September to request inclusion. Casting breakdowns are available via Spotlight. Welcomes letters (with CVs and photographs) from individual actors previously unknown to the company. Also welcomes email submissions and showreels, but will not accept invitations to view individual actors' websites.

Nick Brooke Ltd

The Penthouse, 7 Leicester Place, London WC2H 7RJ
tel 020-7851 0393 *fax* 020-7734 7185
email info@nickbrooke.com
Directors Nick Brooke, Philip Noel

Production details: Founded in 2002 as an independent theatre production company, Nick Brooke Ltd stages 2 productions each year, averaging an annual total of about 280 performances. Tours to approximately 30 theatres throughout England and Wales annually. In general 6-10 actors work on each production. Recent productions include: *Corpse* and *The Shell Seekers*.

Casting procedures: Occasionally employs freelance casting directors. Also holds general auditions; actors should write in January and in the early summer to request inclusion. Casting breakdowns are publicly available via the website and postal application. Welcomes submissions (with CVs and photographs) from actors previously unknown to the company if sent by post, but does not welcome email enquiries. Also accepts invitations to view individual actors' websites.

Cole Kitchenn Ltd

212 Strand, London WC2R 1AP
tel 020-7427 5680 (Switchboard)
tel 020-7427 5681 (Personal Management)
tel 020-7427 5682 (Production Department)
fax 020-7353 9639
email info@colekitchenn.com
website www.colekitchenn.com
Key personnel Stuart Piper, David Cole, Guy Kitchenn

Production details: Production company established in 1970; personal management established in 2005. Has produced more than 60 productions in the West End over the past 35 years. Offers Equity approved contracts. Recent London productions include: *The Female of the Species* (Vaudeville Theatre) with Eileen Atkins; *Lifecoach* (Trafalgar Studios) with Phill Jupitus; *Daddy Cool* (Shaftesbury Theatre) with Javine & Michelle Collins. Current personal management clients include: Helen Lederer (*Ab Fab*), Paul McEwan (*Emmerdale*), Stephen Uppal (*Hollyoaks*), Jess Robinson (*Headcases/Dead Ringers*), Sarah Lark (*I'd Do Anything*), and award-winning West End stars Paul Baker, Graham Bickley, Kim Criswell, Frances Ruffelle, Robyn North, Jimmy Johnston and Caroline O'Connor.

Casting procedures: Casting breakdowns available from *SBS*, Spotlight and Castweb. Welcomes letters (with CVs and photographs) from actors previously unknown to the company sent by post or email. Invitations to view individual actors' websites and showreels are accepted. Rarely has the opportunity to cast disabled actors.

CV Productions Ltd

Hampden House, 2 Weymouth Street, London W1W 5BT
tel 020-7636 4343 *fax* 020-7636 2323
email cvtheatre@aol.com
Director Charles Vance

Production details: Regional touring theatre company.

Casting procedures: Does not use freelance casting directors. Sometimes holds general auditions. Casting breakdowns are not publicly available. Welcomes submissions (with CVs and photographs) sent by post or email. Invitations to view individual actors' websites are also accepted.

Paul Elliot Ltd

1st Floor, 18 Exeter Street, London WC2E 7DU
tel 020-7379 4870 *fax* 020-7379 4860
email pre@paulelliott.ltd.uk
Director Paul Elliott *General Manager* David Bownes

Production details: Large-scale theatre producers, touring no. 1 venues across the UK with plays and musicals. Stages 2-4 productions a year, touring from between 6 weeks to 2 years or more. May use from 3 to 30 actors in each production. Offers TMA SOLT/ Equity approved contracts and subscribes to the Equity Pension Scheme. Recent credits include: *Stones in his Pockets.*

Casting procedures: Casts in-house and also uses freelance casting directors. Actors may write at any time requesting inclusion in auditions. Casting

Theatre

breakdowns are published in *The Stage*, *PCR* and *SBS*, and included in Spotlight Link. Happy to receive CVs and photographs, by post or email, from actors previously unknown to the company. Also happy to receive showreels and invitations to view individual actors' websites. Will consider applications from disabled actors to play characters with disabilities.

Andrew Fell Ltd

4 Ching Court, 49-51 Monmouth Street,
London WC2H 9EY
tel 020-7240 2420 *fax* 020-7240 2499
email hq@andrewfell.co.uk
Directors Andrew Fell, Sally Hoskins

Production details: Theatre production company and general management. Recent productions include: *The Producers*; *Romeo and Juliet*; *The Lieutenant of Innishmore*; and *Taboo*.

Casting procedures: Uses freelance casting directors.

Vanessa Ford Productions Ltd

Upper House Farm, Upper House Lane,
Shamley Green GU5 0SX
tel (01483) 278203 *fax* (01483) 271509
email vfpltd@btinternet.com
website www.vfpltd.com
Managing Director Vanessa Ford

Production details: Founded in 1979. Tours to approximately 30 theatres throughout the UK each year. On average, 14 actors work on each production. Recent productions include: *The Hobbit*, *A Christmas Carol* and *Shirley Valentine*. Offers ITC/Equity approved contracts and does not subscribe to the Equity Pension Scheme.

Casting procedures: Occasionally uses freelance casting directors, and sometimes holds general auditions. Casting breakdowns are available on the website and through *Spotlight*. Welcomes submissions (with CVs and photographs) by post and email. Invitations to view individual actors' websites are also accepted. Will consider applications from disabled actors to play disabled characters.

Robert Fox Ltd

6 Beauchamp Place, London SW3 1NG
tel 020-7584 6855 *fax* 020-7225 1638
email info@robertfoxltd.com
website www.robertfoxltd.com
Director Robert Fox

Production details: Founded in 1980. Theatre and film production company specialising in large-scale theatre productions and musicals as well as feature films. Performances are staged in the West End and on Broadway. Recent theatre productions include: *The Breath of Life*, *The Boy from Oz* and *Gypsy*. Also recently produced the feature films *The Hours* and *Iris*.

Casting procedures: Employs casting directors for specific projects and does not welcome unsolicited

submissions from actors. Casting breakdowns are available on the website, and details of casting directors are sometimes posted there as well.

Sonia Friedman Productions

Duke of York's Theatre, 104 St Martin's Lane,
London WC2N 4BG
tel 020-7854 7050 *fax* 020-7854 7059
email queries@soniafriedman.com
website www.soniafriedman.com
Producer Sonia Friedman *General Manager* Diane Benjamin *Creative Producer* Lisa Makin *Head of Production* Pam Skinner *Associate Producer* Sharon Duckworth

Production details: Sonia Friedman Productions is one of the West End's most prolific and significant theatre producers, responsible for some of the most successful theatre productions in London over the past few years. West End and Broadway Theatre includes: *Dumb Waiter* by Harold Pinter; *Boeing-Boeing* by Marc Camoletti; *Love Song* by John Kolvenbach; *Bent* by Martin Sherman, directed by Daniel Kramer, starring Alan Cumming; *Rock 'n' Roll* by Tom Stoppard, directed by Trevor Nunn; *Eh Joe* by Samuel Beckett, directed by Atom Egoyan, starring Michael Gambon; *Faith Healer*, by Brian Friel, directed by Jonathan Kent, starring Ralph Fiennes, Cherry Jones and Ian McDiarmid (Broadway).

Fresh Glory Productions

59 St Martin's Lane, London WC2N 4JS
tel 020-7240 1941
email info@freshglory.com
website www.freshglory.com

Production details: Established in 2007. Stages 2-3 productions annually, with 175-200 performances in 28-30 arts centres and theatres across England. In general 6-7 actors are involved in each production. Offers Equity-approved contracts as negotiated through TMA and ITC. For recent productions, please consult the website.

Casting procedures: Uses freelance casting directors. Casting breakdowns are available through Castweb and Spotlight Link. Welcomes letters (with CVs and photographs) from individual actors previously unknown to the company, but prefers hard copy to email. Actively encourages applications from disabled actors and promotes the use of inclusive casting.

Ian Fricker (Theatre) Ltd

3rd Floor, 146 Strand, London WC2R 1JD
tel 020-7836 3090 *fax* 020-7836 3078
email mail@ianfricker.com
website www.ianfricker.com
Producer Ian Fricker *Associate Producer* Louise Toeman

Production details: Founded in 2004. West End and touring producer. Stages 4-8 productions each year, with approximately 100 performances in 20 theatres across the UK. In general 1-15 actors go on tour. Offers Equity approved contracts as negotiated through TMA. Recent productions include: *Brief Lives* (Richmond, Brighton, Lincoln, Windsor); *Visiting Mr Green* (13-week tour and West End); Noel Coward's *A Song at Twilight* (10-week tour).

Casting procedures: Uses in-house casting directors; sometimes holds general auditions, and actors should write to request inclusion when advertised in *Spotlight*. Welcomes letters (with CVs and photographs) from actors previously unknown to the company sent by post, but not by email. Accepts showreels and invitations to view individual actors' websites. Rarely (or never) has the opportunity to cast disabled actors.

David Graham Entertainment Ltd

72 New Bond Street, London W1S 1RR
tel 0870-321 1600 *fax* 0870-321 1700
email info@david graham.co.uk
website www.davidgrahamentertainment.com
Director David Graham

Production details: Theatre producer and concert promoter. Stages around 8 productions in 70-80 theatres and concert halls on an annual basis, with more than 300 performances per year. Countries covered include Britain, Holland, Germany, Canada, Spain, Norway and Ireland. In general, 12 performers work on each production. Recent productions include: *The Real Monty*, *The Wonderful West End* and *Hold Tight, It's 60s Night*.

Casting procedures: Does not use freelance casting directors or hold general auditions. Casting breakdowns are available via the website, *PCR* and advertisements in *The Stage*.

The Derek Grant Organisation

13 Beechwood Road, West Moors, Dorset BH22 0BN
tel (01202) 855777
email admin@derekgrant.co.uk
website www.derekgrant.co.uk
Director Derek Grant *Administrative Director* Michael Jones

Production details: Producer of nationwide theatre tours, children's shows, comedy, concerts and plays. On average stages 3-4 projects annually, with around 80 performances in arts centres, theatres and community venues across the UK. In general 6 actors are involved in each production. Recent productions include: Hans Andersen's *The Snow Queen* (13 performances at Lichfield Garrick Theatre), *Pinocchio* (at Bolton Albert Halls), Vince Hill in Concert (at North Pier Blackpool); and *Goldilocks and the Three Bears* (nationwide tour).

Casting procedures: Does not use freelance casting directors. Sometimes holds general auditions and actors are advised to write in September and January requesting inclusion. Welcomes letters (with CVs and photographs) from individual actors previously

unknown to the company, sent by post or email. Accepts showreels and will consider invitations to view individual actors' websites. Considers applications from disabled characters to play characters with disabilities. "We treat all our artistes with respect and have a high reputation in the business."

Hiss & Boo Theatre Company

Nyes Hill, Wineham Lane, Bolney,
West Sussex RH17 5SD
tel (01444) 881707 *fax* (01444) 882057
email email@hissboo.co.uk
website www.hissboo.co.uk
Artistic Director Ian Liston

Production details: Established in 1977. Pantomime producers also specialising in touring plays and revues in the UK and overseas.

Casting procedures: Works with a known pool of performers. Casting and auditions are only available via Spotlight Interactive Casting. Does not welcome unsolicited CVs. Offers actors TMA/Equity approved contracts.

Paul Holman Associates

Morritt House, 58 Station Approach, South Ruislip,
Middlesex HA4 6SA
tel 020-8845 9408 *fax* 020-8582 2557
email enquiries@paulholmanassociates.co.uk
website www.paulholmanassociates.co.uk
Directors Paul Holman, Adrian Jeckells, John Ogle
Associate Producer Andrew Lynford

Production details: Established in 1990. Produces pantomimes, summer shows and one-night attractions. See entry under *Pantomime producers* on page 208 for more details.

Thelma Holt Ltd

Noel Coward Theatre, 85 St Martin's Lane,
London WC2N 4AU
tel 020-7812 7455 *fax* 020-7812 7550
email Thelma@dircon.co.uk
website www.thelmaholt.co.uk
Managing Director Thelma Holt *Executive Director* Malcolm Taylor

Production details: Founded in 1990. Theatre producer of classic plays in the West End, on tour and internationally (particularly Japan). Stages 4-5 productions annually with a total of 250 performances. Tours 6 theatres across the UK each year. On average, 18 actors work on each production. Recent productions include: *Hamlet*, *The Taming of the Shrew*, *All's Well that Ends Well*, *Othello*, *Pericles*, *Titus Andronicus* and *Kean*. Offers Equity/TMA/SOLT approved contracts and subscribes to the Equity Pension Scheme.

Casting procedures: Uses freelance casting directors. Does not hold general auditions. Advises that the company does not encourage unsolicited approaches with letters or photographs, as they will be ignored if not in production. When casting, requirements are made well known via casting directors. "I have employed disabled actors and will continue to do so – not necessarily to play characters with disabilities. When an actor's good, it's horses for courses."

Image Musical Theatre

23 Sedgeford Road, Shepherd's Bush,
London W12 0NA
tel 020-8743 9380 *fax* 020-8749 9294
email brian@imagemusicaltheatre.co.uk
website www.imagemusicaltheatre.co.uk
Composer/Lyricist Robert Hyman

Production details: Founded in 1988. Stages 4 productions annually, with around 900 performances in 70 venues including arts centres, theatres, schools and other educational venues throughout the UK. In general 3-4 actors are involved in each production. *Recent productions* include: *The Jungle Book, The Secret Garden, Tom's Midnight Garden, The Snow Queen, The Wind in the Willows,* and *Alice in Wonderland.*

Casting procedures: Sometimes holds general auditions. Actors should write in June, October and late January to request inclusion. Casting breakdowns are publicly available via the website, from Equity Job Information Service, in *PCR,* and from Castnet and Castweb. Welcomes letters (with CVs and photographs) from individual actors previously unknown to the company only if sent by post. No emails and no showreels, but will accept invitations to view individual actors' websites. Rarely (or never) has the opportunity to cast disabled actors.

Colin Ingram Ltd

Suite 526, Linen Hall, 162-168 Regent Street,
London W1B 5TE
tel 020-7038 3905 *fax* 020-7038 3907
email info@coliningramltd.com
website www.coliningramltd.com
Director Colin Ingram *Production Associate* Simon Ash

Production details: Theatrical producers and general managers. The company offers Equity-approved contracts and participates in the Equity Pension Scheme. "Please see the website for details of recent productions and venues."

Casting procedures: Uses freelance casting directors. Does not welcome unsolicited approaches from individual actors previously unknown to the company.

International Theatre & Music Ltd

Garden Studios, Betterton Street, Covent Garden,
London WC2H 9BP
tel 020-7470 8786 *fax* 020-7379 0801
email info@it-m.co.uk
website www.it-m.co.uk

Managing Director Piers Chater Robinson *Marketing* Richard Thomas *Management* Claire Edworthy

Production details: Established in 1994. "Management of artistes with strong singing, dancing and/or instrumental skills; co-production, publishing and composition. We mostly license productions and have issued more than 1000 licences internationally. For more information, please see the website."

Casting procedures: Uses freelance casting directors and sometimes holds general auditions. Casting breakdowns are available from Spotlight. Welcomes letters (with CVs and photographs) from individual actors previously unknown to the company, sent by post or email. Rarely, or never, has the opportunity to cast disabled actors.

Bruce James Productions

68 St George's Park Avenue, Westcliff-on-Sea,
Essex SS0 9UD
tel/fax (01702) 335970
email info@brucejamesproductions.co.uk
website www.brucejamesproductions.co.uk
Artistic Director Bruce James

Production details: Produces dramas, comedies, thrillers, pantomimes, children's shows and 'summer schools' for many theatres all over the UK. Stages around 12 productions a year. Between 2 and 14 actors are involved in each production. Does not offer Equity-approved contracts. Recent productions include: *Cinderella* (Pomegranate Theatre, Chesterfield); *Snow White and the Seven Dwarfs* (Thameside Theatre, Grays); *The Lion, the Witch and the Wardrobe* (Palace Theatre, Southend-on-Sea); and UK tours of *The Mating Game* (farce), *Hi-De-Hi!* (musical) and *The Black Veil* (thriller).

Casting procedures: Casts in-house and holds general auditions. Actors should write in January, May and September to request inclusion. Casting breakdowns are normally advertised through Spotlight Link and sometimes published via *SBS,* Castcall and Castweb. Welcomes letters (by post, not by email) with CVs and photographs from individuals previously unknown to the company. "Do not send unsolicited emails containing large [file-sized] photographs." Does not welcome showreels via post but will accept links via email, and is happy to receive invitations to view individuals' websites. Will consider applications from disabled actors to play characters with disabilities. Advises actors: "Never give up or stop trying to get seen!"

Gareth Johnson Ltd

Plas Hafren, Eglwyswrw, Crymych,
Pembrokeshire SA41 3UL
tel (07770) 225227 *tel* (01239) 891368
fax (01239) 800089
email gjltd@mac.com
website www.garethjohnsonltd.com

Production details: Founded in 2000, this general management company produces (for a client) up to 6

shows a year, West End, UK and overseas. Recent productions include: *Touched* (Trafalgar); *Imagine This* (TR Plymouth and New London Theatre); *Crown Matrimonial* UK Tour; *Miss Bollywood – The Musical* UK and European tour; *The Far Pavilions* Shaftesbury Theatre. Offers Equity contracts.

Casting procedures: Uses freelance casting directors and does not welcome unsolicited contact of any kind from actors. Policy on disabled actors as instructed by client.

Andy Jordan Productions Ltd
Studio D, 413 Harrow Road, Maida Vale, London W9 3QJ
mobile (07775) 615205
email andy@andyjordanproductions.co.uk
Director Andy Jordan

Production details: Founded in 2000. Commercial production company, largely producing new plays of all genres. Stages 2-4 productions annually with 50-100 performances per year. Performs annually in 4-10 theatres across the UK, including Northern Ireland and Eire. Also tours overseas. On average, 3-7 actors work on each production. Recent productions include: *Lies Have Been Told: An Evening with Robert Maxwell* (2 seasons in West End, 2006), *2Graves* (West End 2006), *Worlds End* (Edinburgh Festival), and *Escaping Hamlet* (Edinburgh Festival). Usually offers Equity approved contracts (either TMA or ITC).

Casting procedures: Uses freelance casting directors. Actors may write at any time requesting inclusion. Casting breakdowns are published on Spotlight Link. Welcomes submissions (with CVs and photographs) sent by post and email. Rarely has the opportunity to cast disabled actors but will consider submissions to play disabled characters.

Richard Jordan Productions Ltd
Mews Studios, 16 Vernon Yard, London W11 2DX
tel 020-7243 9001 *fax* 020-7313 9667
email Richard.Jordan@virgin.net
Director Richard Jordan

Production details: Founded in 1998. Produces theatre in the West End, throughout the UK and internationally. Main area of work is new writing and revivals of plays; occasionally produces musicals. Company works as general managers and consultants for a wide range of producers and theatres in the UK and abroad. Stages around 10 productions annually with 300 performances during the course of the year. Recent productions include: *Lady in the Van, Once And For All We're Gonna Tell You Who We Are So Shut Up And Listen!*, and the Tony-nominated *Behanding in Spokane*.

Casting procedures: Uses freelance casting directors. Sometimes holds general auditions. Casting breakdowns are sometimes publicly available in *PCR*. Welcomes letters (with CVs and photographs) but

not email submissions. Applications are particularly welcome if actors are currently in a production that the company can go and see. Advises that applicants should have an awareness of the type of work produced by the company before sending CVs.

Bill Kenwright Ltd
BKL House, 1 Venice Walk, London W2 1RR
tel 020-7446 6200 *fax* 020-7446 6222
email info@kenwright.com
website www.kenwright.com

Production details: Commercial producing management presenting revivals and new works for the West End and for touring theatres. Recent (or current) productions include: in the West End – *Blood Brothers, Hay Fever, Joseph & The Amazing Technicolor Dreamcoat, Whistle Down the Wind, The Crucible*, and *A Man for All Seasons*; on tour – *Blood Brothers, Festen, The Hollow*, and *This Is Elvis*.

Casting procedures: Uses freelance casting directors, but does some casting in-house. Welcomes letters (with CVs and photographs) sent to Josh Andrews.

Limelight Entertainments
Unit 4, The Gateway, 2a Rathmore Road, London SE7 7QW
tel 020-8858 6141 *fax* 020-8805 2684
email enquiries@limelightents.co.uk
website www.limelightents.co.uk
Artistic Director Richard Lewis *Executive Producer* Martin Ronan

Production details: Established in 1996. Stages 2-3 productions annually, touring to 50 theatres and arenas. Roughly 4-6 actors used in each production. Recent productions include: *Sing-A-Long-A-ABBA, The Fimbles, Love Shack* and *Fully Committed*. Offers Equity approved contracts.

Casting procedures: General auditions are usually held in September. Encourages applications from disabled actors and promotes the use of inclusive casting.

Cameron Mackintosh Ltd
1 Bedford Square, London WC1B 3RB
tel 020-7637 8866 *fax* 020-7436 2683
Chairman Cameron Mackintosh *Managing Director* Nicholas Allot *Casting Director/Associate Producer* Trevor Jackson

Production details: Stages musical theatre productions worldwide. Recent productions include: *Les Miserables, Miss Saigon* and *The Phantom of the Opera*.

Casting procedures: In-house casting. Does not hold general auditions. Welcomes letters (with CVs and photographs) but not email submissions. Also accepts showreels and invitations to view individual actors' websites.

Christopher Malcolm Productions Ltd
11 Claremont Walk, Bath BA1 6HB
tel (01225) 445459

Theatre

email cm@christophermalcolm.co.uk
Director Christopher Malcolm

Production details: Founded in 1980, the company works in both licensing and production. Theatre producer for the West End, UK touring and European touring. Stages 1-2 productions annually with 200-300 performances during the course of the year. Recent productions include: *The Rocky Horror Show, Footloose* (in Europe). Current productions include: *Flashdance the Musical* (UK and London), and *Barbarella the Musical* (in development). Offers TMA/Equity approved contracts and does not subscribe to the Equity Pension Scheme.

Casting procedures: Uses freelance casting director, Debbie O'Brien. Sometimes holds general auditions. Actors should write to the casting director only, requesting inclusion. Advises actors to use their agents as a means of contact with the casting director. Unsolicited letters and photographs are not considered. Actively encourages applications from disabled actors and promotes the use of inclusive casting.

Johnny Mans Productions Ltd
PO Box 196, Hoddesdon, Herts EN10 7WG
tel (01992) 470907 *fax* (01992) 470516
email johnnymansagent@aol.com
website www.johnnymansproductions.co.uk
Key contact Johnny Mans

Production details: Founded as a limited company in 1989. Activities include producing and promoting one-night stands, celebrity concerts, musicals and touring productions; casting for television, pantomime and cruise ships; and artiste and personal management for Sir Norman Wisdom OBE, Max Bygraves, Jeremy Spake, Jess Conrad, Leah Bell, Gerry George and many others. Stages about 30 productions annually, totalling around 250 performances during the course of the year. Tours concert productions to more than 300 different theatres and arts centres across the UK and Ireland each year. Recent productions include: *Calamity Jane*; *Beatlemania*; *The Spirit of Pavarotti*; *Yesterday Once More*; *Don't Laugh At Me*; and *Rock Shock Horror*.

Casting procedures: In the first instance, contact johnnymansagent@aol.com by email, or write in with photograph and CV / biography to the address given above. Prospective future clients will then be contacted accordingly. Johnny Mans Productions offers Equity-approved contracts.

Middle Ground Theatre Co
3 Gordon Terrace, Malvern Wells,
Malvern WR14 4ER
tel (01684) 577231 *fax* (01684) 574472
email middleground@middlegroundtheatre.co.uk
website www.middlegroundtheatre.co.uk
Artistic Director Michael Lunney

Production details: Theatre company producing drama to tour No. 1 UK theatre venues and arts

centres. Stages 1 or 2 productions a year with 180 performances across around 25 venues. Covers the whole of Britain and Northern Ireland. Size of cast varies from show to show. Offers actors non-Equity contracts and does not participate in the Equity Pension Scheme. Recent productions include: *Meeting Joe Strummer*; *The Importance of Being Earnest*; *Billy Liar*; *Dial M for Murder*; and *Tunes of Glory*.

Casting procedures: Casts in-house. Casting breakdowns are not publicly available (Spotlight only). Welcomes submissions from actors (with CV and photograph) if sent by post or email. Also welcomes showreels and invitations to view individual actors' websites. Will consider applications from disabled actors to play disabled characters.

Millionth Muse Productions
1st and 2nd Floors, 20 Stansfield Road,
London SW9 9RZ
tel 020-7737 5300 *mobile* (07905) 259060
email info@millionthmuse.com
website www.millionthmuse.com
Director Paul L Martin

Eleven-year-old production house for cabaret and variety shows. Runs a useful database for performers to join free of charge. Previous regular shows produced for Old Vic Pit Bar, Soho Revue Bar, CellarDoor, The Arts Theatre, The Leicester Square Theatre, Theatre Museum and many others.

Norwell Lapley Productions Ltd
Tenbury House, 36 Teme Street, Tenbury Wells,
Worcestershire WR15 8AA
tel (01584) 819005 *fax* (01584) 819076
email info@cdm-ltd.com
website www.cdm-ltd.com
Director Chris Davis *Artist Manager* Kerry Foley

Production details: Produces theatre in the West End and touring productions. Stages 4-5 productions annually and gives 40-50 performances during the course of the year at theatres nationwide. Recent productions include: *Zipp*. Offers TMA/SOLT/Equity approved contracts and subscribes to the Equity Pension Scheme.

Casting procedures: Uses freelance casting directors and does not deal directly with actors. Rarely has the opportunity to cast disabled actors.

Pendle Productions
Bridge Farm, 249 Hawes Side Lane, Blackpool,
Lancashire FY4 4AA
tel (01253) 839375 *fax* (01253) 792930
email admin@pendleproductions.co.uk
website www.pendleproductions.co.uk
Director TS Lince

Production details: Touring professional theatre company. Stages between 10 and 15 productions each year, with 600 performances nationally in 300 venues of all types. Recent productions include: *Cinderella*, *Sinbad*, and *Treasure Island*.

Casting procedures: Sometimes holds general auditions; actors should write in April-June requesting inclusion. Casting breakdowns are publicly available via the usual channels. Welcomes letters (with CVs and photographs) from individual actors previously unknown to the company sent by post or email. Accepts showreels but prefers not to receive invitations to view individual actors' websites. Actively encourages applications from disabled actors, and promotes the use of inclusive casting.

Popular Productions Ltd
18B Hornsey High Street, London N8 7PB
email info@popularproductions.com
website www.popularproductions.com
Directors Lucy Blakeman, John Payton

Production details: International theatre producer. Stages 4-6 productions annually, with around 80 performances in 4 theatres in the UK and Dubai. Anything from 2 to 100 actors may be involved in each production. Recent productions include: *Annie* (International; Middle East Premiere); *Woman in Black* (Dubai).

Casting procedures: Uses freelance casting directors. Sometimes holds general auditions. Casting breakdowns are available from *PCR*, Castweb and Casting Call Pro. Does not welcome unsolicited approaches by actors unknown to the company, but will consider invitations to view individual actors' websites. Rarely, or never, has the opportunity to cast disabled actors.

David Pugh & Dafydd Rogers
Wyndhams Theatre, Charing Cross Road, London WC2 0DA
tel 020-7292 0390 *fax* 020-7292 0399
Directors David Pugh, Dafydd Rogers

Production details: Theatre production company staging 2-3 productions annually in the West End and Broadway, and touring to theatres throughout the UK. Recent productions include: *Art*, *The Play What I Wrote* and *Blues Brothers*.

Casting procedures: Sometimes holds general auditions. Actors should address requests for inclusion to Sarah Bird CDG (see entry under *Casting directors* on page 95), who is responsible for all casting.

PW Productions Ltd
2nd Floor, 80-81 St Martins Lane, London WC2N 4AA
tel 020-7395 7580 *fax* 020-7240 2947
email info@pwprods.co.uk
Chief Executive Peter Wilson

Production details: The company, which Peter Wilson founded in 1983, specialises in the production, general management and bookkeeping/accountancy for theatre presentations. Recent productions include: *The Woman in Black*, Stephen Daldry's production of *An Inspector Calls*, and *Honour* at The Wyndham's Theatre London, starring Dame Diana Rigg, Martin Jarvis OBE and Natasha McElhone.

The Really Useful Group Ltd
22 Tower Street, London WC2H 9TW
tel 020-7240 0880 *fax* 020-7240 1204
website www.reallyuseful.com

Production details: The Really Useful Group (RUG) was founded in 1977 by Andrew Lloyd Webber. It is an international entertainment company actively involved in theatre ownership and management, theatrical production, film, television, video and concert productions, merchandising, records and music publishing.

Rho Delta Ltd
26 Goodge Street, London W1T 2QG
tel 020-7436 1392 *fax* 020-7436 1395
email info@ripleyduggan.com
Director Greg Ripley-Duggan

Production details: Founded in 1991. Produces West End and touring commercial theatre. Stages 1 production annually which tours to 6 theatres. Recent productions include: *The Old Masters*, *Life x 3* and *The Memory of Water*. Offers actors TMA/SOLT/Equity approved contracts and subscribes to the Equity Pension Scheme.

Casting procedures: Uses freelance casting directors and does not deal directly with actors. Will consider applications from disabled actors to play disabled characters.

Suzanna Rosenthal Ltd
PO Box 40001, London N6 4YA
tel 020-8340 4421 *fax* 020-8340 4421
email admin@suzannarosenthal.com
website www.suzannarosenthal.com

Production details: Founded in 2001, the company produces Off-West End shows. Stages 3-5 productions annually with 100 performances over the year in theatres and outdoor venues across London. In general 5-15 actors are involved in each production. Recent productions include: *Henry VIII* and *The Resistible Rise of Arturo Ui*, *Victor/Victoria* and London's Free Open-Air season at The Scoop.

Casting procedures: Uses freelance casting directors. Sometimes holds general auditions. Actors should only write requesting inclusion in response to advertisements. Casting breakdowns are available via the website, *PCR* and advertisements in *The Stage*.

Showcase Entertainments Productions Ltd
2 Lumley Close, Newton Aycliffe, Co. Durham DL5 5PA

Theatre

Managing Director/Executive Producer Geoffrey JL Hindmarch *Director/Choreographer* Paul W Morgan

Production details: A professional theatrical touring company. Stages 5 productions annually, with around 100 performances in 60 theatres across England, Scotland and Wales. In general 10 actors are involved in each production. Recent productions include: *Musical Magic* starring Paul Daniels and full showcase company (Harlow Playhouse, Litchfield Garrick, Palace Theatre Mansfield).

Casting procedures: Sometimes holds general auditions; actors may write at any time to request inclusion. Welcomes letters (with CVs and photographs) from individual actors previously unknown to the company, sent by post or email. Also welcomes showreels. Rarely, or never, has the opportunity to cast disabled actors.

Marc Sinden Productions Group of Companies

1 Hogarth Hill, London NW11 6AY
tel 020-8455 3278
website www.sindenproductions.com,
www.onenightbooking.com,
www.uktheatreavailability.co.uk,
www.montecarlotheatre.co.uk
Director Marc Sinden

Production details: A West End and touring theatre producer, reaching theatres and arts centres across the UK and Europe. For details of recent productions, please consult the website. Also runs the UK Theatre Availability System (**www.uktheatreavailability.co.uk**) which allows touring companies to check the availability and suitability of theatre spaces.

Casting procedures: Uses freelance casting directors and does not welcome casting enquiries and submissions from actors.

Adam Spiegel Productions

Stage Entertainment Ltd, 6th Floor, Swan House, 52 Poland Street, London W1F 7NQ
tel 020-7025 6970 *fax* 020-7734 2613

Please note that Adam Spiegel Productions is now part of Stage Entertainment UK Ltd (**www.stage-entertainment.com**).

Squaredeal Productions Ltd

24 De Beauvoir Square, London N1 4LE
tel 020-7249 5966 *fax* 020-7275 7553
email jenny@jennytopper.com
website www.jennytopper.com
Director Jenny Topper

Production details: Established in 2003. An independent theatre producer staging on average 2-3 productions annually and performing in the West End and 20 theatre venues across the UK. Recent productions include: *The Clean House* (10-week

tour); *Martha, Josie and Chinese Elvis* (12-week tour); *Duet for One* (West End).

Casting procedures: Does not hold general auditions. Will accept letters (with CVs and photographs) from actors previously unknown to the company, sent by post or by email. Offers Equity-approved contracts as negotiated through TMA. Rarely has the opportunity to cast disabled actors.

Barrie Stacey UK Productions

7-8 Shaldon Mansions, 132 Charing Cross Road, London WC2H 0LA
tel 020-7386 6220/4128 *fax* 020-7836 2949
email hopkinstacey@aol.com
Director Barrie Stacey *Stage Director* Tony Joseph

Production details: Founded in 1966. Specialises in children's musicals and songbook concerts. Stages 24 productions annually with 100 performances during the course of the year. Tours to 8 different theatres in Southern England, including the London area. In general 8 actors are involved in each production. Recent productions include: *West End to Broadway* and *Movie Memories*. Offers non-Equity contracts and does not subscribe to the Equity Pension Scheme.

Casting procedures: All casting is done in-house. Holds general auditions. Casting breakdowns are available on request. Welcomes letters (with CVs and photographs) but not email submissions. Advises actors: "Don't be grand when just starting." Actively encourages applications from disabled actors and promotes the use of inclusive casting.

Stage Further Productions Ltd

Westgate, Stansted Road, Eastbourne BN22 8LG
tel (01323) 739478 *fax* (01323) 736127
email info@stagefurther.co.uk
Director Garth Harrison *Producer* David Nott *Artistic Director* Keith Myers

Production details: Founded in 1985. Produces plays and pantomimes for its repertory seasons and national tours. Also provides entertainment and shows to the cruise industry. Stages 10 productions annually and performs in around 18 different venues, including arts centres and theatres nationwide and cruise vessels. In general 6 actors are involved in each production. Recent productions include: *Anybody for Murder* and *Dead of Night*.

Casting procedures: Holds general auditions. Casting breakdowns are available via *PCR*, *The Stage* and from agents. Welcomes letters (with CVs and photographs) but not email submissions. Invitations to view individual actors' websites are also accepted.

Stanhope Productions Ltd

4th Floor, 80/81 St. Martins Lane, London WC2N 4AA
tel 020-7240 3098 *fax* 020-7504 8656
email admin@stanhopeprod.com
Director/Producer Kim Poster

Production details: Founded in 2001. Theatrical producing company. Stages 4-5 productions annually and gives 576 performances during the course of the year. Tours to 2-4 different theatres, primarily in the West End and London area. In general 18 actors are involved in each production. Recent productions include: *All My Sons, A View from the Bridge, Prick Up Your Ears, Carousel, Fiddler on the Roof, Summer and Smoke, Epitaph for George Dillon, A Woman of No Importance,* and *Brand.* Offers SOLT/Equity approved contracts.

Casting procedures: Uses freelance casting directors. Holds general auditions. Casting breakdowns are available via Equity Job Information Service. Will consider applications from disabled actors to play disabled characters.

Tenth Planet Productions
Medius House, 2 Sheraton Street, London W1F 8B
tel 020-7297 9474 *fax* 020-7439 3584
email admin@10thplanetproductions.com
website www.10thplanetproductions.com
Artistic Director Alexander Holt *Literary Manager* Mark Underwood *Associate Directors* Susan Harriet, Alex Scrivenor

Production details: Founded in 1998, the company has produced more than 30 productions to date. Stages 4-6 productions annually and presents 100-150 performances during the course of the year. Tours to 2-6 different regional theatres in the UK; also tours internationally in association with Sh! Productions Co (its sister company), performing dinner theatre in the Emirates. Performs in site-specific locations such as the Rose Theatre in London. For the past few years the company has been resident Upstairs at the Gatehouse in London. In general 4-8 actors are involved in each production. Recent productions include: *Trestle At Pope Lick Creek* (in association with the Royal Exchange); *Kafka's Dick*; *Absurd Person Singular; Bedroom Farce; Playhouse Creatures Keeler* (in association with Paul Nicholas). 2007/8 productions include: *Black Ajax; Our Boys; Les Liaisons Dangereuses; Keeler* (tour). Offers non-Equity contracts and does not subscribe to the Equity Pension Scheme.

Casting procedures: Holds general auditions. Actors should write in response to advertisements only, or consult the website for information on forthcoming productions. Casting breakdowns are available via *SBS, PCR,* CastNet and Castweb (see entry under *The Spotlight, casting directories and information services* on page 367). Showreels and invitations to view individual actors' websites are also accepted. Advises that the company principally casts NCDT-trained actors or well-established actors with demonstrable experience. As it is unable to retain submissions on file, actors should only write in when casting is advertised, or telephone first. Will consider applications from disabled actors to play disabled characters.

UK Productions
Churchmill House, Ockford Road, Godalming, Surrey GU7 0NB
tel (01483) 423600 *fax* (01483) 418486
email mail@ukproductions.co.uk
website www.ukproductions.co.uk
Directors Martin Dodd, Peter Frosdick *Administrator/ Casting Assistant* Derek Raper

Production details: Established 1995. Produce pantomimes and musicals for No. 1 touring. (See entry under *Pantomime producers* on page 210.) Produces 3 musicals a year, each touring around the UK and Ireland to large scale theatres for 30-35 weeks. Cast size is around 27-30 performers. Offers non-Equity contracts ("roughly in line with Equity") and does not subscribe to the Equity Pension Scheme. Recent productions include: *Seven Brides for Seven Brothers, 42nd Street, Disney's Beauty & The Beast, South Pacific.*

Casting procedures: Casting is done in-house. Does not hold general auditions. Casting breakdowns are distributed via Spotlight or direct to agents. Welcomes performance notices but not any other unsolicited form of correspondence. "Unsolicited CVs are generally a waste of time." Will consider applications from disabled actors to play characters with disabilities.

Anthony Vander Elst Productions
The Studio, 14 College Road, Bromley BR1 3NS
tel 020-8466 5580
Director Anthony Vander Elst

Established in 1977. Produces 1-2 productions per year touring the UK. Recent productions include: *Appearances* (Mayfair Theatre, London); *The Teddy Bears Picnic* (Chester Gateway Theatre); and *Last of the Red Hot Lovers* (London). Unsolicited approaches from actors are discouraged. Offers TMA/Equity approved contracts.

West End International
The Old Brewhouse, Chesham Road, Wigginton, Hertfordshire HP23 6EH
tel (01442) 824557
email info@westendinternational.com
website www.westendinternational.com
Directors Martin Yates, Alison Price

Concert and theatre producers. Will accept casting enquiries and letters (with CVs and photographs) from actors previously unknown to the company, sent by post or email. Does not welcome unsolicited showreels.

Mounting a production without a base theatre

Graham Cowley

So. There's a play you're desperate to do, but you have no theatre. You're in one of two situations: either you are a funded company with good relationships with producing or touring theatres, or it's just you on your own.

Out of Joint started ten years ago. Max Stafford-Clark was about to leave the Royal Court after 13 years; he'd spent all his working life up until then producing new plays, and needed an environment in which that work could continue. As the former Artistic Director of The Traverse, Joint Stock and the Royal Court, and with an international reputation, he could have been forgiven for assuming that funding would be readily available for a new venture such as this. But the fledgling Out of Joint was in competition for the meagre Arts Council project funds along with everyone else, and its early years were as hand-to-mouth as those of any new company. There was no office, so Max and Sonia Friedman, the company's first producer, set up productions and booked tours from their front rooms; blind eyes were turned as small quantities of Royal Court stationery disappeared; and friends were persuaded to give help and advice for no payment.

Financially, the early years were a balancing act between Arts Council Touring grants, stretched as far as they would go, and co-production deals with producing theatres. For the first few shows this was the Royal Court, but since then Out of Joint has co-produced with other theatres as well: Hampstead, the Young Vic, the Soho Theatre, the National, the Liverpool Everyman and Playhouse, and the Abbey, Dublin. Out of Joint co-productions usually take a straightforward form. Both partners agree a pre-production budget, covering the rehearsal costs, wages and fees, building the set, acquiring costumes and props and generally assembling the show. They agree to split this cost in some fashion – either 50/50 or in a ratio reflecting how long each company will have use of the play. If Out of Joint is touring for eight weeks and the run at the Soho Theatre is four weeks, there is a case for an unequal split of the cost of mounting the play. Then, each partner takes full responsibility for the running costs and income while the show is under its management. In Out of Joint's case, this means we pay the wages and all other costs while the show is touring, and our co-producer does the same while it plays in London (or Liverpool, or Dublin).

This way of working has many virtues. For both parties, it represents an opportunity to get more value from a pre-production budget – either by saving money, or, more commonly, by enhancing the total budget available. For the company, it brings not only financial stability but also a temporary home. Having an office and a rehearsal room is all very well, but theatre people like to belong to a theatre. For the theatre, it means that their programme is enhanced by a play or project which would not otherwise have been available to them. And whoever was the initiator, both parties feel an ownership of the play. This is vital, although it involves a good deal of give and take on each side. Where will you rehearse? Who builds the set? Can the theatre contribute a stage manager? All these things are important in encouraging a feeling of joint ownership.

Now, happily, Out of Joint receives regular funding from the Arts Council, and has its own office and photocopier. But early habits of frugality remain: the company has tiny overhead costs, employs only five full-time staff and still enjoys co-producing. A touring company cannot run up substantial debts: with the only tangible assets being some lighting equipment and an ageing van, there is no security for an overdraft. So preserving financial security is crucial.

Financial security can seem like a pipe dream for those at the sharper end of producing. Together with some good friends, I have been putting on plays independently for several years, under the banner of Two's Company. This year we received a small Arts Council grant, for the first time. But by then we had established a way of working with some of London's small theatres which enabled us (just) to operate.

So – you have a play. The first thing is to secure the rights. For an existing play in a small theatre, all you'll get is a licence for your production dates. This may well mean that you need to have a theatre. The first question to ask is, where should it ideally go? It's by no means unknown for plays with epic themes and huge casts to be seen in tiny pub theatres, but perhaps this one needs more space, more facilities? Or is this three-hander capable of filling 250 seats? Maybe we should keep it to 70 ... *Time Out* and *Contacts*, between them, have the most complete lists of the theatres available. How many do you know? It's easier to have a view about a theatre if you've seen a show there. If you don't think your play will fit the policies and criteria of the Bush, Hampstead, the Almeida or the Royal Court, or you don't want to wait (sometimes) a long time for them to tell you that, you can approach one of the fringe theatres. If you've thought carefully about the match between your play and the theatre, you'll have a better chance of securing a suitable venue.

Most theatres are unfunded, so if they show interest, and have a production slot that fits your dates, they will charge you a weekly rent. At this point you'll need to finalise your budget. You know how many actors you need and how much you can pay them. The budget for a set, costumes and props – well, how long is a piece of string? Priorities are all-important. If your play needs army uniforms, you'll almost certainly have to hire them, so allow enough for that. On the other hand, to secure a clever designer, it's often worth sacrificing some money from the physical budget to add to his/her fee – inventiveness can add huge value to your budget.

Clarity about exactly what you can expect from the theatre in return for your rent is important to establish. What hours can you use it for? Can you work all night on the get-in, or are there neighbours who object? What staff, if any, will work with you, and what will they do? How long does it take to move the seating, and who knows how it all works? And almost most important of all, what marketing support will the theatre provide? There might be a season brochure, but how many are produced and where do they go? How does the box office operate, and what figures will you get? And so on. Theatres vary enormously in what they can offer, how much they will support you and how welcoming they are.

Even the smallest show needs some sort of funds to operate with. Even though the box office receipts will be an important source of income (you hope), you can't expect the theatre to pay the takings over until they are very sure you've paid everything that you owe them, so you'll need enough money to keep cash flowing. Nothing demoralises a cast of actors more than being told you can't pay them yet. And while a lot can be done with the

Theatre

beg/borrow/steal method, there are some things you just have to pay for. So you apply to the Arts Council, charitable trusts, businesses, ask friends and relations to give you money. This all takes a long time, so start as soon as you can. Please don't remortgage your house.

In London, particularly, press reviews can be of enormous importance as to whether or not your production is a success. It's really worth engaging a press rep who knows his/her stuff. That, by the way, is a very difficult judgement to make until you've worked with somebody, so see if you can get some informed opinions about the person you're contemplating hiring. If s/he can get you advance press publicity, that's wonderful, but what you really need is for the critics to come, and to come early – it's no use their appearing after the run is over. Some shows take off like a rocket; some burn slowly for a bit before catching alight; and lots more need an audience to be laboriously reached and persuaded to come. Sometimes, it seems, one by one. But whichever it is, your job isn't over until every seat is sold.

So why do it? Because there is a play you believe in, a director of genius, stunningly talented actors – or at least, some of those things. I firmly believe that if you're going to produce a play, you've got to love it. The response of the critics and the audience is personal, and therefore unpredictable – so it's important to be able to say at the end, "Well, I liked it." And, of course, there is nothing like the feeling you get when you look round the theatre bar, or the dressing room, or indeed the auditorium, and think, "All these people are here because I brought them together." Good luck!

Graham Cowley is Producer with Out of Joint, and also Two's Company. He was previously with the Theatre of Comedy Company, the Royal Court Theatre (on whose behalf he transferred a string of hit plays to the West End), the Half Moon Theatre, and Joint Stock Theatre Group.

Middle and smaller-scale companies

This section covers a huge range of companies: from the very prestigious, often subsidised (like Out of Joint), which usually only perform in theatres with around 500 seats (or more), to the very small, which frequently have little or no public subsidy and perform wherever they can find a paying audience. The bigger companies operate much like the commercial 'big boys' in the previous section – except they tend to have longer rehearsal periods. The smaller companies rarely use casting directors, tend to do only one or two performances in each venue, and often pay below Equity rates – and it's probable that you'll have to help with get-ins and get-outs. It's very hard work and you have to rise to the peak of performance every time in spite of travelling in cramped vans, sharing unsatisfactory digs and rarely, if ever, being seen by anyone who could advance your career. However, some very prestigious companies have grown from such very small beginnings – and a number of now highly respected directors, playwrights and actors have started this way. It is important to assess the potential quality of the product (as well as the pay, and terms and conditions) before accepting such a job.

As such companies tend to come and go with great rapidity, the listings only contain companies that have been in existence for three years or more.

Note Some of the companies listed are members of the Independent Theatre Council (ITC) – **www.itc-arts.org**.

7:84 Theatre Company Scotland

Film City Glasgow, 4 Summertown Road,
Glasgow G51 2LY
tel 0141-445 7245
email admin@784theatre.com
website www.784theatre.com
Artistic Director Lorenzo Mele

Due to the changing funding structures in Scottish theatre, 7:84 has now ceased trading.

20 Stories High Theatre Company

6 Marmaduke Street, Liverpool L7 1PB
tel 0151-260 5185
email info@20storieshigh.org.uk
website www.20storieshigh.org.uk
Directors Julie Samuels, Keith Saha *Projects Coordinator* Tessa Buddle

Production details: Established in 2006. Creates dynamic, challenging theatre which attracts new audiences, artists and participants. Stages 2 projects annually, with around 80 performances in 60 arts centres, theatres, and educational and community venues in the North West and nationally. In general 2-4 actors are involved in each production. Offers Equity-approved contracts as negotiated through ITC. Also participates in the Equity Pension Scheme. Recent productions include: *Babul and the Blue Bear* by Keith Saha (co-production with Contact Theatre and Horse & Bamboo – national tour); and *Slow Time* by Roy Williams (North West tour).

Casting procedures: Holds general auditions; actors may write in May and October to request inclusion. Casting breakdowns are available from the website, Equity Job Information Service and *PCR*. Welcomes letters (with CVs and photographs) from individual actors previously unknown to the company, sent by post or email, and is happy to consider invitations to view individual actors' websites. Actively encourages applications from disabled actors and promotes the use of inclusive casting.

Actors of Dionysus (AOD)

14 Cuthbert Road, Brighton BN2 0EN
tel/fax (01273) 692604
email info@actorsofdionysus.com
website www.actorsofdionysus.com
Artistic Director Tamsin Shasha *Development Officer* Alice Booth

Production details: National and international touring company founded in 1993. A member of the ITC and Arts & Business, it currently receives no regular funding. Specialises in performing new adaptations of Ancient Greek drama through a fusion of poetry, music and movement. Has a strong educational focus and runs international summer schools. Stages 1-2 productions each year with an average annual total of 120-150 performances. Venues include arts centres, theatres (including Greek and Turkish theatres), and educational venues across the UK, Eire and Turkey. Also performs on cruise

Theatre

ships. In general 4-6 actors work on each production. Recent productions include: *Trojan Women* (2005), *Hippolytus* (2004), and *Oedipus* (2003 & 2006).

Casting procedures: Does not use freelance casting directors. Holds general auditions; actors should write to request inclusion in August and December. Casting breakdowns are available through the website and *PCR*. Does not welcome general submissions from actors but will accept invitations to view individual actors' websites. Offers non-Equity contracts. Actively encourages applications from disabled actors and promotes the use of inclusive casting.

Actors Touring Company (ATC)

The Tab Centre, 3 Godfrey Place, London E2 7NT
tel 020-7739 8298 *fax* 020-7033 7360
email atc@atctheatre.com
website www.atc-online.com
Artistic Director Bijan Sheibani *Executive Producer* Hannah Bentley

Production details: Established in 1979. 2 productions are staged annually, touring to arts centres and theatres and employing roughly 4-6 actors. Offers ITC/Equity approved contracts. Recent productions include: *A Brief History of Helen of Troy* (UK tour).

Casting procedures: Encourages applications from disabled actors and promotes the use of inclusive casting. Unsolicited approaches from actors are discouraged.

Admiration Theatre

PO Box 50255, London EC3A 5WA
tel 0870-765 1584 *fax* 0870-765 1594
email email@admirationtheatre.com
website www.admirationtheatre.co.uk
Director Jon Hewitt

Production details: Founded in 2001, the company stages 3-4 productions each year with an average annual total of 30 performances across theatres in London. Cast size varies from 2-8 actors. In September 2006, Admiration organised a residential theatre retreat in Gascony, in the South of France. An international group of actors was invited to spend 2 weeks in the countryside, working in a natural environment away from the distractions of the big city. The group's work was research into the creativity of the actor, in creating new material and characters, as well as work on more traditional text. Recent productions include: *Ubu Roi* (Courtyard Theatre, London) and *Seasons of Purity* (Theatro Technis, London).

Casting procedures: Uses freelance casting directors but sometimes holds general auditions. Welcomes letters and emails (with CVs and photographs) from actors previously unknown to the company. Will also accept showreels and invitations to view actors' websites.

ARC Theatre Ensemble

PO Box 1146, Barking, Essex IG11 9WB
tel 020-8594 1095
email carole@arctheatre.com
website www.arctheatre.com
Chief Executive Officer/Artistic Director Carole Pluckrose *Creative Director* Clifford Oliver (Olly)
Associate Directors Joss Bennathan, Jim Dunk, Thierry Lawson, Neville Lawrence OBE

Production details: Founded in 1984, Arc has built a strong core Management and Associate team bringing together an exceptional range of creative skills, educational experience and business and social expertise. The company is governed by an equally diverse and committed Board of Management. "We also benefit from a first-class pool of highly skilled, trained actors, storytellers, facilitators, workshop leaders, production managers and designers who are individually hand-picked to suit each programme or bespoke project." See the website for more details of its work.

Casting procedures: "To register your interest in working with Arc, please submit your details via the website. We will keep your details on record and contact you when a suitable opportunity arises. Alternatively you can email your details to our General Manager, Nita Bocking: **nita@arctheatre.com**."

Attic Theatre Company

Mitcham Library, 157 London Road, Mitcham CR24 2YR
tel/fax 020-8543 7838
email info@attictheatrecompany.com
website www.attictheatrecompany.com
Artistic Director Jenny Lee *Associate Director* Merhdad Seyf *Administrator* Teun Timmers *Booking & Finance Manager* Victoria Hibbs *Production Manager* Kate Reynolds

Production details: The company was formed in 1987 to produce high-quality theatre and develop audiences for new plays, musicals, reworked classics and contemporary plays with a cutting edge. Work is presented at Wimbledon Studio Theatre and other venues, and the company tours on average 1 production each year. Tours up to 15 venues across the UK annually; these include arts centres, theatres, educational venues and community venues. Cast size varies from 1-6 actors. For recent productions, refer to the website **www.attictheatre.com**.

Community work is an integral part of the company's vision. In recent years it has developed *Ma Kelly's Doorstep*, an entertaining show with a serious message on the topic of bogus callers, which tours to day centres and lunch clubs in London boroughs. The sequel is a show on home safety – *Ma Kelly Plays it Safe*. In 2004 the company produced a show celebrating age, with music, dance and drama – *It's the Ritz!*; in 2005, it collaborated with Croydon

Clocktower on *Dancing in The Dark* – a celebration of the lives of Croydon people during World War II.

Attic Theatre Young People's Company holds workshops for 11-15 year olds who meet every Wednesday evening in term time.

Casting procedures: Uses freelance casting directors. Does not hold general auditions and does not welcome casting enquiries or submissions from actors.

Badapple Theatre Company

PO Box 57, Green Hammerton, York YO26 8WQ
tel (01423) 339168
email office@badappletheatre.com
website www.badappletheatre.com
Director Kate Bramley

Production details: Founded in 1998. Specialises in new comedy and biography-based drama as well as documentary drama commissions. Stages between 2 and 5 productions per year at a local rural touring level or national arts centre/small- to mid-scale theatre level. Recent productions include: *Back to the Land Girls* (10-week tour 2010 across rural and arts venues; achieved 97% of audience capacity). Uses 6-8 actors per year.

Casting procedures: Uses *SBS* and direct mail castings to agencies. Actors with an interest in the company are free to contact the office at any time. Directors prefer to see actors in performance prior to castings, so welcomes updates of performances in the Yorkshire region that company directors would be able to attend.

Benchtours Productions Ltd

Bonnington Mill, 72 Newhaven Road, Edinburgh EH6 5QG
tel 0131-555 3585
email info@benchtours.com
website www.benchtours.com
Co-directors Peter Clerke, Catherine Gillard *General Manager* Ben Walmsley

Production details: Founded in 1991, Benchtours is Scotland's leading international touring ensemble. The company seeks to extend the boundaries of theatre and open it up to new and diverse audiences, and is committed to new writing, highly visual theatre, rural touring and disability work. Normally stages 2 productions each year with an average annual total of 40 performances. Tours to approximately 25-30 theatres, arts centres, educational venues and community venues across Scotland (including islands and Highlands) and Northern England each year. Benchtours also tours internationally – recently, to Poland and the USA. Recent national tours include: *The Emperor's Opera* and *Crowhurst*.

Casting procedures: Holds casting workshops in December each year, which the artistic directors invite selected actors to attend. Actors are advised to email CVs and cover letters in October/November. Benchtours offers Equity ITC contracts to all performers and actively encourages applications from disabled actors as part of its integrated casting policy.

Big Telly Theatre Company

Town Hall, The Crescent, Portstewart, Londonderry BT55 7AB
tel 028-7083 6473 *fax* 028-7083 2588
email info@big-telly.com
website www.big-telly.com
Director Zoë Seaton

Production details: Big Telly Theatre Company is Northern Ireland's longest established professional not-for-profit theatre company, formed in 1987 and based in Portstewart on the North Coast. The company produces theatre, interactive workshop programmes and community creativity projects, which mainly tour throughout Northern and Southern Ireland and international markets. It concentrates on the visual potential of theatre through fusion with other art forms such as dance, music, circus, magic and film to create a unique sense of spectacle. "Big Telly's work is driven by a determination to offer audiences entertainment that surprises, stimulates and ignites the imagination."

Casting procedures: Does not use freelance casting directors. Casting breakdowns are available through the website and Equity Job Information Service, and are also released to agents. Welcomes submissions (with CVs and photographs) from actors previously unknown to the company sent by post or email. Invitations to view individual actors' websites are also accepted. Offers ITC/Equity contracts, and endeavours to employ disabled actors when casting for disabled characters.

Boilerhouse

Gateway Theatre, The Arts Quarter, 40-44 Elm Row, Edinburgh EH7 4AH
tel/fax 0131-556 5644
email paul@boilerhouse.org.uk
website www.boilerhouse.org.uk
Director Paul Pinson *Producer* Chloe Dear *General Manager* Jon Clarke

Production details: Founded in 1992, Boilerhouse is an Edinburgh-based performance company which has developed a reputation as a leading creator of exciting, high-quality work in non-theatre spaces. Over the last 12 years, work has been produced in clubs, car parks, warehouses, Pacific ocean-front wharves, London's Docklands, derelict buildings, churches and under a motorway bridge. Boilerhouse aims to create performance events of spectacle and meaning. We work with artists from an extensive range of disciplines in the development of medium- to large-scale outdoor and street-theatre productions. Work has involved collaborations with award-

winning novelists (including Irvine Welsh, Alan
Warner and Duncan McLean), poets, playwrights,
dancers, performers, composers, designers,
choreographers, musicians, metal sculptors, pyro-
technicians, DJs, trapeze artists and car mechanics.

The company normally stages 2 productions each
year totalling approximately 15-30 performances, and
tours to a variety of venues across the UK, Europe
and New Zealand. The cast size can be anything from
2 to 12 actors. Recent productions include: *The
Bridge* (large-scale outdoor show, with aerial
choreography, live and pre-recorded film,
pyrotechnics and performed in Scotland and France –
with audiences of up to 10,000 per show); and
Running Girl (large-scale indoor promenade
production with a cast of 8, including a performer
running throughout the show, moving film-screens
and live music).

Casting procedures: Does not use freelance casting
directors; actors may write requesting inclusion in the
next round of auditions at any time. Will accept
letters, emails, showreels, CVs and photographs from
actors previously unknown to the company, but
advises all applicants to do their research first and
only to send details if they are sure that they are right
for Boilerhouse's style of work.

Border Crossings

13 Bankside, Enfield EN2 8BN
tel 020-8829 8928 *fax* 020-8366 5239
email info@bordercrossings.org.uk
website www.bordercrossings.org.uk
Director Michael Walling

Production details: Established in 1995.
International company working in theatre and
combined arts that creates dynamic performances by
fusing many forms of world theatre, dance and
music. Stages 1 or 2 productions per year touring to
up to 15 venues including arts centres and theatres.
Roughly 4-9 actors used in each production. Recent
credits include: *Re-Orientations* (Soho Theatre 2010);
The Dilemma of a Ghost (2007); *Bullie's House*
(Riverside Studios); *Orientations* (Oval House); *Dis-
Orientations* (Riverside Studios) and *Double Tongue*
(UK tour). "We don't offer Equity contracts,
although our own contracts are modelled on the ITC/
Equity contract, and we usually pay above the
minimum." Does not subscribe to the Equity Pension
Scheme.

Casting procedures: Welcomes letters (with CVs and
photographs) from actors previously unknown to the
company if sent by post, but not by email. Invitations
to view individual actors' websites and showreels are
accepted. Actively encourages applications from
disabled actors and promotes the use of inclusive
casting.

Borderline Theatre Co.

North Harbour Street, Ayr KA8 8AA
tel (01292) 281010 *fax* (01292) 263825

email enquiries@borderlinetheatre.co.uk
website www.borderlinetheatre.co.uk
Producer Edward Jackson

Production details: Founded in 1974, the company
stages 2-3 productions each year with an average
annual total of 60-90 performances. Each tour
normally runs for 31 performances across 13 different
venues. Venues include arts centres and theatres
across Scotland. In general 4 actors work on each
production. Recent productions include: *Tally's
Blood*, *Women on the Verge of HRT* and *Angel's Share*.

Casting procedures: Does not use freelance casting
directors. Currently releases casting breakdowns to
agents, but may publish these on the website in
future. Welcomes submissions (with CVs and
photographs) from actors previously unknown to the
company sent by post or email. Also accepts
showreels.

Bottlefed Ensemble

13 Sydney Road, London N10 2LR
mobile (07751) 420344
email info@bottlefed.org
website www.bottlefed.org
Artistic Directors Kathrin Yvonne Bigler, Rebeca
Fernandez Lopez

Production details: A London-based physical theatre
ensemble founded in 2004 and co-run by Kathrin
Yvonne Bigler (writer/director) and Rebeca
Fernandez Lopez (choreographer/performer), who
merge their European tanztheatre background with
British approaches to improvisation and physical
theatre practice. "The ensemble's creative process is
rooted in durational improvisation and telling stories
through the performers' bodies without a big
emphasis on technical support."

In recent years Bottlefed has been run as a laboratory
for regular research, development and
experimentation, and as a platform for cross-art-form
collaborations. In each project the company works
with a defined group of international artists who
commit to the ensemble as freelance collaborators on
a long-term basis. Also works in Education and
Corporate, delivering creative workshops and
performance projects for professional performers,
young people and adults in school and community
settings, theatres and universities across the UK and
internationally. Recent projects include: *Return to
Reason* (London & Edinburgh Fringe Festival, 2007;
nominated for the 'Total Theatre Award for Best
Original Work by an Ensemble'); and *Camille*
(London, 2006; nominated for 'Best Direction' at the
Lost Theatre Festival in the same year).

Casting procedures: Holds general auditions; actors
may write at any time, and are invited to join the
mailing list for information about upcoming
auditions and workshops. Welcomes letters (with
CVs & photographs) from individual actors
previously unknown to the company if sent by post

or email; also accepts showreels but prefers not to receive invitations to view individual actors' websites. Rarely (or never) has the opportunity to cast disabled actors. "We cast performers to join the ensemble on a long-term basis (which includes regular training, public improvisation events and performances) and not just for individual productions."

Bridge House Theatre

Myton Road, Warwick CV34 6PP
tel (01926) 776437
email ask@warwickschool.org
website www.bridgehousetheatre.co.uk
Director Alison Sutcliffe *Performing Arts Manager* Bronwyn Robertson

Production details: Founded in 2005. Professional theatre-in-residence twice-yearly at Warwick School's purpose-built theatre. Stages 2 productions annually with around 35 performances. Up to 10 actors are involved in each production. Recent productions include: *A Christmas Carol, A Doll's House, The Tempest, An Inspector Calls, Educating Rita, Macbeth, As You Like It, Death of a Salesman.*

Casting procedures: Casting breakdowns are occasionally available from Spotlight Interactive. Welcomes letters (with CVs and photographs) from individual actors previously unknown to the company, sent by post only; will consider invitations to view individual actors' websites. Rarely, or never, has the opportunity to cast disabled actors. "We prefer Midlands-based actors for logistical / financial reasons."

Cahoots Theatre Company

St Martin's Theatre, West Street,
London WC2N 9NH
tel 020-8743 7777 *mobile* (07711) 245848
email ds@denisesilvey.com
website www.denisesilvey.com
Artistic Director Denise Silvey

Production details: Founded in 1999. Produces theatre, cabaret and CD recordings, as well as acting as a general management and press agent (see also DS Personal Management entry under Agents). Stages 3-4 productions a year, with 100 performances over 15 venues (arts centres, theatres and cabaret venues) in London, Edinburgh and New York. Productions may have from 1 to 17 performers involved. Offers Equity-approved and non-Equity contracts. Recent credits include: *A Clockwork Orange, Rain Pryor in Concert,* and *The Translucent Frogs of Quuup.*

Casting procedures: Uses freelance casting directors. Also publishes casting breakdowns on the Equity JIS and PCR. Welcomes emails (but not letters) with CVs and photographs from individuals previously unknown to the company. Does not welcome showreels, but is happy to receive invitations to view actors' websites. Will consider applications from disabled actors to play characters with disabilities.

Cambridge Shakespeare Company

11 Crossways House, Anstey Way, Trumpington,
Cambridge CB2 9JZ
tel (01223) 842293
email cambridgeshakespeare@hotmail.co.uk
website www.cambridgeshakespeare.com
Artistic Director Dr David Crilly *Associate Directors* Simon Bell, David Rowan

Production details: The Festival Company was established in Oxford in 1988 by Artistic Director Dr David Crilly. The main focus for the Company is the annual Cambridge Shakespeare Festival, which runs throughout July and August. Situated in the gardens of the Colleges of Cambridge University, its pastoral setting is one of the loveliest in the world.

Cardboard Citizens

26 Hanbury Street, London E1 6QR
tel 020-7247 7747 *fax* 020-7650 0002
email mail@cardboardcitizens.org.uk
website www.cardboardcitizens.org.uk
Artistic Director Adrian Jackson *Associate Director* Sarah Levinsky

Production details: The UK's only homeless people's professional theatre company. Specialises in making forum theatre, but has broadened its scope to the provision of a range of performance-based cultural actions with, for and by homeless and previously homeless people. Productions include: *Woyzeck* – national tour; *Timon of Athens* – national tour with RSC; *Visible* – national tour, 'down and out' community production.

Casting procedures: Uses in-house casting directors. Holds general auditions; actors may write at any time requesting inclusion. Casting breakdowns are publicly available. Welcomes letters, CVs and photographs from individual actors previously unknown to the company, sent via post or email. Also welcomes showreels and invitations to view individual actors' websites. Offers Equity approved contracts. Actively encourages applications from disabled people and promotes the use of inclusive casting.

The Castle Players

PO Box 17, Barnard Castle, Co. Durham DL12 9YS
tel 0800-074 7080 *fax* (01325) 321473
email fred.traice@googlemail.com
website www.castleplayers.org.uk
Artistic Director Simon Pell *Associate Director* Jill Cole
Commercial Director Frederick Traice

Production details: A community theatre company limited by guarantee. Established in 1987. Undertakes major open-air summer productions in specially constructed tiered-seat theatre. Stages 1 outdoor production and 1 touring production annually. Recent productions include: *Measure for Measure, The Two Gentlemen of Verona* and *Twelfth Night* in the main house; and *Wind in the Willows, Shakespeare – the Cabaret* and *Dracula Revamped* in the studio.

Theatre

Casting procedures: Uses in-house casting directors and holds general auditions; actors should write in January to request inclusion. Will accept unsolicited CVs and photographs sent by email only. Rarely or never has the opportunity to cast disabled actors.

Cavalcade Theatre Company

57 Pelham Road, London SW19 1NW
tel 020-8540 3513 *fax* 020-8540 2243
Directors Graham Ashe, Kim Joyce, Carol Crowther
Touring Manager Colin Agate

Production details: Founded in 1972. Stages an average of 5 productions each year – an annual total of around 200 performances. Tours approximately 20 venues per year, including arts centres, theatres, and outdoor, educational and community venues throughout the UK and Ireland. Also performs at conferences and exhibitions and covers publicity and PR events. In general 8 actors work on each production. Recent productions include: *Alice in Wonderland, The Adventures of Brer Rabbit,* pantomimes, musicals and some small-scale plays.

Casting procedures: Does not use freelance casting directors. Sometimes holds general auditions; actors may write at any time to request inclusion. Casting breakdowns are available in *PCR, The Stage* and through agents. Welcomes submissions (with CVs and photographs) from actors previously unknown to the company if sent by post, but does not welcome email enquiries. Also accepts invitations to view individual actors' websites.

Chain Reaction Theatre Company

3 Mills Studios, Sugar House Yard, Sugar House Lane, London E15 2QS
tel 020-8534 0007 *fax* 020-8534 0007
email mail@chainreactiontheatre.co.uk
website www.chainreactiontheatre.co.uk
Key personnel Tuhina Ahmed (Administrator), Anjali Rundle (Project Manager)

Production details: Established in 1994. An award-winning theatre company producing informative, entertaining and thought-provoking theatre, workshops and video productions for people of all ages. Aims to create quality accessible theatre experiences, and engage audiences with writing and performances that explore contemporary issues and perceptions of everyday life. Currently has 12 educational shows in its repertoire, each designed for a specific age range from 5 to 16 years. Performances tackle sensitive and controversial topics including drugs awareness, sexual health, bullying, healthy eating and exercise, and emotional wellbeing. Also designs bespoke pieces of theatre and video productions for a range of professionals, which may be used at corporate workshops, training events and conferences, and works too in TIE and Outreach.

Since 2003 has produced original musical theatre for adult audiences. Its first production, *Everyone Loves*

Me, won an award for best musical and its most recent production, *Pretty Please,* premiered in London in 2007.

Tours up to 4 shows each year. Recent productions include: *Food 4 Thought; It's Your Body; Movin' On Up;* and *Totally Together.* For more information, contact Sarah Choppen.

Casting procedures: Uses freelance casting directors and sometimes holds general auditions. Actors may write in July to request inclusion.

Chalkfoot Theatre Arts

c/o Channel Theatre Productions, Penistone House, 5 High Street, St Lawrence, Ramsgate, Kent CT11 0QH
tel (01843) 587950
email info@chalkfoot.org.uk
website www.chalkfoot.org.uk
Artistic Director Philip Dart

Production details: A small-scale touring company making work for a range of venues from village halls to heritage sites. Artistic programme is subject to funding.

Casting procedures: "We regret that we are unable to hold general auditions or see actors outside of designated casting periods (unless local to Kent). Agents' information services such as Spotlight are normally supplied with casting breakdowns. We cannot mail individuals with submissions. Please send an sae if you would like us to return your photo."

Channel Theatre Productions

Penistone House, 5 High Street, St Lawrence, Ramsgate, Kent CT11 0QH
tel (01843) 587950
email info@channel-theatre.co.uk
Directors Philip Dart, Claudia Dart

Production details: A creative production company making work for many different venues and communities.

Casting procedures: "We regret that we are unable to hold general auditions or see actors outside of designated casting periods. Agents' information services such as Spotlight are normally supplied with casting breakdowns. Please send an sae if you would like us to return your photo."

Cheek by Jowl

Stage Door, Barbican Theatre, Silk Street, London EC2Y 8DS
email info@cheekbyjowl.com
Artistic Directors Declan Donnellan, Nick Ormerod

Production details: The company was founded in 1981 by Declan Donnellan and Nick Ormerod. The name conveys an intimacy between the actors, the audience and the text; the phrase 'cheek by jowl' is quoted from *A Midsummer Night's Dream* ("Follow! Nay, I'll go with thee cheek by jowl" (Act III Sc II))

Recent productions include: *Cymbeline* and *Three Sisters*.

Casting procedures: "Like the vast majority of other British theatre companies, our actors are on fixed-term contracts. However, many actors come back regularly to work with us. For each new Cheek by Jowl production, a Casting Director is appointed. Please do not send unsolicited CVs as we are unable to accept them."

Cherub Company London
9 Park Hill, London W5 2JS
tel 020-8723 4358 *fax* 020-8248 0318
email mgieleta@cherub.org.uk
website www.cherub.org.uk
Director Michael Gieleta *Producer* Rebecca Miller

Production details: Founded in 1973, Cherub stages an average of 3 productions a year, with 40 performances across 5 theatre venues in the South East region. Roughly 10 actors are employed for each production. Does not offer Equity approved contracts.

Casting procedures: Uses freelance casting directors; also holds general auditions from time to time. Casting breakdowns are available by sending the company an sae. Welcomes letters (with CVs and photographs) from actors previously unknown to the company, but does not welcome these by email. Happy to receive both showreels and invitations to view actors' websites. Actively encourages applications from disabled actors and promotes the use of inclusive casting.

Chicken Shed Theatre
Chase Side, Southgate, London N14 4PE
tel 020-8351 6161 *fax* 020-8292 0202
email info@chickenshed.org.uk
website www.chickenshed.org.uk
Artistic Director Mary Ward *Associate Director of Music* David Carey *Associate Director & Education Manager* Jonathan Morton *Director of Education & Outreach* Paul Morrall *Artistic Development Director* Louise Perry *Director of Dance* Christine Niering *Key personnel* John Bull (Executive Consultant), Jo Collins (Director of Music), David Balcombe (Chief Executive)

Production details: An inspirational theatre company that produces "beautiful and memorable" performances by working on the basis that everyone should be included, regardless of background, age, race or ability. Runs a Children's and Youth Theatre for 800 young people, operates 3 nationally accredited Education courses, engages in community Outreach projects, and has established a growing network of satellite 'Sheds' across the country (plus 2 in Russia).

Produces on average 3 productions in the main house (seats 300) and 4 in the studio theatre (seats 100). Recent productions include: *A Christmas Carol*; "as

the mother of a brown boy ... "; *Vanity Fair*; *Tales from the Shed*; and *Seachange*.

Casting procedures: Uses in-house casting directors. Does not hold general auditions; actors may write at any time to request inclusion. Welcomes letters (with CVs and photographs) from actors previously unknown to the company if sent by post or email, but no showreels please. Accepts invitations to view individual actors' websites. Offers Equity approved contracts. Actively encourages applications from disabled actors, and promotes the use of inclusive casting.

Clean Break
2 Patshull Road, London NW5 2LB
tel 020-7482 8600 *fax* 020-7482 8611
email general@cleanbreak.org.uk
website www.cleanbreak.org.uk
Executive Director Lucy Perman *Administrative Producer* Helen Pringle

Production details: Clean Break was founded in 1979 by 2 women prisoners at HMP Askham Grange. The company commissions professional writers to produce new work looking at issues faced by women with experience of the criminal justice system. The company generally stages 1 production, presenting 35 performances each year. Tours to around 5 theatres and prisons across England and Scotland annually. The average cast size is 3-4. Recent productions include: *Black Crows* by Linda Brogan (Arcola Theatre), *Mercy Fine* by Shelley Silas (Southwark Playhouse, Birmingham Rep, York Theatre Royal, Salisbury Playhouse) and *Compact Failure* by Jennifer Farmer (Arcola Theatre, Contact Manchester, York Theatre Royal, Traverse Edinburgh). Offers ITC/Equity approved contracts and does not subscribe to the Equity Pension Scheme.

Casting procedures: Uses freelance casting directors but also holds general auditions in Oct/Nov. Casting breakdowns are available via the website, Equity Job Information Service, *PCR* and *The Stage*. Welcomes letters, CVs and photographs from actors, but prefers not to be contacted by email and does not accept unsolicited showreels. "Clean Break only employs women (section 7(2)(a) of the Sex Discrimination Act applies). We also actively seek to work with artists with an offending background." Actively encourages applications from disabled actors and promotes the use of inclusive casting.

Clod Ensemble
Unit 1-2 Crown Works, Temple Street,
London E2 6QQ
tel 020-7749 0555 *fax* 020-7749 0597
email admin@clodensemble.com
website www.clodensemble.com
Artistic Directors Suzy Willson, Paul Clark *General Manager* Anneliese Graham

Production details: A small to midscale company established in 1996. Creates theatre, music and performance events, workshops and courses in London, the UK and internationally. Stages on average 1 production each year in the main house; also works in Outreach and Community. Recent productions include: *Red Ladies* and *Greed*.

Casting procedures: Producer does the casting. Sometimes holds general auditions and actors should write in winter and spring to request inclusion. Welcomes unsolicited CVs and photographs if sent by email. Also accepts invitations to view individual actors' websites. Offers Equity approved contracts as negotiated through ITC. Actively encourages applications from disabled actors and promotes the use of inclusive casting.

Close for Comfort Theatre Company
34 Boleyn Walk, Leatherhead, Surrey KT22 7HU
tel (01372) 378613
email close4comf@aol.com
website www.closeforcomforttheatre.co.uk
Director Janet Gill *Co-director* Glenn Johnson

Production details: Founded in 2001. "Takes theatre to living rooms across the country." Stages 3-4 productions each year, averaging an annual total of 30-40 performances in the same number of private homes in the South East, South West and the Midlands. 2 actors work on each production. Recent productions include: *Dossier: Ronald Ackerman in a House in Bristol.*

Casting procedures: Does not use freelance casting directors or hold general auditions.

Cloud Nine Theatre Productions
5 Marden Terrace, Cullercoats,
North Shields NE30 4PD
tel 0191-253 1901
email cloudninetheatre@blueyonder.co.uk
website www.cloudninetheatre.co.uk
Artistic Director Peter Mortimer *Associate Director* Colette Stroud

Production details: Established in 1997. Dedicated to commissioning and producing new work from Northern playwrights. Has produced plays by more than 20 Northern dramatists, in leading North-East venues. On average stages 2 productions in the main house and 1 in the studio each year. Recent productions include: *Selkie – A Modern Myth with Live Sea Music* by Valerie Laws (The Sage, Gateshead then touring the North); *The Laughter Factory* (2007, Touring Sketch Show).

Casting procedures: Uses in-house casting directors. Holds general auditions and actors may write at any time requesting inclusion. Casting breakdowns are available from the website; also from the company's quarterly newsletter. Welcomes letters (with CVs and photographs) from actors previously unknown to the company if sent by post, but not by email. Does not accept showreels or invitations to view individual actors' websites. Offers Equity approved contracts as

negotiated with ITC. Will consider applications from disabled actors, but opportunities to cast disabled actors are rare. "As a North East based company, we tend to cast with actors from this region, and generally would not encourage other actors to apply unless specifically requested."

Company of Angels
126 Cornwall Road, London SE1 8TQ
tel 020-7928 2811
email info@companyofangels.co.uk
website www.companyofangels.co.uk
Director John Retallack *General Manager* Vanessa Fagan

Production details: Established in 1999. New and experimental work for young audiences, with a particular focus on new European writing. Stages 1-4 productions annually, performing in arts centres, theatres, educational and community venues throughout the UK. In general 4-6 actors are involved in each production. Offers Equity-approved contracts as negotiated through ITC. Recent productions include: *Truckstop* (Edinburgh Festival and 3-month small- to mid-scale tour); Theatre Cafe Festival (venues including Unicorn Theatre and Southwark Playhouse); and *Sense* (Southwark Playhouse).

Casting procedures: Sometimes holds general auditions, and actors may write at any time to request inclusion. Casting breakdowns are available from the website, *The Stage*, SBS, the Arts Council mailing list, and ITC. Welcomes letters (with CVs and photographs) from individual actors previously unknown to the company, sent by post only. Also welcomes showreels and invitations to view individual actors' websites. Actively encourages applications from disabled actors and promotes the use of inclusive casting.

Compass Theatre Company
St Jude's Parish Hall, 175 Gibraltar Street, Sheffield S3 8UA.
tel 0114-275 5328 *fax* 0114-278 6931
email neil@compasstheatrecompany.com
website www.compasstheatrecompany.com
Artistic Director Neil Sissons

Production details: The company's credo is: "Theatre is at the heart of a vibrant society. People are interdependent and have a common responsibility. Theatre expresses our commonality and resists the notion that we are separate and alone. It has faith in human beings. It acknowledges our weaknesses and failings but believes in our possibilities. It offers the possibility of redemption and satisfies the overwhelming human urge for renewal. It addresses the question of how we should live. It connects the everyday with the eternal." Recent productions include: *The Price* by Arthur Miller, *Happy Days* by Samuel Beckett, and *Peer Gynt* by Ibsen.

Complicite

14 Anglers Lane, Kentish Town, London NW5 3DG
tel 020-7485 7700 *fax* 020-7485 7701
email email@complicite.org
website www.complicite.org
Artistic Director Simon McBurney *Producer* Judith
Dimant *Education & Marketing* Natasha Freedman

Production details: Award-winning theatre company
founded in 1983. Constantly evolving its ensemble of
performers and collaborators. Work ranges from
entirely devised pieces to theatrical adaptations and
revivals of classic texts. On average presents 2
productions annually. The average cast size is 7 but
can be up to 18. Recent productions include: *The
Elephant Vanishes, Measure for Measure* and *A
Disappearing Number.* Contracts vary: some are
TMA/Equity approved; some (as for *The Elephant
Vanishes*) are non-Equity.

Casting procedures: Occasionally uses freelance
casting directors. Welcomes letters (with CVs and
photographs) sent by post rather than email. "We are
always more inclined to meet actors previously
unknown to us if they are familiar with our work (i.e.
if they have seen a Complicite show or participated in
an Open Workshop). Complicite's Education
Department programmes up to 2 Open Workshop
seasons for actors each year. Contact us to join the
Open Workshop mailing list." Actively encourages
applications from disabled actors and promotes the
use of inclusive casting.

Comyns Carr and Tyger's Heart

18 St Ann's Terrace, London NW8 6PJ
tel 020-7586 5252 *fax* 020-7722 1945
email enquiries@comynscarr.co.uk
website www.comynscarr.co.uk
Artistic Director Melissa Holston *Associate
Producer* Victoria Walker

Production details: Originally founded in 1995,
Comyns Carr now includes a new division, Tyger's
Hart, founded in 2003. Stages 1-4 productions each
year, averaging an annual total of 40-70
performances. Tours up to 22 venues per year,
including arts centres, theatres, and outdoor,
educational and community venues throughout
London and the South East. In general 5-8 actors
work on each production. Recent productions
include: *Fair Maid of the West* and *The Way of the
World.*

Casting procedures: Uses freelance casting directors.
Actors should only write to request inclusion when
auditions have been announced. Casting breakdowns
are available through Equity Job Information Service
and *PCR.* Welcomes letters (with CVs and
photographs) from actors previously unknown to the
company, but not email submissions. Also accepts
invitations to view individual actors' websites.

Concordance

Finborough Theatre, 118 Finborough Road,
London SW10 9ED

tel 020-7244 7439
email admin@concordance.org.uk
website www.concordance.org.uk

Production details: Concordance is a theatrical
production company, founded by Neil McPherson in
1981, and is resident at the Finborough Theatre,
London – see entry under *Fringe theatres* on
page 236. The company presents new writing, revivals
of neglected work and music theatre. "We currently
offer non-Equity contracts but sometimes at Equity
minimum rates." Actively encourages applications
from disabled actors and promotes the use of
inclusive casting.

Cragrats Theatre

Cragrats Mill, Dunford Road, Holmfirth,
West Yorkshire HD9 2AR
tel (01484) 686451 *fax* (01484) 686212
email lauren@cragrats.com
website www.cragrats.com
Director Mark Greenop *Head of Casting* Lauren
Tritton

Production details: Established in 1989. Cragrats is a
theatrical communications company that uses
performance to inspire learning. It is a values-driven
creative organisation, offering an immense variety of
work in TIE, corporate training and in its in-house
venue. 300+ productions per year are performed in
Educational venues, touring in the UK, France and
the Middle East. Offers Equity approved contracts.
Roughly 4 actors are used in each production.

Casting procedures: Casting breakdowns are
available on the website, and in *PCR* and *The Stage.*
Welcomes letters (with CVs and photographs) from
actors previously unknown to the company, sent by
post and email. Accepts invitations to view individual
actors' websites and showreels. Actively encourages
applications from disabled actors.

Cragrats are now part of the Speakeasy4schools
family – **www.speakeasy4schools.com**.

Creation Theatre Company

2nd Floor, Kennett House, 108-110 London Road,
Headington, Oxford OX3 9AW
tel (01865) 761393 *fax* (01865) 245745
email enquiry@creationtheatre.co.uk
website www.creationtheatre.co.uk
Director David Parrish

Production details: Produces site-specific
Shakespeare. Stages 2-5 productions annually in
unusual, non-traditional theatre venues (e.g. open air
shows in parks, factory spaces, and a spiegletent) with
approximately 150 performances per year, mostly in
Oxford. 8 actors work on each production. Recent
productions include: *The Snow Queen* and *King Lear.*

Casting procedures: Does not use freelance casting
directors or hold general auditions. Casting
breakdowns are available by postal application (with

Theatre

sae) and via *PCR* and Castfax. Welcomes letters and emails (with CVs and photographs) from actors previously unknown to the company at any time of year.

Dead Earnest Theatre

Applied Theatre Specialists, Sheffield Design Studios, 40 Ball Street, Sheffield S3 8DB
tel 0114-321 0450
email info@deadearnest.co.uk
website www.deadearnest.co.uk
Artistic Director Ashley Barnes *Drama Project Leaders* Vic Roberts, Stacey Sampson, Charlie Barnes *Operations Manager* Greg Morrall *Administrative Assistant* Agnes Wolinska

Production details: Dead Earnest is an applied theatre company, using theatre techniques to pursue social goals and in particular to impact on how people act and interact. The main focus of activity is in 3 key areas: Creative Learning (working with schools and universities and developing new techniques); Health and Well-being (CPD with health professionals and service user delivery focused on mental well-being); and Changing Communities (community consultation and looking at issues such as equality and diversity). The company works through forming strong partnerships with clients in the Public, Voluntary and Community sectors in order to bring creative thinking and theatre techniques to their specific needs. Clients are spread the length and breadth of the country. There is also a strong link to Sheffield Hallam University, where Artistic Director, Ashley Barnes, teaches in Applied Theatre.

Stages around 30 productions each year (mainly forum theatre), which all rehearse in Sheffield but are shown throughout the country, and supplies roleplay simulators to local hospitals. Does not offer Equity approved contracts and does not subscribe to the Equity pension scheme.

Casting procedures: Uses freelance casting directors. Sometimes holds general auditions. Welcomes postal or email submissions (with CVs and photographs) from actors previously unknown to the company. Applicants should live locally or have a local base, since company resources do not often extend to assistance with accommodation. The company aims to employ 1 new actor per project. Actively encourages applications from disabled actors.

Debut Theatre Company

New Greenham Arts, 113 Lindenmuth Way, New Greenham Park, Berkshire RG19 6HN
mobile (07979) 541964
email info@debut-theatre.org.uk
website www.debut-theatre.org.uk
Artistic Director Elizabeth Park *Associate Directors* Ciaran McConville, Daniel Weyman

Production details: Aims to create the best possible theatre, specialising in new writing and adaptations.

Work has a narrative, ensemble quality, addressing 20th- and 21st-century ideas and challenging audiences. Focuses on "telling the story". To date has created 11 productions – 1-2 on average each year, most recently *Snowbound* by Ciaran McConville at Trafalgar Studios (London, April 2008; Critics' Choice, *The Independent*).

Casting procedures: Sometimes uses a casting director; actors are invited to write in at any time to request inclusion. Casting breakdowns may be publicly available, via Castweb and Castnet and in *PCR*. Welcomes unsolicited letters from actors, especially if they have seen a Debut production, but prefers not to receive emails or showreels. Will accept invitations to view individual actors' websites.

Dirty Market Theatre Company

6 Grace's Mews, Camberwell, London SE5 8JF
tel 020-7701 8429
email info@dirtymarket.co.uk
website www.dirtymarket.co.uk
Co-directors Georgina Sowerby, Jon Lee

Production details: A collective of theatre makers with classical training; aims to integrate classical backgrounds with contemporary practice to create imaginative and exciting live performance. Applies for funding on a project to project basis, and is a member of ITC.

Casting procedures: Uses freelance casting directors. Casts from open workshops, and actors are advised to participate in these to get to know the company's work. Advertises via the website, *PCR*, Casting Call Pro, agents, SPF, etc. Welcomes approaches by actors by post and by email, but prefers to receive showreels by website link. Actively encourages applications from disabled actors.

DV8 Physical Theatre

Toynbee Studios, 28 Commercial, London E1 6AB
tel 020-7655 0977 *fax* 020-7247 5103
email dv8@artsadmin.co.uk
website www.dv8.co.uk
Artistic Director Lloyd Newson

Production details: Stages 1 production annually in the main house. Recent productions include: *To Be Straight With You* (Verbatim Theatre production); *Just for Show* (stage production); *The Cost of Living* (film); *Living Costs* (stage production); *Enter Achilles* (film/stage); *Strange Fish* (film/stage).

Casting procedures: Uses in-house casting directors. Actors should write in when advertised. Does not welcome unsolicited approaches but will accept showreels and invitations to view individual actors' websites. Offers Equity approved contracts as negotiated through ITC, and participates in the Equity Pension Scheme. Actively encourages applications from disabled actors and promotes the use of inclusive casting.

Eastern Angles Theatre Company

Sir John Mills Theatre, Gatacre Road, Ipswich IP1 2LQ

tel (01473) 218202 *fax* (01473) 384999
email info@easternangles.co.uk
website www.easternangles.co.uk
Director Ivan Cutting *General Manager* Jill Streatfield

Production details: Founded in 1982, the company tours theatre productions around East Anglia. New writing and a flavour of the region colour all of its original work. Stages 4-5 pieces each year, with an average annual total of 220 performances at 80 different venues. These include arts centres and theatres, educational and community venues, and site-specific locations. Tours mainly to East England but also nationally on occasion. In general 6 actors work on each production. Offers ITC/Equity contracts; does not subscribe to the Equity Pension Scheme.

Casting procedures: Does not use freelance casting directors or hold general auditions. Casting breakdowns are not publicly available but may occasionally be posted on the website. Welcomes letters (with CVs and photographs, but not saes); email attachments will not be opened. Advises applicants to consult the website to get an idea of the sort of work the company produces. Applicants should only write once and should specify in their letter if they are local or native to the region. Will consider applications from disabled actors to play characters with disabilities.

English Chamber Theatre
6 St Simon's Avenue, London SW15 6DU
mobile (07951) 912425
email jane@janemcculloch.com
website www.englishchambertheatre.co.uk
Artistic Director Jane McCulloch *President* Dame Judi Dench

Production details: A theatre company "without a building". There are 25 productions on the list, which go wherever they are requested. Mainly biographical plays and entertainments with small casts and star actors in leading roles. Recent productions include: a tour of Irish castles with *Dearest Nancy, Darling Evelyn* – the dramatised letters of Evelyn Waugh and Nancy Mitford, with Fenella Fielding.

Casting procedures: Uses only in-house casting directors. Will not consider unsolicited submissions: "Casting is always done when the drama is being written, and roles are tailored for particular actors." Rarely or never has the opportunity to cast disabled actors.

English Touring Theatre
25 Short Street, London SE1 8LJ
tel 020-7450 1990 *fax* 020-7633 0188
email admin@ett.org.uk
website www.ett.org.uk
Director Rachel Tackley

Production details: As one of England's foremost theatre companies, ETT creates emotionally and intellectually engaging theatre of outstanding quality, imagination and ambition. The company works with the country's leading directors and practitioners to produce artistically ambitious theatre that is vigorous, popular and challenging, and tours to large-scale venues nationwide. 4-15 actors are involved in each production. Offers ITC/Equity contracts and subscribes to the Equity Pension Scheme.

Casting procedures: Uses freelance casting directors and does not welcome unsolicited submissions from actors.

European Theatre Company
39 Oxford Avenue, London SW20 8LS
tel 020-8544 1994 *fax* 020-8544 1999
email admin@europeantheatre.co.uk
website www.europeantheatre.co.uk
Directors Adam Roberts, Jennie Graham

Production details: Founded in 1992, the company produces French-language theatre which tours the UK. Stages 3 or more productions a year, with around 250 performances in arts centres, theatres, schools and community venues. Normally employs 5 actors for each production.

Casting procedures: Casts in-house, and publishes its casting breakdowns via *PCR* and *SBS*. Welcomes letters (not emails) with CVs and photographs from French-speaking actors previously unknown to the company.

Feather Productions Ltd
137 Sheen Road, Richmond, Surrey TW9 1YJ
tel 020-8439 9848
email anna@featherproductions.com
website www.featherproductions.com
Artistic Directors Tim Whitnall, Anna Murphy

Production details: Has produced 2 new plays at the Old Red Lion, Islington. Welcomes scripts from new writers.

Casting procedures: Uses in-house casting directors. Sometimes holds general auditions; actors should write in Jan-Feb to request inclusion. Welcomes letters (with CVs and photographs) from individual actors previously unknown to the company sent by post or email. Also accepts showreels and invitations to view individual actors' websites. Offers Equity approved contracts as negotiated through PACT. Will consider applications from disabled actors to play characters with disabilities.

Forbidden Theatre Company
20 Rupert Street, London W1D 6DF
tel 0845-009 3084
email info@forbidden.org.uk
website www.forbidden.org.uk
Education Co-ordinator Linda Baker *Ensemble Production Team* Steve Brownlie, Mark Reid

Production details: Physical and visual theatre company. Produces small-scale productions of adaptations of classics and devised work. Stages 1 production annually and gives approximately 40 performances per year. Tours 2 venues on average and performs in arts centres and theatre venues in London and Scotland. In general, 4-6 actors work on each production. Recent productions include: *Goddess, Stung,* and *Mrs Wobble the Waitress and Friends.*

Casting procedures: Does not use freelance casting directors. Sometimes holds general auditions. Actors can write at any time requesting inclusion. Welcomes letters (with CVs and photographs) but not email submissions. Advises that the company will only reply to actors if inviting them to audition. CVs are kept on file.

Forced Entertainment
The Workstation, 15 Paternoster Row, Sheffield S1 2BX
tel 0114-279 8977 *fax* 0114-221 2170
email fe@forcedentertainment.com
website www.forcedentertainment.com
Key personnel Tim Etchells (Artistic Director), Robin Arthur, Richard Lowden, Claire Marshall, Cathy Naden, Terry O' Connor

Production details: Since forming the company in 1984, the 6 core members of the group have sustained a unique artistic partnership, confirming their position as "trailblazers in contemporary theatre". The company's substantial canon of work reflects an interest in the mechanics of performance, the role of the audience, and the machinations of contemporary urban life. Its work, framed and focused by Artistic Director Tim Etchells, is distinctive and provocative, delighting in disrupting the conventions of theatre and the expectations of audiences. Forced Entertainment's trademark collaborative process – devising work as a group through improvisation, experimentation and debate – has made them pioneers of British avant-garde theatre, and touring all over the world has earned them an unparalleled international reputation. Vist the website for a full archive of work.

Forest Forge Theatre Co
The Theatre Centre, Endeavour Park, Crow Arch Lane, Ringwood, Hants BH24 1SF
tel (01425) 470188 *fax* (01425) 471158
email info@forestforge.co.uk
website www.forestforge.co.uk
CEO/Artistic Director Kirstie Davis *Associate Director* David Haworth

Production details: Tours 3 productions a year into studios, village halls and arts centres, and has a large Creative Learning programme attached. The company is particularly interested in commissioning new work, with rural or regional themes and second productions. Recent commissions include: *Free Folk* by Gary Owen, and *For the Record* by Joyce Branagh.

Forkbeard Fantasy
PO Box 1241, Bristol BS99 2TG
Production details: Founded in 1974; an artist-led, multimedia film and performance company. Stages 1-2 productions and performs about 50 times per year. Tours to 10 venues both nationally and internationally on an annual basis. As this is an artist-led company, actors are only occasionally involved in productions. Performed recently at the Blackpool Puppet Festival, Warwick Arts Centre and The Lowry, Salford.

Casting procedures: Never holds general auditions. Advises actors that the company usually performs with artists who are already in the core team.

Found Theatre
The Byways, Church Street, Monyash, Derbyshire DE45 1JH
tel (01629) 813083
email found_theatre@yahoo.co.uk
website www.foundtheatre.org.uk
Artistic & Casting Director Simon Corble
Administrator Judy Meetham

Production details: Small-scale touring and site-specific theatre.

Casting procedures: Sometimes holds general auditions; actors should write in August to request inclusion. Welcomes unsolicited CVs and photographs sent via email, and invitations to view individual actors' websites. Does not accept showreels or approaches by post. Rarely (or never) has the opportunity to cast disabled actors.

Foursight Theatre
Newhampton Arts Centre, Dunkley Street, Wolverhampton WV1 4AN
tel (01902) 714257 *fax* (01902) 428413
email admin@foursighttheatre.co.uk
website www.foursighttheatre.co.uk
Co-Artistic Director Frances Land, Sarah Thom
Administrator Abigail Prosser

Production details: National touring theatre company. Emphasises the need for "total theatre" combining word, movement and music. Specialises in biographical plays about women in history and runs a strong education programme. Stages 1 production annually in addition to its regional and education work. Performs at arts centres, theatres and educational venues. Cast size varies according to production needs. Recent productions include: *Can Any Mother Help Me?, The Corner Shop, Six Dead Queens & An Inflatable Henry* and *Thatcher The Musical!.* Offers ITC/Equity approved contracts and does not subscribe to the Equity Pension Scheme.

Casting procedures: Casting breakdowns are not publicly available. Actors are advised to keep an eye on the website for information posted prior to productions. Welcomes submissions (with CVs and photographs) by post and email. Invitations to view individual actors' websites are also accepted. Actively encourages applications from disabled actors and promotes the use of inclusive casting.

Frantic Assembly

31 Eyre Street, London EC1R 5EW
tel 020-7841 3115
email admin@franticassembly.co.uk
website www.franticassembly.co.uk
Artistic Directors Scott Graham, Steven Hoggett
Executive Producer Lisa Maguire *General Manager* Laura Sutton *Administrator* Fiona Gregory

Production details: Established in 1994. Produces thrilling, energetic and uncompromising theatre. The company's work reflects contemporary culture and attracts new audiences. In collaboration with a wide variety of artists, the Artistic Directors create new work that places equal emphasis on movement, design, music and text. Has toured extensively throughout the UK and abroad, building a reputation as one of the country's most exciting companies.

Casting procedures: Does not hold open auditions. Does not accept unsolicited CVs. External casting directors are used to cast for productions.

Frantic Theatre Company

32 Wood Lane, Falmouth TR11 4RF
tel (01326) 312985 *fax* (01326) 312985
email info@frantictheatre.com
website www.frantictheatre.com

Production details: Founded in 1990. Stages 2 productions annually with around 1500 performances in 1500 venues throughout the UK and Ireland every year. Venues include arts centres, village halls, theatres, outdoor venues, educational and community venues, private homes and hospitals. On average 4 actors work on each production. Recent productions include: *Can I Do You Now, Sir?* and *Don't Dilly Dally.*

Casting procedures: Holds general auditions. Actors should write in May and November to request inclusion. Casting breakdowns are available by postal application (with sae), Equity Job Information Service, *PCR* and advertisements in *The Stage.* Welcomes submissions (with CVs and photographs) by post or email. Showreels and invitations to view individual actors' websites are also accepted. Actors are advised not to telephone, and to send their details only when they have researched the company's very specific work and can explain their suitability.

Freedom Studios

Bradford Design Exchange, 34 Peckover Street, Little Germany, Bradford BD1 5BD
tel (01274) 730077
email hello@freedomstudios.co.uk
website www.freedomstudios.co.uk
Director Madani Younis *Creative Producer* Deborah Dickinson

Production details: Established in 2007. A national touring, devising theatre company. Stages theatrical events and experiences at arts centres, theatres and outdoor venues across the UK. In general 2-4 actors are involved in each production. Offers Equity-approved contracts as negotiated through ITC. Recent productions include: *Street Voices 2.* Also holds the Asian Theatre School for a 15-week period each year, for aspiring Yorkshire British Asian, Black and ethnic minority artists; and Unit 4, "a twice-yearly platform event for some of the most exciting voices in the UK contemporary arts scene".

Casting procedures: Sometimes holds general auditions. Welcomes letters (with CVs and photographs) from individual actors previously unknown to the company, sent by post or email; also accepts showreels and invitations to view individual actors' websites. Will consider applications from disabled characters to play characters with disabilities.

Full Body & The Voice

Lawrence Batley Theatre, Queen's Street, Huddersfield HD1 2SP
tel (01484) 484441 *fax* (01484) 484443
email fullbody@lbt-uk.org
website www.fullbody.org.uk
Artistic Director Vanessa Brooks

Production details: Established in 2000. Production company exploring a range of projects that include actors with learning disabilities and promote inclusive working practices. Approximately 1 production per year touring to 10-15 venues, including arts centres and theatres in Yorkshire, the North West and internationally. Roughly 5-8 actors are used in each production.

Casting procedures: Occasionally uses freelance casting directors. Does not welcome unsolicited CVs. Actively encourages applications from disabled actors and promotes the use of inclusive casting. Offers Equity approved contracts.

Galleon Theatre Company Ltd

Greenwich Playhouse, Greenwich Station Forecourt, 189 Greenwich High Road, London SE10 8JA
tel 020-8858 9256
email boxoffice@galleontheatre.co.uk
website www.galleontheatre.co.uk
Artistic Director Alice de Sousa *Theatre Director* Bruce Jamieson

Production details: Founded in 1990. Stages 12-14 productions annually and presents 282 performances at its own venue, Greenwich Playhouse. Has toured throughout Britain in previous years. On average 15 actors work on each production. For recent productions, please see the website. Also has a film company, Galleon Films Ltd, which is developing a slate of 4 feature films.

Casting procedures: Uses in-house casting director. Holds general auditions; actors should write to

Theatre

request inclusion when the company is casting for a specific project. Casting breakdowns are available through *PCR*, *SBS*, Castnet and advertisements in *The Stage*. Welcomes letters (with CVs and photographs) but not email submissions. Showreels and invitations to view individual actors' websites are also accepted.

David Glass Ensemble

96 Teesdale Street, London E2 6PU
tel 020-7734 6030 *fax* 020-7734 0365
email info@davidglassensemble.com
website www.davidglassensemble.com

Production details: Founded in 1990, the company tours nationally and internationally, especially in South East Asia – recent productions have toured to Cambodia, Vietnam and Korea, as well as performing at the Portsmouth New Theatre Royal and the Battersea Arts Centre in London. Stages 2 productions a year, and tours to roughly 10 theatre venues, with a company of around 5 actors. Offers ITC/Equity approved contracts.

Casting procedures: Does not issue casting breakdowns. Welcomes CVs and photographs from actors whose work is not known to the company, and also welcomes showreels and invitations to view actors' websites. The company actively encourages applications from disabled actors and promotes the use of inclusive casting.

Godot Company

operating from the Bookshop Theatre, 51 The Cut, Waterloo, London SE1 8LF
tel 020-7633 0599
email info@godotcompany.com
Administrator John Calder

Production details: An actors' cooperative performing at theatres and other suitable venues, including its own headquarters in Waterloo (behind the Calder Bookshop, opposite the Young Vic) and at British, Irish and European theatres and festivals. Stages between 10 and 30 productions in the main house, and the same in the studio, each year. Also works in TIE, Outreach and Community: contact John Calder for details. Recent productions include: many plays by Beckett and similar authors; also readings and adaptations.

Casting procedures: Uses in-house and freelance casting directors. Sometimes holds general auditions; actors may write at any time to request inclusion. "Policy, repertory, casting etc. is the joint decision of the cooperative, which votes when necessary."

Graeae Theatre Company

Bradbury Studios, 138 Kingsland Road, London E2 8DY
tel 020-7613 6900 *fax* 020-7613 6919
email info@graeae.org
website www.graeae.org
Artistic Director Jenny Sealey

Production details: Founded in 1980. Produces theatre made by disabled people (actors, directors and other theatre practitioners) with physical and sensory impairments. Stages 3 productions annually and gives 70 performances at 50 venues each year. Venues include arts centres and theatres in England, Scotland, Wales and Ireland. 3-6 actors are involved in each production. Recent productions include: national tour of *Blasted* by Sarah Kane, and *Whiter Than Snow* by Mike Kenny, which was a co-production with Birmingham Rep. Graeae/New Wolsey Theatre co-produced *Flower Girls* by Richard Cameron in Autumn 2007, and Graeae/Suspect Culture co-produced a new play in Spring 2008.

Casting procedures: Sometimes holds general auditions. Welcomes postal or email submissions (with CVs and photographs) from actors with physical and sensory impairments. Also accepts showreels and invitations to view individual actors' websites. Offers ITC/Equity approved contracts.

Into The Scene is a new Arts Council England initiative led by Graeae. Works with leading drama schools on inclusive practice to encourage drama schools to recruit more disabled actors onto their training courses.

Scene Change is a Graeae initiative working with venues, drama schools and colleges offering taster workshops to encourage more young people to apply to drama schools.

The company offers Continued Professional Development workshops for actors. Past workshops have included Comedy Acting with director Gordon Anderson (ATC/Catherine Tate), and Singing with Barb Jungr.

Grassmarket Project

1 Harley Street, London W1G 9QD
tel 020-7307 8734
email info@grassmarketproject.org
website www.grassmarketproject.org
Artistic Director Jeremy Weller

Production details: Founded in 1989. Independent theatre company producing new work in theatres across Europe, USA and the UK. Stages 2 productions annually and gives 30-40 performances every year. On average, 5-6 actors work on each production. Recent productions include: *De Andre (The Others)*; *Fathers & Sons* (Betty Nansen Theatre, Copenhagen); *Bus Stops* (Glasgow); and *The Foolish Young Man* (Roundhouse Theatre, London).

Casting procedures: Productions are cast by freelance casting directors or the company's artistic director. Sometimes holds general auditions. Employs a mixture of trained and untrained actors. Welcomes letters (with CVs and photographs) by post or email. Showreels and invitations to view individual actors' websites are also accepted. Offers non-Equity contracts. Will consider applications from disabled actors to play characters with disabilities.

Grid Iron Theatre Company

Suite 4/1, 2 Commercial Street, Edinburgh EH6 6JA
tel 0131-555 5455
email admin@gridiron.org.uk
website www.gridiron.org.uk
Director Ben Harrison *Producer* Judith Doherty
General Manager Fiona Watson

Production details: Founded in 1995. Produces new writing and site-specific theatre. Stages 1-3 productions annually and gives 20-50 performances every year. Performs in theatres, outdoor and site-specific venues in Scotland, England and Northern and Southern Ireland. Recent productions include: *Huxley's Lab, Barflies, Once Upon a Dragon*, and *Roam*.

Casting procedures: Sometimes holds general auditions. Actors may write requesting inclusion at any time throughout the year. Welcomes submissions (with CVs and photographs) sent by post and email. Showreels and invitations to view individual actors' websites are also accepted.

Handstand Productions

13 Hope Street, Liverpool L1 9BH
tel 0151-708 7441 *fax* 0151-709 3515
email info@handstand-uk.com
website www.handstand-uk.com
Director Han Duijvendak *Producer* Nicholas Stanley
Co-producer Lucy Dossor

Now working almost exclusively in documentary, film, TV and video production. Rarely requires actors, so please do not submit anything unless a specific casting requirement has been made available on the website.

Headlong Theatre

3rd Floor, 34-35 Berwick Street, London W1F 8RP
tel 020-7478 0270 *fax* 020-7434 1749
email info@headlongtheatre.co.uk
website www.headlongtheatre.co.uk
Artistic Director Rupert Goold *Key contact* Henny Finch

Production details: Formerly Oxford Stage Company. Established in 1974. National touring theatre company dedicated to new ways of making theatre by exploring revolutionary writers and practitioners of the past, present and future. Stages 4-6 projects annually, performing 24-32 weeks of the year. Tours nationally and internationally to arts centres and theatres. Recent productions include: *Earthquakes in London* (co-produced with the National Theatre); *ENRON* (Chichester Minerva/ Royal Court/West End/UK Tour); and *Six Characters in Search of an Author* (Chichester Minerva/West End/Sydney & Perth Festivals).

Casting procedures: Accepts submissions (with CVs and photographs) from actors previously unknown to the company sent by post or email. Invitations to view individual actors' websites are accepted, as are showreels. Offers TMA/Equity approved contracts.

Hidden Talent Productions Ltd

109 Drakefell Road, Brockley, London SE4 2DT
mobile (07905) 175934
email info@hiddentalent.org.uk
website www.hiddentalent.org.uk
Artistic Director Adam Linsson *Associate Directors* Evan Regueira, Alex Hughes, Ben Wiles *Casting Directors* Adam Linsson, Evan Regueira, Alex Hughes, Ben Wiles *Key personnel* Ben Wiles (Resident Musical Director), Samantha Zoe-French (Resident Choreographer)

Production details: Established in 2006 as a not-for-profit, small-scale theatre producing company. Stages primarily musical theatre productions and cabarets. Aims to raise the profile of musical theatre in the community as a recognised art form, by producing new works alongside established 'classic' musicals. Tours to small fringe venues and halls, and provides interactive performances in local schools and other education establishments across the UK. Offers closed workshop performances and readings through to fully staged musical productions in larger theatres. Stages on average 1 production in the main house and 2 in the studio each year. Also works in TIE and Community, for which the key contact is Adam Linsson. Recent productions include: *Heaven Sent, A New Musical Comedy* (Workshop); *Nights on Broadway* (Cabaret); and *Changing Direction* (TIE).

Casting procedures: Uses in-house casting directors. Sometimes holds general auditions; actors may write in at any time, but preferably when the company is casting specific projects. Casting breakdowns are available via the website or on postal application with an sae. Welcomes letters (with CVs & photographs) from individual actors previously unknown to the company sent by post or email. Accepts showreels and invitations to view individual actors' websites. Will consider applications from disabled actors to play characters with disabilities.

Highly Sprung Performance Company

49 Abercorn Road, Chapelfields, Coventry CV5 8EE
tel 020-7667 0141
email mail@sprunghq.fsnet.co.uk
website www.highlysprungperformance.co.uk
Artistic Director Sarah Hunt *Company Director* Mark Worth

Production details: Founded in 1999. Aims to create original and innovative performances exploring the relationship between dance, text and physical theatre. Also runs community and educational activities alongside productions. Stages 1 production annually with 25 performances every year. Tours 10-15 venues annually: these include arts centres, theatres, outdoor and educational venues in the West Midlands, London, Manchester and Edinburgh. On average 2-8 actors work on each production. Recent productions include: *Pretend I'm Not Here* and *More Than Kisses*.

Casting procedures: Holds general auditions. Actors should send CVs and photographs by post or email. These will be kept on file for future auditions. Casting breakdowns are available on the website, by postal application and via Equity Job information Service and advertisements in *The Stage*. Showreels and invitations to view individual actors' websites are also accepted.

Hijinx Theatre

Wales Millennium Centre, Bute Place,
Cardiff CF10 5AL
tel 029-2030 0331 *fax* 029-2063 5621
email info@hijinx.org.uk
website www.hijinx.org.uk
Artistic Director Gaynor Lougher *Associate Director*
Louise Osborn *Administrative Director* Val Hill

Production details: Founded in 1981, the company stages at least 2 professional productions a year on a one-night-stand basis across Wales and England, for community and theatre venues. In general the Spring show is aimed at a learning-disabled audience and their communities, while the Autumn and Winter tours target the general public.

The company has developed a strong commitment to new writing over the years, commissioning plays from many of Wales' leading playwrights. On average, 4 actors work on each production, which includes a strong musical element. Recent productions include: *Chasing Rainbows* (touring day centres, gateway clubs, community centres and colleges); and *The Other Woman* (Wales Millennium Centre, Torch Theatre and community venues). Offers ITC/Equity approved contracts and does not subscribe to the Equity Pension Scheme.

Casting procedures: Shows are cast by the artistic and associate director. Welcomes letters, CVs and photographs from actors previously unknown to the company. Does not accept emails or showreels. Welcomes applications from disabled and non-disabled actors.

Historia Theatre Co

8 Cloudesley Square, London N1 0HT
tel 020-7837 8005 *fax* 020-7278 4733
email kate@kateprice.org
website www.historiatheatre.com
Artistic Director Catherine Price

Production details: Established in 1997. "Historia presents plays that have their source or inspiration in history." 1 production annually with 20-30 performances. Touring productions visit theatres, arts venues, National Trust houses, museums, churches, schools and village halls both nationally and in London. Roughly 6-8 actors are used in each production. Recent productions include: *Judenfrei: Love and Death in Hitler's Germany* (2010 – Henley

Fringe Festival and Tour); *An African's Blood* (2007, and a limited season in 2008; Tour); *Five Eleven or the Powder Treason* (2005; Tour), and *Evelina* (2004; Pentameters Theatre). Offers ITC/Equity rates where possible.

Casting procedures: Does not use freelance casting directors or hold general auditions. Breakdowns are published via *PCR*, *SBS*, Equity's Job Information Service and via Spotlight Link. Unsolicited approaches from actors are discouraged. "Watch *PCR/SBS*/JIS and apply accordingly." Will consider applications from disabled actors when casting for characters with disabilities.

Hoipolloi Theatre

Office F, Dale's Brewery, Gwydir Street,
Cambridge CB1 2LJ
tel/fax (01223) 322748
email info@hoipolloi.org.uk
website www.hoipolloi.org.uk
Director Shôn Dale-Jones *Associate Director* Stephanie
Müller *Production Manager* Richard Couldrey

Production details: Founded in 1994, the company creates visually and physically dynamic, imaginative and comic work which tours to small- and middle-scale theatres and arts centres throughout the UK. It is also involved in educational work. Stages 1-2 productions annually, presenting 100 performances every year at 60-70 venues. On average 4-5 actors work on each production. Recent productions include: *My Uncle Arly*.

Casting procedures: Sometimes holds general auditions. Actors may write at any time requesting inclusion. Welcomes letters (with CVs and photographs) but not email submissions. Invitations to view individual actors' websites are also accepted. Advises actors approaching the company to have some knowledge of its work.

Hollow Crown Productions Ltd

2 Norfolk Road, London E17 5QS
mobile (07930) 530948
email enquiries@hollowcrown.co.uk
website www.hollowcrown.co.uk
Artistic Director Peter Adshead *Associate Directors*
Andrew Jarvis, Carl Jacobs

Production details: "A theatrical production company with a difference. Provides an extension to the young graduate actor's training through the professional production experience." Offers ongoing vocational support to develop and enhance the foundation skills conferred through recognised drama school training, so that each company member may achieve their full potential. Stages 3 productions (Classical, Modern Classics) annually.

Casting procedures: Uses in-house casting directors. Sometimes holds general auditions via workshops; actors may write in at any time. Casting breakdowns are available from the website, in *PCR*, and from

CastNet. Welcomes letters (with CVs and photographs) from actors not previously known to the company if sent by post; no email submissions. Does not accept showreels. Offers own contract based on Equity Fringe/TMA. Will consider applications from disabled actors to play characters with disabilities. "The company is especially keen to hear from actors whose philosophy/approach to text resonates with its artistic policy, and who would be keen to explore often neglected classical texts – including Shakespearean texts in their quarto/folio forms." Consult the website for more details.

Horse and Bamboo Theatre

The Horse and Bamboo Centre, Waterfoot, Rossendale, Lancashire BB4 7HQ
tel (01706) 220241 *fax* (01706) 831166
email info@horseandbamboo.org
website www.horseandbamboo.org
Key personnel Richard Hall, Alison Duddle

Production details: Established in 1978. A visual touring theatre using masks, puppetry, video and movement in theatre. Produces approximately 3 productions per year, touring to 60 venues including arts centres and outdoor venues in the UK, Europe and the USA. Performers must have mask/puppetry or dance experience to a professional level. Offers non-Equity contracts and does not subscribe to the Equity Pension Scheme. Members of ITC.

Casting procedures: Welcomes letters (with CVs and photographs) from actors previously unknown to the company if sent by post, but not by email. Invitations to view individual actors' websites are also accepted. Will consider applications from disabled actors to play characters with disabilities.

Ibsen Stage Company

434 Hornsey Road, London N19 4EB
tel 020-7281 4322
email ask@ibsenstage.com
website www.ibsenstage.com
Director Terje Tveit *Company Co-ordinator* Rosalind Stockwell

Production details: Productions are characterised by a "different and revitalised" approach to Ibsen. Stages 1-2 productions each year, plus workshops and readings, with 40-60 performances annually in theatres in London and Europe. In general, 5-15 actors are involved in each production. Does not offer actors Equity-approved contracts, but will pay Equity rates when funding allows. Recent productions include: *Little Eyolf* (Riverside Studios); *Peer Gynt* (Pleasance Theatre, Islington); *A Doll's House* (National Theatre, Oslo); and *The Nightingale Mystery* (Rosemary Branch Theatre).

Casting procedures: Holds general auditions; actors may write at any time to request inclusion. Casting breakdowns are publicly available via the website, *PCR*, Casting Call Pro and CastNet. Welcomes letters

(with CVs and photographs) from actors previously unknown to the company sent by post or email. Is happy to receive showreels and invitations to view individual actors' websites. Rarely (or never) has the opportunity to cast disabled actors.

Icarus Theatre Collective

32 Portland Place, London W1B 1NAO
tel 020-7998 1562 *mobile* (07792) 428820
fax 0871-528 9755
website www.icarustheatre.co.uk
Artistic Director Max Lewendel *Associate Director* Rosa Wyatt

Production details: "Explores the the harsh, brutal side of contemporary and classical drama." Aims to produce 2 mid-scale and 3 professional fringe productions of theatre every 2 years, using new writing and under-appreciated classics in diverse performance formats. Teams artists from the international community with British artists, and experienced artists with promising young professionals. Also works in TIE, Outreach & Community, for which the key contact is Rosa Wyatt. Recent productions include: *The Lesson* by Eugene Ionesco; *Albert's Boy* by James Graham; *Othello* by William Shakespeare; and *Vincent in Brixton* by Nicholas Wright.

Casting procedures: Uses in-house casting directors. Holds general auditions; actors should write in when advised to do so by the company's newsletter. Casting breakdowns are available from the website and are advertised in *PRC* and *SBS*. Welcomes letters (with CVs and photographs) sent by post, but not email, and does not accept showreels or invitations to view individual actors' websites.

Ichiza Theatre Company

2 Bradford Court, Bloxham, Oxon OX15 4RA
tel (01295) 720500 *fax* (01295) 722118
email office@ichiza.co.uk
website www.ichiza.co.uk
Artistic Director Togo Igawa *Associate Director* Masumi Kako *Administrator* Nao Miyauchi

Production details: Established in 2007. Produces Japanese plays, from traditional theatre to contemporary works, in collaboration with artists from different backgrounds. Recently completed its first production, *The Face of Jizo* by Hisashi Inoue, at Arcola Theatre, to acclaim from wide audiences. Plans to start work in TIE/Outreach in the near future.

Casting procedures: Uses in-house casting directors and holds general auditions; actors are advised to write in only when auditions are announced. Casting breakdowns are available from Equity Job Information Service, *PCR* and *The Stage*. Does not welcome unsolicited approaches by email, but will accept letters (with CVs and photographs) and showreels sent in response to specific, announced auditions. Actively encourages applications from disabled actors and promotes the use of inclusive casting.

Incisor
41 Edith Avenue, Peacehaven, East Sussex BN10 8JB
mobile (07979) 498450
fax 020-8830 4992
email sarahmann7@hotmail.co.uk
website www.theatre-company-incisor.com
Artistic/Casting Director Sarah Mann *Associate Director* James Madden

Production details: Recent productions include: *Pinters People*, *The Odd Couple* and *Abigail's Party*.

Casting procedures: Uses in-house casting directors and does not hold general auditions. Casting breakdowns are published in *PCR* and available from Casting Call Pro / Castweb / Castnet. Welcomes letters (with CVs and photographs) from actors previously unknown to the company, sent by post or by email. Does not accept showreels but will respond to invitations to view individual actors' websites. Actively encourages applications from disabled actors and promotes the use of inclusive casting. "Incisor's style is big and bold, especially as a lot of our work is outdoors. Large characters and voices needed."

Indigo Entertainments
Tynymynydd, Bryneglwys, Corwen,
Denbighshire LL21 9NP
tel (01978) 790211
email info@indigoentertainments.com
website www.indigoentertainments.com
Director Emma Hands

Production details: Founded in 2000. Takes existing small-scale theatre productions, usually with a literary theme, and tours them around the UK and internationally. Stages 5-10 productions annually with 50 performances in 50 venues every year. These include arts centres, theatres, outdoor and educational venues, community venues and hotels all over the UK and in the Middle East and Far East. On average 1-3 actors work on each production. Recent productions include: *The Tale of Beatrix Potter*, *Testament of Youth*, *Hic! The Entire History of Wine (Abridged)*, *Red Wings*, *Richard Bucket Overflows*, *Emily Dickinson & I*, *My Darling Clementine*, and *How Pleasant to Know Mr Lear*. Offers non-Equity contracts and does not subscribe to the Equity Pension Scheme.

Casting procedures: Does not welcome unsolicited CVs. Will accept showreels if they demonstrate productions of interest and are not just an actor's general showreel. Advises that the shows presented are usually intelligent, light, witty commercial pieces rather than experimental work.

Jasperian Theatre Company
29 Harvard Court, Honeybourne Road,
London NW6 1HL

tel (01736) 740907 *mobile* (07941) 616177
email jasperiantheatre@mac.com
website www.jasperian.org
Artistic Director Tony Jasper *Production Directors* Kenneth Pickering, Peter Moreton, Harry Gostelow, Clare Davidson

Production details: Founded in 1992, JTC specialises in plays and revues that have a religious underpinning and/or deal with the human condition. The company is a member of ITC and casts all shows on artistic ability – not on any religious affiliation. Normally stages 3-5 productions each year with a total of around 100 performances. Tours to a variety of different venues including theatres, churches and private houses across the UK. In general 3-7 actors work on each production. Recent productions include: *Charles Wesley 1707* (100 venues), and *Stories of Grace*, *It happened One Friday* and *God's Trombones*.

Casting procedures: Uses freelance casting directors. Actors may write requesting inclusion in the next round of auditions at any time, but the beginning of February, June and September are normally good times. Casting breakdowns are available through *SBS* and CastNet. Prefers actors to send in their details by post but will accept the occasional email. Showreels are also accepted. Advises actors to read audition notices carefully and only come if suitable and available over the time period specified. A member of ITC, offers non-Equity contracts; however: "Apart from usually £250-£350 I also offer all accommodation and meals paid, and in some instances this is better than a basic Equity contract. I attempt to cast only Equity members. In 18 years, no-one has been owed money [by me]." Actively encourages applications from disabled actors and promotes the use of inclusive casting.

Kabosh
The Old Museum Arts Centre,
7 College Square North, Belfast BT1 6AR
tel 028-9024 3343 *fax* 028-9023 1130
email kabosh@dircon.co.uk/info@kabosh.net
website www.kabosh.net
Artistic Director Karl Wallace *Company Touring Manager* Azucena Avila

Production details: Founded in 1994. Produces innovative physical and visual theatre for local, national and international touring and site-specific work. Stages 2-4 productions annually with 56 performances during the course of the year. Tours to around 30 venues annually, including arts centres and theatres, and site-specific locations. In general 2-6 actors are involved in each production. Countries covered include Northern Ireland, Republic of Ireland, England (including London), Scotland, Wales, parts of Europe and North America. Recent productions include: *Rhinoceros* and *Todd*.

Casting procedures: Auditions are by invitation only. Actors should write requesting inclusion in July (for autumn productions) and November (for spring productions). Welcomes applications (with CVs and photographs) sent by post and email. Also accepts invitations to view individual actors' websites. Any actor known to the company is welcome to send a CV and headshot (which will be kept on file), and to notify the director of performances where their work may be seen. The director will endeavour to see new actors. Any unseen actor who has sent a CV will be notified of open auditions, should they arise.

Kali Theatre Company

20 Rupert Street, London W1 6DF
tel 020-7494 9100
email info@kalitheatre.co.uk
website www.kalitheatre.co.uk
Artistic Director Janet Steel *General Manager* Chris Corner

Production details: Founded in 1990 to encourage, support and promote new writing by Asian women. "We focus on content and ideas as much as style, aiming to present memorable theatre events based on challenging and innovative ideas." Stages on average 1 production in the main house and 1 in the studio each year, playing to audiences that are increasingly diverse. Nurtures novice playwrights through its Kali Shorts and Kali Futures initiatives, and has worked with writers such as Tanika Gupta, Rukhsana Ahmad, Gurpreet Bhatti and Shelley Silas among others. Recent productions include: *Azmeen, Another Paradise* and *Bhena*. The company also runs a regional Outreach programme and a Talk Back Festival for Asian Women – consult the website for further details.

Casting procedures: Welcomes letters (with CVs & photographs) from actors previously unknown to the company if sent by post, but not by email. Does not accept showreels or invitations to view individual actors' websites. Rarely (or never) has the opportunity to cast disabled actors.

"Phone to find out what we are casting before sending CVs and photos."

Kaos Theatre

39-41 North Road, Islington, London N7 9DP
tel 020-7700 3885 *fax* 020-7700 3885
email xavier@kaostheatre.com
website www.kaostheatre.com
Director Xavier Leret

Production details: Founded in 1994. Working ensemble of actors, musicians, designers and artists working with text-based theatre. Stages both new writing and contemporary adaptations of existing work (classic and modern). Receives funding from Arts Council England. Stages 1-2 productions annually with 80 performances during the course of the year. The company tours on average to 30 different venues across the UK (excluding the Highlands and Islands) each year. Recent productions

include: *Titus Andronicus* and *The Kaos Importance of Being Earnest.*

Casting procedures: In-house casting. Does not hold general auditions. Casting breakdowns are publicly available via the website, postal application (with sae), Equity Job Information Service, *PCR* and advertisements in *The Stage*. Sometimes welcomes letters (with CVs and photographs) but not email submissions. Accepts invitations to view individual actors' websites. Advises that the company mainly works with a regular ensemble of performers and only occasionally meets or auditions newcomers. Members of the ensemble come from a diverse training background (rarely straight from drama school). Does not welcome over-persistent enquiries; the company will make contact if interested in an applicant.

Kneehigh Theatre

14 Walsingham Place, Truro, Cornwall TR1 2RP
Artistic Director Emma Rice

Production details: Stages 3 productions annually with 130 performances during the course of the year. On average tours to 15 venues annually. Performs in arts centres, theatres, outdoor and "out of the ordinary" indoor venues across the UK and internationally. Recent productions include: *A Matter of Life and Death, Cymbeline, Rapunzel,* and *Brief Encounter*. Offers ITC/Equity approved contracts but does not subscribe to the Equity Pension Scheme.

Casting procedures: Does not hold general auditions. Advises that the company works with a pool of performers, but is interested in meeting new actors – either by personal recommendation or by seeing their work. Actively encourages applications from disabled actors and promotes the use of inclusive casting.

Ladder to the Moon

Unit 105 Battersea Business Centre,
99-109 Lavender Hill, London SW11 5QL
tel 020-7228 9700
email info@laddertothemoon.co.uk
website www.laddertothemoon.co.uk
Artistic Director Chris Gage

Production details: Uses staff coaching and interactive theatre to improve quality of life for older people in care, especially those living with dementia. Employs professional actors trained in interactive theatre to come in as 'character visitors', engaging residents, staff and visitors in their world (anything from a Shakespeare play to a Hollywood movie). Characters respond sensitively to what is said, playing out their story over the course of the show, and are directly influenced and affected by the people they are with. Offers Equity contracts as negotiated by the ITC.

Casting procedures: Casting is done in-house by the Artistic Director. Details of actor recruitment are advertised on the website and artsjobs. Ladder to the Moon is an equal opportunities employer.

LipService

The Comedy Suite, 116 Longford Road,
Manchester M21 9NP
tel 0161-881 0061 *fax* 0161-881 0061
email info@lip-service.net
website www.lipservicetheatre.co.uk
Joint Artistic Directors Sue Ryding, Maggie Fox

Production details: Over the past 20 years, LipService has established itself as one of the leading comedy touring companies, producing shows for the theatre which have a strong base in popular culture. These include: *Jane Bond* (blonde and dangerous; a spoof of all things Bond); *Very Little Women* (a comic version of Louisa May Alcott's *Little Women*); *Hector's House* (an epic tale of togas and taramasalata); *The Importance of Being Earnest* (a trivial comedy for serious people); *Women on the Verger* (a hilarious look at romantic women's fiction); *Move Over Moriarty* (an impenetrable case for Sherlock Holmes and Doctor Watson); and *Withering Looks* (a slice of life with the Bronte Sisters).

LipService attracts audiences from a wide social mix and age range. Based in Manchester, the company has built up a solid touring circuit in the North of England and throughout the rest of Britain. Challenges its audience by setting up a recognisable form and subverting it. This is partly achieved by two women playing all the characters, but also by ingenious theatrical surprises. "Along with the National Theatre of Brent, LipService is one of our great 2-person ensembles." (*The Guardian*)

Casting procedures: Uses casting directors of co-producing venue. Does not hold general auditions. Actors should write requesting inclusion when extra performers are needed for a new production. Casting breakdowns are available direct from the co-producing theatre; details of these are available via the website. Welcomes invitations from actors to view their work, and information from actors familiar with the company's work. Offers TMA/Equity approved contracts. Rarely (or never) has the opportunity to cast disabled actors.

London Actors Theatre Co

Unit 5a, Spaces Business Centre, Ingate Place,
London SW8 3NS
tel 020-7978 2620 *fax* 020-7978 2631
email latchmere@fishers.org.uk

Production details: Founded in 1987 and normally stages 1-2 productions annually, employing 6-8 actors on non-Equity contracts.

Casting procedures: Casting breakdowns are published in *PCR* or *The Stage*. Any approaches not relating to a specific breakdown are discouraged.

London Bubble Theatre Co

5 Elephant Lane, London SE16 4JD
tel 020-7237 4434 *fax* 020-7231 2366
email admin@londonbubble.org.uk
website www.londonbubble.org.uk
Artistic Director Jonathan Petherbridge *Associate Director, Community* Sylvan Baker *Associate Director, Education* Sonia Hyams *Associate Director, New Projects* Karen Tomlin

Production details: The company's mission is "to attract and involve a wide range of audiences and participants, particularly those experiencing theatre for the first time, to inventive and unpredictable events that reflect the diversity of our city and its people".

To this end, the company has the following aims:

• To work particularly with and for people who do not normally have access to theatre for geographical, financial or cultural reasons
• To encourage and enable people to develop their own theatre and related skills
• To work to create a popular theatre form which is open, exciting and accessible
• To produce events which demonstrate and celebrate the creative abilities of all those taking part
• To examine issues of common concern to all those involved through the choice of material for workshops, projects and professional performances
• To challenge prejudice and bigotry through the company's organisation, working processes and final product
• To achieve a diversity of influence that is discernible throughout the company's work and consciousness

Recent productions include: *Spangleguts, Metamorphoses, Myths, Rituals And Whitegoods, Jumping The Gap* and *My Home.*

Mad Dogs and Englishmen

The Old Post Office, Green Lane, Quidenham,
Norfolk NR16 2AP
tel (01953) 888499 *fax* (01953) 888499
email info@mad-dogs.org.uk
website www.mad-dogs.org.uk
Director Ann Courtney *Administration* Jacqui Merryweather

Production details: Founded in 1995. Theatre company based in Norfolk, whose policy is to provide well-balanced, entertaining and educational drama. Main areas of work are new writing, adaptations and classical work. Stages 2 productions annually with 70 performances during the course of the year, plus 30 workshops for schools. Tours to rural venues (churches, public houses) as well as arts centres, theatres, outdoor venues, educational venues, and community venues. On average 4-9 actors are involved in each production. Recent productions include: *As You Like It* and *Outrageous Nonsense.*

Casting procedures: Sometimes holds general auditions. Audition criteria are published in *PCR* at the appropriate times of the year. Welcomes letters (with CVs and photographs) but not email submissions.

Magnetic North Theatre Productions

18 Brandon Terrace, Edinburgh EH3 5DZ
tel 0131-556 3299 fax 0131-556 3299
email mail@magneticnorth.org.uk
website www.magneticnorth.org.uk
Director Nicholas Bone

Production details: Founded in 1999. Commissions
and produces new plays: 5 full productions and 1 film
have been produced. Also produces 'Rough Mix', a
creative development programme for writers and
other practitioners. Stages 1-2 productions annually
and gives 20-40 performances during the course of a
year. Tours on average to 12 venues annually. About
5 actors are involved in each production. Recent
productions include: *After Mary Rose*, *Walden* and
My Old Man.

Casting procedures: Sometimes holds general
auditions. Actors should write to request inclusion
when productions are announced on the website.
Casting breakdowns are publicly available through
the website, postal application (with sae) and *PCR*.
Welcomes submissions (with CVs and photographs)
sent by post or email. Also accepts invitations to view
individual actors' websites. Advises that the company
has a low turnover of productions and a small staff,
and finds it difficult to respond to general enquiries
about available work.

Manchester Actors Company

c/o Administration, PO Box 54,
Manchester M60 7AB
tel 0161-227 8702 fax 0161-227 8702
email s.s.boyes@btinternet.com
website www.manactco.org.uk
Artistic Director Stephen Boyes Administrator Brian
Lavers

Production details: Established in 1980 and now the
North West's leading provider of theatre in schools.
"We are emphatically *not* a TIE company." Reaches
well over 80,000 young people each year with around
6 touring productions. Recent productions include:
The Tempest, *Of Mice and Men*, *The Pirate Queen*,
Much Ado About Nothing, and *Poetry in Motion*.

Casting procedures: Uses in-house casting directors
and sometimes holds general auditions. Actors may
write in June/July requesting inclusion. Casting
breakdowns are available via Equity Job Information
Service and specific casting websites, for example
www.castingcallpro.com. Welcomes letters (with
CVs and photographs) from individual actors
previously unknown to the company, sent by post or
email; also welcomes showreels and invitations to
view individual actors' websites. Actively encourages
applications from disabled actors and promotes the
use of inclusive casting. "We give priority to formally
trained actors who have completed recognised
courses at drama school. We like actors who can face
the rigours of touring with good humour!"

Guy Masterson Productions

Millfield House & Theatre, Silver Street, Edmonton,
London N18 1PJ

Director Guy Masterson

Production details: For more than a decade, a
successful producer of small- to mid-scale work.
Stages 4-6 productions annually with 400
performances during the course of the year. Tours on
average to 350 different national and international
venues, including arts centres, theatres, and outdoor,
educational and community venues. Recent
productions include: *Twelve Angry Men*, *Animal
Farm* and *Under Milk Wood*.

Casting procedures: Sometimes holds general
auditions. Only works with actors seen on a previous
occasion, and then only by invitation.

Meeting Ground Theatre Co

4 Shirley Road, Nottingham NG3 5DA
tel 0115-962 3009
website www.meetingground.org.uk
Director Tanya Myers

Production details: At the heart of the company's
artistic policy and vision is the theatrical exploration
of what the company calls "the politics of the
imagination". Work is based on the belief that, by
taking artistic work across barriers and frontiers –
whether they be national, psychological, intellectual,
cultural, spiritual or disciplinary – new sources of
energy and creativity can be engendered.

Since 1985 Meeting Ground has been celebrating the
meeting of artists from different disciplines and
cultures. Building a strong international reputation
for new production work of the highest innovative
standards and qualities, the company has toured
extensively throughout Germany, Poland, Italy and
the UK, also appearing at numerous festivals.

Casting procedures: Offers ITC/Equity contracts and
does not subscribe to the Equity Pension Scheme.
Actively encourages applications from disabled actors
and promotes the use of inclusive casting.

Midland Actors Theatre (MAT)

25 Merrishaw Road, Northfield,
Birmingham B31 3SL
tel 0121-608 7144 fax 0121-608 7144
email news@midlandactorstheatre.co.uk
website www.midlandactorstheatre.co.uk
Director David Allen Associate Director Gillian
Adamson Secretary Judith Aston

Production details: Founded in 1999. Produces
classics and new work. Stages 2-3 productions
annually with 90 performances during the course of
the year. Tours on average to 75 different theatres,
schools, and other venues in the West Midlands, East
Midlands, and nationally each year. Around 4-5
actors are involved in each production. Recent
productions include: *Macbeth*, *Prospero's Island*, *The
Children* and *The Mothers*. Offers ITC/Equity
approved contracts and does not subscribe to the
Equity Pension Scheme.

Casting procedures: Sometimes holds general auditions. Actors should write requesting inclusion when auditions are advertised; general casting enquiries are most welcome in January and June. Casting breakdowns are publicly available via Equity Job Information Service and *PCR*. Advises that the company is primarily interested in actors who are Midlands-based. Actively encourages applications from disabled actors and promotes the use of inclusive casting.

Mikron Theatre Company
Marsden Mechanics, Peel Street, Marsden, Huddersfield HD7 6BW
tel (01484) 843701 *fax* (01484) 843701
email admin@mikron.org.uk
website www.mikron.org.uk
Artistic Director Richard Povall *Associate Director* Mike Lucas *General Manager* Peter Toon

Production details: Has been touring for 38 years: "a little touring company with the reputation for tackling large-scale subjects and turning history into vivid and dramatic entertainment". Tours on Tyseley, the company's Narrowboat, on the inland waterways of Britain in the summer, and by road in the autumn months. Almost unique in writing and presenting 2 new plays with original music and songs each year. Tours to every conceivable type of venue, reaching audiences that other companies cannot. Recent productions include: *Married to the Job* and *The Lacemakers* (2007); *Debtonation* and *Fair Trade* (2008).

Casting procedures: Uses in-house casting directors and does not hold general auditions. Actors may write in Dec/Jan to request inclusion, and are strongly advised to keep an eye on the website. Casting breakdowns are publicly available from the website, via Equity Job Information Service and Castweb, and in *PCR*. Welcomes letters (with CVs & photographs) from individual actors previously unknown to the company if sent by post, but not by email, and does not accept showreels. Welcomes invitations to view individual actors's websites. Rarely (or never) has the opportunity to cast disabled actors "because of the nature of our tour – however, our Artistic Director is disabled". Asks actors to "please bear in mind that this is a hard tour: boating all day and shows and get-ins every night. Do consult the website before applying".

Mokita Productions
54 Canning Road, London N5 2JS
mobile (07980) 564849
email mail@mokitaproductions.org
website www.mokitaproductions.org
Artistic Director Emily Agnew *Associate Director* Jane Lesley *Other key personnel* Alfie Talman (Assistant Producer), Lucy Leigh (Funding Manager)

Production details: Established in 2007 "to promote work of an exciting, raw, passionate and original

nature". Specialises in new writing and developing work with new and emerging writers; also aims to encourage new and emerging practitioners in directing, producing, design, technical theatre and acting. In general stages 6 productions each year; also works in TIE (contact: Emily Agnew). Recent productions include: *Involution* by Rachel Welch (Pacific Playhouse, London; Pleasance Theatre, Edinburgh); *Pluto* (co-produciton, Blue Elephant Theatre); and Pages (co-production, Pacific Playhouse, London).

Casting procedures: Uses in-house casting directors. Sometimes holds general auditions; actors may write in at any time and details are filed for future reference. Casting breakdowns are available from the website, *PCR*, *The Stage*, Castnet, Castweb and Castingcallpro. Welcomes letters (with CVs and photographs) from individual actors previously unknown to the company sent by post, but not by email. Accepts showreels and invitations to view individual actors' websites. Will consider applications from disabled actors to play characters with disabilities.

MonStar Productions
65A Huddleston Road, London N7 0AE
email monstar@fsmail.net
website www.monstarproductions.co.uk
Artistic Director Monique Briggs

Production details: A freelance producer (own shows, co-productions and sole producer). Also works in TIE. Recent productions include: *Love & Human Remarks* by Brad Fraser, directed by Dominic Leclerc at the Warehouse Theatre.

Casting procedures: Uses in-house casting directors. Holds general auditions; actors should write when a casting call goes out. Casting breakdowns are usually available via agents, or by direct email. Welcomes letters (with CVs and photographs) from actors previously unknown to the company sent by post, but not by email. Prefers not to receive invitations to view individual actors' websites, although may accept showreels. Actively encourages applications from disabled actors, and promotes the use of inclusive casting. Offers Equity approved contracts as negotiated through ITC. "An agent is advised."

Mu-Lan Theatre Company
The Albany, Douglas Way, London SE8 4AG
tel 020-8694 0557 *fax* 020-8694 0618
email mailbox@mu-lan.org
website www.mu-lan.org
Director Paul Courtenay

Production details: Founded in 1988. Stages 1 production annually and gives 30 performances during the course of the year. Tours have covered the North West, South and South West England. About 8 actors are involved in each production. Recent productions include: *Sun is Shining, Romeo and Juliet* and *Takeaway*.

Casting procedures: Uses freelance casting directors. Does not hold general auditions. Casting breakdowns are publicly available via *PCR*. Welcomes submissions (with CVs and photographs) sent by post or email. Also accepts invitations to view individual actors' websites.

New Perspectives Theatre Co
Park Lane Business Centre, Park Lane, Basford, Nottingham NG6 0DW
tel 0115-927 2334 *fax* 0115-927 1612
email info@newperspectives.co.uk
website www.newperspectives.co.uk
Artistic Director Daniel Buckroyd *Key personnel* Chris Kirkwood (General Manager), Emma Morley (Administrator), Mandy Ivory-Castile (Production Manager)

Production details: Founded in 1972. A leading East Midlands touring theatre company; also tours nationally. On average stages 3-4 productions each year, giving 200 performances in 190 arts centre and community venues in the East and West Midlands, Wales, London, the South West, and the North. Offers Equity approved contracts as negotiated through ITC. Recent prodcutions include: *On Saturdays This Bed Is Poland* (Lakeside Arts Centre); *The Iron Man* (Darlington Arts Centre; Riverhead Theatre, Louth); *Saturday Night and Sunday Morning* (Lakeside Arts Centre).

Casting procedures: Does not welcome unsolicited approaches. Actively encourages applications by disabled actors and promotes the use of inclusive casting. "Casting breakdowns are available through Spotlight Link and from the website."

New Shoes Theatre
mobile (07972) 395634
email admin@newshoestheatre.org.uk
website www.newshoestheatre.org.uk
Artistic Director Nicolette Kay

Production details: A new company set up in 2009 to produce *Hurried Steps* by Dacia Mariani. The Board, Artistic Director and Artistic Associates ran Muzikansky for 15 years (**www.mzky.co.uk**). The company stages 1 production annually with around 20 performances to arts centres, theatres, educational and community venues. In general 5 actors are involved in each production.

Casting procedures: Uses in-house casting directors. Casting breakdowns are available via the website, *PCR*, *The Stage*, Spotlight, Casting Call Pro and artsjobs.

NITRO
6 Brewery Road, London N7 9NH
tel 020-7609 1331 *fax* 020-7609 1221
email info@nitro.co.uk
Artistic Director Felix Cross *Executive Producer* Matthew Jones *Administrator* Laura Tomlinson

Production details: Founded in 1978; formerly known as Black Theatre Co-operative Ltd. National touring theatre company that generates and produces contemporary black musical theatre. First established to provide training for black writers, directors and artists. Aims to explore ways of using black music as a means of attracting new audiences to theatre. Stages 1-2 productions annually with 1-2 performances during the course of the year. Recent productions include: *Nitrobeat* and *A Nitro at the Opera*.

Casting procedures: Sometimes uses agents when casting. Also holds general auditions; actors should write at the start of the year to request inclusion. Welcomes submissions (with CVs and photographs) sent by post or email. Accepts invitations to view individual actors' websites. Advises that the company keeps an up-to-date catalogue of black actors and would particularly welcome CVs from actors of different ethnic backgrounds. Offers TMA/Equity approved contracts and does not subscribe to the Equity Pension Scheme. Actively encourages applications from disabled actors and promotes the use of inclusive casting.

No Limits Theatre
Dundas Street, Monkwearmouth, Sunderland SR6 0AY
tel 0191-565 3013 *fax* 0191-565 3015
email info@nolimitstheatre.org.uk
website www.nolimitstheatre.org.uk
Artistic Director/Chief Executive Janet Nettleton
Technical Director Alan Parker

Production details: Founded in 1995, No Limits is a touring theatre company that works with adults with and without learning disabilities. Aims to produce high-quality, devised work that challenges traditional perceptions of theatre and disability, staging 1 production in 20 different venues across the UK each year. It also has a strong commitment to outreach and development work. In general 5-8 actors work on each production. Recent productions include: *I Catch Your Breath* (The Lowry, Manchester); *Silver Street* (The Maltings, Berwick) and *Wall of Whispers* (Blackfriars, Boston).

Casting procedures: Welcomes letters, CVs and photographs from actors previously unknown to the company, but does not accept emails or unsolicited showreels. Advises that the company already has a core acting team but often takes on new actors in workshop training sessions.

Non Stop Cabaret Theatre Company
22 Hall Street, Walshaw, Bury, Greater Manchester BL8 3BD
mobile (07967) 636475
email admin@nonstopcabaret.co.uk
website www.nonstopcabaret.co.uk
Artistic Director James Layton *Associate Director* Simon Winterman

Production details: Formed in 2007. Focuses on re-working classic and 20th century texts. Also produces live art works and offers a range of educational workshops. Recent productions include: *The Maids* by Jean Genet (2008 National Tour, Winner of Best Theatre Production at Buxton Festival Fringe 2008); *Faustus* adapted by Benjamin Cooper (2009 National Tour, Nominated Best Theatre Production and Best Performer at Buxton Festival Fringe 2009); and *Peep(le) Show* (six-hour durational performance exploring endurance, responsibility and transformation).

Northern Broadsides

Dean Clough, Halifax HX3 5AX
tel (01422) 369704 *fax* (01422) 383175
website www.northern-broadsides.co.uk
Artistic Director Barrie Rutter *Associate Director* Conrad Nelson

Production details: Formed in 1992 by Artistic Director Barrie Rutter, Northern Broadsides is a multi-award winning touring company based in the historic Dean Clough Mill in Halifax, West Yorkshire. The company has built up a formidable reputation performing Shakespeare and classical texts with an innovative, popular and regional style, often in unconventional locations (The Tower of London, cattle markets, churches, indoor riding stables, Victorian mills). As well as touring extensively in the UK, the company has delighted audiences across the world, touring to India, Brazil, the USA, Greece, Cyprus, the Czech Republic, Poland, Germany, Austria and Denmark.

The company repertoire consists mainly of Shakespeare and classical texts. These plays possess a timeless resonance and their universal exploration of the human condition has currency in any day and age, appealing directly to the soul, the emotions and the imagination. Northern Broadsides are dedicated to interpreting the classics in a manner which makes what is often regarded as 'difficult' work extremely accessible. Their lively 'no frills' approach, with simple storytelling and minimal sets, has not only won the company many plaudits and awards, but enabled both established and new audiences to enjoy Shakespeare regardless of language or theatrical convention.

Northern Broadsides' work is characterised by its vitality and humour; the passion of the performers, whose acting style is far less 'mannered' than conventional theatrical productions; an ensemble style which adds coherence to the performances (the result of working with a group of actors over a period of time, in some cases many years) and precise direction which results in work of remarkable clarity.

NOT the National Theatre

116 Dalberg Road London SW2 1AW
tel 020-7771 0009
email info@notthenational.com
website www.notthenational.com
Artistic Directors Pete Colley, Lilian Evans, Michael Fry and Daniel Leatherdale

Production details: The company was founded in 1984 by 3 National Theatre actors, with the aim of presenting contemporary plays to varied audiences across the UK and beyond. The productions have always been sufficiently flexible to be performed in both conventional and non-conventional theatre spaces in a repertoire which mixes new plays with revivals of modern classics.

The company has now played over 300 venues nationally and internationally. It has toured on consecutive days from the Swan in Stratford to Holloway Jail, and in consecutive weeks from Brazilia to Bucharest. NOT The National Theatre was the first British company to visit Communist Romania and Czechoslovakia, and the first company to play in Argentina after the Falklands War.

Most tours now play between 30 and 50 dates throughout Britain and Ireland on the small and middle-scale circuits. The company has established strong relationships with theatres and audiences across the UK and beyond, which has allowed it widen the scope and boldness of its programming.

In recent years the company has focused on the second productions of new plays that may have had only a limited first run, or the work of a new or established playwright whose work has not been seen on the national circuit. NOT The National Theatre produced the first national tours of (among others) *Hysteria, Two, The Beauty Queen of Leenane, Not a Game for Boys* and *My Mother Said I Never Should.*

NTC Touring Theatre Company

The Playhouse, Bondgate Without, Alnwick, Northumberland NE66 1PQ
tel (01665) 602586 *fax* (01665) 605837
email admin@ntc-touringtheatre.co.uk
website www.ntc-touringtheatre.co.uk
Director Gillian Hambleton *General Manager* Anna Flood *Tour Administrator* Hilary Burns

Production details: Founded in 1978 as Northumberland Theatre Company. Small-scale touring theatre company performing at village halls, small theatres and community venues in predominantly rural areas. Main areas of work are new writing and ensemble physical theatre pieces. Stages 3-4 productions annually with more than 120 performances during the course of the year. Tours on average to 120 different venues nationally. 5 actors are usually involved in each production. Recent productions include: *Bedazzled, Great Expectations* and *Alex, The Warrior & The Winter Star.* Offers ITC/Equity approved contracts but does not subscribe to the Equity Pension Scheme.

Casting procedures: Sometimes holds general auditions for locally based actors (best time to write is early June or September), but most casting is done through agents via *SBS*. Casting breakdowns are available on request via postal application (with sae) and on the website. Welcomes submissions (with CVs and photographs) sent by post. Also accepts invitations to view individual actors' performances and will always reply to individual actors. Particularly interested in locally based actors or actors with local origins, and will keep details on file for future reference unless requested to do otherwise. Actively encourages applications from disabled actors and promotes the use of inclusive casting.

Off the Cuff Theatre Company Ltd
91A Rivington Street, London EC2A 3AY
tel 020-7739 2857 *fax* 020-7739 3852
email otctheatre@aol.com
Artistic Director Paul Dubois

Production details: Stages 1-2 productions annually, with around 30 performances in 2 arts centres and theatres in the UK and internationally. In general, 4-6 actors are involved in each production. Offers Equity-approved contracts as negotiated through ITC, and participates in the Equity Pension Scheme. See the website for details of recent productions.

Casting procedures: Holds general auditions; actors may write in January to request inclusion. Casting breakdowns are available via the website. Welcomes letters (with CVs and photographs) from individual actors previously unknown to the company, sent by post or email. Also welcomes showreels, but prefers not to receive invitations to view individual actors' websites. Actively encourages applications from disabled actors, and promotes the use of inclusive casting.

The Okai Collier Company Ltd
The Bell Tower, St Barnabas Church, Grove Road, Bow, London E3 5TG
tel 020-8981 6511 *fax* 020-8983 0858
email info@okaicollier.co.uk
website www.okaicollier.co.uk
Artistic Director Omar F Okai

Production details: The Okai Collier Company was formed in 1994 by artistic director Omar F Okai and producer Simon James Collier to explore and push the boundaries of everyday ideas, opinions and opportunities in the creative arts: music, theatre, dance, painting and the written word. Using a variety of media including IT, the company aims to break down contemporary social barriers and encourage new talent by developing a range of projects in this field. These projects include award-winning theatrical productions, opera, creative writing with young people, exhibitions for new artists and community arts projects, as well as its innovative publishing division. Okai Collier is committed to maintaining a balanced portfolio of work, divided between the commercial and charitable spheres and drawing on a diverse range of people and disciplines.

Open Clasp Theatre Company
Level 2, 36 Lime Street, Ouseburn Valley, Newcastle upon Tyne NE1 2PQ
tel 0191-230 1698 *fax* 0191-261 7144
email info@openclasp.plus.com
website www.openclasp.org.uk
Artistic Director Catrina McHugh *Company Development Manager* Roma Yagnik

Production details: Uses theatre and drama to give a voice to women of all ages. The company works in partnership with community groups, running issue-based drama workshops with women's and girls' groups to create theatre that is taken to community and mainstream venues. "We work with many women whose voices have never before reached the stage, and whose stories are worth telling. They share them with us, and we create new stories that reflect those experiences and bring them back to the community. We make sure everyone involved has a great time and a good laugh." On average stages 1 touring production per year, usually in Feb-March, with 16-35 performances in 16-30 arts centres, theatres, and educational and community venues in North East UK, Scotland, North West UK and Yorkshire. Recent productions include: *Rattle & Roll*, *Stand 'N' Tan*, and *A Twist of Lemon*.

Casting procedures: Sometimes holds general auditions; actors requesting inclusion should write in September. Casting breakdowns are available from the website, by postal application with sae, and from online casting services. Welcomes letters (with CVs and photographs) from individual actors previously unknown to the company, sent by post or email, but does not accept showreels. Will consider invitations to view individual actors' websites if accompanied by a full CV. Will also consider applications from disabled actors to play characters with disabilities. "It is paramount that our actors share the ethos of the company. Open Clasp ensures that casting is representative of the diverse groups we work with, the issues explored, and the characters they have created."

The Original Theatre Company
Dovedon Hall, Chedburgh Road, Whepstead, Bury St Edmunds, Suffolk IP29 4UB
tel (01284) 735447
email info@originaltheatre.com
website www.originaltheatre.com
Director Alastair Whatley *Technical Manager* Alan Valentine

Production details: Established in 2004. Stages 3-4 productions annually, with 120-150 performances in 40-50 arts centres, theatres and outdoor venues across the UK. In general 8-13 actors are involved in each production. Offers Equity-approved contracts. Recent productions include: *Vincent in Brixton* (Yvonne Arnaud, Theatre Royal Windsor, Northcott Exeter); *Othello* (Harrogate Theatre, Buxton Opera House).

Theatre

Casting procedures: Sometimes holds general auditions; actors may write in March and July to request inclusion. Casting breakdowns are available from the website, by postal application with sae, and from Spotlight. Welcomes letters (with CVs and photographs) from individual actors previously unknown to the company, sent by post only. Also welcomes showreels and invitations to view individual actors' websites. Actively encourages applications from disabled actors and promotes the use of inclusive casting.

Out of Joint

7 Thane Works, Thane Villas, London N7 7PH
tel 020-7609 0207 fax 020-7609 0203
email ojo@outofjoint.co.uk
website www.outofjoint.co.uk
Director Max Stafford-Clark Administrator and Education Manager Natasha Ockrent Producer Graham Cowley

Production details: Stages 2 productions annually with approximately 230 performances during the course of the year. Tours both nationally and internationally playing to around 12-15 arts centres and theatres each year. Recent productions include: Duck, The Permanent Way, Macbeth and Talking to Terrorists.

Casting procedures: Welcomes letters (with CVs and photographs) but not email submissions. Also accepts performance notices from individual actors. Offers Equity approved contracts. Will consider applications from disabled actors to play characters with disabilities.

Ovation Productions

Upstairs at The Gatehouse, Highgate,
London N6 4BD
tel 020-8340 4256
website www.ovationtheatres.com
Director John Plews Casting Director Katie Plews

Production details: Founded in 1985. Owns and operates Upstairs at the Gatehouse, a fringe theatre in North London (see entry under Fringe theatres on page 234). Recent productions include: Into the Woods and Cooking with Elvis.

Casting details: Casting breakdowns are publicly available via PCR and advertisements in The Stage. Welcomes letters (with CVs and photographs) and email submissions. "Castings are always posted on www.upstairsatthegatehouse.com." Offers non-Equity contracts. Will consider applications from disabled actors to play characters with disabilities.

The Oxford Shakespeare Company

3 Gunter Grove, London SW10 0UN
tel 020-7351 5417
email info@oxfordshakespearecompany.co.uk
website www.oxfordshakespeare.company.co.uk
Directors Kevin Hosier, Charlotte Windmill, Nick Green

Production details: Founded in 2001. Took over from Bold and Saucy (established in 1992), staging Shakespeare plays in Wadham College Gardens, Oxford. Also has a residency at North Garden, Lincoln's Inn, London. Stages 3 productions with 90-100 performances during the course of the year. 9-10 actors are involved in each production. Tours have reached Oxford, London and Basingstoke. Recent productions include: Merry Wives of Windsor and Macbeth.

Casting procedures: Actors requesting inclusion should write in March or April. Casting breakdowns are released to agents and are available via PCR. Welcomes letters (with CVs and photographs) but not email submissions. Actors applying should be able to demonstrate experience of Shakespeare and the rigours of open-air performing.

Oxfordshire Theatre Company

The Annexe, SS Mary & John School, Meadow Lane, Oxford OX4 1TJ
tel (01865) 249444
email info@oxfordshiretheatrecompany.co.uk
website www.oxfordshiretheatrecompany.co.uk
Artistic Director Karen Simpson Administrative Director Louise Wiggins

Production details: Tours high-quality, challenging, entertaining and accessible theatre to audiences in Oxfordshire and beyond. The company has a unique reputation for taking theatre to non-theatre venues, especially in rural areas. Creates a minimum of 3 productions each year, each of which has a resonance with both adults and younger audiences. The autumn production appeals to families with young children; the spring show embraces narratives that challenge, engage and excite adult audiences. From 2009 the company is producing a summer production that will actively encourage young people and older people to become a more prominent part of its audience.

Casting procedures: The company casts by audition. Breakdowns are published on the website as well as in PCR, SBS, Castcall, and Casting Call Pro, among others. Is unable to consider unsolicited submssions at other times. Actively encourages applications from disabled actors and promotes the use of inclusive casting.

Paines Plough

4th Floor, 43 Aldwych, London WC2B 4DN
tel 020-7240 4533 fax 020-7240 4534
email office@painesplough.com
website www.painesplough.com
Artistic Directors James Grieve, George Perrin General Manager Anneliese Davidson Literary Director Tessa Walker Administrative Assistant Clare Martynski

Production details: Founded in 1974, the company is dedicated to producing new writing. Stages 3-4 productions annually across the UK and internationally. Recent work includes: Mark

Ravenhill's *Shoot/Get Treasure/Repeat*, and Steve Thompson's *Roaring Trade*.

Casting procedures: Uses freelance casting directors. Does not accept unsolicited CVs or photographs, as there is no facility to store such information.

Pentabus

Bromfield, Ludlow, Shropshire SY8 2JU
tel (01584) 856564 *fax* (01584) 856254
email thom@pentabus.co.uk
website www.pentabus.co.uk
Development Director John Moreton *Artistic Director* Orla O'Loughlin *Administrative Producer* Thomasina Carlyle

Production details: "Pentabus Theatre believes in asking questions and telling stories that resonate with audiences locally, nationally and internationally. At the heart of our work is our rural location in Shropshire, which affords us a unique perspective on, and relationship to, the world. Our aim is to pioneer engaging, provocative and surprising new work that connects people and places".

Pentabus Theatre is celebrating its 35th year as a producer of innovative, contemporary work. The last few years have been the company's most successful yet. Recent projects have included: *Silent Engines*: Pleasance, Arcola Theatre (Fringe First for Best New Play), *White Open Space*: Pleasance, Soho Theatre, Riksteatren Sweden (Shortlisted for a South Bank Show Award), *Kebab*: Dublin International Festival, Royal Court, and a number of large scale site specific pieces including: *Shuffle*: with the NYT at Merry Hill, one of Europe's largest shopping centres, *Underland*: performed 200 feet underground in a series of caves in the Forest of Dean and *Precious Bane* by Bryony Lavery performed in a number of stately homes across the UK.

In 2009/10, Pentabus performed *Origins* (Pleasance Edinburgh and Theatre Severn Shrewsbury), by Steven Canny and Jon Nicholson, *Tales of the Country* (rural tour) an adaptation by Nic Warburton of Brian Viner's book, and *Pigs, The Hunting Season*, and *The Sleep Affair*.

Casting procedures: Occasionally uses freelance casting directors. Casting breakdowns are available via Equity Job Information Service, *PCR* and the website. Welcomes letters (with CVs and photographs) but not email submissions.

The People's Theatre Co

12E High Street, Egham TW20 9EA
tel (01784) 470439 *fax* (01784) 470439
email admin@ptc.org.uk
website www.ptc.org.uk
Director Steven Lee

Production details: Established in 2003. 4 productions are staged annually. All work is new and original, and the company has built an international reputation for its unique brand of sophisticated pop musicals. Stages 120 performances per year, touring across the country to Receiving Houses and number 1/number 2 venues. The company does *not* play to educational or community venues ("Please do not apply to us for TIE."). 7 actors are generally involved in each production. Recent productions include: the award-winning *Head*; *The Witch's Bogey*; *Bink and the Hairy Fairy*; and *Bink and the Riddle of the Sphinx*.

Casting procedures: Casting is done in-house. Hold general auditions. Actors should only write requesting inclusion in response to casting calls. Actors can also register on PTC's website for first alerts to castings. Casting breakdowns are obtainable via Castweb, Casting Call Pro, CastNet and through the PTC mailing list. Accepts submissions (with CVs and photographs) from individual actors previously unknown to them. Submissions sent by email are also accepted. Invitations to view showreels and individual actors' websites are welcomed. Applications from disabled actors are considered to play disabled characters.

"We want a well-presented CV with personal information, training, experience and detailed skills – particularly singing, as most of our work is musicals. New actors and recent graduates welcome."

People Show

Pollard Row, London E2 6NB
tel 020-7729 1841 *fax* 020-7739 0203
email people@peopleshow.co.uk
website www.peopleshow.co.uk
Steering Group Chahine Yavroyan, Mark Long, George Khan, Gareth Brierley, Sadie Cook, Fiona Creese, Jessica Worral *General Manager* David Duchin

Production details: The longest-running experimental theatre company in the UK, touring nationally and internationally for 43 years. In general stages 1-2 productions each year, with 20-40 performances at 10 venues including arts centres, theatres, and outdoor and site-specific venues. Anything from 3 to 65 actors are involved in each production. Offers Equity-approved contracts as negotiated through ITC. Recent credits include: *People Show 118: The Birthday Tour* (Northern Stage, Contact Theatre, Arena Theatre, Lighthouse, Tobacco Factory, New Cut Arts Centre, Alsager Arts Centre, Gardner Arts Centre, Windsor Arts Centre, Unity Theatre); and *People Show 119: Ghost Sonata* (site-specific show commissioned for Liverpool Capital of Culture at Sefton Park Palm House, Liverpool).

Casting procedures: Does not use freelance casting directors or hold general auditions. Welcomes letters (with CVs and photographs) from actors previously unknown to the company sent by post and email. Is happy to receive showreels and invitations to view individual actors' websites. Actively encourages applications from disabled actors and promotes the

Theatre

use of inclusive casting. "People Show is an ensemble company with a core group of 8 artists, and an extended network of 45+."

Pilot Theatre Co

York Theatre Royal, St Leonards Place,
York YO1 7HD
tel (01904) 635755 *fax* (01904) 656378
email info@pilot-theatre.com
website www.pilot-theatre.com
Artistic Director Marcus Romer

Production details: Pilot Theatre Company is a national touring theatre company based in Yorkshire. The company was launched in 1981 by a group of students from Bretton Hall College and established itself in Wakefield. Throughout the 1980s worked as a devising collective responding reactively to requests for work. The projects that followed ranged from playscheme activities to workshop sessions to touring issue-based work in schools. In 1994, underwent an internal restructuring which resulted in the appointment of a new Artistic Director, Marcus Romer.

"Between 1994 and 1997 Pilot developed its touring circuit nationally. The last 3 schools' touring shows showed an increase of earned income by 600% and an increase in audiences from 5000 to over 18,000 per tour. *Lord of the Flies*, our first midscale touring project, reached an audience of 50,000 per tour. Collaborating with nationally significant venues the Theatre Royal York and the Lyric Theatre Hammersmith, the project has enabled Pilot to reach more young people than ever before, with a full workshop programme available to every tour venue, and teacher resources available to every teacher through the Pilot website."

Casting procedures: The company regularly posts casting information online. "Please try and avoid sending surface mail for casting, as we are trying to minimise wastage and energy usage." Please email your details to: **casting@pilot-theatre.com**.

Playbox Theatre (Generator)

The Dream Factory, Shelly Avenue,
Warwick CV34 6LE
tel (01926) 419555 *fax* (01926) 411429
email stewart@playboxtheatre.com
website www.playboxtheatre.com
Artistic Director Stewart McGill *Directors* Emily Quash, Mary King

Production details: Established in 1986, Generator is the professional acting company of Playbox Theatre, reworking classic drama for contemporary audiences. 2 productions staged annually, touring nationally to arts centres, theatres, outdoor venues and educational venues. Based in Warwick. Up to 12 actors used in each production. Offers Equity approved contracts. Recent productions include: *A Doll's House*, and *Henry VI – The Wars of the Roses*.

Casting procedures: Accepts submissions (with CVs and photographs) from actors previously unknown to the company sent by post or by email. Actively encourages applications from disabled actors and promotes the use of inclusive casting.

Point Blank

Unit 2, 67 Earl Street, Sheffield S1 4PY
tel 0114-249 3650/51 *fax* 0114-249 3655
email info@pointblank.org.uk
website www.pointblank.org.uk
Directors Liz Tomlin, Steve Jackson *Company Manager* Bianca King

Production details: Established in 1999. Small-scale national touring theatre producing new work, devised, physical theatre and new writing. Stages 1 production annually. 30-60 performances per year touring 18 venues which include art centres, theatres, outdoor venues, educational and community venues. Regions covered include North, North West, Yorkshire, West Midlands, South East, London, Scotland, Ireland and Wales. 2-4 actors are involved in each production. Actors are employed under Equity approved contracts negotiated through ITC. Recent productions include: *Operation Wonderland* (15 venues including The Crucible, Latchmere and The Traverse); *Roses and Morphine* (18 venues including The Crucible, Royal Exchange and Aberystwith Arts Centre); and *Last Orders* (Sheffield, site-specific).

Casting procedures: Casting is carried out by in-house casting director. Hold general auditions. Actors can write at anytime to request inclusion; details will be kept on file. Casting breakdowns are obtainable via casting websites. Accepts submissions (with CVs and photographs) from individual actors previously unknown to the company. Applications from disabled actors are considered to play disabled characters wherever possible.

"Research the company first to check it's appropriate. We will get back with details of shows as appropriate. Yorkshire-based actors are particularly welcome to apply."

Prime Productions

54 Hermiston Village, Currie, Midlothian EH14 4AQ
tel/fax 0131-449 4055
email primeproductions@talktalk.net
website www.primeproductions.co.uk
Artistic Director Martin Heller

Production details: Founded in 1985, operates small-scale touring of mainstream drama throughout Scotland; project funded by Scottish Arts Council. 1 production is staged each year, touring around 30 venues – arts centres, theatres, educational and community venues. Between 4 and 10 actors are involved in each production. Recent productions include: *Great Expectations, Further than the Furthest Thing, Romeo & Juliet, Mary Queen of Scots Got Her Head Chopped Off* and *Sunset Song*.

Casting procedures: Casts in-house. Casting breakdowns are not publicly available, and the company does not welcome unsolicited approaches from actors, although it is happy to receive invitations to view individual actors' websites. "We stage productions with very specific casting requirements, which we seek at the time."

Primecut Productions

285A Ormerth Road, Belfast BT7 3GG
tel 028-90645101 *fax* 028-90645101
email info@primecutproductions.co.uk
website www.primecutproductions.co.uk

Production details: An independent touring company based in Belfast and bringing the best of contemporary international playwrights to Irish audiences. Recent productions include: a double bill of *The Mercy Seat*, and *Ashes to Ashes* at the Belfast Lyric; and touring productions of Caryl Churchill's *A Number* and Owen McCaffery's *Cold Comfort*. The company stages 2-3 productions per year and tours to 10-15 venues across Northern and Southern Ireland.

Casting procedures: Does not publish casting breakdowns, but welcomes CVs and photographs from individual actors whose work is previously unknown to the the company; also welcomes invitations to view actors' websites. Will consider applications from disabled actors when casting for characters with disabilities. Offers ITC/Equity approved contracts.

Proteus Theatre Co

Queen Mary's College, Cliddesden Road,
Basingstoke, Hants RG21 3HF
tel (01256) 354541 *fax* (01256) 350186
email info@proteustheatre.com
website www.proteustheatre.com
Artistic Director Mary Swan

Production details: Established in 1981. Touring theatre company operating in the South. Stages 2-3 productions annually touring to 80 venues including arts centres, theatres, outdoor venues, educational and community venues and churches. Recent credits include *Peter Pan* and *Whatever Happened to Bette and Joan?*

Casting procedures: Casting breakdowns available via the website, Equity Job Information service and PCR. Does not welcome unsolicited CVs. Actively encourages applications from disabled actors and promotes the use of inclusive casting. Offers ITC/Equity approved contracts.

Purple Fish Productions

197 Goldhawk Road, London W12 8EP
mobile (07976) 809693
email info@purplefishproductions.co.uk
website www.purplefishproductions.co.uk
Directors Michelle Seton, Luan de Burgh

Production details: Founded in 2001. Aims to produce both established work and exciting devised pieces for adults and children. Michelle Seton and Luan de Burgh both trained in London and at Le Coq in Paris. Stages 3 productions with 75 performances during the course of the year. Tours to 20 different arts centres, theatres, educational and community venues annually. Tours have covered Greater London, Ireland and Canada. In general 2 actors are involved in each production. Recent productions include: *Told by a Dodo* and *The Two of Us*.

Casting procedures: Casting breakdowns are available via *PCR* and the website. Welcomes letters (with CVs and photographs) but not email submissions. Actors should write only when the company advertises. Invitations to view individual actors' websites are also accepted.

Pursued by a Bear

The Maltings, Bridge Square, Farnham,
Surrey GU9 7QR
email pursuedbyabear@yahoo.co.uk

Production details: Theatre company touring new writing across the UK. Stages 2 productions annually and gives 60 performances during the course of the year. Tours to around 10 different arts centres, theatres, educational and community venues each year. Tours have covered the East, North East, South East, South West and London. In general 2 actors are involved in each production. Recent productions include: *Double Helix*, *You Don't Kiss* and *All Fall Away*.

Casting procedures: Welcomes submissions (with CVs and photographs) sent by post or email.

Raised Eyebrow Theatre Company

Low Hall Cottage, Carr Lane, Brompton,
Scarborough YO13 9DH
tel/fax (01723) 850538
email lizipatch@aol.com
website www.raisedeyebrow.co.uk
Artistic Director Lizi Patch *Associate Director* Jon Stokes

Production details: A community and TIE company staging 2-3 productions each year and presenting approximately 220 performances in schools and community venues across England. The company also runs youth theatres and workshops. In general 5 actors work on each production. Recent productions include: *Farmer Charles*, Raised Eyebrow Youth Theatre; *Destination 2014*, for Capacity Builders conference in Birmingham; *The Street Never Ends* and *The Wave*, Filey Festival; *The Past on Your Doorstep*, Chaddeston Park and Osmaston Park, Derby; *A Midsummer Murder*, The Old Mill, Langtoft Abbey House (in partnership with Derbyshire-based Orange Box Design); *Space Pirates – Adventures on Planet Maths*, Tour; *Spike* (in partnership with Scarborough Safer Communities); and *A Midsummer Night's Dream* (Raised Eyebrow Youth Theatre).

Casting procedures: Casting is done in-house and with the help of freelance casting directors. Casting breakdowns are available by postal application (with sae), and in *PCR* and *The Stage*. Welcomes letters and emails (with professional CVs and 10x8 photographs) from actors previously unknown to the company. Will also accept showreels and emails. Advises that professional applications will be given priority over photocopies, passport photos and holiday snaps.

Real Circumstance Theatre Company
100 Lexden Road, West Bergholt,
Colchester CO6 3BW
email info@realcircumstance.com
website www.realcircumstance.com
Artistic Director Dan Sherer *Creative Producer* Anna Bewick *Key personnel* Suresh Patel, Ruth Brock

Production details: Established in 2006 with 3 aims: to produce innovative theatre consisting of new writing by emergent authors, and new plays created by the Company through long-term real-time improvisation; to help young theatre-practitioners develop their crafts (both before and after professional training) and investigate new ways of working; and to raise the profile of Essex and the Eastern Region as a national centre of creative artistic work. Tours 1 Studio Production each year, to the community. Recent productions include: *LIMBO* by Declan Feenan, and *Lough/Rain* by Declan Feenan and Clara Brennan (both co-produced with York Theatre Royal).

Casting procedures: Uses in-house casting directors. Sometimes holds general auditions; actors may write at any time to request inclusion. Welcomes letters (with CVs and photographs) from actors previously unknown to the company, and accepts submissions by email. Welcomes showreels and invitations to view individual actors' websites. Offers Equity approved contracts negotiated through ITC.

Red Ladder Theatre Co
3 St Peter's Buildings, York Street, Leeds LS9 8AJ
tel 0113-245 5311 *fax* 0113-245 5351
email rod@redladder.co.uk
website www.redladder.co.uk
Artistic Director Rod Dixon

Production details: Red Ladder's mission is to make theatre which celebrates, inspires and challenges young people, developing in them the desire and ability to express ideas and strengthen social and cultural cohesion. The company, founded in 1968 in London, has a colourful history. It spans 40 years, from the radical socialist theatre movement in Britain known as agitprop, to its current position.

The company moved to Leeds in the 70s and is still based in the city. During the 80s it redefined itself, changing its cooperative structure to a hierarchy and specialising in targeted work for youth audiences. Acknowledged today as one of Britain's leading national touring companies producing high-quality new plays for youth audiences.

Recent productions include: *Where's Vietnam?* by BAFTA-nominated writer Alice Nutter, and *Forgotten Things* by Emma Adams.

The Red Room
Garden Studios, 11-15 Betterton Street,
Covent Garden, London WC2H 9BP
tel 020-7470 8790 *fax* 020-7379 0801
email info@theredroom.org.uk
website www.theredroom.org.uk
Artistic Director Topher Campbell *Producer* Bryan Savery

Production details: Founded in 1995. Produces new theatre and film work which frees the imagination to challenge the status quo. Creates groundbreaking collaborations between writers, artists and communities to provoke and influence wider social debate. Engages in cultural activism, including bi-monthly RRPlatform events. Stages 1-2 productions annually with 25-50 performances during the course of the year. Tours to international and national locations. In general, fewer than 5 actors (often with ability to work in a devised way) are involved in each production. Recent productions include: *Unstated*, July 2008 (sold out at the Southwark Playhouse, London), *Journeys to Work*, *Hoxton Story*, *Animal*, *The Bogus Woman* and *Stitching*.

Casting procedures: Accepts emailed CVs and photographs – no letters or telephone enquiries, please. Offers ITC/Equity approved contracts where possible. Does not subscribe to Equity pension scheme. Actively encourages applications from disabled actors and promotes the use of inclusive casting.

Red Rose Chain
1 Fore Hamlet, Ipswich, Suffolk IP3 8AA
tel (01473) 288886 *fax* (01473) 288682
email info@redrosechain.com
website www.redrosechain.com
Directors Joanna Carrick, David Newborn, Jimmy Grimes

Production details: A film and theatre company which spends every summer outdoors with its theatre-in-the-forest event. Runs workshops and develops new writing. "Our diverse work all serves to underpin Red Rose Chain's aim: to use theatre and film to challenge thinking and make connections with those who are normally ignored or avoided by mainstream arts." Stages 4 productions annually, with 50 performances in 20 venues including arts centres, theatres, and outdoor, educational and community venues in East Anglia. In general 3-12 actors are involved in each production. Recent productions include: *A Winter's Tale* (Rendlesham Forest); *Slide Down the Rainbow* (Nowton Park); and *I love Kitkats* (Red Rose Chain).

Casting procedures: Sometimes holds general auditions; casting breakdowns are available via the website. Welcomes letters (with CVs and photographs) from individual actors previously unknown to the company, sent by post or email. Also welcomes showreels and invitations to view individual actors' websites. Actively encourages applications from disabled actors and promotes the use of inclusive casting.

Red Shift Theatre Company

67 Marlborough Road, London SW19 2HF
tel/fax 020-8540 1271
email jonathan@redshifttheatreco.co.uk
website www.redshifttheatreco.co.uk
Artistic Director Jonathan Holloway

Production details: Red Shift is a London-based company which tours nationally to small-scale theatres (under 300 seats) and middle-scale (300+ seats) venues throughout the UK. The company also plays London, and has an enviable reputation established over many years as successful participants in the Edinburgh Festival. The company has toured abroad to Alexandria, Cairo, Santiago de Chile and Hong Kong, under the auspices of the British Council. Red Shift has a very distinctive style which has evolved out of the interests of its founding director, Jonathan Holloway.

Casting procedures: Casting breakdowns are advertised on the company's website. Submissions should be made in writing including CV, photo (not returnable) and covering letter stating why you want to work with Red Shift. Applicants must possess a full clean driving licence and be prepared to drive company vehicles. "Bulk submissions from agents not welcome."

Rejects Revenge Theatre Company

The Annexe, 15 Hope Street, Liverpool L1 9BH
tel 0151-708 8480 *fax* 0151-708 8480
email rejects.revenge@virgin.net
website www.rejectsrevenge.com
Director Ann Farrar *Administrator* Adrian Watts

Production details: Founded in 1990. Tours physical comedy to small and midscale venues in the UK and abroad. Stages 1-3 productions annually with 60-90 performances during the course of the year. Tours to 50-70 different arts centres, theatres, educational and community venues across the UK each year. In general 3-4 actors are involved in each production. Recent productions include: *Peasouper* and *Bicycle Bridge*.

Casting procedures: Uses freelance casting directors. Sometimes holds general auditions. Casting breakdowns are available via Equity Job Information Service and the website. Welcomes letters (with CVs and photographs) but not email submissions. Invitations to view individual actors' websites are also accepted.

Reveal Theatre Company

The Creative Village,
Staffordshire University Business Village,
72 Leek Road, Stoke on Trent ST4 2AR

tel (01782) 294871
email enquiries@revealtheatre.co.uk
website www.revealtheatre.co.uk
Creative Director Robert Marsden *Director of Productions* Julia Barton

Production details: Established in 1999. A professional small to middle-scale producing company for touring and residency. Also has a strong Outreach deparment. Stages on average 4 productions each year. Recent productions include: *Silent Anger* (tour directed by Patrick Connellan) and Deborah McAndrew's *King Macbeth* (tour directed by Robert Marsden).

Casting procedures: Uses in-house casting directors; casting breakdowns are available via the website and in *PCR*. Actors may write at any time requesting inclusion. Welcomes submissions (with CVs and photographs) sent by post, but not by email. Also welcomes showreels, and invitations to view individual actors' websites. Offers Equity approved contracts as negotiated through ITC. Will consider applications from disabled actors to play characters with disabilities.

Richmond Productions

47 Moor Mead Road, St Margaret's, Twickenham TW1 1JS
Director Alister Cameron

Production details: Founded in 1993. International touring company producing small-cast comedies. Stages 2 productions annually. Tours to hotels in the Middle East and Eastern Europe. Offers non-Equity contracts. Rarely (or never) has the opportunity to cast disabled actors.

Casting procedures: Advises that the company only uses actors already known to it.

Riding Lights Theatre Company

Friargate Theatre, Lower Friargate, York YO1 9SL
tel (01904) 655317
website www.ridinglights.org
Artistic Director Paul Burbridge *Artistic Associates* Sean Cavanagh, Bridget Foreman

Production details: Initially a community theatre project founded in York in 1977, today Riding Lights is touring up to 3 diverse companies simultaneously throughout the UK and abroad. The company is recognised both as a pioneer in reinstating the value of theatre in Christian communication and for significant original and artistic achievement. Recent productions include: *Flight Cases* and *African Show* (co-production with York Theatre Royal).

Rifco Arts

The West Wing Arts Centre, Stoke Road, Slough, Berkshire SL2 5AY
tel (01753) 570700
website www.rifcoarts.com
Director Pravesh Kumar

Theatre

Production details: An international multicultural touring theatre company that "wants audiences to deal with contemporary and at times taboo subjects whilst still being able to laugh at the world we live in". Stages 1 production annually, with around 70 performances in 6 arts centres and theatres in the UK and Pakistan. In general 2-17 actors go on tour. Offers Equity-approved contracts as negotiated through ITC. Recent productions include: *Where's My Desi Soulmate* (Theatre Royal Stratford East; Arts Depot, North London); and *It Ain't All Bollywood* (Alhambra Studio, Arts Depot).

Casting procedures: Sometimes holds general auditions; advises actors to keep an eye on the press for casting calls. Welcomes letters (with CVs and photographs) from individual actors previously unknown to the company, sent by post or email; also accepts showreels and invitations to view individual actors' websites. Will consider applications from disabled actors to play characters with disabilities.

Rocket Theatre

32 Baxter Road, Sale, Manchester M33 3AL
tel 0161-969 1444 *mobile* (07788) 723570
email martin@rockettheatre.co.uk
website www.rockettheatre.co.uk
Director Martin Harris

Production details: Rocket Theatre was set up in 1995 and for 10 years produced work in Manchester and toured throughout the North of England with regional premieres of work originally staged by some of London's new-writing venues (particularly the Royal Court, the Bush and the National). The company has also produced some completely new plays and has won various awards for its work over that time. Previous productions include: *I Licked a Slag's Deodorant* by Jim Cartwright; *Howie the Rookie* by Mark O'Rowe; *A Skull in Connemara* by Martin McDonagh; and *Dealer's Choice* by Patrick Marber – as well as several new plays by Jim Burke. The company is currently looking to re-launch with several new projects over the next few years: see the website for details. Rocket Theatre is interested in hearing of any interesting collaboration opportunities with other companies or individuals.

Casting procedures: Casting breakdowns are available on the Rocket website and through various industry casting resources. Does not welcome applications from actors unless casting is called for specific parts. No emailed applications.

Scamp Theatre Ltd

44 Church Lane, Arlesey, Bedfordshire SG15 6UX
tel (01462) 734843 *fax* (01462) 730878
email admin@scamptheatre.com
website www.scamptheatre.com
Directors Jennifer Sutherland, Louise Callow

Production details: Established in 2003. An independent production company staging 4 shows annually, with more than 100 performances in the same number of theatres across the UK. In general 3 actors are involved in each production. Offers Equity-approved contracts as negotiated through ITC. Recent productions include: *Private Peaceful* by Michael Morpurgo (West End, Edinburgh); and *Aesop's Fables* (UK, Australia & New Zealand tour).

Casting procedures: Uses freelance casting directors. Welcomes unsolicited CVs and photographs sent by email only, and accepts invitations to view individual actors' websites. Will consider applications from disabled actors to play characters with disabilities.

Scarlet Theatre

Studio 4, The Bull, 68 High Street, Barnet EN5 5SJ
tel 020-8441 9779 *fax* 020-8447 0075
email admin@scarlettheatre.co.uk
website www.scarlettheatre.co.uk
Director Grainne Byrne

Production details: A touring theatre company founded in 1982 which stages between 2 and 6 productions each year. On average the company tours to 10 venues across the UK, Ireland and the rest of Europe annually, with anywhere between 2-10 actors working on each production. Recent productions include: *The Chair Women* (Riverside Studios and Traverse Theatre) and *The Wedding* (Southwark Playhouse).

Casting procedures: Casting is done in-house and actors are welcome to write or email with their CVs and photographs. The company prefers not to receive showreels unless it has requested them.

Sgript Cymru

Chapter, Market Road, Canton, Cardiff CF5 1QE
tel 029-2023 6650
email chris.ricketts@shermancymru.co.uk
website www.sgriptcymru.com
Director Simon Harris *Administrative Director* Mai Jones

Production details: Founded in 2000 and funded by the Arts Council of Wales, Sgript Cymru is a strategic new writing theatre company. Stages 3 productions annually and gives 75 performances during the course of the year. Tours to 25 different arts centres, theatres, and community venues in Wales, Scotland, London and the North West. In general 5 actors are involved in each production. Recent productions include: *Crossings* by Clare Duffy and *The Life of Ryan... and Ronnie* by Meic Povey.

Casting procedures: Uses freelance casting directors. Welcomes letters (with CVs and photographs) but not email submissions. Offers ITC/Equity approved contracts. Will consider applications from disabled actors to play characters with disabilities.

Shakespeare at The Tobacco Factory

Raleigh Road, Southville, Bristol BS3 1TF
tel 0117-936 3054

email office@sattf.org.uk
website www.sattf.org.uk
Artistic Director Andrew Hilton *General Manager* Sophie Jerrold

Production details: Established in 2000. 2 productions staged annually with 80 performances. Up to 18 actors used in each production. Performances in Bristol and London. Recent productions include: *Julius Caesar* and *Antony and Cleopatra*.

Casting procedures: Casting breakdowns available via the website. Accepts submissions (with CVs and photographs) from actors previously unknown to the company if sent by post and via email. Invitations to view individual actors' websites are also accepted. Actors writing to request inclusion should make contact in Oct/Nov. Rarely has the opportunity to cast disabled actors.

Shared Experience
13 Riverside House, 27-29 Vauxhall Grove, London SW8 1SY
tel 020-7587 1596 *fax* 020-7735 0374
email admin@sharedexperience.org.uk
website www.sharedexperience.org.uk
Joint Artistic Directors Nancy Meckler, Polly Teale
Administrative Producer Jon Harris

Production details: An award-winning theatre company founded during the 1970s, Shared Experience stages 2-3 productions annually and tours to different arts centres and theatres in the UK and abroad. In general 6-10 actors are involved in each production. Recent productions include: *The Caucasian Chalk Circle*, *A Passage to India*, *Jane Eyre*, *Kindertransport* and *War and Peace*.

Casting procedures: Uses freelance casting directors. Advises that actors should contact Hanna Osmolska by phone to enquire about the current casting director. "Please do not send unsolicited mail." Offers TMA/Equity approved contracts. Actively encourages applications from disabled actors and promotes the use of inclusive casting.

Sphinx Theatre Company
13 Riverside House, 27/29 Vauxhall Grove, London SW8 1SY
tel 020-7587 1596
email info@sphinxtheatre.co.uk
website www.sphinxtheatre.co.uk
Artistic Director Sue Parrish *Administrator* Louisa Fitzgerald

Production details: Established 30 years ago, the company specialises in writing, directing and developing roles for women. Recent productions include: *Blame* by Judith Jones and Beatrix Campbell, and *The Berlin Cabaret*.

Casting procedures: Casting breakdowns are available via email and/or postal application (with

CVs and photographs). Offers Equity approved contracts. Will consider applications from disabled actors to play characters with disabilities.

A Stage Kindly
7 Northiam, Cromer Street, London WC1H 8LB
mobile (07947) 074887, (07909) 884386
email astagekindly@aol.com, katylipson@astagekindly.com, gileshowe@astagekindly.com
website www.astagekindly.com
Co-founders & Artistic Directors Giles Howe, Katy Lipson

Production details: Founded in 2008. Aims to enthuse about, advocate and help develop new musical theatre. Stages new-writing revues, feature-length and showcase presentations of new works, and offers services specific to writers creating new MT such as translation, appraisal, demos, etc. Also holds workshops for performers with a focus on new musicals. Recent productions include: UK Premiere of *Ballets Russes*; preview showcase of *Soviet Zion*; and tour of international new-writing revue *Bravo*. Stages around 5 productions annually, with 25 performances in venues including theatres, bars, clubs, halls and arts centres. In general 6 actors are involved in each production.

Casting procedures: Audition information is posted on the website, as are casting breakdowns (also available from Casting Call Pro, artsjobs, etc.). Welcomes letters (with CVs and photographs) from actors previously unknown to the company, sent by post or email. Also accepts showreels and invitations to view individual actors' websites.

Ed Stephenson Productions
7 Hawthorn Road, Little Sutton, Cheshire CH66 1PR
tel 0151-339 6145
email roger@edstephensonproductions.co.uk
website www.edstephensonproductions.co.uk
Company Administrator Diane Barker

Production details: Founded in 2004. Stages on average 1 production every 1-2 years; plans to stage shows in historic buildings in the future. Recent productions include: *The Charnwood Sisters* and *Wrens at War*. Recent short film: *A Quiet Night In*.

Casting procedures: Uses in-house casting directors. Sometimes holds auditions; actors should write in prior to each show, if advertised on the Equity Job Information Service. Also uses casting agencies for auditioning. Welcomes letters (with CVs and photographs) from individual actors previously unknown to the company, sent by post or email. Accepts showreels and invitations to view individual actors' websites. Will consider applications from disabled actors where appropriate for the role. "Our contracts are heavily based on ITC/Equity contracts."

Suspect Culture
CCA, 350 Sauchiehall Street, Glasgow G2 3TD
tel 0141-332 9775 *fax* 0141-332 8823

Theatre

email info@suspectculture.com
website www.suspectculture.com
Director Graham Eatough *Administrative Producer*
Purni Morell

Production details: Suspect Culture was formed in
1990 by Graham Eatough, David Greig and Nick
Powell. Early productions include: *One Way Street*
(1995), *Airport* (1996), *Timeless* (1997) and
Mainstream (1999). The company is based in
Glasgow and tours 1-2 productions throughout
Scotland and internationally each year. Generally uses
2-6 actors on each production. Recent productions
include: *8000m* (Tramway, Glasgow) and *One-Two*
(Traverse, Edinburgh; Contact Theatre, Manchester;
MAC, Birmingham; Tron, Glasgow; Byre Theatre, St
Andrews; Lemon Tree, Northampton; Tolbooth,
Stirling and Paisley Arts Centres).

"To us, a collaborative approach means giving text,
design, music and performance equal weight in all
our work. The director, writer, designer and
composer are involved from the very beginning of
each new idea, which is then developed through a
long process of workshops and rehearsal before being
presented to an audience. This emphasis on
collaboration is reflected in the way we credit artists
and assign authorship, which is always shared among
the artistic team."

Casting procedures: Suspect Culture does not hold
formal auditions, but rather open workshops which
are by invitation. This gives the company a chance to
meet practitioners it hasn't worked with before (and
vice versa). The company welcomes letters, emails,
showreels, invitations to view actors' websites, CVs
and photographs from actors – but asks all applicants
to gain a full understanding of Suspect's particular
working methods before writing. Only rarely employs
actors who have not seen at least some of Suspect's
work.

TABS Productions
57 Chamberlain Place, London E17 6AZ
tel 020-8527 9266
email adrianmljames@aol.com
website www.tabsproductions.co.uk
Directors Adrian Lloyd-James, Karen Henson

Production details: Founded 15 years ago, the
company stages approximately 6 productions each
year totalling around 300 performances. It has
produced No. 1 and middle-scale tours and has co-
produced with repertory theatre companies.
Generally tours to about 45 different arts centres,
theatres and outdoor venues across the UK annually.
The average cast size is 4-8 actors.

Casting procedures: Welcomes letters, CVs and
photographs from actors previously unknown to the
company, but does not accept emails or showreels.
Actors should only write when a job has been
advertised to agents through *SBS*. Occasionally offers
Equity approved contracts. Rarely (or never) has the
opportunity to cast disabled actors.

Taking Flight Theatre Company
79 Kings Road, Canton, Cardiff CF11 9DB
tel 029-2064 5505
email takingflighttheatre@yahoo.co.uk
website www.takingflighttheatre.com
Directors Beth House, Elise Davison *Chair* Clark Baim

Production details: Established in 2007. Holds
residential workshops with physically disabled adults.
Accessible, professional promenade productions with
integrated casts/support teams. Stages 1-2
productions annually, with around 30 performances
in 20 outdoor venues across South Wales. In general
6-10 actors are involved in each production. Recent
productions include: *Romeo and Juliet*, and *Gwion
and the Witch*.

Casting procedures: Sometimes holds general
auditions and actors may write at any time to request
inclusion. Casting breakdowns are publicly available
via the website, Equity Job Information Service and
Casting Call Pro, as well as from the Disability Arts
Cymru site. Welcomes letters (with CVs and
photographs) from individual actors previously
unknown to the company sent by post or email, as
well as showreels and invitations to view individual
actors' websites. Actively encourages applications
from disabled actors and promotes the use of
inclusive casting. "We are very eager to hear from
disabled and/or sensory impaired actors."

Talawa Theatre Company
Ground Floor, 53-55 East Road, London N1 6AH
tel 020-7251 6644 *fax* 020-7251 5956
email hq@talawa.com
website www.talawa.com
Director Patricia Cumper *Executive Producer*
Christopher Rodriguez

Production details: Founded in 1986, Talawa is one
of Britain's leading Black Theatre companies. "We
give voice to the Black British experience and we
nurture, develop and support talent. We cultivate
Black audiences for Black work. In doing so we
enrich British theatre." Offers ITC/Equity contracts
and does not subscribe to the Equity Pension
Scheme.

Casting procedures: Welcomes submissions (with
CVs and photographs) sent by post or email. Actively
encourages applications from disabled actors and
promotes the use of inclusive casting.

Tamasha Theatre Company
Unit 220 Great Guildford Business Square,
30 Great Guildford Street, London SE1 0HS
tel 020-7633 2270 *fax* 020-7021 0421
email info@tamasha.org.uk
website www.tamasha.org.uk
Artistic Directors Kristine Landon-Smith, Sudha
Bhuchar

Production details: Founded in 1989. Produces
"untold stories" in mainstream theatre venues. Stages

1-3 productions annually and gives approximately 60 performances during the course of the year. Tours annually to small- and mid-scale theatre venues in London and regionally (e.g. Yorkshire, the Midlands and the South West). In general 2-15 actors are involved in each production. Recent productions include: *Wuthering Heights, A Fine Balance, The Trouble with Asian Men* and *Strictly Dandia.*

Casting procedures: Only holds auditions when casting for a specific production. Tends to use own files when inviting people to audition plus possibly SBS breakdown and Casting Director on specific projects. Welcomes CVs and headshots by post at any time; these will be kept on file and looked at afresh during each casting process. Also runs professional artist development scheme: Tamasha Developing Artists – see website for details. Offers ITC/Equity approved contracts.

Tara Arts Group
356 Garratt Lane, London SW18 4ES
tel 020-8333 4457 *fax* 020-8870 9540
email tara@tara-arts.com
website www.tara-arts.com
Artistic Director Jatinder Verma

Production details: "Positioned between East and West, the company champions creative diversity through the production, promotion and development of work that defies all barriers to the imagination. The creative health of modern diverse humanity demands *no passports.*

• *No passports* for the stories we tell
• *No passports* for the artists we work with
• *No passports* for our audiences."

Founded in 1977, the company tours vibrant adaptations of European and Asian classics, develops new writing and brings the great stories of the world to children in junior schools. The company tours annually to England, Scotland and Wales, and has also toured the Netherlands, Ireland, France, Belgium, Spain, Turkey, Egypt, Hong Kong, Singapore, Japan and Australia. Recent productions include *The Genie of Samarkand, When the Lights Went Out* and *A Taste For Mangoes.*

theatre-rites
The Warehouse, 12 Ravensbury Terrace, London SW18 4RL
tel 020-8946 2236 *fax* 020-8946 0965
email info@theatre-rites.co.uk
website www.theatre-rites.co.uk
Artistic Director Sue Buckmaster *Associate Artist* Sophia Clist *General Manager* Natalie Highwood

Production details: Founded in 1995, theatre-rites is versatile in its approach, creating theatre shows which tour the UK and abroad and pieces set in unusual spaces such as an old tidal mill, a disused corner shop and an empty ward of a real working hospital. theatre-rites also creates interactive exhibitions and

installations in galleries, museums and other public spaces. Drawing on a rich fusion of performance, installation art, puppetry, video and sound, theatre-rites creates work, which stirs the imagination of children and adults alike. Recent productions include: *Hospitalworks, The Thought that Counts* (part of the Young Genius season at the Barbican), and a national re-tour of *In One Ear.*

Casting procedures: Welcomes letters (with CVs and photographs) from actors previously unknown to the company. "Multi-disciplined performers are always very welcome." Offers ITC/Equity approved contracts.

Theatre Absolute
Institute for Creative Enterprise, Technology Park, Puma Way, Coventry CV1 2TT
tel 024-7615 8340
email info@theatreabsolute.co.uk
website www.theatreabsolute.co.uk
Artistic Director Chris O'Connell *Producer* Julia Negus

Production details: Founded in 1992, the company develops, produces and tours new plays. In 2009, Theatre Absolute opened the UK's first professional Shop Front Theatre in Coventry. Work includes performances, play readings and writing classes.

Casting procedures: Actors should consult the website for details of the next project, and for casting breakdowns and information. Welcomes letters (with CVs and up-to-date photographs) but not email submissions. Advises actors not to send blanket letters and CVs. "Find out about our work first – we always see actors who have seen our work if they're suitable for the role offered." Also happy to give advice to new/emerging actors.

Theatre Alibi
Northcott Studio Theatre, Emmanuel Road, Exeter EX4 1EJ
tel/fax (01392) 217315
email alibi@eclipse.co.uk
website www.theatrealibi.co.uk
Artistic Director Nikki Sved *Marketing Director* Annemarie Macdonald *Administrative Director* Jenny Lawrence

Production details: Founded in 1982, the company works with existing and commissioned stories to create work that is physically and visually inventive and often enriched by other art forms – original music, film, puppetry, dance and photography, for instance. Stages 2 productions a year, with a total of around 130 performances. Tours 20 theatres and arts centres as well as schools and community venues, although the nature of the venue depends on the individual show. There are generally 5 actors in each show, and the company offers ITC/Equity approved contracts.

Past work includes: *Birthday* (based on the work of Marc and Bella Chagall, which was nominated for a

Fringe First); *Little White Lies* (*Time Out* Critics' Choice); and *Shelf Life*. Recent productions include: *The Crowstarver* (mid-scale national tour for 8-13 year-olds); *Bonjour Bob* (tour of South West for 5-10 year olds and their families); and *One in a Million* (national tour of small-scale venues aimed at adults).

Casting procedures: Casts in-house. Does not publish casting breakdowns, but welcomes letters (not emails) with CVs and photographs from individuals previously unknown to the company at any time of year. Does not welcome showreels or invitations to view individuals' websites. Actively encourages applications from disabled actors and promotes the use of inclusive casting.

Theatre Babel

PO Box 5103, Glasgow G78 9AR
tel 0141-416 0051
email admin@theatrebabel.co.uk
website www.theatrebabel.co.uk
Director Graham McLaren *General Manager* Kate Bowden *Producer and Casting Director* Rebecca Rodgers

Production details: Founded in 1994, the company stages 1-2 classical theatre productions each year which tour to 10 venues across the UK and internationally. Normally presents approximately 60 performances annually with an average of 8 actors working on each production. Recent productions include: *Macbeth, A Doll's House, Thebans* and *Uncle Vanya*.

Casting procedures: Welcomes letters, CVs and photographs from actors previously unknown to the company, but does not accept email applications or showreels.

Theatre Hebrides

71-77 Cromwell Street, Stornoway,
Isle of Lewis HS1 2DG
tel (01851) 701193
email info@theatrehebrides.com
website www.theatrehebrides.com
Artistic Director Muriel Ann Macleod *Administrator* Donnie Macdonald

Production details: Works mainly in film and multimedia. Commissions new plays and devises scripts. All work is based on Western Isles historic and contemporary culture. Also works as a TV production company and is currently producing comedy drama. Recent productions include: *The Callanish Stoned* by Kevin Macneil; *Kinoch ... Somewhere* by Eric John Macdonald (1-man show); and *Lostbost* by Billy Matheson.

Casting procedures: Uses in-house casting directors and holds general auditions. Actors may write in at any time requesting inclusion. Casting breakdowns are available via Equity Job Information Service or by postal application with sae. Welcomes letters (with CVs and photoraphs) sent by post, but not by email.

Will accept showreels and invitations to view individual actors' websites. Offers Equity approved contracts as negotiated through ITC and PACT. Actively encourages applications from disabled actors and promotes the use of inclusive casting. "We are working in Gaelic and English at present, and are also developing international collaborations. Check the website for details."

Theatre Is

The Innovation Centre, College Lane,
Hatfield AL10 9AB
tel (01279) 461607 *fax* (01279) 506694
email info@theatreis.org
website www.theatreis.org

Production details: Established in 2006. Challenging and creating new models of live performance by, with and for young audiences across the East of England and beyond. 3 productions are staged annually touring East of England, London, Midlands, North West and Wales. 50 performances per year at an average of 20 venues. Types of venue include: arts centres, theatres, outdoor venues, educational and community venues. 4 actors are generally involved in each production. Actors are employed under ITC/Equity approved contracts. Recent productions include: *Master Juba* (Hackney Empire, Norwich Playhouse); *Claytime* (New Wolsey Theatre, Lyric Hammersmith, Unicorn Theatre).

Casting procedures: Casting is done by an in-house casting director. Casting breakdowns are only available to agents via the Spotlight Link. Does not welcome individual submissions from actors. Actively encourages applications from disabled actors and promotes the use of inclusive casting in new writing productions.

Theatre Lab Company

76 St Dunstan's Avenue, London W3 6QJ
mobile (07958) 4048806
email anastasia@theatrelab.co.uk
website www.theatrelab.co.uk
Director Anastasia Revi

Production details: Established in 1997. Stages 1 production annually, with around 20 performances in 3 theatres in the Midlands and South East, and abroad. In general 4-6 actors are involved in each production. Offers Equity-approved contracts as negotiated through ITC "when funded". Recent productions include: *Velvet Scratch* (Prague Festival 2007; Edinburgh Festival 2007; Greek tour 2008; New York Fringe Festival 2008).

Casting procedures: Uses freelance casting directors. Holds general auditions, and actors may write to request inclusion when advertised. Casting breakdowns are available from the website, by postal application (with sae), and in *PCR* and *The Stage*. Welcomes letters (with CVs and photographs) from individual actors previously unknown to the company, sent by post or email. Also welcomes showreels and invitations to view individual actors' websites. Will consider applications from disabled actors to play characters with disabilities.

Théâtre Sans Frontières

Queen's Hall, Beaumont Street, Hexham, Northumberland NE46 3LS
tel (01434) 652484 *fax* (01434) 607206
email sue@tsf.org.uk
website www.tsf.org.uk
Artistic Directors Sarah Kemp (CEO), John Cobb
Administrator Sue Maltby *Finance Officer* Gabby Keaveny *Marketing & Development Officer* Alison Maw

Production details: Founded in 1991. Set up by former students of Philippe Gaulier and Monika Pagneux. Specialises in physical theatre and stages texts in different languages for adults and children using international performers. Stages 2-3 productions annually with 60-100 performances in venues including arts centres, schools and theatres. In general 3-6 actors are involved in each production. Recent productions include: *Como Agua Para Chocolate* (*Like Water for Chocolate*); *Lipsynch* (co-produced with Robert Lepage and Ex Machina, touring internationally); and *La Pelota Magica*, an engaging introduction to Spanish for children aged 6 to 11 years. Touring nationally: autumn 2009 – *Les Trois Mousquetaires*; UK schools January to March 2010 – *Contes Dores* (for childred aged 8 to 12 years); June/July 2010 – *La Pelota Magica*.

Casting procedures: Sometimes holds general auditions. Actors may write at any time requesting inclusion. Casting breakdowns are available on request. Welcomes submissions (with CVs and photographs) sent by post or email. Invitations to view individual actors' websites are also accepted. "We are usually looking for actors who have languages other than English (especially French, Spanish or German), and who have a clear physical theatre training (i.e. Le Coq, Gaulier, Pagneux or Complicite)."

Theatre Set-up

12 Fairlawn Close, Southgate, London N14 4JX
website www.ts-u.co.uk
Charitable Director Wendy Macphee

Production details: Founded in 1976. Presents Shakespeare productions in historic and beautiful sites. Stages 1 production annually with 55 performances over the course of the year. Tours to 35 different outdoor venues annually in the UK, Norway, the Netherlands and Belgium. In general 8 actors are involved in each production. Recent productions include: *The Winter's Tale*. Offers non-Equity contracts and does not subscribe to the Equity Pension Scheme.

Casting procedures: Actors should write in February requesting auditions. Welcomes letters (with CVs and photographs) but not email submissions. Advises actors that "the tour is rigorous and not for the faint-hearted".

Theatre Without Walls

Forwood House, Forwood, Gloucestershire GL6 9AB
mobile (07962) 040441
email hello@theatrewithoutwalls.org
website www.theatrewithoutwalls.org
Directors Jason Maher, Genevieve Swift

Production details: Established in 2002. Award-winning theatre company specialising in forum, education and new writing. Productions represent only one-fifth of its output; also produces television and corporate films. 2 productions are staged annually with 60 performances per year, touring to 20 venues including arts centres, theatres and outdoor venues. Tours cover the UK, Ireland and Europe. 3 actors are involved in each production. Actors are employed under ITC/Equity approved contracts. Recent productions include: *Don Quixote* (Banbury Mill); *The Hold* (Cheltenham Everyman); and *The Plant Hunters* (National Trust).

Casting procedures: "We cast mostly through agents and our own knowledge/word of mouth/recommendations. We sometimes post casting information via Equity JIS and other 'freely available resources'. We never use casting services which actors have to pay for, except for The Spotlight. Any information obtained via paid-for services has simply been copied from another source. Please don't send us any information (such as photos, CVs, showreels, etc.) unless we have requested it. We regularly hold actors' labs and often cast from them." Theatre Without Walls is a member of ITC and most of its work is undertaken using Equity contracts. Those working with vulnerable adults or children must have a current enhanced Criminal Record Bureau/Police Check and hold full insurance equal or greater than that provided by Equity for its members." Considers applications from disabled actors to play disabled characters.

See also the company's entry under *Role-play companies* on page 286.

Theatre Workout

13A Stratheden Road, Blackheath, London SE13 7TH
tel 020-8144 2290
email enquiries@theatreworkout.co.uk
website www.theatreworkout.co.uk
Director Adam Milford

Production details: Established in 2006 to produce bespoke theatre workshops, theatre-based training programmes and productions. Currently working alongside several major West End productions including *Chicago*, *Dirty Dancing*, *The Lion King*, *Wicked*, *Sister Act* and many more. Recent productions include: *Much Ado About Nothing* for the English Theatre in Venice 2007.

Casting procedures: Casting breakdowns are publicly available from casting breakdown services and via the website.

Theatre Workshop
34 Hamilton Place, Edinburgh EH3 5AX
tel 0131-225 7942 *fax* 0131-220 0112
email afleming@twe.org.uk
website www.theatre-workshop.com
Artistic Director Robert Rae *Company Manager* Anne Fleming

Production details: Founded in 1965; stages 4 productions a year with around 60 performances across 2 theatre venues. Occasionally tours internationally. Employs an average of 5 actors on each production, using ITC/Equity approved contracts. Recent productions include: *The Jasmine Road* (No Limits International Theatre Festival, Berlin); and *The Threepenny Opera* (Edinburgh Festival Theatre & Tramway, Glasgow).

Casting procedures: Casting breakdowns are available from the website and Equity Job Information Service. Welcomes letters and emails (with CVs and photographs) from individuals previously unknown to the company. Also happy to receive showreels and invitations to view individuals' websites. Encourages applications from disabled actors and promotes the use of inclusive casting. "Theatre Workshop casts both disabled and non-disabled actors in all our productions."

Third Party Productions Ltd
81 Braybrooke Road, Hastings, East Sussex TN34 1TF
tel (01424) 436149 *mobile* (07768) 694211/694212
email gleave@thirdparty.org.uk
website www.thirdparty.org.uk
Joint Artistic Directors Anthony Gleave, Nicholas Collett

Production details: Established in 1992. A UK and International touring theatre company. Work is based on classic plays which are deconstructed and re-imagined during the rehearsal process, and given a contemporary and experimental vitality. Currently working with John Wright – founder of Trestle Theatre and co-founder of Told By An Idiot – and co-producing work with French company BordCadre and Galician clown company Macquinaria Pesada. Stages 1-3 productions annually with around 40-120 performances at 30-90 venues of all types. In general 3-7 actors are involved in each production. Recent productions include: *The Tragicall History of Dr Faustus – A Damned Fine Play* (New Diorama, London), and *La Fausse Suivante/The False Servant* (Café de la Danse Paris and UK tour).

Casting procedures: Auditions by invitation only. May advertise for certain projects through various publications and websites. Welcomes unsolicited CVs and photographs, and invitations to view individual actors' websites, if sent by email only. Actively

encourages applications from disabled actors when advertising for casting.

Tinderbox Theatre Company
Imperial Buildings, 22 High Street, Belfast BT1 2BE
tel 028-9043 9313 *fax* 028-9032 9420
email info@tinderbox.org.uk
website www.tinderbox.org.uk
Artistic Director Michael Duke *General Manager* Kerry Woods

Production details: Founded in 1988. Produces, develops and stages new work which interrogates life in Northern Ireland. Stages 2-3 productions and tours to 12 different venues annually, including arts centres, theatres and site-specific locations in Ireland, England and Scotland. In general 6 actors are involved in each production. Recent productions include: *Revenge* and *Family Plot*.

Casting procedures: Sometimes holds general auditions. Welcomes letters (with CVs and photographs) but not email submissions. Invitations to view individual actors' websites are also accepted. Offers ITC/Equity approved contracts; only contributes to the Equity Pension Scheme for permanant staff. Encourages applications from disabled actors and promotes the use of inclusive casting.

Told by an Idiot
The Print House, 18 Ashlin Street, London E8 3DL
tel 020-7978 4200 *fax* 020-7978 5200
email info@toldbyanidiot.org
website www.toldby.dircon.co.uk
Directors Hayley Carmichael, Paul Hunter, John Wright *General Manager* Ghislaine Granger *Associate Producer* Nick Sweeting

Production details: Founded in 1992, the company tours to arts centres and theatres throughout England.

Casting procedures: Sometimes holds general auditions. Actors may write at any time throughout the year. The company will make contact if and when a relevant project arises. Welcomes submissions (with CVs and photographs) sent by post or email. Invitations to view individual actors' websites are also accepted. Offers ITC/Equity contracts. Actively encourages applications from disabled actors and promotes the use of inclusive casting.

TOSG Gaelic Theatre Company
Sabhal Mor Ostaig, Sleat, Isle of Skye IV44 8RQ
tel (01471) 888542 *fax* (01471) 888542
email tosg@tosg.org
website www.tosg.org.uk
Artistic Director Simon Mackenzie *General Manager* Janet Ward

Production details: Founded in 1996. Professional Gaelic Theatre Company producing theatre for both adults and children. Also runs a new writing scheme.

All productions are performed in Gaelic. Stages 2 productions annually and gives 50 performances per year. Tours to 30 different venues annually, including arts centres, theatres, educational and community venues in Scotland. In general 5 actors are involved in each production.

Casting procedures: Sometimes holds general auditions. Gaelic-speaking actors can write in May requesting inclusion. Welcomes letters (with CVs and photographs) but not email submissions. Invitations to view individual actors' websites are also accepted.

Trestle Theatre Company

Trestle Arts Base, Russet Drive, St Albans AL4 0JQ
tel (01727) 850950 *fax* (01727) 855558
email admin@trestle.org.uk
website www.trestle.org.uk
Artistic Director Emily Gray *Executive Director* Alison Young

Production details: Founded in 1981 as a touring theatre company, now also with a home venue (Trestle Arts Base) and national workshop programme (Taking Part). Performers/facilitators used across all 3 areas of the company. All projects concentrate on new, devised or commissioned work, incorporating text, physical theatre, dance and other movement forms, storytelling, puppetry, music and song. 1 small to mid-scale tour annually, to 50 venues including arts centres and theatres in Britain, Europe and other international locations. In general 2-5 performers are involved in each project. Offers ITC/Equity contracts.

Casting procedures: Rarely holds general auditions. Does not welcome on-spec CVs. Will consider invitations to see actors in shows if the performance style is relevant to the way in which Trestle works. If looking for suggestions, casting breakdowns will be posted on the website. Usually casts actors with strong physical/visual theatre acting training or experience. Actively encourages applications from disabled actors and promotes the use of inclusive casting.

Triangle Theatre Company Ltd

c/o The Herbert, Jordan Well, Coventry CV1 5QP
tel (02476) 294730/1 *fax* (02476) 294790
email office@triangletheatre.co.uk
website www.triangletheatre.co.uk
Joint Artistic Directors Carran Waterfield, Richard Talbot

Production details: Since 2001, company-in-residence at The Herbert Art Gallery & Museum. Won the UK Museums & Heritage Award for excellence and the Roots & Wings Award for performance and interactive projects in response to museum collections. Runs performances and talks for conferences, schools and colleges as well as collaborations with academics and researchers contributing to the ongoing dissemination of

Triangle's method of extended and immersive play with character, personal biography and history. Stages on average 2 major original productions each year, including studio and site-specific situations. Studio work is actor-centred and scripted from lengthy, devised rehearsals. Site-specific work is experimental and participatory, and developed in partnership with universities and local authorities. Recent productions include: *The Last Women* and *Knickers and Vests* (part of the Cultural Olympiad to London 2010).

Casting procedures: Casting and contracts agreed by Artistic Directors. Triangle holds frequent ensemble auditions and training workshops to develop material, generate ideas and employ associate artists. Actors are advised to consult the website for detailed information and to approach the company regarding specific, relevant projects. Does not welcome unsolicited submissions by post or by email, or showreels, but will accept invitations to view individual actors' websites. Offers independent contracts based on ITC. Actively encourages applications from disabled actors and promotes the use of inclusive casting.

UK Arts International

2nd Floor, 6 Shaw Street, Worcester WR1 3QQ

Production details: Stages 1 production annually which tours to approximately 70 different venues, including arts centres, theatres, education and community venues across the UK.

Casting procedures: Does not hold general auditions and does not welcome submissions from actors previously unknown to the company.

Unlimited Theatre

Studio 11, Aire Street Workshops, 30-34 Aire Street, Leeds LS1 4HT
tel 0113-234 5400
email unlimited@unlimited.org.uk
website www.unlimited.org.uk
Artistic Director Jon Spooner *Development Director* Liz Margree

Production details: Founded in 1997. Creates work intended to "explore how personal experience can illuminate political debate, and which puts marginalised voices centre-stage". Stages 1-2 productions annually with 50-100 performances. Tours to 10-20 different venues each year, including arts centres and theatres throughout the UK (including Glasgow, Edinburgh and Belfast) and overseas. In general 4-6 actors are involved in each production. Recent productions include: *Safety*, *Neutrino* and *Zero Degrees and Drifting*.

Casting procedures: Sometimes holds general auditions. Welcomes letters (with CVs and photographs) but not email submissions. Invitations to view individual actors' websites are also accepted. "We are a small- to middle-scale organisation and only occasionally employ freelance actors. We are always interested in hearing from potential new collaborators." Offers ITC/Equity approved contracts. Actively encourages applications from disabled actors and promotes the use of inclusive casting.

Vayu Naidu Company Ltd
Unit C5, Old Imperial Laundry,
71 Warriner Gardens, Battersea, London SW11 4XW
tel 020-7720 0707
email vayu.naidu@vayunaiducompany.org.uk
website www.vayunaiducompany.org.uk
Artistic Director Dr Vayu Naidu

Production details: The only performing arts company in the UK dedicated to promoting Storytelling Theatre. Seeks to establish a unique base from which a multi-racial cast of theatre writers, musicians, dancers, storytellers and performers can collaborate, bringing together various art forms to create "contemporary, enriching and diverse cultural experiences". Stages on average 3 small-scale productions each year: these can take place in traditional performance venues utilising technical resources, or in workshop settings in schools, colleges, libraries and museums. Creates new works to tour mainstream venues, as well as small-scale programmes 'in repertoire' and tailor-made for specific events. Also works in TIE, Outreach and Community, for which the key contact is Emily Parrish. Recent productions include: *Mistaken* (Annie Besant in India); *Nine Nights* (stories from the Ramayana); and *License to Tell* (pub-storytelling evenings.)

Casting procedures: Applications from experienced storytellers and musicians wishing to work with the Company, or from those wishing to learn/improve storytelling skills via Company workshops should be sent to Dr Vayu Naidu by post.

Volcano Theatre Company
Swansea Metropolitan University, Townhill Road,
Swansea SA2 0UT
tel (01792) 281280
email paul@volcanotheatre.co.uk or
claud@volcanotheatre.co.uk
website www.volcanotheatre.co.uk
Directors Paul Davies, Fern Smith *General Manager* Carys Shannon *Marketing Manager* Claudine Conway

Production details: Original theatrical productions and site-specific events. Small-scale national and international touring company based in Wales. Devised and collaborative work, physical theatre, new writing, adaptations/deconstructions of classics. Stages 2-4 productions and gives 50-80 performances each year. Venues include arts centres and theatres in the UK, Europe and worldwide. Usually 2-8 performers per production. Recent productions include: *i-witness*, *Dead Cat Bounce*, *A Few Little Drops*.

Casting procedures: There are no casting breakdowns. Performers are selected through workshops and invited auditions. Unsolicited admissions are read but not held on record.

Keith Whitall
25 Solway, Hailsham BN27 3HB
tel (01323) 844882
Director Keith Whitall

Production details: Founded in 2000. Produces revues, small-scale musicals and occasionally plays and one-person shows. Stages 2-3 productions annually with 20 or more performances in theatres in Brighton and the South East. So far has only toured to 1 arts centre. In general 9-10 actors are involved in each production. Recent productions include: *Broadway Calling.*, *The Pleasure of Your Company* and *Noel Coward & Cole Porter Revisited*. Offers non-Equity contracts and does not subscribe to the Equity Pension Scheme.

Casting procedures: Sometimes holds general auditions. Actors may write at any time requesting inclusion. Casting breakdowns are usually made available to casting directors or actors seen in a production. Welcomes letters (with CVs and photographs) but not email submissions. "In my revues I usually use 3-4 experienced artistes plus new young artistes in whom I am especially interested." Musical theatre experience is preferable. Rarely has opportunity to cast disabled actors, but "possible in future depending on backstage access".

Wildcard Theatre Company
PO Box 267, High Wycombe, Bucks, HP11 2WB
tel 0870-760 6158 *mobile* (07092) 024967
website www.wildcardtheatre.org.uk
Creative Producer Jo Salkilld

Production details: Recent productions include: *Titus Andronicus*, *Wicked* and *Greek*.

Casting procedures: Casting information is published on the website.

The Wrestling School
42 Durlston Road, London E5 8RR
tel 020-8442 4229
website www.thewrestlingschool.co.uk
Director Howard Barker

Production details: Founded in 1988. "Develops ways of presenting complex ideas in the theatre through the work of Howard Barker." Stages 1 production annually; in general 5-7 actors are involved in each production.

Casting procedures: Sometimes holds auditions. Welcomes letters when casting (with CVs and photographs) but not email submissions. Actors should telephone in late July, or consult the website, to find out if the company is casting.

Y Touring Theatre Co
One KX, 120 Cromer Street, London WC1B 8BS
tel 020-7520 3090 *fax* 020-7520 3099

email info@ytouring.org.uk
website www.ytouring.org.uk
Artistic Director Nigel Townsend *General Manager* Martin Ball *Tour Producer* David Jackson *Associate Director, Creative Learning* Jenny May While

Production details: Y Touring is Central YMCA's award winning professional touring theatre company for young people and adults. Produces 2-4 tours per year in the UK. Offers ITC/Equity approved contracts and does not subscribe to the Equity Pension Scheme.

Casting procedures: Uses freelance casting directors and publishes casting breakdowns through various agencies including, *PCR, SBS*, Castcall, etc. Does not hold general auditions. Will accept CVs and photos by post at any time of year to be held on file for consideration. Please do not send showreels or unsolicited scripts. Will consider applications from disabled actors to play characters with disabilities.

Yellow Earth Theatre

20 Rupert Street, London W1 6DF
tel 020-7734 5988 *fax* 020-7287 3141
email admin@yellowearth.org
website www.yellowearth.org
Artistic Directors Philippe Cherbonnier, Jonathan Man

Production details: In London in 1995, 5 British East Asian performers came together and Yellow Earth was born. Over the years the company has grown into the UK champion for British East Asian theatre, nurturing talents from Britain and the Far East. The company tours nationally and internationally with text-based plays that are characterised by striking visual and physical language. Sets are designed with touring in mind, and the company is used to the logistics of touring to tight deadlines. Detailed technical requirements are provided along with the on-site support of a production manager. Yellow Earth is a member of both ITC and TMA, and uses the ITC and/or TMA Equity contracts.

Casting procedures: Casts in-house. Sometimes holds general auditions; the best time to write requesting inclusion is in the Spring. Welcomes letters (not emails) with CVs and photographs from East Asian actors only. Accepts invitations to view individual actors' websites, but not showreels. Actively encourages applications from disabled actors and promotes the use of inclusive casting. "As an East Asian company, we only keep on file details of actors with East Asian backgrounds (everywhere east of India: for example, China, Japan, Korea, and the Philippines)."

Pantomime is not just for Christmas – it's for life!

Nigel Ellacott

From the audience's point of view, Pantomime is a perennial entertainment, unique to this country, and it happens over the Festive Season when the nights draw in, and the Yule logs crackle on an open fire.

The audience knows it is a "safe" place to take the family – the kids, Gran and Grandad. They know it will always be there, warm and comforting, and that it will never change.

Ah! But of course it does change, and it has changed over its peculiar development into one of Great Britain's intrinsic art forms. It is our art form, even though we stole a bit here and there to make it so. If Pantomime didn't change, I doubt it would be one of the all-time money-spinners and popular entertainments we have today. Pantomime has constantly changed. It has evolved and adapted, and in doing so it has ensured audiences for the future, made managements and theatres a fair bit of profit and, in some cases has enabled theatres to fund the forthcoming rep season well into the summer months.

This Panto season alone, over 360 professional pantomimes will be staged in this country, and a great many actors, musicians and technicians will be employed for periods of up to eight or nine weeks in many cases. Annually it provides regular work for an army of artistes and techies, it employs musicians (although, it has to be said, in ever-decreasing numbers) writers, directors, choreographers and a vast army of outworkers – scenic artists, wardrobe and prop makers, footwear suppliers and wig makers. Pantomime monopolises the transport industry, as pantechnicans travel the length and breadth of the land collecting wardrobe boxes, crystal coaches and giant inflatable beanstalks!

The preparation for the annual onslaught from Fairyland begins, on average, while the current pantomime is half-way through. The Pantomime 'Giants' are not looking for Daisy the Cow to make a Daisy-Burger; they are the 'Big Boys' who control the largest number of productions around the country. In this year of writing Qdos hold the poll position as pantomime employers.

Qdos produced twenty pantomimes this season, with two in Scotland, one in Belfast and three in Wales, and the others ranging from The Hippodrome Birmingham to The Alhambra Bradford.

First Family Entertainment, a recent newcomer to Pantoland, produced nine major productions. FFE is the combined umbrella of Ambassadors Theatre Group and Live Nation (formerly Clear Channel).

UK Productions has Eleven pantomimes around the country, the same number as PHA (Paul Holman Associates), whilst Evolution, Hiss & Boo, Duo Productions, John Spillers and Pantoni are just a few of the many producing managements providing pantomimes around the UK.

A helpful place to search out these companies would be on the diary section of my website: **www.its-behind-you.com**; every pantomime in the UK is listed there.

If you consider that Qdos will employ, on average, ten principals, six to eight dancers, six musicians, a director, choreographer, company manager and three stage management in each of their twenty venues, the numbers begin to mount up. In addition, the venue will provide a stage crew, electricians, sound and wardrobe staff, as well as the combined efforts of in house marketing, publicity, box office and FOH staff.

Pantomime is often the longest running show in the provinces during the year. Seasons can run between four to nine weeks. The Grand Theatre Wolverhampton runs until February 4th, as does a smaller venue like The Kenneth More Theatre in Ilford.

Major star names adorn the posters. The Managements increasingly trying to outdo their rivals with bigger names, more lavish productions – with standards constantly rising, panto is no longer the poorer relation of the theatre world. Admittedly there was a lull somewhere in the 1960s and 70s when it seemed as if an air of complacency had settled in pantoland, but over the past few decades the genre has taken on a new lustre.

The newspapers were delighted to announce that a Theatrical Knight, one Ian McKellan was to don the skirts of Widow Twankey and perform panto at the Old Vic no less! The lure of the Golden Egg has brought soap stars from Australia and Hollywood stars to strut their stuff on the stages of Richmond and Milton Keynes.

There's nothing new in this – Panto has simply done what it does best. It has constantly taken on board the new, the novel and the 'Now' and the 'Wow' factors to keep its position as our premier family entertainment.

Augustus Harris employed the 'star' system at the Drury Lane Pantomimes of the 1890s. Pantomime sucked in Music Hall stars and the odd sporting celebrity in the Edwardian era, just as today it might embrace a *Big Brother* 'Celebrity' or a bone fide classical actor from the RSC.

Desmond Barritt, much loved at the RSC, was performing as Dame many years before Sir Ian McKellan. Sir George Robey was doing the same sixty years earlier.

Pantomime has always had its stars, from Dan Leno to Danny La Rue. It has always had its impresarios, from Augustus Harris, Francis Laidler and Emile Littler to Paul Elliott. It has also been a home to many artistes starting out in the business, and still remains so today. In this day and age it may be difficult to solve a problem like a first job, but with pantomime as a major employer of actors, singers and dancers, it is a very good place to start!

Pantomime is the place to specialise. The traditional characters of the plots are tailor made for this. There are the comics – the younger comedians who follow the origins laid down in commedia d'ell arte – those of Harlequin, who evolved into Buttons or Muddles or Simple Simon. There are the Principal Girls who, like Columbine before them, are expected to be the epitome of femininity, but unlike Columbine are expected nowadays to have a 'belter' of a voice – sweet ballads have evolved into this year's Girls Aloud hit!

The Dame role appeals to both the older comic and the character actor; the 'Sisters' to character actors with a penchant for villainy and high camp. Sadly today the role of Principal Boy is more likely to be cast as a male. Up until Norman Wisdom played Dick Whittington at the London Palladium, the role seemed safely held by the ladies. However, things change, and eventually we might see the resurgence of the fishnets and swagger that personified the role. For now the requirements are Hollyoaks looks and a strong singing voice.

Pantomime is not ageist. As well as encouraging the newcomer, it welcomes the elder statesmen of theatre. There are roles for Villains, Kings, Fairy Queens and of course Dames, as well as Wicked Queens and Baronesses. Maturity, and the well-crafted skills learnt in a lifetime of performing and observing are more than welcome in Pantoland.

The route to appearing in a pantomime production is the usual double-edged sword that newcomers to the business face constantly. It used to be that if you wanted to be a member of Equity you had to have a job. To get a job you had to be a member of Equity. This may no longer apply, but often managements casting for pantomime prefer artistes who have previously appeared in a pantomime.

'Word of mouth' is employed very often by pantomime producers. They visit many productions (not just their own) during the panto season, and will note down artistes who they are interested in. They will look at a track record of where an artiste was the previous year, and will most likely make enquiries to see how they fared in the last pantomime before making a decision on the next one.

Panto producers rarely (if ever) employ a casting director. Some have their own in-house casting department, but mostly they employ their artistes through agents, and, on some occasions, they will hold auditions – these are often secured via agents rather than an 'open' audition.

For pantomime dancers the audition process is somewhat different. The panto companies frequently hold auditions, generally in the early autumn. These are usually advertised in *The Stage* a few weeks beforehand. At these auditions dancers will often be asked to dance first, and then sing. The managements are often looking for 'covers' and understudies at the same time as ensemble. Certainly it helps both dancers and actors to be general all-rounders.

Securing a job as a dancer and understudying a leading role will certainly add to a pantomime CV for the following year. This is often a door of opportunity that will open to allow the transition from ensemble to lead role in a future production.

If you want to pursue a pantomime contract, it helps to know into which category you want to be placed. In the past, an actress who stood over five foot six knew that her height and a fine singing voice would earmark her as a Principal Boy. Nowadays these female-to-male roles are rare. You need to know your strengths: comic ability and timing would make for a role as Henchman or Chinese Policeman. A tall character actor would be aiming at Abanazar or the Sheriff of Nottingham. Pantomime by its very nature places you into one of these traditional and stereotyped roles, and knowing what roles you are most suited for enhances the audition process. But having secured the part, what else do you need?

If I had to use just one word to describe the chief requirement a performer needs in Panto, it would be this: energy.

Energy is required both in performance on stage, and, if it is well controlled and paced, offstage as well. The audience is young. The attention span of the average child is getting shorter. Panto has evolved to meet this new challenge. The pace is faster, the dialogue sharper, the effects more transfixing. However – woe betide the performer who lacks energy. The children will not be fooled by a lack of energy, and a lack of truth; truth is the second requirement.

Pantomimes may be lavish and spectacular. They should also be comical and magical, but the entire structure is based on one solid and immovable thing – the plot. It is the story that will transfix the audience. It is what drives the pantomime onward to its inevitable conclusion – the knowledge that good will always overcome evil.

That simple retelling of what is essentially a morality play can only be held together by truth. If the performer believes in their character, be it good or evil, then the audience and the child in every audience will believe in it too. In panto we have no 'Fourth Wall'. We talk directly to the audience at times (well, certain characters can; others shouldn't). Barriers you find in plays are broken down. Direct contact is encouraged. A pantomime is, after all, the original interactive game.

To create the magic that IS pantomime, we onstage must believe in that magic. We must do it with a truth and a great deal of energy if that magic is to work.

Pantomime is larger than life. When we are on that stage, we become almost cartoon characters. Gestures are broad, expressions are big, and the excitement of the storyline is expressed by our excitement in performing it. Twice a day. Every day. Six days a week. Twelve shows a week for perhaps eight weeks. That energy must be controlled and it must be paced. Above all, every word that you speak must sound as if it is the first time you have ever spoken it. After all, the audience have never heard it before. That audience of children must be nurtured. If their pantomime experience is a joyful and enlightening one, then they will continue to come to the pantomime. In time, they will bring their own children, then their grandchildren ... you see ...

Pantomime is not just for Christmas – it's for life. OH YES IT IS!

Nigel Ellacott began his career with the Welsh Drama Company (part of Welsh National Opera) having trained as a Drama Teacher. He has worked in theatre and in television for the past thirty-five years. Nigel has performed in over thirty pantomimes across the country. Until Christmas 2008 he spent a happy 27 years as Ugly Sister with his stage partner Peter Robbins – for both E&B Productions (Paul Elliott) and Qdos Entertainment. They have appeared in theatres around the UK from Aberdeen to Plymouth, and recently completed the record breaking season of "Cinderella" with Brian Conley at the Hippodrome Birmingham. Nigel has written over twenty-two pantomime scripts. Each year he writes for the Kenneth More Theatre, and in addition has written pantomime scripts for companies both in Great Britain and in Canada, America and South Africa. He established "The Pantomime Roadshow" ten years ago. This production tours schools, taking the "Magic of Pantomime" to three thousand school children in a week. The show aims to attract young audiences to the theatre, and to pantomime in particular, and apart from entertaining, it reveals some of the history and traditions of British Panto. He created the pantomime website **www.its-behind-you.com** a few years ago. This site aims to encourage new audiences for the genre, as well as providing a current data base for performers, and a resource for pantomime and theatre historians. This website is currently sponsored by Qdos. Nigel was the feature of a Channel 4 documentary "Pantoland – The Biz", produced by Iambic Productions, and, together with Peter Robbins became the faces of the Royal Mail Christmas Campaign throughout the UK.

Theatre

Pantomime

This section lists some of the major pantomime producers and some of the theatres and arts centres that produce their own pantomimes. These latter (often subsidised by a local authority) largely present touring and (sometimes) amateur productions. However, a number of these do mount their own professional pantomimes and it can be useful to look through the Theatres & Provincial/Touring section of *Contacts* to check which. Many have websites.

Another way of finding out is to check through the listings and reviews in *The Stage* every Christmas. (Also look at **www.its-behind-you.com** which lists forthcoming pantomimes.) Pantomimes in such theatres will often be directed by the resident director, and usually cannot afford the services of a casting director.

Some of these theatres occasionally produce their own shows throughout the year, especially as part of the work of their Education departments. Where possible we have included this information in each entry, but it is also worth visiting the theatre's website for further details.

PANTOMIME PRODUCERS

Chaplins Ltd
Chaplins House, The Acorn Centre, Roebuck Road, Hainault, Essex IG6 3TU
tel 020-8501 2121 *fax* 020-8501 3336
email fun@chaplinspantos.co.uk
website www.chaplinsentertainment.co.uk
Directors Mr J Weborne, Mr J Holmes *Productions Manager* Emma Newland

Production details: A touring pantomime and theatre-in-education company which also works in film and television production. Stages 28 productions annually, performing in small theatres, schools, social clubs and community centres.

Casting procedures: Uses freelance casting directors and holds general auditions; actors requesting inclusion are asked to write from August until the end of October only. Casting breakdowns are publicly available from the website, by postal application (with sae), in *The Stage* and via Casting Call Pro. During the period specified, the company welcomes letters (with CVs and photographs) from individual actors previously unknown to them, sent by post or email, and will accept showreels and invitations to view individual actors' websites. Rarely or never has the opportunity to cast disabled actors.

Duggie Chapman Associates
The Old Coach House, 202 Common Edge Road, Blackpool FY4 5DG
tel (01253) 691823 *fax* (01253) 691823
email duggie@chapmanassociates.fsnet.co.uk
website www.duggiechapman.co.uk
Director Duggie Chapman *Artiste Bookings* Kim Holmes

Production details: Established in 1970. Producers of pantos, concerts and plays. Annually produces 6 resident pantos including Billingham (Forum Theatre), Blackburn (Thwaites Empire Theatre), Bolton (Albert Halls), Boston (Blackfriars), Barrow-in-Furness (Forum 28) and Bedworth (Civic), plus tours.

Casting procedures: Casting is carried out by in-house casting director. Occasionally holds general auditions. For the pantos, actors should write from March onwards to request inclusion. Casting breakdowns are obtainable through *PCR* and *The Stage*. Accepts submissions (with CVs and photographs) from individual actors previously unknown to the company. Invitations to view showreels and individual actors' websites are welcomed. Rarely has the opportunity to cast disabled actors.

Duo Entertainment
5 Market Place, London W1W 8AE
tel 020-7580 9070 *fax* 020-7580 9060
email office@duo.uk.net
website www.duo.uk.net
Directors Barrie C Stead, Richard Cadell, Carina Skinner *Administrator* Brian Sandford

Produces pantomimes for The Ashcroft Theatre, Croydon; Grove Theatre, Dunstable; Ipswich Regent Theatre; and Embassy Centre, Skegness.

Evolution Productions
Hampton Lodge, 183 Hanworth Road, Hampton TW12 3ED

tel 020-8941 2227 *fax* 020-8255 4273
email emily@evolution-productions.co.uk,
paul@evolution-productions.co.uk
website www.evolution-productions.co.uk
Directors Emily Wood, Paul Hendy

Production details: Founded in 2004 and run by
husband-and-wife team, Emily Wood and Paul
Hendy. Produces pantomimes and occasional
musicals (recently produced *Oliver!* at The Central
Theatre, Chatham). Stages 5 pantomimes a year: The
Marlowe Theatre, Canterbury; The Central Theatre,
Chatham; Yvonne Arnaud Theatre, Guildford;
Lyceum Theatre, Sheffield; and Gordon Craig
Theatre, Stevenage. Offers non-Equity, in-house
contracts ("Equity equivalent") and does not
subscribe to the Equity Pension Scheme.

Casting procedures: Casts in-house – all casting
enquiries should be addressed to Paul Hendy. Holds
general auditions; the best time to write to request
inclusion is March/April. Casting breakdowns are
published via Spotlight and Castweb, and current
casting requirements can be found on the website.
Welcomes letters (with CVs and photographs) and
performance notices from actors previously unknown
to the company, sent by post or email. Happy to
receive appropriate showreels and invitations to view
individual actors' websites. Will consider applications
from disabled actors to play disabled characters.

Extravaganza Productions
PO Box 25, Boston, Lincolnshire PE21 8YE
tel (01205) 355978 *fax* (01205) 354094
email chandler@extravaganza.wanadoo.co.uk
website www.panto-mime.co.uk
Directors David Vickers, Richard Chandler *Casting*
Mike Holoway

Production details: Established in 1995, and
associated with Mike Fisher Associates. Presenting
Pantomimes for The Plaza, Stockport and
Middlesborough Theatre. Number of productions
staged annually varies.

Casting procedures: Casting is carried out by in-
house casting director Mike Holoway. Actors can
write at any time to request inclusion. Accepts
submissions (with CVs and photographs) from
individual actors previously unknown to the
company. Will also accept CVs and photographs sent
via email, invitations to view individual actors'
websites, and showreels. Applications from disabled
actors are considered to play disabled characters.

First Family Entertainment
Fortune Theatre, Russell Street, London WC2B 5HH
tel 020-7010 7890 *fax* 020-7010 7899
email casting@ffe-uk.com
website www.ffe-uk.com
Chief Executive Kevin Wood *Casting Consultant* Scott
Mitchell *Production Co-ordinator* Jamie Taylor

Production details: Produces large-scale
pantomimes. Venues include: Theatre Royal,

Brighton; Churchill Theatre, Bromley; The King's
Theatre, Glasgow; Milton Keynes Theatre, Richmond
Theatre, Regent Theatre, Stoke on Trent; New
Wimbledon Theatre; New Victoria Theatre, Woking;
Opera House, Manchester; Sunderland Empire.
Offers Equity-approved contracts and subscribes to
the Equity Pension Scheme.

Casting procedures: In-house casting director is
Scott Mitchell. Does not hold general auditions: only
write in response to a specific breakdown.
Breakdowns are published in February on Castweb,
CastNet and direct to agents. Welcomes letters (with
CVs and photographs) from actors previously
unknown to the company if sent by post, but not by
email. ("Please do not phone!") Happy to receive
appropriate showreels, invitations to view individual
actors' websites and performance notices. Actively
encourages applications from disabled actors and
promotes the use of inclusive casting.

Hammond Productions
211 Piccadilly, London W1J 9HF
tel 020-7917 2767
email hftm@btopenworld.com
website www.hammondproductions.co.uk
Director Paul Hammond *Casting* Ruth Langridge

Production details: Produces 4 pantomimes: Victoria
Theatre, Halifax; Hazlitt Theatre, Maidstone; Pavilion
Theatre, Worthing; and Drayton Manor Big Top.
Offers actors non-Equity contracts and does not
subscribe to the Equity Pension Scheme.

Casting Procedures: Casts in-house. Actors should
write to or email Ruth Langridge (with CVs and
photographs) between February and July. Casting
breakdowns are published in *The Stage, SBS*, Castweb
and Entsweb. Welcomes CVs and photographs from
actors previously unknown to the company. Happy
to receive appropriate showreels, invitations to view
individual actors' websites and performance notices.
Will consider applications from disabled actors to
play disabled characters.

Hiss & Boo Theatre Company
1 Nyes Hill, Wineham Lane, Bolney,
West Sussex RH17 5SD
tel (01444) 881707 *fax* (01444) 882057
email email@hissboo.co.uk
website www.hissboo.co.uk
Artistic Director Ian Liston

Production details: Established in 1977. Pantomime
producers also specialising in touring plays and
revues in the UK and overseas. Pantomime venues
include: The Riverfront Theatre, Newport; The Corn
Exchange, Newbury; Hall for Cornwall, Truro;
Queens Theatre, Barnstaple; Garrick, Lichfield.
Actors are employed under TMA/Equity-approved
contracts. The company subscribes to the Equity
Pension Scheme. See also entry under *Independent
managements/theatre producers* on page 151.

Theatre

Casting procedures: Casting is done in-house. Casting breakdowns are only available to agents via Spotlight Interactive. Does not welcome unsolicited CVs and photographs. Rarely has the opportunity to cast disabled actors.

Paul Holman Associates

Morritt House, 58 Station Approach, South Ruislip, Middlesex HA4 6SA
tel 020-8845 9408 *fax* 020-8839 3124
email enquiries@paulholmanassociates.co.uk
website www.paulholmanassociates.co.uk
Directors Paul Holman, Adrian Jeckells, John Ogle
Associate Producer Andrew Lynford

Production details: Produces Pantomimes, Summer Seasons, Tours and other commercial projects. Stages between 10-15 productions annually. Venues where productions are staged include: Bridlington, Aylesbury (Civic), Catford (Broadway) Derby (Assembly Rooms), Leeds (Carriageworks), Newark (Palace), Redditch (Palace), Weston Super Mare (Playhouse). Summer Seasons: The Pier Theatre (Bournemouth), Princess Theatre (Hunstanton). Offers non-Equity (Variety) contracts and does not subscribe to the Equity Pension Scheme.

Casting procedures: Casting is done by in-house casting director. Occasionally hold general auditions; Spring is the best time to write requesting auditions. Casting breakdowns are available on Castweb and *SBS*. Accepts submissions (with CVs and photographs) from individual actors previously unknown to the company, sent by post or email. Invitations to view showreels and to attend other productions are also accepted. Will consider applications from disabled actors to play disabled characters, but in practice rarely has the opportunity to cast them.

Imagine Theatre Ltd

Unit F4-F6, Little Heath Industrial Estate, Old Church Road, Coventry CV6 7ND
tel 024-7668 8122
email casting@imaginetheatre.co.uk
website www.imaginetheatre.co.uk
General Manager Stephen Boden *Office Manager* Sarah Boden

Production details: Imagine Theatre (since 2009; formerly Wish Theatre) produces pantomimes and children's theatre for No. 1 tours, including *The Tweenies* and *Fun Song Factory*. Venues for pantomime include: Grand Pavilion, Porthcawl; Eden Court, Inverness; Victoria Theatre, Halifax; Belgrade Theatre, Coventry; Lyceum Theatre, Crewe; Palace Theatre, Kilmarnock; Town Hall, Loughborough; Roses Theatre, Tewksbury. Offers in-house contracts ("enhanced Equity") and does not subscribe to the Equity Pension Scheme.

Casting procedures: Casts mainly in-house. Holds general auditions; actors should email the company

in March-May to request inclusion. Casting breakdowns are not published except on Spotlight. Welcomes CVs and photgraphs from actors previously unknown to the company; prefers these to be emailed rather than posted. Will consider applications from disabled actors to play disabled characters. "Panto isn't a cop-out: it's a serious business. We use actors who can engage with the audience and have fun. It is really useful if actors can indicate their location/home town, which helps with accents and knowing if an individual is local to one of our pantomime venues. Please do not send showreels or invitations to view websites, as unfortunately we just don't have time to deal with them."

Bruce James Productions Ltd

68 St George's Park Avenue, Westcliff-on-Sea, Essex SS0 9UD
tel/fax (01702) 335970
email info@brucejamesproductions.co.uk
website www.brucejamesproductions.co.uk
Directors Bruce James, Martin Roddy

Production details: A touring and repertory company that plays musicals and thrillers together with numerous pantomimes since 1995. Stages on average 8-12 productions annually, touring to a range of venues (pantomime at Thameside Theatre, Grays, and Pomegranate Theatre, Chesterfield). Offers Equity approved contracts; does not subscribe to the Equity Pension Scheme.

Casting procedures: Uses in-house casting directors. Holds general auditions and actors should write in to request inclusion in January, June and October. Casting breakdowns are available from the website, by postal application with sae, or from *Spotlight*. Welcomes letters (with CVs & photographs) from individual actors previously unknown to the company, sent by post or email. Also accepts showreels and invitations to view individual actors' websites. Will consider applications from disabled actors to play characters with disabilities. "Please do not email large photo or CV files (i.e. over 1MB) as they just clog up our system."

Owen Money Productions

4 Westgate Close, Porthcawl CF36 3NP
tel (07896) 258893
email owen.money@btinternet.com
Director Owen Money *Company Manager* Roger Bell

Production details: Established in 2000. Produces 3-4 family pantomimes a year, touring to 7-8 theatres and community venues around Wales between the end of November and the end of February. Also produces a Brian Rix-style 'adult' panto in April (2007 production was *Buttons Undone*). Offers non-Equity contracts and does not subscribe to the Equity Pension Scheme.

Casting procedures: Casts in-house. Casting notices are published in *The Stage*. Actors wishing to audition for the company should write (with CV and photograph) between November and January. Does not welcome unsolicited CVs and photographs by email. Happy to receive appropriate showreels and invitations to view individual actors' websites. Will consider applications from disabled actors to play disabled characters.

New Pantomime Productions
27 Shooters Road, Enfield, Middlesex EN2 8RJ
tel 020-8363 9920
email simonbarry@nppltd.freeserve.co.uk
Director Simon Barry

Production details: Produces pantomimes at 7 venues: Theatr Colwyn, Colwyn Bay; Brindley Arts Centre, Runcorn; Southport Theatre; Kings Theatre, Southsea; Princess Theatre, Torquay; Grand Opera House, York. Offers non-Equity contracts and does not subscribe to the Equity Pension Scheme.

Casting procedures: Casts in-house. Holds general auditions; actors should write in July to request inclusion. Casting breakdowns are not publicly available. Welcomes emails only (with CVs and photographs) from actors previously unknown to the company. Does not welcome showreels or invitations to view individual actors' websites. "Make sure you're suitable for the job you're applying for. We have employed disabled actors – and not just to play disabled characters. So long as the actor is good, that's all that matters."

Pantoni Pantomimes
205 Bexhill Road, St. Leonards on Sea,
East Sussex TN38 8BG
tel (01424) 443400 *fax* (01424) 714847
email david@pantoni.com
website www.pantoni.com
Directors David Lee and Rita Proctor

Produces pantomimes for the Doncaster Civic Theatre; Empire Theatre, Consett, New Floral Pavilion, New Brighton; The Leatherhead Theatre; Library Theatre, Luton; and Octagon Theatre, Yeovil.

The Proper Pantomime Company
6 Empress Avenue, Farnborough,
Hampshire GU14 8LX
tel (01252) 547547
email chris@properpantomime.com
website www.properpantomime.com
Producers Chris Lillicrap, Paul Harvey *Choreographer* Nicola Miles

Production details: Produces pantomimes for: Hexagon Theatre, Reading; Dorking Halls; The Connaught Theatre, Worthing. Also produces children's shows (TIE) and corporate entertainment. Offers actors non-Equity contracts and does not subscribe to the Equity Pension Scheme.

Casting procedures: Casts in-house. Holds general auditions; actors should write or email (with CV and

photograph) in Feb/March to request inclusion. Casting breakdowns are published in *SBS* only. Happy to receive letters (with CVs and photographs) from actors previously unknown to the company, but prefers emails. Happy to receive showreels and invitations to view individual actors' websites, but does not welcome performance notices. Will consider applications from disabled actors to play disabled characters, especially for the TIE tours.

Qdos Entertainment (Pantomimes) Ltd
Qdos House, Queen Margaret's Road,
Scarborough YO11 2SAT
tel (01723) 500038
email info@qdosentertainment.plc.uk
website www.qdosentertainment.co.uk
Producer Jonathan Kiley

Production details: The largest of the commercial pantomime producers with 21 pantomimes across the UK: His Majesty's, Aberdeen; Grand Opera House, Belfast; Hippodrome Theatre, Birmingham; The Alhambra, Bradford; New Theatre, Cardiff; The Hawth, Crawley; Civic Theatre, Darlington; The Orchard, Dartford; Kings Theatre, Edinburgh; Beck Theatre, Hayes; Wycombe Swan, High Wycombe; Hull New Theatre; Venue Cymru, Llandudno; Theatre Royal, Newcastle upon Tyne; Derngate Theatre, Northampton; Theatre Royal, Nottingham; Theatre Royal, Plymouth; Cliffs Pavilion, Southend; Alban Arena, St Albans; Wyvern Theatre, Swindon; Grand Theatre, Wolverhampton. Offers Equity-approved contracts and subscribes to the Equity Pension Scheme.

Casting procedures: Actors should send CVs and photographs by post to Jonathan Kiley in March (star-casting only in February). Welcomes performance notices. Send to: Qdos Entertainment (Pantomimes) Ltd, 1st Floor, 18 Exeter Street, London WC2E 7DU (020-7379 0405)

Spillers Pantomimes
The Old Post Office, Honey Tye, Leavenheath,
Suffolk CO6 4NX
tel (01473) 810100
email jkspillers@talktalk.net
Managing Director John Spillers *Casting* (Mr) Bev Berridge

Production details: Established 1989. Produces pantomimes for Alexandra Theatre, Bognor Regis; Epsom Playhouse; Woodville Hall Theatre, Gravesend; Motherwell Theatre; Majestic Theatre, Retford; Civic Theatre, Rotherham; The Music Hall, Shrewsbury; Pavilion Theatre, Weymouth. Offers actors non-Equity contracts and does not contribute to the Equity Pension Scheme.

Casting procedures: Casting is done in-house. Holds general auditions. Best time for actors to write (with CV and photograph) to request inclusion is March/April. Casting breakdowns are published in *PCR* and

The Stage. Welcomes CVs and photographs from actors previously unknown to the company, sent by post or email. Will consider applications from disabled actors to play disabled characters.

UK Productions

Lime House, 78 Meadrow, Godalming,
Surrey GU7 3HT
tel (01483) 423600 *fax* (01483) 418486
email mail@ukproductions.co.uk
website www.ukproductions.co.uk
Directors Martin Dodd, Peter Frosdick *Production Manager* Andy Batty *Administrator/Casting Assistant* Derek Raper

Production details: Established 1995. Produce pantomimes and musicals for No. 1 touring. (See entry under *Independent managements/theatre producers* on page 157.) Pantomime venues include: The Anvil Theatre, Basingstoke; Bath Theatre Royal; The Grand Theatre, Blackpool; The Pavilion Theatre, Bournmouth; Mansfield Palace Theatre; Malvern Festival Theatre; The Pavilion Theatre, Rhyll, The Grand Theatre, Swansea; The Assembly Hall Theatre, Tunbridge Wells. Offers non-Equity contracts and does not subscribe to the Equity Pension Scheme.

Casting procedures: Casting is done in-house. Does not hold general auditions. Casting breakdowns are distributed via Spotlight or direct to agents. Welcomes performance notices but not any other unsolicited form of correspondence. "Unsolicited CVs are generally a waste of time. Very occasionally suggestions for a specific character – e.g. Dame – can be useful." Will consider applications from disabled actors to play characters with disabilities.

IN-HOUSE PANTOMIMES

Buxton Opera House

Water Street, Buxton, Derbyshire SK17 6XN
tel (01298) 72050 (admin) *fax* (01298) 27563
email admin@boh.org.uk
website www.buxtonoperahouse.org.uk
Chief Executive Andrew Aughton *Theatre Secretary* Pat Russell

Production details: A receiving theatre presenting around 450 performances each year including dance, comedy, children's shows, drama, musical concerts, pantomime and opera as well a Fringe Theatre and Community and Education Programme. Edwardian theatre designed by Frank Matcham, restored in 2001.

Casting procedures: Commissions Channel Theatre Company to produce its annual pantomimes. Philip Dart, the artistic director of Channel Theatre, is responsible for casting. Please see the entry under *Middle and smaller-scale companies* on page 166.

Cambridge Arts Theatre

6 St Edwards Passage, Cambridge CB2 3PJ
tel (01223) 578903 *fax* (01223) 578929
email slowe@cambridgeartstheatre.com
website www.cambridgeartstheatre.com
Theatre Administrator Sue Lowe

Production details: Seating capacity 665. A receiving theatre which presents a wide range of work, including children's theatre, music, dance and drama. Produces in-house panto annually.

Casting procedures: Engages a freelance director who, together with the producer and choreographer, is responsible for casting the panto. Actors should contact the theatre to request an audition for the pantomime in March/April. These submissions will be forwarded to the director, and marked for the attention of Sue Lowe. Actors are employed under Equity approved contracts. Invitations to see actors in other productions are only welcomed from actors in whom the director has already shown interest. Will consider applications from disabled actors to play disabled characters.

The Capitol

North Street, Horsham, West Sussex
tel (01403) 756080 *fax* (01403) 756092
website www.thecapitolhorsham.com
Artistic Director Michael Gattrell

Production details: Seating capacity 423. Produces a professional pantomime each year. Offers TMA/ Equity approved contracts.

Casting procedures: Uses in-house casting director. Optimum time to write requesting an audition is in Spring/Summer. Casting breakdowns are publicly available on the website, in *SBS* or by postal application (with sae). Accepts letters (with CVs and photographs) from individual actors previously unknown to the company, sent by post or email. Also welcomes invitations to view showreels and to attend other productions. Will consider applications from disabled actors to play disabled characters.

The Theatre, Chipping Norton

2 Spring Street, Chipping Norton,
Oxfordshire OX7 5NL
tel (01608) 642349 *fax* (01608) 642324
email administration@chippingnortontheatre.com
website www.chippingnortontheatre.com
Director John Terry *General Manager* Christopher C Durham *Community & Education Officer* Anneke Hay

Production details: The Theatre is a pivotal part of the artistic life of the area, and takes care to programme as diverse a range of performances – theatre, film, dance, comedy and opera – as possible. Its Community & Education programme takes film and opera out to village halls.

An intimate space, it seats 217 (including 4 wheelchair spaces) in either proscenium (end-on) or in-the-round configurations. While predominantly a receiving house, The Theatre produces an annual pantomime which runs for around 80 performances over the Christmas period, as well as occasional smaller ventures. Recent productions include: *Mother Goose* and *Puss in Boots*, new pantomimes by Simon Brett; and *Taste*, a new play which toured Normandy. The Theatre offers TMA/Equity approved contracts and subscribes to the Equity Pension Scheme.

Casting procedures: Does not use casting directors. Welcomes unsolicited CVs and photographs from actors unknown to the company, as well as invitations to view actors' websites. Casting breakdowns for the pantomime are available from mid-summer – via the website, postal application (with sae), the Equity Job Information Service, and occasionally *The Stage*; this is the best time to write to request inclusion. Actively encourages applications from disabled actors, and promotes the use of inclusive casting.

City Varieties

Swan Street, Leeds LS1 6LW
tel 0113-391 7777 *fax* 0113-234 1800
email info@cityvarieties.co.uk
website www.cityvarieties.co.uk
Artistic Director Peter Sandeman

Production details: Seating capacity 531. Grade II listed building, built in 1865. World-famous as the home of BBC TV's *Good Old Days.* Produces a professional pantomime each year, running from the end of November to mid-January. Also continues to produce *Good Old Days* music hall entertainment. Actors are employed under Equity approved contracts and the theatre subscribes to the Equity Pension Scheme.

Casting procedures: Optimum time to write requesting an audition is between February and May. Accepts submissions (with CVs and photographs) from individual actors previously unknown to the company. Invitations to attend other productions are also welcome, depending on distance. Rarely has the opportunity to cast disabled actors (the venue is not currently wheelchair accessible).

Connaught Theatre

Union Place, Worthing, West Sussex BN11 1LG
tel (01903) 231799
website www.worthingtheatres.co.uk
Admin Officer Rosie Gray

Production details: Seating capacity 506 with 6 wheelchair spaces. The Connaught Theatre was built in 1914, but was originally called the Picturedrome. For 20 years it was an early cinema, until 1935 when the Worthing Repertory Company outgrew its own premises and came into the venue, bringing with it the name Connaught Theatre.

Casting procedures: A receiving theatre, but from 2007 has been co-producing its annual panto with The Proper Pantomime Company (see entry on page 209.) Casting enquiries should be through Chris Lillicrap at The Proper Pantomime Company.

The Courtyard

The Courtyard Centre for the Arts, Edgar Street, Hereford HR4 9JR
tel (01432) 346500 *fax* (01432) 346349
email martyn.green@courtyard.org.uk
website www.courtyard.org.uk
Artistic Director Martyn Green *Administrator* Mel Langford

Production details: Seating capacity 436. The Courtyard opened in September 1998 and was the first Lottery-funded theatre to be built in England. It provides "an eclectic programme of work, from produced to received, and offers something for the whole community". Produces a professional pantomime each year, from end November to mid-January. Provides actors with Equity-approved contracts as negotiated through TMA.

Casting procedures: Uses in-house casting directors; actors may write in June to request an audition. Casting breakdowns are available from the website, in *PCR*, or via CastNet Ltd, Castweb and SBS. Welcomes letters (with CVs and photographs) from individual actors previously unknown to the company, sent by post or email. Also accepts showreels and invitations to visit other productions. Actively encourages applications from disabled actors and promotes the use of inclusive casting.

Cumbernauld Theatre

Kildrum, Cumbernauld, Glasgow G67 2BN
tel (01236) 737235 *fax* (01236) 738408
email info@cumbernauldtheatre.co.uk
website www.cumbernauldtheatre.co.uk
Artistic Director Ed Robson

Production details: Established in 1978. A year-round producing theatre with a broad range of artist development and creative learning programmes. Produces a professional pantomime each year, together with other in-house plays, musicals and 'seasons'. Recent productions include: *The Wasp Factory* by Iain Banks.

Casting procedures: Casting is done by the Artistic Director. Auditions are held all year round; actors should obtain casting breakdowns from the website only. Welcomes letters (with CVs and photographs) from individual actors previously unknown to the company, sent by post or email. Will consider invitations to visit other productions, but requests that no showreels be submitted. Actively encourages applications from disabled actors and promotes the use of inclusive casting.

The Customs House Trust Ltd

Mill Dam, South Shields, Tyne & Wear NE33 1ES
tel 0191-454 1234 *fax* 0191-456 5979
email mail@customshouse.co.uk
website www.customshouse.co.uk
Executive Director Ray Spencer

Production details: Seating capacity 441. Established in 1994 as an arts centre, gallery, cinema and theatre.

Theatre

Produces approximately 6 in-house shows each year, and is a member of the North East Theatre Consortium. Stages a professional pantomime in early December which runs through to the first week in January, as well as new writing and occasional new musicals. Provides actors with Equity-approved contracts as negotiated through TMA.

Casting procedures: Uses both in-house and freelance casting directors. The pantomime is cast in June, and CVs are received all year. Casting breakdowns are available from *PCR*. Welcomes letters (with CVs and photographs) from individual actors previously unknown to the compay, sent by post or email. Also accepts invitations to visit other productions. Advises actors to "find out about the venue via our website. Mention our work; it makes us feel important and makes you look as if you care!".

The Everyman Theatre

Regent Street, Cheltenham,
Gloucestershire GL50 1HQ
tel (01242) 572573 *fax* (01242) 224305
email admin@everymantheatre.org.uk
website www.everymantheatre.org.uk
Director of ReachOut Paul Milton (new writing)
Production Assistant Deb Dovinson

Production details: Seating capacity: main house 668, studio 60. Built in 1891. A receiving theatre which presents a wide range of work, from stand-up comedy to children's theatre and including live music, dance and drama. Also works with many emerging and established theatre companies from Gloucestershire and beyond, creating partnerships and productions that are performed at the Everyman and on tour across the county. Produces in-house panto as well as promoting new writing.

Casting procedures: A freelance director is engaged to direct the panto. This director is responsible for the casting process and will choose how and where the casting breakdowns are made available. Actors should write in February to request auditions for the panto, as auditions are held in March and April. Submissions (photos & CVs) are welcomed from actors previously unknown to the company for both panto and new writing projects; these should be marked for the attention of Deb Dovinson. The Everyman also runs an Actor's Lab, providing professional training and opportunities to meet and work with established directors. The Everyman Theatre is an equal opportunities employer and gives due consideration to applications from all sectors of the community.

The Gatehouse

Eastgate Street, Stafford ST16 2LT
tel (01785) 253595
website www.staffordgatehousetheatre.co.uk
Artistic Programme Manager Derrick Gask

Production details: Celebrated its silver jubilee in 2007. A receiving theatre which presents a wide range of work, from stand-up comedy to children's theatre, and including live music, dance and drama. Usually produces its own in-house panto; however in 2007/8 the panto was a co-production with The New Wolsey Theatre, Ipswich.

Casting procedures: Casting is done by freelance casting directors. Breakdowns are available via Spotlight to agents only. Will consider applications from disabled actors to play disabled characters.

The Gatehouse also produces the Stafford Festival Shakespeare. See entry under *Festivals* on page 280.

Hackney Empire

291 Mare Street, London E8 1EJ
020-8510 4500 020-8510 4530
email susie.mckenna@hackneyempire.co.uk
website www.hackneyempire.co.uk
CEO Simon Thomsett *Associate Director &*
Pantomime Producer Susie Mckenna

Production details: Grade II listed Frank Matcham theatre built in 1901. Recently renovated and refurbished. Provides a wide range of productions for the local community and London as a whole. Seating capacity is up to 1280. Produces an immensely popular and critically acclaimed traditional pantomime, eschewing 'celebrities' in favour of the core elements of traditional pantomime: a well-conceived narrative line, spectacular sets and costumes, magical spectacle, music, dance and slapstick comedy. Offers TMA/Equity approved contracts.

Casting procedures: Casting breakdowns are not publically available, but actors wishing to audition for the pantomime should contact Susie Mckenna, by post or email, in August/September. Happy to receive appropriate showreels and invitations to view individual actors' websites. Actively encourages applications from disabled actors and promotes the use of inclusive casting.

Kenneth More Theatre

Oakfield Road, Ilford, Essex IG1 1BT
tel 020-8553 4464 *fax* 020-8553 5476
email kmtheatre@aol.com
website www.kmtheatre.co.uk
Manager and Artistic Director Vivyan Ellacott

Production details: Seating capacity 365. Ilford's civic theatre, the Kenneth More, opened on the very last day of 1974 with a preview of *The Beggar's Opera*. The official opening was on January 3rd, 1975.

Balances its commitment to amateur theatre by providing 26 weeks each year for local amateur companies. The remaining half of the programme consists of visiting professional shows and the professional in-house panto production.

Casting procedures: Casting for the panto is done in-house. There is a regular team of actors who perform in the panto but any additional casting is done through preferred agents. The best time to write requesting an audition for the panto is August and September. Welcomes submissions (CVs and photo) from actors previously unknown to them. Actors applying should have song and dance or previous panto experience. Will consider invitations to see actors in other productions on 'word of mouth' recommendations. Has employed disabled performers but the theatre building has a number of accessibility issues for disabled actors. "We will always consider young local performers."

macrobert

University of Stirling, Stirling FK9 4LA
tel (01786) 467155 *fax* (01786) 466600
email info@macrobert.org
website www.macrobert.org
Artistic Director Liz Moran *Operations Director* Bill Armitage

Production details: A busy multi-venue arts centre seating 472, with particular emphasis on work with and for young people. Produces a professional pantomime each year, in November and December. Offers Equity approved contracts as negotiated through TMA. Subscribes to the Equity Pension Scheme.

Casting procedures: Uses freelance and in-house casting directors; actors may write in April and May to request inclusion. Welcomes letters (with CVs and photographs) from individual actors previously unknown to the company, sent by post or by email. Accepts showreels and invitations to visit other productions. Rarely (or never) has the opportunity to cast disabled actors.

Millfield Theatre

Silver Street, Edmonton, London N18 1PJ
tel 020-8887 7301
website www.millfieldtheatre.co.uk
Arts Centre Manager and Producer Ralph Dartford

Production details: Produces panto in-house. Has been a receiving theatre but is now starting to co-produce a couple of productions each year with partners such as Face Front Inclusive Theatre (**www.facefront.org**).

Casting procedures: Casting is done by liaising with show director and in-house producer. Breakdowns for the panto are sent out to agents via Spotlight Link. Contracts offered are negotiated directly with actors or their agents. Actors can write in May to request an audition for the panto, addressing their submission to Ralph Dartford. At present only welcomes submissions (with CVs and photographs) from actors previously unknown to the company at the time of casting the panto (May). As co-productions are still relatively new to the theatre, is considering developing the website to include a casting page. Will only view showreels if they have

been requested. Welcomes invitations to see actors in other productions in the Greater London area. Will consider invitations to shows at The Edinburgh Festival. Encourages applications from disabled actors and promotes the use of inclusive casting.

Theatre Royal, Bury St Edmunds

Westgate Street, Bury St Edmunds, Suffolk IP33 1QR
email sharron.stowe@theatreroyal.org
website www.theatreroyal.org
Artistic Director Colin Blumenau *Artistic Co-ordinator* Sharron Stowe

Production details: Seating capacity 358. Built in 1819, the theatre is the only surviving Regency theatre in the country. Produces an annual pantomime at Christmas and 2 other shows a year – a rural tour in the Spring (2007 production was Ayckbourn's *Intimate Exchanges*) and an in-house production in the Autumn, often from or about the Regency period. Offers non-Equity contracts.

Casting procedures: Casting is done in-house by Sharron Stowe. Casting breakdowns are published via *Spotlight* only. Actors wishing to be considered for the pantomime should write to the theatre in August. (The Spring and Autumn shows are cast in January/February and June/July respectively). Only welcomes letters and emails (with CVs and photographs) from actors previously unknown to the company during these casting periods. Does not welcome showreels, but is happy to receive performance notices. Rarely or never has the opportunity to cast disabled actors.

Theatre Royal, Margate

Addington Street, Margate, Kent CT9 1PW
tel 0845-130 1786 (Box Office)
tel (01843) 293397 (Admin)
email admin@theatreroyalmargate.com
website www.theatreroyalmargate.com
Artistic Director Will Wollen *General Manager* Art Hewitt

Production details: Seating capacity 440. "A dynamic theatre which re-opened in September 2007 under the leadership of Will Wollen. Receives 2 seasons of professional work and produces its own high-quality actor-musician Christmas show." As well as producing a professional pantomime in December each year, the company is developing new work with Associate companies from the South East.

Casting procedures: Uses in-house casting directors. Actors may write in June and July to request inclusion. Casting breakdowns are sometimes available, obtained via Spotlight, Equity Job Information Service and CastNet Ltd. Welcomes unsolicited approaches (by post – letters, CVs and photographs) from actors previously unknown to the company, only if those actors are actor-musicians and/or Kent-based. No emails, please. Will accept showreels (although "these are not necessary") and invitations to visit other productions. Actively encourages applications from disabled actors, and promotes the use of inclusive casting.

Theatre Royal, Norwich

Theatre Street, Norwich NR2 1RL
tel (01603) 598500 *fax* (01603) 598501
email j.walsh@theatreroyalnorwich.co.uk
website www.theatreroyalnorwich.co.uk
Programming Manager Jane Walsh

Production details: Seating capacity 1300. Produces an annual pantomime each Christmas and is a receiving house for the rest of the year. Offers ensemble actors Equity approved contracts (principals are on buy-out contracts) and subscribes to the Equity Pension Scheme.

Casting procedures: Casts in-house. Actors wishing to audition for the pantomime should contact Jane Walsh in Feb/March. Casting breakdowns are not published. Uses *SBS* to recruit chorus/ensemble; principals will generally be star names or performers that the theatre already has some relationship with. Welcomes letters and emails (with CVs and photographs) from actors not previously known to the company. Does not welcome showreels or performance notices. Will consider applications from disabled actors on the same basis as for non-disabled actors. "Take time to research the theatre's needs before sending your CV. Lots of CVs and photographs are wasted because they are sent at a time when they are not required."

Theatre Royal, Nottingham

Theatre Square, Nottingham NG1 5ND
tel 0115-989 5500 *fax* 0115-950 3476

email enquiry@royalcentre-nottingham.co.uk
website www.royalcentre-nottingham.co.uk
Managing Director Mr Robert Sanderson

Production details: Seating capacity 1186. Pantomimes are produced by Qdos Entertainment; those produced in-house are by its education-based Royal Company, which includes members of the community. Offers actors Equity approved contracts but does not subscribe to the Equity Pension Scheme.

Casting procedures: Casts in-house. Actors wishing to request an audition should contact Jimmy Ashworth in April/May. Casting breakdowns are not publicly available. Welcomes letters and emails (with CVs and photographs) from actors previously unknown to the company. Happy to receive appropriate showreels and performance notices. Actively encourages applications from disabled actors and promotes the use of inclusive casting.

Theatre Royal, Winchester

Jewry Street, Winchester, Hampshire SO23 8SB
tel (01962) 844600 *fax* (01962) 810277
website www.theatreroyalwinchester.co.uk
Chief Executive Fiona Burn

Production details: Seating capacity 400. A receiving theatre which presents a wide range of work, from stand-up comedy to children's theatre and including music, dance and classic plays. The theatre was re-opened in 2001 following a major refurbishment. Produces panto in-house.

Casting procedures: Casting is done by the Director of the show. Breakdowns are available publicly mid-June through *PCR*. Only welcomes submissions (with CVs and photographs) from actors previously unknown to the company in response to a casting breakdown. Encourages applications from disabled actors and promotes the use of inclusive casting.

Starting your own theatre company

Pilar Ortí

The first question you should ask yourself before starting a theatre company is – do you really need to set up a company, or do you just want to put on a show? In order to put on a show you don't need to go through all the hassle of setting up a company. If you *do* want to set up a company – why? In some cases this might be as difficult a question to answer as, "Why do you want to act?", but it's worth having an idea of why you want to invest so much time and energy in setting up and running an organisation rather than looking for acting work. Whatever your answer, be honest with yourself. And the clearer you can be, the better, as your answers will affect the kind of organisation you end up creating.

Of course, many companies emerge after a group of actors produce a show together: at some point, someone decides that, as a company of people, you are worth keeping together. If this is the case, then you are ready to run a company of your own. But there are many ways of making theatre, as you well know, and the range of theatre produced is also vast. What kind of work do you want to do? At this point it is worth bearing in mind your 'artistic policy', and coming up with a couple of sentences that describe the work you do. I know that 'policy' sounds dry, but if you end up constituting yourself as a non-commercial organisation and applying to public funds (or trusts and foundations), you will need to learn a whole new vocabulary which seems to have little to do with your art. You should never lose sight of your artistic dreams and ambitions – but you may need to talk about them in terms of policy, objectives, qualitative evaluation, benefits, management structure, cultural diversity, contingency ... the list goes on and on. This article is meant to inspire you, not send you off to sleep, so don't despair: learn the language and then use it in a creative way that makes sense to you.

Allow yourself to dream

Long-term plans are necessary – so learn to dream. (Okay, give it a try in the first instance by putting on a show. Then, if you enjoy it, carry on!) Plans, of course, can change along the way: I suggest that you have an absolutely ambitious dream plan and a let's-try-and-see-what's-possible-now plan. Opportunities arise when you least expect them, and if you know where you are heading, you can grab them without letting them throw you off-course.

I view running a theatre company rather like directing a show: the more theatre you watch, the stronger the idea you will have of what *you* want the show to be, what is unique about it, and what you can realistically achieve. So if you, like me, trained as an actor or actress and suddenly find yourself running a company, seek advice and look at how others operate. If you consider how other people do things, you will be able to adapt the bits you like and which make sense to you. In a sector such as ours, it is not difficult to find those who are pleased to help – and the freshness of people just starting out reminds us all of how much can be achieved when we don't know our limitations.

Seek help

There is an awful lot of free/cheap advice out there. During the year in which we focused on building the administrative foundations for our company, my colleague and I talked to as many consultants, local authority officers, venue managers, etc. as we could. Some of these conversations came about through informal meetings; others, by taking part in official programmes. We found out what funders were really looking for, and what other companies were doing in our area; we learnt to draw up business plans with budgets covering three and five years; and we discovered what our strengths and weaknesses were, and what threats and opportunities exist 'out there'.

A word of warning: take *all* advice (including that which I am giving you now) with a pinch of salt, especially from those who hardly know you and your work. Follow your gut instinct. When we were in pre-production for *Antigone*, a business consultant suggested that we invite Funeral Services to advertise in our programme, "seeing as how they all die in the end". Mmm.

The best consultancies are those which have been carefully structured so that the consultant spends time with you, getting to know you and your plans, and then helps you find your own answers by providing their expertise. Arts & Business's 'Business in the Arts' programme is worth checking out, although you need to have a very definite idea of what you need help with. (To see what else Arts & Business do, check out their website, **www.aandb.org.uk**.)

Making it 'proper'

Once you have decided on the work you want to do and how you want to go about producing it, you will need to find a legal structure for your company. This shows outsiders that you are serious, and it also makes monetary transactions easier.

Forbidden's first show was produced in Edinburgh: the only 'proper' thing the company had was a bank account (and a name!). We then registered the name and became a limited company, and after our first London show, became a registered charity. This was a good idea as our income mainly comes from trusts and foundations (most of which require you to be a charity in order to receive their grants, for tax purposes); it also allows us to claim Gift Aid when we receive donations from individuals. (Gift Aid is great: the donor claims their donation as tax-deductible, and you receive an extra 23 per cent from the Inland Revenue.)

Setting up a charity still allows you to pursue your own artistic programme: making theatre for the public is considered to 'advance education', which is a charitable objective. So you can still run your company as a business, drawing salaries, etc. and making sure that any annual profits stay within the company.

Just like a limited company, a registered charity is governed by a Board. The main difference between the two set-ups is that those who sit on a charity's Board (the Trustees) do so on a voluntary basis. It therefore would make no sense for *you* to be part of the Board (although there is talk of a possible change in the law to allow Trustees to be remunerated for their work). This means that, in theory at least, you are putting the fate of your company in the hands of other people. So choose your Trustees very carefully, and try to include people who have some knowledge of legal matters and accountancy.

This set-up has worked for Forbidden, as we have been extremely lucky: we have managed to find experienced individuals with integrity and a passion for what we do. You might prefer a different kind of set-up which gives you more legal control: banks and Business Links offer free advice on the different options. If you want some focused advice and have a bit of cash to spare, you might attend the Independent Theatre Council's (ITC) seminar on 'Starting a Theatre Company'. And when you have a bit more cash, you might want to join the ITC – membership is bound to come in handy when questions on legal matters arise. (Have a look at the website, **www.itc-arts.org.uk**.)

Learn as you go along

Know your strengths and weaknesses. Setting up a theatre company will involve doing ten thousand things you might never have done before; however, a lot of it can be learnt along the way, and much of it is common sense. It won't take you long to discover those things you are useless at, and those that you absolutely hate. You then have two choices: do them anyway, or find someone else to do them for you/with you.

If there are more than two of you running the company, decide who will be in charge of what. Certain things, like fundraising, might be too daunting for one person to do on their own, but you can break it down into more manageable pieces. Someone might have a clearer head for numbers and can prepare the budget, and someone else can write the description of the show and why it will make a huge contribution to theatre in this country.

Let's talk about money

And seeing that I've come to fundraising, I shall dwell on it. You can't escape it. No matter how much your company grows, no matter how successful you are, no matter how large your staff is – if you are in charge, you will worry about it, so learn to enjoy it. I know that this sounds perverse, but fundraising applications are your chance to enthuse someone else about what you do. To tell them about your plans – about what you want to do and why you want to do it. Tell them how you want to make a difference; about *why* you think it's different; about how it will help you, and others, grow. And yes, you will need to learn some new vocabulary, and be able to distinguish between qualitative and quantitative evaluation, but it helps if you see this as a game with which you have to keep up. (At the last ITC annual general meeting, I found out that 'well-being' is a new way of convincing funders that theatre is necessary to people's lives!) What's really important is to convince funders that you really want to do the work, and that you want to do it well. (When I talk about funders, I am referring to anyone who might want to donate to or invest in your company. I have no experience of commercial deals, but I imagine that these work in a similar way: you find out what it is that people want in return for their money, and then convince them that you can provide it – as well as putting on a really good show.)

This is also where having long-term plans comes in handy: funding applications usually take between six weeks and three months to be assessed. Sometimes, even more: our first successful application for an Education Officer took more than one year from the date on which I sent it to the day the letter of acceptance came through. While I'm on the subject of those who will give you money – *nurture your relationships with them*. We have found that those trusts, foundations and individuals who are willing to help us out once, are likely to do so again.

I have also discovered that funding applications help you plan in detail how you are going to realise a production or a project. Good funding applications might come in useful even if you don't get the money – they will probably provide a good description of your plans, which you can then show others interested in your work. (For books and directories on fundraising, check out the Directory of Social Change's website, **www.dsc.org.uk**. They also have a small bookshop in Stephenson Way, near Euston Square in London NW1.)

Theatre

Final words

I have left the most important thing until last. *Treat those working with you well, especially your actors.* Make working with you an enjoyable experience. If you hold auditions, make them worthwhile for those attending. When you are able to pay your personnel, pay them on time. Treat them like the professionals that they are. And when things go wrong, as they inevitably will, take responsibility for your company and make up for the hassle with a gesture, however small – custard creams work for me!

When I first started running Forbidden, I kept hearing that I should treat it like running a business. What I have discovered is that it is an exercise in people management. Forbidden exists because people have believed in our work and are willing to invest their time and money in what we do. Different organisations work in different ways: I hope these words have helped you find one that will work for you.

After running Forbidden Theatre Company as Artistic Director for seven years, **Pilar** now uses her people management skills to facilitate learning in leaders and in teams. She is director of Unusual Connections, a company which uses theatre-based training to deliver Leadership Programmes and Strategic Team-Away days. She also freelances as workshop leader and voice-over artist, and can be contated via **info@unusualconnections.co.uk**

Finding funding for projects
Sinead Mac Manus

Finding funding for projects is an essential part of the subsidised theatre scene. Unless you are working in the commercial sector, most theatre productions do not generate enough income to cover their costs. Fundraising provides the shortfall. The funding landscape in the UK is wide and varied, and can seem to the beginner to be an impossible terrain to navigate. However, as with most things, there are tricks of the trade that you can learn, and the process *does* get easier with practice.

Starting points
There are two good starting publications that I would recommend for fledging arts fundraisers: the first entitled 'Guide to Arts Funding in England', is an excellent overview of arts funding available to download for free from the Department for Culture, Media and Sport (DCMS) website (**www.culture.gov.uk/what_we_do/Arts/funding_for_the_arts**). Also recommended is Susan Forrester's and David Lloyd's *The Arts Funding Guide* published by the Directory of Social Change in 2002 (**www.dsc.org.uk**), which may be available in your local library. These guides take the user through the areas where you can find funding for projects, such as Government grants including Arts Council funding, Lottery funding, funding from your Local Authority, grants from charitable trusts and foundations, and bursaries.

Research, research, research
Successful fundraising is all about research, and matching available funds to your projects. If you approach fundraising creatively you should be able to adapt projects to available funds while still retaining your artistic integrity. So how do you discover what is out there? Get on the arts mailing lists to find out about new rounds of funds. Research the funding bodies and their criteria. Talk to your local Council about what funds they can offer you and your project. Find out what venues support new work with bursaries, or support in kind such as free space. Find out what trusts and foundations there are and who they give money to. Look up fundraising directories in your local library or one of the resource centres at organisations such as CIDA in east London (**www.cida.co.uk**), the Directory of Social Change (**www.dsc.org.uk**) or Arts and Business (**www.aandb.org.uk**).

The Funder Finder website (**www.funderfinder.org.uk**) features downloadable resources including a handy budget tool and grant application tool. Their cd-rom with details of hundreds of grants can be found in some resource centres or libraries for free use. They also have a free comprehensive advice pack on their website which has downloadable leaflets on areas such as budgeting, planning a funding strategy and tips for successful applications. The website also has a comprehensive A–Z list of trusts and foundations that have available funds.

It is important to research the funder that you are applying to, in order to find the 'essence' of the funder. This is essential so that you can match your projects to the relevant funder. For example, a Lottery Funding scheme such as Awards for All (**www.awardsforall.org.uk**) distributes public money for the benefit of local communities. Therefore any application to them must be for a project that demonstrates clear benefit to an identified community or body of people.

Similarly, the Arts Councils of England, Wales, Scotland and Northern Ireland all distribute public funds and have to be very open and transparent about how their funds are distributed.

Arts Council England (ACE) is the development and funding agency for the arts in England. You can apply to ACE as an individual for funding between £200 to £30,000. Organisations can receive up to £100,000. You can apply any time and there are no deadlines. A decision will be forthcoming within six weeks for grants under £5,000 and twelve weeks for grants over £5,000. ACE set aims every three years which form the basis of their grant-making policy, so it is important for applicants to think about how their project will fit into these aims. As with any funding body, building a relationship is paramount. Even before you approach ACE for funding, you should be inviting them to your productions and telling them about your projects. Full details of how to apply, including guidance notes, are on the website (**www.artscouncil.org.uk**).

The Arts Council of Wales (**www.artswales.org.uk**) has a similar funding system and structure to England, but there are regular funding deadlines throughout the year. The Scottish Arts Council (**www.scottisharts.org.uk**) has a slightly more complicated funding system with deadlines for different funding streams. The Arts Council of Northern Ireland (**www.artscouncil-ni.org**) has different funding schemes for individuals and organisations, and different closing dates for individual schemes.

In contrast to the Arts Councils in the UK, many charitable trusts and foundations only distribute funds to limited companies, and, in some cases, registered charities. Some can fund individuals, but they are not many. When applying to trusts and foundations, it is important to remember they were usually set up to address an issue or problem. You will need to identify what this is and ensure that your project addresses this.

Find out what you can about the funding body that you are applying to and what their funding priorities are. Make sure you fit into their guidelines and that you are eligible to apply. Remember that all funders have agendas – they do not give money away for nothing. For example, many Local Authority arts funding schemes usually look for local projects that impact on the community and have public benefit. View researching and applying for funding as you would looking for a job. You would not apply to a company if you did not think you were qualified. Similarly, you are wasting your time and theirs if you apply for funding that you are not eligible to get, e.g. your theatre company is not a registered charity, or they only fund work with older people and you work with children.

The proposal

An easy to read guide on writing funding proposals is Tim Cook's *Avoiding the Wastepaper Basket – A practical guide to applying to Grant Making Trusts* (LVSC, 1998). The book is written from the perspective of the funding body, and looks at examples of good and bad funding proposals.

If there is no application form, write a clear and concise (2 x A4 page) proposal. Write in plain English and do not use jargon. Find what the 'grain' of the funding body is. Do their work for them. Show in your funding application exactly how you meet their criteria and fit into their funding policy. Again to use the analogy of applying for a job, use the exact wording of the guidelines in your application when you are talking about your project, much in the way you would use the wording in the Person Specification when you are applying for a job. You can even highlight their criteria in bold or italics to make it stand out.

Follow the guidelines of the fund to the letter – supply all the information that they require but do not add in additional information if it is not requested. If you have something that you think may be of interest to them, mention in your application that this is available on request. Convey your enthusiasm and passion for your project and your belief in yourself and/or your company. Show how the project will be successful. Funders like to back winners.

When you are finished, show your finished application to a non-arts person and ask them to read it for clarity. If you do get a grant, remember to say thank you! Start to build a relationship with the funder and keep them updated on progress with the project. If you are not successful, ask for feedback from the funder on why.

Business sponsorship

Business sponsorship can be a useful way of raising funds for projects if you are not eligible to apply for grant project funding. Business sponsorship is where a company gives your organisation or project cash, or support in kind, in exchange for publicity for their product or service. It is important to remember that businesses will not give you money or support for nothing – they will require something in return. Sponsorship is essentially a commercial deal between yourself and the business, and therefore there should be a clear exchange of benefits, e.g. advertising benefit for the company and monetary benefit for the arts organisation, and there should be a value to the benefit given or received.

Arts & Business is the leading agency for bringing business and the arts together in the UK. Their website provides valuable information about building relationships between the arts and business, including details of investment schemes such as *Read* and *Invest*. They also publish an essential guide to business sponsorship entitled *Arts Business Sponsorship Manual,* which is included when you book on their Arts & Business Sponsorship Seminar – held regularly around the UK. The guide and other resources on sponsorship can also be read at their free resource centre in London (**www.aandb.org.uk**).

Income generation

An important part of finding funding for projects is generating your own income. Income can be earned or generated from a number of different sources: venues can pay you a fee or share the box office receipts of a production. They can also commission or co-produce a work. You can sell merchandise such as programmes, t-shirts or postcards at your events. You can generate income through education work including fees for workshops and residencies. Individuals can give you money for your projects (angels) or they can invest in your work and expect (or not!) a return. You can also raise funds through events ranging from theatre related events such as benefit performances and cabarets to 'fun' events such as sponsored walks to parachute jumps.

Creative thinking

When you are starting out, it can be difficult to see where you can obtain the money for projects. The Arts Council do prefer to fund artists or organisations with a track record, and therefore you may have to find alternative funding initially for your productions or projects. Trusts and foundations tend to only fund limited companies or registered charities, and so again this may not be an area of funding that you can tap into immediately.

Therefore it is important to think of ways of funding your work outside the traditional funding system. In many cases, this may mean that you have to fund your work yourself and hope that you can get a return on it, or at least break even. This is how the majority of companies fund their Edinburgh Fringe Festival run – by investing the money upfront in the hire of the venue, the accommodation and travel and the cost of the production and hoping that the take at the box office will cover these costs and give everyone involved in the production some wages. If you are using your own money to mount a production, you need to be able to assess what level of risk you are willing to accept and think of ways of lessening this risk. Examine your budget and see where you can reduce or cut costs. You could try to get free rehearsal space from a local school in exchange for workshops or use a local printer for your flyers in exchange for advertising in your programme. Consider sharing your venue with another company for a double bill (check that this is acceptable to the venue in advance) to halve the costs of the hire. Book a venue in your local area that you know so that you can at least invite friends and family to have a guaranteed audience. Ask friends and family to invest small amounts of money in your production. This can be done as a gift or on an investment and return basis e.g. an individual invests £100 and is guaranteed a return of £75 or an amount above £100, depending on how well the show does. Offer credits for purchase in the production as gifts – purchasers get credit in the publicity material, and an invitation to a performance.

There are many examples of artists and companies that have used creative ways to get their projects up and running. One company sold performances in the customer's sitting room on eBay for cash. Another company raised the money for a string of rural performances by doing a sponsored walk from venue to venue. Another company raised the money for a production by offering to do up a local community centre – they got free rehearsal space and a venue as part of the deal.

Remember that you are a creative individual! Use some of that creativity to think outside the box when it comes to finding money for projects.

Sinead Mac Manus has worked for a wide range of arts organisations, including Frantic Assembly, Tall Stories and Mimbre. She is currently a freelance creative business consultant and trainer, and has many years of experience working with and training creative entrepreneurs. She is the author of *eVolve Graduate Handbook: a practical guide to producing performance*, and founder of **StartaTheatreCompany.com** – an online guide to starting a performing arts company. Her activity in developing new business models around the idea of e-learning for creative entrepreneurs using web 2.0 tools and social media led her to be chosen this year as one of the Courvoisier: Future 500 to watch.

English-language European theatre companies

This small section seems to be populated by companies set up by enthusiasts who have kept on going with very little subsidy – and sometimes with none at all. Although living away from home and isolated from auditions, it can be fun working for such companies. It is important to note that the work often involves educational projects and/or touring.

ACT Company
25 Avenue du Marechal Leclerc, 92240 Malakoff, France
tel (33) 1 4656 2050
email andrew@actheatre.com
website www.actheatre.com
Artistic Director Andrew Wilson Administrator Anne Wilson Secretary Marie Christine Bento

Production details: Founded in 1981. An English-language theatre company focusing on research and development to make theatrical experiences in English accessible to a non-native-speaking public. Runs theatre in Education projects, workshops, performing for adults and young French native speakers learning English. Takes a physical approach to theatre - regularly working with actors from L'Ecole Internationale de Théâtre Jacques Lecoq. See the Act website for recent and present productions. "As we are based in France we do not follow the Equity system of salaries. However, our system of payment follows the recognised system here in France, paying actors by the performance. This 'French system' however requires actors to be registered here in France, so casting is mainly with French registered bilingual actors."

Casting procedures: Casting is during the months of May and June and CVs (by post) are welcome just before this period. "Please note we are a small company and engage no more than eight actors per season. We are completely open to casting disabled actors, but we are a touring company and a reasonable arrangement needs to be made between us and the actor concerning travel arrangements."

Dear Conjunction Theatre Company
6 Rue Arthur Rozier, 75019 Paris, France
tel (33) 1 4241 6965
email dearconjunction@wanadoo.fr
Artistic Directors Leslie Clack, Patricia Kessler

Production details: Founded in 1991, this bilingual company is composed of professional actors, directors and writers who are resident in Paris and who present productions in both French and English. Past productions include: Pinter's Ashes to Ashes and The Hothouse; and Someone Who'll Watch Over Me by Frank McGuinness.

Casting procedures: Welcomes letters and emails (with CVs and photographs) from actors previously unknown to the company. Contact Leslie Clack for more information.

The English Speaking Theatre Oslo (TESTO)
Jacob Aalls Gate 30, 0364 Oslo, Norway
tel (47) 22 466248
email testo-no@online.no
website home.tiscali.no/testo.no
Artistic Director Simon Lay Director Kristin Zachariassen

Production details: Founded in 1996 by actors Simon Lay and Kristin Zachariassen. Main focus of work is Theatre in Education. Produces theatre adaptations targeted at Norwegian students but also appealing to the general Norwegian public. Recent productions include: How High Is Up?, Too Much for Punch and Judy, Pygmalion and The Woman in Black.

The English Theatre Company Ltd
Nybrogatan 35, 114 39 Stockholm, Sweden
tel (46) 8 662 4133 fax (46) 8 660 1159
email etc.ltd@telia.com
website www.englishtheatre.se
Artistic Director Christer Berg

Production details: Founded in 1981. Stages 2 productions annually. Recent productions include: Shirley Valentine and A Christmas Carol.

Casting procedures: Uses freelance casting directors. Holds general auditions; actors requesting inclusion should write between August and September. Casting breakdowns are not publicly available. Welcomes postal enquiries from actors previously unknown to the company.

English Theatre Frankfurt
Kaiserstrasse 34, D-60329 Frankfurt, Germany
tel (49) 69 242 31615 fax (49) 69 242 31614
email mail@english-theatre.org
website www.english-theatre.org
Artistic Adviser Clive Paget Managing Director Daniel Nicolai

Production details: Founded in 1979. Presents contemporary plays, musicals and classics. 5

Theatre

productions performed in the main house each year, totalling 260 performances.

Casting procedures: Uses London-based freelance casting directors. Does not hold general auditions. Actors should write in April to request inclusion. Casting breakdowns are only available via Spotlight.

The English Theatre of Copenhagen

The London Toast Theatre, Kochsvej 18, 1812 Fred C, Copenhagen, Denmark
tel (45) 3322 8686
email mail@londontoast.dk
website www.londontoast.dk
Artistic Director Vivienne McKee *Administrator* Soren Hall

Production details: Founded in 1982. The largest English-speaking theatre company in Northern Europe. Presents theatre productions and provides corporate entertainment, stand-up comedy and Murder Mystery shows in Scandinavia and abroad. The company's voice-over bureau, 'Speaker's Corner', provides English and American voices for films and commercials. Recent productions include: *Dracula – A Pain in the Neck!* and *The Importance of Being Earnest.*

The English Theatre of Hamburg

Lerchenfeld 14, 22081 Hamburg, Germany
tel (49) 40 227 7089 *fax* (49) 40 229 5040
email ETHamburg@onlinehome.de
website www.englishtheatre.de
Contact Robert Rumpf, Clifford Dean

Production details: Founded in 1976 by 2 Americans, Robert Rumpf and Clifford Dean, who originally trained and worked professionally in the USA. They share general management responsibilities, plan the artistic programme and direct productions. Since 1981 the theatre has occupied its present premises at Mundsburg, 22081 Hamburg. Performs 8 times per week from September to June. A typical season at the English Theatre includes a classic American or British drama, a comedy and a thriller. Recent productions include: *Quartet, Birthday Suite, The Subject Was Roses,* and *Deadly Game.* Also runs Education programmes.

Light Nights – The Summer Theatre

Baldursgata 37, IS-101 Reykjavik, Iceland
tel (354) 551 9181 *fax* (354) 551 5015
website www.lightnights.com
Artistic Director Kristín G Magnús

Production details: Runs a summer theatre show at the Idnó Theatre in Reykjavik. Previous productions have included: *Light Nights* and *On The Way to Heaven.*

Casting procedures: Sometimes holds general auditions. The best time to write requesting inclusion is February/March. Casting breakdowns are not publicly available. Welcomes letters (with CVs and photographs) from actors previously unknown to the company, but not via email. Does not welcome showreels, but is happy to receive invitations to view actors' websites. Offers non-Equity contracts; rarely (or never) has the opportunity to cast disabled actors.

Merlin International Theatre

1052 Budapest, Gerloczy Utca 4, Hungary
tel (36) 1 317 9338 *fax* (36) 1 266 0904
email angol@merlinszinhaz.hu
website www.szinhaz.hu/merlin/english
Director Laszlo Magacs *Associate Director* Emma Vidovsky

Production details: Founded in 1991; Hungary's first and currently its only international theatre. Recent productions include: *The Importance of Being Earnest, Don't Drink the Water, Stones in His Pockets* and *Twelfth Night.* Resident companies at the Merlin Theatre are the Atlantis Company, Junion Group and Madhouse.

Simply Theatre

8B Chemin des Couleuvres, 1295 Tannay, Switzerland
tel +41 22 860 0518
email info@simplytheatre.com
website www.simplytheatre.com
Artistic Director Thomas Grafton

Production details: Founded in 2005. A Professional English Theatre for Switzerland and Continental Europe; and an English-speaking Drama Academy. Stages 3 productions a year in the Main House (plus 3 Academy productions). Recent productions include: *Private Lives, Educating Rita,* and *Sleuth.*

Casting procedures: Holds general auditions and actors may write in at any time. Casting breakdowns are available from *Spotlight* and Casting Call Pro. Welcomes letters (with CVs & photographs) from actors previously unknown to the company, sent by post or email. Accepts showreels and invitations to view individual actors' websites.

Theatre From Oxford

B.P. 10, F-42750 St Denis de Cabanne, France
tel/fax 00-334-77-66-20-42
email theatre.oxford@virgin.net
Artistic Director Robert Southam

Production details: Founded in 1984, the main aim for the past 20 years has been to introduce audiences on the continent to the best of theatre in English. The company has toured plays by Shakespeare, Shaw, Wilde, Willy Russell, Tennessee Williams and Arthur Miller, among others. Touring for 3 months from September to Christmas in 7 European countries, the company plays in anything from the best theatres to school gyms – but nearly always to full houses. Tours again in the spring to many of the same venues, providing theatre workshops. Half of the spectators are students; the other half, adult theatre-goers. The company is shortly to have its own theatre in France.

Casting procedures: Actors are advised that the tours are enjoyable but demanding, and that the company seldom accepts anyone straight from drama school. Casts often include actors with RSC and RNT experience. Recently has been working with African, Asian and Latin American actors and writers, which has meant less work for British and American actors. Casting breakdowns are available by postal application (with sae) and actors are welcome to write letters or emails with their CVs and photographs. Showreels, however, are not welcomed. Offers non-Equity contracts. Will consider applications from disabled actors to play characters with disabilities.

Vienna's English Theatre

UK address: VM Theatre Productions Ltd, 16 The Street, Ash, Canterbury CT3 2HJ
tel (01304) 813330 *fax* (01304) 813330
email vanessa@vmtheatre.demon.co.uk
Theatre address: Josefsgasse 12, A-1080 Vienna, Austria
tel (43) 1 4021 2600 *fax* (43) 1 4021 26042
website www.englishtheatre.at

Production details: Founded in 1963 it is the oldest English-language theatre in continental Europe. It stages 5 shows each year in the Main House and sends 4 Theatre-in-Education tours around the schools of Austria. The season runs from September to July each year.

Casting procedures: Casting breakdowns are posted on the website and actors may write to the UK address above with their CV and photograph at anytime. Emails not encouraged, and showreels not accepted. "All contracts are especially written for us by Equity."

White Horse Theatre

Bördenstrasse 17, 59494 Soest-Müllingsen, Germany
tel (49) 2921 339339 *fax* (49) 2921 339336
email theatre@whitehorse.de
website www.whitehorse.de
Artistic Director Peter Griffith *Casting Director* Michael Dray

Production details: Founded in 1978. Tours schools in Germany with occasional visits to neighbouring countries. Contracts are for 10-11 months. 6 companies of 4 actors each perform 3 plays. Recent productions include: *The Glass Menagerie, Oliver Twist, A Midsummer Night's Dream* and numerous plays for 10-13 year-olds and for 14-16 year-olds.

Casting procedures: Does not use freelance casting directors. Holds general auditions; actors should write in April requesting inclusion. Casting breakdowns are available through the website, postal application (with sae), Equity Job Information Service, *PCR* and advertisements in *The Stage*. Welcomes postal and email enquiries from actors previously unknown to the company. Invitations to view individual actors' websites are also accepted. Contracts are approved by GDBA (the German equivalent of Equity). Rarely has the opportunity to cast disabled actors since "all our actors must take part in 3 different plays, and they must also cope with the rigours of touring".

A touring actor's survival guide

Maev Alexander

Touring is more tiring, harder work, more all-consuming and more relentless than playing in one house. In order to give your best to it and get the best from it, you need to be thoroughly organised and disciplined. The main differences are, of course, the travelling and the accommodation. If you arrange these well in advance, you're on your way to having a happy and rewarding experience and saving yourself angst and money.

Getting there

At the beginning of rehearsals, or even before, you'll be given a schedule of dates and venues and a sheaf of digs lists. Work out as early as you can how you will travel and where you will stay.

If you have your own transport you can plan your journeys on a week-by-week basis, pulling maps and route finders and estimated journey times off the Internet – if you have access – both to digs and to theatres. A good company manager will supply maps of town centres with the venue clearly marked. A satnav can be reassuring, but don't rely on it in big town centres – we had to hold the curtain for a leading lady in Sheffield when her instructions were impossible to follow in a new road layout, so it's a good idea to keep your map-reading skills honed. It's amazing how they improve when you *have* to find digs and theatres within a tight timeframe.

If you don't have your own transport, ask around the company and find out if anyone lives close enough to you, and is willing, to give you lifts. Make it clear that you will contribute to petrol costs, be punctual and not bring too much luggage. If you are using public transport, book as far in advance as you can: Apex (or the equivalent) on trains and low-budget airlines will save you huge amounts of money. The touring company will expect you to do this, and will calculate the amount they give you in fares as economically as possible. Be aware that fares are worked out from venue to venue, and not to your home and out again. Remember also that you may get stuck on a Saturday night if your show comes down after the last train, which is more likely than not; this may add to your accommodation expenses. It also eats into your only day off; most No. 1 tours play Monday to Saturday, running for a week in each venue.

The rule for fares and touring allowance is: outwith 15 miles of your permanent base to qualify for fares only, and 25 miles to qualify for touring allowance. This is calculated from postcode to postcode – not by the most convenient or quickest route. Equity has negotiated sharp rises in the level of touring allowance over the last few years, and this is now reasonable. It's meant to cover accommodation and living expenses – and if you're frugal and careful, it can. You have to balance the level of comfort and convenience with which you need to live happily with the budget on which you have to do it.

Finding the right digs

Digs lists cover hotels, guesthouses, self-contained flats, houses for sharing, B&Bs and rooms in private houses. They normally tell you the price (per night or per week), the type of accommodation, the facilities, the prohibitions (i.e. no smoking, no pets), the extras (TV, kettle in room) and the distance from the theatre. The headliners can probably afford to stay in hotels (and many hotels do deals for touring actors), but other ranks will have to juggle their priorities. If you can feel comfortable in a room in a private house, sharing a bathroom and having access to a kitchen, you can do so remarkably cheaply. If you can't do without an en suite or need to be self-contained, this will obviously be more expensive, and so on up the scale; but read the list carefully and you will find something that will tick most of your boxes without too much compromise. The people who do the letting are generally friends of the theatre in some way, and the standard of accommodation is usually pretty high. I have heard horror stories of rooms booked in hotels on last-minute websites – all-night disco music and overpowering 'room fragrancers'.

Start ringing the most promising-sounding digs as soon as possible, before everyone else does. Good options are places within a 15-minute walk (obviating cabs or long, lonely walks or parking problems), or a house or cottage that is further out, possibly in country-side, to share with fellow company members, both in terms of rent and transport. Beware of landlady-speak for 'a 15- to 20-minute walk' – some landladies clearly have seven-league boots! The level of rates varies from place to place: locations like Bath and Malvern tend to be more expensive across the board than, say, Southampton and Coventry. In big centres like Glasgow, Manchester, Birmingham and Leeds you will probably have to travel to the outskirts unless you can afford hotels.

When you've agreed terms with a landlord/lady, write to confirm the booking and the dates, and arrange to ring a couple of days in advance of the stay to negotiate a mutually convenient time to arrive (leave half an hour's leeway so you don't panic about getting lost). It's wise to at least drop off your luggage before the show so that you know you know where the place is, have keys and don't disturb anyone at a late hour – especially on the first night when there are likely to be drinks front-of-house afterwards. Sorting out digs gets easier the more you tour and the more contacts you acquire. If you're new to it, do ask experienced tourers – most actors are very generous about sharing the secrets of top digs. For future reference, keep records of where you've stayed and what it was like. Pay up front, and remember to leave keys when you leave; get a receipt and behave well enough for the landlord/lady to wish to stay on the digs list. You represent future tourers.

What to take

It's important to pack well. Travel as light as you can, and have as much of your luggage on wheels as possible. You need enough clothes for a week, or longer if you need to go straight to the next venue; keep it simple, remembering to have something warm and something cool (because this is Britain) and something smart for the first-night drinks often provided by the host management or friends of the theatre. A towelling robe doubles as a dressing gown and post-shower gear. Take comfortable, reasonably weatherproof shoes, since you'll spend a lot of time walking. Remember your phone charger (it's worth having a spare for touring), and a toothbrush charger and adapter in case there are no shaving points. It's also worth having an emergency kit containing plasters and painkillers and cold remedies. In most places towels are provided, but pack a hand towel just in case. Travel with a hottie in winter: the only miserable digs I've had were very smart but *freezing*. I complained – do complain; you're not paying to freeze. A pocket torch is useful for unfamiliar, unlit keyholes. Don't forget comforts like books or a radio or iPod.

If you have to be away from your base for extended periods, negotiate doing your laundry with the wardrobe department. If you're home on Sunday, it saves time and hassle

Theatre

if you've put what needs washing into a separate bag in your case so that repacking is straightforward and quick. I was told early in my career that no proper actor has less than three weeks' worth of underwear!

You can generally transport your make-up and other dressing-room necessities, comforts and amusements in a bag or box on the truck transporting the set and props, etc. This is not an automatic right, though, so check with your company manager. Some reasonably rigid receptacle is optimum to avoid breakage; label it clearly with the name of the production and your own name, and do not expect anyone else to lug it to or from your dressing room week by week. Pack it as soon as you can on Saturday night, and check where you can leave it so it's not in the way of the get-out.

Eating and drinking

It's easy to be lazy about eating sensibly on tour – financially and nutritionally. Even if there are cooking facilities in your digs, it's not always convenient to be there and it's tempting to eat out all the time or grab burgers. You're going to need all your energy, so make a point of eating healthily.

In most theatres you'll have access to a microwave and possibly a fridge: ring the stage door and check. They're often in the crew room, so ask if you may use them and be considerate about clearing up after yourself. Making an interesting dressing-room picnic is a worthy challenge even if everything has to be cold. Supermarkets do better and better ranges of salads and sushi. Invest in a mini kettle for your touring box and pack a plate, a mug and cutlery. Set yourself a daily budget for food and then you'll know if you can splash out on a restaurant meal.

It's also tempting to do a great deal more after-show drinking when you're away from home: it can feel as if you're living in a bubble, out of the real world. Ask yourself if you're getting jaded/broke, and limit alcohol to within sensible limits. (The same sense of not being quite in the real world can lead too to the most unlikely affairs: be discreet, whether it involves other people or yourself.)

Bonding and recreation

After-show company meals, weekly or fortnightly, are good bonding exercises providing you all get on. Remember that it's not only part of your job to get on, but also in your best interests. It's even more important in the living-in-each-others'-pockets world of touring to be a good company member; leave your troubles firmly at the stage door and don't moan or gossip. If there's someone you find tricky, keep out of their way. In my experience, touring companies bond well and form even more of a parallel family than usual.

That said, getting away by yourself for a time is restoring. Find the local Tourist Information Office and find out about places of interest and specialist shopping. There's bound to be something that appeals to you, even if you're not a galleries/museums/castles/cathedrals person (the ABC of touring is famously, "another bloody cathedral"). I am lucky – and not alone – in regarding touring as being paid to go sightseeing. Stage door, or your company manager, can tell you of gym and leisure facilities and often arrange temporary membership; they can also point you in the direction of the nearest supermarkets and best-value restaurants.

Sussing out the theatre

One of the interesting and rewarding things about touring is playing the same show in lots of different theatres – from 900-seaters to 2000-seaters, from raked stages to flat ones, from Victorian to modern, from those with acres (seemingly) of orchestra pit to those where the front row is looking up your nose. You'll be called early in the first day of each new venue, generally at about 5 or 6pm, to walk the stage, get to know the backstage layout and take note of significant differences. The presence or lack of a rake may mean more or fewer steps on a staircase, for instance; furniture may be closer together or further apart; wing space may be tight; prop tables may be in different places; dressing rooms will be varying distances away and you may be sharing in one venue and by yourself in another. Take time to absorb these differences, test the acoustic and plan how you're going to accommodate any changes you personally will have to make. Discuss these changes too with anyone else they may affect. Bear in mind that the audiences are always different, as well: it's amazing that what makes people laugh or weep in Cardiff is not the same as what makes people laugh or weep in Hull.

Find out when stage door opens; most theatres allow you access to your dressing room from quite early in the day, which is useful for dumping shopping or 'nesting' when it's tipping with rain. A few don't open until much later, though, which is a great bore and makes it good to have digs close by.

Money matters
On a business level, keep a work diary and note down all your expenses (and mileages if you're driving). Have an envelope or plastic wallet in which to file all your receipts and payslips: it's easy to lose track of these when you're away from home.

Tax offices vary in what they will allow you to claim on tour. Travel and accommodation expenses above your allowances are OK, but some accept claims for all eating expenses (again over and above), some for restaurant/cafe receipts only, and some – including my own – clearly expect you not to eat at all.

Research a mobile phone tariff that will let you keep in touch with family and friends, and your agent, as cheaply as possible.

Finally ...
More and more of the available work involves touring at some level. You might just as well maximise your chances of having a good time and making a decent profit. Regard it as an adventure.

Maev Alexander trained at the Royal Scottish Academy of Music and Drama and has been working in theatre, television and radio for 40 years. She has performed in Rep all over the country, playing everything from Cleopatra to a French poodle, been a member of the RSC, and holds the record as the longest-serving Mollie in *The Mousetrap*. She has starred in two TV series and guested in many others, presented the Newsdesk on *That's Life*, and played in dozens of radio dramas. After completing her 7th No. 1 tour in as many years, and transferring the last but one – *A Man for All Seasons* – to the Theatre Royal Haymarket in 2006, she has filmed *Death Defying Acts* with Catherine Zeta Jones and Guy Pearce, and recorded the second series of *The Eliza Stories* for BBC Radio 4.

Editors' note There are a number of websites that can help you plan your journeys to and from the locations on your tour; they may also save you money. Here are some of the major ones:
• *Maps*: **www.streetmap.co.uk**, **www.multimap.com**, and **maps.google.co.uk**. If you have a mobile phone capable of web browsing, point it to **www.google.co.uk/mmp** to access Google Maps for Mobile. Rather cleverly, if you tell it where you are, it can even give you directions to all the nearest pubs. (If you're going to be using this a lot, check how much

Internet access you have on your call plan. Google does not charge you for the service, but you may find yourself with some hefty Internet usage bills if you're not careful.)

• *Driving*: **www.theaa.com** and **www.rac.co.uk** both offer route-planning and maps, as do Google Maps and Google Maps for Mobile (see above).

• *Trains*: **www.nationalrail.co.uk** for timetables and **www.thetrainline.com** for booking the cheapest tickets available. Also worth looking at **www.megatrain.com** to check for promotional fares. In addition to these, **www.jplanner.org.uk** and **www.traveline.org.uk** are good ways of exploring options (train, coach, plane, etc.) for getting to a location. And of course, the number that the 118 companies get the most requests for: National Rail Enquiries is **08457 48 49 50**; if it's not in your phone already, why not put it there now?

• Coaches: **www.nationalexpress.co.uk**, **www.citylink.co.uk** (Scotland), **www.megabus.com/uk** (which often has promotional fares), and **www.eurolines.com** (destinations around Europe). In addition there are some local companies offering low-cost services to major cities such as London, which a little research should uncover.

• *London Transport*: **journeyplanner.tfl.gov.uk** or, from your mobile, text 60835 (60TFL) with 'a to b' (where 'a' and 'b' are stations, stops or postcodes in London) to find out the best way – tube, train or bus – of getting to where you're going. For example: 'Clapham Junction to The Old Vic'. Common sense and some knowledge of the geography of London may need to be applied to the directions given: in this example the text service recommends a bus journey from Waterloo Station to The Old Vic – a walk of three minutes at most.

• *Flying*: **www.travelsupermarket.com** or **www.skyscanner.net** will search out all available flights to a given destination, sorted by price.

'Vanning it': the golden rules

Andrew Piper

Maev Alexander's article covers pretty much all you need to know about large-scale touring, and many of these principles carry over into small-scale touring too. However, the major difference between the two levels of touring is … The Van.

On a large-scale (or No. 1) tour you are generally responsible for getting to the venue yourself, since these are often in large towns with good transport links. By contrast, much of the work of mid- and small-scale companies is done in venues rather more 'off the beaten track' (a.k.a. The Middle of Nowhere), and often with only one performance in each venue. Most of these companies will transport their actors around the country in a mini-bus, coach or van, which may also contain the set and lighting rig. Whereas the large-scale companies employ stage crew to do the get-ins and get-outs, on such productions it's often the actors and the stage manager who do everything.

'Vanning it' presents an additional set of challenges for the actor. If you don't get on with a fellow actor in a large-scale show, then you may be able to limit the amount of contact you have with them, other than your interaction on stage. If you're on a small-scale tour you will spend most of your waking hours in their company, so it's important that all company members work hard to keep a harmonious atmosphere. Van etiquette is similar to dressing-room etiquette – balancing your needs with the cast's collective needs, and the individual needs of cast members. You can never legislate for a happy company, but here are some of the 'Golden Rules' that will help enormously in that direction:

• *Pull your weight.* This kind of touring is very hard work – you may be travelling, doing a get-in, a show, and a get-out every day for several weeks or months, and slacking off is the one thing guaranteed to make you as popular as herpes. Don't dawdle in the get-out, either; being the cause of not getting to the pub in time for last orders will also not endear you to your colleagues.

• *Be punctual.* The call time is when the van *leaves*, not the time you start to leave your accommodation. Be sitting in your seat, bag stowed, ready to leave at least 5 minutes before the call time. As with almost anything in this business, you're wasting several people's time by keeping them waiting, so respect your fellow actors by being on time.

• *Music.* Bring a personal stereo or MP3 player; don't expect everyone in the van to like your taste in music. One stage manager I know resorted to telling the cast that the stereo had broken rather than sit through yet another argument about whose music to listen to. You might also want to consider a portable DVD player, either for the journeys (unless you're susceptible to travel sickness) or for something to do when you get to your accommodation. Check whether these would be covered by the company's insurance in case anything happened to them, and remember that very few pieces of electronic equipment are built to withstand the rigours of touring.

• *Mobile phones.* Keep conversations short, even (perhaps especially) with loved ones. There are few more irritating things to be forced to listen to than someone cooing to their lover for hours on end. If you're someone who gets a lot of calls, consider setting your phone to silent vibrate; there are only so many times one can listen to the Nokia tune before being overwhelmed by the urge to throw the offending phone out of the window.

Theatre

• *Smoking. Never* smoke in the van, even if the windows are rolled down – it's inconsiderate, and most companies operate a no-smoking policy anyway. (Since the van is considered your workplace, it will also be covered by recent anti-smoking legislation.) Remember, too, that if you're puffing away seconds before climbing aboard then you will carry a strong smell of smoke with you into the van. Be considerate, too, about smelly food – curry, chips, fish, etc. – unless you're all tucking in.

• *Personal hygiene.* Important at all times in this business, but especially so when you're stuck in a confined space with the rest of the cast for what may be hours at a time, perhaps after a particularly physical show and/or get-out. Your fellow actors may be upfront enough to tell you if you're pongy – but don't rely on it. If someone else in the company is niffing, don't gossip behind their back: just tell them, in as direct and as kind a way as possible. Don't let it fester (in more senses than one!).

• *Games.* It's worth bringing a few travel games for when the conversation runs out, even if it's just a pack of playing cards – although not everyone will want to play at any given moment. A good book can help while away the time, although not everyone can read in a van without getting travelsick.

• *Sweets.* The 'tub of love'. It does wonders for morale if someone takes it upon themself to buy a big tub of sweets for the van.

• *Alcohol.* Check the company's policy. If it's permitted, then it's probably best that you either buy your own (sharing around if you desire) or join up with one or two other members of the cast. It's generally preferable not to have a kitty for the whole cast, because not everyone will want to drink the same stuff or the same quantities. If you are getting merry in the back of a van, be considerate to the driver: don't distract them (dangerous!) or be unreasonably raucous. S/he will have had a hard evening too, and tunelessly drunken renditions of football chants will hardly make the journey more pleasant. Remember that requests for toilet stops when everyone's tired and wants to get home may not be popular.

• *Make the most of solo time.* When you do get some time to yourself, make the most of it. Go for a walk, listen to music, read, exercise, meditate, call friends or just sit in a coffee shop and watch the world go by. Camaraderie and team spirit are important in this kind of work, but don't be afraid to take time for yourself when you need it.

• *Plan your meals.* You may be performing in some village hall miles from the nearest source of food, so be prepared. Sometimes – in village halls, especially – sandwiches are provided by the locals, but not always, so stock up before heading off for the day's performance, and keep an emergency supply of biscuits/fruit/pot noodles in your bag just in case. Make the most of the hotel or B&B breakfast.

• *Travel light.* Remember that you will be probably be checking into several different hotels or B&Bs a week, so only take with you what you can comfortably carry by yourself in one go. For ease of access when you want to find that one pair of socks or pants, wheeled suitcases or large hold-alls are preferable to rucksacks. While you may want to have more stuff back at your base, when you're on the road stick to one large bag and a day bag.

• *Finally, keep a sense of humour and a sense of perspective.* Not always the easiest thing to do on some jobs, but you're all in this together so have a good laugh at the absurdity of it all – it may just save your sanity.

Andrew Piper trained at Bristol Old Vic Theatre School. This piece was written in the van belonging to Northumberland Theatre Company (NTC) while he was playing Herbert Pocket, Uncle Pumblechook and Orlick in their production of *Great Expectations*.

Fringe theatres

Essentially, the idea of 'fringe theatre' began at the Edinburgh Festival more than half a century ago. It really started taking off (especially in London) in the late 1960s as an arena for 'alternative' and 'experimental' theatre. The 1990s saw a huge expansion in the number of venues being used, and a downturn in the exploration of theatre forms: the 'fringe' became more commercial and much more competitive – and not just in London and Edinburgh. Today, the terms 'alternative' and 'experimental' are far less frequently used, and the Fringe is now largely seen as a way for actors, directors and writers to showcase their work.

Casting for Fringe productions is usually advertised by one or more of the casting information services, and agents and casting directors do scout for new talent in them. However, it's highly unlikely that you will make any money from participating in such a production – you might end up with a net loss after deducting your expenses. Also agents and casting directors get blitzed with so many invitations that the chances of getting one of them to see you are not high. The only reasons for being in a Fringe production are (a) you might be 'seen'; (b) you fundamentally believe in the production's potential; and (c) it could help keep your acting-juices flowing. But you might find classes less time-consuming and possibly more beneficial.

The Edinburgh Fringe Festival

There is a real sense that every actor should try this 'Carnival of theatre' experience – 'the biggest theatrical lottery in the world' – at least once. You'll meet lots of new people, make contacts and it's a great few weeks, even if your own production doesn't hit the heights.

Good advice on mounting a production on the Edinburgh Fringe is available from the Festival Office (details below).

The listings that follow are restricted to the more 'established' venues, with performance spaces for hire. Some Fringe theatres only programme-in work known to them.

Note If you are thinking of mounting a Fringe production and/or starting your own theatre company, start researching and planning well in advance. It is well worth consulting the Independent Theatre Council (ITC) – **www.itc-arts.org**.

UMBRELLA ORGANISATIONS

Edinburgh Festival Fringe
The Fringe Office, 180 High Street,
Edinburgh EH1 1QS
tel 0131-226 0026 *fax* 0131-226 0016
email admin@edfringe.com
website www.edfringe.com

The Fringe Society was formed in 1959 to coordinate publicity and ticket sales, and offer a comprehensive information service both to performers and to audiences. It compiles information about venues, press and suppliers, and produces a series of publications designed to answer frequently asked questions. Its brochure contains details for 183 Fringe venues in Edinburgh. The office is open all year round and the staff are available to help by phone, email or personal appointment.

Fringe Theatre Network (FTN)
Unit 5A, Ingate Place, London SW8 3NS
tel 020-7627 4920
email helenoldredlion@yahoo.co.uk
website www.fringetheatre.org.uk
Co-ordinator Helen Devine

The FTN provides services, support and a network of contacts for venues, producing companies and individuals working on the London Fringe with the aim of increasing the level of professionalism in Fringe theatre. Acting as an umbrella organisation, the FTN puts forward the interests of Fringe theatre in its dealings with statutory authorities, funding bodies, policy-makers and other arts organsations.

OffWestEnd.com

19 Eugene Cotter House, Beckway Street,
London SE17 1QS
website www.offwestend.com

A London UK theatre information and bookings site that makes it easy to find plays and performances in some of London's innovative theatres outside the West End. Tickets are sold directly from these Off West End theatres, with no fees and no commission beng charged.

LONDON FRINGE VENUES

The Albany

Douglas Way, Deptford, London SE8 4AG
tel 020-8692 4446 *fax* 020-8469 2253
email boxoffice@thealbany.org.uk
website www.thealbany.org.uk
Chief Executive Gavin Barlow

Production details: A multi-use digital arts centre programming music, spoken word, dance, comedy and family shows. The Albany is an artistic and community resource with a fully equipped theatre space, studio theatre, cafe and rehearsal and meeting rooms for hire. Has a strong commitment to working collaboratively with the diverse communities of London and encouraging participation, especially by young people and disabled communities, in the arts. As well as programming performances, the centre provides seasonal participation programmes working with young people, and is a social hub and facilitator for partnership working. Seats 300 (500 standing); 2 secondary spaces seat 60 or 70. Performances also take place in the cafe – capacity 80. All spaces have fully configurable seating; there is also seating on the balcony. Shows usually run from 1 night to 2 weeks. Hire rates may be subsidised depending on community or charity status – see website for rates of different spaces. There is disabled access. Recent productions include: *Lipsticks and Lollipops* by Deafinitely Theatre; *A Warwickshire Testimony* by April de Angelis (Mountview Theatre School); and transfer from the Royal Court of *Gone Too Far!* by Oliver Award Winner Bola Agbaje.

Casting procedures: Does not produce in-house shows.

Arcola Theatre

27 Arcola Street, London E8 2DJ
tel 020-7503 1645
email info@arcolatheatre.com
website www.arcolatheatre.com
Artistic Director Mehmet Ergen

Founded in 2000 by Artistic Director Mehmet Ergen and Executive Producer Leyla Nazli, Arcola Theatre is now one of the most respected arts venues in the UK, "blazing a trail in artistic excellence and innovative management from the outset". Housed in a converted factory in Hackney, Arcola is a favourite of established theatre literati as well as young, upwardly mobile innovators. London's largest theatre studio, it has become well known for the variety of its programming, from new writing to classic drama, music and comedy.

Arcola has staged work by some of the best living actors, writers and directors, including productions by William Gaskill, Timberlake Wertenbaker, Ariel Dorfman, Sean Holmes, Dominic Domgoole, Max Stafford-Clark and Frank McGuinness, among others. 2 Studio theatres and 4 other spaces suitable for rehearsals and other events.

artsdepot

5 Nether Street, North Finchley, London N12 0GA
tel 020-8369 5455
email info@artsdepot.co.uk
website www.artsdepot.co.uk

The only professional arts venue in the London Borough of Barnet. Committed to providing a diverse range of high-quality visual and performance arts for everyone. artsdepot has brand new, state-of-the-art facilities in the form of the large Pentland Theatre, smaller Studio Theatre and Education Spaces, for the provision of drama, dance and visual arts, and a gallery, as well as an excellent cafe and bars.

BAC (Battersea Arts Centre)

Lavender Hill, London SW11 5TN
tel 020-7326 8219
email liab@bac.org.uk
website www.bac.org.uk
Artistic Directors David Jubb, David Micklem

BAC aims to help create and promote exciting, high-quality, collaborative arts activity. The emphasis is on devised rather than script-based work, and especially on the collaboration between different artforms. On the first Sunday of every month, *Scratch Nights* are held at which artists present no more than 10 minutes of material at a very early stage in its development – sometimes stopping in the middle for advice. The audience pays what it can to watch 3-4 of these projects and has a chance to offer feedback to the artists in the bar afterwards. Often presented as part of BAC's Opera Festival or OctoberFest are 2- or 3-night runs of *Scratch Performances*; these are rough show drafts and usually last between 40 minutes and 1 hour. Again, the audience is invited to the bar to give feedback after the show.

The next stage of development comprises 2- or 3-night runs of *Showcase Performances*, at which work is marketed to wider audiences, and is usually presented in the context of one of BAC's annual festivals. Following this, artists may be offered 3- to 6-week runs of *Showcase Performances* for which national reviews will be actively sought.

Artists can get on the BAC ladder of development at different stages and can progress at different rates as appropriate. Work is rarely programmed on the strength of a proposal alone, and the theatre's staff do not have time to read unsolicited scripts. Instead they prefer to build up a relationship with artists over time, viewing their work outside of BAC initially.

At certain times of year the theatre-spaces are hired out to drama schools for showcase events, but all theatre companies must go through the programming process. The BAC has 3 flexible black-box theatre spaces: Studio 1 and Studio 2 (average capacity 43/56) and the Main House (average capacity 150). For all programming enquiries, contact Lydia Spry.

Barons Court Theatre

The Curtain's Up, 28A Comeragh Rd,
West Kensington, London W14 9HR
tel 020-8932 4747
email londontheatre@gmail.com
Artistic Director Ron Phillips

A central London 62-seat theatre in the basement of the Curtain's Up public house and restaurant. Offers 1- to 5-week runs and can be booked up to 12 months in advance at a moderate rental. Also available for 1-day actors' showcases.

Blue Elephant Theatre

59A Bethwin Road, Camberwell, London SE5 0XT
tel 020-7701 0100
email info@blueelephanttheatre.co.uk
website www.blueelephanttheatre.co.uk
Theatre & Programme Manager Jasmine Cullingford

The only theatre in Camberwell. A vibrant arts venue aiming to nurture new and emerging artists across the performing arts. Promotes cross-art-form work and all forms of theatre, from physical and dance theatre to new writing and classics.

Co-produces all shows and is particularly interested in supporting new and emerging London-based artists across the perfoming arts with work that complements the black box performance space. Those interested in bringing a project to the Blue Elephant should submit a written proposal with suggested dates and a full background to Jasmine Cullingford.

The Bridewell Theatre

Bride Lane, Fleet Street, London EC4Y 8EQ
tel 020-7353 3331
website www.stbrideinstitute.org/theatre.html

The Bridewell Theatre is a versatile space, which provides both an atmospheric entertainment venue and an unique conference facility in the heart of the City. In addition to a 12x8m performance space, there is a modular tiered seating system that in standard configuration can accommodate a raked audience of 134 people. The theatre also offers

dressing rooms with en suite amenities, as well as a box-office/reception area and a fully equipped bar. All areas of the theatre are accessible to disabled users via lift.

The Broadway Studio Theatre

Catford, London SE6 4RU
tel 020-8314 9472
email martin@broadwaytheatre.org.uk
website www.broadwaytheatre.org.uk
Artistic Director Martin Costello

Originally opened in 1932, the venue is Grade II listed by English Heritage as a beautiful example of 1930s art deco architecture. There are 2 venues: the Main Theatre seats 800, and the Studio Theatre seats 100. "The Broadway Studio Theatre has extremely limited availability; please contact Martin Costello to check availability and prices."

Camden People's Theatre

58-60 Hampstead Road, London NW1 2PY
tel 020-7419 4841 or (08700) 600 100 (Box Office)
fax 020-7813 3889
email admin@cptheatre.co.uk
website www.cptheatre.co.uk

A 60-seat flexible performance space, available for single nights as well as full runs. Also has rehearsal studio.

Canal Café Theatre

The Bridge House, Delamere Terrace, Little Venice, London W2 6ND
tel 020-7289 6056 *fax* 020-7266 1717
email mail@newsrevue.com
website www.newsrevue.com

A 60-seat café theatre situated above the Bridge House pub next to the canal in Little Venice. Welcomes comedy.

Chelsea Centre Theatre

World's End Place, King's Road, London SWl0 0DR
tel 020-7352 1967 *fax* 020-7352 2024

A 110-seat theatre which can be booked-up 6 months in advance. Particularly welcomes new writing.

Cockpit Theatre

Gateforth Street, London NW8 8EH
tel 020-7258 2920 *fax* 020-7258 2921
email mail@cockpittheatre.org.uk

Theatre seats 180 (60 seats on 3 sides) and should be booked 6 months in advance. Welcomes classics, foreign-language theatre and other niche market work.

The Courtyard Theatre

Bowling Green Walk, 40 Pitfield Street, London N1 6EU
tel/fax 020-7739 6868
email info@thecourtyard.org.uk
website www.thecourtyard.org.uk

Theatre

Flexible seating arrangements, 2 theatres, rehearsal rooms.

Drill Hall

16 Chenies Street, London WC1E 7EX
tel 020-7307 5060 *fax* 020-7307 5062
email admin@drillhall.co.uk
website www.drillhall.co.uk
Chief Executive & Artistic Director Julie Parker

Since opening in 1977, the Drill Hall has supported the development of unusual, unexpected and daring theatre and performance. The creation of new work, the development of new audiences and the provision of new opportunities to participate in the arts are all central to the Drill Hall's mission. Both of the fully accessible theatres and bars may be hired, as may 4 studios and 4 smaller meeting rooms.

Etcetera Theatre

Oxford Arms, 265 Camden High Street, London NW1 7BU
tel 020-7482 4857 *fax* 020-7482 0378
email etc@etceteratheatre.com
website www.etceteratheatre.com

A black-box studio space with 42 raked seats, the theatre particularly welcomes new writing and comedy. Presents an early and a late show Tuesday to Sunday (usually running for 3 weeks or more), with one-off performances on Monday nights.

Finborough Theatre

The Finborough, 118 Finborough Road, London SW10 9ED
tel 020-7244 7439 *fax* 020-7835 1853
email admin@finboroughtheatre.co.uk
website www.finboroughtheatre.co.uk
Artistic Director Neil McPherson

Founded in 1980, the Finborough is "one of London's leading new writing venues" (*Time Out*). It also presents rediscoveries of neglected work from 1800 onwards, music theatre and UK premières of foreign work, particularly from the US and Canada. The 50-seat theatre is available for hire for 4-week runs and 1-night performances: more information is available on the website.

See entry for Concordance, its resident company, under *Middle and smaller-scale companies* on page 169.

Greenwich Playhouse

Greenwich Station Forecourt,
189 Greenwich High Road, London SE10 8JA
tel 020-8858 9256 *fax* 020-8310 7276
email alice@galleontheatre.co.uk
Artistic Director Alice de Sousa

Theatre seats 84 and boasts state-of-the art facilities. Available for hire for short seasons at very affordable weekly rates. Visiting productions benefit free of charge from the advice and support of the resident

Artistic Director – see entry for Galleon Theatre Company Ltd, under *Middle and smaller-scale companies* on page 161.

Hackney Empire Studio Theatre

291 Mare Street, London E8 1EJ
tel 020-8510 4500 *fax* 020-8510 4530
email info@hackneyempire.co.uk
website www.hackneyempire.co.uk
Interim Chief Executive Claire Middleton *Creative Director* Susie McKenna

80-seat studio attached to the historic, Grade II* listed, Matcham-designed Hackney Empire. Contact Frank Sweeney for booking details.

Hen & Chickens Theatre

Above Hen & Chickens Theatre Bar,
109 St Paul's Road, Islington, London N1 2NA
tel 020-7704 2001

A 60-seat theatre welcoming new writing. Directly opposite station. Offers 3- to 4-week runs with Monday nights available separately.

Jacksons Lane Theatre

269A Archway Road, London N6 5AA
tel 020-8340 5226
email kate@jacksonslane.org.uk
website www.jacksonslane.org.uk

Rooms are available for hire on a daily or hourly basis for private parties, rehearsals and performances. The Lavender Room seats up to 40; the Primrose Room seats up to 40; a multipurpose space seats up to 80; the Youth Space seats up to 25; and the Main Theatre seats 125-163.

Jermyn Street Theatre

16B Jermyn Street, London SW1Y 6ST
tel 020-7434 1443 *fax* 020-7287 3232
email info@jermynstreettheatre.co.uk
website www.jermynstreettheatre.co.uk
Artistic Director Gene David Kirk

Hire rates: Theatre seats 70, 5 rows facing, 2 rows on side. Stage space is 8 metres long x 4 metres deep x 3.5 metres high (to grid), 2 dressing rooms with fridges, sofas, microwaves, kettles, iron + ironing board. The theatre is air conditioned.

• Main Shows – Weekly rental is £2450 (this includes get-in, fit-up time, technician operating/rigging, also operates sound as well as lights). A 30% non refundable deposit is required when the contract is signed.
• Showcases / Rehearsed Readings / Seminars – £80 per hour. Theatre is available on Tuesdays / Wednesdays / Thursdays between 10am and 3pm (includes technician)
• Sunday Nights (Cabaret Evenings) – £380 for the evening, available from 6.30pm on the night for 8pm show, includes rehearsal Friday before (includes technician)

Theatre

King's Head Theatre

115 Upper Street, Islington, London N1 1QN
tel 020-7226 8561
website www.kingsheadtheatre.org
Artistic Director Adam Spreadbury-Maher

Famous for helping to launch the careers of many new writers, directors and actors including Stephen Berkoff, Anthony Sher and Victoria Wood. The theatre is situated at the back of a public house with flexible seating for up to 120.

The Landor Theatre

70 Landor Road, London SW9 9PH
tel 020-7737 7276
email info@landortheatre.co.uk
website www.landortheatre.co.uk

A 60-seat theatre situated above a public house.

Lion & Unicorn Theatre

42-44 Gaisford Street, Kentish Town,
London NW5 2ED
email info@giantolive.com
website www.giantolive.com

The Lion & Unicorn is the home of Giant Olive theatre company. Founded in 2008, the company has quickly developed a reputation for high-quality and imaginative theatre and dance. Giant Olive produces classical productions as well as supporting and developing new work and talent. "The Lion & Unicorn Theatre Space is available to hire at the 'Best Fringe Theatre Rates in London'. Giant Olive doesn't just offer a black box, they can provide full production support, with everything from rehearsal space to flyer and poster design. For prices and details, and to view the venue, please contact **info@giantolive.com**."

Menier Chocolate Factory

51/53 Southwark Street, London SE1 1RU
tel 020-7907 7060
email info@menierchocolatefactory.com
website www.menierchocolatefactory.com
Artistic Director David Babani

2900sq ft of highly versatile and atmospheric theatre space, with lighting rig, sound, and video projection. Capacity 200. Recently transferred its production of Sondheim's musical *Sunday in the Park with George* (starring Daniel Evans and Jenna Russell) to the Wyndhams Theatre in the West End.

New End Theatre

27 New End, Hampstead, London NW3 1JD
tel 020-7472 5800 *fax* 020-7472 5808
email info@newendtheatre.co.uk
website www.newendtheatre.co.uk
Artistic Director & Chief Executive Brian Daniels

Theatre seats 84 and has a strong tradition of presenting new plays and musicals, as well as reviving works from the classical canon. Recent productions include: Sondheim's *Assassins*; *A Dangerous Woman* (starring Fenella Fielding); and *Weill & Lenya* (directed by Ken Russell).

New Players Theatre

The Arches, Villiers Street, London WC2N 6NG
tel 020-7930 6601 *fax* (08456) 382102
website www.newplayerstheatre.com

The recently renovated New Players Theatre is a valuable addition to the London theatre scene and business community in the heart of the West End. Already a popular and well-known venue within the theatre, music and entertainment industries, the New Players now offers producers the opportunity to present a diverse and eclectic range of productions in an Off-Broadway-style, well-equipped, high-specification theatre, complete with on-site bars and a restaurant. It is also a distinctive setting for screenings, conference and corporate hires.

Old Red Lion

418 St John Street, Islington, London EC1V 4NJ
tel 020-7833 3053 *fax* 020-7833 3053
website www.oldredliontheatre.co.uk
Managing Director Damien Devine

Founded in 1979, the Old Red Lion Theatre is a 60-seater Fringe theatre primarily dedicated to new writing. Companies wishing to hire the venue should post a script, some company information and a production proposal to the Artistic Director. Normally programmes 3 months ahead.

Oval House Theatre

52-54 Kennington Oval, London SE11 5SW
tel 020-7582 0080
email Karena.Johnson@OvalHouse.com
website www.ovalhouse.com
Director Deborah Bestwick

Comprises 2 spaces; the upstairs theatre seats 50 and the downstairs theatre seats 100. Presents a diverse programme of work.

Pentameters

28 Heath Street, Hampstead NW3 6TE
tel 020-7435 3648
website www.pentameters.co.uk
Founder & Producer Léonie Scott-Matthews

Located in the heart of Hampstead village, among an abundance of cafes, restaurants, bars, pubs and shops and just a minute's walk from Hampstead tube. Aside from the choice of venues to have pre- or post-theatre drinks or dinner, Hampstead is also well-known for its artistic character, offering a supportive, interactive and thriving local community, making it an ideal spot to promote live theatre and creative arts events. To discuss requirements, please telephone Leonie Scott-Matthews directly on the above number: "Please leave a message, and we will respond."

Theatre

Pleasance Theatre London

Carpenters Mews, North Road, London N7 9EF
tel 020-7619 6868 *fax* 020-7700 7366
email info@pleasance.co.uk
website www.pleasance.co.uk/LONDON
Director Anthony Alderson

The Pleasance now has 2 spaces: the Main Theatre, seating just under 300; and the Pleasance Stage Space, a new venue created to nurture the best in new theatre writing and emerging comedy talent, seating 54.

Rich Mix

35-47 Bethnal Green Road, London E1 6LA
tel 020-7613 7490 *fax* 020-7613 7499
email info@richmix.org.uk
website www.richmix.org.uk
Chief Executive Pawlet Brookes

A 132,000 square foot flagship arts and cultural centre, boasting "the best in art, performance, fashion, design, music, dance, film, theatre and comedy – 5 floors of vibrant creativity and excellence".

Riverside Studios

Crisp Road, London W6 9RL
tel 020-8237 1111 (Box Office) 020-8237 1000 (Admin) 020-8237 1015 (Hire Enquiries)
website www.riversidestudios.co.uk
Artistic Director William Burdett-Coutts

Riverside Studios is an arts centre with a varied programme of both domestic and international performance, theatre, dance, music, comedy and other events. Considers work – either hires or co-productions – within the context of its artistic policy.

Studio 2 is a medium-sized black box space suited to all types of production. Comprehensive motorised grid. Flexible seating configuration, up to 400. Studio 3 is a smaller-sized black box space suited to all types of production. Comprehensive motorised grid. Retractable raked seating, up to 156. Other spaces available for hire: cinema, television studio.

Recent companies include: Forced Entertainment, LOVE&MADNESS Ensemble, Rosemary Butcher, Batsheva Dance Company, Bill Bailey, Ed Byrne, Damien Dempsey, Duran Duran, Albert & Friends – Youth Circus Festival, Tete a Tete – Opera Festival.

Rosemary Branch Theatre

2 Shepperton Road, London N1 3DT
tel 020-7704 6665
email cecilia@rosemarybranch.co.uk
website www.rosemarybranch.co.uk
Artistic Director & Theatre Manager Cecilia Darker

Under the same management since 1996, the theatre has recently been expanded to hold a maximum of 65 seats. Presents a diverse programme including opera, classics, new writing, musicals and cabaret. A

rehearsal space is also available. Normally books 3-week runs but this is negotiable. The theatre offers all visiting companies lots of support and goodwill.

Soho Theatre

21 Dean Street, London W1V 6NE
tel 020-7478 0117 *fax* 020-7287 5061
email hires@sohotheatre.com
website www.sohotheatre.com

Soho Theatre + Writers' Centre aims to discover and develop new playwrights, produce a year-round programme of new plays, and attract new audiences. Founded in 1972, the company premiered the early work of such playwrights as Caryl Churchill, David Edgar, Hanif Kureishi, Tanika Gupta, and Timberlake Wertenbaker; more recently it has presented new plays by Laura Wade, Will Eno, Adriano Shaplin, Debbie Tucker Green, Matt Charman, Rebecca Lenkiewicz and Toby Whithouse.

Soho Theatre + Writers' Centre is now a key producing venue of new plays and comedy. Offering the nation's most extensive unsolicited script-reading service, the Writers' Centre provides a range of developmental schemes including: the Writers' Attachment Programme; Launch Pad Workshops; The Verity Bargate Award; The Westminster Prize; a thriving Young Writers' Programme; commissions and seed bursaries; Writers' Rooms; and an extensive Research & Development programme of readings, workshops, script surgeries, seminars and initiatives, all of which "enable us to attract and nurture the most outstanding writers from our local community and throughout the country".

Three writers' rooms are available free of charge, complete with computer, printer and access to a growing script library. They are available to writers free of charge from 10am – 6pm, Monday to Friday and can be booked for as little as an hour or up to a month; priority will be given to writers whose work is being developed by STC.

Soho Theatre + Writers' Centre includes a flexible 144-seat theatre, a large self-contained Studio space with 85-seat capacity, theatre bar, restaurant, offices, rehearsal, writing and meeting rooms. All spaces are accessible and available for hire. For bookings and general information, please visit **www.sohotheatre.com**.

There are 4 spaces to hire at Soho Theatre. Each is air-conditioned, has full disabled access and can be set up to specific requirements. The theatre seats 144 and has a maximum stage area of 11m wide x 6m deep. The studio measures 9m x 11m and is a self-contained and sound-proofed space with an acoustic wall dividing the room into 2. The studio is equipped with a PA system and mini disc; seating is flexible with a capacity of 85. The writers' seminar room measures 7m x 3.5m; it is a light, airy room with a balcony looking over Dean Street. The terrace measures 4m x 3m and has a glass-fronted balcony. It includes a separate waiting area and is suitable for castings and small meetings. For more information, please visit the website, or telephone.

See also entry under *Producing theatres* on page 129.

Southwark Playhouse
Shipwright Yard (Corner of Tooley St & Bermondsey St), London SE1 2TF
tel 020-7407 0234 *fax* 020-7407 8350
email admin@southwarkplayhouse.co.uk
website www.southwarkplayhouse.co.uk

Southwark Playhouse's central vision is that of a vibrant theatre in the heart of the London Borough of Southwark, serving the widest possible constituency within the Borough and beyond, providing a platform for emerging theatre practitioners and a programme of performance, education work and community drama.

Tabard Theatre
2 Bath Road, Turnham Green, London W4 1LW
tel 020-8994 5985
website www.tabardweb.co.uk
Artistic Director Fred Perry

Situated above the Tabard pub, close to Turnham Green tube. Offers 3- to 4-week runs which are programmed 4-5 months ahead.

The Space
269 Westferry Road, London E14 3RS
tel 020-7515 7799
website www.space.org.uk
Centre Director Adam Hemming

A multi-arts centre on the Isle of Dogs, programming a mixture of theatre, music, comedy and dance. Converted from a 19th-century church, with stained glass windows, a Steinway grand piano and flexible seating, the venue provides a uniquely atmospheric environment. The Space is also available for rehearsals and private hire.

Theatre 503
The Latchmere, 503 Battersea Park Road, London SW11 3BW
tel 020-7229 8530 *fax* 020-7229 8140
email mail@theatre503.com
website www.theatre503.com
Artistic Directors Tim Roseman, Paul Robinson

Situated above a public house, Theatre 503 aims to provide a venue for new playwrights, comedians and directors to develop their shows. It has a working relationship with television commissioners and producers, literary managers of established theatres and literary agents, and tries to offer a stepping-stone from Fringe to 'big' theatres.

Theatro Technis
26 Crowndale Road, London NW1 1TT
tel 020-7387 6617 *fax* 020-7383 2545

email info@theatrotechnis.com
website www.theatrotechnis.co.uk

Theatro Technis' ideas and policies are realised for anyone who is interested in the development of individuals and communities. The theatre maintains a balance between classic and contemporary work, and serves to embrace a variety of diverse artforms, ranging from theatre and dance to art, photography, music and film.

Toynbee Studios
28 Commercial Street, London E1 6AB
tel 020-7247 5102
email admin@artsadmin.co.uk
website www.artsadmin.co.uk/toynbeestudios

Toynbee Studios is Artsadmin's unique centre for the development and presentation of new work. The Studios comprise a 280-seat theatre, rehearsal spaces, technical facilities, and the Arts Bar & Cafe, all of which host performances and events throughout the year. Office facilities are also provided for a range of small arts organisations.

Toynbee Studios has 6 spaces catering for professional work, ranging from intimate spaces where artists can experiment to high-spec dance and theatre studios for larger productions/rehearsals, as well as ideal and unusual spaces for meetings and events. Any requests for hires for public events will be considered by Artsadmin, but must be approved by the programming team as fitting with Artsadmin's artistic objectives.

About Artsadmin: Founded in 1979, it is a unique producing organisation for contemporary artists working in theatre, dance, live art, visual arts and mixed media. Based at Toynbee Studios since 1995, the organisation offers a free advisory service for artists, mentoring and development programmes, and a number of bursary schemes.

Tristan Bates
1A Tower Street, London WC2H 9NP
tel 020-7632 8010
email itbt@actorscentre.co.uk
website www.tristanbatestheatre.co.uk
Artistic Director Matthew Lloyd

The Tristan Bates Theatre (TBT) is a venue for new work and groundbreaking experiments. The artistic policy reflects the mission of the Actors Centre, where the training of performers co-exists with the making of new work. "TBT is a launchpad for the talent we discover, and we make relationships with other organisations, producers and theatres to give further life to the work we present. We provide actors, writers and directors with a space in which they can test new ideas and be daring, at a time when the industry demands quick results on tight budgets – i.e. safe choices and tame products."

Union Theatre
204 Union Street, Southwark, London SE1 0LX
tel 020-7261 9876 *fax* 020-7261 9876

Theatre

email sasha@uniontheatre.freeserve.co.uk
website www.uniontheatre.freeserve.co.uk

Primarily a new writing venue, the theatre aims to present a diverse programme featuring the best new talent. Guest performances are supplemented by regular in-house productions. Normally offers 3-week runs.

Upstairs at the Gatehouse

The Gatehouse Pub, North Road, London N6 4BD
tel 020-8340 3477
email events@ovationproductions.com
website www.upstairsatthegatehouse.com
Directors John Plews, Katie Plews

Seats 132 (140 in cabaret style). A rehearsal room is also available. See entry for Ovation Productions under Middle and smaller-scale companies.

White Bear Theatre

138 Kennington Park Road, London SE11 4DJ
tel 020-7793 9193
website www.whitebeartheatre.co.uk
Artistic Director Michael Kingsbury

An L-shaped studio space with seating for up to 50. Generally prefers new writing but occasionally accepts revivals.

Wimbledon Studio Theatre

In Wimbledon Theatre, 103 The Broadway, London SW19 1QG
tel 0870 060 6646 (Box Office)
tel 020-8545 7900 (Admin) *fax* 020 8543 6637
email sambain@theambassadors.com
website www.ambassadortickets.com/Wimbledon-Studio

A black box Studio theatre with flexible seating for up to 80. Normally offers 1-2 week runs which are programmed 6 months ahead. The auditorium is wheelchair accessible.

EDINBURGH FRINGE VENUES

Many of these venues are only available for hire during the Edinburgh Festival Fringe in August. For a full list of venues, contact the Fringe Society (see **www.edfringe.com**).

Assembly Rooms

Assembly Theatre, 250 George Street, Edinburgh EH2 2LE
tel 0131-624 2442 *fax* 0131-624 7131
email info@assemblyrooms.com
website www.assemblyrooms.com

The Assembly Rooms have presented more than 1000 productions featuring most of the major names in British comedy – as well as a huge array of theatre, dance and music events which have been seen by more than 1.5 million people over the last 20 years of the Edinburgh Festival Fringe. The daily programme runs from 11.00am to 3.30am with exhibitions, a café, 2 public bars and a club bar. Aims to programme a balance of theatre, comedy and new work.

Augustine's

Augustine United Church, 41 George IV Bridge, Edinburgh EH1 1EL
tel 0131-220 1677

During the rest of the year this venue is known as Augustine United Church. It is adapted during the Festival to house 2 performance spaces (the upper venue seats 110; the lower venue seats approximately 105). Programmes theatre, musicals, dance and children's theatre from the UK and elsewhere.

Bedlam Theatre

11B Bristo Place, Edinburgh EH1 1EZ
tel 0131-225 9873
email info@bedlamtheatre.co.uk
website www.bedlamtheatre.co.uk

A 90-seat black-box theatre in central Edinburgh housed in a neo-gothic church. The theatre is available for hire when not in use by the Edinburgh University Theatre Company.

C venues

Administration Office: C Venues Limited, 5 Alexandra Mansions, Chichele Road, London NW2 3AS
email info@cvenues.com
website www.cvenues.com

Comprises 4 theatre venues in Edinburgh: C; C too; C central; C cubed. Presents drama, physical theatre, comedy, music, musicals, dance, opera, children's shows and visual arts with an emphasis on new and dynamic work. C's 4 locations include a 203-seat thrust space, 2 end-on black-box studios seating 95 and 144, and a permanent 160-seat proscenium-arch auditorium in the basement. There is also a platform stage in the bar and extensive exhibition space on each foyer level. In total there are 10 spaces including a new basement cabaret bar and 3 intimate black-box theatres at C central.

Gilded Balloon

25 Greenside Place, Edinburgh EH1 3AA
tel 0131-226 6550 or 0131-622 6555

Has a very strong comedy programme; also presents live music.

Greyfriars (Studios 1 and 2)

Greyfriars Kirk House, 86 Candlemaker Row, Edinburgh EH1 2QA

Studio 1 (upstairs, seats 60) and Studio 2 (seats around 40) are intimate spaces suited to 1- to 3-

handers, storytelling or poetry. Applications should be made by February for hire during the Festival Fringe.

Hill Street Theatre

Hill Street Theatre, Universal Arts, Gateway Theatre, Elm Row, Edinburgh EH7 4AH
tel 0131-478 0195 *fax* 0131-478 0185
email hillstreet@universal-arts.com

Presents a programme of well-known works alongside new writing, musicals, dance, mime and physical theatre. Theatrical production includes comic writing but not stand-up comedy. The main theatre seats 120 while the studio theatre is a more intimate space, seating a maximum of 73. Suited to 1-handers, the studio can accommodate up to 8 performers comfortably.

The Netherbow Scottish Storytelling Centre

43-45 High Street, Edinburgh EH1 1SR
tel 0131-556 9579
website www.scottishstorytellingcentre.co.uk

Intimate 100-seat theatre presenting drama, poetry, storytelling and puppetry events. Offers a strong programme of family shows. The whole building, being new-build from 2005, is very wheelchair-friendly both for the public and for actors.

The Pleasance

The Pleasance Courtyard: 60 The Pleasance, Edinburgh EH8 9TJ
tel 020-7619 6868
The Pleasance Dome: 1 Bristo Square, Edinburgh EH8 9AL
The Pleasance Administration Office: Carpenters Mews, North Road, London N7 9EF
website www.pleasance.co.uk

The Pleasance presents more than 160 shows across its 16 venues during the 4 weeks of the Festival Fringe. With more than 190,000 visitors, it remains one of the most popular venues of the Fringe, offering a mix of comedy, theatre, dance and music.

The Underbelly

Off Cowgate,
Edinburgh Permanent Office: 25 Greenside Place, Edinburgh EH1 3AA
tel 0131-622 6566 *fax* 0131-622 6576
email ed@smirnoffunderbelly.co.uk
website www.theunderbelly.co.uk
Venue Manager Ed Bartlam

Comprises 6 spaces over 4 floors with 3 bars. Venues cater for audiences of 60-200 with different seating configurations available. Programmes new writing, theatre, dance and comedy.

Traverse Theatre

10 Cambridge Street, Edinburgh EH1 2ED
email linda.crooks@traverse.co.uk
website www.traverse.co.uk
Administrative Director Mike Griffiths

Centre for new plays in Scotland. All-year-round venue in underground purpose-built theatre with 2 auditoria and off-site rehearsal facilities. Has staged many premieres, including work by David Greig, David Harrower, Rona Munro, Zinnie Harris and Gregory Burke.

OTHER FRINGE LOCATIONS

Komedia

44-47 Gardner Street, Brighton BN1 1UN
tel (01273) 647101 *fax* (01273) 647102
email info@komedia.co.uk
website www.komedia.co.uk

An upstairs and downstairs cabaret bar serving hot food and drinks, each with a capacity of 230 seated around tables, and a 160-seat theatre. Komedia presents a programme of theatre, world music, cabaret, comedy and children's shows. Has been host to names such as Graham Norton, Mel & Sue, League of Gentlemen and The Right Size.

Sevenoaks Stag Theatre

London Road, Sevenoaks, Kent TN13 1ZZ
tel (01732) 451548
email enquiries@stagesevenoaks.co.uk

The theatre can seat up to 453 and has provision for wheelchair-users. Companies should book the space up to 6 months in advance. Programmes a wide range of theatre and dance events.

Watermans Arts Centre

40 High Street, Brentford, Middlesex TW8 0DS
tel 020-8847 5651 *fax* 020-8569 8592
email info@watermans.org.uk
website www.watermans.org.uk

An arts venue comprising 239-seat theatre, 125-seat cinema, studio 1 (large), studio 2 (small), gallery, restaurant and bar, and river views of the Thames. Programmes across a range of different artforms including Asian arts, new media, children's theatre, cinema and participative arts. The studios have a nominal capacity of 80 and 30 seats respectively, but these spaces are mostly used for workshops, meetings and rehearsals.

Theatre

To fringe, or not to fringe

Simon Dunmore

Although it is generally regarded as 'professional' work, there is a tendency in Fringe productions for professional standards (and facilities) to be somewhat lacking – and that is sometimes an understatement. Poor technical back-up, indifferent front-of-house arrangements and general unreliability are too often the case, almost inevitably damaging the quality of the final product.

Some potential problems to watch out for

• *The ego trip.* A number of productions are set up by individuals wanting a starring vehicle for themselves – much like the old actor-managers. It is generally better to avoid such enterprises unless you can be fairly sure that the central 'ego' will not be damaging to your contribution. Ask around for objective advice before accepting a part in such a production.

• *What else will you have to do?* Will you have to do other things – like paint the set, distribute posters, help with the get-in, and so on? You may think that you can make time to do things like this, but are you sure you want to be thus distracted in the last few days before opening night?

• *Is the script good enough?* There really is no point in doing a production that's flawed before it leaves the page.

• *Can you work well with the director?* This is a highly subjective judgement, but since you are not being properly paid, it is important that you feel as sure as you can be that it'll be a worthwhile experience.

• *Can you actually afford to do it?* There is no point in taking time out from paid work in order to rehearse and perform a Fringe production unless you really think that you'll get something out of the experience. (It can be worth asking if your rehearsal-calls can be arranged around your work commitments.) Also, check whether your participation will affect your benefits in any way.

• *Your agent.* If you have one, will s/he be happy for you to do the production?

• *Contracts.* In 2005, Equity published a set of guidelines (working hours, etc.) and a suggested contract for Fringe producers. This is not intended as an alternative to Equity's other agreements; rather, it is designed to help Fringe companies develop good employment practices. Some companies issue their own contracts; it is important to read these carefully and check with Equity if you have any doubts.

• *Will the production get reviews?* A good review equals good publicity – important for any production. Some productions in the most prestigious venues get reviewed in national newspapers. However, because there are so many productions at any one time, the press has strict rules (length of run, for instance) about what they will send reviewers to. It is important to note that the perceptiveness of some of the latter is somewhat shallow (that's not sour grapes; it's a fact).

• *Will the publicity and marketing be sufficient?* After the cost of hiring the venue, publicity and marketing represent the next major cost of a Fringe production. Too many productions try to skimp on these. In such a competitive environment, they are very, very important.

• *Does the venue have a good reputation?* It is much, much harder to get people into less prestigious ones.

• *Promises.* While enthusiasm for a project is wonderful, beware of promises when they seem over-the-top. Too much optimism can blind people to important practical realities.
• *Is it going to be properly organised?* There is far more to putting on a production than most actors realise (see below). Ask questions based on the above and, if you don't feel sufficiently satisfied, politely back away. There is no point in being miserable, as well as unpaid, for several weeks.
• *If I'm not being paid, can I not just pull out if something better comes along?* Legally, you can; morally and professionally it's an extremely dubious thing to do without the full understanding of your fellow participants – and you never know who, among them, might gain 'casting clout' in the future.

Setting up your own production

Too many people think that mounting a production is just a matter of getting a few friends together, borrowing some props and costumes, and getting on with it. What about the costs of hiring a venue, a rehearsal space, the publicity and marketing, the author's royalties (if still in copyright), and so on?

You may be lucky enough to get some, or even all, of these for free, or you might find a rich auntie. But however you fund the above essentials, you have got to do a lot of careful planning before rehearsals start. Will the playwright (and/or translator) allow you to do a production of the play in the first place? Just because a play is in print, it doesn't mean that anyone can perform it. Is the rehearsal room available for enough of the time? What is the deadline for getting the poster design to the printers, so that they can get the result back to you in time for the distributors to get them displayed in good time before opening night? And so on, and so on, and so on … Oh, and it is essential to plan and budget with contingency in both time and money – there are always several things that take more time than you'd thought, and several things that cost more than you'd thought (or forgotten to budget for in the first place).

Doing it yourself is far more complex than most people realise, but can be incredibly satisfying if you succeed. For a technically simple production you probably need to find at least £5000 – and that's without paying any of the participants. The chances of recouping this through the box office are very low; the average audience on the Fringe is about 30 per cent. A recent report stated that: "Theatres are among the most over-regulated businesses in the UK." Legal requirements like Health & Safety, VAT and performance rights cannot be neglected.

Note: For interesting discussion on the whole business of working for little or nothing, go to **http://actorsminimumwage.wordpress.com**.

Simon Dunmore has been directing productions for over 30 years – nearly 20 years as a resident director in regional theatres and, more recently, working freelance. In that time there have been over 200 productions (of all styles, colours, shapes and sizes) – recently: several Drama School Showcases, Maugham's *Home and Beauty* and new plays about sex, WB Yeats' up-and-down relationship with Maud Gonne, one set inside a pyramid and another about Bismarck. Past favourites include: *The Promise* (Alexei Arbuzov), *Antigone* (Jean Anouilh), a seven-handed version of *Antony & Cleopatra* and too many others to mention. He also teaches acting and has worked in many drama schools and other training establishments around the country. He has written several books: *An Actor's Guide to Getting Work* (now in its fourth edition), the *Alternative Shakespeare Auditions* series and is the Consultant Editor for *Actors' Yearbook*. **www.simon.dunmore.btinternet.co.uk**

Theatre

Edinburgh or bust: is it worth it?

Shane Dempsey

The Edinburgh Fringe was established in 1947 and has grown into one of the world's most renowned and diverse arts festivals. From its humble beginnings as an alternative to the Edinburgh International Festival, the Fringe has continued to increase and multiply, and, despite the growing costs to companies and performers alike, it still remains high on the agenda of many. The Fringe can be incredibly daunting and at times even crippling. My aim is not to shatter you, but to ensure that you are armed with as much knowledge as possible before you decide if it's worth it.

In 2009 there were 2098 shows performed in Edinburgh and an estimated 18,901 performers in 265 venues. These figures give you an idea of the level of competition for audiences during the three weeks of August. This is an aggressive and over-saturated market. In the Fringe environment, the efforts of many go unrewarded and often even unnoticed. So, can you break through with your production?

Evaluate your work honestly and realistically

The first thing to do is evaluate the production itself. Ask yourself, "What is the appeal of my particular production? What is it about my show that will make it stand out from the crowd? Do I have permission from the author or their estate to perform the piece? If so, what percentage of my overall income will this take, and what are the possibilities of extending this performance licence post-Edinburgh?"

If the piece is new writing or devised then there are fewer issues with performance rights, but it is crucial to discuss billing and authorship, as these can potentially cause problems later. Circumstances change, so with new work it is essential to secure written agreement over the intellectual copyright of the piece – and this also extends to directorial concepts and vision. Get it down on paper so you always know where you stand and can avoid or deal with any issues that may arise.

As well as fledgling companies taking new work to Edinburgh, the festival is also a testing ground for many established, heavyweight companies and producers. They have years of experience, and they have the economic power to invest large sums in PR and marketing. So ask yourself what will bring an audience to your venue, and why. The reality is that you are in direct competition with these established companies as well as with the other thousands who are newer to the game.

Choose the right venue

There are many venues associated with the Fringe. You need to be clear about the kind of work they are interested in programming; some are very specific as to their requirements, while others have a broader remit. Consider not only the price, but also the reputation and the location of a venue, as they vary considerably.

Your time slot is another point of negotiation: late evenings tend to be dominated by comedy, and a great deal of theatre now plays during the day and late afternoon. A general rule is that the more established venues have the best reputations and tend to charge significantly more for their services than smaller, up-and-coming venues. All venues will require you to sign a contract, and you need to be aware of the small print, as it has been known for companies to skim over this only to discover that they were not aware of all the terms and conditions.

Consider venue costs and other expenses

Many venues offer either a box-office split or ask for a flat fee. Almost all will require a deposit in advance. The average cost of mounting a production in Edinburgh is £8,000-10,000, and deposits will often be required months in advance – so unless you have access to sufficient funds, consider seriously if there is a more cost-effective way of getting your work out there.

And there are other expenses, including music performance rights, public liability insurance and VAT. Accommodation costs soar during the festival, and local landlords take advantage of the influx of artists and tourists, but if you're organised it is possible to secure a deal by booking early. Many companies choose to stay in Glasgow, which is an hour-long commute, but the time and energy required to do this needs to be weighed up against the convenience and cost of staying in Edinburgh.

What do you want from the experience?

Ask yourself early on what you want to achieve out of the experience. Too often this is not given enough thought, so that it is difficult, if not impossible, to achieve any significant outcomes. Remember that Edinburgh is a massive arts market, and that within any market you need to be specific about your audience – be it the general public or producers who can potentially remount your work post-Edinburgh.

If you want a London transfer, regional tour or international tour, target your promotions pack specifically to relevant individuals and always research their programming tastes. Invite them to the show, ensure that they are given complimentary tickets and try to set up a meeting after they have seen your work. Many international producers are seeking work that would be programmed two to three years after the festival, so you have to have a long-term plan for the production and ensure that it has the necessary factors that will support its longevity.

Network!

Many deals in Edinburgh are set up over late-night drinks and midnight meetings, often to fit in with the schedules of producers who are seeing work all day long. They can be fairly informal, but keeping your professional hat on is essential to any success. There are incredible opportunities to meet new people in Edinburgh, and there are numerous events specifically aimed towards networking, including the Producers' Breakfast.

In addition you can take part in a range of informal activities in which you can make connections that may lead to future work and collaborations. This is often triggered by seeing a company's work: the research trip I made recently to Russia to investigate ensemble practice has been greatly aided by contacts I met in Edinburgh. The key to any networking is to find the common links between you and the other practitioner, and then to develop them into a cohesive relationship. Be honest about what you do and why you do it, and people will usually respond positively.

Press officers have essential contacts with the media and could be a valuable asset to your production. They can not guarantee that your work will be reviewed, but having a person working on your behalf can give you a major advantage over the competition. If, like many companies, you are bringing the show to Edinburgh on a very tight budget,

Theatre

allocate one member of the company to be the designated press officer as this makes life a lot easier for all parties. Again, reputation means a lot in the world of the press and some papers will hold more influence than others. Target the ones that you believe will be interested in your work and be sure to read the reviews every day to get a flavour of what the festival has to offer.

Design, marketing, and word-of-mouth

In a market such as the Fringe, the role of good graphic design and web design is often overlooked, but it is essential to ensure that your work is seen – and seen at its best. Ensure that your production pack has strong imagery. The old cliché of a picture painting a thousand words still rings true, especially to overtired editors at the busiest time of their year. The array of flyers that are seen on the streets of Edinburgh is mind-boggling, but eye-catching design can really aid your marketing campaign.

Over and above marketing, however, is word-of-mouth – one of the key influences in persuading people to see your show. Such recommendations are difficult to achieve, and are dependent on your getting healthy, happy audiences early in your run. The majority of companies spend their days marketing their work, sending emails, chasing the press and leafleting: this is the Fringe, and if you're not prepared to do this to the point of exhaustion, stay at home!

For inclusion in the much-coveted Fringe Brochure you will be asked to submit 50 words of copy to describe your production. Keep it simple and clear, and remember that you are going to have to live with this for the life of your show in Edinburgh, so make sure it really sums your work up. It can be useful to have a quote in there from previous work – after all, everybody wants to see a show from a five-star company – but if it's not true, don't claim it to be so! Fabrication rarely, if ever, helps. The Fringe website provides comprehensive guidelines on producing work in Edinburgh: see **www.edfringe.com/take-part**. The information is there if you look for it, so take the time to investigate. It could save you much stress and money.

Dreams can come true ...

The likelihood of your company or show being picked up for a transfer or tour is extremely slim. The financial burden on companies is very high, and you have to weigh this up against the potential exposure and the possibility of gaining other work after the festival. There has been a recent rise in smaller fringe festivals happening outside of the main Fringe, partially in response to its overtly commercial nature. Notably, the Free Fringe and the Big Red Door are proving to be hugely popular and offer far better deals to the artists. Fragments' production of *The Bay* by Hannah Burke was performed at the Big Red Door, Te-Pooka; we also managed to be seen by representatives of the Traverse, Manchester International Festival, and were transferred into London's prestigious Theatre 503. So yes, dreams can come true ... but only after a serious amount of hard graft, and no little luck too.

Shane Dempsey trained as a director at E15 Acting School and runs Fragments, an international ensemble of theatre and video artists (fragments.ie). His work has been staged in Ireland, London, Scotland and Belgium. In 2008 he filmed the groundbreaking documentary *Mothers of Modern Ireland*. His production of *The Bay* toured extensively in 2009, and he is currently preparing to stage a new adaptation by Hannah Burke of Mikhail Bulgakov's *The Master & Margarita*. He has strong Russian connections, and was invited to observe rehearsals by Lev Dodin of the Maly Theatre of St Petersburg in Paris, November 2009 as well as observing acting workshops at GITIS and Vakhtangov Institute, Moscow 2010.

Theatre

Children's, young people's and theatre in education

Paul Harman

Work in this very large sector of employment for actors in the UK varies greatly – both in the style of theatre created and presented, and in the wages and conditions offered by employers. Anyone taking work in the field should always be clear about the aims and status of their prospective employer.

Most producing theatres offer plays for young audiences as part of a season, and Christmas shows and pantomimes are mounted by a large number of receiving theatres and commercial touring companies. Some 200 independent touring companies regularly present original theatre productions, usually in schools, reaching a total audience of at least five million annually. Smaller touring companies may operate for profit, or as profit-share partnerships. Companies which are members of ITC (Independent Theatre Council) offer pay and conditions agreed with the performers' trade union, Equity.

Reality check

There is no official agency that collects reliable statistics or regulates the quality of what is offered. Your work may never be publicly reviewed – and it can be hard and demanding. Casts are often small, and living conditions on the road are sometimes difficult. The work may involve a lot of driving (if you are over 25 and insurable) as well as humping sets in and out of vans. However, the rewards for good-quality work conscientiously presented lie in the warmth of welcome from audiences and bookers alike, and a directness and openness of audience response which is often less evident at more formal, adult-orientated theatre events. In schools, you will perform in daylight, very close to children – so it helps if you like them. They can see every blemish on you, and you can see every reaction on a hundred faces.

You will need physical stamina; the ability to play many parts convincingly; and the facility to hit a peak of performance two or more times in a day, six days a week. You may need skill in playing a musical instrument. In addition, other aptitudes may be called upon. A play may be preceded or followed by workshop activity with young people – from 'hot-seating' in character to involving children in a performance. An understanding of drama education techniques is therefore an advantage, and experience of Youth Theatre useful.

What shows?

For good economic and marketing reasons, most theatre for children presented in larger houses is based on well-known stories by established authors, or on characters from TV shows. Companies may receive financial support from official agencies to present plays on health and social issues. Plays related to the National Curriculum, such as science topics, are in great demand from schools.

Theatre in Education (TIE) is a term commonly used to mean many kinds of theatre in schools. In the strict sense, TIE implies an extended theatre event, combining performance and participatory elements and designed to engage pupils in exploring their own knowledge, feelings and attitudes. This is quite a different process from explaining how magnets work, or presenting an account of an historical event. Very few companies nowadays can afford the time and staffing needed to support real TIE, but there are many opportunities to create and present challenging educational plays on a wide variety of subjects.

Independent touring companies receiving public subsidy from Arts Councils in England, Wales, Scotland and Northern Ireland generally aim to present original, commissioned drama. A small group of writers specialises in this field, addressing personal and social topics, from fear of the dark or the break-up of families to genetics and migration. This group of companies – whose aims are primarily artistic, rather than just to entertain or deliver educational messages – find like-minded companies in 70 countries through ASSITEJ (International Association of Theatre for Children and Young People). Overseas tours and international collaborations are increasing.

Above all, don't look upon this field as an easy step towards something else. Your first experiences may well be tough, but an apprenticeship served with a supportive company will open an area of work that you can return to with growing enjoyment and professional satisfaction.

Paul Harman has worked as an actor and director in professional theatre since 1963. He joined Belgrade Theatre in Education team in 1966, headed Education work at Liverpool Everyman from 1970, and founded Merseyside Young People's Theatre Company in 1978. Since 1994 he has been Artistic Director of CTC Theatre, Darlington. In 1994 he became Artistic Director of CTC Theatre, Darlington and is now the Chair of TYA (Theatre for Young Audiences) – the UK Centre of ASSITEJ.

Children's, young people's and theatre-in-education companies
Note Some of the companies listed are members of the Independent Theatre Council (ITC) – **www.itc-arts.org.uk**.

Action Transport Theatre
Whitby Hall, Stanney Lane, Ellesmere Port, Cheshire CH65 9AE
tel 0151-357 2120 *fax* 0151-356 4057
email info@actiontransporttheatre.org
website www.actiontransporttheatre.org
Director Sarah Clover *Producer* Jessica Egan *General Manager* Karen Parry *Associate Writer* Kevin Dyer *Associate Director* Nina Hajiyianni *Production Manager* Mike Francis

Production details: "A new writing company creating brave, collaborative theatre for, by and with young people." Stages 3 projects annually, with around 60 performances in 10 venues including schools, arts centres, theatres and community venues across the UK. In general 4-5 actors go on tour, playing to family (5+) and adult audiences. Incoming actors should have singing, musical instrument and physical theatre skills, and may be expected to lead workshops. Recent productions include: *Generations*; *The Bomb*; *Scratches in the Earth*; and *Night Train*.

Casting procedures: Holds general auditions and actors may write at any time to request inclusion. Casting breakdowns are available from the website, by postal application (with sae), through Equity Job Information Service and Casting Call Pro, and in *PCR* and *The Stage*. Welcomes letters (with CVs and photographs) from individual actors previously unknown to the company, sent by post or email. Will consider invitations to view individual actors' websites. Offers Equity-approved contracts as negotiated through ITC. Actively encourages applications from disabled actors, and promotes the use of inclusive casting.

Actionwork TIE
PO Box 433, Weston-Super-Mare, Somerset BS24 0WY
tel (01934) 815163
email info@actionwork.com
website www.actionwork.com
Artistic Director Andy Hickson *Production Manager* Cath Davis

Production details: Founded in 1990. Between 2008 and 2009 toured 5 shows in the UK and abroad. Stages on average more than a hundred performances annually, touring to schools, arts centres, theatres, outdoor and community venues. In general 2-8 actors go on tour, playing to audiences aged 10 to 18. Actors may be expected to lead workshops, and it is an advantage to possess additional singing, musical instrument, dance and physical theatre skills; they should hold a current driving licence. Recent productions include: *Clash!*, *33 Skins*, *WWW*, and *Silent Scream*.

Casting procedures: Holds general auditions; actors may write in at any time to request inclusion. Welcomes letters (with CVs and photographs) from individual actors previously unknown to the company, sent by post or email, as well as showreels and invitations to view individual actors' websites. Actively encourages applications from disabled actors, and promotes the use of inclusive casting.

Aesop's Touring Theatre Company

The Arches, 38 The Riding, Woking,
Surrey GU21 5TA
tel (01483) 724633 *mobile* (07836) 731872
fax (01483) 724633
email info@aesopstheatre.co.uk
website www.aesopstheatre.co.uk
Director Karen Brooks L.L.A.M. (Hons.) Dipl. *Other key personnel* Albert Brooks A.C.I.I. (General Manager)

Production details: Established in 1999, a professional Theatre in Education company specialising in National Curriculum based plays for the nursery and primary age range. Tours extensively on a daily basis and at the time of writing is performing 7 2-hander interactive plays and associated drama workshops. Plays are mostly performed in schools but also embarce theatres, community centres, village halls, arts centres and party venues. On average stages 300 performances each year, in 225 venues across London, in the Home Counties and further afield. 2 actors usually go on tour, plus occasionally a driver or stage manager. Applicants should be fit, versatile all-round actors with a good grasp of comedy, and should have their own transport to easily reach base for early morning starts in the company vehicle.

Casting procedures: Sometimes holds general auditions and actors may write in at any time: "We reply to all enquries." Rarely (or never) has the opportunity to cast disabled actors.

Ape Theatre Company

32 Brook Road, Epping, Essex CM16 7BT
tel (01992) 574843
email mail@apetheatrecompany.co.uk
website www.apetheatrecompany.co.uk
Artistic Director Mr Matt Allen *Assistant Artistic Director* Mr Andrew Mulquin *Company Director / Manager* Mrs Yvonne Allen

Production details: Established in 1980. Stages 4 projects annually, with 800 performances at the same number of schools and community venues nationwide. In general 4 actors go on tour with each project, playing to audiences aged 10-plus. Actors are sometimes expected to lead workshops and should

hold a clean driving licence. Dance and physical theatre skills may be an advantage. Recent productions include: *Too Much Punch for Judy*; *Legal Weapon II*; *Pills, Thrills and Automobiles*; and *Viscous Circle*.

Casting procedures: Holds general auditions, and actors are advised to write in July and November to request inclusion. Casting breakdowns are available by postal application (with sae), and via Equity Job Information Service and *PCR*. Welcomes letters (with CVs and photographs) from individual actors previously unknown to the company, sent by post and email, but does not accept unsolicited showreels or invitations to view actors' websites. Offers Equity-approved contracts as negotiated through ITC. Rarely or never has the opportunity to cast disabled actors.

Arty-Fact Theatre Co

18 Weston Lane, Crewe CW2 5AN
tel 070-2096 2096 *fax* 070-2098 2098
email artyfact@talktalk.net
website www.arty-fact.co.uk
Artistic Director Yvonne Peacock *Co-director* Brian Twiddy

Production details: Has been performing in schools since 1993, running history workshops, original plays and classics. Performs 6-7 projects annually, with an average annual total of 500-600 performances in 200-300 schools across England. In general 2-4 actors go on tour and perform to audiences aged 7-18. Physical theatre skills and a driving licence are required. Actors may be expected to lead workshops. Recent productions include: *Of Mice and Men*; *Much Ado About Nothing*; *Eureka!*; and *The Inventive Miss Violet*.

Casting procedures: Sometimes holds general auditions; actors are advised to write in April and July to request inclusion. Casting breakdowns are available via the website, Equity Job Information Service, *PCR* and the Actors' Centre. Welcomes letters (with CVs and photographs) from individual actors previously unknown to the company sent by post or email. Does not accept showreels or invitations to view individual actors' websites. Rarely or never has the opportunity to cast disabled actors. "Include a letter stating why you would like to work for us in particular."

Big Wheel Theatre in Education

The Institute, PO Box 18221, London EC1R 4WJ
tel 020-7689 8670 *fax* 020-7689 8670
email info@bigwheel.org.uk
website www.bigwheel.org.uk
Artistic Directors Roland Allen, Jeni Williams

Production details: Since 1984 has developed interactive theatre for use in education and training in the UK and abroad. Normally tours 10 projects each year, with an average annual total of 400 performances and 200 different venues. Venues

Theatre

include schools and conference centres across the UK, Europe, Japan, Kenya and South Africa. In general 2 actors go on tour and play to audiences aged 7 upwards. Actors are required to hold a driving licence and to lead workshops. Experience in teaching or training is also useful. Recent productions include: *Introduction to Shakespeare*, a game-show-based interactive workshop; *Breakfast with Big Wheel*, a show to teach English in European schools; and a variety of workshops for the NHS about communication, partnerships and peripatetic working.

Casting procedures: Sometimes holds general auditions; actors may write at any time requesting inclusion. "It's quite specialist work. Best to have a good look at the website and only send us your stuff if you think it really is your cup of tea."

Big Wooden Horse Theatre Company Ltd

30 Northfield Road, London W13 9SY
tel 020-8567 8431
email info@bigwoodenhorse.com
website www.bigwoodenhorse.com
Artistic Director Adam Bampton-Smith *Technical Director* Will Evans

Production details: Aims to present high-quality theatre to younger audiences across the UK and to represent the best of British theatre craft abroad. Strives both to entertain and to inform young people, drawing from different cultures and traditions. On average 3 actors tour 3 projects annually, with 400 performances at around 80 venues including arts centres and theatres in the UK, US and Canada. Audiences range from 3 to 11 years. Recent productions include: *The Life and Adventures of Santa Claus*, *The Way Back Home*, *Don't Let the Pigeon Drive the Bus!* and *The Night Before Christmas*.

Casting procedures: Casting breakdowns are available from Equity Job Information Service, *PCR* and SBS. Welcomes approaches from actors previously unknown to the company, sent by post or email.

Bitesize Theatre Company

8 Green Meadows, New Broughton, Wrexham LL11 6SG
tel (01978) 358320 *fax* (01978) 756308
email admin@bitesizetheatre.co.uk
website www.bitesizetheatre.co.uk
Artistic Director Linda Griffiths *Administrator* Bill Robertson

Production details: Founded in 1992, the company strives to provide high-quality, entertaining theatrical productions for young people, from children's classics to Shakespeare and pantomime to new works. Also runs Theatre in Education projects and bespoke workshops across the UK. The company performs in schools and community venues across the Northwest.

Rehearsals take place in North Wales. Between 3-6 actors work on each show and play to audiences aged 3-19 years. Actors are required to be able to sing, dance and drive and may also be expected to participate in workshops. Recent productions include: *Cinderella*, *The Golden Voyage of Sinbad*, *Much Ado About Nothing*, *Red Riding Hood*, *Where There's a Will There's a Play*.

Casting procedures: The company holds general auditions; actors requesting inclusion in these should write in July. Casting breakdowns are available in *PCR*, *The Stage*, Castcall and SBS. Although actors are welcome to write with their CVs and photographs, the company prefers not to receive emails or showreels. Mainly takes actors from recognised drama schools; actors aged over 25 years are preferred for jobs requiring driving. All employees must pass a CRB (Criminal Records Bureau) check for work with children. Offers non-Equity contracts. Actively encourages applications from disabled actors and promotes the use of inclusive casting.

Bloom Productions

tel (0845) 680 9395
email info@bloomproductions.org
website www.bloomproductions.org
Directors Siân Morrison, John McKinney *Associate Director* Michael Buffong

Production details: A social enterprise, bringing together young people and communities with an evolving ensemble of arts practitioners and educators. Creates new work in film, theatre and the creative arts and is committed to widening access to and participation in the arts through creative learning. Offers Equity approved contracts as negotiated through ITC. Tours 12 projects annually to schools, arts centres, theatres and community venues in the South East, playing to audiences aged 5-19. Offers training to actors wishing to develop skills in education. Recent productions include: Journeys Film Project (28 primary schools in Camden, 9-11 year olds); Great Escapes Film Project (5 film shorts linked thematically, 10-15 year olds).

Casting procedures: Uses in-house casting directors. Casting breakdowns are available from the website. Please do not make approaches by post; send CVs and photographs by email. Welcomes showreels and invitations to view actors' websites. Promotes the use of inclusive casting.

Blue Moon Theatre Company

20 Sandpiper Road, Blakespool Park, Bridgewater, Somerset TA6 5QU
tel (01278) 458253
email info@bluemoontheatre.co.uk
website www.bluemoontheatre.co.uk
Artistic Director Steve Apelt *Writer* Mark Scott-Ison *Administrator* Sue Squire

Production details: A producing "fun-packed" children's theatre with lots of participation and involvement – mainly incorporating workshops and after-show discussions. Stages on average 2-3 projects annually. In general 4 actors go on tour, staging around 50 performances for young audiences at 40 UK venues including schools, arts centres, theatres, outdoor and community venues. Singing and physical theatre skills are required, as well as a clean driving licence.

Casting procedures: Sometimes holds general auditions, with casting breakdowns publicly available. Welcomes letters (with CVs and photographs) from individual actors previously unknown to the company, sent by post or email. Also welcomes showreels, and invitations to view individual actors' websites. Offers Equity-approved contracts. Actively encourages applications from disabled actors and promotes the use of inclusive casting.

Blue Star Productions

7-8 Shaldon Mansions, 132 Charing Cross Road, London WC2H 0LA
tel 020-7836 6220/4128 *fax* 020-7836 2949
email Hopkinstacey@aol.com

Production details: Blue Star Productions specialises in first-class children's musicals and Songbook Concerts. These shows tour theatres nationally. They include 8-10 performers, beautiful costumes and scenery, and always feature 'live' music. Recent productions include: *The Wonderful Wizard of Oz*; *The Adventures of Pinocchio*; *Tales from the Jungle Book*; *Alice in Wonderland*; *Snow White and the Seven Dwarfs*; and many others. Songbook Concerts include at least 4 singers, depending on venue and finance. One-man shows include: *Life Upon the Very Wicked Stage*, an audience with Barrie Stacey. Barrie Stacey was voted "Best Children's Show Producer of the Year 2009" at the Encore Awards.

Casting procedures: All casting is done in-house through Blue Star Associates, also at the above address. Holds general auditions annually, or for specific productions. Welcomes letters with CVs and photographs, and also email submissions.

Bournemouth Theatre in Education

BCCA, 93 Haviland Road, Bournemouth BH7 6HJ
tel (01202) 395759 *fax* (01202) 399597
email shaz.watkins@bournemouth.gov.uk
Artistic Directors Tony Horitz, Sharon Muiruri
Administrator Shaz Watkins

Production details: Founded in 1967. "Theatre in Education service within a lifelong learning framework." Works in schools, presenting theatrical performances and facilitating drama; is also actively involved in the field of social inclusion. Normally tours 10-15 projects each year to schools, arts centres, outdoor venues, community venues, prisons and hospitals in the South of England. In general 3-4 actors go on tour and play to audiences of all ages. Actors are required to have good workshop skills and

the ability to relate well to people. Recent productions include: *My Name Is Savitri*, an anti-racism play for Year 4 children; *Angel*, with a disabled actors theatre company; and *Sleeping Beauty*, with Tops (actors with learning difficulties).

Casting procedures: Sometimes holds general auditions; actors may write at any time requesting inclusion. Accepts submissions (with CVs and photographs) from actors previously unknown to the company sent by post or email. Will also accept showreels and invitations to view individual actors' websites. "We do use professional actors on a fairly regular basis, but prefer to use those living in or around the Bournemouth area."

Box Clever Theatre Company

12 G1 The Leathermarket, Weston Street, London SE1 3ER
tel 020-7357 0550 *fax* 020-7357 8188
email admin@boxclevertheatre.com
website www.boxclevertheatre.com
Artistic Director Michael Wicherek

Production details: Founded in 1996, the company produces contemporary theatre for young people: new plays, contemporary adaptations of classic texts, and issue-based and educational work. 6 major national tours are staged each year with an average annual total of approximately 600 performances in 500 different venues. The company performs to more than 60,000 young people every year. Venues include arts centres, theatres, and educational and community venues nationwide. Approximately 3 actors are involved in each production. Recent productions include: *Time for the Good Looking Boy* (for theatres); *The Buzz, Driving Ms Daisy, The Hate Plays* and *Boxed Macbeth* (for secondary schools); and *Car Story* for primary schools.

Casting procedures: Does not use freelance casting directors. Casting breakdowns are available via Equity Job Information Service, the website (normally June/July and October/November), and *PCR*. Welcomes submissions (with CVs and photographs) from actors previously unknown to the company if sent by post and if in response to casting breakdowns only. Advises actors that the company receives a huge response to advertisements placed in *PCR*, and is therefore unable to return photographs or respond in writing to applicants not invited to audition. Non-Equity contracts "in line with ITC". Considers applications from disabled actors to play characters with disabilities.

Brief Candle Theatre

Chesterfield Studios, 44 Newbold Street, Derbyshire S41 7PL
tel (01246) 556161
email office@briefcandle.co.uk
website www.briefcandle.co.uk
Artistic Director David Shimwell *Writer/Director* Paul Whitfield

Theatre

Production details: Established in 2002. Produces high-quality Theatre in Education and theatre for young people and family audiences. On average performs 5 projects each year, with 450 performances in 100 venues including schools, colleges, theatres, community venues and occasionally outdoor performances and festivals. Areas covered: Derbyshire, South Yorkshire, Lincolnshire and Wigan. On average 4 actors go on tour, playing to audiences aged 11 to adult. "We seek to work with actors who are committed to working with young people, and who have the skills required to build fast, effective working relationships with company and audience." Actors may be required to lead workshops. Recent productions include: *The Tower* – a play looking at domestic abuse and power in relationships; *Tight* – a play for 14 year olds looking at use and misuse of alcohol; *An Evening with Mallet and Ming* – a dark comedy for adults and older children, set in a Victorian Music Hall; and *No Place for Dreams* – a family show for the Edinburgh Festival.

Casting procedures: Holds general auditions and actors may write in at any time; the company keeps all submissions for consideration. Casting details are available via Spotlight Link and from the website. Prefers email applications. An approved Manager member of the ITC; all contracts are ITC Equity approved. Encourages applications from all actors, regardless of ability or disability, and promotes the use of inclusive casting.

C&T

University College Worcester, Henwick Grove, Worcester WR2 6AJ
tel (01905) 855436
email info@candt.org
website www.candt.org
Artistic Director Paul Sutton

Production details: Founded in 1988. A theatre company incorporating performance, learning and digital media. Works in schools, colleges and universities in the UK and across Europe. Normally tours 2-3 projects each year with an average annual total of 50-100 performances at 50-100 different venues. In general 2-3 actors go on tour and play to audiences aged 5-65. Dance/physical theatre skills, proficiency with computers and digital media, and a driving licence are required. Actors are also expected to lead workshops. Recent productions include: *Living Newspaper.com*, a docu-drama project online for schools.

Casting procedures: Sometimes holds general auditions; actors should write in September requesting inclusion. Accepts submissions (with CVs and photographs) from actors previously unknown to the company sent by post or email. Will also accept showreels and invitations to view individual actors' websites.

Cahoots NI

109-113 Royal Avenue, Belfast BT1 1FF
tel 028-9043 4349
email info@cahootsni.com
website www.cahootsni.com
Artistic Director Paul McEneaney

Production details: Creates world-class, inspirational theatre for children aged 4 to 11 years. Aims to "expand the imagination of children, and to stimulate their artistic creativity through the visual potential of theatre and the age-old popularity of music, magic and illusion". On average tours 3 productions to schools, special schools, respite centres, councils, arts centres and theatres both nationally and internationally. 4-8 actors go on tour, performing to audiences aged 6-11. Actors should have singing, musical instrument, physical theatre, circus and magic skills, and are sometimes required to lead workshops. Recent projects include: *The Flea Pit Circus*; *The Family Hoffmann's Mystery Palace*; *The Snail and the Whale*; and *The Musician*.

Casting procedures: Sometimes holds general auditions; actors may write at any time to request inclusion. Welcomes letters (with CVs and photographs) from actors previously unknown to the company sent by post or email, and is happy to receive showreels. Does not welcome invitations to view individual actors' websites. Actively encourages applications from disabled actors, and promotes the use of inclusive casting.

Cambridge Touring Theatre

29 Worts Causeway, Cambridge CB1 8RJ
email info@cambridgetouringtheatre.co.uk
website www.cambridgetouringtheatre.co.uk
Artistic Director Rosie Humphreys

Production details: Founded in 2002. A family fun touring theatre. Stages 1 production each year, with 35 performances in 35 theatres and outdoor venues in the South, South East and East of England. In general 6 actors go on tour, playing to audiences aged 2-11 and their families. Incoming actors will be required to lead workshops; some singing, dance and driving ability is an advantage. Recent productions include: *Alice in Wonderland*, *Robin Hood*, *Wind in the Willows*, and *Sword in the Stone*.

Casting procedures: Casting breakdowns are available via the website, Spotlight, postal application with sae, *PCR* and CastingCallPro. Welcomes letters (with CVs and photographs) from individual actors previously unknown to the company, sent by post only.

Changing Faces Theatre Company

PO Box 57877, London SE26 9AN
tel 020-8776 8706 *fax* 020-8778 4079
email info@changingfacestheatre.com
website www.changingfacestheatre.com
Artistic Director Nicholas Kessler *Company Manager* Heather Code

Production details: A not-for-profit theatre company that is young, vibrant and ready to bring the highest quality of interactive, literacy-based theatre and workshops to primary-aged children. With classroom experience, a passion for language, a little bit of glue and a lot of imagination, Changing Faces was formed as a direct response to the challenges of teaching literacy in the classroom in the 21st Century. On average stages 6-10 projects per year, with around 300 performances and 250 workshops in 100-150 schools, community venues, theatres and libraries in London and the South East. In general, 2 actors perform an interactive, audience-actor collaborative show and /or workshop, working with audiences aged 4-11. Musical instrument, vocal and physical theatre skills are required, as is a clean driving licence. Puppetry, workshop skillls and classroom experience are an advantage.

Casting procedures: Sometimes holds general auditions. Casting breakdowns are available via the Spotlight. Rarely or never has the opportunity to cast disabled actors.

Channel Theatre

See entry under Chalkfoot Theatre Arts under *Middle and smaller-scale companies* on page 166.

Creaking Door Productions

Rhys Jones House, St Peter's School, Harefield, Lympstone, Devon EX8 5AU
mobile (07711) 931768
email office@creakingdoor.co.uk
website www.creakingdoor.co.uk
Artistic Director Tom Sherman *Producer* Alix Sherman

Production details: Established in 2005. Specialises in small-scale children's theatre productions in schools and venues throughout the South West; in 2010 the company will implement its new Education Programme. Stages 2-4 productions annually with around 40 performances. In general 2-4 actors go on tour, playing to audiences aged 4 to 13, plus family audiences. Incoming actors should have singing and good basic movement skills, as well as a current driving licence. Actors may be expected to lead workshops. Recent productions include: *Cindarella*; *The Life and Times of Isambard Kingdom Brunel*; KS2 History workshops – *From Time to Time*; *Just So Stories*; *Frogs, Kings and Golden Wings*; *Tales of Bread and Golden Thread*; and *Beauty and the Beast*.

Casting procedures: Sometimes holds general auditions; actors may write in July and October to request inclusion. Casting breakdowns are available from the website, via Equity, and from Theatre Bristol and Theatre Devon. Welcomes letters (with CVs and photographs) from individual actors previously unknown to the company, sent by post only. Rarely or never has the opportunity to cast disabled actors.

Cwmni Theatr Arad Goch

Stryd Y Baddon, Aberystwyth, Ceredigion SY23 2NN
tel (01970) 617998 *fax* (01970) 611223
email post@aradgoch.org
website www.aradgoch.org
Artistic Director Jeremy Turner *Administrative Manager* Nia Wyn Evans

Production details: Founded in 1989. Main focus of work is Theatre in Education. Normally tours 6 projects each year with an average annual total of 150 performances and more than 100 different venues. Venues include schools, theatres and community venues across Wales and occasionally abroad. In general 3-6 actors go on tour and play to audiences aged 4 upwards. Singing ability, proficiency with a musical instrument, fluency in Welsh and a driving licence are required. Actors may also be expected to lead workshops. Recent productions include: *The Impossible Parents Go Green*, for 7-11 year olds, *Winter Pictures,* for young children (4-8 year olds) and *Crash*, a community theatre piece for young people. Offers ITC/Equity approved contracts and does not subscribe to the Equity Pension Scheme.

Casting procedures: Sometimes holds general auditions; actors requesting inclusion should write before the start of the academic year. Accepts submissions (with CVs and photographs) from actors previously unknown to the company by post or email. Will also accept showreels and invitations to view individual actors' websites. Will consider applications from disabled actors to play disabled characters.

Daylight Theatre

66 Middle Street, Stroud, Gloucestershire GL5 1EA
tel (01453) 763808
website www.daylighttheatre.co.uk
Artistic Director Hugh Young *Key personnel* Roger Burfield

Production details: Founded in 1977. Tours educational theatre into schools. Topics have included drugs, HIV/AIDS, Shakespeare, history and mythology, and have been linked to the National Curriculum. Normally tours 7 projects each year with an average annual total of 200 performances and 150 different venues. Venues include schools (mainly primary but some secondary), arts centres and theatres across the UK, Germany and Luxembourg. In general 2-3 actors go on tour and play to audiences aged 4-18. Actors are required to hold a driving licence and may also be expected to lead workshops. Recent productions include: *Can You Take It?* – drugs, alcohol and tobacco education for 9-11 year-olds; *A Midsummer Night's Dream* and *Macbeth* for Key Stage 2 level; and *Ghostcliff Grange*, a World War II drama, also for Key Stage 2.

Casting procedures: Advises that the company rarely needs new actors.

Fevered Sleep

c/o Young Vic, 66 The Cut, London SE1 8LZ
tel 020-7922 2988

email admin@feveredsleep.co.uk
website www.feveredsleep.co.uk
Artistic Director David Harradine *Associate Director* Samantha Butler

Production details: Established in 1996. Creates original performance, visual art and publications, for children and for adults. "Whether in theatres, galleries or other places, our work provides exciting and intimate experiences for our audiences, and encourages people to see the world in new and unexpected ways." Tours 3 projects annually, in around 14 venues (theatres, arts centres, galleries, and site-specific) in the UK, 3 internationally, and 4 in London. In general 2-3 actors go on tour, playing to audiences aged 3-8 and 17+. Incoming actors may be expected to lead workshops, and may require dance, physical theatre and /or musical instrument skills, depending on the project. Recent productions include: *Brilliant, An Infinite Line: Brighton*, and *Stilled*.

Casting procedures: Sometimes holds general auditions, and actors may write at any time. Welcomes letters (with CVs and photographs) from individual actors previously unknown to the company, sent by post or email, as well as invitations to view individual actors' websites – but prefers not to receive showreels. Offers Equity-approved contracts as negotiated through ITC. Will consider applications from disabled actors "in line with our equal opportunities policy".

Freshwater Theatre Company
Channelsea House, Canning Road, Abbey Lane, London E15 3ND
tel 0844-800 2870
email info@freshwatertheatre.co.uk
website www.freshwatertheatre.co.uk
Directors Helen Wood, Carol Tagg *Key personnel* Brooke Gallagher (Operations Manager)

Production details: Established in 1996 with the aim of offering high-quality, affordable, innovative drama opportunites to primary school children and teachers. Runs workshops and storytelling sessions addressing a range of curriculum areas including history, geography, Shakespeare, citizenship, multicultural studies and the needs of early years pupils. Also runs drama in-service training courses for teachers. Does not tour, but provides around 40 sessions all year round at nurseries, schools and community venues in Greater London, Cambridgeshire, Suffolk, Essex, the West Midlands conurbation, and Greater Manchester. Around 40 freelance facilitators work with audiences aged 3 to 11. Relevant experience is required, and actors are expected to lead workshops. Recent workshops include: *Florence Nightingale, Leap into Language, Early Years Story Hunt*, and *An Indian Village*.

Casting procedures: Holds general auditions; actors may write in at any time. Welcomes letters (with CVs

& photographs) sent by post or email, but only from experienced workshop facilitators. Does not accept showreels or invitations to view individual actors' websites. "We only engage dedicated, experienced workshop leaders to undertake our drama sessions, and will only consider those who can provide regular and ongoing availability within the areas we cover."

Fuse: New Theatre for Young People
13 Hope Street, Liverpool L1 9BH
tel 0151-708 0877 *fax* 0151-707 9950
email info@fusetheatre.com
website www.fusetheatre.co.uk
Artistic Producer Andrew Raffle *General Manager* Michael Quirke

Production details: Established in 1978. Performs 3-4 projects annually, with approximately 50 performances in schools, arts centres, theatres and community venues in the North West. In general 2-5 actors go on tour, playing to audiences aged 3 to 18 years. May require singing, musical instrument, dance and physical theatre skills; actors should hold a current driving licence, and may be expected to lead workshops. Recent productions include: *A World Away, Treasure, Portrait of a Nation*, and *Shadow Companion*.

Casting procedures: Sometimes holds general auditions: actors may write at any time to request inclusion. Casting breakdowns are available through the website and via the Arts Council's 'Artsjobs' service. Welcomes letters (with CVs and photographs) from individual actors previously unknown to the company, sent by post or email, and invitations to view individual actors' websites. Offers Equity-approved contracts as negotiated through ITC. Will consider applications from disabled actors to play characters with disabilities.

Gazebo Theatre in Education Company
Bilston Town Hall, Church Street, Bilston, West Midlands WV14 0AP
tel (01902) 497222 *fax* (01902) 497244
email admin@gazebotie.org
website www.gazebotie.org
Artistic Director Michael O'Hara *Strategic Director* Pamela Cole-Hudson

Production details: Founded in 1979. Normally tours 3-5 projects each year plus workshops, with an average annual total of 300 performances and 250 different venues, these are mainly schools and community venues in the West Midlands and South Shropshire. In general between 1 and 3 actors go on tour and play to audiences aged 4-25. Musical ability and movement skills are sometimes required, as is a driving licence. Actors may also be expected to lead workshops. Recent productions include: *Billy No Mates!* (Special Needs); *If you see a crocodile* (Nursery & Reception); *Presents from the Past*; (KS2) *Doing our Bit* (KS3).

Casting procedures: Casting breakdowns are sometimes available by postal application (with sae) or through Equity Job Information Service. The company website will also show details of auditions and artists opportunities. Accepts submissions (with CVs and photographs) from actors previously unknown to the company if sent by post. Open auditions take place over the summer months. Will accept invitations to view individual actors' websites. Does not welcome unsolicited emails. Offers non-Equity contracts. Actively encourages applications from disabled actors and promotes the use of inclusive casting.

Gibber Theatre Ltd
The Old Library, 2A Woodleigh Road, Whitley Bay, NE25 8ET
tel 0191-252 2039 *fax* 0191-252 4833
email hello@wearegibber.com
website www.wearegibber.com
Artistic Directors Victoria Blackburn, Tim Watt

Production details: Founded in 1999. An educational theatre company specialising in drama-based experiential learning programmes for young people of all ages. The company has built a reputation for making a difference in education, by delivering high-quality presentation, performance, workshop, road show and special events. On average performs 10 projects each year, with approximately 300 performances in 250-300 schools across the UK. Also tours to outdoor and community venues, hospitals and theatres. In general 3-4 actors go on tour, playing to audiences aged 5 to 18-plus. Actors may be required to lead workshops, and should have singing and physical theatre skills as well as a driving licence. Recent productions include: bespoke performances and workshops for London Learning Skills Council (Year 10 careers tour exploring post-16 learning and voluntary opportunities), and Newcastle Healthy Schools (KS4 tobacco education tour with a focus on tobacco-industry tactics).

Casting procedures: Sometimes holds general auditions; actors may write at any time. Casting breakdowns are available from *The Stage*, *PCR*, and Castingcallpro.com. Welcomes letters (with CVs & photographs) from actors previously unknown to the company, sent by post or email. Accepts showreels and invitations to view individual actors' websites. Will consider applications from disabled actors to play characters with disabilities.

The Derek Grant Organisation Ltd
Beechwood House, 13 Beechwood Road, West Moors, Dorset BH22 0BN
tel (01202) 855777
email admin@derekgrant.co.uk
website www.derekgrant.co.uk
Artistic Director Derek Grant *Administrative Director* Michael Jones

Production details: "We present traditional children's/family shows and pantomimes. A strong storyline features in every show, along with colourful costumes and scenery, bright musical numbers and lots of joining in!" Normally tours 4 productions each year, with an average annual total of 80 performances in numerous different venues. Venues include arts centres and theatres across the UK, including Northern Ireland. In general 5-6 actors go on tour and play to audiences aged 3-93. Singing ability, dance/physical theatre skills are required. Recent productions include: *Goldilocks and the Three Bears*, *Pinocchio* and Hans Andersen's *The Snow Queen*.

Casting procedures: Sometimes holds general auditions; actors can write at any time requesting inclusion. Accepts submissions (with CVs and photographs) from actors previously unknown to the company sent by post or email. Will also accept showreels and invitations to view individual actors' websites.

Greenwich & Lewisham Young People's Theatre (GLYPT)
The Tramshed, 51-53 Woolwich New Road, Woolwich, SE18 6ES.
tel 020-8854 1316
email info@glypt.co.uk
website www.glypt.co.uk
Artistic Director Jeremy James *Education Officer* Claire Newby.

Production details: GLYPT creates theatre for, with and by young people. It runs Youth Theatre workshops for 8-21 year-olds, and specialist programmes for young people with learning difficulties. The company also runs a comprehensive programme of workshops for young refugees and new arrivals. Tours 2 productions a year to young audiences across South East London and beyond; these visit schools as Theatre in Education programmes, and also play at community and arts centres and at theatres. The work explores current and provoking issues that affect the lives of young audiences, and offers a platform for aesthetic and educational debate. Recent productions have included: *The Inquiry*, *Mud City*, SK8 *Angel* and *Master Juba*.

Casting procedures: Operates the ITC/Equity contract and works with actors committed to the young people's theatre sector. "We actively encourage applications from disabled actors and promote the use of inclusive casting." Welcomes letters and emails (with CVs) from actors and skilled workshop facilitators.

Gwent Theatre
The Drama Centre, Pen-y-Pound, Abergavenny NP7 5UD
tel (01873) 853167 *fax* (01873) 853910
email gwenttie@uwclub.net
website www.gwenttie.co.uk

Theatre

Artistic Director Gary Meredith *Administrator* Julia Davies

Production details: Founded in 1976. Tours at least 4 projects each year with an average annual total of 180 performances. Venues include schools, theatres, outdoor venues and community venues in Gwent and across Wales. In general 3-5 actors go on tour and play to audiences aged 6 upwards. Singing ability, proficiency with a musical instrument and dance/physical theatre skills are required. Actors may also be expected to lead workshops. Recent productions include: *Pa Mor Uchel Yw Fyny?*, *Home Front*, *The Watching* and *Shadow Seeker* (all for schools).

Casting procedures: Sometimes holds general auditions and actors can write at any time requesting inclusion. Accepts submissions (with CVs and photographs) from actors previously unknown to the company if sent by post. Does not welcome unsolicited emails. Will also accept invitations to view individual actors' websites.

Half Moon Young People's Theatre
43 Whitehorse Road, London E1 0ND
tel 020-7265 8138 *fax* 020-7709 8914
email admin@halfmoon.org.uk
website www.halfmoon.org.uk
Artistic Director Chris Elwell *Administrative Director* Jackie Eley

Production details: Founded in 1989. "Young people's theatre touring in London and nationally with a reputation for high-quality work. Also a receiving venue for young people's work." Normally tours 2 projects with an average annual total of 170 performances and 45 different venues. Venues include schools, arts centres, theatres and community venues. In general 2-3 actors go on tour and play to audiences aged under 17. Offers ITC/Equity approved contracts and does not subscribe to the Equity Pension Scheme.

Casting procedures: Casting breakdowns are available through the website and Equity Job Information Service. Sometimes holds general auditions; actors can write at any time requesting inclusion. Accepts submissions (with CVs and photographs) from actors previously unknown to the company sent by post or email. Will also accept invitations to view individual actors' websites. Actively encourages applications from disabled actors and promotes the use of inclusive casting.

Hopscotch Theatre Company
2nd Floor, 7 Water Row, Glasgow G51 3UW
tel 0141-440 2025 *fax* 0141-440 2025
email info@hopscotchtheatre.com
website www.hopscotchtheatre.com
Artistic Director Ross Stenhose *General Manager* Susan McGregor

Production details: Founded in 1988. A Theatre in Education company touring 4 productions each year to primary schools with an average annual total of 520 performances. Venues include schools, arts centres, theatres and community venues across Scotland. In general 4 actors go on tour and play to audiences aged 5-12 years. Singing ability and some proficiency with a musical instrument would be beneficial, but are not necessary. Recent productions include: *Brand New Andrew & Fair Trade Fred*, *The Life & Times of Robert Burns*, and *Tam O' Shanter*.

Casting procedures: Accepts CVs, photographs and covering letter from actors previously unknown to the company sent by post or email. Will also accept showreels. Offers non-Equity contracts. Rarely (or never) has the opportunity to cast disabled actors.

Impact Universal
Hope Bank House, Woodhead Road, Honley, Holmfirth, West Yorkshire HD9 6PF
tel (01484) 660077 *fax* (01484) 660088
email jill.beckwith@impactuniversal.com
website www.impactuniversal.com
Creative Director Ian Townsend *Creative Manager* Rosie Perkin

Company's work: Established in 1994. A communications and training provider using theatrical techniques. The company's work is delivered live, fully interactive and topical, making its impact highly memorable and effective. Presentations, workshops and training events are delivered by experienced, professional actors and facilitators. In an average year tours 33 projects, staging more than 900 performances in the same number of schools, sports halls and conference centres nationwide. In general 3 actors go on tour, playing to audiences aged 11-19. Incoming actors may be expected to lead workshops; physical theatre and impersonation skills are an advantage, as is a clean driving licence. Recent productions include: *Pathways to Healthcare* (any year); *Opt Into Learning* (Year 9); *HE 4 All* (Year 10); *Stay In Learning* (Year 11); and *Stay On Course* (Year 12).

Recruitment procedures: Holds general and specific auditions and actors may write at any time to request inclusion. Casting breakdowns are available from Equity Job Information Service, Spotlight and Casting Call Pro. Welcomes letters (with CVs and headshots) from individual actors previously unknown to the company, sent by post or email, as well as invitations to view individual actors' websites. Rarely, or never, has the opportunity to cast disabled actors.

In Toto Theatre Company
The Colombo Centre, 34-68 Colombo Street, London SE1 8DP
tel 020-7261 1515
email sarah@in-tototheatre.co.uk
website www.in-tototheatre.co.uk
Artistic Director Sarah Carter *Associate Director* Lennie Charles

Production details: Founded in 1989 and became a charity in 2000. Provides inclusive theatre for all ages using a combination of puppetry, live music, storytelling and dance. Specialises in creating 'total theatre' by, with and for young audiences – "a highly visual musical style of theatre approach which is inclusive and accessible to a wide range of ages and abilities". Also runs participatory arts activities for families, children and young adults to make their own performance. Has completed 7 projects to date with an average of 50 performances in up to 30 venues (schools, community venues and outdoor festivals, including site-specific). On average 2-3 performers/actors tour in the company's small-scale productions devised for age groups from 18 months upwards. An additional skill is usually required of actors; playing a musical instrument and puppetry are especially valued.

Casting procedures: Does not hold general auditions. Will accept email enquiries, but unsolicited letters by post are not welcomed. Sometimes advertises casting breakdowns via Arts Jobs or Equity information line. Rather than showreels, prefers to receive links to actors' websites by email. Offers Equity approved contracts through ITC. Actively encourages applications from disabled actors and promotes the use of inclusive casting.

"We usually recruit artists with an interest and proven experience in making theatre collaboratively, with an interdisciplinary approach. Being able to facilitate workshops is a very important requirement, and those with a background in arts therapy, social work, education or working with special needs, in addition to professional performance or visual arts training, are far more likely to be considered."

Jack Drum Arts

43/44 Gladstone Terrace, Sunniside,
Bishop Auckland, Co Durham DL13 4LS
email info@jackdrum.co.uk
website www.jackdrum.co.uk
Co-Directors Paddy Burton, Helen Ward, Julie Ward

Production details: Founded in 1986. "Delivers a strong programme of participatory arts for all sectors of the community." Normally tours 2 projects each year with an average annual total of 40 performances at up to 40 different venues. Venues include schools, arts centres, theatres, outdoor venues and community venues across the UK and abroad, with a focus on rural touring. In general 3-4 actors go on tour and play to audiences of pre-school age and upwards. Singing ability, proficiency with a musical instrument and a driving licence are required for some shows. Actors may also be expected to lead workshops. Recent productions include: 2 shows for young audiences created as part of Children & the Arts START scheme - *From Cinders to Tatters* and *Three Bears Out & About.*

Casting procedures: Accepts submissions (with CVs and photographs) from actors in the North East area only. "We like to know who is around in the North East, especially if based in County Durham. Can help access local networks and professional development." Offers Equity & non-Equity contracts. Rarely (or never) has the opportunity to cast disabled actors, but would be interested in developing projects which can make this possible. Particularly interested in actors who have BSL skills.

Kazzum

Oxford House, Derbyshire Street, London E2 6HG
tel 020-7749 1123
email info@kazzum.org
website www.kazzum.org
Artistic Director Daryl Beeton

Production details: Established in 1989. "We create playful theatre and participative arts activities for young people, using art forms that reflect diverse cultural influences." Stages 1-2 productions each year, with around 40-70 performances in 30 arts centres, theatres, and outdoor and community venues across the UK. In general 3 actors go on tour, playing to audiences aged 4-8 and 10+. Incoming actors should have singing, musical instrument, dance and physical theatre skills and may be expected to lead workshops. Recent productions include: *The Boy Who Grew Flowers*; *Hunt*; *The Sorcerer's Apprentice*; and *Beginning with Blobs.*

Casting procedures: Actors may write in January through to April to request inclusion. Casting breakdowns are available from the website, through Equity Job Information Service and Arts Jobs, and in *PCR*. Welcomes letters (with CVs and photographs) from individual actors previously unknown to the company, sent by post or email. Also accepts showreels and invitations to view individual actors' websites. Offers Equity-approved contracts as negotiated through ITC. Actively encourages applications from disabled actors, and promotes the use of inclusive casting.

Kinetic Theatre Company

Suite H, The Jubilee Centre, 10-12 Lombard Road, London SW19 3TZ
tel 020-8286 2613
email paul@kinetictheatre.co.uk
website www.kinetictheatre.co.uk
Artistic Director Graham Scott *Key personnel* Paul Dunn (Production Office Manager & Casting Director)

Production details: Established in 1988. One of the country's most prominent Theatre in Education companies. Performs plays geared to the National Curriculum for Science, to schools and theatres throughout the UK. Has 9 shows, 4 of which are on the road at any one time. All shows are self-contained musical comedies, all being very different in style. On average performs 12 tours every year with around 900 performances to 600 venues in England, Scotland,

Theatre

Wales and Northern Ireland. All shows are 2-handers, and actors play to audiences aged 5 to 12. Actors require reasonable singing and dancing skills and a driving licence is essential. Recent productions include: *The Hospital Force, Down to Earth, Lady Cecily's Sound Box,* and *Robin & the Withering Wood.*

Casting procedures: Does not hold general auditions; lets actors know when to write in, via the usual casting breakdown sites. Casting breakdowns are widely available: consult the website for full details. Contracts are based on Equity/ITC guidelines for small-scale touring. Will consider applications from actors with disabilities to play characters with disabilities. "We cast for our productions 3 times a year, usually around February, June and October, and we always put out castings for our workshop-style auditions. We cannot consider applications outside these times and due to limited space do not hold details on file. Please do not send unsolicited CVs/photos as it will just waste your money. We recommend that actors check the auditions page on our website for general information on when auditions are coming up, and also for more detailed information to prepare for our auditions."

Krazy Kat Theatre Company

173 Hartington Road, Brighton BN2 3PA
tel (01273) 692552 *fax* (01273) 692552
email krazykattheatre@ntlworld.com
website www.krazykattheatre.co.uk
Artistic Director Kinny Gardner

Production details: A children's theatre company founded in 1972, specialising in highly visual forms of theatre that are accessible to deaf children. Normally tours 4-6 projects each year with an average annual total of 150 performances and 75 venues. Venues include schools, arts centres, theatres, outdoor venues and community centres in Essex, Sussex, Kent and London. In general 2 actors go on tour and play to audiences aged 3-7. Singing ability, physical theatre skills, sign language and a driving licence are required. Actors may also be expected to lead workshops. Recent productions include: *Three Pigs, Jack & The Beanstalk,* and *The Very Magic Flute.*

Casting procedures: Sometimes holds general auditions; actors can write at any time requesting inclusion. Accepts submissions (with CVs and photographs) from actors previously unknown to the company if sent by post. Does not welcome unsolicited emails. Will also accept invitations to view individual actors' websites. Offers non-Equity contracts. Actively encourages applications from disabled actors and promotes the use of inclusive casting.

The London Bus Theatre Company

37 Chestnut Close, Hockley, Essex SS5 5EQ
tel (01208) 814514 *fax* (01208) 814514
email kathy@londonbustheatre.co.uk
website www.londonbustheatre.co.uk
Principal Chris Turner *Chair* Katherine Austen

Production details: One of the most respected theatre-in-education companies in the UK, supported by the National Theatre, Arts Council, National Lottery, police and private companies as well as the Home Office. Provides innovative workshops on the subjects of drugs, bullying, anti-social behaviour, alcohol, domestic abuse, job interview techniques and knife crime. Also provides schools and colleges with the celebrated 'Kick It – Bullying', 'Kick It – Smoking' and 'Kick It – Binge Drinking' DVD series. In 2008 the company produced the award-winning 'Nutter' anti-bullying DVD. Stages an average of 20 projects each year, with approximately 200 performances in 200 venues including leisure centres, colleges and youth detention centres all over England. In general 6 actors go on tour and play to audiences aged 8-18. Actors may be expected to lead workshops and should possess singing, dance, and physical theatre skills as well as holding a driving licence. Recent productions incude: *2 Smart* (Essex police/Essex FM tour of Essex theatres in 2008): and *Nutter* (tour of schools 2008, Arts Council project 2008).

Casting procedures: Holds general auditions and actors may write in at any time. Welcomes letters (with CVs and photographs) from individual actors previously unknown to the company, sent by post or email. Accepts showreels and will consider invitations to view individual actors' websites. Considers applications from disabled actors to play characters with disabilities.

Loudmouth Education & Training

The Friends' Institute, 220 Moseley Road, Highgate, Birmingham B12 0DG
tel 0121-446 4880 *fax* 0121-440 3940
email info@loudmouth.co.uk
website www.loudmouth.co.uk
Company Directors Chris Cowan, Eleanor Bryson
Operations Manager Caroline Bridges

Production details: Founded in 1994. Supplies interactive education and training programmes for young people on personal, social and health education issues, and accessible training for adults to aid personal and professional development. On average 4 teams of 2 actors tour 14 projects around 236 UK venues each year; venues include schools, community venues and youth centres. Actors are expected to lead workshops and must have a full driving licence. Recent productions include: *Trust Me* – an interactive theatre programme focusing on STIs, contraception and unplanned pregnancy.

Casting procedures: Holds general auditions. Welcomes letters with CVs and photographs from individual actors previously unknown to the company. Will accept unsolicited CVs and photographs sent by email. Does not welcome showreels or invitations to view individual actors' websites. Rarely or never has the opportunity to cast disabled actors.

M6 Theatre Company

Studio Theatre, Hamer County Primary School,
Albert Royds Street, Rochdale OL16 2SU
tel (01706) 355898 *fax* (01706) 712601
email info@m6theatre.co.uk
website www.m6theatre.co.uk
Artistic Producer Dorothy Wood *General Manager*
Deborah Palmer

Production details: M6 Theatre Company specalises
in producing and touring high-quality, accessible and
emotionally engaging theatre for young audiences.
Founded in 1977, the company tours 3-5 productions
each year, through approximately 300 performances /
workshops. Touring venues include theatres, schools,
festivals, prisons and early years settings across the
North West and nationally. Cast sizes are generally 2-
4; actors may be expected to participate in workshops
accompanying productions. Recent productions have
included: *Best Friends* for audiences aged 4+ (an
imaginative fusion of dance, theatre and original
music in collaboration with Ludus Dance Company);
Family Business for audiences aged 13+ (exploring
parent / child relationships and intergenerational
offending); and *One Little Word* (a sensitive and
moving production for children aged 3+ exploring
friendship and conflict resolution, underscored with
original music and with only one spoken word). Also
delivers a wide-ranging participatory programme
with local young people.

Casting procedures: Accepts submissions (with CVs
and photographs) from actors previously unknown
to the company. Unfortunately the company is
unable to return photos. Actor contracts are ITC /
Equity approved.

Magic Carpet Theatre

18 Church Street, Sutton on Hull,
East Yorkshire HU7 4TS
tel (01682) 709539 *fax* (01682) 787362
email jon@magiccarpettheatre.com
website www.magiccarpettheatre.com
Artistic Director Jon Marshall *Company Manager*
Steve Collison

Production details: Professional young children's
theatre company presenting shows and workshops in
the UK and abroad. Tours 3-4 productions annually,
with around 250 performances in 250 venues
including schools, arts and community venues, and
festivals. In general 3 actors go on tour, playing to
audiences aged 5-11. Actors may be expected to lead
workshops. Recent productions include: *The Wizard
of Castle Magic*; *Magic Circus*.

Casting procedures: Does not hold general
auditions; actors may write in the autumn to request
inclusion. Advises actors to "ring us rather than
sending CVs, etc., to see when we are casting".

MakeBelieve Arts

The Deptford Mission, 1 Creek Road,
London SE8 3BT

tel 020-8691 3803 *fax* 020-8691 3880
email info@makebelievearts.co.uk
website www.makebelievearts.co.uk
Artistic Director Trisha Lee *Creative Projects Co-
ordinator* Alice Edwards *Company Adminsitrator*
Pippa Taylor

Production details: Established in 2002 and gained
charitable status in 2006. A leading provider of high-
quality arts and education programmes, for
Foundation Stage, Primary and Secondary School
pupils and their parents and teachers. Based in South
London but works in other boroughs. In general 4-6
actors stage 1 project a year, with around 50
performances at 40 schools. Skills required depend on
the production, and actors may be asked to lead
workshops. Recent productions include: *The Woman
Who Cooked Everything*, and *Gulliver's Travels*.

Casting procedures: Holds general auditions. Casting
breakdowns are available from the website and in
PCR and *The Stage*. Welcomes letters (with CVs and
photographs) from individual actors previously
unknown to the company, sent by post or email.
Does not however accept showreels or invitations to
view individual actors' websites. Offers Equity-
approved contracts negotiated through ITC. Rarely
has the opportunity to cast disabled actors.

Moby Duck

12 Reservoir Retreat, Birmingham B16 9EH
tel/fax 0121-242 0400
email info@moby-duck.org
website www.moby-duck.org
Artistic Director Guy Hutchins

Production details: Founded in 1999. Performs 2
projects annually, with more than 50 performances at
the same number of schools, arts centres, theatres
and community venues across all regions. In general
3-4 actors go on tour, playing to audiences aged 4 to
80. Requires actors to have "an understanding of the
other cultures we work in". Actors may be expected
to lead workshops. Singing, musical instrument,
dance and physical theatre skills are an advantage,
and actors should hold a clean driving licence. For
details of recent productions, see the website.

Casting procedures: Sometimes holds general
auditions, and actors may write at any time to request
inclusion. Welcomes letters (with CVs and
photographs) from individual actors previously
unknown to the company, sent by post or email. Also
welcomes showreels and invitations to view
individual actors' websites. Offers Equity-approved
contracts as negotiated through ITC. Rarely or never
has the opportunity to cast disabled actors.

Monster Theatre Productions Ltd

Buddle Arts Centre, 258B Station Road, Wallsend,
Tyne & Wear NE28 8RG
tel 0191-240 4011 *fax* 0191-240 4016
email info@monsterproductions.co.uk
website www.monsterproductions.co.uk

Theatre

Artistic Directors Chris Speyer, Ieuan Einion
Operations Manager Doreen Ford

Production details: Set up in 2000 to continue the work for children under 7 begun by the directors at Northern Stage. Creates new music theatre for young children and runs a youth theatre programme for North Tyneside. Normally tours 2 projects each year with an average annual total of 150 performances and 30 different venues. Venues include schools, arts centres, theatres and community venues across the UK, Wales and Ireland. In general 3-5 actors go on tour and play mainly to audiences under 7 years old. Actors may also be expected to lead workshops. Recent productions include: *The Terrible Grump* and *Trouble Under Foot* (both for under-7s); and *Street of Strangers* for young people and adults.

Casting procedures: Sometimes holds general auditions; actors should write requesting inclusion when advertised in *PCR*. Accepts submissions (with CVs and photographs) from actors previously unknown to the company if sent by post. Does not welcome unsolicited emails. Will also accept invitations to view individual actors' websites. "Due to our scale of work we only employ a small number of actors each year. We favour multiracial casts to reflect our audiences. Musical and movement skills are a great advantage."

Newfound Theatre Company

mobile (07753) 237209
email newfoundtheatre@gmail.com
website www.newfoundtheatre.co.uk

Production details: Theatre in Education company touring/performing several projects each year, with around 200 performances annually to schools in London and the North West. In general, 3 actors go on tour playing to audiences aged 5 to 16. Actors are sometimes expected to lead workshops. Recent productions include: *Making Monologues*, *Rewind*, and *Thinspiration*.

Casting procedures: Uses in-house casting directors; does not hold general auditions. Casting breakdowns are available via Casting Call Pro. Welcomes unsolicited CVs and photographs from actors previously unknown to the company if sent by email; also accepts invitations to view individual actors' websites. Encourages applications from disabled actors and promotes the use of inclusive casting.

Nimble Fish

30 Wilton Square, London N1 3DW
mobile (07939) 522518
email getnimble@nimble-fish.co.uk
website www.nimble-fish.co.uk
Directors Samatha Holdsworth, Greg Klerkx

Production details: "An evolving collective of creative individuals who actively pursue collaborations with disadvantaged communities to foster positive social change." Performs 1 project

annually with around 13 peformances in 14 venues, including schools, outdoor and community venues, and other site-specific venues in London, the South East and Edinburgh. Around 3-6 actors go on tour performing to adult audiences. Actors may be expected to lead workshops. Recent productions include: *The Container* (winner of a 2007 Edinburgh Fringe First and a 2007 Amnesty International Freedom of Expression Award), and *Einstein's Dreams*. Current productions in development include: *The Trial of Wernher von Braun*.

Casting procedures: Sometimes holds general auditions. Does not welcome unsolicited approaches from individuals not previously known to the company. Offers Equity-approved contracts via ITC. Actively encourages applicatinos from disabled actors and promotes the use of inclusive casting.

Nottingham Playhouse Roundabout TIE

Nottingham Playhouse, Wellington Circus, Nottingham NG1 5AF
tel 0115-947 4361 *fax* 0115-947 5759
email andrewb@nottinghamplayhouse.co.uk
website www.nottinghamplayhouse.co.uk
Director Roundabout & Education Andrew Breakwell
Administrator Roundabout & Education Kitty Parker

Production details: Established in 1973. Has toured plays for schools and young people locally, nationally and internationally for the last 36 years. In that time hundreds of thousands of children, young people, parents and teachers have seen the company's work. Its policy is to encourage new writing, and Roundabout has "an enviable record" of adding to its repertoire of work. The company is now part of a much larger Theatre Education department of the Playhouse, and last year it offered 18 different programme strands to more than 14,000 people in over 600 different sessions.

Usually stages 4 new pieces of work each year, with 180-200 performances in over 100 schools, arts centres and small theatres in the East Midlands, East Anglia, and London. In general 3-4 actors go on tour, playing to audiences aged 4-18. It would be useful for incoming actors to have singing and musical instrument skills and a driving licence; BSL and/or Makaton desirable. Actors may be required to lead workshops. Recent productions include: *The Whale's Tooth* (for young people with profound and multiple learning difficulties); *Can You Whistle, Johanna?* (for 8-11 year olds; a new play about 2 boys who 'adopt' a grandfather); and *The Little Mermaid* (for 4-8 year olds).

Casting procedures: Holds general auditions, and actors may write in spring/summer to request inclusion. Casting is conducted by Playhouse Casting Director Sooki McShane when specific skills/types are required. Welcomes letters (with CVs and photographs) from individual actors previously unknown to the company, sent by post only. Will see shows when in the area. Offers Equity-approved contracts as negotiated through TMA. Encourages enquiries from actors with disabilities, and promotes the use of inclusive casting. "We welcome mature (in every sense of the word) actors for our work with young people, and candidates should be ready for a 'life on the road' with very early mornings and the 'dinner ladies'! A genuine liking of children and young people helps. In auditions I ask actors to prepare a text, chosen by myself, which we then work on together. I would expect to spend around 40 minutes with each person."

Oily Cart Company

Smallwood School Annexe, Smallwood Road, London SW17 OTW
tel 020-8672 6329 *fax* 020-8672 0792
email oilies@oilycart.org.uk
website www.oilycart.org.uk
Artistic Director Tim Webb *General Manager* Kathy Everett *Administrator* Sarah Crompton

Production details: One of the leading theatre companies in the UK, creating highly interactive multi-sensory performances for the very young (6 months to 6 years) and for young people (aged 3-19) with Profound or Multiple Learning Disabilities (PMLD) or an Autistic Spectrum Disorder (ASD). Tours national and international venues like theatres and arts centres with early years shows, and takes its special needs work to special schools around the UK. Recent productions include: *Baby Balloon* for audiences aged 6 months to 2 years; *If All The World Were Paper*; *Blue*; and *Pool Piece* – an interactive hydrotherapy pool show for young people with PMLD or ASD.

Casting procedures: Casting breakdowns are available on the website **www.oilycart.org.uk** and the Artsjobs website **www.artscouncil.org.uk/pressnews/mailinglists.php**. Offers ITC/Equity approved contracts. Actively encourages applications from disabled actors and promotes the use of inclusive casting.

Onatti Productions Ltd

9 Field Close, Warwick, Warwickshire CV34 4QD
tel (01926) 495220 *fax* 0870-164 3629
email info@onatti.co.uk
website www.onatti.co.uk

Produces foreign-language productions performed at Primary and Secondary schools throughout the UK, France and Spain. Plays are produced in French, German, Spanish and English; all are written by the company and used as an exciting way of promoting and enhancing languages in schools. Onatti produces around 8 tours each year. Employs native foreign actors for contracts from 3 to 10 months. Actors are sourced from the UK and Europe..

Passe-Partout

13 Stanford Avenue, Brighton BN1 6AD
tel (01273) 557595

email p@sse-partout.com
Artistic Director Michele Young *Manager* Richard Crane

Production details: Founded in 1986. "Theatre for social change – assisting people to have a voice about an issue which concerns them." Normally tours 3 projects each year, with an average annual total of 20 performances and 20 different venues including schools, outdoor centres, community venues and office spaces in the UK and abroad. In general 4 actors go on tour and play to audiences of all ages. Any additional skills that actors may have will be put to use. Actors may also be expected to lead workshops. Recent projects include: *Anti-bullying Strategy Development* (prisons, UK); *Social Capital* (various schools, Europe); *Street Children* (Nairobi, Kenya); *Bio-diversity* (Toulouse, France); and *Silkworm Journey* (France). Has an alliance with Inedit Films to produce 3-minute dramas (fact-based) for educational purposes.

Casting procedures: "We cast from the group of people who have proposed an issue they want to take forward. We sometimes build-in 1 or 2 people from outside that group who have interest and energy."

Pied Piper Theatre Company

1 Lilian Place, Coxcombe Lane, Chiddingfold GU8 4QA
tel (01428) 684022 *fax* (01428) 684022
email twpiedpiper@aol.com
website www.piedpipertheatre.co.uk
Artistic Director Tina Williams *Associate Director* Nicola Sangster

Production details: Founded in 1984, Pied Piper has toured nationally and internationally. Currently project-funded by Arts Council South East and Sure Start, the company is now concentrating on new writing for the age range 3-7. Combination of school and theatre touring.

Casting procedures: Holds general auditions; actors requesting inclusion should write during the summer. Casting breakdowns are available through Equity Job Information Service. "Actors must be happy to tour. Most music is live. Must have a passion for children/young people's theatre." Offers ITC/Equity approved contracts.

Pilot Theatre

York Theatre Royal, St Leonard's Place, York YO1 7HD
tel (01904) 635755
email info@pilot-theatre.com
website www.pilot-theatre.com
Artistic Director Marcus Romer

Production details: A national midscale touring company producing a programme of education resources for young people. Stages on average 3-6 projects annually, with 150 performances in 20 arts centres and theatres across the UK. In general 6-10

Theatre

actors go on tour, playing to audiences aged 11-25. Actors are sometimes expected to lead workshops.

Casting procedures: Actors may write in May and August to request inclusion. Casting breakdowns are available on the website or via Spotlight. Welcomes unsolicited CVs and photographs if submitted by email. Also accepts showreels and will consider invitations to view individual actors' websites. Offers Equity-approved contracts as negotiated through TMA/ITC. Actively encourages applications by disabled actors and promotes the use of inclusive casting.

The Play House

Longmore Street, Birmingham B12 9ED
tel 0121-464 5712 *fax* 0121-464 5713
email info@theplayhouse.org.uk
website www.theplayhouse.org.uk
Artistic Director Deborah Hull *Chief Executive* Gary Roskell

Production details: Established in 1986. An educational theatre charity that creates opportunites for young people to explore and make sense of the world they live in. Best known for its *Language Alive!* theatre-in-education tours, which bring the curriculum to life, and *Catalyst*, which uses theatre and drama to explore real-life issues and dilemmas. Tours an average of 15-20 projects annually, with around 1000 performances in 60-70 schools, outdoor and other venues in the West Midlands. In general 2-3 actors go on tour, performing to young audiences aged 0-18. Skills required vary according to the project and a clean driving licence is required. Actors may be expected to lead workshops.

Casting procedures: Sometimes holds general auditions; actors should write in when these are advertised. Rarely or never has the opportunity to cast disabled actors.

Playtime Theatre Company

18 Bennell's Avenue, Whitstable, Kent CT5 2HP
tel (01227) 266272 *fax* (01227) 266648
email Playtime@dircon.co.uk
website www.playtimetheatre.co.uk
Artistic Director Nicholas Champion *Administrator* Sara Kettlewell

Production details: Established in 1983 with the aim of bringing imaginative and innovative professional theatre to children and young people. Has grown to become "one of the leading children's theatre companies in the South East", and tours both nationally and internationally. Normally tours 2-4 projects each year with an average annual total of 200 performances and 190 venues. Venues include schools, arts centres, theatres, community venues and festivals. Tours have covered the South East, Yorkshire and Humberside and various countries in Europe and the Middle East. In general 2-4 actors go on tour and play to targeted audiences of 5-7, 4-11,

7-11 and 9-13. Actors are expected to offer 1-2 additional skills. Singing ability, proficiency with a musical instrument, physical theatre, puppetry and mime skills and a driving licence are all useful. Actors may also be expected to lead workshops. Recent productions include: *A Tale O' Two*, an adaptation of *The Canterbury Tales*; *Secrets*, a fairy-tale; *Big Red*, an environmental play; and *The Wish*, a traditional-type tale. All have audience participation.

Casting procedures: Holds general auditions; actors should write in August requesting inclusion. Casting breakdowns are available through the website, postal application (with sae), Equity Job Information Service, *PCR*, *The Stage* and Castcall (see entry under *The Spotlight, casting directories and information services* on page 367). Welcomes submissions (with CVs and photographs) from actors previously unknown to the company sent by post or email. Also accepts showreels and invitations to view individual actors' websites (if actor is shown performing). Advises actors to: "Be truthful. Tell us about the things that make you stand out. Tell us briefly why you want to work in children's theatre and why you like touring. Seriously consider the implications of living away from your base for months on end!" Offers non-Equity contracts. Will consider applications from disabled actors to play characters with disabilities.

Polka Theatre

240 The Broadway, Wimbledon, London SW19 1SB
tel 020-8545 8320 *fax* 020-8545 8365
email info@polkatheatre.com, casting@polkatheatre.com
website www.polkatheatre.com
Artistic Director Jonathan Lloyd *Associate Director* Roman Stefanski

Production details: Established in 1979. A theatre for children aged 0 to 13. 6 productions staged annually with 700-800 performances per year. The following skills are required from actors: singing, musical instruments, dance, puppetry and physical theatre. Offers TMA/Equity contracts.

Casting procedures: Casting breakdowns sometimes available via *SBS*. Actors are invited for specific shows. Accepts submissions (with CVs and photographs) from actors previously unknown to the company if sent by post, but not by email. Showreels and invitations to view individual actors' websites are also accepted. Actively encourages applications from disabled actors and promotes the use of inclusive casting. "Find out in advance what we're doing, come and visit Polka and see the work."

Pop-Up Theatre

27A Brewery Road, London N7 9PU
tel 020-7609 3339 *fax* 020-7609 2284
email admin@pop-up.net
website www.pop-up.net

Artistic Director Michael Dalton *Theatre & Administration Manager* Clare Knights

Production details: Founded in 1982. Produces and tours theatre for young people to an annual audience of more than 25,000 across theatres, arts centres, schools and nurseries both in the UK and overseas. Normally tours 3 projects each year, with an average annual total of 150 performances at 75 different venues. In general 2-4 actors go on tour and play to audiences aged under 11.

Casting procedures: Accepts submissions (with CVs and photographs) from actors previously unknown to the company sent by post or email. Also accepts invitations to view individual actors' websites. Offers ITC\Equity-approved contracts. Actively encourages applications from disabled actors and promotes the use of inclusive casting.

Q20 Theatre

19 Wellington Crescent, Shipley,
West Yorks BD18 3PH
Artistic Director John Lambert *Administrators* David Smith, Gillie Kerrod

Production details: Normally tours 10 projects each year with an average annual total of 350 performances. Venues include outdoor venues, corporate workspaces and shopping centres in the North East, Yorkshire and Cambridge. In general 2 actors go on tour and play to audiences of all ages. Singing ability and dance/physical theatre skills are required. Recent productions include: *Pirate Pranks* at Wakefield Shopping Centre; *Metro Gnomes* at Metrocentre.

Casting procedures: Sometimes holds general auditions; actors should write in May or October to request inclusion. Accepts submissions (with CVs and photographs) from actors previously unknown to the company only if sent by post. Does not welcome unsolicited emails. Will also accept invitations to view individual actors' websites.

Quantum Theatre

The Old Button Factory, 1-11 Bannockburn Road,
Plumstead SE18 1ET
tel/fax 020-8317 9000
email office@quantumtheatre.co.uk
website www.quantumtheatre.co.uk
Artistic Directors Michael Whitmore, Jessica Selous *Administrator* Gideon Escott *Production Manager* Rachel Hogden

Established in 1993. 15 productions performed annually. National touring productions visit schools, arts centres, theatres and outdoor venues. Casting breakdowns available. Holds general auditions. Accepts submissions (with CVs and photographs) from actors previously unknown to the company if sent by post, but not by email. Showreels, voicereels and invitations to view individual actors' websites are also accepted. Offers TMA/Equity approved contracts.

Quicksilver Theatre

The New Diorama Theatre, 15-16 Triton Street,
Regents Place, London NW1 3BF
tel 020-7241 2942 *fax* 020-7254 3119
email talktous@quicksilvertheatre.org
website www.quicksilvertheatre.org
Artistic Directors Guy Holland, Carey English

Production details: Founded in 1977, Quicksilver, since 2008, produces 1 new production every 2 years, which is presented at a London venue as well as at partner venues around the UK, mostly small and middle-scale. Cast numbers change from production to production and vary between 1 and 5. Most of the work is aimed at young audiences, and skills required from actors varies depending on need; can include the playing of musical instruments, singing, puppeteering and dance. Actors may also be expected to lead workshops, as Quicksilver has in recent years expanded its artistic and education projects involving participation by children. Recent productons include: *Winter's Tale* (2007, adapted by None Shepphard); *Water Colours* (2007); *Primary Voices* (2007 and 2009, a playwriting project with children and professional actors; and *Ladidada* (2008 and 2010, a co-production between Quicksilver and Indefinite Articles).

Casting procedures: Casting breakdowns are available though the website, postal application (with sae), *PCR* and advertisements in *The Stage*. Accepts submissions (with CVs and photographs) from actors previously unknown to the company sent by post or email. Will also accept showreels and invitations to view individual actors' websites.

Replay Productions

Old Museum Arts Centre, 7 College Square North,
Belfast BT1 6AR
tel 028-9032 2773 *fax* 028-9032 2724
email info@replaytheatreco.org
website www.replaytheatreco.org
Artistic Director David Fenton *Administrator* Ali Fitzgibbon *Development Manager* Eimear Henry *Operations Manager* Fiona Bell

Production details: "Founded in 1988, Replay aims to produce high-quality theatre and related activities that entertain, educate and stimulate children and young people." Normally tours 3 projects each year with an average annual total of 100 performances. Venues include schools, arts centres, theatres and community venues in Northern Ireland and occasionally the Republic of Ireland. In general 4 actors go on tour and play to audiences aged 3-18. Recent productions include: *Macbeth*, a site-specific production at the Crumlin Road Gaol; and *New Kid* by Dennis Foon for 8-11 year olds.

Casting procedures: Sometimes holds general auditions; casting breakdowns are available through the news section of the website. Accepts submissions (with CVs and photographs) from actors previously unknown to the company sent by post or email. Will also accept invitations to view individual actors' websites.

Scene Productions

14 Curl Way, Wokingham, Berks RG41 2TJ
tel/fax (01483) 821005
email info@sceneproductions.co.uk
website www.sceneproductions.co.uk
Artistic Directors Katharine Hurst, Kelly Taylor-Smith

Production details: Founded in 2004. Specialises in exploring new and imaginative ways of examining political contexts and social relationships, using storytelling, audience interaction, mime, puppetry and multimedia. Stages 2 projects annually, with around 80 performances in the same number of schools, arts centres and theatres. In general 3-4 actors go on tour, playing to audiences aged 17+. Requires singing and physical theatre skills from incoming actors, who should hold a driving licence and may be asked to lead workshops. "You should be a good all-rounder who can cope with the pressures of small-scale touring." Recent productions include: *Fear & Misery of the Third Reich*, *The Threepenny Opera*, *The Good Person of Szechwan* (all by Brecht); *The Other Side*, a devised production which premiered at the 2009 Edinburgh Festival.

Casting procedures: Sometimes holds general auditions and actors may write in May to request inclusion. Welcomes letters (with CVs & photographs) from actors previously unknown to the company, sent by post or email. Does not accept showreels, but will consider invitations to view individual actors' websites. Rarely (or never) has the opportunity to cast disabled actors.

Shakespeare 4 Kidz

Drewshearne Barn, Crowhurst Lane End, Oxted, Surrey RH8 9NT
tel (01342) 894548 *fax* (01342) 893754
email office@shakespeare4kidz.com
website www.shakespeare4kidz.com
Producer & Director Julian Chenery *Producer* Carolyn Chenery

Production details: Founded in 1997. "Recognised as the national Shakespeare company for children and young people, it has pioneered its Music Theatre & Shakespeare and Creative Shakespeare Education Programme both in the UK and abroad." Normally tours 2 projects each year with an average annual total of 230 performances across 60 different theatres; now tours internationally from March to June. In general 13 actors go on tour and play to audiences aged 8 upwards. Singing ability and dance/physical theatre skills are required; marketing skills are also advantageous. Recent productions include: *S4K's Romeo and Juliet*; *S4K's Hamlet*; *S4K's A Midsummer Night's Dream*; and *S4K's Macbeth*.

Casting procedures: Holds general auditions; actors should write in March requesting inclusion. Casting

breakdowns are available through the website, *PCR* and *The Stage*. Accepts submissions (with CVs and photographs) from actors previously unknown to the company sent by post or email. Will also accept showreels and invitations to view individual actors' websites.

Sixth Sense Theatre for Young People

c/o The Wyvern Theatre, Theatre Square, Swindon SN1 1QN
tel (01793) 614864 *fax* (01793) 616715
email sstc@dircon.co.uk
website www.sixthsensetyp.co.uk
Artistic Director Benedict Eccles *General Manager* Mervyn Heard

Production details: Founded in 1986. Tours to schools and small-scale venues in the South and South West. Receives funding from Swindon Borough Council and Arts Council England, South West and has an "excellent reputation in the region". Normally tours 3 projects each year with an average annual total of 150 performances across 90 venues. Venues include schools, arts centres and community venues. In general 3-5 actors go on tour and play to audiences aged 5-18. Singing ability, proficiency with a musical instrument, dance skills and a driving licence may be required. Actors are usually expected to lead workshops. Recent productions include: *The Rime of the Ancient Mariner* (for 7-11 year olds), and *Sk8 Angel* (co-pro with Greenwich and Lewisham Young People's Theatre for 12-16 year olds).

Casting procedures: Accepts submissions (with CVs and photographs) from actors previously unknown to the company sent by post or email. Will also accept invitations to view individual actors' websites. Issues ITC/Equity contracts for 5- to 10-week tours. "Happy to receive actors' details but can't always respond. Please don't chase us; if we're interested we'll contact you."

Solomon Theatre Company

Penny Black, High Street, Damerham, Fordingbridge, Hants SP6 3EU
tel (01725) 518670
email office@solomon-theatre.co.uk
website www.solomontheatre.co.uk
Artistic Director Mark Hyde *Managing Director* Forest Paget *Marketing Manager* Jo Coleman *Administrator* Gail Newell

Production details: Founded in 2003. Specialises in communicating messages that result in crime reduction, improved community safety and the promotion of healthy schools and healthy lifestyles. Has performed award-winning plays to tens of thousands of people in schools and community locations across the country, as well as producing films and support material for national programmes. Performs around 7 projects annually in more than 300 venues, including schools, theatres and community venues in the South West, South East, Midlands, Wales and Northern Ireland. On average 12 actors go on tour, performing to audiences aged 12-16 to over 60. Actors must have a driving licence and may be required to lead workshops. Recent projects include: *Last Orders* (alcohol education); *Trickster* (burglary education); *Gemma's Wardrobe* (drugs education); and *Power of Love* (domestic violence education).

Casting procedures: Holds general auditions; actors may write in July, November and April to request inclusion. Welcomes letters (with CVs and photographs) from actors previously unknown to the company sent by post or email. Also welcomes showreels and invitations to view individual actors' websites. Does not offer Equity-approved contracts but does offer Equity rates. Will consider applications from disabled actors to play characters with disabilities.

Spare Tyre Theatre Company

Unit 3.22, Canterbury Court, 1-3 Brixton Road, London SW9 6DE
tel/fax 020-7061 6454
email info@sparetyre.org
website www.sparetyre.org
Artistic Director Arti Prashar *General Manager* Bonnie Mitchell *Administrator* Vicky Tweedie

Production details: The company has 3 principal strands of work:

• Work with elders: the 'HotPots' are a group of people over 60 who perform work, often from personal experience and using humour, about the treatment of elders. They are committed to educating audiences about the potential of older people.
• Work with people with learning disabilities: the 'inc.Theatre' course is a full-time, OCN (Open College Network) approved partnership with Redbridge College for people of all ages with learning disabilities.
• Work with schools: professional TIE productions for school pupils tackling homophobia in schools. Also: 'Dealing with Difference', a workshop for school staff which looks at approaches to tackling homophobia within schools.

Each strand of work has 1 major production a year, touring to roughly 100 venues – from schools, theatres and community venues to hospitals, GP surgeries, residential homes, special needs schools and public sector venues. Primarily covers the London area, but also Yorkshire, Manchester, Kent and Wales. Skills required from actors include (ideally) a driving licence, but also workshop-leading and facilitation skills, experience of working with community groups, and a sensitivity to, and understanding of, relevant issues.

Casting procedures: Casting breakdowns are published in *The Stage* and on the website. Unsolicited approaches at other times – including CVs, showreels and invitations to view individuals' websites – are discouraged. Offers ITC/Equity approved contracts. Actively encourages applications from disabled actors and promotes the use of inclusive casting.

Splendid Productions

1 Lownes Courtyard, Boone Street, London SE13 5TB
tel 020-8318 6469 *fax* 0871-750 2166
email info@splendidproductions.co.uk
website www.splendidproductions.co.uk
Artistic Director Kerry Frampton

Production details: Founded in 2003. A theatre company and an education company creating "challenging, vibrant theatre for young people". Also provides expert training in all areas of drama, from Practitioner theory to Presentation skills. In the last 7 years the company has gained an excellent reputation for the inventiveness of its performances and the clarity of its teaching. Tours 1 main project per year (September through to March), staging on average 100 performances in 100 venues across England and Wales, including schools, arts centres and theatres (always attached to schools or colleges). 3 actors go on tour, playing to audiences aged 13 years and beyond. Actors require singing skills, strong physicality and a driving licence; workshop-leading experience is desirable. Recent productions include: *The Trial*; *Dr Faustus*; *Woyzeck*; *Good Woman of Szechuan*; *Antigone*; *Animal Farm*; and *The Resistible Rise of Arturo Ui*.

Casting procedures: Does not hold general auditions. Actors may write during April-June to request inclusion. Welcomes letters (with CVs & photographs) from actors previously unknown to the company, sent by post or email. Does not accept showreels but is happy to receive links to individual actors' websites. Will consider applications from disabled actors to play characters with disabilities. "We work hard and are very passionate about working with young people. You need to be flexible, approachable and keen to create good theatre in education. Look at our website to see what we do before getting in touch."

StopWatch Theatre Company

Unit 318 Solent Business Centre, Millbrook Road West, Southampton SO15 0HW
tel 023-8078 3800
email info@stopwatchtheatre.com
website www.stopwatchtheatre.com
Artistic Director Adrian New

Production details: Established in 1990. A theatre-in-education company specialising in safety and health programmes. Stages 6 productions annually, with around 800 performances in 700 schools UK-wide. In general 4 actors go on tour, playing to audiences aged 5-16. Actors are expected to lead workshops, and driving is an advantage but not essential. Recent

Theatre

productions include: *Chicken!*, *Arson About*, *Footsteps the Movie*, and *The Road Race*.

Casting procedures: Holds general auditions; actors may write in June and October to request inclusion. Casting breakdowns are available from Equity Job Information Service and Casting Call Pro, and in *PCR*. Welcomes letters (with CVs and photographs) from individual actors previously unknown to the company, sent by post or email, and will consider invitations to view individual actors' websites. Rarely, or never, has the opportunity to cast actors with disabilities. "We always look favourably on those who have done some research and are evidently committed to working in quality theatre-in-education."

The Take Away Theatre Company

10 Millbank Street, Dalrymple, Ayrshire KA6 6FE
tel 0800-158 3840
email admin@takeawaytheatre.co.uk
website www.takeawaytheatre.co.uk
Artistic Director Lee O'Driscoll

Production details: Founded in 2007. A theatre-in-education company delivering "high-impact and dynamic drama projects in schools and other venues throughout the UK". Tours 9 projects annually with 270 performances at schools, arts centres, theatres and community venues. In general 4 actors go on tour, playing to audiences aged 1 to 101. Actors may be expected to lead workshops and should hold a current driving licence; singing, musical instrument, dance and physical theatre skills are an advantage. Recent productions include: *The Jungle Book*, *Scotland (an' a' that)*, *The Wind in the Willows*, and *Hansel & Gretel*.

Casting procedures: Sometimes holds general auditions; actors may write at any time to request inclusion. Casting breakdowns are available via the website, by postal application (with sae), and from Casting Call Pro and CastNet Ltd. Welcomes letters (with CVs and photographs) from individual actors previously unknown to the company, sent by post or email. Also accepts showreels and invitations to view individual actors' websites. Will consider applications from disabled actors to play characters with disabilities.

Ten Ten Theatre

PO Box 49063, New Southgate, London N11 1YU
tel 0845-388 3162 *fax* 0845-388 3167
email office@tententheatre.co.uk and
casting@tententheatre.co.uk
website www.tententheatre.co.uk
Artistic Director Martin O'Brien

Production details: Established in 2006. Specialises in young people's theatre in primary schools, secondary schools, young offender institutions and the local community. Stages 4-6 productions annually with around 400 performances in 200 schools, arts

centres, theatres and community venues across England, Scotland and Wales. In general 2-4 actors go on tour, playing to audiences aged 5 to 21. Actors may be expected to lead workshops. Recent productions include: a six-month tour of secondary schools with 3 separate plays; and a one-week residency at Feltham Young Offender Institution.

Casting procedures: Does not hold general auditions; actors may write at any time to request inclusion. Casting breakdowns are available from the website or via Equity Job Information Service, *PCR* and Spotlight. Welcomes letters (with CVs and photographs) from individual actors previously unknown to the company, sent by post or email, and will accept showreels and invitations to view individual actors' websites. Offers Equity-approved contracts as negotiated through ITC. Will consider applications from disabled actors to play characters with disabilities. "Please view our website to look at our projects and ethos before sending details."

Theatr Iolo

The Old School Building, Cefn Road,
Cardiff CF14 3HS
tel 029-2061 3782 *fax* 029-2052 2225
email admin@theatriolo.com
website www.theatriolo.com
Artistic Director Kevin Lewis *Administrative Director* Wendy York

Production details: "Formed in 1987, Theatr Iolo aims to produce and programme the best of live theatre, making it widely accessible to children and young people in Cardiff and the Vale of Glamorgan to stir the imagination, inspire the heart and challenge the mind. Theatr Iolo works alongside teachers and advisers to enhance teaching and learning across the curriculum." Normally tours 5 projects each year with an average annual total of 150 performances across 120 venues. Venues include schools, arts centres and theatres in Wales and occasionally England, and international festivals. Cast sizes vary, playing to audiences aged 3-18. Singing ability, proficiency with a musical instrument, dance/ physical theatre skills and a driving licence are frequently required. Actors may also be expected to lead workshops. Recent productions include: *Grimm Tales* by Carol Ann Dufy, *Lenny* by Francis Monty (trans. Paul Harman), and *Under the Carpet* by Sarah Argent.

Casting procedures: Sometimes holds general auditions; actors should write in June requesting inclusion. Casting breakdowns are available through Equity Job Information Service. Accepts submissions (with CVs and photographs) from actors previously unknown to the company if sent by post. Emails are also welcome, as long as the file is not too big. Offers ITC/Equity approved contracts. Actively encourages applications from disabled actors and promotes the use of inclusive casting.

Theatr Na N'Og

Unit 3, Millands Road Industrial Estate,
Neath SA11 1NJ
tel (01639) 641771 *fax* (01639) 647941
email drama@theatr-nanog.co.uk
website www.theatr-nanog.co.uk
Artistic Director Geinor Styles *Administrator* Janet
Huxtable *Education Officer* Rachel Lloyd *Outreach
Officer* Samantha Timmins *Production & Touring
Manager* Ceri James

Production details: "The company has been
producing high-quality original theatre for young
people for more than 25 years. We provide a first-
class Theatre in Education service to schools in 3
county boroughs, and tour to general audiences in
venues across the UK." Normally tours 3 projects
each year with an average annual total of 200
performances. In general 3 actors go on tour. Singing
ability is required and actors may also be expected to
lead workshops.

Casting procedures: Holds general auditions; actors
may write at any time requesting inclusion. Accepts
submissions (with CVs and photographs) from actors
previously unknown to the company sent by post or
email. Will also accept invitations to view individual
actors' websites. "Please learn to spell the names of
the company's personnel properly!"

Theatr Powys

The Drama Centre, Tremont Road,
Llandrinod Wells, Powys LD1 5EB
tel (01597) 824444 *fax* (01597) 824381
email theatr.powys@powys.gov.uk
website www.theatrpowys.co.uk
Artistic Director Ian Yeoman *General Manager* Nikki
Leopold

Production details: Founded in 1976. Has an average
annual total of 250 performances across 150 different
venues. Venues include schools, arts centres, theatres
and community venues across Wales. Recent
productions include: *The Giant's Embrace*, *Gafael y
Cawr* and *Angel*.

Casting procedures: Holds general auditions; actors
may write at any time requesting inclusion. Casting
breakdowns are available through postal application
(with sae), Equity Job Information Service, *PCR* and
advertisements in *The Stage*. Accepts submissions
(with CVs and photographs) from actors previously
unknown to the company sent by post or email. Will
also accept invitations to view individual actors'
websites. Offers TMA/Equity contracts and does not
subscribe to the Equity Pension Scheme. Actively
encourages applications from disabled actors and
promotes the use of inclusive casting.

Theatre-Rites

Unit EH612, Erlang House, 128 Blackfriars Road,
London SE1 8EQ
tel 020-7928 4875 *fax* 020-7928 4347

email info@theatre-rites.co.uk
website www.theatre-rites.co.uk
Artistic Director Sue Buckmaster *Executive Producer*
Claire Templeton *Project Manager* John Johnston
Administrator Roisin Caffrey

Production details: Committed to creating
challenging productions which push the boundaries
of theatrical form by experimenting to combine
different artistic disciplines. Highly imaginative visual
experiences for families to share together. Stages 2
productions annually, with around 45 performances
in 12 arts centres and theatres across all English
regions, in Scotland, and internationally. In general
5-8 actors go on tour, playing to audiences of various
ages, often 5+. Actors are sometimes expected to lead
workshops; singing, musical instrument, dance,
physical theatre and puppetry skills may all be
advantageous, depending on the project. Recent
productions include: *Mischief* – Dance Theatre; *Hang
On* – Circus Collaboration; and *Salt* – Site Specific.

Casting procedures: Sometimes holds general
auditions; actors may write at any time to request
inclusion. Casting breakdowns are available via the
website and Spotlight. Welcomes letters (with CVs
and photographs) from individual actors previously
unknown to the company, sent by post or email. Also
welcomes showreels and invitations to view
individual actors' websites. Offers Equity-approved
contracts as negotiated through ITC. Actively
encourages applications from disabled actors, and
promotes the use of inclusive casting. "The work is
devised and often physical, so we frequently look for
performers with previous experience of this kind."

Theatre Centre

Shoreditch Town Hall, 380 Old Street,
London EC1V 9LT
tel 020-7729 3066 *fax* 020-7739 9741
email admin@theatre-centre.co.uk
website www.theatre-centre.co.uk
Artistic Director Natalie Wilson *General Manager*
Charles Bishop *Associate Artist (Education)* Michael
Judge

Production details: Founded in 1953. A new writing
company commissioning, developing and producing
new plays which are toured nationally and
internationally to schools, arts centres and theatres.
Normally tours 3 projects each year with an average
annual total of 180 performances across 100 different
venues. In general 3-4 actors go on tour and play to
targeted groups aged 4-18. Singing ability, proficiency
with a musical instrument and dance/physical theatre
skills may be required. An affinity with new writing
and touring audiences is an advantage. Offers TMA/
Equity approved contracts and subscribes to the
Equity Pension Scheme.

Casting procedures: Casting breakdowns are
available through the website, postal application
(with sae), Equity Job Information Service, *PCR* and

Theatre

advertisements in *The Stage*. Accepts submissions (with CVs and photographs) from actors previously unknown to the company sent by post or email; actors should write around New Year or Easter. "We keep all unsolicited CVs on file and do consult them when casting – therefore do send refreshed CVs! Get to know us and our work; there are regular free open day/showcase performances to which people on the mailing list are always invited." Actively encourages applications from disabled actors and promotes the use of inclusive casting.

Theatre Company Blah Blah Blah!
West Park Centre, Spen Lane, Leeds LS16 5BE
tel 0113-274 0030
email admin@blahs.co.uk
website www.blahs.co.uk
Artistic Director Anthony Haddon

Production details: A Leeds-based Theatre in Education company founded in 1985; also produces theatre for young people with integrated workshops. Normally tours 2-3 projects each year with an average annual total of 100 performances across 60 different venues. Venues include schools, arts centres, community venues and youth centres in Yorkshire. In general 3-4 actors go on tour and play to audiences aged 5 upwards. Singing ability, proficiency with a musical instrument, dance/physical theatre skills and a driving licence are all potentially useful. Experience of TIE work is also helpful, as actors are generally expected to lead workshops. Recent productions include: *Barkin'*, a play for teenagers based on the novel *Lady – My Life as a Bitch* by Melvin Burgess, which toured youth centres; *Hansel and Gretel*, a series of workshops for Primary schools; *Silas Marner*, touring to rural community venues and schools with related workshops. Offers ITC/Equity approved contracts and does not subscribe to the Equity Pension Scheme.

Casting procedures: Sometimes holds general auditions; actors may write at any time requesting inclusion, as CVs are kept on file for 1 year. Accepts submissions (with CVs and photographs) from actors previously unknown to the company only if sent by post. Does not welcome unsolicited emails. Will also accept invitations to view individual actors' websites. "We are particularly interested in hearing from people with both acting and facilitation skills." will consider applications from disabled actors to play characters with disabilities.

Theatre Exchange Ltd
The Old NAAFI, Weston Drive, Caterham, Surrey CR3 5XY
tel (01883) 331545
email info@theatre-exchange.org.uk
website www.theatre-exchange.org.uk
Artistic Director Katy Potter *Education Director* Stephen Cordwent

Production details: An educational theatre company focusing on the creative exchange between young

people, artists and those who work with young people. Works on up to 21 projects each year, with an average annual total of 650 performances across 400 different venues. Venues include schools, arts centres, theatres and community venues across the South East of England. In general 6 actors go on tour and play to audiences aged 4-13. Interest in and some experience of working with young people is necessary; a driving licence is also useful. Actors are also expected to lead workshops. Recent productions include: *Monsters, Myths & Legends, Luverly Jubilee* and *The Greeks*.

Casting procedures: Holds general auditions; actors requesting inclusion should write between May and July. Casting breakdowns are available by postal application (with sae), on Equity Job Information Service and through advertisements in *The Stage*. Accepts submissions (with CVs and photographs) from actors previously unknown to the company sent by post or email. Will also accept invitations to view individual actors' websites. "Please send a letter detailing why you are interested in working with young people, along with your CV."

Theatre Hullabaloo
Darlington Arts Centre, Vane Terrace, Darlington DL3 7AX
tel (01325) 352004
email info@theatrehullabaloo.org.uk
website www.theatrehullabaloo.org.uk
Creative Producer Miranda Thain

Production details: Founded in 1979. A specialist producer of theatre for young audiences. Tours regionally, nationally and internationally for audiences aged 3 to 16 years. Recent productions include: *My Mother Told Me Not to Stare*, a deliciously dark operetta for everyone aged 8 and above; and *Five* – a contemporary dance installation for 3 to 5 year olds (also touring in Ontario).

Casting procedures: General auditions are sometimes held; actors are advised to write in the Autumn to request inclusion. Welcomes letters (with CVs & photographs) from individual actors previously unknown to the company, sent by post or email. Also accepts showreels and invitations to view individual actors' websites. Offers Equity approved contracts as negotiated through ITC.

Ticklish Allsorts
57 Victoria Road, Wilton, Salisbury SP2 0DZ
tel (01722) 744949
email garynunn@ntlworld.com
website www.ticklishallsorts.co.uk
Artistic Director Gary Nunn

Production details: Children's entertainers since 1981, using puppets, songs, live action, pantomime and comedy. Tours 5-6 projects annually, with 300-350 performances in 80-100 schools, arts centres, theatres, outdoor and community venues, and festivals throughout the UK. In general 1-2 actors go on tour, playing to audiences aged 4-11. Actors should possess singing and musical instrument skills, and must like comedy and working with children. They may be required to lead workshops. For details of recent productions, see the website.

Casting procedures: Actors may write to request inclusion at any time; "summer is always busy, and Christmas". Casting breakdowns are available through local drama schools. Welcomes letters (with CVs and photographs) from individual actors previously unknown to the company, sent by post or email. Rarely, or never, has the opportunity to cast disabled actors.

Travelling Light Theatre Company

Barton Hill Settlement, 43 Ducie Road, Barton Hill, Bristol BS5 0AX
tel 0117-377 3166 *fax* 0117-377 3167
minicom 0117-377 3168
email info@travellinglighttheatre.org.uk
website www.travellinglighttheatre.org.uk
Producer Jude Merrill *General Manager* Cath Greig

Production details: "Since 1984 the company has produced innovative and inspiring work for young audiences. Uses live music, visual and physical performance in its work." Normally tours 2 projects each year with an average annual total of 200 performances across 25 different venues. Venues include schools, arts centres, theatres, community venues and festivals across England, Northern Ireland, Scotland, Wales, North America and the Republic of Ireland. In general 2-3 actors go on tour and play to audiences aged 3-18. Singing ability, proficiency with a musical instrument and physical theatre skills are required. Actors may also be involved in education workshops. Recent touring productions include: *The Ugly Duckling* (for 3+ years) and *Lenny* (for 12 years upwards).

Casting procedures: Casting breakdowns are available through Equity Job Information Service, *PCR* and Castweb (see entry under *The Spotlight, casting directories and information services* on page 367). Accepts submissions (with CVs and photographs) from actors previously unknown to the company only if sent by post. Does not welcome unsolicited emails. Will also accept invitations to view individual actors' websites.

Unicorn Theatre for Children

147 Tooley Street, More London, London SE1 2HZ
tel 020-7645 0500 *fax* 020-7645 0550
email stagedoor@unicorntheatre.com
website www.unicorntheatre.com
Artistic Director Tony Graham *Associate Director* Rosamunde Hutt *Associate Director & Literary Manager* Carl Miller *Education & Youth Director* Catherine Greenwood

Production details: Founded in 1947. "The UK's professional children's theatre company has recently

opened, near London Bridge, the first purpose-designed theatre for children in the UK." Performed 9 projects in 2005/06 with a total of 460 performances. Has produced site-specific works across England and in Cardiff, Glasgow and Edinburgh. In general up to 8 actors are involved in each production and play to audiences aged 4-11. Singing ability, proficiency with a musical instrument and dance/physical theatre skills are desirable. Past productions include: *Clockwork*, an opera of Philip Pullman's novel of the same name, for the Linbury Studio, Royal Opera House and touring; *Journey to the River Sea*, a co-production with Theatre Centre, adapted for the stage from the Eva Ibbotson novel. Offers TMA and ITC/Equity approved contracts and subscribes to the Equity Pension Scheme.

Casting procedures: Accepts CVs and photographs from actors previously unknown to the company only if sent by email. Advises actors to send an interesting covering note detailing why they are interested in working with Unicorn in particular. Actively encourages applications from disabled actors and promotes the use of inclusive casting.

Whirlwind Theatre Productions with Whirlwind Children's Theatre Company

54 High Road, Halton, Lancaster LA2 6PS
tel (01524) 812851
email enquiries@whirlwindtheatre.org.uk
website www.whirlwindtheatre.org.uk
Artistic Directors Myette Godwyn, Mike Whalley
Associate Artistic Director Alistair Ganley *Patron* David Wood OBE

Production details: Formed in 2000 to produce a community play for the Museum of Cannock Chase in association with Illyria Theatre Company, and a South of England tour of a music-based show for 5-10 year-olds – *Goldie Locks and the Three Bears*. The company has close ties with the Palm Court Theatre Orchestra, and productions are period-music-based with physical and visual performance aimed at the 4-10 year age-group. Whirlwind runs a performance summer school; also has a Saturday youth theatre club and a programme of workshops.

Normally undertakes 2-3 projects each year with a total of around 150 performances. Venues include churches, arts centres, fields, schools, theatres, outdoor and community venues across England. In general 3 actors go on tour and play to audiences aged 4 upwards. Actors must be proficient in workshop-leading for this age-group; will also need singing, dance/physical theatre skills and preferably the ability to play an instrument to a high standard. A driving licence is also required and actors must be prepared to help with get-ins and get-outs. Whirlwind Theatre has a strong Christian ethos, and most rehearsals and community work are carried out at King's Community Church in Lancaster. Although the company welcomes applications from actors of all different beliefs and backgrounds, they should feel at ease with this when applying. Recent productions include: *King's New Clothes* (TIE); *Hamish Bear and Storytelling Magpie* (TIE); *Toad of Toad Hall* (summer-school production in Ryelands Park, Lancaster).

Casting procedures: Sometimes holds general auditions; these are always held in Lancaster. Casting breakdowns are advertised in *PCR*. Welcomes letters and emails (with CVs and photographs) from actors previously unknown to the company. All actors are required to be CRB (Criminal Records Bureau) checked.

Wizard Theatre

175 Royal Crescent, Ruislip, Middlesex HA4 0PN
tel 0800-583 2373
email leon@wizardtheatre.co.uk
website www.wizardtheatre.co.uk
Artistic Director Leon Hamilton *Company Manager* Emmy Bradbury *Associate Producer* Oliver Gray

Production details: Established in 2002. Produces plays, message-based shows and workshops, conferences and training films. On average stages 10 projects annually, with more than 300 performances in 100 community and conference venues across London and the Home Counties. In general 3 actors go on tour, performing to audiences aged 2 to 80.

Actors may be required to lead workshops. Good facilitating, impro and devising skills are useful. Recent productions include: *Robin Hood*; *Tipping the Scales* (obesity conference); *Staying Safe* (Community Safety Workshop); *Pinocchio*; *OUCH!* (one-man show); and *Wind in the Willows*.

Casting procedures: Sometimes holds general auditions; actors are welcome to write in at any time. Casting breakdowns are available via Casting Call Pro. Welcomes unsolicited approaches by actors by post or email. Also accepts showreels and will consider invitations to view individual actors' websites. Does not offer Equity-approved contracts: "Usually we pay well above Equity rates. Excellent facilitators and workshop leaders always desirable!"

Young Shakespeare Company

31 Bellevue Road, Friern Barnet, London N11 3ET
tel 020-8368 4828 *fax* 020-8368 6713
email youngshakespeare@mac.com
website www.youngshakespeare.org.uk
Artistic Directors Christopher Geelan, Sarah Gordon

Production details: One of the best-established and respected educational theatre companies in the UK. Currently performs Shakespeare to more than 100,000 young people each year, working in schools, theatres and professional development centres to provide a year-round programme of performances, workshops and INSET courses. On average stages 10 productions each year, with around 1000 performances in 25 theatres/arts centres and 1000 schools in most regions throughout England. In general, 5 actors per show perform to audiences aged 6 to 16. Actors may be expected to lead workshops and must have a clean driving licence. Recent productions include: *Romeo and Juliet*, *Macbeth*, *The Tempest*, *Hamlet*, and *A Midsummer Night's Dream*.

Casting procedures: Holds general auditions and actors may write at any time to request inclusion. Cassting breakdowns are available via Spotlight Link. Welcomes letters (with CVs and photographs) from individual actors previously unknown to the company, sent by post or by email, but does not accept showreels or consider invitations to view individual actors' websites. Rarely has the opportunity to cast disabled actors: "All applications are considered, but please note that our touring schedule is physically demanding."

Zip Theatre

Newhampton Arts Centre, Dunkley Street, Wolverhampton WV1 4AN
tel (01902) 572250 *fax* (01902) 572251
email admin@ziptheatre.co.uk
website www.ziptheatre.co.uk
Artistic Director Jon Lingard-Lane *Administrator* Sunita Dass

Production details: Founded in 1980. Normally tours 6 projects each year with an average annual total of 300 performances. Venues include schools, arts centres, theatres, outdoor venues and community venues in the West Midlands and nationally. In general 5-6 actors go on tour and play to audiences aged 5 upwards. Singing ability and dance skills are required. Actors are also expected to lead workshops. Recent productions include: *Packers* – arts centre tour of a new play by Alex Jones; *Sparx* – TIE piece about arson; and *The Promise* – for secondary schools on post-16 options.

Casting procedures: Sometimes holds general auditions; actors may write at any time requesting inclusion. Accepts submissions (with CVs and photographs) from actors previously unknown to the company sent by post or email. Does not welcome unsolicited emails.

Casting calendar

Many companies are happy to receive CVs and photographs from actors at any time of the year, but some – such as those listed below – have a regular, annual schedule of casting and as such are most receptive to approaches in certain months. The table below shows the best time to approach companies, and gives information about whether their casting breakdowns are published on their website; whether they will send out breakdowns on receipt of an sae; where they publish their breakdowns (other than via the Spotlight Link); and in what section of this book their details may be found. ('JIS' is the Equity Job Information Service. Details for most of the casting breakdown services can be found under *The Spotlight, casting directories and information services* on page 367.)

Read the company's entry carefully before contacting them, to ensure that you are not wasting either their time or yours by making an inappropriate submission. The letters in brackets after the company name indicate the section in which their details may be found.

Euro = *English-language European theatre companies* (page 223)
IHP = *In-house pantomimes* (page 210)
IM = *Independent managements/theatre producers* (page 148)
MSS = *Middle and smaller-scale companies* (page 161)
PP = *Pantomime producers* (page 206)
PT = *Producing theatres* (page 117)
YP = *Children's, young people's and theatre in education* (page 247)

COMPANY	BREAKDOWNS PUBLISHED
December/January	
Chichester Festival Theatre (PT)	
Shakespeare's Globe (PT)	
January	
The Castle Players (MSS)	
The Derek Grant Organisation (IM)	
Bruce James Productions (IM)	SBS, Castcall, Castweb
Image Musical Theatre (IM)	Website, JIS, PCR, CastNet, Castweb
Midland Actors Theatre (MSS)	JIS, PCR
Nick Brooke (IM)	Website, Post
Nitro (MSS)	
Off the Cuff Theatre Company (MSS)	Website
Theatre Centre (YP)	JIS, PCR, The Stage
Traverse Theatre, Edinburgh (PT)	
January/February	
Theatre Royal, Bury St Edmunds (PT)	
January-March	
Kazzum (YP)	Website, JIS, PCR
Sheringham Little Theatre (PT)	
February	
Everyman Theatre, Cheltenham (IHP)	
First Family Entertainment (PP)	Castweb, CastNet
Jasperian Theatre Company (MSS)	SBS, CastNet
Kinetic Theatre Company (YP)	PCR, Castweb, CastNet, Castcall, CCP, JIS

Theatre

COMPANY	BREAKDOWNS PUBLISHED
Manor Pavilion Theatre, Sidmouth (PT)	Post
Theatre Set-up (MSS)	
February/March	
Light Nights, Iceland (Euro)	
The Proper Pantomime Company (PP)	SBS
Theatre Royal, Norwich (IHP)	SBS
February-May	
City Varieties (IHP)	
February-July	
Hammond Productions (PP)	The Stage, SBS, Castweb, Entsweb
March	
Andy Barnes Productions (IM)	
Duggie Chapman Associates (PP)	PCR, The Stage
Qdos Entertainment (PP)	
The Original Theatre Company (MSS)	Website, Post
Shakespeare 4 Kidz (YP)	PCR, The Stage
March/April	
Cambridge Arts Theatre (IHP)	
Evolution Productions (PP)	Castweb, Website
Library Theatre, Manchester (PT)	
Oxford Shakespeare Company (MSS)	PCR
Spillers Pantomimes (PP)	PCR, The Stage
Theatre Centre (YP)	JIS, PCR, The Stage
March-May	
Imagine Theatre (PP)	
Wish Theatre (PP)	
Spring	
Dundee Repertory Theatre (PT)	
April	
Arty-Fact Theatre Company (YP)	JIS, PCR
English Theatre Frankfurt (Euro)	
Soloman Theatre Company (YP)	
White Horse Theatre, Germany (Euro)	Post, JIS, PCR, The Stage, Website
April/May	
Macrobert (IHP)	
Queen's Theatre, Hornchurch (PT)	
Theatre Royal, Nottingham (IHP)	
April-June	
The Capitol, Horsham (IHP)	Website, SBS, Post
Nottingham Playhouse Roundabout TIE (YP)	
Pendle Productions (IM)	
Splendid Productions (YP)	
May	
20 Stories High Theatre Company (MSS)	JIS Website, PCR
Frantic Theatre Company (MSS)	JIS, PCR
Bruce James Productions (IM)	SBS, Castcall, Castweb
Millfield Theatre, Edmonton (IHP)	
Pilot Theatre (YP)	Website
Q20 Theatre (YP)	
Scene Productions (YP)	
TOSG Gaelic Theatre (MSS)	

COMPANY	BREAKDOWNS PUBLISHED
May/June	
ACT Company, France (Euro)	
Nick Brooke (IM)	
Gazebo Theatre in Education Company (YP)	JIS
May-July	
Greenwich Theatre (PT)	Website
Theatre Exchange Ltd (YP)	Post, JIS, The Stage
June	
Bitesize (YP)	PCR, The Stage, Castcall, SBS
The Courtyard (IHP)	Website, PCR, CastNet, Castweb, SBS
The Customs House Trust Ltd (IHP)	PCR
Image Musical Theatre (IM)	Website, JIS, PCR, CastNet, Castweb
Bruce James Productions (PP)	Website, Post
Jasperian Theatre Company (MSS)	SBS, CastNet
Kinetic Theatre Company (YP)	PCR, Castweb, CastNet, Castcall, CCP, JIS
Midland Actors Theatre (MSS)	JIS, PCR
NTC Touring Company (MSS)	SBS, Post
Orange Tree Theatre, Richmond (PT)	Post
StopWatch Theatre Company (YP)	JIS, Castingcallpro, PCR
Theatr Iolo (YP)	JIS
Theatre Royal, Winchester (IHP)	PCR
Torch Theatre, Milford Haven (PT)	Post, JIS
Traverse Theatre, Edinburgh (PT)	
June/July	
Box Clever Theatre Company (YP)	JIS, PCR, Website
Manchester Actors Company (MSS)	JIS, Castingcallpro
Pied Piper Theatre Company (YP)	JIS
The Theatre, Chipping Norton (IHP)	Post, JIS, Website
Theatre Royal, Bury St Edmunds (PT)	
Theatre Royal, Margate (IHP)	JIS, Castnet
July	
ApeTheatre Company (YP)	Post, JIS, PCR
Arty-Fact Theatre Company (YP)	JIS, PCR
Bitesize Theatre Company (YP)	PCR, The Stage, Castcall, SBS
Chain Reaction Theatre Company (MSS)	
Creaking Door Productions (YP)	Website, JIS
Kabosh (MSS)	
New Pantomime Productions (PP)	
Solomon Theatre Company (YP)	
The Original Theatre Company (MSS)	Website, Post
The Wrestling School (MSS)	Website, Phone
August	
Actors of Dionysus (MSS)	PCR, Website
Found Theatre (MSS)	
Pilot Theatre (YP)	Website
Playtime Theatre Company (YP)	Post, JIS, PCR, The Stage, Castcall
Theatre Royal, Bury St Edmunds (IHP)	
August/September	
Cwmni Theatr Arad Goch (YP)	
English Theatre, Stockholm (Euro)	
Hackney Empire (IHP)	

Theatre

COMPANY	BREAKDOWNS PUBLISHED
Kenneth More Theatre, Ilford (IHP)	
August-October	
Chaplins Ltd (PP)	Website, The Stage, Castcall
September	
Andy Barnes Productions (IM)	
C&T (YP)	
The Derek Grant Organisation (IM)	
Jasperian Theatre Company (MSS)	SBS, CastNet
NTC Touring Company (MSS)	SBS, Post
Open Clasp Theatre Company (MSS)	Website, Post
Pitlochry Festival Theatre (PT)	Post
Traverse Theatre, Edinburgh (PT)	
September/October	
Magic Carpet Theatre (YP)	
October	
20 Stories High Theatre Company (MSS)	JIS, Website, PCR
Bruce James Productions (PP)	Website, Post
Creaking Door Productions (YP)	Website, JIS
Image Musical Theatre (IM)	Website, JIS, PCR, CastNet, Castweb
Kinetic Theatre Company (YP)	PCR, Castweb, CastNet, Castcall, CCP, JIS
Q20 Theatre (YP)	
StopWatch Theatre Company (YP)	JIS, Castingcallpro, PCR
October/November	
Benchtours Productions Ltd (MSS)	
Box Clever Theatre Company (YP)	JIS, PCR, Website
Clean Break (MSS)	JIS, PCR, The Stage
Shakespeare at The Tobacco Factory (MSS)	Website
Theatre Hullabaloo (YP)	
November	
ApeTheatre Company (YP)	Post, JIS, PCR
Frantic Theatre Company (MSS)	JIS, PCR
Kabosh (MSS)	
Owen Money Productions (PP)	The Stage
Solomon Theatre Company (YP)	
Southwold & Aldburgh (PT)	Phone
December	
Actors of Dionysus (MSS)	PCR, Website

Festivals

These are populated by all kinds of companies listed in previous sections. Some are hired-in by a festival's organisers; others 'hire' space in order to participate – the latter predominate at the most famous festival of all, in Edinburgh. Participation in a festival can be enormous fun, and a great opportunity to meet other actors and see other productions. However, the chances of such a production transferring, let alone making money, are limited.

UMBRELLA ORGANISATIONS

British Arts Festivals Association (BAFA)

3rd Floor, The Library, 77 Whitechapel High Street, London E1 7QX
tel 020-7247 4667 *fax* 020-7247 5010
email info@artsfestivals.co.uk
website www.artsfestivals.co.uk

Provides information and a professional network for the festivals movement in the UK, working to promote the profile and status of arts festivals. As well as the arts festivals website, which catalogues festivals in the UK and provides links to festivals in Europe, BAFA also publishes a free Calendar and Directory of the 105 festival members in print, and produces an advance festivals press pack each January. Members have the opportunity to attend BAFA conferences, training courses and focus meetings. Membership is open to all arts festivals in the UK and associate membership to other arts organisations. Does not promote individual artists, companies or tours.

The European Festivals Association

General Secretariat, Kleine Gentstraat 46,
B-9051 Gent, Belgium
email info@efa-aef.eu
website www.efa-aef.eu

Represents more than 90 high-quality festivals and 13 national festivals in 38 European countries. The website offers a general overview of these festivals, together with a detailed list of thousands of events and performances in its annual calendar.

UK ARTS FESTIVALS

24:7 Theatre Festival

PO Box 247, Manchester M60 2ZT
tel/fax 0845-408 4101
email info@247theatrefestival.co.uk
website www.247theatrefestival.co.uk

An annual festival of new writing based in Manchester. The Festival operates an adjudication process, and then invites selected writers to participate. All submitted scripts must be under 60 minutes, original, never performed before and capable of being staged in non-theatre spaces. Venues are selected to provide the best combination of technical facilities and audience experience, with reasonable production costs. Participation fees are subsidised to allow both experienced theatre companies and first-time solo writers to take part. The Festival seeks to provide opportunities for emerging actors, directors and technicians to showcase their talents in the invited productions, and arranges events before and during the week in order to encourage new networks and collaborations to be forged.

Arundel Festival

tel (01903) 883474
email arundelfestival@btopenworld.com
website www.arundelfestival.co.uk

For 10 days each August, the market town of Arundel is host to a multi-arts festival which began in 1977. Street theatre and a festival Fringe are regular features, as are concerts, exhibitions, fireworks and jazz. The festival culminates in an open-air production of a Shakespeare play in the grounds of Arundel Castle. Each production is led by a cast of experienced professional actors, and extended with members of the local community, who work with the professionals throughout the 6-week rehearsal period.

Barbican International Theatre Event (BITE)

Barbican Centre, Silk Street, London EC2Y 8DS
tel 020-7638 4141
email theatre@barbican.org.uk
website www.barbican.org.uk/bite

Since its first programme in 1998, BITE has sought to create a venue in London dedicated to presenting some of the most significant and innovative artists around the world. The Spring 2005 season featured music, theatre and dance pieces from many different

Theatre

countries. Events included: Theatre O's *Astronaut*; Peter Brook's *Ta Main dans la Mienne*; and Fabulous Beast Dance Theatre's production of *Giselle*.

Bath Shakespeare Festival

Theatre Royal, Sawclose, Bath BA1 1ET
tel (01225) 448844
website www.bathshakespeare.org.uk

Presenting premières, international productions and new commissions, the Bath Shakespeare Festival takes place over 2 weeks in March. In addition to full-scale Shakespeare productions there are workshops, film screenings and education events.

Belfast Festival at Queens

Ulster Bank Belfast Festival at Queens,
8 Fitzwilliam Street, Belfast BT9 6AW
email g.farrow@qub.ac.uk
website www.belfastfestival.com
Festival Director Graeme Farrow

Founded in 1963, the Belfast Festival is an annual 3-week international arts festival held in October and November each year. The largest festival of its kind in Ireland, it covers all artforms including theatre, dance, classical music, literature, jazz, comedy, visual arts, folk music and popular music, attracting more than 50,000 visitors. Theatre performances in 2004 included: the Belfast Theatre Company's production of *A Most Notorious Woman*; Theatre Royal Bath's production of *Blithe Spirit* with Penelope Keith. Artists wishing to participate in the festival should submit a written proposal to the address listed above.

Birmingham ArtsFest

Birmingham City Council Events Section,
c/o Manor House, 40 Moat Lane, Digbeth,
Birmingham B5 5BD
tel 0121-464 5678
email artsfest@birmingham.gov.uk
website www.artsfest.org.uk

ArtsFest is one of the UK's largest free arts festivals and is held in venues across Birmingham for 2 days in September. It programmes a range of free performances including theatre, jazz, opera and dance events. Street theatre also features heavily, with musicians, jugglers, visual artists and stand-up comedians all presenting their work outside. There are also a variety of workshops on offer, ranging from screenwriting to Bollywood dancing.

Brighton Festival

email info@brightonfestival.org
website www.brightonfestival.org

Founded in 1967. For 3 weeks in May, there are more than 300,000 attendances at 800 separate arts events taking place in venues across Brighton and Hove. Artists from a number of different countries are represented in theatre, dance, music, opera, books, events and outdoor spectaculars.

Running alongside Brighton Festival, Brighton Festival Fringe (previously called 'the Open') has been in existence for 37 years, and is the biggest in England, showcasing a variety of artforms and activities. Applicants for the Fringe should first read the 'How to be in Brighton Festival Fringe' document available on the website, and then register online.

Cambridge Hotbed Festival

Junction CDC, Clifton Road, Cambridge CB1 7GX
tel (01223) 578000
email cat@junction.co.uk
website www.hotbedfest.co.uk

Following the success of the original Hotbed 2002, Menagerie Theatre Company (**www.menagerie.uk.com**) and Junction CDC (**www.junction.co.uk**) joined forces to present Hotbed 2004 and 2006, Cambridge's New Writing Theatre Festival. Over 3 weeks in July, venues around Cambridge – including CB2, Cambridge Drama Centre and Cambridge Arts Theatre's Playroom – hosted a variety of new plays by a selection of regional and national writers. Productions ranged from 15-minute lunchtime shorts to full evening performances, with a selection of workshops, talks, masterclasses and seminars also included in the programme.

The festival presents opportunities both for writers and for actors to get involved. Any writer may submit a complete play for 2 actors lasting 15-20 minutes. Successful writers will see their production professionally developed and performed at various central Cambridge venues throughout the 3-week festival. A repertory company based around the members of Menagerie Theatre Company supports the festival, and actors are welcome to audition for the company a few months in advance. For further information about the next Hotbed and how to get involved, contact Cat Moore by phone, email or post.

Canterbury Festival

Christ Church Gate, The Precincts, Canterbury,
Kent CT1 2EE
tel (01227) 452853
email info@canterburyfestival.co.uk
website www.canterburyfestival.co.uk

Founded in 1929, the Canterbury Festival takes place over 2 weeks in October. The festival features music, dance, drama, opera, film, community events, talks, walks and visual arts.

The Marlowe and Gulbenkian Theatres in Canterbury and the Theatre Royal in Margate are host to major dance, drama and opera companies. Many small professional and amateur companies perform in the smaller venues and present a wide variety of drama and dance during the 2 weeks of the festival. These have included local companies as well as small foreign companies such as the Brazilian company Teatro Sao Paulo Fabrica, and Hungarian children's theatre Kolibri Theatre.

Other drama companies that have appeared at the festival include the Royal Shakespeare Company, the National Theatre Company, Actors Touring Company, Trestle Theatre, Compass Theatre, Shared Experience and Yellow Earth Theatre.

Chichester Festivities

Box Office, 45 East Street, Chichester,
West Sussex PO19 1HX
tel (01243) 780192
email info@chifest.org.uk
website www.chifest.org.uk

The Box Office is open for making reservations a month in advance of the festival. At other times consult the website or make contact by email.

Chichester Festivities are programmed over 2 weeks in July and have included performances of classical, jazz and world music, talks, contemporary sculpture in the Cathedral Cloisters, fireworks at Glorious Goodwood Racecourse and outdoor theatre productions. Founded in 1975, the festival celebrated its 30th anniversary in 2005.

The event has attracted performers such as Dame Judi Dench, Jools Holland, Fay Weldon and Nigel Kennedy.

Dumfries and Galloway Arts Festival

Gracefield Arts Centre, 28 Edinburgh Road,
Dumfries DG1 1JQ
tel (01387) 260447 *fax* (01387) 260447
email info@dgartsfestival.org.uk
website www.dgartsfestival.org.uk

An annual 9-day festival at the end of May, established in 1979. Founded with the aim of bringing high-quality international events to community audiences that would not otherwise have the opportunity to experience such talent, the festival now also presents local talent of international standing.

The festival programmes a wide range of events covering music – including classical, jazz and folk – dance, theatre, literary, children's and the visual arts. Events take place in a range of venues throughout the region.

The Ealing Comedy Festival

Festivals and Events, 1st Floor SE Perceval House,
Uxbridge Road, Ealing, London W5 2HL
tel 020-8825 6640 *fax* 020-8825 6069
email events@ealing.gov.uk
website www.ealing.gov.uk/services/leisure/
ealing_summer/index.html

The Ealing Comedy Festival takes place in Walpole Park over 1 week in July and reaches audiences of over 1000 each night. The festival has played host to some of the leading names in modern British comedy – including Ricky Gervais, Harry Hill, Al Murray, Rob Brydon and Jimmy Carr– and generally features around 25 comedians each year.

Edinburgh Festival Fringe

The Fringe Office, 180 High Street,
Edinburgh EH1 1QS
tel 0131-226 0026 *fax* 0131-226 0016
email admin@edfringe.com
website www.edfringe.com

The Fringe was started in 1947 to complement the first Edinburgh International Festival. It now breaks its own record every year as the largest arts festival on the planet, bringing thousands of performances of hundreds of shows in more than 200 venues across Edinburgh each August.

The Fringe Society was formed in 1959 to coordinate publicity and ticket sales and offer a comprehensive information service both to performers and to audiences. It compiles information about venues, press and suppliers, and produces a series of publications designed to answer frequently asked questions. The office is open all year round and the staff are available to help by phone, email or personal appointment.

Edinburgh International Festival

The Hub, Castlehill, Edinburgh EH1 2NE
tel 0131-473 2001 *fax* 0131-473 2003
email eif@eif.co.uk
website www.eif.co.uk

Founded in 1947, the Edinburgh International Festival is an annual event held over 3 weeks in August, using all the major concert and theatre venues in the city. With music, opera, theatre, film, dance, and the Military Tattoo at the Castle, the festival is now recognised as one of the world's most important celebrations of the arts.

Also offers a programme of year-round activities, with courses and workshops on diverse subjects from playwriting to the use of digital video, and one-off projects for school children, students and adults collaborating with actors, directors, choreographers and musicians involved in the festival. Performance at the Edinburgh International Festival is by invitation only, issued by the Festival Director.

Exeter Summer Festival

Exeter City Council, Civic Centre, Paris Street,
Exeter EX1 1JJ
tel (01392) 265205 *fax* (01392) 265366
email general.festivals@exeter.gov.uk
website www.exeter.gov.uk/summerfestival

The city's celebration of contemporary and classical music, theatre, dance, comedy and visual arts.

Over 2 weeks in June/July, Exeter Summer Festival programmes diverse arts events, exhibitions and firework displays. Artists interested in performing should contact **artist.enquiries@exeter.gov.uk**.

Fierce!

608B The Big Reg, 120 Vyse Street,
Birmingham B18 6NF

Theatre

tel 0121-244 8080 fax 0121-244 8081
email contact@wearefierce.org
website www.wearefierce.org

Annual festival of performances and events in theatres, bars, clubs, galleries and public spaces across the West Midlands. The festival takes place over 1 month in May/June.

Grassington Festival

The Festival Office, Grassington Festival, Grassington, North Yorkshire BD23 5AU
tel (01756) 752691
email arts@grassington-festival.org.uk
website www.grassington-festival.org.uk

A multi-disciplinary festival featuring contemporary and classical music, theatre, poetry and film, and taking place over 2 weeks in June/July.

Greenwich and Docklands Festivals (GDF)

The Borough Hall, Royal Hill, London SE10 8RE
tel 020-8305 1818 fax 020-8305 1188
email admin@festival.org
website www.festival.org

Taking place over the 4 weekends of July, the Greenwich and Docklands Festival programmes multi-disciplinary arts events around East London each summer. As well as programming large-scale, visually impressive work, the festival places emphasis on educational projects and participatory arts.

The International Festival of Musical Theatre in Cardiff

Market Chambers, 5/7 St Mary Street, Cardiff CF10 1AT
tel 029-2034 6999 fax 029-2037 2011
email enquiries@CardiffMusicals.com
website www.CardiffMusicals.com

The festival aims to present the best of musical theatre, old and new, large and small. Its new-writing programme, 'The Global Search for New Musicals', showcases new musicals selected from a year-long search; many of the musicals showcased in 2002 Global Search have gone on to enjoy success around the world. In addition, there are masterclasses enhancing the work being shown in the festival programme; in 2005 these included a Cole Porter Day, a Stephen Sondheim Symposium and a performance masterclass from Broadway musical director, Don Pippin. Also presented as part of the festival is the BBC Radio 2 Voice of Musical Theatre, where young professional singers from around the world compete for a substantial cash prize and BBC broadcast engagements.

International Playwriting Festival

Warehouse Theatre, Dingwall Road, Croydon CR0 2NF

website www.warehousetheatre.co.uk/ipf.html
Festival Administrator Rose Marie Vernon Casting Sally Vaughan

The International Playwriting Festival has been in operation since 1986 and has consolidated the Warehouse Theatre Company's role in discovering and developing new writing talent. Launching the career of many successful playwrights, the festival has seen many of its plays transferred to the West End, the Royal Court, Hampstead Theatre and Stratford-upon-Avon.

Taking place over a few days in November, the festival is held in 2 parts. The first is a competition (for which entries must be received by June) which is judged by a panel of distinguished theatre practitioners; the second is a showcase of the selected plays in November.

The festival has received applications from writers in the USA, Hong Kong, Croatia, Holland, Australia, Estonia, Sierra Leone, Italy and New Zealand, as well as from the UK.

Lichfield Festival

7 The Close, Lichfield, Staffordshire WS13 7LD
tel (01543) 306270
email info@lichfieldfestival.org
website www.lichfieldfestival.org
Administrator Peter Bacon

Annual 10-day multi-arts festival in early July, Literature Weekend in September/October, plus occasional seasonal events.

London International Festival of Theatre (LIFT)

Trinity Buoy Wharf, 64 Orchard Place, London E14 0JW
email info@liftfestival.com
website www.liftfestival.com
Artistic Director Mark Ball

Started in 1981, LIFT is a biennial summer festival introducing some of the world's most exciting artists and theatre-makers to London. LIFT events have been staged in more than 30 London venues as well as in a number of site-specific venues such as streets, disused buildings, the river, parks and open spaces.

Also runs developmental and educational programmes exploring the nature of exchange and creativity for a range of audiences including schoolchildren and industry leaders.

London International Mime Festival

35 Little Russell Street, London WC1A 2HH
tel 020-7637 5661 fax 020-7323 1151
email mimefest@easynet.co.uk
website www.mimefest.co.uk
Directors Joseph Seelig, Helen Lannaghan

Founded in 1977 by Joseph Seelig and Nola Rae, the London International Mime Festival presents contemporary visual theatre. Events are non text-based and can include animation theatre, circus skills, mask, mime, clown and visual theatre. Most work will be either a UK or a London premiere.

The festival takes place over 16 days each January with the deadline for submissions in mid-July. Participation is by invitation only. To be considered, send a DVD to Helen Lannaghan and Joseph Seelig at the address above with an sae enclosed for the return of material.

Ludlow Festival

email info@ludlowfestival.co.uk
website www.ludlowfestival.co.uk

Running for more than 45 years, the Ludlow Festival takes places over 2-3 weeks in June/July with a range of music, theatre and exhibitions on offer. Each year it features open-air Shakespeare productions which are staged in the grounds of Ludlow Castle.

The Mayor's Thames Festival

website www.thamesfestival.org

The Mayor's Thames Festival is a free annual event that takes place on and around the River Thames between Westminster and Southwark Bridges. Using the river as a powerful unifying symbol for the whole of London, one of the festival's main aims is to enable more collaborations between artists and community groups. Over 1 weekend in September it programmes events such as night carnivals, fireworks spectaculars, mass choirs, music stages, a range of participatory activities, and both artist-led and river-orientated events.

Merseyside International Street Festival

tel 0151-709 3334 *fax* 0151-709 4994
email info@brouhaha.uk.com
website www.brouhaha.uk.com

Established in 1990, the Merseyside International Street Festival brings a mix of dance, drama, acrobatics, music, comedy, puppetry and street theatre to around 30,000 spectators in Liverpool each July/August.

Minack Theatre Summer Festival

Porthcurno, Penzance, Cornwall TR19 6JU
tel (01736) 810694 *fax* (01736) 810779
email info@minack.com
website www.minack.com

Founded in 1932. An annual, 17-week summer season of plays, musicals and opera held at Minack's unique open-air theatre carved into the Cornish cliffside. Created in 1929 by Rowena Cade and her gardener Billy Rawlings, the Minack lends itself to large-cast plays. Most companies involved are amateur, although approximately 3 each year are professional.

National Student Drama Festival (NSDF)

19-21 Hatton Garden, London EC1N 8BA
tel 020-7831 6400
email info@nsdf.org.uk
website www.nsdf.org.uk
Director (CEO) Holly Kendrick

The festival showcases and nurtures innovative theatre by young people, and offers masterclasses, workshops and forums for debate and discussion. NSDF is open to colleges, youth theatres, community organisations and universities, and takes place each spring in Scarborough. Professionals who have attended include Mike Leigh, Willy Russell, Mark Ravenhill, Sir Alan Ayckbourn and Michael Billington. The NSDF Ensemble is a company of talented young theatre practitioners from all over the UK. Supported by professional artists, Ensemble members take part in a one-off training/residency, culminating this year in performances at Latitude Festival. On the recommendation of the NSDF selection team, members are invited to audition each year from the wide range of shows entered for the festival.

National Theatre's Watch This Space Festival

Royal National Theatre, South Bank, London SE1 9PX
tel 020-7452 3333
email wts@nationaltheatre.org.uk
website www.nationaltheatre.org.uk/wts
Watch This Space Producer Angus MacKechnie

Takes place outside the National Theatre over the summer. The festival features theatre, music, dance, variety, film and circus from Britain and abroad. All events are free and run for about 8 weeks from late June to early September.

Pride of Place Theatre Festival

c/o Eastern Angles, Sir John Mills Theatre, Gatacre Road, Ipswich IP1 2LQ
website www.prideofplace.org.uk

International festival held every 2 years to celebrate the work of theatre companies involved in rural touring and to debate the role of theatre in rural communities. Features seminars, discussions and performances from many of the major rural touring companies, including Eastern Angles, Farnham Maltings, Forest Forge, New Perspectives, Northumberland Theatre Company (NTC), Oxfordshire Touring, Pentabus and Proteus. In 2008 the festival was hosted in Alnwick, Northumberland by NTC Touring Theatre. See NTC's entry under *Middle and smaller-scale companies* on page 184.

Royal Court Young Writers Festival

Royal Court Theatre, Sloane Square, London SW1W 8AS

Theatre

website www.royalcourttheatre.com/ywp.asp

A biennial festival, the Royal Court Young Writers Festival presents full professional productions and script-in-hand readings of the best new plays by British writers under 25. The festival has launched the careers of playwrights such as Leo Butler, Simon Stephens, Lucy Prebble and Laura Wade. For information about the festival, please see the Royal Court website. For casting procedures, please see the entry for the Royal Court under Producing Theatres.

Salisbury Festival

87 Crane Street, Salisbury, SP1 2PU
tel (01722) 332977 fax (01722) 410552
email info@salisburyfestival.co.uk
website www.salisburyfestival.co.uk

Established in 1973, for 20 years the festival consisted mostly of classical music events. It is now multi-disciplinary and combines prestigious Cathedral concerts with family street entertainment, circus, theatre and other arts events. There are normally between 30-50 different programmes and projects and a total of some 100 different events which take place at the end of May and beginning of June.

Shrewsbury Summer Season

tel (07709) 685156
website www.shrewsburysummer.co.uk

The first Shrewsbury Summer Season took place in June, July and August 2004 with a programme of visual arts, music, drama, dance, spoken word and comedy events.

Stafford Festival Shakespeare

c/o Gatehouse Theatre, Eastgate Street, Stafford ST16 2LT
tel (01785) 253595
website www.staffordfestivalshakespeare.co.uk
Artistic Programme Manager Derrick Gask

As well as an annual pantomime, The Gatehouse Theatre, generally a receiving house, produces the Stafford Festival Shakespeare, an open air production at Stafford Castle every summer. Casting breakdowns for The Festival Shakespeare are sent out in January and casting is done by freelance casting directors. Rehearsals for The Shakespeare Festival start in June. Photos and CVs sent to the theatre by actors wishing to be considered for audition will be forwarded to the casting director. Invitations to see actors in other productions are welcomed and should be addressed to Derrick Gask. Will consider applications from disabled actors to play disabled characters.

See entry under In-house pantomimes on page 212 for details of the annual pantomime.

Role-play companies

Actors have long used their craft in promotional areas like selling products and services over the phone and in department stores; work opportunities in these fields are advertised in *The Stage*. More recently, the idea of using theatre skills deeper inside the world of business (and the service professions, like medicine) has grown considerably. Essentially, the high level of co-operation ('interactivity') and the excitement, creativity and inspirational power of good theatre is being grasped by hierarchies 'outside the proscenium arch'. Role-play practitioners today are using techniques evolved by the Theatre in Education movement in the 1960s and 70s – but with far better-paying 'customers'.

The established companies – mostly created by actors – have built up a great deal of expertise in this new world, and do not take on new 'role-players' lightly. It is therefore especially important to research each individual company's *modus operandi* before spending time and money in contacting them. However, this is a world well worth exploring as an exciting and lucrative alternative area of work.

A Corporate Act

172D Woodside Green, London SE25 5EW
tel 020-8405 5674 *mobile* (07798) 718321
email info@acorporateact.com
website www.acorporateact.com

Company's work: Has several years' experience working in the corporate events industry. From initial concept to effective fulfilment of a brief, the company has built its reputation by listening to iindividual needs and client requirements, so that "whatever the occasion, a fresh, creative and dedicated approach is guaranteed. We have assembled a reliable, knowledgeable and experienced team that will make impact at all corporate events".

Acting Out Ltd

Regal Chambers, Cavendish Street,
Chesterfield S40 1UY
tel (01246) 520014 *mobile* (07852) 320788
fax (01246) 558396
email info@acting-out.co.uk
website www.acting-out.co.uk
Artistic Director Claire Ashcroft, BA (Hons)

Company's work: Supplies professional role-play actors for training for all kinds of staff, from medical and legal to bar staff and corporate training. All actors must have professional role-play experience. Clients include: NHS Trust and the National Trust.

Recruitment procedures: Periodically extends its actor-base, monthly to annually, via agents, websites, PCR and Equity. Welcomes letters (with CVs and photographs) from actors previously unknown to the company sent by post or email; is happy to receive showreels and invitations to view individual actors' websites. Will consider applications from disabled actors to play characters with disabilities.

Activation

Riverside House, Feltham Avenue, Hampton Court, Surrey KT8 9BJ
tel 020-8783 9494 *fax* 020-8783 9345
email info@activation.co.uk
website www.activation.co.uk
Director Paul Gilmore

Company's work: A leading provider of bespoke interactive training. Services include forum theatre, role-play, scriptwriting and performance, and the design and delivery of training programmes. Incoming actors are trained by the company, according to the requirements of the project. Strong acting and listening skills are required of all the actors. Recent clients include: Diageo, Barclays, and Lloyds TSB.

Recruitment procedures: Periodically extends its actor-base, often by word-of-mouth but also using the Internet. Welcomes letters (with CVs and photographs) from actors previously unknown to the company if sent by post, but not by email. Does not welcome showreels, but is happy to receive invitations to view individuals' websites. Will consider applications from disabled actors to play characters with disabilities.

Actors in Industry Ltd

Talbert House, 52A Borough High Street,
London SE1 1XN
tel 020-7234 9600 *fax* 020-7357 0915
email enquiries@actorsinindustry.com
website www.actorsinindustry.com
Directors Bill Cashmore, Carry Clubb, Roger Ayres, Lorraine Brunning *Head of Operations* Jeni Giffen

Company's work: Established in 1992. "We are the foremost interactive training company in the UK, using role play, facilitation and interactive training and coaching to create meaningful skills improvement and behavioural change for individuals and organisations." Requires incoming actors to possess a good knowledge of business, feedback skills, and the ability to use their "third eye – i.e. the ability to put yourself in another person's position". Provides training for actors in the form of an induction, group workshops and one-to-one sessions. Recent clients include: PWC, Linklaters, Lovelli, Barclays, Lilly, Kraft, Johnson & Johnson, IBM, and Rolls-Royce.

Recruitment procedures: Extends its actor-base twice yearly, and recruits via emailed / posted CVs (business and acting) and covering letter. Rarely has the opportunity to cast disabled actors. Advises actors to "be honest about your experience; over-elaboration will be discovered very quickly".

AKT Productions

18 Grosvenor Street, London W1K 4QQ
tel 020-7495 4043 *fax* 020-7495 0692
email info@aktproductions.co.uk
website www.aktproductions.co.uk
Directors Tim Bannerman and Andy Powrie

Company's work: Established in 1996. Provider of theatre-based learning resources, developing quality learning and development programmes. Incoming actors are expected to have experience of corporate role-play. Clients include: KPMG, Transport for London, Linklaters, HMPS, Shell, BP, Royal Mail. Actor-base is extended every 8-12 months via recommendations and applications.

Recruitment procedures: Accepts submissions (with CVs and photographs) from actors previously unknown to them. Will also accept CVs and photographs sent via e-mail. Invitations to view individual actors' website, are also accepted. Applications from disabled actors for specific projects are considered

Apropos Productions Ltd

2nd Floor, 91A Rivington Street, London EC2A 3AY
tel 020-7739 2857 *fax* 020-7739 3852
email info@aproposltd.com
website www.aproposltd.com
Director Paul Dubois

Company's work: Established in 1999. Provides training for local, national and international clients. Key focus is on Organisational Behaviour. Training is provided for incoming actors through an induction process: client briefings. Training is given to become facilitators. Corporate experience is useful but not essential for incoming actors. Actor-base is extended annually through agents, website, Equity Job Information Service and *PCR*. Clients include: Local Government Association, Thompson Scientific, Colchester Borough Council.

Recruitment procedures: Accepts submissions (with CVs and photographs) from actors previously

unknown to the company. Disabled actors regularly form part of its teams, and are actively encouraged to apply.

Barking Productions Ltd

Note: No longer trading under this name. For training and development services, they are trading as Frank Partners. For comedy improvisation and corporate entertainment, they are trading as Instant Wit.

Blue Beetle

First Floor, Aspect Court, 4 Temple Row,
Birmingham B2 5HG
tel 0870-325 7000
email enquiries@bluebeetle.co.uk
website www.bluebeetle.com
Contact Graham David

Recruitment procedures: A core group of 15 people, with others brought in when required. "We have a really simple statement, that tells you exactly what our training is like: Work hard. Play harder. Learn more."

Michael Browne Associates Ltd

The Cloisters, 168C Station Road, Lower Standon,
Beds SG16 6JQ
tel/fax (01462) 812483
email enquiries@mba-roleplay.co.uk
website www.mba-roleplay.co.uk
Directors Michael Browne, Angie Smith

Company's work: Established in 1997. Holds an extensive database of more than 500 professional, corporate actors. Works closely with clients to cast, devise, manage and interpret events and assessments to inform, challenge, develop, assess and train. Will provide training for incoming actors on particular clients' material as and when required. Actors should have Professional Drama training and experience in the corporate world using roleplay for assessment, training and development. Clients include: MoD, HMRC, Nationwide, Coors Brewers, Costain, VW, RBS, DVLA and Open University.

Recruitment procedures: Periodically extends its actor-base when required "via interview after personal application and recommendation". Welcomes letters (with CVs & photographs) from actors previously unknown to the company, sent by post or email. Accepts showreels and invitations to view individual actors' websites. Will consider applications from disabled actors for specific projects.

CentreStage Roleplay

The Stables, White Cottage, Cheapside,
Ascot SL5 7QE
tel (01344) 876800
email info@centrestage-roleplay.com
website www.centrestage-roleplay.com
Contact Pippa Shepherd

Company's work: A leading development consultancy specialising in the use of drama to enhance learning. Combines extensive business experience with a background in professional theatre and communication skills development. Uses roleplay, forum theatre, issues-based plays and other theatrical techniques "to bring learning to life without sacrificing professionalism or diluting messages".

Recruitment procedures: In the first instance, actors should send a CV outlining their acting and business experience, along with a recent photograph and covering letter, to Pippa Shepherd. Details will be kept on file until an audition slot becomes available. "We receive many CVs: if we don't contact you, this doesn't mean we've forgotten about you."

Characters
12 Stillness Road, Honor Oak Park,
London SE23 1NG
tel 020-8856 4005 *mobile* (07710) 493483
website www.characters.uk.com
Contact Catherine Hamilton

Company's work: A well-established roleplay company with 14 years' experience. Owned by Catherine Hamilton, whose background combines a professional acting career with community health experience. Initially, the company focused on working with police forces and social services departments. It has now begun to expand into the NHS and private sector, more than doubling its client base.

Cragrats
The Cragrats Mill, Dunford Road,
Huddersfield HD9 2AR
tel (01484) 686451 *fax* (01484) 686212
email enquiries@cragrats.com
website www.cragrats.com
Creative Director Mark Greenop *Business Director* David Bradley

Company's work: A theatrical communications company founded in 1989; specialises in corporate training, TIE and issue-based theatre nationwide. Employs 500 actors per year. Project managers and facilitators are trained in-house. Clients include: ASDA, NHS, Learning & Skills Councils, and the Royal Bank of Scotland.

Recruitment procedures: Extends its actor-base each month. Recruits actors through the website and through agents, Equity Job Information Service and advertisements in *The Stage*. Welcomes submissions (with CVs and photographs) by post or email from actors with at least 3 years of training at an approved drama school. "We regularly recruit actors aged 21-60. Please contact us. All rehearsals are Yorkshire-based, though work can be anywhere in the UK."

Cragrats are now part of the Speakeasy4schools family: **www.speakeasy4schools.com**.

DramAnon
Langtons House, Templewood Lane,
Farnham Common, Bucks SL2 3HD
tel (01753) 647795 *mobile* (01753) 647783
email info@dramanon.co.uk
website www.dramanon.co.uk
Directors Steven Brough, Melanie Nicholson

Company's work: A leading provider of drama-based training in the UK. In operation for more than 11 years, the company has built up a client base including many police and fire services, councils and NHS Trusts within the public sector, together with professional companies, law firms, retailers, construction and pharmaceutical companies within the private sector. DramAnon expanded its activities in 2007 and now offers a wide range of services including roleplay, forum theatre, assessment, evaluation, consultation and full DVD production alongside conventional training models.

Dramatrain
1st Floor, Reform Place, North Road,
Durham CH1 4RZ
mobile (07595) 220255 (Chas);
(07595) 219951 (Diggy)
email info@dramatrain.co.uk
website www.dramatrain.co.uk
Directors Chas Thomason, Diggy Wilson

Company's work: Established in 1994. Interpersonal and management skills development, using forum theatre. Provides incoming actors with in-house and on-the-job training; work experience and life skills required. Clients include: BP, Conoco, Rolls Royce and the NHS.

Recruitment procedures: Periodically extends its actor-base as needed, through personal recommendation and via the website. Welcomes letters (with CVs and photographs) from actors previously unknown to the company, sent by post or email. Welcomes showreels and invitations to view individual actors' websites. Will consider applications from disabled actors for specific projects.

Frank Partners
website www.frankpartners.co.uk
Key personnel Neil Bett, Anna Carus

Company's work: "We work in a variety of ways, including role play, forum theatre, facilitation, games, coaching, making films ... in fact, any kind of creative, bespoke intervention from fronting conferences (at Deloitte) to enabling creative, strategic thinking (at BBC Worldwide)."

Impact Universal Ltd
Hope Bank House, Woodhead Road, Honley,
Holmfirth, West Yorks HD9 6PF
tel (01484) 660077
email getintouch@impactuniversal.com
website www.impactuniversal.com

Theatre

Creative Manager Ian Townsend *Assistant Creative Manager* Dave Taylor *Creative Administrator* Jill Beckwith

Company's work: A communications and training provider using a range of powerful and emotive techniques selected to best fulfil a client's brief. Work is delivered live, fully interactive and topical, making its impact highly memorable and effective. Incoming actors should possess knowledge of Hot Seating and Forum Theatre. Recent clients include: National Grid, NHS Yorkshire, and Spectrum Housing Group.

Recruitment procedures: Regularly extends its actor base. Uses in-house casting directors and holds general auditions; actors may write at any time to request inclusion. Casting breakdowns are available from Spotlight, Casting Call Pro and Equity Job Information Service. Welcomes letters (with CVs and photographs) from individual actors previously unknown to the compay, sent by post or email. Also accepts showreels and invitations to view individual actors' websites, or to visit other productions. Rarely has the opportunity to cast disabled actors, but strongly encourages applications.

Instant Wit

6 Worrall Place, Worrall Road, Clifton, Bristol BS8 2WP
tel (0117) 974 5734 *mobile* (07808) 960826
email info@instantwit.co.uk
website www.instantwit.co.uk
Directors Chris Grimes, Stephanie Weston

Company's work: "A quick-fire comedy improvisation show packed full of sketches, gags, songs, surreal situations, flying packets of 'Instant Whip' and prizes! The show is completely improvised and shaped around audience suggestions. Because of this, each show is unique and takes the form that you – the audience – want it to take."

Interact

138 Southwark Bridge Road, London SE1 0DG
tel 020-7793 7744 *fax* 020-7793 7755
email info@interact.eu.com
website www.interact.eu.com
Directors Derek Hollis, Ian Jessup *Company Administrator* Jamie Wright

Company's work: Founded in 1996, the company aims to bring theatre skills to business, using the abilities of professional actors, writers, directors and facilitators. Role-play constitutes just 30% of output. Provides incoming actors with some training in the form of a briefing for basic role-play, rehearsal and guidance for complex work. Offers facilitators specific training in project management. Clients include: ACAS, the Foreign & Commonwealth Office, the BBC, and Royal and Sun Alliance.

Recruitment procedures: Periodically extends its actor-base. Recruits actors through the website and through agents, Equity Job Information Service, *PCR*

and direct contact. Fluency, confidence and strong acting and improvisation skills are required. Business and forum theatre experience can also be an advantage. Welcomes letters (with CVs and photographs) but not email submissions. Invitations to view individual actors' websites are also accepted. Advises actors that: "Those with previous experience are most likely to be interviewed. We are unable to reply to submissions. If you are of interest to us, you will be contacted."

LADA Management

Sparkhouse Studios, Ropewalk, Lincoln, Lincs LN6 7DQ
tel (01522) 837243
email management@lada.org.uk
website www.lada.org.uk
Agents Jennifer Birch, Richard Boschetto

Company's work: Personal management established in 2005. "LADA understands the demands and pressure of business; we also appreciate that each business is unique and has its own objectives, and so will tailor and create bespoke training programmes to suit each individual situation."

Maynard Leigh Associates (MLA)

Victoria House, 64 Paul Street, London EC2A 4NA
tel 020-7033 2370
email info@maynardleigh.co.uk
website www.maynardleigh.co.uk

Company's work: MLA is essentially a community of about 25 people who share common values, are committed to their own and other people's personal growth, and are passionate about their work affecting an increasing number of individuals and organisations. They are required to be expert workshop leaders with an interest in the psychological aspects of human potential development. Clients include: Hewlett Packard, Halifax plc, Ernst & Young, BBC TV, Barclay, and Visa.

Recruitment procedures: All new consultants and leaders go through a rigorous and lengthy process, regardless of their professional experience. It can take up to 18 months of participation in MLA activities before being allowed to represent the consultancy with clients. There are regular personal development sessions in which people explore how they are doing in MLA and how they need to develop further. As MLA invests heavily in its existing Associates, its pace of growth is limited. Professional actors with a good working knowledge of business and corporate life should submit their details by email.

Pearlcatchers Ltd

Claremont House, 70-72 Alma Road, Windsor SL4 3EZ
tel (01753) 624985 *fax* (01753) 830855
email enquiries@pearlcatchers.co.uk
website www.pearlcatchers.co.uk

Director Sharon M Young *Key personnel* Melanie Wright (Business Operations Manager), Karen Hanley (Business Development Manager)

Company's work: An event and training consultancy offering a fresh approach to learning, teambuilding and conferences. Provides actors with opportunities to shadow at events, and offers regular training afternoons and briefing sessions. Requires business skills/knowledge and prior experience in role playing and forum theatre. Clients include: AWE, BT, Ernst & Young, London Underground, Cisco, Bupa, DVLA and the RAF.

Recruitment procedures: Extends its actor base every 2 years, recruiting via *The Stage*. Welcomes letters (with CVs & photographs) from individual actors previously unknown to the company, sent by post or email. Does not accept showreels or invitations to view individual actors' websites. Considers applications from disabled actors for specific projects.

The Performance Business
78 Oatlands Drive, Weybridge, Surrey KT13 9HT
tel (01932) 888885
email info@theperformance.biz
website www.theperformance.biz
Directors Michael McNulty, Lucy Windsor

Company's work: Provides incoming actors with personal assessments and one-to-one coaching. Requires excellent feedback skills and experience of working in business. Clients include: organisations in the financial, pharmaceutical, engineering, and manufacturing & public sectors.

Recruitment procedures: Periodically extends its actor-base, recruiting via the website and CastNet Ltd. Welcomes letters (with CVs and photographs) from individual actors previously unknown to the company, sent by post or email. Will consider invitations to view individual actors' websites. Actively encourages applications from disabled actors and promotes the use of inclusive casting.

Power Train (UK) Ltd
15 Colston Street, Bristol BS1 5AP
tel 0117-922 1500 *fax* 0117-922 1550
email recruitment@powertrain.co.uk
website www.powertrain.co.uk
Managing Director Jill Dean Business *Support Manager* Rebecca Green

Company's work: Established in 1996. Leads the way in delivering dramatic customer service performance programmes for frontline staff and their managers. The training is high impact and challenging, relevant and insightful, and deliver results that stick. Following a selection day, incoming actors will be expected to attend 2 days of training/development/ workout prior to being accepted onto Power Train's approved register. No fees are paid for these days. Requires actors to have an acting qualification, and to possess experience in forum theatre and corporate

role play. Clients include: Mercedes-Benz, Aviva, British Gas, Virgin Media, Virgin Trains, and Visa.

Recruitment procedures: Extends its actor-base around 4 times a year. Recruits via the website, *The Stage*, and personal recommendations. Welcomes letters (with CVs and photographs) from individual actors previously unknown to the company, sent by post or email. Does not accept showreels but will consider invitations to view individual actors' websites. Rarely has the opportunity to cast disabled actors. "Being an approved Power Train associate does not guarantee work. We select teams to suit the assignment. We also expect a high degree of professionalism."

Roleplay UK
2 St Mary's Hill, Stamford, Lincs PE9 2DW
tel (01780) 761960 *fax* (01780) 764436
email actors@roleplayuk.com
website www.roleplayuk.com
Director James Larter *Commercial Manager* Ferlin Barnard *Creative Director* Andy Blair

Company's work: Established in 1994. Drama-led communications and training. Provides training for incoming actors in the form of workshops.

Recruitment procedures: Periodically extends its actor-base every six months or every year, depending on demand. Recruits via Equity Job Information Service. Does not welcome unsolicited approaches by individuals unknown to the company, but actively encourages applications from disabled actors and promotes the use of inclusive training.

Simpatico Roleplay Agency
8 Manor Park, Histon, Cambridge CB24 9JT
tel (01223) 575259
email steve.attmore@ntlworld.com
website www.simpaticoagency.org
Director Steve Attmore

Company's work: Founded in 2002. Focuses on medical roleplay, and will provide 1-day initial training for incoming actors. Requires self-awareness in particular. Clients include: Royal College of Surgeons; East of England Deanery; and University of East Anglia Medical School.

Recruitment procedures: Extends its actor-base 6-monthly, and generally recruits via word-of-mouth. Welcomes letters (with CVs & photographs) from actors previously unknown to the agency, sent by post or email. Also welcomes invitations to view individual actors' websites, but does not accept showreels. Considers applications from disabled actors for specific projects.

Steps Drama Learning Development
Unit 4.1.1 The Leathermarket, Weston Street, London SE1 3ER
tel 020-7403 9000 *fax* 020-7403 0909
email mail@stepsdrama.com
website www.stepsdrama.com

Theatre

Account Directors Robbie Swales, Richard Wilkes, Simon Thomson, Mark Shillabeer, Angela McHale

Company's work: Founded in 1990, the company supplies training to a wide variety of corporate companies through the use of drama. The work includes role-play, forum workshops and drama facilitation. Incoming actors receive training in the areas of feedback skills, forum workshops, coordinator workshops, facilitation skills and 'train the trainer'. Clients include: JP Morgan, NHS, AXA PPP, and The Audit Commission.

Recruitment procedures: Extends its actor-base once or twice a year, selecting 2-3 people in each round. Actors should submit their CV via the website. Actors should have excellent improvisation skills and be able to present themselves realistically as part of the business world in both their dress and language. Requires actors to behave in a professional manner both in their dealings with Steps and with their clients. Must be organised, reliable and good team players.

Theatre&

Church Hall, St James Road, Huddersfield HD1 4QA
tel (01484) 532967 *fax* (01484) 532962
email cmitchell@theatreand.com
website www.theatreand.com
Directors Kath Hirst, Dan Alexander, Carol Sibbald, Russell Watters *Casting & Events Manager* Clare Mitchell

Company's work: Founded in 2005. An innovative training, development and creative presentation company working all over the UK. Designs and develops a variety of learning and communications interventions, which incorporate drama-based training techniques in order to deliver the client's desired outcomes. Theatre& Development focuses on public and private sector organisations; Theatre& Learning works within the education sector, delivering careers-based information to schools; and Theatre& Events provides larger-scale events, such as

conferences and company product launches. Offers some training to incoming actors, who should possess some touring or corporate training experience, strong improvisation skills, and the ability to use a variety of accents. Clients include: NHS, Careers Scotland, AimHigher, Scottish Enterprise, and ECITB.

Recruitment procedures: Regularly holds auditions to increase its database of actors, and employs up to 100 actors per year. Contract lengths range from a few weeks to 6 months. "Please send your CV and a photo, along with a covering letter detailing why you think you are a suitable candidate. We are unable to respond to everyone, but will be in touch to invite you to audition if you are successful." Accepts showreels and invitations to view individual actors' websites, and will consider applications from disabled actors for specific projects.

Theatre without Walls

Forwood House, Forwood, Gloucesterhire GL6 9AB
mobile (07962) 040441
email hello@theatrewithoutwalls.org.uk
website www.theatrewithoutwalls.org.uk
Directors Genevieve Swift, Jason Maher

Company's work: Established in 2002. Award-winning producing theatre company with an active training/corporate wing, working in the public and private sector. Also produces television and corporate films. Clients include: National Trust, Gloucestershire Local Authority, Apollo, BBC, The Prince's Trust. Training is provided for incoming actors in the form of workshops and rehearsals in forum, role play and interactive drama. Incoming actors require good improvisational skills.

Recruitment procedures: Actors are recruited through agents and Equity Job Information Service. Disabled actors regularly form part of the team and are actively encouraged to apply. See also the company's entry under *Middle and smaller-scale companies* on page 197.

Professional role-playing

Robbie Swales

In 1992 an actor rang me and asked if I would do a job with him, which he had been offered through another actor. The job was to do a role-play with some accountants. I said, "What's role-play?" My friend explained that I had to role-play a demotivated worker, and that the purpose of the role-play was to help the accountants learn how to motivate members of their team. I did the job and enjoyed it. Since then – my first experience of role-play – this area of work for actors has expanded enormously. Although there are still networks of individual actors gaining role-play assignments, the bulk of the work for actors is provided by drama-based training companies, which provide organisations with role-players and actor/facilitators.

So why has this sector grown, and why is there a need for drama-based training companies, rather than individual actors applying directly to the end-user to offer their acting skills?

Trainers and developers within organisations have discovered that when they deliver behavioural skills training, an experiential interactive session provides better learning opportunities for the participants than the traditional talk-and-chalk approach. Because actors can put different behaviours on and take them off like a coat, they have become a valuable resource to the trainers; they make the sessions lively, interesting, interactive and memorable. Participants remember the learning, and then go and use the skills in the workplace. Training and development in the workplace is only carried out if a company or organisation believes that it will improve efficiency, and therefore productivity. The use of actors for training is no exception; they help to make the behaviour of people in organisations more effective.

Drama-based training companies are what one might call one-stop shops. If an organisation, such as a high street bank, wants to employ actors to role-play on a series of development centres, the training department in the bank will find it easier to approach a role-play company. The trainer from the bank can explain their needs, check how that role-play company guarantees the quality of their actors, and then negotiate a fee. The role-play company can book the actors, brief them appropriately, and arrange for them to be in the right place at the right time.

The field of drama-based training is growing more and more sophisticated, and some of these companies are becoming more like consultancies, with entire interactive theatre programmes being researched, designed, written, rehearsed and delivered by the drama-based company. For such companies to be effective at this type of work, they need a core team of full-time staff, while maintaining a freelance team of actors trained in the appropriate skills whom they can employ on a project-by-project basis.

There are, very broadly, two types of role-play work: role-playing one-to-one with a participant; and role-playing with another actor in front of an audience, with whom the actors then interact. Most role-play work is improvised; however, there are some types of interactive theatre which kick off the session with a scripted scene, before the actors then start improvising the suggestions of the audience.

One-to-one role-play

The range of work performing one-to-one role-play with a participant requires different levels of skill from the actor. An example of the simplest type of role-play is improvising a patient for an assessment centre, where no feedback is required from the actor to the participant. The Royal College of Anaesthetists requires candidates for their anaesthetist qualifying exams to role-play with a simulated patient (an actor), so that the communications and empathetic skills of the candidate can be assessed. The role-play lasts about five minutes and is not complex.

An example of a one-to-one role-play at the more challenging end of the scale would be role-playing a Senior Tax Manager being interviewed for a job. It is important to remember that an actor is used, primarily, to display different types of behaviour (e.g. being nervous, arrogant, aggressive, etc.). However, for the actor to be a convincing Senior Tax Manager for a behavioural role-play, they need to have an overall grasp of what the job entails, and they may need to throw in a few technical phrases to add reality to the situation. This kind of role-play requires a day of training for the actor, so that they can learn about the role of the Tax Manager, memorise a few key technical words and phrases and rehearse the role-play encounter.

Actors are also required to give each participant with whom they role-play some high-quality feedback about their performance. At this highly sophisticated level of role-play, being able to deliver such feedback is an essential skill. Remember to frame the feedback with affirmative and supportive language.

The skills required to be a good one-to-one role-player are: the ability to go into character instantly; the ability to improvise well; the ability to understand and interpret the brief; the ability to memorise some technical terms; the ability to adjust your performance in relation to the quality of the input from the participant; and the ability to give feedback that is communicated sensitively and is useful to the participant.

Delivering an interactive theatre session

This technique has been used in schools by Theatre in Education companies for many years, and is now being used increasingly in the workplace. There are many different variations in the way that interactive theatre, or forum theatre, is delivered, but the principle is quite simple. Actors playing a scene will break out from that scene and talk to the audience, in character, asking for advice. This advice is then taken back into the scene by the actor and played out to see if it is effective.

Many aspects of development and learning can be addressed via interactive theatre: managing difficult conversations; feedback skills; diversity awareness; assertiveness skills; customer service; influencing skills; leadership; performance management; coaching; recruitment; and employment law awareness.

The skills necessary for performing high-quality forum theatre are: good improvisational skills; the ability to gain a thorough understanding of the objectives of the programme; being an able facilitator in order to confidently handle the responses from the audience; and the ability to hang onto a character while improvising and facilitating.

Applying for work

There are many different types of role-play/drama-based training companies. When we created Steps in 1992, we were one of only a handful of role-play companies; I have now lost count of the number of similar organisations! They all have different cultures and different ways of approaching the work, and each individual company's style probably reflects the personalities of their creators. Some companies may only provide actors to do one-to-one role-play, while others may concentrate on providing interactive theatre. Companies may have a large database of actors; others may have a small pool of actors who work on a fairly regular basis.

My advice would be to browse through the websites of the companies listed and get a feel of what they all claim to be offering. Find out from other actors who have worked in this area about their experiences. Ask them what they think of the company who employed them. At Steps we look at all actor CVs that we receive, and run audition workshops as, and when, we need to select new actors onto our team.

Role-playing for learning is no less a professional activity than professional acting. Punctuality, wearing the appropriate business/work clothes, maintaining confidentiality, interacting in an exemplary way with clients and participants, and working effectively as a member of a high-performance team with fellow role-players, are all behaviours that are required during a role-play assignment.

Being a role-player is a fascinating way for an actor to use their skills in between acting assignments while maintaining an income. Also, from the feedback I have received from role-players, the benefits are not only one-way: actors can learn a great deal from the organisations in which they role-play. The work they do can build their confidence and help them to discover new ways of managing their own careers.

Robbie Swales attended the Bristol Old Vic Theatre School from 1968 to 1970. During the 1970s he acted in Rep, toured and appeared in the West End; during the 1980s he made most of his income from TV commercials. In 1994 Robbie joined Steps – Drama Learning Development, and is now one of six directors who manage the company. In 2002 and 2003 Steps was one of the hundred fastest-growing inner-city companies in the UK, appearing on the HM Treasury-sponsored Inner City 100 Index.

Theatre

Cabaret for the 21st century

Paul L Martin

Mention the word 'cabaret' and the vast majority of people will think of Bob Fosse's 1972 movie of the same name which shot Liza Minnelli to fame. Like the art-form itself, 'Cabaret' has been through many incarnations, having originally been a 1966 Kander and Ebb stage musical which was based on the writings of Christopher Isherwood which, in turn, were based on the 1951 play 'I am Camera'.

To find the origins of cabaret the art-form, we must go back to 1881 and Montmartre, Paris, where the first 'cabaret artistique' was opened. Shortly after it was founded it was renamed Le Chat Noir (The Black Cat). It became a locale in which up-and-coming cabaret artists could try their new acts in front of their peers before they were acted in front of an audience. The place was a great success, visited by important people of that time. The term 'cabaret' is indeed a French word for the taprooms or cafés where this form of entertainment was born, as a more artistic type of *café-chantant*. It is derived from Middle Dutch *cabret*, through Old North French *cambrette*, from Late Latin *camera*, and basically means 'small room'. These modest beginnings were trumped by commercial success at venues such as Moulin Rouge and The Folies-Begeres, which continued to attract a large number of people until the start of the 20th century.

Twenty years later, Ernst von Wolzogen founded the first German cabaret, later known as 'Buntes Theater' ('colourful theatre'). All forms of public criticism were banned by a censor on theatres in the German Empire; however, this ban was lifted at the end of the First World War, allowing the cabaret artists to deal with current social themes and political developments. This meant that German cabaret really began to blossom in the 1920s and 1930s, but when the Nazi party came to power in 1933, they started to repress this intellectual criticism of the times. Cabaret in Germany was hit badly and nearly all German-speaking cabaret artists fled into exile in Switzerland, France, Scandinavia, or the USA.

For the past decade I have been part of a cabaret resurgence which began in London, in its own reincarnation of the art-form. The current interest in an art-form that is over 100 years old and has been ignored or ridiculed by generation after generation of punter is all mixed in with the changes to our economy, class system, attention span and sense of humour.

I left drama school 12 years ago, having done Acting and Musical Theatre at Mountview Academy. One of the things I remember most keenly from my time there was a certain teacher telling us that there were too many actors in the world and not enough jobs, and advising us to think about creating our own work. This advice was instrumental in my producing cabaret shows under the company banner of Millionth Muse Productions (now MMP Ltd) some time later, programming regular events at Theatre Museum, Lost Society, Battersea Barge, The Space, Leicester Square Theatre, Arts Theatre and many more.

I quickly became more and more interested in cabaret as a genre, and in how intimate, raw and dangerous it can be for both performer and audience. There is no fourth wall, and the script – if there is one at all – can be thrown out the window at any moment. Many cabaret artistes who sing, tell jokes and spin stories will work for the most part from a place of truth about themselves and their experiences, and this is where the rawness and the danger comes in. Put them in a cabaret room, and many of the world's greatest actors are completely at a loss without a character and a script to hide behind. There is also very often a much more informal relationship between performer and audience member, with audiences often sat around tables drinking and sometimes even eating. I believe this is one of the key elements which makes cabaret a more desirable evening's entertainment for our modern minds and short attention-spans. Why go to the theatre and sit in the dark silently for three hours with no leg room when you can have dinner, drinks and a show all at the same time, right? Right, but it can make for an evening of unruly revelry and the cabaret artist must always have one eye on this and be ready with a quick response to control the crowd. Your best Hamlet monologue is not advisable in a cabaret room.

As well as a sense of instant gratification and the opportunity to multi-task your social time, cabaret offers a night of live entertainment at a much reduced cost compared, say, to going to a West End musical. And, although the production values will undoubtedly be a great deal lower, you may very well hear the same songs performed in cabaret by the same artists who are working round the corner in that very West End show – musical theatre being a natural slip-road from which to arrive at cabaret. This is not surprising, given that many great musical theatre songs lend themselves perfectly to the first-person storytelling material that we cabaret artists find a wonderful 'in' with our audiences. Having said that, I have met people who have come to cabaret from careers in circus, dance, stand-up comedy, pop and rock, classical music and even therapy!

I believe that cabaret is a very specific skill, not suited to everyone, and a genre in itself. It is too often lumped together with jazz or comedy or – even more bizarrely – contemporary dance in one instance. On a marketing basis, and for fans to find events they may be interested in, this lack of acknowledgement of the craft is disastrous. Part of my work over the past decade has been to raise awareness of this fact, and in 2006 I ran a campaign to lobby *Time Out London* to start a listings section for cabaret. Although they initially ignored me and later treated my enquiries with much contempt, I am proud to say that the enormous support shown by my contacts and mailing list meant they could no longer ignore public demand. In 2009 my colleagues began a similar campaign at the Edinburgh Festival, whose brochure does not differentiate the genre. The good people at the festival offices were immediately forthcoming and are trying out a new way of categorising in 2010 in order to gauge exactly how to move forward. Lastminute.com has also began categorising cabaret separately on its ticketing website, recognising the growing demand for burlesque, variety and circus events in the UK.

Following changes in licensing laws and the smoking ban, clubs, bars, restaurants and theatres are finding platforms for live, raw and in-your-face entertainment wherever they can, needing new and innovative ways of getting punters through the door and keeping them there longer and later than ever. It would be a shame for any performer to not at least consider whether there might be a place for them within the cabaret art-form, whether that be to earn some extra cash, keep their hand in with a live audience, or hone a new skill – or indeed all three! Think about it – can you juggle? Sing? Fan-dance? Eat fire? Tell a joke? Do you excel at clowning? Hanker to drag up? Have an outlandish character you always wanted to show the world? All of these things – and more – can be classed as cabaret. The sky really is the limit. The Oxford English Dictionary definition of cabaret does not mention what is happening on stage – it is all about the way the audience are seated and how they experience the event.

Theatre

• If you are interested in finding out about performance opportunities in cabaret, I would recommend researching the following production companies and entrepreneurs, which are all easy to find on Google:
• LONDON: Tim MacArthur and Katherine Ives at Trilby Productions; Alexander Parsonage for Finger in the Pie Cabaret; Kitty Klaw at The Ministry of Burlesque; Tobias Fauntelroy at White Mischief
• BRIGHTON: Amanda Blanch at The Hanbury Club
• GLASGOW: Rufus and Louise at Rhymes with Purple
• EDINBURGH: Lily White
• BIRMINGHAM: Claire Hearne at Lulu Spanx
• DUBLIN: Sara Colohan at The Tassel Club
It is still difficult for cabaret to stand out in magazine and Internet listings, so it is hard to give advice as to how to find the relevant information. I would recommend checking out *Time Out*'s cabaret listings on a regular basis, and researching venues and performers that identify with the genre. This will open door after door and link after link for you. It is also worth looking into what's happening in Berlin, Sweden, Paris, Amsterdam, Melbourne, Adelaide, and New York, all of which have burgeoning scenes at the moment.

In 2010 I celebrated 20 years of working as a cabaret performer, promoter and producer, and I am proud of and excited by what a thriving sub-culture I have helped to build. I began by running lectures and workshops on cabaret in drama schools and at The Actors Centre, and then in 2007 acquired the cabaret and burlesque agency Better Chemistry to add to our portfolio. Burlesque has been enormously fashionable in the last few years, and cabaret is sure to become even more popular. I still work as an actor on television and on stage, and always have – but what started as a side-line to keep me going has become the passion of my life. After all, it *is* a cabaret.

Paul L Martin is founder and director of the biggest cabaret agency and production house in the UK. He is also a cabaret performer in his own right, having worked extensively as a compere, cabaret singer and raconteur all over the world for the past 20 years.

Media
Introduction

The last twenty years have seen incredibly rapid advancements in recording technology, computers, digital media and the Internet. There has also been an enormous growth in the principal broadcasting companies contracting-out much of their output; this in turn has led to an increase in the number of independent companies employing actors. (There are also companies whose output does not include drama – these have not been included in the listings.)

Most film and television companies use casting directors, and it's usually a waste of time and money writing to anyone else unless you have a personal contact. It is worth remembering that many companies do work for businesses – training and promotional films, for instance.

Student films may be a somewhat poor relation to Hollywood blockbusters, in terms of pay (if any) and exposure, but they can provide useful experiences, be a good addition to your CV, and have the potential to lead onto something that is properly paid and much more prestigious. Extracts from such a film could also be useful for your showreel.

Casting for radio is much more akin to that for theatre, although often without the use of a casting director.

Countdown to 'Action!'

Edward Hicks

The shooting process will vary slightly from production to production, and will present different challenges. But the one element that is certain – be it multi-camera studio or single-camera location – is the waiting. It's hardly surprising that actors have a reputation for story-swapping; it helps to pass the time! However, as actors spend the day unable to fully relax, in a permanent state of standby ready for 'Action', the waiting can be strangely tiring.

The average shooting day is long, and even though a finished shot lasts seconds on-screen, setting up a shot and lighting takes hours. If the sequence involves stunts, special-effects, animals or supporting artistes, it can take several days. For the actor, this means intense moments of concentrated activity (lasting minutes) followed by long periods of waiting (lasting hours). This balance between being relaxed, yet at the same time remaining focused and energised, can be difficult to achieve. Then, when things fall behind schedule (which inevitably they do), the pressure to get it right intensifies – making it even harder to relax.

A small role in an episode of a long-running television programme can frequently be far more nerve-racking than a larger part. I've often seen actors sitting around all day waiting to do a few lines, only to discover that their little scene is to be covered in one shot ... which is to be the last shot of the day. The director knows that the crew (who have worked flat-out all day) must finish on time, as there's no money in the budget for overtime; a good 1st AD won't be shy about reminding the director of this. So with only ten minutes to get the scene in the can, you're frantically called to the set (not a good moment to leave a jacket or prop in your dressing room!); you're introduced to the 1st AD (the person responsible for keeping the director on schedule); you do a rough block with the director, followed by final make-up and wardrobe checks; then someone screams "turn over", the board is read out and the director yells "Action!" Suddenly, with all eyes on you (not to mention a camera), the pressure to get it right first time is enormous. This kind of scenario may sound extreme, but every actor will experience it.

Every production will be slightly different, but the countdown to a standard shoot (if such a thing exists) will probably be as follows.

Firstly, the audition. Remember that getting one is an achievement in itself – so make the most of it. It's hard to get seen for TV and films, and even if you don't land this job, the audition may lead to others. Nearly all castings are handled by a casting director who liaises with the agents and assembles various actors to meet the director. These castings are more like an interview than an audition, involving a brief chat followed by a reading. Arrive early, as you may find a couple of pages waiting for you at reception. Don't be surprised if you only get to read the scene a couple of times; that's quite normal and the casting director usually reads the other roles. It will probably be filmed and may only last ten minutes or so.

Having been cast, you'll be sent a script (possibly a revised draft) and a schedule. Read them both carefully. The schedule is an important document and should help to answer a lot of your questions. At the very least, it will contain a call sheet with details of where you need to be and when; most are far more detailed than that, and include cast lists, crew lists, phone numbers, maps, directions to locations, travel arrangements, health and safety regulations, etc. Check that your contact details are correct and that the dates on the schedule are the dates you were booked for. It's rare for them to be wrong, but it's always best to check as you may start work before your contract arrives. Your agent would have the original booking dates from when the company first checked your availability.

Next you'll receive several phone calls. Firstly, one from the 2nd AD or a production assistant confirming your call. If you have any questions that the schedule can't answer, this is the time to ask. For instance, if by this stage you've not received a script, mention it. They listed me as the wrong character on a schedule once and when I mentioned it to the 2nd AD, it turned out that some of the lines and my character's name had been changed. Nobody had told me and I had learnt the wrong role. Luckily, I still had time to learn the right one! Then, you'll probably get calls from someone in the Costume and Make-up departments. Depending on the scale of the production they may arrange fittings and make-up tests. Either way, make sure you know all your measurements for Costume, including hat and glove sizes. (Incidentally, it's not uncommon in TV for you not to try on your costume until you arrive for the shoot – so give them your real sizes, not the sizes you wish to be!) Also, if your hair is different from your Spotlight photo, tell them, as they might be making decisions based on it.

While waiting for your shooting day to come around, work on your script; familiarise yourself with the lines and characters. Any work you do at home that better prepares you before the shoot could prove useful, especially as less and less time is allocated for rehearsing on set. Don't forget to work on the standby scenes too; these are scenes that are held in reserve in case the schedule is changed at the last minute. They'll be on the call sheet listed as standby scenes or wet weather scenes. You'll probably then hear nothing until a day or two before you start, when they'll ring to confirm your call.

When you arrive at the unit base, the first person you'll meet will most likely be the 2nd AD who, among other things, is responsible for your whereabouts during the shoot. Make sure that they or someone else knows where you are at all times: 2nd ADs are full of stories about wandering actors bringing shoots to a grinding halt because they decided to look around a location. Remember, you'll end up looking foolish – but the 2nd AD gets the blame.

Having arrived at the unit base or the studios, and provided the shoot is running to schedule, you'll be shown to a dressing room or green room. If the schedule has been changed (it often is), you'll be taken straight to Costume and Make-up. If on location, the unit base will either be a building or various trailers and trucks. You'll probably be left on your own as most people will be shooting somewhere else, but there may be other actors around (and if on location, catering people and various drivers). However, at some point you'll be collected and taken to Costume and Make-up. First thing in the morning these places are a hive of activity, so look out for the other actors in your first scene that day. The chances are that some of them will be in make-up at the same time as you.

Depending on the size of the production, you may have your own make-up artist and your own dresser who will be responsible for your costumes. As you will end up spending a lot of time with these people, they'll be a large factor towards your enjoyment of the shoot. I know one director who judges the mood of his cast and crew by the atmosphere in the Wardrobe, Make-up and Catering trailers.

Media

Once you are in costume and have been to Make-up, you'll probably get sent back to your dressing room or trailer. How long you spend waiting to be called will depend on how well they are sticking to the schedule ... and how you pass the time is up to you. Every actor I've met has their own way (I know of one actor who used to spend his time trying to write sitcom scripts, and ended up becoming a very successful writer). Some actors (but not all!) like to get together and run lines, which is great if you are inexperienced as it can help calm the nerves. However, the important thing to remember is that you have to be ready, so that whenever you are called to the set, you are able to do the best you can when the director yells, "Action!"

Every actor knows that work generates work. So no matter how small your role is, never forget that you've been given an opportunity many other actors would relish. I can't think of a more exciting place than a film set full of talented technicians and actors, who are all pulling together to create something. So make the most of it and enjoy it, because if you're lucky, you can work in some amazing places with some incredibly talented people.

Edward Hicks is currently Head of Film, TV and Radio at RADA – a post sponsored by Warner Bros. He has directed numerous Shorts, commercials and promos, is a graduate and former governor of LFS, has various film projects in development, and has written articles on screen acting in addition to being a regular contributor to *Actors' Yearbook*. Ed has taught at various Drama Schools including East 15, where in 2001 he created the first media-based acting course to gain NCDT accreditation. Under the name Edward Rawle-Hicks he started his professional career as a child actor (from the age of ten), appearing at the RSC, in the West End and in numerous commercials, films and television projects.

Television companies

These almost always use casting directors who, in turn, will circulate casting breakdowns to agents they trust. However, a carefully timed (and crafted) submission from an individual can occasionally excite interest.

BBC NETWORK TELEVISION

BBC (Drama)
BBC Television, Drama Room, Wood Lane, London W12 7RJ
tel 020-8743 8000
BBC Elstree, Neptune House, Clarendon Road, Borehamwood WD6 1JF
website www.bbc.co.uk/drama
Controller, Drama Production & New Talent John Yorke *Director, Drama Production* Nicolas Brown *Controller, Series & Serials* Kate Harwood *Executive Producer, EastEnders* Diederick Santer *Head of Drama (Children)* Steven Andrew

Note that while most of these senior programme makers are based at Wood Lane, many BBC Casting Directors are based at the Elstree site.

Casting information: The BBC no longer has a central casting department. Casting advisers are appointed to each specific programme as required. Output includes: *Casualty, Holby City, Doctors, EastEnders* and much else. The various programmes' casting departments will accept letters from actors previously unknown to them (with CVs, photographs, showreels and performance notices); however, actors are advised that while casting personnel are on the lookout for new talent and do attend shows, they are extremely busy and tend to use agents while casting. See the Casting Directors section on page 95 for more information.

Birmingham
BBC Birmingham TV Drama Village, Archibald House, 1059 Bristol Road, Selly Oak, Birmingham B29 6LT
tel 0121-432 8888
website www.bbc.co.uk/birmingham
Executive Producer Birmingham Drama Will Trotter

Manchester
New Broadcasting House, Oxford Road, Manchester M60 1SJ
tel 0161-200 2020
website www.bbc.co.uk/manchester
Editor, Entertainment & Features Helen Bullough

BBC Northern Ireland
BBC Broadcasting House, Ormeau Avenue, Belfast BT2 8HQ

tel 028-9033 8000
website www.bbc.co.uk/ni
Head of Drama Patrick Spence

BBC Northern Ireland produces a broad spectrum of radio and TV programmes, both for the BBC's networks and for its home audience. Output includes news and current affairs, documentaries, education, entertainment, sport, music, Irish language and religious programmes. It also has a thriving drama department which reads unsolicited scripts across all genres, i.e. single, serials, series, feature films and the short-film scheme Northern Lights, which is aimed at new talent from within Northern Ireland.

In addition to making network radio programmes, broadcasting on BBC Radio 1, 2, 3, 4, and 5 Live and BBC World Service, BBC Northern Ireland also makes programmes for its local radio listeners.

BBC Scotland
40 Pacific Quay, Glasgow G51 1DA
tel 0141-339 8844
website www.bbc.co.uk/scotland
Head of Drama, Television Anne Mensah *Head of Drama, Radio* Patrick Rayner

BBC Scotland is the BBC's most varied production centre outside London, providing BBC TV and radio networks and BBC World Service with pivotal drama, comedy, entertainment, children's, leisure, documentaries, religion, education, arts, music, special events news, current affairs and political coverage. Internet development is also a key element of production activity.

In addition to making network output, more than 850 hours of TV programming per year are transmitted on BBC1 Scotland and BBC2 Scotland. BBC Radio Scotland is the country's only national radio station, and is on air 18 hours a day, 7 days a week. Local programmes are also broadcast on Radio Scotland's FM frequency in the Northern Isles, and there are daily local bulletins for listeners in the Highlands, Grampian, Borders, and the South West. BBC Radio Nan Gaidheal provides a Gaelic service on a separate FM frequency for around 40 hours a week.

The BBC offices are wheelchair accessible.

BBC Wales
BBC Broadcasting House, Llandaff, Cardiff CF5 2YQ
tel 029-203 22000
website www.bbc.co.uk/wales
Head of Drama Piers Wenger

Media

BBC Wales provides a range of services in both English and Welsh, on radio, television and online.

The Drama department produces programmes for local and network BBC television channels and local and network radio stations. Notable recent successes of the department include *Doctor Who*, *Torchwood*, *The Sarah Jane Adventures*, *Life on Mars* and *Ashes to Ashes* for television, and the serialised and single dramas for radio, *The Wooden Overcoat*, *Investigating Mr Thomas*, and *Solo Behind the Iron Curtain*.

INDEPENDENT TELEVISION

ITV (**www.itv.com**) is the biggest commercial television network in the UK. It is made up of a network of 15 different regional licences, each with its own set of obligations and conditions designed to reflect the particular character of their region and the interests of their viewers. Eleven of the licences in England and Wales are owned by ITV Plc (**www.itvplc.com**), formed in 2004 following the merger of Carlton and Granada. SMG owns the two Scottish licences, Scottish Television and Grampian; UTV and Channel Television own the licences for Northern Ireland and the Channel Islands respectively.

Note Channel 4, Channel 5 and S4C don't make their own programmes, so do not have casting departments.

Channel Television
The Television Centre, St Helier, Jersey JE1 3ZD
tel (01534) 816816 *fax* (01534) 816777
website www.channelonline.tv

Provides programmes for the Channel Islands during the whole week, relating mainly to Channel Islands news, events and current affairs. Does not produce any in-house drama.

ITV Anglia
Anglia House, Norwich NR1 3JG
tel 0844-881 6900 *fax* 0844-556 3931
website www.itv.com/anglia

Provides programmes for the East of England, daytime discussion programmes, documentaries and factual programmes for UK and international broadcasters. Does not produce any in-house drama.

ITV Central
Gas Street, Birmingham B1 2JT
tel 0121-643 9898 *fax* 0121-643 4897

website www.itv.com/central
Provides ITV programmes for the East, West and South Midlands every day.

ITV Granada
Granada Television Centre, Manchester M60 9EA
tel 0161-832 7211
email casting@itv.com
website www.itv.com/granada
Casting Director, Coronation Street Gennie Radcliffe
Casting Director June West

The ITV franchise-holder for the North West of England. Produces programmes across a broad range for both its region and the ITV network.

Welcomes submissions (with CVs and photographs) from actors previously unknown to the company sent by post or email. As the Casting Department is extremely busy, it cannot guarantee to respond to all submissions. Advises actors to call to find out what projects are being cast, and to send in their details as and when appropriate.

ITV London
South Bank, London SE1 9LT
tel 020-7827 7000
website www.itv.com/london

See ITV Yorkshire and ITV Granada for casting contacts.

ITV Meridian
Forum One, Solent Business Park, Whiteley, Hants PO15 7PA
tel (08448) 812000
website www.itv.com/meridian

The ITV franchise-holder for the South and South East coast of England. Does not produce any in-house drama.

ITV Tyne Tees & ITV Border
Television House, The Watermark, Gateshead, Tyne and Wear NE11 9SZ
tel 0844-881 0100
website www.itv.com/tynetees; www.itv.com/border

Broadcasts to the North of England 7 days a week, 24 hours a day.

ITV Wales & ITV West
ITV Wales, The Television Centre, Culverhouse Cross, Cardiff CF5 6XJ
tel 0844-881 0100
ITV West, Television Centre, Bath Road, Bristol BS4 3HG
tel 0844-881 2345
website www.itv.com/wales; www.itv.com/west

Provides programmes for Wales and the West of England during the whole week. Produces programmes for home and international sales.

The ITV West Television Workshop, aimed at young people (up to 26), offers experience in the performance and production skills required for TV, film, theatre and radio. See **www.itvworkshop.co.uk** for more information.

ITV Yorkshire (YTV)

The Television Centre, Leeds LS3 1JS
tel 0113-243 8283 *fax* 0113-244 5107
website www.itv.com/yorkshire
Casting Director Faye Styring

Established in 1968, YTV is one of the biggest ITV companies. Following the new Communications Act and the merger of Granada and Carlton, it is part of the new single ITV plc which began life on 2nd February 2004.

YTV continues to produce a range of drama and light entertainment programmes, including: *A Touch of Frost*; *Emmerdale* (shown on the network every weekday night); and *Heartbeat* – ITV1's most popular long-running drama series. In 2003 a new sister programme, *The Royal*, attracted 11.3 million viewers and a 41.3% share of the television audience. In addition to its drama series, YTV has made a number of one-off dramas for the ITV network, including: *Booze Cruise* and *Brides in the Bath*. With an audience of 9.7 million viewers and a 44% audience share, *Booze Cruise* ranked as the best performing Single Drama from any channel for the whole of 2003.

The Casting Department generally works through agents, but will accept submissions (with CVs and photographs) from actors previously unknown to the company if sent by post. As the Department is very busy it cannot guarantee to acknowledge all submissions, but advises actors to enclose an sae for a quicker response. Prefers not to be contacted by telephone or email.

STV Productions

STV Central, Pacific Quay, Glasgow G51 1PQ
tel 0141-300 0300
STV North, Television Centre, Graigshaw Business Park, West Tullos, Aberdeen AB12 3QH
tel (01224) 848848
website www.stv.tv
Head of Drama Eric Coulter

STV Productions (formerly SMG Productions) is the television production arm of STV Group Plc, and incorporates Ginger Productions. Its client list includes all terrestrial networks and major satellite and cable channels. Output includes drama, factual/factual entertainment, entertainment and children's programming.

The Drama Department has more than 20 years' experience of producing network drama for ITV1. Credits include: *Taggart*; *Dr Finlay*; *Rebus* and *Goodbye Mr Chips*. The Drama team is based at Glasgow offices. Casting procedures differ from project to project; generally uses independent casting directors, but also accepts letters from actors 'on spec' (with CVs and photographs). Where appropriate these will be passed on to a relevant programme or project.

UTV

Havelock House, Ormeau Road, Belfast, Northern Ireland BT7 1EB
tel 028-9032 8122 *fax* 028-9024 6695
email info@u.tv
website www.u.tv

Provides programmes for Northern Ireland. All drama is produced by the ITV network.

Media

Casting for television

Janie Frazer

There are now many casting directors working in television, and each will have their own way of working. This is my own viewpoint and may not be shared by others, but I hope it may be helpful.

I came into casting by way of the theatre. When I was a schoolgirl I fell in love with the theatre and, being good at English, thought perhaps I could become a drama critic. However, some wise person suggested that before writing about the theatre I should work within it, and so I managed to get a job – at first unpaid, sweeping the stage and as a dresser, and subsequently as an ASM and then handling publicity for the Citizens Theatre Glasgow. I had also been involved in the big auditions held at the start of each season for the Citizens, and had come to realise that the actors were the thing that interested me most about the theatre. Subsequently I moved to London and incessantly badgered LWT for a job as a casting assistant, which finally transpired. I have worked there, through several mergers which have resulted in the company currently known as ITV, for many years. I have cast for all types of television productions; mainly drama, comedy drama and situation comedy, but also sketch comedy, factual drama, hidden camera, animation (voice-over), and various others programmes which defy definition.

Each production has its own specificity, but there are basic requirements that apply to all of them.

The script

This is the first principle and the foundation for everything else, even though the script may change beyond recognition during the process of getting the production to the screen. The script contains the characters, their descriptions, and the dialogue; from this, in consultation with the director and producer, I will put together a list of suggested actors for the roles.

Casting for television carries with it certain commercial considerations. The casting of the main characters is often crucial to a programme getting commissioned in the first place, since in commercial television the advertisers need to be assured of getting a specific audience for the programmes around and within which they buy advertising space. This is the reason for the often-heard grumble that the same well-known faces crop up again and again, and the reason for it is that they have good form – i.e., the programmes they appear in produce good viewing figures, which is what both ITV and the BBC are striving to maintain.

Beyond the 'name' casting, the casting for other roles involves interpreting the director's vision, style, ideas and the tone of the piece to come up with suggestions that will best express the way in which the director wants to portray the material. Therefore, the same script may elicit different suggestions from me, according to the individual director.

Suggestions for actors

How do I arrive at these? I have many lists, and many files, sorted in an idiosyncratic fashion over the years and added to constantly after seeing actors' work on stage and screen. Also there is *Spotlight*, which is the casting director's invaluable and indispensable tool. If there was only one piece of advice I could offer to an actor, it would be to appear in *Spotlight*, and to keep one's entry accurate and up to date. I now use *Spotlight* almost exclusively via the Internet, as the information contained on the website is wonderfully comprehensive and well organised, and allows me to do cross-reference searching (e.g. for a 30-year-old Punjabi speaker with a Manchester accent) which is extremely swift and useful. The information contained on the site does however rely entirely on the input of the actors who subscribe to *Spotlight*, and it is therefore very important that actors keep their credits and personal details current.

Also and most importantly, their photographs. To state the crashingly obvious, television is a visual medium. It's vital that an actor's photograph is up to date and actually looks like them. Vanity should not be the issue, as television requires all types and ages to be portrayed; moreover, an inaccurate photograph can be misleading and time-wasting. The Spotlight's website has now progressed to offer audio and video clips of each actor, and I have found that these can be really useful to play to a director when discussing casting. Therefore, I would strongly recommend that actors make full use of all the opportunities offered by *Spotlight* to show their wares.

Via the Spotlight Link I am also able to send out a breakdown of characters to the agents, who then relay back their suggestions, which I can order, prioritise and follow up. I will discuss with the director and producer the various suggestions we have made between us, and those that have come from agents; I will then arrange casting sessions for the various roles.

Getting in touch

I would love to be able to say that receiving letters with photos and CVs, or emails with all those attachments, is always a boon – but I'm afraid it's not usually the case. More useful is to be notified of actors' forthcoming performances: even if it's not always possible to cover these, it's good to know what work you are doing, and one may ask other casting directors if they have seen you in the piece.

Showreels can be useful to view as examples of an actor's work, but tend not to be so significant if they arrive unsolicited – there are simply not enough hours in the day to watch everything that is sent in. I find I am most likely to watch them if they are directly relevant to a current project (for instance, if I am looking for young Northern actors, or working on a sketch comedy show, I will select to watch those that might fall into the relevant categories).

When you are called for audition

Almost invariably now, casting sessions for television dramas and comedy are video-taped. This allows for greater scrutiny of the actor, and assessment of their presence on screen away from the social context of the audition. It does not mean that the actor has had to produce a flawless reading, but many things emerge from watching an actor on screen which may have been missed during the live reading. The camera is sensitive to minute changes in thought-processes and expression as the actor is being filmed in close-up; this is something the actor needs to bear in mind during a television casting audition – that the performance will be watched at close hand, and therefore a loud voice and large expressions will convey considerable impact which may need to be scaled down.

Whatever an actor's looks, the most important feature on screen is the eyes. The people casting the programme need to see yours. Therefore, it will help enormously if you are able to absorb, familiarise yourself with, or best of all learn the scene so that you are able to raise your eyes from the script. Almost all 'sides' or scenes for reading will have been emailed to your agent or yourself prior to audition. Make sure you have an email address. Acquaint yourself with script formats such as Final Draft (at the time of writing, a free download for viewing scripts in Final Draft format is available from the website **www.finaldraft.com**). If you wear glasses, print the scene in a large font so that you can still read it if at the casting they would prefer to see you without glasses.

Other basic things to bear in mind are to arrive on time; make sure you know the specific whereabouts of the casting venue, and how long it is likely to take you to get there. You may be unavoidably kept waiting, in which case make sure you let the casting director know if you have another appointment you need to get to. If you can, do some prior research, both about the project, and also about the producer and director of the programme. You can find out about their previous work via the IMDb website, **www.imdb.com** – and since they will after all be looking at your CV, they may be impressed and flattered if you also know something about theirs.

Spend some time thinking about the material you've seen, so you have something to say about it. Many actors would be surprised at how much their observations have contributed to the final version of the script. In television as in film, time is money. Pre-production periods have been reduced to the minimum, which means that there is often very little time for rehearsal once shooting begins. Directors often therefore use the casting process to try out ways in which they would like to scenes to play – this can be rewarding for the actor, and useful even if they do not finally land the part; often directors keep their interview lists and bear actors in mind whom they've liked but who haven't been quite right for the part in question.

If you look good, I look good

Sometimes actors view casting interviews as an exam, or as some sort of test they have to pass. However, there is at least one person in the room who is completely on your side – the casting director. The casting director's reputation relies on the calibre of the actors invited for interview, and if the actors aren't up to it then the casting director is the one who's on the line. Therefore, by getting you in for audition, the casting director is demonstrating faith in your ability and rightness for the part.

Know your value

Everyone has their own USP – their unique selling point. Even if you are Mr/s Ordinary, then that's it. It's valuable. Get to know what it is that is most intriguing about you, and play to your strengths. Ask your colleagues for constructive criticism and listen to it. Emphasise your strengths and don't pretend to be what you are not. Whereas the theatre can thrive on disguise and artifice, the camera takes no hostages and is ruthless in its exposure.

Did you get it?

If you got the part, then congratulations! But an actor is often confused as well as disappointed about not getting a part. They will ask: should I have done it like this, dressed like that, what did I do wrong? It's hard to explain to an actor that the choice is not dependent on something they did or didn't do, but often is the result of someone else being more right for the part than they are. This is a nebulous assessment which I can appreciate is very unsatisfactory to hear, but it is nevertheless the truth. Those actors who have ever been on the other side of the casting process often remark how they now understand what this means, but it doesn't help much with the feeling of frustration. One can only suggest that by the law of averages, eventually the part will come up for which you are the most right; that you've done pretty well to get the interview in the first place; that the director may well have clocked you for the future – and that the whole experience stands you in good stead.

For most of her professional life **Janie Frazer** worked as a casting director for ITV Productions, the programme-making division of ITV. She is now working freelance. Janie's career in casting has covered all the genres of single drama, drama series, continuing drama, factual drama, comedy drama, situation comedy, single comedy and sketch comedy. Amongst the many productions she has cast are *Spaced*, the cult comedy series with Simon Pegg; *Coronation Street*, Britain's longest-running soap; and *Blue Murder*, the detective series starring Caroline Quentin.

Working in a soap

Susan Penhaligon

I had never been in a soap. When I started back in the seventies, doing a soap was seen to be a bit down market and selling out. If you wanted to be considered a 'serious actor' you avoided them like the plague – a bit grand maybe, but that was the perceived wisdom then. Now, all that has changed. With the nature of TV – reality shows, multi channel choices, repeats - most actors today would be very happy to get a few episodes or even a long term engagement on a prime time terrestrial channel performing in front of an audience of ten million. For an established actor like me, it's a chance to let everyone know I'm not dead! And for a young actor it can be a fantastic way of upping your profile and introducing yourself (let alone earning some money to put in the bank) so when the call came for me to get on the train to Leeds to audition for *Emmerdale* I was both delighted and very nervous. I was lucky and got the part and a six month contract which was then extended for another six months. The work process was completely new to me and after thirty years in the business it was a challenge. My observations are obviously personal and about *Emmerdale*. Another actor might have a different view, but hopefully they will be useful to you.

Auditioning often means you have to travel to either Leeds or Manchester, or if it's *Eastenders*, to Elstree. Make sure you arrive on time. This is very important as it tells the casting director you are punctual and reliable (very important for soap schedules). I went by train to Leeds which allowed me to look at the script on the way up.

Do try to learn the scenes they send you and to go in with confidence, different actors have different methods, I convince myself I don't want the job, apparently producers and directors feel uneasy if someone is needy and desperate! Sometimes you are handed the script when you arrive so try and get there early to pick up the pages, take them away and learn as much as you can. This shows you can learn lines quickly, a useful tool for soap acting. Often, if it's going to be a long-term contract, they will give you an emotional scene and a funny scene and it can be hard to do without preparation. I focus on the lines and the emotion, trying to make the lines come off the page, but don't be surprised if you come away thinking you've done badly. Its part of the process. If you get the part, the ability to learn quickly and focus emotion without much discussion will be very handy.

Don't worry about accommodation. Most TV companies have lists of hotels and B&Bs for your initial weeks. If you are going to be a long term character you might want to rent a flat or, after you get settled, share with another actor. At the *Emmerdale* studios there is a notice board outside the actors' Green Room where people advertise rooms and flat sharing.

I found most of the regulars on *Emmerdale* had moved within commuting distance and had families. This can make you feel a bit lonely. After a day's work they go back to their cosy homes while you sit in a hotel room. But the young actors on the show had a great social life and I found most people to be extremely friendly and welcoming. Given time, you find a life for yourself. It's a help if you know friends in the area you can visit who are not in the show, so you can debrief. It's not a good idea to let off steam with people you are working with. Tread carefully to begin with. Keep your own counsel.

A word of warning: when I was in *Emmerdale*, the way expenses were paid was changed after much consultation between Equity and management. The result was that individual expenses are now paid on top of your fee. The flat-rate expenses for everyone became redundant. Your agent needs to sort this out for you. Also I found that the expenses were sent a few weeks after I had to pay my rent, so be prepared to have those funds available or have your agent arrange an advance.

You will probably be asked to go on a costume trip with the costume supervisor before you start. I would advise that you have a good idea of how you would like the character to look, particularly if you are on a long contract, as the bulk of your wardrobe will be bought at the beginning (obviously if you are involved in a wedding scene or special occasion, another shopping trip will be done). In fact I would go as far as having a chat with the producer about how you see the character and what they have planned for you.

A good producer will suggest that you go to them if you have any problems. Be bold about doing this, it's important. I foolishly didn't clarify some issues I had, and for me there was always a grey area about where my character came from, what social band she belonged to and how she fitted in with the three main regulars – the family she joined. *And* I never discussed with the producer what kind of clothes she wore.

This also goes for later on, when you might feel strongly about a speech change or story line you're not sure about. The names and extension numbers of the script editors are in the Green Room and they don't mind if you ring to discuss any lines you feel don't work.

The layout of the *Emmerdale* studios is a bit like a factory! The management are on top, the workers are on the shop floor, so it's easy to get to see someone. I'm sure it's true for the other soaps.

I have to say that my first day passed in a flurry of nerves, meeting people, attempting to remember names, constantly changing costume and trying to figure out which camera was on me. Most of the soaps do what they call a multi camera set up, i.e. you have four cameras recording the scene at the same time. If this is a new experience for you, it can be a bit nerve-wracking – but don't worry. Actually you don't have to know which camera is on you, and if the director needs you to be aware for whatever reason, he will make a point of telling you on the appropriate line. Eventually it becomes like second nature; you kind of see the red light going on in the corner of your eye and it won't throw you. On location you will only have at most, two cameras – it's easier.

In the studio, which is more like a warehouse, the different sets are lined up side by side. This is very confusing for a beginner, and it's easy to get lost. Even after a year, I could still be found wandering aimlessly around muttering, "Where's the Woolpack?" Try not to feel a fool just because the long-termers know exactly where they are going. I used to follow the herd, but sometimes ended up in the wrong set! The runners (or third assistant directors), who give you the morning calls, will tell you the number of the next scene and come and get you when you are needed on set. They are wonderful. They're young and keen; anything you need to know – ask them.

Emmerdale does three blocks of four scripts every fortnight. You may be involved in four or five episodes, but no more than eight, over two blocks. Each block has its own crew, A/Ds and director. There are three units working at all times, but you will only be involved with two units. One unit is usually out at the *Emmerdale* village, the other in the studio and during the day you will be taxied between the two. Most soaps do between 20 and 30 scenes a day (*Emmerdale* tries to do 38). You won't be involved in all those scenes, but you could do up to 20.

Your scenes will be out of sequence and in different blocks, so you might be changing your costume from scene to scene (when you start, it's best to ask the costume department after each scene if you need to change). This sounds simple, but I found that when I had a lot to do, the speed at which you finish a scene, rush back to your dressing room, change and then rush back to the studio can be very confusing at first. The costume department will choose your clothes for the scenes and are on the ball with continuity. They are usually willing to bring you something else out of your wardrobe if you are unhappy, but generally it's best to wear what they have chosen for you; otherwise you can spend the whole day discussing or even arguing, and it's not worth it.

I did find the make up, costume department, production team and crew amazing. They worked the longest hours of anybody, with professionalism and good humour. And the latter is one of the essential ingredients to creating a happy work atmosphere. Particularly in the hot house environment of a soap!

This brings me on to another important problem: how to divide your script up. I found that every actor had their own method. Some of them had large folders with each filming day, date and episode cross-referenced with the director's name and a short break-down of the story order. (People called the blocks by the director's name.)

I found my own way, which was to put the scenes together in a daily shooting order with the day and date at the top. I made sure I read the episode thoroughly before I split it up, hoping I would remember the story order on the set. I did come a cropper once, forgetting that in a scene I had shot the week before I was tearful and vengeful, only to be too sunny and smiley in the following scene. A pitfall of shooting out of sequence. Some of the directors are very good at reminding you of the story order. The regulars seem to have an uncanny ability to make every scene work as well as it can with the minimal amount of effort and worry about story order.

The changing nature of soap story lines has no logic. To begin with it's frustrating, particularly if you've been lucky enough to work in an environment where all the right questions are asked about your character's motivations and behaviour. I advise you to give all that up; there just isn't time. A soap is about narrative, so your lines are taking the story forward (not necessarily revealing anything about your character). This is why people are always seen in the same sort of costume or hat – it identifies them (if you start off carrying a dog you'll probably carry the dog in every scene!).

Unlike a play, or an episode of *Casualty*, there is no beginning, middle and end. You step onto the roller-coaster and you go with it until you leave. I found if you play the emotion in the scene for what it is, as real and as truthfully as possible, without thinking about what has happened to the character in the past or what's coming up in the future, it saves you a lot of angst and time trying to talk to the director about your motivation while the first assistant is looking at her watch, making, 'got to GET ON' noises. The shooting schedules are such that directors rarely have time to discuss the scenes in depth (although there are exceptions) and a lot of the time the scenes can't take too much analysing.

Obviously if the only line you have all week is, "Pull us another pint, Val," then there's not much you can do except arrive on time, be friendly, have a laugh and know your words.

If you have a short stint in the soap then you might only work with one director, but if it's a year or so you can work with a lot more. I found this to be the single most confusing part of being in a soap. After years of working on productions where you build a relationship with a director, acknowledging that they are team leader, taking notes from them, trying to collectively put their vision on the stage or screen, I discovered that in a soap this is all topsy turvy. Directors come and go. They do a block at a time, which will involve three or four story lines, then go away to edit while the story machine rolls on with another director. There are often first-time directors and you will know more about your character than they do. If a director has been away for six months on other jobs, they can't possibly catch up on all the story lines – so you end up explaining that no, you can't get in the car and drive out of the village because two episodes ago you lost your licence. Having said that, I worked with some very good directors who did a lot of other TV work, so it's best you understand that they can be as frustrated as you. For both of you it's the nature of the format that describes your working methods.

A typical day would be getting up at 6am, either driving yourself to the studio or paying for a taxi (if you are on location, a studio car will pick you up). You arrive in your dressing room to put on costume, then into make up to be ready on set for 8am. You might work through the day until 7pm (not necessarily in every scene). So you wait either in your dressing room or in the Green Room to be called. The A/Ds don't like you to leave the building or location. Such is the nature of schedules that you can have one scene first thing in the morning and five more starting at 6pm – be prepared for this. I used to take a book; some actors spend the time learning their lines. I always preferred to learn my lines the night before, even if I got in late. And a word on learning: don't over learn, it's not like a play. And learn to learn quickly. It's quite possible that you could be given a new piece of script just before going into the studio ... this happens, and there are always rewrites. Don't feel bad about drying on set either. Everyone does it. Obviously if you dry all the time people will get fed up with you. But I discovered that fluffing and drying is very much part of a day's work.

More than likely you will have blocks out when you can get home. I had a month out when I came back from Leeds to London. On top of that you are entitled to two weeks' holiday a year. At Emmerdale the blocks are posted up on a notice board with the episode numbers running along the top and the characters names involved down the side, so you can have some idea of your work pattern. But, not only did I need a degree to understand this schedule, I also found that it changed, so don't take it as gospel. There is always a friendly soul nearby to explain everything to you but don't expect to be told. Ask, ask, ask would be my motto. *Nobody sits you down and says this is how it all works.* Including when the canteen opens and shuts. Find out to avoid disappointment! (The canteen is subsidised, by the way, so really OK food is very cheap.)

Although most people know how to behave, just a little word. Too much ego is frowned on. Without losing your own identity, it's common sense that you should acknowledge there are actors who have been doing the show much longer than you. A modicum of humility is appreciated, along with a bit of respect. They will respect you in return. Being able to laugh or make people laugh is at a premium. I had a day when I had 18 scenes and by mid-afternoon I couldn't remember my own name. So a bit of banter relieves the pressure.

Believe me, it's hard work doing a soap. It's not a doddle, like a friend of mine suggested. The days can be long with a lot of scenes to remember, or very tedious, when you have little or no story line and you are needed for a non-speaking background appearance. You can be playing high emotions one minute and a lighter moment the next, and there is very little feedback apart from 'that's fine, next scene'. There's no audience to clap you and producers are busy people, so they can't be on the studio floor the whole time telling actors how good they are. don't expect it. If it happens, and it can, be happy. I found that it was the other actors who encouraged me. They were kind and supportive, a lovely crowd.

Now, there is that thing called FAME. After about six months, depending on your story lines and the success of your character, you will be noticing people looking oddly at you on the train, or someone comes up and says, "Didn't I meet you on holiday in The Himalayas last year?" Six months on and the general public think they know you. They'll call you by your soap name, ask for your autograph and generally be pleased to see you.

Along with all this good feeling comes publicity. If you are young and good looking, the soap publicity machine will want to use you. It's part of the job – but if you feel adamant that you don't want the readers of *Heat* magazine to know what underpants you wear, then don't do it. I personally think there is a way of doing the publicity while keeping your private life intact, but be careful. If you become a successful soap actor you have to watch your back. There will always be a photographer when you least expect it, or a member of the public will snap you staggering legless out of a club. There is nothing wrong with getting your name known; the problem with a soap is that you become known as your character. That's ok if you are happy to stay in the show for as long as they'll have you, but if you have ambitions to play other parts, it can take time to erase the memory of the character you played. Of course there are some actors who come out of soaps and do very well. But there are more young actors who seem to fall by the wayside. And some, sadly, hardly work at all. If you do go down the celebrity route, I would say go for it big time. Make sure your *own name* is printed large in the paper and in people's minds.

And please, please don't believe your own publicity. It's a fickle game. If it's decided that your character has run its course, they will write you out and the publicity stops. So keep your feet on the ground, however famous the attention makes you feel.

And there's something else. If you are good in your part and show you are serious about the process of acting, people take notice; the word goes around. You can be in a soap and still be rated as a good actor. Sometimes you'll get the chance to play a well-written scene with substance so you can show what you're made of. I found that the actors in *Emmerdale* worked hard to keep the standard of acting high, sometimes against all odds. They cared about it and wanted it to do well in the ratings.

I had a wonderful year and I learnt a lot. That's very satisfying when you've been working for as long as I have.

Susan Penhaligon's first appearance in theatre was playing Juliet in *Romeo ond Juliet* at the Connaught Theatre, Worthing. Since then stage appearances include two seasons with the Royal Exchange Theatre (Manchester) and parts in productions at the Nuffield Theatre (Southampton), Birmingham Rep and the Palace Theatre (Watford). In the West End her appearances include Natasha in *The Three Sisters*, a leading role in Richard Harris' *The Maintenance Men,* and Annie in *The Real Thing*. She has appeared many times on television; early work included *The Taming of the Shrew, Doctor Who, Upstairs Downstairs, Tales of the Unexpected* and *Dracula* with Louis Jordan. She is best known to viewers as Pru in *Bouquet of Barbed Wire* and as Judi Dench's sister in *A Fine Romance*. Among other film parts Susan played Mae Rose Cottage in the movie of *Under Milk Wood* and appeared in Paul Verhoven's film *Survival Run*. She has published her first collection of poems in collaboration with Sara Kestelman, called *Two Hander* (Do-Not Press).

The world of children's television

Iain Lauchlan

What are the special skills you need for this murky world of children's TV? Well, to answer that I would have to divide my reply into three sections: children's drama, children's presenting, and animation voice-over work.

Children's drama has to be tackled like an adult drama. You have to commit to the part, find and play the truth of the part and be sure to play the relationships with the other characters in a believable and truthful way. Children are not a separate race; they are just like little adults with less experience. They tend to like the same things – good quality storytelling and characters that entertain.

Children's drama is like any other kind of drama. You need to be able to act, audition well and be handy with a pen and paper to write to the producers and commissioning editors. There is so little drama done for children that you need to be sending letters to these people constantly, as they need to be reminded of your existence. The truth of the matter is that there is no money around for big children's drama productions anymore: as a result the producers never get to know many actors, so you need to keep writing to them.

There is a move to increase the drama output by the BBC and by Channel 5 for children, so hopefully the possibility of doing a drama may increase.

Children's presenting is another story altogether. Not every actor can present ... it's a different skill. Some actors master it easily, and some have great difficulty. If you are an actor that likes pantomime and enjoys breaking the fourth wall to contact the audience directly, then the chances are you will enjoy presenting.

Finally the voice-over artiste. There are many opportunities in this field, as voices are always required for animation characters, puppet characters and costume characters.

As an actor it can be a very enjoyable experience exploring what your voice can do. I often get voice CDs sent to me that only explore the different accents that an actor can do, but it is important to explore the different qualities of voice you can achieve, because these are the artistes that get the work.

You must explore how high a voice you can sustain, how low you can go, how odd you can make it. Where in your mouth, throat or nose you can place the voice so that you can switch voices when asked to in a session.

I find that if you study pictures of characters from children's books and give them the voice you think suits them, then you can begin to expand the limits you have set on your voice. It will amaze you the different qualities of voice you can achieve without falling back on accents.

There are many animations made every year in this country and they all need voices. Once you have settled on some crazy voices as well as a selection of normal ones, then get them down on a clear CD. Not a tape done in your living room, as these are painful to listen to when you are searching regularly. And get them out there. Send them to everyone. Tell people you exist and that you have a very useful collection of voices.

Here are three 'C's' which are important to remember when acting presenting and performing voices for children– whether it is in the theatre, recording studio or in a TV studio… **Commitment, Contact and Communication.**

Media

Firstly you must **commit** to whatever age range you are presenting to or acting for. This means getting to know your audience, whether it be pre-school, 7-10 year olds, 10-12 year olds, or teenagers. Each age range needs to be spoken to in a way that is not condescending, that is truthful and that seems to treat them as older than they are. All children are aspirational and will only engage with a presenter, actor or programme if they feel that it caters for older children as well.

Contact is the most important aspect of presenting and acting. Particularly presenting. You have to commit to the audience and let your performance either cross the footlights or drive its way down the lens of the camera to contact and connect with your young audience. Many actors are more comfortable with their performance staying within the fourth wall and allowing the audience to have a passive experience enjoying the relationships, together with the twists and turns in the plot.

Presenters must contact the audience directly and have a dialogue with them. The experience must be an active one from the audience's point of view, and is a commitment by the presenter to the audience with a similar commitment back to the presenter. If I can mention the actor in the pantomime again, this is a half-way house for a character like Idle Jack. Although he is playing a character and telling a story, his performance will not be complete until he has an audience and builds a rapport with them. The audience is the final member of the cast. This is also true for a presenter.

If you are performing with others on stage then the process of communication must be an imaginary triangle that begins with you and travels to the other presenter via the audience. This is just as important if you are having a dialogue on stage between two presenters. It is essential that you have contact with your audience at all times. This contact is most important when presenting to a pre-school audience. There must be a trust, a respect and an entertaining rapport built up that should never falter.

Communication is therefore a key factor in performing to children. If you are not communicating – be it dialogue, a song or a comedy routine – then the audience will not be engaged and will get bored. They will either chat if they are in a theatre, or walk away from the screen if they are in a cinema. Children will give a very honest response.

If you feel that you are one of those actors that could be a successful presenter, then how do you break into the world of children's television?

There are many types of children's programming, like animations, live action with costume characters, live action with presenters, documentaries, game shows and magazine programmes. Some of them do not require presenters, but others do – and ask presenters to offer information, facts, link songs and comedy routines. Experience as an actor will come in very useful when required to do these things and should be played up when writing for work. Time spent as a Holiday Camp host is also invaluable; you experience at first hand the reaction children have to you and to your material. When I audition for presenters or costume characters, I often see Red Coats.

How do they know I exist?

It is the old story here yet again. You must write to the producers who make children's programmes and tell them you exist. This will be all of the major children's broadcasters like BBC, ITV, Channel 5 and Nickelodeon, plus many of the Independent Production Companies that now produce a large percentage of children's programming for the above broadcasters.

You must tell them you are around and what you are capable of and keep telling them. Every time they are casting for their latest production your letter must be on their desk, otherwise they will not think about you. A good clear CV with relevant information including your height, age, weight, experience and skills, together with a professional looking letter showing clearly your contact details and a good, truthful photograph, is all that is required. I am not a great lover of showreels as they often show the limitations of the artist rather than their true capabilities. They are also way too expensive to produce.

Yes, there is a children's TV world out there, and it is possible to break into it. The advice you must keep in mind at all times is this: make sure that people know about you and what you can do. Don't just tell them – *keep* telling them.

Start collecting a list of production companies and who runs them. They keep changing, so keep up to date with them. *Contacts* should be able to provide you with the broadcasters information, and PACT should have a list of Independent Producers. Good luck!

Iain Lauchlan has been involved with children's television since 1980, when he fell into being a presenter on *Playschool* which he did regularly for eight years. During this time he also presented *Fingermouse* and a selection of children's radio programmes. Iain then ran his own company, which created children's programmes such as *The Tweenies*, *Boo*, *BB3B* and latterly *Jim Jam and Sunny*. During most of this time he has tried to keep his 'acting' career going, which is a challenge if you make it as a presenter. The most important thing he has learned is to make sure people know you exist.

Independent film, video and TV production companies

Media

Companies in this field start up and close down all the time, and it is very important to have a proper contract if offered work with an independent. If in doubt, check with Equity.

Absolutely Productions
Unit 19, 77 Beak Street, London W1F 9DB
tel 020-7644 5575
email info@absolutely-uk.com
website www.absolutely-uk.com
Managing Director Miles Bullough

Founded in 1988. Produces drama and comedy for cinema and TV, and TV entertainment programmes. Recent credits include: *Dead Air* (C4), and *Skin and Blister* (short film).

Actaeon Films Ltd
50 Gracefield Gardens, London, SW16 2ST
tel 020-8769 3339 *fax* 0870-134 7980
email info@actaeonfilms.com
website www.actaeonfilms.com
Company Director/Producer Daniel Cormack *Producer* Matt Gunner *Head of Development* Becky Connell

Production details: A London-based production company established in 2004 to develop and produce theatrical motion pictures, both drama and comedy. Recent productions include: the Tiscali Award-winning *Amelia and Michael* (35mm, 2007) starring Anthony Head; the UK Film Council completion-funded *A Fitting Tribute* (HD/Super 8mm, 2007); and the micro-short comedy *Nightwalking* (HD, 2008) starring Raquel Cassidy.

Casting procedures: Uses freelance casting directors and publishes casting breakdowns in *PCR*. Offers PACT/Equity approved contracts and does not subscribe to the Equity Pension Scheme. Actively encourages applications from disabled actors and promotes the use of inclusive casting. "We welcome invitations to showcases, screenings and theatrical productions and will view showreels, but we don't advise sending CVs/headshots unless in relevant response to a current casting call."

Anglo-Fortunato Films Ltd
170 Popes Lane, London W5 4NJ
tel 020-8932 7676 *fax* 020-8932 7491
email anglofortunato@aol.com
Contact Luciano Celentino (Managing Director)

Produces action drama, comedy and psychological thrillers. Offers Equity approved contracts and does not subscribe the the Equity Pension Scheme. Actively encourages applications from disabled actors.

The Ashford Entertainment Corporation Ltd
20 The Chase, Coulsdon, Surrey CR5 2EG
tel 020-8660 9609 *fax* 0870-166 4142
email info@ashford-entertainment.co.uk
website www.ashford-entertainment.co.uk
Managing Director Frazer Ashford

The Ashford Entertainment Corporation Ltd was established in 1996 by producer Frazer Ashford with the aim of developing film and television programming for the international marketplace. The company is also the major shareholder in The Reel Thing Ltd, a UK-based corporate television and events company.

Avalon Television Ltd
4A Exmoor Street, London W10 6BD
tel 020-7598 7280 *fax* 020-7598 7300
website www.avalonuk.com
Directors Jon Thoday, Richard Allen-Turner, Sally Debonnaire

Production details: TV, film and radio company producing drama, comedy and documentaries. Recent credits include: *The Frank Skinner Show*, *Shane*, *Harry Hill's TV Burp*, and *The Sketch Show*.

Casting procedures: Always casts through freelance casting directors and does not issue public casting breakdowns. Does not welcome unsolicited contact of any kind from actors previously unknown to the company. Offers Equity approved contracts.

Bentley Productions
Pinewood Studios, Pinewood Road, Iver, Bucks SL0 0NH
tel (01753) 656594 *fax* (01753) 652638
website www.all3media.com/companies.php?company=3
Managing Director Brian True-May

Specialises in high-quality drama, and has completed productions for both ITV1 and BBC1, including *Midsomer Murders*. Bentley followed the success of *Midsomer Murders* with an action thriller for ITV1, *Ultimate Force*.

Big Bear Films
Gable House, 18-24 Turnham Green Terrace, London W4 1QP

tel 020-8996 5062 *fax* 020-8996 5182
email office@bigbearfilms.co.uk
website www.bigbearfilms.co.uk
Producer/Directors Marcus Mortimer and John
Stroud *Head of Development* Suzi McIntosh

Established in 1998. Makes comedy, drama, and
factual entertainment programmes for all networks.
Recent productions include: *My Hero* (BBC1), *Get A
Grip* (ITV with Ben Elton), *Strange* (BBC1), *The
Hairy Bikers Cookbook* (BBC2). Casting done by
freelance casting directors Tracey Gillham and Sara
Crowe. Actors are employed under Equity approved
contracts. Actively encourage applications from
disabled actors. "Please come to auditions with some
knowledge of the part and the production."

Big Red Button Ltd
91 Brick Lane, London E1 6QL
email hello@bigredbutton.tv
website www.bigredbutton.tv
Key personnel John Burns, Pier Van Tijn, Sagar Shah

Production details: Established in 2002. Specialises
in short films and music videos. Works in live action,
puppetry and animation. Also employs actors in
drama, comedy and commercials.

Casting procedures: Holds general auditions and
actors can write to request inclusion at anytime.
Casting breakdowns are available on the website and
in *PCR*. Welcomes letters (with CVs and
photographs) from actors previously unknown to the
company if sent by post, but not by email. Invitations
to view individual actors' websites are not accepted,
but showreels are welcome. Does not offer Equity
approved contracts. Rarely has the opportunity to
cast disabled actors.

Blakeway Productions
6 Anglers Lane, London NW5 3DG
tel 020-7428 3100 *fax* 020-7284 0626
email admin@blakeway.co.uk
website www.blakeway.co.uk

Established in 1994. In 2004 the company was bought
by Ten Alps PLC and in 2007 it merged with 3BM
Television and Ten Alps TV, bringing together strong
track records of successful production across the
genres of documentaries, docu-dramas, current
affairs and factual entertainment formats.

Has produced more than 200 hours of prestigious
programming for the BBC, Channel 4, More 4, ITV1
and Five in the UK, and leading US broadcasters
including PBS, National Geographic, HBO, The
History Channal and Discovery. Recent hits include:
the Emmy nominated docu-drama *9/11: The Twin
Towers*, a co-production with Dangerous Films for
BBC1 and Discovery; *The Clinton Years* for Radio 4;
and the Bafta winning docu-drama *Nuremberg:
Goering's Last Stand* for Channel 4 and The History
Channel.

Blue Wand Productions Ltd
2nd Floor, 12 Weltje Road, London W6 9TG
tel 020-8741 2038 *mobile* (07885) 528743

fax 020-8741 2038
email lino@bluewand.co.uk
Managing Director Lino Omoboni *Executive
Producer* Paola Omobomi

Established in 1990, the production company works
exclusively in feature film production. Recent credits
include: *Camelot*.

Box TV
151 Wardour Street, London W1F 8WE
tel 020-7297 8040 *fax* 020-7297 8041
email info@box-tv.co.uk
website www.box-tv.co.uk
Executive Producer Gub Neal

Founded in 2000 by award-winning producer Gub
Neal, formerly Head of Drama at Channel 4 and
Controller of Drama at Granada Television. Produces
film and television of the highest quality and vision
for markets throughout the world. The company was
joined in 2006 by Adrian Bate, formerly Head of Film
& Drama at Zenith Entertainment.

Bryant Whittle Ltd
49 Federation Road, Abbey Wood, London SE2 0JT
tel 020-8311 8752
email romy@bryantwhittle.com
website www.bryantwhittle.com
Directors John Bryant, Amanda Whittle *Assistant*
Romy Tennant

Production details: An independent production
company working in feature film production, with a
slate of live action and CGI animated movies. Also
offers a script editing service. Employs actors in
drama and voice-over.

Casting procedures: Uses freelance casting directors
and actors may write at any time to request inclusion;
details will be kept on file. Offers Equity-approved
contracts.

Cactus TV
Cactus TV Studios, 373 Kennington Road,
London SE11 4PA
tel 020-7091 4900 *fax* 020-7091 4901
email touch.us@cactustv.co.uk
website www.cactustv.co.uk
Joint Managing Directors Amanda Ross, Simon Ross

Specalises in broad-based entertainment, features and
chat shows. Since its inception in 1994 Cactus has
produced 41 distinct titles in the UK, for 10 different
channels.

Carlton Television Productions
35-38 Portman Square, London W1H 0NU
tel 020-7486 6688 *fax* 020-7486 1132
Director of Programmes Steve Hewlett

Comprises Carlton Television Productions, Planet 24
and Action Time. Makes drama programmes for all
UK major broadcasters (ITV, BBC, Channel 4,

Media

Channel 5 and Sky) and regional programmes for Carlton Central, Carlton London and Carlton Westcountry.

Carnival Film & Television Ltd

Oxford House, 76 Oxford Street, London W1D 1BS
tel 020-7307 6600
email info@carnivalfilms.co.uk
website www.carnivalfilms.co.uk
Managing Director Gareth Neame Creative Director Sally Woodward-Gentle

Production details: Founded in 1978. Works mainly in TV production, creating drama with a popular and international feel. Employs actors for drama. Commissioned by major UK broadcasters including BBC, Channel 4 and ITV. Has received various prestigious awards/nominations, including Oscars and BAFTAs. Recent credits include: Whitechapel, Enid, Hotel Babylon, and Material Girl.

Casting procedures: Uses freelance casting directors, does not deal directly with actors. Offers PACT/Equity contracts. Will consider casting disabled actors to play disabled characters.

Celador Films Ltd

39 Long Acre, London WC2E 9LG
tel 020-7845 6800 fax 020-7845 1147
website www.celador.co.uk
Chairman Paul Smith Managing Director Christian Colson

Works also in television and radio. TV output is mostly non-fiction and light entertainment – e.g. Who Wants to be a Millionaire? and You Are What You Eat – although the company produced the sitcom, All About Me, starring Jasper Carrott and Meera Syal.

"The company is developing a number of other projects, including a further Neil Marshall project for production; BAFTA-winner Adrian Hodges' adaptation of Claire Tomalin's Whitbread Award-winning biography of Samuel Pepys, The Unequalled Self; Farang, a low-budget road movie set in Thailand – a collaboration with writer Richard Cottan and director Peter Webber; an original screenplay from Paul Webb, based on events following the accession of Lyndon Baines Johnson to the United States presidency in the aftermath of Kennedy's assassination; and Big Deal, a comedy about a hapless English journalist attempting to navigate the shark-infested waters of the international poker circuit."

Celtic Films

3–4 Portland Mews, London W1F 8JF
tel 020-7494 6886 fax 020-7494 9191
email info@celticfilms.co.uk
website www.celticfilms.co.uk

Production details: Established in 1986, Celtic Films has acted as a co-producer for 15 feature-length episodes of Sharpe for ITV, and for the award-winning The Girl from Rio.

Casting procedures: Accepts submissions (with CVs and photographs) from actors previously unknown to the company if sent by email. Showreels, voicereels and invitations to view individual actors' websites are also accepted. Offers Equity approved contracts. Will consider applications from disabled actors to play characters with disabilities.

Chatsworth Television Ltd

97-99 Dean Street, London W1D 3TE
tel 020-7734 4302 fax 020-7437 3301
email television@chatsworth-tv.co.uk
website www.chatsworth-tv.co.uk
Managing Director Malcolm Heyworth

Founded in 1980, the company produces entertainment, factual programmes and drama. Has sister companies in TV distribution and licensing.

Coastal Productions

25B Broad Chare, Quayside,
Newcastle upon Tyne NE1 3DQ
tel 0191-222 3160
email coastalproductions@msn.com
website www.coastalproductions.co.uk

Created in 1997 by Sandra Jobling and Robson Green with the aim of making feature films and TV dramas in the North East of England – and supporting local young people wanting to get into the industry. The company's many production and co-production credits include: Take Me, Blind Ambition, The Last Musketeer, Touching Evil, Close and True, Grafters 1 & 2, Rhinoceros, Hereafter, Unconditional Love, Rocketman, and Wire in the Blood.

Collingwood O'Hare Productions Ltd

10-14 Crown Street, London W3 8SB
tel 020-8993 3666 fax 020-8993 9595
email info@crownstreet.co.uk
website www.collingwoodohare.com
Head of Development Helen Stroud

Founded in 1988. Animation series and specials for children. Does not deal directly with actors: prefers to deal with agents.

The Comedy Unit

Glasgow: 6th Floor, 53 Bothwell Street,
Glasgow G2 6TS
tel 0141-220 6400 fax 0141-220 6444
London: 3-6 Kenrick Place, London W1U 6HD
tel 020-7317 2230 fax 020-7317 2231
email info@comedyunit.co.uk
website www.comedyunit.co.uk
Managing Director April Chamberlain Creative Director Colin Gilbert

Produces some of Scotland's best-loved television and radio shows, as well as a range of programmes for transmission across network and satellite channels. Formed in 1996, became part of the RDF Media Group in 2006.

Company Pictures

Suffolk House, Whitfield Place, London W1T 5JU
tel 020-7380 3900 *fax* 020-7380 1166
email enquiries@companypictures.co.uk
website www.companypictures.co.uk
Managing Directors George Faber, Charlie Pattinson
Head of Film Robyn Slovo *Executive Producer (TV)*
Suzan Harrison

Does not accept unsolicited submissions; proposals
should be submitted through agents.

Cowboy Films

40 Langham Street, London W1W 7AS
tel 020-7580 2982
email info@cowboyfilms.co.uk,
charles@cowboyfilms.co.uk
website www.cowboyfilms.co.uk
Managing Director Charles Steel

Until recently, Cowboy Films represented a range of
top-quality commercials and music video directors,
and also worked on feature films such as *The Hole*
and *Goodbye Charlie Bright*. Sister company
Crossroads Films in the US has taken over the roster
of music video and commercial projects, while
Cowboy continues to work on features. Kevin
Macdonald's *The Last King of Scotland* is the
company's most recent project.

Create Media Ventures (formerly Create TV & Film)

52 New Concordia Wharf, Mill Street,
London SE12 2BB
tel 020-7154 6960
email assistant@cmventures.co.uk
website www.createmediaventures.com
Key personnel Vanessa Chapman, David Kerney

Production details: Originally established in 2000 (as
Create TV & Film) and relaunched in 2005 as Create
Media Ventures. Specialises in TV and film in the
areas of drama, children and animation. Recent
credits include: *Little Robots* and *Bionicle* (employing
voice cast).

Casting procedures: Casting breakdowns can be
obtained via the casting director. General auditions
are held, and actors are advised to apply in January
and September for inclusion.

Welcomes letters (with CVs and photographs) from
actors previously unknown to the company if sent by
post, but not by email. Invitations to view individual
actors' websites are also accepted. Actively encourages
applications from disabled actors and promotes the
use of inclusive casting.

Dalton Films Ltd

127 Hamilton Terrace, London NW8 9QR
tel 020-7328 6169 *fax* 020-7624 4420

Production details: Established in 1987. Working
mainly in film drama. Recent credits include: *Oscar
and Lucinda, Country Life, Madame Sousatzka*.

Casting procedures: Casting is carried out by
freelance casting directors. Actors should only make
contact in response to announcements in the trade
press – does not welcome any form of unsolicited
communication from actors. "Do not waste time or
postage until a film is actively being cast or being
developed." Rarely or never has the opportunity to
cast disabled actors.

Don Productions Ltd

2 Foskett Mews, Shackwell Lane, London E8 2BZ
tel 020-7254 0044 *fax* 020-9227 3283
email london@donproductions.com
website www.donproductions.com
Director Donald Harding

Japanese/English bilingual TV and media production
company based in London. Produces TV drama,
documentaries, news and sports programmes. Clients
include: Japan Broadcasting Corporation, Nippon
Television and Channel 4. Recent work includes: *The
Life of Charles Darwin*.

The Drama House

The Clockhouse, St Mary Street,
Nether Stowey TA5 1LJ
tel (01278) 733336
email jack@dramahouse.co.uk
website www.dramahouse.co.uk
Chairman/Chief Executive Jack Emery

Produces drama and drama-documentaries for film
and TV. Recent credits include: *Inquisition* for
Channel 5, one of the first HD drama shoots –
starring Derek Jacobi; also *Breaking the Code, Witness
Against Hitler, Little White Lies* and *Suffer the Little
Children*. Commissioned by major UK broadcasters:
BBCTV, Channel 4 and C5. Also international PBS
and HBO. Winner of many international and
national awards. Hopes that high-profile work will
encourage writers and other professionals to come to
the Drama House.

Ecosse Films Ltd

Brigade House, 8 Parsons Green, London SW6 4TN
tel 020-7371 0290 *fax* 020-7736 3436
email info@ecossefilms.com
website www.ecossefilms.com
Director Douglas Rae *Head of Drama* Robert
Bernstein

Founded in 1988. Works mainly in TV and feature
film production and employs actors in dramas and
comedies. Recent credits include: *Mrs Brown,
Charlotte Gray, Monarch of the Glen* and *Amnesia*.
Uses freelance casting directors and does not deal
directly with actors.

Extra Digit Ltd

10 Wyndham Place, London W1H 2PU
website www.extradigit.com

Production details: Founded in 2002. Works in film
and television and employs actors in drama, comedy

Media

and documentary. Recent credits include: *Somewhere*, starring Hugh Cornwell, and *Life is a Circus*, starring Steve Ryland.

Casting procedures: Occasionally uses freelance casting directors. Welcomes approaches by actors by post only, with CVs and photographs. Will accept showreels if these do not require a response. Has no equal opportunities policy: "If you can do the part better than anyone else, you get the job – regardless."

Eye Film and Television

Epic Studios, 112-114 Magdalen Street, Norwich NR3 1JD
tel 0845-621 1133
email production@eyefilmandtv.co.uk
website www.eyefilmandtv.co.uk
Managing Director Charlie Gauvain

Independent producers of film and TV drama and documentaries. Also produces corporate, commercial, education and training material. Clients include: BBC, ITV1/Anglia, Channel 4, Five, and First Take Films. Recent credits include: *The Secret of Eel Island* and *POV*.

The Farnham Film Company

34 Burnt Hill Road, Lower Bourne, Farnham GU10 3LZ
tel (01252) 710313 *fax* (01252) 725855
email info@farnfilm.com
website www.farnfilm.com
Key personnel Ian Lewis, Melloney Roffe

Production details: Areas of work include film, TV, video, documentaries and corporate. Recent productions include: *Children of the Lake*, *The Chef's Apprentice*, and *Mona the Vampire*.

Casting procedures: Casting breakdowns are available via the website and in *PCR*. Offers Equity contracts. Does not welcome unsolicited CVs. Actively encourages applications from disabled actors and promotes the use of inclusive casting.

Feelgood Fiction Ltd

49 Goldhawk Road, London W12 8QP
tel 020-8746 2535 *fax* 020-8740 6177
email feelgood@feelgoodfiction.co.uk
Managing Director Philip Clarke *Drama Producer* Laurence Bowen

Producers of film and TV drama.

Film & General Productions Ltd

4 Bradbrook House, Studio Place, London SW1X 8EL
tel 020-7235 4495
email cparsons@filmgen.co.uk
Directors Clive Parsons, Davina Belling

Founded in 1971, the company produces a wide range of feature films, television drama and children's drama. Work includes: *Gregory's Girl*, *Scum*, *I Am David*, *Tea with Mussolini*, *The Queen's Nose* and

Green-Eyed Monster. Does not accept unsolicited submissions. Producers may send short synopsis by email to Clive Parsons, but the company only accepts showreels from agents.

Flashback Television Ltd

58 Farringdon Road, London EC1R 3PB
tel 020-7490 8996 *fax* 020-7490 5610
email mailbox@flashbacktv.co.uk
website www.flashbacktelevision.com
Managing Director & Executive Producer Taylor Downing *Creative Director & Executive Producer* David Edgar *Director of Production* Tim Ball

Flashback Television has been in continuous production since 1982 and is one of the top rated production companies in the UK. The company has a reputation for the quality of its work, for high visual standards and powerful story-telling. Flashback produces factual, factual entertainment and drama programming for broadcasters in the UK and around the world. In the UK Flashback has worked for all the other major British broadcasters including the BBC, Channel Four, ITV, Five and BSkyB. Recent credits include *Nigella's Christmas Kitchen* (BBC), *Married to the Prime Minister* (C4), *Secrets of the Classroom* (C4) and *Beau Brummell: This Charming Man* (BBC). Flashback also produces many hours of programming each year for the UK Government-backed channel Teachers' TV.

Flashback has a long track record of production in the international market. For over a decade the company has been producing series direct for North American broadcasters Arts & Entertainment Television Networks and Discovery. They have also co-produced several major projects with FR2 in France. Recent credits include *The Lost Evidence* (The History Channel), *Superhomes* (Discovery), *Top Tens* (Discovery), and *Weaponology* (Discovery).

Flashback also produces interactive material including the website *History Quest* for Channel 4 Learning, and educational podcasts for the British Council.

Flashback Television is based in London and Bristol. More information can be found at **www.flashbacktelevision.com**.

Focus Films Ltd

The Rotunda Studios, rear of 116-118 Finchley Road, London NW3 5HT
tel 020-7435 9004 *fax* 020-7431 3562
email focus@focusfilms.co.uk
website www.focusfilms.co.uk
Director David Pupkewitz *Head of Production* Lucinda Van Rie

An independent feature film development and production company founded in 1982 by David Pupkewitz and Marsha Levin. Early successes with TV documentaries and dramas preceded a transition to feature films in the 1990s. Recent productions include: *51st State* with Robert Carlyle and Samuel L Jackson; *Book of Eve* with Claire Bloom and Julian Glover; and *Crimetime* with Stephen Baldwin and Pete Postlethwaite. Upcoming projects include: *Heaven and Earth* and *Chemical Wedding*.

Focus Productions Ltd
4 Leopold Road, Bristol BS6 5BS
tel 0117-230 9726
email martinweitz@focusproductions.co.uk
website www.focusproductions.co.uk
Directors Ralph Maddern, Martin Weitz

Production details: Established 1993. Specialising in TV features and documentaries. Employs actors in TV, radio and film. Also for presentation and voice-overs. Recent credits include: *The Real Rain Man* (C5), *Painting the Mind* (C4), *The Piano Player* (C5) and *Vivaldi's Fantasia* (film).

Casting procedures: Holds general auditions. Actors are advised to apply requesting inclusion at any time. Casting breakdowns are available by telephone. Welcomes letters (with CVs and photograph) from actors previously unknown to the company if sent by post, but not by email. Also accepts invitations to view individual actors' websites. Offers Equity approved contracts. Rarely has the opportunity to cast disabled actors.

Mark Forstater Productions Ltd
11 Keslake Road, London NW6 6DJ
tel 020-8933 5475

Works in film and TV production.

Fremantle Media
1 Stephen Street, London W1T 1AL
tel 020-7691 6000 *fax* 020-7691 6100
website www.fremantlemedia.com

Leading producers of prime-time drama, serial drama, entertainment and factual entertainment, programming in around 43 territories. Runs production operations in more than 25 countries worldwide. Brands include: Pop Idol, Grand Designs and Never Mind the Buzzcocks.

Funny Face Films Ltd
8A Warwick Road, Hampton Wick, Surrey KT1 4DW
Director Steven Drew

Production details: Works mainly in Film/Video.

Casting procedures: Uses in-house Casting Director. Sometimes holds general auditions. Welcomes letters (with CVs & photographs) from actors previously unknown to the company, sent by post or email. Accepts showreels and will consider invitations to view individual actors' websites. Will consider applications from disabled actors to play characters with disabilities.

Galleon Films Ltd
Greenwich Playhouse, 189 Greenwich High Road, London SE10 8JA

tel 020-8310 7276
email alice@galleontheatre.co.uk
website www.galleonfilms.co.uk
Chief Executive Alice De Sousa

Production details: An independent film and drama production company.

Casting procedures: Uses freelance casting directors and sometimes holds general auditions. Casting breakdowns are publicly available via all actor-accessible publications and the website. Does not welcome unsolicited letters and CVs or showreels, but will consider invitations to view individual actors' websites. Actors are employed under Equity approved contracts.

Green Umbrella
2 Home Farm Court, Shillinglee, Surrey GU8 4SY
tel (01428) 707933 *fax* (01793) 778212
email jules@gumedia.co.uk
website www.gupublishing.co.uk
Producers Steve Gammond, Bruce Vigar *Managing Director* Jules Gammond

Founded in 1990. Works in DVD and book publishing and distribution. Recent credits include: *Destination South Africa, Easyfit*, and *Betjeman's Britain*.

Greenwich Village Productions
Greenwich Village Productions,
14 Greenwich Church Street, London SE10 9BJ
tel 020-8853 5100 *fax* 020-8293 3001
email info@greenwichvillage.tv
website www.fictionfactory.com/gvtv
Producer/Director John Taylor

An established producer of documentaries for the BBC World Service and BBC Radio 4, Greenwich Village Productions specialises in "intelligent entertainment". Recent credits include: *Adlestrop* and *Love & The Art of War*.

Hat Trick Productions Ltd
33 Oval Road, London NW1 7EA
tel 020-7184 7777 *fax* 020-7184 7778
email reception@hattrick.com
website www.hattrick.co.uk
Joint Managing Directors Denise O'Donoghue, Jimmy Mulville

Founded in 1986, Hat Trick Productions is one of the UK's most successful independent production companies working in situation and drama comedy series and light entertainment shows. Recent credits include: *The Kumars at No. 42, Worst Week of my Life, Have I Got News for You* and *Room 101*.

Heavy Entertainment Ltd
111 Wardour Street, London W1F 0UH
tel 020-7494 1000 *fax* 020-7494 1100
email info@heavy-entertainment.com
website www.heavy-entertainment.com
Director David Roper

Established in 1992. Audio and video producers. Areas of work include drama, corporate, commercials and audiobooks. Offers Equity approved contracts. Welcomes showreels, voicereels and invitations to view individual actors' websites.

Hurricane Films Ltd

17 Hope Street, Liverpool L1 9BQ
tel 0151-707 9700 *fax* 0151-707 9149
email sol@hurricanefilms.co.uk
website www.hurricanefilms.net
Managing Director Solon Papadopoulos

Founded in 2000, produces single films and documentary series from original ideas. Recent credits include: *Warship* (in association with Granada TV); *Comm-Raid on the Potemkin* (FilmFour); and *Wrecked* (BBC2).

J I Productions

90 Hainault Avenue, Giffard Park, Milton Keynes, Bucks MK14 5PE
mobile (07732) 476409
email jasonimpey@live.com
website www.jasonimpey.co.uk
Director Jason Impey

Production details: Works mainly in film, making feature horror films. Also employs actors in the fields of drama, comedy and documentary. Recent credits include: *Tortured, Troubled, Home Made* (1 & 2), *Revenge of the Dead, Demon Scroll, Lust, The Bridge*, and *Woods of Terror*.

Casting procedures: Uses freelance casting directors and holds general auditions; actors may write in at any time requesting inclusion. Casting breakdowns available via postal application with sae. Welcomes letters (with CVs and photographs) from individual actors previously unknown to the company, sent by post or email. Also accepts showreels and invitations to view individual actors' websites. Actively encourages applications from disabled actors and promotes the use of inclusive casting. "Always on the lookout for new talent."

Kelpie Films

227 St Andrews Road, Glasgow G41 1PD
tel 0871-874 0328 *fax* 0871-874 0329
email yearbook@kelpiefilms.com
website www.kelpiefilms.com

Independent production company that produces a range of broadcast and corporate/commercial work, from computer-animated children's programmes to documentaries in the Middle East and low-budget feature films. Credits include: BAFTA-nominated animation, *Cannonman*; Grierson Award-winning documentary, *And So Goodbye*; and large-scale corporate work for global clients such as Shell and the UK Government.

Left Bank Pictures

33 Foley Street, London W1W 7TL
tel 020-7612 3299, 020-7612 3132

email info@leftbankpictures.co.uk
website www.leftbankpictures.co.uk
Chief Executive Andy Harries

An independent television and film production company founded in July 2007 by Andy Harries, Marigo Kehoe and Francis Hopkinson. "We are working with the UK's leading writing, directing and on-screen talent to produce bold, innovative feature films, television dramas and cutting-edge comedy. We also pride ourselves on nurturing and championing exciting new talent set to create the hits of tomorrow."

Lexitricity Ltd

15-25 Vereker Road, West Kensington, London W14 9JU
tel 0870-840 4466
email alexandra@lexitricity.com, production@lexitricity.com

Founded in 2006. An independent production company making short films, music promos, documentaries and actors' showreels. Comprises a writer, director, producer and storyboard artist, teamed up with an experienced professional crew employed on a freelance basis. Work includes experience on feature films, BBC dramas and documentaries as well as award-winning short films. Will take clients through the entire production process, from concept and storyboard to a creative shoot and edit. Works closely with photographers, illustrators and graphic artists to produce original marketing material including flyers, posters and DVD cover designs.

LWT and United Productions

London TV Centre, Upper Ground, London SE1 9LT
tel 020-7620 1620
Controller of Drama Michele Buck

Founded in 1996. Producers of TV and film.

Maverick Television

Units 1-4 Progress Works, Heath Mill Lane, Birmingham B9 4AL
tel 0121-771 1812 *fax* 0121-771 1550
website www.mavericktv.co.uk
Casting Director Alexandra Fraser *Executive Producer* Jim Sayer

Production details: Established in 1994. Television production company producing broadcast and non-broadcast content to all terrestrial and specialist channels. Recent productions include: *10 Years Younger, The Property Chain, VEETV, Born Too Soon* and *The Comedy Lab*.

Casting procedures: Accepts submissions (with CVs and photographs) from actors previously unknown to the company, sent by post only – no emails please. Welcomes invitations to view individual actors' websites; does not accept showreels. Offers Equity approved contracts. Actively encourages applications from disabled actors.

Maya Vision International Ltd

6 Kinghorn Street, London EC1A 7HW
tel 020-7796 4842 *fax* 020-7796 4580
email info@mayavisionint.com
website www.mayavisionint.com
Producer/Director Rebecca Dobbs *Producer* Sally
Thomas *Writer* Michael Wood

Maya Vision International is an independent film and
television production company, founded in 1983.
Since then it has won many awards, and become
renowned for making work of the highest quality.

Specialising in producing "original, landmark
documentaries, features and drama for film and
television", Maya Vision has developed a unique
style, making some of history's great stories accessible
to a wider public.

Working alongside many broadcasters and funders,
including the BBC, ITV, Channel 4, five, PBS, UK
Film Council and Arts Council England, Maya
Vision's acclaimed catalogue has been screened in
more than 140 territories worldwide. Since 2002 the
company has been managing the UK Film Festval's
successful Short Film Completion Fund, and has
helped support nearly 60 titles that have gone on to
win more than 150 awards and appeared in at least as
many festivals worldwide. See the website for how to
apply for funds.

Met Film Production (formerly APT Films)

Ealing Studios, Ealing Green, London W5 5EP
tel 020-8280 9127 *fax* 020-8280 9111
email info@metfilmproduction.co.uk
website www.metfilmproduction.co.uk
Managing Director Jonny Persey, *Director* Paul
Morrison, *Producers* Stewart le Maréchal, Al Morrow

Enterprise dedicated to the development and
production of feature films for national and
international audiences. Also produces short films.
The company has a number of feature films in
development.

Recent credits include: *Deep Water, Wondrous
Oblivion* and *Soloman & Gaenor.* Upcoming work
includes: *Heavy Load* and *The Pied Piper of
Hutzovina.*

NFD Productions Ltd

PO Box 76, Leeds LS25 9AG
tel/fax (01977) 681949
email alyson@nfdproductions.com
website www.nfdproductions.com
website www.film-tv-casting.com
website www.film-tv-agency.com
Director Alyson Connew

Production details: Production company producing
Adverts, Exhibition Video, Corporate Video,
Educational content, Training Videos, Wedding
videos, Streaming Video and Multi-Media.

Casting procedures: Casting is done via an online
agency and actors are encouraged to register their
details at **www.film-tv-agency.com**. Note that
commission will be charged on work obtained
through the agency.

On Screen Productions Ltd

Ashborne House, 33 Bridge Street,
Chepstow NP16 5GA
tel (01291) 636300 *fax* (01291) 636301
email action@OnScreenProductions.com
website www.OnScreenProductions.com
Director and Producer Richard Cobourne *Producer
and Director* Alison King *Assistant Producer and
Production Manager* Esther Prosser

Production details: Established in 1992. Creative,
business-led, integrated visual communications
company producing the full range of broadcast and
non-broadcast TV, video, TV commercials,
interactive media, training, live events, conferences,
exhibitions etc. Frequently uses actors across many of
its productions – the majority of which are non-
broadcast (60% for Health and Pharmaceutical
companies).

Casting procedures: Casting is done by freelance
casting directors as needed, or in-house by Joe
Allansen. Accepts submissions (with CVs and
photographs) from individual actors previously
unknown to the company if sent by post or email
(postal submissions are preferred). Invitations to view
showreels and individual actors' websites are also
accepted. Deals in 'buy out' contracts (except
broadcast and theatrical). "We do not discriminate
either positively or negatively against disabled
actors."

OVC Media Ltd

88 Berkeley Court, Baker Street, London NW1 5ND
tel 020-7402 9111 *fax* 020-7723 3044
email eliot@ovcmedia.com
website www.ovcmedia.com
Director Joanne Cohen

Production details: Established in 1982. Areas of
work include TV, film, video and documentary
production. Recent credits include: *History of the
World Cup, African Odyssey* and *My Matisse.*

Casting procedures: Accepts submissions (with CVs
and photographs) from actors previously unknown
to the company if sent by post, but not by email.
Showreels, voicereels and invitations to view
individual actors' websites are also accepted. Offers
Equity approved contracts and does not subscribe to
the Equity Pension Scheme. Will consider
submissions from disabled actors to play disabled
characters.

Park Village Ltd

1 Park Village East, Regents Park, London NW1 7PX
tel 020-7387 8077 *fax* 020-7388 3051

email reception@parkvillage.co.uk
website www.parkvillage.co.uk
Managing Director Tom Webb *Directors* Thor, Sven
Harding, Simon Burill, Mark Brozel, Mark
Emberton, Andy Welch, Marek Losey, Nuno Dias,
Max Rocket, Rowena True

Established in 1972. Commercials production
company working mainly in commercials and
content/interactive. Casting is done by freelance
casting directors. Recent credits include Marks &
Spencer Food. Actors are employed under Equity
approved contracts. Will consider applications from
disabled actors to play disabled characters.

Penumbra Productions Ltd
80 Brondesbury Road, London NW6 6RX
tel 020-7328 4550 *fax* 020-7328 3844
email nazpenumbra@compuserve.com
Contact HO Nazareth

Founded in 1981. Independent film and TV producer
making contemporary social-issue drama and
documentaries. Also produces non-broadcast videos
when commissioned.

Picture Palace Films Ltd
13 Egbert Street, London NW1 8LJ
tel 020-7586 8763 *fax* 020-7586 9048
email info@picturepalace.com
website www.picturepalace.com
Producer & Chief Executive Malcom Craddock

Founded in 1972. Works mainly in feature films and
TV drama production. Recent credits include:
Sharpe's Peril, Sharpe's Challenge, Frances Tuesday
and *Extremely Dangerous* (all ITV); *Rebel Heart*
(BBC); *A Life for a Life* (*The True Story of Stefan
Kizko*); and the *Sharpe* series.

Pinball London Ltd
56A Riversdale Road, London N5 2JZ
tel 020-7226 6490
email info@pinballonline.co.uk
website www.pinballonline.co.uk
Director Paula Vaccaro

Production details: Founded in 2009. Independent
film production company assembled by creative and
business entertainment industry professionals with a
common goal of producing independent auteur-
oriented films. Film is main area of work, but may do
music promos, TV and Internet content. Recent
credits include: *A Day in Two Lives* (short); *Margo &
Max* (long feature); and Perempay & Dee Feat. Shola
Ama (DJPLAY music video).

Casting procedures: Uses freelance casting directors.
Sometimes holds general auditions; actors may write
at any time to request inclusion. Only accepts postal
submissions, which *must* include CV, professional
actor's reel on DVD, and head shot photos.

Red Rose Chain
Gippeswyk Hall, Gippeswyk Avenue, Ipswich,
Suffolk IP2 9AF

tel (01473) 603388 *fax* (01473) 601102
email info@Redrosechain.com
website www.redrosechain.co.uk
Director Joanna Carrick *Key personnel* David
Newborn (Producer), Jimmy Grimes (Designer)

Production details: Established in 1997, a theatre
and film company that focuses on tackling
challenging subjects such as domestic violence,
teenage pregnancy and child abuse. As well as being
screened at international festivals and winning a
number of awards, the company's films – which are
used in 50% of UK schools – aim to raise awareness
and train health and social care professionals and
young people. Recent productions include:
Valentine's Day, Friday Night Shirt, and *Walking
Away.*

Casting procedures: Sometimes holds general
auditions: actors may write in Jan/Feb to request
inclusion, but are asked to "please check the website
regularly for information regarding upcoming film or
theatre work". Welcomes letters (with CVs &
photographs) from actors previously unknown to the
company sent by post, but not by email. Accepts
showreels but prefers not to receive invitations to
view individual actors' websites. Actively encourages
applications from disabled actors and promotes the
use of inclusive casting.

The Reel Thing Ltd
20 The Chase, Coulsdon, Surrey CR5 2EG
tel 0845-357 6393
email info@reelthing.tv
website www.reelthing.tv
Key personnel Frazer Ashford, Chris Day

Established in 2001. Specialising in corporate and
business TV production. Working the UK and
worldwide for small, local clients and large
multinationals. Recent credits include: *Fire Safety*
(Homebase Ltd) and *Lake Avalon* (US). Does not
welcome unsolicited CVs. Offers non-Equity
contracts and does not subscribe to the Equity
Pension Scheme. Actively encourages applications
from disabled actors and promotes the use of
inclusive casting.

Replay Film & New Media
25 Museum Street, London WC1 1ST
tel 020-7637 0473
email solutions@replayfilms.co.uk
website www.replayfilms.co.uk
Directors Dave Young, Stuart Slade *Production
Manager* Danny Scollard *Creative Director* Tim
Copsey

Established in 1990. Activities include: drama,
documentary, corporate, E-learning, training,
consultancy. Involved in all aspects of film and new
media, web design, working mainly in TV, video and
computer media production. Casting breakdowns are
available publicly on the website and Castweb.

Invitations to view individual actors' websites are accepted.

September Films

22 Glenthorne Road, London W6 ONG
tel 020-8563 9393 *fax* 020-8741 7214
email september@septemberfilms.com
website www.septemberfilms.com
Chairman David Green *Director of Production* Elaine Day

September Films is a leading UK independent television and film production company with offices in London and Los Angeles. It was founded in 1992 by feature film director, David Green, who devised the groundbreaking *Hollywood Women* series that launched the company. Having produced over 1000 hours of primetime television during the last 13 years, September is an established specialist in factual entertainment, features, reality programming and entertainment formats.

Seven Stones Media Ltd

The Old Butcher's Shop, High Street, St Briavels, Gloucester GL15 6TA
tel (01594) 530708 *fax* (01594) 530094
email info@sevenstonesmedia.com
website www.sevenstonesmedia.com
Managing Director Adam Alexander *Creative Director* Jeremy Gibson

Established in 2005. Recent productions include: *Return to Tuscany* and *Urban Chef*. Does not welcome unsolicited CVs.

Sightline

Dylan House, Town End Street, Godalming, Surrey GU7 IBQ
tel (01483) 861555 *fax* (01483) 861516
email keiththomas@sightline.co.uk
website www.sightline.co.uk
Director Keith Thomas *PA to Director* Alex Hayes

Production details: Established in 1985. Complete in-house multimedia production company specialising in corporate videos, CD Roms, DVDs and websites. Employs actors in corporate work and commercials. Recent credits include: Edexcel, BAA and London and Quadrant HT.

Casting procedures: Welcomes letters (with CVs and photographs) from actors previously unknown to the company – please send by email, not by post. Invitations to view individual actors' websites are welcome. Does not offer Equity approved contracts or subscribe to the Equity Pension Scheme. Rarely has the opportunity to cast disabled actors.

Sixteen Films

2nd Floor, 187 Wardour Street, London W2 5SH
tel 020-7734 0168 *fax* 020-7439 4196
email ann@sixteenfilms.co.uk
website www.sixteenfilms.co.uk
Director Ken Loach *Producer* Rebecca O'Brien

Sixteen Films was set up by Ken Loach and Rebecca O'Brien following the dissolution of Parallax Pictures in Spring 2002. They are joined by Paul Laverty as Associate Director.

Speakeasy Productions Ltd

1-2 Henrietta Street, London WC2E 8PS
tel 020-7836 0866 *fax* 020-7240 9623
email info@speak.co.uk
website www.speak.co.uk
Director Jim Adamson *Head of Production* Jeremy Hewitt *Head of Post-production* Magnus Wake *Production Manager* Simone Bett

Production details: Corporate media production company and event management company based in London and Perth. Works mainly in video production, employing actors in documentary, corporate, and commercials. Occasionally holds general auditions. Recent credits include: Royal Bank of Scotland *Raid Video* with Fiona Bruce; *Recipe for Success* events for Food Standards Agency with Phil Vickery.

Casting procedures: Accepts submissions (with CVs and photographs) from actors previously unknown to the company. Will also accept CVs and photographs sent via email. Invitations to view showreels and individual actors' websites are also accepted. Promotes inclusive casting and applications from disabled actors are considered.

Spellbound Productions Ltd

90 Cowdenbeath Path, Islington, London N1 0LG
tel 020-7713 8066 *fax* 020-7713 8066
email phspellbound@hotmail.com
Producer Paul Harris

Small independent production company specialising in feature films and drama for television. Current projects include: *Twist of Fate*, a romantic comedy in development with Columbia Pictures (LA). Other projects in development include an animated feature, a drama series for television, and other 'genre' pieces.

Stagescreen Productions

Suite 92, One Prescot Street, London E1 8RL
tel/fax 020-7481 4810
Director Jeffrey Taylor *Development Executive* John Segal

Founded in 1986, Stagescreen is a film and TV production company with offices in London and Los Angeles. Recent credits include: *What's Cooking*, directed by Gurinder Chadha (Lionsgate); *Alexander The Great* directed by Jalal Merhi (ProSeiben); and *Jekyll*, directed by Douglas Mackinnon and Matt Lipsey (BBC). Forthcoming work includes: *Young Cleopatra*.

Offers PACT/Equity approved contracts and does not subscribe to the Equity Pension Scheme. Will consider applications from disabled actors to play disabled characters.

Table Top Productions

1 The Orchard, Chiswick, London W4 1JZ
tel/fax 020-8742 0507
email top@tabletopproductions.com
website www.tabletopproductions.com
Director Alvin Rakoff *Production Manager* Ben Berry

Production details: Established in 1967. Credits
include: *A Voyage Round My Father, Romeo and
Juliet, Liberty Tree, Don Quixote, Dance to the Music
of Time* (C4) and *Separate Tables* (Mill at Sonning
Theatre).

Casting procedures: Casting breakdowns are
available via the website; apply only when in
production. Offers Equity approved contracts. Does
not welcome unsolicited CVs. Rarely has the
opportunity to cast disabled actors.

Talkback Thames

20-21 Newman Street, London W1T 1PG
tel 020-7861 8000 *fax* 020-7861 8001
website www.talkbackthames.tv

Founded in 1981. Produces TV situation comedies
and comedy dramas, features, and straight drama.
Credits include: *Property Ladder, Jamie's Kitchen,
Smack the Pony, The 11 O' Clock Show* and *Da Ali G
Show*. TalkBack is part of the Fremantle Media
Group (see page 317).

Tiger Aspect Productions

Drama address: 5 Soho Square, London W1V 5DE
tel 020-7434 0672 *fax* 020-7544 1665
email general@tigeraspect.co.uk
Comedy address: 7 Soho Street, London W1D 3DQ
tel 020-7434 0700 *fax* 020-7434 1798
website www.tigeraspect.co.uk
Head of Drama Greg Brenman

Founded in 1993. Produces TV drama, comedy and
sitcoms with the aim of "investing in and working
with the leading writers, performers and programme-
makers to produce original, creative and successful
programming". Credits include: *Teachers* (C4), *My
Fragile Heart* (ITV), and *Playing the Field* (BBC1).

Trafalgar 1 Limited

153 Burnham Towers, Adelaide Road,
London NW3 3JN
tel 020-7722 7789 *fax* 020-7483 0662
email t1ltd@blueyonder.co.uk

Production details: Established 1985. Produces
feature films, music videos, documentaries and short
films. Recent productions include: *Rough Cut and
Ready Dubbed, Art of the Critic* and *11th Dimension*.

Casting procedures: Welcomes letters (with CVs and
photographs) from actors previously unknown to the
company sent by post or email. Showreels, voicereels
and invitations to view individual actors' websites are
also accepted. Offers Equity approved contracts. "We
rarely have the opportunity to cast disabled actors."

Twenty Twenty Television

20 Kentish Town Road, London NW1 9NX
tel 020-7284 2020 *fax* 020-7284 1810
email triciawilson@twentytwenty.tv
website www.twentytwenty.tv
Managing Director Peter Casely-Hayford *Executive
Producer* Claudia Milne *Head of Development* George
Kay

Twenty Twenty Television is one of the UK's leading
independent television production companies,
making award-winning documentaries, hard-hitting
current affairs, popular drama and attention-
grabbing living history series. Its recent primetime
children's shows are also bringing success in an
exciting and challenging genre. *The Choir* won a 2007
BAFTA Award; the series *That'll Teach 'Em* won an
Indie Award and was nominated for a British
Academy Award. The *Lads Army* series gained the
Royal Television Society primetime features award as
well as a BAFTA nomination, and the international
factual hit *Brat Camp* brought home an International
Emmy from New York in November 2004.

Formed in 1982 by 'hands on' programme-makers,
Twenty Twenty Television has always grown
organically. Its industry-wide reputation for quality,
intelligence and rigour was built in factual
programmes. Twenty Twenty remains truly
independent and is still run by creative and
enthusiastic programme-makers. Its work has been
broadcast by networks around the world including
the BBC, CBBC, ITV, Channels 4 and Five in the UK,
and ABC, The Discovery Channel, Turner Original
Productions, Sundance Channel, CNN, The Arts and
Entertainment Channel and WGBH in the USA.

TwoFour Productions Ltd

TwoFour Studios, Estover, Plymouth PL6 7RG
tel (01752) 727400 *fax* (01752) 727450
email enquiries@twofour.co.uk
website www.twofour.co.uk
Director of Broadcast Melanie Leach *Press & Publicity*
Amanda Wood

Production details: Established in 1987. Independent
television production company specialising in factual,
lifestyle and documentary programming. Recent
credits include: *Accidents Can Happen* (BBC1); *Cruise
with Stelios* (Sky); *The Hotel Inspector* (C5); *Why Men
Wear Frocks* (Channel 4) and *Life Begins Again* (C4).

Casting procedures: Welcomes actors' showreels.
Offers Equity approved contracts. Will consider
applications from disabled actors to play characters
with disabilities.

Video Enterprises

12 Barbers Wood Road, High Wycombe,
Bucks HP12 4EP
tel (01494) 534144 *mobile* (07831) 875216

email videoenterprises@ntlworld.com
website www.videoenterprises.co.uk
Director Maurice R Fleisher

Video Enterprises is a UK-based video production and crewing company specialising in Broadcast, Corporate, Industrial, Theatrical and Social Events programme-making.

Videotel Productions

84 Newman Street, London W1T 3EU
tel 020-7299 1800 *fax* 020-7299 1818
email mail@videotelmail,com
website www.videotel.co.uk
Casting Directors Stephen Bond, Peter Wilde, Kathrein Guenther

Production details: Established in 1975, Award-winning Videotel is "the world leader for the production of DVD/video, multimedia and web-deliverable training material for the maritime industry".

Casting procedures: Hold general auditions, casting information available via the website, Spotlight, Talent Circle, Casting Call Pro and CastNet UK. Offers Equity approved contracts. Accepts submissions (with CVs and photographs) from actors previously unknown to the company sent by post or email. Showreels, voicereels and invitations to view individual actors' websites are also accepted. Rarely has the opportunity to cast disabled actors due to the fact that most of the company's work is filmed aboard ships.

Walking Forward Ltd

Studio 6, The Aberdeen Centre, Highbury Grove, London
tel 020-7359 5249
email info@walkingforward.co.uk
website www.walkingforward.co.uk
Director Gavin Payne *Casting Directors* Sarah Noll, Rory Thersby *New Business* William Pretsell

Production details: An educational theatre and film company specialising in dramatic road safety productions. Produces theatre tours and short films for the British Armed Forces, TFL and many local borough councils. Recent credits include: *Wasted* (schools tour, Transport for London); *Welcome Back* (theatre production, Cyprus, British Army Land Command); and *Zoom Wales* (multimedia film and theatre tour, WLGA).

Casting procedures: Sometimes holds general auditions; actors may write in July/August to request inclusion. Casting breakdowns are available via Spotlight. Welcomes letters (with CVs and photographs) from actors previously unknown to the company sent by post or email, and accepts showreels and invitations to view individual actors' websites. Offers Equity-approved contracts. Has an equal

opportunities policy – all are welcome as long as an actor is able to complete what is required.

Walsh Bros Ltd

29 Trafalgar Grove, London SE10 9TB
tel 020-8858 6870 *mobile* (07879) 816426
email info@walshbros.co.uk
website www.walshbros.co.uk

BAFTA-nominated productions range from television series and dramas for BBC 'Sofa Surfers', Channel 4's *Don't Make Me Angry*, and feature film production *Monarch*. The BBC documentary series *Headhunting the Homeless* was shortlisted for the Grierson Awards 2004.

Wilder Films

21 Little Portland Street, London W1W 8BT
tel 020-7631 3417 *fax* 020-7636 4439
email molliehalford@wilderfilms.co.uk
website www.wilderfilms.co.uk
Director Paul Gowers *Managing Director* Richard Batty

Production details: Established in 2003. Works mainly in film and video production, especially corporate, brand and short films, and commercials. Recent credits include: *Ripple* – a comedy short film; British Gas recruitment; Aston Martin corporate; and Olympic bid films.

Casting procedures: Uses in-house and freelance casting directors and holds general auditions – but "will look for people if needed". Does not welcome unsolicited approaches but may accept invitations to view individual actors' websites.

Michael Winner Ltd/Scimitar Films

219 Kensington High Street, London W8 6BD
tel 020-7603 7272 *fax* 020-7602 9217
email winner@ftech.co.uk
Directors Michael Winner, John Fraser

Production details: Established in 1956. Specialises in film and television commercial production. Employs actors in drama, comedy and commercials.

Casting procedures: Welcomes letters (with CVs and photographs) from actors previously unknown to the company if sent by post, but not by email. Offers Equity approved contracts.

Working Title Films

76 Oxford Street, London W1N 9FD
tel 020-7307 3000 *fax* 020-7307 3003
email dan.shepherd@unistudios.com
website www.workingtitlefilms.com
Chairmen Tim Bevan, Eric Fellner *President* Liza Chasin *President UK Production* Debra Hayward

Recent films include *Atonement* (with James McAvoy, Keira Knightly, Romola Garai, Saoirse Ronan and Vanessa Redgrave) and *The Golden Age* (with Cate

Blanchett and Geoffrey Rush, who reprise the roles they orginated in the award-winning *Elizabeth*, joined this time by Clive Owen).

World Productions Ltd
Lasenby House, 32 Kingly Street, London W1B 5QQ
tel 020-3179 1800, 020-3179 1801
email helen@world-productions.com
website www.world-productions.com
Executive Producer Tony Garnett *Executive Producer/ Head of Development* Simon Heath *PA & Office Manager* Helen Saunders

Produces TV drama features, series and serials. Recent credits include: *Between the Lines*, *Ballykissangel* and *Love Again* – a film about Philip Larkin (BBC).

Zenith Productions Ltd
43-45 Dorset Street, London W1U 7NA
tel 020-7224 2440 *fax* 020-7224 3194
email general@zenith-entertainment.co.uk
website www.zenith.tv.co.uk
Managing Director Ivan Rendall *Casting Director* Matt Western *Head of Drama* Adrian Bate

Founded in 1984. Part of the Zenith group, which comprises Zenith North and Zenith Productions. Works mainly in producing a wide range of programmes for terrestrial, satellite and cable television and feature films for worldwide theatrical distribution.

Film schools

Although the work is minimally paid (if at all), it is well worth contacting film schools for casting consideration. Despite the fact that you'll often find yourself in the hands of a director with no idea about actors and acting, the potential of gaining something from the experience is possibly greater than that of participating in a Fringe theatre production – and the end result could contain material worthy of use in a showreel. Some schools keep files of actors' CVs and photographs for students to refer to when casting.

Castings for many low- or non-paid films are advertised on Shooting People (**www.shootingpeople.org**) – see entry on page 435.

The Arts Institute at Bournemouth
Wallisdown, Poole, Dorset BG12 5HH
tel (01292) 533011
Key contact/Lecturer Mike Fisher

Students do not only consider local actors for their short films. Actors are generally offered their expenses and a DVD copy. Welcomes enquiries (containing CV, photograph and covering letter) from new actors; actors' details are kept on file.

Brighton Film School
Administration, 13 Tudor Close, Dean Court Road, Rottingdean BN2 7DF
tel (01273) 302166 *fax* (01273) 302163
email info@brightonfilmschool.org.uk
website www.brightonfilmschool.org.uk
Key contact Franz von Habsburg

Film-industry-recognised. Provides training in all aspects of motion pictures production: screenwriting, directing, cinematography, editing and production management. More than 30 student short films are made each year; students generally recruit actors through Shooting People (**www.shootingpeople.org**). There is no formal agreement with Equity. Students do not only consider local actors. Actors are generally offered their expenses and a DVD copy. Welcomes enquiries (containing photograph and 1-page CV) from new actors if sent by post.

International Film School Wales
University of Wales College, Caerleon Campus, PO Box 179, Newport NP18 3YG
tel (01633) 432677 *fax* (01633) 432680
email uic@newport.ac.uk
website www.ifsw.newport.ac.uk
Head of School Humphry Trevelyan

A recognised Welsh national institution for the production and development of the audiovisual culture of Wales, through training, education and postgraduate research. On average 60-80 student short films are made each year. Students generally recruit actors through agents, casting directors, Equity Job Information Service and public notices at the Royal Welsh College of Music & Drama. There is no formal agreement with Equity. Actors' details are held on file. Welcomes enquiries (with CV, photograph and covering letter) from new actors. Students at BA and MA level increasingly work in production groupings and cast professionally. "As the main centre for film education and training in Wales, we seek, encourage and support the casting of professional actors wherever possible. We also require actors to teach part-time on our BA Hons in Performance course."

London College of Communication
Elephant & Castle, London SE1 6SB
tel 020-7514 7935 *fax* 020-7514 6843
email s.jeans@lcc.arts.ac.uk
website www.arts.ac.uk
Course Director Sarah Jeans

A long-established film and television course with both BA and FdA programmes. Students work on 16mm, video and HD, and cast for projects throughout the year. Letters and CVs are welcome. Expenses only are offered, but a copy of finished work is supplied for showreels.

London Film Academy
52a Walham Grove, Fulham, London SW6 1QR
020-7386 7711 020-7381 6116
email info@londonfilmacademy.com
website www.londonfilmacademy.com
Key contact Laura Tovey

Specialise in professional full-time film training. Students make a series of short graduation films and commercials using both professional and non professional actors. Students train in all areas of filmmaking.

"Students use agents, casting directors, and the various Internet websites and paper casting publications to recruit actors." Accept submissions (with CVs and photographs) from actors previously unknown to them. Actors' details are kept on file for the student's reference and the actor is contacted directly. Payment to actors depends on the individual project budgets. Expenses will usually be paid and the actor will receive a copy of the showreel.

The London Film School

24 Shelton Street, London WC2H 9UB
tel 020-7240 0161 *fax* 020-7240 0167
email c.bright@lfs.org.uk
website www.lfs.org.uk
Librarian/Casting Chrissy Bright

London Film School offers a 2-year MA Course in the art and technique of filmmaking, with approximately 120-130 student short films being made each year. Students generally recruit actors through Spotlight, *PCR*, Star Now, Talent Circle, Acting Faces. Expenses and a DVD copy of the film are normally offered to actors cast in student films. The School welcomes enquiries from actors (with CVs and photographs) and will be happy to keep their details on file for future productions. We also have a 1-year MA Screenwriting Course.

National Film and Television School

Beaconsfield Studios, Station Road,
Beaconsfield HP9 1LG
tel (01494) 671234 *fax* (01494) 674042
email admin@nftsfilm-tv.ac.uk
website www.nftsfilm.ac.uk
Key personnel Shakil Mohammed

Offers 2-year MA courses including fiction direction, cinematography, production design, editing, sound, animation, and documentary. Students generally recruit actors through casting directors, *Spotlight*, Shooting People (**www.shootingpeople.org**) and from actors' files kept by Shakil Mohammed. Has a formal agreement with Equity. Students do not only consider local actors. Actors are generally offered their expenses. Welcomes enquiries (with CVs and photographs) from new actors which should be

marked for the attention of Shakil Mohammed. Actors' details are held on file. Actors are also required throughout the year for workshops, and files are kept for this purpose. Graduation projects are cast by external casting directors.

UCCA Farnham (Surrey Institute of Art and Design)

Falkner Road, Farnham GU9 7DS
tel (01252) 722441 *fax* (01252) 892787
email sjeans@ucreative.co.uk
website www.ucreative.ac.uk
Director of Studies (Media) Sarah Jeans

The course, accredited by the British Kinematograph, Sound & Television Society, offers a broad grounding in film and video practice. Students work on both 16mm productions and video. The course emphasises film as social practice, and the study of issue-based work is a dominant theme. An average of 40-50 student short films are made each year. Actors are recruited through *Spotlight*, *PCR* and Shooting People. Only local actors are considered. Travel expenses and a copy of the film are offered, although it is not always possible to provide transfers of 16mm projects. Welcomes CVs and photographs (sent by post, not email) from actors.

University of Westminster

University of Westminster, Watford Road,
Northwick Park, Harrow, Middlesex HA1 3TP
email P.S.Hort@wmin.ac.uk
website www.westminster.ac.uk/filmschool
Key personnel Peter Hort, Malcolm Mowbray, Simon Passmore, Zoe Allsop

Makes around 40 short films per year from 3 minutes to 20 minutes in length, on 16mm film and video. Expenses and DVD copy of the film to actors. Welcomes letters (including CV and photograph) from actors previously unknown to the school.

The essentials of screen acting

Mel Churcher

The first question I always ask when I run a film acting workshop is, "What are the differences between screen acting and theatre acting?" The first and most fundamental difference is always the last one that actors tell me, and yet it is the most crucial.

In theatre, there is an audience. In film, there is no audience.

It sounds so simple and obvious but this awareness has a deep and subtle effect on your work. When you perform for the stage, you are always sharing with the people out there in the darkness, even if it is a tiny space with an audience of one. Even in the most intimate production, there is live interplay between you and the audience – the watchers and the watched.

In film, you do your work surrounded by technicians but they are not your audience. They are there to do their own important tasks and, apart from making sure that their aspect of the work is as good as they can get it, most have little interest in, or knowledge about, what you are doing. In fact only a few key people like the director, the producer, script supervisor, sound crew and dialogue coach are wearing headphones to hear what you are saying!

Certainly, the camera isn't your audience. It is an inanimate object that is there to record your secret life. You need to open yourself up to being minutely scrutinised by it, but you share with it at your peril: once you start to 'show' to it, you will be perceived as false.

In other words, you have to believe that this weird world full of cameras, microphones and people is a form of real life. You have to believe that there is no one there but the other characters who also inhabit this strange reality. You have to think extremely hard at every moment and trust that the camera sees that. And it will. Martin Scorsese calls it 'the physic strength of the lens'. Thinking is enough and you have to trust it. You must never 'show' us what you are thinking. If you do that, we won't believe you are living this real life that we are privileged to observe from our safe position in the darkened cinema or from the corner of our sofa. That explains why it would be possible to move a close-up of a good actor from one film situation to another. The camera can see you thinking – but it doesn't know what you are thinking. You can test this out. Look around you in the tube and watch someone closely who is just sitting and thinking. Now, in your imagination, try putting them into different situations. Perhaps they are looking at a loved one, worrying about a bill or thinking about a hidden secret. You will see how, in life, they could be in any of those scenarios and yet look the same. Of course, I don't mean you should be consciously deadpan. We can see emotion when you feel and think. Your eyes literally shine with all the thoughts that light them up. Too often, this light dims when an actor is speaking learned text. You need all the thoughts, memories and pictures in your head to be as specific and extra-ordinary as they are in life, but not 'acted'.

One day you hope that an audience will see the assembled jigsaw of your film flickering on a screen, but that audience has nothing to do with your work at the time of shooting.

The next most important difference between screen and live work is that a film is shot out of order. You may bury your lover before you've met them or murder your boss before you've interviewed for the job. Each scene is done from many different angles (or set-ups). The bigger the production, the more of these set-ups there will be. Then each set-up can involve many takes and each take needs to be fresh and spontaneous. So film takes tremendous imagination and focus, not to mention stamina.

You also need to know where you are in the story. You, as the role, can only live in the moment, but you, as the actor, need to know exactly where you are in the story. How long ago did you hurt your knee? Do you know about that affair yet? Exactly how drunk are you?

I have a quick tip for this. Take a pack of filing cards. Now write a card for each scene you are in, including the ones where you don't have any dialogue. Write the scene number at the top of the card. Then put down where you've come from and, at the bottom of the card, put where you're going to. Write who is in the scene with you and what you know or feel about them at this time. For example, is this before or after you're pregnant? Do you know about the robbery yet? Then put down anything else that's important – I'm feeling hungry, I've just run a mile, it's a heat wave, etc. Now tie all your cards together and you have a flickbook of your journey through the film.

Now when they pick you up at 5am and tell you you're not doing scene 32 but scene 64 because the set blew down in the night, you won't spend the next hour in a panic, thumbing through the script trying to find out where you are in the story and how bad your limp is!

You don't need to write down your dialogue – that's in your script. Why can't you write these notes there too? Because, in a big film, that script will change a dozen times and you'll end up with a rainbow-coloured script of re-writes. You'll never have the energy to keep transferring your notes. Also, it is bulkier than your little carry-around flickbook. And doing this work really makes sure you read the script thoroughly!

Of course the technology makes filming so different to live theatre. It comes hard to realise that no matter how well you act, if the camera doesn't see it, it doesn't exist. There's only one reality and that's what ends up on that screen. That means hitting your mark or you'll be out of focus, watching your continuity or the shot can't be used, having to be closer than you want to be to your partner because the camera, with its two-dimensional nature, changes spatial relationships and enduring long hours of waiting for that technology to work properly.

You need tremendous, specific imagination. You may have to imagine strange alien creatures whilst staring at a blue or green screen, Your partner may not be able to be in your eye-line for your close-ups. And you need to be thinking the whole time and visualising what you talk about.

Which brings me to rehearsal. There's not much rehearsal for film – well, not as we know it in theatre, If you're very lucky, there may be a few weeks of pre-production but it is unusual for all the cast to attend at the same time. You'll have a script reading of sorts (where everyone will want to change the text), and meetings with the director. You'll have costume fittings, make-up tests, horse-riding, sword-fighting and dialect coaching where applicable. But, until you arrive on that set for shooting, you may never have rehearsed with, or even met, the person you are going to play the scene with.

And yet you do need to do a tremendous amount of preparation before you get to that stage. But it must be the right kind. Beware of imposing a 'character', as the camera will read it as overdone and false. You really do need to 'inhabit' the role. It needs to be you 'as if' you were in that situation or living in that time. And that 'as if' could mean a complete change of physicality, depending on the life you've led in the role. You might be a medieval peasant who digs the ground or an astronaut who has trained for a weightless environment. So 'Who am I?' and 'Where am I?' will take the life you've led and the period into account. But you have to reach it organically through research, work and specific imagination.

Now you need to ask. 'What do I want? Your needs must be powerful and strong. You may not show those needs to the other people in the story (that's sub-text), but strong needs must drive you.

Beware of deciding how you get what you want. If you plot a course or decide how to play the scene, you will not be open to react in the moment. And you don't know what the other people will bring to the scene yet. Until you have that short but valuable rehearsal on set before shooting, you need to stay open to all possibilities.

What you can also do on your own or with a willing partner is to improvise scenes that fill in the gaps. You can't break up with someone till you've met and loved them. So if your only scene is a divorce, improvise your first meeting at home. Or imagine waking up and thinking of them the morning after the first date. Act out stories you're going to tell in the dialogue so that you've already lived through the events and have powerful specific pictures in your head when you come to tell them on the screen.

You are a unique, exciting human being – don't let your character be less engaging than you are!

So keep open, really listen, think hard and react in the moment. And also sit back. This sounds silly but nerves and a desire to please will often make you crane forward. Good actors are comfortable in their own skins and we are drawn to people who show a little 'attitude'. We shy away from people who are needy, insecure or sorry for themselves.

Find out the size of the shot from the camera crew so that you can work out technical problems and know how much you can move to stay in shot.

Remember to warm up. Your breathing should be relaxed and centred. Make sure you're releasing your abdominal area as you breathe in and not holding it tight and breathing high up in your upper chest. When you are relaxed, you will feel your stomach gently moving away from you as you breathe in and flattening back as you breathe out. You need to make sure that you continue to breathe like this when, with the excitement of shooting, adrenalin is pumping round your body. This will keep you relaxed and your face clear. It will put you in touch with your feelings, so that you don't 'push' emotions. If your face keeps screwing up or overworking, it is a sure sign that you are not centred and you're manufacturing emotion. The breathing work will also help to keep your voice warm and resonant. You only need to use the level of voice you'd need in life but don't choose a half-whispered sound that doesn't carry any emotional life and will mean you'll need to record it again in post-production because no-one could hear you! This is an expensive business and it is much harder to re-find your performance months later, standing in a recording studio trying to match your lip-movements to your image on screen.

Finally, forget anything you've ever heard about theatre work being big and screen work being small. Films and TV plays are about extreme situations, emotions or characters. How can that be small? If you are truly rooted in truth, you can be as big as you'll need to be (allowing for the technical aspect of where you can move in a close-up). If the director says it's too big, then sure thing, you're sharing or manufacturing or signalling what you want us to feel and it's not too big – it's just not truthful.

Mel Churcher was an actor for many years but now works as a director and international acting and voice coach. Her theatre voice work includes The Royal Shakespeare Company, Shakespeare's Globe and The Open Air Theatre, Regent's Park, where she was resident voice and text coach from 1996 to 2007. Mel has coached on dozens of major movies including *Control* (BAFTA nominated), *The Count of Monte Cristo*, *King Arthur*, *The Fifth Element*, *The Hole*, *Lara Croft: Tomb Raider*, *Tristan & Isolde*, *Danny the Dog*, *Eragon* and *Incendiary*. She runs regular film acting workshops at the Actors Centres and leading drama schools. She has an MA in Performing Arts (Mddx), and Voice Studies (CSSD) Her book *Acting for Film: Truth 24 Times a Second* is published by Virgin Books. **www.melchurcher.com**

Fringe film: low-budget shorts, student films and web-based work
Edward Hicks

Media

A challenging and changing environment
Fringe theatre is familiar to most actors as an area for potential work that may be low-paid, but which can give you the chance to experiment and/or stretch yourself more than you might in commercial theatre. The equivalent is happening in screen work, with a growing area of possible opportunities that splits into two categories: Short films (including Student films), and web-based work. It is to this new and expanding area of potential screen work that I am referring, under the umbrella title of 'fringe film'. Is it time to take this work more seriously, or is it just another example of how actors are poorly paid and sadly exploited?

With filmmaking equipment being more accessible than ever before (even phones now have cameras), more and more people are 'Shooting'. The days of needing to hire expensive equipment and a huge crew to make a film are now behind us, thanks to digital technology. A reasonable digital camera from your local high street and a computer with an editing program (some even come with free editing software) is all you need to shoot and edit a film that could be of sufficiently high technical quality to be broadcast (provided the filmmakers know what they are doing!). But remember, just because a person can use a computer does not mean they can write a novel. The technology may have opened the doors to more filmmakers, but the abilities and artistic choices of everyone involved in the project, and how the equipment is used, are – and always will be – the most important factor.

Thus this changing environment of 'fringe film' presents a dilemma for the professional actor. On the one hand, there is more potential screen work out there; on the other, the quality of this work varies hugely. In the past, some of this work was seen as being a little amateur, not taken too seriously and perhaps considered not really appropriate work for the professional actor. However, it could also be argued that just as fringe theatre may not be as well paid as the more traditional commercial theatre, it can still prove a worthwhile commitment for an actor to take on – after all, a few West End shows started on the fringe. There is also a popular misconception that this area of work is always expenses-only and unpaid, whereas in reality that is not always the case.

Short films
Film schools and websites such as Shooting People (**www.shootingpeople.org**) are a good place to start finding work in Shorts. Although the majority are Student films listed under the Lo/No Budget category (usually meaning expenses-only), don't presume that the film will be rubbish. The script is all-important, and I'm often amazed by the creative ideas of young filmmakers who are desperate to make their films despite the lack of funds.

It's also worth noting that despite the new HD technology, some of the best-regarded film schools shoot some films on 35mm (celluloid), which is far more expensive; they see it as fundamental to the film training. These films can provide a fantastic opportunity for an actor to experience being surrounded by expensive equipment and a large crew – an opportunity that might not present itself with projects that are shot digitally. And there's always the additional chance that the student director you work with today will be a successful feature-film director tomorrow.

However, be under no illusion. The vast majority of Shorts (and indeed web-based work) will be expenses-only, and therefore as a professional actor you need to consider carefully if working for free is something that you wish to do and/or promote. Some actors argue that working for free should not be allowed, and that actors are being unfairly treated – taken advantage of, in fact. I can understand this point or view, since nobody wishes to see anyone being exploited. That said, it is a reality of the world we live in that there are budding, often very talented, filmmakers out there who are also struggling and failing to secure funding. Funding for film is extremely competitive, and can be a simple matter of a particular film or filmmaker not fitting one single criterion. They are then left with no choice but to fund the film themselves – which goes some way to explaining the lack of money available with which to pay crew and actors. Simply put, for some projects, paying both actors and crew can mean that the Short does not get made. For more advice on this, and with any specific queries or concerns, contact Equity (**www.equity.org.uk**).

So don't rule out an expenses-only Short if the project provides you with an exciting challenge: an opportunity to stretch yourself and experiment, gain more experience on camera, make material for a showreel, and forge new contacts. One advantage of Shorts is that the shooting process is quick (not just for budgetary reasons) – often only taking a few days. Therefore your time commitment is minimal, and you can squeeze it around any castings that may come up. Most people working in this area will try to accommodate you (especially if they are not paying you), because they understand that, just like them, you have to earn a living and can't turn down a casting or a paid job. I've known several actors who have even managed to work on a Short during the day while performing in the theatre at night, as the shooting schedule was designed around the performance times.

There is a huge international film festival circuit for Short films, which caters to every level – from the more established and respected events that include a Short film section, to festivals that are aimed purely at Shorts. It's not unusual for some of the better Shorts that win prizes at the biggest festivals to end up being broadcast on television. However, if the filmmakers claim they are submitting the Short to Cannes as an incentive to get you on board, remember that *submitting* a film to a festival does not mean that it will automatically be accepted.

Make sure you fully understand what it is you are getting involved in, and, if the filmmakers are new and you don't know them, do some research (consult IMDB, the International Movie Database; browse via various search engines; talk to fellow actors and so on). You could ask to see examples of the director's work, find out if any of his or her films have ever been selected for a festival, and then research the festivals (there are some that take anything and everything!).

I would also recommend that you always ask to see the script before a meeting, especially if they are not paying you. The best advice I ever heard given to actors about Shorts was, *"If the script and project do not excite you, walk away."* Remember, if you commit to a project like this, you have a responsibility to take it as seriously as you would anything else you do, regardless of salary. If your professionalism is not reciprocated by the people you are working with, word will soon spread – and you cannot afford to be tarnished by the wrong kind of association.

Bear in mind too that not all Shorts will be Student films, expenses-only or made by the DIY filmmaker. Some will have competed for funding, and the criteria for gaining funds may include paying a fee to the actors and crew. It's not uncommon for Shorts to win funding, provided this is matched by the production company – and some film schools have been known to pay a token fee to the actors. Peter *'Lord of the Rings'* Jackson made a Short in order to test a new type of camera; directors often make a Short in order to help gain funding for a feature film project. Shorts at this level are more likely to be funded, and to have an established production company on board to produce them, as well as a casting director to cast them.

Web-based work

You only have to look at the number of Shorts, commercials, virals (web content that is aimed at triggering an online following which builds its own momentum as it spreads – a commercial of sorts) that are posted on sites like YouTube to see how the web has become a huge growth area for screen work. However, it also highlights how quality standards can vary massively. At one end of the scale are huge, multinational companies with budgets to match, employing production companies to make virals, commercials and Short films; and at the other is the DIY filmmaker filming his dog on a skateboard. Just as with the Short film market, do your research, make sure you know what you are getting involved in, and check with Equity.

Advertising agencies continue to look for less traditional outlets for their work, and the web is becoming an important area for them – which in turn means more potential screen roles for actors. I know one actor who has been able to establish himself as a cabaret act, based on a character that he originally helped to create for a web-based advertising campaign. More recently, too, web-based TV shows have started to spring up: projects that are made exclusively for the web and not broadcast on traditional TV. The first web-based soap was sold not long ago to a TV network, having established a large initial following on the Internet. With more and more of the population now watching TV over the web rather than on traditional TV sets, this phenomenon looks set to grow and grow over the next few years; actors will need to be especially careful as to what they sign in terms of agreements over future sales.

So, if you're a new actor who has just left drama school and wants more screen experience, or a more experienced actor keen to stretch yourself, this growth area I refer to as 'Fringe Film' might be worth considering. However, like all new growth areas, approach with caution. Despite people's best efforts and intentions, quality is never guaranteed. You must be realistic about what it is you are doing – and be honest with yourself about why.

Edward Hicks is currently Head of Film, TV and Radio at RADA – a post sponsored by Warner Bros. He has directed numerous Shorts, commercials and promos, is a graduate and former governor of LFS, has various film projects in development, and has written articles on screen acting in addition to being a regular contributor to *Actors' Yearbook*. Ed has taught at various Drama Schools including East 15, where in 2001 he created the first media-based acting course to gain NCDT accreditation. Under the name Edward Rawle-Hicks he started his professional career as a child actor (from the age of ten), appearing at the RSC, the West End and in numerous commercials, film and television projects.

Radio and audio book companies

Unlike in the visual media, many radio directors have their roots in theatre and will go to stage productions to inform their future casting. And, unlike their visual media counterparts, they have a far greater understanding of actors and acting, and are far more open to casting against obvious physical type.

The BBC has by far and away the biggest radio drama output, and it also uses actors to read poetry, narrations and stories. Some of this 'output' is made in-house; a good proportion is contracted-out to independent companies. This is one area of work that doesn't very often use casting directors. It is a good idea to listen to radio drama in order to become aware of its ways – you won't hear much swearing, for instance. Also see 'Voice-over agents' (page 90) and 'Showreel and voice-demo companies' (page 395); some of the latter have excellent advice on making a voice demo on their websites.

BBC Radio Drama
Bush House, The Strand, London WC2B 4PH
tel 020-7557 1013
website www.bbc.co.uk/soundstart
Head of Radio Drama Alison Hindell *Coordinator, Drama Company* Cynthia Fagan *Production Executive, Radio Drama* Rebecca Wilmshurst

BBC Radio Drama Department is the biggest producer of drama on radio in the world. It provides more than 700 hours of drama a year for Radio 3, Radio 4, BBC World Service, BBC7 and the BBC Asian Network. Plays are broadcast every day of the week and can be heard at any time, either on air or on the website. An audience of about half a million people is listening every time a play is aired. Output includes: *Westway* (drama set in a London health centre); *The Archers* (countryside soap opera); the Friday and Saturday plays (thrillers, mysteries and love stories); afternoon plays, classic serials, Woman's Hour Drama (weekday drama serial); play of the week (from around the world); book of the week (non-fiction); book at bedtime (fiction, including modern classics).

The Radio Drama Company was founded in 1940 as the BBC Repertory Company, and is still frequently referred to as The Rep. The company's focus allows new acting talent to work alongside established actors in a variety of radio productions. Actors joining the RDC have already worked with many eminent artists such as Julia Mackenzie, Derek Jacobi, Richard Griffiths, Cheryl Campbell, Anna Massey and Daniel Day-Lewis.

Past members of the company have included Stephen Tompkinson, Alex Jennings, Adjoa Andoh, Norman Bird, Emma Fielding, Anthony Daniels, Ben Onwukwe, Joanna Monro, Ann Beach, Janet Maw, Suzanna Hamilton and Carolyn Pickles.

The RDC does not use freelance casting directors and casting breakdowns are not publicly available.

Sometimes holds general auditions and actors can write at any time requesting inclusion. Welcomes postal submissions from individual actors previously unknown to the company, but does not accept email enquiries. Voice demos and invitations to view individual actors' websites are also accepted. More information can be found under 'FAQs' at **www.bbc.co.uk/soundstart**

The Norman Beaton Fellowship is part of BBC Radio Drama's commitment to place integrated casting at the heart of its output. The NBF aims to provide access to BBC Radio Drama for talented actors from non-traditional training backgrounds, and particularly those from minority ethnic backgrounds who are currently under-represented in radio drama.

The Radio Drama Company will also be forging links with theatre companies all over Britain to help develop and nurture new talent for both radio and the stage and to find new NBF bursary winners. Consult the website for information about the next Norman Beaton Fellowship and for details of eligibility requirements.

The Carleton Hobbs Bursary is aimed at students graduating from accredited drama courses across the country. Looks for distinctive, versatile radio voices to form the next season's Radio Drama Company. It aims to recruit 4-6 winners annually. Students will be seen through an audition process, from which an equal mix of men and women will be selected. Winners receive a 6-month binding contract as members of the Radio Drama Company. Up to 4 runners-up will be engaged as freelance actors in one-off productions.

Belfast
BBC Broadcasting House, Ormeau Avenue, Belfast BT2 8HQ
tel 028-9033 8000

website www.bbc.co.uk/ni
Head of Drama Patrick Spence

Birmingham
BBC Birmingham TV Drama Village, Archibald
House, 1059 Bristol Road, Selly Oak, Birmingham
B29 6LT
tel 0121-432 8888
website www.bbc.co.uk/birmingham
Editor, Radio Drama, The Archers Vanessa Whitburn

Cardiff
BBC Broadcasting House, Llandaff, Cardiff CF5 2YQ
tel 03703 500 700
website www.bbc.co.uk/wales
Senior Producer, Radio Drama Kate McCall

Glasgow
40 Pacic Quay, Glasgow G51 1DA
tel 0141-339 8844
website www.bbc.co.uk/scotland
Head of Radio Drama Patrick Rayner

Manchester
New Broadcasting House, Oxford Road, Manchester
M60 1SJ
tel 0161-200 2020
website www.bbc.co.uk/manchester
Executive Producer, Radio Drama North Susan
Roberts

INDEPENDENT RADIO COMPANIES

Above the Title Productions
50 Lisson Street, London NW1 5DF
tel 020-7916 1984 *fax* 020-7722 5706
email mail@abovethetitle.com
website www.abovethetitle.com
Chief Executive, Executive Producer Simon Clegg

Founded in 1998, Above the Title Productions has
made over 500 hours of radio programming covering
a range of genres, from comedy to factual
programmes, drama, discussion programmes, and
music and the arts. See the website for detailed
programme credits.

All casting is done through agents; direct contact with
actors is not welcomed. Is no longer able to accept
voice demos and CVs, as the company has received
such a large number of applications in the past.

Art and Adventure Ltd
L'Ocean Ltd, 5 Darling Road, London SE4 1YQ
tel/fax 020-8692 0145
email roger@artandadventure.org
website www.artandadventure.org
Creative Director Roger Elsgood

A production company specialising in making high-
production-value, location-recorded long-form
drama for BBC Radio 3 and 4 with international casts

and directors. Recent work includes: *The Two
Gentlemen of Valasna* and *The Mrichhakatikaa* for
Radio 3, both recorded entirely on location in India;
To the Wedding for Radio 3 – a collaboration with
Complicite; *Shooting Stars*, for Radio 3 (directed by
Mike Hodges and starring Michael Gambon, Michael
Sheen and Clive Owen); *King Trash*, the second play
in Mike Hodges' radio trilogy; and *Inferno* with Corin
Redgrave, Alex Jennings and Laurie Anderson.

The company is always happy to receive submissions
and voice demos from actors (preferably as hard
copy), and auditions as necessary. It sometimes offers
Equity contracts. Actively encourages applications
from disabled actors and promotes the use of
inclusive casting.

The Comedy Unit Ltd
6th Floor, 53 Bothwell Street, Glasgow G2 6TS
tel 0141-220 6400 *fax* 0141-220 6444
email info@comedyunit.co.uk
website www.comedyunit.co.uk
Producers/Directors Colin Gilbert, Niall Clark, Rab
Christie

Founded in 1996. Works in TV and radio
productions – has produced approximately 30 hours
of TV and 25 hours of radio. Areas of work include
drama, sitcoms, comedy and other light
entertainment. Recent drama credits include: *Ronan
the Amphibian* and *Coming Home*.

Sometimes holds general auditions. Actors can write
at any time requesting inclusion. Submissions from
actors previously unknown to the company are
accepted, sent by post or email. Voice demos and
invitations to view individual actors' websites are also
accepted.

CSA Word
6a Archway Mews, 241a Putney Bridge Road,
London SW15 2PE
tel 020-8871 0220 *fax* 020-8877 0712
email info@csaword.co.uk
website www.csaword.co.uk
Key personnel Victoria Williams, Clive Stanhope

Founded in 1991. Producer of audiobooks, drama,
readings, feature programmes and documentaries for
BBC Radios 4, 2 and BBC World Service.

Does not hold general auditions, as the company
tends to use agents for casting. Invitations to view
individual actors' websites are accepted. Equity
contracts are not used, "but we usually pay above
Equity minimum." Happy to consider disabled
actors: "We work mainly in speech, audio and radio
work, so rarely an issue with regard to physical
disability."

Culture Wise
1 Chiswick Staithe, London W4 3TP
Key personnel Mukti Jain Campion, Chris Eldon Lee

Founded in 1988. Areas of work include TV and

Media

radio documentaries. Does not hold general auditions. Invitations to view individual actors' websites are accepted. The company rarely employs actors, as the primary focus is on factual output: actors are generally used for short readings only, within a feature programme.

Curtains for Radio

1-3 Middle Row, London W10 5AT
tel 020-8964 0111
email contactus@curtainsforradio.co.uk
website www.curtainsforradio.co.uk
Producers/Directors Andrew McGibbon, Jonathan Ruffle, Nick Romero

Established in 2001. Specialises in comedy, comedy drama, comedy archive and music. The ability to perform in foreign languages, regional dialects and singing are among the skills required by actors. Records one play annually. Recent titles include: *Wheeler's Fortune* (2003), *Wheeler's Wonder* (2004), I *Was Morrissey's Drummer* (2005), *Reality Is An Illusion Caused By Lack Of N.F.Simpson* (2007). Casting is carried out by freelance casting director Rachel Freck.

Accepts submissions from actors previously unknown to them. Voice demos and invitations to view individual actors' website are also accepted. "Voice demos should only be sent on a CD that can be played in any CD player." Voiceover artists are employed under Equity approved contracts. Actively encourage applications from disabled actors.

Devlin Morris Productions Ltd

97b West Bow, Edinburgh EH1 2JP
Key personnel Morris Paton

Producers of theatre, radio and cultural tourism projects. Areas of work include drama and light entertainment. Recent drama credits include: features for BBC Scotland, Radios 4 and 3, and the World Service. Does not hold general auditions. Actors can write at any time requesting inclusion. Submissions from actors previously unknown to the company are accepted if sent by post. Voice demos and invitations to view individual actors' websites are also accepted. Does not accept email enquiries.

Falling Tree Productions (formerly Alan Hall Associates)

20 College Approach, Greenwich, London SE10 9HY
tel 020-8858 8118 *fax* 020-8305 6939
email info@fallingtree.co.uk
website www.fallingtree.co.uk
Executive Director Alan Hall

Founded in 1998, Falling Tree Productions is an independent supplier to BBC Network Radio (3 and 4 principally) and foreign broadcasters, crafting documentaries and music feature productions. Winner of the Sony Gold in 2004 feature category,

and previously, in the music feature category too. Has also been awarded the Prix Italia (twice) and the Prix Bohemia. The company has employed actors in documentaries, music features, anthology programmes and museum guides. Recent credits include: *Song on the Death of Children, Brahms' Beard* and *Something Understood*.

Will accept submissions (written or emailed) and voicereels from actors previously unknown to the company. Welcomes invitations to view an actor's website. Advises that actors are used mainly for readings in radio productions, but also in the production of numerous voice-overs for museum and art gallery audioguides.

The Fiction Factory

14 Greenwich Church Street, London SE10 9BJ
tel 020-8853 5100 *fax* 020-8293 3001
email production@fictionfactory.co.uk
website www.fictionfactory.co.uk
Key personnel John Taylor, Celia de Wolff, Joanna Green, Roland Jaquarello, Marina Calderone

Founded in 1993. Makes radio drama and features for the BBC and has recently expanded into video production. Areas of work include drama, documentaries, light entertainment and voice-overs. Recent drama credits include: *In Search of Lost Time*; *Markheim*; *Abrogate*; *London, This is Washington* (Radio 4).

Does not hold general auditions. Submissions from actors previously unknown to the company are accepted if sent by post. Voice demos are also accepted. Does not welcome email submissions or invitations to view individual actors' websites. "It is helpful if showreels contain material appropriate to the kind of work sought; for example, corporate voice-overs or radio advertisements don't necessarily show off acting skills."

First Writes

1 Stables Yard, Waterbeach, Cambs CB25 9FN
tel (01223) 861750
email info@firstwrites.co.uk
website www.first-writes.co.uk
Key personnel Ellen Dryden, Richard Blake, Jonathan Dryden Taylor

Established in 1992. Areas of work include BBC Radio Drama for Radios 3 and 4, and World Service. Recent credits include: *The Franchise Affair, I Was Born There* and *The Eliza Stories*. Offers Equity approved contracts and does not subscribe to the Equity Pension Scheme. Accepts submissions from actors previously unknown to the company if sent by post, but not by email. Welcomes voice demos and invitations to view actors' websites. Aims for inclusive casting where possible.

Heavy Entertainment Ltd

111 Wardour Street, London W1F 0UH
tel 020-7494 1000 *fax* 020-7494 1100

Media

email info@heavy-entertainment.com
website www.heavy-entertainment.com
Director David Roper

Established in 1992. Audio and video producers. Areas of work include drama, corporate, commercials and audiobooks. Offers Equity approved contracts. Welcomes showreels, voicereels and invitations to view individual actors' websites.

Ladbroke Productions
17 Leicester Road, East Croydon, Surrey CR0 6EB
mobile (07590) 555458
email neilgardner@ladbrokeradio.com
website www.ladbrokeradio.com
Producers/Directors Neil Gardner, Richard Bannerman, Neil Rosser, Adam Fowler, Anna Scott-Brown *Assistant Producer* Anna Van Dieken

Founded in 1975, Ladbroke Productions produces for all BBC networks in many genres, including drama, documentaries, music, light entertainment and features. Its studio and production facilities are also used by BBC Drama, BBC Readings and BBC Factual Learning. Actors are mainly employed by the company in its drama and documentary production. Recent credits include: *Sitting in Limbo* (BBC World Service) and *In the Company of Men* (BBC Radio 3).

Will accept unsolicited submissions (written or emailed), voice demos and invitations to view actors' websites. April and September are generally better months to write.

Loftus Audio Ltd
2A Aldine Street, London W12 8AN
tel 020-8740 4666 and (01620) 893876
website www.loftusaudio.co.uk
Directors Joanne Coombs, David Smith

Small award-winning audio and radio production company based in West London specialising in features, documentaries and readings for BBC Radio. Requires plain narration and poetry from actors. Records several audiobooks a year. Recent titles include: *Family Britain* by David Kynaston for Bloomsbury, and Michael Chabon's *Manhood for Amateurs* for Radio 4's Book of the Week. Accepts submissions from individual actors previously unknown to the company. Will also accept submissions sent via email. Straight narration is preferred on voice demos and should be sent as an MP3. Actors are employed under Equity approved contracts. Applications from disabled actors are welcomed.

Pennine Productions
17 Crimicar Lane, Sheffield S10 4FA
tel 0161-427 1460
website www.pennine.biz
Contact Janet Graves

Founded in 2000. Has made documentaries and features for BBC Radio 4 since 2001, and

programmes for BBC Radio 3 since 2004. Has produced book readings for Radio 4 since 2005. Broadcasts northern, national and international stories. Main areas of work include documentaries and readings. Recent credits include: *Israel in East Africa*, *When Jesus Rode into Bristol* and *Land of the Oval Ball* (all Radio 4, 2003). Offers Equity approved contracts and does not subscribe to the Equity Pension Scheme.

"We only welcome unsolicited approaches from actors with significant broadcast experience, particularly of book readings – or other audiobook productions. We are too small to be useful to actors trying to break into the network radio or TV." Happy to consider applications from disabled actors: "radio experience is the over-riding concern."

Pier Productions
8 St Georges Place, Brighton BN1 4GB
tel (01273) 691401 *fax* (01273) 693658
Managing Director Peter Hoare

Founded in 1993, an award-winning Brighton-based company and a significant supplier of factual and drama productions to BBC Radio 4. The company employs actors for drama productions and is keen to work with talent located in Brighton and the surrounding area. Does not hold general auditions. Submissions from actors are accepted by post and email, but invitations to view individual actors' websites are not welcomed. It must be emphasised that opportunities in radio drama are limited and that the company does not use the services of voice-over artists.

Shell Like
81 Whitfield Street, London W1T 4HG
tel 020-7255 5224
email enquiries@shelllike.com
website www.shelllike.com
Producer Mike Blunt *Production Assistant* Richard Donaghue

Production details: Specialises in audio production and radio commercials. Works mainly in radio. Employs actors for corporate and commercials. Recent credits include: T-mobile and NSPCC (both radio).

Casting procedures: Sometimes uses freelance casting directors and may hold general auditions. Does not encourage unsolicited approaches but will accept invitations to view individual actors' websites. Actively encourages applications from disabled actors and promotes the use of inclusive casting. "We are happy to advise actors on how to get into voice-over work, and how to get a showreel made."

So Radio Ltd
18 Hatfields, London SE1 8GN
tel 020-7960 2000 *fax* 020-7960 2095

Media

email info@sotelevision.co.uk
website www.sotelevision.co.uk
Producer/Director Graham Stuart

Founded in 2003 as the radio arm of So Television Ltd. Recent credits include: *The Storyman with Andrew Clover* and *It's that Jo Caulfield Again* for BBC Radio 4. The company has employed actors mainly for light entertainment productions.

Does not accept unsolicited written submissions. As the company is small it cannot promise to reply to all enquiries. Offers Equity approved contracts (where applicable). Actively encourages applications from disabled actors and promotes the use of inclusive casting.

Lou Stein Associates Ltd
email info@loustein.co.uk
Producer/Director Lou Stein *Co-Director* Deirdre Gribbin

Lou Stein founded the Gate Theatre, Notting Hill, and was Artistic Director of the Palace Theatre, Watford. Lou Stein Associates was formed in 2002 to continue Lou's interest in new work, adaptations, music theatre and media. Employs actors for drama programmes. Recent drama credits include: *My Month with Carmen* (starring Miriam Colon and Julian Glover); *Embers* (adapted by Lou Stein from the novel by Sandor Marai and starring Patrick Stewart); *The Possessed* (written and directed by Lou Stein from the Dostoevsky novel, starring Paul McGann); *Performances* by Brian Friel (Wilton's Music Hall, starring Henry Goodman and Rosamund Pike); *Crossing the Sea* (a new opera by Deirdre Gribbin).

Voice demos and invitations to view individual actors' websites are accepted, but actors are requested to email in the first instance. Please note that no reply will be given unless the actor is suitable for immediate casting. Names will be retained on file. Offers Equity approved contracts. Actively encourages applications from disabled actors and promotes the use of inclusive casting.

Tintinna Productions
Summerfield, Bristol Road, Bristol BS40 8UB
tel (01275) 333128 *fax* (01275) 332316
email tintinna@aol.com
Producer Ian Bell *Research & Production* Sandy Bell

Founded in 1998. Specialises in factual documentaries including history, lifestyle and human interest. Main area of work is documentaries. Does not hold general auditions. Submissions from actors previously unknown to the company are accepted if sent by post. Voice demos are also accepted. Does not welcome email submissions or invitations to view individual actors' websites.

Unique
50 Lisson Street, London NW1 5DF
Executive Producer: Drama & Entertainment Frank Stirling

Produces drama, documentaries, comedy and light entertainment for radio. Recent drama credits include: *Zazie* (World Service), *A Confidential Agent, Fragile!* (Radio 4), *Professor Bernhardi, Bajazet* (Radio 3), and *Something Understood* (poetry and prose readings for Radio 4).

Submissions from actors previously unknown to the company are accepted sent by post or email. Voice demos are also accepted. Does not welcome invitations to view individual actors' websites. Advises actors to "include radio work on demo". "We regret that we cannot reply to all submissions, but your details will be kept on file."

Whistledown Productions
8A Ayres Street, London SE1 0AS
tel 020-7407 8001
email davidprest@whistledown.net
website www.whistledown.net
Producers/Directors David Prest, Sarah Cuddon

Founded in 1993. One of the largest independent suppliers to BBC Radio, with a background in features and landmark documentaries, as well as programme strands such as *The Reunion, Traveller's Tree,* and *Questions Questions.* Also produces voice demos in custom-build studio.

AUDIO BOOKS

Barefoot Audio Books Ltd
123 Walcot Street, Bath BA1 5BG
Director Tessa Strickland *Group Project Manager* Emma Parkin

Recent titles include: *Mrs Moon, Animal Boogie* and *Tales of Wisdom and Wonder.* Does not use freelance casting directors. Accepts submissions from actors previously unknown to the company if sent by post, but does not welcome email enquiries. Voice demos and invitations to view individual actors' websites are also accepted. Singing ability is required from actors, and Caribbean and African voices are needed in particular.

HarperCollins Audio
77-85 Fulham Palace Road, London W6 8JB
tel 020-8307 4630 *fax* 020-8307 4517
email enquiries@harpercollins.co.uk
website www.harpercollins.co.uk
Director Rosalie George *Editorial/Production Manager* Nicola Townsend

Has produced more than 1000 titles for both children and adults over the last 15 years. Work spans all genres including crime, comedy, literary fiction, mass market fiction, non-fiction, poetry and classics. Recent titles include: *Brick Lane* by Monica Ali; *Sharpe's Havoc* by Bernard Cornwell; and *Lovers and Liars* by Josephine Cox.

Foreign languages and regional dialect skills are required from actors. Does not use freelance casting directors. Advises actors to make contact by email or telephone, or preferably through an agent. Also accepts invitations to view individual actors' websites.

Isis Audio Books

7 Centremead, Osney Mead, Oxford OX2 0ES
tel (01865) 250333 *fax* (01865) 790358
email sales@isis-publishing.co.uk
website www.isis-publishing.co.uk
Audio Production Manager Catherine Thompson

Founded in 1975. Publishes unabridged audiobooks. Recent titles include: *Twelve Sharp* by Janet Evanovich; *The Vanishing Act of Esme Lennox* by Maggie O'Farrell; *Tenderness of Wolves* by Stet Penney; and *The Good Husband of Zebra Drive* by Alexander McCall Smith.

Does not use freelance casting directors. Accepts submissions from actors with proven audiobook experience if sent by post or email, but does not welcome telephone enquiries. Actors should have a range of voices and good sight-reading ability. Offers non-Equity contracts and does not subscribe to the Equity Pension Scheme. Actively encourages applications from disabled actors and promotes the use of inclusive casting.

Macmillan Audio Books

20 New Wharf Road, London N1 9RR
Audio Publisher Alison Muirden *Audio Editorial Coordinator* Rebecca Folkard-Ward

Casts in-house. Accepts submissions from actors previously unknown to the company if sent by post, but does not welcome email enquiries. Voice demos are also accepted. Does not offer Equity contracts or subscribe to the Equity Pension Scheme. Will consider applications from disabled actors to play disabled characters.

Naxos Audio Books

40A High Street, Welwyn, Herts AL6 9EQ
tel (01438) 717808 *fax* (01438) 717809
email nicolas.soames@naxosaudiobooks.com
Producer/Director Nicolas Soames

Founded in 1984. Produces classic fiction, modern fiction, drama, poetry and children's classics for CD and download. Recent titles include: *The Canterbury Tales*, *Heidi* and *King Lear*. Regional dialect skills are required from actors. Accepts voice demos.

Orion Audio Books

5 Upper St Martin's Lane, London WC2H 9EA
tel 020-7240 3444 *fax* 020-7379 6158
email audio@orionbooks.co.uk
website www.orionbooks.co.uk
Audio Manager Pandora White *Audio Assistant* Victoria Nicholl *Audio Publicity Manager* Jonathan Weir

Started in 1996, Orion audio draws mainly on the Orion Group lists, but also acquires elsewhere. With notable authors such as Ian Rankin, Maeve Binchy, Michael Palin, Francesca Simon, Antonia Fraser, Michelle Paver, Terry Wogan, Raymond Khoury, Kate Mosse, Michael Connelly, Miss Read, and Dan Brown. Orion Audiobooks prides itself on its diversity with continued success at creating and using new packaging. Orion's strong marketing skills allow its titles to reach a very wide range of non-traditional outlets, and it is now firmly established in the digital download market. Produces 50-60 audiobooks a year. Recent titles include: *Horrid Henry's Christmas Cracker*, *Grizzly Tales: Nasty Little Beasts 1.1*, *The Naming of the Dead*, *Whitethorn Woods*, *Salmon Fishing in the Yemen*, *Love and Louis XIV* and *Young Stalin*.

Casts in-house. Useful skills include regional dialects and occasionally singing ability. Welcomes submissions and voice-demos from actors previously unknown to the company. Offers Equity approved contracts. Happy to receive submissions from disabled and non-disabled actors with the right skills for the job.

Random House Audio Books

20 Vauxhall Bridge Road, London SW1V 2SA
tel 020-7840 8400 *fax* 020-7834 2509
email jlewis@randomhouse.co.uk
Editorial Director Zoe Howes *Editorial Assistant* Jenni Lewis

Created in 1991, the Audiobooks division of Random House publishes writers such as James Patterson, John Grisham, Andy McNab, Ruth Rendell and Kathy Reichs.

Uses freelance casting directors. Accepts submissions from actors previously unknown to the company, sent by post. Voice demos and invitations to view individual actors' websites are also accepted.

Soundings Audiobooks Ltd

Isis House, Kings Drive, Whitley Bay,
Tyne & Wear NE26 2JT
tel 0191-253 4155 *fax* 0191-251 0662
website www.isispublishing.co.uk
General Manager Gillian Bell

Founded in 1984, the company records around 190 audiobooks a year. Recent productions include: Robert Ludlum's *The Ambler Warning*; Anna Jacobs' *Seasons of Love*; and Alexandra Connor's *The Tailor's Wife*.

Casts in-house and does not issue casting breakdowns. Welcomes letters (not emails) with voice demos or invitations to view individuals' websites. Prefers voice demos without commercials. Uses non-Equity contracts. "We rarely (or never) have the opportunity to cast disabled actors."

TalkingPEN books

Global House, 303 Ballards Lane, London N12 8NP
tel 020-8445 5123 *fax* 020-8446 7745
email info@talkingpen.co.uk
website www.talkingpen.co.uk
Producers/Directors R. Dutta, D.M. Chatterji,
Henriette Barkow

Established in 2002. Produces Audiobooks, E-books,
Talkingpen books and posters. The ability to perform
in foreign languages, singing and storytelling are
often required of actors. Voice demos should include
short story telling in English or other language.
Records 20 audiobooks annually. Recent titles
include: *Hansel and Gretel, Jill and the Beanstalk,
English Terms Explained.*

Accepts submissions from actors previously unknown
to them. Voice demos and invitations to view
individual actors' website are also accepted. Actively
encourages applications from disabled actors.

Acting for radio

Gordon House

I remember once, in a burst of evangelical enthusiasm at having decided never to touch a cigarette again, upbraiding a distinguished member of the Radio Drama Company for her constant disappearances to the Green Room to light up. (Nowadays, of course, all BBC Green rooms are smoke-free, and your poor cigarette-smoking actor has to shiver in the car park.) "My dear man," she wheezed grandly. "The only reason you employ me on the wireless is because of my nicotine-nourished, port-soaked larynx. Living badly has made me the radio actress I am today!"

Well – it's a point of view. Just as the camera relishes certain skin textures, so the microphone may embellish the actor or actress who has lived a little – resulting in, shall we say, an idiosyncratic oesophagus. But as a way of getting a radio part, it's not a course of action I'd recommend. Radio simply doesn't pay enough to sustain a life of alcoholic debauchery.

So how do you get into radio? "It's a closed shop," moaned one actor to me the other day. "You hear the same names, time and again – and there's no way of breaking into this magic circle." I personally have worked with well over 800 actors, so it can't be that much of a closed shop ... although it's true that given the ruthless time constraints of the medium (a 60-minute play will be rehearsed and recorded in two days), there's a natural tendency for producers to work with those actors whom they know can 'deliver' quickly. There's no joy to be had in the seventh take of a difficult scene when your nervous newcomer is finally coming to grips with the ambiguities of his or her character, as well as the technical demands of this strange new medium, while everyone else's performances have long-since peaked and are now beginning to sound tired and lacklustre.

But that said, new writers and new actors are the lifeblood of the medium. And what do you need to be a good actor on radio? It's simple. You need to be a good actor. If you're successful in the theatre, in film, on TV – then of course you can be successful on radio. A good actor is a good actor. It obviously helps if your voice doesn't sound like a creaking door (given that creaking doors are a staple diet of many a radio play), and the medium has no place for prima donnas. With every producer sparingly counting his or her loose change, there's no such happy luxury as a radio 'extra'; so if you're cast as Hamlet, you can also expect to do your fair share of off-mic mumbling in Claudius' court. And if that doesn't appeal, don't do radio.

You also have to be prepared to work fast and make almost instant decisions. Over the years I've worked with a few actors whom I admire hugely; whom I've seen – in other media – give performances of rare charm and intelligence; but who in radio have simply been unable to 'come off the page' – make the character they're playing sound truthful and real. Of course this may simply be attributed to the crass inadequacy of the director. But for some actors the sheer speed at which they have to make decisions about character, motivation, sub-text and so forth is incredibly daunting. And then there's the physical absurdity of much of what they have to do: "How the xxx do you expect me to be 'truthful' when I'm carrying a xxxing great script in my left hand, a glass of water, masquerading as gin, in my right, and you want me to walk through a carpet of scrunched-up audio tape and pretend it's a meadow," shrieked one despairing actor to me a couple of years ago.

Media

And yet that's exactly what we expect – truth. There's no medium as unforgiving for exposing over-acting or over-emoting (or worse – simple 'reading'). A radio play – and particularly a contemporary, naturalistic play – should make listeners feel that they are eavesdropping on real conversation. It's a medium that may owe much to theatre for providing it with great writing and acting talent (though the reverse is equally true), but the technique of radio acting is far closer to that of film than of theatre. "Less is more! Less is more!" as my erstwhile colleague, Martin Jenkins, one of Radio Drama's finest practitioners, used to impress on his casts. (It was Martin, incidentally, who uttered the memorable phrase: "Good Luck – Please!" before the umpteenth take of one particularly stressful scene.)

How do you bring yourself to the attention of radio producers? Well – there's no denying the fact that a lovingly crafted CD arriving on your desk just as you're in the process of casting your next play, and can't for the life of you think who you can get to play the embittered Glaswegian ex-shipbuilder who's contemplating a sex change, can make all the difference. But choose the pieces you record with care – and keep them short. If varied accents are not a speciality, there's no point in doing all sorts of varied accents. Obviously, it's a great asset to be master – or mistress – of many different voices, this being a medium where 'doubling' and 'trebling' is done with impunity. But a CD where the truthfulness of most of your extracts is undone by your game but doomed attempt to do a passable Geordie, won't help anyone. Many years ago I remember auditioning Jeremy Sinden for a part. "What accents do you do?" I asked him. "I do two actually," he said. "I do posh. And I do very posh." Well a mere two accents didn't stop Jeremy getting a load of work in every medium – including radio – in his all-too-brief, but exhilarating, career.

Having recorded your tape or (preferably) CD, you can, of course, circulate it to every producer who's ever made a radio play. But my advice would be to be a little more discerning. Listen to some radio plays (a great way of determining for yourself what works and what doesn't) and note the names of the producers whose productions particularly appeal to you. You can then write a personal note to them – you know the kind: "I must say, Mr House, I really enjoyed your fascinating and unusual interpretation of *Hedda Gabler* on Radio 3 last night, and incidentally Hedda is a part I've always yearned to play myself,"(etc.). I'm not saying it will get you a part, but producers are as vain as the next person (I should know) and it may well make them more inclined to slip your CD into the CD player, on the basis that anyone with such discerning judgement as yours must be worth hearing.

Radio is a fantastic and hugely under-rated medium, and actors, by and large, love working for it. It can also be the stepping-stone to fame and fortune. For many years we've been running our own radio bursary scheme for accredited drama schools – the Carleton Hobbs Competition (named after one of the great 20th century radio actors) – and the role-call of actors who have been winners, from Richard Griffiths to Stephen Tompkinson, from Nerys Hughes to Emma Fielding, is hugely impressive. Our new bursary scheme, the Norman Beaton Fellowship, for actors who didn't go to an accredited drama school, is also providing us with some excellent new talent. Details of both these schemes can be found on the BBC website.

And of course we producers don't simply wait to receive your CDs, but are constantly on the lookout for new and exciting talent from wherever we can find it. You may not need to approach us – we may approach you! As World Service Drama producers, Hilary Norrish and myself gave a young actor called Ewan MacGregor his first two professional jobs, having seen him in a drama school showcase. And Ewan – if you ever get to read this – where are the invitations to those glamorous film previews you promised you'd send us when you were famous? Remember – it was radio that gave you your first break!

Gordon House is the former Head of the BBC Radio Drama Department. He joined the BBC as a studio manager in 1972, working in Children's Television and Radio Sport before becoming a drama director. For 14 years he headed the small BBC World Service Drama team, during which time the Unit won more than 30 national and international awards. In 1998 Gordon won the Writers' Guild Special Prize for services for his work with new writers, and has twice won the Sony Drama Award. He is a founder member of The Worldplay Group, a radio association of drama directors from broadcasting stations around the world, which initiates a yearly season of international radios dramas broadcast on BBC World Service, ABC, CBC, RTE, Radio New Zealand and Radio Television Hong Kong.

Media festivals

These are geared towards showcasing directors, rather than actors. However, they can be useful places to network, learn and (if your film is short-listed) to gain extra exposure.

Belfast Film Festival
The Exchange Place, 23 Donegal Street,
Belfast BT1 2FF
tel 028-9032 5913 *fax* 028-9032 5911
email info@belfastfilmfestival.org
website www.belfastfilmfestival.org

Normally held in March/April each year, the Belfast Film Festival brings the best of independent, world, local and classic cinema to screens across Belfast. In addition there are panel discussions, workshops, music events and a series of related club events in venues across the city.

Candidates may submit features, shorts, animation and documentaries for inclusion in the festival. The deadline for submissions is normally early December. While all categories will be considered for screening, the only competitive category is the Irish short film. To be eligible for the £1000 Kodak Short Film Prize, films must have been shot in Ireland during the previous year and last no longer than 20 minutes.

BFM International Film Festival
tel 020-8531 9199
email festival@bfmmedia.com
website www.bfmmedia.com

Presenting the UK's premier black film event each September across venues in London, the BFM promotes the range and diversity of black cinema and television around the world. Showcasing an array of award-winning features, documentaries, animation and short films by established international talent alongside black British film-makers, the BFM also screens a substantial amount of high-quality work from up-and-coming filmmakers. In addition, there are exclusive preview screenings, seminars, workshops and masterclasses on offer. Awards are presented to winners in the following categories: best actor, best actress, best film, best cinematography, and best screenplay.

Bite the Mango
National Media Museum, Bradford BD1 1NQ
tel (01274) 203308
email ben.eagle@nationalmediamuseum.org.uk
website www.nationalmediamuseum.org.uk/btm

Founded in 1994, Bite the Mango aims to promote the best in world cinema, with an eclectic mix of features, shorts and documentaries from many countries around the world. The festival runs for 1 week in September, and features premières, previews, retrospectives, masterclasses and seminars by leading figures in world cinema.

Bradford Film Festival
National Media Museum, Bradford BD1 1NQ
tel (01274) 203308
email ben.eagle@nationalmediamuseum.org.uk
website www.nationalmediamuseum.org.uk/biff
Director Tony Earnshaw *Contact* Ben Eagle

Held each year in March, the Bradford Film Festival presents a number of special guests, tributes, screentalk interviews, masterclasses, spotlights, the Crash symposium and the Widescreen weekend over a 15-day period.

Features, shorts, documentaries and experimental work submitted for competition must have been completed during the previous 2 years.

Brief Encounters Festival
Watershed Media Centre, 1 Canon's Road,
Harbourside, Bristol BS1 5TX
tel 0117-915 0186 *fax* 0117-930 9967
email info@brief-encounters.org.uk
website www.brief-encounters.org.uk

Brief Encounters is an international short film festival which runs for 1 week in November and promotes new talent in the film industry. With more than 20 screenings of diverse new shorts from around the world, special guests and events, parties, awards, seminars, masterclasses, surgeries and focus sessions, the festival offers insights and advice from industry professionals about every aspect of film. For advice about funding and submitting your work, visit the website.

Cambridge Film Festival
Arts Picture House, 38-39 St Andrew's Street,
Cambridge CB2 3AR
tel (01223) 500082 *fax* (01223) 462555
email info@cambridgefilmfestival.org.uk
website www.cambridgefilmfestival.org.uk

Established in 1977, the festival was relaunched in 2001 after a 5-year hiatus, and now runs for 10 days in July. Aiming to screen the best of current international cinema and to rediscover neglected films of the past, it also runs a programme for children, supported by events and workshops, and organises free outdoor screenings and touring events across the Eastern region. The festival is attended by many actors and directors and is complemented by parties, receptions, drive-in movies and educational events. Recent visitors include Cate Blanchett, Richard Harris, Timothy Spall and Joel Schumacher.

Directors such as Peter Greenaway, Patrice Chereau, Philip Kaufman and Francesco Rosi have also presented work at the festival, and many acclaimed films – including *Reservoir Dogs, Intimacy, Bowling for Columbine, Goodbye Lenin!* and *La Haine* – received their UK première in Cambridge.

Cardiff Screen Festival
10 Mount Stuart Square, Cardiff CF10 5EE
tel 029-2033 3324 *fax* 029-2033 3320
email via form on website
website www.iffw.co.uk
Festival Manager Sarah Howells

Celebrating film, TV and new media from Wales and further afield, the festival offers a wide selection of screenings, special guest appearances, debates and programmed industry events for 10 days each November.

The DM Davies award is open to any short-film director who is of Welsh origin or has been a native of Wales for 2 or more years. It is one of the largest short-film prizes in Europe; previous winners have included Justin Kerrigan (*Human Traffic*) and Sara Sugarman (*Very Annie Mary*). Entries are screened towards the end of the festival, with many of the directors in attendance. The winner receives a comprehensive package of funding, facilities and assistance to shoot a 10-minute film in Wales.

Celtic Media Festival
249 West George Street, Glasgow G2 4QE
tel 0141-302 1737
email info@celticmediafestival.co.uk
website www.celticmedialfestival.co.uk

The Celtic Media Festival celebrates the cultures and languages of Cornwall, Brittany, Ireland, Scotland and Wales in film and in television broadcasting. Awards include: Short Drama Award, Drama Feature Award and Drama Series Award. The festival is attended by producers, directors, commissioning editors, film executives, media students, distributors and schedulers.

Chichester International Film Festival
Chichester Cinema at New Park, New Park Road, Chichester PO19 1XN
tel (01243) 786650 *fax* (01243) 790235
email info@chichestercinema.org
website www.chichestercinema.org/film-festival
Director Roger Gibson

An 18-day festival in August/September presenting more than 70 feature films, Q&As with visiting directors, and related talks. More than half the films shown are previews and premières; the remainder form retrospectives on important contributors to the film world.

The Commonwealth Film Festival
Unit 9, Greenheys Business Centre, Manchester Science Park, 10 Pencroft Way, Manchester M15 6JJ
tel 0161-342 0044 *fax* 0161-342 0055
email info@commonwealthfilm.com
website www.commonwealthfilm.com
Director Mathieu Ravier

The festival promotes filmmaking talent in the Commonwealth and seeks to develop new audiences for their work. Committed to inclusivity and excellence, it also aims to promote respect for human rights, equality, freedom and sustainable economic development. Founded in 2001, the festival presents documentaries, short films, seminars, workshops, industry networking events and parties during its 10-day run across April/May, and is the largest festival showcase for Indian, Canadian and South African cinema in Europe. Submissions must be made in, or co-produced with, one of the 72 nations of the Commonwealth.

Disability Film Festival
London Disability Arts Forum, 20-22 Waterson Street, London E2 8HE
tel 020-7749 4352 *fax* 020-7749 4363
email info@ldaf.org
website www.disabilityfilm.co.uk
Festival Coordinator Caglar Kimyoncu

Showcasing the talent of disabled filmmakers, the Disability Film Festival takes place over 4 days in December, and is hosted by the BFI Southbank (formerly the National Film Theatre). The festival offers filmmakers, film-goers and industry professionals the opportunity to meet, exchange feedback, network and socialise. It has also become a forum for debate, challenging the exclusion of disabled people either on screen or as filmmakers. Submission forms and guidelines are available to download from the website.

Edinburgh International Film Festival
Filmhouse, 88 Lothian Road, Edinburgh EH3 9BZ
tel 0131-228 4051 *fax* 0131-229 5501
email info@edfilmfest.org.uk
website www.edfilmfest.org.uk
Artistic Director Hannah McGill *Managing Director* Ginnie Atkinson

Celebrating cinema for over 60 years, the festival aims to entertain, challenge and inspire audiences for 10 days each August. The programme covers a range of different areas such as British Cinema, red carpet gala events, live interviews with cinema greats, retrospectives, debuts and second films from new filmmaking talent, short films and special events. Previous events have included the National 48 Hour Film Challenge, Script Factory masterclasses and performed readings, a BAFTA-sponsored interview with Sir Sean Connery, and a Skillset event on Careers in Film.

Submissions should be received by April; all the forms, rules and regulations can be downloaded from the website. Films submitted from outside the UK must have been produced during the 2 years previous to the festival, and British films during the year beforehand. All films must be UK premieres.

Foyle Film Festival

The Nerve Centre, 7-8 Magazine Street, Derry-Londonderry BT48 6HJ
tel 028-7137 3456 *tel* 020-7126 0562
email bernie@nerve-centre.org.uk
website www.foylefilmfestival.org
Festival Director & Programmer Ms Bernie McLaughlin

Established in 1987, the annual Foyle Film Festival is the flagship project of the multi-media Nerve Centre. For 9 days in November, the Foyle Film Festival capitalises on all the technical expertise of the Nerve Centre to produce a unique programme of film, music, digital technologies, and education. The festival is themed and delivers a programme of art house cinema: international and local premieres, foreign language, documentaries, classic film, industry workshops, presentations, outreach events, as well as a stand-alone education programme which is curriculum focused and targets all local primary and secondary schools, colleges, and universities.

The festival competition has received Oscar recognition for its Light In Motion (LIM) Film Awards. Foyle Film Festival is renowned for attracting top industry professionals to the city, with past guests including high-profile names such as: Julie Christie, Neil Jordan, Wim Wenders, Kenneth Branagh, Jenny Agutter, Julien Temple, Christiane Kubrick, Andrew Eaton, Brenda Blethyn, Roddy Doyle, Irvine Welsh, Stephen Frears, Ronan Bennett, Jimmy McGovern, Rob Coleman, Sam Taylor-Wood, Kate Adie, Jonathan Rhys Meyers, Cillian Murphy, Ardal O'Hanlon and Dervla Kirwan.

Hull International Short Film Festival

Hull Film, Danish Buildings, 44-46 High Street, Hull HU1 1PS
tel (01482) 381512 *fax* (01482) 381517
email office@hullfilm.co.uk
website www.hullfilm.co.uk
Director Esther Johnson

Held over 5 days in late September, the festival shows short narrative, documentary, animated and experimental films. The aim is to show international and local short films as an innovative and exciting artform, as well as to provide training opportunities in the region. The festival also includes outdoor screenings, music and film events, international speakers and archive events.

Leeds International Film Festival

PO Box 596, Leeds LS2 8YQ
tel 0113-247 7952 *fax* 0113-247 8397
email filmfestival@leeds.gov.uk
website www.leedsfilm.com
Director Chris Fell

Leeds International Film Festival has been presenting extensive programmes of new and unseen cinema from around the world since 1987, supported by a number of events and workshops for those wanting to get into film and TV. The Yorkshire Short Film Competition highlights emerging new filmmaking talents in the Yorkshire region, while the Louis Le Prince International Short Film Competition promotes some of the best fiction completed in the last year around the world. The key features of the festival include UK Film Week, an annual showcase of emerging talent; Film Festival Fringe, where the bars and clubs of Leeds host human rights films, music documentaries and special events; the Main Programme; and Unique Retrospectives.

The festival is complemented by the Leeds Children's and Young People's Film Festival held in April each year, with an award for National Young Filmmaker of the Year.

London Film Festival

BFI South Bank, London SE1 8XT
tel 020-7815 1322 or 020-7815 1323
fax 020-7633 0786
website www.lff.org.uk

The BFI London Film Festival is Europe's largest public film event, screening an average of 280 films from 60 countries in October/November each year. Leading figures in the film industry present their work at the festival, and the programme is supported by a number of interviews, industry and public forums, lectures, education events, Gala films and special screenings promoting the best in cinema across the world.

London Lesbian & Gay Film Festival

c/o BFI Southbank, Belvedere Road, South Bank, Waterloo, London SE1 8XT
tel 020-7928 3535 or 020-7928 3232 (Box Office)
website www.bfi.org.uk/llgff
Senior Programmer Brian Robinson *Head of Festivals (bfi)* Sandra Hebron *Festival Producer* Helen de Witt

The London Lesbian and Gay Film Festival presents the best of British and international Queer Cinema in all its forms – mainstream and avant garde. Features and shorts are complemented by discussions and interviews with writers and filmmakers. The London run of the festival is based at the BFI Southbank (formerly known as the National Film Theatre), with other screenings taking place in Leicester Square. Following this run in March and April, it continues on tour around the UK until the autumn. See the website for programme details, including the tour schedule, or contact the BFI box office for a brochure of the London run.

Manchester International Short Film Festival

Kinofilm, 42 Edge Street, Manchester M4 1HN
tel 0161-288 2494 *fax* 0161-281 1374
email john.kino@good.co.uk
website www.kinofilm.org.uk
Director John Wojowski

British New Wave and an International Panorama of film provide the main focus to the festival, with a regional showcase, 'Made up North', aimed at promoting films from local and regional filmmakers. Education and Professional Development events are also hosted by the festival and are presented by external curators and organisations.

The festival is open for film submissions each year from January to June, with shortlisted entries being screened at the festival itself in October. Short films on any theme, subject or category and made on any format are eligible, as long as they run no longer than 20 minutes and have been made within the 18 months prior to the festival. The Kinofilm Awards acknowledge outstanding achievements in short film, with awards in many categories. Rules, regulations and application forms are available on the website.

Raindance Film Festival Ltd

81 Berwick Street, London W1F 8TW
tel 020-7287 3833 *fax* 020-7439 2243
email info@raindance.co.uk
website www.raindance.co.uk
Producer Jesse Vile

Running for 2 weeks in October, Raindance is the UK's largest independent film festival and is committed to screening the boldest, most innovative and challenging films from the UK and from around the world. Weighted heavily towards new talent, the festival offers more than 100 features (many of which are directorial debuts), 20 shorts programmes and a wide range of events, workshops and parties.

Rushes Soho Shorts Festival

66 Old Compton Street, London W1D 4UH
tel 020-7851 6207
email info@sohoshorts.com
website www.sohoshorts.com

Taking place for 1 week in July/August, shortlisted films are screened free of charge throughout Soho's cafes, bars and cinemas, as well as other special events and screenings being held. In addition, Vue cinemas around the country will also be holding screenings throughout that week. The festival culminates in an awards cremony with winners being announced in the following categories: Short Film, Newcomer, Animation, Music Video, and Title Sequence & Idents. Patrons of the festival include BAFTA and the Directors' Guild of Great Britain.

Films for submission should be no longer than 12 minutes, and should have been produced in the 12 months prior to the deadline.

UK Jewish Film Festival

5.09 Clerkenwell Workshops,
27-31 Clerkenwell Close, London EC1R 0AT
tel 020-3176 0048
website www.ukjewishfilmfestival.org.uk

Established in 1997, the festival is committed to showing a wide variety of films which celebrate the diversity of Jewish cultures and identity, and which reach both Jewish and wider audiences. In addition to film screenings there are education projects and talks with directors. The UK Jewish Film Festival Short Film Fund offers a grant of up to £15,000 for the production of a short film or video (drama, animation or factual) of a Jewish theme and with a significance both to Jewish and to general public audiences. For application details, consult the website.

Disabled actors
Introduction

This section brings together companies and organisations of specific interest to disabled actors. It should also be noted that (a) some agents and companies now welcome enquiries from disabled actors (see listings), and (b) the Conference of Drama Schools (CDS) states that, "All members of the Conference of Drama Schools are committed to a policy of widening access, to reflect the social and cultural diversity of society." Some drama schools have more detail on their disability admissions policies on their websites.

In television, there are some positive efforts to encourage the representation of disabled performers and contributers in programme-making. Have a look at: **www.bbc.co.uk/commissioning/diversity** and **www.channel4.com/4disabledtalent**.

In addition, disabled Equity members can add their details to the *Disability Register*, which is published by The Spotlight. Casting directors looking for disabled actors can search this register via the Spotlight website.

Note The UK Government recognised BSL as an official language in March 2003, and the editors acknowledge that many deaf people consider themselves to be members of a linguistic and cultural minority – Deaf with a capital 'D' – rather than disabled people. For the sake of simplicity, however, this book uses a broad definition of disability to encompass Deaf people (although an individual entry will retain the distinction if present in the material provided to us by that company).

The editor would like to thank Silvie Fisch (of The National Disability Arts Forum) and the staff of Graeae Theatre Company for their help in compiling this section.

TRAINING

Apart from the training offered by drama schools, a number of theatre companies and organisations operate training schemes or courses for disabled actors. Many of these schemes are relatively short – a few days or weeks – but Lawnmower's Liberdade, Chicken Shed's BTEC National Diploma, Mind the Gap's Staging Change, and Shysters' ShysterShadows operate over a longer term. Shorter courses are run by (among others) Birds of Paradise, Blue Eyed Soul, Candoco, and Oily Cart. These are often advertised through the NDAF's email newsletter, EtCetera – **www.ndaf.org** has more information about how to subscribe – or contact the company concerned for more information. (Details for all the theatre companies listed here can be found in the *Sources of work* section below.)

SOURCES OF WORK

Amici Dance Theatre Company

Turtle Key Arts, Ladbroke Hall, 79 Barbly Road,
London W10 6AZ
tel 020-8964 5060 *fax* 020-8964 4080
email tkas@amicidance.org
website www.amicidance.org
Artistic Director Wolfgang Stange

Dance theatre company integrating disabled and
non-disabled artists and performers.

Anjali Dance Company

The Mill Arts Centre, Spiceball Park, Banbury,
Oxfordshire OX16 8QE
tel/fax (01295) 251909
email info@anjali.co.uk or education@anjali.co.uk
website www.anjali.co.uk
Artistic Director Nicole Thomson *Admin Officer*
Adrienne Szabo

Production details: A professional contemporary
dance company. All Anjali's dancers have a learning
disability. The company produces and tours
performances, and undertakes Educational and
Outreach work; it is one of the first of its kind in the
world. It aims to show that disability is no barrier to
creativity. Stages 1-2 productions a year with up to 10
performances over 6-8 venues around the country,
such as the Mill Arts Centre (Banbury), Stratford
Circus (London), and the Pegasus Theatre (Oxford).

Casting procedures: Casts in-house, does not issue
casting breakdowns, and welcomes letters (but not
emails) from individuals previously unknown to the
company. Welcomes invitations to view individuals'
websites, but not showreels.

Apropos Productions Ltd

2nd Floor, 91A Rivington Street, London EC2A 3AY
tel 020-7739 2857 *fax* 020-7739 3852
email info@aproposltd.com
website www.aproposltd.com
Director Paul Dubois

Company's work: Established in 1999. Provides
training for local, national and international clients.
Key focus is on Organisational Behaviour. Training is
provided for incoming actors through an induction
process: client briefings. Training is given to become
facilitators. Corporate experience is useful but not
essential for incoming actors. Actor-base is extended
annually through agents, website, Equity Job
Information Service and *PCR*. Clients include: Local
Government Association, Thompson Scientific,
Colchester Borough Council.

Recruitment procedures: Accepts submissions (with
CVs and photographs) from actors previously
unknown to the company. Disabled actors regularly
form part of its teams, and are actively encouraged to
apply.

art+power

Centre Gate, Colston Avenue, Bristol BS1 4TR
tel 0117-317 8099
email info@artandpower.com
website www.artandpower.com
Key contact Joanne Goldsworthy

Bristol-based organisation that uses the arts to
empower disabled people and build a more equal,
inclusive and creative society. art+power produces
theatre, dance and live art projects.

Birds of Paradise Theatre Company

333 Woodlands Road, Glasgow G3 6NG
tel 0141-339 1155 *fax* 0141-339 1177
email all@birdsofparadisetheatre.co.uk
website www.birdsofparadisetheatre.co.uk
Artistic Director Morven Gregor *Projects Manager*
Shona Rattray *'Agent for Change'* Robert Softley

A professional touring theatre company which
produces adventurous and challenging work that
places disability issues in the public arena. The
company has toured throughout Scotland for 12
years with inventive programmes of performances
and workshops, both for traditional theatre-going
audiences and people who have difficulty
experiencing theatre due to disability or geographical
isolation.

Birds of Paradise shares its knowledge of good
practice across the arts and disability sector with a
clear objective: to increase the number of disabled
professional theatre practitioners working in
Scotland. The company recognises that in order to
reverse hundreds of years of discrimination against
disabled people, it needs to present high-quality work
and positive role models for contemporary Scottish
Theatre, its audiences and practitioners. These role
models are also engaged to support the company's
work with physically disabled young people, who
continue to be excluded from participating and
engaging in the arts.

Since 1995, the company has intensively trained 150
people over 22 acting courses and technical skills. 400
general Outreach and Taster Workshops have been
run, involving approximately 4800 people, and there
have been 7 inclusive touring productions with
disabled and non-disabled performers and stage
workers. 23 disabled actors have been employed; 12
non-disabled actors have also been employed. 4
disabled people were employed in technical jobs.

Previous productions include: *The Farce of
Circumstance* by Tom Lannon (1995); *The Resistible
Rise of Arturo Ui* by Bertolt Brecht (1996); *Tongues* by
Sam Shephard and Joseph Chaikin (1997); *Working
Legs* by Alistair Gray (1998 commission); *Playing for
Keeps* by Archie Hind (1998 commission); *Merman*
by Susan McClymont and Dave Buchanan (2000
commission); *Twelve Black Candles* by Des Dillon
(2001); *The Irish Giant* by Garry Robson (2003);

Brazil 12 Scotland 0 by Ian Stephen (2005 commission); *Mouth of Silence* by Gerry Loose (2006 commission); and *Beneath You – Spider Girls are Everywhere!* by Kathy McKean (2007 commission). Birds of Paradise Theatre Company in association with The Citizens' Theatre produced *Offshore* by Alan Wilkins, directed by Morven Gregor, in September 2008.

Blue Eyed Soul Dance Company

The Lantern, Meadow Farm Drive, Sundorne, Shrewsbury SY1 4NG
tel (01743) 210830 *fax* (01743) 466854
email admin@blueeyedsouldance.com
website www.blueeyedsouldance.com
Artistic Director Rachel Freeman

Production details: Founded in 1994, Blue Eyed Soul is a successful inclusive dance company, which offers a dance repertoire, and education and training programmes. It embraces difference, and actively seeks out creative partnerships between disabled and non-disabled people. It stages 1 production a year, with an average of 20 performances in a wide range of locations including arts centres, theatres, outdoor venues, educational and community venues. Areas covered have included the West Midlands, London, the North West and the South East.

Casting procedures: Uses freelance casting directors, and holds general auditions. Casting breakdowns are available by postal application (with sae). Does not welcome unsolicited CVs, showreels or invitations to view individuals' websites from dancers unknown to the company. Offers non-Equity contracts.

Candoco Dance Company

2T Leroy House, 436 Essex Road, London N1 3QP
tel 020-7704 6845 *fax* 020-7704 1645
email info@candoco.co.uk
website www.candoco.co.uk
Co-Artistic Directors Stine Nilsen, Pedro Machado

Candoco Dance Company is the contemporary dance company of disabled and non-disabled dancers. By producing creatively ambitious dance performances, the company aims to push the boundaries of contemporary dance and to broaden people's perception of what dance is and who can dance.

Candoco was founded in 1991, and through its performances and education work has developed into the world's leading exponent of inclusive dance practice. The company regularly commissions artists and choreographers to create new dance work that tours nationally and internationally. It also runs a variety of training courses, residencies, workshops and 3 Youth Dance Companies.

Chicken Shed

Chase Side, Southgate, London N14 4PE
tel 020-8351 6161 *minicom* 020-8350 0676
website www.chickenshed.org.uk
Artistic Director Mary Ward

Children and young people's theatre company producing shows that are inclusive and accessible to all. Performs a wide range of works, spanning experimental pieces to full-scale productions; original works to Shakespeare. In addition the company runs:

• An inclusive theatre education workshop programme for nearly 700 members from the ages of 5 to 24 (550 up to the age of 18)
• The only inclusive BTEC National Diploma in Performing Arts in the country
• Special interactive performances for pre-school children and their parents and carers
• Training and work experience in performance and all aspects of theatre production to young people
• Training in inclusive practice through workshops and seminars for a range of professionals from the fields of education, social services and health
• A community facility that is completely accessible physically and has a warm and welcoming ambience
• A national training and development programme with mainstream and special educational needs schools; this has already established 15 new inclusive children's and youth theatre companies across the country, with more on the way

Common Ground Sign Dance Theatre

32-36 Hanover Street, Gostin's Building (4th Floor), Hanover Street, Liverpool L1 4LN
tel/fax 0151-707 8033
textphone 0151-707 8380
email info@signdance.com
website www.signdance.com
Artistic Director & Choreographer Denise Armstrong
Administrative Director Simeon Hart

Founded in 1986, Common Ground is a dance theatre company creating unique performances (through the fusion of sign language, dance and physical theatre) which are accessible to all audiences.

Deafinitely Theatre

Unit 20, Deane House Studios, 27 Greenwood Place, London NW5 1LB
tel 020-7424 7360
email paula@deafinitelytheatre.co.uk
website www.deafinitelytheatre.co.uk

Artistic Director Paula Garfield *General Manager* Mark Sands

Founded in 2002 to produce performance ideas by Deaf people. All the company's work is Deaf-led but is accessible to hearing people as well. The company runs projects and workshops for Deaf people and colleges in writing, acting and technical theatre. Recent productions include: *Dysfunction* (Soho Theatre); *Children of a Greater God* (Jackson's Lane); *Motherland* (Jackson's Lane); *Two Chairs* (Oval House).

Full Body & The Voice

Lawrence Batley Theatre, Queen's Street, Huddersfield HD1 2SP

Disabled actors

tel (01484) 484441 fax (01484) 484443
email fullbody@lbt-uk.org
website www.fullbody.org.uk
Artistic Director Vanessa Brooks

Production details: Established in 2000. Production company exploring a range of projects that include actors with learning disabilities and promote inclusive working practices. Approximately 1 production per year touring to 10-15 venues, including arts centres and theatres in Yorkshire, the North West and internationally. Roughly 5-8 actors are used in each production.

Casting procedures: Occasionally uses freelance casting directors. Does not welcome unsolicited CVs. Actively encourages applications from disabled actors and promotes the use of inclusive casting. Offers Equity approved contracts.

Graeae Theatre Company

Bradbury Studios, 138 Kingsland Road,
London E2 8DY
tel 020-7613 6900 fax 020-7613 6919
email info@graeae.org
website www.graeae.org
Artistic Director Jenny Sealey

Production details: Founded in 1980. Produces theatre made by disabled people (actors, directors and other theatre practitioners) with physical and sensory impairments. Stages 3 productions annually and gives 70 performances at 50 venues each year. Venues include arts centres and theatres in England, Scotland, Wales and Ireland. 3-6 actors are involved in each production. Recent productions include: national tour of *Blasted* by Sarah Kane, and *Whiter Than Snow* by Mike Kenny, which was a co-production with Birmingham Rep. Graeae/New Wolsey Theatre co-produced *Flower Girls* by Richard Cameron in Autumn 2007, and Graeae/Suspect Culture co-produced a new play in Spring 2008.

Casting procedures: Sometimes holds general auditions. Welcomes postal or email submissions (with CVs and photographs) from actors with physical and sensory impairments. Also accepts showreels and invitations to view individual actors' websites. Offers ITC/Equity approved contracts.

Into The Scene is a new Arts Council England initiative led by Graeae. Works with leading drama schools on inclusive practice to encourage drama schools to recruit more disabled actors onto their training courses.

Scene Change is a Graeae initiative working with venues, drama schools and colleges offering taster workshops to encourage more young people to apply to drama schools.

The company offers Continued Professional Development workshops for actors. Past workshops have included Comedy Acting with director Gordon Anderson (ATC/Catherine Tate), and Singing with Barb Jungr.

Grid (part of Inter-Action MK)

The Old Rectory, Waterside, Peartree Bridge,
Milton Keynes MK6 3EJ
tel (01908) 678514
email info@interactionmk.org.uk
website www.interactionmk.org.uk
Project Manager Hannah Kitchen

Inspired by the work of Chicken Shed Theatre Company (see page 351), Shed MK runs various inclusive performance projects – among them, youth theatre projects for 7-11 and 12-16 year-olds.

Hijinx Theatre

Wales Millennium Centre, Bute Place,
Cardiff CF10 5AL
tel 029-2030 0331 fax 029-2063 5621
email info@hijinx.org.uk
website www.hijinx.org.uk
Artistic Director Gaynor Lougher Associate Director Louise Osborn Administrative Director Val Hill

Production details: Founded in 1981, the company stages at least 2 professional productions a year on a one-night-stand basis across Wales and England, for community and theatre venues. In general the Spring show is aimed at a learning-disabled audience and their communities, while the Autumn and Winter tours target the general public.

The company has developed a strong commitment to new writing over the years, commissioning plays from many of Wales' leading playwrights. On average, 4 actors work on each production, which includes a strong musical element. Recent productions include: *Chasing Rainbows* (touring day centres, gateway clubs, community centres and colleges); and *The Other Woman* (Wales Millennium Centre, Torch Theatre and community venues). Offers ITC/Equity approved contracts and does not subscribe to the Equity Pension Scheme.

Casting procedures: Shows are cast by the artistic and associate director. Welcomes letters, CVs and photographs from actors previously unknown to the company. Does not accept emails or showreels. Welcomes applications from disabled and non-disabled actors.

IMPACT Theatre Company

The Stirling Road Centre, Stirling Road, Acton,
London W3 8DJ
tel/fax 020-8896 3682
email impact-theatre@btconnect.com
website www.impactondisabilityarts.com
Artistic Directors Kim Mughan, Amanda Braggins

IMPACT (IMagine, Perform And Create Together) Theatre Company was founded in 1999. It was set up by and for adults with learning disabilities facilitated by two Artistic Directors. While not a professional company, IMPACT helps to develop skills of performance and self-expression for its actors.

Krazy Kat Theatre Company

173 Hartington Road, Brighton BN2 3PA
tel (01273) 692552 *fax* (01273) 692552
email krazykattheatre@ntlworld.com
website www.krazykattheatre.co.uk
Artistic Director Kinny Gardner

Production details: A children's theatre company
founded in 1972, specialising in highly visual forms of
theatre that are accessible to deaf children. Normally
tours 4-6 projects each year with an average annual
total of 150 performances and 75 venues. Venues
include schools, arts centres, theatres, outdoor venues
and community centres in Essex, Sussex, Kent and
London. In general 2 actors go on tour and play to
audiences aged 3-7. Singing ability, physical theatre
skills, sign language and a driving licence are
required. Actors may also be expected to lead
workshops. Recent productions include: *Three Pigs*,
Jack & The Beanstalk, and *The Very Magic Flute*.

Casting procedures: Sometimes holds general
auditions; actors can write at any time requesting
inclusion. Accepts submissions (with CVs and
photographs) from actors previously unknown to the
company if sent by post. Does not welcome
unsolicited emails. Will also accept invitations to view
individual actors' websites. Offers non-Equity
contracts. Actively encourages applications from
disabled actors and promotes the use of inclusive
casting.

Lawnmowers Independent Theatre Company & Liberdade

Swinburn House, Swinburn Street,
Gateshead NE8 1AX
tel/fax 0191-478 9200
email info@thelawnmowers.co.uk
website www.thelawnmowers.co.uk
Arts Director Geraldine Ling *Apprenticeship
Coordinator* Rob Huggins

Theatre company addressing issues of concern for
people with learning difficulties, often with an
international dimension. Uses theatre and drama as a
means for people with learning difficulties to explore
and develop ideas, and help plan and take control of
their futures.

Also runs the Liberdade Apprenticeship Scheme, a
3-year physical theatre apprenticeship scheme for
young adults with learning difficulties who aim to
form their own theatre company.

Louise Dyson at VisABLE People

PO Box 80, Droitwich WR9 0ZE
tel (01905) 776631
email louise@visablepeople.com
website www.visablepeople.com
Agent Louise Dyson

Production details: Founded in 1994, VisABLE is the
UK's first agency representing only disabled people

for professional engagements. It represents artistes
with a wide range of impairments and in every age
group, including children. 1 agent represents around
50 artistes in all areas of acting, including presenting.

Casting procedures: Does not welcome performance
notices: "Sorry, usually no time to get out and see
them; existing clients only." Happy to receive other
enquiries (with CVs and photographs) from disabled
actors via email only. Showreels should always be
accompanied by an sae for return. Also happy to
receive invitations to view individual actors' websites.
Recommends the photographer Simon Donnelly.
Commission: 10-17%

Magpie Dance

The Churchill Theatre, High Street,
Bromley BR1 1HA
tel 020-8290 6633
email info@magpiedance.org.uk
website www.magpiedance.org.uk
Artistic Director Avril Hitman *General Manager* Laura
Riches

Magpie Dance is a company for people with learning
disabilities; based in Bromley, Magpie can also deliver
workshops to any region in the UK. With an
emphasis on ability rather than disability, the
company has a national reputation for its exciting
approach to inclusive dance.

Mind the Gap

Mind the Gap Studios Bradford, Silk Warehouse,
Patent Street, Bradford BD9 4SA
tel (01274) 544683 *fax* (01274) 544501
email arts@mind-the-gap.org.uk
website www.mind-the-gap.org.uk
Artistic Director Tim Wheeler *Administrative Director*
Julia Skelton

Production details: Founded in 1988, Mind the Gap
is a theatre company with a belief in quality, equality
and inclusion, and a mission to dismantle barriers to
artistic excellence so that learning-disabled and non-
learning-disabled actors can appear as equals. The
company has 5 main areas of activity:

• National Touring: in 2000, Mind the Gap
progressed from devised work to adaptations of well-
known texts. In recent years the company has
produced: *Of Mice and Men* (2000 and 2005); *Dr
Jekyll and Mr Hyde* (2001); *Pygmalion* (2002); *Don
Quixote* (2003 – collaboration with Northern Stage);
and *Cyrano* (2004). Total audiences for the 2005 tour
were approximately 6700.
• Learning & Skills: each year Mind the Gap runs a
full-time accredited training course for people with
learning disabilities. In addition, as part of the DaDA
awards scheme, the company runs Staging Change –
a residential, nationally recruited training course for
people with learning disabilities, working in
partnership with 5 of the country's leading
mainstream drama schools.

Disabled actors

• Acting Company: comprising 7 learning-disabled graduates of Mind the Gap's training courses who work on National Touring productions and their own programme of local and regional performance work and workshops.
• Outreach: each year, Mind the Gap's Outreach programme works with 300 young learning-disabled people from West Yorkshire on short-term drama training and performance projects.
• Advocacy: Mind the Gap advocates for people who are traditionally excluded or marginalised from mainstream practices. Mind the Gap is also commissioned to do a variety of performance projects: e.g. *Finding their Feet* – a production commissioned by Bradford School of Health Studies; and *Inside Knowledge* – commissioned by Tonic as part of a consultation to provide guidance for the design of a new cancer care centre in Leeds.

Stages 1 or 2 national tours annually (25-30 performances each), 1 large-scale regional performance project (3-6 performances), and 1 or 2 regional schools tours (12 performances). The national tour visits 15-20 venues: in 2005 these included West Yorkshire Playhouse; The Theatre, Chipping Norton; Ustinov Studio, Bath; Norwich Playhouse; Rose Theatre, Ormskirk; New Vic, Newcastle-under-Lyme; and Jackson's Lane Theatre, London. 3-5 actors are involved in the national tour, up to 7 actors in the schools tour, and over 20 performers in the regional performance project.

Casting procedures: Casts in-house. When the company is seeking to recruit an actor from outside the core company, it contacts agents, and advertises in *The Stage* and on its website. Casting breakdowns are available on request. Welcomes letters (with CVs and photographs) as well as showreels and invitations to view individuals' websites, "although we do not often employ actors who are not known to us. For national touring work we rarely cast outside our core Acting Company, but we do keep on record details which have been sent to us. We are particularly interested in hearing from disabled artists". Offers TMA/Equity approved contracts.

Nasty Girls
email redcunningham@btinternet.com
website www.nasty-girls.co.uk

Disabled/Deaf women who devise, write and perform their own material specialising in cardboard characters, overblown egos, cheap laughs and slapstick.

Oily Cart Company
Smallwood School Annexe, Smallwood Road, London SW17 OTW
tel 020-8672 6329 *fax* 020-8672 0792
email oilies@oilycart.org.uk
website www.oilycart.org.uk
Artistic Director Tim Webb *General Manager* Kathy Everett *Administrator* Sarah Crompton

Production details: One of the leading theatre companies in the UK, creating highly interactive multi-sensory performances for the very young (6 months to 6 years) and for young people (aged 3-19) with Profound or Multiple Learning Disabilities (PMLD) or an Autistic Spectrum Disorder (ASD). Tours national and international venues like theatres and arts centres with early years shows, and takes its special needs work to special schools around the UK. Recent productions include: *Baby Balloon* for audiences aged 6 months to 2 years; *If All The World Were Paper*; *Blue*; and *Pool Piece* – an interactive hydrotherapy pool show for young people with PMLD or ASD.

Casting procedures: Casting breakdowns are available on the website **www.oilycart.org.uk** and the Artsjobs website **www.artscouncil.org.uk/pressnews/mailinglists.php**. Offers ITC/Equity approved contracts. Actively encourages applications from disabled actors and promotes the use of inclusive casting.

Pride of Place Theatre Festival
website www.prideofplace.org.uk

The Pride of Place group of Rural Touring theatre companies hold a general audition each summer specifically to see disabled actors that they have not met before. As general auditions, they do not necessarily result in immediate work, but are about establishing a relationship with the companies for future opportunities.

See the entry on page 279 for more details of the Pride of Place Festival and the companies involved.

Contact Brendan Murray of Oxfordshire Theatre Company or visit the OTTC website for more information about the auditions. Contact details for Brendan Murray and OTTC can be found on page 186.

Salamanda Tandem
14-16 Bridgford Road, Nottingham NG2 6AB
tel/fax 0845-293 2989
email info@salamanda-tandem.org
website www.salamanda-tandem.org
Artistic Director Isabel Jones

Producer of contemporary art works, creative environments and sensory performances, where people can choose to observe or become part of the artwork itself. It works with a wide spectrum of people, and in particular people with disabilities. Strong advocate for ethical practice in arts and health. Publishes articles and conducts training and professional education.

Shoot Your Mouth Off
Unit B, Cromwell Business Park, Cromwell Street, Hartlepool TS24 7LP
tel (01429) 42349 *mobile* (07960) 532554
email karensheader@aol.com
Director Karen Sheader

Shoot Your Mouth Off is a film company run by a disabled producer/actor, Karen Sheader. SYMO began making films with a local professional video production company, Carpet Films, in 2001; Carpet Films has since become part of SYMO. The company has made 12 films to date, many of which have been screened at both disability and mainstream festivals in the UK and internationally, including San Francisco and Moscow. An award-winning production company based in the North-East of England, it works with actors who consider themselves to be disabled – "all our films explore some aspect of the experience of being a person with impairments in a disabling society". Makes comedies, dramas, documentaries and interactive digital media.

the shysters (part of open theatre company)

Room 17, Steeple House, Percy Street, Coventry CV1 3BY
tel/fax (024) 7623 9186
email shysters@opentheatre.co.uk
website www.theshysters.co.uk
Artistic Director Richard Hayhow *Associate Director* Kathy Joyce *Company Manager* Sue Walker

The shysters theatre company was set up by open theatre company (otc) in partnership with the Belgrade Theatre, Coventry in 1997, but is now incorporated fully into the work of otc. "The company uses an ensemble way of working that reflects our unique characteristics (which we call 'shysterness') and which has its roots in learning disability". The shysters are keen to collaborate with others and are always looking for new ways to develop and make theatre.

In 2002 the shysters set up the shystershadows to offer training in performing arts skills and 'shysterness' to young people with learning disabilities.

Spare Tyre Theatre Company

Unit 3.22, Canterbury Court, 1-3 Brixton Road, London SW9 6DE
tel/fax 020-7061 6454
email info@sparetyre.org
website www.sparetyre.org
Artistic Director Arti Prashar *General Manager* Bonnie Mitchell *Administrator* Vicky Tweedie

Production details: The company has 3 principal strands of work:

• Work with elders: the 'HotPots' are a group of people over 60 who perform work, often from personal experience and using humour, about the treatment of elders. They are committed to educating audiences about the potential of older people.
• Work with people with learning disabilities: the 'inc.Theatre' course is a full-time, OCN (Open College Network) approved partnership with Redbridge College for people of all ages with learning disabilities.

• Work with schools: professional TIE productions for school pupils tackling homophobia in schools. Also: 'Dealing with Difference', a workshop for school staff which looks at approaches to tackling homophobia within schools.

Each strand of work has 1 major production a year, touring to roughly 100 venues – from schools, theatres and community venues to hospitals, GP surgeries, residential homes, special needs schools and public sector venues. Primarily covers the London area, but also Yorkshire, Manchester, Kent and Wales. Skills required from actors include (ideally) a driving licence, but also workshop-leading and facilitation skills, experience of working with community groups, and a sensitivity to, and understanding of, relevant issues.

Casting procedures: Casting breakdowns are published in *The Stage* and on the website. Unsolicited approaches at other times – including CVs, showreels and invitations to view individuals' websites – are discouraged. Offers ITC/Equity approved contracts. Actively encourages applications from disabled actors and promotes the use of inclusive casting.

Spiral

See entry for First Movement on page 357.

Starfish Theatre Company (formerly Jumpstart)

See entry for Prism Arts on page 358.

StopGAP Dance Company

Farnham Maltings, Bridge Square, Farnham, Surrey GU9 7QR
tel (01252) 718664
email vicki@stopgap.uk.com
website www.stopgap.uk.com
General Manager Abi Reeve

A vibrant integrated dance company that includes disabled and non-disabled dancers. It challenges traditional notions about dance by using each dancer's physical and intellectual potential as a starting point for creating new work. "We work from a philosophy of physical, psychological and social integration. In so doing, we recognise and celebrate individuality and the differences between people, while continually seeking artistic and technical excellence in all that we do."

Theatre without Walls

Forwood House, Forwood, Gloucesterhire GL6 9AB
mobile (07962) 040441
email hello@theatrewithoutwalls.org.uk
website www.theatrewithoutwalls.org.uk
Directors Genevieve Swift, Jason Maher

Company's work: Established in 2002. Award-winning producing theatre company with an active training/corporate wing, working in the public and private sector. Also produces television and corporate films. Clients include: National Trust, Gloucestershire Local Authority, Apollo, BBC, The Prince's Trust. Training is provided for incoming actors in the form of workshops and rehearsals in forum, role play and interactive drama. Incoming actors require good improvisational skills.

Recruitment procedures: Actors are recruited through agents and Equity Job Information Service. Disabled actors regularly form part of the team and are actively encouraged to apply. See also the company's entry under *Middle and smaller-scale companies* on page 197.

Theatre Workshop

34 Hamilton Place, Edinburgh EH3 5AX
tel 0131-225 7942 *fax* 0131-220 0112
email afleming@twe.org.uk
website www.theatre-workshop.com
Artistic Director Robert Rae *Company Manager* Anne Fleming

Production details: Founded in 1965; stages 4 productions a year with around 60 performances across 2 theatre venues. Occasionally tours internationally. Employs an average of 5 actors on each production, using ITC/Equity approved contracts. Recent productions include: *The Jasmine Road* (No Limits International Theatre Festival, Berlin); and *The Threepenny Opera* (Edinburgh Festival Theatre & Tramway, Glasgow).

Casting procedures: Casting breakdowns are available from the website and Equity Job Information Service. Welcomes letters and emails (with CVs and photographs) from individuals previously unknown to the company. Also happy to receive showreels and invitations to view individuals' websites. Encourages applications from disabled actors and promotes the use of inclusive casting. "Theatre Workshop casts both disabled and non-disabled actors in all our productions."

Touchdown Dance

Waterside Arts Centre, Sale M33 7ZF
tel 0161-912 5760 *fax* 0161-912 5783
email info@touchdowndance.co.uk
website www.touchdowndance.co.uk
Director Katy Dymoke

Touchdown Dance provides dance workshops for visually impaired and sighted people of all ages and ability, ranging from 'jam' weekends to more intensive courses.

Wolf + Water

The Plough, 9-11 Fore Street, Torrington,
Devon EX38 8HQ
tel (01805) 625533
email w+w@eclipse.co.uk
website www.wolfandwater.org

Co-founders Steve Newton, Philip Robinson
Administrator Peter Smith

Since establishing itself independently in 1991, after 3 years as the Beaford Centre's 'Common Sense Project', Wolf + Water Arts Company has brought its creative and therapeutic approaches to a wide variety of groups locally, nationally and internationally. These groups have included people with learning difficulties; people with mental health issues; people in conflict situations; offenders; communities; young people at risk; children with life-threatening illnesses and their families; and staff groups working with all the above. The company produces original topical performances for conferences and for tour, and provides a wide range of training courses for those wishing to use drama and arts techniques in special-needs situations. Work has taken the company throughout the UK, Eire, Scandinavia, the Middle East and the Balkans.

FESTIVALS

Disability Film Festival

London Disability Arts Forum,
20-22 Waterson Street, London E2 8HE
tel 020-7749 4352 *fax* 020-7749 4363
email info@ldaf.org
website www.disabilityfilm.co.uk
Festival Coordinator Caglar Kimyoncu

Showcasing the talent of disabled filmmakers, the Disability Film Festival takes place over 4 days in December, and is hosted by the BFI Southbank (formerly the National Film Theatre). The festival offers filmmakers, film-goers and industry professionals the opportunity to meet, exchange feedback, network and socialise. It has also become a forum for debate, challenging the exclusion of disabled people either on screen or as filmmakers. Submission forms and guidelines are available to download from the website.

ARTS ORGANISATIONS

Ableize Arts

website www.ableize.com/disabled-arts

A selection of disabled arts sites, from theatre and dance to visual arts. The Ableize site also features links from accommodation and travel to support groups and employment and benefits. A fantastic, wide-ranging site.

Acadea

MEA House, Ellison Place,
Newcastle upon Tyne NE1 8XS
tel 0191-222 0708 (*mobile & text*) (07932) 304241
email info@arcadea.org
website www.arcadea.org

Arcadea aims to promote the artistic and cultural equality of disabled people in the North East region, serving Co. Durham, Northumberland, Tees Valley and Tyne & Wear.

Artlink Central
Cowane Centre, Cowane Street , Stirling FK8 1JP
tel (01786) 450971 *fax* (01786) 465958
email info@artlinkcentral.org
website www.artlinkcentral.org

Established in February 1988, Artlink Central is a registered charity founded in the belief that involvement in the arts is life-enhancing and should be available to all. It enables a wide range of disabled and/or marginalised people to work with experienced professional artists on high-quality arts projects in the Stirling, Falkirk and Clackmannanshire areas of Central Scotland.

Artlink Edinburgh
13A Spittal Street, Edinburgh
tel 0131-229 3555 *fax* 0131-228 5257
website www.artlinkedinburgh.co.uk

As Artlink Central, but based in Edinburgh and the Lothians.

Artsline
c/o 21 Pine Court, Wood Lodge Gardens, Bromley BR1 2WA
tel 020-7388 2227 *fax* 020-7383 2653
minicom 020-7388 2227
email admin@artsline.org.uk
website www.artsline.org.uk

Founded in 1981 with the aim of increasing disabled people's participation in the arts, and to provide them with accurate information about access to arts and cultural events in London. In collaboration with the London Disability Arts Forum, it began producing *Disability Arts in London (DAIL)* magazine in 1986, and now provides a newly launched access database with details for arts and entertainment venues across London, including: theatres, cinemas, museums, art centres, tourist attractions, comedy, music venues and selected restaurants. For details of other publications, projects and services available, consult the website.

Carousel
Community Base, 113 Queens Road, Brighton BN1 3XG
tel (01273) 234734 *fax* (01273) 234735
email enquiries@carousel.org.uk
website www.carousel.org.uk
Artistic Director Mark Richardson *Executive Director* Liz Hall

Carousel was founded in 1982, and operates primarily in the South East of England. It is a Brighton-based arts organisation that works with people who have learning disabilities. Among its

projects are the High Spin Dance Company and the Oskabright Film Festival.

DaDa-Disability & Deaf Arts
The Bluecoat, School Lane, Liverpool L1 3BX
tel 0151-707 1733 *minicom* 0151-706 0365
fax 0151-708 9355
email info@dadahello.com
website www.dadahello.com
CEO Ruth Gould

DaDa-Disability & Deaf Arts is a disabled and Deaf led organisation. It aims to facilitate the active participation of disabled and Deaf people in all aspects of the arts and creative industries, and to promote and celebrate disability and Deaf arts and culture. Based in Liverpool City Centre, the company's work covers the whole of the North West and the UK, as well as operating on an international scale.

Disability Arts Cymru
Sbectrwm, Bwlch Road, Fairwater, Cardiff CF5 3EF
tel 029-2055 1040 *textphone* 029-2055 1040
fax 029-2055 1036
email post@dacymru.com
website www.dacymru.com
Director Maggie Hampton

Disability Arts Cymru is the only organisation in Wales providing Disability Equality Training (DET) specifically for arts providers; it lists among its clients the Arts Council of Wales and the Royal Welsh College of Music and Drama. A number of documents are available from its excellent website, which offer advice on a range of subjects including access issues for touring companies. In June 2006 the company ran 'The Unusual Stage School', a free 11-day course aimed at disabled would-be actors living in Wales.

Disability Arts Online
9 Jew Street, Brighton BN1 1UT
tel (01273) 771878
email info@disabilityartsonline.org.uk
website www.disabilityarts.org

Aims to assist the professional development of disabled and deaf writers and artists, working across all art forms.

Diverse City
The Grayston Centre, 28 Charles Square, London N1 6HT
tel 020-7193 9684
website www.diversecitylondon.org

Advocates for and delivers diversity and equality of opportunity in culture and learning.

First Movement
Level Centre, Old Station Close, Rowsley, Derbyshire DE4 2EL

tel (01629) 734848
email fmt@first-movement.org.uk
website www.first-movement.org.uk

First Movement is an experimental arts organisation developing projects which uniquely reflect the experiences, choices and abilities of groups of people with severe and profound learning disabilities. Runs a performance company called Spiral.

National Disability Arts Forum (NDAF)

59 Lime Street, Newcastle upon Tyne NE1 2PQ
tel 0191-261 1628 *minicom* 0191-261 2237
fax 0191-222 0573
email ndaf@ndaf.org
website www.ndaf.org

The National Disability Arts Forum aims to create equality of opportunity for disabled people in all aspects of the arts. It does this by:

• Supporting the development of Disability Arts Agencies, both regional and local, throughout the UK
• Maintaining and developing a network through which these Agencies can support and assist each others' development
• Establishing favourable conditions within which disabled people can explore and express the condition of disability through the arts
• Promoting the value of art by disabled people

It also:

• Promotes and supports examples of good and/or innovative practice that encourages the participation of disabled people in the arts
• Assists organisations in developing good and/or innovative practice that encourages the participation of disabled people in the arts

The members of the Forum believe that it should be disabled people themselves who determine where and with whom responsibility for decision-making and advocacy on their behalf should lie. Hence, the organisation is accountable to, and controlled and managed by, disabled people.

Like other 'self-led' disability organisations in the UK, NDAF is committed to promoting equal opportunities, and prioritises the employment of disabled people, as well as operating an ethical fundraising programme to finance its projects. It works to promote similar practices throughout the arts community, and supports other arts organisations with corresponding policies.

The Forum's main strategy for delivering its mission is to support and work with others whose work involves making their products or services more accessible or attractive to disabled people, those who are engaged in producing and promoting Disability Arts, and those who provide specialist arts services to disabled people, such as workshops or exhibitions.

NDAF aims to undertake at least 1 major arts project a year that is targeted directly at disabled people. Usually these are 'model' projects, or projects that are designed to break new ground.

Note Visit the website to sign up to *EtCetera*, NDAF's email newsletter, which contains (among other things) job opportunities, training and workshops, and a Pick-of-the-Week for television and radio. Also on the website you can listen and subscribe to its Disability Arts podcast.

Northern Ireland Arts & Disability Forum

Cathedral Quarter Managed Workspace,
109-113 Royal Avenue, Belfast BT1 1FF
tel 028-90 239 450
email info@adf.ie
website www.adf.ie
Chief Executive Officer Chris Ledger

A non-profit-making voluntary organisation that aims to provide:

• Information to disabled people and organisations – both inside and outside the arts sector
• A body that advocates on behalf of disabled people in the arts sector
• A networking, developmental and coordinating body
• A body that identifies and fills gaps in training provisions for disabled people working in the arts
• A focus for campaigning

Also runs a gallery to exhibit the work of disabled artists.

Prism Arts

Unit 003, Warwick Mill Business Village,
Warwick Mill, Carlisle, Cumbria CA4 8RR
tel (01228) 564571 *fax* (01228) 564433
email office@prismarts.org.uk
website www.prismarts.co.uk
Director Catherine Coulthard

Promotes disabled people's access to creative arts activities in Cumbria. Runs Starfish Theatre Company, a group of learning-disabled performers.

Shape

Deane House Studios, 27 Greenwood Place,
London NW5 1LB
tel 0845-521 3457 *minicom* 020-7424 7368
fax 0845-521 3458
email info@shapearts.org.uk
website www.shapearts.org.uk

Shape is based in North London with offices in Hammersmith and Fulham, Wandsworth and Islington. It is a charity that opens up access to the arts, enabling greater participation by disabled and older people.

Theatre Resource

Great Stony, High Street, Chipping Ongar,
Essex CM5 0AD
tel (01277) 365626 *minicom* (01277) 365003
email info@theatre-resource.org.uk
website www.theatre-resource.org.uk
Director/Chief Executive Jeff Banks

"Theatre Resource is a dynamic and forward-looking professional arts organisation, specialising in the area of disability arts and social inclusion. Our work promotes the creativity, culture and heritage of disabled people and socially excluded groups, for the benefit of all."

RIGHTS, ADVICE AND SUPPORT

Broadcasting & Creative Industries Disability Network (BCIDN) – see
Employers' Forum on Disability below

Directgov
website www.direct.gov.uk/disability

The government's Public Services portal, with links to information and advice on employment, home and housing options, financial support, health, education and training, rights and obligations, transport, travel and holidays, leisure and recreation, and caring for someone.

Employers' Forum on Disability
Nutmeg House, 60 Gainsford Street,
London SE1 2NY
tel 020-7403 3020 fax 020-7403 0404
minicom 020-7403 0040
email enquiries@efd.org.uk
website www.efd.org.uk

The leading employers' organisation focused on disability as it affects business. Funded and managed by more than 400 members, the Forum works to make it easier for companies to recruit and retain disabled employees and to serve disabled customers. Umbrella organisation for the Broadcasting & Creative Industries Disability Network (BCIDN), a forum for the UK's major broadcasters to explore and address disability as it relates to the media industry. It is advised by a panel of associates – 14 disabled people with considerable media experience who work in different areas of broadcasting and the media in general.

Equality and Human Rights Commission
England: Freepost RRLL-GHUX-CTRX,
Arndale House, Arndale Centre, Manchester M4 3AQ
tel 0845-604 6610 textphone 0845-604 6620
fax 0845-604 6630
email englandhelpline@equalityhumanrights.com
website www.equalityhumanrights.com

Having taken over from the Disability Rights Commission in 2007, the Equality and Human Rights Commission's role is to:

• ensure that people are aware of their rights and how to use them

• work with employers, service providers and organisations to help them develop best practice
• work with policymakers, lawyers and the Government to make sure that social policy and the law promote equality
• use its powers to enforce the laws that are already in place.

Wales
Freepost RRLR-UEYB-UYZL, 3rd Floor, 3 Callaghan Square, Cardiff CF10 5BT
tel 0845-604 8810 textphone 0845-604 5520
fax 0845-604 5530
email waleshelpline@equalityhumanrights.com

Scotland
Freepost RRLL-GYLB-UJTA, The Optima Building, 58 Robertson Street, Glasgow G2 8DU
0845-604 5510 0845-604 5520 0845-604 5530
email scotlandhelpline@equalityhumanrights.com
(The helplines are open Monday-Friday 8am-6pm.)

Ouch!
website www.bbc.co.uk/ouch

The BBC's online disability magazine, including weblogs, message board, and a monthly podcast.

Skill: National Bureau for Students with Disabilities
Unit 3, Floor 3, Radisson Court, 219 Long Lane, London SE1 4PR
tel 020-7450 0620 fax 020-7450 0650
minicom 020-7450 0620
Freephone helpline: (0800) 328 5050
email skill@skill.org.uk
website www.skill.org.uk
Chief Executive Barbara Waters

Informs and influences key policy makers to improve legal rights and support for disabled people in post-16 education and training. Skill works together with individual disabled people, professionals working in education, training and careers, employers and disability organisations to influence government.

Opening hours: Tuesdays 11.30am – 1.30pm and Thursdays 1.30 –3.30pm.

Promotes best practice through:

• Membership – keeping professionals up to date and informed about policy changes, providing the opportunity for exchanging information and ideas for closer involvement with its work
• Running topical conferences and seminars
• Producing informative and practical publications
• Providing consultancy and staff training for colleges, universities and other organisations.

Disabled actors

Opportunities for disabled actors

Jamie Beddard

The plethora of journeys and experiences of disabled performers over the past 30 years has ranged from the lonely, demoralising, and depressing to the downright bizarre. The barriers encountered far outreach the regular obstacles preventing non-disabled actors from learning, and plying their trade. Performance attributes of technique, voice, improvisation and movement seem distant concepts when you cannot get through the doors of drama school, producers baulk at the idea of employing disabled performers, and most training and employment opportunities are based around strict notions of 'the classical actor'. This is altogether surprising in the creative industries, which should surely celebrate uniqueness, individuality and diversity. However, where once black actors were denied access to stage and screen, so those with different bodies have fought similar battles for opportunity, acknowledgement and representation. This, against a backdrop in which esteemed, non-disabled actors regularly pick up Oscars for their touching portrayal of characters with disability: Daniel Day Lewis in *My Left Foot*; Jamie Foxx in *Ray*; John Voight in *Coming Home*; Tom Hanks in *Forrest Gump* – there's a long list, and they are one-dimensional replications of impediments, far outweighing any considerations around full and meaningful characterisations. Authenticity has been a label seldom attached to the portrayal of disability in the mainstream.

Personal anecdotes are perhaps best served by exploring the issues faced by disabled performers, as until recently, there have been no formal routes of progression into the industry. Those few who have made the periphery have tended to have random and short-lived paths based around such indeterminates as maverick directors, word of mouth or, as in my particular case, luck. The groundbreaking film *Skalligrigg* – a road movie in which a rag tag of disabled characters take to the road on a mythical quest – threw my staid career path into chaos, and levered a window (previously boarded up!) into performance. In the absence of disabled actors, many first-timers with no experience were suddenly thrust onto a film set; I thought the sound-boom was a cheap prop! 'Rough diamonds' probably most accurately described those of us fortunate enough to get such a break, and, for me, the film opened up a completely new, and exciting, world. A mixture of bluff, wide-eyed enthusiasm and no little begging had to suffice in the absence of any formal training.

This 'new and exciting world' was also populated by baffling and disheartening prejudices, and initial enthusiasm soon became tinged with disappointment and anger. A casting director for *Eastenders* once informed me that a disabled character – played by a disabled actor, heaven forbid! – would place the programme in the realm of freak show. So much for diverse communities and gritty realism! This attitude is unfortunately still painfully prevalent and theatre directors are worried that their audiences will be put off by seeing a disabled person on stage.

I contacted Graeae Theatre Company – a company that had been going since the early 1980s, and was run by, and for, actors with sensory and physical disabilities. Graeae had become accustomed to (and was hardened by) irksome battles against prevalent prejudices and barriers. I found a group of like-minded individuals who were challenging these ridiculous, outdated and offensive attitudes, and were determined to pursue careers considered impractical and unrealistic. They were developing, writing and performing theatre as does any small-scale company; sometimes very good, and sometimes not so good. However, the normal critical faculties brought to bear on other companies seemed strangely absent from assessment of Graeae's work, with emphasis on the 'oh so strange impairments' rather than art. The *Independent*, when reviewing Graeae's 2002 production – *Peeling* – came up with such helpful insights as, "Beaty is four feet tall; Coral has tiny limbs and a torso about the same size as her head." Apart from gross inaccuracies, the obvious offence to the individual actors involved and the banality of such revelations, what relevance has this to the art? Hopefully, the paying public didn't recoil in shock at this assembled collection of bizarre physical specimens!

I always yearned for a bad – rather than ignorant, ill informed and avoiding – review, because this would suggest a considered judgement based on the same criteria as any other performer. Undoubtedly, I have been involved in a few 'turkeys', and they should be recognised as such! However, fascination with individual impediment always seems the central tenet of any assessment of performance. Perhaps it would be interesting to apply such criteria to the wider acting fraternity – solely judging Woody Allen on his glasses, Tom Hanks on his stature, or Kenneth Williams on his nasal inflection.

Over the years the profile of Graeae, and of disabled performers in general, has grown, and there has been a gradual acceptance that it is no longer acceptable to marginalise their talents, aspirations and contributions. In many ways the Arts have lagged behind society in taking the first steps towards embracing and committing to diversity. Although, there has, in many quarters, been a genuine will to broaden participation, the stick of the Disability Discrimination Act has been instrumental in initiating fundamental appraisal and change. The possibility of legal challenges has shaken many organisations, venues and makers from their comfy inertia. Even tokenism is preferable to apartheid!

Drama schools, in particular, have found the concept of students with disability difficult to grasp, but the introduction of the Dance & Drama Awards has started the process of drama schools thinking not only about the physical access to their buildings, but also about the attitudinal access and ways to promote inclusive teaching. This is very exciting and will no doubt pave the way for young disabled people to go through mainstream training rather than be reliant on Graeae.

While the process of change will take time (especially the attitudinal aspect), Graeae has had to respond to the obvious demand by setting up the training course in conjunction with London Metropolitan University. This course offers all the elements found in drama schools, and provides the skills, disciplines and training that were denied people of my age. Lack of sufficiently trained and experienced disabled actors has long been an excuse for the 'cripping up' of non-disabled actors, while training providers continually stress the unlikelihood of disabled graduates sustaining careers in the industry. A classic chicken-and-egg situation, in which aspirant disabled performers are denied entrance at all levels. However, the percentage of those who have graduated through Missing Piece, and gone into the industry, compares favourably with other drama schools, and Graeae is frequently approached by casting directors looking for disabled talent. So, young people with disabilities do share the same aspirations as any others; there is an increasing demand for such actors; and the institutions are failing to shoulder responsibility.

Missing Piece is fulfilling this vacuum, and has now been running since 2000. The nine-month (September to May) intensive training allows disabled students to work with a wide range of theatre practitioners – both specialist and mainstream. The course can act as a foundation course to further education or drama school – access and will permitting! – or, as is often the case, a direct gateway into the industry. Academic and practical elements of performance are covered, and opportunities for showcasing and touring afforded. Recent years have culminated in professional touring productions of *Mother Courage* and *George Dandin*, and many relationships have been brokered between Graeae's performers and directors, producers and casting directors. There is a crossover with the Performing Arts degree at London Metropolitan, with disabled performers working alongside and in collaboration with tutors and students at the University. As well as the main Missing Piece course, Graeae run a series of taster workshops throughout the year for prospective actors.

So strides are being made by Graeae, and by other companies; the excuses and barriers preventing inclusion are slowly being dismantled. There are viable careers for those with the talent, determination and thick skin when necessary.

BBC has set up a talent fund for disabled actors to try and address dated attitudes, and to encourage writers to write storylines which are not always hospital-based or about the whole 'disability thing'!

However the failure of mainstream films such as *Inside I'm Dancing*, which continue to propagate stereotypes and exclusion – with all the main disabled characters played by non-disabled actors – will hopefully mark a sea-change in attitudes and imaginations among creators. The existing, and perspective, body of talent out there no longer allows for petty excuses or wilful misrepresentation. Disabled people, like any others, can make good, bad or indifferent performers, and should be judged as such. However, we have a right to expect the same opportunities, treatments and prospects as all. Banging the door down has become boring – just let us in. It's not rocket science!

Jamie Beddard is an actor, writer and director. Involved with Graeae since 1991, he was Associate Director of the company for some years. He is currently working as a freelance director and co-editor of *DAIL* magazine. Graeae productions 2006/7 include *Blasted* by Sarah Kane, touring March to May; *Once Beyond These Walls, A Girl* by Richard Cameron, touring October to November; and *Whiter Than Snow* by Mike Kenny – a co-production with Birmingham Rep, touring February to April 2007. For full details, visit the website **www.graeae.org**. For information on Missing Piece, contact: **ellie@graeae.org**.

Resources
Introduction

This section covers those practical items (and sources of more detailed help and advice) that are, to the actor, what tools and a first-aid kit are to a carpenter. Some may be irrelevant to you – for instance, you may feel as though you could never have the organisational skills to set up your own company. Others are essential to all actors: good photographs, for example. Whatever your needs, time taken to formulate clearly your requirements before approaching any of the contacts listed below will be time well spent.

Equity

Louise Grainger

Equity is the only Trade Union to represent performers and people working creatively across the entire spectrum of arts and entertainment, both live and recorded. The main function of Equity is to negotiate minimum terms and conditions of employment throughout the entire world of entertainment, and to endeavour to ensure that these take account of social and economic changes. We look to the future as well, negotiating agreements to embrace the new and emerging technologies which affect performers – so satellite, digital television, new media and so on are all covered, as are the more traditional areas. We also work at national level by lobbying government and other bodies on issues of paramount importance to the membership. In addition we operate at an international level through the Federation of International Artists which Equity helped to establish, the International Committee for Artistic Freedom, and through agreements with sister unions overseas.

As well as these core activities, Equity strives to provide a wide range of services for members so that they are eligible for a whole host of benefits which are continually being revised and developed. These include helplines, job information, insurance cover, members' pension scheme, charities and others. (For more information, visit the Equity website **www.equity.org.uk**. For details of Equity's Job Information Service, see entry under The Spotlight, casting directories and information services.)

Louise Grainger is a Marketing & Membership Services Officer for Equity.

Equity
Head Office, Guild House, Upper St Martins Lane, London WC2H 9EG
tel 020-7379 6000 *fax* 020-7379 7001
email info@equity.org.uk
website www.equity.org.uk
• Job Information Service: 0870-901 0900
• Theatre, Variety, Opera & Dance Helpline: 020-7670 0237
• Film, Television, Radio & Audiovisual Helpline: 020-7670 0247
• Tax & Benefits Helpline (Tuesdays & Thursdays only): 020-7670 0223
• Bullying Reporting Line: 020-7670 0268
• Subscription Enquiries: 020-7670 0219

Regional offices:

Midlands
Office 1, Steeple House, Percy Street, Coventry CV1 3BY
tel (02476) 553612
email info@midlands-equity.org.uk

North East
The Workstation, 15 Paternoster Row, Sheffield, S1 2BX

tel 0114-275 9746
email njones@sheffield.equity.org.uk

North West and Isle of Man
Express Networks, 1 George Leigh Street, Manchester M4 5DL
tel 0161-244 5995 *fax* 0161-244 5971
email info@manchester-equity.org.uk

Scotland and Northern Ireland
114 Union Street, Glasgow G1 3QQ
tel 0141-248 2472 *fax* 0141-248 2473
email igilcrist@glasgow.equity.org.uk

South East
Guild House, Upper St Martins Lane, London WC2H 9EG
tel 020-7670 0229 *fax* 020-7379 7001
email jainslie@equity.org.uk

Wales and South West
Transport House, 1 Cathedral Road, Cardiff CF1 9SD
tel 029-2039 7971 *fax* 029-2023 0754
email info@cardiff-equity.org.uk

Resources

Equity Pension Scheme

Did you know that you could get your theatre employer to contribute to your Equity Pension Scheme?

Successful negotiations by Equity in 1997 saw the launch of the EPS. Initially it catered for members working mainly in television, but further negotiations meant that by January 2001 the EPS had been expanded to include actors, actresses and stage management working in theatre.
• Firstly the EPS was launched in the West End with SOLT Managers participating. These were quickly followed by the RNT, the Globe on the Southbank and Walt Disney Theatrical (UK). The RSC joined in January 2002.
• 1st April 2004 saw further expansion of the EPS with the inclusion of Subsidised Repertory Theatre (TMA, Grade 1) and Commercial Theatre Managers.
• From 1st April 2005 this extended to Grade 2 and 3 theatres.
• Most recently, for the 2005/06 season onwards QDOS Entertainment is also party to the EPS.
This means that the majority of theatre engagements will benefit from contributions to the EPS.

What is the EPS?
• The EPS is a Stakeholder compliant product, which is administered by First Act, the appointed insurance intermediaries to Equity and its members.
• The funds are managed by Norwich Union; the UK's largest insurer with over £230 billion of funds under management. The EPS has access to over 60 investment funds, catering for all attitudes to investment risk including ethical funds. Details of these funds can be supplied upon request.
• You have total flexibility. You can contribute when you are working, and when you are not; you can take a break.
• The EPS is penalty free and has a maximum charge of 0.75% per annum of the funds under management i.e. £0.75 for every £100 in your fund.

How the EPS works
As an EPS member you benefit from a contribution paid by your employers, equal to a percentage of your weekly rehearsal of performance fee. Details of these and the participating employers are shown below.
To qualify, you agree to make a contribution from your weekly fee. Again details are shown below.
The employer contribution is added to your salary and then deducted together with your personal contributions.
There is no need for a direct debit or chance of spending the contributions by mistake as both yours and the employer contributions are sent directly by the employer to First Act, for investment on your behalf.
Once with Norwich Union, basic rate tax relief is added.

An example (SOLT)
If your weekly performance fee was £400:
• Your contribution £10 per week

Resources

• Employer contribution £20 per week
• Total Net contribution £130 per month
• Total Gross contribution £166.67 per month

As you can see, you would have paid £40, but a monthly investment of £166.67 is achieved.

The EPS can work in a number of ways.

1. You can make contributions related to your engagement only, this way you can pay in when you are working but freeze payments when you are not, **and**

2. you can make additional personal payments by direct debit on a monthly basis, **and**

3. you can make additional personal contributions by cheque on an add hoc basis.

As you would expect, this document is only a brief introduction to the EPS and not a full explanation.

If you are already a member of the EPS, you must make sure that you have inserted your EPS membership number onto your contract/addendum **or** advised your Company Manager of your EPS membership number.

More information – including an application form – can be found on the Equity website. If you have any questions please contact Andrew Barker of First Act, *tel* 020-8686 5050, *fax* 020-8686 5559, *email* **eps@firstact.co.uk**.

The Spotlight, casting directories and information services

Spotlight is a fundamental part of the fabric of the acting profession, and it is essential to have an entry. (It is a false economy not to have one.) The growth of the Internet has seen a rise in companies offering similar services – usually, for a lower subscription. Once again it is important to research thoroughly the value to you of investing in one of these. As well as trying to assess whether such an investment will really enhance your visibility to employers, an essential part of that research is to read the 'small print' properly.

With some exceptions (major musicals, for instance), many employers do not openly advertise the properly paid acting work they have to offer. It's simpler to contact agents whom they know and trust for casting suggestions. This limits the number of submissions, largely prevents (time-wasting) unsuitable applicants, and goes some way towards ensuring that those suggested for consideration are really suitable for the parts available. Consequently, the time required to consider all the CVs and photographs submitted is contained within reasonable limits. It can take a day's work to go through a thousand submissions to select whom to interview; it can take another day's work to interview just 30 of these.

Casting information services – often allied to Internet casting directories – glean their information from all kinds of sources. The important thing to remember is that some of the information about 'properly paid acting work' is of a second-hand nature – that is, it was not sent directly to them in the first instance. Consequently, it is important to research reputations for accuracy (and 'up-to-dateness') before committing your funds to such companies. However, many Fringe production and student film opportunities are directly advertised in such publications, and such opportunities might lead on to 'properly paid acting work'.

The Spotlight

Head Office, 7 Leicester Place, London WC2H 7RJ
tel 020-7437 7631 *fax* 020-7437 5881
email info@spotlight.com
website www.spotlight.com

The Spotlight was founded in 1927 and has since become world-famous for its casting directories. Today more than 30,000 performers appear in the book and Internet versions of *Spotlight*, including actors and actresses, child artists, presenters, dancers and stunt artists. As the industry's leading casting resource, *Spotlight* is used by TV, film, radio and theatrical companies throughout the UK, and many worldwide. Its Internet casting services have become an essential communication tool, uniting actors, agents and production professionals more quickly and easily than ever before.

Membership of The Spotlight means that a performer is promoted to casting opportunities in a number of ways. Firstly, each artist has a photo and contact details in the *Spotlight Directories*, which are printed once per year. Their details are also held on an Artists' Records telephone database, so that casting/production professionals know immediately where to call when they want to get in touch.

Additionally, every performer is promoted on Spotlight Interactive (**www.spotlight.com**) – the online version of *Spotlight*. Here, casting professionals can search performers' details according to very specific criteria. For example: "Show me all actors with black hair, aged 35–40, who can speak French and play the guitar." In 2006, The Spotlight website received over one million artist searches, and actor CVs were viewed a total of 5,753,312 times.

Performers can upload showreels, voice-clips and additional photos to enhance their online CVs, which is a far quicker and more cost-effective way of promoting themselves than sending out endless copies to casting directors and agents in the post. Artists are also issued with a pair of unique PIN numbers which allow them respectively to access their CV whenever they wish – keeping credits and

Resources

skills up-to-date – or to email to others, a link to their *Spotlight* CV.

Spotlight is also used on a daily basis by production professionals sending out casting briefs to agents. In 2006, a weekly average of 160 casting breakdowns was sent out via The Spotlight Link, with more than 33,370 artists submitted weekly for an average of 541 individual roles, spanning a wide variety of TV, film, theatre, radio and commercial work. This makes The Spotlight by far the busiest casting service in the UK. The Spotlight also offers a job information service which goes directly to artists themselves: see the website for the latest details.

The Spotlight also publishes *Contacts* every November. This is a directory of companies and individuals working across TV, film, stage and radio, and costs £12.50.

To join The Spotlight, visit the website **www.spotlight.com**, call 020 7437 7631, or email **info@spotlight.com** for application forms. Entry is strictly limited to professionally trained and/or professionally experienced performers, and applications are always vetted.

AT2 UK (Actors-Inc)

FREEPOST RLZY-TBYA-UATX, Sandhurst GU47 0FR
email info@actors-inc.co.uk
website www.AT2Global.co.uk

Details of casting information services: Casting breakdowns are delivered instantly via email, in addition to a weekly newsletter which is sent every Friday afternoon. Members can search the website for information, advice and details of workshops and events, as well as a full listing of virtually all theatrical agencies in the UK. Job advertisements for casual temporary work geared towards resting actors are also posted on a daily basis.

Details of actors' Internet Directories: Actors' details are included in a fully searchable database which is accessible to casting professionals, and a personal profile and web address which may be used for easy self-promotion, networking etc. Audio samples and video showreels can also be incorporated. AT2 is an expanding global company, with offices in the UK, South Africa, Australia and New Zealand. As part of your membership, you may easily transfer your profile to different host countries if you are travelling abroad.

The annual membership fee is £60 for the standard package, or £75 if you would like to incorporate video and audio samples. Recent productions cast include Skins (E4 – Sally Broome Casting), Crimewatch (BBC – Vital Productions), Grease (West End – Debbie O'Brien Casting), Sony (Commercial - Casting Unlimited), Nike (Commercial – Ali Fearnley Casting) along with student films, profit share, TIE etc.

Castcall

106 Wilsden Avenue, Luton LU1 5HR
tel (01582) 456213 *fax* (01582) 480736
email info@castcall.co.uk
website www.castcall.co.uk

Details of casting information services: Established in 1986. Information service is available by email, with regular updates throughout the week. Actors should be professionally trained or experienced to be included. Charges £65 for 25 weeks, or £120 for 50 weeks. Allows actors to put subscriptions on hold if required and to resume when appropriate. Also offers general advice and free image scanning.

Sources of casting breakdowns have included: Crocodile Casting, Casting Unlimited, Panto People, Layton & Norcliffe, Pippa Ailion, Jayne Collins, Vital Productions, the BBC, Greenwich Films, Nina Gold and many repertory theatres.

Casting Call Pro

c/o Blue Compass Ltd, Unit 1, Waterloo Gardens, Milner Square, London N1 1TY
tel 020-7700 0474
email info@castingcallpro.com
website www.uk.castingcallpro.com

Details of casting information services: Established in 2004, Casting Call Pro is an online service now used by over 14,000 professional actors. The site is updated daily with a wide range of casting breakdowns which include films, theatre tours, corporate work and commercials. Details of appropriate opportunities are sent directly to users as they become available. Users can select which types of opportunities (e.g. film, theatre) they wish to receive information about. Members can then apply for opportunities through their CCP profile. CCP profiles feature actors' headshots and basic details along with their work history and skills and can include a showreel or voicereel if required. Casting Call Pro also fosters a lively community of actors. Whether you need advice on how to handle problem situations, want feedback on your new head shots or need the right audition piece, CCP's 'Green Room' and other features help users keep control of their career. Casting Call Pro's unique interface even allows users to keep track of old contacts, and forge new ones by giving you access to the company, agency and service provider directories. More information and a full breakdown of features are available online.

The standard service from Casting Call Pro is entirely free. They also offer a Premium Service offering a wider range of features. To discover more about the benefits of using Casting Call Pro as well as current subscription rates and latest updates to the service, please visit the website at **www.uk.castingcallpro.com**. All members are also included in their online directory which is viewed over 30,000 times each week.

To join Casting Call Pro you must have graduated from an NCDT accredited course, be a current Equity member or have at least 3 professional acting credits (no extra, or non-speaking roles).

The Casting Scene

The Real Casting Couch Ltd, Workstation,
Paternoster Row, Sheffield, South Yorkshire S1 2BX
tel 0161-265 7698
email admin@thecastingscene.com
website www.thecastingscene.com

The Casting Scene is the brainchild of award-winning writer/director Virginia Heath, and web developer James Russell, who were inspired by using the immediacy of the web to bring actors, directors and producers together. "We aim to discover, promote and facilitate the casting of talent in film, TV and 360-degree content creation." The innovative online casting service has been developed in consultation with directors, producers, casting directors, content creators and actors alongside experts at the forefront of interactive web and mobile technology.

The Casting Scene is supported by Melt. Melt is a programme of The Culture Company working with the BBC, Channel 4, Orange, PACT and Screen Yorkshire, and is funded by Yorkshire Forward, Objective 1 South Yorkshire and Arts Council England.

With a 3-month subscription (costing £30) to **www.thecastingscene.com** you can audition online for as many projects as you like, upload and share your showreel and gain access to their unique showreel editing tool. For more details, see the website.

CastNet Ltd

20 Sparrows Herne, Bushey,
Hertfordshire WD23 1FU
tel 020-8420 4209 *fax* 020-8421 9666
email admin@castingnetwork.co.uk
website www.castingnetwork.co.uk
Key contact Alyson Sharron

Details of casting information services: Established in 1997. The information service is only available online, with information circulated to members by email every day. Casting information is tailored to the exact requirements of the actor; if an actor is not interested in working in certain areas, such as student films or TIE, they will not be sent details of those projects. Information is also filtered according to the skills and physical characteristics of actors. When suitable casting opportunities do arise, CastNet will send actors free text messages and emails. Actors may make a submission for any project via the website or by telephone; CastNet will then send their CV, headshot and a covering letter to the casting director.

All reproductions of photos and postage costs are included in the subscription charge. Sends a weekly summary report by email, detailing every production

for which actors have been submitted. CastNet receives casting breakdowns from a range of clients including Fringe theatre, mainstream films and TV.

Details of actors' Internet directories: All actors must meet the following criteria to be included: have graduated from an NCDT-accredited course; have a minimum of 3 professional theatre, film or acting credits (does not include extra or drama school work); be able to use 1 UK-based accent to a 'native' standard; have full membership of Equity (or be eligible); have a professionally taken b&w publicity photograph; and be at least 18 years old at the time of application.

Admits new members every week. CastNet has more than 4,000 casting professionals registered on the site, and supports the casting of around 2,500 productions each year. Actors' CVs are included on the website, with instant messaging facility for casting directors to contact them by email or text message. Will also include up to 4 photos, showreel and voice demo at no extra charge. Registers personal domain name for each actor and points it directly to their online CV. Anyone can access online directory. Members' online details are updated daily. For details of current clients (both actors and casting professionals), consult the website.

The weekly subscription rate is £6.50 and includes all the services listed above.

Castweb

7 St Luke's Avenue, London SW4 7LG
tel 020-7720 9002
email info@castweb.co.uk
website www.castweb.co.uk
Key contact Patrick Warrington

Details of casting information services: Established in 1999. A daily information service is available online, with casting breakdowns circulated to subscribers throughout the day. Subscription starts at £17.95 per month. Castweb has circulated casting opportunities for over 1200 production companies and casting directors, and subscription is strictly for the use of professional actors and established agents only. It is now received by more than 1000 agents across Europe, as well as over 400 in the UK. At just 39p per day, it remains the essential source of casting opportunities for professional performers in the UK.

Equity Job Information Service (JIS)

Guild House, Upper St Martin's Lane,
London WC2H 9EG
website www.equity.org.uk

Details of casting information services: Launched in 1999, this service is now available (to members only) 24 hours a day via the Equity website; the phone line was discontinued in August 2007. It is available free of charge to all members. The service provides details of job opportunities in the wide range of fields in which Equity members work. Users of the service can search for jobs in acting, singing, dance, variety, light entertainment and circus, and in non-performance work such as stage management. All the work listed is at least reasonably paid (although not necessarily at full Equity-agreed rates), thoroughly checked for accuracy, and the job-providers checked for their record of fair treatment of employees.

The effectiveness of this service relies on members only submitting themselves for suitable roles. Too many unwanted applications will make employers reluctant to advertise on JIS in the future, and reduce the number of opportunities for actors.

Internet Movie Database (IMDb)
website www.imdb.com

This is not just a comprehensive database of film and television around the world, but also an opportunity for actors to post their photos and CVs ('resumés') for a fee (currently, $15.95 per month) if they have a profile of work listed there. Once you've subscribed, you also have access to a huge international contact database of people and companies, and the facility to track film and television projects from development to post-production.

Mandy.com
website www.mandy.com

Posts casting calls for actors for film. See entry under *Publications, libraries, references and booksellers* on page 433.

Production & Casting Report (PCR)
PO Box 11, London N1 7JZ
tel 020-7566 8282
email info@pcrnewsletter.com
website www.pcrnewsletter.com

Details of casting information services: Established in 1968. Available in print and online, *PCR* is a weekly newsletter which carries details of casting and crew opportunities in film, television and theatre. Information is checked carefully by staff and always comes directly from the production company or casting director – *PCR* never prints second-hand information. A free telephone information line is also available to help subscribers track down casting leads, and for news of last-minute auditions there is a free email alert service. Every week, dozens of opportunities are featured from such sources as Hubbard Casting, David Grindrod, Lucinda Syson, Birmingham Stage, Red Shift and Jeremy Zimmermann, among others. Low-budget film, voice-over, pop promo, commercial, corporate video and Fringe casting calls are also featured.

The subscription rate is £22.46 per month by direct debit (£80 for 12 weeks, £145 for 26 weeks, £280 for 52 weeks).

Other publications include:

• *Filmlog*: lists feature films in pre-production and

development, with details of studios, locations, key people and addresses (£40 for 12 months)

SBS (Script Breakdown Services)
Suite 204, 254 Belsize Road, London NW6 4BT
tel 020-7372 6337
website www.sbscasting.co.uk

SBS is a publication giving casting breakdown information. It is circulated to agents *only*, and is not available to individuals. However, in 2009 a new service was introduced for recently trained actors from CCD, NCDT and CDS schools, called SBS-Graduates. For more details, visit **www.sbs-graduates.co.uk**.

Shooting People
email contact@shootingpeople.org
website www.shootingpeople.org
Co-founders Cath LeCouteur, Jess Search *Casting Editor* Andrew Robertson

Shooting People allows thousands of people working in independent film to exchange information via a range of daily email bulletins, including a daily UK Casting Bulletin. This allows actors to discuss their craft and receive casting calls from directors, producers and casting directors. Shooting People's overall membership is currently more than 34,000. Actors can create a public casting profile as well as getting significant discounts off key film products and services.

Part-membership allows subscribers to receive email bulletins only, and is free. Full membership costs £20 per year and entitles users to a range of other services. See entry under *Publications, libraries, references and booksellers* on page 435 for further details.

The Stage
47 Bermondsey Street, London SE1 3XT
tel 020-7403 1818 *subscriptions* (01858) 438895
email newsdesk@thestage.co.uk
website www.thestage.co.uk
Managing Director Catherine Comerford *Editor* Brian Attwood

Online and weekly print publication for the entertainment industry. News, reviews, features and recruitment for theatre, light entertainment, opera, dance, TV, radio, backstage and technical, management, education and training. Established 1880

Talent Circle
website www.talentcircle.org

Details of casting information services: Established in 2003. Provides a free online casting information service and resource where emails are circulated to members on a daily basis.

Details of actors' Internet directories: Directory is open to all actors free of charge and is publicly accessible. Casting directors can select level of experience required at sign-up, as no minimum criteria are demanded of members. Members can update their own entry (to include photograph, voice sample and CV) at any time.

UK Theatre Network
PO Box 3009, Glasgow G60 5ET
tel 0870-760 6033 *fax* 0870-760 6033
email editor@uktheatre.net
website www.uktheatre.net

Details of casting information services: Established 2001. A weekly magazine in PDF, Kindle and Ebook format is circulated to members by email. In addition the company offers webmail, website hosting, reviews, contacts and listings of what's on. All services are provided free of charge. New members should contact **subscribe@uktheatre.net**.

Details of actors' Internet directories: This service is available free of charge to all active performers aged 16 upwards. Members' details are available publicly and can be updated by the actor at any time. Actors can include their CV, photograph and voice sample on the directory.

Please note that the new website requires a login prior to seeing other members' profiles.

Marketing and the Internet: maintaining your online presence

Nancy Bishop

Where do you go when you want find something? To the Internet. Casting directors do the same. Today, casting happens quickly and initially online: casting directors post their breakdowns on search engines, such as Spotlight, and agents submit actor suggestions electronically. As a casting director, I receive hundreds of submissions in the first hour after a breakdown is posted. Only moments after an actor auditions, I pop the clip on a site that shares it with production. Any actor in these times must have an Internet presence 24/7, so that casters anywhere anytime have the information to cast you.

If I can immediately access an actor's showreel online, during a brain-storming session with a director, he's that much closer to the job. When the director can see your work at the click of a button, he's more likely to short-list you for a role. Yes, it is your agent's job to market you, but by getting your own materials online you're giving them the tools they need to help you book the job.

I suggest a three-pronged strategy to boost your Internet presence:

1) Register on the major quality casting sites, and search engines.
2) Construct and maintain a website that uniquely markets you.
3) Be Google-able and YouTube-able.

1. Casting sites and search engines

The most ubiquitous entertainment website is the Internet Movie Data Base (IMDB.com). Serious actors exploit all of the possibilities that it offers. Once you have professional film or TV credits, join its professional sister site, IMDB.pro, which allows you to insert contact details so that professionals can find you, and you can find them.

Keeping your material updated on IMDB is also essential; you can do it yourself. Although it costs, posting your headshot on IMDB is a solid investment. A director may see an actor in a film, but not know the name of the role he played. With your photo posted, there's no doubt.

In the UK, Spotlight membership is essential, as it is the first and last website that many casting directors use. My pet peeve, when using Spotlight, is when actors don't include a showreel. By all means, use all of the options available to you: CV, reel, photo gallery, voice clips. If I don't know your work, I will most definitely want to see tape on you.

Suggested websites:

Spotlight (www.spotlight.com)
Casting Call Pro (www.castingcallpro.com)
The Casting Scene (www.thecastingscene.com)
Cast Web (www.castweb.co.uk)
Shooting people (www.shootingpeople.org)

2. A website

A website, properly designed, is a worthwhile investment. The actor search engines are necessary, but not enough; there are directors who are looking outside the box. A website

enables you to uniquely brand and market yourself because you can control the content and presentation. Make sure that your pages are designed to strategically market you as a professional actor, not as a vanity site. The central questions in a marketing campaign are:
1. What do you do?
2. Who are your customers?
3. Why do they buy from you?
Let these marketing questions guide the content of your website.

What do you do? You're a professional actor. Don't confuse your viewers with too many images or superfluous interests. If you are expert in something that enhances your acting, such as singing, horse-back riding, or dance, then devote some space to it. But make sure it's not too prominent or it will look like you're a singer who acts, rather than an actor who sings.

Who are your customers? They are casting directors, producers, directors. Figure out what information they would need to cast you. Ensure your site's usability for all customers by testing it on different systems and browsers like Mac and PC, Firefox and Outlook.

Why should they buy from you? This is a good question. Why should they cast you? What are you selling? Since YOU are the product, identify your image and the range of roles that you play. Through your own personal style you will reflect, on the site, what you have to offer, how you look, what your experience is, how you've trained. "All things spring from the client's identity," claims web designer Deborah Dewitt, "which incorporates, logo, fonts, colours, graphics, photos and layout – all of these combine to visually represent their offering, personality and communication style." An effective actor's website will include the following:

Home page

The home page features the actor's one main headshot. Don't muddle it with multiple images; they're for the gallery. Change the content on your home page often; announce news, like a new show, or snippets of good reviews on the front page. Not only will this keep us up to date but it will make your site easier for search engines to find.

Menu items

CV – hone down your résumé to the most impressive selected credits, rather than bombarding your viewers with everything you've done since secondary school. Provide a downloadable PDF version with contact info, so casting directors can print it.

Biography (optional) – this is a short prose section that includes where you were born and how you've got to where you are. It is a way to emphasise your background, and what makes you unique. If you witnessed 9/11, or lived in the wilds of Borneo, for example, that could inform your experience for a given role.

Gallery – here's a chance to show the range of roles you can play and to offer additional information. Make sure the images are truly representative of you and what you look like now. Supplement your headshot with a wider shot, so we can see your wonderfully round, or modestly slim, frame. If your main headshot is quite serious, consider including a comedic photo. A variety of production stills are helpful but be selective about what images you choose: web expert Ellen Treanor Strasman notes that "The average visit time per page is less than one minute, so people won't look at that many photos. The rule of lists is that people will look at the first three and the last one." So put the strongest photos in these positions.

Showreel – don't miss this part. There is no substitute for the moving picture. Some actors separate their work by project, showing a few clips from each. Others divide their clips by type – for example, comedy, drama, action – and make mini-reels. Ordinary showreels with a variety of clips should be no longer than 2-3 minutes. Start the reel and each clip with your image so we know exactly who we should be watching. If you have clips in different languages, separate them.

Other sections that you might include are:

Voice-over – if you do voice work, and have a voice reel, include it.

Blog – this is an opportunity to express, in journal form, your own notes on projects or work. Keep it professional. Political blogging or personal information can go on a separate site. If you use Facebook, keep two separate accounts; one for business and one for personal.

Links – link your page to a professional search engine, your agency or a project you're working on, and ask them to link back to you. The more links there are to your site, the more traffic you'll get, which will push your site further up in the search engines.

3. Be Google-able and YouTube-able

If you are not already famous, no one will know to Google your name. So how will casting directors find you? If you're shopping on the Internet for roses in Prague, what do you Google? "Roses, Prague." If I'm looking for an actor who can juggle, what will I type in? "Actor, juggler."

Google needs text and key words in order to index and find your site. Think about your specific skills and what makes you unique. Use these as keys words that link to other pages on your webpage. Keep the important keywords towards the top of the page; this will help casters find you. If you have a special marketing point, you can even name your website accordingly – for example, www.kenchu.karateactor.com or www.kiwi-actor-in-london.com.

Name your video clips specifically as well, such as "Ken Chu, Karate fight" and load it onto YouTube. I love it when I can type an actor's name into YouTube and immediately a showreel or clip surfaces. I can then paste the link into an email and send it as a suggestion to a director.

The Internet has changed the way casting happens. It allows casting directors to sweep the far corners of the earth for talent at the click of a button. I recently cast a film with actors from four different countries, and never left my office to do it. The director was in South Africa, and interviewed actors on Skype, as the budget didn't allow him to meet them in person. Maintain an online presence and be ready to put your audition on tape and upload it for us to view. Don't be a technophobe and throw away the many wonderful possibilities that the Internet offers.

Nancy Bishop is a Casting Society (CSA) casting director, who casts from her base in Prague. She is also the chair of the Prague Film School Acting Department, and the author of Methuen Drama's *Secrets from the Casting Couch*. For more information see www.nancybishopcasting.com

Photographers and repro companies

Good photographs (and quality reproductions of same) are an essential part of an actor's professional armoury and there is absolutely no point in trying to scrimp on them. ('A picture is worth a thousand words.')

Your photograph is a silent, static, two-dimensional representation of vocal, mobile, three-dimensional you. It should be of your head down to your shoulders, reasonably stylish and well produced without necessarily being too glamorous. It should look natural and have life, energy and personality – especially in the eyes, the most important part of your face. Your photo should say, 'Here I am; I know who I am; I'm OK with who I am.' Also, it is very important that your photograph really looks like you when you arrive for interview.

Crucial to the final result is finding a good photographer (a) who understands the world that the end result is intended for and (b) with whom you can work well. In the listings that follow, you'll find a wide range of prices and deals. It is important to research as many of these as possible, without making cost your prime consideration. Ask friends, teachers and your agent (if you have one) for recommendations, and check through *Spotlight* and websites to see samples of work. Read the details under each listing to get a 'feel' for who might produce the 'goods' for you. Once you have a shortlist of possibilities, phone each with appropriate questions (what to wear, studio or natural light, and so forth) in order to get a sense of how well you might be able to work with him/her. Only *after* you've done all this research should cost be a consideration. Even then, a cheap deal could mean that the photographer will spend much less time, and take fewer photographs, than a more expensive one. You might be lucky with the former, but you'll enhance your chances of getting really good results with the latter.

Note Allow plenty of time for this research. Also, bear in mind that as the deadline for *Spotlight* gets nearer, photographers become increasingly busy and it becomes more difficult to book a session.

Copyright

Under the Copyright, Designs & Patents Act 1988, the photographer owns the copyright on any new photograph, even though you've already paid for the original. That means that you have to obtain his/her permission to have new photographs reproduced in *Spotlight* or anywhere else. Your photographer may be happy to approve such reproduction, but may not be so happy about any cropping or other alterations: you must get permission if you intend to do this. The other important new legal requirement is that your photographer must be credited on any reproduction of the original. Some of the repro companies are now doing this as a matter of course.

Repros

You could get subsequent, high-quality reproductions done by your photographer or by someone else nominated by him/her. However, these will be expensive. The specialist repro companies can do this significantly more cheaply with minimal loss of quality. Once again, check with others about the quality (and service and reliability) of individual companies before taking costs into consideration. It is also useful to overestimate the number of copies you might need over the lifetime (generally, about two years) of your chosen photograph – because (a) you'll almost always find that you underestimate that number in the first place, and (b) you can take advantage of cheaper unit costs.

Note It is often preferable to send a 10x8in (25x20cm) photograph for submissions; however, good-quality 'jpegs' (around 400 pixels wide) inserted into your CV are becoming increasingly acceptable. If you're planning to email a CV containing your photograph, make sure that the total document size is not more than about 200kb, or you'll end up clogging up the casting director's mailbox. (Most image editing software will have a menu option to allow you to reduce the image size if required.) It is important to check the current charges of each photographer (and repro company) that interests you, as some will change during the lifetime of this edition.

10 out of 10 Photography
Forest Hill Business Centre, Clyde Vale,
London SE23 3JF
tel 0845-123 5664
email pauljneed@hotmail.com
website www.pauljneed.co.uk
Photographer Paul J Need

Services & rates: Charges £80 for a photo shoot. Photographer has a background in theatre, film, concert and television lighting, as well as teaching lighting design at RADA. Offers digital photography.

Abacus Photography
156 Kingshill Road, Swindon SN1 4LN
tel (01793) 537257 *mobile* (07966) 551909
fax (01793) 344208
email nick@abacus-photography.co.uk
website www.abacus-photography.co.uk

Services & rates: Charges £50 for a photo shoot which includes photographer's fee and studio and equipment costs. This does not include the cost of any 10x8in (25x20cm) prints which are priced at £5 each. A variety of packages is also available. Offers discounts for group bookings. Digital photography is also available at a charge of £50 for 24 images. Always advises clients to bring a change of clothing and discuss their requirements before the shoot.

Work portfolio: Established in 1992. Photographs can be viewed on the website. Has taken publicity shots for around 20-30 actors.

The Actor's One-Stop Shop
First Floor, Above The Gate Pub, Station Road,
London N22 7SS
tel 020-8888 7006
email info@actorsonestopshop.com
website www.actorsone-stopshop.com

Services & rates: Charges £195 for a photo shoot which includes photographer's fee, studio and equipment costs, processing of 1 b&w 36exps, contact sheet and 4 10x8in (25x20cm) prints. Offers 10% discount for group (2 or more) bookings. Offers both pre-shoot and post-shoot consultancy, advising

clients on clothing, image projection and selection of photos, as well as general advice on how best to promote themselves within the acting industry.

Work portfolio: Established in 1997. Photographs can be viewed on the website or in person by visiting the studio. Has taken publicity shots for around 250 actors. Recent clients include: Tagforce (an actor register), Omar Khan, Samuel L Jackson, Anna Friel and Rachel Watkins.

Adrian Gibb
44A Wallbutton Road, Brockley, London SE4 2NX
tel 020-7639 6215
email adriangibb@googlemail.com
website www.adriangibb.co.uk

Established in 1995. Charges £130 for a photoshoot, which includes photographer's fee, studio, processing and contact sheets. Takes 1-2 rolls of film at 36exps; digital also offered (100-200 images). Price includes 4 8x10in prints. Discounted rates for students of between £60 (1st year) or £100 (2nd year). Works at home in studio and/or garden. Studio is wheelchair accessible. Has taken publicity shots for 60-100 actors, including Tamara Beckwith and Sophie Monk.

Stuart Allen
mobile (07776) 258829
email info@stuartallenphotos.com
website www.stuartallenphotos.com

Services & rates: Charges £150 for a digital photo shoot which includes 360-500+ images, your own website for proof viewing the whole shoot with email links to you and your agent, contact sheets emailed to you as Adobe PDF files, updated contact sheets emailed to you as you narrow down your selection, cost of retouching four images, photos prepared for *Spotlight*, Casting Call Pro and Castnet, images emailed to *Spotlight*, Casting Call Pro and Castnet (if applicable). Shoot taken in natural light and typically last 2-3+ hours. All the images can be in black & white and/or colour. "The photos are captured in uncompressed high resolution 'RAW' format so as to give you the best possible quality and maximum control over the final image. This is the digital equivalent of a negative. It is superior to the other smaller and lower quality digital formats."

Film shoots also available at £130 for two 36 exp films and contact sheets. Competitive print service available. Offers full advice on clothing, makeup and hair.

Areas that are covered in the UK for headshots are London, Bath, Bristol, Brighton, Cardiff, Cheltenham, Guilford, Oxford, Warwick and Winchester. If you do not live near one of these cities please check on availability.

Work portfolio: Stuart studied photography at Salisbury College of Art and Design. Since then he has worked in numerous spheres of the entertainment industry taking photographs. Shooting headshots of actors for almost a decade his work can be seen on his website, Casting Call Pro website and *Contacts*. Please check website for latest prices.

AM-London Photography
3A Godolphin Road, London W12 8JE
tel 020-7193 1868 *mobile* (07974) 188105
email studio@am-london.com
website www.am-london.com

Offers 2 types of headshot session; please see details below (student discount price is given in brackets):
• 1.5 hr Headshot Session (Studio and Natural Light) at £340 (£270). The package includes: 1.5 hour shoot in studio and natural light (outdoor). Variety of portraits and character shots. 250+ images supplied colour and black & white high res on disc. 4 retouched 10x8in prints
• 50 min Headshot Session (Studio only) at £270 (£220). The package includes: 50 min shoot – studio shots & variety of portraits. 150+ images supplied colour and black & white high res on disc. 2 retouched 10x8in prints

"With both sessions we make sure we get lots of variety. This means using different lighting setups, different backdrops and a number of outfit changes."

Matt Anker
London
mobile (07835) 241835
email matt@mattanker.com
website www.mattanker.com

Services & rates: Charges £235 inc. VAT for a photoshoot. Takes 300-350 shots and will provide a complete set in colour and black and white on disc, plus 2 x 10x8in prints and any simple re-touching needed. Discounted rate for students is £117.50 inc. VAT. All photography is digital. The shoot takes place at a home studio and on location. Has taken publicity shots for around 40+ actors.

Ric Bacon
30 Fortis Green Road, Muswell Hill,
London N10 3HN

mobile (07970) 970799
website www.ricbacon.co.uk

Services & rates: Charges £280 for a photo shoot which includes photographer's fee, processing of 2 b&w 36exps, 6x4in print of every shot (rather than a contact sheet) and all negatives. Offers reduced rates to students. Shoots in a very relaxed manner, in natural light or studio, and offers advice on all aspects including clothing and make-up. Prints are ready to view in 1 hour and will be reviewed with the client, offering advice on selection of images for self-promotion if needed. Happy to look at old photographs of the client that they particularly like or dislike. Works with film or digital.

Work portfolio: Established in 1999. Photographs can be viewed on the website and has a comprehensive portfolio at The Spotlight offices. Has taken publicity shots for around 500 actors.

Chris Baker
tel 020-8441 3851
email chrisbaker@photos2000.demon.co.uk
website www.chrisbakerphotographer.com

Service & rates: A photographer since 1974, charges £245 for a photo shoot including 2 b&w 36exps, contact sheets and 5 10x8in prints. Student rate is £210 for the same service. Also offers a digital service at the same rates for around 60 digital images and 5 retouched photos on disk. Shoot takes place in a studio or outdoor location – only the outdoor location is wheelchair-accessible.

Work portfolio: Examples of work can be seen on the website or at The Spotlight offices. Has taken photographs for several thousand actors, among them Sally Anne Triplett, Julia Sawalha, Kim Medcalf, Todd Carty, and David Griffin. "Informality and relaxation are the secret to a successful photo session. Clients get 2 hours, giving us time to have a cup of tea and discuss their requirements.

I recommend that clients look as natural as possible, and discourage the use of make-up artists as it's far more important that my subjects look 'like themselves'! Tops should be unfussy and typical of the wearer. If in doubt, a simple black shirt is hard to beat.

I shoot digital or film, depending on the preference of my client, and am happy to advise on which will work best for you. I retouch the final selected images whether they're prints or on disc, eliminating stray hairs, spots or anything else that distracts from the real you.

I've been doing this for 30 years and am a full-time professional – not someone just dabbling as a sideline! My work is of the highest technical quality, but more importantly reflects the personality and potential of my clients; that's why so many of them come back."

Sophie Baker
tel 020-8340 3850
email sophiebaker@totalise.co.uk

Services & rates: A photographer since 1972 initially

working in theatre front of house – National Theatre, Royal Shakespeare Theatre and many West End shows – no relation to Chris. Rate is £190 plus £10 for digital for two rolls of film and five 10x8in photographs. Student rates are £150 solo sitting (including digital and four 10x8in photographs) and £200 for a shared sitting providing three 10x8in photographs each. Photographs taken mostly in natural light in third floor studio overlooking Hampstead Heath and outside in the park.

Work portfolio: Work portfolio can be seen at the Spotlight offices. A website is planned!

"As a former student at the Central School of Speech and Drama (after the first year I realised that 'acting' wasn't for me – I would be happier behind the camera) I am aware of the discomfort and tensions the sitter can feel so I attempt to empathise and look to make the subject feel as comfortable as possible. The sessions are therefore relaxed and tailored to create a calm atmosphere. I have seen many directors and casting agents looking through books of photographs and therefore aim for a 'bright eyed and bushy tailed look' but not to overglamorize. It is important that a portrait photo attracts the eye of the director but it must be an honest reflection of the sitter. I suggest the client has a good night's sleep before hand and comes with a mixture of tops and necklines. It is not easy to dictate what will work over the phone."

Taken photographs for as many as 14,000 actors, among them Judi Dench, Ian Holm, Nigel Hawthorne, Ben Whitrow, Hugh Bonneville, Jane Horrocks, Rachel Weisz and John Lynch. "As I have been working for over 35 years the list is long. Over a period of 25 years I was also a film stills photographer working with Ken Loach, Stephen Frears, Louis Malle, Denys Arcand, Atom Egoyan to name a few but now prefer working on my own and not at the dictate of crazy film scheduling hours."

Paul Barrass

Unit 6, Ellingfort Road, London E8 3PA
mobile (07973) 265931
email paul@paulbarrass.co.uk
website www.paulbarrass.co.uk

Services & rates: Session price is £120. Includes four 10x8in prints. Special student rate of £100. All photography is digital. Photos can be taken either in the studio or outdoors. All locations have wheelchair access. Images are viewed during the photo session on a monitor. Has photographed in excess of 1000 actors.

Helen Bartlett Photography

Based in London and Cambridge
tel 0845-603 1373
email info@helenbartlett.co.uk
website www.helenbartlett.co.uk

Services & rates: Established in 2003. All photography is digital. Cost of headshot photo shoot

is £150; £185 for headshots and full length. Photos are proofed online by way of a private gallery for the client. Usually around 30 images to choose from. The cost includes three photographs which are provided digitally on a CD so the client can make their own prints. Additional images are available at £35 each and a set of printed contact sheets are available for £40. Photos taken in outdoor locations or client's home. Photo sessions can be arranged at a mutually convenient location in either London or Cambridge so locations that are wheelchair accessible can be organised.

Work portfolio: Has photographed approximately 45 actors. Has photographed many of the clients of Rhino Management. Sessions take approximately 2 hours and can include a variety of locations.

"I recommend bringing a selection of tops with simple necklines, avoiding white."

A Beautiful Image Photography & Design (Debal Bagachi)

31 Church Walk, Brentford, Middlesex TW8 8DB
tel 020-8568 2122 *mobile* (07956) 861698
email debal@abeautifulimage.com
website www.abeautifulimage.com

Services & rates: Charges £150 for a photo shoot which includes photographer's fee, studio and equipment costs, processing of 2 b&w 36exps, contact sheets and 2 10x8in (25x20cm) prints (either hand- or digitally printed). Occasionally offers 10% discount for clients sharing a shoot. Digital photography is also available at the same rate; images can be supplied on CD Rom. Also able to provide website and print publicity. Advises actors to keep make-up simple for b&w photography and wear unfussy, unpatterned tops with simple necklines.

Work portfolio: Established in 1994. Photographs can be viewed on the website and at The Spotlight offices. Has taken publicity shots for around 50 actors. Recent clients include: Elizabeth Alexander, Patrick Regis, Fiona Marchant and Diane Cracknell.

Marc Broussely

South West London
mobile (07738) 920225
email info@10x8headshots.com
website www.10x8headshots.com

Services & rates: Established in 2008. Charges £150 for a photoshoot at home studio: this includes 4 edited shots delivered in high-res digital files. 10x8 prints are extra at £20 each, although a discount is available for larger quantities. Student price is £130. Has taken pictures for around 30 actors.

Sheila Burnett

email sheilab33@ntlworld.com
website www.sheilaburnett-photography.com

Services & rates: Charges £200 + VAT (£180 + VAT for students) for a photo shoot. Includes 4 10x8in prints. Offers digital photography. Photos taken in studio. Works with 170 actors per year, including Imelda Staunton, Catherine Tate, David Soul, Paul Freeman, Simon Pegg, Anita Harris and Jackie Clune.

"Appointments can be made either online or by phone. I always advise on what is good to bring to the session. I'm open to any questions and happy to have a chat about what it is you want to achieve. My sessions always start with a 10-minute warm-up, this is mainly for me to adjust the lights and find the best position. It is also a good time for you to acclimatise to my studio and the tungsten lights. Because we are indoors, this makes it possible for you to freshen up upon arrival and to change outfits, apply make-up etc., and, for the boys, to shave if you want. I also rather like to have a cup of tea and a chat before we start. "

Will C
Studio 55d Dartmouth Road, London NW2 4EP
tel 020-8438 0303 *mobile* (07712) 669953
email billy_snapper@hotmail.com
website www.theukphotographerexhibition.co.uk
website www.billysnapper.com
website www.london-photographer.com

Services & rates: Established in 1968. £160 includes 80 colour, 80 b/w and 2 high-res CDs with all photos at 14 million pixels, delivered to the client in the studio. All photos are seen at the moment of taking on a large screen. Make up and hair can be provided in full attendance for the whole photo session for £80. Prints are obtained from an independent printer for £5.00 (b/w) and £7.00 (colour). Majority of photos taken in studio (home studio), other location prices are available on request. No wheelchair access to studio.

Work portfolio: Has photographed approximately 6500 performers including: Dame Judi Dench, Will Young, Charles Dance. Advice: "Neutral colours for clothes, no patterns, simplicity".

Jon Campling Headshots
206 Ellison Road, London SW16 5DJ
tel 020-8679 8671 *mobile* (07941) 421101
email photo@joncampling.com
website www.joncamplingheadshots.com

Services & rates: Established in 2004. All photography is digital. £100 includes online contact sheet, CD of all images in full resolution, and full digital correction of 4 images, only payable if client uses the images. Uses instant full size preview at session. Happy to give free advice via email or telephone. Prints of images are available at £1.99 each or 99p if order 20 or more of each. Photos are taken in home studio. No wheelchair access. Has photographed over 150 actors which include: Shenna Ellis, Dominic Cazenove, Charlotte Graham. "I am an actor myself ... I advise a simple approach to make up and clothing."

Robert Carpenter Turner Photography
The Studio, 62 Hemstal Road, London NW6 2AD
tel 020-7624 2225
email robert@carpenterturner.co.uk
website www.carpenterturner.co.uk

Services & rates: Charges £225 for a photo shoot which includes all costs and at which at least 70 high-quality digital photographs are taken. These are then displayed on the web with a private code for only the customer and agent to view. From these are ordered 6 pictures, which are corrected and improved as required, or changed to high-quality b&w images before being written to CD Rom. 2 10x8in prints are included. Time allowed for photoshoot is 2 hours.

Work portfolio: Established in 1960. Portfolio of photographs, latest rates and other information can be viewed on the website. He has taken publicity pictures for many hundreds of actors and performers over the past 40 years. Studio contains a grand piano for use by musicians.

Charlie Carter
tel/fax 020-8222 8742
email charlie@charliecarter.com

Services & rates: Established in 1998. Charges £375 for photo shoot including 3 x 36exps films and 4 x 10x8in prints. Starting to work with digital, but still mostly film. Sessions are in a home studio on the second floor, so not wheelchair-accessible. Examples of work can be viewed at The Spotlight offices. Clients include: Kenneth Branagh, Tom Hollander, Roger Allam, Emily Blunt, Isla Blair, Eve Best, Harry Enfield, Eleanor Bron, Martin Shaw, Kerry Condon, Paul McEwan, Serena Evans and Charlie Condou – as well as agents Ken McReddie Ltd, Rebecca Blond Associates, Conway van Gelder, ICM, PFD, Hamilton Andrews, Elinor Hilton, and Billboard.

Advises clients to start preparing several days beforehand – timing haircuts so that there's time for it to grow out a little, cutting out alcohol, drinking lots of water, taking exercise – so that skin and eyes will look their best. "Ladies, please check your diaries to avoid your session clashing with the worst part of PMT – mad to have pictures done when you are not at your loveliest ... By the time you add together the cost of photographs, repros and *Spotlight*, it's a lot of money – so protect your investment by doing everything you can to feel as good about yourself as possible. The session will take as long as it takes."

Andrew Chapman
198 Western Road, Sheffield S10 1LF
tel 0114-266 3579 *mobile* (07779) 861921
email andrew@chapmanphotographer.eclipse.co.uk
website www.andrewsphotos.co.uk

Services & rates: Charges from £125 for a photo shoot, which includes all photography and computer labour charges, studio and equipment costs. The session includes 100+ photos, b&w and/or colour) which are transferred to the computer; you may select any or all images and these are written to a CD for you to take away for immediate use. Prints and contacts are available (e.g. a 10x8in is £15) if required, but in most cases images are emailed directly to *Spotlight* and for repros. Also gives clients a 'release note' so that photos can be used for PR, repros, agents, *Spotlight*, etc.

Black and bright colours work well in b&w, and higher necklines are usually better than low: "I always advise people on an individual basis. Ideally, allow about 2 hours for the session."

Work portfolio: Has more than 3500 actors on database as well as singers, dancers, models, martial artists and others. Clients are from agents across the country; they include: Philippa Howell, Sharron Ashcroft, Jane Hollowood, Liberty Management, David Daly, Direct Line, and Act One. "Qualified member of BIPP, SWPP, BPPA with over 20 years' experience."

John Clark Photo Digital

tel 020-8854 4069
email info@johnclarkphotography.com
website www.johnclarkphotography.com

Services & rates: Charges £145 per hour for digital photography.

Work portfolio: Established in 1982. Photographs and advice can be found on the website. Has taken publicity shots for around 500-600 actors. Recent clients include: actors represented by Roger Carey Associates, Collis Management, Crawfords, Rossmore and Langford Associates.

Anna Isola Crolla

London & Hemel Hempstead
mobile (07980) 551468
email annaisolacrolla@hotmail.com
website www.annaisolacrolla.co.uk

Established in 1997. Charges £175 for a photoshoot (includes a CD of selected edited images). Client receives 3 rolls of 120mm film – total 36exp taken. Additional cost of £10 per 10x8 thereafter. Digital photography is available priced at £150. Home studio and outdoor location available. Has taken publicity photos for around 100 actors.

CW Photos

Southampton
tel (02380) 732550
email cwp@cwphotos.co.uk
website www.cwphotos.co.uk

Services & rates: Charges from £55 for a photo shoot, which includes fees, studio, processing and prints (2 selected from 40 taken). An option of either 10x8in prints or files on CD. Special packages for actors (including students) include a 10-image

portfolio disc from £125 (head shots, 3/4 length, full length, different backgrounds and lighting, and 10 selected finished images from 100 taken). Other packages are available to suit all budgets. All locations are possible: the main studio is wheelchair-accessible.

Work portfolio: Established in 1990. Has photographed more than 100 productions and of more than 60 actors. Clients include: Ros Liddiard, Steven Fawell, Susannah Steadman, James Norton and Joanna Russel. Each client gets a personal assessment and recommendation."

Grant David Photography

34a Manor Park Road, London N2 0SJ
tel 020-8815 9789
email grantdavidphotos@tiscali.co.uk
website www.grantdavid.co.uk

Services & rates: Charges £100 for a photo shoot: this includes all fees and studio costs, processing of 2 b&w 36 exps, contact sheets and 2 10x8in prints. Offers the same package to students at the reduced rate of £60. Digital photography is also available at the same rates and will enable the client to leave the session with all the shots on CD. Advises clients to use very little make-up and to bring 3 tops, keeping patterns and jewellery to a minimum. Post-production includes air-brushing on blemishes/spots for free.

Work portfolio: Established in 1992. Photographs can be viewed on the website and at The Spotlight offices. Has photographed around 600 actors, with recent clients including: Janine Smith, Amanda Fulton and Luke Long.

Nicholas Dawkes Photography

London W10
mobile (07787) 111997
website www.westbournestudios.com

Services & rates: Charges £150 for head shots (£135 for students) and £200 for portfolio shots (£185 for students); prices start at £175 for corporate head shots. Includes a full consultation and a 2-3 hour session, with both outdoor and studio shots as standard. Up to 300-400 pictures taken, with full review of images on a large screen throughout. Same-day uploading of online contact sheet in colour and b&w, with email links to the client and their agent. Retouching 3 images on CD with your selected high-resolution photos.

"Before becoming a full-time photographer I worked as an actor in television, film and theatre, which gives me an in-depth understanding of the the creative industry. The aim of my sessions is to not put pressure on you to 'perform'; I want you relaxed and only then can we capture some life in the image."

Angus Deuchar

PO Box 25799, London SW19 1WQ
tel 020-8286 3303 *mobile* (07973) 600728
email angus@actorsphotos.co.uk
website www.actorsphotos.co.uk

Services & rates: Charges £230 for a photo shoot taken in natural light. Price includes approximately 120 proofs viewed on a website, 4 finished b&w 10x8in (real!) photographic prints and a CD with various electronic versions. Student deals available. Telephone or email for further information.

Work portfolio: Photographs and "advice to actors seeking photographs" can be viewed on the website. Has around 20 years' experience of taking actors' portraits, and used to be an actor himself. Clients include: Neil and Adrian Rayment (*The Matrix Reloaded*), Anne Reid, James Bolam, John Alderton and Richard Lumsden.

DF: Photographer
Studio 29-31, Stafford Road, Brighton BN1 5PE
tel (01273) 549967 *mobile* (07958) 272333
email info@image2film.com
website www.image2film.com
Photographer David Fernandes

Has worked as a photographer since 1995, and has taken photographs for roughly 500 actors. Charges £85 for a photo shoot including 2 10x8in prints, using either film or digital. Special 'shared sitting' rates are available to students. Works in a studio, outdoors or in the client's home. Shoots and edits actors' showreels; please phone for prices. The studio is not wheelchair-accessible. Advises clients to "bring a selection of tops with different necklines. Not too 'fussy'. A black top always works well".

Mike Eddowes
tel (01903) 882525 *mobile* (07970) 141005
email mike@photo-publicity.co.uk
website www.theatre-photography.co.uk
Services & rates: Established in 1975. Services offered include: headshots, editorial publicity shoots, editorial portraits, poster images and theatre production photography. Cost of portrait photoshoots is £225. This includes 6 10x8in prints plus CD with 50 images. Special discount of £30 is offered to clients who mention *Actors' Yearbook*. Studio in Kennington, London SE11, or natural daylight outdoor shoots in West Sussex. London studio is not wheelchair accessible. More details are available from the website.

Work portfolio: Examples of photography can be seen on the website. Has photographed several hundred actors. Testimonials are available on their website along with examples of photography.

"Don't wear too much makeup; bring clothes which are you as yourself (not dressing up!); and have an early night before the photography session. Try and build a relationship with a photographer and stick with him or her. Don't get a keen amateur friend to try and take your photos – acting is a very tough career and you need all the help you can get!"

Elliott Franks Photography Services
PO Box 29801, London SW19 1WW
tel 020-8544 0156 *mobile* (07802) 537220

email frankse@aol.com
website www.elliottfranks.com

Services & rates: Charges £85 (reduced from £160 for *Actors' Yearbook* readers) for a 2-hour photo shoot in Wimbledon studio with 5 changes of tops, 3 rolls of medium-format film (high quality) with 12 shots per roll, and 3 contact sheets. Usually shoots a fourth roll for fun which is supplied on CD Rom. One-off 10x8in (25x20cm) prints are priced at £11.31 each; repros of 12 10x8in prints are priced at £1.85 each.

Work portfolio: Established in 1997. Photographs can be viewed on the website and at The Spotlight offices. Has taken publicity shots for more than 300 actors. Recent clients include: actors represented by ICM and Wendy Lee Management Ltd.

James Gill
6 Hanover Gardens, London SE11 5TL
tel 020-7735 5632

Services & rates: Charges £85 for a photo shoot which includes photographer's fee, studio and equipment costs, processing of 1 b&w 36exps, contact sheet and 2 10x8in (25x20cm) prints. Increases to £130 for 2 rolls and 4 10x8in prints. Extra 10x8in prints are priced at £12.50 each. Advises actors to keep it simple. Will take photos of actors as they wish to be presented, and will take all the time necessary.

Work portfolio: Established in 1992. Photographs can be viewed at The Spotlight offices. Has taken publicity shots for around 500 actors and in addition has more than 40 years' experience of working in theatres, both in casting and as company manager.

Nick Gregan Photography
Unit 3, 10A Ellingfort Road, London Fields, London E8 3PA
tel 020-8533 3003 *mobile* (07774) 421878
email info@nickgregan.com
website www.nickgregan.com

Services & rates: Charges £145 for a photo shoot, which includes fees, studio, processing and contact sheets (around 300 shots are taken). The first two 10x8in prints are free; £10 per print thereafter. Students are offered an extra discount of £35 on production of a valid student card. Also offers digital photography, for which the same rates apply. Photos are taken in a studio or outdoor location and both are wheelchair-accessible.

Work portfolio: Established in 1992. Has taken publicity photos for more than 3000 clients, including Paul Danan, Lucinda Rhodes and Henry Luxemburg. "My website offers '7 secrets to a great head shot' – check it out for loads of useful information."

Charles Griffin Photography
PO Box 36, Deeside, Chester CH5 3WP
tel (01244) 535252

email studio@charlesgriffinphotography.co.uk
website www.charlesgriffinphotography.co.uk

Services & rates: Photographer since 1993. Charges £149 for photo shoot, which includes processing of 2 x 12exps medium-format (high-quality) rolls, contact sheets and 2 10x8in prints. (Offers this service at £92.83 if client mentions *Actors' Yearbook* when booking a 2-hour session. Student rates are also available – telephone or email for information.) Digital service also available at the same rates, although an extra charge is made to provide the images on CD. Uses studio and outdoor location (both wheelchair-accessible).

Work portfolio: Examples of work can be seen on the website. Has taken photographs for around 250 actors, among them Raquel Lee, Gemma Gray, Sam Gratton, Paul Draw. "Sessions are conducted in a relaxed atmosphere: I will shoot images of actors as they wish. Clients should bring a variety of plain tops: those with high neckline or v-neck in red, grey or black are most useful."

Claire Grogan

12 Calverley Grove, London N19 3LG
tel 020-7272 1845
email claire@clairegrogan.co.uk
website www.clairegrogan.co.uk

Services & rates: Charges £225+vat for photo shoot including photographer's fee, studio and equipment costs, 2 roll B&W 36 exps contact sheets and 4 10x8s. This shoot can be either outdoors, studio or combination of both. Also offers 1 roll 36 exps and 2 10x8s studio only for £150+vat. Special rates for full time drama students are £170+vat for 2 roll session or £110 for 1 roll session. Offers full advice on clothing and make-up when a booking is made. Sessions last approx 2 and a quarter hours in a relaxed atmosphere. "I make a point of capturing shots that really reflect the actor's personality and casting potential."

Work portfolio: Established in 1991. Photographs can be viewed on the website and at Spotlight offices. Takes around 400 publicity shots for actors each year and is recommended by a number of agents. Clients have included Steve McFadden, Lindsey Coulson, Stephen Tompkinson, Heather Peace, Nicola Blackman, Ben Richards, Debbie Arnold, Chris Walker, Caroline O'Neill, Phil Whitchurch, Tiffany Chapman, Philip Brown.

"Sorry no wheelchair access at present."

Jamie Hughes Photography

mobile (07850) 122977
email jamie@jamiehughesphotography.com
website www.jamiehughesphotography.com/headshots

Services & rates: Charges £285 for a bespoke photoshoot lasting up to 2 hours in a relaxed

atmosphere. Over 300 images are shot with the best supplied on CD to take away, plus re-touching and processing of 3 10x8in prints and digital originals. Additional prints (including re-touching) are available for £15 each. Uses a studio and outdoor location, both of which are wheelchair-accessible. Please see website for examples.

Remy Hunter

Flat 2, 9 Belsize Park, London NW3 4ES
tel 020-7431 8055 *mobile* (07766) 760724
email remy_hunter@hotmail.com
website www.remyhunter.co.uk

Services & rates: Established in 2003. Charges £190 and £140 for a 4 hour and 2 hour Actors session respectively. Includes 80 digital shots taken for 4 hour session and 40 shots for 2 hour session. Also includes CD of all shots given to client at end of session and a further CD of 6 high resolution images for 4 hour session and 4 images for 2 hour session. Student discount available as follows: £150 for a 4 hour session and £120 for a 2 hour session. Shared sessions available for half of the above prices per person. Also includes two CDs. Studio and outdoor shots available during same session. Free retouching of images where necessary. Uses a studio that is not accessible to wheelchair users.

Work portfolio: Has taken photographs for roughly 500 actors, including (with Spotlight PIN in brackets): Freya Dominic (2211-8979-4470), Gemma Harvey (0615-5643-5877), Julie Pollin (0459-1206-3661), Jonathan Grace (aka James Dillinger – 2517-8940-4373). Advises clients to "bring a range of tops with varying necklines. Black tends to come out best, so a couple of black tops are a good idea. For make-up bring what you'd wear from day-to-day".

David James Photography

mobile (07808) 597362
email info@davidjamesphotos.com
website www.davidjamesphotos.com

Established 2001. Charges £230 for photo shoot including processing of 2 x 36bw films, and four 10x8in prints. Also offers digital shoot at the same price. Uses studio, outdoor locations and client's own home for the shoot; the studio is not accessible for wheelchair users. Has taken photographs for around 200 actors including clients of ICM, PFD and Markham & Froggatt.

Matt Jamie

London W6
mobile (07976) 890643
email photos@mattjamie.co.uk
website www.mattjamie.co.uk/portraits

Services & rates: Established in 2000. Digital photography. Cost of photo shoot is £145. This includes an indoor and outdoor session with well over 100 images taken (viewable on camera during the shoot and then an online gallery same day), with 3 finalised images in high resolution sent via email. Further images may be purchased any time. Offers 100% satisfaction promise – a free re-shoot or refund if not satisfied with shots taken. Prints are not included, these are charged at £1 per print for orders of 20 or more images (10x8in). Further details are available on the website. Special packages include: £100 for individual student rate or £90 per person for bookings of 3 or more students. Photos taken in studio or outdoor locations. Will travel to outdoor locations selected by client for small extra fee to cover expenses. Local outdoor locations used are wheelchair accessible. Studio sessions at drama schools can also be arranged.

Work portfolio: Examples of photography can be seen in portfolio at Spotlight offices. Highest rated photographer on Casting Call Pro. Has photographed hundreds of actors, including commissions from Ambassador Theatre Group, Whats On Stage.com, TheatreMAD and *Theatregoer Magazine* to photograph stars including Kevin Spacey, Kristin Scott Thomas, Patrick Swayze and John Barrowman.

"I offer a relaxed, informal shoot which can take as long as you need. You can bring a variety of different clothes (I suggest at least 2 different necklines, and generally plain colours – bring something you feel confident in), wigs, friends, or anything else you might want with you to make you feel relaxed."

JK Photography
17 Delamere Road, West Wimbledon, London SW20 8PS
mobile (07816) 825578
email jkph0t0@yahoo.com
website www.jk-photography.net

Services & rates: Established in 1997. Charges £145 for a photo shoot in studio or outdoor location (includes 100 shots plus fee, studio, processing and contact sheets). £10 per print. Offers a 10% discount for students.

Work portfolio: Has taken photographs for around 300 actors. "Stick to plain colours with no patterns or logos, and bring a range of different necklines. Professional hair and make up will be provided on the day."

Steve Johnston
mobile (07775) 991834
email steve@stevejohnstonphoto.com
website www.stevejohnstonphoto.com

Services & rates: Established in 1994. Based in London, offering bespoke casting photography service to actors, musicians and dancers. Shoot lasts 1-2 hours either on location, in the studio or the client's home. Only outdoor locations are wheelchair accessible. Only shoots digitally. This enables critique as images are taken. A 1-2 hour session would normally result in around 40-60 final images.

Contacts are either presented on secure online website or printed off. Images can be colour or black and white. Price per session is £165 incl. VAT. This includes online contact sheet and light retouching of 4 selected images. Prints of any selected/retouched images cost £8.00 each. Any further retouching is charged at £10 per image. Also offers free online upload of images to Spotlight and Castingcallpro. Special student rate £130.

Work portfolio: Examples of photography available on website. Has photographed approximately 20 actors. Recent clients include: Janet Jefferies, Davina Silver, Carrie Jones and Julie Ford. "Bring along a change of tops, black or white would be best, with no patterns or stripes and simple uncomplicated necklines (shirts work well). Keep makeup as natural looking as possible. Keep hair as you would normally wear it. Feel free to bring along any images showing styles you particularly like and any previous spotlight/ casting images."

JustActors
118A Woodfield Road, Leigh on Sea, Essex
tel (01702) 478281
email yearbook@justactors.co.uk
website www.justactors.co.uk

Charges £139.99 for a photoshoot, which includes all pre-artworked images on CD and 6 final artworked images uploaded to clients'-only website for print ordering. More than 11 years of photographic experience; photographer is also a working actor. Sample shots may be viewed on the website.

Neil Kendall Photography
19 Oakfield Court, Haslemere Road, London N8 9RA
tel 020-8340 4214 *mobile* (07776) 198332
email mondo.nez@virgin.net
website www.neilkendallphotography.com

Services & rates: Charges £135 for a photo shoot which includes photographer's fee, studio and equipment costs, processing of 3 b&w 36exps, contact sheets and 2 10x8in (25x20cm) prints. Uses both studio and natural light.

Work portfolio: Photographs can be viewed on the website. Has taken publicity shots for around 30-35 actors. Recent clients include: Vanessa Earl, Peter Ackyroyd, Graham Norton and Liberty X.

Jack Ladenburg Photography
mobile (07932) 053743
email info@jackladenburg.co.uk
website www.jackladenburg.co.uk

Services & rates: Established in 2006. Only digital photography. Cost of photo shoot is £195. This includes three 10x8in prints. Student discount of £30; further discounts for group bookings. Will retouch and resize according to clients' wishes and send them previews of their selected shots before printing. Photos taken in studio or outdoor locations. Only outdoor locations are wheelchair accessible.

Work portfolio: Portfolio is available to view at the Spotlight offices. Has photographed approximately 200 actors. Recent clients include Julian Rhind-Tutt, Nicholas Day, Tara Summers and Katherine Tozer. "I place a big emphasis on making sure that my clients are happy and relaxed before we start the shoot, and that they enjoy themselves on the day. I never rush through a session and always devote either a morning or an afternoon to one shoot. I don't set a limit on how many photos I'll take in a session, and make sure we concentrate on the casting needs of each actor."

Carole Latimer
113 Ledbury Road, Notting Hill, London W11 2AQ
tel 020-7727 9371
email carole@carolelatimer.com
website www.carolelatimer.com

Services & rates: Professional photographer for over 25 years. Charge for actors' headshots is £300 inc. VAT (student rate is £250). This includes three 10x8in prints. Extra prints are charged at £16 each. Digital photography is also offered. Photographs are taken in a studio and occasionally outdoor locations. The studio does not have wheelchair access.

Work portfolio: Provided publicity photos for approximately 2000 actors including: Kate O'Mara, Alistair McGowan, Maureen Lipman, Zoe Lucker and clients from the following agencies ICM, Conway Van Gelder, Narrow Road. "No large patterns, if black and white shoot, at least one black top always bring a selection of tops so I have a choice. I have an exceptional daylight studio with full lighting equipment. Good facilities for make-up."

Steve Lawton
134 Randolph Avenue, Maida Vale, London W9 1PG
mobile (07973) 307487
email stevelawton2@msn.com
website www.stevelawton.com

Services & rates: Charges £280 for a photo shoot, which includes A3 contact sheets; CD of all shots in colour and b&w; and 4 touched-up 10x8in prints. The same package is offered to students at the reduced price of £250. Additional 10x8in prints are priced at £12.50 each. A traditional b&w film service is also available. Advises clients not to bring patterned tops; fitted t-shirts and v-necks in blue, grey or black are most effective.

Work portfolio: Established in 2001. Has taken photographs for more than 2500 actors and is recommended by Curtis Brown, Independent Talent Group, United Agents, Lou Culson, Jorg Betts, Shane Collins, International Artists and Bronia Buchanan, amongst others. A full portfolio and price information is available on the website.

LB Photography
36 Nutley Lane, Reigate, Surrey RH2 9HS
tel (01737) 224578 *mobile* (07885) 966192

email labowerman@hotmail.com

Services & rates: Charges £160 for a photo shoot (£150 student rate), which includes photographer's fee, studio and equipment costs, processing of b&w 36 exposures and poster-sized contact sheet, and 2 10x8 prints. Price increases to £185 for 2 sheets; additional 10x8 prints are £10 each. There is no VAT charged at any stage. CD transfer also available. 6-7 Hi Res shots for £25.Photographs may be viewed at The Spotlight offices, in *Contacts* and on the Castingcallpro website.

Work portfolio: Photographs may be viewed at The Spotlight offices, in *Contacts*, and on the Castingcallpro website. Has taken publicity shots for over 3000 actors. More than 50 agencies send clients on a regular basis, including Narrow Road, Evans & Reiss, Brown and Simcocks, Hatton & McEwan and CAM.

Pete Le May
mobile (07703) 649246
email pete@petelemay.co.uk
website www.petelemay.co.uk

Services & rates: Based in London and established in 2002. Typically charges £250 (£200 for students) for a session lasting 2-3 hours, a disc of all the photographs – allowing you to make as many prints as you want – and minor re-touching of your favourite 6 images. All photography is digital, allowing you to review and discuss photos during the session. Photos are taken using natural light, both indoors and outdoors, and can be taken at a location of your choice. Examples of previous work and a full price-list are available from the website.

Murray Lenton
2 Toll Bar Barn, High Hesket, Near Carlisle, Cumbria CA4 OHR
tel (01697) 475442 *mobile* (07941) 427458
email murray.lenton@btinternet.com

Services & rates: Digital or film as required. Rates to be discussed at time of booking. Theatre photography and portraits since 1997. General photography since 1983.

Work portfolio: Established as a general photographer in 1983, and as a theatre photographer in 1997. Recent clients include: Tamsin Greig, Simon Dormandy, Luke Sorba and Wild Girls.

MAD Photography
200 Gladbeck Way, Enfield EN2 7HS
tel 020-8363 4182 *mobile* (07949) 581909
email mad.photo@onetel.net
website www.mad-photography.co.uk

Services & rates: Charges £185 for actors' photo shoot which includes photographer's fee, studio and location shoot, 75 proofs contact sheets emailed same day and 4 10x8in prints. Offers discounted rate of

£125 to students (includes as above, but with 2 10x8in prints); also offers student shared shoots at £85 each (includes as above, but with 50 proofs contact sheets and 2 prints). Extra 10x8in prints are priced at £15.95 each and images on disc are £20. "Hair and make-up should be natural. Bring 4 tops in any colours: one v-neck, one collar, one t-shirt and one jacket. No white!"

Work portfolio: Established in 1997. Photographs can be viewed on the website and in *Contacts* and CastingCallPro. Has taken publicity shots for over 6000 actors and student actors. Clients include: Shane Richie, Michelle Ryan, Susan Penhaligon, Michael Knowles, Jessica Wallace, John Partridge, Tom Law, Belinda Owusu, Janie Dee and Phoebe Thomas.

Gemma Mount Photography
1st Floor, 3 Torrens Street, London EC1V 1NQ
mobile (07976) 824923
email gemma@gemmamountphotography.com
website www.gemmamountphotography.com

Services and rates: Charges £190 for a photo shoot, which includes 60-100 shots on CD. Rates are reduced to £125 for students, and to £150 if you book with a friend. Prints are charged at £5 each. All photos are taken with natural light, indoors and outdoors.

Advises clients as follows: "Simple clothes are best; nothing should distract from the face or limit the casting. Bring a variety of tops – it is always better to have too many. V-necks are generally most flattering for women, because round necks tend to make a face look broader. A dark shirt is often good for guys and a selection of plain t-shirts. White can be great outside and often makes an actor look younger. If you have long hair, avoid colours that are a similar tone, or your hair won't stand out. Matte make-up is good; avoid anything shiny, as you want to look as natural as possible."

Work portfolio: Established in 1998. Has taken photos of around 400 actors, including Adam Borzone, Stephen Riseborough, Anya Vinci, Elizabeth Holmes, Daniel Saldin, Sarah Scowen, Dee Lapido and Samantha Pearl.

Adam Parker
1 Hoxton House, 34 Hoxton Street, London N1 6LR
tel 020-7684 2005 *mobile* (07710) 787708
email actors@adamparker.co.uk
website www.adamparker.co.uk

Services & rates: Established in 1996. Rates: £200-250 for a photo shoot; includes retouching and four 10x8in prints. Lower rates for students and groups. Photos taken in studio or at an alternative location by arrangement. Offers digital photography.

"I shoot fashion and beauty and will use this experience to make you look good but still look like you! I use the highest quality equipment and take great care to deliver a top service. Make-up / hair and fashion stylists can be arrangement if desired."

Michael Pollard Photographer
Manchester-based
tel 0161-456 7470 *mobile* (07800) 989457
email info@michaelpollard.co.uk
website www.michaelpollard.co.uk

Services & rates: Charges £110 for a 50-60 shot contact sheet including the first 3 images chosen to CD. Additional images are charged at £9 each, either to CD or print. Student rates are available. Shoots can be studio or outdoors or a mixture of both. As many shots as necessary are taken and these are later carefully edited down to give the actor the very best and most varied images from the shoot. These images are printed on contact sheets and posted out to the actors, and additional b&w and colour electronic contact sheets can be emailed to agents or actors free of charge.

Actors can bring a number of tops ranging from lighter to darker tones. "Tops should be simple and comfortable with generally a round or V-neck. Hair needs to be tidy but avoid going to the hairdresser the day before to have it cut. For women, make-up should be simple and sparing, avoiding lip liner or lipstick that is too dark or too red. The key is to keep things simple and natural and to be positive and be prepared. Think how you want to look and how you don't want to look. Enjoy it and be yourself!"

Work portfolio: Established in 1982 (1993 for actors). Photographs can be viewed on the website and at the Northern Actors Centre, Manchester. Has taken publicity shots for around 3000 actors. Recent clients include: Darren Day, Lucy-Jo Hudson, Samantha Siddall (*Shameless*), Sophia Di Martino (*Casualty*), Caroline Strong (*Emmerdale*), Vicky Binns (*Coronation Street*) and Bruce Jones.

David Price Photography
69 Pevensy Road, London SW17 0HT
mobile (07950) 542494
email info@davidpricephotography.co.uk
website www.davidpricephotography.co.uk

Services & rates: Prices start from £150. Informal sessions shooting in daylight and studio light. Session includes: 2-3hr shoot, CD with 6 final edited images and two 10x8in prints. Uploading of final images to an actor's agent is also included. Online ordering from **www.photoboxgallery.com/davidpricephotography** (prints are no longer available through Visualeyes). Film sessions available; please refer to website for prices.

"Portable studio equipment allows me to visit clients' homes at special request." Hair and make-up available if booked in advance at £40. 10% student discount available.

Studio is not accessible for wheelchair users.

Work portfolio: Clients include, Narrow Road,

Hobson's International, Stephanie Evans Associates, Jackie Palmer Stage School, Bristol Old Vic Theatre School, Lamda, RAM and Central School of Speech and Drama, and commissions from theatres across the country.

David has connections with The Actor's Workshop Youth Theatre and also does Headshot Introduction workshops for acting students.

"Your headshots should be a fair and flattering portrait of the professional that you are. I aim to achieve a strong, confident image that represents the person that will walk through that door at the audition or casting. I am more than happy to give advice on the nature of the industry and the best way in which to market yourself."

Prices are subject to change. Please check the website for the latest prices.

Robin Savage Photography

North London
mobile (07901) 927597
email contact@robinsavage.co.uk
website www.robinsavage.co.uk

Services & rates: Established in 2000. Charges £175 for actors' headshots: this includes 100 proofs as well as 12 finished images supplied as high-res copies on CD. Student rate is £150. Shoots mostly outdoors, but also around home and home studio (all are wheelchair accessible).

Work portfolio: Clients include: Grant Burgin, Shobu Kapoor, Haruka Kuroda and Kate Terence.

Howard Sayer Photography

tel 020-8123 0251
email howard@howardsayer.com
website www.howardsayer.com

Services & rates: Casting head shots £225 inclusive of VAT for sitting; includes CD with high res images released for printing. Studio or location setting.

Work portfolio: Recent clients include: BBC, Teddington Studios and Benedict Promotions.

Karen Scott Photography

London
mobile (07958) 975950
email info@karenscottphotography.com
website www.karenscottphotography.com

Services & rates: Charges £175 for a digital shoot, which includes b&w portfolio and a selection of colour images also. Approximately 80 images selected, cropped and finished, slight re-touching applied if necessary and provided on CD. All photographs provided as high-resolution. Includes contact sheets for reference and can advise on prints. Session is relaxed and unlimited in time, allowing several clothing changes and shot using flattering natural light, be that outdoors or indoors. £125 discounted rate is offered to all full time students.

Live performance and publicity shoots undertaken for individuals and theatre companies for an arranged fee. Your individual needs within any discipline in the arts is discussed before each shoot and advice on clothing and make-up offered. "An honest yet striking image, portraying the qualities behind the photograph."

Work portfolio: Portfolio can be viewed on the website and in The Spotlight offices, and also in *Contacts.*

Catherine Shakespeare Lane

The Monsell Stores, 43 Monsell Road,
London N4 2EF
tel 020-7226 7694
email cat@csl-art.co.uk
website www.csl-art.co.uk

Services & rates: Charges £390 for a photo shoot which includes photographer's fee, studio and equipment costs, processing of 2 b&w 36exps, contact sheets and 4 10x8in prints. Offers a student package for £270 (1 roll of 36 and 2 10x8in prints). In special circumstances this package is also available to non-students for £280. Uses natural light inside and favours a natural look. "My aim is to show my clients at their most interesting."

Work portfolio: Established in 1975. Photographs can be viewed at The Spotlight offices and in *Contacts.* Has taken publicity shots for more than 2000 actors.

Peter Simpkin

17 Grove Avenue, London N10 2AS
tel 020-8883 2727
email petersimpkin@aol.com
website www.petersimpkin.co.uk

Services & rates: Charges £411.25 (inclusive of VAT) for a photo shoot which includes photographer's fee, studio and equipment costs, processing of 3 b&w 36exps, contact sheets and 6 10x8in (25x20cm) prints (also supplied with a CD). Student price is £352.50 inclusive of VAT.

Work portfolio: Established in 1973. Photographs can be viewed on the website. Has taken publicity shots for thousands of actors. Recent clients include: actors represented by ARG, Curtis Brown, Christina Shepherd Associates; students from Webber Douglas (now Central School of Speech & Drama), LAMDA, Mountview and Bristol Old Vic.

Rosie Still

391 Sidcup Road, London SE9 4EU
tel 020-8857 6920
email rosie391@talktalk.net
website www.rosiestillphotography.com

Services & rates: A professional photographer for 35 years. Charges a special price for actors of £120 for a portrait session (normally £150). This includes session fee, proof sheet and two 10x8in b&w prints of the client's choice. The price accommodates up to 4 changes of top. Also offers a special reduction for students to £80, which includes all of the above but accommodates 2 changes of top.

Takes as many shots as are necessary, depending on the client's needs. Offers an airbrushing service at no extra cost; for an additional £10 can also provide the whole shoot on CD for the client to take home (normal price, £20). Additional prints are £5 each, but the price is reduced if a number of the same prints are required. Also does repros, z-cards, photo business cards and photo CVs. All sessions are carried out in own South London studio, approx. 15 minutes' train journey from London Bridge station and with parking spaces directly outside. The studio is wheelchair accessible.

Work portfolio: Portfolio includes many pop stars and TV celebrities, but specialises now in publicity shots for actors and drama students. Clients include: Ami Metcalf, Debra Stephenson, Charlie Clements, Liz Frazer, Bella Emberg, Christopher Parker, Chris Jarvis, Zoe Heyes, Maureen Sweeney, John Leyton, Gabrielle Bradshaw and Mia McKenna-Bruce. Examples of work can be seen on the website **www.rosiestillphotography.com** and on Castingcallpro.

"Ladies should keep make-up to the minimum – as if going out for the evening, nothing heavier. Men should wear none at all. My priority is to finish a shoot with the client 100% satisfied with their results."

Philip Thorne
Dorset
tel (01929) 554872 *mobile* (07799) 350329
email enquiries@philipthorne.co.uk
website www.philipthorne.co.uk/filmandportraits

Services & rates: Established in 2005. Charges £150 for a photoshoot (online contact sheet of images plus 6 retouched high res images of choice on CD – p&p extra at £2.50). Includes around 36 shots. 10x8in prints are available at a cost of £10 each plus p&p. Student rate is £100.

Work portfolio: Has taken publicity shots for around 50 actors, including John Altman, Katherine Parkinson, Ian McNeice, Joe Absolom and High Bonneville.

TM Photography & Design
Suite 228, Business Design Centre, 52 Upper Street, Islington, London N1 0QH
tel 020-7288 6846
email info@tmphotography.co.uk
website www.tmphotography.co.uk

Services & rates: Established in 1995. All photography is digital. Cost of photo shoot is £70. The cost includes one 10x8in print which can be

taken away on the day of the shoot. Images can be viewed by the client as they are taken. Images are loaded on to a private webpage to be viewed. Orders can be placed online. Student photoshoot is discounted at £40. Photos taken in studio or outdoor locations or client's home. Studio is wheelchair accessible.

Work portfolio: Has photographed approximately 3000 actors, walkons and background artists. Has photographed many of the clients of Allsorts Agency, Ray Knight, G2, Guys & Dolls. Actors photographed include: Fraser Hines, Antonia Okonma. Photoshoots can be booked at short notice. Also offers repro service and promotional products such as websites, model cards and CV creation.

ToShoot.Com (formerly 7LA Studios)
42b Medina Road, London N7 7LA
tel/fax 020-7686 2324
mobile (07960) 726957
email hi@toshoot.com
website www.toshoot.com
Photographer Carlos Cicchelli

Services & rates: Established in 2003. "Actors' and models' headshots and portfolios done on digital of film. Prices vary depending on the job. Email for quotation."

Steve Ullathorne
London
tel (07961) 380969
email steve@steveullathorne.com
website www.ullapix.com

Services & rates: Charges £185 for a digital photo shoot; this covers all fees and studio costs, contact sheets and 5 10x8in prints. Will offer a discount to students, negotiable at the time of booking. All clients receive an online contact sheet with a web address that they can pass on to their agent. Prior to the shoot, clothing and locations will be discussed with the client on the telephone. All photos are retouched in Photoshop to remove any blemishes plus any other light retouching required by the actor. Email proofs are sent of each chosen image. Rather than specifying a number of images, prices are dictated by duration of the shoot, which is 1.5 hours. Actors usually end up with more than 100 shots to choose from.

Work portfolio: Please see website for samples. Agency recommendations include: Brown and Simcocks, Mike Leigh Associates, and Conway van Gelder.

Martin Usborne Photography
mobile (07747) 607930
email mail@martinusborne.com
website www.martinusborne.com

Services & rates: Established in 2000. Shoots exclusively on high end digital cameras so all shots can be seen directly after the session on a computer.

Clients select prints which are then processed immediately and printed off on professional lab printer. Images can be colour or black and white. Charge for photo session is £200. This includes two 10x8in prints and CD of all shots at full resolution. Touch up service is offered at an extra cost of £50. Photo session lasts 2 hours. Student discount £175. Photos taken in studio or outdoor locations. Only outdoor locations are wheelchair accessible.

Luke Varley

mobile (07711) 183631
email luke@lukevarley.com
website www.lukevarley.com

Established in 2004. Charges £210 for a photo shoot, which includes approximately 130 shots and 4 10x8in prints. Shoots take place in a studio (inc. home studio) or at an outdoor location that is wheelchair-accessible. Has taken publicity photos for several hundred actors, including clients from the following agencies: Ken McKreddie, Troika, McFarlane Chard and Bronia Buchanan.

Robin Watson

tel 020-7833 1982
email robin@robinwatson.biz
website www.robinwatson.biz

Services & rates: Charges £180 for a photo shoot. This includes all fees and studio costs, processing of 2 b&w 36exps, contact sheets and 2 10x8in prints. Digital photography is also available and costs an additional £10 for transferring images to CD. Advises clients to keep clothing simple with unfussy necklines and mid-tone single colours, not black and white. Make-up should also be simple, perhaps a little eye-liner and some foundation powder if the complexion is shiny.

Work portfolio: Established in 1994. Photographs can be viewed on the website or in *Spotlight*. Has taken photographs of hundreds of actors, with recent clients including: Rula Lenska, Christopher Timothy and Finty Williams.

Caroline Webster

North London
mobile (07867) 653019
email caroline@carolinewebster.co.uk
website www.carolinewebster.co.uk

Established in 2009. Charges £85 for studio or outdoor shoot, and £150 for both studio and outdoor shoot. Approximately 100 digital shots are taken, and final photos provided in colour and black and white, as jpegs and tiff files on disc. Offers a student rate of £60 for studio or outdoor shoot. Has taken publicity photos for 25 actor clients, including Siobhan Dillon, Paul Merton, Geraldine Fitzgerald and Kate Duchene.

Robert Workman

32 West Kensington Mansions, Beaumont Crescent, London W14 9PF
tel 020-7385 5442
email bob@robertworkman.demon.co.uk
Studio address: Studio 103B, The Business Village, Broomhill Road, London SW18 4JQ
website www.robertworkman.demon.co.uk

Services & rates: Charges £250 plus VAT for a photo shoot which includes photographer's fee, studio and equipment costs, processing of 2 b&w 36exps, contact sheets, 5 10x8in (25x20cm) prints and a CD for digital submissions to casting directors and *Spotlight* online. Special student portrait session costs £150 plus VAT.

Work portfolio: Photographs can be viewed on the website. Has been taking around 200 publicity shots for actors every year for 20 years. Recent clients include: Caroline Quentin, Jude Law and Philip Middlemiss.

REPRO COMPANIES

Denbry Repros Ltd

57 High Street, Hemel Hempstead, Herts HP1 3AF
tel (01442) 242411
email info@denbryrepros.com
website www.denbryrepros.com

Charges £7.20 plus VAT for the initial copy of a b&w negative. Can also reproduce from a digital image.

Repros of a b&w 10x8in (25x20cm) are priced as follows:
£26 for 25, £47.05 for 50, £89.05 for 100, £178.10 for 200, £200.40 for 250 and £393.75 for 500.

Repros of a b&w postcard print are priced as follows:
£19.50 for 25, £36.30 for 50, £66.05 for 100, £132.10 for 200, £133.75 for 250 and £234.95 for 500.

All prices exclude VAT. Colour repros are also available at an increased price.

Other services include a studio for casting photography, downloading images from the Internet and supplying images on CD in colour or b&w.

Denman Repros

Burgess House, Main Street, Farnsfield, Nottinghamshire NG22 8EFF
tel (01623) 882272 *fax* (01623) 882272

Initial scan of a 10x8in (25x20cm) print is free. Can also work with CDs, negatives and transparencies.

Repros of a b&w 10x8in are priced as follows:
£48 for 100, £64 for 250 and £88 for 500.

Repros of a b&w postcard print are priced as follows:
£34 for 100, £39 for 250 and £64 for 500.

Note Please ring for latest prices for colour repros.

Faces Prints

10 Avondale Road, Carlton, Nottingham NG4 1AF
tel 0115-847 5640 *fax* 0115-847 5640
email facesprints@ntlworld.com

Initial scan is free.

Repros of b&w 10x8in are priced as follows:
£28 for 25, £43 for 50, £56 for 100, £73 for 200, £85 for 250 and £99 for 500.

Repros of a b&w postcard print are priced as follows:
£22 for 25, £32 for 50, £37 for 100, £49 for 200, £59 for 250 and £85 for 500.

Will also provide a free gloss on quantity of 25, free photo retouch, free design on 'z-cards', and email proofing and free name/caption insertion.

Moorfields Photographic
Old Hall Street, Liverpool L3 9RQ
tel 0151-236 1611
email info@moorfieldsphoto.com

Established in 1981. Please refer to the website, and to the separate advertisement in this Yearbook, for full details.

Profile Prints
Unit 2, Plot 1A, Rospeath Industrial Estate, Crowlas TR20 8DU
tel (01736) 741222 *fax* (01736) 741255
email sales@courtwood.co.uk
website www.courtwood.co.uk

One-off charge of £2.75 for negative from email, CD or original. All media accepted.

Repros of 10x8in b&w or colour are priced as follows:
£29.75 for 24, £52.25 for 50, and £94.25 for 100.

Credit card-sized self-adhesive 'minis' (great for CVs):
£13 for 50, and £18.25 for 100.

Produces all sizes, postcards and z-cards. Prices include p&p and VAT.

Visualeyes Imaging Services
95 Mortimer Street, London W1W 7ST
tel 020-7323 7430 *fax* 020-7323 7438
website www.visphoto.co.uk

Reproducing actors' headshots for more than 30 years. True photographic printing from 6x4in to 16x12in. Other services include digital printing, scanning, retouching and image archiving. Visit the website for full information on services, prices, ordering and despatch options. Offers a discount to students, free clean-up of images, and free transmission of image to *Spotlight*.

Getting the most from your photographs

Angus Deuchar

When searching for actors, most casting directors or directors start with a pile of photographs. Their time is limited, so they really only want to see the people who stand a chance of being right for a part – and the picture will be a vital part of their decision-making process. It's important therefore, to ensure that the photographs you use are as good as they can possibly be.

Have a flick through *Spotlight*. As well as being compulsive entertainment for any actor, it can be a great way to decide what works and what doesn't. If *you* were the casting director, who would (and wouldn't) you see? Try it for different types of production: a musical, a Shakespeare play, a TV drama. You may be surprised at the assumptions you make based on the photographs.

I'm going to look at what makes a good actor's photograph; help you think through how to choose a photographer; and discuss how you can get the best results from a photo session. Here is a list of, in my opinion, some important qualities to look for in a good headshot. It should be:

• **Honest.** This to me is the key to a good actor's photograph. Decisions at interviews are often largely made in the first few seconds, so it's important that the person who walks through the door is the person they saw in the photograph. If an actor looks different in some way, the interviewer's first reaction may well be disappointment. Which can't be a good start!

• **Well lit.** The face and hair should be well lit. If there are excessively bright areas or shadows on the face, the photo is probably not doing the actor any favours.

• **In focus.**

• **A good connection with the eyes.** These are possibly the most important feature, as these are what we generally look at first. We make a connection with the eyes. They should be well lit, in focus, looking *at* the camera and not squinting. They should also be 'alive' and not glazed over.

• **Well framed.** Ideally just head and shoulders. Not too close up, as it can look a bit overbearing. Likewise, not too far away as the face becomes too small.

• **Nothing 'tricksy'.** No fake hand-gestures, and certainly no props!

Can't I just get my friend to take some pictures in the back garden? Well, you could (in fact, some do). But what kind of image of yourself would that portray? You can always see such pictures in *Spotlight* – the actor looking awkward, squinting into the sunlight or the picture out of focus. Again, if you were the casting director, would you consider that actor to be serious? There's no point in cutting costs here. Decent photographs can more than pay for themselves.

Finding a photographer

Assuming you've decided to employ a photographer, how do you find the right one? Professional photographers are not all alike. Some who may be fantastic at, say, press or fashion, may not be good at actors' portraits. It's important that the photographer knows the business of Acting. There are countless listings of specialist actors' photographers – in publications like this one; as adverts in *Contacts*; or on posters in Actors Centres; but the style of photographs, and the ability of the photographers, are as varied as the prices and packages. It is therefore essential to check out their work for yourself. Have a look at their website if they have one, or at least try to see several different examples of their work.

Don't make a choice based solely on price. The amount a photographer charges is not necessarily an indication of how good (or bad) they are. Wherever possible, make your decision about a photographer based mostly on the *work* they produce, rather than how much they charge. It's important ultimately that you get the best possible photographs.

Find out the following:

• **Studio or natural light?** Studio light is easier to standardise and can be used at any time of the day or night and during any weather. It can be made to flatter someone, but won't necessarily show what they will look like in 'real life'. I prefer natural light, as I believe it to be generally more honest. Good natural light can still show someone at their best, but it won't deceive. It can also be more relaxing for the subject to be outside for the session. Casting directors often prefer natural light as it gives a better indication of who is actually going to walk through the door.

• **Film or digital?** Digital technology has moved on to such an extent that the quality of either format is comparable. Digital tends to produce a cleaner, less grainy image *and* you can check the results as you go along. It is essential however, that whoever is preparing the final photograph knows how to convert the image into a good-quality black and white print, with decent contrast and without loss of detail. This takes a reasonable amount of skill and know-how.

• **How much do they charge?** Does that include VAT? If relevant, you may want to ask about concessions for students.

• **How many photos do I get?** Find out how many photos will actually be taken at the session and how many different, finished 8x10 prints you can choose.

• **How will I view my proofs?** Some photographers will put your proofs onto a website enabling you to view them blown up on the screen. You may prefer a paper contact sheet, which, although much smaller to view, is more portable. If you want both, you may need to pay extra – so ask.

• **How long until I see my proofs?** Websites can often be published the same day as the session, while a paper contact will usually need to be produced and posted, so will take a few days. Some photographers will show you pictures on a computer straight away. This can be useful as a guide, but you probably shouldn't try to make final decisions without a bit of time to think.

• **How long will it take until I get my finished prints?** Try to get an indication of how long you should expect to wait after placing your final order. Hopefully, no more than a few days.

• **Do I get a CD?** As well as the prints, a few electronic versions of the final photos are extremely useful. They can be used on a website, to send a submission via email, to send to The Spotlight, to print out yourself, or to act as the master-copy for your 'repros'. Find out if the photographer will provide you with a few different versions on a CD, and if it's included in the price.

The session itself

Here are some important things to prepare before – or think about during – your photo session.

• **Your 'look'.** Do you want to appear neutral or as a particular 'type'? For instance, earrings (on men especially) or other piercings, may limit you to modern or even 'alternative' characters. A formal jacket might suggest a business person or MP. Any of these looks may be fine, as they can make you 'ideal' for a particular type of role – but it's likely that that's all you'll ever be seen for while using that photograph! You decide – it really depends upon how you are marketing yourself.

• **Make-up and hair.** Preferably little or no make-up, but certainly no more than you would wear normally, day to day. Some photographers provide a 'hair and make-up' service but I would strongly discourage actors from using this. Don't confuse actors' portraits with having a glamorous photo to stick on top of the piano! If someone else prepares you, you're unlikely to look like the 'normal' you and it may be difficult to recreate that look in the future. Likewise, if you're planning to get a new hairstyle before your session, do so several days in advance to give you a chance to get used to it.

• **What to wear.** Concentrate on the neckline. Wear something you feel comfortable in, but avoid distracting patterns or logos. Most colours are fine, and black often works well. Bright white can affect the exposure so is less helpful. A jacket of some sort for some of the photos can often work well. Jewellery can be distracting so is usually best avoided.

• **Facial expression.** A big smile is often great for musicals or front-of-house pictures, but for other casting purposes it can seem a little over the top. Any kind of 'emoting' can seem over-earnest or, worse, corny. I tend to favour a good neutral expression with 'spark' behind the eyes. A kind of a relaxed, open look with the smallest hint of a smile.

Ultimately, photographs play an important part in helping you get a foot in the door. But once you've been called for the interview, it's over to you ...

Angus Deuchar trained as an actor, during which time he subsidised his grant by taking photographs of his fellow students. When he left drama school in 1987 he soon realised that this was an ideal way to make a living between jobs! He pursued both careers for the first seven years, but has continued with just the photography since then. A website showing examples of his work can be seen at **www.actorsphotos.co.uk**.

Voice-overs

Bernard Shaw

'Voice-overs' are very buoyant, with more available work than ever before and more opportunities for 'newcomers' to find their place in this exciting world. The voice business is strictly that – business! Learn how it works and learn how to earn your place within it. Focused and targeted effort will be rewarded; a business-like approach might well open lucrative doors for you.

You are unlikely to make any professional progress without a 'demo' CD showing the quality and range of your natural voice. Newcomers are more likely to be booked for their 'own' voice than for their ability to perform a multitude of doubtful regional accents and unrecognisable impressions. Given that very few employers actively seek a 'versatile voice', there is little point in marketing yourself under this rather old-fashioned banner. Identify your natural strengths and market them in places where they might be in demand. Demonstrate, briefly, what you can do well.

Historically, actors had interminable voice-demo cassettes designed to be all things to all listeners, with many of them containing up to 20 tracks ranging from Shakespeare to coffee ads. These are no longer acceptable: anyone sending out such a thing will be regarded as out of touch with current reality and will not be taken seriously. The medium of choice is now CD and the preferred running length is three minutes! The BBC and other companies producing Radio Drama will tolerate eight or nine minutes. Voice Actors (the cool way to describe yourself) should have a master CD containing a range of material which can be 'picked and mixed' to suit a variety of recipients. Home computers make it very easy to create a different content and running order for each CD produced.

This master CD ought to be produced and recorded by one of the few reputable studios specialising in this work and should contain only genuine material. Do not write your own scripts or rely on 'spoofs'. Your recordings need to sound as professional as the real thing and should be complete with music and sound effects. For work voicing ads you should have three or four 30-second commercial scripts such as hard sell, soft sell, real person, and 'character' voice. For documentary work, you could have a two-minute 'wildlife' read together with a contrasting piece 'explaining' a concept or process. This material is easily found as there are thousands of scripts available on the Internet.

If you have specialised knowledge (perhaps from a former profession or hobby), you should include a recording demonstrating this. Computer games are now bigger business than Hollywood films so it would be wise to record some material for this market. You might be possessed of the deep tones of a Super Hero or discover the ability to voice cutesy cuddly toys – or both! The voices required for these games are similar in range and extremes to those heard in cartoon films and children's stories. Games companies do not normally cast on the strength of a 'demo' CD, but professionally produced recordings might well get you a place on their audition list.

Radio Drama producers expect to receive a CD containing four pieces no longer than two minutes each. The material should be one 'classical', one 'contemporary', one 'comic' and a poem. The ideal is to produce a balanced listen which gives an overall glimpse of your range and abilities, but without straying into the trap of attempting to demonstrate your skill (or lack thereof) in producing large numbers of accents and characters. Be yourself!

Your CDs should be well and imaginatively labelled and packaged. Ideally they should be as impressive, interesting and memorable as anything bought in a high street shop. Full-time Voice Actors spend much time, effort and money on designing their packaging. It should be memorable enough for the CD to be found from within a pile of 100 others long after the name of the artist has faded from memory. Use a memorable 'catch phrase' with a coordinated picture or design. You cannot rely solely on the quality of your voice, nor on the open-mindedness of employers and agents, to get you a hearing. High-quality, imaginative packaging is essential. The software which helps you produce it is to be found in most modern computers; if it is not resident on your desktop, it can be bought for only £10.

There are two ways to find work. You can either ask an agent to put you on their books, or you can contact the employers yourself. Before a voice-over agent agrees to represent you, it will be necessary for you to demonstrate that you can provide them with a new income stream. The primary function of any agent is to make money for themselves; it is a waste of time and effort to approach agents who already represent someone who sounds the same as you. Agents have Internet sites where their clients' voices can be heard; visit these sites, and if you hear someone sounding like you, don't waste your time and energy on a pointless phone call. When you find someone who does not already represent what you have to offer you will be able to call them from a position of strength and confidence.

Many successful Voice Actors choose to represent themselves. They enjoy the challenge of running what is essentially a 'Small Business' from home. Their core reference book is Mr Osborne's *Voice-Over Contacts*, which is a most useful and reasonably priced publication containing details of a large number of employers and other important contacts within the voice business. Full details can be found at **www.voiceovercontacts.co.uk**. Newcomers may be surprised to find their phone calls meeting with a much warmer response from the advertising agents than from the voice agents.

Treat the voice world in a professional and business-like manner, and it will, at the very least, listen to what you have to offer. Always present yourself as a 'solution' rather than a 'problem' and, above all, try to match your strengths to their needs. Good luck!

Editor's note Since this article was written, the term 'voicereels' (for 'voice demo') has become more common.

Bernard Shaw, who died peacefully in December 2008, was the author of *Voice-Overs: A Practical Guide* – a popular training manual on both sides of the Atlantic. He ran regular Voice-Over and Radio Acting workshops at the Actors Centres in London, Birmingham, Manchester and Newcastle. He worked full time in the voice business and was one of the most experienced producers of voice demos in the world.

Showreel and voice demo companies

The rapid growth in recording technology has seen an explosion of such companies over the last decade. There has also been a significant increase in the amount of (sometimes contradictory) advice offered on content, length, and so on. Much of this 'advice' is available on individual companies' websites, where you can sometimes also find samples of their work.

Voice demos (also known as 'voicereels' and, sometimes confusingly, 'showreels') have been around for several decades, and a good one could attract the attention of a voice agent. However, the world of voice-overs is hard to break into and so a quality-produced demo is very important. Showreels (applied to videoed performances) are a more recent innovation and are not yet quite the 'norm' – some agents and casting directors insist on seeing you perform live. However, a good one might just tip the balance in your favour.

If you intend to travel down these routes, check the details (including pricing) of each possible company and the quality of their work. You should also assess whether the financial investment(s) involved could produce sufficient return. These additional 'calling cards' need to be of broadcast quality and professionally packaged to have any impact. As with photographers, it is very important to research as thoroughly as possible before committing your meagre funds. Is there a real possibility that one (or both) will enhance your chances of acting work?

Note It is very important that you have permission from the copyright-holders of any material that you intend to use, and some companies will help with this. It is also important to check the current charges of each company that interests you, as some will change during the lifetime of this edition.

Accent Bank
420 Falcon Wharf, 34 Lombard Road,
London SW11 3RF
tel 020-7223 5160
email enquiries@accentbank.co.uk
website www.accentbank.co.uk
Director Lisa Paterson

A voice-over portal distributed to an international market. Acts as a shop window for experienced voice-over talent specialising in authentic regional and international voices. "Accent Bank provides bespoke one-on-one coaching and workshops for those new to the business. We pride ourselves on a very personal service, using the best coaches and directors, original material and excellent production facilities to bring out the best in your voice. For more information, or to have a chat, contact us by phone or email."

Actor Showreels
97B Central Hill, London SE19 1BY
tel (07853) 637965
email post@actorshowreels.co.uk
website www.actorshowreels.co.uk

Key contact Hugh Lee
established 2007

Showreel services: Each actor works with an editor to select the material from pre-existing clips. The editor uploads the edited material online, so that the actor's agent can also view the edit. The DVDs go to print as soon as the actor is satisfied with the final edit. Charges a flat fee of £120 for producing a showreel. 5 colour printed DVDs are included in the cost. The average duration of a showreel is 5 minutes. Recent clients have included: Jennifer Hennessy (Curtis Brown), Nathalie Armin (Lou Coulson), Stephen Hogan (CAM), Suzanne Burden (MacFarlane Chard).

The Actor's One-Stop Shop
First Floor, Above the Gate Pub, Station Road,
London N22 7SS
tel 020-8888 7006 *fax* 020-8888 9666
email info@actorsonestopshop.com
website www.actorsonestopshop.com
established 1997

Showreel services: Offers broadcast-quality, professionally packaged reels. Scenes are crafted like

Resources

film/TV excerpts rather than being 'audition pieces'. Actors can choose either monologue or dialogue scenes, in any combination they wish. A single scene (monologue) reel costs £310 (including final copy in box DVD presentation).

Also edits reels from past work at a cost of £60 per hour; clients sit-in on the edit and receive the finished product the same day. Price includes full archiving of material so that the reel can be easily and affordably updated in the future. Actors can order DVD, CD Rom or VHS copies. The company also supplies 'streamed' copies for agency and The Spotlight websites.

Recommended by several agents, The Spotlight and CastingCall Pro. See website for reel samples.

Ben Crowe
23 John Aird Court, Little Venice, London W2 1UY
mobile (07952) 784911
email bencrowe@hotmail.co.uk
Key contact Ben Crowe

Charges £65 for producing a voice demo from scratch (or £55 with Spotlight card, and for students). Includes 2 additional CD copies. Average duration of the demo is 60-90 minutes. "Select 4 30-second speeches for Spotlight voice clips."

Crying Out Loud Productions
mobile (07809) 549887
(Simon) *mobile* (07946) 533108 (Marina)
email simon@cryingoutloud.co.uk
website www.cryingoutloud.co.uk
Key contacts Simon Cryer, Marina Caldarone

Voice demo services: Established in 1999. Charges from £280 to produce a bespoke voice demo from scratch; this includes a face-to-face consultation with Marina Caldarone to select material, studio time with both producer and director, full editing and production, a 2-minute MEGAMIX, a 2-year archive, a Master Audio CD and a data CD containing MP3 files and Contacts Brochure. There are no hidden costs. Clients will record a selection of material consisting of around 4 Commercials, 2 Narratives, 1 Documentary and 2 Dramas.

Each client meets with the director, Marina Calderone, for a consultation to select the most suitable material for their voice. Clients should aim to leave at least 7 days between consultation and recording session so they have sufficient time to prepare.

Recent clients have included: Charles (Lord) Brocket, Andrew Castle, Sky, Elizabeth Norman (the voice of BT 1571), the Disasters Emergency Committee (DEC), Ubisoft, and Sally Gunnell OBE. Both Simon Cryer and Marina Caldarone are practitioners in the industry working in Radio Commercials and Radio Drama.

Cut Glass Productions
Studio 185, 181-187 Queens Crescent, Camden, London NW5 4DS

tel 020-7267 2339
email info@cutglassproductions.com
website www.cutglassproductions.com
Producer Phil Corran

Voice-demo services: Three package options:
• £210 'Revive' – created for artists who wish to update or make changes to an existing showreel.
• £250 'Create' – for actors/artists who need a completely new reel. A lot of support and advice is given to beginners. Includes script consultation and 4 hours' studio time.
• £350 'Raw Talent' – this package is for complete newcomers to the voice industry who feel they are going to need the freedom of unlimited time in the studio.

Once each actor's showreel expectations are established, there is a detailed pre-consultation by phone – this enables Cut Glass to get to know you and select material suitable for your playing age/range. Cut Glass doesn't recycle scripts – each piece (4-5 commercials, 2 narrations or documentaries, maybe an animation/story piece) will be unique to you. There is also a detailed consultation on the day to discuss selected material. The recording session itself is a creative experience in terms of ideas and performance, with Phil Corran directing and producing the session. You will be guided throughout the production, and go home with your mastered reel and 1 extra copy. Showreels are around 4 mins long, with an option to produce a 90-second punchy 'montage' which sits at the beginning of your reel and can be emailed to casting directors as an MP3 or used on Spotlight.

As well as specialising in creating high-quality voice-over showreels, Cut Glass is a digital voice-over production studio and creative voice agency. As such, the company has a diverse range of clients – both professional voice-over jobs and showreel customers – and works with animation/computer games companies, corporates, the BBC and independent production companies. It regularly produces audio guides and comedy podcasts, and produces showreels for other agencies as well as its own. See the website for examples of 'montages' of the agency's showreels.

Advice to beginners: As voice-over agents (see entry on page 90), Cut Glass recommends that your showreel be no longer than around 4 mins; any longer and you will have lost the casting director/agent's attention. Talk to people who work in the voice industry, and listen to recommendations. It's so important to get your showreel production spot-on, because it's your one chance to showcase your vocal talent.

MyClips
Flat 1, 2 Blackdown Close, London N2 8JF
tel 020-8371 9526
email info@myclipsdvd.co.uk
website www.myclipsdvd.com
Key personnel Ruth Hutchinson, Alex Perkins

Showreel services: Edits showreel credits into individual clips. Because a myclips DVD is non-linear, the casting director or agent can choose the order of the clips they wish to view. Footage can be supplied in DVD, VHS or 8mm video format. The company can also improve the quality of the clips, for example by altering the colour balance or removing some of the hiss from VHS credits. Charges £199 to provide a showreel including 5 DVD copies, each presented in a clear slimline myclips DVD case. Also designs and prints print full-colour, photographic quality, double-sided DVD case inserts with more information about the client. The standard insert includes photo, CV, biography and contact details. On request, the company can include further details to suit individual needs, including a promotional flyer for an upcoming performance. Prints a full-colour, photographic quality design directly onto the DVD face: "No more sticky labels." Each DVD also has animated menus so that the viewer can see a preview before choosing which clips they wish to watch. "A myclips DVD is incredibly user-friendly." An upgrade package is also available at £99.

Opus Productions Ltd
9a Coverdale Road, London W12 8JJ
tel 020-8743 3910 *fax* 020-8749 4537
email via form on website
website www.opusproductions.co.uk
Key personnel Claire Bidwell, Neil Wilkes

Established in 1999. Works mainly in computer media production. Specialises in video and audio encoding, DVD authoring, video editing, graphic design and website design. Will edit, produce and encode video and DVD showreels for actors.

The Reel McCoy
4 Kirkdale, Sydenham, London SE26 4NE
mobile (07708) 626477
email reelmccoyservice@aol.com
website www.reelmccoy.moonfruit.com

Key contact James Hyland

Established in 2005. Offers a highly specialised service in which existing material is re-edited so that the actor becomes the primary focus of each of his or her chosen segments, while still maintaining the narrative of the scene. Also specialises in creating non-verbal montages with music. Clients include: Nick Bartlett (Narrow Road), Hassani Shapi (Nancy Hudson Associates Ltd), and Jonathan Rigby (JLM Personal Management). Charges £20 per hour for producing a showreel with an average duration of 5 minutes. This includes 1 DVD, with further copies charged at £4 each. Offers a free consultation session and portfolio photo-reel included on the completed DVD. Recommends actors to "make sure they have noted the time in which their chosen footage appears on their voicereels or DVDs; this will save time in the editing room".

The Reel Deal Showreel Co
6 Charlotte Road, Wallington, Surrey SM6 9AX
tel 020-8647 1235
email info@thereel-deal.co.uk
website www.thereel-deal.co.uk
established 2003

Showreel services: Has 2 rates for editing a showreel: £199 for a full day's editing, which includes 2 free hours to update the reel, and 2 free DVDs; or the hourly rate of £35 for actors who don't have a lot of material. A discount of 15% is offered if you mention this publication when booking your edit. Clients include: James McAvoy, Rory Kinnear, Rula Lenska, Shane Richie and Shobna Gulati, amongst others.

Replay Film & New Media
25 Museum Street, London WC1 1ST
tel 020-7637 0473
email solutions@replayfilms.co.uk
website www.replayfilms.com
established 1991

Showreel services: Although Replay can record presentations and performances from scratch, for most clients the task is to produce a carefully constructed compilation of highlights from existing TV and film performances. Advises that the correct selection and juxtaposition of these clips is essential, and it is therefore vital that clients sit-in on the editing process to ensure that they are happy with the final result. Most showreels last 4-7 minutes. Will supply scripts if requested, but does not organise for copyright clearance.

As most showreels take around 4 hours to edit, Replay has put together the following package for a fixed fee: up to 4 hours in the edit studio with the editor (digitising existing clips from VHS, capturing digitised clips onto an Avid editing suite, editing the captured clips and inserting titles where required); and 3 VHS copies. The digital master tape will be archived at 2 sites. Exact prices are available on application only. Discounted rates are available to actors, presenters, students and non-commercial theatre companies. Overtime (anything over 4 hours) is charged at approximately 50% of the commercial editing rate.

Recent clients include: Donald Standen, Julian Hanshaw, Justine Waddel, Michael Mears, Patsy Kensit, Shared Experience Theatre Company and Vicky Johnson.

The Showreel Ltd
Knightsbridge House, 229 Acton Lane, Chiswick, London, W4 5DD
tel 020-7043 8660 *fax* 020-8995 2144
email info@theshowreel.com
website www.theshowreel.com

Showreel overview:
• Free pre-session telephone/video consultation.

Resources

• Free access to our script archive and voice-over resource centre.
• 1x 90-second commercial showreel.
• 1x 90-second narrative showreel.
• One of London's top demo producers to record your reel.
• Full-day one-to-one recording session at our top London studios.
• Free digital editing, post-production and mastering.
• 5 Master CDs ready for duplication.
• Free MP3 files for easy email and web distribution.
• Free audio archiving service.
• Free marketing CD containing priceless information to get you started.

Special offer: £350 plus VAT. For other services, please visit the website.

Showreelz

28 Eastbury Road, Chiswick, London W4 2JZ
mobile (07885) 253477
email brad@showreelz.com
website www.showreelz.com
established 1998

Showreel services: Showreelz.com has been filming and editing showreels for performers for more than 10 years. The company now has a base in Chiswick, London W4. Rates are £50 per hour for filming and £30 per hour for editing.

• Shooting reels from scratch: total cost approx. £200-250. This includes company fee, studio and equipment costs, recording and editing of new material and 2 DVDs with full colour print on the DVD. Offers free consultation to actors shooting from scratch, ascertaining the roles they are most likely to be cast in and selecting pieces accordingly.
• Editing: produces reels lasting on average 2-5 minutes. Charges £30 for editing from existing material and can accept most formats. £40 DVD mastering charge to include menu design if required, full colour print on the DVD, clamshell cases and 2 copies. Further copies from £3 each. Can also put reels online or prepare reels for uploading to casting services.

Also films showcases, productions and auditions. Recent clients include: Ricci Harnett, Tamer Hassan, Rosemary Ashe, Justine Glenton, Isabel Losada, JC Mac, Eugene Washington, Abbin Galeya, Satnam Bhogul, Amy Darcy. Online payment now accepted. Offers a 15% discount on editing to actors mentioning this publication.

Voice-demo services: Supplies scripts for actors to use if desired. Total cost approx. £120 to produce a voice demo from scratch. This includes the company fee, studio and equipment costs, recording and editing of material and 2 CD copies. Rates are set at £30/hour. Normally produces voice demos lasting 2-3 minutes. Will offer a 10% discount to actors quoting this publication. Recent clients include: Kelsey Cameron, Kal Mansoor, David Lee, Brian Scoltock and Eugene Washington.

Silver-Tongued Productions

178 Ramillies Road, Sidcup DA15 9JH
tel 020-8309 0659
email contactus@silver-tongued.co.uk
website www.silver-tongued.co.uk
established 1996

Voice-demo services: Prices start at £120, depending on length of time required in studio. Silver-Tongued Productions is a small independent company. They will guide you through the whole process of recording your voice reel, from choosing scripts to directing you during the recording session, making it as simple and as easy as possible. They supply the commercials which are selected in consultation with the actor, taking into consideration the style of the voice, age etc., showing as much variety as possible. The readings are the actor's choice and can be from plays, books, poetry or prose. Again, try to show a variety. For a free brochure and a sample CD, visit their website and fill in the brochure request form on their "Contact Us" page, or give them a call.

Recent clients include: Philip Glenister, Aiden McArdle, Robert Duncan, Pip Torrens, Guy Masterton, and Jeremy Edwards. Agency recommendations include: Ken McReddie Ltd, Hobson's Voices, Foreign Voices, Break-A-Leg.

Small Screen Showreels

17 Knole Road, Crayford, London DA1 3JN
tel 020-8816 8896
email info@smallscreenshowreels.co.uk
website www.smallscreenshowreels.co.uk
Key contact Anthony Holmes

Established in 1999. Supplies scripts, premises are wheelchair-accesssible. Does not organise copyright clearance. Recent clients include: Andrew Sachs and Daisy Aitkens (both MacFarlane Chard), Frank Scantori and Vidal Sancho (both Narrow Road). Charges £40 per hour for editing with client present, or £250 (package price) for editing-by-mail. Charges up to 10 copies £3 each, up to 30 copies £2.50 each, up to 100 copies £2 each, over 100 copies price on request. Average duration of a showreel is 3.5 minutes. Spotlight members, or those who quote *Actors' Yearbook* when booking, will receive a 10% discount. Also offers assistance with selection of material for existing footage if required. Does not record voice demos, but is able to edit existing ones if required.

SonicPond Studio

70 Mildmay Grove South, Islington, London N1 4PJ
tel 020-7690 8561
email martin@sonicpond.co.uk
website www.sonicpond.co.uk
Key contact Martin Fisher

Showreel services: Supplies scripts for actors to use if desired. Charges £200 (£175 for students) to film a showreel from existing material only, with 3 copies included in the price and extra copies charged at £2.50 each. The average duration of a showreel is 4 minutes. Clients include: Edmund Kente and Annie Cooper (Felix de Wolfe); Zoe Lister (Williamson & Holmes); Rhian Green (Emptage Hallett); and Shaun Prendergast (Brown & Simcox). Advises actors: "Don't worry that you may not have enough material; you most likely do. Less is truly more with showreels. Also, don't wait for that copy of the student film you have been waiting to be sent, think of the reel as an organic growing thing which you will add to and change for the whole of your career. Just get it started."

Voice-demo services: Supplies scripts for actors to use if desired. Charges £295 to produce a voice demo from scratch; working from existing material the hourly rate is £40. 3 CDs are included in the package, with extra copies charged at £2 each. Average total duration of the demo is 7-8 minutes. Students receive a discounted package of £250 for a full voicereel; for actors, Spotlight clips (4x30-second pieces) are charged at £85. Voice clients include: Bob Golding (Hobsons); Nicholas Keith (Yakety Yak); Kellie Bright (Sue Terry Voices); Sam & Mark (Harvey Voices); Zoe Lister (Harvey Voices); and James Alexandrou (Earache). Advises actors: "Don't worry about the pieces – everyone does. We will work together to find you the best material; it's much more about finding the tone for each piece on the day, which is our job in directing you. In the meantime, listen to as much voiceover as possible, and think about what works and why."

Take Five
37 Beak Street, London W1F
tel 020-7287 2120 *fax* 020-7287 3035
email info@takefivestudio.com
website www.takefivestudio.com
Key contact Charlie Lort-Phillips
established 1995

Showreel services: Charges £70 per hour for filming and £45 per hour for editing (this includes all studio and equipment costs). VHS copies are priced at £6 each, DVDs at £13 each and CDs at £6 each. Discounts are offered for bigger quantities.

A script consultation is held with each actor, preferably 7 days prior to filming. Scenes can be shot in the studio or on location and benefit from professional direction, lighting and cameramen. Most showreels last around 5 minutes. The company advises actors who are sending in existing material only to cue scenes on the tape or to have the timecodes written down to speed up the capturing process.

Recent clients include: Siobhan Hewlett (Hamilton Hodell), Harry Eden (ICM), Lee Ingleby (Conway van Gelder) and Tim Barlow (Paul Becker).

Twitch Films
22 Grove End Gardens, 18 Abbey Road, London NW8 9LL
tel 020-7266 0946
email post@twitchfilms.co.uk
website www.twitchfilms.co.uk

Established in 2006; offices are fully wheelchair-accessible. Working with existing material, charges a flat fee of £200, which includes editing, design of DVD interface and discprint, 10 professionally printed and packaged DVDs, digital files for use on the Internet, websites and for emailing, and full archiving. For shorter edits and updates the hourly rate is £40; additional discs can be ordered from £2.50 each, depending on quantity. The average duration of a showreel is 3-5 minutes.

"We advise recording material from scratch only in exceptional circumstances, primarily when an aspect of the actor's range, which would be key to their castability, is under-represented in their existing footage. We do not provide scripts, but will give detailed advice on what scripts may be appropriate, and assist in making the selection." Recent clients include: Darren Boyd and Eleanor Matsuura (Amanda Howard Associates); Colin Salmon (GMM); Jane Perry (Andrew Manson Personal Management); Kevork Malikyan (United Agents); and Trevor White (Price Gardner Management).

Ken Wheeler
Sound, 4 St Pauls Road, Clifton, Bristol BS8 1LT
tel 0117-973 4595
email kenwheeler@mac.com
website www.soundat4.com

Established in 1987. Supplies scripts. Recent clients include: Jaguar, The Co-Op, Alfa Romeo, Scholastic Education and Bristol City Council.

Details of voice demo services: Normal hourly rate is £100. For £350 will produce a voice demo from scratch, working with new material and including direction, recording, editing and mixing – work can take up to 8 hours. During a pre-production meeting, commercial and corporate scripts, narration, prose and poetry will be selected that are suited to the particular voice to provide a varied and balanced demo.

Performers careers advice service

Give your career the attention it deserves, with this invaluable advice from Beverley Hills, one of only three Equity-accredited performance careers advisers in the country.

As an actress, I'm lucky to have carved for myself what has been termed a 'freelance portfolio career'. This means that I do several freelance jobs in between performing.

My own journey in the Arts began working backstage at the Birmingham Rep, moving on to dressing at the RSC, then designing Opera in Italy, before becoming a jazz singer and finally an actress. I am also a commissioned writer with a Masters Degree, which gives me knowledge of Higher and Further Education opportunities, plus the funding issues that face freelancers. Experiencing all these different backgrounds at first-hand gives me a wider than average skills-base when it comes to my work as an accredited careers adviser.

What is the service, and who is it for?

The Performers Careers Advice Service was piloted by Equity and Skillset, and is now fully supported by Equity. It is an advice service that is available to all performers, regardless of their area of specialism. You might be a circus performer, dancer, actor, singer, variety performer, DJ, VJ (Video Jockey) or burlesque stripper – anything you can do in front of an audience is termed 'performance' (steady now!), and as a performer you are eligible to benefit from the service.

The service is available to everyone, no matter what their level of experience or expertise. I have advised new entrants, returners, and those who simply feel that their career is stuck in a rut. My clients have included those at the very top of their game: big TV and film celebrities, who perhaps need no help to find work, but instead are trying to rediscover their passion for performing.

How does it work?

There are three accredited advisers (two in London and one in the North West) who offer the service on a freelance basis. All three of us are working practitioners with a wealth of shared experience, covering stage, TV, radio and theatre, plus our own specialisms – so we're not stuck behind a dusty computer terminal looking at stats and telling you how to do your job; we're out there in the field, working ourselves as we gather vital practical information about the wonderful, ever-changing business of performing. Furthermore, we're experienced in the age-old problem of how to survive when you're not working!

After contacting one of us directly (our biographies and email addresses can be found at **www.skillset.org/careers/services/access_careers_advisors/**), you will be sent an online application form to complete. This gives us an idea of where you are in your career, and what you would like to achieve. A number of performers are returners, having been out of the business for a while for whatever reason; some people haven't worked for a spell, or need to know how to find an agent; and some are seeking permission to leave the business. Whatever your position, as your adviser I will help facilitate movement or change.

After I receive your completed application form, I will do some research into how best to help your achieve your goals. You will then be invited to attend a one-to-one session. My sessions take place in London and last for 60 minutes. During the session together we devise a tailormade action plan, which is specifically designed to encourage progression.

Subsequent to this initial meeting there is a follow-up service, where you have the opportunity to see the same adviser for the sake of continuity, or to talk to another in order to get a fresh perspective. Once you've seen an adviser you can also take advantage of the free email service for any questions that may subsequently spring up. There's no need to feel isolated any longer, which is a common trait in our business. You are fully supported for as long as you want to be.

The wonderful thing about being an accredited adviser is that I have privileged access to the profession, with links to casting directors, agents, directors, producers, etc. that are usually denied the working actor. I can ask direct questions, and pass on information to you, the client, 'from the horse's mouth'. I can tell it like it actually is, rather than reverting to mere speculation or outdated hearsay.

What if I change my mind?
Occasionally, performers do change their minds between filling out an application form and meeting me – and that's fine. Often, simply writing down your list of goals can help clarify the muddy waters. It's hard for performers to talk rationally about their careers: spouses and agents have heard it all before, and other actors are probably in the same boat. It can all end up with a collective moan down the pub, which may be therapeutic but is not necessarily productive! Our service is objective, confidential and based in extensive experience. We look honestly at your career and give you up-to-date advice about CVs, photos, agents, marketing and all the other elements involved in being a performer.

But does the service work?
That depends on how much effort you think your career is worth. Last time my acting work was once again thin on the ground, I took a long, hard and *objective* look at myself as a performer, and noted where I could make some changes (some of the same changes I also encourage my clients to make, by the way). It took a year to fully make all the adjustments, which included some classes, a revamp of my marketing strategies and, most of all, a significant weight loss. Did it work? Put it this way: I got my first theatre job in a long time, playing Shirley Valentine at The Garrick, which sold out every night and broke all box office records.

What will it cost me?
The current prices are:
• For a 60-minute session: £40.00
• For a 60-minute follow-up session: £35.00

How can I apply?
You can find the advisers' full biographies and contact details at www.skillset.org/careers/services/access_careers_advisors/. Otherwise, visit **www.equity.org.uk** – and give your career a boost.

Beverley Hills has a wide-ranging portfolio career as an actress, voice-over artiste, TV presenter and writer, Equity careers adviser and workshop leader, Skillset course accreditor and workshop leader, NCDT performance reviewer, ITC trainer and University/Drama School lecturer. She was recently appointed Creative Adviser for the Westminster-based charity 'Dream Arts'. For more information, visit **www.beverleyhills.co.uk**.

Resources

The five steps to successful networking

Shaun Prendergast

There are two qualities required to become successful in this business. One is talent, the other the willingness to learn about the business of being an actor. Networking daunts most of us, but it is essential in acting, where the normal career pattern consists of short-term contracts for a variety of employers interspersed with meetings which may bear fruit in the future. Once you have met and worked with someone, chances are you'll do it again and again. But networking is how you initially meet new people, and meeting people for the first time is how you get that first, all-important job with them. Nothing will get you work like personal contacts – by people thinking of you *before* they go to the casting directories.

But of course, you hate networking. A lot of people feel like this even in the commercial world, but the problem is exacerbated in the arts, where there is a lingering feeling that an actor who approaches their career with a strategy is somehow compromising their artistic standards. This is amateurish rubbish. It matters hugely in this business who you know, not because it is ruled by nepotism, but because personal recommendation lies at the heart of all casting. Basically, no-one recommends you for a job unless they've seen your work themselves, or met you in person. Contacts are all, so follow these five simple networking rules and you'll gain in confidence, form a wider circle of contacts and get more work.

1. Be charmed, not charming

Remember, everyone you meet while networking is also networking too – and is probably as ambivalent about it as you are. Where most actors slip up is in thinking that networking is about selling themselves as performers to strangers, without the comfort of a character to hide behind. It isn't, and once you acknowledge this, you'll relax.

Of course, you must be positive about your talents but you don't need to 'perform' in any way – just be yourself. Successful networkers know that networking isn't just about making other people interested in you; it's about you being interested in them. People like to be able to make a personal recommendation, because it increases their own status as someone who possesses a wide circle of contacts. But you will only spring to mind if they've had some form of comfortable contact with you. The surest way of making someone uncomfortable is to foist yourself or your career details on them without first establishing a bond between you. So listen rather than speak.

And as you listen, you'll be gaining a deeper understanding of how the business works: who runs theatres or TV departments, who commissions, how finance is raised, how a series is created, what a film storyboard is. The value of this is simple – the more you know, the better you'll be able to appreciate what your own role is. You'll also be ahead of the game when it comes to understanding changes in direction within the industry, and be able to plan your strategy accordingly. Remember, your career is *your* responsibility – not your agent's (they are part of your strategy, not the sum of it), but you. You are only as good as your contacts. So you must cultivate contacts in every aspect of the business, because they in turn will provide you with more contacts.

2. Be businesslike

Adopting the right tone when you communicate is essential, as are correct spelling and grammar – no text-speak or slang. And don't fall for the 'make your message stand out by adding a poem/petal/aphorism' school of thought. Such devices make you look like a needy child, not a fellow professional. Keep messages brief, polite, businesslike and to the point.

You will meet thousands of contacts throughout your career, and forget most of them, unless you keep a record. Create a contacts file on your computer, and a profile for each person you have ever met in the business – every fellow student, tutor, playwright, actor, director, etc.; what they look like, where you met them and so on. Add new people every week, and update once a month. I'm not talking about stalking here, just creating an *aide memoire* for the future.

Has the casting director called you in before? Have you appeared in or studied other work by the author? Checking this stuff means you don't insult someone by forgetting them – which can easily happen – and it also gives you something to talk about, should you be asked. It helps enormously to know a director's work – have you seen a production of theirs you can talk about?

You need business cards, good quality, giving your agent or contact details. You also need really good photos, which actually look like you. Join social networking sites (such as Facebook) and become allied to as many theatre, film and TV organisations as you can. Create a Wikipedia entry, and update it. Create links to favourable reviews of your work or the shows you are in. Check if any film or TV work you do is included in an IMBD rating, and update it. Get excellent showreels and a website. Work at it. This is not school, where it's cool to do as little as possible; this is the business where graft counts. To stay in the game for the long term, it's important to remember to cultivate contacts in the generation before you as well as the established figures you meet. In ten years' time the fresh-faced wunderkind you vaguely remember could be producing a movie with you in it – if they know who you are.

3. Start with those you know

You already have a network. The people you train with are your most valuable asset – there is a bond there which may survive a lifetime, so stay in contact and share those contacts. This is not just a matter of swapping names, it's about going to see people in shows, meeting casting directors and writers and theatre directors, and then keeping a log of those you've met.

If you hear of a job going for someone you know, tell them. If you can recommend them, even better. Like for you, these initial contacts will gradually widen their own circles of contact and influence. Some of the people you share grotty flats with and see at old school reunions will end up running the very companies you're both desperately trying to get work with now. Staying in contact with each other and promoting each other throughout your careers is essential.

4. Never turn down an invitation

Most actors tend to isolate themselves when they're not working, and then reconnect when they are. But it is impossible to tell when you will make a valuable contact – and for that reason you must go to any gathering you can, to learn, and to network. This is especially true of something you've actually been invited to, and can gain entry to free!

Resources

Get out there, and meet people in the flesh. Go to first nights, to talks, to festivals. If you are invited to a play reading, be there, and stay and talk afterwards. Somewhere out there are people who could employ you, and would do so if they know you existed. Go find them.

5. Be the first to keep in touch

If you go to see a show you like, send a message of thanks to the director. Again, keep messages brief (two lines is good), businesslike and positive. If you get a casting, ditto: a short message of thanks to the director, producer and casting director. Let people know if you have a show on – send emails to everyone on your contact list.

One of the best ways you can increase your profile is to create new work and get it seen. This is where the Internet is in its infancy and where the rules change by the week. Where once the only chance of spreading the word was by persuading people to see you in Rep or Fringe shows, this is now no longer the case. YouTube, podcasts and whatever other forms of self-broadcasting come along next are incredibly effective methods of establishing a profile cheaply and getting it to a wider audience. Learn to use them. Write your own stuff (or persuade someone else to write it for you) and get it out there.

Finally, a word of warning. These five rules are not to be applied sometime, or next week, or when you feel like it. If you are serious about this career, they should be applied now, today, every day. Tomorrow depends on it.

Shaun Prendergast is an award-winning actor and writer. Recent acting work includes Mr Boo in *The Rise and Fall of Little Voice* in the West End (directed by Terry Johnson), Detective Superintendant Mike Evans in *Collision* for ITV (directed by Mark Evans), and Heinrich in the feature film *Fast Track No Limits* (directed by Axel Sand). His writing credits include *Eastenders*, *Roman Mysteries* and *The Lightning Kid* (all BBC), and *Rocket Man* (ITV Coastal).

Do actors need to live in the South-East?

Nigel Collins

I was appalled to be asked to write this article as I did not realise that here in Wakefield in West Yorkshire we were not in the South-East. Actually, fellow professionals who live in Northumberland would claim that we are just about a suburb of London. In fact, it is possible to be in the heart of London within a couple of hours of leaving home via GNER and tube or cab. If there is enough notice of auditions it is also possible to buy fairly cheap train tickets online (yes, we have entered the 21st century oop North!).

Having left drama school in Manchester nearly 28 years ago and only living in London when needing to do so when working there, I feel confident in being able to say that it is possible to live outside the southeast and have an acting career. However, wherever we live as actors, we all depend on the contacts we make, the hard work of our agent, good fortune and to a large extent our network of friends in the business locally. There are many such networks outside London. For instance, many actors in Newcastle or Liverpool can and do have rewarding and busy careers without ever having to consider leaving their home cities as there is plenty of work around in local theatres and regional television dramas and series. Speaking personally, as a 'regional actor', i.e. what film-school hot-shot directors refer to as 'General Northern', I have done pretty well playing the 'Yorkshire' card over the years, a card that could well be trumped if played anywhere but in the relevant area. The resultant casting opportunities are almost always in the north – Manchester or Leeds generally for ITV, but increasingly over recent years the BBC have been casting in London productions to be shot in the regions; during the 80s and 90s they seemed to cast away from headquarters, but alas not as often these days. There was probably some money-saving memo from a corporate suit who had never been further north than Hampstead. Of course, I am willing to withdraw this slur immediately for the sake of a casting opportunity. No use upsetting people unnecessarily.

Earlier I mentioned the need for a good agent. Vital anywhere, but perhaps more so in the regions; in the south-east and London it is possible to keep up with all the latest tittle-tattle, gossip, rumour and speculation if one is a skilled networker, being physically remote from London means that one is very reliant on the hard work of an agent to keep up with all the latest casting news and to act on it.

We can all supplement the work that our agent does by looking at theatre websites and writing suggesting our suitability for whatever is coming up in the next season. Obviously, this can be done from anywhere, but, if the casting breakdown is for certain theatre companies it is a positive advantage to be northern based. Barrie Rutter at Northern Broadsides and John Godber at Hull Truck are just two directors who discriminate positively in favour of northern-based northerners. In part, this is to do with cost savings that are available by employing an actor who does not qualify for subsistence but more usually because directors have long realised that there is a large 'pool' of good performers on their doorstep. So there is no real need to trudge down the M 1 to spend a couple of days in some overpriced

Resources

church hall with no heating, a comedy reverberating echo and a steady stream of RADA and Central graduates doing their 'Ee bah gum, I'll go to t' foot of our stairs' salt-of-the-earth types when they know very well that they only have to whistle down the nearest Actor's Centre workshop in Manchester or Leeds to have half a dozen potential David Threlfalls or Judi Denches champing at the bit to give their 'Now is the winter..' in their best Brighouse dialect. None of this is intended to give the impression that we regional types regard ourselves as somehow 'special' or more, how shall I put it, gifted, than our fellow strugglers marooned in the congestion zone that is the southeast, but we know what we know. But you knew that already didn't you?

Within an hour's drive of our affordable three bedroom mid-nineteenth century cottage there are at least a dozen theatres creating new and interesting work alongside the usual rep fare needed to guarantee their continued existence. I am thinking about places with international reputations such as West Yorkshire Playhouse in Leeds, The Royal Exchange in Manchester, Crucible Theatre in Sheffield, Hull Truck and Pilot Theatre in York. A little further afield there is NTC National Touring in Northumberland (which in 2008 will be hosting the Pride of Place festival for touring theatre companies), Theatre By The Lake in Keswick and Duke's Playhouse in Lancaster amongst others.

There is not a great deal of fringe theatre around out of London; which many of us think of as rather a good thing! In-between jobs are also more difficult to come by in parts of the country with higher unemployment, with proportionately more people competing for what few opportunities there are. In the past it was always possible to 'pick up' a job for a while, leave to fulfil a theatre contract and return to the same employer. More recently, those same employers are likely to recruit permanent staff that can be relied on to be there all the time. In these days of ongoing employee development, staff appraisals and one-to-ones actors do not seem to fit into the corporate structure. Except when we are employed by that same organisation to enter the workplace to role-play during training days!

Fortunately, many corporate videos and training films are made around the country in addition to a constant stream of TV and film commercials, usually cast (in my case) in Manchester or Leeds. Of course the usual ratio of castings to jobs applies – about 50 to 1! To a certain extent the availability of such jobs depends on the economy and the willingness of companies to spend money. In times of recession it is noticeable that this aspect of the business tends to withdraw back to the southeast.

On a practical level there are plenty of photographers, voice coaches and singing teachers available. I travel 30 miles down the M1 to Sheffield for my publicity shots, but due to the joys of the internet am able to have the repros printed in London and mailed direct to my agent in Manchester. I mentioned the Actor's Centre earlier; there are many and varied workshops that take place in Manchester and Leeds, which are very popular with us northerners. There is not yet a voice class to help get rid of the RP that seeps into our natural speech from time to time but I'm sure it is on the cards.

Most actors would answer 'quality of life' if asked why they choose to live away from London. The cost of living, housing, insurance and travel are all far lower. It is possible to find a good state school without too much trouble. A car journey is measured in minutes and hours, not days and weeks. We have fantastic open spaces in our cities, most of which have undergone regeneration that puts them on a par with many of our European neighbours. The Lake District, North York Moors, Yorkshire Dales and the Peak District National Parks are all an easy drive. The rugged coastline of North Yorkshire and the pleasures of Blackpool are 90 minutes away.

The one thing that the vast majority of we 'distance-theatricals' accept is the need to be prepared to travel to London at short notice for auditions and interviews (on occasion, for theatres or TV companies not far from home!). This can be expensive if there is no time to purchase cheaper tickets, making a £150 hole in the weekly budget, but that is the price one has to be prepared to pay to stay in the mainstream of the business. There are actors, as I mentioned above, who manage to work consistently in their local areas and have no desire to travel elsewhere. For instance, in Newcastle, some actors have been in the ensemble at Northern Stage for approaching 8 years. This consistency of employment benefits local theatres and TV companies who have a reliable pool of experienced actors to choose from and the actors themselves who do not need to worry about chasing every job prospect in other 'circles' of the industry.

The reader must understand that all of the above is written from the standpoint of a Tyke and all that that entails. In no way should any of this piece be construed as an invitation to sell up and move to the regions. We're not very welcoming and we can do without any upward inflation on house prices, thank you very much.

Editor's note: Since this article was written, there has been a rapid expansion in opportunities to audition via the Internet – see Nancy Bishop's article *Marketing and the Internet: maintaining your online presence* on page 372.

Nigel Collins was born in the late 1950s at the correct side of the Pennines, and grew up in the Heavy Woollen District of the West Riding of Yorkshire in an area famed as the World capital of mungo and shoddy manufacture. Not having much clue as to what these (allegedly) textile processes might entail, he took the safe option and went to Manchester Poly School of Theatre. Not having much clue what that entailed either. However, learning the intricacies of collar studs, phonetics and 5&9 has been a boon ever since, especially useful for small scale touring. Realising that it WAS possible for 'Oop Northerners' to work in theatre and television despite what he had been told, Nigel has assiduously extended his playing age from 23 to 63. By the time you come to read this it may be old news as Nigel fully expects the industry to come to its senses, so you will probably have heard him telling his story on *Desert Island Discs*, *Parky* or at the very least *Friday Night with Jonathon Ross*.

Tax and National Insurance for actors
Philippe Carden

Actors enjoy a rare hybrid status. They are treated as self-employed for income tax purposes but as employees for National Insurance. This combination brings with it a number of advantages, but also certain complications. Many actors choose to instruct an accountant to benefit from those advantages, and to avoid the pitfalls created by the complications.

The income tax advantages include being able to claim a deduction for expenses against income in arriving at taxable net profit (or allowable loss), provided that those expenses are incurred "wholly and exclusively for the purposes of the trade". *The Equity Advice and Rights Guide*, available free of charge to its members, provides a very helpful list of usually allowable expenses, with suitable notes to restrain the enthusiasm of actors to stretch definitions to their limits. Self-imposed restraint in claiming for expenses is sensible in minimising the risk of being selected for an Inland Revenue enquiry. Some accountants produce their own list.

It is helpful to assess the types of expense according to the risk of being challenged by the Revenue. Here are some examples:

Low risk or No risk
• Commission paid to agent (including VAT)
• Annual subscription to Equity
• Travel and subsistence on tour
• Photographs and publicity (repros, *Spotlight* entry)
• Classes to maintain skills, e.g. voice, movement
• Business stationery and postage
• Fee paid to accountant

Medium risk
• Professional library – scripts, books, CDs
• Publications – *The Stage, Time Out*
• Travel and subsistence when not on tour
• Visits to theatre and cinema

High risk
• Wardrobe – renewal, dry cleaning and repair
• Hairdressing and make-up
• Gratuities to dressers and stage door-keepers
• Home as office

As the risk rises, so too must the care taken in deciding which to claim and which to discard. Engaging an accountant to use his or her experience, skill and judgement in carrying out a review of expenditure claims is a source of considerable reassurance to many actors. It is worth noting that entertaining, as in paying a meal for another person (even if a casting director), is never allowed.

An accountant's review may also be key in calculating the business proportions of motor car expenses, land-line and mobile telephone charges, and television and video hire and television licence. An accountant's help in computing capital allowances for expenditure on capital items (computer, motor car, musical instruments) is appreciated by all but the most self-confident.

The emphasis so far has been on the income tax advantages of being self-employed. Whilst many actors are happy to register themselves as self-employed within the three-month time limit, others enlist the help of an accountant even at that stage to provide a buffer-zone between themselves and the Inland Revenue. Once registration is done, a Unique Taxpayer Reference ('UTR') will be issued, often still referred to as a Schedule D number. Unless preventative action is taken at the time of registration, or very soon afterwards, a costly national insurance (NI) pitfall will trap the unwary actor.

If an actor is to be treated as an employee for NI, s/he certainly does not want to be seen as self-employed for NI as well. Such duplication is costly and usually brings no additional benefits. A common solution is to apply for small earnings exception (SEE) from the flat-rate weekly NI paid by 'normal' self-employed people – Class 2 – by completing and submitting form CF10.

For actors who do some work abroad and/or who write and direct as well as perform, the solution is more likely to involve paying Class 2 but applying for deferment of Class 4. That class of NI is the earnings-related charge borne by 'normal' self-employed people in addition to the flat-rate Class 2. It confers no benefits to the payer and is collected by the Inland Revenue as part of the self-assessment system.

The complexities of the NI regime, and especially the interaction of its different classes, encourage co-operation between actor and accountant at least as much as does the application of the criteria for acceptability of expenses for income tax purposes.

So, the basic bundle of services provided by an accountant includes the following:
• Annual income and expenditure account
• Capital allowances computations
• Advice on NI and the necessary form-filling
• Completion of the annual Tax Return
• Preparing a tax calculation and checking the Revenue's version
Additional services would include completing quarterly returns for actors successful enough to be registered for VAT, and advice on the tax and NI implications of performing abroad.

Most accountants charge according to time spent and the seniority and expertise of the persons doing the work. Here is an example of how this might work in practice for a young actor: he would need four hours of a book-keeper at £30 per hour (£120), plus an hour for a manager's review and tax return (£50); an hour of the manager's time to sort out the NI (£50); and finally half-an-hour of the principal's/partner's time for overall review and quality control (£50). With perhaps a few telephone calls or a shortish meeting, the annual fee would typically be £340 plus VAT, i.e. £399.50.

In my experience, as the cost of the initial meeting is rarely charged for, I make a loss in year 1 of a new client. I break even in year 2, and only make a profit in year 3 and subsequent years. It is not a surprise therefore that I see my relationship with a client as a long-term one, one which has time and effort invested in it by both actor and accountant.

To an actor in the early years of his career, the accountant's annual fee of about £400 represents a significant expense. The decision to instruct an accountant is a personal one. Some actors are much more comfortable and confident than others in dealing with money matters, taxation and National Insurance. Others shy away from such a course of action and choose to have an ally in the form of an accountant.

In general terms, for an actor with gross earnings of less than £15,000 but who still makes a profit, having an accountant is optional. For one with smaller earnings and who makes a loss, having an accountant could be worthwhile to use that loss effectively. For those with gross earnings in excess of £15,000, the choice is compelling.

Having made the decision to use an accountant, choose the firm carefully. The most desired method is word of mouth. A personal recommendation from another actor, from your drama school or indeed from the company manager works well. It is important that the accountant selected know about the taxation and NI of actors rather than being a general practitioner. It is also important that the accountant be a member of one of the professional bodies of accountants as an indication of quality – and just in case a dispute arises which cannot be resolved amicably. Most of the institutes have a system of arbitration for fee disputes, for example, which can be used as a last resort.

Another factor in the choice of accountant is the size of the firm. The range is huge: from a sole practitioner to a multinational firm employing thousands. The former will be suitable for an actor of modest means, while the latter might be a good match for a performer with very considerable earnings and royalties from several countries around the world. In between those extremes are smaller firms with one to five partners and which specialise in the tax affairs of those who work in theatre, television and film, and larger firms which have an entertainment and media department with a similar specialism. The smaller firms are likely to provide a more personal service and lower fees. The larger are likely to have access to a greater breadth of related expertise (such as film finance, production accounting) but fees will be correspondingly higher.

Each accountant will have his or her favoured way for actors to keep records. The most important point is that an actor must co-operate with his or her accountant to save time and maximise the return on effort. Here are some guidelines and handy hints:
• Keep all agent's remittance advices, payslips and invoices.
• Only claim expenses incurred "wholly and exclusively for the purposes of the trade".
• Use the Equity list of usually allowable expenses for guidance.
• Keep receipts for all expenses and write explanatory notes on them (for example, "for audition with X")
• File away carefully details of any interest or dividends received, jobseeker's allowance claimed, Gift Aid payments made and any other item which may be needed to complete your tax return.
• Deliver your accounts papers to your accountant as soon as you can after the end of the tax year – never leave it until close to the 31st January deadline! (*Note* From 2008, all paper self-assessment returns must be received by 30th September. If you file online, you will have another two months until 30th November. Deadline for payment of any tax owing remains 31st January.)

Philippe Carden is a chartered accountant specialising in the taxation of actors and other individuals working in theatre, film, television and dance, onstage and backstage, artistic and technical. He co-wrote *Investing in West End Theatrical Productions* (Robert Hale, 1992) and has written articles for *The Guardian*, *The Stage* and other publications.

Accountants

M Barnfather & Co
15 Birley Street, Blackpool FY1 1DU
tel (01253) 622519 *fax* (01253) 294179
email mike@mikebarnfather.co.uk
Accountant Michael Barnfather

Founded in 1974. Charges between £150 and £250 for preparation of accounts and submission of tax return. Provides support by means of face-to-face meetings, phone and email (mostly phone and email). Provides Excel spreadsheets and Money Manager (cashbook accounting software, compatible with most PCs but not Mac or Linux) if necessary. 3 clients are actors, but other clients include circus artistes, magicians, singers and dancers. Offices are not wheelchair-accessible (2nd floor). "We encourage all clients to keep proper accounting records (we advise them on their specific requirements), and to forward tax correspondence (including Self-Assessment return forms) directly to us as soon as received."

Breckman & Company
49 South Molton Street, London W1K 5LH
tel 020-7499 2292 *fax* 020-7408 1151
email info@breckmanandcompany.co.uk
website www.breckmanandcompany.co.uk
Accountants Kevin Beale, Graham Berry, Robert Breckman, Richard Nelson

Established for more than 40 years. Costs are dictated by complexity and time spent. Initial meeting is free during which the fee structure will be discussed. Client support includes face-to-face meetings, phone and email (included in the price).

P O'N Carden
56-58 High Street, Ewell, Surrey KT17 1RW
tel 020-8394 2957 *fax* 020-8394 2722
email philippe@poncarden.com
Accountants Philippe Carden, Manine Head

Founded in 1977. Charges £400 ("in the early years") for a complete set of accounts and tax return. "Time and complexity increase this – up to £2000 to include quarterly VAT returns. Tailor-made packages for really complex cases." Provides face-to-face meetings in central London. "My actor clients make clear how much support they feel they need, and the programme of work is tailored accordingly." Provides Excel spreadsheets appropriate to the client's needs. 40% of clients are actors; 45% are other entertainment industry professionals. The offices are not wheelchair accessible, but meetings can be held in wheelchair-accessible locations. Advises actors *not* to "just give your accountant bags of receipts. Provide information about why you are claiming particular expenses. Do be obsessive about keeping payslips and remittance advices".

Mark Carr & Co
Garrick House, 26-27 Southampton Street, Covent Garden, London WC2E 7RS
tel 020-7717 8474
email info@markcarr.co.uk
63 Lansdowne Place, Hove, East Sussex BN3 1FL
tel (01273) 778802 *fax* (01273) 778822
website www.markcarr.co.uk
Accountant Mark Carr (FCCA)

Provides individual service according to the client's requirements. Annual accounts for the HM Revenue & Customs tax return as well as a whole range of services are offered. Fees can be calculated on time spent basis or a fixed fee – £250 upwards, depending on the complexity. Payment terms can be varied to suit the client. First meeting is free of charge. Free advice service on a one-to-one basis on tax and book-keeping are offered at The Actors Centre. Very popular free downloadable Excel spreadsheets available from the website to clients and non-clients. 50% of client base are actors, 50% are other entertainment professionals. The London office has wheelchair access. "We have over 370 clients, who range from those starting out to those with celebrity status."

Count & See Limited
219 Macmillan Way, London SW17 6AW
tel 020-8767 7882 *fax* 0845-004 3454
email info@countandsee.com
website www.countandsee.com

Charges an annual fee of £250 (plus VAT) upwards, depending on the amount of work involved. Provides actor clients with face-to-face, phone and email support. The trading office is wheelchair-accessible. "Before setting up my own practice, I worked for a number of firms specialising in the entertainment industry, so I have experience in advising such clients."

Dub & Co
7 Torriano Mews, Torriano Avenue, London NW5 2RZ
tel 020-7284 8686 *fax* 020-7284 8687
email office@dub.co.uk
Accountants George Dub, Joyce Davies

Chartered, certified accountants established in 1979. Charges from £400 + VAT for preparation of accounts for a tax return. Provides face-to-face meetings, phone and email support included in this fee. Does not provide software or spreadsheet templates to clients. Handles the tax and accountancy affairs of around 50 actors and 100 other entertainment industry professionals. The company's offices are wheelchair accessible.

Dunbar & Co
70 South Lambeth Road, London SW8 1RL
tel 020-7820 0082 *fax* 020-7820 0806
email mason@equitax.co.uk
Accountants Nick Mason (Senior Partner), Bob Long

Founded in 1896. Fees are on a time-cost basis, depending on the complexity of the client's tax affairs, but a typical fee range for an actor would be £330-£420 p.a. Support is provided via various means, including face-to-face meetings, phone and email. Provides spreadsheet templates for clients, which require Microsoft Excel. 50% of clients are actors, with a further 15%, other entertainment-industry professionals. Offices are wheelchair-accessible.

"We offer a full accountancy service, including bookkeeping, VAT, tax returns, tax advice, assistance with Revenue investigations, limited company accounts, personal and corporate tax planning. Our sister company, Sandford Dunbar, is authorised by the FSA as an independent financial adviser specialising in personal financial and pension planning."

Fisher Berger & Associates
Devonshire House, 582 Honeypot Lane, Stanmore, Middlesex HA7 1JS
tel 020-8732 5500 *fax* 020-8732 5501
email nik@fisherberger.com
website www.fisherberger.com
Accountant Nik Fisher FFA FCCA

Established in 2005. Charges between £250 and £750 on average, depending on the amount of work involved. Offers actors face-to-face and email / phone support: "as much as they require; our policy is to teach actors how best to keep their books and records, to save on accountancy fees". Provides spreadsheet templates in Excel and for VAT analysis, suitable for a range of software platforms. Around 15% of clients are actors, and 25% other professionals in the entertainment industry.

Jonathan Ford & Co
The Coach House, 31 View Road, Rainhill, Merseyside L35 0LF
tel 0151-426 4512
email info@jonathanford.co.uk
website www.jonathanford.co.uk
Accountant Jonathan Ford

Charges from £275 to £450, depending on the level of bookkeeping the client has done themselves. All fees are agreed in advance. Client service is comprehensive and includes face-to-face meetings, telephone and email support, all included within the fee. "Using the Internet we can meet the needs of clients all over the country." Supplies Excel spreadsheet templates, so MS Office is required; the software is suitable for all operating systems. Has around 10 actor clients and 40 other entertainment

industry professionals. Offices are not wheelchair-accessible. Advises actors to "see our 10 tax commandments!".

Goldwins
75 Maygrove Road, London NW6 2EG
tel 020-7372 6494 *fax* 020-7624 0053
email aepton@goldwins.co.uk
website www.goldwins.co.uk
Accountant Anthony Epton

Established in 1987. Specialises in the entertainment industry, handling the tax and bookkeeping affairs of around 200 actors. Charges around £400 for preparation of an actor's tax return, although this can vary from £250 up to £1000 depending on the complexity of the job. Provides face-to-face meetings, phone and email support included in this price. Does not provide software or spreadsheet templates. The company's offices are wheelchair accessible.

Goodman Jones LLP
29/30 Fitzroy Square, London W1P 6LQ
tel 020-7388 2444 *fax* 020-7388 6736
email jrf@goodmanjones.com
website www.goodmanjones.com
Partner Julian Flitter

Founded in 1934. "Each person is different and we tailor our support to the clients needs, so costs can range from £250 to £500 for more complex returns involving international aspects and multiple categories of income." This amount would include any support required in the form of face-to-face meetings, phone calls, letters and emails. "The range of services we offer includes tax compliance services from personal tax returns and VAT returns, advice on whether or not to incorporate as a limited company, when to register for VAT, how to deal with working abroad, bookkeeping services, preparation of financial accounts (limited company, sole trader, LLP or partnership) as well as full personal tax planning and company secretarial and payroll services." Can supply software templates to clients as required, but recommends "keeping it simple". Offices are wheelchair accessible.

Hard Dowdy
23-28 Great Russell Street, London WC1B 3NG
tel 020-7436 2171 *fax* 020-7436 4923
email info@harddowdy.com
website www.harddowdy.com
Accountants Tim Waters, Jacqui Lee Foster

Fees are charged on a time-spent basis and on average range between £450 and £750, depending on the complexity and quality of the records provided. Client support includes face-to-face meetings, telephone and email services. The company is based in the West End and currently acts as auditors and advisers to Equity – "a specialist firm, offering a comprehensive service". Depending on the size of a client's business, offers Sage accounting packages to tailored Excel spreadsheets. Has around 350 actor clients and 50 other entertainment industry professionals. Offices are wheelchair accessible. "Accurate records, maintained regularly, will save time, tax and accountancy fees!"

Harris Coombs & Co

5 Jaggard Way, London SW12 8SG
tel 020-8675 6880 *fax* 020-8675 7017
email mailbox@harriscoombs.co.uk
website www.harriscoombs.co.uk
Partners Graham Harris FCCA, Richard Coombs FCA

Charges to prepare actors' accounts for annual Inland Revenue tax returns range from £500-£1000. Charges vary depending on figures and VAT. Client support includes: face-to-face meetings, phone, email (all included in the price). Personal service in all financial matters: tax, NI, VAT etc. Of client base 15% are actors and 20% are other entertainment industry professionals.

Harveys LLP

The Old Winery, Lamberhurst Vineyard, Lamberhurst, Kent TN3 8ER
tel (01892) 890388 *fax* (01892) 891892
email tax@harveysllp.com
website www.harveysllp.com
Accountants Damian McGee, Lynnette Lawrence

Established in 2008. Charges £600 plus VAT per annum. Client support includes face-to-face meetings, telephone and email, as well as fee protection insurance and freepost record envelopes. Accounts support is charged at £40 per hour; tax compliance at £60 per hour; and partner at £90 to £150 per hour. Supplies clients with MS Excel spreadsheet templates suitable for Windows XP and Vista. 50% of the client base comprises actors, and 30% other entertainment industry professionals. Offices are wheelchair-accessible.

Hayles & Partners Ltd

39 Castle Street, Leicester LE1 5WN
tel 0116-233 8500 *fax* 0116-233 7288
email via form on website
website www.hayles.co.uk
Accountants Geoff Banks, Amanda Jelley

Charges from £150 for preparation of a basic tax return. Provides face-to-face meetings, phone and email support. Initial consultation or advice is offered free of charge. Does not supply software or spreadsheet templates to clients. Advises actors to "open a separate business bank account and identify all receipts and payments, retaining all supporting documentation".

Horwath Clark Whitehill

St Bride's House, 10 Salisbury Square, London EC4Y 8EH

tel 020-7842 7100
website www.horwathcw.co.uk
Accountants David Ford, Tim Norkett

Established in 1982. Provides flexible solutions to clients' tax problems; initial meeting is offered free of charge. Supports clients via meetings, phone and email. Will supply software and/or spreadsheet templates that are tailor-made to individual requirements. Current client list includes 20 actors and 20 other entertainment industry professionals. Offices are wheelchair-accessible. Fees vary according to the complexity of the service(s) required: £400 + VAT is the minimum. "The better the quality of the client's recordkeeping, the lower the fees."

J Morris and Co

17 St Ann's Square, Manchester M2 7PW
tel 0161-832 4841 *fax* 0161-835 2539
email johne@alexander.co.uk
website www.alexander.co.uk
Accountant John Evans

An accountant since 1969, John Evans merged the J Morris & Co practice with Alexander & Co in 2005. Charges for completion of accounts and submission of tax return start at £250 "dependent on complexity of case". Provides support by means of face-to-face meetings, phone, email and written correspondence, and can offer introduction to further specialist advice (e.g. legal) where required. Provides PC (Windows) compatible software or spreadsheets as required. Offices are not wheelchair accessible. "We deal with a number of actors and entertainers, and we are on Equity's list."

Nyman Libson Paul

Regina House, 124 Finchley Road, London NW3 5JS
tel 020-7433 2400 *fax* 020-7433 2401
email entertainment@nlpca.co.uk
website www.nlpca.co.uk

75 years in the entertainment industry.

Shaw Walker

26 Great Queen Street, London WC2B 5BB
tel 020-7242 1134 *fax* 020-7831 7232
email alison@shawwalker.co.uk
website www.shawwalker.co.uk
Accountants Mrs A McCarthy, Mr P Skinner, Mr T K Chong

Established in 1925, charges from £400 to prepare actors' accounts for the tax return, depending on the complexity of the accounts. Provides a face-to-face initial meeting; support thereafter is as convenient to the client, and this is included in the fee. Provides a complete range of accounting services – VAT, tax, PAYE, business support, book keeping *et al.* Software and/or spreadsheets are provided to the client as required. Offices are not easily wheelchair-accessible. Advice to actors: "Seek a *qualified* accountant."

David Summers & Co

Argo House, Kilburn Park Road, London NW6 5LF
tel 020-7644 0478 *fax* 020-7644 0678

Resources

email dsummersfca@hotmail.com
website www.dsummers.co.uk
Accountants David Summers and Chet Haria

Established in 1982. Charges start from £200 + VAT
for preparation of annual self-employed accounts and
the self-assessment tax return. A quote is given at the
initial meeting, which is free of charge. The services
offered also include preparation of limited company
accounts and corporate tax returns, VAT registration,
payroll, tax planning advice, etc. Client support
includes face-to-face meetings, phone, email, and
dealing with day-to-day queries as they may arise (all
included in the price). Approximately 10% of clients
are actors or members of the entertainment industry.
"We tailor advice to each individual's requirements."

TWD Accountants
Grosvenor House, St Thomas Place,
Stockport SK1 3TZ
tel 0845-058 2223 *fax* 0845-059 2292
email sarahb@twdaccounts.co.uk
website www.twdaccounts.co.uk
Director Mike Parkes

Founded in 1996, formerly Tax Watchdog Direct. A
fixed-fee tax and accountancy service, charging £169
+ VAT (£198.58) per year. TWD provides phone and
email support to all clients, as well as a first year free
online bookkeeping system, TWD Online. TWD
Online is a new, easy-to-use web-based bookkeeping
program available on a 14-day free trial (1 year if you
sign up for the accountancy package). The system can
be accessed at www.twdaccounts.co.uk/services/
online-bookkeeping and is ideally suited to
entertainment professionals. 15% of clients are actors;
5% are other entertainment-industry professionals.
For useful tips and advice visit the FAQ page,
designed specifically for actors (www.
twdaccounts.co.uk/clinic/frequently-asked-tax-
questions/actors).

Vantis
66 Wigmore Street, London, W1U 2SB
tel 020 - 7467 4000 *fax* 020 - 7467 4040
email mediagroup@vantisplc.com
website www.vantisplc.com
Accountant Cliff Crown

Vantis plc is the AIM listed leading UK accounting,
tax and business recovery and advisory group. We are
experienced, pro-active tax advisers, with an extensive
media client base, including actors and entertainment
industry professionals, that extends both nationally
and internationally. This has resulted in Vantis being
known as one of the leading firms with specialist
media accountants and advisers.

Client support includes: face to face meetings, phone,
email (all included in the price). Level of client
support ranges from proactive advice, regular
meetings, seminar programmes and a direct phone
link to a dedicated professional. Excel spreadsheets/
templates are provided to clients.

We advise clients "keep it simple; keep records of
expenditure as you go; pass it over as soon as possible
after tax year end; keep talking to us – we can take
the strain off you."

Wyatts Accounts
18 Highbury New Park, London N5 2DB
mobile (07710) 160442
fax 020-7226 0211

Friendly and clear service. Specialists with actors,
artists and performers. Reasonable and transparent
scaled fees and charges. Provides software and/or
templates for Sage, Excel, Quickbooks and Money
Manager for Apple or PC. Client base is 100 per cent
arts and entertainment industry professionals. Offices
are not wheelchair-accessible.

Between engagements

or 'How to survive until the next job'
Andrew Piper

All the articles in this publication are one person's perspective, and as such need to be tested against your own judgement and experience. None more so than this article, because like you I'm an actor. Unless you are extremely lucky (or have only just graduated from drama school), you will have experienced periods of unemployment, and will have come up with your own strategies for coping with this. What follows is a collection of thoughts on what seems *to me* to be good advice for any actor finding themself temporarily out of work. I don't always follow this advice, but it does seem to help when I do. Not everything here will be right for you, but I hope that some of it will make it easier for you get to your next acting job with body and soul intact.

I've grouped the suggestions in this article under four headings: stay solvent, stay employable, stay visible, and stay sane. Do all these things, and acting work should never be too far away.

Stay solvent

It might surprise you that I start with this, but money problems can make all the other suggestions in this article so much more difficult to do. Your first priority as an actor, therefore, is to make sure that you can keep a roof over your head, food in your fridge, and your creditors (if any) off your back. Without these things it becomes next to impossible to present a confident face to the world, to maintain the self-esteem and self-belief that one needs to survive as an actor, and to plan any strategies for finding acting work. So with this in mind – and recognising that this is the least interesting bit – here are my tips for staying solvent:

• Save money when you are working. That's not easy if you're on the sort of wages that are common in theatre, but the more money you can save now, the more you'll have in reserve for the lean times ahead. Even if you have another job to go onto after this one, the chances are that there will be a few weeks between finishing one and starting the next, and that's time that potentially no one will be paying you for. Remember too that your wages will rarely have tax deducted from them, which means you will need something in reserve for when the tax bill is due. If you're doing a long theatre job, then consider setting up a standing order to a savings account – even if you only manage to save a few pounds a week, you may be glad of it further down the line.

• Live as cheaply as you can. The lower your overheads, the more you can save and the longer you can ride out a period of reduced income.

• Make your extravagances count. If you've been frugal during the week, then you can treat yourself at the weekend. Something as simple as making your own sandwiches may save you enough to pay for a meal out in as little as a few days. Skipping two or three nights of drinking and clubbing could even save you enough for a weekend in Paris or Prague.

• Probably the largest single expense you'll have is your rent or mortgage. This is generally unavoidable – unless of course you're still living with your parents – but if you're someone who does a lot of touring then it can be frustrating to be paying some exorbitant London rent for a room that you're hardly using. (Mortgages are different, of course, because at least you'll own something at the end of it.) However, for most people, having a place you can call home and look forward to returning to is immensely important. Whether or not you feel there are savings that can be made – by subletting while away, say, or moving to a cheaper area – don't leave it out of the equation when looking at keeping your costs down.

• Get a second phone. That might seem perverse, but if you don't have access to a landline (for example, if you're away from home) and you have an 'anytime minutes' contract with one of the operators, get yourself an old mobile phone (eBay is quite good for this) and put a pay-as-you-go SIM card in it for making all your off-peak calls. That way, all your long off-peak chats to your mum/partner/best mate won't eat up your valuable 'anytime' minutes. Shop around, and see what will work out best for you.

• Have a look at **www.moneysavingexpert.com**. Run by the journalist Martin Lewis, this website has all sorts of tips and tricks for making your money go further.

• Get a 'day job'. Even Kenneth Tynan's actor mistress once observed that "the worse thing about not working is having to work". And ain't that the truth! Sooner or later most of us – especially those who work mostly in theatre – have to knuckle down to something unrelated to acting in order to pay the bills. What form this takes will depend on your particular skills – it doesn't hurt to get some IT and typing skills under your belt when you get the chance – but consider office temping, waiting and bar work, call centres (one company, RSVP – **www.rsvp.co.uk** – is even run by actors), and shop work, for starters. If you have a teaching qualification, then you could make some slightly better money by doing 'supply teaching', covering for full-time teachers in case of illness. Many of the photographers listed in this book are (or were) also working actors – although this shouldn't be regarded as a way to a quick buck: those guys have worked long and hard at perfecting their skills. One of the most popular ways of earning cash between jobs is promotions work. Have a look at these sites for more information: **www.stuckforstaff.com**, **www.turns.net**, **www.ays.co.uk** and **www.promojobspro.com** (this last one is run by the same people as CastingCall Pro). I've even turned my hand (if that's the right expression) to artists' life-modelling, although I've never managed to earn more than beer money for it. One friend of mine took a course in massage in order to have another string to his bow – although I'm generally cautious about diverting money, time and energy into training that won't actually improve your employment prospects as an actor. One job I wouldn't recommend is 'extras' work, unless what you aspire to be is a background artiste. Never did a job so eloquently encapsulate the meaning of the phrase, 'so near, and yet so far'. (*Note* This point doesn't really belong in the 'stay solvent' section, but while we're on the subject of day jobs: Never take a job that you couldn't in good conscience drop at short notice to go to an audition or accept acting work, unless you want to be stuck doing that job for the rest of your life. Alas, almost any job that one could describe as 'interesting' or 'stimulating' also requires a degree of commitment. For this reason, most 'day jobs' that are suitable for actors are tedium incarnate. I wish it were otherwise. I really *really* wish it were otherwise.)

• Don't sit around waiting for the money to run out. If you have managed to bring in a good chunk of money, paid off your debts, set aside enough for your tax bill, had a holiday, and still have enough left not to need to work for a while ... get a part-time job. Your savings will last you longer, and instead of turning into a couch potato (which can happen frighteningly quickly) you will retain a sense of yourself as a working, earning person. By all means do the other things you never had time to do before – take classes, see films, visit galleries, meet friends – but do these on your days off.

• Know what State Benefits you're entitled to, and claim them (and if you're not entitled, then don't). I loathe and detest signing on – Jobcentres are rarely beacons of hope and optimism – and will do almost any kind of work rather than do so, but if you do find yourself without work then it is worth taking the time to fill in the forms. Talk to Equity if the Jobcentre is sniffy about you signing on as an actor.

• Act quickly if you do get into financial trouble. If you find yourself borrowing money for your day-to-day living expenses (including using credit cards) or to make payments on existing debts, then you have a problem, and one that must be dealt with as soon as possible. This is too big an issue for me to tackle here, but you can get advice on dealing with unmanageable debts from your local Citizens' Advice Bureau, **www.citizensadvice.org.uk** (in Scotland this is **www.cas.org.uk**); from National Debtline, **www.nationaldebtline.co.uk** or *tel* 0808-808 4000; and from Consumer Credit Counselling Service, **www.cccs.co.uk** or *tel* 0800-138 1111. Whatever you do, don't be tempted to take out another credit card (even a zero interest one) or another loan unless this will allow you to cancel your existing credit cards, because you'll spiral even further into debt. Never *ever* touch those 'debt consolidation', 'one-easy-payment' companies that advertise on daytime TV – they just want to make money out of you and will make matters worse. It doesn't have to be scary – you have more power than you might think. The banks want their money back, of course, but would much prefer to accept a repayment plan which fits your budget, than go through the expense of legal proceedings when they know you can't pay.

Stay employable

This is perhaps the easiest section for me to write, because, well, we all know it all already. But do we do it? No, neither do I. Time and money are big factors, of course, but so are simple inertia and laziness. "Chance," said Louis Pasteur, "favours the prepared mind," so here's my list of best practices, given in the knowledge that I rarely get around to more than a handful of them when I'm between jobs.

• Brush up your skills – voice, dance, singing, stage combat, Shakespeare, Alexander Technique, etc. – and learn new ones. There are various places in London and around the country that offer professional-grade courses in these, such as the London and Manchester Actors Centres, The City Lit, and the drama schools and universities listed in the Short Courses section of this book. Get a driving licence if you don't already have one.

• Keep fit, whatever your preferred means is. Sport, gym, dance, swimming, walking, martial arts – even regular bouts of acrobatic sex would do it, I suppose, as long as afterwards you didn't light up or order pizza. Aerobic fitness is most important as this provides both the stamina to get through an evening's performance (I'm talking theatre now, not sex) and the twinkle in the eye that says 'energy and vitality' to an auditioning director. (A twinkle that says 'regular, acrobatic sex' is probably quite effective too, in certain circumstances.)

• Brush up on your audition speeches and songs. How would you feel if, at short notice, you got an audition for a great job, and you fluffed it because your speeches or songs were rusty or tired? It's happened to me; don't let it happen to you.

• Read plays. Not because you *should* (because if that's your reason then you won't) but because they're *fun*. A lot of us came into this business because we loved plays – it's odd that once we got here we read so few of them. (Keep an eye open for good audition speeches while you're reading.)

• Keep in touch with what's going on in the business. Read *The Stage*, talk to your agent and your actor friends, keep your finger on the pulse. Know which theatres have new artistic directors, which casting directors are working on which projects, and so on. Remind yourself that you're an actor – not always easy after the umpteenth week of photocopying and filing in some awful temp job.

• Watch TV. And no, I don't mean *Trisha* or *Cash in the Attic* – watch drama on TV, and go to the theatre and cinema. Remind yourself of how it's done, and make a note of the performers, directors, casting directors and production companies whose work you most admire.

• Visit your dentist. That smile of yours is important, so look after it. You don't have to go getting expensive cosmetic work done (unless your gnashers are particularly hideous, or unless you're up for a lot of romantic leads in film and television), but get a check-up with your regular dentist and make sure any problems are spotted early. I had an abscess while on tour once, and was in agony for several days. This pain was as nothing, though, compared to the shock of the bill I had for a (private) emergency dentist to perform root canal surgery. Don't let it happen to you: get them sorted before you go away.

• Lastly, but perhaps most importantly: keep yourself **available**. Remember what your real job is. As I mentioned in the previous section, it's a sad fact that almost any job that's interesting will require a degree of commitment, but if you are so committed to your 'day job' that you can't drop everything for an audition or acting work then you are putting yourself and your acting career at a real disadvantage. Talk to your agent (if you have one) when you're planning a holiday – he or she must know your every movement, even if it's only a long weekend, because both you and your agent will look stupid if an audition is arranged for a time when you're actually going to be sunning yourself on some Mediterranean beach, or giving the Best Man's speech at your brother's wedding. Talk to your agent, too, if you're considering applying for Fringe work. In some circumstances this can be a good showcase for your talents, but this must be offset against the fact that it will put you out of the running for any paid work – talk it through with your agent and discuss what you hope to get out of it. Keep your mobile phone switched on whenever possible, and return calls from your agent immediately.

Stay visible

All the preparation in the world won't count for much if nobody knows you're there. There are thousands of us out there, all chasing too few jobs, and it can be hard enough to get noticed even when you're doing everything right. That means that being a wallflower just isn't an option, however much you might hate the idea of marketing yourself. So here are a few (relatively painless) suggestions for keeping your name and face in employers' minds.

• Keep your *Spotlight* CV up to date. An entry in *Spotlight* is essential for film, television and increasingly also theatre jobs. Unless your CV is up to date then (a) the casting director's picture of you is incomplete and (b) it will look like you haven't worked for the last x years.

• Keep your photo up to date. Angus Deuchar's excellent article on page 390 will tell you why, and what to do if it's not. It's significant that all the casting directors who have written for this book have stressed how important it is that your photograph actually looks like you.

• Keep in touch with past employers. Unless you've disgraced yourself while working for them, these people represent your best chance for further work. Send a friendly email or postcard to let them know what you've been doing, with perhaps a mention that you'd love to work with them again and would appreciate a call next time they're casting.

• The best time to write to other potential employers and casting directors is when you're working and can invite them to see you. Of course there's a pretty slim chance that any London-based employers will travel up to Pitlochry to see your Stanley Kowalski or Blanche Dubois, but that's not the point: they will see that you are working – not 'just finished' working (the meaning of which can be curiously flexible) – but actually working, right now.

• Keep covering letters brief, but as individual as possible. Most companies get stacks of CVs from actors with nothing but the baldest of covering notes, so a sentence along the lines of "I'm hoping to see your *Macbeth* when it comes to Leeds" or "My friend John Smith is having a great time working for you at the moment" may make yours stand out from the rest.

• Think about your marketing materials: photo, CV, covering letter. Are they well presented? They represent you: do they do a good job? Are the CV and letter on good-quality paper or the nasty, cheap stuff you get in photocopiers? Get someone who knows what they're talking about to give constructive criticism about them. There are differing opinions about this, but I think it's always worth printing your photo onto the CV itself. If it's well printed then many theatre companies are quite happy with this instead of a full 10x8. If you're sending out a lot of letters and CVs, then it might be worth asking your local printer to quote for some headed notepaper with your photo at the top. Don't get him to print the whole CV – it will go out of date long before you get round to mailing them all. (I should say that my agent completely disagrees with this idea – he reckons you should always send 10x8s, and leave printing your photo on your CV for when you've run out of photos. As I said, opinion is divided.)

• Additional marketing tools. Websites can be quite a good way of getting someone to spend time finding out about you, and of putting across a particular image. The cost of commissioning one from scratch can vary wildly, but someone with only a modicum of computer know-how should be able to knock together something quite presentable using a site like **www.moonfruit.com** or **www.easily.co.uk** (this latter also allows you to register quite cheaply your own domain name – e.g. andrew-piper.com). Don't fret if you haven't got one – your *Spotlight* web page already carries all the important information. Personal websites are currently a 'nice-to-have' not a 'need-to-have'.

• Postcards and business cards. Not a substitute for the CV and photo, but quite a useful additional tool – something to give or send someone who has met you, as a reminder of who you are. Postcards can also make quite good performance notices – something a casting director can read easily while eating breakfast. Have a look at **www.vistaprint.co.uk** (and there are many others) for business cards, including ones with your photo on. There are a number of companies which can produce postcards quite cheaply: **www.justpostcards.co.uk** and **www.goodprint.co.uk** are two but there are others if you hunt around.

• Apply for jobs. Sounds obvious, but plenty of actors wait for their agent to submit them for everything. Even if the agent is doing their job, in practice this will mean that your CV arrives with a pile of others, with little or nothing to indicate why you are (a) particularly good for this job or (b) interested in working for this company. Find out what's casting – the listings in this book will tell you how best to do that for each company, and your agent may also be happy to tell you – and make your own applications. Tell your agent who you're writing to, and make sure that the CV your agent sends out on your behalf is accurate and up to date.

• On the subject of agents, stay visible to yours. Quite a number of agents have far too large a client list (30 to 35 per agent is about right, I reckon) so it's easy for them to forget about those they haven't heard from in a while. Some form of contact – phone or email, say – every week or two isn't unreasonable when you're not working. Make it a constructive call – not just "have you got me any auditions?" – and talk about what you can be doing to generate work: what's casting, who to write to, ideas for people to approach for general auditions (especially if you're travelling), and so on. Remember that they work for you, so make the most of their skills.

• Write to directors, producers and casting directors whose work you have seen, and tell them how much you enjoyed or admired it.

• Network. Go to see friends in plays, especially first nights, and get yourself invited to the party or pub afterwards. No need to be pushy – just be sociable. When you meet the director don't be tempted to 'do an audition' – casting is almost certainly the last thing on his or her mind right now, and you'll just alienate them. Conversely, don't *not* talk to them just because they're the director – that can be just as irritating. Remember that they're human beings. You won't be able to forget that they're the director, but try to see them as just someone you're meeting at a party. Then follow it up with a CV or showreel in the post. (Have one to hand in case they ask for one.)

• Showcase your talents. The Actors Centres run showcase evenings to which casting professionals are invited, and there are various others around – although be careful, before you stump up too much cash, that they are reputable. One recent addition to the collection is London Bites, which is monthly at Turnmills in Clerkenwell (**www.standupdrama.com**). Also worth considering is Fringe theatre. It is a huge commitment in terms of time and money (in lost earnings alone) to embark on a Fringe production, so make sure you'll get something out of it. If you want to work on *Holby City*, ask yourself if a Fringe production of *Godspell* is really the best showcase for you. Also, if you want casting directors to travel to see you, is it going to be worth your while doing something dark and disturbing in some tiny, God-forsaken flea-pit in the middle of nowhere? More problematic is the question, 'Is it likely to be any good?' – and for that you'll have to do your homework. Find out what the director (and writer if it's a new play) has done before, because you may not want to give up several weeks' earnings to work with a first-time director straight out of college. Everyone has to start somewhere, but you've a right to be able to make an informed judgement if you're working for next to nothing. Google, Whatsonstage.com and Theatre Record may be helpful here. (See the introduction to the Fringe theatre section for more pitfalls to watch out for.)

• Do a short film. These can be useful camera experience, and occasionally provide material for a showreel. Some of these are paid (often badly); a great many are not. These days every kid with a media studies degree wants to be the next Guy Ritchie, so again if you're working for nothing, make sure you have confidence in your director and producer before committing yourself. You're not a charity, and you're not an amateur who just does it for fun.

Stay sane

Being an actor should carry a mental health warning – working away from home, unemployment, rejection, failure, insecurity, poverty: all of these can take their toll on your psychological health and on your relationships. And the worse thing about that is that it makes it even harder to find and get acting jobs – few things kill your chances in an audition quicker than the smell of desperation. After all, if *you* don't have confidence in yourself, why should they? So look after yourself, and take responsibility for your own wellbeing. Here are my suggestions for psychological pick-me-ups ...

• Be sociable, even if you don't feel like it. It can be a lonely business when you're out of work – and often even when you're working – so make the most of the time to see as much of friends and family as possible. This is particularly important with partners, especially if the kind of work you tend to get means being away from home. Throw parties or invite your friends to dinner when you're feeling up, and call your actor friends for an understanding shoulder to cry on when you're not.

• Make time for things you enjoy, that make you feel good about yourself. Perhaps this may mean setting yourself challenges – do the garden, DIY around the home, learn French, run a marathon – or may just mean setting aside 'me' time. Yoga and meditation are particularly good for this, and some people draw great strength from religious observance.

• If (like me) you are a naturally anxious person, and meditation or yoga don't appeal, then consider getting some relaxation music and spend some time every day listening to it. If anxiety and self-image are your problem, don't go buying some motivational 'You too can be rich and famous' hypnosis tape or you could make things worse: deal with the problem in hand. Have a look at **www.relax-uk.com** or **www.relaxaudio.com** for some examples.

• Get out in the fresh air. Remember when you were younger, when adults urged you to switch off the telly and get outdoors? Well, they were right – exercise and sunlight are vitally important for both your physical and mental health, particularly in the winter months when daylight is in short supply. Even when we're working, often much of our time is spent in windowless boxes, so make the most of a nice day and go for a walk.

• Take a holiday. That's really not easy to do, especially at the start of one's career. A week away from the 'day job' is a week not earning money, which can be expensive if you've already used up your holiday pay subsidising those days or weeks of involuntary unemployment that often occur just before or just after an acting job. But everyone needs to recharge their batteries from time to time, even if it's just a long weekend visiting old friends.

• Detox. Most actors drink – I think it was Gene Hackman who once observed that all actors eventually become either directors or drunks – but if your last job involved a lot of boozing (or if you're currently waking up with one or more hangovers a week), then try a few weeks off the sauce. Drink two litres of water a day, get plenty of early nights, and try to make fruit and fresh veg a good fifty per cent of everything you eat. Some people also find it beneficial to give up bread or go veggie or vegan for a while. Go back to beer-

and-burgers after that if you want, but notice the difference in your mood and concentration when you do.

• Keep a positive attitude. Remember, you're in this for the long term, so although six months or more can feel like a long time, compared with the 30- or 40-year career you have ahead of you, it's really not so long. Almost all actors are out of work for periods in their career – even very good ones – so don't panic.

• Don't give yourself a hard time about past failures: learn the lesson and move on. Make here and now your starting point, and plan for the future based on what *is* rather than what *might have been*.

• Silence your inner critic. Brendan Behan wrote that "Critics are like eunuchs in a harem: they know how it's done, they've seen it done every day, but they're unable to do it themselves." We all have a critic within us, but the less room we give it, the less we'll feel like eunuchs ourselves. Be generous to your fellow professionals, understanding of what they go through, and don't be threatened by their success. A friend of a friend of mine is doing very well for himself – very good-looking, great agent, lovely telly and film roles coming his way – and I so wanted to dislike him. But meeting him again at a party recently he was warm, relaxed, interested in what I was doing, remembered things I'd told him last time we met – in short, utterly charming. And I realised that that's actually what made him the star. Not just the looks or the talent – both of which he does have in spades – but also the generosity of spirit, the belief that 'I'm ok, you're ok'. It might be the acidic queen with the barbed tongue who gets the laughs at the party, but it's people like that actor who will in the end do well. So resist pressure to join in bashing reputations or impugning characters, and learn compassion for yourself and for others.

• Don't just wait for your agent to call. Be proactive. Take charge of your career. Keep doing the things listed above that will improve your chances of finding work.

• Finally – and you may be surprised that I give this advice in an actors' yearbook – if it really is getting too much for you, then it may be time to call it quits. Acting can be a very cruel business, and not everyone is built to withstand the emotional battering that visits most actors from time to time. If there is anything at all that you could be happy doing instead of acting, then do it: there is no shame at all in looking after your sanity. A very talented friend of mine who left the business after years of frustration described her new situation to me thus: "I'm doing a job that I hate and I'm happier than I've been in years." Many people who leave acting find related work – teaching, for example, or work in some aspect of production – but I know some who have found that proximity to what they've left behind to be too painful, and have opted for entirely unrelated occupations. In the end, it comes down to what makes you happy, where you feel at home, and what ultimately brings you peace. Enjoying acting is not the same as enjoying being an actor.

There's a 'prayer' that runs, 'Grant me the serenity to accept the things I cannot change, courage to change the things I can, and wisdom to know the difference.' This seems to me to be a good motto for any actor. A great many decisions affecting our lives as actors are out of our hands, but a great many more we *do* have control over. The trick to staying sane in this business seems to be knowing (and accepting) which are which.

Andrew Piper trained at the Bristol Old Vic Theatre School. More information can be found at **www.andrew-piper.com**. He edited the 2007 and 2008 editions of *Actors' Yearbook*.

Physical and mental fitness for actors

Alex Caan

The instrument or tool of the actor is the body. Like a musical instrument, if it is left idle it will become out of tune and lose its ability to function effectively.

Actors need to constantly develop their instrument to get the best out of it. Unlike a musical instrument, we carry our tool with us every day. With good habits and practice we can alleviate many of the problems that need to be fixed before they start. The work required to have a positive ongoing effect is not as great or as demanding as one would expect. Before we look at what we can do to make our bodies outstanding, let's look at what our bodies really are.

In a person of average weight and build, 70 per cent of the mass of the body is muscle and bone. Therefore we can have a large effect on our bodies, by focusing on our muscles and bones. Before we can affect change in our muscles and bones we need to understand how they work and what relationships they have with each other.

The structure of the body is extremely complicated but can be viewed in quite a simplistic manner. Originally we would have walked on all fours, which is why our upper limbs have very similar corresponding joints to our lower limbs. Each hand has five digits, with a dominant thumb; our corresponding lower body part is the opposite foot, with the big toe as the dominant digit. The wrist and ankle are similar multi-directional joints, whereas the elbow and knee are both hinged joints. The shoulder and hip are ball and socket joints.

The upper and lower limbs are also connected by corresponding groups of muscles. The quads, which are in the front of the thigh, are related to the upper body through the triceps, which are in the back of the upper arm. The hamstrings, at the back of the upper leg, are related to the biceps. The gluteus or buttocks are related to the pectorals or chest muscles. So rather than looking at muscular activity in isolation, we must see muscles as groups working together.

When the body moves forward, the opposite arm and leg swing. The combination of muscles working together propels our bodies. Muscles move limbs by shortening.

Muscles work together synergistically and in a healthy, well-maintained body are balanced. If bad habits occur, this simplicity of movement can lead to long-term health problems by over-use of some muscles, and under-use of others. This constant over-use/ under-use will lead to a tired or sore body part in a specific area, often one side of the neck or lower back.

As we move forward, the chain of movements pass through the centre of the body. This passing through the centre is a clue to the focus of long-term fitness and wellbeing for the actor.

The centre of the body is the place where all life stems from. It is here that a baby is connected to its mother through the placenta, that later becomes the belly button. In the centre of the body is the diaphragm, from which, through correct training, all breath should originate.

The movement of our bodies creates heat and energy. Contrary to what some directors believe, we are not beings that live in our head or brain space. We live in our bodies and

Resources

movement produces powerful emotional responses. This is encapsulated in the phrase 'Motion creates Emotion'. This is why actors talk about getting the walk of the character, because this allows them to get into the body of the character, which in turn allows them to get into the personality of the character. Some actors do this instinctively, but it is and can be a learned skill.

Actors communicate thoughts in the vast majority by speaking. There are, of course, actors who use mime and dance to communicate, but mainly thoughts are communicated verbally, using speech or song. Words are merely a manipulation of breath using the tongue, mouth and vocal cords. Without breath we have nothing to carry our thoughts over large theatrical space.

Coincidentally, breath or oxygen is the most important nourishment our bodies need. Without food one can live for 40 days or more; without water one can live for 7-10 days; but if you don't breathe for five minutes you will die.

Using this as our guide, the focus of the actors' fitness should be built around the development of a robust powerful tool that can create large amounts of powerful breath. Not just large volumes of breath, but outstanding control of the mechanism that delivers that breath.

The mechanism that delivers the breath is the lungs and diaphragm and their supporting muscles. These muscles need to be strong, but also need to be mobile and have excellent endurance.

Lastly, the value of water cannot be underestimated. A 5 per cent drop in hydration can lead to mild dehydration, which can lead to a large drop in bodily function, both mental and physical. Even a 2 per cent drop in hydration can have a very damaging and negative effect on our voice. In temperate climates we lose 2.5 litres of water throughout an average day. If we are performing, rehearsing or undertaking strenuous physical activity we will use much greater amounts of water than this. Therefore we must monitor our bodies and increase water intake when needed. Passing clear urine is a good indicator of hydration – if not first thing in the morning, then definitely throughout the day.

So where does one start in the nitty-gritty of training the actor's body? Actors come in all shapes and sizes. I am not advocating that all actors try to become slim and pert: who would play all the non-slim, non-pert roles? Equally, I am not advocating that all actors develop muscular physiques. We need to be limber in the joints and muscles, but there is no point in the serious actor developing big muscles at the expense of range of movement. I believe that you can be tall, short, slim, rotund, lanky or squat and at the same time be very fit. Olympic shot putters are very large but all can run great distances and move like ballet dancers.

Fitness for actors doesn't require a massive overloading of the body. To reach Olympic-standard fitness we would need to break the body down systematically over a period of time, in order to allow the body to regenerate stronger than before. This regeneration occurs during periods of rest. But this overloading is not really needed for general fitness for actors.

In all of our fitness development we need to place breath control and posture at the forefront. The ideas and concepts of the Alexander Technique are pivotal to this. Its values are based on excellent posture and good use of muscles, rather than overuse and bad postural habits. So when performing any movement, be aware of the alignment of the head, neck and back. Often actors strain their voices because they are tight in another part of their body, which pulls the head and neck out of alignment, resulting in a sore throat or strained voice. For those of you who are not familiar with the Alexander Technique, I would recommend that an awareness of posture and balance is vital to long-term fitness.

A simple starting point for general fitness for actors is walking. Walking is the most underused and undervalued exercise we can do. It involves a good pair of training shoes and a place to go! Between 20 and 60 minutes' continuous walking a day will increase lung capacity and make our heart a great deal stronger. I know many actors say that they walk at least that in a day – going shopping, walking to the bus or train, and so on. I am not discounting that, but I am advocating a steady brisk walk with arms swinging back and forth in time with the opposing leg. By doing this, the whole body is being exercised and the core muscles through the centre of the body are activated. It is akin to the phase of human development, that we know as crawling. The same benefits cannot be achieved through passive day-to-day walking.

Walking has a very effective return for the amount of effort expended, because there is little detrimental impact on the joints of the lower limbs. The swinging of opposing arms and legs also helps reinforce correct neurological pathways. This helps us to move our bodies more effectively and efficiently as a kinetic chain, rather than as disjointed isolated movements.

A walking regime three days a week is a good place to start. You will not only build your lungs and heart, but also the tissues around your joints in the legs, arms and back. These need time to adapt and grow to the new stresses being placed on them. Taking a day off in between will allow the tissues throughout your body to regenerate during the periods of rest.

If you are a fitness novice, then building up to an hour-long walk is an achievable goal. Start with a ten-minute walk that builds systematically over a period of between four and six weeks, rather than blazing into a brisk hour-long walk initially. Increasing your walks by three minutes each walk will let you achieve an hour-long walk from a ten-minute starting point in just six weeks. Three minutes may sound a lot, but since it requires adding just one and a half minutes to your outward journey, it is not an unrealistic amount.

Swimming is also an excellent way to work the heart and lungs without placing any stress on the joints, as it is a non-weight bearing form of exercise. However, it is important to swim using the front crawl and backstroke rather than predominantly using the breast stroke, so that we continue to move opposing upper and lower limbs to work our core muscles. A mixture of all swimming strokes would be best to work the greatest range of muscle groups and minimise the likelihood of housemaid's knee (a common breast stroke-related injury)! Learning to swim with your head partially submerged in the water is vital, in order to maintain correct alignment of the spine.

The same incremental approach to developing fitness through walking, as recommended above, should be applied when undertaking a swimming regime. Rather than using the increment of time, the number of lengths swum is a very simple starting point. Do bear in mind the length of each pool that you may swim in may vary! It is likely that the more often you swim, the quicker you will become. So increasing the number of lengths that you swim each session may require little or no extra time in the pool.

We have exercised the heart and lungs with walking and swimming. We need now to develop our range of movement and strength. Basic Yoga movements are also a simple

Resources

and effective way to increase inner strength and develop range of movement and good posture. I am not looking at the more physical jumping around or sauna types of Yoga. I am advocating basic Yoga moves.

Yoga has many positive effects, which include large ranges of movement and mobility. By getting into certain Yoga positions we are not only stretching the muscles, but also massaging the internal organs. Yoga also has the benefit of establishing excellent breath control. The breath floods into the centre of the body and has to be released with control and in a sustained manner. This has a very relaxing and meditative effect. This helps us switch off our overactive minds, the value of which cannot be underestimated.

Buying a book or DVD on Yoga or joining a Yoga class is an excellent place to start. If Yoga doesn't appeal to you, then Pilates is an excellent alternative. Both Yoga and Pilates are fantastic for developing breath control and posture control techniques.

Let us look at a sample week's exercise programme – for example, walking or swimming on Monday, Thursday and Saturday, with Yoga or Pilates on Tuesday and Friday. This gives you two days off, on Wednesday and Sunday, which follow either two or three days of activity. Rest is vital to regeneration. We only become fitter and stronger by allowing our bodies to recover and grow. These days off give the individual physical downtime, which can then be filled with mental stimulation of some kind, including meditation, vocal and singing practice, reading or other pursuits that aid the actor's development as a whole.

> **Further information**
>
> For more information about any of the suggested forms of exercise, see the websites listed below:
>
> Alexander Technique www.alexandertechnique.com
> Walking www.thewalkingsite.com
> Swimming www.britishswimming.org
> Yoga www.bwy.org.uk (British Wheel of Yoga)
> Pilates www.pilatesfoundation.com

This is a brief overview of the most suitable and simple exercises to cover what is required for the stresses and strains of most acting jobs. All of these suggestions can be carried out from home or on tour. The time and effort required to train in this manner will not be detrimental to the actor's performance. By starting small, and increasing gradually, the actor will feel more invigorated and energised from undertaking an exercise programme.

The actor's body should be viewed as a communication tool. Bodies require stimulation to develop. Without stimulus, the body and mind will deteriorate. Permitting this to happen is an injustice to the craft of acting. We all only have one body, and we need to look after it and maintain it for our specific needs.

Alex Caan was an international athlete before training at RADA for three years. Since graduation, he has worked extensively in theatre, TV and radio. Alex works as a business consultant, teaching powerful communication through effective use of the body. He also teaches acting for animators to the world's leading computer games company. Alex has coached Premiership football and rugby players to international level, and advised several Premiership football academies on their development programmes. He is currently coaching sportsmen and women at Olympic and World level in a range of different athletic disciplines. www.raiseyourbar.com

Funding bodies

The competition for funding is so fierce that it is important to allow sufficient time for research, planning and proper presentation of your proposed project. It is well worth checking to see what information is available on the websites listed in this section. Many funding bodies are happy to advise on form-filling, what kind of projects stand a chance and what could constitute a realistic amount to ask for. It is also well worth going on one (or more) of the Independent Theatre Council's (ITC; see page 443) courses for assistance in the complex world of funding applications.

Bodies that offer individual funding should be approached with similar care and attention.

NATIONAL ARTS COUNCILS

Arts Council England

14 Great Peter Street, London SW1P 3NQ
tel 0845-300 6200 *fax* 020-7973 6590
textphone 020-7973 6564
email enquiries@artscouncil.org.uk
website www.artscouncil.org.uk

Arts Council England is the national development agency for the arts in England, promoting excellence, innovation and diversity within the arts. It awards grants to individuals, arts organisations and national touring projects using public money from government and the National Lottery.

Grants for individuals are generally between £200 and £30,000, while those for organisations range from £200 up to a maximum of £100,000. Most grants, however, will be under £30,000. National touring grants are available for individuals and organisations touring to 2 or more Arts Council England regions, and normally vary between £5000 and £200,000. Grants for individuals, organisations and national touring can cover activities lasting up to 3 years.

All applicants should apply to the region in which they are based. Application forms, guidance notes and information sheets can be downloaded from the website. A wide range of resources, publications, links and information about other funding sources is also accessible on the website.

Arts Council of Northern Ireland

MacNeice House, 77 Malone Road, Belfast BT9 6AQ
tel 028-9038 5200
email publicaffairs@artscouncil-ni.org
website www.artscouncil-ni.org

The prime distributor of public support for the arts, the Arts Council of Northern Ireland is committed to increasing opportunities for artists to develop challenging and innovative work. In addition to funding schemes for organisations and community

groups, the council has developed a special programme of schemes to extend support for the individual artist. This programme includes the General Arts Award, which provides funding for specific projects, specialised research and personal artistic development; and the Major Individual Award, which supports established artists in the development of ambitious work.

Arts Council of Wales

Bute Place, Cardiff CF10 5AL
tel 0845-8734 900 *fax* 029-2044 1400
email info@artswales.org.uk
website www.artswales.org.uk

Responsible for funding and developing the arts in Wales using money from Welsh Assembly Government and the National Lottery. Provides arts organisations and individuals in Wales with the opportunity to apply for funding towards clearly defined arts-related projects. Scheme Guidelines for the funding programmes are available on the website. Anyone applying for funding should speak to an Arts Development Officer in their local office to discuss how well the project aligns with national and regional priorities. Contact information for all local offices can be found on the website.

Creative Scotland

249 West George Street, Glasgow G2 4QE
tel 0141-302 1749
12 Manor Place, Edinburgh EH6 7BG
tel 0131-240 2404
website www.creativescotland.com

In April 2010 the Scottish Arts Council merged with Scottish Screen to become Creative Scotland.

Creative Scotland will:

- invest in ideas
- invest in talent
- invest in education
- invest in places

"We are committed to investing in and developing the arts, screen and creative industries in Scotland

and playing a lead role in promoting the value and importance of these to everyone."

REGIONAL ARTS COUNCIL OFFICES

Arts Council England, East
Eden House, 48-49 Bateman Street,
Cambridge CB2 1LR
tel 0845-300 6200 *fax* 0870-242 1271
textphone (01223) 306893

Area covered: Bedfordshire, Cambridgeshire, Essex, Hertfordshire, Norfolk, Suffolk.

Arts Council England, East Midlands
St Nicholas Court, 25-27 Castle Gate,
Nottingham NG1 7AR
tel 0845-300 6200 *fax* 0115-950 2467

Area covered: Derbyshire, Leicestershire, Lincolnshire (excluding North and North East Lincolnshire), Northamptonshire, Nottinghamshire, Rutland.

Arts Council England, London
2 Pear Tree Court, London EC1R 0DS
tel 0845-300 6200 *fax* 020-7973 6564

Area covered: Greater London.

Arts Council England, North East
Central Square, Forth Street,
Newcastle upon Tyne NE1 3PJ
tel 0845-300 6200 *fax* 0191-230 1020
textphone 0191-255 8585

Area covered: Durham, Northumberland, Tees Valley, Tyne and Wear.

Arts Council England, North West
The Hive, 49 Lever Street, Manchester M1 1FN
tel 0845-300 6200 *fax* 0161-934 4426
textphone 0161-834 9131

Area covered: Cheshire, Cumbria, Greater Manchester, Lancashire, Merseyside.

Arts Council England, South East
Sovereign House, Church Street, Brighton BN1 1RA
tel 0845-300 6200 *fax* 0870-242 1257
textphone (01273) 710659

Area covered: Berkshire, Buckinghamshire, East Sussex, Hampshire, Isle of Wight, Kent, Oxfordshire, Surrey, West Sussex; and unitary authorities of Bracknell Forest, Brighton & Hove, Medway Towns, Milton Keynes, Portsmouth, Reading, Slough, Southampton, West Berkshire, Windsor and Maidenhead, Wokingham.

Arts Council England, South West
Senate Court, Southernhay Gardens, Exeter EX1 1UG
tel 0845-300 6200 *fax* (01392) 229229
textphone (01392) 433503

Area covered: Cornwall, Devon, Dorset, Gloucestershire, the Isles of Scilly, Somerset, Wiltshire; unitary authorities of Bath and North East Somerset, Bournemouth, Bristol, North Somerset, Plymouth, Poole, South Gloucestershire, Swindon, Torbay.

Arts Council England, West Midlands
82 Granville Street, Birmingham B1 2LH
tel 0845-300 6200 *fax* 0121-643 7239
textphone 0121-643 2815

Area covered: Herefordshire, Shropshire, Staffordshire, Warwickshire, Worcestershire; metropolitan authorities of Birmingham, Coventry, Dudley, Sandwell, Solihull, Walsall, Wolverhampton.

Arts Council England, Yorkshire
21 Bond Street, Dewsbury,
West Yorkshire WF13 1AX
tel 0845-300 6200 *fax* (01924) 466522
textphone (01924) 438585

Area covered: Yorkshire and the Humber, which includes North and North East Lincolnshire.

NATIONAL FILM AGENCIES

Northern Ireland Screen
3rd Floor, 21 Alfred House, Belfast BT2 8ED
tel 028-9023 2444
website www.northernirelandscreen.co.uk

Northern Ireland Screen is the national screen agency for Northern Ireland. Its aim is to accelerate the development of a dynamic and sustainable screen industry and culture in Northern Ireland.

Scottish Screen
In April 2010 Scottish Screen merged with the Scottish Arts Council to become Creative Scotland.

UK Film Council
10 Little Portland Street, London W1W 7JG
tel 020-7861 7861
email info@ukfilmcouncil.org.uk
website www.ukfilmcouncil.org.uk

Established by the Government in 2000, the UK Film Council supports the development of the British film industry and film culture. Offers a variety of funding schemes to nurture new filmmaking talent and provides money to regional film agencies for distribution to local projects.

For general enquiries about any of the UK Film Council's short film schemes, and to be kept informed of future opportunities, contact **shorts@ukfilmcouncil.org.uk**.

Note Just as this edition of *Actors' Yearbook* went to print, the Department for Culture, Media & Sport (DCMS) announced that they were proposing to abolish the UK Film Council as part of a cost-cutting drive. The DCMS said that film funding would continue, but would be distributed through other bodies.

Wales Screen Commission (formerly Sgrin Media Agency for Wales)
33-35 West Bute Street, Cardiff Bay,
Cardiff CF10 5LH
tel 0800-849 8848
email enquiry@walesscreencommission.co.uk
website www.walesscreencommission.co.uk

The Wales Screen Commission is the location service for Wales, offering comprehensive information and support on locations, facilities, crew and local services throughout Wales.

REGIONAL FILM AGENCIES

EM Media
Antenna Media Centre, Beck Street,
Nottingham NG1 1EQ
tel 0115-993 2333
email info@em-media.org.uk
website www.em-media.org.uk

EM Media is the Screen Agency for the East Midlands region of England, and invests in East Midlands based creative talent, supporting and developing projects and activities that meet its business aims.

Film London (formerly London Film & Video Development Agency)
Suite 6.10, The Tea Building,
56 Shoreditch High Street, London E1 6JJ
tel 020-7613 7676 *fax* 020-7613 7677
email info@filmlondon.org.uk
website www.filmlondon.org.uk

Film London is the capital's public agency for feature film, television, commercials and other interactive content, including games. "Our aim is simple: to ensure that London has a thriving film sector that enriches the capital's businesses and its people." Film London is supported by the UK Film Council and the London Development Agency, also receiving significant support from Arts Council England London, the Mayor of London and Skillset.

Northern Film & Media
Northern Film & Media, Studio 3, The Kiln,
Hoults Yard, Walker Road,
Newcastle upon Tyne NE6 1AB
tel 0191-275 5930 *fax* 0191-275 5931
email info@northernmedia.org
website www.northernmedia.org,
www.northeastmovies.co.uk

Northern Film & Media is the screen agency for the North East of England. "Our vision is to create a strong commercial creative economy in the North East, by investing in talent and ideas."

Screen East
1st Floor, 2 Millennium Plain, Norwich NR2 1TF
tel (01603) 776920
email info@screeneast.co.uk
website www.screeneast.co.uk

Screen East is the regional screen agency for the East of England, dedicated to developing a vibrant and flourishing film, TV and digital media industry. "We do this through the activities of our four departments: Locations, Production, Enterprise and Skills, and Audiences and Education. We allocate Lottery Funding on behalf of the UK Film Council through the Regional Investment Fund for England. (RIFE)."

Screen South
The Wedge, 75-81 Tontine Street, Folkestone,
Kent CT20 1JR
tel (01303) 259777 *fax* (01303) 259786
email info@screensouth.org
website www.screensouth.org

Screen South is the film and media agency for the South East of England. "We aim to be a resource that helps people get their ideas off the ground, whether they want to make a short film, learn how to write successful scripts, set up a film festival or shoot a major movie here. We promote talent, preserve our film heritage and find ways of presenting exciting film to new audiences. Screen South is a Lottery distributor. The funding we distribute is primarily from the UK Film Council's Regional Investment Fund for England (RIFE)."

Screen West Midlands
Screen West Midlands, 9 Regent Place,
Birmingham B1 3NJ
tel 0121-265 7120 *fax* 0121-265 7180
email info@screenwm.co.uk
website www.screenwm.co.uk

Screen WM is the lead agency for film, television and digital media in the West Midlands; a region that is driving innovation and excellence in content creation and cross-media collaboration. "Our remit is to develop the economic, social and cultural wealth of the region through supporting the screen media industries." Screen WM's new partnership with Channel 4, to deliver the channel's new 4iP fund, has positioned the West Midlands at the centre of the digital media revolution in the UK, with the agency now supporting the games, online and interactive sectors.

Screen Yorkshire
Studio 22, 46 The Calls, Leeds LS2 7EY
tel 0113-294 4410
email sally@screenyorkshire.co.uk
website www.screenyorkshire.co.uk

Screen Yorkshire's mission is to inspire, promote and support the development of a successful long-term film, broadcast, games and interactive media sector to grow the economic, social and cultural wealth of the region.

South West Screen
St Bartholomews Court, Lewins Mead,
Bristol BS1 5BT
tel 0117-952 9977
email info@swscreen.co.uk
website www.swscreen.co.uk

"We are the organisation that supports and develops creative media industries in the South West. We can offer funding and assistance to encourage innovation, grow creative businesses, develop talent, reach new audiences and develop the skills necessary to move forward."

Vision+Media (formerly North West Vision)
100 Broadway, Salford Quays, Manchester M50 2UW
tel 0844-395 0385
website www.visionandmedia.co.uk

Working on behalf of the digital and creative industries in the North West, Vision+Media aims to grow a world-class digital and creative economy within the North West region.

OTHER SOURCES OF FUNDING

Additional information about various entertainment charities and benevolent funds can be found on the website of The Actors' Charitable Trust **www.tactactors.org**. Unless explicitly mentioned, most of the organisations listed below and on the TACT website do not provide assistance with drama school fees or maintenance.

Actors' Benevolent Fund
6 Adam Street, London WC2N 6AD
tel 020-7836 6378 *fax* 020-7836 8978
email office@abf.org.uk
website www.actorsbenevolentfund.co.uk

For more than 125 years the Actors' Benevolent Fund has provided financial assistance to actors unable to work due to poor health, an accident or old age. To be eligible for assistance, applicants need several years of professional acting experience.

The Actors' Charitable Trust (TACT)
58 Bloomsbury Street, London WC1B 3QT
tel 020-7636 7868
email robert@tactactors.org
website www.tactactors.org
General Secretary Robert Ashby

Grant, advice and support for the children of professional actors. Also administers TACT

Education Fund: Maintenance grants for students on arts courses who have a parent who is or was a professional actor.

Calouste Gulbenkian Foundation
50 Hoxton Square, London N1 6PB
tel 020-7012 1400 or 0845-872 9930
fax 020-7739 1961
email info@gulbenkian.org.uk
website www.gulbenkian.org.uk

Awards grants to professional organisations or professional artists, working in partnerships or groups, developing new art in any artform.

Department for Business, Innovation & Skills
Castle View House, East Lane, Runcom WA7 2GJ
tel 020-7215 5555
website www.bis.gov.uk

This new (as of June 2009) organisation now covers Further & Higher Education. Its work was formerly the responsibility of the Department for Education & Skills.

Equity Charitable Trust
Plouviez House, 19-20 Hatton Place,
London EC1N 8RU
tel 020-7831 1926 *fax* 020-7242 7995
website www.equitycharitabletrust.org.uk

The trust seeks to further education through support and development of the performing arts, and to provide for the welfare and health of professional performers, former performers, their relatives and dependants. Also offers free debt counselling and benefits advice.

Evelyn Norris Trust
222 Africa House, 64 Kingsway, London WC2B 6BD
tel 020-7404 6041
website www.equitycharitabletrust.org.uk/
evelynnorris.php
Secretary Keith Carter

The Evelyn Norris Trust is a charity that accepts applications for grants from members of the concert and theatrical professions. The Trust aims to help with the cost of convalesence or a recuperative holiday following illness, injury or surgery.

First Light
Studio 28, Fazeley Studios, Fazeley Street,
Birmingham B5 5SE
tel 0121-224 7511

First Light is the UK's leading initiative enabling young people to realise their potential via creative digital film and media projects. It operates a number of youth funding schemes, including:

• The Young Film Fund – the UK Film Council's Lottery-funded filmmaking initiative for 5-19 year

olds. For guidelines and information on how to apply, go to **www.firstlightonline.co.uk**
• Mediabox – a Department for Children, Schools & Families fund to help young people establish a positive voice in the media. It offers disadvantaged 13-19 year olds the opportunity to develop and produce creative media projects using film, print, television, radio or online platforms. There are grants of up to £40,000 available now. For more information, visit **www.media-box.co.uk**
• Second Light – a talent development scheme which, through production-based training, will give 30 talented young people aged 18 to 23, from BME backgrounds, supported opportunities to move into the film industry. For more information go to **www.firstlightonline.co.uk**

The Foyle Foundation

Rugby Chambers, 2 Rugby Street, London WC1N 3QU
tel 020-7430 9119 *fax* 020-7430 9830
email info@foylefoundation.org.uk
website www.foylefoundation.org.uk

The Foyle Foundation makes grants to registered charities in the UK whose core remit covers the arts, learning or health. It has supported tours, festivals and education projects, and helped to develop new work. It will also consider funding the building or updating of arts facilities. The average size of grant is between £5000 and £20,000. Application forms and guidelines are available to download from the website.

The Jerwood Charitable Foundation

171 Union Street, London SE1 0LN
tel 020-7261 0279
email info@jerwood.org
website www.jerwood.org

Awards grants to young people, mainly aged 20 to 35, who have demonstrated achievement, commitment and excellence, particularly in the performing arts. Financial support has been offered to young actors, dancers, choreographers, playwrights, filmmakers, singers and musicians and others in the performing and visual arts. The charity seeks to make grants which will produce tangible and visible results and whose beneficial effects will extend beyond the immediate recipient of the grant.

National Theatre Foundation

c/o National Theatre, South Bank, London SE1 9PX
tel 020 7452 3366 *fax* 020 7452 3364
email foundation@nationaltheatre.org.uk
website www.nationaltheatre.org.uk/foundation
Administrator Lucy Francis *Welfare Counsellor* Mary Hill

The Royal National Theatre Foundation exists to help anybody who works or has worked at the National Theatre and is in need of help – usually in

circumstances where he or she cannot afford the normal things of life which most people take for granted. This may take the form of a loan or a one-off grant towards a range of things, depending on the individual's circumstances. Each case is treated on its merit and involves the applicant submitting a confidential application form which includes details of savings and a statement of regular income and expenditure. More information including an application form is available at **www.nationaltheatre.org.uk/foundation** or email foundation@nationaltheatre.org.uk. The Welfare Counsellor can be contacted directly on 020-7452 3737.

NESTA (National Endowment for Science, Technology and the Arts)

1 Plough Place, London EC4A 1DE
tel 020-7438 2500 *fax* 020-7438 2501
email nesta@nesta.org.uk
website www.nesta.org.uk

Offers a variety of funding schemes to promote innovation within the fields of science, technology and the arts.

The Oxford Samuel Beckett Theatre Trust Award

PO Box 2637, Ascot, Berks SL5 8ZN
email info@osbttrust.com
website www.osbttrust.com
Director Romilly Walton Masters

The purpose of this annual award is, in particular, to help the development of emerging practitioners in the field of innovative theatre/performance and, in general, to encourage the new generation of creative artists. Artists from all disciplines are encouraged to apply.

The award is for a site-responsive, non-traditional show to take place in one of the 5 host Boroughs for the Olympic and Paralympic Games. The show will be part of the Barbican BITE season and CREATE Festival in East London.

Performance Initiative Network

School of Arts, Brunel University, Uxbridge UB8 3PH
tel (01895) 266505
email kerry.irvine@brunel.ac.uk
website www.performanceinitiative.co.uk

Contact Kerry Irvine

Supporting the professional small theatre company and theatre artist to make and produce their work. Runs the GroundWork Festival, eVolve, and the PiLab series of projects.

The Royal Theatrical Fund

11 Garrick Street, London WC2E 9AR
tel 020-7836 3322 *fax* 020-7379 8273
email admin@trtf.com
website www.trtf.com

432 Resources

Founded in 1839, the Royal Theatrical Fund makes grants which will alleviate the suffering, assist the recovery, or reduce the need, hardship or distress of theatrical artists or their families/dependants. To be eligible to receive a grant, a person must have professionally practised or contributed to the theatrical arts (on stage, radio, film or television) for a minimum of 7 years.

Sophie's Silver Lining Fund

c/o Tony Scott Andrews, At Aplin Stockton Fairfax, 36 West Bar, Banbury, Oxon OX16 9RU
tel (01295) 251234
email office@sslf.org.uk
website www.sslf.org.uk

Provides assistance to needy acting and singing students with the cost of their training. "Please note that regretfully, we are no longer able to accept applications for funding from individual students. Awards are only made to students put forward by a small number of drama and music colleges selected by the trustees."

TACT Educational Fund

See entry under The Actors' Charitable Trust

The Wellcome Trust

Arts Awards, 210 Euston Road, London NW1 2BE
email arts@wellcome.ac.uk
website www.wellcome.ac.uk/arts

The Wellcome Trust Arts Awards is the Trust's new funding scheme, which continues to support arts projects that engage with biomedical science.

"The Arts Awards provide funding for a range of projects that bring together any art form and any area of biomedical science. We encourage collaboration between professionals from different disciplines, between adults and young people, and between experts and the public. The scheme builds on the success of previous schemes such as Sciart, Pulse and Science on Stage and Screen, and is part of the Trust's £3.2million Engaging Science programme. 2 levels of funding are available – small to medium sized projects (up to and including £30,000) and large projects (above £30,000). Full details are available on our website, including details of pending deadlines for large and small grants, application guidelines, examples of previously funded projects, and the application form."

Publications, libraries, references and booksellers

This section lists the major sources for scripts and sheet music – and routes to finding that elusive script or score. While Internet search engines can be extremely useful in such a quest, it sometimes requires some lateral thinking to find what you want. It is possible to find out-of-print plays via libraries or book-finding services and by combing second-hand book shops. Some publishers (even a few playwrights' agencies) will organise a photocopy – for a fee. Also, the British Library (in theory) has a copy of every play ever performed in this country, but there can be complications in actually getting hold of a copy. Start with your local library if you're determined to find a specific play; if they don't have it, they may well be able to get it from another library (via the inter-library loan system), but be prepared for it to take a long time. Another route is to try to find a theatre at which the play has been performed: they may be able to help.

AbeBooks.com
website www.abebooks.com
Excellent website which will search the catalogues of hundreds of secondhand booksellers in this country and around the world.

Amazon.co.uk & Amazon.com
website www.amazon.co.uk or www.amazon.com
UK and US sites (respectively) for books, DVDs, CDs and all sorts of other things. Secondhand items are listed alongside the new, so often a good place to find cheap scripts.

Arts Oracle
website www.artsoracle.com
A comprehensive online directory that quickly puts you in touch with the services you need. Agents to art centres, casting directors to costumiers, photographers to promotional services, training to tutors. Thousands of companies, services and individuals, listed in over 100 categories, updated daily. For those searching it is a resource that is accurate, fast and totally free of charge. For those listed it presents numerous opportunities – from free listings to a targeted banner campaign. All content can be updated at any point.

Barbican Library
Barbican Centre, London EC2Y 8DS
tel 020-7638 0569
website www.cityoflondon.gov.uk/barbicanlibrary
Situated on level 2 of the Barbican Centre, this is the largest lending library in the City of London. In addition to the general library, the strong arts and music sections reflect the Barbican Centre's emphasis on the arts. The library is fully accessible by wheelchair and has a number of other access facilities including hearing induction loops and a reading magnifier machine. *Opening hours*: Monday and Wednesday: 9.30am – 5.30pm; Tuesday and Thursday: 9.30am – 7.30pm; Friday: 9.30am – 2pm; Saturday: 9.30am – 4pm.

Bookbarn International
White Cross, Somerset BS39 6EX
tel (01761) 451777
website www.bookbarninternational.co.uk
"The UK's largest used book warehouse," with many thousands of cheap secondhand scripts and a searchable catalogue online.

The British Library
96 Euston Road, London NW1 2DB
tel 0843-208 1144
(Switchboard), 020-7412 7676 (Advance Reservations, St Pancras Reading Rooms and Humanities enquiries), 020-7412 7702 (Maps), 020-7412 7513 (Manuscripts), 020-7412 7772 (Music), 020-7412 7873 (Asia, Pacific & Africa Collections)
website www.bl.uk

The British Library is the national library of the United Kingdom and contains a substantial collection of plays and manuscripts from the UK and Ireland, as well as from other parts of the world. The sound archive also includes just about everything from the sound of Amazonian tree frogs to classic recordings of Shakespeare's plays. Users need a Reader's Pass (details on how to acquire same is on the website) to access and read particular publications. The library will, for a fee, allow photocopying – subject to copyright legislation.

Resources

Chappell of Bond Street

152-160 Wardour Street, London W1F 8YA
tel 020-7432 4400 *fax* 020-7432 4410
email enquiries_bs@chappell-bond-st.co.uk
website www.chappellofbondstreet.co.uk

Stocks the largest range of printed music anywhere in
Europe, covering everything from popular chart
books to medieval instrumentals, exam pieces to
orchestral scores. *Opening Hours*: Monday to Friday:
9.30am – 6pm; Saturday: 9.30am – 5pm.

Contacts

See separate section on The Spotlight.

Doollee.com

website www.doollee.com

An excellent free online guide to modern playwrights
and theatre plays which have been written, or
translated, into English since the production of *Look
Back in Anger* in 1956.

The Drama Student

Top Floor, 66 Wansey Street, London SE17 1JP
tel 020-7701 4536 *fax* (07092) 846523
email editor@thedramastudent.co.uk
website www.thedramastudent.co.uk
Editor Phil Matthews

Recently launched as the only magazine dedicated to
drama students across the UK. Published quarterly,
the first issue appeared in January 2009. The
magazine brings together an exciting community of
current and prospective students actively pursuing a
career in theatre, film, television or radio, either as an
actor or behind the scenes. *The Drama Student* is
their essential reference, a publication with both
enthusiasm and substance.

Dress Circle

57-59 Monmouth Street, Upper St Martin's Lane,
London WC2H 9DG
tel 020-7240 2227 *fax* 020-7379 8540
email info@dresscircle.co.uk
website www.dresscircle.co.uk

Dress Circle was founded over 25 years ago to supply
the widest possible selection of Musical Theatre and
Cabaret-related products from around the world –
CDs, cassettes, videos, DVDs, posters, cards, mugs,
collectibles and more. Opening Hours: Monday to
Saturday: 10.00am – 6.30pm. "If we can't get it – no
one can!"

Samuel French Theatre Bookshop

52 Fitzroy Street, London W1T 5JR
tel 020-7255 4300 *fax* 020-7387 2161
website www.samuelfrench-london.co.uk

Samuel French has been publishing, selling and
leasing plays for performance since 1830. Today it has
more than 2000 playscripts available, covering all

elements of performing theatre – from comedies to
tragedies, sketches to full-scale musicals. In addition,
the bookshop stocks a comprehensive range of
playscripts and technical books on all aspects of
theatre. Publishes *The Guide to Selecting Plays*, which
lists plays according to genre and cast size. Bookshop
is wheelchair-friendly, staff are helpful and signage
suitable for visually-impaired. Enlarged print
catalogue & lists on demand.

Internet Movie Database

website uk.imdb.com

A comprehensive database and news round-up of
film and television around the world.

The Knowledge

WLR Media & Entertainment, 2nd Floor,
Paulton House, 8 Shepherdess Walk, London N1 7LB
tel 020-7549 8666
email knowledge@wilmington.co.uk
website www.theknowledgeonline.com

Covering all aspects of production, The Knowledge
Online contains contacts and services for the UK
film, television, video and commercial production
industry. Its *Know-How* section contains studio and
post-production charts, production guidelines,
articles and maps, and in 2003 it introduced an
overview of international co-production by the
British Film Commission.

Limited access can be gained by registering online,
but for full access to over 18,000 entries and to the
Know-How, users must pay a £50 annual
subscription.

London Arrangements

30 Maryland Square, London E15 1HE
tel 020-8221 2381 *fax* 020-8926 2724
email enquiries@londonarrangements.com
website www.londonarrangements.com
Director Stephen Robinson

Specialises in the production of hard-to-find backing
tracks. Main genres covered are big band, theatre,
film, easy listening and classical. Samples of all tracks
can be listened to online, and the majority may be
ordered in any key at no extra charge.

London Theatre

website www.londontheatre.co.uk

A website containing news, reviews, events, booking
information and seating plans for London's theatre
scene plus maps, hotels and general tourist
information.

Mandy.com

website www.mandy.com

An online service providing a directory of 40,000
technicians, facilities and producers and a vacancy list
for jobs in production, crew, art departments and

post-production. Also posts casting calls for actors, classified ads and information about films for sale and distribution on its website.

Musicroom

email info@musicroom.com
website www.musicroom.com

The world's largest online retailer of sheet music, tutor methods, instructional DVDs & videos, music software and instruments & accessories.

National Theatre Bookshop

National Theatre, South Bank, London SE1 9PX
tel 020-7452 3456 *fax* 020-7452 3457
email bookshop@nationaltheatre.org.uk
website www.nationaltheatre.org.uk/bookshop

Opening Hours: Monday to Saturday: 9.30am – 10.45pm (this varies on certain public holidays); 12pm – 6pm on Sundays when there is a performance. David Hare once described it as "the most varied and complete performing arts bookshop in the English-speaking world".

PlayDatabase.com

website www.playdatabase.com

US site that helps theatre-lovers find monologues and plays for production.

Playregistry.com

email info@playregistry.com
website www.playregistry.com

A database containing thousands of well- and lesser-known plays; the list is growing all the time. "Search through our vast database to find detailed information about the plays and playwrights, including synopses, biographies, character breakdowns, production histories and much more."

Project Gutenberg

website www.gutenberg.org

An online library of more than 18,000 books – and many classic plays – which have gone out of copyright in the US. Also a growing collection of music recordings and scores. Possibly the largest of its kind in the world.

Rogues and Vagabonds

13 Elm Road, London SW14 7JL
tel 020-8876 1175
email contact@roguesandvagabonds.co.uk
website www.roguesandvagabonds.co.uk

"*Rogues & Vagabonds* is an online publication for everyone who loves theatre with news, reviews (plays, books, exhibitions), interviews, comment and debate from freelance contributors, and is as much about our theatrical heritage as the present and future of the performing arts. There are specific resources for professionals, including free casting information,

links to useful websites and information on a range of services for actors."

Rogues and Vagabonds is no longer being published. However, the site will remain fully accessible as a valuable resource.

Royal Court Theatre Bookshop

Sloane Square, London SW1W 8AS
tel 020-7565 5024
email bookshop@royalcourttheatre.com
website www.royalcourttheatre.com

Offers a diverse selection of contemporary plays and publications on the theory and practice of modern drama. The staff specialise in assisting with the selection of audition monologues and scenes. Royal Court playtexts from past and present productions cost £2. The Bookshop is situated in the downstairs Royal Court Bar & Food area. *Opening Hours*: Monday to Friday: 3pm – 10pm; Saturday: 2.30pm – 10pm.

Screen International

Greater London House, Hampstead Road, London NW1 7EJ
tel 020-7728 5000
email mike.goodridge@emap.com
website www.screendaily.com

International news and features on the film business. Subscriptions cost £135 p.a. for 48 issues plus unlimited access to **ScreenDaily.com**.

Script Websites

Although subject to rules on copyright, a number of websites make the scripts for films and television shows, and suggestions for audition speeches, available online. These sites tend to come and go, but here are some that are current at the time of going to press:

- **www.script-o-rama.com**
- **www.sfy.ru**
- **www.imsdb.com**
- **www.playscripts.com**
- **www.simplyscripts.com**
- **www.whysanity.net/monos**
- **www.singlelane.com**

The Sheetmusic Warehouse

email pianoman@globalnet.co.uk
website www.sheetmusicwarehouse.co.uk

Specialists supplying old music, rare music, music from the shows, musicals and operetta, popular music, wartime music, jazz music, Deep South American music. Music Hall music, classical music, modern music ... "You name it, we've probably got it. Music to play, music to sing to or music to frame and hang on your wall!"

Shooting People

27 Hedingham Close, London N1 8UA
email contact@shootingpeople.org
website www.shootingpeople.org

Shooting People allows thousands of people working in independent film to exchange information via a range of daily email bulletins. These include:

• Daily UK Filmmakers Bulletin – for directors, producers and crew to share information on the latest technologies, get advice, find crew, locations, production deals, events & screenings, training and more. Currently more than 22,000 members
• Daily UK Screenwriters Bulletin – writers all over the UK use this email network to discuss writing, share ideas and hear about competitions, opportunities and training. Currently more than 13,000 members
• Daily UK Casting Bulletin – for actors to discuss their craft and receive casting calls from directors, producers and casting directors. Currently more than 14,000 members
• Weekly UK Script Pitch Bulletin – a weekly collection of script pitches offered to producers and directors by the writers on the Screenwriters Network. Currently more than 11,000 members

Both part and full membership are available. Part membership allows subscribers to receive email bulletins only, and is free. Full membership costs £20 per year and entitles users to a range of other services. Full members can create an actors' personal profile with a photograph and be listed in the online directory, post to any bulletin and download guides on various confusing aspects of film-making such as actor contracts, health & safety and distribution. They are also entitled to create member cards and browse other member cards to find potential local collaborators.

Shooting People also organises a number of parties, screenings, workshops and other events for which full members receive advanced notice.

Skoob Books
66 The Brunswick, Marchmont Street, London WC1N 1AE
tel 020-7278 8760
website www.skoob.com

An excellent collection of secondhand plays, including many translated works and as-new titles at half RRP. Strong theatre, film, music and TV sections in a very large basement bookshop. All academic areas covered, and masses of paperback fiction. Lift access and knowledgeable, friendly staff. Thousands more books in its Oxford Warehouse, sent to the shop on request. Experienced in set-dressing, offering advice, samples and loan or purchase of books and ephemera.

The Stage
47 Bermondsey Street, London SE1 3XT
tel 020-7403 1818 *subscriptions* (01858) 438895
email newsdesk@thestage.co.uk
website www.thestage.co.uk
Managing Director Catherine Comerford *Editor* Brian Attwood

Online and weekly print publication for the entertainment industry. News, reviews, features and recruitment for theatre, light entertainment, opera, dance, TV, radio, backstage and technical, management, education and training. Established 1880

Theatre Record
131 Sherringham Avenue, London N17 9RU
email (subscriptions) ruth@trsubs.co.uk
website www.theatrerecord.com

Established in 1981 as *London Theatre Record*, the magazine was renamed in 1990 to cover work across the UK. *Theatre Record* publishes the complete, unabridged reviews of all new shows covered by national press and leading listing magazines. Fringe shows get extra attention from the critical teams of *Time Out* and *Metro* (London), while special supplements cover festivals and seasons such as Edinburgh (official and Fringe), LIFT and the London International Mime Festival.

As well as reviews, each show is represented by a full listing of cast, technical credits and, where possible, production photographs. Also lists opening nights for forthcoming productions. Issued fortnightly.

Theatrevoice
website www.theatrevoice.com

The leading site for audio content about British theatre, featuring journalists from across the UK press, and practitioners from across the theatre industry. It was set up in 2003 to see if theatre could be talked about in a new way: allowing critics to be more expansive than the usual space constraints of the print media allowed; to enable actors, writers, directors and designers to be heard talking in detail and at length about their work; and to help members of the public interact more directly with theatre-makers and commentators. The Theatre Museum, now V&A Theatre Collections, which provided technical assistance and a place for recording from the site's inception, assumed management responsibilities for the site in the summer of 2005, to ensure that Theatrevoice's growing archive of material would be preserved for posterity. In April 2008, V&A Theatre Collections and Rose Bruford College agreed to support the site in partnership. Theatrevoice acknowledges with gratitude all the input that has been and still is freely given.

Theatricalia
website theatricalia.com

Theatricalia is aiming to become "the repository of theatre productions on the Internet". In doing so, it will enable people to discover theatre that is going on around them, follow actors they have seen in previous productions, and record memorable events of productions they have seen.

Virtual Library of Theatre & Drama
website www.vl-theatre.com

Lists online versions of plays and resources in more than 50 countries.

Westminster Reference Library

35 St Martin's Street, London WC2H 7HP

tel 020-7641 5253

website http://www.westminster.gov.uk/services/libraries/special/perform/

General reference library with 15,000 volumes on the performing arts, including *PCR*, *Spotlight* and *The Stage*. *Opening Hours*: Monday to Friday: 10.00am – 8.00pm; Saturday: 10.00am – 5.00pm.

Wikipedia

website en.wikipedia.org

A free, online encyclopedia with over one million articles. Originally created by an army of volunteers in 2001, it can be added to or edited by anyone at all – a very democratic publication. This democracy can sometimes mean that contentious or politically sensitive issues are not always presented in the most balanced way, although some measures are in place to prevent flagrant abuse of the system. Occasionally too, the editing process makes for some slightly disjointed articles. However, as a free source of information on just about any topic, it is unsurpassed. The theatre section can be accessed via the following link: **en.wikipedia.org/wiki/Portal:Theatre**.

The World of Musicals

website www.mtishows.com

A great resource for researching songs – some of which can be partially listened to and read about on this site.

Organisations, associations and societies

This section contains details of all kinds of ways (not listed elsewhere) of getting involved, sourcing useful information, learning, finding interesting lectures, networking, and simply keeping in touch with what's going on. It is important for the 'jobbing' actor to keep up-to-date with developments within the industry, and getting involved in related activities can pay dividends in the future.

Actors' Church Union
St Paul's Church, Bedford Street, London WC2E 9ED
tel 020-7240 0344
email actors-church.union@tiscali.co.uk
website www.actorschurchunion.com
Administrator Libby Shaw *President* Bishop Jack Nicholls *Senior Chaplain* The Revd Rob Gillion

Provides pastoral support for all members of the entertainment world, regardless of beliefs. Runs a network of voluntary chaplains for theatres, clubs and studios, in the UK and overseas. Also runs a charitable trust for children of parents in entertainment.

The Agents' Association (GB)
54 Keyes House, Dolphin Square,
London SW1V 3NA
tel 020-7834 0515 *fax* 020-7821 0261
email association@agents-uk.com
website www.agents-uk.com

Established in 1927 to represent and enhance the interests of entertainment agents in the United Kingdom and to standardise practice. Boasts a membership of more than 430 agencies, covering all fields of the entertainment industry.

Arts & Business
Nutmeg House, 60 Gainsford Street, Butlers Wharf,
London SE1 2NY
tel 020-7378 8143 *fax* 020-7407 7527
email info@aandb.org.uk
website www.aandb.org.uk

With support from the Department for Culture, Media Sport and Arts Council England, Arts & Business delivers a range of services to arts organisations of all sizes across the UK promoting the effectiveness and creativity of business and arts partnerships.

Services include sponsoring seminar workshops, training courses, a resource centre, development forums, one-to-one advice sessions and a wide range of publications. Contact details for regional offices are available on the website.

ASSITEJ International
Preradoviceva 44, 10000 Zagreb, Croatia
tel +385 1 4667034 *fax* +385 1 4667225
email sec.gen@assitej-international.org
website www.assitej-international.org/english/home.aspx

ASSITEJ International (Association Internationale du Theatre pour l'Enfance et la Jeunesse) states: "Since the theatrical art is a universal expression of mankind, and possesses the influence and power to link large groups of the world's people in the service of peace, and considering the role theatre can play in the education of younger generations, an autonomous international organisation has been formed which bears the name of the International Association of Theatre for Children and Young People." Also see Theatre for Young Audiences (TYA), below.

British Academy of Film and Television Arts (BAFTA)
195 Piccadilly, London W1J 9LN
tel 020-7734 0022 *fax* 020-7292 5868
email membership@bafta.org
website www.bafta.org

Founded in 1947, BAFTA provides facilities for screening and discussions, runs a popular and varied events programme coverings all aspects of film, television and interactive entertainment, encourages research and experimentation, and presents the annual Orange British Academy Film Awards.

Approximately 4 events are available to members each month. These range from major industry debates to pre-release screenings of film or television productions, followed by a question-and-answer session with the producer, director, writer and/or cast. A series of Networking Evenings was launched in 2001 to facilitate informal meetings and the exhange of ideas between industry professionals. One of the key events in the programme is the annual David Lean Lecture which has been given by such luminaries as Woody Allen, Ken Loach, John Boorman, Robert Altman and Sidney Pollack.

Applicants must have a minimum of 4 years' professional experience in the film, television or video games industries (or any combination of these) and must be able to demonstrate a significant professional contribution to the industry.

British Association for Performing Arts Medicine

4th Floor, Totara Park House,
34-36 Gray's Inn Road, London WC1X 8HR
tel 020-7404 8444 (London Helpline)
tel 0845-602 0235 (Helpline elsewhere)
tel 020-7404 5888 (Admin) *fax* 020-7404 3222
website www.bapam.org.uk

The British Association for Performing Arts Medicine is a specialist charity, founded in 1984. It deals with the occupational health field of performing arts medicine.

BAPAM aims are to:

• Assist performers either by seeing them in the advisory clinics run by BAPAM or directing them on to appropriate places for treatment.
• Undertake research into the particular medical and psychological problems that afflict performers, in order to build up knowledge and skills in the treatment of these problems.

BAPAM keeps a database of healthcare practitioners to whom patients can be referred after a free assessment. This includes conventional and complementary therapies, physical and psychological expertise: GPs and consultants, physiotherapists, chiropractors, osteopaths, Alexander practitioners, counsellors, voice-therapists, all of whom take a special interest in the needs of performers.

BAPAM also administers AMABO (The Association for Medical Advisers to British Orchestras). This scheme ensures that there is appropriate medical treatment available for orchestral musicians. The scheme is run on a similar basis to the provision of medical care available to football, rugby and cricket teams. Doctors provide, on an honorary basis, the kind of specialist advice and medical care specifically geared towards musicians, which might not normally be available from a patient's own GP.

All calls are treated in confidence. Information and referral to the assessment clinics is free. Most often, even if it is then necessary to refer on to a specialist consultant, the appointment is available quickly, either free or at reduced cost.

British Council

Arts Group, 10 Spring Gardens, London SW1A 2BN
tel 020-7389 3194 *fax* 020-7389 3199
email arts@britishcouncil.org
Norwich Union House, 7 Fountain Street, Belfast BT1 5EG
tel 028-9024 8220 *fax* 028-9023 7592
email nireland.enquiries@britishcouncil.org
The Tun, 3rd Floor, 4 Jackson's Entry, Holyrood Road, Edinburgh EH8 8PJ

tel 0131-524 5714 *fax* 0131-524 5714
email scotland.enquiries@britishcouncil.org
1 Kingsway, 2nd Floor, Cardiff CF10 3AQ
tel 029-2092 4300 *fax* 029-2092 4301
email wales.enquiries@britishcouncil.org
website www.britishcouncil.org/new/arts

The British Council is the UK's public diplomacy and cultural organisation and works in 100 countries, in arts, education, governance and science. The Arts Group supports around 2000 arts events every year encouraging international collaborations, performances and exchanges with some of the top UK artists. In addition they support arts-based workshops, seminars and online events.

The form of support which is offered varies according to the project. In most cases the Council acts as an advisory body and brokers partnerships with overseas contacts such as artistic programmers and producers, venues, choreographers and festival directors. Although most work is geared towards young people aged 16-35, this isn't an exclusive emphasis and classic or traditional work is supported, especially if it has a modern slant.

Resources available on the website include an annual directory of UK drama, dance, live art and street art companies that have work suitable for overseas touring; specialist information about drama/performing arts education in the UK; and *Britfilms* **www.britfilms.com** – a portal site for the UK film industry with information about international film festivals, UK film directors and films, making a film in the UK, training and careers advice.

Not open to the public except by appointment. Write, phone or email to establish contact or get in touch with an artform specialist.

British Film Institute (BFI)

BFI National Library, 21 Stephen Street, London W1T 1LN
tel 020-7255 1444
email library@bfi.org.uk
BFI Southbank, Belvedere Road, South Bank, Waterloo, London SE1 8XT
tel 020-7928 3535
email nft@bfi.org.uk
website www.bfi.org.uk

Established in 1933, the BFI strives to increase the level of understanding, appreciation and access to film and television culture. In addition to the BFI National Library which holds the largest film archive in the world, the organisation runs BFI Southbank (formerly the National Film Theatre) and London Film Festival (see entry under *Media festivals*), and the BFI IMAX Cinema. It also publishes books, releases films in cinemas, on video and DVD, runs educational programmes and has one of the largest collections of film stills and film posters in the world.

British Music Hall Society

82 Fernlea Road, London SW12 9RW
tel 020-8673 2175

Resources

website www.music-hall-society.com
Secretary Daphne Masterton

Founded in 1963 and with offices across England, the society aims to preserve the history of music hall and variety, to recall the artistes who created it and to support entertainers working today. Members receive copies of the society's quarterly magazine *The Call-Boy* containing news, views and information about the sector; they also have the opportunity to attend evening and weekend study group meetings. Arranges live theatre shows and it is possible for members to take part in such performances on these occasions.

Casting Directors Guild
website www.thecdg.co.uk

A professional organisation which represents casting directors working in film, television, theatre and commercials. The Casting Directors Guild aims to standardise professional working practice and to enable the exchange of information and ideas between members.

Election to the Guild is at the discretion of the Committee. Full members must have worked in 1 or more areas of the industry for at least 5 years and are entitled to use the initials CDG after their name. Probationary members must have worked as an assistant to a casting director for 3 years.

Members are listed on the website with information about their areas of work and recent credits.

Casting Society of America
website www.castingsociety.com

The Casting Society of America is the premier organisation of theatrical Casting Directors in film, television, and theatre. Although it is not a union, its members are a united professional society that consistently set the level of professionalism in casting on which the entertainment industry has come to rely. Its more than 350 members are represented not only in the United States, but also in Canada, England, Australia and Italy.

Co-operative Personal Management Association
email cpmauk@yahoo.co.uk
website www.cpma.coop

Founded in 2002, the CPMA works to further and promote the interests of its members, who are acting agencies located across the UK. Backed by Equity, it seeks to raise the profile of co-ops with both employers and actors, and to represent the interests of co-ops with external bodies. Also works with members to identify and assist in solving the unique problems of a co-operative, to encourage good practice, to develop training skills and opportunities, and to act as an advocate for co-operative working.

The John Colclough Consultancy
tel 020-8873 1763
website www.johncolclough.co.uk

Practical independent guidance for actors & actresses. When The Spotlight decided to end their advisory service in March 2005, John Colclough decided to carry on an 'advisory' service independently using the knowledge he had gained at The Spotlight and also from his shop-floor experience as an actor, director and producer.

Sessions take place over the telephone. Please refer to the website for current charges. Payments may be made either by cheque or credit/debit card after the consultation has taken place. Telephone calls are free to landlines. Calls to mobiles will be charged for, unless the caller offers to return the call. For a consultation, telephone John on 020-8873 1763.

Conference of Drama Schools (CDS)
PO Box 34252, London NW5 1XJ
email info@cds.drama.ac.uk
website www.drama.ac.uk

Founded in 1969 to strengthen the voice of member drama schools and encourage the highest standards of training, the CDS also helps students understand the range of courses on offer and how to apply for them. The CDS played a key role in the negotiations which led to the formation of the National Council for Drama Training (see entry below).

The 22 member schools offer courses in Acting, Musical Theatre, Directing and Technical Theatre training. CDS members offer courses that are professional, intensive and vocational. They are often mentally and physically demanding and, unlike most degree courses at universities and colleges, do not generally contain a high proportion of academic work.

Produces the *Guide to Professional Training in Drama and Technical Theatre* for careers officers, teachers and applicants, providing a description of each member school, its policy and the courses it offers together with information about funding. It also provides details of summer schools. The printed version is available free of charge from French's Theatre Bookshop (see entry on page 434). Alternatively it can be downloaded from the CDS website. (CDS also publishes *The Guide to Careers Backstage* which is also available from French's and from the CDS website.)

Conservatoire for Dance and Drama (CDD)
Tavistock House, Tavistock Square,
London WC1H 9JJ
tel 020-7387 5101 *fax* 020-7387 5103
email info@cdd.ac.uk
website www.cdd.ac.uk

The Conservatoire is one of the newest and most exciting higher education institutions in the country, established in 2001 to secure the future of conservatoire-level vocational training in dance and drama in England. It has a unique structure, made up of 8 affiliate schools. All are small, specialist, vocational training institutions with international reputations for high-quality training in dance, drama or circus arts. Through the Conservatoire, all the affiliates receive funding from the Higher Education Funding Council for England, which helps to ensure that the most talented students benefit from vocational training, to which access can given regardless of background or financial circumstances.

The Conservatoire welcomes applications from disabled people and judges applicants solely on their talent and potential to develop the skills required for their chosen profession. "We are committed to admitting and supporting disabled students and warmly encourage you to inform the school so that appropriate support can be put into place as soon as possible."

The eight Conservatoire affiliate schools are: Bristol Old Vic Theatre School, Central School of Ballet, Circus Space, The London Academy of Music and Dramatic Art (LAMDA), London Contemporary Dance School, Northern School of Contemporary Dance, Rambert School of Ballet and Contemporary Dance, Royal Academy of Dramatic Art (RADA)

Council for Dance Education and Training (CDET)

Old Brewer's Yard, 17-19 Neal Street, Covent Garden, London WC2H 9UY
tel 020-7240 5703 *fax* 020-7240 2547
email info@cdet.org.uk
website www.cdet.org.uk

The Council for Dance Education and Training is the national standards body of the professional dance industry. It accredits programmes of training in vocational dance schools and holds the Register of Dance Awarding Bodies – the directory of teaching societies whose syllabuses have been inspected and approved by the Council. It is the body of advocacy of the dance education and training communities, and offers a free and comprehensive information service, *Answers for Dancers*, on all aspects of vocational dance provision to students, parents, teachers, dance artists and employers.

Culture.info

website www.culture.info

The aim of Culture.Info is to be the first port-of-call for users seeking cultural information on a particular topic. Each Culture.Info sub-portal provides a carefully researched set of listings of links to information that is more focused and useful than can usually be obtained from the vast majority of existing listings or search engines.

Dance UK

The Urdang, The Old Finsbury Town Hall, Rosebery Avenue, London EC1R 4QT

tel 020-7713 0730 *fax* 020-7833 2363
email info@danceuk.org
website www.danceuk.org

Dance UK was founded in 1982 and works with and on behalf of dance, providing information, publications, networks, forums for debate and conferences and a unified voice for all its members. It has about 130 corporate members, including most of the major dance companies, venues, agencies, funders and educational institutions. Individual members include individual dance artists, choreographers, administrators, managers, technicians, teachers, students, writers and members of dance audiences.

The organisation is active in 3 main areas: Communication, Professional Development and Healthier Dance. As well as the website, Dance UK manages email groups for choreographers, dance managers and independent dance artists, and produces *Dance UK News* which is mailed quarterly to members. Has set up a number of practical initiatives to promote longer-lasting careers and professional development in dance including insurance schemes for teachers, the UK Choreographers Directory, and books and information sheets on floors, pensions, insurance and copyright.

Promoting the health and well-being of dancers, it also generates research, educational talks and events, posters, information sheets and books. The Practitioners Register is a telephone help-line providing contact information for local medical and complementary therapists with experience of working with dancers. For information about other dance organisations and performing companies, visit the links page on the website.

Denville Hall

62 Ducks Hill Road, Northwood, Middlesex HA6 2SB
tel (01923) 825843 *fax* (01923) 841855
website www.denvillehall.org.uk

The care home for elderly actors, including residential, nursing and dementia care and short respite stays.

Department of Culture, Media and Sport (DCMS)

Information Centre, 2-4 Cockspur Street, London SW1Y 5DH
tel 020-7211 6200
email enquiries@culture.gov.uk
website www.culture.gov.uk

The DCMS is responsible for Government policy on the arts, sport, the National Lottery, tourism, libraries, museums and galleries, broadcasting, film, the music industry, press freedom and regulation, licensing, gambling and the historic environment.

Arts policies are carried out in partnership with Arts Council England and its Regional Arts Councils,

Resources

other government departments such as the Department for Education and Skills, and with regional bodies such as local authorities.

Directors Guild of Great Britain & Directors Guild Trust

Studio 24, Royal Victoria Patriotic Building, John Archer Way, London SW18 3SX
tel 020-8871 1660
email emma@dggb.org
website www.dggb.org

The Directors Guild of Great Britain and Directors Guild Trust work together to promote and support directing across all media: film, television, theatre, radio, opera, commercials, music videos, corporate film, multimedia and new technology. The Guild hosts events and training, produces and sponsors publications, has a respected public voice on arts and media policy, and is a Forum for members to meet and share experiences and skills. "We welcome professional directors in all media, students of directing and associated studies, educational establishments teaching directing in theatre, film and television, corporate members who would like access to our facilities, and everyone interested in the art and craft of directing."

Actors can obtain information about the Guild's members and their career profile using the online searchable database. For information on directors who are not members of the Guild, the DGGB has a number of suggestions on their website. Actors may wish to consult the following websites for information on international directors:
• www.dga.org (Directors Guild of America)
• www.dgc.ca (Directors Guild of Canada)
• www.asdafilm.org.au (Australian Screen Directors Association)

Directors UK

Inigo Place, 31-32 Bedford Street, London WC2E 9ED
tel 020-7240 0009 *fax* 020-7269 0676
email info@Directors.UK.com
website www.directors.uk.com

Directors UK (formerly the Directors' & Producers' Rights Society (DPRS)) is the collecting society which represents British film and television directors. It collects and distributes money due to directors for the exploitation of their work. The Society is also a campaigning organisation, working to establish and protect directors' rights in the UK and abroad. It works closely with the Directors Guild of Great Britain (DGGB) and the Broadcasting, Entertainment, Cinematograph and Theatre Union (BECTU) to improve the conditions and terms under which directors are employed. The current membership runs to 4000 directors and estates, working in all fields of film and television: from features to soap, from fly-on-the-wall to natural history.

Drama Association of Wales

The Old Library, Singleton Road, Splott, Cardiff CF24 2ET
tel 029-2045 2200 *fax* 029-2045 2277
email teresa@dramawales.org.uk
website www.dramawales.org.uk
Key contact Teresa Hennessy

Founded in 1934 and a registered charity since 1973, the Drama Association of Wales aims to increase opportunities for people in the community to be creatively involved in high-quality drama.

Its main activities are an extensive mail-order library service with more than 300,000 volumes of plays, biographies, critical works and technical theatre books, and training courses in all aspects of theatre, including a 7-day residential summer school.

Also runs several new writing schemes offering a script-reading service, a playwriting competition, workshops and support for first productions, and organises the Welsh National Drama Festival from March to June, culminating in the Wales One Act Festival.

UK membership costs £20 per year for individuals and £42 for groups, both professional and amateur.

Dramaturgs' Network

69 Hounslow Road, Twickenham, Middlesex TW2 7HA
tel (07939) 270556
email info@dramaturgy.co.uk
website ee.dramaturgy.co.uk

The Dramaturgs' Network is a professional organisation which promotes the role of the dramaturg in the UK. Providing members with a network of support, the organisation brings dramaturgs, literary managers and script editors together to create opportunities for debate and sharing of information and experiences. In collaboration with other professional bodies such as the Directors Guild of Great Britain and Equity, the organisation seeks to standardise the definition and working practice of dramaturgs in the UK.

The website contains details of members, activities, a newletter archive and other information.

Euclid

website www.euclid.info

Euclid provides a range of European and International information, research and consultancy services. It has been appointed by the UK Department for Media, Culture & Sport and the European Commission as the official UK Cultural Contact Point, in particular to promote the EU's funding programmes for culture.

Federation of Scottish Theatre

c/o Royal Lyceum Theatre, 30B Grindlay Street, Edinburgh EH3 9AX

tel 0131-248 4842
email fst@scottishtheatre.org
website www.scottishtheatres.com

The Federation of Scottish Theatre is a membership and development body which advances the interests of professional Scottish theatre and dance at home and abroad.

Highlands & Islands Theatre Network (HIN)

c/o HI-Arts, Suites 4 & 5, 4th Floor, Ballantyne House, 84 Academy Street, Inverness IV1 1LU
tel (01463) 717091
website www.hitn.co.uk

HITN has the following agreed aims:

• to promote the advancement of education and the arts in the Highlands and Islands of Scotland area for the benefit of the public;
• to promote the professional theatre sector in the Highlands and Islands of Scotland area at regional, national and international levels;
• to work with other organisations to encourage wider access to theatre across the Highlands and Islands of Scotland area.

Independent Theatre Council (ITC)

12 The Leathermarket, Weston Street, London SE1 3ER
tel 020-7403 1727 *fax* 020-7403 1745
email admin@itc-arts.org
website www.itc-arts.org

Founded in 1974, the Independent Theatre Council (ITC) is the management association and political voice of around 700 performing arts professionals and organisations. ITC provides its members with legal and management advice, training and professional development, networking, regular newsletters and a comprehensive web resource. Additionally ITC initiates and develops projects to enrich, enhance and raise the profile of the performing arts.

Working across a variety of art forms including drama, dance, opera, music theatre, puppetry, mixed media, mime, physical theatre and circus, ITC members usually operate on the middle and small scale and are dedicated to producing innovative work, often in unconventional performance spaces.

ITC has commissioned a wide range of publications which offer guidance on potentially difficult aspects of working in the performing arts, advice on good practice and further sources of information. For more than 20 years the Independent Theatre Council has been organising training for managers and staff across the performing arts. ITC now runs nearly 50 different courses each year. In addition it has broadened its service to become leader in the field providing Action Learning sets, team building events and Executive Coaching.

For details of how to join and other benefits available to members, consult the website.

International Federation of Actors (FIA)

Guild House, Upper St Martin's Lane, London WC2H 9EG
tel 020-7379 0900 *fax* 020-7379 8260
email office@fia-actors.com
website www.fia-actors.com

The FIA currently represents 105 performers' unions and guilds in 75 countries around the world. Membership is limited to unions, guilds and professional associations – individual actors may not join. FIA works internationally to represent and co-ordinate the interests of performing artists and their professional organisations.

Services: Lobbying at European and international level on behalf of performers; defence of artists' freedom; trade union development; information exchange through conferences and meetings; networking.

Objectives: To promote a better understanding of performers' concerns and challenges around the world; the ensure that all main decision-making processes take due consideration of the specific needs of performers; to contribute to improve the social and professional conditions of performers worldwide; to facilitate the sharing of knowledge and experience on all issues of common interest between member organisations.

International Network of Casting Directors (INCD)

The idea for an informal international network was floated during a meeting of casting directors during European Film Promotion's ShootingStars event at the Berlinale. Until now, casting directors have only been organised in national associations, but INCD would offer them "the chance to exchange ideas on an international level about their different ways of working, to take advantage of synergies with international co-productions and to attract greater attention to the work of casting a film."

National Council for Drama Training (NCDT)

249 Tooley Street, London SE1 2JX
tel 020-7407 3686
email info@ncdt.co.uk
website www.ncdt.co.uk

The National Council for Drama Training is a partnership of employers in the theatre, broadcast and media industry, employee representatives and training providers who work together to increase support for professional drama training and education.

It seeks to maintain the highest standards and provides a credible process of quality assurance through accreditation for vocational drama, reassuring students that the courses they choose are recognised and respected by the drama profession.

National Operatic and Dramatic Association (NODA)

58-60 Lincoln Road, Peterborough PE1 2RZ
tel (01733) 865790 *fax* (01733) 319506
email info@noda.org.uk
website www.noda.org.uk
Patron The Lord Lloyd Webber

Founded in 1899, NODA is the main representative body for amateur theatre in the UK. It has a membership of around 2500 amateur/community theatre groups and 3000 individual enthusiasts throughout the UK, staging musicals, operas, plays, concerts and pantomimes in a variety of performing venues, ranging from professional theatres to village halls.

Produces a quarterly national magazine, *NODA National News*, containing advice and information for the amateur theatre sector, listings of performances in the National Theatre Diary and classified ads. Also holds area and national conferences, workshops and summer schools.

National Rural Touring Forum (NRTF)

mobile (07901) 812306
email admin@nrtf.org.uk
website www.nrtf.org.uk

The NRTF is the organisation that represents a number of mainly rural touring schemes and rural arts development agencies across England and Wales. "Our touring scheme members work with local communities to promote high quality arts events and experiences in local venues."

National Theatre Platforms

South Bank, London SE1 9PX
tel 020-7452 3333
email angus@nationaltheatre.org.uk
website www.nationaltheatre.org.uk/platforms
Platforms Producer Angus MacKechnie

An eclectic programme of pre-performance events celebrates all aspects of the arts, offering the chance to learn about the National's work and discover more about theatre in general. Platforms usually start at 6pm, lasting for 45 minutes – there are occasional afternoon events, usually starting at 2.30pm. Tickets: £3.50 (£2.50 concessions).

New Media Scotland

Informatics Forum, 10 Crichton Street, Edinburgh EH8 9AB
tel 0131-650 2750
email hello@mediascot.org
website www.mediascot.org

New Media Scotland is a national development agency fostering artist and audience engagement with all forms of new media practice.

North American Actors Association (NAAA)

mobile (07873) 371891
email admin@naaa.org.uk
website www.naaa.org.uk
Administrator Kelly Jeffreys

The North American Actors Association is a network serving the entertainment industry by supporting North American actors with a base in Britain.

Membership is open to professional actors who can work on both sides of the Atlantic without restriction, are full members in good standing of at least one entertainment union, and have proof of professional contracts. To those involved in casting, we act as a resource of genuine North American actors, and are happy to provide agent and other contact details of our members.

Northern Ireland Theatre Association (NITA)

12 Islandboy Road, Moyarget, Ballycastle, Co. Antrim BT54 6JP
tel (07825) 913844
email info@nitatheatre.org
website www.nitatheatre.org
Coordinator Bronwen Williams

NITA is the body for professional and semi-professional theatre in Northern Ireland.

Pact (Producers' Alliance for Cinema and Television)

3rd Floor, Fitzrovia House, 153–157 Cleveland Street, London W1T 6QW
tel 020-7380 8230
email info@pact.co.uk
website www.pact.co.uk

The UK trade association that represents and promotes the commercial interests of independent feature film, television, animation and interactive media companies. Headquartered in London, it has regional representation throughout the UK, in order to support its members. An effective lobbying organisation, it has regular and constructive dialogues with government, regulators, public agencies and opinion formers on all issues affecting its members and contributes to key public policy debates on the media industry, both in the UK and in Europe. It negotiates terms of trade with all public service broadcasters in the UK and supports members in their business dealings with cable and satellite channels. It also lobbies for a properly structured and funded UK film industry and maintains close contact with the UK Film Council and other relevant film organisations and government departments.

Personal Managers' Association

PO Box 63819, London N1 1HL
tel/fax 0845-602 7191

email info@thepma.com
website www.thepma.com

Founded in 1950, the PMA is an association of artists' and dramatists' agents which provides members with a forum to exchange ideas and information. The association maintains a code of conduct and acts as a lobby when necessary.

The Radio Independents Group (RIG)

c/o Square Dog Radio, Kilmagadwood Cottage, Scotlandwell, Kinross KY13 9HY
email chair@radioindies.org
website www.radioindependentsgroup.org
Chair Mike Hally

A non-profit-making trade body funded through membership fees and other fund-raising activities, representing the interests and needs of the UK's independent radio production industry. Formed in July 2004, RIG currently represents two-thirds of the industry, and membership continues to grow – recently (June 2010) topping 100 for the first time, to include globe-spanning commercial giants through to one-person companies, partnerships and sole traders. As well as representing members' and the industry's needs in negotiations with the BBC, commercial radio and other groups, and the government, RIG offers support, resources, information, access and training. Its aim is to bring together the knowledge of the thousands of dedicated and skilled people in the independent radio production sector, and to make as much of it available to all as is possible.

Royal Television Society (RTS)

Kildare House, 3 Dorset Rise, London EC4Y 8EN
tel 020-7822 2810 *fax* 020-7822 2811
email info@rts.org.uk
website www.rts.org.uk

Provides the leading forum for discussion and debate on all aspects of the television industry, with opportunities for networking and professional development for people at all levels and across every sector. The RTS has 14 national and regional centres in the UK which draw up an annual programme to suit the needs of their members.

Events organised by the RTS include dinners, lectures, conventions, conferences and awards ceremonies. In addition it produces a monthly magazine, *Television*, outlining key industry debates and developments.

Society of London Theatre (SOLT)

32 Rose Street, London WC2E 9ET
tel 020-7557 6700 *fax* 020-7557 6799
email enquiries@solttma.co.uk
website www.solt.co.uk

Founded in 1908 by Sir Charles Wyndham, the Society of London Theatre is the trade association which represents the producers, theatre owners and managers of the major commercial and grant-aided theatres in central London.

Today the Society combines its long-standing roles in such areas as industrial relations and legal advice for members with a campaigning role for the industry, together with a wide range of audience-development programmes to promote theatre-going.

The Society of Teachers of Speech and Drama (STSD)

73 Berry Hill Road, Mansfield, Nottinghamshire NG18 4RU
email stsd@stsd.org.uk
website www.stsd.org.uk

Protecting the professional interests of qualified, specialist teachers of Speech & Drama, the STSD encourages good standards of teaching and promotes the study and knowledge of speech and dramatic art in every form. Has established close links with drama schools and examination boards and its publications are read worldwide.

Members receive copies of its newsletters, information sheets and the journal *Word Matters*. They are entitled to free advice, to be included in a register of members and to attend its summer conference.

Students of Speech & Drama can search for suitable teachers using the online database.

The Stephen Sondheim Society

265 Wollaton Vale, Wollaton, Nottingham NG8 2PX
email administrator@sondheim.org
website www.sondheim.org
Chair Mandy Dixon *Administrator* Lynne Chapman

Society to promote the works of the composer and lyricist Stephen Sondheim. Keeps track of all productions (professional and amateur) of Sondheim's musicals, publishes a newsletter, arranges theatre visits, and from time to time also sponsors appropriate productions.

At the time of writing, membership is £15 (single), £10 (concession) or £20 (joint) but please consult the website for the latest rates.

StartaTheatreCompany.com

email admin@startatheatrecompany.com
website www.startatheatrecompany.com

An online guide to starting and developing a performing arts company. An e-learning course with 6 comprehensive modules, covering all you need to know about building a successful and sustainable enterprise. Delivered through fortnightly video and audio lessons, the guide is presented by tutor Sinead Mac Manus. Sinead has many years of experience working with and training performing arts companies, and has brought this experience to the world of e-learning.

Studio Salford

King's Arms, 11 Bloom Street, Salford M3 6AN
website www.studiosalford.com

Studio Salford is an umbrella group representing and promoting several theatre companies, raising the profile of Salford as a viable artistic location and promoting artists from all over Salford and Manchester. Their performance venue is the intimate and unique space upstairs at The King's Arms.

The Society of Teachers of the Alexander Technique (STAT)

1st Floor, Linton House, 39-51 Highgate Road, London NW5 1RS
tel 020-7482 5135 *fax* 020-7482 5435
email office@stat.org.uk
website www.stat.org.uk

The Alexander Technique has been taught for more than 100 years. In 1958, the Society of Teachers of the Alexander Technique (STAT) was founded in the UK by teachers who were trained personally by FM Alexander. STAT's first aim is to ensure the highest standards of teacher training and professional practice.

Teaching members of STAT:

• Are registered (MSTAT) to teach the Technique after completing a 3-year, full-time training course approved by the Society or one of the Affiliated Societies overseas
• Are required to adhere to the Society's published *Code of Professional Conduct and Competence*, and are covered by the professional indemnity insurance.

There are currently more than 2500 teaching members of STAT and its Affiliated Societies worldwide. Graduates of STAT training courses are assessed by a system of external moderation; the Society also runs a postgraduate programme of Continuing Professional Development. STAT's further aims are to promote public awareness and understanding of the Alexander Technique, and to encourage research. The Society publishes a regular newsletter, *STATNews*, and *The Alexander Journal*.

The Standing Conference of University Drama Departments (SCUDD)

website www.scudd.org.uk

Represents the interests of Drama, Theatre and Performing Arts in the Higher Education Sector in the UK. Acts as a mediating body with organisations such as funding councils, the AHRC and the Arts Councils, and is consulted by such organisations when matters of future policy are discussed and decided.

Theatre for Young Audiences (TYA)

16 Victoria Embankment, Darlington DL1 5JR
tel (01325) 483259
email paul.harman63@ntlworld.com
website www.tya-uk.org
Contact Paul Harman

TYA (UK Centre of ASSITEJ) is a network for makers and promoters of professional theatre for young audiences, linking the UK to theatres, organisations and individual artists around the world. Works for a fuller awareness of the value of theatre for young audiences.

Theatre in Wales

website www.theatre-wales.co.uk

"The only comprehensive Welsh theatre and performance website."

Theatres Trust

22 Charing Cross Road, London WC2H 0QL
tel 020-7836 8591 *fax* 020-7836 3302
email info@theatrestrust.org.uk
website www.theatrestrust.org.uk

The National Advisory Public Body for Theatres, protecting theatres for everyone. Operates nationally in England, Wales, Scotland and Northern Ireland, providing an authoritative and knowledgeable source of expert advice and information on theatres. The Theatres Trust provides a range of advisory services, is a statutory consultee on planning applications, and provides guidance on design, conservation, property and planning matters to theatre operators, local authorities and official bodies, and also runs an information service. Its archives include records of over 3500 theatre buildings and some 30,000 images, as well as plans and other documents.

Theatrical Management Association (TMA)

32 Rose Street, London WC2E 9ET
tel 020-7557 6700 *fax* 020-7557 6799
email enquiries@solttma.co.uk
website www.tmauk.org
Chief Executive Julian Bird

TMA is the pre-eminent UK wide organisation dedicated to providing a professional support network for the performing arts industry. Founded in 1894 by Sir Henry Irving, it is now an association of people and throughout the UK professionally involved in the production and presentation of the performing arts. Its members include repertory and producing theatres, arts centres and touring venues, major national companies and independent producers, opera and dance companies, and associated individuals and businesses.

TMA is run by a Council elected from and by the membership. This Council represents all sectors of the business and employs the professional staff team who provide the services for members. Diverse as they are, TMA members share a common conviction that the professional and social advantages of membership increase their ability to run successful businesses. Member organisations are encouraged to follow best professional practice and are given advice to enable them to do so. Individuals can benefit from training and networking opportunities to help develop their careers.

TMA shares a common staff with the Society of London Theatre (SOLT).

Total Theatre

University of Winchester, Faculty of Arts, Winchester SO22 4NR
tel (01962) 827107
website www.totaltheatre.org.uk

Total Theatre is a national agency with an international focus, developing contemporary theatre for both theatre makers and theatre audiences.

V&A Theatre & Performance Collections (formerly The Theatre Museum)

tel 020-7942 2697
email tmenquiries@vam.ac.uk
website www.vam.ac.uk/tco

The V&A's Theatre & Performance Collections hold the UK's national collection of material about live performance in the UK since Shakespeare's day, covering drama, dance, musical theatre, circus, musical hall, rock and pop, and other forms of live entertainment. In March 2009, the new Theatre & Performance galleries at the V&A opened to the public. The galleries replaced those at the Theatre Museum in Covent Garden, which closed in 2007. The new displays explore the process of performance, from the initial conception, through the design and development stages, to audiences' reactions.

Women in Film and Television (WFTV)

4th Floor, Unit 2, Wedgwood Mews, 12-13 Greek Street, London W1D 4BB
tel 020-7287 1400 *fax* 020-7287 1500
email info@wftv.org.uk
website www.wftv.org.uk
Membership & Events Manager Emily Compton

A membership association open to women with a minimum of 1 year's professional experience in the television, film or digital media industries. With more than 800 members including writers, actresses and directors, the WFTV promotes the interests and diversity of women working at all levels in these industries. Offers a network of national and international contacts with an online directory of members, and provides a number of social forums, workshops, seminars and preview screenings.

The Writers' Guild of Great Britain

40 Rosebery Avenue, London EC1X 4RX
tel 020-7833 0777
email admin@writersguild.org.uk
website www.writersguild.org.uk

A trade union for professional and aspiring writers in TV, radio, film, theatre, books and videogames. 2,300 members, affiliated to the Trades Union Congress. The Guild negotiates collective minimum terms agreements with the main broadcasters and trade bodies for producers and subsidised theatre – these cover fees, advances, royalties, residuals, pension contributions, rights, credits and other matters. Guild members have access to free contract vetting, legal advice and representation in work-related disputes, and the Writers' Guild Welfare Fund gives emergency assistance to members in financial trouble. Also offered are professional, cultural and social activities to help provide writers with a sense of community, making writing a less isolated occupation. Members receive *UK Writer*, a quarterly magazine, plus a weekly email bulletin containing news and work opportunities. The Writers' Guild Awards, presented every November, recognise the best writing across all arts and entertainment media. The Writers' Guild Books Co-operative helps authors to self-publish and market their works. Further information can be found in *Writers' & Artists' Yearbook* (A&C Black).

An actor's guide to keeping sane

Tim Bentinck

This is not a flippant title. The psychological battle of being an actor/breadwinner is the war; doing the job is just the fighting.

If you're a good builder and you're not getting work, it's probably because you're being undercut by the East Europeans, but you still know you're a good builder.

If you're an actor, you have no such objective take on the matter. In order to be a professional actor, you *have* to believe you're bloody good, or you can't even get started, let alone continue. The problem is that your own estimation of your talent is inherently biased, because when a builder has finished a roof conversion that looks beautiful and doesn't leak, no one rings him to complain. When an actor has done a part on telly and no-one rings, is it because (a) they weren't watching? (b) they thought you were good but didn't bother to ring? (c) they thought you were crap? or (d) they didn't like you anyway and turned over the minute you appeared? Even when your best friends think you're crap, they almost never say.

Therefore, you have to rely on your own judgement, and as an actor it's extremely difficult to be objective, disinterested and honest about your own performance. On stage you get a good idea when your jokes fall flat and people talk about the set in the bar afterwards, but on screen and on radio, you really are not the best judge. Everyone, myself included, can believe they're being brilliant when they're not. When you start off as an actor you *have* to have at heart a naïve belief that your originality, eccentricity, new interpretation of a text, your life experience, your pain, your joy, your discovery of sex for the first time in history, your raw talent, or your chutzpah and charm will blow them all away.

This, dear actor, we all have. You can't *be* an actor without empathising with some part of the above.

The reality, *quelle malheur*, is mostly down to luck – the right place, the right time, and almost nothing more. Oh, and probably being unconventionally good-looking or sexy. Being good at it is an added bonus.

I'm 52. About 25 years ago someone I knew fairly well said to me drunkenly at a party, "Oh I saw you in that thing on telly last night, you were *awful*! Jeremy did you see it? Wasn't Tim dreadful?! Ha ha ha." At the time I was really hurt. I was shocked and rocked to the core. I had to find a way to deal with it, so I just decided she was a cow and mad and had no taste and didn't get it, and got on with life. About a year ago, when I watched the episode in question again on DVD, I realised she was painfully closer to the truth than I'd realised. I'd never done telly before and had just done nine months as a pirate in the West End and I was way OTT — lots of *acting* going on. I hadn't learned the 'do nothing' rule. In my defence I was fairly dishy and the swordfights were good. Yes she was a rude cow for saying it, but the point I'm circumlocutorily trying to reach is this: At the time, everyone said I was brilliant. No – I was *alright*. Beware the flatterers. Make people tell you the truth and then do something about it. Never be afraid of criticism; it's usually well founded, and sometimes well meant.

So in order to remain sane in this business, it is important that you have a very strong belief – backed up by some rigorous interrogation of your most trusted friends, your family, your loved ones and your fans – that you have what it takes, if given the chance, to be an astonishingly brilliant actor. Because unless you're very lucky, you are going to be hurt, rejected, abused, disrespected, talked down to, patronised, dismissed, ignored, not appreciated, paid badly, not paid at all, taken for granted and generally ground down for the rest of your life ... so if you can't face that, forget it.

From then on, one of three things is going to happen. The first is that you become a megastar. End of story, read a different book. The second is that you become a professional actor, earning some kind of living. The third is that it's a total bloody disaster. Here are some suggestions for how to remain sane with option two.

About five years ago, I spent a good six months of that year worrying about what things were going to be like five years in the future. Here I am today and everything's pretty fine. So I had effectively *wasted* all that time of my life worrying about something that didn't happen. Absurd. You have got to seize the day, or the night if that's your thing – *carpe noctem*, even!

Depression is a killer; it killed someone close to me, and I've been down that road too. But you can talk yourself out of it. You can bully yourself. Buy a bike and ride it, swim, have more sex, go to the pub and meet new people, get drunk with them and solve the problems of the world, sign up for a rally driving course, use the credit card to pamper yourself and don't worry about tomorrow (if that doesn't work, take Prozac but don't do the drinking thing – it's unhealthy, expensive and doesn't work). Do that until you've stopped being depressed, then you can worry about the debt with a more sanguine view – sanguine and proactive (dreadful word but can't think of an alternative).

You have *got* to treat it as a business. You're the product and if someone else isn't selling you (PR or agent), then it's down to you. My very first agent came from the world of PR and said to me that he knew nothing about acting, but aimed to get my name on the desks of everyone who mattered, every day of the week. He made me a lot of money. You're up against the PR might of comedians, footballers, models, weather-girls, body-builders, basketball players, TV presenters, extras, personal fitness coaches to the stars, drunks, reality-show winners, reality-show runners up, Pop Idols, and specifically Jade (insert adjective of choice, like 'talented', 'intelligent', 'thin', 'attractive') Goody.

Get a website, make a voicereel, make a video compilation, send them to Spotlight, send them to your agent, send a DVD to casting directors. Get yourself in the press, get yourself on radio, write plays, write songs, drive trucks, plant gardens, do classes, keep fit, look good, raise a family, change the nappies. Live a life, the experience of which you can bring to your acting. Be in trim and ready to grab the bits of luck that come your way with bold confidence.

Another thing: work on your memory, or carry a notebook. Remember the names of the casting directors; remember the directors you work for; be pleasant to the runner, because s/he'll be the producer/director in six year's time; remember what your agent looks like when you meet him/her at parties; remember the voice-overs you did and who directed them; also, get a copy of everything to add to your showreel. Remember to keep all your receipts and put money aside for tax; if you're VAT registered, you're being paid to be a tax collector, so do it yourself – keep the money and have a holiday.

If you're young – *do it now do it now*! Over 40? – you've learned the game, so play it; you're just a more mature version of you at 20. If you're over 50, this is the time to strike:

be bold, we've learned it all, we've got it all to give. Young filmmakers take heed: we are what you will be in 30 years' time, so we represent what you aspire to. You're pretty bright now, but don't you reckon that after 30 years you'll have learned a whole shed-load more? Well that's *us*. Welcome to Saga and the days of low insurance, paid-off mortgages and, finally, the bus pass, which I admit is still hard, at my age, to contemplate. It's eight years away though. Hmmm.

All the bloody pain and insecurity and rejection is mitigated, though, by this:

You could face a cavalry charge in the Crimea. You could star in a West End musical. You could fly an F3 Tornado simulator. You could fight duels and fire machine guns. You could sit on a rubber pad on the top of a mountain inside the Arctic circle in Norway for three days waiting for the fog to clear to shoot a commercial for beer and get frostbite. You could be protected at night from elephant and tiger by armed guards in the Masai Mara, filming an ad for ice cream – and get sunstroke. You could dice for the lead with Damon Hill in a Formula One Kart. You could re-voice Gerard Dèpardieu in a movie, be the voice of James Bond in a computer game and say "Mind The Gap" on the Piccadilly Line. You could be kissed by Kevin Kline or thrown overboard by Roger Moore. You could die in the arms of Sean Bean and snog loads of beautiful women. You could have Claudia Schiffer looking into your eyes saying, "Ich liebe dich, ich liebe dich...". You could dub the lucky guy who shags Sharon Stone in *Basic Instinct 2*. You could earn your living with an earring in your ear and a sword around your waist. You could star in sitcoms, television series and radio soaps. You could do live improvisation games on stage and be filmed on horseback, scuba diving, canyoning, parachuting and piloting a flying boat. You could time a kiss, on a beach on the Great Barrier Reef, so that the setting sun shines between your closing lips as the waves lap around your suntanned body.

Sorry, but look we're all bloody show-offs after all, and if after 30 years I couldn't give a list like the above, I'd have given it up.

It's a great, great adventure. It's a business and you have to run it. If it isn't working, give it up. I know plenty of ex-actors who are hugely successful at their new jobs. When I was training at Bristol, I remember thinking that *everybody* should do this course – not just actors, but everyone. If you've acted professionally for a while, it's a brilliant intro to everything else. Look at politicians – crap actors. Local government – the same. Most businessmen talking to their staff – abysmal. Actors can turn their hands to anything, so if you give it up, it wasn't wasted; it was part of your life-training.

Downer. What I mean is this: I've seen the highs and I've dived down deep with the lows. I know the reality but I'm still fired by the dream. That's what keeps us going.

Churchill said it most accurately, with all the power of the struggle of the war behind him: "Keep Buggering On."

See you on the green.

More about **Tim Bentinck** can be found at **www.bentinck.net**.

Bibliography

Books for aspiring, student and young actors

Margo Annett, *Actor's Guide to Auditions and Interviews* (3rd edition, A & C Black, 2004). A useful guide outlining some of the techniques needed for success.

Simon Dunmore, *An Actor's Guide to Getting Work* (4th edition, A & C Black, 2004). A practical, comprehensive guide covering all aspects of marketing yourself as an actor.

Simon Dunmore, *Alternative Shakespeare Auditions for Women* (A & C Black, 1997). A collection of 50 less-well-known speeches for women.

Simon Dunmore, *MORE Alternative Shakespeare Auditions for Women* (A & C Black, 1999). Another collection of 50 less-well-known speeches for women.

Simon Dunmore, *Alternative Shakespeare Auditions for Men* (A & C Black, 1997). A collection of 50 less-well-known speeches for men.

Simon Dunmore, *MORE Alternative Shakespeare Auditions for Men* (A & C Black, 2002). Another collection of 50 less-well-known speeches for men.

Ellis Jones, *Teach Yourself Acting* (Hodder & Stoughton Ltd, 1998). A good overview of acting and the profession.

Jennifer Reischel, *So You Want to Tread the Boards: The Everything-you-need-to-know, Insider's Guide to a Career in the Performing Arts* (JR Books Ltd, 2007)

Anna Scher, *Desperate to Act* (Lions, 1988). Brilliant, basic advice for those so 'desperate', from a lady who should know.

William Shakespeare, *Hamlet, Prince of Denmark*. Especially Hamlet's advice to the players (Act 3, scene 2), which is some of the best advice on acting ever given.

Malcolm Taylor, *The Actor and the Camera* (A & C Black, 1994). Another good 'primer' for the beginner.

Other career advice books for actors

Ed Hooks, *The Audition Book* (3rd edition, Back Stage Books, 2000). Excellent reading if you're thinking of trying your hand in the USA. It's also worth looking at Ed's website for his excellent 'Craft Notes' (**www.edhooks.com**).

Peter Messaline and Miriam Newhouse, *The Actor's Survival Kit* (3rd edition, Simon & Pierre, 1999). Well worth reading if you're thinking of trying your hand in Canada.

Books for any actor

Stephen Aaron, *Stage Fright: Its Role in Acting* (University of Chicago Press, 1986). Fascinating book, written by a psychotherapist who is also an experienced director and teacher.

Brian Bates, *The Way of the Actor* (Century Hutchinson, 1986). Very interesting insights into the inner workings of the actor's psyche.

Nancy Bishop, *Secrets from the Casting Couch* (Methuen Drama, 2009). A practical workbook written from the point of view of a very experienced casting director.

Peter Brook, *The Empty Space* (Penguin, 1990). Written in the 1960s, but still essential reading.

Adrian Cairns, *The Making of the Professional Actor* (Peter Owen Publishers, 1996). A fascinating study of the history, and possible future, of the art of acting.

Resources

Simon Callow, *Being an Actor* (Penguin, 1995). Autobiographical books by famous actors are generally useless in terms of practical career advice. However, this one – part autobiography and part advice – has a great deal of down-to-earth common sense. His famous 'manifesto' on directors' theatre is spot on.

Mel Churcher, *Acting for Film: Truth 24 Times a Second* (Virgin Books, 2003). Invaluable insights into the specific techniques involved.

Nicholas Craig, *I, an Actor* (Pavilion Books, 1988). A very funny send-up of the starry actor's autobiography. A must.

Declan Donnellan, *The Actor and the Target* (Nick Hern Books, 2005) A fresh approach to the actor's art from the artistic director of Cheek by Jowl

John Gillett, *Acting on Impulse: reclaiming the Stanislavski approach* (A&C Black, 2007). An excellent demystification of Stanislavski.

Uta Hagen, *A Challenge for the Actor* (Macmillan, 1991). One of the best books on acting ever written.

Richard Hornby, *The End of Acting: a radical view* (Applause Books, 1992). Revelatory insights into the processes of acting.

David Mamet, *True and False* (Faber & Faber, 1998). This book cuts through much of the mythology that surrounds acting.

Fintan O'Toole, *Shakespeare Is Hard, But So Is Life: A Radical Guide to Shakespearean Tragedy* (Granta Books, 2002)

Kenneth Rea, *A Better Direction* (Calouste Gulbenkian Foundation, 1989). A very thorough inquiry into directors and the need for more training opportunities.

Patsy Rodenburg, *An Actor Speaks* (Methuen, 1997). An entirely practical guide with excellent advice and exercises to help develop the performer's voice.

Michael Sanderson, *From Irving to Olivier – A Social History of the Acting Profession* (Athlone Press, 1984). A very expensive, but nevertheless fascinating, study of the actor's world over the last century.

Edda Sharpe & Jan Haydn Rowles, *How to Do Any Accent: The Essential Handbook for Every Actor* (Oberon Books, 2007)

Bernard Graham Shaw, *Voice-Overs, A Practical Guide* (A & C Black, 2000). A useful guide which explains and teaches the skills of voicing radio and television commercials.

Michael Shurtleff, *Audition* (Walker & Company, 1984). An American book which should be read. It contains brilliant insights and thoughts to help any actor.

The Spotlight, *Contacts* (The Spotlight, annually in October). Contact details for everything you can think of (and more) that relates to the performing arts in general.

Webography

What follows is a selected collection of the most important websites for aspirants and professionals, and some others which the editors have found extremely useful, but don't quite fit elsewhere in this book.

Important websites for aspirants and professionals

www.actorscentre.co.uk – Actors Centre London
www.agents-uk.com – Agents' Association of Great Britain
www.bbc.co.uk – BBC homepage
www.bbc.co.uk/drama/radio – BBC Radio Drama
www.bis.gov.uk – Department for Business, Innovation & Skills, now covering universities; formerly the job of the Department for Education & Skills (www.dfes.gov.uk)
www.thecdg.co.uk – Casting Directors Guild
www.cpma.coop – The Co-operative Personal Management Association
www.drama.ac.uk – Conference of Drama Schools, with links to member schools' websites
www.eif.co.uk – Edinburgh International Festival
www.edfringe.com – Edinburgh Festival Fringe
www.equity.org.uk – Equity
www.fringetheatre.org.uk – Fringe theatre network, with listings of and links to London Fringe venues
www.itc-arts.org – Independent Theatre Council homepage with links to member companies' websites
www.imdb.com – Internet Movie Database; catalogues all sorts of information on more than 250,000 films and the 900,000 people who helped to make them
www.ncdt.co.uk – National Council for Drama Training
www.northernactorscentre.co.uk – Northern Actors Centre
www.thepma.com – Personal Managers' Association
www.scudd.org.uk – Standing Conference of University Drama Departments
www.spotlight.com – The Spotlight publishes the most important actors' directories
www.thestage.co.uk – *The Stage*, contains news, information and job advertisements which are updated each Thursday
www.ucas.ac.uk – UCAS, the central organisation that processes applications for full-time undergraduate courses at UK universities and colleges

Other useful websites

http://accent.gmu.edu – the speech accent archive uniformly presents a large set of speech samples from a variety of language backgrounds
www.artsline.org.uk – Arts-Line, provides access information on arts venues
www.bfi.org.uk/filmtvinfo/ftvdb – the British Film Institute's film and television database
www.britfilms.com – an extensive source of information on the UK film industry
www.britishtheatreguide.info – lots of articles, reviews and links about British theatre
www.companieshouse.gov.uk – Companies House: useful for checking background details (like date of foundation) of individual companies
www.edhooks.com – contains some interesting articles on acting

www.excellentvoice.co.uk – information and advice for voice-over artists with examples of good voice demos online

www.hiddenextra.com – a useful online guide for those looking to become supporting artistes

www.its-behind-you.com – seemingly a comprehensive list of pantomimes and their producers

www.ku.edu/~idea – the International Dialects of English Archive (IDEA) is a useful collection of English-language dialects and English spoken in the accents of other languages

www.officiallondontheatre.co.uk – Society of London Theatre website with news, reviews and booking information

www.royalist.info – a database that provides biographical details of thousands of individuals who have either belonged to, or been connected with, the royal family of England and Scotland during more than 1000 years of history

www.shakespeare-online.com – electronic copies of the plays and poems, along with other related material of interest. These copies of the texts should be checked against published editions before use in audition or performance, in order to gain the benefit of modern scholarship

www.simon.dunmore.btinternet.co.uk – advice on many aspects of the profession, including auditioning, marketing and good professional practice

www.sound.co.uk – information and advice for voice-over artists with links to many other sites

www.susan.croft.btinternet.co.uk/Supplements/Blackplays.htm – lists the work of those Afro-Caribbean and Asian playwrights whose work has been published, and in most cases produced, in Britain

www.theatredigs.com – a site aimed solely at touring professionals within the UK entertainment industry

www.theatrenet.com – news, events and special offers and links to agents, producers, theatre companies, venues and more

www.uksponsorship.com – an online database of UK sponsorship opportunities

www.uktw.co.uk – UK Theatre Web, with information, events and tickets for theatre in the UK

www.usefee.tv – a site which lets performers, their representatives and employers quickly calculate the appropriate use fee for featured players in TV commercials based on the established, industry-endorsed method approved by the Personal Managers' Association, the Association of Model Agents and Equity

www.visit4info.com – a site where you can see recent television and cinema commercials and get details of the companies who created them

www.vocalist.org.uk – a site for singers, vocalists, singing teachers and students of voice of all ages, standards and styles. The site contains useful information on aspects of singing, performance, plus free online singing lessons and articles for vocalists related to singing and getting into the music industry

www.voicefinder.biz – lots of useful information about the world of voice-overs

www.voiceovers.co.uk – a forum for voice-over artists to advertise themselves

www.whatsonstage.com – a UK theatre listing service with search facilities, a ticket-ordering service, reviews, news and debate

Index

Index

19.95

20185337T

CLACKMANNANSHIRE COUNCIL

ook is to be returned on or before the last date stamped below.

THE JUDAS HEART

THE
JUDAS HEART

INGRID BLACK

ISIS
LARGE PRINT
Oxford

First published in Great Britain 2007
by
Penguin Books Ltd.

Published in Large Print 2008 by ISIS Publishing Ltd.,
7 Centremead, Osney Mead, Oxford OX2 0ES
by arrangement with
Penguin Books Ltd.

British Library Cataloguing in Publication Data
Black, Ingrid
    The Judas heart. – Large print ed.
    1. Saxon (Fictitious character) – Fiction
    2. Murder – Investigation – Ireland – Dublin – Fiction
    3. Detective and mystery stories
    4. Large type books
    I. Title
    823.9'2 [F]

ISBN 978–0–7531–8036–5 (hb)
ISBN 978–0–7531–8037–2 (pb)

Printed and bound in Great Britain by
T. J. International Ltd., Padstow, Cornwall

Dangerous conceits are in their natures poisons
Which at the first are scarce found to distaste
But, with a little act upon the blood,
Burn like the mines of sulphur.

Othello, Act III, Scene iii

Prologue

The last time I'd seen Leon Kaminski, I had almost shot him. It would've been a mistake if I had, but I doubt that would've been much consolation to his family afterwards.

In those days I was a Special Agent with the Federal Bureau of Investigation, working out of upstate New York. I was part of a team hunting a fruit cake known to the press as the White Monk, who'd murdered three women in the woods round Saratoga.

It was my last case as a Special Agent, though I didn't know it at the time.

It was one of those things that become significant only in retrospect.

I don't get along with woods. And I don't get along with mountains or fields. Take me more than ten minutes from the nearest deli and I'm lost. Some people like to sleep within range of the sound of waves washing the shoreline. I like to sleep with the sound of traffic coming in through an open window: the shriek of tyres, howling sirens, raised voices.

I need to be reminded I'm alive.

Consequently I was already freaked out before we even got out of sight of the road. What made it worse was that it was late in the year, dark too early; one of those days when the day barely seems to have roused itself before it's closing down and putting up the shutters.

Soon I got separated from the others.

Great start.

All I could see were shadows, with more shadows behind. Sound was muffled in the trees. Things scurried. Branches snapped. The birds sounded like human voices, mocking.

Then there were no birds either.

That was worse.

I didn't know where I was going. Didn't know what I was doing. All I knew was what I was looking for. That was a local man called Paul Nado who, it was rumoured, knew the geography of these woods better than he knew the layout of his own yard.

He also had priors for indecent assault, and no alibis for the time of the three killings. He fitted the profile. He matched the witness description. The few friends he possessed also said that Nado had been obsessed since he was at school with the original White Monk, the ghost of a monk from way back who was supposed to haunt the area and who had given the killer we were now hunting his ridiculous alter ego. Nado even used to dress up in an old white robe like St Francis and sneak around peering into people's windows after dark.

More to the point, he'd gone AWOL after being questioned by police investigating the three killings.

2

Altogether Nado looked promising — and, as it turned out, he was more than promising. He was indeed the White Monk.

The only problem at that moment was finding him.

How long could a being hide out there in the woods without being caught?

I didn't want to find out.

That's why I was getting ready to throw my hard-won reputation as a hardass to the winds and call for help. Instead I saw a figure through the trees, walking silently.

Nado.

It had to be.

I reached for my gun, cocked the hammer, got ready to call on him to freeze.

And if he didn't, I knew what I had to do.

I didn't intend taking any chances.

Then the figure turned round and looked in my direction, like he could sense the gun trained on him, and I saw that it wasn't Nado.

Wasn't the phantom White Monk either, which in a way was a bigger relief.

It was JJ.

JJ was what we always called Kaminski, though I never did find out why. Nicknames obey strange rules. Sometimes they just stick and then everyone forgets where they came from. Kaminski himself always hated it and begged us to stop using it, but we never did.

Probably because of the begging.

He was part of the same FBI team. In fact, it was his profiling work which had led the way to Paul Nado's

door. He'd thrown himself into that case like no other agent I'd ever known. He breathed it. It consumed him. *But where the hell was he going now?*

"JJ?" I whispered.

Then louder.

"Jesus, JJ, are you trying to get yourself killed? What are you —"

Kaminski simply looked at me, smiled and raised his finger to his lips to shush me.

Then he turned and disappeared into the trees.

By the time I'd made my way back to the others, it was completely dark and the search had been called off an hour ago. "Where's JJ?" they said. And when I told them what I'd seen, some of the other agents thought I was crazy. No change there, then.

He must've got lost, they reckoned, and enjoyed a good laugh at his expense.

It wasn't that cold, after all.

It wasn't like he'd freeze.

Next morning, when Kaminski still hadn't returned, *that*'s when they started to believe me. That's when they stopped laughing.

Not surprisingly, his disappearance caused something of a stir. That's me using deliberate understatement. His disappearance sent the whole unit into turmoil for a time. Some of the other agents even wondered if he'd become Nado's latest victim. Maybe he was following a lead. Maybe he'd heard something and gone after the White Monk by himself.

He'd always craved the credit for closing a case.

4

Maybe this time he'd just taken his thirst for glory a step too far.

The only problem with that theory was that, at the exact time we were combing the woods, Nado himself was on a Greyhound bus heading toward Michigan, where the big hero later turned himself in after seeing his ugly mush on the TV news in his motel room.

It was a year to the day before the mystery of Kaminski's whereabouts was finally cleared up, when the man himself was discovered hanging out in a trailer park in North Carolina which, if you knew Kaminski, was the last place in the world you'd have expected to find him.

A five-star hotel in Vegas, maybe, but not a trailer park in North Carolina.

Not a trailer park *anywhere*.

What I heard is that he'd had some kind of breakdown, that the strain of working the White Monk case had caused him to crack up; and, looking back, I could see that all the signs had been there. And I say I heard about it because by that time, I'd left the FBI too.

I'd had enough.

I guess that case took its toll on all of us.

The straw that broke the camel's back.

I'd called him personally a few weeks after he was brought back to the city to ask if he was all right, if there was anything I could do to help. The conversation was strained. He was on medication. His voice kept drifting in and out like the stations on a cheap radio.

He said he was fine. He said he simply couldn't take it any more. He thought if he just walked and kept walking, he wouldn't have to deal with all the crap that came with being in the FBI and having your head invaded by those dark images and memories.

He just wanted to get away, he said.

To disappear.

To stop thinking.

I could relate to that.

We promised to keep in touch, but of course we never did. I wrote a book about my experiences and moved on. As for him, I never did hear what he was doing, though a couple of years ago I saw a news report from back home about a murder case which quoted a Special Agent Leon Kaminski, so whatever it was that had made him crack up they'd managed to put the pieces back together again. Like Humpty-Dumpty.

Unless there was another Leon Kaminski out there, taking up where the old one had left off. Maybe the FBI makes replicas of us all and stores them in a huge basement in Quantico, ready to take over when the real one's used up.

Nothing would surprise me.

Nothing, that is, except for what happened when, by chance, I caught sight of Kaminski in Dublin one day about ten years after I'd last seen him.

CHAPTER
ONE

Someone once said the best cities are those that a man can walk out of in a morning.

How long it should take a woman to walk out of them, the author of the quotation never got around to explaining. I guess women didn't count in those days. Or maybe he thought women should be too busy preparing a banquet for twelve and dreaming up new ways to please their man when the lights go out to have much time left over for mere walking.

It could be that he even believed encouraging women to take to the road was a dangerous practice because once they started, how could you be sure they'd come back?

If so, he had a point. Sometimes the view is better far from home.

Dublin certainly fits the definition, whoever's doing the walking. There may be more people living here than in Boston, my home town — plenty more, and every year the city grows. But it rarely feels like it. Dublin remains what they call in the guidebooks compact.

That means small.

I don't hold that against it. I've never exactly been a giant myself. And good things, as my mother always

used to assure me before I got too old to be reassured by lies, come in small packages. Besides which, there are more than enough places to hide out if that's what you need. As in any city, you could live here a lifetime and still find roads you hadn't noticed before leading to places you hadn't expected. Hidden places. Secret corners.

There are nearly sixty pages in the city's A to Z guide, from Abbey Cottages to Zoo Road and all points in between — and that day, as it passed five o'clock and headed sluggishly to evening, I could have been anywhere in those sixty pages.

I could have taken any turning in that maze of possibilities.

Instead I was making my way up into the heart of the city, away from the river, toward the place where I'd arranged to meet Grace once she finished work, and taking my time about it, because it was summer and the city was stretching out around me as lazily and contentedly as a cat, unselfconsciously itself, and there was no sense in hurrying anywhere when the day was like this, the streets glinting golden from the slowly descending sun, the squares all leafy shadows and silence, the tower blocks turned into cathedrals of glass and chrome, shining like promises, the whole place tingling with life.

The plan was to catch something to eat before heading to the theatre later to watch some hotshot young American actor I'd never cared for in some play I didn't want to see — Shakespeare, of all things. Not my scene at all. And that might've been why I was

taking my time as well. The upshot was that at that precise moment when I could have been anywhere I was actually emerging out of the soothing coolness of Crown Alley into the bright glare of Temple Bar. A couple of minutes later, or earlier, and I might never have seen him.

Likewise if I'd take a different route that day.

So call it chance.

Call it a sixth sense.

Whatever you call it, there I was.

It was Sunday, which meant the book market was just winding down for the day. There were stalls laden down with old paperbacks, and more books in rickety cases standing at angles on the cobblestones. First editions. Only editions. People were milling around.

It was a scene I'd witnessed a hundred times before, and there was nothing very extraordinary about this one, except . . . except that something made me look over, and I found myself looking at my own face staring out from the picture on the back of one of my books.

And I was looking good, if I say so myself.

It sure is amazing what they can do with computers these days.

The book was a study I'd written a few years ago on criminal profiling, and I felt a little irritated, as I always do when I see my books for sale in second-hand stores. Not least because it's another book that someone somewhere didn't want. Didn't want it so much that they just had to get it out of the house. What can I say? I'm a delicate flower of innocent maidenhood. Rejection hurts. The other reason it bugs me, of course,

is because I don't get a cent on the resale. Your book can go on being sold on for ever, with everyone else getting a cut on it each time, and none of it ever gets back to me. It offends my sense of fair play.

What am I saying? To hell with fair play. It offends my pocket.

So it was the book I noticed first rather than the man leafing idly through it.

He was standing leaning up against the side of the stall, using the shelter of the overhead canopy as a shadow for reading. He had the book in one hand, and with the other he was shielding his eyes from the sunlight. It was a very JJ way of standing.

At first I couldn't say for sure that it was him. I'd spent the day playing poker with Thaddeus Burke and some of his friends down by the quays, and, yes, I'd been drinking a little too. The fog of whiskey had combined with the thicker fog of the heat. I'm not at my best in summer as it is. My brain doesn't function properly once the temperature hits 20 degrees. My head felt simultaneously light and heavy. The two together could easily make me believe I was seeing things, or at the least that I couldn't immediately trust what I saw.

Plus there is something about Dublin itself, I've always thought, that makes misidentification a constant danger. In Dublin I'm constantly half seeing people who look half familiar, and I'm never sure if they really are who I think they are at all.

There was a moment of uncertainty like that when I first saw the figure holding my book. And yet I felt sure

it must be him. He looked a little older than I remembered, but then that could be because he *was* older. So was I. So was everyone. He looked a little more crumpled too, a little darker at the edges. Even, I found myself thinking, a little sadder. He'd dyed his hair, but he looked like he didn't much care any more what he looked like, and that wasn't like him at all. All the same, I knew there could be no doubt.

It was him all right.

No one else could be so JJ-like without being JJ.

For a moment I found myself wondering if he was waiting here for me. But that was absurd. *I* hadn't even known I'd be coming this way myself. How could he have known it?

And he soon disproved that theory, anyway, because he looked up and saw me standing on the other side of the square, and there was no mistaking his surprise. He stared as if it was my presence here that was unlikely, not his — and then, in a gesture that made me shiver with the memory, he lifted a finger and placed it flat against his lips.

Ssh.

Then he looked up suddenly at something high up behind my back, and his eyes widened, before taking the same finger that he'd placed against his lips and pointing up with it, urging me to look. And, like the fool I was, I turned my head to see what it was.

All I could see was the grey façade of an old building. A long-haired redhead in a white dress was sitting on the ledge of a window near the top, one leg dangling out, and smoking a roll-up cigarette which,

from the abstracted expression on her face, suggested there was possibly more in it than tobacco. What was I supposed to have seen? What had he —

As I turned my head back toward him, I saw what the pointing had been for.

My book now lay discarded on the cobblestones.

Kaminski was gone.

I had no idea which way he'd fled, but there was an alleyway to the left of where he'd been standing which led away from the square, and I took that, running quickly, hardly knowing why or what I would do or say if I caught him. I had no right to do or say anything.

I'd have to figure those little details out later.

It wasn't long before I saw him. *He* wasn't running but he had quickened his pace so that he had now almost reached Dame Street, where the road shimmered hotly with traffic.

"JJ!"

He glanced back, and for a moment looked like he might stop.

But no. He was on the move again, and I saw his hand shoot up above the other heads, like a child in school eager to answer a question from the teacher.

He was hailing a cab.

The crowd seemed to thin out as I got nearer the road, almost as if they were clearing a path for me. It meant I had a good view of him as his cab pulled to the side of the kerb and he slipped smoothly into the back seat, slamming the door.

"*JJ, wait!*"

The cab pulled away, leaving me standing, breathless and uncomfortably hot, watching as it accelerated down Dame Street toward Trinity College.

My first thought was to flag down the next cab, and yell: "Follow that car!"

I'd waited my whole life to do that. I guess that's what comes of watching too many bad movies.

But there weren't any other cabs around. And, even if there had been, I was too astonished to act fast enough. Of all the reactions I could have imagined to the sight of me, that was the last one I could've expected. I hadn't let myself go that much, had I?

Paralysed by confusion, I stood and watched as the cab got further away.

Any other day it would've been stuck in traffic, but today was Sunday and it was gone in moments. At the lights on College Green, it turned left.

The last sight I had of Kaminski this time was of his face, peering out the back window, watching me watching him, making sure the brief pursuit was over.

Then that sight faded too.

He had melted into the city.

The old magician had pulled a disappearing trick on me for a second time.

CHAPTER
TWO

"There are lots of Americans in Dublin," said Fitzgerald. "The place is full of Irish-Americans looking for their roots."

"JJ isn't Irish," I said. "He's Polish. If he wanted to visit the old country, he'd have booked a flight to Warsaw, not Dublin."

"Maybe he's lost. Or making a connection," she quipped. Then, when I didn't smile, she continued: "Then what if he's over seeing relatives? There are plenty of Poles in Dublin right now. They've even set up their own cable TV channel, you know. And don't you remember, I actually arrested a Polish man for murder last month. That's the seventh nationality I've arrested in the past three years. I like to think of it as a sign that we're getting very tolerant and multicultural. We welcome murderers now from all parts of the globe."

This time, I couldn't help smiling.

"They should put that on the holiday brochures," I suggested. "Think of the boost it'd give to tourism. You could even offer a discount for block bookings by psychopaths."

"There you go," she added to that. "Your friend could simply be here on holiday."

"People like JJ don't take holidays."

"He could have changed since you knew him."

"People like JJ don't change either. It'd be too quiet for him here anyway."

"Dublin's too quiet for you too," said Fitzgerald, "but you're still here."

"What can I say? Love makes us all do strange things."

"That's it. He must be in love."

We were catching that bite to eat in a tiny Italian place in Wicklow Street. That is, we'd got past ordering and on to the first glass of wine, but not so far as to actually start eating, unless the bread basket that I was quickly making my way through counted.

Fitzgerald was doing what Fitzgerald did best. She was being rational. I needed that sometimes. Counterpart to my craziness. Though it still didn't explain why Leon Kaminski had run from me, as I lost no time reminding her.

"True," she conceded. "That's not what you'd call normal behaviour. Not that you're exactly a practitioner of the fine art of behaving normally yourself."

"I'll ignore that remark."

I looked across the table at her, and once again my dominant thought as I watched her was how well named she was. She did have grace, a poise and elegance that had always eluded me. I was lucky to have gotten her. There were days when I thought she was way out of my league. I didn't deserve her. She put up with a lot, and she rarely complained.

Grace Fitzgerald was a Detective Chief Superintendent with the Murder Squad of the Dublin Metropolitan Police, and she was the very reason I was in Dublin at all.

I'd met her shortly after coming to the city for the first time. She was a source for a book I was writing at the time about a serial killer called the Night Hunter who had killed five women. Somehow we were still together — and, with my talent for screwing up relationships and getting people hacked off with me, that ought to be considered something of a miracle.

Without Fitzgerald, I doubted I'd still be here at all. Dublin was a great place to hang out, but I would never have stayed here longer than a couple of months if it hadn't been for her. Because of her, I'd now been here much longer than I'd ever stayed in one place. Before I knew it, I was living here and I couldn't even recall when I passed the line from passing through to actually living in the place. That was a line you crossed before you knew you'd crossed it, and then sometimes it was too late to get back to the other side.

She was perfectly integrated into the city in a way I'd never been in any place. Boston, maybe, but even there I don't remember ever being entirely comfortable. Maybe I was just uncomfortable in my own skin, and you couldn't change that, couldn't slough and shrug out of it like a snake when the weight of everything became too much.

Fitzgerald wore her own skin like it was a silk gown. It fitted her exactly, and through her it was like a thousand invisible lines radiated out and criss-crossed

the whole city, so that she and it became inseparable. I found myself able to get a connection to the city through her; otherwise I'd merely have been drifting, ghost-like, through the streets, rootless, pointless.

Right now, I was trying to explain to her why I felt so unnerved by seeing Kaminski.

I was failing because she still didn't get it.

"How do you know him, anyway?" she said.

"He was in the same FBI field office as me in upstate New York," I explained. "He was senior to me, obviously. I'd only just left Quantico, and he was the golden boy, fast-tracked to the top, his path laid out. He was good-looking, always well dressed. His parents came from Poland after the war and settled in New Jersey, and they'd instilled that into him. He had to look the part. He had to blend in. Be anonymous."

She nodded. "I know the type."

"Kaminski played his part to perfection," I said. "He'd effortessly erased whatever traces remained of his European genes and become the true all-American college kid. You know, teeth so bright you had to wear shades, and so straight you'd think they were put in his mouth with the help of a spirit level. Not a hair out of place. His skin was so perfect you'd swear he must have had the DNA of new-born babies injected into the nape of his neck every morning at seven sharp, and twice a day at weekends for that extra glow. He probably thought he looked like Tom Cruise. He certainly had to wear heels like Tom Cruise, because he wasn't much taller than I am, and *everyone's* taller than I am. The Seven Dwarfs included."

"You didn't get along with him?"

"I got along with him fine. Hey," I said, when I saw her looking at me sceptically across the table, "don't be so cynical. I get along with people all the time."

"I'll take your word for it."

"It surprised a lot of other people too," I admitted with a shrug. "They had a system when you were starting out in the FBI. You didn't have a job as such, but fully fledged agents could take whichever younger inexperienced agents they took a shine to along on operations. Hence the newcomers tended to ingratiate themselves with the older ones. Well, you know me. I was never one for ingratiation. Something insolent is encoded in my DNA. Despite that, JJ took me under his wing. I don't know what tricks he thought I brought to the party, but he must've thought I brought some because he was always picking me."

"He must have seen you as a challenge," said Fitzgerald.

"That's what I reckoned. I certainly got a lot of experience thanks to him, worked on a lot of cases that would otherwise have passed me by, or which I might've waited years before coming into contact with. I was grateful. It could be tough for women in those days. I thought we were friends. That's why I couldn't understand why he didn't tell me what he was feeling in the run-up to his disappearance. I always felt I could've helped."

"And afterwards it was too late because by then you'd left the Bureau too?"

"Precisely."

Left. That makes it sound so simple. In fact, nothing could be further from the truth. I was only in the FBI five years, which is only a quarter of the recommended period before retirement, but I burned out faster than I'd expected. I'd had enough of death. I didn't realize then that death has a habit of following you around, no matter how hard you try to escape it.

Whatever the reason, I ended up resigning my post and writing a book about my experiences in the Bureau. The book did well enough to lead to other books, I got a movie deal, I had real money for the first time in my life, and by a circuitous route I finally found myself here in Dublin, where I continued to write the odd book now and then.

Very odd books, some might say. Crime books, books on profiling, sketches of old cases, unsolved murders, forgotten killers. I had a new life, but people in the FBI had never forgiven me. They felt betrayed. I'd had angry calls from former colleagues demanding why I'd done it. Personally, I think they overreacted. But that's the way it goes.

I didn't hold it against them.

I moved on.

Or I thought I had. Now here he was, back in my sights.

Acting suspiciously.

"You should find out where he's staying, go round and say hello," said Fitzgerald. "You don't always have to make things more complicated than they really are. There are a million innocent explanations as to why he could be here."

"I don't think so," I said confidently.

"You sound pretty confident."

"That's because," I said, leaning across the table with a smile of triumph, "I took down the number of the cab JJ got into and managed to track down the driver."

"And?"

"And it turns out that Leon Kaminski isn't Leon Kaminski at all. Or rather he isn't calling himself that. He's staying at a hotel under an assumed name."

"That's not a crime. Not technically."

"You haven't heard the name he's using yet. Want to take a guess what it is?"

"I don't like the odds."

"Buck Randall III."

Fitzgerald laughed so hard that diners at the other tables turned to look at her disapprovingly.

"*That* is one great name," she said, shaking her head.

"Isn't it?" I said. "Sounds like the hero of some fifties Western series on TV. Now what would JJ be doing creeping round Dublin calling himself Buck Randall III?"

"You got me," she said. "I give up. Tell me."

"I don't know, that's the point. It was a rhetorical question."

"Is that what you call it?"

"He must be here on FBI business. *That*'s why he ran. He didn't want me knowing. He didn't want me interfering."

"You? Interfere in things that are none of your business? The very thought."

20

"I'll ignore that remark too," I said, and as I spoke I realized there was nothing left in the bread basket but crumbs. I'd probably spoiled my appetite for dinner now.

"Do you want me to make some calls?" said Fitzgerald, taking pity.

"You'd do that?"

"Anything for a quiet life," she said. "But you know, if he *is* in Dublin on FBI business, then I'd be the last person to find out about it. You Americans rarely believe in sharing information about what you're up to with we unsophisticated locals."

I was about to rise to the bait, as I always did when people in Dublin started reeling off their litanies of anti-Americanisms, when Fitzgerald's cellphone went off.

The smile vanished from her lips, and the same diners who had disapproved of her laughing were now openly muttering rebelliously.

"Shit," she said. "What now?"

She took it out of her pocket and looked at it.

"It's Healy," she said. She meant Sean Healy, a fellow detective on the Murder Squad and the one she felt closest to in the whole department. They'd worked together on cases from the first day she joined. "I'd better go see what he wants. Don't be going anywhere now."

Fitzgerald pushed back her chair and rose. By the time she reached the lobby, she was already through to Healy. The glass door swung shut and cut off her voice, but I could still see her through the glass, talking

quickly. I refilled my glass with wine and swirled it around just for something to do with my hands and tried to suppress the feeling that the evening had come to an abrupt end.

"Duty calls?" I said when she got back.

"A woman's body's been found."

"Murdered?"

"Would they be calling me on my night off otherwise?" She sighed. "The City Pathologist's already on his way over. I guess that puts paid to *Othello*."

"I'll try not to be too disappointed," I said.

I hadn't even realized it was *Othello* we were going to see.

"Are they sending a car?"

She nodded.

"Five minutes' time. And I've been looking forward to dessert all day. Oh, well, it'll be good for my figure." She caught my eye. "I'm sorry for ruining your evening."

"It can't be helped. Don't go beating yourself up about it."

"Will you be OK on your own?"

"I think I can manage to find my way home," I smiled. "If I get lost, I'll call 999. Don't worry about *me*. There's no point getting hooked up with a garbage man and then complaining when he has to go and take out the trash. That's part of the job description."

"What a charming way you have with words."

"You know what I mean."

"I do. I wish I didn't, but I do."

CHAPTER
THREE

I made my way home alone through the warm evening streets only to find that the elevator was broken again. That meant I had to climb the seven flights of stairs to my apartment, and by the time I got there I couldn't deny that I'd been in more agreeable moods.

To make matters worse, the door had started getting temperamental lately and I had to kick it a few times before it opened. The woman who lived alone across the hallway from me came out to ask if everything was all right. What she meant was that I should shut up.

I told her everything was fine. What I meant was that she should get back to bed and mind her own business. It wasn't much after ten and the woman was in her pyjamas.

And I thought *my* social life left something to be desired.

I'd spent the last couple of hours since Fitzgerald was summoned to the scene of another death just walking round, idly following a haphazard circuit of streets that were so familiar to me by now that I could have walked them with my eyes blindfolded.

Not that I intended to try.

You never know what you might step in.

Cities in summer always come into their own after the sun goes down. During the day it's too hot to stir, too hot to care, but at night the dark takes the edge off the heat that has gathered in the streets. People come out and experience the city with an immediacy impossible at other times of year. Usually they just regard the streets as passages to connect the places they need to get to. In summer, people become a part of the city instead of intruders in it. Temple Bar tonight had been humming with voices and music and the clatter from the open windows of restaurant kitchens. Tables and chairs had spilled from every doorway, and people were drinking wine and flirting with one another. Without Grace, I felt disconnected from it all. It seemed a waste to be spending the night alone.

Death has no consideration for people's lives.

Once inside my apartment, I put a CD on low without even looking at what it was, then took a beer from the fridge and carried it out to the balcony, sitting with my feet on the balustrade, surveying my kingdom. I lit a cigar to keep the beer company. Cuba's greatest gift to civilization, though since its other contributions included political repression, censorship, and a way of life so wretched that huge numbers of its own citizens would rather risk shark-infested seas to cross to Florida than remain, that's not necessarily saying much.

Far across the river on the Northside, I could see the light at the top of the Dublin Spire glowing, a personal Pole Star for everyone like me who had nothing else of their own to look at that night. The rising smoke from the cigar made the light quiver.

Somewhere out there was Kaminski.

Or should that be Buck Randall III?

Fitzgerald was right, she usually was right. I shouldn't let what Kaminski was doing in Dublin bother me. He had a right to go where he wanted and to call himself whatever he liked. And if he *was* on FBI business, then I had even less right to know.

I'd relinquished the right to be involved in those matters a long time ago.

But it's never been my nature to let things go. That's what gets me into trouble. And it wasn't like I'd asked for this reminder of my past life to barge its way in unceremoniously.

Nor had I asked to be reminded of it in so bizarre a fashion.

All he'd had to do that afternoon was wave a greeting, say: "Hello, Saxon, how's things?" A couple of moments of polite conversation, then: "I have to scoot, but you keep in touch now, you hear?" Even if both of us knew it was a lie.

Instead, he'd raised his finger to his lips as if imploring my silence, just like before, and it was like he was mocking me. Though why I should feel mocked by the memory of *his* disintegration was unclear. It wasn't me who'd lost it. Though some of my former colleagues certainly thought otherwise when they read my book — and lost no time telling me.

Sitting here so far from the world where I'd originally known Kaminski, I couldn't help being perplexed at how it had come to this. Why did things have to get so *weird*?

25

What made it worse was that our dealings with each other had always been so uncomplicated. Most of the time, at any rate. There was one little incident between us that I didn't much care to dwell on which had made the atmosphere awkward for a time, but even that hadn't been allowed to poison what had always been a straightforward relationship.

We'd always been able to laugh too.

Usually at my expense, it's true, but that was fine by me. I'd never made the mistake of taking myself too seriously. Doing what we did every day, you couldn't afford to.

One time, I recalled, we'd been swapping ghost stories, late at night with a beer and a cigar, and I'd make the mistake of telling JJ about something which happened to me as a child. The incident itself had stayed with me since childhood, the kind of thing you find yourself remembering in unexpected moments or revisiting in dreams.

I must have been eight, nine, something like that. I'd been playing hide-and-seek with friends in a broken-down rooming house at the end of the street in Boston where I lived with my mother and brother and sister — my father had never been around much in those days, or any days, come to that, and I can't say I'd ever missed him much — and I'd seen a little girl like myself, dark-eyed and sad, sitting on a chair in an empty room where wallpaper was peeling from the walls and foul water was dripping from a leak in an overhead pipe and making a large pool at her feet.

26

She'd stared at me and smiled and held out her hand, as if for help.

When I walked toward her, she vanished.

I don't think I've ever run so fast.

My friends all laughed and said I was crazy, said I was seeing things. Maybe I was. All I know is that I never dared go back there to play again — and neither did they.

Years later I tried to find out whether anything had ever happened in that house, whether what I'd seen was a trace of something bad that had happened there long ago, but of course there was nothing of the sort. It was just a regular house on a regular street in Boston. I don't know what I expected. To learn that the house had been built on the site of an old Native American burial ground or something, I guess.

Like I say, sometimes I think I've watched too many movies.

The last time I was home briefly, I saw they'd pulled the house down, and nothing had been put up in its place. I saw my mother shuffling to the corner store in her slippers too, though I didn't approach or stop to say hello. I hadn't come to see her.

That was an ordeal I tried to avoid as much as possible.

Kaminski, needless to say, had found the whole incident in the house when I was a kid hilarious. Serves me right for telling him about it. Next day he and another friend of his in the Bureau by the name of Lucas Piper had made up a mock old-style black-and-white Hollywood cinema poster with my

picture on it and the words *Saxon is Back as . . . Claire Voyant — The Girl Who Saw Ghosts* written along the bottom like the title of a movie. Then they'd posted it on to the wall of the office above my desk, where I couldn't miss it.

And nor could anyone else.

Boys will be boys.

I smiled now, remembering it, as I made my way to the fridge for another beer. Being in the FBI had taken its toll, but there were happier moments too. I shouldn't forget that.

And then I stopped, feeling foolish.

Of course, why hadn't I thought of it before?

Lucas Piper had been Kaminski's closest friend in the Bureau. Perhaps his only true friend, the only one who penetrated the surface and got to meet the real Kaminski underneath.

I know I certainly never had.

The two men had grown up together in Ohio, though Piper's family was as blue collar as Kaminski's was trying desperately to be white bread. Half of Piper's folks worked in the steel mills. The other half didn't work at all. Despite all that, they were inseparable at high school, went on to the same college, joined the Academy at the same time. They'd double dated, gone on skiing holidays each winter, even shared an apartment together for a while. They were nicknamed the Siamese Twins, and some people even used to joke that they should get married and be done with it. If

28

anyone knew what JJ was doing in Dublin, it would be Piper.

Though whether he chose to tell me was another matter. I'd never gotten on as well with Piper as I had with Kaminski. Never gotten on with Piper much at all.

I'm not saying he had a problem with women, but he was always competitive with me. Like he felt threatened. He once admitted that he thought I'd only gotten where I was because I was a woman, which would've made me laugh if it hadn't been so ridiculous.

Then, as now, the Bureau had certainly been pulling out the stops to get more women to apply, but once they applied it was another matter. There were still more than enough of the old guard at the training academy who considered it a personal failure if they gave a woman an easy time, making a female graduate rarer than a Bigfoot in downtown Manhattan.

You simply didn't get through an intensive course mastering a range of disciplines from behavioural science to criminal law to firearms tuition on some kind of half-baked politically correct favouritism. So much as even fall short on the two-mile sprint and the push-ups, and you were out. Gender didn't come into it.

Piper's kneejerk hostility had eased over time, but he'd never truly accepted my right to be there. No matter how many cases I worked, he never stopped insinuating behind my back that I was only where I was because I'd gotten *on* my back for the right people at the right time. He made it clear I'd never be an equal in his eyes.

That never bothered me particularly, since I didn't like the way the world looked from his eyes anyway. But right now it left me with a potential problem.

Would Piper talk to me?

I'd just have to call him and see what happened.

But what was his number? I could remember the old number for his house in New Jersey, but what were the chances he was still living there? No, I knew a better way to contact him. I left the beer perched precariously on top of the fridge and went to the closet at the end of the hall where I kept my junk — or what, for insurance purposes, I called my papers. Basically it was all the crap I'd accumulated from ten years of researching and writing books. And in my case, that's a lot of crap. I accumulate so many bits of paper that I should really open a recycling facility in my apartment.

The cranky woman with no sex life across the hall would love that.

I knew Piper's cellphone number had to be in here somewhere, because I'd written it down a couple of years ago when it had been given to me by a source I'd contacted about a book I was writing on infamous unsolved missing persons cases. He hadn't been able to help — that was his excuse, at any rate — but gave me Piper's number to fob me off.

Either that, or he just didn't like Piper.

Piper was known as an authority on missing persons. It was said, usually by Piper himself, that there wasn't anyone he couldn't track down.

Same as Kaminski, he wasn't short on self-belief.

That might've been what drew them together.

It was Piper who'd found Kaminski in North Carolina, and my source told me there was one particular case Lucas had worked on lately in Pennsylvania which would be perfect for my book. A witness in a mob murder trial had fled in fear of what would happen to him if he testified against his former associates. Piper found him and brought him back within hours of the trial. The prosecution got their conviction.

The man himself got a bullet in the back of the head three weeks later, when he was supposed to be starting a new life on the witness protection programme.

That's showbusiness.

Perfect the case may have been, but I hadn't felt up to calling anyone from the old days at that time, and certainly not Piper, so reluctantly decided the book would have to manage without Piper's input. But I knew his number had to be in here somewhere.

Dig hard enough and I'd probably find the Lost Ark of the Covenant too, not to mention Indiana Jones himself searching for it.

Consequently, by the time I found what I was looking for and returned to the kitchen, it was after midnight, the CD was long finished and the beer was warm.

I poured it down the sink and took a cold one from the fridge, perching on a stool and draining most of the new bottle in one swig. Clearing out my junk was thirsty work. Then I finished off a half packet of potato chips I'd left sitting out last night, before picking up the

remote and flicking idly through the channels as I drank.

It was only when I found myself wondering if I should watch a rerun of *Taxi* that I realized I was doing anything I could think of to put off making the call to Piper.

Damn, I hate it when I run out of excuses.

Not giving myself time to dream up another evasion, I snatched up the American cell phone I kept for such purposes and tapped in the number I'd spent so long digging for in a dark hole. I knew I didn't have to worry about the time, since New Jersey was five hours behind Dublin.

The night was still young over there.

I just hoped that, after all this trouble, he hadn't changed his number.

He hadn't. On the fifth ring, Lucas Piper answered. I recognized his deep, rich, slightly sardonic voice at once, though I hadn't been prepared for what he was going to say.

"You're late," he said.

CHAPTER
FOUR

"That's a nice way to greet an old friend, I must say," I remarked when an awkward pause made it clear that I wasn't exactly who he'd been expecting to hear from.

"I'm sorry, I was waiting for a call from someone else," he answered eventually, gruffly, pointlessly. I'd figured that much out for myself. "Who is this, anyway?"

"It's Saxon," I said.

There was another uncomfortably long silence.

"You remember me, don't you, Piper?"

"Oh, I remember you all right, Saxon. How could anyone forget you?"

"I'm a hard woman to forget."

"You're a hard woman, period," Piper said. "What you calling for? Old times' sake?"

"In a way. How are things at the FBI?"

"You want to know that, you'll have to talk to someone in the FBI."

"I thought that's what I was doing," I said.

"Not me, sister. Not any more. You know that old proverb about what to do when you're in a hole? Well, I stopped digging."

"So what're you at now?"

"I set up my own company. Surveillance. Phone tapping. That kind of thing."

That fit. Piper had always been a bit of a communications boffin. His house had been like something out of an electronics catalogue. Closed-circuit TV in every room. Switches everywhere. He was obsessed by security. Never felt safe. Some people thought he was paranoid, but then paranoid is arguably a good thing to be when you're a Special Agent. He'd even hooked up some kind of system which meant he could phone home and turn on his lights in New Jersey even if he was in Nebraska, Europe, wherever. Why he'd want to turn his lights on in New Jersey if he was in Nebraska is another matter.

I guess geniuses don't get where they are without thinking outside the box.

"Best decision I ever made," he said.

"Yeah?"

"I got tired of being passed over for promotion. Every other agent seemed to be going places while I was running faster than ever to stay in the same place."

"I'm sorry to hear it."

"It's the curse of service. Besides, you know what the pay's like. Sucks. Now I'm bringing in more money than I know what to do with. Guess that makes two of us, huh?" He laughed, but there was no pleasure in it. It was more like a cough or a sneeze, just a sound his body gave out to release pressure. "You going to tell me what you want from me?"

He sounded suspicious.

I can't say I blamed him. It had been a long time.

"I'm looking for a number," I said. "For Kaminski."

The silence this third time went on even longer.

"I can't help you," was the answer that came at last. "I haven't spoken to Kaminski in over a year. Last time I tried to phone him, he'd changed his number. I don't have his new one. I'm sorry."

Not as sorry as I was. Piper had been the one person I was sure would know what was happening with Kaminski. Now it turned out he knew as little as I did.

Nevertheless, I pressed on.

"Do you at least know what field office he's working out of these days?"

"Listen, Saxon, you've been out of the loop a long time —"

"I'm only asking for a number, Piper," I said testily. "I'm not looking for the lowdown on all the Bureau's secrets. I won't even tell him it came from you if it makes you uncomfortable."

"It's not that," Piper said. "Kaminski's not with the FBI any more either."

"JJ quit?"

I couldn't have been more astonished if he'd told me Kaminski had taken a vow of celibacy. He'd had FBI sewn into his being the way a kid on his first day in school has his name sewn on the inside of his jacket. He was wedded to the FBI the way the Pope is wedded to the Catholic Church. The idea of his leaving it was like John Paul Getty announcing he'd had enough of being rich and was giving it up for, well, a trailer park in North Carolina.

"What happened?" I said.

"It's a long story. He went a bit, how shall I put this, loco. His wife died."

"I didn't even know he was married."

"You do now. She was abducted after visiting some store not far from where they lived. Her body was found later. Strangled. They'd only been married a couple of months."

Suddenly it didn't look so inexplicable that JJ looked frazzled.

"They ever find who did it?"

"No. That was the problem. Kaminski was convinced he knew who'd killed her. He wanted the Bureau to go after the guy. They thought he was losing it. Getting unstable. It was suggested gently that he take a break from work to help him get over his wife's death. Instead he handed in his shield and walked. That was the last anyone saw of him. I don't know what he's done since. I tried phoning a couple of times, but he never returned my calls."

"So where'd he go? Where's he now?"

"No idea."

"You haven't been able to find him?" I said. "That's not like you. What happened to the man who could find the proverbial needle in any field of haystacks?"

"I didn't *try* to find him," retorted Piper, bridling at the implied criticism.

"You didn't?"

"I was out of the loop myself by that point. I didn't have the resources. And, in addition," he sounded more reluctant now, as if he didn't know whether he ought to be saying what he *was* saying at all, "we'd not been

getting along so well before it happened. Things had changed. And *after* it happened . . ."

"Let me guess," I said. "You told him the same as the FBI."

"More or less. I hadn't seen him for months, then out of the blue he calls and wants my help tracking down his wife's killer. I told him he needed to take it easy. That he was heading for a breakdown. Let's just say it wasn't what he wanted to hear."

"And that was the last you saw of him?"

"That was the last anyone saw of him," said Piper. "Soon after, he disappeared."

"Like last time."

"Exactly like last time, only this time I don't think he intends coming back. I know Kaminski better than anyone. If he doesn't want to be found, he won't be."

"You found him in North Carolina."

"That's my point. The only reason I found him then was because he was *ready* to be found. This time, it's different. This time I think he's gone for good." He stopped abruptly, as if the thought had only just occurred to him. "Why do you want to speak to him anyway?"

I wondered what he'd say if I told him I'd seen JJ that afternoon in Dublin, but decided I'd have to go on wondering because I wasn't going to tell him.

I don't know what held me back. Maybe it was what Piper said about Kaminski wanting to be lost. That afternoon, he had run away. Maybe he didn't want to be found.

"It's nothing," I said carelessly instead, hoping it wouldn't be obvious to Piper I was lying. He'd always been perceptive when it came to picking up on all those signs a speaker unwittingly gave away when they were being evasive. I trusted in the fact he could only hear my voice, and all the non-verbal clues I was probably giving off right now were only being transmitted to my empty apartment. "I wanted to ask him about a case we worked on together years ago. There were a few details I'd forgotten that I needed to clear up."

Piper gave no indication that he thought my answer was incomplete.

"You're not writing another book, are you?" was all he said.

"What else is there to do these days?"

He laughed the same hollow laugh. "Speak for yourself, Saxon. I have plenty of things to be doing with my time these days. Life is good."

"You don't miss it?"

"The FBI? Are you kidding me? That's like asking a guy who's just found out his VD's cleared up whether he misses the itch. You saying you do?"

"Every minute of every day," I said before I could stop myself.

If bafflement could communicate itself down a phone line, Piper's did right then.

"What's to miss?" he said.

"I don't know," I admitted. "The feeling that you're making a difference. That you're not just standing by and handing the keys of the world to the bad guys."

"Last time I looked, there were still bad guys everywhere."

"All the more reason to stick at it," I said.

"I stuck at it long enough," he said. "I gave the Bureau twenty years. Now all I want is for whatever time I got left on this earth to be mine. That's not much to ask, is it?"

"It isn't."

"But listen," he went on unexpectedly, "since it's you, I'll do you a favour. I'll make some calls, ask about Kaminski, see if anyone's heard from him recently."

"You will? That'd be great."

"I'm not promising anything," said Piper. "These days I'm nothing but a civilian with a business to run, remember? It may take a little time."

"Whatever you can get for me," I said, "I'd appreciate it. Here, I'd better give you my cellphone number so you know where to reach me. And then I'll get the hell out of your ear. Leave the line free for that other call you're waiting for. I'm probably keeping you from something more interesting."

"You are, since you mention it."

"What can I say? My timing always was lousy."

"At least some things never change," said Piper, as he took down my number. "That's almost reassuring. Nothing else stays the same. All it does is get older. But, hey, enough of my problems. I'll talk to you again when I have something. Goodnight."

"Goodnight," I said, and felt happier as I replaced the phone. Piper had said: "I'll talk to you when I have

something." Not if, but when. His self-belief hadn't changed either.

Unless . . . the thought struck me at that exact moment . . . unless he *already* knew where JJ was. Unless they were in this — whatever *this* was — together.

Promising to call me back might've simply been a way of playing for time.

I groaned. It was too late for figuring through all the possible permutations of a situation. Sometimes you had to stop thinking so much and leave things to work themselves out. And with that piece of fortune cookie wisdom, I locked up and made my way to bed.

Lying in the dark, I found my mind coming full circle back to earlier that evening when I'd been sitting at my window, looking out at the city, wondering where JJ was.

Lives unravel so easily. He had everything, and then it comes to pieces in his hands, all for a perversity of fate, and for that, JJ's life turns 180 degrees in an instant and he's looking in an entirely different direction than before.

Instead of looking into the future, he's trapped in the past.

Everything stops.

But I still wanted to know what he was doing here in Dublin, and I had a couple of places where I could start. I was tired but also impatient to begin. I checked the clock. It was after 2a.m. Piper had been right, without knowing it, when he said: "You're late."

I really needed to start getting some early nights.

CHAPTER
FIVE

The phone rang early the next morning, waking me up. Still half asleep, I snatched at it, anxious to know if it was Lucas Piper ringing back with information about Kaminski, though I didn't for one moment believe he could've gotten anything for me that quickly. What's more, it would now be the middle of the night in New Jersey. Lucky New Jersey. I'd had a restless sleep. The heat had made me uncomfortable. Even kicking off the sheets hadn't helped.

The caller, though, was Fitzgerald, and I had to suppress a faint disloyal feeling of disappointment as I lay back against the pillow.

"Sorry, did I wake you?"

"No," I said. "I mean, yes, but it doesn't matter. You know me, I'm always up with the lark, eager to throw myself into the joy of another Monday morning. How's it going?"

"I've had better nights."

"You manage to snatch any sleep?"

"Ten minutes in the car."

"It must be bad."

"How do you quantify bad?" replied Fitzgerald. "Sometimes I think that's the worst part of this job.

Death no longer surprises you. It's just another night's work."

For investigator and investigated alike.

Call it the banality of evil.

"She was definitely murdered, then?"

"I think we can safely say it wasn't suicide. But you know Alastair Butler," she said, meaning the City Pathologist. "Until he's completed the autopsy, he's not willing to say for certain that it's murder. A victim could've been seen by a roomful of witnesses taking seventeen bullets in the back, but, until he's satisfied himself there's no chance the cause of death could really have been smoke inhalation, he's not going to commit himself."

"Pathologists are all the same," I said.

"Tell me about it," she sighed. "All the signs are that she was tied naked by the wrists and ankles to the bedposts, mouth taped over, before the bastard put a plastic bag over her head and tightened it with cords until she suffocated. There were some signs of genital bruising too, suggesting a possible sexual assault. He also" — and here she hesitated slightly before continuing softly — "cut off one of the fingers of her right hand."

"Post-mortem?"

"Thankfully so."

"Trophy?"

"Doesn't look like it. He left the finger behind."

"Then why cut it off in the first place?"

"A friend we spoke to says she always wore a ring on that finger. It belonged to her mother. It was left to the

42

victim after her mother died. It hasn't turned up, so it looks like it was the ring he really wanted."

"He couldn't just take it off?"

"In this case, apparently not. According to Butler, the victim suffered some sort of cadaveric spasm. Her fingers were clenched tight. He wouldn't have been able to just unfold them to get the ring off. Cutting would have been the only way."

Now I understood. It usually takes between two and eight hours for rigor mortis to develop in a dead body. In cases of cadaveric spasm, however, rigor mortis sets in immediately, sometimes in all the muscles of the body, but generally in a smaller group of muscles. It's a rare enough phenomenon, but most pathologists were bound to come across it from time to time. The point was that a tightened fist would take considerable effort to open.

Though that didn't mean this killer only cut off the finger because there was no other way of getting the ring. Cutting off the finger may have been what he intended to do all along.

Hence my next question.

"Did he bring the knife with him?"

"I see what you're getting at, but no, he got it from the kitchen."

"Making himself at home," I said grimly. "Did he take it with him?"

"It was left lying on the floor by the bed. He wiped it clean first on the bedsheet."

"Fingerprints?"

"Gloves," she said. "There was also no sign of a break-in. So either he knew the victim and she let him into the house, or he had a key, or knew where to get one. Plus it turns out she had a secret camera hidden at her front door, recording who came and went. The tapes have been taken away. Whoever killed her must have known the camera was there. You can't even tell it's there from the doorway outside. But until Butler finishes his report and makes it official, we're not going to be able to release any further details to the press. That's why they're going crazy. He can't be hurried."

"You're the one who'd better hurry up and make an arrest, then," I said. "Give them something to report. I'm disappointed in you. You must be slowing up in your old age."

"Give me a chance. We only got a positive ID from her father an hour ago."

"Are you allowed to tell me her name?"

"She was called Marsha Reed."

"Reed?"

Fitzgerald must've heard something in my voice.

"You know her?"

For a moment, something had flashed into my head. The trace of a memory, though it was gone as quickly as it arrived.

"Her name sounds familiar," I answered feebly.

"It would make things a damn sight easier if you could tell us something about her," Fitzgerald said. "We don't have that much on her. She only moved into the area about three months ago. The neighbours know nothing about her. Hardly anyone seemed to speak to

44

her. Some of them don't even recognize her picture. And none of them heard a thing, naturally."

"How long had she been dead?"

"No more than twenty-four hours," Fitzgerald said. "We've got a taxi driver who remembers dropping her at the door on Saturday night about ten o'clock. He says she was drunk, kind of giddy, in high spirits, you know. She needed help to the front door. He had to unlock it for her. He says when she opened her bag to get out the key, there was a large amount of cash inside. He couldn't say how much, but a few thousand certainly. It wasn't in the house when the body was found, but he insists he didn't take it."

"That's what they all say," I remarked.

"Don't worry, Healy and I are heading over to speak to him as soon as the forensic team are finished here. But his story seems to stack up in all other respects. Unless he's the kind of man who's capable of killing a woman, cutting off her finger and then returning to continue the night shift without any outward signs of stress or disturbance."

"Stranger things have happened," I said. "But look on the bright side. If the house was locked and there are no signs of a forced entry and the tapes from the hidden camera are gone, then at least you're narrowing down the possibilities. It does sounds pretty much like it was someone she knew."

"That might not necessarily narrow it down," said Fitzgerald cryptically.

"It doesn't?"

"It's a long story. I'll tell you about it over lunch. Give you something to look forward to."

"Can't wait. I didn't think you'd be able to get away."

"I'll be here a few hours yet," she conceded. "You know how long the forensic work can take. They're vacuuming the place now, and then the fingerprint section will come in, and they'll have to lift soil and grass samples from the garden, and make shoeprint moulds, and check for tyre marks, and take apart the plumbing to look for traces of blood in the pipes. But I'll have to take a break eventually unless they want a basket case with severe exhaustion heading up this investigation. It'll have to be out at my place, though."

"Sure. Any reason it has to be there? My apartment's closer."

"I have to go back and pick up some stuff," said Fitzgerald. "I'm meeting the Commissioner later this afternoon, remember? I need to get the right outfit. You can't have Detective Superintendents going into meetings looking like they've spent the night at a crime scene, after all," she added sarcastically. "Might give the wrong impression."

"I forgot about the Commissioner," I said. "Your place it is, then. And listen, I'll pick up some food before heading out there."

"Sounds good. I'll be there around one, OK?"

"One it is," I said.

I put down the phone, cursing myself for forgetting about Fitzgerald's meeting with the Commissioner. She'd only been given final word of it three days ago,

and since then her preoccupation with the impending meeting had been making her unusually distracted.

Unusually, because being distracted had always been *my* job.

The reason for the meeting was the retirement some months previously of Assistant Commissioner Brian Draker, former head of the Murder Squad, the search for whose replacement had dragged on so long now that Fitzgerald had taken to joking how she was almost tempted to ring up Draker and beg him to come back. Yeah, in the same way that people in London might be tempted to ring up the Great Plague and ask it to return because they missed it so much. Now it seemed the DMP had finally found their man, and Fitzgerald was going to be told at the meeting who she'd be working under for the foreseeable future.

I'd tried to persuade her to apply for the job herself. Draker had given her plenty of trouble in his time as Assistant Commissioner, and I resented the thought of her having to go through it all again with the next jerk who felt threatened by a strong, intelligent woman.

But throughout Fitzgerald insisted she'd rather take redundancy and stay home listening to me gripe all day than be stuck behind a desk — or, worse, schmooze her way round Dublin with officials, politicians, civil servants and other wastes of oxygen, assessing budgets, holding meetings, allocating resources, shuffling paper, as any responsible, career-minded Assistant Commissioner was expected to do. Investigations on the ground were all that mattered to her, all that ever *had* mattered,

and if I was honest I couldn't have felt the same way about her if her priorities had been any different.

I don't know what that said about the two of us. A therapist would probably conclude that our single-mindedness was a sign of some personal or social dysfunctionality. A masquerade to conceal some inner loss.

That was yet another good reason to stay well clear of therapists.

CHAPTER
SIX

Hugh, the old guy who minded the door of the building and sorted the mail and banged the pipes half-heartedly when something went wrong with the heating, was sitting on his usual chair in the lobby when I got downstairs. He was reading a newspaper. To be exact, he was reading the sports pages at the back of the newspaper which meant I had a clear view of the front-page story: *Girl Brutally Murdered in Inner City Tragedy*.

Reporters didn't hang around like pathologists, waiting for every detail to be meticulously checked out before deciding what had happened.

"That's a bad business," he murmured with a shake of the head when he saw what I was looking at. He had a vaguely reproachful look in his eyes, like he blamed me in some mysterious way for what had happened. "If you ask me, the whole town's going downhill. There never used to be things like this when I was younger."

"There have always been murders," I pointed out mildly.

"Not like this," Hugh said, turning the newspaper over and jabbing a bony finger at the front page. "Says here he sliced her up." There was a relish in his voice

now. Nothing gives people more satisfaction than wallowing in the world's wickedness. "It makes me glad I'm old. At least I won't have to live to see it getting even worse. And it will, you mark my words. Dublin's getting as bad as that place you come from. What do you call it again?"

"America?" I offered.

"That's the one," he said. "You're always killing each other over there, aren't you?"

"Not all of us," I said. "A few of us manage to get through each day alive."

But he wasn't really listening. I hoped I wasn't about to get a lecture from Hugh as well on all the things that were wrong with America.

In my experience, lectures like that were rarely brief.

I stopped him in his tracks by handing him a piece of paper.

"What's this?" he said suspiciously.

"The name of a locksmith," I told him. "He's coming over to take a look at my door. I've been having a few problems with it."

"I could take a look at it, if you like. Save you some money."

Think fast, girl. Let Hugh near the door and it wouldn't open till the Second Coming.

"That's OK," I said quickly. "The locksmith's a friend of mine. I just wanted to make sure you let him in. He'll be here about eleven. You'll be here?"

"I'm always here," Hugh declared grumpily. "Nowhere else to go, have I? They'll have to carry me out of here feet first in a box." And for the second time

50

that morning, it almost sounded like he was relishing the prospect.

"Well, if you could just hang on until you've let in the locksmith, I'd appreciate it."

"Very amusing," said Hugh as I headed to the door. "You should be on TV."

I waved goodbye as I stepped out into the morning's sharpness, but Hugh had already retreated back into his newspaper. The crossword this time.

He seemed to be coping well enough with the disintegration of Dublin society.

Soon as I hit outside, I could tell it was going to be another hot one. The sun hadn't yet blistered the day, but the air was tense with trepidation, waiting, expecting the assault. It was already growing bright. The trees in St Stephen's Green were ablaze with colour. Windows shone like silver on fire. The edge of things was furred with light. I slipped on my sunglasses to dim the world into bearability. Last thing I needed right now was a headache.

I'd woken that morning with a purpose. I knew what I had to do. I was going to head straight round to JJ's hotel and say hello. And if that turned out to be as easy as it sounded, I'd be lucky. But what was the worst that could happen? He could tell me to take a hike. Plenty of people had told me to do that before. He could join the list. Alternatively, he might've been thinking about what happened yesterday, regretting it even. He might be glad to see me.

And that might be a pig I could see coming into land at Dublin Airport . . .

Whatever his reaction, I wasn't going to think about it beforehand, I was going to plough on and let happen whatever was going to happen.

And if he did tell me to take a hike, I'd have gotten him talking at least.

That'd be progress.

I walked down Kildare Street and turned right at the end, following the flow of the traffic round by Lincoln Place and into Westland Row, getting caught up in the tide of passengers streaming out of Pearse Street Station, inexorable as always, sheltering as best they could in the shadows of buildings, relieved at every breath of wind, while workmen hung from the scaffolding like half-wild monkeys, shirtless, wolfwhistling every woman who passed below. The hotel where Kaminski was staying wasn't far beyond the station, hiding down a lattice of neglected and purposeless streets, but at first sight I felt certain that this mean, faded building couldn't be the right one.

The cab driver had said the Caledonian, right?

The building looked like it was waiting for the wrecking ball. There was a jagged crack right down the centre of the outer wall like a stroke of lightning. Metal bars hugged the front as if holding the bricks back from throwing themselves down on to the street below.

Half the letters in the hotel's painted sign had peeled off, and the railings at the front were buckled inward, as if a car had recently mounted the kerb and rammed into them. Or had it happened years ago and it was

simply that no one had got around to fixing the damage?

The hotel was a reminder that, however much I might imagine I knew the city, the unexpected was still possible. I don't think I'd ever noticed the place before in all my circuits of the streets. One thing was certain. Either Kaminski had fallen on some seriously hard times, or he was deliberately staying in a place where no one who knew him would ever anticipate finding him. I took a deep breath and walked in through the front door.

The inside of the hotel was even shabbier and dingier than it looked from the outside, and that was some achievement. It never ceased to amaze me what people would put up with when they booked into a hotel. If they wanted to live like pigs in their own homes, I could respect that, that's their choice. But why they wanted to live with the accumulated filth of strangers was a total mystery. The place looked like it hadn't been dusted since the hotel went up over a hundred years ago. The chairs were unpicking themselves with age. The carpets were held together with threads. Come to think of it, the threads were all that was left. Heavy velvet curtains guarded the windows like bouncers, stopping the light from coming in.

A woman at reception looked up as I came in.

She was sitting on a stool behind the desk, smoking a cigarette with one hand and turning the pages of a magazine with the other, though her eyes were actually focused on a TV at the other end of the counter on which some grim morning chat show was playing.

She had large breasts and a floral patterned dress that was way too tight for the strain her chest was asking it to take. She looked flustered and sweaty, and her make-up could have been photographed from space. She had that exaggerated femininity that ends up displaying the opposite effect to the one intended. She was . . . forty? Fifty? Pick a number. Whatever the real age, it was more years than she cared to acknowledge. Her hair hung loose, and blonde as the bottle it came from had made it. Her roots were showing, in more ways than one.

She regarded me suspiciously.

"Yes?" she managed eventually.

"You have a guest staying here by the name of Buck Randall."

I couldn't bring myself to add the last part of his chosen title.

"I'm afraid Mr Randall left word that he was not to be disturbed," the woman answered with a look of satisfaction, like she'd won some battle I hadn't even realized was being fought. Maybe she had a soft spot for Kaminski and wanted to keep him to herself. Her voice oozed a fake gentility that people often affect this side of the Atlantic. Though why they bothered was an answer that escaped me every time.

"He won't mind being disturbed by me," I said.

Like hell he wouldn't.

A look of deflation passed across her features, but she was still reluctant. "Mr Randall was very specific about not being disturbed."

"What if it's an emergency?"

"Is it an emergency?"

"It might be."

She considered the point carefully, before deciding: "I'll call his room. Wait there."

She eased herself down from the chair, adjusted her clothes awkwardly around her hips and squeezed through a narrow door into a back room, where I heard the sound of a telephone being picked up, followed by silence. A few moments later she returned.

"Mr Randall must be out," she said, glancing at the rack of room keys behind the chair where she'd been sitting when I first walked in. She frowned. "That's funny, he didn't leave his key. I must have missed him. If you want to leave a message for him —"

"I'll call back later," I said, and I was halfway across the lobby to the door when an idea suddenly occurred to me.

There was another way of finding out what JJ was up to.

Near the door was a stand of leaflets and flyers telling visitors what cultural delights awaited them in the city: shows, exhibitions, museums, stores. The ones that caught my eye were advertising the Shakespeare performance that Grace and I had missed last night.

Othello, starring Zak Kirby as Iago, 8p.m. at the Liffey Theatre.

I took one, digging out from my pocket the pen that I always carried, in the unlikely event that creative inspiration should strike me on the hoof, and scribbled down the first number that came into my head.

The number didn't matter, what mattered was what the leaflet would show me.

I folded it in two, then walked back to the reception.

She'd been watching me the whole time from the side of her eye and gingerly took the leaflet between her long red fingernails as I handed to her.

"On second thoughts, leave this for Buck," I said. "Ask him to call me. I wrote down the number. As long as you're sure it's not breaking the no disturbing rule —"

"I'll leave it in his pigeonhole, madam."

And she turned round and popped the leaflet into a small space marked with the number thirteen. Thirteen. That was the room where JJ was staying.

"Thanks," I said and flashed a smile.

It wasn't returned.

Satisfied, I turned round and headed to the door to leave.

Except, of course, I didn't leave.

Thankfully, finding Kaminski's room was a lot more straight-forward than getting up the stairs without the female impersonator on reception realizing I hadn't gone.

And, once I found it, getting inside was easier still.

A chambermaid was pushing a cart piled high with towels and clean sheets and boxes of soap along the corridor. I flashed my sweetest, most benign smile and told her I was Buck's wife, that I'd forgotten my key and needed to get back inside.

She looked Malaysian, and I'm not sure she understood much English. But she obviously followed what I was trying to say because she fished for the right key from the string at her waist and unlocked the door without objection. She didn't appear to care either way once she'd established that I was unthreatening. And why should she care? She was one of that international army of foreign workers that keep half the Western world going.

Overlooked, overworked, despised and receiving little for it in return but a total absence of security and a pay cheque that wouldn't keep a dog in comfort — not to mention the same dog's basket of abuse from all and sundry into the bargain. The last few years had seen more of these people arriving in Dublin than in the entirety of the city's history. Generally the traffic of misery had gone the other way.

That didn't mean the city's population was any more willing to be sympathetic to those forced to travel far from home in order to make a meagre living. Instead, as in any city, there were always people who chose to believe that immigrants were coming only to steal their jobs, conveniently forgetting the fact that these were mostly the jobs the natives didn't want to do in the first place because they considered themselves too good for them. That's what they call stealing? If these people were thieves, then they were the kind who broke into your house, before tidying up, cleaning the bathroom, taking out the trash, and putting a roast in the oven to slow cook in time for your arrival back home.

I tried offering the woman some money for opening the door, but she just smiled awkwardly and shook her head, backing off toward the cart, looking a little bemused.

And then I felt ashamed for trying to use money to make myself feel benevolent.

By the time I was inside JJ's room, I could already hear the cart rattling down the corridor, like a miniature version of the trams that now ran below the windows of my apartment, clanging round St Stephen's Green into the night. I stood with my back to the door, just making sure there really was no one in here with me. What if JJ had a woman in the room? That would've been something, stumbling into JJ's love nest uninvited.

Not that it looked much like a love nest, I thought, as I got used to the room and satisfied myself it was empty. The nest of some neglected old eagle who didn't much care where he spent his time, perhaps. The room was dingy and smelled faintly of damp, and the drawn curtains only added to the seedy atmosphere. I tiptoed across the floor to draw them back. Bright light poured through the gap I'd made and instantly lost its power.

Never mind, it was sufficient for my purposes.

Though as I quickly realized, there wasn't much to see.

It had looked better with the curtains pulled over. There was a TV, a chair, a double bed with a table next to it on which sat a kettle, a scattering of tea bags in paper envelopes, cartons of UHT milk, an unopened packet of biscuits and a copy of the *Dublin Street Guide*, essential reading for a stranger in town.

The bed didn't look like it had been slept in.

And I wouldn't have slept in it either. I'd have taken my chances with the armchair.

JJ was a fastidious man. Least he had been when I knew him. I couldn't see him willingly picking a place like this. Was it all he could now afford? Or did he figure this was the kind of place where a man could hide out as long as he wanted without being disturbed?

It was certainly the place for hiding things. There were probably a few tropical diseases which had been hiding out here since the world began. They say there are undiscovered species even now deep in the Amazon jungle, but I'd bet the Amazon had nothing on the species of unmentionable life that were to be found in this room.

That made it all the more important I find out why JJ was putting up with it.

Starting with the wardrobe, I began to hurriedly search the room, stopping only once as I heard footsteps in the corridor outside. Voices. A laugh. They passed by.

I pulled open a few drawers. Underwear. T-shirts. A couple more pairs of shoes over by the window. Pants and shirts in the wardrobe. Nothing fancy, and he'd always been fussy about how he dressed. There was also a case on the top shelf of the wardrobe, but there was nothing in that either, and shaving stuff in a bag in the bathroom together with an aerosol deodorant and some headache pills. There was nothing under the bed, or in the drawers of the bedside cabinet save for the traditional Gideon Bible left by missionary-minded

souls who, for some peculiar reason, had concluded that hotels were the best places to find converts.

In my experience, lonely men left alone in hotel rooms were more likely to switch to the subscription porn channels than open up the Acts of the Apostles.

Apart from that, the room held nothing of interest but a copy of a local listings magazine folded and left in the waste-paper basket. I tried flicking through the pages to see if Kaminski had marked anything, but the pages remained as the printer intended them.

I sat on the bed, defeated.

So much for my plan for searching.

Then I noticed a piece of paper poking out from inside Kaminski's copy of the *Dublin Street Guide* on the bedside table.

Eureka.

What Kaminski had slid inside the book was a scrap torn from a newspaper and folded over so many times that the creases had begun to pull apart. Opening the paper out to lay it flat on the bed was an operation which required patience, care and delicacy.

So naturally I tore the damn thing immediately.

It hardly seemed worth all the effort when the unfolding was done.

On one side of the newspaper was an ad for a sale of discount porn DVDs and videos at a store in Capel Street, north of the river, and another for a closing-down clearout at a wholesale pet supplies outlet on the outskirts of town. Talk about an unlikely combination. I doubted that either had much to command Kaminski's attention, unless he'd developed

a taste for porn or poodles since we'd last met. Hopefully not both at the same time.

It must be this on the other side, then — but how?

Woman Killed in Accident — a small news item, undated, though I could tell by the print that it came from the *Dublin Evening Press*, and the pet store ad mentioned something about closing down at Easter, which meant it had to be at least four months old.

The woman who was knocked down and killed in a southside suburb of Dublin yesterday evening has been named as 42-year-old Cecelia Corrigan of Priory Crescent, Donnybrook. The unmarried teacher died instantly after being struck by a car in Herbert Road shortly after 7p.m. and was pronounced dead at the scene. The driver of the car was questioned by police and later released without charge. "There was nothing he could do to avoid hitting her," said a witness. "She just stepped out in front of him." A frontseat passenger in the car involved in the fatal accident was later treated in hospital for shock but was not kept in overnight. The dead woman's remains will be removed from her home tomorrow evening at 8p.m. for burial at Glasnevin Cemetery on Friday. Police have asked for any further witnesses to contact them at their nearest Metropolitan Police station.

And that was that.

There wasn't even a photograph of her.

I felt weary all of a sudden. I was more at sea now than I'd been before I tricked my way into Kaminski's room. And that was saying something.

What interest could JJ have in the accidental death of a fortysomething schoolteacher in Dublin months ago? If tracking down the man who killed his wife was the reason he left the FBI, how had he ended up checking out the accidental deaths of spinsters in the suburbs? Had Kaminski known this . . . what was her name again . . . Cecelia Corrigan? How could he? Or was there simply more to her death than met the untrained eye, but which had caught Kaminski's? I scanned the scrap of newspaper again for a hint of anything untoward, but if there was any suggestion of mystery in the text, it was completely lost on me. Was I putting two and two together and getting ninety-nine? It wouldn't be the first time.

Maybe I was losing my touch.

Maybe I never had a touch to lose.

But I folded it up carefully and replaced it all the same. He'd taken the trouble of inserting it there. He must have had his reasons. I just wished I knew what they were.

I checked my watch.

Ten.

Time enough if I hurried.

CHAPTER
SEVEN

Once outside, I began to feel a touch ashamed of myself for being so inquisitive.

Even if Kaminski was interested in this Cecelia Corrigan's death, what of it? It was someone else's story, someone else's jigsaw, not mine. Things often have private meanings to an individual that shouldn't be communicated to any other human being.

That lost meaning if they *were* communicated.

I should go home, forget I ever saw him, forget I'd ever heard the name of poor dead Cecelia Corrigan in whom Kaminski might or might not have an interest. And yet I couldn't. I had a hunch there was some connection here to what Piper had told me on the phone. Or was I conveniently imagining I had a hunch as a way of legitimizing my curiosity?

Grace had warned me about that before.

All I knew is that I was going to give it one more shot, to try to make sense of things before I gave up. Before I learned to mind my own business.

Next stop was Pearse Street, a short walk from the hotel. The road — once grand, now a shabby, seedy main thoroughfare where no one lingered long if they could help it and certainly not after dark — ran all the

way from Trinity College down to the Grand Canal, where it crossed the bridge and broke up into Ringsend and Irishtown. Halfway along the street there was a library, home of the City Archives, some dating back to the twelfth century.

Closer to my own purposes, the battered brown building also housed the Dublin Collection, incorporating thousands of local, national and international newspapers, some stored bound, most on microfilm. In the past I'd spent hours in these rooms. Now I came here rarely. Soon I was seated at a desk in a corner of the library, near an old man in a threadbare tweed jacket despite the warm, who sat with his eyes closed, obviously asleep, though his head didn't droop once. He was obviously practised in the art of dozing unobtrusively.

I settled down to the tedious business of going back through back issues of the city evening newspaper to see if I could find more details of Cecelia Corrigan's fate.

Local newspapers never cease to astound with the sheer cascading avalanche of pointless details they manage to include about stuff that no one else would surely consider of any importance. Flower shows. Summer fêtes. Lost animals. Things that could be of interest only to people who lived in the city, and not to so many of them either. It was the same everywhere. Each city was a capsule separated from the world and existing in some bubble of its own. Each person who lived there had their own map of the city in their heads, and it warped their vision so that the city was always

larger to them than the surrounding country, no matter how huge, no matter how important. It was what happened on each street and in each neighbourhood, rather than in the world beyond, which mattered. We are all solipsists.

Reading them at times could be like trawling for one solitary fish in the ocean.

Without a net.

That morning I was lucky. I found the fish. Cecelia Corrigan had died in March. There was a handful of reports on the accident which killed her, a few days of silence, then fewer reports of her funeral. Nowhere was there the slightest hint of any suspicious circumstance surrounding her death. The driver of the car which killed her had even attended the funeral. There was a blurry picture of him in one of the news reports, standing next to a young woman named in the caption underneath as Cecelia Corrigan's niece, Becky. His name, it seemed, was Mark Hudson. The woman's surviving family obviously bore him no ill-will.

There wasn't much more in the deaths notices. *In loving memory . . . with deepest sympathy . . . fondly remembered . . .* the standard formulae of grief.

As far as I could see, only one item stood out from the printed huddle of mourners. That was a message offering commiserations to Becky Corrigan on the death of her aunt from "your colleagues at *Dublin Eye* magazine". That was the same magazine I'd noticed in Kaminski's waste-paper basket at the hotel.

Not that owning a magazine was a crime. Even I had to admit that.

Then I saw it. A couple of weeks after Cecelia Corrigan's funeral, thanks to some overzealous security man, there'd been a brief security alert at Dublin Airport when a parcel had arrived with her name on the front and a return address from the Terrell Unit in Livingston, Texas.

The Terrell Unit was where Death Row prisoners were housed, though it wasn't where they were executed. That happened forty miles away in Huntsville, Walker County, in the east of the state. I'd flown down there once to interview an inmate, and a more unnerving town I'd never known. They called it Prison City because one in four of the population is an inmate, and the Texas Department of Criminal Justice is the town's biggest employer.

Outwardly, everything looks ordinary, unexceptional, quiet.

Inwardly, it feels like the whole place is built on bones.

Don't get me wrong. I've never been some hand-wringing bleeding heart who thinks the state has no right to take life. It's just like all the misery the prisoners have caused has been dragged along there with them and holed up in the walls. Some of it is bound to leak out and poison the air. I couldn't live some place like that. I couldn't breathe.

Cecelia Corrigan evidently saw things differently. She'd been writing to one of the prisoners on Death Row in Texas and campaigning for his conviction to be overturned.

That wasn't so uncommon. There was an unending supply of gullible . . . sorry, compassionate women, usually past their prime and unmarried, who wanted to strike up relationships with men behind bars. Some were simply lonely. Some were looking for romance. For soulmates, God help them. Having gone so long without the real thing in their lives, they were grasping in desperation on to this meagre, obscene, long-distance substitute. Ironically, the fact these men were behind bars made it safer to love them. Nothing would ever come of the romance, so any fantasy could be projected on to it.

Some women went further. They were actually turned on by the thought of what these men had done. They wanted the sordid glamour of a close association with evil.

Others still were motivated by a principled opposition to the taking of life — though why this should manifest itself via an attachment to men who had taken life in far more perverse and brutal ways than any gas chamber ever had was something they'd have to explain. I certainly couldn't do it. The folks who gathered outside prison gates on the night of each execution, lighting candles and sobbing like it was Mahatma Gandhi who was being put down inside, should try visiting some crime scenes. Ask them then if they still want to idealize men for whom murder lies somewhere between a hobby and a vocation.

Cecelia Corrigan's correspondent had been a man by the name of Jenkins Howler.

The name meant nothing to me, but then why should it? There were plenty of prisoners on Death Row and plenty more being added every year.

Murder is a business that never seems to go into recession.

The parcel detained at Dublin Airport purported to be from Howler, though of course it couldn't actually have come from him. Death Row inmates are not even allowed to smoke, let alone send mysterious parcels to their dead penfriends. Inside was a rough, hand-made bouquet of flowers. Howler had obviously found some way of getting the flowers sent in tribute to his late penfriend via a third party. Who it was I had no idea, but that wasn't so important as the fact I had finally found some thread of a story which it made a semblance of sense for Leon Kaminski to pursue. Was Howler the man that JJ suspected of killing his wife?

Had Kaminski come to Dublin looking for evidence to prove it?

Whatever the reason, I had something to work with at last. It was at this point I realized, no matter how guilty I felt about interfering with things that were none of my concern, that it had gone too far now for me to turn back. Kaminski — Cecelia Corrigan — Jenkins Howler — I simply had to keep following the trail to see where it led.

And I knew just who to ask.

Back home, I switched on the radio and weaved in and out of signals along the dial in search of more information on Marsha Reed's death, but there was

nothing apart from the usual diet of cheesy pop music for those whose attention span started to struggle after three minutes, and talk radio stations where people were encouraged to drown themselves in whatever sea of complaint was lapping at their personal shore at any particular moment.

That day, like most days, the voices were mainly spitting out the usual diet of bile about the United States. Here we go again. I'd learned soon after coming to Dublin that, though the welcome was friendly enough on the surface, you didn't have to dig down very far to find that the people who passed as the foremost thinkers in Dublin, the ones whose voices whined out of every screen and every radio, considered the United States to be little better than the Third Reich, imperialist overlords imposing their savage and depraved values on the world. Values like, oh, democracy and free speech and respect for women.

Scary stuff, huh?

I'd quickly grown tired of being expected to show humility in the face of my country's alleged litany of sins, or to parrot the carping as some precondition of membership of a club that I didn't want to belong to anyway. There were plenty enough Americans in Dublin willing to do that. We were expected to whisper our nationality apologetically, like it was shameful. Being American and proud of it was the new love that dare not speak its name.

Not that I've ever felt proud of being American either. Being proud of where you're born makes no more sense than being proud of having blue eyes.

There's nothing you can do about it either way. But I damn sure wasn't going to be made to be ashamed of it.

Eventually I found a news station, but all they said was what'd been in the newspapers that morning: that a woman's body had been found in a house in Dublin and that police were trying to contact members of her family before naming her.

In the end I snapped off the radio impatiently.

"Is that where the Chief is?" came Boland's voice from over by the door.

Until about a year ago, Niall Boland had been a member of the Murder Squad alongside Fitzgerald, though he'd never really been cut out for murder, if that's the right way of putting it. He knew that himself better than anyone.

There are plenty of fine police officers who should never be allowed near a murder investigation, and Boland was most definitely one of them. The writer Brendan Behan once said that the police in Dublin looked like they'd had to be coaxed down out of the mountains with raw meat, and I guess it was men like Boland he was thinking of. There was a thick-set roughness about his appearance that spoke more of the farms and hills than it did of the city. It sometimes felt like some cosmic joke that he had been born in Dublin at all. Everything about him betrayed a man who ought to have been rising at dawn to inspect his own fields and reclining at night with his feet stretched toward a peat fire.

But that country boy solidity masked a sensitivity that meant he was always going to find working the Murder Squad too damaging. Murder affected everyone, of course, unless they were chiselled out of stone, nursing hearts dead to the business of being human, but it was true that it took a certain sliver of ice in the heart to be able to go on doing it, day after day, murder after murder, and if Boland ever had ice in his heart it had melted long ago.

Eventually he gave up the battle against reality and jumped ship. With his girlfriend, he opened a locksmith's store in the indoor market that ran between South Great George's Street and Drury Street. It was Boland's name I'd given to Hugh that morning.

I'd gotten back from the library to find him already at work. It said something for how much I trusted him that I didn't mind his being here without me. There weren't many people I could say that about. Like Lucas Piper, I was a little paranoid about security.

"You don't have to call her Chief now," I pointed out, walking over to the front door where he was kneeling, tightening screws. "You're a free man."

"She'll always be Chief to me."

"Don't tell Cassie."

"She's Chief No. 2," he said with a grin.

"A man cannot serve two mistresses. Unless you're one of those men who like being bossed about by big dominatrixes in leather masks and tight lederhosen with whips and chains," I said. "I've read about your sort in the Sunday newspapers."

"My secret is out," Boland said. "That must be why I'm so good with locks."

"Speaking of which," I said, "how much longer are you going to be?"

"Didn't you ever hear that old saying about patience being a virtue? I'm nearly done. These are fascinating old locks you have. Seems a pity to replace them."

"As long as they work," I shrugged.

"Give me five minutes, then, and I'll be out of your hair."

"You meeting Cassie for lunch?"

"Not today," he said. "I have to stay in and mind the shop."

"Just imagine," I said. "If you hadn't left the Murder Squad, you could be over there now with the rest of the team instead."

"No thanks," said Boland firmly.

He was another one, getting on with their lives, like Piper.

Another one who'd been able to leave it behind.

"Do they have any idea who did it?" he asked now.

"No," I said. "But there doesn't seem to be any sign of a forced entry, and it was a bit late at night for the killer to be posing as the gasman or a courier to get inside, so either it was someone she knew and she let them in, or it was someone with a key."

"The Chief should check her locks," said Boland.

I frowned. What did Fitzgerald's locks have to do with this woman's murder?

"The dead girl's locks," explained Boland when he saw my blank look.

72

"I'm still lost," I said.

"You'd be surprised by the things I've learned since starting this job. One thing I've learned is never to trust a locksmith. Apparently, there's a brisk black market trade in keys."

"There is?"

"Think about it," he said, warming to the theme. "A locksmith gets called in to change someone's locks, and when he's in the house he sees a few nice pieces scattered about, maybe he even knows a bit about antiques or collectables and realizes what they're worth. More to the point, he knows other people who might be interested in getting their greedy hands on the stuff. So he makes a couple of extra keys of the place he's just fixed up, and Bob's your uncle. He sells them on and a few weeks later the people come home to find there are considerably fewer things in the house than there were when they went out."

"This is a bit more serious than a robbery."

"Same difference, as far as the methodology goes. You never know, her locksmith could've taken a shine to her and cut himself an extra key for when he summoned up the courage to act on it. Locksmiths make spares illicitly all the time, though they don't like to shout about it, for obvious reasons. There was even a case in Japan recently of a writer who was murdered after publishing a book exposing what they were up to."

"I guess that's how you could afford a new car," I teased him.

I'd seen the new people carrier parked on the kerb when I got back from the library. It looked impressive,

though it wasn't going to look so impressive once the clampers got to it.

"I got that entirely legit," Boland said. "Just because I know some of the wicked ways of the trade doesn't mean I take after them. Besides, I don't need to. We're doing so well now we've just taken a young lad on to work with us. Wish I'd done it years ago instead of plodding along, playing at being a real policeman. I hardly do the locks myself now. I just sit in the shop and send the new boy out. I'm only here doing these ones because it's you."

"I'm honoured," I said. "Not to mention relieved. At least I can trust you not to go selling on my keys to the criminal underworld."

"The bad guys wouldn't stand a chance against you even if I did."

"I wouldn't say that. My karate's a little rusty these days," I joked. "It's an intriguing idea, though. I'll tell Fitzgerald what you said. It might be worth following up. At least it would explain how the killer got in and out without any sign of a break-in."

"You really think it's worth checking out?"

He looked pleased to have come up with a useful suggestion.

"I wouldn't say it if I didn't. You know, Boland, sometimes I think you'd make a good policeman. You're wasted in your new life."

CHAPTER
EIGHT

"Your Ceceilia Corrigan had an interesting taste in friends," said Burke.

Thaddeus Burke, that is to say: owner of, and sole worker at, Burke and Hare's, a radical (at least that's what he called it) bookstore down by the quays, where the water slapped continually at brown stone, lingering idly on its way to the sea.

Decorated former US marine, lifelong communist, cat lover, whiskey connoisseur, truly execrable poker player — there was something in Burke's overcrowded personality for everyone. And, speaking for myself, it was the terrible poker that I liked best, plus the fact that he seemed to effortlessly gather a whole bunch of equally terrible poker players round him. For a girl who paid her way through college back in Boston playing poker, they made for easy, if not so rich, pickings. Sometimes I truly wished he'd get to know some rich people for a change and invite them along on one of his poker nights. Sadly, Burke was drawn to the marginalized and the penniless, and there's only so much hard cash you can snatch from these people before you start feeling bad about it. Guilt takes all the pleasure out of winning.

Well, some of it.

All the same, I had to admit that playing poker with Burke's inner circle of Dublin's dissolute was less stressful than those far-off days in college when I'd spent my nights in darkened downtown rooms across a table from the kind of men my mother had always warned me to stay away from. And she was right. Those were the days when, if you played poker, you were never really sure if you wanted to win. Losing might've meant poverty, but you didn't know *what* winning might mean. Chances were it wouldn't be pleasant.

No one ever asked any questions about what anyone else there did from nine to five. That was one of the rules. But they didn't need to wear badges to signal that these were men who were less used to handing over their own money than taking other people's money off them. Whether the other people wanted to hand it over or not.

It was inevitable that an exile like me would find my way to Burke eventually, and so it had proved. I counted him now as one of my few genuine friends in the city, and I hoped he could say the same about me. His politics I wasn't so crazy about, but I figure that a man's politics are his own concern. More important than any ideological differences was how he carried himself as a human being, and Burke had a dignity and self-possession in his bearing that you often see in the best soldiers.

I'd never seen him lose his temper, not even when he came down from his room above the store some

mornings to find the word *Nigger* painted across the front window.

The continuing suspicion of a black face in some quarters of the city was one of those hidden parts of life in Dublin that they never get around to mentioning in the guide books.

It was Burke I'd asked to check up for me on Jenkins Howler, since he had a computer hooked up to the internet, where he could track the progress of the workers' revolution across the globe (current status: way behind schedule), and I didn't. He also needed it for his business. Half his sales were online now, he'd told me not so long ago when I was complaining at the permanent hum the computer made behind the desk. Most of his customers never even came into the store. My relationship with technology, by contrast, was almost as bad as my relationship with other people. Almost, but not quite.

It's true that logging on to the internet would probably have made researching my books a whole lot more straightforward, but I still didn't want to. I know my personality, my weaknesses. I'm too easily distracted. I wouldn't trust myself with that much opportunity not to do any work. No, I preferred to stay with my usual methods of online research, namely getting Burke to do it. Besides, it gave me an excuse to come round and drink his whiskey.

That clinched any remaining argument.

"She's not my Cecelia Corrigan," I said now in answer to his earlier remark about the dead woman's choice of friends. "She wasn't anybody's. That was the

problem. Who'd choose to have a guy on Death Row for a friend if there were other available options?"

"What have you got against prisoners on Death Row?" said Burke.

"What have I got against them?" I repeated incredulously. "You mean, apart from the fact that they're a collection of murderers, rapists, gangsters, armed robbers, cop killers, drug addicts and child molesters?"

"Who says? The Texas Department of Criminal Justice?" said Burke. "That ain't exactly the testimony of the angels. They make mistakes. Innocent men get strapped to the table too, you know, while the doc injects them with that crap."

"I know that, Burke, but you —"

"And have you ever looked at those statistics?" he interrupted. "Only 11 per cent of the population of Texas is black, and you wanna guess what the percentage is of black offenders on Death Row in the state? 40 per cent. 40. Over 50 per cent of Texas is white, but white prisoners only make up 30 per cent of the inmates on Death Row."

"That doesn't excuse what they've done."

"I'm not saying it does. I spent twenty years as a soldier. I don't have any illusions about human nature. But you can't divorce the issue of capital punishment from the social, political and racial context in which it's implemented by the government," Burke said.

"Shooting dead the cashier so you can take twenty bucks from the cash register isn't making a political statement."

"No, but giving thirty years to a white guy who shoots a cashier, and a one-way trip to the prisoners' graveyard in Huntsville to a black guy whose does exactly the same, *is* a political statement. The whole system stinks."

"Look, not even I'm crazy enough to say the system's perfect," I said. "I just can't think of an alternative. The dead deserve justice. It's the only thing we've got left to give them. And those men, they carry on spreading evil even when they're behind bars. It's their nature. They *should* be dead." I paused. "Is Jenkins Howler black?"

Burke grinned. "You think I'm fooled by the way you just sidestepped the argument about capital punishment there and tried to switch the talk back to the reason you came round here?"

"Obviously not."

"You're damn right I'm not. But for your information," said Burke, "Jenkins Howler isn't anything any more, black, white, Hopaki Indian or Eskimo. He's dead, and there are no segregated buses in hell."

"Dead?" I said.

"That's the usual outcome when you're executed."

Burke placed a sheet in front of me, showing a headline from a three-month-old copy of the *Texas Ranger* which said: *Rapist-Murderer Executed in Huntsville*. It even featured a picture of him. Howler had been a weaselly man with a pinched, mean-looking face, scrappy moustache, bad teeth.

And no, he wasn't black.

"Good-looking guy," I remarked.

"And with a personality to match," Burke stressed. "I don't want to give you any more ammunition for your simplistic and unrepentant right-wing views on the American criminal-justice system, but I seriously doubt if this guy's passing is going to be much loss to the world. Not if this stuff is anything to go by, at any rate."

This stuff turned out to be a pile of press cuttings and write-ups about Howler that Burke had downloaded and printed out for me from the internet.

He laid them down on the table, then sat back, watching the world go by outside his window, as I began to flick through the sheets. Burke, bless him, had even put the collection into chronological order — oh, what it must be like to have a logical mind — starting with a ten-year-old news item about Howler's arrest for the rape and murder of a female hitchhiker whose body had been found in shrub-land by the side of the road near Austin three weeks earlier.

The gun which had been used to kill the girl was found in the glove compartment of Howler's pick-up truck. Not exactly a criminal genius, then.

When DNA testing, as a later news report confirmed, also linked Howler to the scene, he soon confessed. Though not to the murder of a young black woman shot dead at a crack house in Tyler two years previously, which tests showed was also carried out by the same gun. His story was that he'd bought the gun in a bar in Galveston, which was possible, I guess. Few guns being passed around on the black market had a clean history. Each one was corrupted by its history and corrupted by those who had held it. Having too

little evidence to go on, the prosecutor decided not to pursue that charge. The rape and murder was sufficient for a conviction as it was, especially when DNA tests also matched Howler to three further rapes of students in the university town of Austin some years previously.

There were further reports, growing more intermittent as time passed, of Howler's trial and sentencing, then of the various appeals launched by his attorneys against the capital sentence, all of whom seemed to talk as if it was Howler who was the true victim of all this.

Finally came the execution.

There seemed to have been quite a campaign to have Howler's sentence commuted to life imprisonment. He'd been a particular favourite of the nuns. He'd found Jesus when he was inside — don't they all? — and his new religious friends were gathered outside the night he died, praying, singing hymns, lighting candles, bleating to reporters about the cruelty and injustice of taking human life. Pity Howler hadn't embraced that creed a bit earlier.

"Did he make a last statement?" I said, noticing it wasn't in the pile.

"He did," said Burke. "I thought I printed it out for you. Isn't it there?"

I rifled quickly back through the pages.

"I can't see it."

"I'll print you another one off," he said. "It was very touching. He said he was very sorry for all that he'd done, and all the hurt he'd caused, and he asked the family of the dead girl for their forgiveness. He said that he was going home now to the Lord, where he would

answer for his sins, and he hoped they'd find some comfort in his death."

"Your dictionary obviously has a different definition of touching than mine."

"And your dictionary obviously doesn't acknowledge the existence of the word repentance," said Burke.

"I believe in the *word*," I said, "I just don't know whether it amounts to much."

"At least he was facing up to what he'd done," said Burke. "That's something. Some of these men keep the families of the victim on the rack right to the end. They enjoy it. I guess that's why there was such a campaign around Howler. The sinner repenteth and all that. There was even a documentary about the campaign to save him on one of the public access networks. I could try and get hold of a copy, if you like, but I wouldn't raise your hopes too high."

"My hopes are never high. That way everything is a pleasant surprise."

"This is definitely the guy you wanted to know about, then?"

"It's him all right," I admitted.

"And you think this is the same guy your old friend JJ has an interest in?"

I'd told him when I called earlier from outside the library on Pearse Street about seeing Kaminski in Temple Bar.

"I not only think it," I said, "I know."

"How do you know?"

"I just know, is all."

"You just know? So it's that kind of knowing, is it?" he said. "That's the kind of knowing I think I'm better off not knowing too much about. That's the kind of knowing that could get a girl into a lot of trouble."

"I like being in trouble."

"You do, don't you?" said Burke. He shook his head with mock sadness. "It's a wonder to me you never wound up in the next cell to a guy like Howler."

"I'd need a sex change first."

"You know what I mean. Still," he said, shrugging, "you know your own business, and I know how to mind mine. Though I must admit I'm curious as to how an ex-Bureau man's presence in Dublin is supposed to be connected to an execution in Texas."

"I'm curious too," I said. "All I know is that this Howler was writing to Cecelia Corrigan and now she's dead too and Kaminski's sniffing around her corpse. It was nothing, an accident, but I can't help feeling there must be some connection."

"And you thought the key to the code was Howler?"

"That was the idea."

He was silent a moment, considering.

"Maybe," he suggested in due course, "Kaminski thinks this Howler might have passed on information to her before he died, and he wants to know what it was."

"Maybe's a big country."

"Then take this stuff with you as your guide," said Burke. "You haven't had a chance to study it properly yet. Though, if you want my advice, I don't like the way it looks."

"Explain yourself, soldier."

Burke shrugged. "It just feels wrong. You be careful."

"What could happen?" I said. "Howler's dead, the woman he was writing to is dead."

"But the guy who got you interested in this is still very alive and running round the city, and you don't know what the hell he's doing. I don't want anything to happen to you."

"Nothing can happen to me. I'm indestructible."

"That's what all the folks in the graveyard thought."

Burke looked up as the bell on the door jingled and a small fat guy in an ill-fitting T-shirt with a hammer and sickle on the front was framed against the sunlight in the door. I recognized him. He was known as Red Ned, though I doubted that was what it said on his birth certificate. He was one of Burke's poker circle, though far as I knew it wasn't the night for poker. Unless the cowards had started organizing games without me.

"Am I early?" he said as he came in.

"You're early," confirmed Burke, "but come in anyway."

"Saxon," the newcomer nodded. "You're the last person I expected to see here."

"Don't worry," I said. "I'm just off. I didn't realize the time. What am I missing?"

"We're having a meeting here later on," said Burke. "We get together a couple of times a week to plan the overthrow of the capitalist system."

"Aren't you boys a little old for all that bullshit?" I teased.

"We're giving capitalism until next Tuesday to crumble, and if it doesn't we're taking up embroidery.

You're welcome to join us," Burke said. "Having you on board during the revolution might just tip the balance."

"It's a tempting offer, but I promised Fitzgerald I'd go round and prepare lunch."

"Listen to you," said Red Ned with a wink. "You're starting to sound like a housewife."

"That's what I hate about you pinkos," I said with staged offence. "Soon as you start to lose the argument, you immediately resort to insults."

"Words are the only weapons we have against the oppressors," he said solemnly.

"You're breaking my heart. I'd better get out of here before you have me weeping with more hard-luck stories about the workers."

"It's your loss, comrade."

"I doubt that, but I'll make you a deal. You start the revolution without me, and if things start going your way I'll make sure to switch sides in time for the victory parade."

"Spoken like a true mercenary," said Burke.

CHAPTER
NINE

I picked up some food that could be heated later from a tiny Middle Eastern place I'd discovered once while walking near Fownes Street. It wasn't far out of my way. I didn't know if Healy liked this kind of food, but he'd have to put up with it. Fitzgerald had sent me a message earlier that he'd be coming too. Briefly I considered walking back to my apartment and taking the Jeep out from the underground car park, but by the time I'd gotten up there and taken the car from its place, I'd have wasted another fifteen minutes. By the time I struggled through the traffic to her house, I'd have wasted even longer. I decided to take the train instead.

Tara Street was near. A train rattled over the bridge above as I approached the station, filling the air with its thunderous clang, making the air seem hotter somehow as it disgorged a bellyful of carbon fuels into the atmosphere and melted another iceberg, if you believe all that jazz about global warming. Typical that I'd missed the train. Then I saw with relief that it was going the other way. Trains were fairly regular, but even so I didn't want to be kept hanging around longer than necessary.

It was a relief to turn off the street into the Stygian gloom of the station. It felt like the last remnant of coolness in the city. Oasis in the desert. Inside, I bought a ticket at the booth, and then pushed through the turnstile to take the escalator up to the crowded platform.

I stood with my back to a pillar and lost myself in the buzz of conversation that rose and receded like a tide around me. I avoided catching anyone's eye. I didn't feel like being dragged into conversation. My body might've been in Dublin, but my brain was in Texas. I was with Jenkins Howler, and I have to admit I've enjoyed better company.

To keep focused, I let my eyes fall to the platform.

There, just before the drop on to the tracks, a line had been newly drawn, along which was also painted a warning: *Do Not Cross the Yellow Line*.

I smiled.

Crossing the line was what I was best at. What I'd always done. I had crossed the line this morning again in JJ's room. I shouldn't have intruded on his privacy like that. Another twinge of guilt came, but I suppressed it impatiently. It was important to suppress guilt or you'd never get anything done. Never get anything interesting done, at least.

But there were other lines I'd crossed, throughout my life, and it was only after you crossed them that you realized nothing would ever be the same again. And by then it was always too late. There was no going back. Sometimes it was for the best. Sometimes not.

The biggest line I'd ever crossed was when I joined the FBI. Behind me then was one world, and the new world I entered made me see everything in an entirely different light.

Or perhaps light is the wrong word, since what I saw was so dark.

Those experiences tainted my mind and made it impossible for me to go back to feeling positive or trusting about things again. I lost my faith in human nature. I lost my faith in people doing the right thing or stopping bad things from happening.

Leaving the FBI was another huge step, because now my mind had been battered and changed, but there was nothing I could do with my thoughts any more but brood on them, impotently. There is less that can be done in the FBI than you hope, disappointment is perpetual, a feeling of inadequacy pervades the soul. But at least you can do *something*, even if it is never enough. Once outside, I was permanently barred from that world I had come to know. I'd dwelt there once. Now it was a foreign country. I was across the border.

Perhaps if I'd taken a different path and tried, I mean really tried, to put it behind me, I could have made things work. I could have moved on. But no. With my great talent for screwing up, I had carried on writing about that life and hanging round its edges, even wound up with a woman who still worked in the investigation of murder, which meant that it was constantly within my orbit, though there was nothing I could do about it but look on.

From the other side of the line.

And yes, I had killed a man once. That was another crossing of the line, albeit one I tried to revisit in my memory as little as I could, easier said than done though it was.

Dreams were the worst.

They're beyond rational control.

I was grateful when my melancholy thoughts were interrupted by the snaking arrival of the train around the bend into the station.

That is, I called it a train, but the locals knew it as the DART. The letters stood for Dublin Area Rapid Transport, though there were times when the Rapid part of the acronym sometimes felt more like a vague aspiration than an iron-clad promise. Still, it was a good way to get around certain parts of the city if you didn't feel like driving. I climbed aboard.

No seat, it was too busy, so I simply grabbed a pole that connected floor to ceiling and held on as the carriage jerked forward, trying to concentrate on where I was going, because I didn't want to start daydreaming and miss my stop. I'd done that before.

Instead I stared out of the window and watched them go by, the names of the stations ticking off in my head like the beat of a metronome.

Pearse.

Grand Canal Dock.

Lansdowne Road.

Sandymount.

Sydney Parade.

It was only as the train pulled out of Sydney Parade that I realized it was where I was supposed to get out.

I'd been staring at the station's name written on a metal sign, feeling hollow. Sydney had been my sister's name. She was dead now. Her funeral was the last time I'd been home to Boston, and sometimes I didn't know if I'd ever go back again.

After Sydney died, there was nothing there worth going back *for*.

I stepped off at the next station, which had been saddled with the singularly ugly name of Booterstown, and began walking back along the seafront. The tide was out. A wide expanse of sand and flatness stretched into the distance, the monotony of the view broken only by occasional walkers, like drawings of stick men, lingering among the pools of stranded water. The sea beyond was as still as a lake. The masts of sailing boats scarcely moved.

I was on Strand Road.

Not far now.

Fitzgerald lived in a cul-de-sac across the sea with a view of Howth Head from her bedroom. Cul-de-sac: they had to be the three most terrifying words in any language, next to *I love you* and *it's a boy*. The houses had been put up about five years ago, and they didn't look like they'd last much longer than the stuff I'd bought for lunch. They were the sort of houses that a child would make out of Lego. Front door, four windows, chimney, like a sketch of something that might one day be a house rather than the real thing. I hated it here.

So did Fitzgerald, but for her it was just a place to eat, a place to sleep, a place to take a shower. It was like a hotel without chambermaids to root around in your underwear drawer and use your toothbrush to clean the toilet. She kept irregular hours. It was all she needed.

We'd often talked about getting a house together. It made no sense to keep two places going when as often as we could we were both either at one or the other. Living in two places simply multiplied the time we spent travelling between them, and travelling was getting more difficult round the city with every month that passed. Fitzgerald said she could remember a time when you could get from one side of Dublin to the other in a half-hour. Now you'd have no chance of doing that unless you grew wings. Traffic choked the city more tightly than a noose. But still, somehow, we'd never gotten beyond talking about it. There was always something else that pushed house-hunting on to the back burner.

We wanted different things, that was the problem. She may have hated her house, but cross the road and there was the Strand and the wide sweep of Dublin Bay, Howth Head opposite and Bray Head in the distance. This is where she liked to walk. If she could have her way, she'd live out in the country, with roaring fires, and logs piled by the stone hearth, and seven dogs sleeping at her feet. She should've married a farmer, and they could've gotten themselves a smallholding out West, where they could tend pigs and grow parsnips and make wine out of nettles. My longing had always been for the city, for bustle and noise. Trying to find a

compromise between the two extremes was like negotiating an end to the Cold War. Not that we were likely to come to blows about it, just that what we wanted was so far apart as to make any chance of finding a happy medium pretty much impossible.

It was complicated by the fact that houses in Dublin were so expensive.

I had enough money not to have to worry about it, and Fitzgerald had her house to sell. Pooled together, we had plenty. But it never ceased to shock me what people in Dublin paid for what in any other city would've been regarded as unremarkable properties.

That was why people were moving further and further out of the city and commuting in each morning, just so they could afford a place of their own, and houses in the centre of town that would once have been lived in were now offices for insurance brokers and lawyers — Dublin was full of lawyers, and I used to think the States was overrun with them — and were locked up and dark at night, giving an eerie, otherworldly quality to the streets. The gardens in the middle of the old squares were dark and deserted. Take a small turn off the main street and the city, which a moment ago had been thronged and noisy, had almost ceased to exist at all. A vista emptier than the post-nuclear winter landscape had taken its place.

Yet even that had to be preferable to this, I thought, as I walked up the path to Fitzgerald's house and a curtain twitched in response in the window next door.

It was that kind of place. The kind where they keep tabs on you to make sure you never have any privacy.

Your privacy offends them. And the fact that Fitzgerald wasn't married to a chartered surveyor and spending her days rearing three kids probably offended them too. I resisted the childish temptation to stick out my tongue at the neighbours, and let myself in. There was no sign of her yet, but then I hadn't expected there to be.

A murder investigation doesn't watch the clock.

I stacked the food in the fridge to keep for later.

Whenever later turned out to be.

To pass the time, I lifted a Coke from the ice box and turned on the large fan which Fitzgerald had set up on the worktop in an effort to keep cool, and I sat with the news reports about Jenkins Howler that Burke had printed off for me fanned out on the kitchen table, held down with various pieces of silverware to stop them blowing away.

And there was his last statement. The page must've gotten stuck to the back of another sheet. That was how I'd missed it. It was only the breeze from the fan that made it work loose. I read it through slowly, ending at Howler's last words.

"*Warden, I'm ready.*"

Well, bully for him.

That's what many condemned men said when the time came, and it always made me angry. They had no right to be ready. Their victims hadn't been given the chance to prepare themselves for death, to find Jesus or to make their peace with the world.

They had simply been snatched away from life, violently.

The Texas Department of Criminal Justice was certainly thorough, I'll say that. For each execution, there was not only a record of the offender's last statement but a sheet detailing their previous criminal convictions, history of education, height, weight, eye colour, the country they came from, you name it, as well as an account of the crimes for which they were being punished. There was even a note of the ethnic origins of their victims. Killers tended to stay within their own ethnic group. It was black on black, white on white, Hispanic on Hispanic. Burke would say that proved him right when he argued how every act had its origins in the social, economic and racial circumstances out of which it had been born.

My own view was that killers simply took their opportunities for fun where they could find them, and in a country as segregated as the United States they were inevitably going to find most of those opportunities in the particular subgroup they belonged to. There was nothing profound about it, it was merely a reflection of where they were at.

Or was that just an example of the two of us finding different ways to describe the same phenomenon?

In addition to all this, there was a list of those who had been present at the execution of each prisoner, and there used to be a description of the prisoner's chosen last meal until the publication of that information was deemed insensitive and ordered to be kept secret. Though why the revelation of a psychopath's Big Mac and fries should be considered out of the bounds of decency, while the final degradation and suffering of

victims at the hands of these same losers with a grudge against society was published for all to see, was beyond me.

Depressed, I read through Howler's final statement again — the expressions of regret, the best wishes for the future for his friends and fellow inmates and guards, the born-again claptrap — looking for something I couldn't be certain I would recognize even if I saw it. Whatever Howler had done to get Kaminski on his scent, I still didn't have enough information to determine. All this effort, and I was no closer to an answer.

I scraped back my chair in frustration and roughly yanked open the door of the fridge to get another Coke. Or, better still, a beer. The fridge shook in protest at my delicate, ladylike touch, dislodging some further sheets of paper which had been pushed into the gap between the top of the fridge and the microwave that sat up there.

I caught them as they fell. I saw at once what they were. They were brochures for house sales. Detached Victorian villa in Rathgar and Ranelagh. Edwardian semi-detacheds in Dalkey and Sandycove. Period features, orginal fireplaces, en suite bathrooms, fitted kitchens. I guess house-hunting wasn't as on the back burner as I'd thought.

CHAPTER
TEN

"You're going bald," I said, when they finally arrived at the door an hour later.

"Bald is sexy," growled Healy.

"Whoever told you that must've had one sick sense of humour."

"Stop talking nonsense, woman, and bring me some food."

It was after two and Healy's car had just pulled into the driveway with Fitzgerald in the passenger seat, and I'd gotten up from the kitchen table, where I was still reading, to open the door for them. The scent of the sea was in the breezeless air.

They both looked spent. Not sleeping tends to have that effect. But, as it happened, Healy was right. His hair may have been thinning and greying a little, but it made him look more attractive. These days he almost looked distinguished.

He was nearly fifty now, a veteran of many cases, and remained the person in the department that Fitzgerald probably felt most comfortable with, the one she related to and could talk to. He'd never had the same problem working for a female Chief Superintendent that some of the other members of the team did, and

just as important he'd never had a problem with our relationship. Plenty of the others found it either threatening or a vehicle for trademark crude humour. Healy just regarded ours as a normal relationship like any other.

We often found ourselves eating together when they were working a case.

He headed through to the tiny kitchen and threw himself into a chair.

"What a day," he said.

I saw Fitzgerald's eye move to the pile of real estate brochures which had fallen on me from the top of the fridge, and then look at me sharply, like I'd caught her out.

"It's fine," I said in a low voice.

"What's fine?" said Healy, not noticing anything was wrong.

"Lunch," I said.

"I should think so," he said. "A man comes in after working hard, he expects to find some decent chow waiting for him at the table."

"I'll get your pipe and slippers later, good master of mine," I said. "Meanwhile, why don't you help yourself to a cold drink while I get the food ready?"

"Beer?" he said hopefully.

"You're driving," said Fitzgerald.

"Drat."

I took the various trays of pre-prepared food from the fridge and began to scoop them out on to plates — cold chicken, falafels, olives, houmous, pitta bread.

Red Ned was right. I was turning into a housewife.

"What's all this?" said Healy, lifting a sheet and peering at it.

"Just some research I've been doing," I said.

"*Death Row Killer in Final Appeals to Texas Governor*," he read aloud. "You know, I sometimes think it wouldn't be such a bad idea if we had the electric chair here too."

"They don't have the electric chair in Texas," I said, taking it neatly from him.

"They don't?"

"Lethal injection," I said. "Sodium thiopental to sedate the prisoner, pancuronium bromide to relax the muscles and collapse the lungs, potassium chloride to stop the heart."

"You really know how to make a girl look forward to her food," said Fitzgerald.

"Oh, I don't know. It doesn't sound too bad," said Healy. "Not compared to what they've usually done."

"All assuming you get the right man," Fitzgerald pointed out.

"That's true," he admitted. "Do you remember that guy in Churchtown?"

"Parker?"

"No," said Healy. "Parker was Islandbridge. The Churchtown one was supposed to have killed his wife. Maybe it was before your time. They all merge into one after a while. Anyway, everything checked out. He did five years before the real killer was finally picked up. Standish something, that was his name. He's remarried now. Owns a pub. Bought it with his compensation

money. If we'd had capital punishment, he'd probably have been hanged."

"Exactly," said Fitzgerald. "The graveyards in Texas must be filled with men like Standish something."

"But you can't help wishing sometimes," said Healy, "that there was *some* punishment in place that even came close to matching the crime. You kill someone now, and what do you get? Ten years, if you're unlucky. And it's not exactly a Siberian gulag when they're in there. More like a holiday camp."

"Don't let's go there again," said Fitzgerald, raising an eyebrow across the table at me. "He gets so bad sometimes he even starts to sound like you."

"I'm serious," said Healy. "It makes you wonder what the point is of catching them when all they get is a slap on the wrist and a few years somewhere warm and cosy, with all their meals cooked and paid for. And what then? Freedom, so they can do it all again."

"And as I've told you a hundred times before," said Grace, "it's not our business to worry about that. We can only do our job. If the courts and the government don't do theirs, that's not our fault. We've done all we can."

"I know, I know," said Healy. "It just pisses me off."

"Sounds like you've both had a rough twenty-four hours," I said.

"The first twenty-four hours are always the worst," said Fitzgerald. "Then routine kicks in."

"You manage to find out anything more about her?"

"Did we?" asked Fitzgerald, talking to herself. She frowned. "I suppose we must have done. We're building

up a picture, let's put it that way, but I still couldn't honestly say that I have the slightest idea what she was like. She was twenty-eight. Blonde. Single. Not much by way of family. Good-looking. Drove a Ferrari. Lived in a recently converted chapel. She worked for one of those small theatre companies down in Temple Bar, off Fishamble Street."

"An actress?"

"She had ambitions to be an actress, she'd taken a few small parts in some plays, even got her name on to some of the posters, but her day job was in publicity, PR, fundraising. To be honest, I don't know what she did exactly. You know what these groups are like, everyone does a bit of everything, it's hard to pin them down."

"There can't be that many small theatre companies in Temple Bar doing so well that their part-time actresses can afford to drive a Ferrari and live in a converted chapel," I said.

"It's not in such a terrific area. It's in the Liberties. But I take your point. The money came from her father," explained Fitzgerald. "He's a widower, made his money in the building trade, she was an only child. I think he probably spoiled her a bit."

"Was it the father who found her?"

"No. That pleasure went to a girl she worked with in the theatre company. Name of Kim Denning. She was the one who told us about the ring. She says she hadn't heard from Marsha for a couple of days, so she went round last night to see what was wrong. When there was no answer, she made her way round the side of the

100

church, climbed up to look through a window, and saw what seemed to be a body lying across the bed. That's when she spoiled our plans for an evening at the theatre by calling 999."

"A starring role at last," I said sadly.

"My words exactly," said Fitzgerald.

"Did she have a boyfriend?"

"Did she ever," said Healy between mouthfuls of food.

"Busy lady?"

"Seems like Marsha Reed was something of a swinger," Fitzgerald explained. "And not just your average swinger. From what we've been able to learn, she was heavily into the whole S & M scene. She belonged to some private members' club in town that puts on parties for broad-minded citizens who like to get their kicks in the modern equivalent of a medieval torture chamber. I exaggerate slightly but only slightly. She was a regular visitor."

"Plus there was a diary," said Healy, "with dates and details of a whole bunch of men she'd been with, some women too, and what she'd been doing with them."

"Names?"

"Mainly initials," said Fitzgerald.

"Meaning it'll be all but impossible to trace each one," I said.

"I certainly doubt they'll be lining up at HQ to identify themselves to the police."

"It's a lead, at any rate," I said. "You've had less to work on in the past. What's your feeling? You think she met her killer that way?"

"Hard to tell. It's certainly a dangerous world to be getting into. On the other hand, it could be simpler than that. You know what it's like."

"Sado-masochistic sex, or murder?"

Fitzgerald smiled.

"Both. But, seriously, sometimes we make things more complicated than they have to be. It could be unrelated. We're going to try to track down her movements, who she was seen with last, that sort of thing. We have statements coming out of our ears already, but nothing much that leaps out of the chart as yet. If anything, the club complicates things."

"How?"

"Because how do we know what was part of her consensual sex life and what was part of her murder? Butler couldn't even say for sure whether Marsha was sexually assaulted. There were certainly signs she'd had some very rough sex a few hours before she died, but there were also old vaginal and anal abrasions that had healed up, suggesting she wasn't exactly a stranger to rough sex. Then there're the cords around her ankles and wrists. Were they restraints used to keep her under control or just a part of her usual lovemaking routine?"

"I see what you mean."

"Butler says the cords were tied quite lightly, considering. The bindings weren't excessive. They were sufficient to render her helpless, but not any more than was needed to restrain her from getting away. Tying her to the bed looks like a means to an end rather than an aim in itself. As for the bag over the head, it's not exactly the stuff of romantic fiction, but it's not

unheard of in the kind of circles the victim was moving in to use partial suffocation as an aid to orgasm. What if this was just a sex game that went horribly wrong?"

"Sex games don't generally involve one party cutting off the other one's finger," I pointed out. "If she died accidentally while having weird sex, and he panicked, that's one thing. But post-mortem mutilation's something else. So is theft. You didn't find the ring?"

"No," said Healy. "And that wasn't all that was missing."

"It wasn't?"

"She also had a necklace that she'd started wearing the last three months or so," explained Fitzgerald. "Never took it off, apparently. The taxi driver confirms she was wearing it when he dropped her off. That wasn't at the scene either."

"So your guy took a ring *and* a necklace?"

"Maybe we're looking for a psychopathic jeweller," said Healy.

"That's not funny," said Fitzgerald.

"Never said it was."

"And that's not even mentioning the cash," I said. "You don't really think theft was a motive, do you?"

"Right now, I can't see a motive at all. We just have to concentrate on eliminating names. The reasons why can come later."

"Unfortunately," said Healy, "the swabs came back clean for semen, so that's not going to help. Either whoever she had sex with that night wore a condom, or else they were using some other kind of object for penetration. And let's face it, from what we saw and

103

learned today, that could be practically anything, animal, vegetable or mineral."

"We're just going to have to put the frighteners on all those bondage-type groups around the city," said Fitzgerald. "Crank up the pressure on them to come up with names."

"Surely there can't be that many of them around," I said.

"Where have you been?" said Healy. "The things people get up to are limitless. When I was in Vice, we raided this place that made the club Marsha belonged to look like a kids' playground. There were all these men there chained up like slaves."

"You see everything in this job."

"You're not lying," said Healy. "They were even wearing these tight loincloths that made them look like babies with nappies on, and they had pins and chains stuck in places you wouldn't believe. Or places you probably would believe, knowing you. And you want to know the worst thing about it? They'd all paid for the privilege of being there. There were businessmen, priests, teachers."

"Men are nuts," I said. "You're only realizing this now?"

"What can I say?" said Healy. "Everyone needs a hobby. You women have shopping, we have perversion."

"Give me shopping any day," said Fitzgerald with feeling.

"Marsha Reed obviously didn't think so," I said darkly.

"No," she acknowledged.

104

"Do you have a picture?" I asked.

"Of Marsha?" she said. "I've got one somewhere."

"Here," said Healy, reaching into his pocket and taking out his wallet. He opened it up and slid out a small snapshot. "Her friend Kim gave me this one."

I took the picture from his fingers — and gasped. A blonde-haired woman smiled shyly out of the photograph at me, and I was struck again by incomprehension at how the dead could not know what was going to happen to them. How could they be so unsuspecting?

How could they smile?

But it wasn't that which had made me gasp.

"I do know her," I said.

"You knew Marsha Reed?" said Healy.

"I told you she recognized her name," Fitzgerald reminded him.

"So where'd you meet her?"

"She was in my class," I said. Then, realizing Healy probably didn't know what the hell I was talking about, I explained: "I took an evening class for aspiring writers last year at a college in York Street. I was meant to be showing them the disparity between real police and FBI procedure and what you read in the books and see in the movies. But I'm not much of a teacher. We spent most of the time just shooting the breeze and eating chocolate-chip cookies. One of the other students used to bring them in each week."

"What about Marsha?" said Fitzgerald.

"It's like you were saying earlier," I said. "I never felt I really got to know her at all. She did plenty of talking,

105

don't get me wrong, she was real fascinated by the whole subject, used to ask detailed questions, take notes. But she never talked about herself, except to say that she was writing a novel." I looked again at her photograph and shook my head. "I'd never in a million years have pegged her as the kinky swinger type."

"Do you still have a list of the other students?" asked Fitzgerald.

"Somewhere."

"Try to dig it out," she said. "The more people we can find who knew Marsha, the better the picture we can draw up of her."

"I'll do it when I get home. And if I can't find anything, I'll ring the college. They should have contact addresses and telephone numbers. Ironic, isn't it? They wanted to know more about authentic police procedure, and now they're going to get a lot closer experience of it than they ever imagined."

"Hence the old proverb about being careful what you wish for," said Fitzgerald.

CHAPTER
ELEVEN

I hitched a ride back with Healy. He was taking Fitzgerald to Dublin Castle for her meeting about the new Assistant Commissioner and where I wanted to go was on the way. She looked the picture of efficiency in her best suit, though she said she felt uncomfortable, and didn't even understand why she had to make this effort at all. It wouldn't make her any less of a detective if she turned up in pair of torn Levis and a Grateful Dead T-shirt.

I got him to stop and let me out near the Showgrounds on Merrion Road. Fitzgerald didn't ask why I wanted to be dropped off in that particular spot; I guess she was a little distracted and didn't have space in her head for queries about my own plans for the rest of the day. Or maybe she didn't think it was any of her concern. Fitzgerald and I had always known how to give one another space. That was one of the reasons our relationship worked.

I certainly didn't offer the information unprompted. It wasn't a secret as such, just something I wanted to keep to myself for now. Or maybe that's what a secret is, I don't know.

We made arrangements to meet up later; I stood on the sidewalk as the car pulled back into the traffic, watching until it was through the next set of lights. Then I turned and made my way along the narrow path that led between the sparkling narrow water of the Dodder on one side and the green haven of Herbert Park on the other.

The Dodder looked almost appealing that afternoon. Almost clean.

As for the weather, there was still no prospect of a break in the sun's campaign yet. Rare breaths of wind stirred the leaves on the trees, but mostly the afternoon was as motionless as an oil painting.

Cecelia Corrigan's house, or the house which had been Cecelia Corrigan's before her death, was in a leafy backstreet off Morehampton Road on the other side of the park, where all was in blessed shadow from overhanging trees and the houses sheltered under the branches like they were sunshades. As I turned into the street, I could hear a dog barking in one of the gardens. A cat lay sleeping on a wall. It opened one eye with a blink as the dog barked and regarded me as if to share a bewilderment that anything could bother making such an effort on a hot day like this.

I checked along the gates.

Here it was.

Number 8.

The gate swung open with a protest of a squeak, and I walked up to the front door, which was surrounded with roses like some country cottage on a picture postcard.

The brass door knocker was in the shape of a cat and there was a grey stone cat sitting on the step too, with a spider's web constructed neatly in the gap between its ear and shoulder. The garden looked small but neat, and a little overgrown. I guessed it must have been Cecelia Corrigan's concern, and now she had gone the garden had been left to its own devices and was declining gently into a quiet chaos of tangled growth.

I knew the feeling.

I knocked.

Waited.

Traffic buzzed by distantly on the main road, and a closer buzzing denoted a bee that was hovering round the roses at the door, moving from flower to flower.

Apart from that, there was no other sound.

I knocked again, and this time a shadow abruptly loomed into view behind the glass, startling me. A moment later, the door swung open, and there stood a young woman, tall and slim with close-cropped dark hair, dressed in flat shoes and a loose-fitting summer dress with no bra. She was girlish-looking, with a tiny pointed nose, and definitely seemed younger than her mid twenties. I knew she was in her mid twenties because I knew who she was.

I'd seen her picture in the newspaper.

It was Cecelia Corrigan's niece.

Becky stopped in surprise when she saw me. She clearly hadn't realized I was there at all. She was wearing a shoulder bag, through which she had been rummaging for what I could only presume were her car

keys, because that's what she was lifting out when we met.

"Oh," she said.

It was a start.

"Becky Corrigan?" I said. "I scared you. Didn't you hear me knocking?"

She didn't answer. She just looked at me and said, half to herself: "Another American." That threw me. "I suppose you're here about dear departed Aunt Cecelia?"

If I was expecting to find a woman in mourning, I'd clearly come to the wrong place. She certainly didn't talk about her aunt as if the memory of her death was a painful one.

"If I'm not in your way."

"You'd better come in," she said with a sigh. "But I'm warning you, I haven't got much time, I'm late for an appointment already."

Before she could change her mind, I stepped inside to a long narrow hall in which stacks of boxes and old furniture were arranged untidily, virtually hiding a grandfather clock in the corner. Through doorways I could see more boxes, more chairs upended, piles of books and half-emptied shelves along the walls.

"I'm selling up," she declared. "Aunt Cecelia was a bit of a collector, but there's not much point keeping the place like a mausoleum just because she's dead."

"I guess not," I said non-committally, though her attitude seemed a little heartless, even to me.

"Did you know Aunt Cecelia?" asked Becky.

"Not as such."

"She was a harmless old bag, I suppose. But I wouldn't say I was very close to her. I just started living here while I was studying at UCD. Afterwards, I sort of stayed on."

"Did she leave you the house in her will?"

"She left me everything in her will," she said. "Apart from a few thousand which she wanted the Cats' Protection League to have. She was mad about cats. She had seven of them. They used to drive me mad." *Used to?* She must have seen the confusion in my face. "I had them put down after she died. I can't look after seven cats. I don't have the time."

"I see."

"What else was I supposed to do?" she said defensively. "I'm not going to sit in every night looking after a bunch of cats that I never asked to be left in charge of in the first place. If you ask me, that's where Aunt Cecelia went wrong. If she'd spent more time with real human beings instead of her cats, maybe she wouldn't have gone so batty in the end. I don't intend to make the same mistake. I'm going to enjoy myself while I'm young."

She smiled a little too brightly, and then the smile was replaced by a frown.

I'd been waiting for this moment.

"What did you say you wanted again?" she asked.

"I didn't."

"I suppose it's about her old friend Howler?" she went on.

I was thrown a second time.

"Do lots of people come round to ask about him?"

"No. But it's what the other American wanted to talk about too. And I told him the same thing I'm going to tell you. I don't know anything about Jenkins Howler, and I don't *want* to know anything. I knew my aunt wrote to him, and I knew about her campaign for him. She was always writing to the Minister for Justice demanding that he intervene and save lover boy from the electric chair, but of course he wasn't interested. Why should he be?"

"You didn't support her campaign?"

"No." She shook her head firmly. "As far as I was concerned, they could have torn him apart limb from limb and I wouldn't have given a flying fuck. After what he did to those women . . ." So she knew *something* about Howler at least. "Of course, *she* never told me what he'd done," Becky added. "I had to look him up on the internet. We had quite a row about it."

"What did you aunt say?"

"That every sinner deserves a second chance. That's the kind she was. Always off to mass. She said Howler had found Jesus." She rolled her eyes. "Whatever."

"But you didn't fall out permanently over him?"

"No, no, nothing like that. She was lonely. This was her obsession. She was only in her forties, but you'd think she was sixty or something from the way she used to go on. I don't know what she expected. That he'd be out one day and they'd get married, probably."

"Had they talked about marriage?"

"I only looked at a couple of his letters. Maybe he meant it. Who knows? Someone like that, you wouldn't know what was really going on in their heads, would

you? I don't know why there's such a fuss about the whole thing, really. He's dead now. She's dead."

She regarded me oddly. It was as if she kept getting distracted by the sound of her own voice and then having to remind herself that there was someone else there.

"He was a reporter too," she said.

"Jenkins Howler?"

"No, not Howler. Not as far as I know anyway. I meant the other American who came here. He worked for the *New York Post*. Or was it the *New York Times*? I can't remember. He said he was doing a piece on my aunt for the newspaper."

So Kaminski was posing as a reporter now, and she obviously thought I was one too.

I chose not to put her right.

"When was this?" I asked.

"About a week ago," she said. "To be honest, I couldn't understand what was so interesting about my aunt's death. It's not like she was murdered or anything. And it was months ago." She said it like months ago was another century. Sometimes it is when you're young. I wondered if she expected me to enlighten her as to why Cecelia Corrigan's passing should excite such intrigue. I only wished I knew.

"Are you so sure," was all I said instead, "that there really *was* nothing more to your aunt's death than meets the eye?"

Once more, she regarded me oddly.

"He asked me that as well. And, as I told him, my aunt was knocked down. It was an accident, that's all.

Unless you both know something you're not telling me?"

"Me?" I said. "I don't know anything."

She continued staring at me for a moment, trying to read my expression. Then she jumped as the half-hidden grandfather clock chimed a muffled hour.

"And now I really am late," she mumbled crossly. She glanced at her watch to back up the clock's unwelcome news. "Look, Ms . . . I'm sorry, I didn't catch your name."

"Er, Kaminski."

"Then I wish I could be more help, Ms Kaminski, but I really have to scoot."

"There *was* one more thing before you go."

"Yes?"

"I wanted to ask if I could read the letters Jenkins Howler wrote to your aunt."

"You can't."

"Don't get me wrong. I realize they're private," I said. "I won't make them public if you'd rather —"

"You misunderstand me," she said. "I haven't got them any more."

"You haven't got the letters?"

"I sold them," she confessed. "The reporter I told you about, he offered to buy them and I couldn't see any reason to refuse. He mentioned something about a book he wanted to write on women who struck up friendships with convicted killers. He said Aunt Cecelia's letters would be invaluable to him. I didn't think any more of it. They meant nothing to *me*."

But they clearly meant something to Kaminski.

114

What could be in those letters that he was so desperate to get his hands on?

"I know it must be frustrating if you wanted to look at them," Cecelia's niece said, her voice becoming tetchy now as if sensing my disapproval, "but they do belong to me."

"*Did*, you mean," I pointed out.

CHAPTER
TWELVE

My American cellphone rang the moment I sat down on the tram heading back into town. There was only a handful of other passengers, so thankfully talking openly wasn't a problem.

"Good morning," said a voice.

It was Lucas Piper, calling from New Jersey.

"Piper, I thought you'd forgotten me."

"How could I forget you, Saxon? The thought of talking to you again has been the only thing keeping me going."

"I was beginning to think you wouldn't call back."

"You jump to conclusions too quickly. Things take time."

"You have to admit, it's not like we were ever best buddies."

"No," he said, "we weren't. That's true. But we *were* both friends of JJ. I thought if I managed to get you back in touch with him, you might be able to help him."

"Help him?"

"He's in a dark place right now. He needs all the friends he can get."

"Why don't you get in touch with him yourself?"

"It's too late for that now. Too much was said. I wish it hadn't been, but it was. You can't simply wave a magic wand and make everything right again." He stopped. "Where the hell are you? I can hardly hear you speak."

"I'm on a tram," I said.

"San Francisco?"

"That's right. How did you guess?"

"I never guess," he said. "I simply used a process of logical deduction."

"Is that what they call it?"

"I guess you just want me to shut up and tell you what I found out about Kaminski?" said Piper.

"That's the general idea."

"Then I'll get straight to the point. I'm afraid the news isn't good. I haven't been able to find out where JJ is. He hasn't been back to his apartment for five months, and he's not been getting his mail forwarded anywhere either."

"Terrific," I said sarcastically. "You must be losing your touch."

"Hold on there," Piper replied. "I said I didn't know where he *is*, I didn't say I didn't find out where he went after New York." He paused, like he was waiting for applause.

"Are you going to tell me," I said, "or do we have to play twenty questions?"

"He went to Texas."

"*Texas?*"

"Yeah, Texas, you know, twenty-eighth state of the Union, big place, lots of oil?"

"I've heard of it, thanks for the geography lesson. Why'd he go there?"

"Maybe he liked the climate. Maybe he inherited an oil well. Or it could just be because the guy he suspected of killing his wife lived in Huntsville."

"What kind of person lives in Huntsville?"

"The kind who works as a guard on Death Row," said Piper.

"You're joking?"

"Do you hear me laughing? He worked at the Terrell Unit. Ten years' dedicated service. You want my opinion, Kaminski went down there to try to track him down."

"For what purpose?"

"I wouldn't like to speculate," said Piper.

"OK, so you're telling me he's in Texas?"

"I'm telling you he *was* in Texas. He was renting a cheap room on the outskirts of Huntsville. One day he cleared out and he hasn't been seen there since."

"How do you know all this?"

"I spoke to the landlord of the house where he was staying. He told me Kaminski was a little wired, a little nervous, drank a bit too much, but was harmless enough. He didn't know where he'd gone. Kaminski certainly didn't tell him where he was going, didn't even say he *was* going. One week, the landlord went round for the rent money and he wasn't there."

"And he definitely didn't return to New York?"

"Not so far as his old neighbours know. I left word for them to contact me if he turns up again. If I hear

anything, I'll let you know. But I wouldn't go getting my hopes up."

"What about the guard on Death Row?"

"That's the thing," said Piper carefully. "He's gone AWOL too. I spoke to the local cops down there. They told me he didn't turn up for work one morning about three months ago. When they went to search his house, they found him gone."

A chill took hold of me, like it was January in July.

"Kaminski caught up with him, then?" I whispered.

"Like I say, I wouldn't like to speculate. The cops say they'd spoken to Kaminski a couple of weeks before. The guard had made a complaint. Said Kaminski was harassing him. They'd tried to warn him off, and, as far as they were concerned, it had had the desired effect. No more complaints. Then the complainant vanishes into thin air."

"They didn't bring in JJ again?"

"They brought him in, all right, but they didn't have anything on him. Plus there was some doubt about the other guy's disappearance. Seems like he packed a case before he vanished, which suggests he intended to leave town. He also had some serious money issues. So they had to let Kaminski go. Apparently, he promised to stay in town in case they needed to speak to him again. Next thing, he vanishes as well."

"Christ, what a mess."

"You said it," agreed Piper. "So now you see why Kaminski might have good reason to want to make himself hard to find. And whatever he did, I hope it stays that way."

119

"Even if he's got blood on his hands?"

"Not innocent blood," he pointed out.

"You've only got Kaminski's word for it that this man killed his wife."

"That'll have to be good enough for me."

"It wasn't good enough when he called you afterwards."

"I didn't say I felt good about it, did I?"

"Wasn't good enough for the FBI either."

"You and I both know," said Piper, "that the FBI make mistakes. Every day. I've made plenty of them myself. But look, if you're so interested in all this, why don't you fly down to Huntsville and pick up the trail yourself? It's not that far."

"It's not?"

"Not from San Francisco," said Piper. I'd forgotten that's where I was supposed to be. "Three hours on the plane, couple hours on the road. You'd be there easily by tonight."

"It's really not that important," I said hurriedly. "I doubt he'd be in much of a mood to discuss a few old cases for my book over a beer. And you said it yourself — if he doesn't want to be found, he won't be."

"I just wish I could've been more help."

"You were help enough. I appreciate it."

"So do I get to buy *you* a drink sometime?" asked Piper.

"What are you going to do — send it by courier?"

"I meant next time we're in the same general time zone."

120

"I know what you meant, I was being sarcastic. Bad habit."

"One of many."

"You said it."

It was getting near my stop now. I was about to end the call and make my way down to the door, when a thought suddenly struck me.

"Hey, Piper, can I ask you one more thing?"

"Shoot."

"What was the name of the guard Kaminski suspected of killing his wife?"

That empty laugh of his rattled in my ear. "It was Buck Randall III, if you can believe that."

Believe it?

I would've put good money on it.

I returned to my apartment, but working was impossible. Thinking was impossible. The only thing that was possible was baking — and not the cakes and cookies type of baking either.

What was baking was me.

The heat in my apartment was hostile, offensive. It was playing rough with me in my own living room. Pushing me around, refusing to let me settle. I tried sitting out on the balcony, looking down at the traffic, but the heat seemed to strike off the ground and upwards and hit me straight between the eyes. Its aim was as clinical and as precise as a laser's.

The city was heating up, and the people were trapped in its embrace. I couldn't bear it and retreated inside, lay down on the couch with an electric fan

turning, pointing at my face. I tried to close my eyes and sleep, but there were too many thoughts in my head.

Through the window drifted the sound of one of the summer concerts that were held most days in St Stephen's Green. Today it was loud and unwelcome but I could hardly close the windows, without any air conditioning to keep the interior bearable.

Instead I had to put up with it.

I was supposed to be reading a script which had been sent to me. A couple of years ago, they'd made a TV movie from one of the cases in my first book. The movie had made me look good, not least because the actress they got to play me was more attractive than I could ever hope to be. It's nice to be flattered. They also made me look good in the sense that I was now being credited with single-handedly solving every crime I'd ever come into contact with.

It had been far more complex than that, but what do complexities matter when it comes to the movies? I was the photogenic one — correction: the actress playing me was the photogenic one — and hence by the infallible logic of Hollywood she had to be the one who caught the bad guy. I wasn't complaining. They'd paid me more for the movie rights than I considered they were worth, and I'd sold a lot of copies of the tie-in edition after it was shown, mainly I suspect because they'd put a picture of the actress who played me on the front cover. I should get her to stand in for me all the time. I'd make a fortune.

Fitzgerald probably wouldn't complain either.

Now they were in the process of making a sequel, which, if this latest script was anything to go by, had left the realms of reality behind and departed for Fantasy Island.

Not that I was objecting to that. I'm with Katharine Hepburn on that score: *Never complain, never explain.* The fact that a second film had come with a second cheque didn't hurt. Plus I'd managed to negotiate a percentage of the profits of the movie. Assuming that there were any. It wasn't a large percentage, but it was large enough to make me not care whether they made a movie claiming I'd personally captured Jack the Ripper.

I was supposed to be reading the new script and making suggestions. That had been my job on the last movie too. My name was listed on the credits as an Expert Consultant. Or was it Special Adviser? One or the other. Special Agent to Special Adviser in a few short years. Did that count as progress or retreat? My mind changed day to day on that question.

Sometimes minute to minute.

In the end, I flung the script aside impatiently and lay back on my couch, eyes closed, trying and failing to imagine that the breeze from the fan was a breeze from the sea.

I was confused.

No surprise there. Confusion is my natural state of mind. But today I was confused like I'd never been confused before.

I don't know why I should've been feeling so defeated. The pieces were finally fitting into shape. Kaminski's wife — Jenkins Howler — the Death Row

guard he suspected of killing his wife — the spinster in Dublin who'd fallen for the condemned man — Kaminski in Dublin. The components were all there, but they wouldn't form any kind of pattern that made sense.

In the end, I knew the only thing I could do was to go round to the hotel and ask him right out what he was doing in Dublin. That had been the plan all along, after all. It's just that breaking and entering had somehow gotten in the way. It generally does.

This time would be different. From what Piper had told me, Kaminski needed a friend. Maybe I could help him out. Maybe I could help him face down whatever demons had brought him to Dublin. At the least, I could have a drink with him and take a human interest in what was happening with his life. All this running around was pathetic. It wasn't for him or for the truth, I was just trying to cover up some emptiness in my own life.

And if he *was* on the run from whatever bad things he'd done?

I'd have to deal with that dilemma when it arose.

It didn't take long to get round to the hotel. Everything inside was exactly the same. The same shabby lobby. The same music playing on the intercom.

Most of all, the same sulky receptionist.

She must've remembered me from last time but kept up the act all the same.

"Good afternoon, madam, can I help you?"

Talk about having a stick up her ass.

124

"I'd like to speak to Mr Randall, please."

"I'm afraid you're too late, madam."

"Too late?"

"Mr Randall checked out this morning."

She seemed aggrieved by that and glowered at me like it was my fault.

I guess it was.

"He's gone?" I repeated blankly.

"I'm afraid so. He meant to stay till the end of the week, but said something had come up and he had to return to the States. Is your name" — she turned to check something on a sheet of paper on the desk behind her — "Mrs Kaminski?"

That sinking feeling in my stomach sank a little lower.

He had some nerve.

"That's me," I said.

I swore her eye dropped to my hand to see if I was wearing a ring. What was she going to do — demand to see a picture of me in my wedding dress?

"He left something here for you to pick up," she said tightly. "I told him you came here looking for him. He said he was sorry to have missed you, but to give this to you if you turned up again." And she slid open a drawer in the desk and lifted out an envelope.

Handed it to me.

For the attention of Mrs Kaminski.

I recognized his handwriting at once.

"Sorry you missed him," said the blonde, smiling slyly.

I knew what she was thinking — if you could describe what went on in her head as thinking. She had me pegged as some flaky, lovesick female chasing the handsome but melancholy and reluctant Buck Randall III. If so, she clearly had me confused with herself.

I didn't bother answering her. I simply took the envelope and went through the revolving door to the steps outside. I stood in the sunshine and tore the envelope open.

I knew without looking what would be inside.

Sure enough, it was the same leaflet from the theatre that I'd left for JJ that morning. Or half of it, at any rate. He'd torn it in two, and along the plain edge of one half of the leaflet he'd written me a message: *Saxon. Looks like our paths are destined not to cross. Hope you found what you were looking for in my room. — Buck.*

CHAPTER
THIRTEEN

"Hey, you! Lady!" he said.

I'd only that moment carried my drink over to my table in this, the latest of a string of bars I'd been reacquainting myself with that day, and now I was looking up to find the barman on the other side of the room pointing at me accusingly.

Me, a lady?

He'd obviously never met me before.

"You can't smoke in here," he said.

I looked down at my hand. I was in the process of lighting a rather fine cigar which, according to the store owner in Smithfield who had them shipped in for me from the States, comprised 50 per cent Dominican and 50 per cent long filter Cuban tobacco exported before the 1962 embargo, though they could've been made from dried Patagonian llama dung and I'd still have smoked them, they tasted so good. Though perhaps only on special occasions. And now, after one solitary puff, I was being told to put it out.

"You want to get me fined?" he said when I began to protest.

I held up my hand in apology. "OK, OK, I'm sorry," I said, "I forgot."

I stubbed it out, feeling as I did so that I was committing an unforgiveable crime against perfection, like scribbling with a ballpoint on the *Mona Lisa*.

That was a sure sign I'd had too much to drink. Not only too drunk to argue, but too drunk to remember that you couldn't smoke in this city any more

Actually, that wasn't strictly true. You could smoke, just not in any of the bars or restaurants. The city had taken a lead from Manhattan and imposed a public ban on tobacco. If you wanted to smoke and drink at the same time these days in Dublin, you had to stand outside, on rooftop terraces or crowded into courtyards with the other social renegades. The rationale behind the ban was to protect employees in bars and restaurants from the effects of passive smoke. My opinion was that if employees didn't want to breathe in someone else's smoke, they shouldn't get a job in a bar, they should go work in a kindergarten or something. But who listened to me? Grace thought the new rule was great, waxing lyrical about how you could go into bars and restaurants and, for the first time in years, not find them wreathed in second-hand smoke. But then she was the kind of woman who wanted to eat organic fruit and knew the carbohydrate and fibre concentration of just about every meal she ever ate. Me, I thought they'd ruined the whole atmosphere of bars — an opinion intensified by drinking, after which nothing seems as good as it used to.

And I was feeling sorry enough for myself as it was.

I got to my feet, took my bottle of Budweiser and wandered out to the beer garden. It was a small place,

not much more room than it took to raise an elbow to bring the cigar to my lips, but it was enough. I lit up for a second time. At least it was warm out here tonight.

Tonight?

Well, nearly. Shadows were creeping in. I could almost see stars.

Where *had* the day gone?

The only company in the garden was an old man sitting on the wall, smoking a pipe. We nodded at one another with the quiet, unspoken solidarity of a despised minority.

The two last smokers in a city of people determined to be the healthiest on the planet.

I wished now I'd gone somewhere else for a drink. There were a few places in Dublin where they knew how to treat a lady who wanted a quiet cigar. There was nowhere you could smoke inside, but there were establishments which put aside great spaces outside where you could destroy your lungs in comfort. It wasn't so great in winter, when the ice on the pipes had frozen or the terraces were ankle-deep in the city's trademark rain, but right now, with the temperature on the thermometer heading high, it could be fantastic.

You got a better quality of people out here too.

Leave the interior for the saints who wanted to feel pious in the worship of their own bodily purity, and come out here with the people who simply wanted to have a good time and be left alone long enough to enjoy life without interference or disapproval.

129

Though I had to admit that, just this minute, me and the old guy were going to be pushed to make a party of it. He looked like the last party he'd been at was in 1947.

I sat down on the edge of the wall and regarded the area round me, lit brightly by overhanging lamps. It seemed like a metaphor for all that had gone wrong in the last twenty-four hours or so. I'd always thought of Dublin as a city of shadows. Not the hard-edged shadows that the sun was casting on the summer streets each afternoon, their edges so sharp on the ground that you felt you should step over them to avoid cutting yourself. Rather I thought of Dublin as a city of the shadows of night, of secrets. Partly that was because I lived much of my life nocturnally. I'd happily sleep all day and spend the night wandering round. I was an owl. A hunter. That made me perfect for hunting out other hunters. They preferred the dark too. It was what I was made for. It was as though I could see the city more truly at night. See it in its own shape. Light distorted rather than revealed. If it got too bright, the city had to step back and give the light room. After nightfall the city shuffled off the burden of daylight and revealed itself to those who shared its passion for concealment.

Dublin, more than most other cities, was a place that came into its own after dark.

Fogged by dark, it was at its most alluring and beautiful.

A little like me.

I smiled.

That was the attraction of the city. It was a place a girl could hide out. You could disappear inside it like an ant inside an old hollowed-out tree, where no one could find you if you didn't want them to. You could be overlooked. And that was what I wanted. I wanted to be a ghost drifting, unnoticed, through the city, just watching, observing, listening.

Now it was like there was too much illumination. The city was overly determined to show itself to the world. To show that it had nothing and nowhere to hide. That it was respectable. It wanted to be liked. I call that a pity. The smoking ban was one part of it. They had attempted to wipe away something they saw as anomalous and in fact had wiped away something that added to the city's charm. At least that's what I thought when I'd started to have too much to drink and remembered I couldn't smoke a damn cigar. It's the way I am. I need to make everything more dramatic than it really is or I feel only half alive.

Right now, I was feeling sorry for myself because of JJ. I might not be able to find anywhere to hide in the city any more, but *he* had managed it. He had hidden from *me*.

And there really wasn't much I could do about it.

Sure, I could try calling a few hotels and hope I got lucky, but I didn't fancy my chances. He wouldn't be using any name I could guess at, so what was I going to do? Ring them all up and say: "Excuse me, by chance have any Americans checked in lately?"

I could have kicked myself for allowing it to happen. Losing him was one thing. Losing him in such a foolish

way only made me feel all the more powerless. Like I'd lost control of my life and everything that counted was being decided by other people.

I should've realized he'd figure the whole thing out. He sees me in Temple Bar, then an American woman turns up out of the blue at his hotel? There was no doubt he'd have guessed someone had been in his room also. Dammit. Being so clever, I had simply been outmanoeuvred, and I had a dreadful premonition as I sat here that I'd never find out what his presence in Dublin had all been about. And not knowing had always been my worst nightmare.

It was strange. I had the definite sense that he'd won some game we were playing, and yet I didn't even know what the game was or how the rules worked.

To hell with it, I said to myself. It didn't matter.

Didn't.

Matter.

And yet I knew that it did. The crust of my defiance was as thin as the ozone layer.

I guess I could've spent all night there, getting more pissed with myself, but at that moment my cellphone went off. The old boy looked at me reproachfully, like I'd broken some unwritten but sacred agreement, like I wasn't the woman he'd taken me for, regardless of the cigar and the bottle of Budweiser. I shrugged a mute apology. He was probably right.

I barked out a hello.

"No need to bite off my nose."

"Fitzgerald?"

"Of course it's me," she said. "Who else were you expecting? A secret lover?" She laughed like the thought was absurd. Which it was. Wasn't it? "Where are you?"

"Last time I looked, I was in the yard of an atmospheric little place off . . . let me think now . . . Baggot Street. I think."

"You're in the pub?"

"I'm in a bar, that's right. Or outside it, I should say, me and my illicit cigar. I'm expecting the tobacco police to swoop any moment and drag me away for questioning."

"Are you drunk?"

"Am I drunk? Of course I'm not drunk. I'm outraged you could ask me such a question. I've hardly touched a drip . . . I mean, I've hardly touched a drop . . ."

"I think that answers my question. Well, listen. Don't go anywhere, I'm coming over. Healy can drop me off on his way home. I'll expect to have a drink waiting for me."

"Are we celebrating?"

"We might be."

"You've not cracked the case yet, have you?"

"No such luck."

"What's the big deal, then?"

"The new Assistant Commissioner, remember?"

"Screw it, I completely forgot. What am I thinking? How did it go? What's he like?"

"I think the new Assistant Commissioner's going to work out just fine," Fitzgerald said with a conspiratorial laugh. "I'll tell you all about it when I get there. Think

you can manage to get me a drink without spilling it? I shouldn't be long."

Soon my mood of self-pity and resentment at Kaminski was replaced by one of bemusement.

"She wants to what?"

"She wants to meet you."

This was the last thing I'd expected. I'd only just got over the shock of learning from Fitzgerald that the next Assistant Commissioner in charge of the Murder Squad was going to be a woman, and now it turned out that she wanted to meet me as well.

It was the same bar, except we were inside now. Fitzgerald had arrived about ten minutes earlier, looking harassed but sensational as always. Didn't matter if she hadn't slept all night or had spent the day at a crime scene, she still always had that elusive glitz that had certainly eluded me most of my life, no matter how hard I tried to nurture it.

I think you must either be born with it or not.

She was sitting on the stool opposite me with her legs crossed, white wine to hand. Men in the bar were watching her purely for the pleasure of seeing her sit there.

I shrugged in incomprehension.

Not at the fact men were looking at her — I understood that part — but because of what she was saying. The words sounded straightforward enough, but they might as well have been in Sanskrit for all the sense they were making in my skull.

"What would anyone want to meet *me* for?"

"Beats me," teased Fitzgerald. "Unless you owed them money."

I raised an eyebrow.

"Or maybe she wants your autograph."

"You're being flippant again," I warned her.

"Or maybe," Grace continued, ignoring the warning, "she wants to ask you out on a date."

"I thought you said she was married."

"Divorced. I said divorced. And you know what these divorced women are like. I've heard a girl can get some of her most successful pick-ups with recently divorced women. Sadly, I was never able to find out. You came along and spoiled things."

"Then it'll be you she's after, not me. You're a better catch."

"I never mix business with pleasure," she said. "Besides, we're both out of luck. She's not the type. If anything, I'd say she's more likely to want to ask you about the case."

Now I really *was* baffled.

"Marsha Reed? How can I help there?"

"I don't know, I'm merely speculating. She's already suggested that I ask Fisher to team up on it." She meant Dr Lawrence Fisher, a celebrated forensic psychologist who had worked on a small number of cases with Fitzgerald before and who'd recently moved to Dublin for tax purposes. He made most of his money now writing popular books on criminal psychology and appearing on TV, and writers pay no tax in Dublin. "I spoke to him this afternoon. He's taking a look at Marsha's journal. There's a lot of nasty

stuff in there, stuff she's written about other people. I thought he might be able to make something of it."

"That'll be right up his street," I nodded.

"What about you?" she said.

"Me?"

"Remember I asked you to draw up a list of the people who were in your class?"

I couldn't believe I'd forgotten about that.

Nor could Fitzgerald.

I considered telling her about Piper's call, which had driven Marsha Reed out of my mind. But it would take too long, and she had too much else on her plate to start worrying about potential fugitives from justice like Leon Kaminski. More than that, forgetting what she had asked me to do was unjustifiable, whatever my other distractions.

"I'll get it for you first thing in the morning," I promised.

"You'd better. Or I'll tell Stella you're not to be trusted."

"You didn't mention that the new Assistant Commissioner Carson and you were already on first-name terms."

"It must have slipped my mind. Like making that list slipped yours."

"Touché."

"You'll be on first names with her yourself after you meet her tomorrow," Fitzgerald said.

"Who said anything about tomorrow?"

"She did. And she's the boss, remember, so don't be late. Ten thirty, on the dot."

I took a deep breath. I hate being backed into a corner.

I hate losing the initiative even more. I didn't even remember agreeing to this meeting, and suddenly I was being warned against being late for it.

"I guess you'd better tell me about her again, then," I said resignedly.

"What can I tell you? She's from the North. Late forties. She comes from a pretty rough background. She has an uncle in jail for armed robbery. From the point of view of her family, joining the police must have been like a little Palestinian girl suddenly deciding that she wants to be a rabbi rather than a suicide bomber. You'll get along," Fitzgerald went on confidently. "She doesn't believe in tiptoeing carefully around for fear of whose nose might be put out of joint. In fact, I think she rather enjoys putting them out of joint."

"I like the sound of her already."

"She's definitely going to ruffle some feathers down here. Not only have they got a woman, but one from the North too. That won't go down well."

"How'd she get the job?"

"Our masters obviously felt they needed to make a radical break to convince the public we're still capable of doing our job. You know what things are like in there."

She didn't have to elucidate. The Dublin Metropolitan Police had been under inquiry for the best part of the last two years. There had been talk for decades of corruption, sharp practice, incompetence, occasional misdirected brutality. A retired judge had been

appointed to investigate allegations of malpractice. His report had uncovered major institutional failings, widespread nepotism and a culture of hapless endemic ineptitude, not to mention evidence of racist and sexist bullying, at the very heart of the force.

Fitzgerald had found out that last part to her cost. Every step she'd taken along the path had been against the force of tradition weighing her down. She knew there were still powerful people in the DMP who didn't think a woman was capable of running a major department, especially one as vital as Murder. That she'd gotten as far as she had was a miracle.

"How do you know so much about her anyway?" I said.

"Policing is a small world. I'd seen her around," said Fitzgerald. "You know, at conferences and the like. We're always being sent on these courses where police from the North and from Dublin are supposed to meet up, share experience, build contacts, that sort of thing. I even worked with her once, but that was years ago, before I knew you and I was only an Inspector. A doorman was shot at a pub in the inner city. Turned out he was a member of the glorious Irish Republican Army and came from Belfast originally, so I ended up liaising with Stella Carson. She was rooting out some suspects who'd fled after the murder."

"You close the case?"

"Are you questioning my professional capabilities, Special Agent? Of course we closed the case. Not that there was very much to it. It turned out he was killed

by one of his paramilitary colleagues in a row over drug money. So much for the revolution."

"Did you like her?"

"She was fine. She's like they all are up in the North. She's hard to get to know. There's a reticence there, a barrier you never quite cross. And they have these voices."

"Most people do."

"Not like these voices," she said. "People from the North have the kind of voices where, even if they're only asking you to pass the salt, it sounds like they're really intending to haul you up an entryway and kneecap you."

I felt immediate empathy.

"People think I'm aggressive because of my voice too," I said.

"No, that's different. You *are* aggressive. *She* only seems like it."

"Everyone's a critic."

"Still," she said, "it'll be worth having her around just to see the looks on everyone's faces. You should've seen Dalton." Seamus Dalton was one of the longest-serving detectives in the Murder Squad. A man with a chip on his shoulder so high that it could probably be seen from Boston Harbor on a clear day. He thought a woman's place was either in the kitchen or in the bedroom. Or just in the wrong. He'd see this as an assault on his entire world. "I thought he'd lost all powers of intelligent speech when he heard the news."

"You mean, he has some to lose?"

"All powers of speech, then. This is going to be a bigger culture shock to him than the day he was told to stop making homophobic jokes in the canteen. That was suffering enough for him, poor thing. This could finish him off. He was no fan of Draker, but Draker was from his world. He has about as much chance of understanding Stella Carson as he does of understanding nuclear physics. In the meantime, how about you get me another drink?"

"Why do I always have to go get them?"

"Because they take notice of you," she answered. "Barmen just ignore me."

"Fair enough. I'll do it, as long as we can go sit outside so I can smoke."

"You win."

So I got us more drinks, fending off the attentions of the pinstriped man on the next stool who was taking the opportunity to talk to Fitzgerald by offering to pay for them, and we sat outside where it was still warm, and drank, and I smoked, and then we had a couple more drinks, until it got too crowded outside with people who'd realized at last that bars are no fun without the smokers, and we made our escape, strolling round to a place in Wicklow Street that sold great tapas, and walked further, eating them, as more people wandered past, enjoying the summer evening. The turquoise sky above the city was speckled with pale stars like glitter, and a busker somewhere was playing a distant protest song.

His angry voice was the only discordant note to the evening.

We talked a little about the investigation into Marsha Reed's death, but mostly we talked about nothing much at all, which is sometimes the best thing to talk about, or else let the city talk to us as we walked in silence, eavesdropping on a thousand other conversations. And then we walked back to my apartment, taking the long way so that the walk would last longer. There was something magical about the city that night. An older spirit suppressed in the relentless commerce of the day had come alive and walked among the living. Lights sparkled and shone all around. Or was it just the thought of possible new beginnings?

The morning would tell me.

For the moment, I tried to savour it for what it was. Tried to feel content. The feeling never lasted long. It was important to hold on to it as long as possible when it came.

CHAPTER
FOURTEEN

He almost collided with me. He was coming down the steps of Dublin Castle as I was climbing up them, and he didn't see me till it was too late. It was nobody's fault, but he scowled at me in annoyance all the same, his high forehead bulging alarmingly.

I stepped aside to let him pass and then watched as he crossed the courtyard.

Fleetingly, I wondered if this was some bigwig in the DMP that I'd never met before, furious at Stella Carson's appointment and determined to take it out that day on any woman he encountered. But he didn't look like a policeman. There was something too casual about his appearance. His grey hair was slightly too long, certainly for a man who must have been in his fifties. He wore brown corduroys. The collar of his shirt was unbuttoned and tieless. He was walking with a kind of defiant sashay, as if he was struggling to contain an energy that was bubbling up inside him. And were those moccasins he had on his feet? They were. No one ever got anywhere in the Dublin Metropolitan Police wearing moccasins and corduroy trousers.

Or sashaying, for that matter.

The younger man accompanying him was having to hurry to keep up. He wore a dark suit — no moccasins here — and his arms overflowed with cardboard files.

At the gate, the older man turned round and threw a *what the hell are you looking at?* glare back in the general direction of the building. Then he turned and was gone.

"What did you make of him?" a familiar voice said behind me.

Fitzgerald was standing at the top of the steps, watching me watching him.

I hadn't seen her come out.

"Who is he?" I said, climbing up to stand by her.

"That's Victor Solomon."

"Should the name mean something to me?"

"Do you remember the night Marsha Reed's body was found, we were supposed to be going to the theatre?" said Fitzgerald. "He's the director of the play we were supposed to see."

"*Hamlet?*"

"*Othello*, actually. But you were close."

"Whatever. What's he doing here? Did he hear you had to miss the play and came round to offer you free tickets?"

"Not exactly. He was sleeping with Marsha Reed."

"I don't know why I'm taken aback. You did say she was sleeping with everyone."

"Not all of them, though, gave her an expensive necklace."

"The missing necklace was from Solomon?"

"The very same," she said, and held the door open for me as I stepped inside.

I knew this place well enough. Dublin Castle was where the Murder Squad of the Dublin Metropolitan Police had its headquarters, along with a number of other major departments, such as Vice, Anti-terrorism and Drugs. There were cells in other parts of the city, local police stations where less serious crimes were dealt with. There was even the main administration block out in the Phoenix Park, where the Commissioner and his cronies were to be found and where most of the important decisions were made. But Dublin Castle was where what really counted went on. Didn't matter how many robberies were solved or how many tax evaders convicted, or how many people the Dogs Division picked up for not having a dog licence, or even how many pickpockets were rounded up for swiping wallets from tourists who seemed to think they were safe in Dublin — it was how a police department dealt with murder cases that made the difference to their reputation and standing.

Dublin didn't exactly have a shining record in this respect, though it was not for lack of trying on Fitzgerald's part. She was a fine detective, just frequently frustrated by the lack of proper structures and resources. Uniformed police in the city couldn't always be relied upon even to preserve a crime scene properly for forensic analysis. Sometimes it felt like the cops were lagging decades behind. Unless Fitzgerald was called in quickly, it was often too late.

144

As always when I came here, I had to suppress the vague feeling that I had strayed into unfriendly territory. It was easy to forget that the police and I were supposed to be on the same side. Too often in the past, I had been made to feel as welcome as an outbreak of bird flu, even when I was meant to be offering a helping hand with particular cases.

Make that *especially* when I was meant to be helping out.

"Here," said Fitzgerald.

"What is it?"

"Your pass," she said, pinning it to my collar. "Now you're official."

"Thanks. Are we going up?"

"Follow me."

And follow her I did, up the main stairway to the upper floors where most of the Murder Squad's real work was done, and wishing we could've taken the elevator instead. Unfortunately, she told me that was broken too, like the one in my apartment building.

Did anything work any more?

I was out of shape. Long gone were the days of my FBI training, when I could do a hundred push-ups without giving it a second thought. Lately I found getting out of bed a struggle.

"So was that his lawyer with him?" I said between breaths as we climbed.

"His solicitor brought him in this morning, said his client wanted to make a statement," Fitzgerald explained, taking the steps with ease. "He knew we'd be digging into Marsha's background and obviously

realized it was inevitable that his name would come up eventually. He decided to take the initiative and present himself for questioning. It wouldn't look good if we'd turned up at the theatre unannounced. Not good for business, I mean."

"*Did* you know he was Marsha's boyfriend?"

"Her friend, who found the body, said Marsha had told her she was sleeping with someone important in theatre circles here in the city, but she wouldn't reveal who it was. Not initially. She badgered her until Marsha eventually admitted it was Solomon."

"What's his story?"

"That he and Marsha had been sleeping together on and off for the last six months or so, but that it was no big affair as far as he was concerned. But then he *would* say that. He's engaged to be married to the actress who's starring in his latest play. They're quite a well-known couple. You can understand why he wouldn't want it getting into the papers that he was seeing Marsha Reed as well. He says he last slept with her about a month ago."

"They'd split up?"

"He says it wasn't even the kind of relationship where you needed to split up," said Fitzgerald. "They just saw one another when they saw one another. I got the impression that if he bumped into her around town in the evening and he didn't have anything else lined up, he was happy enough to appoint her as his temporary bedwarmer, but that he wasn't going to be calling her up to make a date for dinner or drinks or anything like that."

146

"He gave her the necklace, didn't he?"

"A meaningless trinket, if you listen to him."

"Was he part of her little S & M set?"

"He says not," said Fitzgerald. "According to him, he knew nothing about that part of her life and, if he *had* known about it, he'd never have got involved with her in the first place."

"The morally upright type, huh?"

"That's the general picture. Though more upright than moral, if you ask me. You know what these artistic types are like. See? Here we are now. Do try and stop panting. People will think we were up to something."

And she ushered me through the door into the upstairs corridor off which the Murder Squad was housed. Her own office was at the end of the hall. The main incident rooms were down the left. The windows along the other side looked on to the street below.

Patrick Walsh was standing in the corridor, waiting.

What was there to say about Walsh? He was young, lean, ambitious, capable, sharply dressed, good-looking, and those were just a few of the reasons why so many of the other detectives loathed him. I liked him well enough, though I admit there was a cockiness to him that could be jarring on first contact. He considered himself to be God's gift to the women of Dublin, and felt that women should be grateful to the Lord for blessing them with such a gift.

He'd even asked Fitzgerald out once.

Whatever other faults he had, he certainly didn't lack chutzpah.

He did, though, have a bad habit of calling me —

"Babe! If I'd known you were coming in, I'd have put on my best aftershave."

"Save it for someone who doesn't mind being called babe," I said. "Though to do that, I guess you'd have to find a time-machine to take you back to the 1970s."

"I love it when you get angry," Walsh said.

"Break it up, you two," said Fitzgerald. "If you want to flirt, do it on your time."

Flirt? That woman sure knew how to get on my wrong side.

"I heard you wanted to talk to me, Chief," Walsh went on before I could object.

"Yeah, there's something I want you to take a look at for me. Saxon," she said, "did you manage to finish that list?"

"I have it here in my pocket."

I fished it out and passed it to her. She unfolded the sheet of paper and glanced quickly through the names.

"Is this the whole list of people who took your class?" she said.

"There were seven," I confirmed. "Eight, if you include Marsha Reed."

"Popular course," murmured Walsh sarcastically.

I ignored him.

"I put down a few impressions of each one, just as a pointer for you. Sarah O'Leary — that's her there at the top — was the one who seemed to know Marsha best. They sat together, sometimes they left together. I heard them making arrangements once to meet up for a drink."

148

"Has her name come up in the investigation yet?" she asked Walsh.

"It doesn't ring any bells."

"That guy there," I said, pointing to another name on the list, "might be worth talking to as well. He arrived for one class with Marsha. I remember hearing them laughing on the stairs up to the lecture room. They may've only just seen each other as they arrived, but it's probably worth following up anyway to see how well he did know her."

"What about the others?" asked Walsh.

"That's for you to find out," said Fitzgerald.

"Chief?"

"Take this list round to the college and find addresses and phone numbers for all seven. Pay them a call, see if they have any further information about Marsha Reed."

"Will do. And Solomon's alibi? Shall I check that out first?"

"Leave that to me," Fitzgerald said. "I'm just going back to my room to pick up some files, then I'm going over to speak to his fiancée with Healy."

"Solomon claims he was at the theatre until eleven on the night of the killing," Walsh explained to me. "Then with his fiancée until ten the next morning."

"You never know, he might be telling the truth," Fitzgerald said. "It happens."

"Shall I make my own way up to the Assistant Commissioner's office, then?" I said.

"Walsh will take you. Won't you, Walsh?"

A grimace. "Yes, Chief."

"What's the matter with you?" I said after Fitzgerald had gone out of earshot. "Don't you want to take me up there?"

"It's not that, babe. You know nothing gives me more pleasure than spending time with you. I just want to get these interviews over as soon as I can," he explained, waving the list of names Fitzgerald had handed to him a moment earlier. "I have a date tonight."

"From what I hear, you have a date every night."

"But *this* date is something special," he said. "This one I have high hopes for. Her name's Lucy and she works downstairs in Vice."

"Is that part of the attraction?"

"If a woman chooses to works in Vice, she's got to be kind of kinky, right?"

"Walsh, you're a sick man. Logical but sick."

"I'll take that as a compliment," he said. "I just wish I could've gone with the Chief instead of being stuck with the job of tracking down your ex-students. No offence."

"None taken."

"I bet Healy gets to meet Zak Kirby too. I worship that guy."

"Healy or Kirby?"

"Very funny. You should be a stand-up comedian."

"That's what my doorman tells me."

I'd forgotten that Walsh had a thing about the theatre. He'd often admitted that acting was his first love, and police work only came second when it became clear that the acting was going nowhere. He still took part in amateur productions occasionally. Getting a

foot in the door with Victor Solomon's crowd at the Liffey Theatre, even under these circumstances, would've been even more irresistible to him than an evening with Lucy from Vice.

Was Fitzgerald keeping him away from that part of the investigation because she feared he might not be able to keep his mind on the job, or that he might be too starstruck by the people he'd be seeing there to stay objective? If he had any sense, he wouldn't mention his hero worship of Zak Kirby. The American was surely already beginning to wonder what he'd got into, with the cops turning up to interrogate him about the movements of his own director on the night of a brutal murder.

If they started asking for his autograph as well . . .

I was being unfair. Walsh had always shown total integrity when it came to doing his job, even if he did leave his brain in his pants when it came to the rest of his life. He probably just wanted this one rare chance to soak up some of the atmosphere of the real theatre.

It wasn't a crime.

"Come on," he said dolefully. "I'd better get you to the Assistant Commissioner before the Chief comes back and gives me hell."

CHAPTER
FIFTEEN

Stella Carson came out from behind the desk and held out her hand to greet me.

"You must be Saxon."

Now that I was hearing it for myself, the voice didn't sound so bad. It wasn't going to win any prizes for musicality, that's for sure, but I'd been on the receiving end of worse.

"I've heard a lot about you," she added.

"That's what I was afraid of."

She was smaller than I'd expected — smaller than Fitzgerald, that is, if not as small as me — with a sharp, clever face, an impression accentuated by the way she had her dark hair pinned back severely. The smile she offered was warm enough, however, and her eyes didn't have that deceitful look you often saw, where the eyes are sizing you up critically even as the mouth plays the part of smiling. She had a strong, athletic look to her, still looked trim. Most men her age in the force had already succumbed to middle-aged spread, the side-effect of consuming too many long liquid lunches with the other administrative overlords at whatever gentlemen's club they hunkered down in. There was none of that with her.

"Won't you sit down?"

I took my place in the chair she waved me into and watched as she made her way back round to the other side of the desk. There was an open cardboard box on her desk from which she'd been taking out various files and books and diaries — as well as a framed photograph showing a young woman in her mid twenties in a graduation gown and mortarboard hat, holding a rolled-up degree. The photograph had been given pride of place on the desk. Quite a contrast from the way the office had been when Assistant Commissioner Draker had occupied it, when any trace of his ordinary home life had been ruthlessly expunged, like it didn't matter. Either that or Draker had never *had* an ordinary home life of which to be reminded.

"My daughter," Draker's successor explained when she saw me glancing at it. "She recently finished her law degree. She's starting work soon with the Prosecutions Office."

"That's a relief," I said. "For a second there, I thought you were going to say she was becoming a defence lawyer."

"The enemy," agreed Carson. "What a dreadful thought."

"Will she be following you down to Dublin?"

"She's already down here. She went to Trinity. So you could say I'm the one who's following her. I'm staying in her place right now while I look for a house and trying hard not to interfere too much with her life. It's a difficult habit to break."

"At least you're *trying* to break it," I said. "Some mothers never learn to let go."

"Are you speaking from experience?"

"Not me. I think my mother decided to let go approximately five minutes after she gave birth," I said wryly. "I'm not objecting. It suited me fine."

She paused briefly before continuing. "You're probably wondering why I asked to see you."

"It had crossed my mind."

"It wasn't to talk about my family troubles, if that's what you're thinking. I'm saving *that* up for my memoirs. Fitzgerald didn't tell you what I wanted?"

"She said she didn't know," I said.

"I didn't say anything directly," Carson said, "but I think she guessed what I was thinking all the same." Another pause. "Do you want something to drink? Coffee? Tea?"

"I'm good."

"Straight to the point. That's what I would've expected. I read your book. Your first book, that is. I don't get much time for reading, but I did read that. I like your point of view."

"I appreciate it."

"Fitzgerald tells me you knew this woman who died."

Is that what this was about?

"I wouldn't say I knew her."

"You'd met her, though?"

"Dublin's a small town in many ways," I said. "She sat a course I was teaching."

"Do you think she admired you?"

"She gave no hint of it if she did," I said. "Why do you ask?"

154

"She had a lot of books about crime, murder, in her room. Serial killers, you know."

"Novels?"

"Mostly non-fiction. Yours were among them."

"You think that's important?"

"You know how it is, you have to examine every possible lead. If nothing else, it helps flesh out the kind of woman Marsha was. From what I've seen of the initial reports, there's not much else to go on." She paused and picked up a cardboard file from her desk. "Have you seen the crime-scene photographs?"

I shook my head.

That was her cue to slide the cardboard file across the desk toward me.

"Take a look," she said.

The first picture I took out of the file was one of Marsha Reed lying dead where she was found, naked, tied to the bedposts with cords, a bag over her head. Her last desperate breaths had made the bag cling to her face like a second skin. The sheets underneath her body had become tangled with the violence of her struggle to capture air.

There were plenty more of the same. Close-ups, wide-angle shots, panoramas of the interior of the converted church where she'd lived, each photograph overlapping with the next, so that not one inch of the dead woman's final surroundings would be missed.

Most curious to me were a series of snapshots showing Marsha Reed's body lying on the bed covered with a sheet.

"Did one of the police officers at the scene cover her body?" I said.

"No," the other woman said. "She was found like that. Didn't you know?"

I hadn't known. Fitzgerald hadn't mentioned it.

I found myself considering what it meant. Did the killer feel ashamed of what he'd done? Killers sometimes covered the bodies of their victims if they couldn't accept what they'd done. Covering the body was a way of pretending that it hadn't happened. Sometimes too they didn't want the dead eyes of their victims staring back at them accusingly, though in Marsha's case she had died face down. Whatever the reason, covering the body certainly tied in with the investigation's assessment of a sexually motivated killer who knew his victim.

"He didn't cover the body straight away," Carson said.

"He didn't?"

"The blood was dry when it touched the sheet. That meant some time must have elapsed between the killing and the covering."

But why leave the body uncovered so long just to get suddenly squeamish? Had he come back, intending to wrap up the body for transport elsewhere, only to be interrupted?

"You see why we need your help," I heard her say distantly as I leafed slowly and with grim fascination through the crime-scene pictures.

"Sorry?"

For a moment, the pictures were forgotten.

156

"I realize what I'm asking must come as a surprise. But you know what I'm saying makes sense. For years now things haven't been as they should have in this place. The Commissioner knows it. Draker knew it too, but he was too stubborn to do anything about it. Procedures have been lax. Standards have been allowed to slip. Fitzgerald has held the place together for a long while, but there's only so much she can do."

"It's been a struggle, yes."

"Exactly. Every new direction has been resisted. Every last penny of funding has had to be prised out of reluctant fingers. It's no way to run a department. Frankly, I wouldn't have stood for it in Belfast, and I'm not going to stand for it here. I intend to shake things up. We need to be ahead of the game for once and not forever running along behind trying to catch up. At times it feels here like they're still struggling to get to grips with the twentieth century, never mind the twenty-first. I've spoken to Dr Fisher already; he's agreed to get on board."

"Fitzgerald mentioned he was looking at Marsha Reed's diary."

"I hope that'll only be the start of it," she said. "Since he's here in the city permanently now, it makes sense to use his expertise as much as we can. You're smiling."

"I'm imagining Fisher's reaction when he realizes how you're reeling him in," I said. "He protests so much at his workload already, and yet he allows himself to be drawn every time into offering his services. I half wonder if that isn't the real reason he left London, so

that Scotland Yard wouldn't be on the phone to him every week with another case."

"Thankfully, we don't have the same crime rate as London yet," the Assistant Commissioner said. "But the key word there is 'yet'. Long gone are the days when Dublin could console itself that murder was something that happened elsewhere."

"Sounds like Fisher picked the wrong city for a quiet life."

"You too, perhaps."

"The difference is that *I* don't have the same specialist skills to offer as Fisher," I said. "I don't even have a proper job any more. I'm just an inquisitive meddler."

"I don't care what you call the talents you have. All I know is that your experience is something I can't afford to simply throw away. I've already talked this over with Grace. She's totally behind me. She knows the problems we have. Both of us need to know there's a collection of people out there that we can call upon when needs be. That's how it is in most police departments round the world. They understand the value of using the abilities of people with experience to make investigation easier. And you're an outsider here. Like me. Outsiders see things other people can't. They make connections and spot anomalies where others on the inside can't." She raised an eyebrow sardonically. "At least that's the theory."

"And that's what you think I can do?"

"I don't know. What I do know is that Dublin's changing, and the DMP has to change with it. We're

158

already in the middle of a recruitment drive to try to get more non-nationals into the force. Poles. Lithuanians. Nigerians. There are so many different nationalities and cultures out there now that have been thrown together, it creates new problems, but new opportunities as well. The DMP has to reflect the people who actually live here."

She suddenly pulled a face.

"Listen to me," she went on, "I sound like a bloody recruitment ad. Think about it, that's all I ask. Like I say, you can see for yourself why your input could prove invaluable."

And she nodded toward the crime-scene photographs I was still cradling in my hands. I saw what she'd done now. She'd let me see the photographs to soften me up for the approach, knowing I'd be horrified and angry at what I saw but intrigued too.

Intrigued enough not to want to walk away without getting close to the truth.

I took a long time answering, and when my answer came, it sounded weak even to my ears. "I'm not sure I know what I can do," I said.

"Me neither," she said, "but I'm willing to find out. Are you?"

CHAPTER
SIXTEEN

"And what precisely are you asking me for?"

"I wanted the benefit of the esteemed Dr Lawrence Fisher's advice."

"You know what to do," said Fisher. "You don't need me to tell you. You should accept. You've complained often enough about being out of the loop, about never having enough to do. This is the perfect opportunity to put that right. Plus you'd have the chance to work alongside Grace. With me too, for a while. What more could a girl want?"

"I guess you're right," I said a little sulkily.

"Of course I'm right," said Fisher. "Just make sure you get paid handsomely for your efforts. You know what your problem is, Saxon?"

"You mean, there's only one?"

"Let me rephrase that. Do you know what *one* of your problems is? You don't know how to simply take what you want, even when it's being offered to you on a plate. You think because it seems too easy that there must be something wrong with it."

"There usually is."

"But plenty of times there isn't," he retorted. "Sometimes things really are what they seem.

Sometimes there are no hidden catches. You agonize about things too much."

"I don't trust simplicity," I admitted.

"Well, it's about time you started," he said briskly.

The way he said it reminded me so much of Fitzgerald. They were the two people in my life to whose advice I should always listen to stop myself making bad choices. Like he said, Stella Carson was holding out a possibility that I'd longed for, vaguely, hopelessly, for years: the chance to get back into the centre of things, no longer stranded on the sidelines.

The only problem was Kaminski.

If I hadn't seen him a couple of days ago, I would probably have said yes already. But there was something about his presence here in the city which demanded a response from me, and if I did accept the new Assistant Commissioner's invitation, then what would that mean for Kaminski? I couldn't go on sneaking around behind Fitzgerald's back, keeping her in the dark about what I'd learned about his presence here. And yet could I really tell her what I knew, or thought I knew, when the police would inevitably have to become involved? Could I betray him like that? Or should I just back off and forget I ever saw him?

But what then if he did something stupid?

Kaminski could certainly be impetuous. In the past, he could coil himself so tight you didn't know when he might snap. When he did, he himself was usually the one who suffered. His lost year in North Carolina proved that much. But there'd also been one or two rumours I'd heard down the years about him getting

rough with suspects when he felt the situation called for it.

I'd never seen it happen myself, but then nor had I asked him about the rumours. That was the weird thing that happened when you worked so closely with someone. You turned a blind eye to things which, in normal circumstances, would make you distinctly uneasy.

So no, I didn't know if that part was true. But it rang true. When Kaminski got an idea into his head, there was no stopping him. Until I knew what idea he had in his head this time, I didn't feel in all conscience that I could wash my hands of him.

I almost began to wish as I sat there that I hadn't seen him at all.

It would've made the decision I had to make so much easier.

Not that Fisher was to know that.

As it was, right now we were supposed to be having lunch with Miranda Gray, Fisher's new Significant Other, as they say in certain circles. Idiot circles, that is. But then, what else could you call her? *Girlfriend* sounded faintly absurd for a middle-aged man. *Partner* always seemed like the whole thing should come with a business agreement attached. As for *lover*, I really didn't want to picture Fisher in the throes of ecstasy. At least not while I was eating. The two of them had recently dropped the pretence that they were simply good friends and set up home together in a large Victorian house in the mellow, leafy, bourgeois district round the Rathmines Road. He'd left his wife, Laura,

and children, back in London, although he saw them as often as he could, and I know he missed them terribly.

Laura especially, though he'd never admit it.

Miranda's not being here had its advantages, however. It meant he could fill me in on what he'd found in Marsha Reed's journal. Though, as he spoke, I soon realized that it might have been quicker to tell me what *wasn't* in it. As Fitzgerald had said, she had had a busy life.

"I don't even know whether half of what I'm reading is true or not," Fisher said. "I've completed plenty of profiles before on sexual obsessives, people whose entire lives were dedicated to the pursuit of it, but I've never known a woman so fiercely driven by the same impulses as Marsha Reed. Her every waking and sleeping thought seems to have been consumed by sex: its planning, execution and aftermath. Everything was written down in detail from her dreams to her regular encounters at the S & M club in town."

"What makes you doubt the truth of what you've read?" I asked.

"Nothing I can put my finger on exactly, except that Victor Solomon doesn't appear in the pages of her book at all. Why leave him out? Was it because he was her real lover and the rest of them were nothing but figments of her own imagination?"

"They couldn't be. Fitzgerald has already spoken to people at the club. They remember Marsha well. She seems to have been game for anything."

"Was she protecting him, then, by rendering him invisible in her journal?"

"Journals are private. Who would she be protecting him from?"

"Not all journals are private. It could be that she used her journal as part of her erotic life, maybe shared it together in bed with her conquests. She might not have wanted anyone stumbling on the secret of her relationship with Solomon, if secret it was. Also," he noted with a frown, "I have to say that the people I've known previously who shared the same sexual obsessions as Marsha increasingly found it hard to continue any normal sort of social or professional or family life whatsoever, whereas to all outward appearances *her* existence seemed unremarkable. Humdrum even. How she managed that is a mystery. Also there were other manuscripts found in her possession besides her journal which suggested she had a talent for fiction. Or for fictionalizing her actual experiences, perhaps I should say."

"What were they like?"

"Erotic crime fiction, you'd have to call it. Short stories in which sex and murder become inextricably linked, often written in the first person so that it's only small details which make it clear it's not herself directly that she's writing about."

"Did she cast herself as the victim in these stories?" I said.

"Victim or perpetrator, she seemed to have had an equal preference for either role."

"You think she was acting out one of her fantasies the night she died?"

"It's certainly a possibility," Fisher said, "though there was nothing in her writings which corresponded precisely to the circumstances of her own death."

"Maybe she preferred to try them out first before writing them down."

"And this time she didn't get the opportunity? It's possible."

It certainly put a new slant on her presence in my classes on criminal procedure. Something darker than mere curiosity had led her there. I only hoped nothing I'd said had unwittingly led her imagination down that one-way corridor where it was snuffed out for ever.

"You wouldn't be responsible for it even if it had," said Fisher, when I confessed my fear to him. "That's the uncomfortable thing about people. They have minds of their own, and no one else is ultimately responsible for what goes on inside them. Not that I should be talking to you about all this business," he added unexpectedly, "since you insist on still pretending to be undecided about accepting the Assistant Commissioner's offer."

"What do you mean, pretending?"

But all he could say in reply was: "What the —?"

And immediately I discovered what had distracted him.

Some drunk, folded in a filthy coat that seemed more fit for winter than the bright summer's day, had appeared in the street out of my sight through the window of the restaurant and now fell heavily against the glass before slumping in a heap to the ground.

As we watched, he hauled himself with difficulty to his feet, his hands gripping the glass, leaving greasy stains where he touched it, and turned on unsteady legs to face us through the window, looking in as though we were alien fish in an aquarium on which he couldn't quite focus. His hair was matted and bird-nested with unknown filth, and his face was hidden beneath a tangled beard that looked more like a growth of the same dirt than hair.

Silently he mouthed something to us, but whatever it was we would never know because the waiter had appeared belatedly from the direction of the kitchen and was hurrying toward the door, waving a towel in his hands like he was shooing away a fly.

The old hobo took awkwardly to his heels.

"Charming," said Fisher as we watched him hobble away.

"I guess that's what you get for taking a table by the window."

The waiter by this time was standing at the entrance, looking severe and disapproving, arms folded, the picture of a man who has escaped some fight but wants it to be known that he'd have been up for it if only he'd been around when it started.

My eye, though, was fixed on the road down which the drunk was clumsily making his getaway. As he reached the corner, he turned and looked back at the restaurant where we were sitting. I saw him reach into his pocket and take out a bank note. He held it in both hands and kissed it, then did a stiff little jig on the corner with delight.

Then he was gone.

"That's an odd thing," said Fisher.

"What?"

"Look."

He pointed to where the old man had climbed up against the glass.

A scrap of paper was stuck there now with chewing gum. I recognized it at once as the other half of the leaflet I'd left for Kaminski at his hotel and which he, in turn, had left for me. On the edge of this half was scribbled a cellphone number.

"He left you his contact details," said Fisher. "He must want a date. Your lucky day."

"Ever think it might've been you he wanted, Fisher?"

And I laughed to cover my irritation that Kaminski had trumped me again.

I didn't know where *he* was to be found in the whole city, but seemingly he even knew where I was having lunch. Was there anything he didn't know about me?

I finished up with Fisher as quickly as I could, turning down his prompting to accompany him to Marsha Reed's house. As soon as he finished the rest of the wine, he would be heading over there to take a look at the place where she'd died. There were some curious details of her murder, he added, trying to reel me in mischievously, that he thought I might find interesting.

I told him I needed longer to decide whether I should get involved.

"Just make sure you make the right choice," he left me with.

★　★　★

Once I was safely outside, I dialled the number that had been scribbled on the edge of the leaflet on the glass. It rang only once before it was answered.

"You've had your fun, JJ. Now are you going to tell me what you want?"

"I'm not JJ," the voice on the other end answered. "I'm Buck Randall, remember? You can't have forgotten me already. Or do you make a habit of breaking into everyone's room?"

"Oh, *that* Buck Randall? I knew the name sounded familiar. So how are you, Buck?"

"I'm doing terrifically. You?"

"Never been better. A bit tired from chasing old friends through Temple Bar, you know how it is."

"What can I say? I suddenly remembered an urgent appointment I had to get to."

"Was that what it was? And there was me thinking you were trying to avoid me."

"You always *were* on the paranoid side."

"Look who's talking. I'm not the one who's changed my name and dyed my hair."

"Everything changes. Nothing lasts for ever."

"Did you get that little pearl of wisdom from a fortune cookie, JJ?"

"Buck," he corrected me.

"Don't start that again," I sighed. "Are you going to give me a break or not?"

"I'm considering it, what more can I do?"

"*Hey, watch where you're going!*"

"Excuse me?"

168

"I wasn't talking to you," I said. "It's tricky, walking along here and trying to listen to your lectures in philosophy at the same time. You should try it."

"Who says I'm not doing it right now?"

That was true.

Listening hard, I could hear traffic, faint and discordant, on the other end of the line. I wondered if it was the same traffic I could hear in my other ear, the traffic on the street I was walking along. Then I wondered if he was watching me now, if he was near.

I spun round quickly.

There was a short laugh at the other end, but there was nothing of amusement in it.

I guessed I was right.

He *was* watching me.

But if I knew Kaminski, I wouldn't see him no matter how hard I looked. Like me, he knew how to make himself inconspicuous. Or at least like I *used* to.

"I have to admit," I said, "that was a neat trick with the hobo."

"It's amazing what a few crisp new bills will get you," said Kaminski. "I told him you were friends of mine, and I wanted to play a prank on you for your birthday. He didn't even ask any questions, just took the money and did exactly what I asked him to do."

"Maybe he has Americans asking him to fall into windows all the time."

"Could be," said Kaminski. "Still, it got us talking again."

"You wanted that, you could've just walked into the restaurant."

169

"Now look who's talking. I didn't ask for any of this, in case you've forgotten. You started it. You knew where I was staying, why didn't *you* just come round and say hello?"

"That was the initial plan."

"What went wrong?"

"You were out."

"So you broke into my room?"

"Strictly speaking, I didn't break in," I said. "All I did was ask the maid to let me in."

"She told me. Did you really say you were my wife?"

"It was the first thing I could think of."

"I'd have thought being married to me was the *last* thing you'd have thought of."

"I must've been feeling desperate," I said.

"Desperate?"

"To know what you were doing in Dublin."

Silence greeted that remark. I sensed he wanted to ask me if I'd found out what he *was* doing in Dublin, but he didn't want to just come right out with it. Instead he said: "I didn't even know to begin with that you were in Dublin. Didn't know you were still here, that is. I knew you'd come here years ago. It's not like you to stay in one place so long."

"You said it yourself," I reminded him. "Everything changes."

"Not you," he said. "The Saxon I used to know wouldn't have hung around the same city for . . . what is it now? Ten years?"

Ten years. Suddenly I felt old.

"The Saxon I knew was always moving on."

170

"Then we're even, because the JJ I knew wouldn't have picked a name like Buck Randall III to book into hotels under."

"I have my reasons."

"You want to share them with me?"

"Maybe," he said, as if he was learning that fact about himself for the first time. "I just need to be sure I can trust you first."

"Trust me?"

"Yeah, trust. You know, the thing two people have between them that means one of them doesn't go breaking into the other one's bedroom uninvited."

"There you go again. I told you. I didn't break in. I'm sorry it bugged you so much."

And *I* realized as I spoke that I meant it. "I'd no right," I said.

"Not then you didn't," said Kaminski. "No. But now?"

He let the prospect hang like a spider on a thread.

"Now?"

"Like I said, I didn't know you were in Dublin at first. Then I saw you in Temple Bar. It spooked me out. I'd just been passing through and I saw your book lying on a table. I picked it up. The next thing I knew, there you were, standing on the other side of the square. It felt like . . . you'll say this is insane . . . it felt like a sign."

"I don't think it's insane."

"Later, I realized someone had broken into my room, and made it my business to find out who it was. The widow who owns the place told me someone had

been asking for me at the desk. A short, dark American *female*. It didn't take long to figure it out."

"I'm not that short," I protested.

"I'm only telling you what she told me. Plus she said my mysterious caller had bad attitude coming out of her ears. I knew at once it was you."

"She said *I* had a bad attitude?"

"She didn't put it exactly like that. She simply said you were a little . . . what was the word she used again? Argumentative, that was it. Not even you can deny that."

"OK, you got me there."

"So I began to ask myself," said Kaminski, "if that was a sign too. If you were being directed toward me. There was no way I'd expected you to track me down so quickly. I knew you'd do it eventually, I already had plans in place to move on. But that was fast work, Special Agent. I allowed myself to hope there was a reason for it."

"You found me pretty fast yourself," I pointed out.

"That wasn't so hard. *You're* not hiding out under a false name."

"Fair point. But if you wanted my help, why not just come right up and ask me?"

"I could have done that," he conceded. "But then I wouldn't have had all the fun of seeing you put out for once. Of getting one over on you. That's a rare pleasure. Let me indulge it for a while. Besides, I wanted you to realize you weren't the only one who could play games. You can't expect to get your own way the whole time."

If only he knew.

I don't think I'd gotten my own way in years.

How times change.

"So what now?" I said impatiently.

"We meet up, I guess. Talk."

"And you'll tell me what your being here is all about?"

"If you're anything like the Saxon I once knew," he said, "you'll have figured some of it out by now."

"I saw the newspaper clipping, if that's what you mean."

"And?" He sounded apprehensive.

"And I know the woman who died was writing to someone on Death Row in Texas by the name of Jenkins Howler. I know too that Howler has passed over to the great beyond."

"Anything else?"

I hesitated before continuing. "I also know what happened to your wife."

In the long pause before he responded, I became convinced that he'd broken the connection between us. Only the continuing traffic in that ear told me otherwise.

"Who told you?" came his voice finally.

How long did I consider telling him straight that it was Lucas Piper?

Not even one second.

If I asked myself why I held that part back, I couldn't have put it into words. There was something about not wanting him to know that Piper had been talking behind his back. They might have fallen out, but they'd been friends for so long it was bound to feel like

betrayal. There was also a worry in me that telling him that part would lead to all sorts of other questions: what had Piper told me, how much did I know, what was I going to do with the information I had. It would take too long to explain to him where I was at in my understanding, and in the time it took to reach the end of the explanation he might've become unnerved enough to decide I was too high a risk to whatever plan of action he had in mind.

In addition, a part of me liked being able to keep this nugget back from him.

It gave me some reason to believe he wasn't holding all the aces.

"I read about it in the newspaper," I told him in preference to the truth.

I'm not sure he believed me, but he accepted the lie with good grace.

"Then it's all the more important that we meet," he said.

"What about right now?"

"Not so fast," said Kaminski. "I need to prepare the ground first."

"When, then?"

"I'll be in touch," he said.

"You're just going to hang up and disappear again? No. Come on, you can't do that."

I was wrong.

He just had.

I couldn't believe it. He was doing it again, teasing me, taunting me, taking control of me, and I was letting him. *I was letting him.* I stood in the middle of that

summer street, suppressing the urge to kick something, anything, feeling as if everything in existence had been created in that instant just to irritate me. The blaring horns of impatient, overheated drivers as they took out their frustrations on one another. The courier cyclists weaving in and out of the traffic, sinister and silent, looking like aliens peering out through flylike shades. The office girls going by lost in their iPods, frowning slightly as if in concentration to hide the fact they didn't know how to work them. The men in suits walking by almost in slow motion, like they were auditioning for a part in *Reservoir Dogs*, over-compensating for the fact they were accountants. The world was going about its business without asking for permission or approval, but I was letting my every move be controlled by *him*.

I remembered suddenly the way I'd felt when I'd gone round to the hotel and found him gone. How I felt like I'd lost control of my life. That everything was being decided by other people. I was exhausted by being the tumbleweed that gets blown from place to place by someone else's will. I was tired of being other peoples' fool.

That's when I decided I would take back control of my own life. Whatever happened after that, I would deal with it when it happened. Kaminski had no right to expect anything more from me. I turned and made my way back to the restaurant.

Fisher was still at the table, finishing the last of the wine.

175

"Did you forget something?" he said.

"Yes," I said. "I forgot to tell you I'm coming with you."

CHAPTER
SEVENTEEN

West of Aungier Street lay the Liberties. Originally known by the grand designation of the Liberties of the Monastery of St Thomas of Canterbury, this district got its name from the fact that it was self-governing and didn't come under central control until the nineteenth century, though whether it was under effective control even now is a matter for some debate.

At one time the area was outside the city walls. A place of poverty, deprivation and political rebellion, where tanners and weavers and linen-workers from Continental Europe were thrown together to sink or swim. However hairy the modern city could get at times, it had nothing on that Dublin of old, when you took your life into your hands just walking these same streets. In past decades there'd been occasional half-hearted attempts at gentrification, with the small, often one-roomed cottages that lined the narrow streets being knocked together and renovated. But the area still had a rough edge to it. It felt raw. Some of the city's more refined residents wouldn't venture this way if you paid them, let alone live here.

Marsha Reed hadn't been one of them.

This was where she had lived.

More to the point, this was where she had died, and where Fisher and I came after leaving the restaurant, picking up my Jeep on the way since it was quicker than heading over to Dublin Castle and begging a lift. The church stood out among the low houses as incongruously as a Mother Superior in a strip joint, and when I first caught sight of the narrow lane running up between the other houses toward it, I feared my presence here would be more incongruous still. But to hell with my misgivings. It was too late for them.

I found a parking space as near as I could to her house, climbed out and left the car in Ossory Square — initially misreading the sign as Ossuary Square, which was grimly appropriate, considering why we were here — before doubling back to the right entrance.

The cop standing guard at the wooden gate that closed off the lane must have been briefed to expect me, because he didn't seem too troubled when I came along with Fisher. He didn't even ask to see my ID. He simply pushed open the gate and let us through.

Beyond the gate stretched a gravel driveway, wide enough for one car, at the end of which stood the church itself. It was only a small building, barely taller than the crouching terraced houses which surrounded it. The doorway on the facing gable took up most of the front wall, with room above for only one modest stained-glass window.

A small spire pointed crookedly at the sky.

Around the church, the land was laid out in a pretty garden, and the boundary was marked first with trees and then a wall, shielding the house from view. That

may have partly explained why none of the neighbours saw or heard a thing the night she was murdered.

The garden, I noticed as we drew closer, was waiting to be filled by light, like a bowl by water, and right now, in high summer, I doubted there was a more peaceful spot in the whole city. I could scarcely even hear the traffic. I could well understand why Marsha Reed would have wanted to live here, whatever people said about the area's dangers.

Next to the door was a stone nameplate with ST GOBNAT's inscribed upon it, the *o* in the name represented by the shape of a bee. There were plenty more bees cut into the heavy oaken door as well, buzzing round chiselled wooden hives.

I ran my fingers over them, losing count.

"Apparently, she kept bees," said Fisher as he stepped aside to let me in.

"Marsha Reed?"

"St Gobnat," he said with a bewildered look. "Does Marsha Reed strike you as the kind of woman to keep bees? Though maybe they'd have come in handy. There's a legend that says St Gobnat used her bees to see off a band of raiders who were trying to steal cattle."

"You might say she told them to buzz off," I answered.

"For that joke, I'm almost tempted to refuse to let you in," said Fisher. "But since I have no authority to stop you, I'll give you a second chance."

I took a deep breath and crossed the threshold into Marsha Reed's house, pausing briefly before going in because there was always a moment before entering a

place where someone has been killed when you find yourself wondering if you'll be able to tell something bad has happened there from the very air itself. Whether the poisonous aura which you suspect such places must possess as a result of what happened in them will be detectable, or whether it's only there in your own imagination. The truth, of course, was that the places where people die are generally indistinguishable from anywhere else at first glance and scent.

That was what Marsha Reed's house was like.

First impressions? That Marsha Reed had money, and plenty of it. Her father had obviously ensured that she wanted for nothing. Once you stepped out of the small stone hallway behind the door, there was essentially just one large open space, laid out with polished wooden floorboards, and with stained-glass windows all around and a lofty ceiling above ribbed like the inside of a whale. Medieval-style lights hung like descending spiders.

Expensive designer furniture had been arranged at the front of the room to make an improvised sitting area centred around a table strewn with movie and TV magazines bearing the grinning faces of identikit movie stars, the detritus of Marsha's aspirations, together with a huge plasma TV screen and a tottering pile of DVDs. Behind that a bookcase was stuffed with the novels and true-crime paperbacks that Stella Carson had already told me Marsha collected.

A little further on, steps led to a raised section in the centre of the room, surrounded by a wooden railing, like an altar, where the victim's iron-framed bed stood.

This was where Marsha had snatched her final breath before having the next one, and all the others that should have followed it, snatched from her. I recognized the scene from the photographs the Assistant Commissioner had shown me in her office.

The bed had been stripped of sheets since then, bagged up and taken away by forensics, and the bare mattress looked forlorn and exposed. Going up to see where she died, I could still identify traces of white powder on the bedposts where the technical team had dusted for prints, a reminder of how easy it was to turn an ordinary home into a crime scene.

All it took was one random, or not so random, act of violence.

As for the rest of the church, there wasn't much to say.

There were two doors on either side of the far wall. The first led into a small vestry that had been converted into a kitchen, though there was little sign that much in the way of cooking had ever gone on there. Marsha Reed's active social life had seen to that. The other door opened into a short corridor, off which were a number of equally small rooms where Marsha had hung her clothes and stored her shoes. Again, no expense had been spared. Each label carried the mark of some designer whose name was vaguely familiar to me.

The final room on this corridor contained the bathroom, white as heaven.

More bees buzzed in the stained glass above the bath.

I opened the door of the medicine cabinet, knowing it would be bare. Taking away a victim's pills was one of the first things police did following a murder. They had to check what was actually in the bloodstream of the dead against what was supposed to be there.

"What medication was she on?" I asked Fisher.

"Prozac for depression," he said. "Diazepam for stress. There was a small cocktail of other prescription drugs in there too, for which she didn't have a prescription. It seems she was self-medicating, basically taking whatever she could get her hands on."

"Recreational drugs?"

"Some of the surfaces dusted positive for cocaine, and there were a couple of tabs of ecstasy wrapped up and stuffed down the side of a chair in the main room. The lab results aren't back yet, but her friends confirm she indulged chemically on a fairly regular basis."

"Did Daddy know that's where his money went?"

Fisher shrugged. "Who knows what anybody really knows or thinks?"

"That's a reassuring sentiment, coming from a criminal psychologist."

"You know what I mean," said Fisher. "I can make educated guesses with the best of them, but people are always going to spring surprises on you. That's what they do best."

"Did Marsha Reed spring any surprises on you?"

"Only insofar as there's not a trace here of her other more unconventional pursuits."

"What did you expect to find — whips and chains hanging in the closet?"

"I expected to find *something*," he said. "Instead it's as if she worked hard to keep the two parts of her life separate and they're still not on speaking terms now she's gone."

"That's not so unusual."

"No," he acknowledged. "But it's *noteworthy*."

"Maybe she didn't want her father finding out what was really going on in his baby daughter's head," I suggested. "Maybe she feared he wouldn't approve."

"So she keeps things neat and anodyne to stop him cutting off her cash supply, saving it all for the privacy of her journal? It's a possibility."

"Have you come to any other conclusions?" I asked.

"Tell me what you think first."

"Me? I don't know what to think. Everything seems so" — I searched for the word — "unremarkable. You'd never guess anything out of the ordinary had happened here."

"You've hit the nail on the head. Unless I'm missing something blindingly obvious," Fisher said.

"It wouldn't be the first time."

"You keep your sarcastic put-downs to yourself, Special Agent. All I mean is that this looks like one of these rare cases when what you see really might be all there *is* to see."

"That's significant in itself, surely?"

"It's the most significant aspect of the whole business. No one blundered in here unexpectedly and murdered this poor woman. You only have to look at the crime scene to know whoever did this felt

comfortable here. At home even. He wasn't rushed or stressed."

"So you're saying it wasn't one of her casual pick-ups?"

"I'm not saying it couldn't be, but I don't think she would've brought someone she met through the S & M scene back here for sex. The environment is just too sexless and anonymous to match their requirements. I'm assuming she went elsewhere for that. To clubs, or to the men's own houses. Besides, would a casual pick-up have felt so comfortable here?"

"More of a regular boyfriend, then?"

"A boyfriend? Yes, that might work. But the truth is we don't know *who* felt comfortable here. There could have been men in and out of Marsha's house all the time that we don't know about, men who could have become familiar with the layout of the place. They could fit the bill as easily. Till we know who they are, we can't rule anything out."

"It definitely wasn't a random attack, though?"

"No way." Fisher shook his head firmly.

"You mean this was an organized scene?"

"Organized is too simple a description. It's more complex than that."

I knew what Fisher meant. Amateur profilers made much of the differences between organized and disorganized crime scenes and what they meant, but nothing was ever that straightforward. It was one of the things I'd explained in my lectures to my students: the difference between a fictional crime scene, where the evidence and the nature of the attack were signposted

and clear, and an actual crime scene, where things were less absolute.

Not that the classifications were worthless.

Everyone had to start somewhere.

It was all a question of trying to determine how motive affected a crime scene. Basically an organized crime scene reflects the control which the killer brings to the place of killing. The scene shows planning, premeditation. There would be an effort to avoid detection. The killer is aware of what he's doing and does all he can to avoid leaving incriminating evidence behind. Disorganized crime scenes, by contrast, display clear signs of spontaneous action and frenzied assaults. Victims are selected at random. Weapons might be chosen the same way. The attack will be hurried, the crime scene disarrayed.

At least, that's what the textbooks say.

In that sense, Marsha Reed's house fitted the classic organized scene, especially when it came to the use of restraints. Organized killers need to *control* their victims. They need to minimize resistance. On the other hand, organized killers usually picked targeted strangers as their victims, and, if Fisher was right, Marsha was no stranger to her killer.

They also usually took the body away, or made some effort to conceal it. That accorded with the desire to escape detection. The most inexperienced killer would know that the longer a body is kept away from the police, the better his own chances of getting away with the crime. Here, no attempt was made to hide the body at all. In fact, it was openly displayed, making discovery

inevitable. Covering it with a sheet certainly hadn't been a serious attempt at concealment. The significance of that act lay elsewhere.

The body hadn't even been moved after death, though that could simply have been a consequence of necessity. The killer would have found it difficult to shift a body from Marsha's house down the lane and into the street without being seen.

Alternatively, it could be a sign of his confidence again. He didn't *care* whether the body was found, because he didn't expect the police to be able to catch him whatever he did.

Another difference was that Marsha's killer must have lingered on the scene for some time after committing the murder, hence the dried blood on the sheet. Equally, that could point to the killer having returned subsequently to the scene of crime, which in itself was recognized as a reason why a crime scene showed signs of organized and disorganized behaviour simultaneously. But why would he have taken the risk or returning?

Because he'd left incriminating evidence behind?

Or because the need to take some trophy overrode any sense of caution?

Another commonly cited reason for finding conflicting evidence at a crime scene was because there were *two* killers. Could that have been the explanation in this case?

"Or it could be," I said slowly, groping my way through the possibilities, "that this whole scene has been staged to throw investigators off the scent."

"Now you're getting somewhere," Fisher said with a smile.

I realized that he'd been gently leading me to this point the whole time.

"You're saying you think the scene *was* staged?"

"I think there is no doubt that this scene was staged," said Fisher. "The place was arranged to make some point, to tell some story. The question is, what story?"

"To know that, you'd have to know first what it looked like before."

"Now that forensics have finished up, Grace is planning to get some of Marsha's friends in here individually to take a look around. We certainly don't want them coming by in a crowd and confusing one another. If anything has been moved around and changed by the killer in an attempt to convey some message, they're the ones most likely to spot it."

"Sounds like a good idea."

"The only problem," Fisher replied, "is that her friends don't seem to have come round here much. She seemed to socialize with them mainly in town, or at their houses."

"The solitary type."

"In that respect, she was. In others, obviously she was a little less shy. But any friends from her secret life who *did* come here aren't exactly going to be rushing round to help the police make an inventory of the fixtures and fittings. Of course," he added, "I could be wrong about her knowing her killer at all. Maybe he's just the type who feels confident enough to move in

187

spaces that are foreign to him as easily as he moves in his own house."

"Then that makes him all the more dangerous," I said.

"I don't think we need any further proof that the man we're looking for is a dangerous individual," commented Fisher bleakly. "We have his handiwork as evidence."

CHAPTER
EIGHTEEN

Fitzgerald was standing on the gravel drive in front of the church, talking to Seamus Dalton, when we finally stepped outside. It was Dalton who noticed me first — and if I could've anticipated the look of mingled confusion and loathing on his face at the sight of me, it would have single-handedly dispelled any doubts I had about accepting Stella Carson's offer.

He couldn't have been more taken aback if Marsha Reed herself had come out of the church, and made a noise in response somewhere between a worldless moan and a profanity.

The noise alerted Fitzgerald to the fact something was wrong with Dalton, and she followed his gaze until her eyes met mine. She hid her own surprise well, but I could tell she was pleased. That was harder to hide. A smile was flickering on the edges of her mouth.

"There you are, Saxon," she said. "No need for any introductions in present company, at any rate. You both know each other. I did mention Saxon'd be joining us for a time, didn't I, Dalton? The new Assistant Commissioner has invited her to offer her expertise on the investigation."

Dalton didn't answer.

Most likely, he didn't trust himself to answer civilly. I doubt I would've been able to either if the roles were reversed. I tried not to enjoy his discomfort too obviously.

"Detective Dalton's just brought round Marsha's phone records," Fitzgerald went on, pretending not to notice the strained atmosphere which had descended on proceedings.

"I didn't realize you were here," I said.

"Only arrived a moment ago. I spent the morning with Desdemona."

"Desdemona?"

"Solomon's girlfriend. She's playing the main female lead in his latest production."

"Desdemona's the name of the character," Fisher whispered to me helpfully.

"Right. I did wonder. What's her real name?"

"Ellen Forwood. Seems Solomon was either telling the truth, or they're both lying. She says he was with her from after the play ended on Saturday night until the next morning."

"So he couldn't have sneaked over here and killed Marsha?"

"Not unless he has a body double," muttered Dalton.

No chance of Dalton ever getting a body double, that's for sure. Where would they ever find that much excess fat to replicate his waistline?

"Did his fiancée know about Solomon's relationship with Marsha?" asked Fisher.

"Not until this morning, when he confessed all — and not, I hasten to add, out of the goodness of his heart. The press got wind of his relationship with Marsha Reed."

"And?"

"She says she's forgiven him. That everyone makes mistakes. According to her, they were planning on an autumn wedding before all this blew up, and nothing has changed."

"If marriage was in the offing, that would've made it all the more inconvenient," I said, "if Marsha Reed decided to make life difficult for Victor Solomon. It would give him the perfect motive to want rid of her."

"That still doesn't explain how he can be in two places at once," said Fitzgerald.

"True."

"Plus we've been through the records we can find of cars in the area at the time and there's not a sniff of Solomon's presence. Not that that's conclusive proof," she added.

"Any joy with the phone records?" pressed Fisher.

"Sort of. That's why I came round to let you take a look at them."

She handed a bundle of sheets to Fisher.

"The top sheet is a list of the calls she made on the night she died," said Fitzgerald. "Then they go back in reverse chronological order for six weeks."

"The highlighted ones?"

"Those are the calls to Solomon," she explained.

"Did she always call him this often?"

"Quite the contrary. Initially she hardly called him at all. It could be she didn't need to, because she was seeing enough of him. Or it could be she was more careful at the start to maintain his privacy. She must've known about his relationship with Ellen Forwood. Then, as her own relationship with Solomon started to cool off, the calls increased in frequency."

"There must be over a dozen each day," observed Fisher, lifting each sheet in turn.

"And on the last day, more than twenty."

"Few of them lasting more than a few seconds," I said, as Fisher handed me the record.

"Solomon says she kept calling and begging him to meet her again. He kept telling her it was over and to stop harassing him. Harassing was his word. By the end, he was just cutting Marsha off every time as soon as he realized it was her on the other end."

"What about the other numbers?" I said.

"Some are probably men she met through the club she belonged to," said Fitzgerald. "A handful have already come forward to admit they knew her. The others —"

"Are probably married," I finished for her.

"I shouldn't wonder. I've already put Dalton on to the job of tracing them."

And boy, did he look delighted with it.

"And this one?"

"That," Fitzgerald said, "is the last number Marsha Reed ever called."

The call had lasted only a couple of minutes, but the time recorded meant that it must have taken place less

than an hour before the pathologist's estimate of the time Marsha died.

"Who is it?"

"His name is Todd Fleming. And," she said to me, "there's one curious feature I thought might grab you. He used to work as a locksmith. Remember what Niall Boland said about the criminal propensities of errant locksmiths? Here's someone who wouldn't have had any trouble getting in and out of Marsha Reed's house if he wanted to."

"You say he *used* to work as a locksmith?"

"That's right. Currently he's working the night shift at a 24-hour internet café down in Temple Bar."

"Has his name come up in the investigation thus far or not?"

"Not. It's the first we've heard of him," said Fitzgerald. "We're going over there now to have a word with him. Healy's waiting in the car. You can come with us," she added to me.

I didn't need to be asked twice.

I felt Dalton's eyes burning resentfully into the space between my shoulderblades as Fitzgerald and I walked down the lane back to the road. He wasn't going to be pacified by being told my presence was the Assistant Commissioner's idea. That only gave him additional excuses to mistrust her and me together. Like he didn't have enough already.

"Damn," I said.

"What is it?"

"I forgot about my car. I parked it round in Ossory Square earlier."

"Give me the keys," said Fitzgerald. "I'll get one of the drivers to bring it round to Dublin Castle later. If it still has any tyres on it by then, that is. Some of the kids round here can strip a car back to its constituent elements quicker than a school of piranha can strip a shark's carcass back to the bone. What were you thinking of, leaving a car unattended down here? Not that your Jeep being burned out by joyriders would be any loss, you understand."

"You leave my Jeep out of this. That car's like family to me."

"In your case, that's not much of a compliment. The last time you saw your mother more than twice in the same calendar year was when you were in high school. And Saxon?" She checked over her shoulder quickly to make sure we were out of earshot. "I'm glad you decided to accept Stella's invitation," she said. "Really I am. I think this is what you need."

"I don't want to get in your way —"

"You're not in anyone's way."

"Try telling that to Dalton," I pointed out.

"Dalton's just going to have to learn to adjust," Fitzgerald said firmly. "It wouldn't be before time. Though coming on top of the new Assistant Commissioner being a woman as well, the shock of your arrival might just tip him over the edge."

"We can only hope."

"Here," she said.

We were back in the street.

Healy was parked up on the sidewalk, and was sitting with his head back on the seat and his eyes closed.

Fitzgerald rapped on the glass good-naturedly to wake him up.

"Look sharp," she said. "We've got company."

"I see that," said Healy, as Fitzgerald slid easily into the front seat and I clambered more awkwardly into the back. "It's good to have you back on board, Special Agent."

"Don't give me that Special Agent crap, or I might be tempted to change my mind."

"You're the boss."

"No, I'm the boss," said Fitzgerald. "She's not taken the whole place over yet."

"Only a matter of time," said Healy. "Only a matter of time."

It was way too early to find Todd Fleming at work in the café. Instead we headed north, up Francis Street, over the river on to Church Street and Phibsborough Road. At Cross Guns Bridge, we turned right into Whitworth Road and from there took another left into the network of streets that thronged darkly, despite the sunshine, underneath the railway line.

Healy and I waited in the car while Fitzgerald strode to the front door of the house.

She was back within moments.

"No luck," she said. "A neighbour in the flat below says he's usually out around this time picking up his son from nursery school. He should be back in ten minutes."

But ten minutes turned into fifteen.

And fifteen into a half-hour.

Still there was no sign of him.

"Do you think the neighbour warned him we were here?" suggested Healy.

"So he decides not to come home?" said Fitzgerald. "He might as well just tattoo the word GUILTY on to the front of his forehead. No one is that stupid."

"Half our arrests happen because people are that stupid," said Healy.

"Is this him now?" I said.

A man had turned the corner at the end of the road, walking hand in hand with a young child of five or six, a little blond-haired boy in blue shorts, awkwardly carrying a large box underneath his arm with the name of a famous toy store written on the edge.

The man whose hand the boy held was about thirty years old, and he looked, from the rumpled state of his long hair and unshaven cheeks, like he'd only recently gotten out of bed. Maybe he had. If this was the right man, he had the working hours of an owl. The day would be for sleeping. He was dressed casually in jeans and a T-shirt bearing the name of some local football team, and in his free hand he carried a half-empty shopping bag. He had piercing eyes, which he trained on us as he neared the place where we waited.

"Todd Fleming?" said Fitzgerald through the open window.

"Who wants to know?"

She got out and showed him her badge.

"Chief Superintendent Fitzgerald," she said. "I wonder if we could have a word?"

196

Fleming glanced from her to Healy and me in the car, then back to Fitzgerald.

"Wait here. I'll just get someone to look after Jake."

The badge hadn't phased him at all.

I heard the little boy asking what was wrong as his father led him up the path to the front door, and Fleming making some excuse about having to talk to friends of the boy's mother, and then their voices faded as they went indoors.

A couple of minutes later Fleming reappeared.

"What do you want?" he said cagily.

"Don't play games," said Fitzgerald. "It's predictable, it's tedious, and it only wastes your time and ours. You know what we've come here to talk about."

Fleming considered her words.

It didn't take long for him to see sense.

"I knew it was only a matter of time before I heard from you," he said. He was about to say more when he changed his mind. "Can we go somewhere quieter?"

"If that's what you want," said Fitzgerald.

"I don't want to stand on the street like a lemon, that's for sure," said Fleming. "You've already made me the chief topic of conversation round here for the next month as it is. If Jake's mother gets to hear that the police have been knocking on the door, she'll let me see even less of him than she does already."

"In that case, climb in the back. Healy?"

"There's a park not far from here," said Healy. "We can go there."

Fitzgerald walked round to the other side of the car and held the door open for Fleming. He manoeuvred in

next to me, his piercing eyes holding mine dispassionately for a second before Fitzgerald made her way back round to her own door and got back in, forcing him to fumble quickly with his belt before Healy could pull out from the kerb again.

He was in a car with what he thought were three police officers.

He didn't want to make things worse by forgetting his seat belt.

"How did you find out about me?" he said as we drove.

"Your mobile number was in Marsha Reed's phone records," Fitzgerald told him, turning round in her seat so that she could look directly at him where he sat in the seat behind Healy. "In fact, you were the last person she called before she died."

That didn't throw him either.

"I thought I might be," he said. "I mean, I knew I had to be *one* of the last people she spoke to, because of the time. I heard on the news afterwards that she died around midnight."

"Why didn't you come forward and tell the police you heard from her that night?"

"What would've been the point? I didn't know anything."

"You weren't worried it might look suspicious if you kept quiet?"

"Suspicious in what way?"

"Someone killed Marsha," said Fitzgerald. "If I was in your shoes, I wouldn't want to give the police any

198

more reason than necessary to suspect me of being the one who did."

"I wasn't worried about *that*," Fleming said dismissively.

"Why not?"

"She called me at work," he said, as though the answer was obvious. "I was there until after three o'clock in the morning. Scores of people must've seen me there. I knew no one could say *I* killed her."

He had a point. It was certainly a better alibi than Victor Solomon's forgiving fiancée.

"What would I want to kill her for, anyway?" he added.

"Why would anyone?" said Fitzgerald.

"I thought that's what *you* were supposed to find out," Fleming replied testily.

"All in good time," said Fitzgerald. "This'll do."

She was talking to Healy, telling him to stop the car again.

Outside was a playground. Children played on slides and swings. We could hear them laughing through the open windows. Inside the car it was hot.

Fleming was wiping the palms of his hands on his jeans. "I should've brought Jake," he said sardonically, gazing out at the playground. "Made a day of it."

"How did you know Marsha Reed?"

"You mean, how did a badly paid shop worker get to know someone like Marsha with her own Ferrari and little black book filled with the numbers of important people?"

"That's not what I meant at all," said Fitzgerald. "What I meant is, were you one of her whip and leather crowd? Money doesn't come into it. Well? *Is* that how you met her?"

"Christ, no." He actually sounded shocked by the suggestion. "That's not my scene at all. I met her because she used to come into the café some nights. We got talking."

"Were you lovers?"

"I wanted us to be," said Fleming. "I'm not going to deny it."

"She wasn't interested?"

"She only wanted us to be friends," he said, injecting all the sarcasm he could into the last word. "Isn't that what women always say when they don't fancy you? I suppose she was getting her pleasure in other ways."

"Did you know about that side of her life?"

"It wasn't a secret. She used to tell me stories of the men she met at the club she belonged to," he recalled. "The way she talked about it, it sounded like a meat market."

"You didn't approve?"

"I didn't *understand*. There's a difference. I wasn't judging her. She was a nice girl. I cared about her. I didn't want anything bad to happen to her. I told her it was dangerous."

"What did she say to that?"

"That she was a big girl, and she knew what she was doing. She told me it was just a bit of fun," Fleming said, "and that I should come along one night and see for myself. I never did, before you ask. The only time I

ever saw Marsha was in the café. She came in two, three times a week, usually late at night, to use the computers. She said she didn't have one at home. We used to have a coffee together, talk for a while. I hoped one night it might turn into something else. But it never did. I was a shoulder to cry on, that's all."

"What about the night she died?" said Grace. "Why did she call?"

Fleming took a deep breath, as if this was the part he'd been dreading. "She was upset," he said. "She'd been seeing Victor fucking Solomon."

"She told you that?"

"It was no secret. He'd told Marsha he could help her make it as an actress. I told her it was the oldest story in the book, but she wouldn't listen. She'd started sleeping with him, and then, of course, when he got what he wanted he dumped her. Or rather, he stopped sleeping with her as often as he had before. He still used to call her up for sex when he felt horny and there was nothing better on offer, and she always used to oblige."

"She still thought he could help out her career?"

"That's what she *said* it was," Fleming said, avoiding Fitzgerald's eye. "She even tried to say he might be able to help me."

"How could he have helped you?"

"Even shop assistants can have ambitions, you know. I write plays. I had one put on last year at the Dublin Fringe Festival. I'm working on a new one now. I just work at the café to pay the rent. Marsha reckoned if she could make the right connections, we could both get

something out of it. We used to talk about the future all the time, about her starring in a play of mine. Then again," he said thickly, "maybe she just *wanted* to sleep with Solomon. She slept with plenty of others as well as him. It was only me she didn't want to go to bed with."

He didn't try to hide the bitterness in his voice.

"You say she was upset about Solomon the night she died?"

"She said she'd met him earlier that evening, and that he'd demanded she give back some necklace he'd given her. Said now they weren't together any more, that she should return it. He wanted to give it to his fiancée as a wedding present. It was expensive, though what's money to a man like him? I also got the impression that she'd been asking him to get back together, begging him by the sound of it, and he'd turned violent. It was hard to get much sense out of her, she was crying so much."

It certainly didn't sound like the taxi driver's description of Marsha that night.

He'd said she was giddy and excitable.

"What did she want *you* to do?" said Healy. "Go to Solomon's house and rough him up on her behalf?"

"Nothing like that. And believe me, I offered. That only made her cry more. She just wanted me to come round to her place. She said she needed someone to talk to."

"But you didn't go."

"I was working, I told you, I couldn't get away." Fleming sounded defensive now. "It was going to be another three hours before I finished work, and I

202

couldn't just drop everything and run round because she'd summoned me. I didn't want to lose my job. And I was tired of her thinking I could just be dangled like some puppet she could play with."

"You sound angry," said Fitzgerald.

"I *was* angry. I *am* angry. I'm angry with her because she had to die like that. Marsha could've been with me instead of all those creeps she threw herself at, instead of Solomon. She would've been safe with me, but no, she wasn't interested. I didn't turn her on, because *I* wouldn't hurt her like those other sick bastards did. And don't bother looking at me like that, as if you think I killed her out of jealousy because she rejected me. You're not listening. I spent the whole night at the café. You can check up on me on the CCTV."

"Then you have nothing to fear, do you?"

"Did I say I was afraid?" he shot back. "Are you deaf? I don't give a damn what you think you know about me. I'm the one who has to live with the knowledge that if I'd gone round to Marsha's house when she called that night, she might still be alive. Do you have any idea what that's like? I was afraid that night all right. Afraid of losing my job. And because of that, Marsha was the one who ended up losing her life. It's all my fault."

"Then why," said Fitzgerald coldly, "didn't you come immediately and tell us all this when you heard what had happened to Marsha? If you cared for her so much, didn't you want to help put Solomon away for what he'd taken away from you?"

"Don't you worry about Victor Solomon," said Fleming. "I don't intend to let him get away with anything. I have *plenty* of plans for him."

CHAPTER
NINETEEN

Outside Dublin Castle, reporters were massed like cavalry before a battle. Cameras flashed as Healy's car slowed to turn at the gates; there was shouting; a blur of faces through the glass; microphones were pushed forward in the vain hope that a window would be lowered and a few words offered by Fitzgerald. The throng surged forward and was barely held back by the clutch of uniformed officers sent out to keep them at bay. Fitzgerald ignored them all. She scarcely gave any impression of having noticed them. Maybe she was used to it.

Nothing sells newspapers more than a good murder, after all, and the murder of Marsha Reed was one of the more lurid cases to have come to attention in recent months.

Once the pack scented blood, they rarely let up.

Victor Solomon's name had given the case the added glamour of showbusiness too. The lovers of famous Shakespearean directors were not found murdered and mutilated every day. I wondered if his fiancée would be so forgiving when she had to face this barrage.

Nor had the severed finger remained secret for long. Fitzgerald hadn't seriously expected that it would.

Reporters knew where to find Murder Squad detectives after hours. A few drinks, some flattery, maybe even a little money changing hands, and tongues were inevitably loosened, strict instructions to silence forgotten, discretion abandoned.

So would the killer strike again? That was what the reporters had gathered at the gates of Dublin Castle to find out, though they could have learned the answer to the question much more quickly by simply familiarizing themselves with the available literature on murder.

Of course Marsha Reed's killer would strike again. He would keep striking until he was caught. No sexually motivated murderer ever stopped of his own volition.

Why would he?

We climbed out of the car at the back of Dublin Castle and took the rear entrance into the building. It seemed strange to have to move about so surreptitiously, as if we were the ones who'd done something wrong, but I understood Fitzgerald's preference for keeping things low key. She wanted nothing to interfere with the investigation. She needed to stay focused.

Upstairs, she asked me to wait while she went to speak to someone on the desk about getting the uniformed presence outside increased. I stood at the window of her office, looking down at the now distant, silenced crowd gathered for scraps, like gulls on fishing day.

There were others watching the proceedings too. Lone figures at the edge of the larger group, semi-detached from what was happening but still

lingering as if hoping some of the air of suppressed excitement might rub off on them. That was nothing new. The world was full of voyeurs attaching themselves to things that were none of their business, filling the empty spaces in their own existence with the detritus of other people's lives.

Other people's deaths.

Murder always had and always would act as a malignant magnet.

Looking down now, though, I couldn't help wondering who else might be out there, watching. The kind of controlled, organized killer who had taken Marsha Reed's life from her would undoubtedly be anxious to follow the course of the investigation, to know every detail of what was going on. He would listen to each news show, devour each newspaper. He would keep cuttings. He might even find a way to inveigle himself into the proceedings, itching to see the police at work closer to hand, to gain an insight into their thinking on the case.

Often men like that were frustrated would-be policemen themselves.

He might be out there right at this moment, in the street below, getting off on being so close to the heart of the Murder Squad inquiry, on knowing that just behind the grey walls of Dublin Castle the pictures of his handiwork were on display, and that scores of detectives were wrapped entirely in the world that he had created out of the darkness of his own mind. To the killer, it would be like they were paying homage to his work.

Being so close, he might also hope to catch any whisper of new developments. Of possible leads. Reporters talked. They couldn't help it. It wasn't in their nature to be discreet. Sadly, their ceaseless chatter was a highly effective advance-warning system for any killer.

I found myself scanning the loiterers and the watchers below, and even any passer-by who lingered a moment longer than necessary, for signs that they might be the one we were seeking. A young man in an Hawaiian shirt stood smoking in the doorway on the other side of the street, laughing to himself as if at a private joke. What was he doing there?

A businessman driving up Dame Street missed the traffic lights and had to be beeped into action by the cars behind, so preoccupied had he been by the scene at the gate.

What did he find so fascinating?

A streetsweeper leaned on his brush and stared through the gates.

Hadn't he seen reporters here before?

That was the worrying thing. You want the wicked and the damned to bear some kind of mark that distinguishes them from the rest of us. That sets them apart. But they don't. They look as normal as everyone else. Or, that is to say, as abnormal. Because once you started looking at people in a particular light, they almost all began to seem suspicious. To simply not feel right. You stopped believing in anything good or decent. All you saw in the eyes of strangers was some flicker or

flash of inner wickedness struggling to remain under control.

To remain hidden.

"Scavengers," said Fitzgerald behind me, and I turned, not realizing until then that she'd been there. She must've thought I was still watching the reporters.

"It keeps them out of trouble," I remarked lightly.

"And how are we going to keep you out of trouble?"

"You could lock me up."

"And have the American Embassy on my back for mistreating one of their most valued citizens?" said Fitzgerald. "Not likely. I'll try this instead."

She tossed a file down on to her desk.

A man's photograph was pinned to the front, one of those ordinary, unremarkable-looking people whose existence I'd been pondering when she came in.

"His name's Mulligan," she said. "John Arthur Mulligan. Thirty-two. He's got more convictions than you've got grudges. Yeah, that many. Rape. Sexual assault. You name it. One of the officers in Vice, Walsh's bit of stuff that he thinks we don't know about, came up with his name as a possible for Marsha Reed's killing. Apparently, he liked to tie up his ex-girlfriend naked and threaten her with a knife when he was feeling horny."

"They don't teach you that in the Kama Sutra."

"I wouldn't know. Your reading's obviously more varied than mine."

"Have you brought him in for questioning?" I said, ignoring the jibe.

"No need. Turns out he was rearrested two weeks ago for breaching an exclusion order against the same ex-girlfriend and was locked up when Marsha Reed was killed."

"Then I don't —"

"See what I'm getting at? You will," said Fitzgerald. "Mulligan was out of circulation at the time of the murder, but he's very far from being the only man in Dublin with a known penchant for a little light bondage and violence against women. I thought you could head down to Records and check the files, see if anyone else like Mulligan comes back."

"Good idea," I said.

"Nice of you to say so," she answered with a smile. "I was going to ask one of the detectives to do it, but since you're around . . . You do have a sharp eye for deviance."

"That doesn't sound like a compliment," I said.

"It wasn't."

And so, dutifully, if without much enthusiasm, I headed downstairs to Records.

This had been Niall Boland's special domain before he'd fled the Murder Squad for the exciting world of locks and keys. He'd frequently squirrelled himself away here in the basement of Dublin Castle for as many hours as he could manage before his absence was noted, king of all he surveyed — that being mainly row upon row of cold metal shelves, lined with cardboard folders in boxes, all overseen by bare and unforgiving lightbulbs.

For the next couple of hours, I familiarized myself with the contents of the files, at least insofar as they related to the Marsha Reed case. That meant locating any offender or ex-prisoner whose habits or *modus operandi* touched in even the most incidental way upon the manner and circumstances of her death. Rapists who tricked their way into women's homes rather than breaking and entering; attackers who preferred to tie up their victims, for whatever practical or symbolic reasons; those who used or threatened to use knives — they were all here.

It was the same pattern I'd noticed earlier when watching passers-by from Fitzgerald's window. The more you looked, the less light there seemed to be in the world. Everybody became a suspect. The world scarcely seemed large enough to contain the evil that was done in one small city on the edge of Europe like Dublin, let alone in the rest of its swarming farthest reaches. The basement echoed with the voices of the nameless and forgotten victims.

I decided to confine myself to the last three years, otherwise I would have been down there all night and left at the end of it with more files than there was time to process efficiently. Then came the business of sorting the assembled names into more easily manageable categories — Impossibles, Unlikelys, Could Bes and Possibles — and then subdividing them still further the more information I had at my disposal.

A had carved his initials into his pregnant wife's belly, but he'd subsequently been killed in a gangland shooting in North Dublin. *B* had tied up and raped

three women, but he was still in prison. *C* had posed as a policeman to gain access to the homes of numerous women down the years, but he had never done more than steal their underwear.

One by one, the list was whittled down to size.

Eventually I was left with perhaps half a dozen men who could be regarded, without too much stretch of the imagination, as capable of the murder of Marsha Reed or significant aspects of it. And that was a depressing enough number in itself. It's comforting to believe that murder and mutilation are esoteric affairs, of practical interest only to the few. The terrible truth is that there are more people with the required diseased distortions of the brain to carry them through than it is altogether healthy to count, and it is often in administrative caves such as the Records Office that their scent can first be picked up and followed.

That day, it was Terence Dargan's scent that got into my nose.

And in more ways than one.

CHAPTER
TWENTY

A fly was trapped in the gap between the window and the closed curtains of Terence Dargan's house, struggling to escape from its prison in that manic, slightly sinister way flies have.

Fitzgerald and I stood on the doorstep, waiting for the man himself to answer the door. He, however, showed no signs of urgency. Perhaps he was out.

But out where?

Dargan's file had been the one Fitzgerald had seized on when I brought my collection of Possibles back upstairs. She remembered Dargan. She'd worked on his case years ago at the start of her career when he was charged with murdering a woman who lived in the next street and the attempted murder of another woman not five minutes' walk from his home. He wasn't a man who believed in putting too much effort into finding victims. He wasn't fussy.

As long as they were near by, she said, they'd suffice.

That's probably why he was caught so quickly.

What she didn't know was that he'd been released from prison two months ago and was now living in the Liberties, near Marsha Reed's house. The small spire of

St Gobnat's peeked above the house opposite. Dargan must've seen it every day when he opened his curtains.

If he ever *did* open them.

"God knows why they let the creep out," Fitzgerald muttered, her eyes hidden behind dark glasses. "He can't have done more than ten years. Some justice."

"What happened to you telling Healy yesterday that it wasn't your business what happened to offenders after they got to court?"

"Screw that," she said. "And screw Dargan as well. Where *is* he?"

She rapped again impatiently on the front door.

"Maybe he's skipped town," I suggested. "Would *you* hang around waiting for the police to come and pick you up if you really *had* killed Marsha Reed?"

"Dargan wasn't too bright," she pointed out, "and I doubt he's become a brain surgeon in the intervening years. He's probably hiding behind the sofa, hoping we'll go away. For Christ's sake, Terence," she raised her voice, knocking at the door again, "we only want to ask you a few questions." Then she stopped abruptly. "You hear that?"

"No, what?"

"*That.*"

We both pressed our ears to the door and listened. Now that she'd pointed it out to me, I *could* hear it. A low humming, like machinery, coming from somewhere within.

"Maybe that's why he can't hear us," I said.

"The noise isn't that loud," said Fitzgerald.

214

She knelt down and lifted the flap of the letterbox to peer inside.

"Nothing," she said. "You take a look."

I saw a narrow corridor, threadbare carpet, peeling wallpaper. The light inside was yellow, the filtered essence of the few fragments of sunlight that had managed to find their way inside and then been trapped, as surely as the fly in the window.

A small pile of letters lay behind the door, undisturbed.

"What do you think?" said Fitzgerald.

"I'd say he *has* run out on you."

"*Bastard.*"

"He can't have gone far," I reassured her. "Like you said, he's not the sharpest tool in the box, and he's only recently out of prison. He'll not have much money on him."

"Come on, then. No point hanging around."

It only took one phone call from Fitzgerald's car to get the necessary warrant to enter Terence Dargan's property. In that time, a van had arrived with the equipment to break down the door and a couple of extra armed officers in case of trouble, and an ordinary summer's day in the city suddenly took on a new air of curiosity for nearby residents.

They hung on their gates, watching expectantly.

"Soon as you're ready," Fitzgerald told the newly arrived officers.

The muffled bang as the front door of Terence Dargan's house was thrown off its hinges and back into the dingy hallway sounded like distant thunder, but

almost as soon as it had faded it was replaced by that humming again, only it was louder now and less like machinery. Now it sounded more like some kind of demented chanting coming from deep underground, the kind of noise that could drive a being crazy if they listened to it too long, looking for meaning or sense in its relentless rhythm. *What could it be?*

The answer came as soon as Fitzgerald entered the house and opened the door of the front room, where the curtains had been closed against the light.

"Dargan, are you —?"

Through the first crack, flies swarmed out, the hum broken free at last and given shape and form, filling the air and turning it black, a spreading cloud that kept expanding like smoke until the air around us was almost used up greedily by them, and I had to cover my mouth to stop myself swallowing them. The two armed officers who had accompanied us were not so lucky. They bent over, coughing, as their mouths filled up, and they knelt, spitting out what looked like thick black blood but was only the bodies of the flies they hadn't been fast enough to avoid tasting. One ran back to the garden and vomited violently.

The flies caught in our hair, shivered their way inside our clothes.

I felt sick as I watched them, as I *felt* them, but what made me even more nauseous was the acrid stench that they carried out with them from the enclosed room.

The unmistakable sweet smell of the dead.

Slowly the cloud of flies was getting smaller. It had found the open door and headed for light and freedom,

216

and if I was superstitious I could almost have imagined it as the physical manifestation of an evil soul let loose on the world, dispersing to continue its dark work in new homes now that the old one was of no further use as nourishment or shelter.

The old house was Terence Dargan.

At least I presume it had been Terence Dargan once. All it was now was a corpse in the advanced stages of decomposition, sitting by a rusty gas fire set with screws into the wall. By now he was little more than rotting rags hanging from a frame of bone and still looking moist, the corrupted flesh partly fused into the fibres of the chair on which he sat.

This was where the flies had come from.

Sarcophagidae.

More commonly known as flesh flies. They could smell a fresh corpse from several miles away. They were attracted to the bodies of the dead once the maggots and the blowflies had done their work. Not that there was often much left once the maggots had taken their fill. Maggots could devour half a corpse in a week. Up to 300 other insects could also be present, depending on where and when the body was left after death. Spiders. Beetles.

Analysis of the larvae of the flies would help pinpoint exactly when death had occurred in this room. It could take as little as ten minutes before the first blowflies arrived, colonizing open wounds and orifices, and from that moment the parasites appeared in a predictable sequence. All you needed to do was to calculate backwards to the time the victim died.

Studying the insect activity in the bodies of the dead could also determine whether wounds were inflicted pre- or post-mortem, whether the body had been moved, sometimes even the cause of death. Not that it would matter much in this case, I guessed.

I'm no forensic entomolgist, but even I could tell that Terence Dargan, if indeed this was him, must have been dead before Marsha Reed met her killer.

He couldn't be our man.

It was after midnight by the time I picked up my Jeep from Dublin Castle and returned, alone, to my building, turning off the street and down the short ramp into the underground car park that was shared among the residents of this building and the adjoining one.

I never liked coming down here. During the day was not so bad, but after dark it was a claustrophobic, dank, eerie place. Couple of times I'd even heard rats running around. Rats are creatures I just can't stomach. There must be something primeval in the fear, something that goes right back to the time when we squatted in mud huts and rats meant death.

There was also a stale smell that suggested the winos used it as a place to sleep.

And worse.

It was supposed to be patrolled. That was why we paid our service charge, right? But I'd never seen anyone else down here the times I came except fellow residents with whom to pass on the same complaints. And tonight there was no one there at all, and all the

lights but one over by the door leading to the elevator looked like they were broken.

The headlights skittered across the walls as I turned into my usual space and switched off the engine. Then I saw — what?

Something had moved. I'd caught a glimpse of it shifting slightly in the rear-view mirror, but when I turned it was gone. Probably one of the bums, I told myself sternly. Get a grip. But I felt nervous as I climbed out. I paused a moment with the door open under my hand in case I needed to get back in again and lock the doors behind me.

Nothing happened.

I reassured myself there was nothing there, that I was just feeling jumpy after the events at Terence Dargan's house a few hours earlier, and locked the door with a high-pitched beep. The light in the car flashed brightly for a moment, then extinguished itself; and now there was only the pale orange light from the streetlights outside at the top of the ramp leaking in for illumination, and what seemed like the distant haven of the light above the door.

Between the pillars that held up the roof, shadows lurked. The windshields of the parked cars were like black mirrors reflecting blackness back, so that the more you stared at them the more they began to look like holes into which you might fall if you weren't careful.

The air was stifling and hot, even after midnight. It was like all the hot air of the city had fled here during the day to escape and had then become trapped. Now it

was heating up this space like the blast from a restaurant kitchen. I could feel the heat pounding in my head, which in turn dulled my sense of hearing, and that made things seem worse.

Carefully, I began to make my way across the car park.

I could hear the murmur of traffic in the streets above head level, and even the sound of music drifting over from some bar. But in here my footsteps sounded unnaturally loud.

I found myself concentrating on the sound they made, like a monk contemplating the sound of running water as an aid to prayer. My heart was racing in my chest. I didn't know what was wrong with me. It wasn't like me to be so nervous. I didn't usually —

I spun round.

There.

There *was* something, I knew it. Something behind that car over there, the Mini which belonged to the neurotic woman who lived opposite me, who fed the pigeons from her balcony and even let them fly inside, according to Hugh.

Not that you could always believe what Hugh said.

Christ alone knew what he told people about *me*.

But something *was* moving there.

I could see it.

"Come out!" I said with more confidence than I felt. "I know you're there!"

Something shifted slightly in the dark.

I took a step forward.

"Come out, I said."

A couple more steps toward the Mini, quickening my pace to cover my trepidation, wishing that I had something more than keys in my hand to defend myself.

Though you could do worse than have keys for a weapon. There were times in the past when I *had* done worse, and I was still around to tell the tale.

I paused a final moment, before jerking forward quickly to startle whoever was hiding there into revealing themselves — and then I jumped as something rushed out past my feet, and I let out a cry, remembering the rats. Only it wasn't a rat, but a black cat with luminous green eyes which must have wandered in here to get some shelter from the heat.

Or else someone in the building had taken in a cat against regulations.

The cat was now cowering under the next car, staring out at me with wide frightened eyes. Feeling guilty, I got down on my haunches and held out a hand and tried to make some cat-friendly noises, but they obviously didn't convince this cat because he didn't look like he intended coming anywhere near me. And I can't say I blame him.

I wouldn't have trusted me either.

"Go fuck yourself, then, you fleabitten little rag," I muttered to myself irritably as I got to my feet again and turned round.

The cry was out of me before I could hold it in.

Kaminski was standing right behind me.

"What're you playing at?" I yelled at him. "You near scared me to death."

"What were you doing at Marsha Reed's house?" was all he said to that.

I couldn't speak. I saw him in the dimness and he looked half deranged. In fact, forget the bit about being only half deranged. His eyes were wide and staring, like he'd just stuck his finger into a live socket. His skin looked flushed and blotchy. He had the vague, slightly unfocused look of a man who'd been drinking. Though in truth, I only remembered what he looked like afterwards. At the time, all I could think of was what he'd just said.

"Marsha Reed?" I echoed, taking a step back as I did so, not liking anyone to get that close. It makes me uneasy. Especially when they're clearly in an emotionally unsteady mood.

"Yeah, Marsha Reed. The dead woman. You know who I'm talking about," Kaminski said, his voice rising with irritation. "What were you doing there earlier?"

"What were *you* doing there?" I answered.

He paused at that.

"I had my reasons," he muttered.

"Then I had my reasons too. Two can play at that game."

"What game?"

"I haven't a clue. Whatever game it is you're playing here right now, hiding out here, sneaking up on me . . ."

He suddenly looked apologetic.

"Look, I'm sorry about that, OK? I was pissed with you. I just wanted to —"

"Scare the crap out of me. Yeah, I noticed."

222

"I was going to say I wanted to give you a taste of your own medicine," he said quietly. "It was a bad idea, I see that now. I've said I'm sorry."

I took a deep breath. "Look," I said, "we can't talk here. You'd better come up to my apartment. I've been in your hotel room, it's only fair I return the compliment, right?"

He caught my eye and smiled at the reminder. Suddenly he didn't look so unnerving. He was under pressure and I was jumpy, that's all it was.

"And then," I added, "you can tell me what the hell's going on."

"I'm not sure I know the answer to that question myself," Kaminski said.

A loud rattle alerted us to the fact that another car had crossed the grate at the top of the ramp, and in the next second a bright explosion of headlights cut the gloom around us, like an intruder bursting in. I recognized the Mercedes as it turned into a far corner.

"It's just a man who lives on the floor below me. Come on," I said, "why don't we go upstairs where it's quieter and I can fix you coffee or something?"

He didn't say anything on the way up the stairs, nor in the hall as I stood looking in my pocket for my new key. Only when I stepped inside and switched on the lights did he break his silence, whistling appreciatively as he looked around at my apartment.

"So this is where you're hiding out these days," he said. "Nice place."

"You're the one who's hiding, JJ," I said.

"Don't call me that," he said.

"Don't call you what?"

"JJ," he said. "I hate it. I always hated it."

"I'm sorry," I shrugged. "I didn't realize you felt so strongly about it."

"You never bothered to ask," he said, and then, as if to cover his embarrassment for having been so touchy about a mere name, he said: "Nice apartment."

"Make yourself at home," I said. "I'll get the coffee."

From the kitchen, I watched him walk over and take a seat, leafing idly through a pile of academic periodicals on the low table in front of him.

"*The Journal of Research on Crime and Delinquency . . . The Canadian Journal of Criminology and Corrections . . . Advances in Criminological Research*," he read out as he rifled through them. "I can see your reading habits haven't changed much."

"There's a copy of the *National Enquirer* in there somewhere, if the other stuff's a bit too highbrow for you," I said, spooning coffee into the cafetière. "Apparently, the latest issue says that Nixon was an alien. Like this is supposed to be a surprise. Or was it Jerry Springer? I can't remember. One or the other."

"Are you ever serious about anything?"

"Not if I can avoid it. Here."

I handed a cup to Kaminski, then sat down opposite him across the table, taking my chance to get a better look at him in a brighter light. The deranged look had almost entirely vanished now, replaced by something that looked more like weariness. The sort of weariness that makes your bones ache with the misery of the effort of staying awake and the greater misery of not

knowing why it's even worth staying awake to begin with.

"So," I said. "You going to tell me what this is all about?"

CHAPTER
TWENTY-ONE

Kaminski didn't answer directly. For a long time, he didn't answer at all. He just nursed his cup of coffee like it was winter out and he needed the warmth. Eventually he put it down on top of one of the magazines, reached into his pants, took out his wallet and opened it up.

He withdrew a photograph and held it out to me.

Taking it in my fingers, I saw a picture of a woman in her mid thirties, with her hair in dreadlocks and wearing shades. She had just turned round, perhaps someone had called her name, and the camera had caught her unguarded and unposed. She was laughing.

"Is this your wife?" I said.

"Heather," said Kaminski. "Her name was Heather. I met her through work. She was a secretary in one of the field offices. She wanted to be a Special Agent. She was going out with someone at the time, he was in the FBI too, he didn't want her to get involved, said it was too dangerous, but I tried to encourage her. Told her to go for it. You only live once."

The words caught in his throat, and he looked away, to the window, staring out, then took another swig of

coffee. By the time he spoke again, he'd managed to get it together.

"Nothing happened at first because, like I say, she was with this other guy. Then they split up and I took the chance to ask her out. We got married three months later. Had our honeymoon in Vegas."

"I never had you down as the marrying type," I said gently.

"I wasn't. You know me. Girl in every port. Marrying was never on my agenda. Then Heather came along. You said it yourself the other day. People change. We all do."

"You want to tell me what happened?"

"We were living in New York, at my apartment. You remember my apartment?"

"I'll never forget it. Your office had more human touches than that place."

"Heather gave it the human touch. She made it more homely. She bought curtains, new stuff for the bedroom, sheets in pastel colours, all that kind of shit. There were ornaments everywhere too. She filled the place with them. I don't know why women buy them."

"I don't either," I admitted.

"I didn't mind. I was glad she was making the place her own. She was still working as a secretary, but I was trying to see if I could get her on a training programme for the Bureau. I had these visions of our working together. Man and wife crime-fighting team." He smiled at the memory. "It was probably insane, but when you're in love you think insane thoughts. Maybe that's how you *know* you're in love."

"What happened?"

"I was at home. A rare day off. I'd spent the morning pottering around the place aimlessly, enjoying being free. She was at work. On the way home, she called to ask if there was anything we needed. I said we needed milk. That was the last time I spoke to her. She never got home. A couple of days later, they found her. She'd been abducted, murdered. Her body was dumped down by the river. The rats had eaten away half her face. She still had the milk in her bag when the body was found. That and a Hershey's Cookies 'n' Crème candy bar. She knew I loved those. I found out later she'd stopped off at a 7/11 a couple of blocks from the apartment. Somewhere between there and home she disappeared."

The flow of words was halted again. His hands gripped the cup tightly.

"I'm sorry," I said quietly. I hate people who take refuge behind those trite catchphrases, but what else was there to say?

"The man who found the body and raised the alarm," Kaminski said, "was called Buck Randall." He said the name with distaste, like each syllable hurt. "Buck Randall III, for Christ's sakes. He was a prison officer on Death Row down in Texas. The Terrell Unit. You know. He told the police he was up in New York seeing friends and sightseeing, and just saw her body on the mud down by the river when he was passing over the bridge."

"You obviously didn't believe he found it merely by accident."

228

"Nor did the cops initially. They said he was edgy, he kept changing little details of his story, nothing that amounted to anything in itself but taken together set your alarm bells ringing. You know how it is. When they examined the CCTV footage from the store where Heather had bought the milk on the way home, they discovered that he'd been in there around the same time. He left a couple of minutes after she did."

"That's some coincidence."

"Damn right it was. I checked his records and I also found he had priors for assaulting his ex-wife. An ex-wife, what's more, who'd later disappeared herself after moving, supposedly, to Arizona, only no one in Arizona had ever heard of her. He'd also been questioned about another murder in New Mexico five, six years ago. I knew it was him. He probably saw Heather in the store, maybe he'd been looking for the right woman to target and she came along, he decided she was the one. But in the end the cops let him go. They said they had nothing. Forensics didn't match up. He had a witness who said he met him in a bar down the street five minutes after he left the store. What could they do? They held him for a while, questioned him, next thing he's walking out of there, no charges, nothing."

"It was risky," I said, "being the one to discover the body. He must've have known his face would show on the CCTV."

"Some of these bastards get a kick out of taking risks like that. Who knows what goes through these assholes' heads? You were in the FBI. You studied the same stuff

as me. They have impulses we can't even being to fathom. They take trophies, they want to be acknowledged, they play games with the cops."

"But the cops didn't think so?"

"They told me to go home. They even made a complaint about me to the Bureau."

"A complaint?"

"They said I was harassing them. Harassing them. What are they? Choir girls? More like they couldn't stand the fact I wasn't willing to simply let the whole thing go. Sure, what was my problem? It was only my wife."

"How did the Bureau react?"

"I was hauled up and told to drop the whole thing. Take six months off. Go to Barbados. You know the kind of bullshit they pull. They said I'd feel better if I had a break, that maybe I'd be able to put it all in perspective. That's the word they used. Perspective."

"I'm guessing you didn't make it to Barbados."

"I told them to stick their job. I quit. Said I couldn't see the point any more. Upholding justice and going after the bad guys and all that crap when I couldn't even protect my own wife, when a woman's murder could just be put down on the It Can Wait shelf."

"What was your plan?"

"I just wanted to do some digging. I'd been in the FBI. I knew how to find things out. I wanted to find out all I could about him. From what I'd seen of the crime scene in New York, I knew the whole thing had been planned more closely than they thought. There was a determination there. A direction. That kind of

thing didn't come out of nowhere. The guy who did it had done it before. And, even if he hadn't, he'd do it again."

"So you followed him back home?"

"To Huntsville," he nodded. "I got an apartment near the prison where he worked. I didn't need money. I had plenty of that saved. My folks were dead by then, they'd left me some stocks and a house that I could sell quickly if I needed extra cash. I found out where Randall lived. I found out where he went to the gym, where he hung out with his friends, the bars where he drank, the strip joints where he usually went after work. I used to sit a couple of tables away from him and he had no idea who I was. Probably thought I was another pathetic inadequate loser like him. It was hard, though. I had a hunch that maybe he was committing his crimes away from Texas, maybe he took a trip each vacation somewhere new and did what he had to do. I couldn't know if or when he made a booking. What was I to do? All I could do was follow him around and wait for him to make a mistake."

"And did he?"

"He didn't put a foot wrong," said Kaminski. "He went to work, he came home, he visited his little elderly mother in Austin once a week. So that's when I had to start making some new moves. Taking some risks. I found the people he worked with inside the prison and asked a few questions. I found out that Randall was pretty close to a guy inside named Jenkins Howler. Howler had killed several women about ten years back and had spent the whole time in prison since waiting to

get what was coming to him. You know that much. You checked him out. He and Randall were apparently thick as thieves. Randall used to bring him in books, dirty magazines, give him extra rations, that sort of thing."

"Very cosy," I said.

"It'd make you sick," said Kaminski. "Howler was scheduled for execution in two months' time, they were going through the usual appeals and stuff, I used to see crowds protesting outside the prison sometimes, though it wasn't going to do any good. Howler was dead meat. But it didn't surprise me that Randall and Howler were friends. If Randall was the sort of man I thought he was, he was bound to find the company agreeable, right? Those people can smell their own. Could be it was getting so close to Howler that had given Randall the courage to act out his own fantasies, who knows? Maybe Howler had seen his weakness and worked on him, wanting someone to continue the good work after he'd gone. I didn't have it nailed yet, but I knew that I was getting close, that this was the key to where it all lay."

"It sounds like there's a but coming up," I said.

"There was a *big* but. One morning I got a knock on my door from the local police. Someone had tipped them off to where I was, what I was doing. It was my own fault. I took too many risks asking round about Randall. I got too close to him. The cops were there to warn me to stay away from him. He'd taken out an exclusion order on me. I wasn't allowed within half a mile of where he lived or worked. They said he was afraid I was going to do something. I reminded them it

232

was a free country, and I could go where I liked. They reminded me that there was an arrest warrant pending if I stepped one inch out of line."

"So let me guess. You flew straight back to New York and forgot all about it."

Kaminski smiled genuinely for the first time that night.

"You know me well," he said. "I kept my head down for a few days, realized I needed to go more carefully. Only it didn't turn out that way. Couple of weeks later, Randall did a bunk. He didn't come into work one day, or the next, contacted no one to tell them where he was. Next thing I know the police are back, accusing me of having murdered him."

"You must admit you were the obvious suspect."

"Thankfully, like I said, I'd been keeping my head down, hanging out, doing normal stuff, and there were plenty of people who could vouch for me. But it was tricky for a while. They even tried to suggest that I'd paid some hitman to finish him off."

"You hadn't?" I said.

He looked at me across the table.

"If I wanted Randall dead, I'd have finished the job myself," he said starkly, and I believed him. I remembered the similar threats Todd Fleming had made earlier that day about the man who killed Marsha Reed. Kaminski wasn't the only one who felt the need for revenge. "But at least I thought now they'd listen, now they'd know that Randall was up to no good. He'd realized I was on to him and that was why he'd flitted. How obvious did he have to make it before they'd see?

But they *still* wouldn't listen. Told me to forget it again. That I was obsessed. They said *I* was the one who needed locking up. They said it was being afraid of me that had made Randall run, and he'd turn up eventually when he felt safe again. They actually felt sorry for the guy. They said I was persecuting him. They couldn't see I was the victim, I was the one who was suffering. I felt like I was further away from my goal than ever. I wasn't ever going to find him now. He could be anywhere. I couldn't even be sure he was still in the States. For all I knew, he'd gone down to Mexico . . ." Behind Kaminski, the sound of the traffic was dulled, lessened. I realized how long we must have been talking.

I stole a glance at the clock and saw that it was 2a.m. "What did you do?"

"I didn't really have a plan," he admitted. "I thought maybe I'd go back to New York and see if I could persuade some of the guys in the Bureau to help me out, see if they could turn up Randall somewhere in the system. It's not so easy to vanish. There're social security numbers, people need to rent cars, take planes. He was bound to leave a trail some time. Slugs always do. Part of me also thought that if I could get them to provide me with lists of similar attacks on women, maybe women killed in convenience stores, 7/11s, that maybe I'd get a pattern in my head of what he'd done before and be able to predict where he might hit next."

"Sounds like a long shot," I said.

"It *was* a long shot. It was the longest shot I've ever attempted in my life. I was just grasping at straws,

234

trying not to sink. As it happened, what I actually did was just hang around Texas for a few months to see if he came back. I'd reached the end of whatever ingenuity I had. I was spent. And then," he paused for effect, "I got something in the mail."

"The newspaper clipping at the hotel," I said.

"The very same. That clipping told me about the death in Dublin of a woman I'd never heard of; with it was a typewritten note saying *Are you really going to give up that easily?* It said that if I really wanted to meet up with him, I had to fly to Dublin and book into the hotel where you tracked me down under the name Buck Randall and wait. He'd make contact."

"What did you think?"

"What did I think? I didn't know what to think. I couldn't see how a woman being run over in Dublin connected to what Randall had done to Heather, and yet there it was in black and white. He'd sent it to me. It had to mean something."

"You're sure it came from him?"

"By that time, I wasn't sure about anything. But I didn't have the luxury of sitting round waiting to see what would happen. I was out of ideas. It was all I had. I found an internet café and went online to see what I could find out about her, but I didn't find out much more than was contained in the news item I'd been sent. It wasn't exactly the kind of story CNN had covered in depth, put it that way. But I did learn that she'd been writing to Jenkins Howler. And then I was more confused than ever. She'd been writing to Howler, and now she was dead. Had Howler sent

Randall over to kill her? You know what those relationships are like. They're sick enough to start with. They certainly don't want the woman they're writing to striking up another sick romance with the next guy along on Death Row after they've gone. What better way of putting a line under the relationship than to have her done away with?"

"But she hadn't *been* killed," I reminded him. "She died in an accident."

"Exactly. And there was one other flaw to the theory."

"She died while Randall was still in Texas."

"So how could he have done it? Yeah, that was the problem. But there was still the same question. Why then had Randall sent me the note telling me about this woman? I had a few theories about that. That he wanted us to continue whatever game we'd been playing elsewhere. That he hadn't liked the odds back home and preferred to take his chances elsewhere, in a new arena, and that this was the lure to get me to follow him. Equally, I wondered if there *was* more to the woman's death than met the eye, and I knew I wasn't going to learn the answer to that out in Texas. That's why I came to Dublin."

"Why didn't you just give the note to the police in Texas? Or the FBI?"

"They hadn't listened to me all along. Why should they suddenly listen now? They'd just think it was more evidence I was for the funny farm. Or they'd say I sent it to myself or something. I'd be wasting my time — and worse, they'd know what my next move would be.

They'd know I was bound to follow Randall to Dublin. I'd have made it too easy for them."

It sounded fair enough.

I lifted the empty mugs and carried them back into the kitchen.

"I checked out Cecelia Corrigan's death myself," I told him as I rinsed out the mugs and put them into the dishwasher, "and I absolutely don't think there *was* anything more to it than an accident. The local police know who did it, he was never under any suspicion, there were witnesses. There was nothing mysterious about it at all."

"I know," he said. "That's the part that got me. I seemed to be back again where I started. And that's why I thought about contacting you, seeing if you could help. You were on the outside too, like me. The difference was that you know this city and I don't. If anyone could find Randall, I knew it was you. Especially after you found *me*."

"And then what?"

"I just want justice," said Kaminski.

I wondered what exactly he meant, but I was almost afraid to ask.

Did he want justice or revenge of a more immediate kind?

"Don't get me wrong," I said. "I don't have any objection to murderers getting what's coming to them. I'm the last person in the world to take the moral high ground where that's concerned. But making sure you get the right guy is kind of important too."

"That's why I thought working together made sense."

"If it was so important, why give me the brush-off this lunchtime?"

"Like I told you, I wanted to make you sweat it. I wanted to make you wait a while to put you in your place. I thought I had time."

"You're saying you don't?"

"I don't have a single minute to waste any more. When I got back to my hotel after talking to you, there was *another* note from Buck Randall waiting for me."

CHAPTER
TWENTY-TWO

The room was white, anonymous, antiseptic, made almost unbearable by the heat — and even more unbearable by some of the people sitting round the table that morning.

At the head of the table sat Fitzgerald, with Sean Healy on one side of her and Patrick Walsh on the other. Those three, I didn't mind. Dr Fisher was supposed to be there too but hadn't been able to make it, so I felt like a captured cowboy in injun territory. I was sitting down near the other end of the desk, marvelling at how history repeats itself. At school I was always hiding out at the back of the class, hoping not to be noticed, hating the people up front with their hands in the air, desperate for approval. Now here I was lurking near the back again, though my chances of going unnoticed this morning were about as good as a goat's chances of making it to a long and happy retirement when placed in the lions' enclosure at the zoo.

Seamus Dalton, who was sitting at the other end of the table to me, near where the action was, kept shooting sly glances off in my direction, making it clear what he thought of seeing me back again. There were

other detectives there too that I knew by sight — Stack, Kilbane, Ledger. They weren't openly hostile as such, just indifferent to whatever difficulties I might be experiencing or how isolated I felt. And I wasn't going to blame them for that.

No one likes an intruder.

I remembered the first time I'd been here to help on a case. I'd found myself sitting next to Niall Boland, who'd done his best to make me welcome. I'd valued his friendship. This morning I was appreciating him all the more, and simultaneously cursing him for ducking out in search of the quiet life and leaving me to face all this crap alone.

At least this wasn't the full team that had been assembled over the murder of Marsha Reed, only the lead detectives. I couldn't say I was sorry to have missed the whole team, since the scepticism which I could feel coming off this small group was bad enough.

"Let me get this straight," Dalton was saying. "Some screwball that you used to work with in the FBI has been playing hide-and-seek with the man he thinks murdered his wife, and now you want us to believe that the same man murdered Marsha Reed?"

"I'm not asking you to believe anything," I said tightly, for what felt like the thousandth time since the meeting had begun. "I'm just telling you what Kaminski told me. He got a delivery in his box at the hotel where he's staying yesterday morning. Inside was a newspaper clipping on the murder of Marsha Reed with a handwritten message saying: *How many more women have to die before you get your act together?*

He took it as evidence that the man who killed his wife was taunting him about having killed Marsha Reed too."

"And we're supposed to take the word of a guy who's been booking himself into hotels under the name of the man he thinks murdered his wife? Sounds fucked up to me."

"He was only doing what he was told to do," I said as patiently as I could. "He was only following leads. That's why he went round to Marsha Reed's house to check things out."

Which is where he saw me. It was no wonder he'd been confused. He thought I must've worked out myself the connection between what happened to his wife and Marsha Reed's death, but how could I have done that when he'd only been sent the note himself that morning? Had he missed something real obvious? He didn't know that I had no inkling there was any connection between the two strands before he himself pulled that rabbit out of the hat. I *still* didn't know if there was any connection. It all seemed so bizarre.

And now I felt like I was betraying him.

Felt it like a knot in my chest.

Last night he'd sworn me to secrecy. He didn't trust the police with the information, he said. If they got involved now, Randall would know it. He'd vanish again. Kaminski would lose him once more. "*You and me, we can get him, together,*" he'd said. "*We can bring him in. The cops have messed up too many times. They don't deserve another chance. I do.*"

I'd never seen him so desperate.

Instead, after he left, I'd watched him from on high through the window like his guardian angel as he crossed the road below, weaving through the minimal traffic on the road at that late hour. At the far kerb, he looked over his shoulder without breaking stride, glanced back toward the building and waved up at me. I waved back.

Soon as he was out of sight, I picked up the phone and called Grace.

I had no doubt I was doing the right thing. I'd seen the pictures of Marsha Reed's body. I couldn't conceal evidence that potentially might reel in her killer. Moreover, whatever he might think or say once he learned what I'd done, I knew this was the best way to help Kaminski. This was his best chance to catch Randall. No one had believed him before. Now the police were in the middle of an active murder investigation. They'd have to take his story on board. He just wasn't thinking straight right now.

Though if he saw Seamus Dalton that morning, Kaminski would hardly be reassured that the police in Dublin would take him any more seriously than the police in Texas had.

"I'm just telling you what the man said," I found myself telling Dalton and hating myself for even trying to mollify him. "I didn't say Buck Randall actually killed Marsha."

"Too right he didn't fucking kill her," Dalton sneered right back.

"What makes you so sure?" said Walsh.

I was glad to see someone wasn't dismissing the idea out of hand.

"What makes me so sure?" echoed Dalton incredulously, looking at a couple of the other cops for confirmation, as if this was the dumbest thing he'd ever heard. "What makes me so sure is a little thing called evidence. Namely, the lack of it."

"There's not much evidence against Victor Solomon either," Walsh said equably.

"What about what Todd Fleming said?" answered Dalton.

"We only have his word for it that Marsha told him Solomon had beaten her up. And she might have been lying herself. Even if it's true, it doesn't prove he killed her."

"There's still more than there is against this Texan prison guard who might not even be in Dublin for all we know. You're forgetting the report from Dr Fisher." Dalton hated psychological analysis, profiling, all that fancy bullshit, as he called it, but he didn't mind using it when it helped him make a point or put someone down. "Most of what we got was the usual airy-fairy waffle about the killer having an emotionally stunted background and issues to do with self-esteem, like that has anything to do with anything. But one thing his report did say is that this was no stranger-on-stranger killing. You read it. It said the killer felt comfortable at the scene. How was the imaginary Buck Randall III supposed to get familiar with Marsha Reed's house when he didn't know her from a hole in the ground?"

"Imaginary?" I said. "What's that supposed to mean?"

"It means we've got no reason to believe this Buck, Chuck, Fuck, whatever he's called, is even in the country. Since we all lost sleep overnight after being roused by your contribution to the investigation, Special Agent, everything's been checked, and what did we come up with? Zippo. Zilch. A big fat zero. Diddly squat, as you'd probably say."

"He'd hardly come into the city under his own name," I said testily.

"If you ask me, he didn't come into the country at all."

"Then how did he send the messages to Kaminski?" said Walsh, jumping in again.

"Am I the only one who's noticed that there's no evidence anyone sent *anything* to Mr Leon Kaminski? Because strangely enough he didn't bring along the notes he claims he got from his wife's killer to show to Little Ms FBI, and the only evidence he got anything the first time is a scrap torn from a newspaper. I could've got that myself."

"He left them back in his hotel," I said.

"That's right, he conveniently left them in his hotel. But even if there were notes," Dalton went on, his voice getting louder to stop Walsh interrupting again, "even if there were a thousand notes on pieces of parchment, written in gold ink, for all we know they could be coming from himself. For all we know, losing his wife could've sent him loco" — he mimed a twirling motion with his fingers at the side of his ear — "he could have

a whole colony of bats up there in the belfry now. You ever stop to think maybe this whole story about some killer on the run is just a fantasy he dreamed up?"

"You'll be saying next his wife wasn't killed at all."

"She was killed all right," said Sean Healy. "That much we do know. I called the NYPD last night. They confirmed that the body of a woman named Heather Kaminski had been recovered from the side of the river in New York on October 10th last. They told me the case was still ongoing, though I think we can all guess what that means."

"Then maybe *you* sent the notes to him," Dalton said to me, "so that you could get your foot back inside the door here."

"Dalton, you're so full of crap they could use your body for fertilizer."

"I'm serious. How come everything has to be about you? No sooner have you *graced* us with your presence again than the whole fucking case starts to revolve around you. We couldn't have an ordinary murder in the city. Oh no, that'd be too simple. That'd be too boring for you. Instead it has to all centre on you and your fancy American friends again."

"That's enough," said Fitzgerald quietly. "I said enough," she added when I opened my mouth to reply to Dalton. "This isn't getting us anywhere."

She was good at that. Like any good referee, she didn't police passion or argument, but she knew when it had gone too far and needed to be checked back into coolness. Nothing could be gained from Dalton and I sniping at one another like children. There was

something about the man, though, that just made me lose it. His entire existence was calculated to offend me, and it was pretty clear that he felt the same way about me.

We didn't understand each other.

We never would.

What's more, we didn't *want* to.

"Dalton's right," Fitzgerald went on, taking control. "Up to a point," she continued when Dalton started to look smug. "Everything we know about the crime scene, about Marsha Reed's life, about the psychological shape of this crime, makes it unlikely that this man, Buck Randall, is our killer. But that doesn't mean we can casually ignore what Leon Kaminski told Saxon. Every lead has to be checked. Every path has to be followed."

"But this Heather woman was strangled," said Dalton insolently, refusing to let it go. "And she wasn't killed in her house either. The MO's completely different."

"Not entirely," answered Fitzgerald, unruffled. "She was tied up, remember, just like Marsha. What's more, when her body was found, Heather's ring was missing too. That's one connection we can't ignore."

"Kaminski never told me that," I said.

"Why would he? The press might know about the severed finger, but they haven't found out about Marsha's missing ring yet. He had no way of knowing that possibly tied the two crimes together."

Dalton looked unconvinced but settled this time for a resentful silence.

"So you want us to look for this man, Chief?" said Walsh.

"First things first," said Fitzgerald. "That means establishing whether anyone can identify him as having been in the vicinity of the killing. I called the Texas police department this morning. They confirmed that Randall was close to this Jenkins Howler inside, and they also confirmed that Randall was reported missing when he failed to appear for work for a few days running, and was investigated as a missing persons case. But they said that three months later Randall called and said he'd been visiting his brother in Oklahoma and that he was sorry, he hadn't realized people were searching for him, but he wasn't coming back. Seems he had some debts hanging over him he wanted to escape."

"Big debts?" said Healy.

"All debts are big if you can't afford to pay them off. Now whether you believe that or not, he's not wanted for any crime, he's not broken any laws, he hasn't skipped bail, nothing, so as far as they're concerned if he's in Dublin that's his concern. He's free to go where he likes. But I explained the situation, and" — she opened the file in front of her — "they did send through this photograph of him from the prison records to help us look for him."

She handed the picture to Sean Healy, who passed it to Dalton, who passed it down the line till it reached me. I saw a man like any other. Small square face, tiny eyes, neat moustache, untidy scar over his left eyebrow. I glanced at it briefly and passed it on. It went all the

247

way round to Walsh, who tried to hand it back to Fitzgerald to complete the circuit.

She shook her head.

"Give it to Kilbane," she said. "Kilbane, I want you to run up some copies and then pass them round discreetly in the area where Marsha Reed lived. Talk to neighbours, shopkeepers, taxi drivers. Ask them if they've ever seen this man hanging round at all. Might turn out to be a thankless task, but if they *do* recognize him, that changes everything."

"Shall I take it down now, Chief?" said Kilbane.

"Do," Fitzgerald nodded, and Kilbane scraped back his chair and rose to take the picture downstairs to get copies made. "And you, Stack, I want you to take these." Again she handed a loose sheet over. "Those are Randall's fingerprints. You're going to have to check them against the prints we lifted from Marsha Reed's flat. No need to look so happy about it. It's a tedious job but someone has to do it. Besides, if you get a match the effort will have been more than worth while and you can take all the credit for it. Walsh?"

"Yes, Chief?"

"I want you to run over to speak to Mark Hudson."

"Mark Hudson?"

"The man who knocked down Cecelia Corrigan," I said.

"The very same," said Fitzgerald. "If Leon Kaminski is right, and there's a killer on the loose in the city, then this is where it all began. Or didn't. The point is we just don't know. The evidence is even more tenuous in relation to this incident than it is with Marsha Reed's

248

death, but we can't afford to blithely ignore it. It will all have to be checked out."

"It really was an accident," said Healy. "I read the file."

"That's true. But maybe Hudson saw something that could prove crucial. Maybe she stepped in front of the car deliberately. Maybe she was pushed. Maybe she was talking to someone immediately before she died who hasn't been positively IDed."

"Hudson said nothing about it at the time."

"It's a long shot," she confessed, "but people often remember things a long time after they happen. Especially when there's been a traumatic event. They get flashbacks. Memories. Sometimes they see what happened more clearly weeks after the event than they did when it was happening in front of their eyes. The mind makes an imprint of the event and stores it away for future use. Can we take the risk of ignoring the possibility?"

"No problem, Chief."

"What about me?" said Dalton.

He had the correct proportion of insolence he could get away with in his voice worked out perfectly each time. He was a master of the nuances of contempt.

"What have you *been* doing?" said Fitzgerald.

"Checking out Marsha's movements the last few days before she died."

"Then carry on doing that. I said I wanted to check out every lead, I didn't say I wanted to close down old roads every time a new road branches off the main one. This is an augmentation of what we've been doing so far, not a replacement for it. That goes for the rest of

you. Just follow the same lines of inquiry as before. There, we're done for this morning. Meet again here at four to see what you've got. Now go to it. And Sean," she said, as chairs were scraped back and the detectives began to head for the door, "I want you to take over from me here for the next couple of hours and hold the fort. You know what needs done."

"Consider it done. What's the story?" asked Healy.

"I want to speak to this Leon Kaminski myself. And you're coming with me, Saxon. I think you should be there when I introduce myself. He knows you. You know him. I want to hear from him myself what he knows about this whole affair."

"I don't know where he's staying," I admitted ruefully. "Last night he left without —"

"That's OK," said Fitzgerald. "Dalton found him."

"Dalton?"

"It was easy," said Dalton. I hadn't realized he was still there, eavesdropping. He was standing by the door, watching me. "A few phone calls, that's all it took."

He made no effort to conceal his glee at having bested me.

"Don't let him bother you," Healy said to me after Dalton's wide smug ass had made its exit. "He got one of the sergeants to do it this morning. It makes a difference when you tell hotels you're calling from the DMP for information. They take you much more seriously."

"The main thing is we know where he is now," said Fitzgerald. "He's not the one who's in control like he has been hitherto. Let's go see how he likes that."

"Right now that doesn't feel like much of an advantage."

"Every little helps," she replied, unperturbed. "Besides, it's all we've got."

CHAPTER
TWENTY-THREE

It took him so long to answer the door that I began to suspect he wasn't there.

"You think he's moved on again?" I whispered.

"No," said Fitzgerald. "Someone's coming."

A number of emotions crossed Kaminski's face when he opened the door and saw me standing there. First came the shock that I was there at all, then a resigned smile crept into his features, and he murmured: "So you tracked me down. Does this mean you've decided to —"

And then the door swung open wider and he saw who was standing behind me.

The smile vanished.

"Don't tell me," he said. "You're the tooth fairy."

Fitzgerald held out her badge for him.

Kaminski looked at it, rubbing his face as he did so, rubbing away sleep.

He looked ashen. He needed to shave. I wondered again what his former self would think if he could see himself now. Whether he would even recognize himself.

It was as if the outer form remained roughly similiar, but the person inside had been transplanted and couldn't help exposing itself periodically. Some

metaphorical Invasion of the Body Snatchers had taken place in Kaminski. He was like a building whose interior had been ripped out and refashioned. The two halves of himself didn't fit together any more.

"Detective Chief Superintendent Grace Fitzgerald," he read aloud. "I'm honoured." He handed the ID back without looking at Grace after the initial realization that she was there. Instead his eyes were fixed firmly on me. "So you sold me out," was all he said.

"I didn't sell anybody out," I said thickly.

He didn't answer that. Instead he stepped back and waved a hand. "I guess you'd better come in," he said to the both of us. "Unless you're here to put me under arrest?"

This time he did look at her.

"Why would we be putting you under arrest, Mr Kaminski?" asked Fitzgerald.

He shrugged. "For withholding vital information from the police, for being in the country under false papers, for sounding my horn in a built-up area after 11p.m., that sort of thing. I'm sure you can think of something."

"You didn't tell me you were here on a false passport," I said.

"You didn't ask," Kaminski pointed out. "But you didn't seriously think I'd have come here under my own name, did you? I'm a little tired of everyone knowing where I am."

"Right now," said Fitzgerald, stepping into the room briskly, "I don't much care what name you're travelling under. Our priorities are a little different."

Kaminski shut the door behind us.

It was a small room, little more than enough space for a bed and a few sticks of furniture. Grey net curtains were drawn over. The light was so sickly it reminded me of Terence Dargan's house and that was something I didn't care to be reminded about. Those flies had haunted my dreams last night. I'd woken more than once imagining I could hear them humming again. In the corner, a TV was switched on. Kaminski had been watching golf. There were the remains of a meagre room-service lunch on a tray. His bag was on a chair, still only half unpacked, as if it hadn't made up its mind whether it was staying.

The bed was crumpled, like he'd been sleeping when we knocked. A half-empty bottle of Jack Daniel's stood on the bedside table next to a tumbler.

Kaminski made no move to remove it. He clearly didn't care what we saw.

Or what we thought about what we saw.

All he did was pick up the TV remote and snap the sound off. He kept the set on, though, so the sight of long acres of green, interrupted occasionally by flashes of blue sky as the camera followed the trajectory of the ball, remained in the background as we talked, and I found I couldn't help my eye straying unconsciously to the set as we spoke.

Kaminski wasn't distracted by it. He didn't glance at it once. He was still staring blankly at us. I sensed we could've been standing there stark naked, and he would scarcely have noticed. Something was dead inside him. Perhaps it was his own capacity to feel alive.

"You must be leading the investigation into that girl's death," he said finally to Fitzgerald. "Did Saxon tell you what I told her?"

"She did."

"Then what are you doing here?" he asked bluntly "Shouldn't you be out there looking for Buck Randall?"

"We're actively pursuing a number of lines of inquiry, including that one," Fitzgerald said. "I hope it turns out to be fruitful. But these things take time. In the meantime, I thought it might help if I spoke to you myself, heard your side of the story."

"I'm not in the mood to talk right now," Kaminski said with a show of feigned regret. "Besides, I'm sure Saxon here has told you all you need to know. I'm confident she's repeated everything I said last night faithfully. What more needs to be said?"

"I realize this is a difficult time for you, Mr Kaminski —"

"Please," said Kaminski. "Call me JJ."

"I thought you hated being called JJ?" I said.

"It doesn't look like it matters any more what I want or don't want," he said. "Just tell me this," he added, turning to me again. "Did you even give this any thought at all, like I asked you to, or did you just pick up the phone and dial 999 and tell her everything I said?"

"Of course I gave it some thought," I said wearily. "That's why I told her. I was the one who *was* thinking."

"Well, I guess I should've known better than to trust you anyway," he said to that. "You always were an

insubordinate little shit. You were always questioning everything, always dissatsifed with whatever we were doing, always wanting to take over and do things your own way. You always knew better. Though you've obviously changed some now, huh?"

"What does that mean?"

"It means, look at you, running round doing the police's work for them, running to do their bidding, like a dog fetching a stick. You put it down, you get a pat on the head, they throw you another one."

"That's not fair," I said.

"Saxon," said Kaminski, "I am way past caring about fair. No offence," he went on, turning to Fitzgerald, "but you know we used to have contempt for people like you when we were in the Bureau."

"Is that so?" said Grace.

"It was always the same. We'd drop in on some little out of the way place, a town, somewhere, anywhere, Nowheresville most of the time, and then instantly you'd just hit this wall. The local police didn't want you treading on their patch, on this little patch of territory that they'd lovingly cultivated, where they were lords of everything, and suddenly here we were, the FBI, dropping in. It was warfare. Sure, the professional rivalry and creative tension could have its uses, keep us on our toes, but we still knew it was warfare."

"Times change," I said.

"You're telling me," he said wryly.

"This is getting us nowhere," said Fitzgerald. "Whatever problems you have with involving the police in this matter, the fact is that it's too late now. It's out

of your hands. Your best bet is to cooperate as fully as you can with the police in Dublin, whatever you think of our abilities, and see if between us we can't track down this man."

Kaminski didn't answer. It was like the fight had gone out of him with his last defiant speech. He simply nodded mutely, then sat down on the edge of the bed and regarded us as if to say: *OK, then, what have you got?* Grace answered the unspoken challenge by taking out the original photograph of Buck Randall which she had retrieved from Dublin Castle after copies had been made. She dropped it on to the bed next to Kaminski.

"Is this the man you suspect of killing your wife?"

Kaminski looked at the picture for an eternity, almost like he was trying to decide whether this *was* the same man, but I could see how his fingers tightened on it.

"That's him," he said grimly in the end.

"Is it a good likeness?" asked Fitzgerald.

"Randall's lost the moustache," he said. "This must've been taken when he first joined the prison guard. That must be about, let me think, seven years now? Maybe a little longer? He looks a little older now." He took out his wallet and prised out a picture. It was a little battered from being in his pocket so long. In this one, Randall was out of uniform and walking in the sun. It looked more natural than the one we had. "This is the best one I have," he said. "It's the one I show people when I want to know if they've seen him. I took this one of him when he came off duty one night," Kaminski said. "But it's been three months since I saw

him, so I guess he could've changed his appearance again."

"Can I keep this?" said Fitzgerald.

"No. Like I say, it's the best one I have."

"You have more of them, then?"

Kaminski smiled grimly. "You could say that . . ."

Kaminski got to his feet and walked over to the wardrobe. He opened the door and reached inside. He came back carrying a small black holdall. I wondered where he'd been keeping it. It certainly hadn't been in his last hotel room or I'd have found it. He unzipped it and tipped it upside down. A small shower of photographs fell out on to the bed.

There were dozens, all of them of Buck Randall. Kaminski had obviously been watching Randall for a long time. There were shots of him in his car, shots of him outside what I presumed was his front door, shots of him standing at a window, looking out, shots of him pushing a shopping cart piled high with groceries through a parking lot.

"It's lucky the cops never found your collection when they pulled you in," I said. "They'd have had you down as a stalker. Where have you been keeping all these?"

"I usually put them in the hotel safe, if that's what you're wondering," he said. "You never know who might be breaking into your room next."

There was a short uncomfortable silence.

I could feel Fitzgerald looking at me.

"You broke into his room?" she said eventually.

"Didn't she tell you that part?" said Kaminski, and he smiled with genuine pleasure for the first time that

morning. I had to admit it was good to see it, even if it was at my expense. It suggested there was some of the old Kaminski still left in there.

"I wouldn't exactly call it breaking in," I began carefully.

"What would you call it?"

"She bribed a chambermaid to let her in, isn't that right, Saxon?" said Kaminski.

"Shut up, Leon. Who said I bribed her? I spun her a line, is all. I wanted to have a look round, see what he was up to. I didn't know how else to do it. I should've told you," I admitted to Fitzgerald. "It didn't seem like the right time. I'm sorry."

She didn't say anything, just shook her head in disbelief and turned back to the pictures, asking Kaminski: "Do you mind if I take a couple of these?"

"Will you bring them back?"

"Soon as I've made copies," she promised.

"Then be my guest."

Fitzgerald carefully picked out three pictures which showed Randall at his best and slid them into her pocket. Kaminski pushed the other pictures to the side and sat down again on the bed. He made no move to put them away.

"When was the last time you saw this man?" Grace asked him.

"I told you. About three months ago. You're not trying to catch me out, are you, Detective Chief Superintendent? You'll have to try a bit harder than that."

"You definitely haven't seen him since you arrived in Dublin?"

"No."

"Then how do you know he's here?"

"Because he's communicated with me. I thought Saxon told you everything?"

"Don't get me wrong," said Fitzgerald. "I just need to get the facts straight. How do you *know* it was Buck Randall who was making contact with you?"

"Why would anyone else be trying to make me think they were Buck Randall?" said Kaminski, looking confused and still answering a different question. "It doesn't make any sense. It was Randall I had the quarrel with. No one else hates me that much."

"You think he hates you?"

"I'd take a wild guess that a man who takes the trouble to taunt the husband of the woman he murdered probably isn't filled with feelings of great affection."

"Why does he hate you?"

"Because I'm the only one who knows who he is . . . what he is . . . I know his true nature. Everyone else fell for the act, they didn't recognize him. I did."

"Why not just kill you too?"

"You'd have to ask him."

"Take a guess."

"Because this is more fun?"

"It's dangerous, though," I said. "You said yourself that no one else suspects him of being anything other than what he appears to be. That way he gets to carry on doing what he does. By playing games with you, he

runs the risk of being discovered. Of being *stopped*. I still think it would be better to just get you out of the way."

"I've wondered about that," said Kaminksi reluctantly. "I can only think he's getting a kick out of this, that this has become part of the pleasure for him. Killing is a risk-taking business. It's the risk that people like Randall get off on."

"And that's the same reason you think he killed Marsha Reed?"

"He didn't need a reason to do that. Killing women is what he does. But he wanted me to know, yes, he wants to torment me, he wants to show me what he can do. To show me what he's going to carry on doing unless I stop him. Because no one else will. I don't think he's planned this whole thing through. I think he's improvising. He just wanted to kill Heather, but when I began to pursue him then that became woven into it too."

"And now you're connected to him."

"Through Heather, yes. She's what it's all about."

"You're sure that he'll contact you again? That he won't just run now?"

"Why would he run? The only way he runs is if you make a mess of this and let him know the police are on to him. He has to think it's me and me alone. It has to be him and me, no one else. If he gets any hint the police have gotten involved, he'll be gone."

"And you won't get your revenge," I said.

"It's more than that. If he just vanishes now, it's not only me who loses. It's the other women he'll kill,

because he will. He vanishes now more people are in danger. I hope you understand how serious this situation is, Chief Superintendent?"

"I have a long experience of these kinds of investigations," Fitzgerald answered icily. "I know what's at stake. I know how to be discreet. You should also know that the more information I have, the easier it becomes. If I could see the notes Randall sent you —"

"I lost them," he interrupted bluntly.

"You told me you had them last night."

"I'm a careless person, what can I say?"

"You're just keeping them to yourself now to spite me," I said. "Because I squealed on you, as you see it, you're throwing your toys out of the carriage, not cooperating."

"It could make all the difference," said Fitzgerald, more conciliatory.

He didn't waver. "If they turn up, you'll be the first on my list."

"I could have them analysed."

"I'll keep it in mind."

"We're only trying to help," I said quietly.

"Is that what they call it now? Trying to help? It feels more like betrayal."

"I haven't betrayed anyone."

"Of all the people I thought I could trust, it was you. I was the one who gave you your first break. If it wasn't for me, you wouldn't have gotten near a big case for years. With your bad attitude, maybe never. Now the one time I need you, the one time I ask anything of

262

you, you dump on me. I thought we meant more to each other than that."

"I did what I thought was right. Whatever you say, however bad I feel about it, I still think it was the right thing to do. You can't find Buck Randall on your own."

"He found me," said Kaminski simply. "I can find him."

CHAPTER
TWENTY-FOUR

"I forgot to tell you," said Fitzgerald as we made our way downstairs. "Alastair Butler called this morning. He finished the autopsy on Dargan. Nothing official, but he's 80 per cent sure he died from breathing in the fumes of that gas fire we saw screwed to the wall of his room."

"An accident, then?"

"Maybe not. The fire had been tampered with. Whoever did it must have known that, once it was switched on, the effects of inhalation could be fatal."

"Someone wanted him dead?"

"The families of his victims are still out there, remember. Could be they thought Dargan got off too lightly and decided to take justice into their own hands."

"Or feared," I said, "that he might do it again to some other woman now he was free."

"Alternatively," she suggested, "Dargan could've nobbled the fire himself."

"Why would he want to commit suicide?"

"Apparently, he was facing new charges. The Prosecutions Office wanted to pursue him on further allegations made against him at the time of his original

arrest. They weren't happy that he'd been released early. Maybe he just couldn't face going back inside." She paused a moment as a man in a boiler suit passed us on the stairs, heading up. "We'll probably never know for sure," she said. "The world is full of secrets, after all."

Something about the way she spoke caught my attention.

"What do you mean?" I said.

"You and the hotel room," she reminded me. "You haven't forgotten already?"

"Oh . . . *that.*"

I was about to try to justify my actions, though Christ alone knows how I was going to, when Fitzgerald interrupted me with a question so out of left field that it took me a moment or two to recover.

"Do you think he knows about us?" she said.

"How *could* he?" I answered eventually.

"That's not what I asked."

"True. Then I'd say not."

"You didn't tell him?"

"If I did, I didn't mean to," I said. I considered what she'd said for a moment, as we reached the ground floor and crossed the lobby to the entrance. "JJ was always pretty perceptive," I admitted. "He picked up on things that weren't obvious to the rest of us."

"Some people are like that," she agreed. "Maybe it was my reaction when he mentioned your breaking into his hotel room that gave it away."

"I didn't break in."

"Let's not split hairs. It was the not telling me which was the important part."

We went out to the car in silence. I leaned on the roof on one side, resting my chin on my folded hands, as she searched her bag for the keys on the other side.

"I really am sorry," I said.

"Are you?"

"Yes! At least, I don't know." The car beeped open, and I climbed in. "I didn't want to worry you. I still don't. It was nothing. Just me being me."

"You being you will get you arrested one day."

"Do you always do everything by the book?" I said.

"Not always," she admitted.

"Do you always tell *me* when you've crossed the line?"

"Not always."

"There you are, then."

"What we don't know can't hurt us, is that what you're saying?"

"Something like that."

"Does that include not telling me about you and Kaminski?"

Shit, that was the last thing I needed.

"I'm pretty perceptive myself when I need to be," Fitzgerald said.

"There's not much to tell, really," I said resignedly. "One time we were working on a case together. We'd flown down to Denver, Colorado, had a frustrating day. We ended up going to some awful bar and drinking too much. One thing led to another."

"You slept with him."

266

"If you could call it that. It was nothing. Not something I cared to remember, at any rate. I just wanted to forget about it as quickly as possible. Next day I never mentioned it, he never mentioned it, and neither of us ever said a word about it again. Not once. It was . . . embarrassing. I felt I'd lost some contest. JJ was the kind of man that other agents wouldn't have trusted their wives around. He made Walsh look like a monk in comparison. I didn't want him to see what happened as a victory. The melting of the ice maiden, you know. They were always talking, all of them, in the field office, about how frigid I was. I just felt I'd let myself down, and all because I got drunk. I didn't know afterwards if they were talking about it among themselves, but I don't think so. I think I'd have known. There would've been looks, smiles, you know what it's like, sudden silences. They wouldn't have been able to hide it. Since there was nothing like that, I guessed Kaminski hadn't said a word about it."

"You must've been relieved."

"In a way, yeah, I was," I said. "But in another way, it made things worse."

"Why worse?"

"Because by not saying, it made it seem as if it was somehow . . . what's the word? A guilty secret. Something illicit. So the more he didn't say anything, and I didn't say anything, the more it seemed to grow and take on a significance it didn't deserve. I always felt it was back there in reserve, and he could use it against me somehow. You're not mad, are you?"

"Why would I be mad?" she said. "It was a long time before I met you."

"I'd hate you to be jealous, is all. There's no need. My relationship with Kaminski, such as it was, isn't so much dead as never alive. It wasn't relevant."

"At the risk of sounding picky, sleeping with someone is always relevant." She offered a smile of reassurance. "But, even so, I don't want you to feel bad. It was something I sensed up there, that's all. I needed to know. It makes things easier next time we all meet. But I don't deny it's weird. That's the first person I've ever met that you've slept with. The first person I know about, anyway. Unless you've been seeing Dalton behind my back."

"I think we both know that's the least of your worries."

"I'm just wondering," she said.

"Wondering what?"

"Wondering if what you two had was more significant to Kaminski than to you."

"In what way?"

"In this way," she said. "What if he really came to Dublin to see *you* again? What if this whole thing was planned from the start to get him into a position where he could see you? That you were *meant* to see him that day, it wasn't accidental at all."

"That's not possible. Is it? His wife *was* killed. He *did* quit the FBI. He *did* follow Randall back down to Texas."

"But still the only connection between the two events — the one in America and the one here — is him. And *you* are his only connection to Dublin."

"What are you going to do?"

"I'm going to put him under surveillance and see what happens," she said. "Either way, it makes sense. If all this really does have something to do with Marsha Reed's death, I need to know where he goes. I don't think he'll cooperate. If Buck Randall gets in touch again, I think he'll keep it to himself. And if it *doesn't* have anything to do with her death, I have to know that too. The last thing I need on this case at this point, at any point, is distractions. Whichever it is, I want to know what he's doing."

She was picking up her cellphone to give the instruction when it rang.

"Walsh, is that you? Speak up, I can hardly hear you. What is it?" Long pause. "I've got you. I'll be there right away. What's the address?"

She wrote it down, then dropped the phone back in her pocket.

"Mark Hudson's gone," she said.

"The guy who knocked down Cecelia Corrigan?" I said. "What do you mean, gone?"

"Gone. Vanished. He hasn't been seen for over a week. He was reported missing by his cleaning woman to the local police station. Since then, nothing."

"That doesn't make any sense. Her death really was an accident, wasn't it?"

"Maybe that's only what we were supposed to think," she said.

It was only when we turned into the street that I realized where we were.

"Is this the street where Hudson lived?" I said.

"Yes," she said. "Number 11."

"But this is where *she* lived too."

"Where who lived?"

"The woman Hudson knocked down and killed. Howler's penfriend."

"Cecelia Corrigan lived in this street too?"

"The very same."

As we climbed out, I recognized the low white stone wall, the creaking gates, the sleepy summer trees dappling shadows on the ground.

The only difference was that now there was no sign of the black cat.

It was obviously getting too crowded for the poor creature.

I looked up at Cecelia Corrigan's house and thought I saw someone standing at an upstairs window, but, when I raised a hand to shield my eyes from the sun and get a better look, the someone vanished, and there was only the trembling of a curtain.

"Chief," said a familiar voice.

"Walsh," said Fitzgerald, "what have you got?"

The young detective looked glum as he came down the path to meet us.

"Nothing, Chief. The place is empty. One of the neighbours had a key," he said, "so we were able to take a look inside. Everything seems in order, no signs of struggle or a hurried departure. There's someone in there you might want to talk to, though."

He led the way up the path and through the door into Mark Hudson's house. I felt that peculiar

sensation of nervousness you always get on walking into someone else's house when they aren't there. It's like an intrusion. It *is* an intrusion. That it's a necessary one doesn't make it feel any less like a violation of privacy. I felt like a peeping tom.

And yet who was here to feel offended? Something about this house smelled empty, like it had already adjusted itself to the business of being abandoned.

And at least I didn't have to worry about flies this time . . .

In the small rear kitchen stood a young man in a police officer's uniform, looking nervous. It wasn't every day a local cop got to meet the Chief Superintendent of the Murder Squad. This cop's face was slightly flushed. He was fidgeting on his feet.

Walsh introduced him as Sergeant Chase.

"He was on duty when Hudson was reported missing."

"Is that Hudson?" said Fitzgerald. She was pointing to a framed photograph on the shelf above the fireplace, which showed a man of thirty, possibly, wearing dirt-spattered sports gear and holding up a trophy.

"He played rugby for his local club," acknowledged Walsh. "His teammates were the last ones to see him. He'd arranged to meet them mid week for training. When he didn't show and couldn't be contacted and they realized he hadn't been in work, they reported him missing. By which time someone else had reported him missing too. His cleaning lady."

"That's Mrs Emily Nolan," said Sergeant Chase. "She came in at 9 a.m. on Tuesday to begin work. Mr Hudson normally left her wages in an envelope on the mantelpiece, but there was nothing. She thought it was a bit unusual, but did her work as usual. Next day, the money still wasn't there and he hadn't been home, so she called the local station."

"Seems a bit drastic, calling in the police that quickly," said Fitzgerald. "Didn't she know any friends or family of his she could call?"

"She says she couldn't think of anyone else to ring," said Sergeant Chase. "He'd never mentioned any family, and the only neighbour Hudson really had any contact with lived across the way. She was the one who told Mrs Nolan to go the police."

"Number 8," I said quietly.

"How'd you know that?" said Walsh.

"That's where Becky Corrigan lives," I said.

"Corrigan?" said Walsh with a frown. "The old woman Hudson knocked down?"

"She wasn't that old," I corrected him, though it was curious because that was the way I thought about her too. "But yeah, that's Jenkins Howler's late penfriend. Becky was her niece. She still lives in the house. It's over there, see?"

I showed him where, through the window, the house opposite was clearly visible. Mark Hudson probably saw it every day, just as Ceclia Corrigan saw his. It could never have occurred to either of them that one day he would be the unwitting cause of her death.

If it *had* been unwitting.

272

Fitzgerald must have been nursing the same thought, for I heard her say next: "Tell me what happened that day, the day Cecelia Corrigan was killed."

"There's not much to tell really, er, sir," Sergeant Chase answered her awkwardly. "I'd only come on duty, it was about seven in the evening. There was a call-in saying there'd been an accident down on Herbert Park. A woman badly injured, it said. I was sent out to take a look at it. By the time I got there, the woman was already dead. She'd been crossing the road at the traffic lights when she'd been hit by a car turning into the street."

"Was the driver . . . was Mark Hudson . . . still there?"

"Oh, yes, he was still there. He was in a pretty bad way, to be honest. He couldn't stop shaking. He was sitting on the kerb with his head in his hands, crying, shaking. Quite a crowd had built up by then, and they were gathered round asking him what had happened, but he couldn't talk. It was only when we eventually got him back here to the station and got him a cup of tea, that he calmed down enough to tell us what had happened."

"Was he arrested?"

Sergeant Chase looked startled by the question, as if arresting people was the last thing he could imagine himself doing.

"No! He was breathalysed at the scene of the accident, of course, but he didn't have a drop of drink on him, and there was no evidence he'd been driving carelessly or too fast. Plenty of eyewitnesses saw it all

happen. The dead woman didn't stand a chance. She'd just stepped out in front of the car. He couldn't stop. Miss Corrigan said so herself."

"I thought you said she was dead by the time you got there?" I said.

The young cop turned reluctantly toward me, wondering perhaps if he'd said the wrong thing. "I meant the young Miss Corrigan," he said.

"Becky Corrigan was there when her aunt died?" said Fitzgerald in astonishment.

"Not only was she there," said Sergeant Chase, "she was in the passenger seat of the car. Mark Hudson was giving her a lift home when he hit her aunt."

I whistled softly. Funny how she hadn't mentioned that when I spoke to her.

"And you're sure," said Fitzgerald tentatively, "that there was nothing more to what happened? Nothing suspicious? Something that didn't fit?"

"Nothing." He shook his head bemusedly. "It was an accident."

How many times had I heard those words in the past days?

Fitzgerald and Walsh tried more questions, different angles, but they might as well have been speaking Mandarin Chinese for all the impact they were making on Sergeant Chase. As far as he was concerned, he had attended the scene of a routine road-traffic accident and nothing was going to shake him from that conviction. And maybe he was right.

Finally, Fitzgerald told him that would be all, and she went off to check out the rest of the house with

Walsh. I retreated to the garden, found a bench to sit on and lit a cigar.

I had other things to think about. I was feeling guilty about Kaminski. I didn't want to say anything to Fitzgerald about it because she might get the wrong idea. Might think that somehow I still had feelings for him. I didn't. At least I didn't *think* I did. My only feeling for him right now was pity. I was struggling with the awful feeling that I'd taken away the one thing that kept him going, which had sustained him in the days since his wife was murdered, and that was the possibility of reeling in Buck Randall III.

There was something else too. What Kaminski had said hit home. As far as he was concerned, I was the cops' lapdog now. I was the thing we'd always fought against. I was the thing I'd always despised. Somewhere along the way I had become respectable.

Safe.

I still couldn't work out how I felt about that. Part of me needed to be on the outside. It was part of what defined me. Take that away, and what was left? And I was no nearer getting an answer to that when Fitzgerald and Walsh came out to join me.

"Any luck?" I asked.

They didn't need to speak to give me my answer.

Their faces said it all.

Or at least they did until Walsh's face suddenly brightened. "Would you look at that?" he said appreciatively.

I followed the direction of his gaze. On the other side of the street, a slender woman in a revealing summer

dress had emerged from the gate and was glancing over at us with a curious frown. She caught my eye, and there was a vague flicker of recognition on her face before she turned and began to make her way toward the main road.

"That's Becky," I explained to him.

"The girl who was in the car?"

"And the one who inherited the money, don't forget that part."

"Rich and hot with it," he said. "It doesn't get any better than this. Leave her to me." And he trotted to the gate to follow her. "Excuse me, miss," he called after her.

I saw her turn and wait until Walsh caught her up. He showed her his badge before reaching out an arm and shepherding her back toward her house.

"Say *she* did it," I found myself saying.

"What?" said Fitzgerald, astonished.

"I'm serious. Say she was having an affair with Hudson. She gets him into her clutches, has him knock down the aunt so that she can inherit the money and the house, and then, when Hudson's outlived his usefulness, she bumps him off too."

"What an imagination you have," said Fitzgerald. "Do you have any reason for thinking so or is this just one of your legendary intuitions?"

"Neither. Thinking aloud, is all."

"You have the dimmest view of women of anyone I've ever known," said Fitzgerald.

"That's because I am one," I said. "I don't have any illusions."

I didn't really think that. A memory of her coldness on first meeting, the way she'd talked about Cecelia Corrigan, had merely hit me as I looked across at her.

Coldness was no crime, but it provoked mistrust.

"You know," said Fitzgerald indulgently, "you can't send everyone you don't like to the electric chair. The drain on the power supply would be too great."

"Since when did you become so understanding?"

"Oh, I couldn't be compassionate all the time," she smiled. "Just now and again as a special treat. Now what say we get back to looking for the elusive Mr Hudson?"

CHAPTER
TWENTY-FIVE

The search for Mark Hudson was complicated by the small and inconvenient fact that we didn't know exactly what we were looking for. A straightforward missing person?

A fugitive?

A killer?

Or the victim of a killer, who had disappeared from his own life as effectively as he had disappeared from everyone else's? Or was his absence a complete non-mystery which would be solved by his suddenly turning up, unaware of the stir he had created?

The procedure for finding the lost was different in each case. Which one was followed could make all the difference to how successful the search turned out to be. I almost found myself wishing I could call up Lucas Piper and ask him for help. His famous skill in uncovering those who had seemingly been erased from the universe would be invaluable.

Or would it? This was a different city, a different country, a different world, than he was used to. He might be totally at sea here. Then again, he couldn't be any more at sea than I felt. And surely the principles were the same whether you were looking for someone

in this Dublin or Dublin, Ohio? I should send him a postcard. *Wish you were here.*

Where to begin? Mark Hudson didn't have many friends, and the ones he did have knew of no earthly reason why he should have gone off the radar screen. Of a family there was no sign. There was no sign either of a girlfriend or boyfriend. On that score, Hudson's sexuality remained stubbornly indeterminate. His few friends knew of no sexual partners, and there was no pornography in the house to indicate which way his inclinations lay. A study of his computer also found no clue in the websites he'd visited, or the emails that he sent. Most of those were related to his work as a salesman. Most of those sent *to* him were commercial pitches, offering the usual range of bizarre and generally unsavoury services.

Hudson's bank account had also remained untouched since he vanished. The last withdrawal from his account came from an ATM in Talbot Street, near where he worked. The CCTV at the bank had recorded him taking out money the day before he disappeared. Grey and grainy, it represented the last sighting of the missing man. If he had been planning on going away for any length of time, there was no hint of it in this transaction.

Nor were there any unusual patterns in his financial dealings in the months leading up to his disappearance. It wasn't like he was stockpiling money ready for a midnight flit.

His car hadn't turned up either. He'd switched cars after knocking down and killing Cecelia Corrigan.

Popular psychology would suggest that he did so because the car reminded him of that painful memory. Well, maybe. He'd bought a used Honda, metallic blue, 2002 registration. A search of car parks and side-streets in the city had failed to uncover it abandoned. Police patrols remained on the lookout for it but without much hope.

Of course, if his disappearance *was* the result of foul play, whoever was responsible would make every effort to get rid of the incriminating evidence, including the car.

But how to dispose of a car? Bodies can be dumped down abandoned wells, buried under a new patio, put inside existing graves, fed to animals. Generally the best way to get cars out of sight effectively was either to send them to the auto crusher, or to have them resprayed and fitted with fresh number plates. Inquiries were pursued on both fronts.

It all came back to the same question: *why* was Mark Hudson missing? Dublin wasn't like London or New York. Unlike those places, it wasn't a place where the world's detritus came to burrow down, unseen, in the city's cracks, where those who have spent a lifetime cultivating anonymity for usually malicious ends congregate.

But until we answered that question, the rest might remain for ever hidden.

Becky Corrigan hadn't been much help. She recalled seeing Hudson around the weekend he vanished, but they hadn't spoken and she didn't know him well

enough, she claimed, to detect any weirdness in his behaviour that might suggest something was up.

She also flat denied that he could have intended in any way to kill her aunt. She'd been in the car. She *knew* how it had happened. She'd *seen* it — "with my own eyes", as she put it. (Why do people always say that? Like there was a way they could've seen it with someone else's eyes instead.) On this, she was certain. Maybe Hudson had been distracted by talking to her, maybe he'd taken his eyes off the road for a second, but do it deliberately? No way.

I didn't think much of her story, but Fitzgerald had an irritating habit of asking me to prove my hunches with evidence and that wasn't possible, mainly because there wasn't any.

All I knew is that it all seemed a bit too neat that Hudson would've given her a lift that night, but then Becky said he often picked her up on his way home, in fact she suspected he had a thing for her, that he deliberately arranged the times of his journeys in the hope that he'd get the chance to offer her a lift, though she insisted their relationship went no further than casual friendship. He wasn't her type, she said.

And, in truth, I had no good reason to suspect her of lying about it. Becky benefited from her aunt's death, but that didn't mean she'd colluded in it.

I'd benefit from my mother dying too, since I'd get a half share, along with my brother, in the family mansion — OK, so it's a decaying town house in downtown Boston, but I keep up to date with the real-estate prices in New England and it was still worth

getting hold of — but that didn't mean I should be hauled in as a suspect when she finally croaks.

Not that I hadn't seriously considered the attractions of bumping the old girl off in my time. Sure, everyone's had the same thoughts, no? Or is that just me?

The more we delved, the less there seemed to go on. Hudson's mental state remained unfathomable. Was he depressed? Did he feel bad about killing Cecelia? Might he have taken his own life in despair? Guilt could do that to a person, but in Hudson's case such lines of inquiry couldn't be any more than guesswork and speculation. Whoever said no man is an island should have tried meeting Hudson. He wouldn't have been so sure then.

Normally in missing persons' cases, there's a long list of people whose testimony can be sifted for hints of the elusive one's likely whereabouts. Wives, ex-wives, cuckolded husbands, children, business associates, relatives, folks they owned money to, folks who owed *them* money, even the police if they'd ever found themselves on the wrong side of the law.

Hudson's only contact with the police had been following Cecelia Corrigan's death, and, like the dead woman's niece, Sergeant Chase continued to insist that there was no more to that than had been immediately apparent. There was no reason to doubt either of them.

But that still didn't explain where Hudson was right now.

Pictures of Buck Randall were circulated discreetly around the area, to Hudson's few friends, work

colleagues, Becky herself, but they failed to elicit any positive response.

No one had seen Buck Randall here, just as no one had seen him in the vicinity where Marsha Reed died, and none of her friends, either those at the theatre or at the sex club where she'd gone to get her fun, could place his face. His fingerprints were also conspicious by their absence in the converted church where she died. The whole thing looked like one huge red herring, and Seamus Dalton didn't hesitate to remind me of this when I returned to Dublin Castle.

I sat at a borrowed desk, wondering again what the hell I was really doing here. It was early days, but I was painfully conscious of my failure to bring any of those skills to the table that Assistant Commissioner Stella Carson had hoped I would. At least with Kaminski, I would've known what I was doing. At least I would've been doing something useful, especially if, as I was increasingly starting to suspect, there turned out to be no connection whatsoever between Buck Randall's presence in the city and the death of Jenkins Howler's lonely penfriend.

And yet how could there *not* be a connection? The only other explanation was that the two things were a coincidence, and how likely was that? Though maybe I should revise my scepticism in the light of experience. Sometimes chance takes a hand. Like the time I saw Kaminski in Temple Bar. Likewise, if Dermot Bryce hadn't quarrelled with his wife on a particular night, or he hadn't left the house to go walking and calm down, or he'd taken a different path, or gone to a late-night

café instead, or didn't watch the news, or didn't believe in helping the police, we might have floundered a lot longer.

But that was all still to come. At that precise moment, I'd never even heard of Dermot Bryce, and I had no idea how important his recollections would turn out to be.

"You look like you need rescuing," said Healy eventually. "Want to come with me?"

The trip was worth it alone for the look on Todd Fleming's face when we saw us walking into the café. I'd say we were both the last people he'd expected to see — and also the last ones he *wanted* to see, with the one exception of Fitzgerald herself. He'd been spared that at least.

"This is early for the night shift," remarked Sean Healy affably.

"I'm covering for someone," Fleming said.

"Sounds like a confession," said Healy.

Fleming looked momentarily alarmed before recovering his composure.

"If I ever feel the need to confess, I'll go find a priest," he said. "In the meantime, what can I get you? Coffee?"

"Coffee would be good. Black. No sugar," said Healy. "Saxon?"

"Nothing for me."

"You arrest Solomon yet?" Fleming asked as he reached for a cup and poured Healy his coffee. "Or

have you just come here to ask me some more pointless questions?"

"We're still in the middle of our investigation," Healy answered. "But, as it happens, we're not here to see you at all. Your boss left something for us. I'd say that's it up there."

Fleming followed the line of Healy's gaze until it rested on a brown envelope tucked behind a jar on a shelf above his head. The words *FAO Sergeant Healy* were scrawled across the front. Looked like Healy had been secretly demoted somewhere along the line.

Fleming reluctantly lifted down the envelope and slid it across the counter. His curiosity was obviously pricked as to what was inside, but he wasn't going to admit it by asking. All he said was: "Will that be everything?"

"No," said Healy. "We'll need the use of one of the computers. Is that a problem?"

"It's quiet," said Fleming by way of an answer.

"Then lead the way."

Fleming took us to one of the booths in the café. He was right about it being quiet. Apart from us, there was only one other customer, a young woman over by the door checking out cheap flights online. The lure of a foreign sun. Even so, Healy asked for the booth furthest from the counter, in a dim corner where we wouldn't be overlooked.

"This was where Marsha always sat," said Fleming as he switched on the screen and typed in the password, before adding sharply: "But then you probably knew that already."

As it happened, we hadn't known, but it soon made sense that she would have chosen this spot. What Healy had in the envelope was a printout of the websites which Marsha Reed had looked at during her visits to the internet café. Fitzgerald had asked the owner for a list and, once he'd spluttered a little about civil liberties and the Big Brother state, he'd agreed to see what he could do. The internet was a felons' paradise. Terrorists, pornographers, people traffickers, drug smugglers: they all operated under its sheltering wing. And where they went, the law was bound to follow. First Amendment devotees might not like it, but the police couldn't afford to allow any public space to remain out of surveillance. And the internet, as many of its habitual users frequently failed to realize, was the most public space of all. Nothing that happened there was ever truly private. Hence, all it took to locate a record of Marsha Reed's internet use was the computer she had used and the times she had accessed it.

And, like I say, it then didn't take a genius to figure out why she preferred this dim haven in the corner. The kind of websites she'd visited in the café were not the kinds you'd want to share with any casual observer looking over your shoulder as you surfed.

First there were websites set up as anonymous forums where other like-minded souls who shared Marsha's sexual proclivities could make contact, swap stories and tips, arrange to meet up. There were sites listing clubs in other cities — maybe she'd visited them on her own travels, or maybe she was just curious to know what was out there — and weblogs by people

who wanted to record every aspect of their sex lives, in considerable detail, for the benefit of strangers online. Mostly, though, Marsha's interests on the internet had revolved around her private studies into murder, which had also been evinced by her book collection.

From my own reading, I was anecdotally familiar with the content of many of the websites Marsha had regularly visited, but it still made me feel uncomfortable seeing them for myself. These were not forums which had been set up to collate academic research into serial murder, but more like fan sites on which users were invited and encouraged to trade their own enthusiasms for their "favourite" killers or to rank crimes, as in a popularity poll, according to various sick criteria. There were plenty of photographs too, many of which must have come from the original police investigation teams from across the world: the United States, the Far East, Europe. Murder was the ultimate loss of privacy. The bodies of the dead were inevitably reduced to the raw stuff of police work. This, though, added a new and unnecessary dimension to the unavoidable indignity. At the click of a button, the intimacies of the crime scene were now translated into instant entertainment for voyeurs.

There was nothing in the photographs I hadn't seen a thousand times before, and not just through the impersonal gaze of the camera but up close, drawn inexorably into the dark aura that the dead weave around them, near enough to touch, near enough to smell. But it wasn't the content of the pictures which shocked, but the heartless context in which they were

being so casually and thoughtlessly presented. It made me angry, wondering what Marsha Reed had seen in these places, what primitive pleasure she had taken from them, if it was indeed pleasure that she'd been looking for when she visited them. Would the pictures of *her* crime scene end up online too? I wondered what she would've thought of that. Would that have made her understand the violation involved? Or would it have turned her on more?

I didn't know her well enough to answer that.

I didn't know her at all.

Angry or not, I kept my feelings in check. My feelings had no place. This was what investigation was all about. It was about detaching yourself from the passions that surrounded murder so that you could see them more clearly. Getting too involved was fatal.

I should know.

I made that mistake all the time.

Sean Healy barely spoke a word as we worked. His eyes were fixed to the screen, silently taking in what he saw, missing nothing; he only made occasional notes.

His coffee grew cold.

Across the café, I sensed Todd Fleming watching intently whenever he got the chance. The radio had been playing when we walked in. It was now switched off, as if he needed to concentrate and the noise of it had been distracting him.

Did he know what we were looking at?

Did he fear we might find something we weren't supposed to know about?

Once, accidentally, I caught his gaze from across the café.

He didn't look away and I felt like I'd been caught out doing something shameful, without being able to say precisely what the shame was meant to be for.

Before I could say a word to Healy about it, though, he whistled softly.

"Would you take a look at this?" he said.

I found Fisher in the canteen at Dublin Castle, picking half-heartedly through a limp salad. Miranda must've put him on a diet. Poor chump.

"Have you got a moment?" I said.

"For you," he said, pushing away the plate with gratitude, "always. Besides, I have nothing much to do until the reception tonight."

"The reception?"

I'd forgotten. There was going to be some party that night for Stella Carson to let her meet and greet the press and local bigwigs. I was supposed to be going there myself. I guess there wasn't much chance of getting out of it.

"You're not running home to Miranda, then?"

"Miranda won't be home till later," he said, "and I don't fancy being out there by myself. It's not like there's anything there for me when I'm on my own."

He was probably thinking of Laura and the children again.

"You don't like the neighbours?"

"I hardly see the neighbours. Not during the day, anyway. It's a ghost town. They're all at work."

"Not everyone is as fortunate as us. They have to work for a living."

"I know. It's such a bore. But it's not that. It's the kind of people they are. They're all investment bankers, insurance brokers, MDs of their own companies. I have nothing in common with these people. Even when I do bump into them, I have nothing to say to them."

"I'm sure you manage," I observed wryly.

Fisher had never been lost for words for long.

"I manage," he acknowledged, "but with no conviction. Who are these people? Where did they come from? What language do they speak? They're an alien species to me. Still, I suppose that's what work's for, isn't it? To fill the emptiness."

"Speaking of which . . ."

I opened the flap of the folder I was carrying and took out a sheaf of printouts to show Fisher what Healy and I had found on the computer at the internet café.

I soon had his attention.

"She was soliciting strangers online to murder her?" he said.

The merest raise of an eyebrow was the only surprise Fisher allowed himself to show. I guess when you've seen and heard everything, there's not much that can shock you any more. And Fisher had seen just about all there was to see in his time.

"Consensual homicide," he said. "Interesting. There was a similar case in the United States about ten years ago. I don't remember the precise details. A woman from Maryland — a happily married businesswoman, by all accounts — used the internet to arrange for a

stranger to sexually torture and then kill her. Police found that her computer contained hundreds of pages of email in which she'd been trying to convince people to kill her too."

"Sharon Lopatka," I said. "I remember. She was tortured for days before being killed. Christ knows what was going on in her head. There was also a German man who agreed to torture and kill his companion and then eat his remains. He was only arrested when he posted a request for more victims. I'm sure Marsha Reed must've come across the cases."

"And got the idea from that?"

"It's a possibility," I said.

"If she was a willing participant, that would certainly explain why the cords weren't tightened so fast. The ethics of it are fascinating," Fisher added. "If the victim wants it to happen, does that make it murder? If death is what Marsha sought, was she victim or perpetrator?"

"Murder is murder," I said with certainty. "Just because the victim might want what happens to them doesn't mean you have the right to do it. And we can't say for certain that this was what Marsha really wanted. She might've been using the exchanges as an outlet for some private fantasy of hers. We don't know she ever really intended to go through with it. And she never once in all those emails reveals her real name. She only gives a phone number. That hasn't been traced either. There's no evidence it even belonged to her."

"The Mardi Gras phenomenon, they call it," said Fisher. "You assume disguises, masks, to take on various personalities and act them out without

consequences. The internet's the perfect place to do that. It explains, at any rate, why she didn't have a computer in her own house. I did wonder about that. Her father seems to have bought her everything else. This was another part of her life that she wanted to keep secret, separate, neatly fenced off."

"Pretty risky, using a public computer in an internet café."

"Not when you have someone who works there eating out of the palm of your hand. Besides, why should she worry that anyone would be interested in her internet activities? She was just another customer in just another café. Ms Anonymous." He paused. "Did anyone express an interest in taking her up on the offer, by the way?"

"She'd corresponded for weeks with a couple of dodgy characters," I said, "batting scenarios back and forth. There, all the details are on the next page. See? But it seemed to come to nothing. They expressed an initial interest, then backed off."

"Maybe they got scared off when they began to suspect she was serious. Well, it shouldn't be too difficult to trace them and get their version of events. But even if they have a perfectly innocent explanation for what they were doing, that doesn't mean she didn't excite someone else's interest, someone who then managed to track her down independently."

"So it could be anyone in the whole of cyberspace?"

"Practically," said Fisher.

"That doesn't exactly narrow down the suspects, does it?"

292

"Don't forget the money too," he added.

"The money?"

"In her purse the night she died. The taxi driver saw it when she was looking for her key. According to her bank records, Marsha had taken out five thousand in cash that afternoon. What if that money was to pay someone to kill her?"

"The subject of money's never mentioned in any of her emails."

"But she didn't find anyone to do what she asked of them that way, did she? What if she realized she had to make other arrangements? Find a professional?"

"But what — ? Why —?"

I gave up.

"Marsha's lost me," I said. "What was she *doing*?"

"You'll never understand other people's desires, other people's deepest needs," Fisher said. "It's futile to try. That's one thing I have learned. What goes on in people's heads will always be a mystery. That's what makes them so dangerous."

"Victims aren't supposed to be as dangerous as their killers," I said stubbornly.

"When are you ever going to understand that there are no rules when it comes to murder? Everything is chaos and surprise. That's what makes this job so interesting."

"You're saying I should see it as a good thing that nothing makes sense any more?"

"There are worse things than being baffled," he observed placidly.

"There are also worse things than walking stark naked round St Stephen's Green," I said, "but that doesn't mean you have to recommend it as a lifestyle choice. And what if our bafflement leads to some other woman being butchered? Have you thought about that?"

"Saxon, my dear, right now I am thinking about precious little else."

CHAPTER
TWENTY-SIX

"This isn't my idea of a party," said Walsh.

"This isn't anybody's idea of a party," I answered. "And if it *is* somebody's idea of a party, I don't want to have the misfortune of ever meeting them."

We were standing in a large room in the Parliament Hotel, at the top of Dame Street, almost directly opposite Dublin Castle. A wall of windows looked out on to buses passing below. Traffic was heading home. Waiters circulated inside with trays bearing drinks, and there was a free bar until nine. That was something at least. I was clutching a bottle of warm beer and wondering what I was doing here. I knew what Kaminski would say I was doing here. Kissing ass, that's what he'd say. And maybe he was right.

The room was crowded with people I didn't know and didn't particularly want to get to know. Patrick Walsh, who'd grabbed hold of me almost as soon as I'd arrived and saved me from splendid isolation, was taking time to point out a few of them to me.

"See that guy over there with the bad hairpiece? He's in charge of the DMP press office. That short guy who looks a bit like Hitler, only not quite so pleasant? That's the Assistant Commissioner for Traffic." And on he

went, telling me who had screwed who to get what positions and the gossip about the various people in various departments. Some of the guests needed no introduction. I recognized their faces, in particular the huddles of reporters, getting snippets for the weekly social diaries charting who was hot and who was not in Dublin public life. It was certainly good for public relations to have a woman taking over the Murder Squad. They wanted to make sure they got as much capital out of it as they could.

"Here, pass me another one of those beers. I seem to be empty. Thanks. You know, you don't have to stand here with me. You can circulate if you want. I'll be fine."

"No problem. Besides, I'm trying to avoid someone."

"Anyone I know?"

"See the woman over there with the tits?"

"Don't they all have them?"

"Not like those," said Walsh with an appreciative leer, then the smile vanished when he saw the look I returned. "Sorry," he said. "Sometimes I forget you're a woman."

"Thanks, I needed that."

"No, I mean it in a good way," he said quickly. "Usually with a woman these days, you have to watch everything you say or they start looking at you like you've broken some golden rule of the sisterhood. With you, I don't feel like you're judging me. I don't have to be so careful what I say. I can say what I'm really thinking. That's a good thing, isn't it?"

"I guess so." I was still trying to work out whether I'd just been on the receiving end of a compliment or an insult and whether it mattered whether someone actually insulted you when what they'd been trying to do was say something nice. In the end I gave up.

"You were telling me about the woman with the tits," I reminded him. "I presume you're seeing her?"

"And trust me, there's plenty worth seeing," he said.

"So why are you trying to avoid her?"

"She's been moving a little too fast for my liking," he said. "She always wants us to be spending time together, she wants to know where I'm going, what I'm doing, she even asked me a couple of nights ago for my home phone number."

"Women today," I said sardonically. "What are they like? Just because they've let you have ramblers' rights over their bodies, they think they ought to be able to call you."

"She has my mobile phone number, what else does she want? I need my space," said Walsh. "I know the score. They start by asking for your number and then they want to know where you are all the time and then they tell you that you're drinking too much and before you know it they're saying they love you and want to have your baby."

"And you deduced all this from the fact she asked for your home phone number?"

"I can read the signs," he said confidently. "And I figured that if she saw me with another woman, she'd make a scene. She can be . . . fiery. Women can be very vengeful, you know." And that was true enough. "The

truth is I don't believe in monogamy. It's not natural for men and women to stay together for ever, don't you agree?"

"I've never had a problem with monogamy," I said. "When I'm with someone, I'm with them. I don't usually look around for a replacement."

"I couldn't be like that. It's only natural to try out what else is available."

"Maybe it's a male thing," I said with a shrug.

"Most of the women I know are like that too. Maybe there's just something wrong with your sex drive." And he said it so pleasantly that I was again stumped as to how to respond to what sounded like an insult. But I never got the chance, because he suddenly interrupted his own thoughts with a low appreciative murmur: "Hello."

Another woman had caught his eye on the other side of the room. She was tall, dark-haired, with mischievous eyes and prominent cheekbones and a great figure. She was smiling politely at something her companion, a small dumpy man that Walsh had already identified to me as an inspector with the Immigration Office, had said to her.

The smile verged on a grimace.

"Now that's more like it," he said. "Who is she?"

"That's Stella Carson's daughter," I said. "I saw a picture of her in the Assistant Commissioner's office. She's a lawyer."

"What's her name?"

"Sally, I think. You're not going to make a move, are you?"

"Why not?" he said. "It could be good for my career, going out with the boss's daughter. I'd be like one of the family. I'd make Inspector two years tops."

"Unless you cheated on her and broke her heart and the outraged mother decides you're being transferred to the Dogs Division. Mothers can be very protective."

"I never thought of that." Walsh looked disappointed, until another thought struck him: "But it couldn't hurt to just talk, could it? Wait here. I'll not be long. I'm a fast worker."

Walsh checked his appearance quickly in a nearby mirror before starting a nifty sideways dance to where Sally Carson was beginning to look a little less than delighted by the anecdotes of Mr Immigration. I couldn't help smiling at Walsh's talent for getting himself into emotional tangles, until I became aware that someone was staring at me.

I looked over and saw the infamous woman with the tits and the bad habit of asking men for their home phone numbers glaring at me with obvious dislike. I was clearly being put down as the big bad wolf who'd stolen boy wonder away from her.

"It's OK," I wanted to tell her, "I never date anyone who needs to shave their back."

But I doubted she would've believed me.

Suddenly weary, I wondered how long it would be before I could sneak away without my absence being noted. Assuming, that is, that my presence had been noted anyway.

I began to walk slowly round the room because, when you're on the move, you can always pretend that

you have something to do and somewhere to go. I estimated I could spend an hour making my way round and round the room, like a goldfish in a bowl, avoiding conversation, before I got so dizzy I fell over.

I hadn't gone far when I spotted Fitzgerald. She was standing with Stella Carson and Sean Healy and the mighty Commissioner himself at the far end of the room. I hadn't spoken to her since arriving. It was one of those occasions when we both decided it was judicious to stay discreetly apart — so as not to frighten the horses, as it were. The Commissioner knew about our relationship, sure he did, but I sensed it was something he preferred to know about in the abstract, like a mathematical equation, rather than have the evidence in front of him.

They were all laughing at something one of them had said. Probably one of the Commissioner's bad jokes. Fitzgerald had a very expressive mouth. I often found myself watching her talk, not necessarily hearing what she said, but just liking the way it moved.

She'd also loosened her hair so that it hung down her neck. She told me once that she'd had hair down to her waist as a child and having to cut it was the saddest thing she'd ever had to do. It was, she said, like the end of childhood. Me, I couldn't get out of my childhood fast enough, but I could see how the symbolism might've meant more to her.

When she wore her hair loose, it was like she was free in some indefinable way.

It was then that the Assistant Commissioner reached out and touched Fitzgerald's arm. It was nothing, a

gesture to command attention, and yet for a moment it made me angry, and I was surprised at myself. I'd never been the jealous type before. It shocked me.

I turned away in irritation, hating the irrationality of thoughts. The way you had no power over them. The way they just came unbidden and unwanted, and drove out all self-possession. I took a deep breath and told myself not to be so stupid.

It didn't help.

At that moment, I wanted to get out of there.

Be alone.

On the way out, I met Walsh coming back from the men's room. He looked sheepish, but it was too dim at first for me to see what was wrong with him.

"You had enough?" he said.

"I need some air," I told him.

It was a plausible enough lie.

"I'll come with you. I could do with getting some air myself."

"Honestly, I just want some time to myself. What's up with you, anyway? I thought you were moving in on the younger Miss Carson?"

"Let's just say I don't think that's going to work out."

He stepped forward a little into the light and I saw that he had the beginnings of an impressive black eye. So *that's* why he'd looked so sheepish.

"She hit you?" I said, amazed.

"Not Sally. Lucy."

"Lucy being the girl from Vice?"

"She saw me chatting up Sally. I told you she'd make a scene. She just came right over and kapow. The woman's fucking nuts. What did I tell you about them being spiteful?"

"What did Sally Carson say?"

"When she stops laughing, I'll let you know."

"Don't let it bother you. Women can be vengeful, surely you've realized that by now? And I'm sure your male ego will survive. There are plenty more women upstairs for you."

"True," he said, brightening. "You're sure you don't want me to come with you?"

"Walsh, you're a sweet guy, and I appreciate the offer, I do. But I couldn't forgive myself if I came between you and your raging libido. I don't want to cramp your style."

"If you put it like that," he said, "it does seem a shame to deny the women of Dublin the incomparable pleasure of my body on such a warm summer's evening. Wish me luck."

"You don't seem to need it," I pointed out. "Except with Lucy."

"Ouch," he said. "What'd you have to go reminding me about her for?"

CHAPTER
TWENTY-SEVEN

I didn't feel like returning home straight away. I was restless, antsy, disgruntled with myself and the world. Nothing new there, then. I needed to walk. But I scarcely noticed where I was going because I was still thinking about Stella Carson's reception. Had Fitzgerald been trying to make me jealous back there, to punish me in some way for not telling her about Kaminski and me? Was she trying to send me a message not to take her for granted? Telling me that if I didn't appreciate her, there were plenty of other people who would?

No, I was being paranoid. She hadn't even known I was there. She had her back turned to me the whole time. I was making myself unhappy for no reason.

Perhaps I was simply feeling vulnerable. Fitzgerald had always spent more time in work than out of it, it came with the territory, but there'd never been anyone that she worked with before that I could have imagined her having anything other than a professional relationship with. Now there was someone who, given different circumstances, it didn't take a huge leap of imagination to suppose could spark a mutual attraction. Stella Carson was a good-looking woman.

After her recent divorce, she was available. Nothing was unthinkable.

The city that night was hot. Suffocatingly hot. The weather still showed no signs of breaking. The streets were crowded and noisy, like they'd been a couple of nights ago when Fitzgerald and I had walked back to my apartment from the bar. I even thought I recognized some of the same faces, taking advantage of the warm while it lasted — which in Dublin, it rarely did. It was exactly the same scene, except that tonight the city had become infested with a kind of malignancy. Everything which had seemed healthy and vital now seemed rank, rotten, like meat left out in the sun too long. It even felt like it was getting hotter rather than cooler as the night got later, as if everything were conspiring to just feel wrong.

I didn't know how the other people in the streets couldn't feel it too. How it didn't ruin everything for them. Could they not smell the city going bad?

It was the kind of heat that makes people angry. And maybe I'd been touched a little by that myself. It was almost as if something was about to explode or catch fire. The streets needed a dousing of rain to slake their thirst and cool their fever, but there was no chance of that. The sky was drier than an African plain, cloudless and cracked like a dirt track.

Everywhere I walked, I saw signs of the festering mood which had gripped the city. In the crimson sweating faces of the people that I passed. Their exposed roasted flesh. The scent of food in the air, usually so inviting, now sickened me. A man stood on

the corner of Molesworth Street cramming a burger into his mouth like a python greedily swallowing its prey whole, and the juices ran down his chin like blood. Another stood near by, urinating through the bars of a metal grille covering the doorway of an office. A man and a woman stood arguing loudly on the junction of Ely Place and Merrion Row. There was a dead dog decaying on the banks of the Grand Canal. Garbage floated by on the water's oily surface. The smell was bad here, and getting worse. The weeds looked like strips of raw flesh.

Gradually I realized that I wasn't walking without purpose or direction. Without knowing it, I had been making my way to Kaminski's hotel. I found myself standing across the road from its weathered old stone façade, looking up to where I imagined his window to be.

Was he in?

Fitzgerald hadn't mentioned whether she'd put the tail on Kaminski that she'd talked about that morning, but I guessed so. If she said she'd do something, she did it. Even so, I knew any tail on Kaminski would prove fruitless. He'd know he was being followed and adjust his patterns accordingly. He knew how to make his daily existence as anonymous and lacking in trace evidence as Mark Hudson's was looking right now. He'd proved that in North Carolina. I checked out the street in front of the hotel quickly to see if I could detect where the watching officers might be positioned. A stationary silver car a hundred yards away with blacked-out windows looked the most promising.

Unless, I thought, it was Buck Randall himself, keeping an eye on the object he was tormenting. Now wouldn't that be something?

I wandered over and knocked on the car window.

Nothing.

So I knocked again. Louder. This time, the window descended slowly with a whirr. In the driver's seat sat a man who couldn't have been more obviously a police officer had he walked about with the words *Police Officer* tattooed on his forehead in flourescent ink.

"What's he doing?" I said.

"Sorry?" he replied with a show of incomprehension. But he had the look of a schoolboy caught out looking at another kid's test.

"Kaminski," I said. "The guy you're watching. What's he been at?"

There was a long pause.

"Do I know you?" he said eventually.

I explained who I was.

Showed him my nice new shiny ID to prove it.

"I heard about you," he conceded reluctantly.

"Then can I get in?" I said. "Don't worry, I'm not going to ask to play with your truncheon. I just don't want JJ to see me if he's up there."

He looked bemused again.

"JJ?"

"JJ . . . Kaminski . . . look, can we continue this conversation behind blacked-out glass?"

By now anyone walking by would've thought I was a hooker fishing for a client.

306

With a grunt, the surveillance guy finally unlocked the door and let me in, and I slid into the passenger seat, grateful at least for the air conditioning inside.

Cool air played with my hair, and I let it.

"So you know the target?" the driver said to me.

"We used to work together," I said, "back in the States. We were in the same FBI field unit. That's why I thought I'd come along tonight and see what's happening."

Another expressive grunt.

"Nothing is what's happening," he said. "Far as we know, he hasn't left his room all afternoon. He had his dinner brought up, some drinks from the bar, and that's about it."

"Who else is watching?"

"We've got one more keeping an eye on the rear of the building. That's the only exit apart from the firedoors, and they'll set off the alarm anyway if they're opened. He can't get out without our knowing."

"Isn't that what they said about Clint Eastwood in *Escape from Alcatraz*?"

As if on cue, a voice crackled on to the police radio. "*He's moving.*"

And a moment later, we were gazing out of the windshield at the steps of the hotel, where Kaminski could now be seen, still looking dishevelled, ruffling his hair. He barely looked up from the ground as he descended the steps and set off along the sidewalk in the direction of town. He certainly didn't look across at the car in which we sat. Maybe he really hadn't noticed it. He was distracted right now, after all. Or maybe he

was only making it seem as if he hadn't. I couldn't help wondering if he'd seen me climbing inside and this was his way of yanking my chain. Making me think he was going somewhere.

Making me think he was on his way to meet someone.

Someone like Buck Randall.

Chances were he was just going to pick up another bottle of Jack Daniel's, but I still felt as if something was about to happen. Maybe that's what the strange atmosphere in the city that night had been preparing me for.

I reached for the door handle.

"What are you doing?"

"I want to follow on foot."

"You can't follow him, you don't have — Hey, come back!"

I stayed on the other side of the street, keeping Kaminski in view, ready to dodge out of sight if he became suspicious of being followed. But he didn't turn round once. He just walked straight on. A man with a purpose. Or was I simply reading in his actions what I wanted to see? Soon he had crossed the Grand Canal and continued on to Lower Baggot Street. Doubt grew. If Randall had managed to make contact with Kaminski to arrange a meeting, why not somewhere quieter? Or did he want the safety of the crowd around him?

The city began to fill up again, with the same sweating, shouting, laughing, partying summer souls as before, only now they made less impression on me than

the breath of a butterfly. My entire attention was focused on Kaminski and his mission.

Wait.

What was this? Kaminski had approached a man standing in a doorway and was talking to him. Could this be ... Then the man raised his arm and pointed further down the street, and I realized Kaminski had only been asking for directions.

A mute wave of thanks and he was on the move again.

I tried to suppress an ache of disappointment when I saw where Kaminski had apparently been going — an all-night chemist just past Roger's Lane.

Kaminski pushed open the door and disappeared inside.

I edged closer to the glass and looked inside.

Kaminski had stopped in an aisle less than six feet away from me, looking at boxes of painkillers. So much for the big mystery. He was probably just trying to shift a headache from all that Tennessee whiskey earlier. He lifted a packet down and headed to the counter to pay.

I turned and saw the surveillance guy from the car standing across the street at the bus stop, trying his best to look inconspicuous and failing miserably.

He made a gesture as if to say: *What's he doing?*

I shrugged.

I managed to get out of sight before Kaminski emerged from the chemist with his box of pills, and I smiled to myself as his eyes glanced across the street briefly at his pursuer. It would take more than

pretending to check out a bus timetable to fool Kaminski.

Had he seen me too?

I wouldn't be surprised.

He set off again in the direction of his hotel, and I couldn't decide whether to bother following him back there. The whole evening seemed to have been a waste of effort on my part, like I'd been trying to prove something to myself without knowing what it was I was trying to prove. I should just head home. My apartment was close. At that moment, bed seemed like the best idea I'd had in a long while. But soon I was glad I stayed out.

There was some kind of disturbance up ahead on the corner of James Street East. A small huddle of people had gathered round in a ring, like they were getting ready for some impromptu teamtalk. Kaminski's steps slowed as he neared them.

In the gaps between the legs of the people watching, I could see a young woman kneeling on the ground, barefoot, grasping the front of her loose nightdress and pulling it tightly to her frame, in an effort to cover herself. The nightdress was torn. She was crying. As I got closer, unconcerned now whether Kaminski saw me, I heard her voice.

Choking.

Pleading.

The breath catching in her throat.

"Don't let him come back," she was telling them. "Please, keep him away from me."

"What is it?" someone asked her.

Between sobs that racked her body like electric shocks, she finally managed to force out the words.

"He tried to kill me," she said.

He tried to kill me.

And then she started screaming.

CHAPTER
TWENTY-EIGHT

"What happened to *you* last night?" said Fitzgerald when she called next morning.

For a second, I didn't know what she was talking about.

"I was with Rose Downey, remember?" I said, naming the woman that I'd found crouched and frightened on the ground on the road to Kaminski's hotel the previous night.

"That's my point. You'd gone by the time I got there," said Fitzgerald. "I was looking for you. Healy told me you were on the scene when he arrived. Next thing, you were gone."

"I didn't feel so hot."

"A headache?"

"I just wanted to get home."

I guess I didn't sound too convincing.

"You OK?" pressed Fitzgerald. "You sound strange."

"It's nothing. Forget it. Like I said, I don't feel so hot."

"Last time you used that line it was in the past tense," Fitzgerald said. "You've deteriorated quickly. Would you rather stay home today?"

"I was thinking of dropping by the hospital to see Rose again."

"There's not much point. The doctors still have her sedated. They won't let us question her yet. They say she's not strong enough. She had a pretty traumatic ordeal."

"You didn't manage to get anything out of her about what happened, then?"

"All she said last night was that she came back to her apartment in James's Place East after a night out with friends, got undressed and ready for bed, and as soon as she turned out the light he jumped on her. He must've been hiding in her bedroom the whole time. Christ knows how she managed to get out, but somehow she managed to open the door and escape."

"No description?"

"Says she didn't see his face, nor did he say a word. And of course, by the time we got her address out of her, he was long gone."

"You think it's the same guy?"

"Who knows? We'll have a better idea over the next couple of hours, once her apartment's been properly analysed. The lock on the door was already broken, apparently, so there's no sign of any break-in, there was no need for it, and no restraints were used, but then he didn't have time to finish the job, so who knows what way things may have turned out? I'll be able to give you more details over lunch, if you're interested. There's a price, though. I want you to do something for me first. You know Kim Denning?"

"Marsha Reed's friend. The one who found her body."

"That's her. She's going round to Marsha's house today to pick up some stuff. We've finished with it now. The keys are being handed back to the father later this afternoon. Apparently he didn't want to deal with clearing out his daughter's personal stuff, so Kim said she'd do it for him. I said I'd go round this morning to open up for her, but after the attack on Rose Downey and what you found out yesterday about Marsha's trips to the internet café, I've got too much to follow up. So what about it? Would you do it for me? I can pick you up at Marsha's place about one and we can go get something to eat together . . ."

Which is how I found myself walking round to Dublin Castle to pick up and sign for the key to Marsha Reed's house from the desk sergeant, and then continuing on down Patrick Street past the cathedral and over the junction toward Lower Clanbrassil Street.

At least an early night had cleared my head. I was feeling stupid again for allowing myself to be made to feel low by my suspicions. It's just that sometimes when you've lapsed into foolishness, it can be tempting to nurse the foolishness longer than is healthy. In all these years Fitzgerald had never given me a moment's cause to doubt her.

She deserved better than my paranoia.

My moods.

I turned off into Fumbally Lane, relishing, as I always did when I came here, the almost Dickensian quality of the old street names in this area of the city:

Ebenezer Terrace, Marrowbone Lane, Black Pitts. When so much else in the city had been prettified and sanitized, it was good to be reminded of the ancient dark heart still beating here.

Marsha Reed's father, Healy had told me, was blaming himself for his daughter's death for buying her a house in this district. He hadn't wanted her to live here. He could have afforded to fix her up with a place of her own in any part of the city. But St Gobnat's was what she wanted, so St Gobnat's was what she got. I got the impression she was the kind of girl who was used to getting what she wanted. The father had been left a widower when Marsha was still young. She'd been spoiled. I wondered if that was what made her seek out such extremes in her sexual life. Was she punishing herself because life had been too easy?

Then I admonished myself for indulging in this pop psychology.

I should leave that to Fisher's new girlfriend.

It was strange, though, how people had an instinct to blame themselves for things that weren't their fault. It wasn't living in this district which had killed Marsha. Most likely, it was her own bad choices which had done that, and there's nothing parents can do to stop their kids making those once they've flown the coop. Just ask my mother. It wouldn't have mattered where Marsha had lived in the city if her own desires were leading her into danger.

I guessed it would be sold now, I thought as I passed through the front gates and continued up the lane toward the church. Marsha's father would hardly want

to keep the place after what had happened to his only child within its walls. For a moment, the thought crossed my mind that we should buy it, Grace and I. That's what she wanted, wasn't it? A place together. And two weeks ago, maybe, it would've been perfect for us. Close to the city for me, peaceful enough for Grace. Did it make a difference that Marsha had died here? *Someone* would live here again. Why not us? And yet I knew, even as I framed the notion in my brain, that this was a non-starter. The house would be tainted for ever now.

"Oh."

The exclamation came from a red-haired young woman wearing flat shoes and what seemed like jodhpurs, sitting on the steps of the church and clutching a purple shoulder bag on her lap. She had a startled look on her face. I guess she hadn't heard me coming.

"I wasn't really sure what time I was supposed to be here," she explained, scrambling to her feet, once I'd introduced myself.

"You been waiting long?"

"About an hour," she said, considering. "I didn't mind. It's so beautiful in here, isn't it? I can't believe this is the last time I'll ever come here. I can't believe someone else is going to be moving in. Everything about it just reminds me so much of Marsha . . ."

She bit her lip gently. Whether it was simply an involuntary habit, or she was trying to stop herself from crying, I couldn't tell. I fitted the key into the lock to let us in.

"I know it sounds strange," she said, "but I'd buy it myself if I could. I wouldn't live here. I couldn't. I'd just hate someone to come and pull it down. Marsha loved it so much. After what happened, I wouldn't be surprised if her father had the whole place flattened."

"Why *don't* you buy it?"

She laughed hollowly. "I couldn't afford it. I'm an out-of-work actress. The last job I had was the voiceover for a radio ad for toothpaste. My work doesn't even pay my own rent, never mind the mortgage on a place like this."

"You met Marsha through the theatre, right?"

She nodded as she stepped into the hallway "We were appearing together in *A Midsummer Night's Dream* . . ." She stopped. "Listen," she said. "It's so quiet."

It was. The last time I'd been inside the church, Fisher had been talking, detectives had been coming and going, trailing a perpetual echo of footsteps and murmured voices.

Now I knew what the phrase "silent as the grave" really meant.

This must have been what it was like for Marsha when she was on her own. This must have been what attracted her to the place. Once the door was shut, the world ceased to exist. All was still, undisturbed, uncomplicated. What a contrast to her own messy life.

"I should get started," Kim said, but she made no move to do so.

"Do you want me to come with you?" I said.

"Would you?"

We went through, crossing the main floor to the doors at the other end of the church and walking down the narrow corridor toward Marsha's closet. Kim took out a roll of black garbage bags from her shoulder bag and began to tear them off one by one. She started to fill them methodically with the clothes in Marsha's drawers and her shoes.

"I don't know what I'll do with all this stuff. Give it to the charity shop, I suppose. It doesn't seem right somehow," she said. "I know it's not like she has any use for them any more, but she was so passionate about her clothes. She was passionate about *everything*."

"Does that include Victor Solomon?" I said.

She shot me a look of flame.

"Don't talk to me about that bastard," she said. "He's the reason she's dead."

"You think Solomon killed Marsha?"

"He has an alibi, doesn't he? That's what I heard," said Kim. "I didn't mean he physically killed her. Just that if it hadn't been for him, she might still be alive now. All she wanted was to be with him. She was crazy about him. When he rejected her —"

"She put herself at risk trying to forget him?" I finished for her.

"I warned her," said Kim. "I knew she'd been going to that club downtown. She used to tell me about it. It was a giggle, that's all." I recalled that's what Todd Fleming said too. Marsha must have told that to everybody, trying to make the darkness of her desires seem routine and uncomplicated. "It was mostly role-playing, she said, dressing up, pretending to be

318

someone else for a few hours. Putting on a mask. It's like acting, yeah? I mean, I knew she had these *fantasies*," she went on reluctantly, "about being tied up, about being dominated, but if you knew her, you'd understand there was no harm in it. There's nothing wrong with a bit of kinkiness now and then, is there? It's not against the law. Everyone does it these days. They even sell those furry handcuffs on the high street now, don't they?"

From what we now knew of Marsha Reed's sex life, it had gone way beyond a bit of innocent kinky fun with furry handcuffs and silken binds, and I suspected that Kim Denning knew it too, which was why she was subconsciously turning all her statements about her friend into questions, like she was looking to me to back up her need to see all that Marsha did in the best light. I didn't puncture her illusions. I wanted to hear her talk.

"She told me she stopped going to the club after she met Victor," Kim said. "She wanted a different life. She wanted to be with him, but she said he wasn't interested in taking things further than a casual thing. Wham bam, thank you, ma'am. That was his style. He gets his kicks pushing the little people like me around on stage. But he wouldn't leave his adoring wife-to-be, and Marsha drifted back into her old world again. If she'd been with him, maybe she'd have been safe. Though whether he would've been is another matter."

"What do you mean?"

"Marsha was very possessive. I've never met anyone who could get so jealous. She'd just lose it completely

when she was mad. If anyone was going to kill anyone, I'd have said it was Marsha who'd kill him, never mind the other way round. She was furious when he said he didn't want her any more. She actually said she'd kill him. She said she'd kill him and then kill herself. I told her not to talk like that. It's ironic, really. If only she'd been more patient."

"More patient in what way?"

"Didn't you know?" she said, eyes widening in surprise as she paused momentarily from what she was doing. "Solomon's fiancée's dumped him. Everyone was talking about it last night. I met some friends for drinks last night. They're appearing in *Othello* at the moment. They said he was in a foul mood yesterday, and he had a blazing row with her and she ended up throwing his engagement ring back at him."

"So much for her forgiving him for his relationship with Marsha."

"I don't blame her," said Kim. "Marsha was no angel, I told her she shouldn't get involved with a man who was practically married. But Solomon's the one who was cheating, not Marsha. And it wasn't the first time either. He must've screwed most of the young actresses in Dublin. They think he's going to make them famous, but once he's taken what he wants he can't get rid of them fast enough. And yes, before you ask, he did it to me too. That's why I warned Marsha. I told her what he was like. But she wouldn't listen. She was convinced he really cared about her. I'm just glad he's finally got what was coming to him. Now he knows

what it feels like. I'm sorry it didn't come out sooner, that's all."

"What difference would it have made?" I asked.

"Maybe she'd have seen him for the scumbag that he really is," she said. "Maybe she'd have stopped torturing herself over him and found herself a nice guy for a change."

A guy like Todd Fleming, I thought.

Though sadly, as he found out, she didn't seem to want *nice*.

She didn't even seem to have wanted normal.

CHAPTER
TWENTY-NINE

"So where's lunch?" I said, when Fitzgerald finally pulled up in her Rover at the front gate of St Gobnat's. Kim Denning had left ten minutes earlier. She'd ordered a cab so that she could take all the black bags away with her. Now the church was empty of everything except furniture, and that would be taken away and sold soon enough, I guessed. All traces of Marsha would be gone.

"Bull Island," Fitzgerald said.

"Is that some fancy new restaurant I haven't heard of?" I said, already knowing the answer by the frowning look of concentration on her face.

"I'm afraid lunch will have to wait," she said.

"Something happened, huh? Is it Rose?"

"She's still not in a fit state to be interviewed formally. We've got a trauma counsellor on hand in case she feels like talking, but I'm not expecting a breakthrough any time soon. No, it's Mark Hudson. We found out this morning he spent some time in the States before taking up his job here in Dublin. He was living out in New Mexico."

New Mexico.

"Kaminski claimed Randall killed a woman in New Mexico."

"Hudson was staying in the same rooming house as the woman who died. He was questioned by the police and the FBI at the time, but he was never in the frame as a suspect."

"So Randall allegedly kills a woman in the same house Hudson's staying in, then allegedly turns up in Dublin, if Kaminski's to be believed, and now Hudson's gone missing?"

"And there's no allegedly about that part," Fitzgerald pointed out.

"There's something else too, isn't there?" I said.

"I think we may have found Hudson's car."

And that was compensation enough for missing lunch.

My stomach could wait.

As we drove back through the city centre and over the river, up Parnell Street and Summerhill, past Fairview Park and on to the road that snaked round by Clontarf Promenade, she explained to me what had happened that morning.

A man by the name of Dermot Bryce had called Dublin Castle. He'd heard a report on the morning news that police were looking for a metallic-blue Honda with a 2002 registration and remembered seeing one a couple of weeks earlier out along the Bull Wall.

The wall had been constructed, I'd read once, about two hundred years ago on the north side of Dublin Bay to provide shelter for the city port and make the

passage in and out easier for ships. Behind the wall, huge deposits of sand and silt had gradually been left by the tide and merged to form the so-called Bull Island, three miles long and still growing steadily.

The whole area was now a protected nature reserve, home to thousands of migrating birds such as geese and oystercatchers, as well as housing two golf courses (sometimes I think the whole world is being turned into a golf course). Dubliners often went out to walk or swim, crossing the wooden road-bridge that connected the island to the mainland.

It was the way Bryce had gone that night after quarrelling with his wife.

"I wanted to be by myself for a while," he explained when we finally found him waiting for us near the coastguard station, as arranged. He worked as a porter at Central Station and was still wearing his uniform, peaked cap and all. He only had another twenty minutes of his lunch break to go, he informed Fitzgerald grumpily. She told him not to be concerned. If he was needed for longer, she'd make sure the station was kept informed.

He didn't look convinced. He looked, in fact, like he was thinking that a call from the Murder Squad was the last thing to make his boss feel happier about a missing employee.

"The sooner you tell us what you saw," Fitzgerald urged, "the sooner you can go."

"I was over there," Bryce said, pointing further along the road that ran along the Bull Wall and which looked from this angle as if it dropped eventually and

disappeared into the sea. And maybe it did, for all I knew. "Right where that red car is now. You see it? I was just standing there, having a cigarette, looking out, thinking."

It was certainly one hell of a view, if you could ignore the huge container terminals that dominated the foreshore in the middle distance. Blank those out and the great sweep of Dublin Bay stretched before us, sparkling fiercely in the sunlight, with mountains huddled protectively in the distance, heads wreathed in white clouds so perfect they were like drawings, stone guardians watching over the city that crowded untidily at their feet.

"There was hardly anyone about," Bryce said. "It wasn't hot like it is now, it was raining, and it must've been after eleven o'clock. You don't see too many people out here when it's like that. That's probably why he thought I was this Peters fella."

"Why *who* thought you were?" I said, bemused.

"This man who came along. He was an American, like you. Wearing one of those baseball caps. I'd seen him coming over the bridge in this car, just as I told your people earlier, and he parked right next to me down there and got out and asked me if I was Peters."

"What did he say when you told him you weren't?" asked Fitzgerald.

"He laughed, that was all, then he told me they had to meet a man here by the name of Peters, who was supposed to be buying the car off them."

"Them?" I said.

"There was another man in the front seat. I didn't see his face."

Mark Hudson?

"What did you think of his story?" asked Fitzgerald.

"Seemed like a funny place to be selling a car," admitted Bryce, "but it was none of my business. Even if he was up to no good, what was *I* supposed to do about it?"

"So what happened then?"

"To be honest with you, I was worried to start off that the pair of them might be queer, you know? That they might've thought I was that way inclined myself. But he wasn't interested once he knew I wasn't this Peters. He just got back in the car again."

"Did the two men drive off?"

"No," he said, shaking his head, "all they did was sit there, looking out of the windscreen. They were still there when I left to go home about ten minutes later."

"And you didn't think any more about it until you heard on the radio this morning that the police were looking for a blue Honda?"

"Why would I?" he answered, reasonably enough.

"I wonder if anyone else saw them," I said to Fitzgerald.

"I told you," answered Bryce on her behalf, "there was hardly a sinner about."

"You didn't see anyone who might've been this Peters, then?" said Fitzerald.

"Not unless he was disguised as a seagull," he scoffed.

326

I found myself wondering if this Peters even existed, and noticing as I did so that Bryce was glancing down in an obvious way at his watch.

"Can I go now?" he said.

"In a moment," said Fitzgerald. "First I want you to take a look at this."

"Yeah, that's him," said Bryce as he took the picture from Fitzgerald's fingers. "That's the fella I saw that night. So what's he supposed to have done, anyway?"

What had Buck Randall done? Finally proved he really was in the city, that's what.

At least Kaminski wasn't entirely off the wall.

"That'll be all, Mr Bryce," was the only reply Fitzgerald gave him, returning the picture to her inside pocket. "We'll be in touch if we need you again. Thanks for your help."

It was what is officially known as getting the brush-off, and Bryce knew it. He went off muttering about wishing he hadn't bothered. What did he want? A medal?

"Come on," said Fitzgerald when he was out of earshot.

We walked from the coastguard station along to where the red car that Bryce had pointed out was parked, keeping close to the edge to avoid the other cars that crawled regularly on this road toward the golf club.

I tried to imagine the road empty of people and getting dark. It had to be eerie. Somewhere out among the sand dunes, I could hear birds calling, screeching. At night they must sound like something from another

world. I wouldn't like to come here after nightfall, even if I had walked out on a quarrel with my beloved and wanted to clear my head.

It could be cleared just as easily within range of a streetlight.

Immediately to the right of where the cars were parked, the ground dipped unevenly under grass and rocks down toward the sea. Seagulls hopped awkwardly among the stones. They flapped away, crying in protest, as Fitzgerald stepped off the road to join them.

"Let's hope Bryce remembered the right place," she murmured as I followed her.

Together we crouched down to examine the rocks. She didn't need to tell me what she was looking for. Somewhere here might be the end of the search.

The seagulls returned and settled and watched with interest, heads to one side. Had we managed to find some source of food that they'd missed?

It only took a couple of minutes before Fitzgerald gave a low exclamation.

"Saxon, look."

A scratch of metallic-blue paint on the edge of a rock.

"I think we'd better call in the divers," she said softly.

It took them less than an hour to locate Hudson's blue Honda. That is, they found a Honda, though its colour was difficult to determine, the water was so murky down there.

Then came the problem of getting it out.

328

Getting the lifting crane across the wooden road-bridge was a logistical nightmare in itself. The bridge hadn't been built for that kind of punishment and creaked alarmingly under the strain. The engineers brought in by the DMP Water Unit to oversee the operation insisted it would hold, and hold it did, but I wouldn't have been surprised to see the crane go down to join Hudson's Honda under the water and be swallowed inexorably by the same sand and silt.

There wasn't much for me to do but stand around and watch as the crane manoeuvred bulkily into place on the road, and divers descended anew to attach a hook to the car's rear axle. The grinding of gears filled the air as the crane struggled with the bay for possession of the car. The afternoon was tense with the rasp and scrape of machinery. The seagulls had fled.

And slowly, slowly, fighting its fate, the car emerged, dripping and black with filth.

The fenders were buckled and the grill was pulled into a lopsided grin.

"What can it tell us?" said Fitzgerald.

"Not knowing the answer to that question," I said, "is why you have to ask it."

"How very Zen you are today," she replied.

She looked apprehensive, though.

Waiting was always worse than disappointment.

The Honda, which could now be seen to have been metallic blue, even if its colour had now become the subject of negotiation with the sea, was dragged over the rocks like a dog at the end of a leash, reluctant to do as it was bidden, until it sat, defeated, on the road.

Even now no one approached it.

"It won't bite, boys," said Fitzgerald lightly as she stepped up and peered into the windshield and the windshield stared back blackly, guarding its secrets.

The driver's side door was more forthcoming. All the windows had been wound down, presumably to make the car sink more effectively once it entered the water.

Fitzgerald bent down and put her head inside.

There was still water inside and a stench like an open sewer. Christ alone knows what was trapped in the mud that coated the seats. Essence of Dublin Bay: I couldn't see it catching on as a new fragrance. Fitzgerald pulled on a pair of Latex gloves and tried the handle.

It didn't budge.

It was probably just as well, or what was inside the car would've ended up on her shoes.

The other doors wouldn't open either.

Before taking off the handbrake and pushing the car into the water, had Buck Randall crippled the locks to make them harder to open? Why would he have bothered?

Twenty feet down in Dublin Bay was surely barrier enough to the curious?

Fitzgerald shifted round to the back of the Honda and tried the button on the trunk.

Click.

"We're in," she murmured as she lifted it open.

Then she staggered back violently, as the sweet, decadent, obscene smell of death escaped from the trunk where it had been trapped and took ownership of the shore.

I clasped my hand over my face in a futile attempt to stop the smell assaulting me.

Fitzgerald had the presence of mind not to do the same. She wouldn't want to lift the gloves to her mouth now. Instead she protected her face in the crook of her elbow and turned away. "After all this time down there, what will be left?" she'd asked.

Not much, was my guess.

Fitzgerald was soon taking charge. She ordered everyone back while the City Pathologist was summoned. What we had now was a crime scene. Nothing was to be disturbed. The engineers and crane crew were told to return to the city. Uniforms were directed into place to keep unwanted onlookers away from the area. Blue tape appeared from nowhere. A shapeless white canopy was shouldered into place around the car, for the police's privacy rather than the victim's, though for that too. It wouldn't take long for the reporters to appear. We sat, waiting for the pathologist to arrive, in a room at the coastguard station which she had immediately requisitioned for use by the Murder Squad.

A young sergeant was dispatched for coffee.

The coffee he found wasn't going to win any awards for taste, but it sufficed. The smell of it at least offered some relief from the smell of decay. Once it gets into your nostrils, it's hard to shift. You keep imagining you can still smell it even when you're far away.

It clings to you.

You wonder why other people haven't noticed it on your hair and clothes.

She didn't need to tell me what she'd seen. Bodies decay much more slowly when immersed in water than in the air, but the process still ain't pretty. After only a few hours in water, the skin becomes wrinkled and white, especially on the soles of the feet and the palms of the hands. It's as if the dead one has been walking on icing sugar.

Within a few weeks, the skin slips off like clothing. Hair becomes loose and as easily lifted off as a badly fitted wig. The body becomes bloated and filled with gas. It easily breaks apart if not handled correctly. The pathologist would want to make as close an examination as he could out here. By the time the body reached the mortuary, many vital indications could have been corrupted or destroyed. Murderers had relied on this fact for centuries, disposing of bodies in water because it eradicated so much of the evidence against them.

"It was definitely a man?" I asked her as we sipped the coffee.

"I'm pretty sure," she said. "It looked like a man's clothes."

"I wonder if he was dead already when he went into the water?"

Whoever it was, I hoped that he *had* been dead already. The alternative, that the victim drowned while trapped in the trunk of the car, was too grisly to contemplate.

Though would we ever know? Determining absolutely the cause of death in these circumstances could prove impossible. Even determining the identity of the victim

might be beyond the reach of the science, unless there was adequate DNA or dental records to match against the corpse. In many instances, the body fat itself could be transformed into a greasy, pale, soft substance akin to butter or soap. There would be no face to speak of.

The City Pathologist reminded us of each and every one of these provisos when he arrived with Sean Healy about an hour after the car had been dredged out of the bay.

Alastair Butler was a careful man. He lived carefully, he dressed carefully, he spoke carefully, he worked carefully. It could make him frustrating to deal with, but it did mean that when he made a pronouncement it represented his most exact thinking on the matter.

He did not deal in speculation.

He dealt in facts.

Right now he was staring over the top of his half-moon spectacles, having declined coffee, listening while Fitzgerald outlined the circumstances in which the body had been found.

"Whether he was dead when he went into the water, I don't know," she told him, "but I'm assuming the body went into the water the night Bryce met Buck Randall."

"Assuming, Chief Superintendent?" said Butler quizzically.

"Call it an educated guess, then. Why would he drive all the way out here with Hudson's car, only to come back a second time and double his chances of being seen?"

"Trial run?" I offered.

"Too risky," she said.

"Murderers do strange things," Healy said.

"Remember we don't know that he *is* a murderer," pointed out Fitzgerald. "We only have Leon Kaminski's word for that. The police in New York didn't think he'd killed anyone."

"He acts like a murderer," I said. "Sneaking around, nameless, invisible."

"Does that make Kaminski a murderer too?"

"Kaminski?"

"He's been sneaking around as well. Again, we only have his word for it that he's looking for his wife's killer. I don't like it when so much hangs on one man's testimony." She sighed. "For that matter, how do we know it isn't *Randall's* body in the boot? This is totally different from the MO Randall himself's used so far."

"You mean he met . . . what did you say his name was again?" said Healy.

"Peters, according to the witness."

"He's arranged to meet this Peters, then — Peters, whoever he is, murders him — stuffs him in the boot — pushes the car into the water."

"That's what I was considering," said Fitzgerald.

"What about the other man who was seen by Bryce in the front seat?"

"You got me on that one."

"Randall certainly didn't seem to act like a man with something to hide," I admitted grudgingly. "Driving up to a complete stranger out of the blue and starting a conversation with him isn't the best plan of action if

you're trying to dispose secretly of a body in the trunk of the car you've let witnesses see you driving."

But no, Randall couldn't be dead, I told myself firmly, refusing to follow my imagination down that avenue, because he'd subsequently contacted Kaminski to claim Marsha Reed's murder for himself. He mustn't have expected to meet anyone out here, I decided. The line about Peters must've been the first thing that came into his head to cover his back. Though wouldn't killing Bryce have covered it better?

For once, I could see the benefit of Alastair Butler's way of doing things. Speculation wasn't getting us anywhere. First we needed to know who was dead in the trunk.

Everything else would flow from that.

"I'd say it's over to you, Doc," I told Butler.

"Don't expect any miracles," he murmured disapprovingly. "I only perform those on Sundays." And with that, he and Fitzgerald went off to get themselves suitably boiler-suited for the gruesome task ahead. Fitzgerald did not look like she was relishing the prospect.

"I still don't see what any of this has to do with Marsha Reed," said Healy, when we were left alone with the cold coffee and he was standing at the window watching them go.

I couldn't see any obvious connection either but didn't want to admit it.

"One thing at a time," I said carelessly instead.

"You're not wrong there," he said. "In this job, one at a time is more than enough."

CHAPTER
THIRTY

"Is it so absurd?" I asked Fisher later as we sat in Fitzgerald's office in Dublin Castle.

"That Buck Randall would come to Dublin to kill Hudson?" said Fisher. "Not absurd, no. Personally I've never come across it before, but I've certainly read of similar cases."

Late afternoon was mingling into early evening. For the first time in weeks, low clouds had rolled in and were sagging heavily on the tops of buildings. There might even be rain later. I couldn't remember the last time it rained. The city needed it. Already there was relief in the streets below that the incessant jabbing of the sun's rays had eased temporarily.

A moment earlier Fitzgerald had gotten off the phone to Alastair Butler to confirm that the body in the trunk really was that of the missing Mark Hudson. Unsurprisingly, there was no possibility of a visual identification — the water had seen to that — but Hudson's driver's licence had been found in an inside pocket of the victim's jacket, as well as his house keys, and a wallet containing a couple of credit and store cards in his name.

More to the point, since those could have been planted on the body, Fitzgerald had already had the foresight to pull in Hudson's dental records before the body was returned to the mortuary for the autopsy. It was a relatively simple matter once the victim was X-rayed to establish that it was indeed Cecelia Corrigan's unfortunate neighbour dead in his own car.

What Butler also found was a non-fatal wound to the back of the head, probably caused by some ordinary metal household tool such as a poker, as well as high levels of a particular brand of insecticide in the victim's bloodstream. It suggested that Hudson had been poisoned, though whether it would ever be possible to prove completely that this was how he met his death, considering the deteriorated state of the remains, was another matter. He may have been dead already when the wound was inflicted to his head. Butler still couldn't determine whether the wound was postmortem or ante-mortem. More tests would be needed to prove that. All we knew for certain was that Mark Hudson's killer had exhibited an entirely different MO from the man who had killed Marsha Reed. Unless that was the point. Unless the change of tactic was nothing but a ruse designed, *staged*, again, to throw Buck Randall's pursuers off the scent. Presuming, that is, that Buck Randall was the killer.

Right now, he was the only angle we had to go on.

Randall's presence in the city had not been adequately explained.

He was seen with a car belonging to Mark Hudson at the water's edge.

The car was recovered with Hudson's murdered body inside.

Randall's fingerprints were, we had since learned, all over the interior.

Concluding that Buck Randall had serious questions to answer was not jumping to conclusions. It was simply following the evidence to its logical end.

But there was still the small question of why a prison guard from Huntsville, Texas, would come all this way to murder a man who had, apparently accidentally, killed a woman who had been writing to a prisoner the guard had known on Death Row.

Did it have anything to do with the death of the woman in New Mexico? If not, then the whole thing was a coincidence, and I believed in those even less than I believed in fairies.

"Maybe Jenkins Howler just *asked* him to do it," said Fitzgerald.

"Why?" said Healy.

"Why did he agree to do it, do you mean, or why did Howler want him to?"

"Both."

"Starting with the second, Howler might've believed that Hudson deliberately killed Cecelia Corrigan," she said. "We still can't say for definite that he didn't. We've no reason to suppose that he did, but that only means we have no evidence, not that it didn't happen."

"OK," said Healy, "I'll accept that, but why then would this Buck Randall agree to do it? Cecelia wasn't *his* penfriend. She meant nothing to him."

"But Howler meant something to him," I said. "You heard how close the two of them were. They were thick as thieves."

"Thick as murderers even," murmured Walsh, who was sitting with his feet up on the windowsill, drinking a cup of coffee and absently sending text messages on his cellphone as we all talked. From the frequency with which they were coming I suspected it must be one of his latest conquests. I hadn't even thought he was listening properly. Obviously I was wrong.

"Exactly," I said. "If Howler asked him, he might've felt it was his duty to do it."

"A doomed friend's last wish, you mean?" said Fisher.

"That's not so unimaginable, is it?" I said.

"I already told you," said Fisher. "It's not unimaginable at all. Many perpetrators have committed murder in the past in order to please another person, a person who meant a lot to them. That's why we have laws against committing murder by proxy. If it didn't and couldn't happen, there'd be no point having a law against it."

"I thought murder by proxy usually meant contract killings," said Walsh.

"Those are the most common kind of proxy killings, where you simply pay someone to commit the murder that you are either unable or unwilling to commit yourself."

"But you don't think that's what happened in this case?"

"I suppose Jenkins Howler *may* have found some convoluted way of financially reimbursing Buck Randall for committing this murder on his behalf, but it all looks rather implausible," confessed Fisher. "More likely, if he did come all this way to do this last favour for Howler, then it was because of a convergence of interests at that particular moment. They were each getting something out of it. Or he might not even have told Howler that he was going to do it. It might've been a posthumous tribute to a friend who'd died on Death Row."

"You don't think he was under Howler's influence when he acted, then?" I said.

"He might've been," said Fisher, though he was so cool about the idea I guessed it wasn't one he'd entertained for long. "If there is one thing habitual killers are good at, apart from not getting caught, it's finding other human beings' weak spots and exploiting them for their own ends. They use charm, cunning, fear, pity, whatever it takes to get what they want. Making it seem, for example, that they're that person's only friend, or that something bad will happen if they don't do the thing which is being asked of them. They work at people insidiously until they do exactly what they're being directed to do. They act out their will using other people as the weapons. What can I say? It happens. Many are weak, and the few are strong. The few are bound to prey on the many. It's crime as Darwinism. The innocent often fall under the spell of psychopaths until they're completely in their power."

"If Kaminski's right about Randall killing his wife and the other woman in New Mexico," I pointed out, "he's not so innocent."

"I didn't say it was only the innocent," said Fisher. "In fact, if Randall did come to Dublin to kill Mark Hudson, it strongly suggests that he *was* the one who killed those two unfortunate women in the States, as your friend so vehemently suspects. Not least because the hold a killer has over a person who comes into his orbit inevitably diminishes the further away that person gets in time and place from the source of the influence, and Buck Randall's been away from Howler's influence for months now. He'll hardly still be acting under Howler's control."

"In other words, Randall killed Hudson because he wanted to, not because he was being compelled to in some way by Howler's evil eye?"

"Undoubtedly. If he *did* kill Hudson, at any rate — which, I need hardly remind you, remains only a working hypothesis, however superficially attractive. I know, I know," Fisher exclaimed, holding up his hand to repel our objections, "the fingerprints, the witness statements. But it's still circumstantial evidence. It only means he was *there*."

"I wonder if Howler knew Randall was a killer already," I said, half to myself, ignoring his caveats.

"I seriously doubt that Randall would have taken the risk of letting him find out the precise details of his previous adventures," said Fisher pointedly again. "It would have given Howler too much power, and Randall can't be that stupid. In fact, that's another discrepancy

in this whole situation. Usually in these proxy relationships, there's a dominant, clever, manipulative one, and a weaker, more submissive partner. Here it's not so easy to disentangle which was which. It could be that Randall was the dominant one in the relationship all along. He may have been the one who latched on to Howler, feeding off his energy in some malignant way, not the other way round. Or maybe it was simply a meeting of minds, like souls with the same appetites and desires being drawn together."

"Like falling in love," I said.

"Now you mention it, that's another discrepancy," Fisher said. "These kinds of interdependent murderous relationships I'm talking about generally have some sexual basis. The wife or girlfriend of the killer does what he asks of them, even becoming a murderer in their own right, because they want to keep the connection they have with this man going, or to maintain an erotic intensity that needs blood to feed on. There's nothing to suggest there was anything like this between Buck Randall and Jenkins Howler."

"They could've been doing one another through the bars," remarked Walsh appreciatively. He offered the room a wide grin and got stony faces in reply.

"You know, Walsh," said Fitzgerald, "sometimes I worry about you."

"I'm serious, Chief," said Walsh. "I had a drink once with this prison officer who worked up in the women's wing at Mountjoy. There was one girl in for shoplifting who used to offer him all sorts of off-the-cuff services in her cell. It happens all the time."

"I'm surprised you don't quit and put in an application up there yourself," I said.

He looked offended.

"*I* don't need to. This guy was one ugly fucker. He needed all the help he could get." Suddenly he stopped himself. "Oh, sorry for swearing, Chief."

Fitzgerald simply shook her head in bewilderment.

"Can we get back to the subject?" she said wearily.

"To be fair," said Fisher, suppressing a smile, "it's not such an outlandish suggestion. Prisoners and prison officers do often find themselves in inappropriate sexual relationships. You don't stop being a sexual being just because you've been incarcerated. Prison officers have been known to abuse that need for intimacy to satisfy their own desires. It's a power thing. But in this instance? I don't know enough about them to rule it out or in."

"That's why I've asked the police in Texas and the prison authorities there to send us all they have on Buck Randall," explained Fitzgerald. "The more we know about him, the easier it will be to predict his next move. Predict it and, let's hope, prevent it."

"I only hope there's enough in what they send to get some handle on this man," said Fisher. "Right now, I feel like I'm blundering about in a room where all the windows have been blacked out. It's like making a psychiatric assessment of a patient that you've never even met and whose actions and motivations you only ever hear about third and fourth hand."

"Anything that helps find him is an improvement on where we are now," said Fitzgerald. "Though I have to

tell you that, from what I've heard so far, Randall had an exemplary record as an employee. There wasn't a single official complaint against him."

"He did drink, didn't he, according to one report?" I said.

She acknowledged it with a nod.

"There's a possible angle. Drink's a classic disinhibitor," Fisher pointed out.

"Finding an American in the city has to be easier than finding a local, at any rate," I added. "We know from the witness on Bull Island that Randall's making no effort to conceal his accent. How many Americans can there be here? At the very least, he has to be living somewhere, eating somewhere, getting money somewhere. He'll have left a trace."

"Unless he's being sheltered by someone," Healy suggested.

"No object moves through space without causing some disturbance," I said. "And Randall doesn't seem to want to move through it without causing some ripples at least."

"You mean Kaminski?" said Fitzgerald.

"I do. It's no fun for him playing his games alone. He wants others to join in too."

"Two may be company," said Healy, "but he might consider us joining in as well to constitute a crowd."

"Then we'd better do all we can," said Walsh, "to make sure he doesn't know we have joined the game."

"Isn't that going to be a bit difficult," I pointed out, "when he notices on the news that we've dredged up the evidence of his latest handiwork from Dublin Bay?"

CHAPTER
THIRTY-ONE

"There's a message for you," said the doorman, Hugh, when I finally made it through the front door of my building at eight o'clock that evening, looking forward to a shower and a drink.

I recognized Kaminski's handwriting at once when I took the envelope from him.

I tore it open and read the message inside.

I'll pick you up outside at 8.30.

The letters RSVP had been added in, then crossed out.

"When did this come?" I asked Hugh.

Hugh looked uncomfortable. "I've been busy," he said. "Mrs Williams upstairs had a busted cistern again, I had to put out the bins —"

"What time did it come, Hugh?"

"About nine this morning," he said sheepishly.

"In other words, it was already sitting in my mailbox about an hour before I stood here talking to you about your bunions, and you didn't even give it to me?"

"It was my ingrowing toenail actually," said Hugh.

"That's not really the point, is it?"

"I'm sorry, my mind was on other things . . ."

"Forget it," I sighed. "It's done."

I checked my watch.

It was now five after eight. I still had time to get ready if I got moving. There was no question but that I was going to accept the invitation. If Kaminski had decided to end his sulk, I wasn't about to screw it up because my doorman was a certifiable idiot.

I ran upstairs and into my apartment. Quickly checked that there were no messages waiting for me on the phone. There weren't. Another five minutes to shower and pull on a clean pair of jeans and a shirt, and as long as it took to send a hurried and badly spelled text message to Fitzgerald explaining what I was doing, and I was back down in the lobby again before the clock had reached the half hour.

Hugh was sitting with his feet up in his small office, watching soccer on TV.

"Any more messages for me," I asked him, "or are you planning to save them all up and give them to me tied up with a silk ribbon for Christmas?"

"Christmas isn't for months yet," he said blankly.

"That's the point, Hugh, it was a . . . oh, never mind. Go back to sleep."

I pushed open the door and stepped out into the evening air just as Kaminski appeared at the foot of the steps. He'd put on a jacket, shaved, combed his hair. It was an improvement.

"I expected you to be late," he said when he saw me.

"Why?"

"I figured you'd want to make me wait in punishment for having gone cold on you."

346

"It's true I thought you were pissed with me," I said, "but it never crossed my mind to take it out on you. I'm tired of playing games. I want to know what's going on, that's all."

"It wasn't that you couldn't wait a moment longer than necessary to see me, then?"

"Don't flatter yourself, Kaminski."

"I'm way past flattering myself," Kaminski said. "I was just jagging you. Must be the excitement of hitting the social scene again. You know, this is my first night out since my wife died. Most nights I just sit alone in front of the TV flicking channels."

"You sound like my doorman," I said.

"Is that a bad thing?"

"If you'd met him, you wouldn't have to ask. So tell me, where are we going?"

"That's a surprise."

"I hate surprises," I said. "But I'm glad you're talking to me again. I never wanted to make you mad. I only wanted to help find the man who killed your wife, and I thought my way was the best way. I thought you weren't thinking right at the time."

"It's water under the bridge," Kaminski said. "Things have moved on."

"What is it? I can tell from your voice that something's up."

"You could say that."

"What happened?"

"What's happened is I'm making progress at last," he said.

"Tell me, come on, don't make a meal of it."

"Patience," he said infuriatingly.

And he stopped any further questions by hailing a cab, and we climbed in the back while he gave an address written down on a scrap of paper to the driver up front.

The driver took one look at it and then made his way to the lights at the corner. He continued straight on past University College on our right before turning left on to Camden Street and away from town until we were over the canal and on to the Rathmines Road.

As we drove, a light rain began to brush the windshield, the fulfilment of the vague promise in the clouds I'd seen above the bay earlier in the day.

I wondered if the tail was keeping up.

"Here," said Kaminski as we drove along.

He handed me a scrap of newspaper from of his pocket. At first I thought it was the same story I'd found near his bed in his first hotel, until I noticed the typeface was different.

"What is it?" I said.

"Take a look."

I took a look. It was an ad from out the personal columns of a local newspaper. The *In Memoriam* column. It read: *Cecelia, fondly remembered, a friend of a friend from Texas.*

"It was in yesterday's edition," he said.

"Who put it in?" I said.

"A friend of a friend from Texas," said Kaminski. "Can't you read?"

"Why would Buck Randall want to put a message like this in the local rag?"

348

"Because he knows I'll be looking for traces of him everywhere. He wanted me to see it. To show me that he's still in town. Still in the game."

The message would certainly confirm what Fisher had been tentatively suggesting earlier that evening: that Randall might have killed Mark Hudson as a tribute to his late friend Howler. But had Kaminski gotten it confirmed that Randall paid for the message to go in?

"The newspaper wouldn't tell me who placed the message. Customer confidentiality. But I had a hunch. I went along to the cemetery where she's buried, and I was right. There were fresh flowers on the grave. The gardener who tends the place told me that fresh flowers had come for Cecelia Corrigan every morning for the past three weeks."

"Becky might've sent them," I said, though it didn't sound like something she'd do.

"The niece? I thought of that," said Kaminski, "so I went there this morning and talked to the guy who delivered the flowers. He said an American came in three weeks ago, put down a bundle of cash and instructed them to send flowers every day for the next month."

I remembered the rough bouquet of flowers which had been stopped at customs a couple of weeks after Cecelia's funeral, purporting to come from Death Row.

"Randall?" I said.

"None other. The delivery boy IDed the picture."

That man was everywhere.

Where the road forked beyond the Town Hall, we now continued left and soon disappeared into the maze of well-behaved residential streets and squares that dwelt in the enfolding arms of Rathmines Road on one side and Ranelagh Road on the other. A mellow mid-evening mood had settled on the district. Inside the houses, I imagined the city's tribe of urbane, well-dressed, well-paid couples sharing a glass of wine over spaghetti.

But where were *we* going?

I got my answer as we pulled up outside a small wooden door set into a wall and covered with graffiti. The back entrance to the cemetery.

Kaminski sure knew how to show a woman a good time.

The rain was getting harder as we climbed out. It was nothing much by Dublin's standards, but I still wished I'd brought a jacket with me as Kaminski handed money through the window to the driver and the cab pulled away from the kerb, leaving us alone.

"So this is your idea of a night out?" I said to him.

"I thought you'd want to see it for yourself."

"The morning would've been just fine."

"Waiting is for fools," said Kaminski. "Besides, I got a call about an hour ago from someone who works here saying he'd seen someone hanging around the grave. I thought it might be worth checking out and figured you wouldn't mind missing dinner to help me."

"I guess it'd be a silly question to ask how we're going to get in?" I went on, trying the handle and finding it locked.

"Since when did you let a little door get in the way?"

I hoped he wasn't going to suggest we climb over the wall. I'd hate to fall off and have to explain to the docs in the emergency room that I'd been breaking into a cemetery.

People can be funny about things like that.

"Then aren't you glad I have a key?" said Kaminski, and he produced it with a flourish from his pocket like some street-corner card-sharp pulling out an ace from his sleeve. "You're not the only one who knows how to bribe the staff to get inside where they're not supposed to be," he said, and laughed to himself too loudly. I was beginning, I must confess, to find his manner disconcerting. There was something giddy about him.

Excitable.

"Let's get it over with," I said.

Right now, I wanted to be off the street and out of sight, even if the graveyard was the only alternative. The company of the dead had never bothered me. They couldn't hurt anyone. Besides, there were old bones everywhere. Just because you couldn't see them didn't mean they weren't there. Cemeteries were just places to gather the bones up tidily.

Kaminski unlocked the door and we stepped inside. Thankfully, it was still light enough to see by, though the rain was quickly dimming the light as it got heavier. Puddles had started to form on the footpaths between the neatly tended graves.

Kaminski didn't hesitate but headed straight into the heart of the cemetery, ignoring the paths and weaving

instead among the headstones to where he needed to go.

That was a grave in a far corner, by the wall, overhung with the thin rain-dripping branches of a weeping-willow tree. By the time I caught up with him, he was standing mutely in front of it, staring down at the brown mound of earth topped with a large bouquet of flowers that marked the spot where Cecelia Corrigan was buried.

To be honest, I couldn't see why he'd needed to bring me here at all.

There was nothing to see beyond what he'd already told me about in the cab, and I was about to say so scornfully when I became aware that he hadn't moved a muscle since I'd caught up with him at the graveside. After his earlier restlessness, there was something unnerving about that too, and I looked across at him to check that he was all right.

"Kaminski?"

His eyes were wide.

"Someone's disturbed the earth," he said.

"What?"

"Someone's been digging," he said, and suddenly he knelt in front of the mound of soil and began to claw at it with his hands, oblivious to the wet dirt that soon caked his hands.

"Kaminski, stop it, you can't do that."

He only dug all the more furiously.

"What are you —"

My voice failed as he stopped digging and held up something between his fingers.

Something shiny.

It was a ring.

"Marsha," I breathed.

But there were tears in his eyes as he held it up, and I realized it couldn't be Marsha Reed's missing ring. Why would he cry over that? It was Heather's. He didn't need to tell me.

"I have to call Fitzgerald," I said.

I sensed him bristle with alarm.

"What has this got to do with her?" he snarled, and his fingers gripped the ring more tightly as if afraid I was about to take it off him. "This is between Randall and me."

I'd given away too much, but it was too late to back out.

"They found the body of the man who knocked down Cecelia Corrigan today," I said.

"What?"

"His car was lifted out of Dublin Bay," I said. "Hudson was in the trunk."

He clambered to his feet, his knees brown with wet earth, and something of the fight seemed to have gone out of him.

"This changes everything," he said bleakly.

"In what way?"

"Everyone in this damn city is going to know about Buck Randall soon," he said. "How long do you think the press will take before they find out who he is? And how long do you think Randall's going to hang around in Dublin once his cover's blown? I've lost him."

"No."

"Yes! I know what he's like. I've been following his trail long enough. If he sees that Hudson's body's been found, he's going to be out of here faster than a fucking jet plane. It'll ruin everything. He'll not be there, I know he won't."

There was something else going on here that he wasn't telling me about.

"He'll not be *where*, Kaminski?"

Kaminski turned his head away and wouldn't listen.

"He made contact again, didn't he?" I said. "That's what you were hinting about earlier outside my apartment when you told me to be patient? Shit, Kaminski, if you have any idea where Randall is, you have to tell the police, can't you see that?"

"I don't have to tell anyone anything," he said bitterly. "I thought I'd give you a second chance tonight to help me, but there's no way I'm going to let him slip through my fingers a second time." And I knew from the cold way that he spoke that he'd made up his mind. I also knew there was only one way I could get him to change it.

CHAPTER
THIRTY-TWO

"I can't believe you did this to me," said Kaminski.

"I told you once before," I said. "If you're not thinking straight, I'm going to have to do your thinking for you."

It was 2a.m.

The trip to the cemetery had ended abruptly when police called to arrest Kaminski on suspicion of having entered the country using a false passport. It had been my idea. While he knelt at the graveside, I'd silently texted Fitzgerald and told her I thought Kaminski had information on Buck Randall that he had no intention of sharing willingly.

And if he wouldn't share it willingly, then unwillingly was the only other way.

Right now, Kaminski was on the wrong side of an interview desk in Dublin Castle, while Fitzgerald and I sat on the other side, a sergeant at the door on guard, waiting for the realization of his situation to hit him, at which point he might become more cooperative.

There was no sign of it happening yet.

The room was taut with Kaminski's rage.

I couldn't say I blamed him.

"I can't believe you did this to me," he said again. Then he corrected himself. "No, now I think of it, what I really can't believe is that I *let* you do this to me again. It was stupid, stupid, stupid. I should've learned my lesson the first time you betrayed me."

"You use that word too easily," I told him.

"It's the right word."

"It's the wrong word, and you know it," I said. "Come on, Kaminski, stop playing the wounded innocent and start looking at things the right way up. Buck Randall's in the city someplace, *you* don't know where he is, *we* don't know where he is, and even if you do find out where he is he's going to be waiting for you to come to get him. You don't stand a chance."

"And you think your friends in this dump do?"

"They stand a better chance than a guy who's acting like he's lost his mind and suddenly thinks he's Superman or something. Is it a bird? Is it a plane? No, it's Leon Kaminski, flying through the air in search of the man who killed his wife."

"That's a cheap shot," said Kaminski, looking at me with disgust.

"I'm just trying to make you see that you need help," I said. "You can't do this alone."

"I managed to get this far on my own."

"The only reason you managed to get this far was because he *told* you where he was," I reminded him. "If Buck Randall hadn't made contact with you and given you the come-on, you'd still be bumming around Texas trying to pick up his scent."

"I'd have found him," he said thickly.

356

"Maybe you would've, maybe you wouldn't, we'll never know," I said. "What we do know is that he's here someplace in the city right this minute, while we sit here swapping pleasantries, and if you seriously want to bring him down you're going to have to start understanding that we can't let you run around Dublin like a grenade with the pin taken out, ready to blow. If you really want Randall brought in, you're going to have to get over this chip on your shoulder about the police and start cooperating — beginning by telling us what message he's given you this time. And don't bother pretending you don't know what I mean."

"I've told you already, I'm not saying a goddam thing."

Fitzgerald, who'd been sitting quietly the whole time, leafing through a sheaf of papers on her knee, tutted softly at that and shook her head, and she went on tutting softly and shaking her head without raising her eye once from the page, like everything she was reading there was shocking her profoundly, like she'd never known such a miscreant in all her days.

In the end, she sighed melodramatically and threw the papers face up on to the desk, before leaning back in her chair and fixing Kaminski with a faintly amused look.

"Do you know what the penalty is if you're found guilty of entering the country on a false passport?" she asked him.

"No. Should I?"

"If you're going to be travelling round the world on false passports, it's the sort of thing you should

probably bone up on. To be honest, I'm not quite sure myself what the penalty is. Immigration law isn't my specialty, and that department'll be closed till nine this morning. Pity. But it couldn't be that severe, could it? It's not like this is North Korea."

"I'm glad to hear it," Kaminski said sarcastically.

"Then again," she added, "yours *is* a particularly provocative case. I just got a preliminary list of what my officers found when they searched your hotel room." She nodded at the thin sheaf of papers. "It makes fascinating reading. One false passport I can understand, two even, but how many was it you had again? I've forgotten." She picked up the papers and flicked through to the relevant page. "Five, that was it. That's a lot of false passports. Any judge worth his salt is going to think you were up to no good, Mr Kaminski."

"We both know that, once I get an attorney, this case has no more chance of reaching the courtroom than Saxon here has of winning this year's Miss Charm contest."

"True," agreed Fitzgerald. "She probably would struggle, though she's been working hard at her manners lately, haven't you, Saxon? Some of her handlers think they might even be able to start introducing her to polite society in the next few months."

"Is there a point to this pantomime?" groaned Kaminski.

"Just killing time," said Fitzgerald cheerfully. "We've got another two or three days of each other's company to get through, so we might as well enjoy it."

"Two or three days?"

The truth was slowly dawning on the poor klutz.

"That's how long we get to hold you before we either have to charge you or release you," said Fitzgerald. "So even if you're right and there's no chance of your being convicted of travelling on a false passport, or you *are* convicted and given a token fine in sympathy for your situation, the point remains that you'll still be spending the next seventy-two hours here with us."

"You wouldn't do it," said Kaminski but he didn't sound too confident.

"Wouldn't I?"

"You can't," he said, and I thought I detected the first note of panic in his voice. "I can't spend the next three days here. It'll fuck up everything."

"Have somewhere to go, do you?" asked Fitzgerald disingenuously.

"You know I have somewhere to go," Kaminski spat back. "It's what this whole thing has been about. It's what it's all been leading up to. If I don't get out . . . Saxon, help me."

The attempt at persuasion had turned into a plea now.

His desperation was a pitiable sight.

"I'm sorry," I said. "There's nothing I can do for you now."

"It's not Saxon you should be worried about, Mr Kaminski," said Fitzgerald. "It's me. Look at me. I'm a Detective Chief Superintendent with the Murder Squad of the Dublin Metropolitan Police. Do you honestly think I can just let you walk out of here,

knowing that you may have information I need to locate a man that I urgently need to talk to? This isn't just about you and Buck Randall any more and what happened in New York, it's about what's happening right here, right now, outside that door, and what might happen in the future."

"But if you don't let me go," said Kaminski, "you'll never find him."

"And maybe nor will you. That's a risk we'll both be taking — unless you come to your senses and realize that you have to share with us what you know. I know you're afraid he'll slip out between your fingers if we get involved, but that's the last thing I can afford to let happen as well. You must see that. We have to give each other a break."

"How do I know I can trust you?"

"Trust doesn't come into it. This is simply a mutually beneficial arrangement. And the sooner you're straight with us, the sooner you can start taking advantage of it."

In response, Kaminski closed his eyes, considering, silent, still. I caught Fitzgerald's eye as we waited for an answer. She raised her eyebrows in a kind of shrug. She didn't know which way this was going to go either. Kaminski had always been unpredictable.

"OK," he said eventually.

His eyes opened and met hers piercingly.

"You'll tell us what you know?" she said.

"I'll tell you. And in return, you let me go."

"That's the deal," she said.

Kaminski took a deep breath. "Buck Randall sent me another message," he said. "It was slipped under my door when I came back to the hotel two nights ago. He was setting up a meeting."

"There was no note in your room," said Fitzgerald, tapping a finger on the inventory of stuff from Kaminski's hotel room that she'd been consulting earlier.

"I had it with me when you arrested me at the cemetery."

Fitzgerald frowned. "Bring in the box of Mr Kaminski's possessions that were taken from him when he arrived here tonight," she said to the sergeant at the door. "I'm warning you," she added to Kaminski when the other policeman had gone, "if you try anything clever, if you even think about double-crossing us or try to keep us in the dark in some way about what's going on here, I'm going to have you put back immediately under arrest. And this time it won't be for entering the country on a false passport, it'll be as an accessory to murder. I'm just going to have to assume that you *want* this bastard to get away."

"I understand," said Kaminski.

The sergeant returned presently with the box and passed it to Fitzgerald's outstretched hands. She began to sift through the contents. Not that there was much to sort. When he was brought in, Kaminski had been carrying a wallet with the usual assortment of credit cards and cash, some loose change, a cellphone, a book of matches from, of all places, the Mountain House Lodge in Aspen, Colorado, a flyer advertising some

funfair that was opening later tonight down on Merrion Square West, a clipping from the newspaper about Marsha Reed's murder, a packet of mints, a ballpoint pen and a receipt for the headache pills I'd watched him buy when he was being followed the night before.

"I'm not seeing any message here," said Fitzgerald menacingly.

Kaminski reached over and lifted out the flyer for the funfair.

"*This* is the message," he said. "Randall left it under my door. He means this is where I have to meet him."

Fitzgerald took the flyer, unfolded it and read through it quickly, turning it over a couple of times to make sure that she hadn't missed anything.

"There's no writing on it," she said. "How do you know it's a message from him?"

"I put two and two together is how."

"What makes you so sure you haven't come up with five?" I said.

"Or a hundred and one," said Fitzgerald.

"Maybe everyone on your floor got one of these pushed under their door," I added.

"I asked," said Kaminski. "They didn't."

"Still seems a bit weak to me," said Fitzgerald.

"Listen," said Kaminski. "I know this bastard. I've lived with him inside my head for months now. Trying to think like him. Trying to see the world as he sees it. That's what we were taught, right, Saxon? You become one with the killer. That's how you catch him. So when I say I know this came from Randall, you're just going to have to take my word for it."

362

"Very well," said Fitzgerald. "I've got no choice. You're doing no good to me taking up space here. You can go. You can make your date at the funfair. And we'll be there too."

"Just make sure you don't mess up," he warned her.

"It's stopping you from messing up that this is all about," she replied. "You don't have to worry about us. Buck Randall won't know we're there."

He didn't answer that.

I guess trusting the local police was still a step too far for the former FBI man.

"You're not bullshitting us, are you, Kaminski?" I said quietly.

He fixed me with a look of such bitterness that it almost made me gasp.

"You're the expert on everything," he snapped. "You're the one who always knows best. So you tell me, Special Agent. Can I be trusted? Is my word my bond?"

"I honestly don't know any more," I answered.

"Honestly?" he echoed with a harsh laugh. "There's an ironic word from a woman who's just had someone she calls her friend arrested."

"At least I know now that I don't have to worry about you two still harbouring feelings for one another," said Fitzgerald, as, from an upstairs window, we watched, Kaminski crossing the yard of Dublin Castle on his way back to freedom. "If looks could kill . . ."

It had taken a while to get rid of Kaminski. As Fitzgerald had explained to him when he complained about how long it was taking, Dublin wasn't some

Third World dictatorship. You couldn't just arrest and then unarrest someone without finishing the paperwork.

"Do you think he was telling the truth?" I asked her now, as Kaminski turned down Dame Street and disappeared from view.

"You tell me. You know him better than I do. But I'm going to send someone round to personally babysit him until it's time to go to the funfair. There's not much more I can do than that. Letting him go is a risk I have to take. If it gives us Buck Randall, I'll be a hero. If Kaminski's leading us up the garden path, I'll look like a fool. That's life."

We remained at the window, looking out as the rooftops began to lighten. Summer mornings came early, and by now it was well after five. The traffic had begun. At times it felt like it never stopped, not really. The streets still retained a film of wet from the overnight rain, but it would be gone by the time the sun had risen fully. A few hours of rain couldn't stop the summer in its tracks. Already I thought I could detect its intensity rising steadily once more.

"You should try to get some sleep," she said to me eventually.

"What's the point?" I said.

"You'll need to save your strength for tonight, if you intend to be there."

"At the fair?" I said. "Try keeping me away. I love carnivals. That's where I first learned to drive, on the dodgem cars."

"So that's why your insurance premiums are so high."

"What about you?" I asked her. "Don't you need sleep any more?"

"I can't. Not for a while yet," she admitted. "I had a call last night after you left. It was from Victor Solomon's fiancée. Ex-fiancée, I should say. They've split up."

"Marsha's friend told me," I said. "What did she want?"

"She didn't want to talk over the phone," said Fitzgerald. "She asked if I could go round to her place this morning at eight. So you see, there's not much point in my trying to sleep."

"Oh, well, sleep is overrated. We already waste enough of our lives in its grip as it is. One minute out of every three we ever live, we're unconscious. Think of all the things we could be doing with that time instead. It'll do us good to skip it for a night."

"You think so?" said Fitzgerald. "I've always thought it was the other two thirds we spend awake which were really wasted. I'd happily spend the rest of my life in bed."

"Mmm, me too, now you mention it."

"That's not what I meant."

"Spoilsport."

"But since you're so keen to defy the sandman," she said, "why don't you come along with me later to interview the woman who narrowly escaped becoming Victor Solomon's third wife? I'm sure if we get enough coffee inside us between now and eight o'clock, we might even be able to manage to look vaguely human by then."

"I wouldn't bank on that," I said, "but sure. Sounds fun."

"I'm not sure fun's the first word I'd choose, but each to their own." She paused. "You know, I'm really glad you accepted Stella's offer," she went on. "It makes a difference knowing there's another person here I can rely on. I just hope you're not feeling too guilty about abandoning Kaminski. I don't want you to think you've settled for second best."

"I don't," I said. "I know I made the right choice."

I trusted my voice to sound convincing. The truth was that I still wasn't sure I'd made the right choice. Doing everything by the book didn't come easily for me. I always wanted to cross that line and find out what life was like on the other side. Something about Kaminski's intensity appealed to me, thrilled me. I recognized it as the echo of my own heart.

And if it hadn't been for Fitzgerald, I'd be out there with him right now.

Stalking the prey.

Something in me still sensed too that it would be better for us all if I was. Without me, there was nothing to hold Kaminski back and rein him in. No one to tell him when he was going too far. Alone, the ferocity of his hatred for Buck Randall was unchecked and untamed. I dreaded to think what would happen if he finally caught up with him, and there was no one around to stay his hand. How would I feel then about the decisions I'd made?

CHAPTER
THIRTY-THREE

It was Seamus Dalton, of all people, who woke me, knocking thunderously on the door and barging his way into Fitzgerald's office. I must have fallen into my own private nothingness sometime during those early hours, my head on her desk.

So much for that jazz about time spent asleep being time wasted.

I felt hot and disoriented for a moment, not knowing where I was or how I'd gotten there. It's a common sensation. Often on first waking I can't even remember whether I'm back home in Boston, and always feel a sort of longing that it might be true, until the familiar contours of a room melt into shape. Hence Dalton found me at a disadvantage, bemused by sleep, and he looked at me with disgust as though he'd caught me doing something disreputable. He must've known I was there alone. He wouldn't have forced his way so belligerently into Fitzgerald's office if he'd expected her to be there too.

He wouldn't have dared.

"What time is it?" I said, unfurling myself stiffly from the position in which I'd managed to arrange my limbs and rubbing my face in an attempt to bring back some

feeling to my cheekbones. My face must have looked at that moment like a rumpled bedsheet with an imprint of my sleeve pressed into the mould of my skin. Not a good look.

I was glad there was no mirror to confirm my worst fears.

"After eight," Dalton barked. "Here."

If a plastic cup could be slammed on to a desk, Dalton came as close as anyone could to slamming it. A little coffee spilled out over the rim, and he cursed as the hot liquid burned his skin.

He wiped his hand on the seat of his pants.

"You're bringing me coffee?" I looked at him suspiciously. "What is this — your belated contribution to International Women's Day?"

"It's just a cup of coffee, don't make a big issue out of it. Walsh bought it for you from the vending machine downstairs to help you wake up, then the Chief called him away. I was coming this way so he asked me to bring it up to you. He must think I'm your fucking housemaid or something. Feel free not to drink it."

"No, coffee's good, er, thanks."

"You've got five minutes."

He was gone before the fact that I'd just thanked him for something really sank in.

I wondered if this was some kind of peace offering.

Peace offerings weren't what I associated with Dalton.

Five minutes? It must be time to go talk to Victor Solomon's ex-fiancée. I lifted the coffee gingerly and sniffed at it. It smelled harmless enough, but I decided

not to take my chances. I slid back the window and poured it out, making sure there was no one below first. Anything Dalton had been that close to should probably be filed under Best Avoided.

The man himself wasn't so easily avoided, however, because he was waiting in the lobby when I got downstairs. Looked like he was going too. Terrific.

He grunted his second greeting of the morning, but we were mercifully spared the ordeal of trying to make conversation by the arrival of Patrick Walsh, shouldering his way through the front door and coming to a halt when he saw us standing there.

"The Chief's waiting," he said.

"Whose car are we taking?" I asked.

"The Chief said to take one out of the car pool, so I did."

"I'll drive, then," said Dalton.

"But I was going to —"

"I said I'll drive, son. I'd rather not put my life in the hands of someone who probably spent half the night banging some blonde bimbo he picked up in a nightclub."

"She was a redhead actually." Walsh grinned at me as Dalton snatched the keys and pushed his way out of the lobby. "I met her in the bar after work. I don't know what I've got, but whatever it is they all seem to want it. I need a stick to keep them away."

The door swung open again.

"Are you two coming or not?" snapped Dalton.

"There's someone who really *could* do with getting laid," said Walsh when the other detective had

disappeared again. "Don't suppose you want to volunteer, do you?"

"You first," I said. "I haven't had my shots."

The car Walsh had picked out of the car pool was a silver Audi. Even when he was working, Walsh was obviously still looking to impress any passing female. Not that he expected to be on the back seat with me while Fitzgerald and Dalton sat up front.

"Saxon," said Fitzgerald brightly as I clicked my seatbelt into place. "Are we working you too hard? Dalton tells me you were sleeping when he went up to fetch you."

"That's just what it looked like to the untrained eye," I answered slickly.

"Is that so?"

Ellen Forwood lived in North Great George's Street, a steep incline of Georgian terraces whose doorways alone made it a Mecca for architectural groupies. They were certainly impressive, each one flanked by pilasters and crowned with some elaborate shining fanlights above the door. This area of the city, together with Mountjoy Square to the east, had once been the hub of polite Dublin society until the money moved south of the river. Now these houses, where wealthy landed families had dwelt not so long ago, were mainly occupied by language schools, solicitors' offices, art galleries, even a museum dedicated to James Joyce, a writer so beloved of the locals that they drove him into exile during his lifetime and only decided they adored him after he died. The usual story.

Previous years had seen heroic attempts at restoring the street and its surroundings to their former glory, and many of the houses remained in private hands. But there was something rather melancholy about their efforts when the general area around them was as dispiriting and rundown as ever, with a definite, dark criminal undertow to everyday life that meant most people still preferred to keep their distance. In that respect, it reminded me of the district where Marsha Reed had lived too. It took a certain nerve to live here.

What did Ellen Forwood see in it? There were plenty of theatres in the surrounding streets, that might have been one thing, not to mention the undoubted cultural cachet of living in a street immortalized by a great writer. North Great George's Street was still a name to conjure with in the kind of circles that Victor Solomon and company moved in.

We pulled to a stop outside Ellen's front door and Fitzgerald clambered out.

Walsh and I followed.

Dalton turned off the engine but stayed behind.

I'd been right about the weather. The day was growing warm again, like the rain had been nothing but an implausible memory. There was a morning clatter in the air. A hum of traffic from the city's main thoroughfare of O'Connell Street a couple of hundred yards away beyond the high brown buildings, buses and cars on those endless journeys to nowhere.

When Fitzgerald lifted the doorknocker, carved into the shape of an animal's golden head, and rapped the

371

door with it, the sound rang out loudly in the enclosed street, the echo ricocheting from wall to wall.

"Hello," she said curiously to herself in the aftermath of silence.

Hammering the knocker had made the door shiver and open inward slightly, like it had been left open accidentally by someone entering or leaving.

"Ms Forwood?" she called into the gap that had appeared.

There was no answer.

"Ms Forwood, this is Detective Chief Superintendent Fitzgerald."

She knocked again, and the door opened wider, but this time the sound was on the inside of the house, almost like it was going from room to room, looking for an answer.

No answer came.

Fitzgerald stepped into the gap — and stopped.

A woman lay curled on the floor at the end of the hallway.

Fitzgerald rushed forward and knelt down by the woman's side. Careful not to touch anything, she bent a head to the woman's mouth and listened.

"She's breathing," she said to Walsh. "Call for an ambulance."

"Is it Solomon's fiancée?" I said as Walsh hurried out into the street.

Taking a step forward, I could see a knot of blood on the back of the woman's hair, and a further smear of blood on the floorboard near to a rear window and

more on the pane itself. She must have turned herself over after falling there. But what had made her fall?

"It's her all right," said Fitzgerald.

"I think she's trying to speak," I said.

Trying to open her eyes too.

"Lie still, Ellen. Help's on the way."

Another low murmur.

Fitzgerald hooked her hair behind her ear and bent her head once more to the woman's lips. But even I could hear what she whispered when the word finally came out.

"*Victor.*"

"Solomon," I said.

"Did he do this?"

The woman tried to nod her head but winced in pain.

"No more talking," Fitzgerald said.

Ellen Forwood closed her eyes once more. Fitzgerald got back to her feet and hurriedly examined the scene immediately around the prone figure while we waited anxiously for the ambulance. The moments seemed to drag longer than hours.

"What's taking it so long?" said Fitzgerald. "The hospital can't be more than three streets away." But, even as she spoke, the faint howl of a siren could be heard through the open door, approaching, getting louder as it turned the corner at the top of the street.

Doors slammed, footsteps hammered on the sidewalk, paramedics appeared.

Fitzgerald identified herself, then stepped back to let them do their job.

"Come on," she said to me.

"Shall I stay here?" said Walsh.

"Has Dalton called Dublin Castle yet?"

"They're sending another car."

"Then I'm leaving you in charge," she said. "Make sure Ellen Forwood's accompanied to the hospital, we mustn't let her out of our sight. Secure the scene. Search the rest of the house. Find witnesses if there are any. Don't try to talk to Ms Forwood herself until I get back. Leave her to the paramedics."

"Are you going to find Solomon?" I said.

"Who else?"

Dalton already had the car running. I'd barely shut the door behind me when he was away and picking up speed. At the top of the street, he turned left and headed toward Parnell Square. Fitzgerald took out the siren and, winding down the window, attached it to the roof.

"Where does Solomon live?" I shouted above the sudden din.

"Prussia Street," Fitzgerald said.

"Prussia Street?" I said. "I didn't have him down as the Prussia Street sort."

"Solomon hasn't a cent to his name," Fitzgerald said. "We've been checking him out ever since we knew he was involved with Marsha Reed. He's lost hundreds of thousands through gambling in the last few years. He did have a big house out by Killiney Bay, but he had to sell it to pay off his debts. He's been living out this way for the last six months or so. I think his circumstances

being made public was the thing he feared the most. He said that if the press ever got wind of how he was living now, he'd sue us for everything we've got. He's obviously never seen my budget. I'm presuming that's one of the reasons he fixed on Ellen Forwood to marry. He was looking to go up in the world."

"Well," I said, "I'd say a reconciliation's out of the question now."

"Fuck it," cursed Dalton.

The traffic was snarled at the top of Capel Street, and many drivers seemed to consider it a point of honour to wait until the very last moment to pull over and let the police through. By the time we were running down King Street toward Stoneybatter, more precious moments had been wasted. Fitzgerald was on the radio, ordering a second car to meet us at Solomon's place and another unit to head to the theatre in case the director had gone there.

"That must be it," she said, as Prussia Street opened up before us.

A blue-and-white squad car was parked by the side of the road near the 24-hour supermarket, and an officer in uniform was holding up a hand like a traffic cop trying to stop oncoming traffic. Dalton pulled sharply into the left and tugged on the handbrake.

"Is he in?" Fitzgerald asked the uniform as she jumped out.

"There's no answer from inside."

A narrow doorway between two low-rent stores, one with its window boarded up, led to a flight of uncarpeted stairs. Fitzgerald, closely followed by

Dalton, ran up to the second floor, where another uniform was standing guard at the open door. He looked faintly alarmed to see us.

"Any sign of Solomon?" Fitzgerald asked him.

The cop shook his head.

"OK, you can go back downstairs now, we'll take over."

"And remember," Fitzgerald said to us, "careful not to touch anything."

She stepped through the doorway.

A mean little apartment opened up before her.

I couldn't believe a man like Victor Solomon could live in a place like this. He must have fallen on hard times indeed. I wondered if Ellen Forwood knew how desperately the man she had intended to marry must have felt the need to make her his own, regardless of all other considerations. This was the apartment of a man who had sold virtually everything that wasn't nailed down, and would have sold his soul too if only he could have found the right bidder. I'd known plenty of people like it at the poker table, men whose eyes blazed with the violence of the desire not so much to win as to just stop losing.

It certainly wasn't the apartment of a man who could afford to give away necklaces as meaningless trinkets to casual sexual partners that he claimed meant nothing to him.

"He's gone," said Fitzgerald.

The diagnosis was hard to refute. Drawers had been pulled out, doors hung open, dirty dishes were piled high in the sink, all was emptiness and abandonment. A

handful of suits lay in crumpled heaps on the floor of the wardrobe. Shirts had been flung over the backs of chairs. A pair of shoes sat awkwardly on the windowsill. Someone had been packing.

And hurriedly.

"I want theories," said Fitzgerald. "Where is he?"

"He's doing a bunk," said Dalton. "and there are only two places to go."

"The airport."

"Or the boat."

There was no point in trying to escape by road. The country beyond Dublin was too small to hide out in for long.

"The airport," I said firmly. "He needs to get as far away as possible. The boat doesn't go far enough. And it's way too slow. You could have police waiting for him by the time he reaches the other side of the water. He couldn't take the chance. He's banking on being far outside your jurisdiction before you even realize he's gone."

"And the next boat's not till lunchtime," said Dalton. That settled the argument.

"The airport it is, then," said Fitzgerald.

"Are we on the move again?"

We were.

Getting north to the airport was easier once we hit the main road out. The streets became wider, and the drivers took it less personally when commanded by the siren to pull over and let us through. I heard Fitzgerald back again on the police radio, sending more officers

out to the harbour just in case we were wrong about Solomon's preferred escape route.

She also requested back-up, preferably armed, at the airport.

The police would be getting stretched soon if Solomon was not found.

And when we finally reached the airport, not finding Solomon began to look like a distinct possibility. It was summer, after all. The airport's busiest time. There didn't seem to be a square inch of the airport terminal that was not already occupied by someone who was either on their way somewhere else or waiting to greet someone returning from elsewhere. Call it organized chaos, except there were times when it didn't seem very organized at all.

On the board above our heads, destinations fluttered by faster than birds.

Paris.

Chicago.

Rome.

Bangkok.

Toronto.

There was a world to hide out in. Solomon could have been here an hour ago, two hours, we didn't know when he'd attacked his fiancée. He could have paid cash for the first plane out — he didn't even care where. By the time we had been through the passenger lists and established where he'd gone, he could be a continent away, in a place where it might be impossible to find him or to get him back even if we did find him.

And in the back of my mind constantly now there was another thought.

If Solomon had run, it was because he was most likely guilty of Marsha Reed's murder. *And if he was guilty of that, then what about Buck Randall?*

Was that nothing to do with this at all?

Slow down, girl.

One problem at a time.

Fitzgerald had already taken charge of airport security and got them looking for Victor Solomon, though, since it took more than ten minutes to get the theatre director's picture forwarded electronically from Dublin Castle to the airport office, their contribution to the search was more symbolic than practical. She sat in front of a bank of TV screens, scanning faces in the crowds as the cameras picked them out, shouting frequently for the camera to be pulled in closer or further back when she thought she recognized someone.

Dalton couldn't bear to sit watching TV, so he went off to make a circuit of the coffee bars and gift stores in the terminal, restless with an energy that had no release.

Occasionally he appeared on the TV screens in front of us, each time almost prompting a cry of recognition, his face becoming confused in our heads with Solomon's, so desperate were we to find a face we recognized, until we remembered it was only Dalton.

"This is some haystack," murmured Fitzgerald as she scanned another sea of faces.

And the needle in it wasn't giving out so much as a gleam.

I felt the same impatience that had sent Dalton out into the terminal starting to eat at me too. If I sat there much longer, holding myself in. I'd grow a tumour.

"I'm going to see if Dalton needs a hand," I said eventually.

Fitzgerald was so engrossed in the screens that she didn't even acknowledge the unlikelihood of what I'd said. Or maybe she knew it was nothing but words, the first excuse my head could dream up to get me out of that suffocating office.

Whatever it was, I was out.

Everything had slowed right down. The crowds seemed to move and sway in syrup. Sound was a background hum throbbing in my ears. Announcements of flights crackled distantly but might as well have been in a foreign language for all the sense they were making to me. I was trying to tune them all out in order to concentrate on the one thing that mattered — seeing Victor Solomon's face. Or could he be far from here already?

"Dalton," I said.

The detective spun round at the sound of his name.

"The fucker's not here," he said. "I've been round this place a million bleeding times. I'd have seen him. He's gone. What's the Chief doing?"

"She's on the phone to the Assistant Commissioner."

He snorted. "What are they doing?" he said scornfully. "Swapping beauty tips?"

"You know that's not fair, Dalton."

"Don't tell me what's fair and what's not. I'm the one who's trying to search this whole building on my own while she sits in there on her arse talking on the telephone."

I was tempted to inquire what else he expected her to sit on. Her elbow, perhaps? But it was a fair presumption that he wasn't in the mood for jokes. He rarely was. Dalton was one of those people in whose soul humour has never found a welcoming home.

"Chill out," I said instead.

"Chill out?" He pulled his face into an exaggerated grimace of disbelief. "Tell you what, why don't you chill out while I go take a piss?"

The guy had a way with words that made a lady feel real special around him.

"Where're the jacks round here, anyway?"

"If you mean the men's room, it's over there," I said, pointing. "You can't miss it, it's the one with the picture on the door of the stick figure that's *not* wearing a skirt."

He'd only taken one step toward the far door when he stopped.

"Fuck me," he said.

Not an invitation I could ever imagine taking him up on.

The outburst was forgivable this time, because at that precise moment Victor Solomon had emerged from the men's room, clutching a holdall, and was inching his way nervously toward one of the departure gates, his eyes restlessly scanning the airport lounge as if he expected to be challenged at any moment. His face

looked flushed, and the bag kept slipping through his fingers like his hands were damp with sweat.

I guess he didn't have much practice in fleeing the country.

"Get the Chief!" Dalton demanded over his shoulder, as he hastened his step and made to intercept Solomon, who still seemed unaware that his cover was blown.

Fitzgerald, however, was already coming toward us. She must have seen her fugitive on the security cameras. By the time she caught up with Dalton, we were only a hundred yards or so from Solomon and he was almost at the check-in desk for Air Italia.

"This is the last call for the 9.25 flight to Rome."

So that's where he was going.

Solomon reached into the pocket of his pants and pulled out his passport, sliding it across the counter at the blandly smiling girl behind it.

Then the smile vanished as she looked up and saw us approaching.

Fitzgerald held out her hand and took the passport as Solomon turned, the nervous half-smile he'd rustled up for the check-in girl crumbling as he realized what was happening.

"Victor Solomon," she said, "I am arresting you on suspicion of the murder of Marsha Reed and for the attempted murder of Ellen For — ."

"I want my lawyer," said Solomon, interrupting. "I know my rights."

He was still griping when Dalton put the cuffs on him and led him out to the car.

CHAPTER
THIRTY-FOUR

"He swears he didn't mean to hurt her," I told Fisher as we sat together on the steps of City Hall in the sunshine, watching the people go by and sharing some grapes out of a bag, like we didn't have a care in the world, like we were tourists. Which, in a way, we both were.

"That's what they all say," said Fisher. "How does he explain the fact she had a plastic bag over her head if he didn't mean to hurt her?"

"Not Marsha," I said. "Ellen, the fiancée. Or ex-fiancée, I should say. He still totally denies having anything to do with Marsha's murder."

"But I thought they found the necklace in his room at the theatre?"

"Says he has no idea where it came from."

"That's what they all say too."

"Don't they just?"

The discovery of the necklace had certainly been unexpected. A search warrant had been obtained for the theatre following Solomon's apprehension, and, within the hour, it had been uncovered in a plastic supermarket bag stuffed behind a cupboard in Solomon's office. Why he hadn't gotten rid of such

incriminating evidence was anyone's guess, but even his lawyer had looked taken aback when presented with news of it.

That's where Fitzgerald was now with Sean Healy, talking to the director's colleagues and supervising forensics as they made a fingertip search of his office, vacuuming up fibres, dusting for prints, looking for fragments of leaf or soil that could be matched to those taken from the grounds surrounding Marsha's house. Getting a match would undermine Solomon's contention that he'd never been there, which is why the Murder Squad was treating the place where her necklace had been uncovered as respectfully as a crime scene.

They were looking for the missing ring too.

So far, it had failed to show.

That night's performance of *Othello* had been cancelled. With the director in custody on a murder charge, the leading lady in hospital and the theatre itself occupied by scores of grim-faced technical staff in white overalls and face masks, that wasn't so astonishing. A sign outside informed the public that the play would open again tomorrow.

Solomon had refused to speak any further after hearing that the necklace had been found, except to say that he was being stitched up for a murder he hadn't committed and would sue everyone in the building. It was a pity, really, because up until then he'd been doing plenty of talking. This was a man with no intention of exercising his right to remain silent. The police had given him a spade, and he'd kept on digging, digging,

digging, ranting angrily at Marsha for having, as he now claimed, stolen from him the necklace he'd bought with the last of his savings for Ellen Forwood and then refused to return it, taunting him with his desperate financial circumstances, offering one moment to use her father's fortune to help him out if he carried on seeing her, the next moment refusing him a cent.

He didn't seem to appreciate that his palpable anger against Marsha might not exactly be helping his assertion of being innocent of her killing.

Mainly, though, he talked about what had happened that morning at Ellen's house.

How he'd heard she'd contacted the police the night before and was intending to withdraw her alibi following their break-up. He hadn't really been with her the night Marsha Reed died; he'd simply asked her to say that he was in order to take the heat off him.

Ellen hadn't suspected for a moment that he was guilty of the young actress's murder, but she knew that any adverse publicity would be damaging for both of them. There certainly wouldn't be many celebrity magazines interested in the photos of their wedding if the truth had become known. Only after Ellen learned that her husband-to-be had been involved in a sexual relationship with Marsha at the same time as they were planning their own wedding had she decided to call the whole thing off and stopped taking Solomon's calls. The show of forgiveness for the police when they first spoke to her had simply been a front.

She wasn't an actress for nothing.

Soon after, she further decided, whether from a desire for revenge or guilt at having lied in the first instance, to come clean to the police. And not just about his alibi.

Now she was also claiming that Solomon enjoyed tying her up during sex. It wasn't her thing, she said, but she went along with it to please him. Sometimes he hurt her. He claimed to be sorry, but she'd seen the bright look in his eyes when he was doing it.

So much for his offended claim not to share Marsha Reed's appetites.

Somehow, Solomon had found out that Ellen Forwood had been about to come clean about both things to the police. He'd gone round that morning to beg her not to reveal his secret. He told her she was the only woman he'd ever loved. He threw himself on her mercy.

When that didn't work, he threatened to finish off her career as an actress. A ludicrous claim, considering that she was most likely about to bring his own career to a close by blowing his alibi for murder. There was a quarrel, the quarrel had turned into a struggle, she slapped him, he pushed her, Ellen fell and cracked her head against the windowpane, hence the blood smears. She ended up in a heap in the hall. He panicked and ran.

That was his version of events, at any rate.

Fitzgerald was waiting for a chance to talk to Ellen to hear her version.

"Is she going to be all right?" asked Fisher.

"The hospital says she'll be in for a while yet," I told him, "but there should be no permanent damage. She'll have one hell of a headache for a while, though."

"I can imagine," he said. "What I don't understand is why he didn't just call for an ambulance if he really was sorry that he'd hurt her."

"He says he thought she was dead. He thought he'd killed her. And, to be fair, he did look relieved when he learned that she was alive. Then again, he's a former actor too. How much you can take what either of them says and does at face value is anyone's guess."

"You're such a cynic."

"I'm only going by the evidence," I said. "The urge for self-preservation is definitely what kicked in when he thought he'd killed Ellen Forwood. First thing he did was race round to his rooms, pack a bag and head to the airport to get the first flight out of the city. That's what he was doing when we found him. He was hiding in the men's room, waiting for the last call for his flight before coming out. It was pure chance that he came out just at the same moment Dalton was headed to the door. Solomon's just a stage name, apparently. His passport was in his real name of Mahoney. That's why he wasn't coming up on computer records of flight bookings. If he'd gotten on to the plane, we might never have seen him again."

"What was he intending to do once he reached Rome?"

"He grew up in Italy," I said. "Speaks fluent Italian without an accent. He says the plan was to hide out until he had the chance to clear his name."

"Clear him of what? He admits attacking Ellen Forwood."

"It was clearing his name of the murder of Marsha Reed he was interested in. He knew once his alibi fell apart that the police would blame him again for her death. He thought that if he could stay out of sight for long enough, then the real murderer would be found."

"He'd still have to answer for the attack on his fiancée."

"He thought people would understand once they knew what had happened, and the pressure he was under. I know, it's mad, he wasn't thinking straight."

"I know the feeling," said Fisher intently.

"What do you mean?"

"Just that I've obviously had this whole thing the wrong way up from the start. Solomon's behaviour — fighting with his fiancée — making a metaphorical break for the border like that this morning. It doesn't really fit the profile I had in mind of Marsha Reed's killer."

"The careful, methodical, make-no-mistakes kind of guy, you mean?"

"That was the general idea."

"Even methodical types can panic," I pointed out.

"And everyone makes mistakes, I know." He leaned back, extended his arms, folded his hands, and cracked his knuckles softly. The noise always makes me shudder. "You know how it works. You try to insinuate your way into the killer's head, working back step by step until your thought patterns correspond to theirs. When I did that, it was never Solomon's eyes I was

looking out of. Why would such a careful man take the risk of keeping the proof of his guilt badly hidden where police were bound to find it if they searched? And what about Marsha's online requests for someone to kill her? Where do they fit in?"

I said nothing, because Fisher had given a voice to a doubt which I had so far left unspoken and which I wasn't sure I was ready to admit even to myself.

The DMP had everything they needed on Victor Solomon.

He had motive — the need to protect his secret affair from his future wife.

He had opportunity — no alibi for the night of the murder.

He had the necklace back in his possession.

He certainly had a reason for wanting it back. Maybe two reasons. One, because it was proof of his relationship with Marsha. Two, because he needed the money he could get for it.

What's more, he had incriminated himself by running.

So why did catching him not feel better than it did? I'd kept the doubt silent in my mind because I couldn't be sure that I wasn't simply refusing to see the evidence for what it was out of a misguided sense of loyalty to Leon Kaminski, that I wasn't being misled by his aching need to blame Buck Randall for this murder as well as that of his wife. And yet what of the clipping that Randall had sent Kaminski, boasting of Marsha Reed's murder?

Did that now mean nothing?

Or had it meant nothing all along?

★ ★ ★

I tried mentioning the doubts tentatively to Fitzgerald as we walked back to my apartment later, the sun cutting deep shadows into the ground at our backs as we walked into its path, but she had a plausible answer to every one of my questions.

"You know what Dalton would say, don't you?" she said.

"That Kaminski sent the clipping to himself," I said. "But you don't believe that."

"No, I don't. But we haven't found a single scrap of evidence to connect Buck Randall to the murder of Marsha Reed," Fitzgerald said. She paused as we waited for a chance to cross St Andrews's Street. "All we have is Kaminski's conviction that there *must* be a connection somewhere. And how do we know that Buck Randall, even if he did send that clipping to Kaminski, didn't simply *want* him to think he'd killed this woman? If he's playing tricks with Kaminski's mind, it makes sense."

"So you're saying these two strands are entirely separate?" I said.

"Why not? We thought there was some connection between Marsha's secret sado-masochistic life online and what happened to her, between her online fantasy life and her murder, but now we're faced with the likelihood that there wasn't. Why shouldn't these strands be separate too? They make no sense if we try to make them intersect. If we see them as separate strands which merely happened to run together for a while at a given point, then everything falls into place. Solomon killed Marsha. Buck Randall is involved

390

somehow in the disappearance and death of Mark Hudson. Randall simply used Marsha as a weapon in the psychological battle he's waging on Kaminski. *And*," she added hastily before I could object, "even if there is some further connection between the two strands that we are failing to see clearly, the next course of action remains entirely the same. It's about reeling in Buck Randall. Once we have him in custody, we can take it from there."

"OK, I'll buy that," I said reluctantly.

"Then let's get on with it," said Fitzgerald. "We're already searching the city for him. Did you know Randall was a heavy drinker? Practically an alcoholic, according to the reports I got from Texas. That means he has to surface somewhere: bars, off-licences, supermarkets. Most of all, there's tonight. That's still our best chance to apprehend him."

I couldn't argue with that.

Our steps were leading us away from Dublin Castle where, for the last couple of hours, the final briefing before tonight's huge surveillance operation had been taking place. I hadn't got a chance to talk to Fitzgerald during the meeting, the room was so crowded. That had its advantages too. It had been crowded enough that I'd become blessedly invisible again.

A small clutch of officers had tagged along undercover earlier that day as part of a final routine police inspection to check that safety regulations were in order. It had given them a good working knowledge of the layout of the site, which they then proceeded to pass on to the team which would be carrying out that

evening's surveillance. There'd been a tense mood in the air that always came when something major was in the offing.

The presence alone of Finbar Donnelly from the armed-response unit was sufficient to ensure no one took what was happening lightly, though as always on such occasions it seemed like half the room was engaged in a testosterone contest with him. Seamus Dalton in particular had spent the meeting leaning back in his chair, chewing gum, feet up on the table, doing everything bar unzipping himself and slapping it on the table to prove that he was man enough to match any fellow officer with a gun. Dalton's mood was high too because he'd captured Solomon that morning and was currently feeling like a cross between Eliot Ness and Philip Marlowe.

Sometimes you wonder how far man really has evolved from the Stone Age — and when I say man, I don't mean it in the all-inclusive sense of mankind. I mean those members of society who seem to keep half their IQ hidden in their pants. And as to where the other half's hidden, no one knows because they've never managed to locate it.

Donnelly had used a map of the area around Merrion Square that was pinned to the wall, and a smaller rough sketch of the layout of the fair itself, to explain precisely where the armed response officers would be located in case of trouble, stressing all the while that his men were there only as a last resort and the best outcome would be if they went unneeded.

Dalton had snorted scornfully at that.

"That's right," he was heard to mutter. "Leave the hard work to us as usual."

It was, to say the least, a blessing when the meeting was called to an end, and we could head back to my apartment to snatch a shower and something to eat. We didn't have much time. Fitzgerald wanted to see Kaminski one last time before waving him off to the fair.

For me, the night couldn't come quickly enough. I was impatient to begin. An end of sorts seemed tantalizingly close, like we only had to reach out and take it. But the minutes between now and then stretched out like the vastness separating stars, and the light itself seemed to be trying to frustrate us. The day never wants to step aside and hand the world to darkness in summer, but there was no chance of Buck Randall turning up at the fair until it had. Everything until then was just a question of waiting. I'd never been good at that.

I let Fitzgerald climb into the shower first while I found a few fragments of salad hiding out in the corners of the fridge, threw them together with a dressing, cut some bread that didn't feel too stale and tried to make an omelette to go with it all. Unfortunately, there's something about an omelette that always defeats me, and this one was no exception.

"That looks good," Fitzgerald said appreciatively all the same when she appeared ten minutes later from the bedroom with wet hair and clean clothes.

The hot water had knocked some of the exhaustion out of her face, but she still wasn't going to fool anyone

that she'd been giving Sleeping Beauty a run for her money in recent days. Her mouth yawned involuntarily at regular intervals. Her eyes were too wide with the effort of keeping them open.

She groaned as her cellphone made a pleading noise at the exact moment we sat down to eat, and she reached down for the jacket which she'd dropped on the floor next to the couch on her way to the bathroom, rummaging around in the inside pocket until she found it.

She checked her messages cursorily.

"I need to recharge," she said. "The phone and me likewise."

"Any messages?"

"Nothing," she said. "Unless you count the press. No matter how often I change my private number, they always get it. I don't know why they bother going to all the trouble. It's not like I ever tell them anything."

"Have you heard any more about Ellen Forwood?" I asked.

"I dropped in on her at the hospital again before going to Dublin Castle," Fitzgerald explained. "She's in the same hospital as Rose Downey, so I was able to kill two birds with one stone, pardon the expression. Ellen's been in and out of consciousness, so I only managed to spend a few minutes with her, but I've never seen anyone more eager to make a statement."

"She did withdraw her alibi, then?"

"She did. Unfortunately she also *confirmed* his story about what happened between them at her house in North Great George's Street. He came round to

confront her, they argued, grappled briefly, she fell and hit her head. Pure accident, she says."

"So the attempted murder charge will need to be quietly dropped?"

"That was always the icing on the cake anyway," she said. "More important is making the murder charge stick. That, and what happens tonight." She suddenly looked apologetic. "Actually, Saxon, do you mind if I don't finish this omelette?"

"I wasn't aware," I said, "that you'd even started it."

CHAPTER
THIRTY-FIVE

It took me a while to notice later that we were walking down Kildare Street past the front gate of Parliament Buildings and on toward the huge grounds of Trinity College where, behind the railings on College Green, a group of men in shorts were playing cricket for fun in the last of the light, the thwack of the ball hitting the bat hanging dully in the air.

"This isn't the way to Kaminski's hotel," I said.

"How observant you are today," teased Fitzgerald. "I didn't want to take the risk of just turning up at Kaminski's door. For all we know, Buck Randall may be watching the hotel. He always seems to know where Kaminski is. I asked Malachy Stack — you remember him from the crime team meeting? — to bring Kaminski along somewhere quiet near by."

Fitzgerald's definition of quiet was evidently different from mine. A couple of minutes later we were turning into Lincoln Place, and I found myself being led up the steps of the Dublin Dental School and Hospital, into a reception area on the first floor lined with plastic chairs. Luckily, there was no sign of any patients. Either the place was closed or they'd all been put off the idea

of coming in for treatment by the gruesome posters lining the walls.

They made the inside of your mouth look like Vietnam circa 1975.

In the middle of one row, Kaminski was sitting on a chair next to Detective Stack.

He didn't look happy.

Kaminski, that is, not Stack. Though on second thoughts, Stack didn't exactly look the picture of joy either. The conversation had obviously been a little strained.

"Stack," said Fitzgerald, "take the door, will you, check no one comes in after us?"

The detective rose gratefully and did as he was told.

"What's with the babysitter?" asked Kaminski when the other man had gone.

"I had to make sure you were behaving yourself," Fitzgerald said, taking the seat next to him while I sat on the row in front, turning round in my seat to face him.

"I'm a big boy," said Kaminski. "I don't need Mary Poppins holding my hand. And what's with this place? A dental hospital? Do you offer all the people you're holding against their will a free dental check-up, or is this a special offer for me alone?"

"No one's holding you prisoner," said Fitzgerald. "How melodramatic you are sometimes. You remind me of Saxon. You're free to walk away at any time."

"Free to get subsequently arrested for being an accessory to murder, you mean."

"All choices have consequences," she said smugly. "That doesn't mean we're not free to make them. It's one of the perplexities of the human condition."

Kaminski must have decided there wasn't much mileage in that complaint, because he didn't bother answering her. Instead he turned his attention to me.

"What's with the dark rings round the eyes?" he asked. "Didn't you get any sleep last night? Or did you two hit the town to celebrate screwing up all my plans?"

"We were otherwise engaged," I said.

"Actually," said Fitzgerald, "we arrested someone for the murder of Marsha Reed."

Kaminski looked stunned. "You've got Buck Randall?"

"I said we arrested someone for Marsha Reed's murder. I didn't say it was Randall."

"Then who was it?"

"Victor Solomon," I told him.

He wore a bemused expression that said my answer didn't make logical sense.

"So Randall gets away scot-free?" he said.

"He's still wanted in connection with Mark Hudson's murder," said Fitzgerald defensively. "I'd hardly call that getting away with anything."

"Randall won't have been so stupid as to let you pin that one on him."

"He was stupid enough to be seen at the spot where Hudson's body was found."

"Yeah, that was convenient for you, wasn't it?" said Kaminski. He shook his head roughly. "No, there was a

reason for that. There was a reason for everything. He has it all worked out. He's been ahead of you every step of the way."

"His fingerprints were all over Hudson's car," Fitzgerald insisted. "Inside and out."

That silenced him for a moment.

Then he shrugged that off too.

"He'll have an answer," said Kaminski. "He always does. He's going to wriggle off the hook for this the same way he wriggled off it when he murdered my wife. Even if you do pick him up, you'll end up holding him for a couple of days and then wave him off at the airport with a slap on the wrist for breaching immigration rules."

"You don't have much faith in the police here in Dublin, do you, Mr Kaminski?"

"Do you blame me?" he said. "Look at that chump you sent to watch over me." He gestured toward Stack, who was standing by the door looking about as inconspicuous as an elephant at a geisha party. "He has cop written all over him. Did you ever stop to wonder," he continued, "what would've happened if Randall had seen *that* trailing around after me like a devoted puppy all day? He'd know you were going to be waiting for him at the fair tonight. He wouldn't show. Maybe it's already too late. Maybe he already has seen him."

"And I told you, that's a risk we're both going to have to take," said Fitzgerald, though I could tell she understood what Kaminski meant. "I couldn't let you wander about on your own. I don't trust you. I still

don't know that you're even telling the truth about the fair."

"Just make sure you keep well away from me tonight," he warned. "I'm not having you messing up my chance to get Randall after all the work I've put into hunting him down."

"I know how to do my job," Fitzgerald said coldly.

"Make sure you do."

To avoid any further conflict, she showed him the map of the funfair and the surrounding streets, pointing out the relevant details of the surveillance operation to him, but he scarcely glanced at it.

"You've been wired up?" she asked him eventually, giving up on the briefing.

Kaminski nodded.

"Then if you see Randall, simply say the word and we'll take over."

"Yippee," he said sarcastically. "Can I go now?"

Fitzgerald checked her watch.

"It's almost nine," she said. "You can go. But be warned. No games. There are more than enough of my officers around out there to stop you doing something stupid, so don't even bother trying. You'll only embarrass yourself."

I thought he was going to say something in response to that, but whatever it was he decided to keep it to himself. Maybe he felt contemptuous silence was all that we, his tormentors, deserved. Instead he turned and walked away, weaving through the lines of plastic chairs to the door where Detective Stack was waiting.

"Good luck," my voice rose after him, trying to sound encouraging.

He flinched slightly, but that was all.

"Should I follow him?" asked Stack once Kaminski had gone.

"He's on his own now," Fitzgerald replied. "Did you search him before we arrived?"

"Yes, Chief. He wasn't too pleased about that either."

"He wouldn't be. He was clean?"

"He didn't have anything on him."

"Good. There's no way I wanted him taking any kind of weapon along with him tonight. The temptation would be too great. Unless he's received some special Marines training in unarmed combat, I doubt there's much danger of Buck Randall coming to harm."

"Let's hope you're right," I said, but even as I said it I wasn't sure if I believed it. Part of me feared that Kaminski was right. That Buck Randall, even if he was placed in custody, would somehow contrive to ensure that no dirt stuck to him. What was better — for a guilty man to escape justice, or for Kaminski to finish this once and for all?

I didn't trust myself to give the right answer.

By now the shadows were lengthening at last, the sky was fading. Night wouldn't be long.

There was also no sign of Kaminski as we left the building soon after.

"You don't think —"

"That he's run out on us? No, I don't think he's run out on us."

Still, it was a relief when Fitzgerald managed to get through to Walsh and he told her he could see Kaminski approaching Merrion Square from the other direction.

"Why's he going that way?" I wondered aloud as we made our own way to the square. "He must've walked straight past the road leading to Merrion Square, gone the complete wrong way and then turned back on himself further on."

"Probably trying to piss us off," she suggested.

He was succeeding.

"Come on, let's go join the party."

The light was noticeably more strained than it had been before we went into the dental hospital. Night took a long time coming in summer, but once it started it came on fast. I felt a sense of growing expectation gathering inside my chest.

This was it.

Within the hour, we might be face to face with the elusive Buck Randall.

We took a more immediate route than Kaminski, for all the world like two women out for a summer evening's walk to the fair. At least, that's how I hoped we looked. Kaminski's words about Detective Stack practically having the word cop written all over him. Fitzgerald blended in to my eyes, but then I might be too familiar with her to be able to judge her dispassionately. *Did* she look like a cop?

What, for that matter, did *I* look like?

Certainly no one gave us a second glance as we joined the increasing mass of people making their way down toward Merrion Square where, above the rooftops, the top of a Ferris wheel could be seen now turning slowly, lights flashing in the shape of the metal, standing out more sharply against the thickening dark sky. Dark — yes it really was now.

I could hear music thudding, bass and drum, into the warm night, mingled with snatches of laughter, the squeals of the nervous on the fairground rides.

There was a sign above the gate: *Opening Night*.

"You know," Fitzgerald said as we walked through the gate into the square, and looked around all the stalls and rides laid out before us, "it's a shame we have to waste a night like this. I love funfairs. I remember the one we always used to go to out in the West every summer when I was a child. It sat right at the edge of the sea. It probably only had a couple of dodgems and a few arcade games, but to me in those days it was like Las Vegas."

"You mean, hookers and Mafia hitmen everywhere you look, and little old ladies from Idaho feeding their life savings into the slot machines?"

"Something like that," she said. "Only without the hookers and the hitmen."

"And the little old ladies didn't come from Idaho."

"I doubt it," agreed Fitzgerald.

I didn't say anything about what I felt. I'd always hated carnivals, whatever I'd said to Fitzgerald last night. Always seen something seedy and untrustworthy in them. If the carnival was a man, he'd be the kind of

man who could as easily knock you around as show you a good time. There's an air of jollity about them, but underlying that simmers a barely concealed mood of anger and menace and resentment. The people who attach themselves to the wandering carnivals are those who have nothing else left. They've been driven out of the world of light and on to the road in broken-down trucks, the modern-day equivalent of outlaws and renegades. There's always the feeling at the carnival that someone is going to get hurt, and you just hope it isn't you. And, caught up with that, there is the promise, or maybe that should be the threat, of bad sex and sudden intimacies that could feel more like violence. Strange enemies lurk in the shadows, and you're never quite sure if they belong there or not.

People did, admittedly, seem to be having a good time at the fair tonight — stumbling dizzily out of the funhouse and showing off at the test-your-strength machines — so maybe it was just me who got grouchy under their influence. There were plenty of small children running round too, eating candy apples and cotton candy, clinging on to oversized teddy bears that their fathers had won by tossing wonky rings on to hooks on a wall or firing corks out of mounted shotguns at moving yellow plastic ducks. Couples walked arm in arm. Bursts of tinny music competed raucously with each other from every ride that we passed.

I tried to look as if I was there to enjoy myself like everyone else, and to stay alert for any sign of Buck Randall. That wasn't proving so easy. I knew what his

picture was like, but the man himself might've come here tonight in disguise. That was most likely how he *had* come. He wanted to keep the advantage over Kaminski.

The crowds didn't help. I hadn't expected the fair to be so busy, but then why wouldn't it be? It was a mild night, not a chance of rain. The lights and music beckoned.

I began to think half the city had turned out for the fair's first night.

A couple of times I caught a glimpse of someone who might be Randall . . . or was I only projecting Randall's features on to some other stranger because I wanted to see him so badly? And I couldn't stare too long, because if it *was* Randall then I couldn't alert him to the fact that other people besides Kaminski might be expecting him to turn up.

Once I caught myself staring and realized it was Kaminski I was staring at. He was staring back at me like he'd been trapped by the same trick of the mind, his eye latching unconsciously on to something known.

So I had to content myself with sideways glances and stolen looks, and couldn't decide whether they were better or worse than nothing. In fact, I soon realized, I'd have been better placed to see Randall if I was watching the fair from one of the windows in the surrounding buildings. And who knows, that might've been exactly what Randall was doing.

Say he was holed up in one of those apartments. Say he'd rented an office for the week or the month. It was the easiest thing in the world to camp up there tonight

and observe the scene below, god-like, through binoculars. I saw Kaminski, standing by a hot-dog stand, squeezing mustard on to his food and trying to look nonchalant. What if Randall was watching him that very second? What if every move he'd taken had been observed from the moment he'd passed through the gate?

And what if Kaminski wasn't the only one who was being watched?

Everywhere I looked now, I seemed to see one of the surveillance team lingering, lurking, idling self-consciously — a figure here by the coconut shy, another there by the dodgems. Or was it only the fair's own security guards, talking to one another over walkie-talkies, watching out for possible trouble? They were all looking alike to me now, and a kind of panic gripped me temporarily, a sense that the situation was not as much under control as we'd imagined. I turned to speak to Fitzgerald — and found that I'd lost her somewhere along the way. A moment before, I was sure, she'd been there. I'd felt her hand touch my elbow, guiding me in the right direction as the crowd threatened to carry me on the wrong path.

Now there was no sign of her.

And there was no sign of Kaminski at the hot-dog stand.

Where was he?

I pushed my way back into the pressing throng of bodies and on through toward the place where I'd last seen him. The sizzle of meat cooking turned the air

rancid again, as it had the night Rose Downey was attacked. The stench of burning fat was as offensive as stale sweat. The paper in which the food came wrapped, now scrunched into stained, greasy balls, littered the ground around the food stall like flowers at a funeral.

And then I thought I saw not Kaminski but Fitzgerald, a couple of hundred yards away from where I was standing now, her back turned to me, walking toward the helter-skelter.

I resisted the urge to call her name and instead plunged back into the tide.

Waded through the crowd as if through heavy water.

But she wasn't at the helter-skelter. Nor at the carousel beyond. I was walking now without direction, simply going round, searching for some anchor to fasten my fractured impressions of the scene that evening back into place. Light was throbbing in my temples, and with it the screech and whine of machinery. The music was getting louder. The carousel spun crazily, horses hurtling round after one another's tails, mouths pulled back in demonic grins. Indistinct figures stepped expertly among the waltzers as the cars turned in a blur of faces.

And then I heard a voice.

Shouting.

"*Stop!*"

It was Kaminski. And soon other voices had joined his. A murmur was spreading through the crowd, like Chinese whispers. I couldn't catch what it said, but I

could see where it was coming from. The hot-dog stand. The direction I'd come from minutes before.

"It's the police," I heard a woman ahead of me in the crowd say to her companion.

"What the fuck are they doing here?" he answered testily.

The idea that the police might actually have a good reason to be somewhere was one which many citizens of Dublin still considered too implausible to be entertained for a second.

As I got closer, I heard someone else say that the police had some guy on the ground — could it be Buck Randall? — and there was a crackle of police radios. The music continued from the rides but seemed to have fallen back until it was hardly audible any more.

All I could hear was the commotion up ahead.

"Stand back!"

"Let her through," said Fitzgerald, because there she was, standing with a cellphone pressed to her ear and reaching out with her other hand for my arm to drag me into the circle. And the plain clothes cop who'd been trying to keep a boundary between the police who'd grouped together at this point and the restless crowd threw up his hands theatrically in exasperation, as if the futility of the task had just become apparent to him.

"Have you got him?" I mouthed to her, but she was talking so fast and so loud that nothing I said could get through. She simply pointed at Patrick Walsh, who, I now saw, was standing looking somewhat redundant and ineffectual a couple of yards away.

"Walsh," I said, "what's going on? Have you got Randall?"

Before he could answer, Kaminski's voice cut in angrily.

"Don't you tell me to calm down, you fucking incompetent fuckheads!"

He was standing in the middle of a group of police officers who were trying to hold him back. His nose was bleeding. His shirt was torn. Another man I didn't recognize, an unpleasant-looking character with a ring of studs through his lower lip, sat on the grass near by in handcuffs, trying to kick out at Kaminski's legs whenever he got the chance.

"What is it, JJ?"

"They lost him!" he spat when he saw me. "They fucking lost him! How in God's fucking name did you people let him get away? What the fuck were you thinking?"

At which point I considered it safe to assume that no, we hadn't gotten Buck Randall.

CHAPTER
THIRTY-SIX

"I got a call," said Fitzgerald as she lay back on Kaminski's bed next morning, pillow at her back, arms folded behind her head, legs outstretched to the end of her boots. "One of the surveillance team said Kaminski had seen someone who might be Buck Randall. I tried to get your attention, but the place was too noisy and you were distracted, you weren't hearing me."

I'd been surveying the windows round Merrion Square, imagining our every move being watched and missing entirely what was happening right there on the ground.

I guess I must be more out of practice than I knew.

"By the time I reached the place where Randall had apparently been spotted," explained Fitzgerald, "it was too late. Kaminski said he'd lost visual contact. No one else had seen him, so I wasn't sure what to think — or, more to the point, what to do next. Melt back into the crowd again and wait for another sighting? Try to move in and close him down, shutting off the exits and searching the crowd one by one? Well, I knew I couldn't do that. It would've been chaos, there were too many people milling around."

"So what did you decide?" I asked.

"I didn't have the chance to decide *anything*," she said with feeling. "Suddenly there was another shout. I heard someone calling out Buck Randall's name. It was Kaminski again. Next thing a scuffle had broken out. I ran over. It looked like some guy had punched Kaminski and they were grappling together like the worst pro wrestlers you ever saw. It was almost comic. The one thing I *could* see was that it wasn't Randall he was fighting with."

"Who was it?"

"I can't even remember his name. He was just some scanger who'd gone along to the fairground with his girlfriend."

"Scanger?"

"Yeah, a scanger, you must know what a scanger is. Let me think. What would you say? White trash maybe. It's an old Dublin word. Think young person of limited intelligence and even more limited vocabulary, who has an inordinate fondness for shaving his head, dressing in cheap sportsgear and piercing his body with too many pieces of metal."

"I'm following you. It's a new word on me, but I'm following you."

"This particular representative of the species, anyway, was at the fairground last night. Kaminski claimed he saw Buck Randall through the crowd; he tried to push his way towards him, ended up upsetting some popcorn belonging to this delightful individual's girlfriend. Next thing you know he's landed one on Kaminski's nose, and they're rolling around in the dirt trying to knock one another's lights out — the young

scanger to defend his fair maiden's honour for the grievous hurt of losing her popcorn, and Kaminski just so he could get away and pursue what he said was Randall. The surveillance team came running, thinking Kaminski had their man, and instead found the world's most pathetic fight in progress at their feet. By the time it had been broken up, the evening's work was comprehensively ruined."

"And Kaminski?"

"Came right back here, packed his things and made a bolt for it. In all the confusion, I forgot to keep a tail on him." She slid her legs off the bed and walked to the wardrobe, opening the door to show me the empty hangers where Kaminski's shirts had hung, the absence in the corner where his holdall had sat. "I screwed up. I was too tired. And now I can't help asking myself whether the whole thing was a set-up from the start."

"You mean he created the confusion so that he *could* slip away?"

"He was the one who cried out Buck Randall's name. I don't think he saw a damn thing," said Fitzgerald. "I don't think Randall was ever there. There was no meeting arranged at the funfair. Kaminski just made it up to give him a chance to get out of our line of sight."

"We had him backed into a corner."

"He had to think fast."

"And he did."

I remembered that night at Dublin Castle following our visit to the graveyard, when he was brought in for questioning. He had somewhere he needed to be. Buck

Randall had made contact. He was being threatened with a cell for the next three days, he was going to miss whatever appointment he'd made with the man who'd killed his wife. The only way he could get out was to offer us a false meeting instead.

I recalled how he'd closed his eyes in his chair while he considered what Fitzgerald was telling him. He was searching for something inside his mind.

"And then it must've come back to him that he had the leaflet," she said. "Someone probably handed it to him in the street as he walked by; he'd stuffed it in his pocket without thinking, and it gave him the perfect bluff. He could say the leaflet was the message from Randall, go along with the charade, start a fight in the funfair and sneak away under the cover of the ensuing pandemonium, leaving himself free to get to the *real* meeting alone."

"It was my fault," I insisted. "You said it yourself. I knew him better than anyone else in this town. I should've known he was spinning a line."

"He was another good actor. The city seems to be full of them these days. And you know what? I don't blame him for splitting," she said, shutting the wardrobe door and dropping heavily on to the edge of the bed again. "Look how we screwed up last night. Why *should* he trust us to help him find Randall when we fell for a blatant ruse like that?"

"You mustn't blame yourself."

"You're right. There'll be plenty of other people willing to do that on my behalf. *This* certainly isn't

what the Assistant Commissioner was hoping for in her first week in charge."

She stabbed a finger at the newspaper lying thrown on to the bed at her side.

Mystery over Dublin Police Operation in City Fairground read the headline.

"I read it," I said. "The story's thinner than an anorexic ghost."

"It's thin now, but it won't take them too long to flesh out what the surveillance team was really doing in Merrion Square," Fitzgerald said. "They can't be fobbed off for ever."

"The press have the attention span of a cranefly," I said fiercely. "Couple of days and they'll have moved on to the next story. There was some trouble at the fairground, so what? Happens all the time. Just feed them a line about how it was an operation to round up illegal immigrants or crack down on drug trafficking. Reporters love that crap."

"Even the press aren't stupid enough to fall for that one," said Fitzgerald. "Since when did the Murder Squad spearhead trawling expeditions against illegal immigrants? No, they know already there was more to it than that. All they have to do is put the jigsaw together."

"Then be straight with them. Call a press conference. Tell them you're looking for a man called Buck Randall. Give them his picture. Let them put it on the front page. There's no point taking the softly-softly approach any more," I said. "What use is secrecy? Randall will probably guess last night was

about him. The best chance of finding him now is to flush him out of wherever he's been hiding. Make him a celebrity. Deprive him of his anonymity."

"We might drive him underground instead," said Fitzgerald.

"There's always that chance. But it will also make him nervous, and nervous people make mistakes. He'll feel watched wherever he goes. He'll be a wanted man. And even if he doesn't break cover, Kaminski might. He'll know his window of opportunity's running out."

"Do you really think it could work?" asked Fitzgerald expectantly.

"It couldn't hurt," I said.

Fitzgerald got to her feet again.

She was restless, like she wanted to pace to think, but there was scarcely the space in that tiny room for breathing, let alone pacing. She was working out the permutations. Totting up what could go wrong and matching that against the possible benefits.

"Saxon," she said eventually, "you're either a genius or a fool. What say we find out which it is?"

That my genius would be confirmed so fast came as a surprise even to me. Not that I'd ever doubted it, you understand, it just made a pleasing change to have the hard evidence.

There were sightings of Buck Randall at an amusement arcade in Westmoreland Street, a cinema in Poolbeg Street, a bar in Camden Row, and the outpatients clinic at St James's Hospital. Either he was a very busy guy or there were a lot of cases of mistaken

415

identity out there. Most promising of all was the landlord in Kilmainham, not that far from where Marsha Reed had died, who called to say he'd rented a room to a man with an American accent who resembled the photograph of Randall which had been issued.

"Yeah, that's him," he said lazily, lifting the front of his T-shirt to scratch at his overhanging belly — but he wasn't really looking at the photograph Fitzgerald had laid down flat on the desk in front of him. Instead he was staring at a young woman in the road outside, skimpily dressed for the heat, bending down to pick up something she'd dropped.

He was old enough to be her grandfather. For all I know, he *was* her grandfather. He didn't look like he'd let a little thing like that get in the way.

His wife — bloated and sweating and squeezed painfully into a dress that looked like it was begging for mercy — sat next to him, watching him non-judgementally.

She hadn't spoken a word since Fitzgerald, Patrick Walsh and I had arrived.

"Please look closely at the picture," said Fitzgerald, her voice rising to get his attention. "It's very important that you're sure this really is the man who stayed here."

The man sighed and reluctantly forced his gaze away to look at the picture.

"It's him. I already told you it was," he said. "How many more times? He wasn't using the name the police gave on the TV, mind. He called himself . . . what was it now? O'Brien. Said he was an Irish-American over

416

looking into his roots. Soon as I saw his picture on the news at one, I knew it was him. Said to you it was him, didn't I?"

That last remark was addressed to the wife, who suddenly seemed to be jerked out of her lethargy by the words of her loving husband. Roused at last, she managed a nod of agreement and then returned to the semi-catatonic state she'd been in since we got here.

He, meanwhile, narrowed his eyes and peered at Fitzgerald.

"It was you, wasn't it? At that press conference?"

Fitzgerald confirmed stiffly that it was.

"Thought it was. I never forget a face."

"That's a useful habit to have."

"You look a lot younger on TV."

"Is that so?"

"Yeah. Must be all those lights. Still, don't suppose you'd be so high up in the police if you were still nineteen, eh?"

And he chuckled to himself like he'd just told the world's funniest joke.

Seemed like women to him were there to be put in their place, leered at or ground into passive, defeated submission like the one slumped next to him in her chair.

With the patience not so much of a saint as half a dozen saints combined, Grace managed to guide his attention back to the picture. "When did you first meet him?" she asked, stressing each syllable coldly.

"Three weeks ago. I know, because the rent was due Friday."

"How did he pay?"

"Cash. Two weeks' deposit, rent one week in advance."

"Did you ask for any ID?"

"I haven't got time to be asking people for their passports and driving licences," he said scornfully. "As long as they have the money and I've got a room for them to stay in, they're welcome to it. I'm not their bleeding nanny."

"Can you remember *anything* about him?" Fitzgerald asked.

"Not much," he admitted. "I hardly saw him, and when I did he didn't speak. Used to pass him on the stairs occasionally. He didn't keep regular hours."

"Did he say what he did for a living?"

"Didn't ask."

"He didn't let anything slip?"

"Not that I noticed."

"What about visitors?"

"None that I saw."

"Phone calls in or out?"

"There's a payphone out there on the wall." He gestured to the door leading out into the hall. "Couple of times I saw him sitting out there, waiting for a call."

"You ever listen in?" I said.

"I've got better things to do."

Like lust after every young girl who passed the window.

"So you noticed nothing unusual about him, you didn't know who he talked to or about what the whole

time he was here, and then he was just gone?" said Fitzgerald.

"He must've left this morning," the landlord said. "He was definitely here last night. I heard him moving about, didn't I? Then, when I saw your press conference on TV on the news, I went up to check he was still there and found he'd cleared out without a word."

Randall must've seen the press conference when it was televised live that morning. Either that or someone else had alerted him to it. He knew his cover was blown, so he ran.

If only the landlord and his wife had seen the press conference live instead of the highlights on the lunchtime news, he mightn't have had such a head start.

"I suppose all this will get into the papers now, won't it?" the man continued gloomily, starting off on his scratching again. And, to be fair, he had a lot of flesh to scratch. "I almost wish I hadn't picked up the phone. I don't want people getting the wrong impression. I run a respectable business here. Still" — and he brightened visibly as an idea struck him — "at least I can say I've had someone famous staying here."

"Famous?"

I could see that Fitzgerald was getting near to the point where homicide was looking like a good alternative strategy for dealing with this witness.

"This man you're looking for," he said. "He must be famous if you're after him, mustn't he? Stands to

reason. So go on, tell me. What'd he do? Did he murder someone?"

He said the word with such relish, it was like he was tasting it on his tongue.

"I'm afraid I'm not at liberty to discuss that," said Fitzgerald.

The man's eyes opened wide with affront.

"Excuse me for breathing, I'm sure."

He was still muttering under his breath about who did the police think they were, and whose taxes did they think paid their wages, when we finally escaped upstairs to check out the room where the elusive Buck Randall had been staying for the past few weeks.

It made Kaminski's original hotel room look like the Hilton. I was struck by the resemblances between the two men, both hiding out in a strange city in down-at-heel surroundings, their contact with the world around them reduced to furtive, obscure excursions on missions only they fully understood. And now, within the space of twenty-four hours, the two of them had both cut loose and vanished into the city. Where were they now?

Randall had left little behind him, save for a couple of odd socks, a shirt still hanging in the wardrobe and a shaving brush next to the sink in the bathroom.

Not exactly much to go on.

There was a stale smell in the room of sweat and unwashed flesh.

Fitzgerald right now was standing by the TV. There was a tape left in the VCR. She pressed the switch and ejected it.

"*Muff City,*" she read when it came out. "Charming."

"I think I've got that one on DVD," Walsh whispered to me. "It's very good."

"Tragic how the Academy Awards always overlook the best films," I replied.

"Ironic, isn't it?" said Fitzgerald. "He needs to hide out, not make himself too conspicuous, but he still takes the risk of popping along to the local perverts' pleasure palace to pick up a copy of this crap."

"Actually," said the unexpected voice of the landlord from the doorway at our backs, "that's one of mine." He must have followed us upstairs to eavesdrop on the conversation. "Mr O'Brien must've taken it from my library downstairs. Can I have it back?"

In the middle of everything, it was reassuring to see some people still had their priorities in the right order.

CHAPTER
THIRTY-SEVEN

Walsh stayed behind at the rooming house to continue the search while Fitzgerald and I returned to Dublin Castle. She had to brief the Assistant Commissioner later, both on the case against Solomon and also on what had happened last night, and now she had today's events to add to the mix. She needed to make sure she was up to speed on the investigation.

That meant getting through the reports which had been gradually mounting in the last couple of days on her desk. The reports so far covering the attack on Rose Downey were scant. That was still being handled as a simple assault, whatever hunch we might have had about it being connected in some way with Marsha's murder. In that respect, Rose was fortunate it hadn't gone far enough for any possible similarities to emerge.

It was the reports on Marsha Reed which were going to take time to get through.

First up there were statements from confidential informants at the S & M club to which Marsha Reed belonged, and the transcript of an interview with one of the men Marsha had contacted through an internet chatroom to share her fantasies of being murdered. He turned out to be the happily married owner of a

health-food shop in the city centre who had no idea that the woman he'd been corresponding with online was the same one who'd been found murdered less than a week ago. His story was that the whole exchange between the two of them was nothing more than a fantasy, and that he'd stopped once she suggested meeting up and maybe trying out a few scenarios. Lucky for him, the police didn't intend to tell his wife about the matter.

I would have.

Added to that were the profiles on Marsha's fellow students in the class I'd taken, though again it all seemed somewhat redundant in the light of subsequent events, and page after page of messages left on the email hotline which had been set up following her murder.

An accompanying detailed fingerprint analysis of the necklace found in Solomon's office showed, frustratingly, that it had been wiped clean and had no fingerprints of any kind upon it. Forensics did, however, confirm that microscopic traces of mud and grass matching those samples taken from Marsha's house had been picked up in the same office, though the finding of the Shoe Identification and Retrieval team was that there were no footprints matching his at the scene itself. A number as yet remained unidentified.

There was also the psychological report on Solomon from Fisher, who'd interviewed him briefly since his arrest. Solomon had not been forthcoming, to say the least, and indeed found the very idea of being psychologically profiled offensive and absurd.

Fisher could come to few conclusions, save that Solomon was a domineering personality, controlling and narcissistic, which struck me as something which could be said about most of the people in the theatre. As to whether he considered Solomon capable of such extreme violence, he didn't say, but I could read between the lines. Solomon was capable of extreme violence, as we all were, but Fisher did not think him particularly high risk.

There was also a rundown of everything that was known about Solomon's movements in the days before and after the killing of Marsha Reed, and especially his whereabouts on the night itself. There was undoubtedly a black hole in the record now that his alibi had collapsed. He'd left the Liffey Theatre when the night's performance ended shortly after 11 p.m., not staying for his usual drink, and no one could place him anywhere until the following morning when he had a late breakfast at Bewley's coffee shop in town with a postgraduate student who was writing a profile of him for a journal called *Dublin Theatre Studies*. The student revealed that Solomon had been hungover that morning and in bad form, and also that he'd attempted unsuccessfully to lure her into bed, promising that he could help her get her play produced in London. It seemed to be something of a pattern with him.

Like all police reports, getting through them was a thankless task, giving, as they did, the distinct impression of having been written by people with only a passing acquaintance with the English language and rules of grammar. Paragraphs came at random, or not

at all. Spelling was atrocious. Malapropisms abounded. Many simple pieces of information, from dates and times to further contact numbers, were omitted entirely.

It's no wonder so many criminal cases fall down when they come to court because the police reports are so badly written. Often contradictory, and speckled with information which cannot be properly verified, they're a goldmine for unscrupulous defence attorneys.

The most crucial sheet among the multitude on Fitzgerald's desk would have been all too easy to overlook. It was stapled to the end of the report on his movements, almost like an afterthought, and came from the pen of a patrol cop on the night Marsha Reed died. This was about 2.45 a.m. and revealed that Solomon had been seen in the area round Fitzwilliam Place East in a dishevelled and drunken state, not seeming to know where he was. A patrol car had stopped him to make sure he was OK and then let him proceed on his way.

What was interesting about this was not only that it was the only confirmed sighting between his leaving the theatre and the following morning, but that he'd said he was on his way at the time to see the actor Zak Kirby at his apartment block in the same area of the city.

"Kirby isn't staying at a hotel?" said Fitzgerald.

"He doesn't like hotels," said Walsh, and then he flushed slightly as we turned to look at him curiously. "I read an interview with him in one of the American film magazines," he explained sheepishly. "It said he found

them artificial, unreal, and that when he's in a city he likes to get an authentic feel for the place rather than the front they put on for visitors."

Fitzgerald rolled her eyes.

"So where *is* he staying?" I asked.

She checked the notes on the desk in front of her.

"Mullingar Studios, apparently," she said. "You know it?"

I shook my head.

"It's a big fancy building off Leeson Street," she said. "All shiny glass and chrome."

"Very authentic," I said sarcastically. "He'll really get a feel for the rough side of the city there."

"Don't be so dismissive," said Fitzgerald. "A woman pushed her husband off the thirteenth floor last year, don't you remember? It doesn't get much more authentic than that."

"What does Kirby say about all this?"

"That's the thing. He gave a statement to the police when Solomon's name first came up. He said he didn't see Solomon from the time the play ended Saturday night until the following evening."

"You think Kirby was lying?"

"No idea. But you heard what Fisher said about the mixed scene, the different knots, the possibility of two killers. By Kirby's own testimony, he wasn't back at his apartment until after one. That gives him plenty of time to have taken part in the killing."

"You're not saying Zak Kirby is a killer?" I said.

"Why not?"

"Because too many people would recognize him if he suddenly started wandering round the city, slaughtering women," I said. "That's one of the perils of being famous. OJ apart, it severely limits your chances of committing murder."

"I think you'll find that OJ Simpson was found not guilty," said Fitzgerald.

"Whatever. My point is that every step he takes is ten times more likely to be seen and remembered than if it had been someone anonymous like you or me taking it." I paused. "Still, I wonder if he ever came into contact with Buck Randall —"

"Let's not even go there," said Fitzgerald firmly. "I told you, we've got to treat these stories like they're completely self-contained. I can't start trying to make them link up. That way lies madness. It couldn't hurt, though, to pull up the CCTV from the building where our American movie star is staying and see if Solomon ever did arrive there that night."

And it certainly didn't.

"I have absolutely no idea," said Zak Kirby, and if he really was innocent as charged then it was a perfectly reasonable answer to the question Fitzgerald had asked him a moment earlier.

Having said that, Kirby was, like most of the people we seemed to have encountered during this case, an actor, so if he *did* know why Victor Solomon had turned up at the door of his apartment building at 3 a.m. on the night Marsha Reed died, as the CCTV footage had revealed he had, then it wouldn't be so

difficult to pretend ignorance as it might be for the rest of us mere mortals. Though if he *was* lying, it was a damned good act.

We'd found him sitting in his dressing room at the Liffey Theatre, preparing for that night's performance of *Othello*. The show must go on, isn't that what they say? This one had closed for only one night following the near-death of the leading lady and the arrest of the director on a murder charge. The company was clearly taking the old adage literally.

Kirby had an enviable reputation among young American actors. He'd made the transition from obscure off-Broadway shows and small-budget independent, slightly left-field movies to big-screen Hollywood fame without once being dogged by the usual accusations of selling out. He managed to keep his street cred intact while simultaneously beaming out from the cover of every celebrity magazine. He'd mastered the trick of being good-looking enough for teenage girls to want his poster on their walls, but cool enough for teenage boys not to think he was trying too hard, lending his face and name along the way to all the best progressive causes, and hacking his hair into a faux-punky style that fooled enough people into thinking he didn't care what it looked like. Every couple of years, he also stepped off the celebrity carousel to ostentatiously rediscover his artistic roots by treading the boards, giving the showbiz magazines another opportunity to write at length about what an intriguing, unconventional character he was. Hence the summer's sojourn here in Dublin.

Oh, and did I mention that he'd written a novel too? A slim, sensitive, coming-of-age tale set among young actors dreaming of better things in a rooming house in Brooklyn.

It would be.

Right now, he was lighting a cigarette and trying to remember that night.

"Let me think," he said, mussing up his hair self-consciously and creasing his forehead into a photogenic frown. "You have to appreciate that I get a lot of people ringing my buzzer. Lot of people calling my line. Calls all the time. Night. Day. Day. Night. You know how it is," he added to me. He'd recognized my name as soon as Fitzgerald introduced me. Turned out too that he knew some of the people who'd worked on the TV movie of my first book. Now he was drawing me into his story for back-up. "Their names all blur into one after a while. Just this morning, I took what must've been thirty calls from various TV stations and newspapers wanting to hear about this new script I've been working on about the war in Iraq. I'm calling it *American Dream, Arab Nightmare*. I think it's going to totally expose the hypocrisy of what we're doing out there in the Mid-East. It's the new colonialism, it genuinely is. What we're doing now is no better than what the Europeans did in Africa for centuries, carving up the land, stealing the natural resources, keeping down its true owners."

I was beginning to appreciate why Dublin had taken Zak Kirby to their hearts.

He talked their language.

"I've no idea how they found out about it," he continued smartly about his host of morning callers. "I was trying to keep the project under wraps. I loathe publicity."

You could've fooled me.

Having more manners than me, however, Fitzgerald waited till he'd finished his little speech on global geopolitics before pressing on.

"This wasn't some reporter on the hunt for a scoop," she said. "It was your own director. You're saying you don't remember him coming round that night at all?"

"I know I didn't let him in."

"We know you didn't let him in as well," said Fitzgerald. "The CCTV shows he stood there for five or six minutes, ringing the buzzer, before he went away. Were you out?"

"No. I gave a statement about that already. I was asleep. The CCTV shows me coming in, right?"

"It does. It was a little after one."

"Then how could I have left again without being seen?"

"The CCTV on the back entrance is broken," Fitzgerald said. "Anyone could get in and out without being seen."

He looked shocked. "They could? I'll have to get my people on to that. I can't have fans getting into the place where I'm staying that easily. I've had similar problems before in LA."

"You had a stalker?"

"A teenage girl broke in while I was away filming," said Kirby. "Lived in my house for a week before she

was discovered. She'd been sleeping in my bed. Wearing my clothes."

"So you don't remember Solomon buzzing?"

"I don't. That's the gospel truth."

"You're a heavy sleeper."

"Acting takes its toll. More so when it's a part like Iago. Come to think of it," he said, "I shouldn't wonder if that wasn't what Vic wanted to talk to me about that night."

"Did he make a habit of calling round after midnight to discuss your part?"

"As a matter of fact, he did. He must've been round six, seven times since we started rehearsals. He's a very learned man. I could listen to him talk all night. And believe me, sometimes it feels like I have." He laughed indulgently at his own joke. "Solomon must've read virtually every word that's been written about the play. He loved to talk about the part, and the range of different actors down the years who've portrayed Iago. Most of the other great actors through the years have tried their hand at it." I loved that sly use of the word *other* there. "Olivier, Spacey, Branagh, McKellen, we've all had a shot."

"And this is what you used to spend all night talking about?" I asked.

"You could talk about this material for ever and still not get to the bottom of it. The role of Iago is one of the most important parts in the whole of Shakespeare's canon. I'm not boasting when I say the play should really be called *Iago*, not *Othello*. The whole structure of it is about how manipulation and deceit work

together to precipitate tragedy. About how Iago works his will through Othello. I guess Victor and I often got a bit carried away with it."

"But not that night?"

"Like I say, that night I don't have any memory of him coming round. I certainly didn't talk to him. It's always a rough period, coming up to the end of the first week of a show. I generally pop a pill, put on my earmuffs and say goodnight to the world. Particularly when it's a part this demanding. I've never stretched myself so much. Do you know *Othello*?"

"I had a part in it once at drama school," answered Walsh unexpectedly.

I'd forgotten he was there. He'd been so quiet, standing by the dressing-room door the whole time we were talking, not contributing a word, taking in the backstage ambience, if the sound of hammering from the floor above and a radio blaring counted as ambience.

I guess he was a little starstruck. He'd mentioned a couple of days ago how much he admired Zak Kirby. His smile could have lit up the dark side of the moon when Fitzgerald told him earlier that he could tag along to the theatre this time while she interviewed him.

"You were at drama school?" Kirby said to Walsh, and to give him credit he sounded genuinely interested. Walsh flushed ever so slightly.

"Three years," he said, "but it didn't work out."

"Please tell me you haven't given up acting completely."

432

"I'm in a small amateur company. We put on a couple of plays a year. We did *Othello* a couple of springs ago," Walsh said.

"Who were you?"

"Cassio," said Walsh. "I know it's not a huge part or anything."

"Hey," said Kirby, "Cassio's a good role. You should keep going. Never give up. I'm serious. Once you give up wanting to make a difference, that's the day you start to die inside. You never know what's around the corner. I was twenty-six before I got my first lead role."

The pleasure Walsh clearly took from this exchange almost made me ashamed that I'd been giving Kirby such a tough time in my estimation. Maybe he wasn't such a schmuck, after all, even if he was a walking mouthpiece for all those liberal clichés I so despised.

"You should come along to tonight's performance," Kirby was telling Walsh. "I'll get you three tickets, one for each of you, and leave them at the desk. This is a big night."

"You're not missing Victor Solomon too much, then?" said Fitzgerald.

"Don't you folks have a little rule about being innocent until proven guilty?" the actor said in all seriousness. "I know he's been through the wringer lately, but Vic's not such a loser. He lost his way a little, is all. I don't think he murdered anyone."

"Shame for him you're not eligible to serve on his jury," I said.

"I'd rather play the murderer," he flashed me his big-screen grin good-naturedly. "All those weeks centre

stage on the stand, all eyes fixed on you and you alone. It's the ideal role for any actor. It's always more fun to play the villain."

"I doubt Solomon's looking forward to the prospect quite so eagerly," said Fitzgerald.

CHAPTER
THIRTY-EIGHT

"Well, I think you should go," said Burke, refilling my glass. "Zak Kirby's one of the good guys. I saw him on TV talking about a film he's making about the US occupation of Iraq."

"You couldn't have seen him on TV. He hates publicity. You must've imagined it."

"I wouldn't expect *you* to like him," he went on decisively. "Unless someone's a fully paid-up member of the National Rifle Association, you practically write them off as a pinko."

"You're a pinko. I haven't written you off."

"True," he conceded. "You're a mass of contradictions."

"Don't knock them. My inconsistency is my best feature. That and my ass. Only difference is it's my ass that talks most sense some days."

Burke laughed so loud that he made his cat, Hare dart in alarm from the chair where he'd been curled up making preparations for sleep, and the last of the day's customers in his own store turn round in the aisles of books to see what he was laughing at.

They looked blank on realizing it was me.

"I still think you should go," he said. "I know it's a regular poker night, but Shakespeare's more important than poker . . ."

"Blasphemer."

". . . and *Othello* is one great play."

"So everyone keeps telling me," I answered grouchily.

"You know what your problem is, Saxon?"

"Yes," I said, "I do. Fisher asked me that exact same question. In all honesty, I can't remember precisely which of my many faults it was that he proceeded to elevate into the number one position, but I'm sure it was a good one."

"Your problem," said Burke, refusing to be sidetracked from what he intended to say, "is you think because everyone's telling you something that it must, by definition, be wrong."

"How's that a problem?"

"It's a problem because you miss out on too much that way. Like *Othello*."

"If the play's all you're worried about, then have no fear. I'm going," I declared. "Fitzgerald missed it the first time we had tickets because that was the night they found Marsha Reed's body. I'm not lucky enough to get out of it a second time. Unless you know someone who can arrange another murder for me at short notice?"

"Sorry, I sold my last copy of the *Psychopaths' Phone Directory*."

"Pity. Shakespeare it is, then. If she ever turns up, that is."

436

I checked my watch.

There was more than an hour to go before the play started, but in a town where time is notoriously relative and an arrangement to meet someone is regarded by most of the people living here as more of a well-meaning aspiration than a definite commitment, Fitzgerald was one of the few who could be relied upon to be where and when she said she'd be.

But tonight she still hadn't arrived.

There had to be a reason for it.

I wasn't worried about her as such. Fitzgerald was one of the few people I did let myself worry about but not on this occasion. I knew where she was. She'd returned to Dublin Castle to give her briefing to Assistant Commissioner Carson. But that had been more than two hours ago and there'd been no word since. Should I call and make sure she was OK?

"Maybe she just got fed up with your bad moods and decided to dump you for another former Special Agent with a better temperament," suggested Burke helpfully.

"Kaminski's the only other former Special Agent in town, far as I know, and he's not her type. Besides, he's playing hide-and-seek again. She wouldn't know where to find him."

"Then drink your whiskey and relax. She'll be here." And he retrieved the fleeing cat from the store room and made it sit on his lap, using his big hands to stroke the affronted creature into forgiving him for the earlier fright. "You know," he added more softly now so as not to disturb it, "you might even find the evening interesting."

"Want to make a bet on that?"

"I'd sure bet Buck Randall III would find it interesting."

"Buck Randall probably couldn't even spell Shakespeare, let alone understand it," I said. "What's he got to do with *Othello*?"

"He's got everything to do with *Othello*," said Burke. "Or maybe not Othello so much as Iago. Don't you see?" I had to admit that I didn't. "You know the story, right?"

"Vaguely," I said. "I caught the Orson Welles version on TV one night years ago, but I was pretty drunk at the time. I don't remember much about it."

"That was in the bad old days when actors used to black up to play Othello," said Burke. "In some of those old productions, Othello couldn't even touch the fellow actors in case the boot polish came off and stained their nice new costumes."

"Al Jolson, eat your heart out."

"They did everything but give Othello a banjo and get him to sing 'Old Man River' in between eating courses of fried chicken and gumbo," Burke growled disapprovingly.

I resisted the urge to confess that such an alternative sounded like it'd be a lot more fun than the version I'd seen all those years ago after coming home late from the bar.

"All you have to know," he continued, conveniently saving me from my lifelong tendency to put my foot in it, "is that Iago, a soldier, has been passed over for

promotion by Othello, his captain, in favour of another man called Cassio."

"That's the part Walsh played."

"Don't interrupt. In revenge, Iago then plots to make Othello suspect his wife, Desdemona, of having an affair with Cassio so that he'll kill her and ruin his reputation."

"Seems a bit of an overreaction to missing out on promotion," I said. "just as well it never caught on. It'd be a bloodbath out there every time a position was filled."

He ignored me.

It was usually the best way.

"Iago calls it his cunning pattern," Burke explained. "He works on Othello's decent, trusting nature, tormenting him with words, placing one layer of deception on top of another, so that no single character apart from Iago ever knows the truth, they only know their own part in it, until Othello is driven into a kind of temporary insanity by jealousy and murders the one thing he loves best. That's why the play's named after Othello, not Iago. It's his tragedy."

"Sounds to me," I said, "like it was his wife's tragedy for marrying a man who'd kill his supposed beloved just because he thinks she's getting a bit of action elsewhere. Didn't they have divorce in those days? And that's another thing. How come we're supposed to feel sorry for this man when he was the one who murdered his wife? That was his decision."

"It's symbolic," he said. "Think of it as a dark fable of how jealousy and suspicion can corrupt the most honest and noble souls."

"You're starting to sound like one of those cultural programmes I always try to miss on cable," I said confusedly. "So where does the pound of flesh come into it?"

"It doesn't," said Burke patiently. "That's *The Merchant of Venice*."

"Right," I said slowly, running over what he'd said once more in my mind. "So Iago twists Othello's mind and sends him mad and then Othello murders his wife and we're all supposed to feel sorry for him. I can follow that. Apart from the feeling sorry for him part. What I don't see is how that ties in to Kaminski and Randall. Randall isn't trying to get Kaminski to murder his wife. According to Kaminski, it's Randall who did that already."

"You're taking it too literally."

"I am?"

"It's not the details that matter so much as the way Iago sits at the centre of his web, spinning lies and plots. He even compares himself to a spider right at the start of the play. Iago manipulates Othello's weaknesses until he has no control any more over his own mind. He's like the Pied Piper of Hamelin, leading the children on a merry dance into the darkness. Think about it. Isn't that what Buck Randall's been doing to your friend Kaminski the whole time? He's been jerking his strings from the moment their paths crossed. Even Kaminski's weak spot is the same as Othello's: his love for his wife. That's what makes him vulnerable."

"But to what end?" I said. "Why would he want Kaminski to fall for this line about him being the city's

very own killing machine? What does he want him to *do*?"

"Finding the answer to that is your job," said Burke, "not mine."

I considered what he'd told me.

"Maybe," I said, venturing tentatively toward a possible answer, "Randall wanted Kaminski to come after him all along. He wasn't trying to escape. He was the hunted leading the hunter into a trap so that the roles could be reversed. He knew Kaminski would never give up, so why not just face the inevitable confrontation and get it over and done with?"

"Only it's better to do it on your own terms than your enemy's?"

"And in the arena of your choosing. Exactly," I said. "Which means Buck Randall won't simply vanish, whatever else Kaminski feared. He'll stay and finish what he started."

"He's running out of time if that's the plan," Burke reminded me.

"All the more important, then, that we find Kaminski fast. He's our only lead to Buck Randall." I checked my watch again, suppressing irasciability. Though not for long, probably. It wasn't only Randall that time was running out on. "Where *is* that damn woman?"

I was standing on the kerb at Crampton Quay, waiting for a gap in the hurtling traffic to cross over to the Ha'penny Bridge, when I finally got my answer to that question.

"Saxon," she said. "Can you hear me? This signal isn't good."

"You're cracking up," I told her.

"You wouldn't be the first to tell me that."

"Where are you?"

"I'm with Walsh. We're on our way to the theatre as we speak."

"Weren't we supposed to be meeting up at Burke's place?"

"Change of plan," she crackled in my ear.

The rest of the sentence was lost in static.

"Fitzgerald?"

I had my finger in one ear and my cellphone pressed tightly to the other, straining to differentiate her voice from the other noises around me, but I quickly learned that a warm summer's evening on the riverside in Dublin is not the best place to try to conduct a conversation with a woman in a car any number of streets away.

"Hello? Hello?"

In the end, I gave up.

It didn't matter. She'd said she was on her way to the theatre. I could talk to her there. Getting back to the theatre had been the plan anyway when I decided to leave Burke and Hare's five minutes earlier. In the meantime, all I had to do was get across this road.

Preferably without being run over.

Before long, I was striding across the bridge, looking down at the strollers idling down the boardwalk that now ran along this stretch of the river as it slapped and wound through the heart of the city. The evening

442

sunshine cut low shadows over the wooden slats at the walkers' feet and glanced like fire off the steel railings.

Even the water seemed in a better mood than usual that evening, sparkling and blue-green and innocent where usually it was grey-brown and hungry and resentful of the walls that held it back and told it where to go. The city was gazing languorously down at its reflection in the river and liking what it was. The low quayside buildings glowed contentedly.

The fetid, feverish atmosphere of two nights ago seemed to have evaporated again.

Outside the Liffey Theatre, the same easy mood was in evidence. People stood chatting, enjoying the last of the evening sunshine before plunging inside to Othello's tormented world, others merely escaping the smoking ban by having a final deliciously wicked cigarette. Zak Kirby stared out menacingly from the posters.

He was right. *This* version of the play at least should've been named after him. The guy playing Othello peeped out on the posters from behind the great actor's back, almost apologetic for muscling in on his moment of glory.

Kirby's billing was even bigger than Shakespeare's.

Fitzgerald arrived a few moments after me, climbing out of the front seat of a marked police car as it pulled into the kerb. Then Walsh got out the back door too, and they both walked over to me. That certainly got the attention of the waiting theatre-goers.

"Shall we go inside and get a quick drink?" she said.

"You think we have time?"

"There's always time for a drink."

The people around us seemed faintly disappointed. Maybe they'd hoped they were going to see an arrest, namely mine. Instead the three of us now climbed the steps into the theatre, and the police car drove off in the direction of O'Connell Street.

The bar was crowded when we got inside, so we took up a position by the door and sent Walsh to buy the drinks. I didn't waste any time.

"Something happened, didn't it?" I said.

"Am I that transparent?" answered Fitzgerald. "Yes, something happened. Though what it means, I still haven't quite managed to figure out."

"Well, are you going to tell me what it is, or do I have to beat it out of you?"

"You'll have to get a pair of stepladders first," she teased me gently. Then her face became grave, and she lowered her voice so as not to be overheard by the people pressing in around us. "We found something," she said. "Well, I say we found it. What I mean is that her friend Kim found it. You remember you met her at Marsha's house the other day?"

"She was picking up Marsha's stuff," I recalled.

"And inadvertently picking up a mobile phone too," Fitzgerald said.

"I'm guessing the phone was for the number she left on the online chat rooms for people to call?" Fitzgerald confirmed it. "Where was it?"

"It was in the pocket of one of Marsha's dresses. Kim found it entirely by accident. God knows how we missed it. She just happened to notice something hard

when she was packing the clothes away into boxes. She looked to see what it was and then brought it round today to Dublin Castle. That's what kept me. That's why I wasn't at Burke's."

"What was on it?"

"There were calls to only one other number. We don't know who that belonged to, and she hardly ever spoke to him directly, only sent a whole series of text messages covering a period of two weeks. Basically, she was telling him exactly what she wanted him to do when he came to her house that night and making arrangements to pay him."

"The missing money from her purse —"

"Exactly."

"So she *did* set up her own murder?"

"That's the thing," said Fitzgerald. "It seems that Marsha didn't really want to go the whole way. She saw it simply as a kind of play-acting. They were going to carry out a simulation of her murder, so that she could feel what it was like, test the boundaries of her desire, as she put it, but within a controlled environment. The man was to go through with the act exactly as if it was real, right up until the last moment, when he would stop."

"Except he didn't."

"Except he didn't," agreed Fitzgerald. "Either because it all went horribly wrong —"

"Or because he never intended to stop in the first place," I finished for her, "and she walked right into the trap." I sighed. "There was no name? No clues as to his identity?"

"Nothing whatsoever," Fitzgerald said. "She told him she didn't want to know anything about him. I think the mystery of the whole thing turned her on. She talked to him about her pretend murder like they were planning on making love."

"When did he last make contact with her?"

"She called him two nights before she died."

"She was making the final arrangements?"

"That's what it looks like."

I was about to say something else when Walsh returned with our drinks.

Our faces must have said it all.

"No need to ask what you've been talking about," he remarked as he passed cold bottles of beer into our warm and grateful hands. I noticed he also had a programme with him. He must've picked it up at the bar. There was a telephone number scribbled along the edge.

The programme clearly wasn't the only thing he'd picked up.

That boy never stopped.

It's a wonder it didn't drop off.

"Either way," I said, "I don't see how Victor Solomon fits into it."

"Don't say that."

"Someone has to. You can't claim Solomon was trying to silence a woman who was threatening to destroy him and was so desperate for cash he stole her necklace and cut off her finger to get a ring that no one can find anyway, and then admit she'd been sending texts to another man begging him to kill her only days

before she was actually killed. His lawyers will tear your case to shreds."

"Who says Solomon wasn't her mysterious phone caller himself?"

"It didn't sound like it," said Walsh gently. "In one of the texts she wrote to him: *I can't wait to meet you.* She wouldn't use that phrase if she was talking to Solomon."

Fitzgerald groaned. "Don't do this to me. Not tonight," she said. "I'm just bushed, I can't think straight. Tomorrow. We'll talk about it tomorrow. Tonight was meant to be an escape."

"I'm sorry," I said. "Forget I said anything. You know what I'm like. I'm the land that diplomacy forgot. Though you know, I'm not sure *Othello* will be much of an escape."

"What do you mean?"

"Jealousy, murder, sex, lies, revenge — it sounds more like a normal day's work for you than like an escape," I commented.

"I'm impressed," she said. "Since when did you get to be such an expert on Shakespeare?"

"Burke was cribbing me in your absence," I said. "The way he talked about it, he almost made me look forward to seeing the damn thing."

"Only almost?"

"Only almost," I conceded gruffly. "But you know what they say. Every oak tree started out once as a little acorn."

"I see you more as a little nut," said Fitzgerald. "What do *they* grow into?"

"I'll take a look in the mirror when I get home and let you know."

"I think we're going in," said Walsh, and, looking round, I saw that the crowd in the bar had gotten much thinner since we arrived. Either the play was about to start, or they were definitely trying to tell us something. Hastily, I finished my beer and followed him up the steps into the dim theatre, where a half-musical murmur, like an orchestra tuning up, was moving through the massed ranks of disembodied heads, the last remnants of conversation before the evening play began. We took our seats in the centre of one row toward the front, and waited, and I wished I'd gone to the bathroom before sitting down here because there was no way I could ask all these people to move again, especially not now the lights were dimming further, and the voices with it, as though the same switch which turned down the lights was able to turn down conversation at the same time. Neat trick if you could do it.

Oh, well, it served me right for never being able to resist a cold beer.

Gradual as dawn, a pale blue light appeared behind the curtain up on stage, moving, shivering, and, as the curtain drew back, I saw that it was a light like water rippling, which cast restless shadows over the flat façades of frowning buildings.

Venice, wasn't that where the play began?

Moments later there came approaching footsteps, echoes at first, then louder, and Zak Kirby appeared, followed by another man.

"Tush! never tell me . . ."

And so we began.

I settled down in my seat and tried to concentrate.

Kirby was good, I had to give him that. The brash young actor had gone. He was Iago now, the slighted soldier, world-weary and cynical and burning with the need for revenge, angry at seeing others less capable promoted ahead of him.

And I could understand that part at least. I'd seen it often enough in the FBI, as those who came garlanded with qualifications and meaningless academic recommendations strode ahead of the rest, overtaking agents who'd given years of their lives to the Bureau and had worked more cases than the newcomers had even read about. Promotion too often was for the golden circle. If you weren't in it to begin with, you stayed where you were.

Always the outsider.

His face was snarled with resentment at his ill-treatment, then would switch in an instant so that anyone seeing it would think at once they were in the company of a friend.

Someone who only had their best interests at heart.

And then it came to me.

Unexpectedly.

Unclearly as yet.

But undeniably too. At least it was to me. Whether Fitzgerald would be convinced that here lay the lock and key of all the villainous secrets which had occupied us for these past days remained to be seen.

"We have to go," I whispered to her.

"What are you talking about? We can't go. We only just got here."

"I can't explain," I said. "I know who he is. I know who Iago is. At least I think I do. I don't have a name for him yet, but I know where to get one."

Someone shushed me loudly from the row behind.

"You're not making sense," Fitzgerald hissed.

"You have to trust me," I said.

"Shit, why do I hate hearing those words?"

CHAPTER
THIRTY-NINE

"This had better be good," said Fitzgerald as soon as we were outside the door of the theatre and had a chance to talk, "and not just another one of your feeble excuses to wriggle out of improving your mind with a bit of culture."

"Blame Burke," I said. "He's the one who got me thinking."

"Burke?"

"He pointed out the parallels between the play and what was happening with Kaminski and Buck Randall. It all made sense. *Someone* was leading Kaminski on, setting a trap to entangle him, but think about it. Whoever was jerking his chain had to be subtle, clever, manipulative. Like Iago. Does that really fit what we know about Buck Randall III?"

"He never struck me as a candidate for *Mastermind*," she conceded.

"It's like I said to Burke earlier. What does Randall want? In the play, everything's simple. Iago wants Othello to murder his own wife, so he keeps planting suspicions and winding him tighter till he blows, right? But if Buck Randall's the Iago in all this, then he's only planting suspicion against himself. Why would he do that?"

"I take it that's a rhetorical question?"

"If you mean, do I have the answer already, I think so," I said. "It just came to me in there, out of nowhere. Randall's not Iago in all this. He's Desdemona. He's the one against whom suspicion's being planted. And maybe, like her, he's been innocent all along."

That would certainly explain a lot. Why Randall would let himself be seen so openly out at Bull Island. Why should he hide his face if he'd done nothing wrong? It explained too why he didn't care if his fingerprints were found all over the car that was pulled from the water. He had no reason to believe anyone would even be interested in his fingerprints. He probably didn't even know that Mark Hudson's body was in the trunk. Maybe he just drove the car out there because that's what he'd been instructed to do, to meet this mythical Peters perhaps, and someone else came later to dispose of it. Each step along the way, he could've been planting suspicion against himself without even realizing he was doing it.

"The point is," I said, "that he's the one that someone wants to die."

"And they're using Kaminski to do it?"

"Remember how Fisher described the same phenomenon when he spoke of how it was possible for a killer to act out his will using other people as the weapons?"

"But who could hate Buck Randall that much to want him dead?" asked Fitzgerald. "The only person we know who hates Randall sufficiently is Kaminski."

"But it isn't necessary for anyone to *hate* Randall to want him dead. Iago didn't hate Desdemona either. He simply wanted to use her death to bring about the downfall of Othello. It was Othello that he despised. So surely it's Kaminski that our own Iago hates too?"

"Then let me change the question round slightly. Who hates *Kaminski* enough to want to turn him into a killer?

"There was a part in the play early on," I said, trying to recall exactly how it went, "when Iago was explaining his reasons for wanting revenge. How did it go? Something about Othello getting it on between the sheets with his woman."

"*It is thought abroad that 'twixt my sheets he's done my office,*" she quoted effortlessly.

"That was it. It reminded me of something Kaminski told me that night in my apartment when he showed up. He said Heather was going out with someone else when they first met."

"You mean, Kaminski had been doing someone else's office between the sheets too?"

"That's what I'm thinking."

And now I could tell that she was interested.

"You have a plan," she said.

"Follow me."

I couldn't hang about waiting for Fitzgerald to call a car to bring us back to Dublin Castle and walking would take too long. Nor did I have enough power in my American cellphone for what I had to do. That left only one option.

Round the corner on O'Connell Street stood one of the international call centres that had sprung up across the city in recent years to let the thousands of people who'd arrived here from Eastern Europe and elsewhere call home cheaply. Small booths lined the wall like confessionals, and the light shone from the glass out front like a warm welcome.

I was out of breath by the time I'd run round there, then I had to search through my cellphone for the number I needed. I felt I was wasting time. Time I didn't have.

Time Kaminski didn't have.

Certainly time that Buck Randall didn't have.

Then I punched in the number wrongly.

Cursed.

Tried again.

At last it rang.

"Piper," he said when he answered.

"Piper, it's me, Saxon. Listen, I need your help again."

That familiar empty laugh. "Who're you trying to get in touch with now?"

"It's nothing like that," I said. "I've got something to tell you. I found Kaminski."

"You found him?"

He sounded hesitant, like he didn't believe me.

"I found Buck Randall too," I went on. "Leastways, I know he's here, and I know *why* he's here. I *think* I know at last what's been going on."

"Right," he said slowly.

He still didn't sound sure.

"So where are they now?"

"I don't know," I admitted.

"But I thought you said —"

"I know what I said. I had Kaminski, but he's split on me again. Piper, are you listening to me? Buck Randall didn't kill Kaminski's wife."

"He didn't?"

"He couldn't have. Nothing he does makes any sense if he really did kill her. Someone just wants Kaminski to believe that he did."

"I'm not following you," Piper said.

"It's complicated," I said. "You have to trust me. Someone's trying to set up Kaminski. That's what it's been about all along."

"Who?" he said.

"That's the problem. I don't know. I thought you might be able to help me. I know who it is, I just don't know who it is, if you understand what I mean."

"Saxon, there's probably not another soul on the planet right now who understands what you mean."

"I think Heather was seeing someone in the Bureau before she met Kaminski. I think Kaminski was having an affair with her while she was seeing this other guy, and *that's* why he killed her. And now he's making Kaminski pay too."

"Saxon, listen to me, you have to stop this," said Piper. "What you're doing here, it's too dangerous. I don't know what Kaminski's up to, but he's got you involved in it too now. He's been out of his head ever since his wife died, he's just been waiting to blow, and

455

you don't want to be near him when he does. You have to walk away."

"You were the one who told me Kaminski needed a friend."

"It was wrong of me. I shouldn't have let you get involved. I didn't think you'd go this far. Listen to yourself. You sound half crazy. You've got to forget about Kaminski before he drags you down with him."

"It's too late for that," I said. "The only thing I can do now is get to him before he destroys everything. I just need to know, was Heather seeing someone else in the Bureau when she met Kaminski? I need a name, nothing else."

"You're serious," he said.

"I've never been more serious in my whole life."

"Then this is what I'm going to do," said Piper. "I don't want you to do anything until I get to Dublin. I'll get a plane first thing tomorrow morning. We can discuss it then. Together we'll figure out a way to help Kaminski. I shouldn't have left you to do this on your own . . ."

Finally, he noticed my silence.

"Saxon?"

He's like the Pied Piper, Burke had said.

Piper.

I almost laughed. It was so simple. You call a cellphone in New Jersey, you have no idea where it really rings.

"Saxon, are you there?"

"*How do you know I'm in Dublin?*" I said.

★ ★ ★

456

Traffic roared softly down O'Connell Street, the sound dulled by the glass.

It was like a wind rushing in my head.

"I never said I was in Dublin," I said, more loudly.

"What are you talking about?"

"I never said *Kaminski* was in Dublin."

Now it was Piper's turn to go silent.

"It was you, wasn't it?"

"For Christ's sake, what was me?"

"It was you that Heather was going out with when she met Kaminski. It was you she left to be with him. That's why you and Kaminski had fallen out. I am such a fool."

"You're raving."

"You're lying," I said.

"I'm lying? You were the one who said you were in San Francisco."

"Why, Piper? Why did you kill her?"

I counted ten cars passing, and a truck whose brakes squealed like an animal in pain as it came to a belated stop at a red light, before he answered.

Before he stopped pretending.

"They betrayed me," he said simply. "I don't know if you understand what that's like, if you can comprehend what it's like to have your insides torn out by the one person you thought you could trust, but I don't recommend the feeling."

"All she did was fall in love," I said.

"I'm not talking about Heather," he said scornfully. "I'm talking about Kaminski. How could he do that to me? And don't talk to me about love. She made me

puke the way she tried to tell me she couldn't help herself, she had to be with him. Well, she paid the price."

"And Kaminski?"

"I thought killing her would be enough. I thought that would punish Kaminski enough. But it wasn't. It wasn't nearly enough. He had to suffer more. Then he called me and asked for my help in bringing down Randall — after what he'd done to me, he wanted my help! And I knew how easy it would be to lead him by the nose. I remembered Randall from the case down in New Mexico. He was the perfect fall guy. I could've sent Kaminski a leaflet saying Randall was the second gunman in Dallas in '63 and he'd have believed it. All I had to do was make him think, right until the last moment, that he was getting revenge for Heather's death, and then finally let him see the truth: that the one he really should have gone after had gotten clean away, and he'd never have the chance to finish what he'd started. He'd simply sit rotting in a prison cell somewhere, torturing himself with what ifs and guilt at killing Randall. All I had to do was provide the bait and he'd fall right into the trap."

"So that's why you killed Marsha Reed?"

"Don't expect me to feel guilty about that. It's what she wanted. She was the one who made all the arrangements. I simply played my part."

"She thought it was all a pretence," I said thickly.

"Be careful what you wish for," said Piper, "it might just come true." And I remembered that Fitzgerald had used similar words once about Marsha too.

Desires can be dangerous things.

Who knows where they might lead?

"I'd come across people like Marsha Reed before, when I was in the FBI. She wasn't too hard to find. All I had to do was persuade her she'd be safe, and she was up for it. She thought it was a huge joke. Right until the very end . . . It meant coming to Dublin, but that was OK. I knew Randall would be easier to control here anyway. After that, it was easy to get Kaminski to follow us. And once he was here, I just had to convince him that the man who killed his wife had struck again and I knew he'd respond accordingly."

"You took the ring from Marsha."

"I'd taken the ring from Heather's body because I wanted it back. I'd bought it for her. She had no right to have it any more. Therefore I had to take the ring from Marsha too. It proved a little harder to get at than last time, but it had to be done. After that, it was simply a matter of giving Kaminski repeated reminders that Randall had to be stopped."

"The ring in the grave . . . Rose Downey . . ."

"That one didn't work out so well, but, hey, you can't win 'em all."

"And Mark Hudson?"

"He recognized me from New Mexico when I went round to Becky Corrigan's house to buy those ridiculous letters Jenkins Howler had sent her," said Piper bluntly. "I bumped into him as I was leaving. He said hello. What else could I do? I couldn't risk being IDed."

"You didn't strangle *him*."

"I figured I'd make the MO different in his case. Keep you all on your toes. Besides, I didn't want too much heat from the police in Dublin. My purpose was to play out the rest of the game with Kaminski. I only wanted those letters to make him suspicious, to make him wonder what was in them that someone wanted to hide."

Some game.

It wasn't hard to imagine how things might have gone with Hudson. How maybe he saw Piper and got talking, invited him in for a drink, how Piper slipped something into his glass when he wasn't looking . . . Then, when he started feeling groggy, he simply struck him on the back of the head to knock him out, put Hudson's body in the trunk of his Honda and got Randall to come with him out to Bull Island to dump it, making up some story about how they were going to meet some guy called Peters, that way making sure Randall was seen.

"You still haven't won yet," I said.

"How do you figure that?"

"All I have to do is find Kaminski. Once he knows the truth —"

"But I have Kaminski here with me right now. He's sleeping in the next room. He has a busy night ahead of him. Why do you think he was so keen to get out from under your watching eye at the fair? I'd arranged the real rendezvous with Randall for him. You can't imagine how grateful he was when I turned up to make amends and offer my help. Buck's looking forward to it too. I told him I knew someone who could help him. He

seems to have got the idea from your press conference this morning that he's in some kind of trouble."

And he laughed.

I felt the panic rising inside me.

"Piper, don't do it. Randall doesn't deserve this. Kaminski doesn't deserve it."

"Goodbye, Saxon. No hard feelings," he said. "I never intended for you to get involved. I tried to warn you off, but once you got involved I knew you'd be useful. You're even crazier than Kaminski. Once he got you involved, you were bound to reinforce his sense of what he had to do. He just needed a little push. But you know, Saxon, despite everything I always liked you. Maybe that's why we were always at each other's throats. We were too alike. And maybe we *can* still have that drink someday, huh? I'd enjoy that."

Those were the last words I ever heard him speak. I never heard his voice again. Never saw his face. In fact, I realized as I sat there in the booth and watched Fitzgerald, unaware of the truth, gesturing me outside to ask what I'd learned, I hadn't seen his face this whole time except in a picture. The last time I'd seen him face to face was ten years ago, and yet he'd been directing my whole life in these last days. Now he'd vanished more completely than ever, like Kaminski had vanished into the trees in New England. Only Piper knew how to do it properly. He wouldn't be found again. The only other contact I had with him at all was one night, couple of days later, when I came home to find Marsha Reed's missing ring dangling from a frayed piece of string and slung around my door handle . . .

I took it as a warning from Piper to stay well away from him.

And the world would keep on turning in his absence, the sun would keep on shining, the rain keep on falling. That was the thing about murder. It didn't disturb normality, it scarcely even scratched the surface of it. The dead went into the ground, and the living forgot them. Thousands every day, killed a hundred different ways. Lucas Piper had gone, but there were always Lucas Pipers, just as there were always innocent fools like Leon Kaminski and Buck Randall III. None of us amounted to much in the end. A hundred years from now, we'd all be forgotten. There was a strange kind of comfort in it.

In the meantime, as Kaminski had known and had tried to make real in his wrong-headed way, there was always justice and there was always vengeance. In one way or another, one place or another, I hoped Piper would get what was coming to him.

The rest of that evening passed largely in a haze. There were phone calls and questions. I was distantly aware of voices. But something in me had become detached. I couldn't make sense of what had happened. It was like everything I'd thought was true was now lined up against the wall, laughing at me. Fitzgerald said I shouldn't blame myself. She said you never really know what these people are thinking, and I thought: is that what he was now? One of those people? And I realized I didn't even know any more what kind of person Lucas

Piper was. Everything I thought I'd known about him turned out to be as insubstantial as cigar smoke.

If only, I found myself wishing futilely, I'd been straight with Kaminski from the start. I hadn't wanted to say too much because Lucas Piper told me that first night I called him how he and Kaminski were no longer friends and I didn't want to complicate things by admitting to Kaminski how I knew about his wife's death. *Who* had told me.

I didn't want to make him mad.

Hence I said nothing. Maybe together we would have seen through Piper's lies. I'd never know.

All I can say is that it seemed like a good idea at the time.

That's the story of my life. Things look like a good idea at the time, and they rarely are. In fact, I would go so far as to advise running like a cat out of a rabid dogs' home from anything which seems like a good idea at the time. Most of the greatest disasters in history have started out that way. But then that was part of what I was too. What I'd done, what I'd become, where I was now — none of it had been part of any plan. There hadn't been a plan. Maybe that was the problem. Everything in my life had been accidental.

Even seeing Kaminski in Temple Bar a week ago.

None of it had been planned.

But I was still finding it difficult to accept that it was the FBI man who'd been leading Kaminski by the nose, ass-like, into the darkness. But Becky Corrigan had confirmed that it was Lucas Piper who'd tried to buy Jenkins Howler's letters to her aunt.

One photograph.

That's all it had taken in the end to confirm his identity.

She also told us that it was Hudson's talking about the time he was questioned by the FBI in New Mexico for the murder of a woman that had got her aunt interested in the whole subject in the first place. Hudson had talked up how easy it would be to end up on Death Row for something that you'd never done. Something in his words tugged at her bleeding heart.

Soon after, she'd started writing to Jenkins Howler.

Strange how everything turned out to be connected in some way.

By this time Piper's fingerprints, which had been sent over from the personnel division at the FBI, had also been matched up to those found all over the inside of the trunk of the car in which Mark Hudson's rotting body had been found.

As for Buck Randall, it soon became clear that he was indeed as much of a dupe as Kaminski. The only difference was that he was being paid for his stupidity.

Fitzgerald had managed to pull up his bank records from back home and found that round about the same time Kaminski was following Randall round Huntsville, Randall had deposited a cheque for nearly thirty thousand dollars into his account.

The money came from a company run by Lucas Piper.

After he was persuaded of the seriousness of the situation, Randall's brother in Oklahoma confirmed the rest. Before he left Texas, Buck had told him that he'd

been given the money by Piper in order to take a job with his electronics company. He didn't know what kind of job it was. Didn't know what it entailed. All Piper told him was that it would be well paid and that he would be back in Texas before the end of the summer.

Randall was in debt. He didn't feel like he was in any position to refuse. Besides, it seemed like easy money. All Piper asked of him was that he not reveal his whereabouts to anyone else, the police included, no matter what story they spun him.

Randall knew Kaminski was after him.

He knew why.

He was afraid.

Lucas Piper's offer represented a way out. If only he'd known that he was walking straight into Piper's trap. That in running away from Kaminski he was actually running straight toward him.

Randall's brother also confirmed that he'd spoken to Buck a couple times since he arrived in Dublin. Piper was acting strangely, Buck had told him. He'd been booked into some mean rooming house in a part of town far from the bright lights, big city atmosphere he'd been expecting, and he was being sent out around the city on pointless errands, buying flowers, turning up to meet people who turned out not to be there.

And Randall's drinking had also gotten out of control, his brother revealed. He could hear it in Buck's voice. He wasn't thinking clearly any more. Most likely that was Piper's plan too. To keep Randall so drunk

that he didn't know what the hell was going on half the time.

Maybe he was drugging him too.

Randall certainly had no idea Kaminski was in the city, still pursuing him. He was just doing what Piper told him. Despite all that, he was getting suspicious.

He'd had enough, he'd told his brother in his last call.

He wanted to come home.

He didn't care about the money any more.

How he must've panicked when he saw that news report this morning and realized that he was still being hunted, not just by Kaminski this time, but by every cop in town. I guess he ran to Piper, looking for guidance, wanting to know what was happening. And how grateful he must've been when Piper said he knew someone who could help.

His brother told us that Randall had been twitchy around cops ever since he was questioned in New Mexico about the murder of a woman. They'd given him a hard time, apparently, which was why he'd been so nervous when he came across the same treatment in New York. Piper must've told him he could keep him away from the cops this time. Maybe he said he knew someone at the American Embassy who could clear up the misunderstanding.

By then it was too late. All the time, Piper had been laying the final pieces of the trail for Kaminski to follow, until finally he pulled the biggest rabbit of all out of the hat: himself.

He'd made contact with Kaminski.

Offered to help.

I recalled the book of matches Kaminski had in his pants the night he'd found the ring in Cecelia Corrigan's grave and been arrested. The Mountain House Lodge in Aspen, Colorado. I should have remembered this was where he and Piper had gone skiing together during their vacations. That had probably been Piper's sign to Kaminski that he was back in touch, that he'd forgiven him for taking Heather from him, and he wanted to help find the man who killed her. That was what Kaminski had been talking about that night. "*I'm making progress at last,*" he'd said. But his only progress had been right into Piper's hands.

And how would it end?

I thought I knew the answer to that, but I was almost afraid to form the thought in my head. Almost afraid that thinking it would make it true.

For now, only one thing mattered.

Finding Kaminski.

CHAPTER
FORTY

Shortly after midnight, a woman returning home late from work noticed that the wooden gates leading into Marsha Reed's house in the Liberties had been forced open.

She called the local police station, and the dispatcher sent out an order that the nearest patrol car was to go round to check it out. We heard the crackling message over the radio as we were returning to town along Morehampton Road from Becky Corrigan's house.

"It's probably just a coincidence," said Walsh.

"Better check it out all the same," said Fitzgerald, and she took the next left on to Marlborough Road, heading to Ranelagh, and from there to the Grand Canal.

The night still looked unfeasibly new, despite the lateness of the hour. No one was going to bed. The warm lights of the city kept them from wanting to go home. On the side of the canal, a group of young men, giddy from the evening's merrymaking, stood cheering round a lamp-post as one of their number shinnied up to place a traffic cone at the top like a hat.

Lovers embraced on bridges.

The streets were bleaker and more deserted once we crossed on to Clanbrassil Street, because here the city was less inviting, and there was less to stay outside for. The only other sign of life as we came to the place where Marsha Reed had lived was the patrol car, which was now arriving at her gate in answer to the radio's summons.

The uniformed cop looked almost startled to see us, until Fitzgerald waved her badge at him. Then he looked relieved when she told him we'd be taking over.

"Just wait in the car in case we need you," she said.

"See," I said.

The gates had been forced with a crowbar. Splintered wood flowered from the wound. I pushed them open a fraction and peered into the shadowy alley, trying to make out movement, shapes, anything. The darkness wasn't cooperating.

It certainly didn't look so pleasant a spot as it had the other day when I came here to meet Marsha's friend Kim. The night may have been warm, but there was a harder edge now.

"Walsh, have you got a torch?"

"In the boot, Chief."

"Go get it."

Walsh walked to the car and returned quickly with a flashlight. He handed it to Fitzgerald, and she switched it on, pointing the beam down the alley, probing for any signs of movement, like a searchlight picking out enemy aircraft.

The beam was bright enough to reveal the whole scene ahead as luridly as though lit by a blast of

lightning, only this lightning didn't burn itself out instantly. Way down the end of the lane, light reflected against a window and disturbed the bats in the trees. They squeaked in protest as they flapped out of the way of the light. Leaves were exposed like negatives.

"It's probably nothing," said Fitzgerald. "Kids. Or some drunk looking for a place to sleep. But there's only one way to find out for sure."

She pushed the gate and we stepped inside and began to walk the path down to Marsha's house. The church loomed up in the darkness, more ominous now than it had seemed in the daytime. This must have been what it looked like that night Marsha Reed was murdered. This must have been what Lucas Piper saw as he approached.

Or maybe that night there'd been a light ahead, shining by the front door, forming some destination to aim at. Maybe the stained-glass windows had glowed from within.

Maybe Marsha had even been waiting at the door.

When we reached the end of the lane, where the grounds opened out around the church, Fitzgerald stopped and pointed the flashlight into the corners of the garden.

Just to be sure.

Emptiness gaped back.

That left only the church itself.

I heard Fitzgerald gasp as the light spread across the doorway.

The door was open.

"Should I get back-up?" whispered Walsh.

470

Fitzgerald took a moment, composing herself.

"I want to take a look first," she answered.

We crossed quietly to the door and climbed the steps. Fitzgerald reached out a hand and pushed at the door. It opened smoothly, without a sound. The stone hallway behind it was cleared of furniture now. It looked more like a church again than a place to live.

"Let me go first, Chief."

Fitzgerald raised her finger to her lips.

"Can you hear it?" she asked him.

I heard it too.

A whispering like her own, only this sound was continual, a voice talking to itself softly in the dark ahead, without any alteration in tone, as if in prayer. Someone else was still inside the church, and it sure didn't sound like kids or some drunk.

Only one more door to go.

My skin was taut with tension.

Fitzgerald's too, I realized, as her arm accidentally brushed against mine, and an electric shock passed between us. When did it suddenly get so cold? Wasn't it summer?

Her hand closed around the door handle.

Turned it.

Click.

The sound of the lock releasing was like a gun hammer cocking.

"Police," warned Fitzgerald, raising her voice.

Then she entered.

The flashlight in her hand broke into the church first, bright as an angel appearing out of nowhere. But

471

there was no angel standing ahead of us, only a man with his arms raised in front of his face to shield his eyes from the unexpected illumination, hands facing outwards.

His hands were stained red.

Behind him his shadow surged against the stone, huge as a monster.

He was standing on the altar where Marsha Reed's bed had stood.

The bed where she'd died.

And I saw now that the bed was still there. Her father must have wanted it left untouched, as though it was cursed somehow. Fitzgerald dipped the light so that the man standing there could lower his hands, and the beam of light spread across the bed — and found something else. Another figure, except this one was not standing, and would never stand again. Instead it was doubled over, arms clutched under a belly that must have been seared with agony at the moment of death but which was now far beyond the reach of pain. Blood pooled out on the mattress underneath the body, black as treacle in the flashlight's gaze.

A knife, coloured in the same black along the blade, lay discarded on the floor.

"JJ?" I said, because the figure standing in front of the bed had now lowered his arms, and I could see that it was Kaminski, and he was smiling, his lips still moving in whispers.

"Kaminski," said Fitzgerald. "What have you done?"

"I killed him," he said, and the smile grew wider.

472

"Killed who?" she demanded. "Who have you killed?"

"Randall," he said, frowning like the question was so ridiculous as to not even deserve an answer. "Buck Randall — he's dead. It's over. He thought he could get away with it. He thought he could kill Heather and I'd just let him get away with it."

I couldn't speak.

Piper had told Randall he'd be back in Texas before the end of the summer.

What he hadn't told him was that he'd be returning in a casket.

I saw now that this had been the linchpin of his plan.

Our last hope — that Kaminski would learn the truth, and that Piper could take Randall's place, the place that should have been his — was gone.

Fitzgerald's voice was cold. "You fool," she said. "Buck Randall didn't kill your wife."

Kaminski started to laugh, and then the laugh became angry when he realized he was laughing on his own.

"What are you talking about?" he demanded. "What are you — Are you fucking crazy or something? Do you think I don't know what this bastard did to me?"

"Buck Randall did not kill your wife," repeated Fitzgerald.

Kaminski looked from her to me.

"Saxon?" he pleaded.

"She's right."

"Then who — Who killed her?"

"It was Lucas," I told him.

Kaminski began shaking his head violently "No," he said. "He was helping me."

"Kaminski, stop."

"No."

"He wanted you to suffer for taking Heather away from him."

"No. He told me he'd find Randall. You know what Piper was like. He could find anyone. *You* wouldn't help me. He said we'd do it together for Heather. No," he said. "No."

But the word wasn't a denial any more, and it wasn't disbelief. The word was the sound of a man who had just seen every reality on which he had built his life crumble.

A man who had suddenly woken up from a dream, and now understood that everything he had accepted as right was actually wrong. He was where Piper had wanted him. He was at the end of the line, with nowhere left to go. He'd crossed that invisible line and made himself a killer, for the sake of what he thought was justice, but it had all been in vain.

He had murdered an innocent man.

And now Kaminski knew it.

And he'd know it for ever.

His eyes were wild with strange truth.

"I'm sorry," I said.

Kaminski didn't hear me. Instead he dropped to his knees. He was mumbling something under his breath as his hands felt around the floor.

A moment too late, I saw what he was looking for.

The knife.

Just as I realized what was happening, Kaminski's fingers closed around the handle of the knife and he turned it round and pointed it to his chest. He closed his eyes.

He thrust the knifepoint toward him.

I watched it all as if in slow motion — but Walsh was quicker. He'd seen what Kaminski was about to do and had managed to make up the space between. As Kaminski's grip tightened on the knife, preparing himself for what was to come, the young detective threw himself forward to snatch at the handle. The knife still entered Kaminski, but not where he'd wanted it to go, not where the decision would have been irreversible.

Kaminski gave a low moan of pain that swiftly turned into a lower moan of despair as Walsh cheated him of the knife and stopped him finishing what he'd started.

"Let me die," he begged. "Please, let me die."

I often wondered afterwards if it wouldn't have been kinder to let him do just that.

Epilogue

The following evening we repaired to Shanahan's on the Green. A restored Georgian town house now transformed into an American-style steakhouse, and best known, apart from the fact that the body of a young woman had been found in the foundations sometime in the eighteenth century, for the rocking chair behind the bar in the basement where we were now sitting.

The chair had once belonged to President Kennedy. He took it everywhere with him, including Air Force One. Now it presided over drinkers in the suitably named Oval Office Bar. It was Stella Carson who'd suggested we all meet up here — Fitzgerald, Healy, Walsh, herself and me — and I didn't complain. It was one of my favourite places in the whole city.

We were sitting now on red velvet armchairs around a table on which perched an antique lamp surrounded by champagne glasses, as though they were guarding it.

The champagne had been Fitzgerald's idea. She'd long been of the opinion that champagne was for celebrations and commiserations and all points in between. Me, I'd have preferred a beer, but when

someone else is paying, you don't complain about that either.

So which was it? Celebration or commiseration? Two cases which I'd convinced myself were connected, and then been forced to admit might have nothing to do with one another, turned out to be connected after all, but neither in the way we expected, and the angle which had seemed to most of the investigating team like an absurd distraction turned out to be the heart of it all. Meanwhile the only person behind bars was Leon Kaminski. I didn't know what would happen to him. Even if a judge and jury took pity on him in the end for the murder of Buck Randall, he was locked now in a prison of his own making, and Piper had the key. As long as Piper was out there, Kaminski could never be free again, never be at peace.

As for Solomon, he'd been released earlier that day. There was no chance of pursuing a case against him for murder any more, not after all that had happened, and Ellen Forwood was refusing to press charges against him for the incident in which she'd been injured.

He was a free man, though I doubted his career would exactly flourish in future.

Mud sticks.

"If you close a case, then it's a celebration," the Assistant Commissioner ruled in the end. "Even if you feel utterly crap about it. That should be the first rule of detective work."

"Hear, hear," said Healy. "I'll drink to that."

And he reached out a hand and lightly touched the back of Stella Carson's own. It was a tiny gesture,

scarcely noticeable. Walsh didn't even see it — though that could've been because he was eyeing up the waitress as she weaved her way slinkily among the tables.

I looked at Fitzgerald and saw her smiling.

Silently, I managed to ask if what I was seeing was what I thought it was.

Silently, she managed to answer that it was.

I couldn't have been more astonished. All this time, I'd been tormenting myself with the possibility that something might develop between Fitzgerald and Stella Carson, and all the while the one the Assistant Commissioner was getting close to was Healy. That was fast work for a week.

Othello should have taught me the dangers of jealousy.

It was like Fitzgerald said. You saw what you wanted to see, you made connections where your mind made them, making things appear that were not really there.

You started seeing the world through the wrong eyes.

"There's just one thing I don't understand," said Fitzgerald.

"The necklace," said Healy.

"Exactly. If Marsha really did inadvertently arrange her own murder, and Solomon had nothing to do with it, then how did the necklace end up hidden in a bag in his office? Piper never said anything about either of them. I'd swear he didn't know they existed."

"I can answer that," said a voice behind us, and we turned to find Todd Fleming standing close by, looking nervous and carrying a small holdall . . .

★ ★ ★

478

Fleming had followed us to Shanahan's that evening to make a confession. He wanted to tell us what really happened on the night of Marsha Reed's murder.

She'd called him at the internet café, he said, and told him what she planned to do. Told him about her arrangement with her anonymous caller. What he was going to do. He told her she was mad. Told her it was dangerous. Warned her about all the things that could go wrong, but she wouldn't listen. It was all an act, she assured him, nothing more.

Where was the harm in that?

She told him that she'd planned the whole thing to scare Solomon into thinking that he'd almost lost her. She'd tried everything. She'd tried begging and blackmail and a plentiful supply of easy sex and even the prospect of some of her father's money to try to lure him back to her, but Solomon was having none of it. He wanted out of their relationship once and for all. He was going to marry Ellen Forwood and nothing Marsha could do would change that. The only thing she could think of now to bring him back was to make him believe that she had almost been killed. Surely once he saw how close he had been to losing her for ever, he would realize that he loved her and had to be with her and how much she needed him?

She had it all worked out.

She was to be roughed up a little and tied to the bed. The bruises would make it look good afterwards. The cuts would heal. She didn't mind. Didn't she enjoy pain? Didn't it turn her on? She was happy as she told him what was in store. Excited.

She certainly wasn't afraid.

She just needed Todd's help to make the deception complete. His role was to call round later after work and let himself into the house. The story would be that he had disturbed the killer in the act and the monster had fled. Then he was to call the police. Marsha would take it from there. She was an actress, after all. She knew how to lie convincingly.

Todd Fleming was terrified, he was confused, he was angry that she was still thinking about getting back with Solomon after the way he'd treated her. But she managed to talk him round. He agreed to call at her house after he finished work. How could he refuse? He loved her. Whatever she asked of him, he had to do it. He couldn't help himself.

What he actually found when he got there and let himself in with the spare key she'd left on the doorstep for him was Marsha's lifeless body lying on the bed.

A severed finger next to it.

The night had clearly not gone according to plan.

Fleming was distraught. For a time he couldn't think straight. All he could do was blame himself for allowing Marsha to talk him into taking part in her insane scheme. He should have walked out of work the moment she called, it didn't matter if he was fired, nothing else mattered except that he should have gone round to protect her.

He knew one thing.

It was his fault she was dead.

But then another, stronger thought began to gnaw at him. It wasn't his fault at all. Solomon was the one who

was to blame. He'd driven Marsha to this last insane act. In a way, he *had* killed her. And Fleming wanted him to suffer for it. He longed for that more than anything he'd longed for in his life. *He* was the one who'd driven Marsha to put her life at risk, so he was the one who had to pay. Fleming already loathed Solomon because Marsha had wanted him so badly. Now he had even more reason to hate him. To want him punished.

Fleming even convinced himself that if it hadn't been for Solomon, maybe there'd have been a chance for him and Marsha to be together. That it was Solomon, rather than her own dark appetites, which had kept them apart. And he thought he knew exactly how to get his revenge on this man who had made him suffer so much.

He would frame him for her death.

He took the necklace, planning to plant it in Solomon's office when he had the chance, wearing the same shoes he was wearing that night so that the physical evidence traces would match. It wouldn't be difficult to get inside. Theatres are open places, like Zak Kirby said. So that's what he did, first covering her obscenely displayed dead naked body with a sheet because he couldn't bear to see what had been done to her. And then he took the tapes from the hidden camera at Marsha's door too, knowing they could clear Solomon's name. (Piper thought he had everything figured. He hadn't seen that one. The expert in surveillance had become the victim of it.)

His hurt at being denied kept him going for days, consumed him, sustained him, and then he stopped sleeping and lay awake remembering her brutalized body, and repeating to himself over and over that the man who did that to her, and would surely do it to other women too if he was not stopped, was still out there. He couldn't go through with it any more.

He didn't want to be the kind of man who crushed someone just because they'd had what he himself had wanted so badly. He wanted to be better than that. So he confessed — and brought along with him a holdall containing the missing surveillance tape.

Later, we sat in Fitzgerald's office, as Walsh took Fleming downstairs to make a statement, and watched the grainy black-and-white tape, seeing the clock ticking down and Marsha coming home, unsteady on her feet; the taxi driver helping her with her keys; and, once they had vanished from view, a cat, sleek and dark, out hunting, tiptoeing carefully across the path in front of the door before halting, startled by a new arrival, and fleeing.

Then there he was, Piper, strolling to the door like he was on some social call, entirely unaware that he was being filmed, and disappearing inside.

The surveillance footage told us nothing we didn't now know already, but there was still a grim fascination in watching the seconds tick by on the tape's own clock, while inside the church, in one of those seconds, Marsha Reed's life was snuffed out.

Was it that second?

482

Or this?

Eventually, Piper reappeared, and he walked down the path and out of sight. We fast-forwarded to see Todd Fleming himself arrive at 2a.m., stepping nervously, not knowing what to expect, and finally there was only the cat again, tail raised, distrustful and alert, back to sniff the porch where these strangers had been, rubbing itself against the stone to replace their scent with its own. It sat on the path and looked up at the camera, as if it knew it was there, and its eyes glinted like mirrors in the dark. Then nothing, as the camera was switched out.

Case closed.

"More champagne?" said Fitzgerald.

She'd brought the half-empty bottle with her from the restaurant.

"I'd say there're about two glasses each left. We'll have to drink it out of paper cups from the coffee machine," she added, "but champagne's champagne. Just one condition."

"Yeah?"

"Not a word about Marsha Reed. I've had quite enough of her for one night, the stupid girl. What do you say?"

"Consider it done," I said with feeling. "I don't know about you, but I'm in the mood for getting seriously drunk. When the world ceases to make sense, you might as well join it."

It was only afterwards, when we'd gone back to my place to sit on the balcony and start on another bottle, and I was savouring a cigar and blowing the smoke

defiantly across the rooftops of the piously non-smoking city below, that it occurred to me how similar Lucas Piper and Marsha Reed had been. What they had in common was that neither could cope with a situation most of us have to learn how to handle at least once in our lives: being dumped. Not being wanted. Their inability to cope with it had made one a killer and the other a victim.

It was on the tip of my tongue to share this nugget of dubious wisdom with Fitzgerald when I remembered what she'd said. Not a word about Marsha Reed.

A deal's a deal.

It could wait.

Second Shot

Zoë Sharp

Charlie Fox is fast becoming the must-read heroine of mystery   **Ken Bruen**

There are thrills and twists aplenty in an absorbing mystery   **Telegraph**

Charlie Fox has a new client: a multi-millionaire mother who is looking for protection from a nuisance ex. When Simone decides to escape his unwanted attentions and the scrutiny of the press by going to America, it should make Charlie's job easier. But Charlie has some very bad memories from her last time in the US and from the moment they arrive, Simone seems to undermine all of Charlie's measures for her security. As the action culminates in a shoot-out in the snow, Charlie struggles to get to the bottom of what is jeopardising her assignment.

ISBN 978-0-7531-8074-7 (hb)
ISBN 978-0-7531-8075-4 (pb)

Die With Me

Elena Forbes

You could find your new best friend on the net . . . or discover your worst nightmare.

For 15-year-old Gemma it is already too late. Her body is found in the nave of a church in Ealing, west London. At first, all the signs were that it was a suicide. But then the autopsy suggests otherwise, and Detective Inspector Mark Tartaglia and the Barnes murder squad are called in.

For Tartaglia and his team it is just a matter of time before the tragedy repeats itself.

ISBN 978-0-7531-7918-5 (hb)
ISBN 978-0-7531-7919-2 (pb)

Cross

Ken Bruen

Cross — an ancient instrument of torture.

A boy has been crucified in Galway. People are
shocked. The Church is scandalised. Jack Taylor agrees
to help his old friend Ridge search for the killer. His
investigations take him to many old haunts, where he
encounters ghosts — dead and living. Everyone seems
to want something from him, but Jack isn't sure that he
has anything left to give. He wonders if he should sell
up, pocket his euros and get the hell out of Galway like
everyone else seems to be doing.

Then the sister of the murdered boy is burned to death.
Jack knows that he must stay and hunt down the killer,
if only to administer his own brand of rough justice.

ISBN 978-0-7531-7874-4 (hb)
ISBN 978-0-7531-7875-1 (pb)

The Wrong Kind of Blood

Declan Hughes

Ed Loy hasn't been back to Dublin for 20 years. Now his mother is dead and he has returned home to bury her. He soon realises that the world waiting for him is very different from the one he left behind all those years ago.

An old classmate, Linda Dawson, pleads with him to find her missing husband, Peter. She doesn't want the police involved. As if a worried wife with a seductive persona weren't enough to keep Loy occupied, his childhood pal turned small-time criminal, Tommy Owens, shows up on Loy's doorstep with a hard-luck story and a recently fired gun.

When Loy finds an old photograph of his long missing father on Peter Dawson's boat, and a corpse is discovered in the foundations of the local town hall, things begin to get personal. Suddenly, in this place where he grew up, he finds himself thrown into a world of organised crime, long hidden secrets, corruption, violence and murder.

ISBN 978-0-7531-7664-1 (hb)
ISBN 978-0-7531-7665-8 (pb)

The Dead

Ingrid Black

. . . pray for her soul . . . seven days . . . will begin with Mary . . .

Five years ago Ed Fagan disappeared and since then nothing has been heard from the serial killer known as the Night Hunter. Now a Dublin newspaper has received a letter claiming to be from Fagan with a chilling message: he's going to kill again.

At first the Dublin Metropolitan Police are inclined to dismiss the letter as the work of a crank. Then the body of prostitute Mary Lynch is found and it's only too clear that a murderer is at large again.

But is it Fagan?

Saxon, a former FBI agent, was writing a book about Fagan when he disappeared and is certain that the killings are not the works of Fagan. But how can she convince the police to look beyond the obvious and to go after the real killer . . .

ISBN 978-0-7531-7239-1 (hb)
ISBN 978-0-7531-7240-7 (pb)